ROGUES OF BINDAR

Other books by Chris Turner

Fantastic Realms

Future Destinies

Denibus Ar

ROGUES OF BINDAR

Chris Turner

Innersky Books

This is a work of fiction. All the characters and events portrayed in these stories are either fictitious or are used fictitiously.

© 2011 Chris Turner

Cover Art: Jessica Scholze

Published by Innersky Books
Canada
www.innersky.ca

ISBN 978-1-927117-56-9

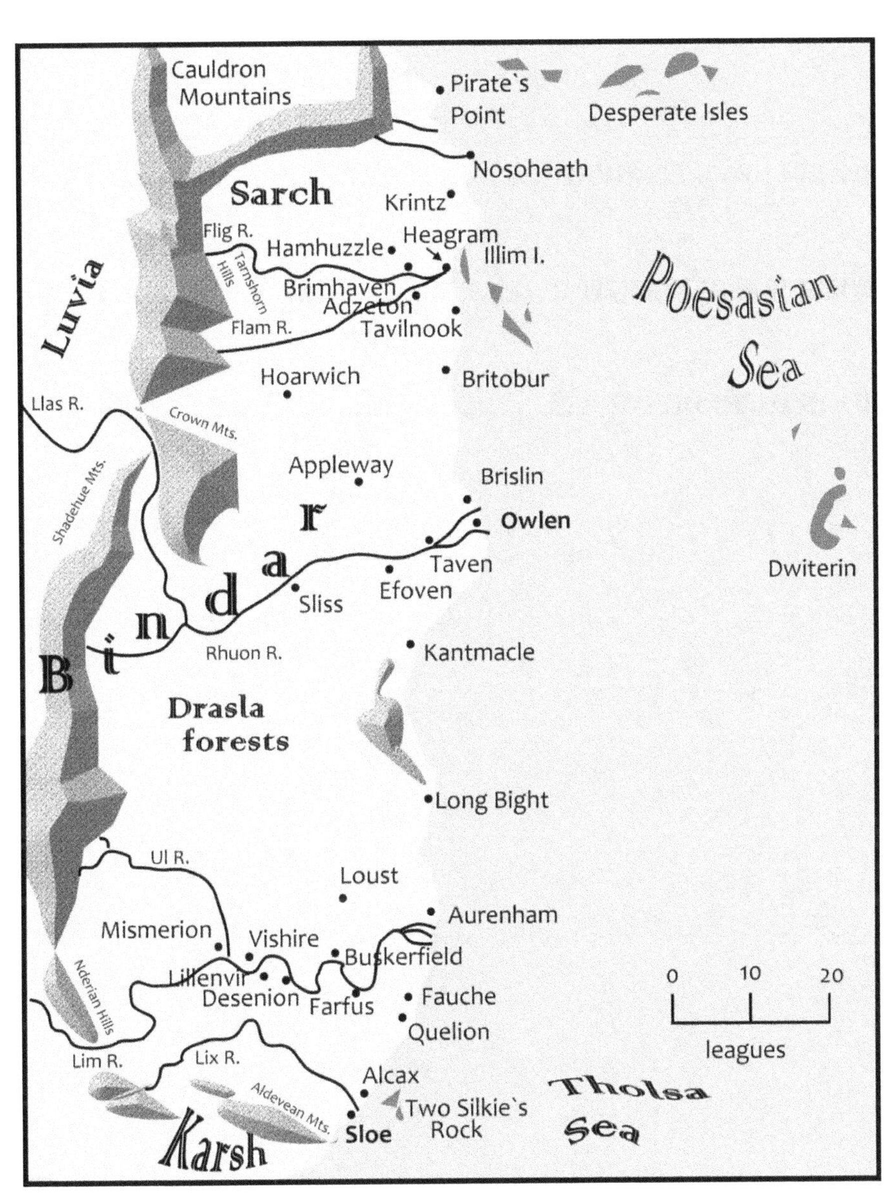

Cauldron Mountains
Pirate`s Point
Desperate Isles
Nosoheath
Sarch
Krintz
Flig R.
Hamhuzzle
Heagram
Illim I.
Tamshorn Hills
Brimhaven
Adzeton
Luvia
Flam R.
Tavilnook
Poesasian Sea
Hoarwich
Britobur
Llas R.
Crown Mts.
Appleway
Brislin
Shadehue Mts.
r
Owlen
Dwiterin
a
Taven
Sliss
Efoven
n
d
Rhuon R.
Kantmacle
Bï
Drasla forests
Long Bight
Ul R.
Loust
Mismerion
Aurenham
Vishire
Buskerfield
Nderian Hills
Lillenvir
Desenion
Farfus
Fauche
0   10   20
Quelion
leagues
Lim R.
Lix R.
Alcax
Two Silkie`s Rock
Tholsa Sea
Aldevean Mts.
Sloe
Karsh

CONTENTS

BOOK I : WOLF'S-HEAD 9

BOOK II : FREEBOOTER 213

BOOK III: REDEEMER 431

WOLF'S-HEAD

BOOK I

It was in a dream that illumination dawned in him. Escape was so simple! Humiliating months of hard labour in a rag-tag gang of scoundrels including the insane neomancer responsible for this incarceration had made him grim and cunning. As he chipped away at the mortar of the wall's one loosened rock, the magical gladius gleamed, and he reflected on how his curiosity for the arcane, and his thirst for adventure had brought him and his former friend to such an unexpected pass.

If only the cursed allure of the circus tents, the low-level sensory entertainments and diversions had not that day made him play truant and drawn him into these sinister forces beyond his control!

The stone gave way. The first step of his plan had succeeded! Now there was no turning back . . .

CHAPTER 1

MARVELS AND MIRACULA

AT

HEAGRAM FAIR

From Chaplain's modern guide to misconceived terms:

"Enchanter: One who brings plausibility to the most farfetched acts, fascinates eye, ear, and creates a sense of 'suspended disbelief'.
Common methods: sleight of hand, illusion, hypnotism, dissembling, alteration. Held in general contempt are hoaxing, snake-charming, trained owls, talking amulets and the like..."

I

Grey listless morn. A questionable time to be out catching rockgobblers on the beach in northern Bindar, but here he was, Baus, a handsome swain, watching the surf lick the sand like mischievous serpents' tongues. He had sea-green eyes, a tinge of swarthiness, a jauntiness to step, a canniness to gaze, an affability of voice, edged with a more poignant subtlety to baffle the shrewdest of listeners. Not far from Heagram's port, the beach stretched languidly, as too did the sea, a quilt of deepest aqua. The drab, chill stillness promised nothing to improve Baus's spirit.

While his creative faculties wandered over his less-than-optimal circumstance, he scuffed at the low tow line anchored fast in the sand. Only yesterday he had been upbraided by Harky the shoremaster for inadequate productivity: a measly dredging up of four rockgobblers and two nibblers. He had impressed on the shoremaster's mind the damaging effect of negative affirmations, but had received only stern reprimands and fist-waving in return.

He thrust himself back to his grey reality. The matted tangle of nets at his feet stunk of rotten fish; the joints were braced with iron, fickle with rust, causing his fingertips to bleed. Swoops of lavender cloud hung in swirls of muted colour. Northward ran a shoreline the hue of wharf planks; to the south, a broad expanse of mud flats, dark and slick in low tide.

Almost at the edge of his vision, he discerned smoke rings—dragging above the low cluster of stone and timber buildings, the salt-washed precincts of Heagram.

Scowling, Baus pulled back at the dark masses of his hair. Was there any way to be out of this dreary loop? He had a quick mind, deft hands, even a sensitive soul—how could he not try his luck at another seaside locale?

The idea seemed grandiose. He fingered his loose ponytail trailing at his back. Who was to say he would be any better off elsewhere?

Grimacing, he looked down at the pair of brickboar breeches clinging to his thighs, grunting at their sea-drenched and patched quality. Despite their disrepair, they fitted him admirably, accentuating his lean figure. A sea charm of translucent green hung on a cord about his neck. The charm was won in a dice match of 'Varlets and Vixens' on Heagram's quayside in *Snogmald Tavern*, from a pair of ribald Brislin boatswains.

Cursed, or blessed, Baus's sense of self-appreciation was excessive. Unlike his slewed situation (which implied a disproportionate degree of drudgery in relation to his spiritual skills) it was not outside of his powers to control his pride. As for the individual, one made his own destiny.

Or so went common opinion.

Normally he would be out sailing the *Calaan*—sheeting the one-masted fishing sloop and trawling for gallfish or snogmald, but the boat was currently raised on the wharf, facing repairs—the underbelly had been recklessly driven too close to Fiddler's reef and a hole was staved in her stern. As a result he was relegated to baiting the rockgobbler traps, repairing the gallfish nets, searching for razor clams and the odd mollusc that happened to wash upon the shore . . .

A league out to sea blossomed Illim Island whose cypress-rich mystery cast poor shadows upon the swells.

Baus lay down his paltry basket of catches and slumped himself down on a wet rock gleaming from the withdrawing tide. A few lubberly scows bobbed out in the harbour—odd shapes which he recognized at once as Mesmelter's cog, Jubben's *Gobblerbane* and Leaster's *Windfall*. A large carrack rode the deeps—her high hull riding proudly on the water; her polished oaken masts shafted high, her white sails hung limply in a near non-existent wind. Likely one of Prince Arnin's scouts—a presence, which, outside of the capricious wind itself proved an unnerving coincidence, indicating the presence of freebooters troubling the seas.

The vessels continued in their courses, moving like sluggish turtles confined to a grievous march across a trackless waste.

A week passed and Baus stood rooted in almost identical hollowness, staring out over the ocean. How many days had passed without anything of significance taking shape in his life? Was he really living—eking out his existence on the wearisome mud flats? Scratching his stubbly cheek in frustration, he realized that there was no more time for waiting . . .

A distant clank of metal issued from afar. Following came the faint trickle of laughter and a forlorn call of an ekloon dipping in the wind.

Perking up ears, Baus saw past the crumbling sea wall a score of figures stretching tarps along the communal flats. Men hoisted tepee-like canopies upon sturdy poles. Why were they so animated at this early hour?

Uncertainty changed to understanding. The fall fair was in play!

He trooped his way back along the beach. Surprise and purpose had him catching sight of the pencil-gaunt shapes of Harky and Nillard struggling awkwardly in the shallows, wresting a substantial wrack of tangled nets from the sea and heaving the nets in their own idiosyncratic rhythms.

Baus gave the pair wide berth, manoeuvring closer to the pier.

The mud flats stretched out to the water's edge where sounds of activity from Heagram waxed louder and in more insistent spurts. A sandier strip of beach graced the bluff's toes further inland.

Baus strode on, arriving at a box-shaped shelter of ill-fitted yew which rose out of the sand like a sore wound. A lurid sign was pasted above a copper goat's bell and a club, reading 'B-E-A-C-H M-O-N-I-T-O-R'. An individual of no great stature sat on a high stool, wearing a mauve and black pin-striped uniform. His hair was straight and brown, stiff as rope, plastered to both sides of his head; a leather cord, outfitted with black pearls and gull feathers, was wrapped about his neck. Neither brittle nor exuberant, the youth sported a pair of squirrelly ears, a flat nose, moon-grey eyes and a disagreeable overbite which fixed his expression into a perpetual grin.

Baus allowed himself a smile. Weavil—town poet, laureate of odes, also known as 'beach monitor' . . . whittling a limb of sea-beech with innocent absorption. At his side clumped a tangle of nets and a basket of sharp stakes. In his spare time, the poet was obliged to weave nets and whittle wood for the weirs, which at present were failing.

Baus tipped his head in a formal salute.

The poet inquired with lofty courtesy, "And where be we off to in such a mood of peccadillo? Tormenting limpets and cockles as usual?"

"My greatest bondage," replied Baus. "And you? Still on guard for Vrang, our elusive sea drake?"

"Never a sign!" admitted Weavil. Mock unhappiness traced an unpleasant crinkle on his sea-lined face. "Though the legend says the monster will fly one day, crimson, mighty-scaled, past the Wistish Isles beyond the rim of the world."

Baus made a guttural sound. "Bah! I shouldn't be giving energy to this legend, or holding my breath for any drakes."

"Really!" Weavil grunted. "Are they all monkey-tales? A duty is a duty." He cocked his head to one side and seemed more a weasel poking its neck out of a hole than a young man. "I wonder about your wisdom, Baus . . . you still have not answered my question."

Baus signalled impatiently. "I journey to Heagram's fair—to reckon what is to be reckoned."

"A plan of providence!" Weavil jumped down from his perch, crowding his companion with eager boyishness. "Perhaps I shall taste the annual festivities too." He smoothed out his pin-striped vest. With anticipation, he blurted out his thoughts. "Not on this instant though. I am engaged in 'shore duty', upon which I must wholly focus."

"A sensible dictum," declared Baus. "Dipping in the waters of the Flam while on duty would be unthinkable."

Weavil protested. "The razor clam and dogtooth fern surely slice the flesh and sting the bones! You know well that Prefect Barth has instructed me to monitor all people who approach the water. 'Tis a known fact that my sole agency is to spy out drakes and inform the masses of possible hazards and perils."

"Only too evident by your modest signage. Yet my remarks remain unaltered—I advance to the fair! With that, I bid you good day." Baus sauntered off, whistling a happy tune while Weavil gazed enviously after him.

II

The port of Heagram was populated with folk of many qualities. It hosted a venerable, old-style architecture rich with stone-carved fountains, flagstoned plazas, vined archways, antique buildings and monuments. An old bell tower stood off to the centre of *Beerstrom's plaza*. Curiously, a phalanx of varnished boats and retired seacraft flanked the cool, cobbled *Sea Alley*. Tending toward the river tumbled an array of pilings in the harbour, pot-darkened at their bottoms and supporting a collection of wide wooden slats. A host of sailcraft, including the swift two-masted *Wind Stallion* and the voluptuous *Latitude Fey* lay moored, while farther along the pier, in somewhat murkier waters, dories and lighters were berthed, along with fishing boats, scows, cogs, paint-peeled and barnacled. Since the beginning, Heagram harbour had been shaped in the form of a sickle where the two rivers, the Flig and the Flam joined the Poesasian. Now Baus saw narrow wooded peaks piling past the conjunction of the two watercourses, several warehouses, the boatwright's yard, a collection of foundries and Durgen's scrapyard, and the old gravel road, *Castaway's Trail*, which wound its way past Muoffen's mill and up the Flam's nearest foreshore. Inland past the pubs and valestone residences loomed the grand town hall and a picturesque schoolhouse, with freshly painted yellow roof, behind which rose ranks of woody briar-oak, tinged with a late summer green. On top of the bluffs the old lighthouse shone from a glassy beacon, heralding visitors from the sea.

People were arriving from all quarters: by sailboat, along the inland road, in wagons, carts, on wegmor mounts or carriage. Folk, primarily from Brimhaven, Tavilnook, Adzeton, Britobur and Hamhuzzle, were eager to mingle. They were of mixed sorts, though some ventured from as far as Owlen and the seaport of Brislin, realms of Prince Arnin. There was no small opulence or lack of breeding here!

The river ferries buzzed. At this hour, three new caravans clacked their way down the boarding ramps, saddled with a ragtag of bumpkins. Atop their beat-up wheelbacks and rickety, clattering carts, banjo players beat out jangly tunes. A larger three-masted sailship lay anchored in the harbour, from which at a distance, an elegantly-polished pennoned skiff pushed its way brightly to shore, ferrying grandees from Owlen.

Booth tenders continued to load goods into drays which were hauled over to the fairgrounds with the help of town dogs. Wares and accoutrements, horns, bugles, cauldrons, cages, wooden baskets, easels, poles, banners and flags moved as one. Odours of fried eels, oil-cake, pogo kelp and sausage signalled a grand feast planned for the afternoon which Baus hoped to attend, estimating that there would be a record turnout today. The streets were clogged with carping animals, beasts and carts and it was hardly noon. Through the seaborne cloud, patches of blue sky presaged fair weather. The day's festivities were now in motion, rich with golden sunbeams; flagpoles and steel-tipped masts were a-glow.

Pausing to critique the fairgrounds, Baus turned a watchful eye toward a sprawl of new tents. Balloons and flagpoles rippled freely in the salty breeze. Thirty five aisles stretched over Glane's Glade like pathways through canopied gardens. They were clustered with excited people and their pets: tinkers, salespersons, hawkers, gamesters and performers. There were fine displays of fire, animal roars, booms, a cacophony of riotous voices, shouts and calls—presumably intentioned to impress the new visitor, touting the excellence of certain entertainment and exhibits. Baus ducked as a firecracker ripped through the sky, heralding the launch of a circus act. Hot smoke rose above the tents ten aisles down.

Baus cocked his head: there was more than a usual gaggle of stiltwalkers, fire-blowers, sword-swallowers, acrobats, clowns, jugglers and tricksters this year. Of late Heagram fair had become more of a carnival than a local exposition.

A sidewise glance confirmed that visitors were converging on a central lane. Baus nodded to a group of retired fishermen, including an old sea geezer with a greasy pipe hanging out of his tobacco-stained mouth. He passed a clot of children who smacked down candy floss, then to a huddle of women dressed in blue caps and white gowns. They were tittering over a mass of embroidery, discussing the latest fashions, while in separate soap and flower booths, Baus recognized three maids with whom he had made recent intimate connections. To avoid any awkward confrontations, Baus made a wise detour, ducking into an oddment booth where he acquired a moustache of black straw, felt hat, and wide-brimmed glasses which he expertly angled over his eyes from experience. He recalled the last time he had bumped into Tersa, the foremost of the trio who had reacted very unkindly to his association with Salys and the significantly more buxom Roxa. Ah . . . what to do with all these petty grievances?

Moving along in unobtrusive fashion, Baus skipped several booths, amazed and appalled at the abundant display of bric-a-brac and bells fastened to wire, dancing puppets in water jugs, glow figures on pogo sticks, garish glue-paper costumes, an endless variety of house ornaments. Kiosks were packed with knickknacks, gewgaws of all sorts; nothing triggered any profound interest.

Half way along the third aisle, he stumbled upon a booth of ancient relics: primarily shells and glass and pewter. Something of more substance!

He found the booth manned by a pair of merchants from the west—denizens of Ikule or Hilgimi. The foremost vendor, completely bald and sporting an out-moded waxed moustache, snapped to attention. His partner, an individual of great corpulence and arm, darker of complexion and attentive of eye, remained placidly composed.

With languid ease, Baus examined the wares with a scholar's eye. The centre piece loomed twice the size of a man's skull. A large shell inscribed with a hanged man's corpse comprised the outer bulk, around which several primitives engaged in curious ritual.

"Aha, Seigneur, I see you are eyeing the Dulfiog special. A remarkable piece of antiquity this is, even for eyes as old as mine! Migor, my colleague and brother, has no idea from where it came."

Baus acknowledged the information with academic interest. "The article is intriguing— yet doubtless of origin that can be traced as faraway as Zanderland." He scratched his brow, barely noticing the approach of Migor with large hands spread wide: "Perhaps one may argue a different claim," said the imposing vendor. "Uyu and I are in a muddle over which primitive caste the relic may have been born to. The Koyo? The Negir? The cannibalistic Recendu? All are equally plausible. The world is a tribal mishmash of cultures, societies and traditions."

Baus tapped a finger of uncertainty to the object. "My conviction would be that of the Negir."

"A high-minded guess," chirped Uyu with a flourish. "Recall! The bygone era with which we are dealing is obscure, even to polymaths. The roots of the rare item are real. In the rare witness texts of the god Yarma, the period involved is barbaric, as that of the Zelthoxian age, its peer." Leaning forward to better assess the customer's perspicacity, he confided, "I must say that this piece is selling for an affordably low price of sixty-nine cils."

Baus croaked. "A piece like this may go for as high as thirty-four cils in a market of monarchs! If I harboured enough funds to spare the trinket, I would offer you five cils, nothing more."

Uyu uttered a squeaking cry. "Trinket? Are you so parsimonious that you would spare not a few tawdry coins for an authentic relic? You would be driven out with scourges in my land for disrespecting the offer. The item is worth a king's ransom! Regard the obscurity of the ritual. The primitives embark in an abomination of curious proportions." He skipped about, tapping the inscription with animation.

"The ritual is not in question," declared Baus flatly. "Just the price. Five cils—my final offer."

Uyu looked up, his tone stretched to an abominable whine. "You are not grasping the inestimable worth of the Dulfiog! It is a treasure beyond price! Why are you so intransigent?—we are offering you a boon at a paltry cost. We find you a valued, principled customer!"

"I accept the remark, unconditionally; however—" Baus eased back on his heels, floating closer to the nearby wall. His eyes were suddenly riveted to a barbaric chain suspending a curious monstrosity at eye level. The object was reminiscent of a bird-cage, topped with an irregular bird of petrified beobar and gave off an air of eldritch antiquity. The black beast was some kind of harniforous, possibly a psudoferous, equipped with drooping beak, serrated claws, bovine eyes and a hint of foul flair. The cage itself was bizarrely outfitted with several realistic-looking, terracotta figures in which the representations showed inherent human qualities, accompanied by grazing animals, bunched in groups and clusters and gathered around a wicket fashioned of birds' nests.

Baus screwed up his face into a perplexed grimace. To decipher the actions or angles of engagement of the figures in relation to the animals, including goats and ruminants, was not comforting.

"The guardian fowl," Uyu intoned, "is none other than the god Tuskou who watches benignly over the gentle, but mischievous 'Zmoo' and their ruminants."

"Intriguing," remarked Baus.

"The chronicles of Zmoo are detailed in Rovsmip's *Encyclopediax*, as I'm sure you're acquainted with."

"Naturally. Though in no way in any expert fashion."

"You admit to humbleness . . . ha! Very well, then you must know that 'Tuskou' tutors his subjects on the vagaries of fate when the primitives commit indifferent acts?"

"So much is only just."

Uyu seemed to find the response affected and curled his lip.

Somewhat repulsed by the flavour of Uyu's dogmatism, Baus scrutinized the vendor with mounting dislike. Uyu hopped closer. A markedly more flushed animation entered his cheeks. The vendor urged Baus to touch the artifact.

"I daren't!" Baus cried. Scratching his ear, he felt somewhat annoyed at the foolish grin etched on the vendor's face. The garlicy odour wafting from his body gave Baus stimulus to leap closer to the 'birdcage'. Curiously, he overshot his mark; he held out a hand to stabilize his precarious flight.

Fingers clutched a rung of the artifact. A lever switched. A clay figure was released from the cage with astonishing speed. An inexplicable waft of gas was followed by a negligible explosion. One of the clay figures hopped forward with urgency. It butt a hip into Baus's finger, which had wormed its way through the cage. By means unknown, Uyu had initiated a prank through means of a controlling mechanism.

Scrambling back, Baus hissed. The action jostled Uyu, who in turn cannoned into Migor. There was a windmilling, a vertigo. The glittering yuyuks and shellames on the far wall came down in an ear-piercing clatter of chert, shell and glass.

Uyu sprang back in horror. Migor remained speechless. The big man launched himself to his feet, covered in glass and debris, with the speed of a cobra.

Baus watched the display with composed placidity. Dispassion shone in his eyes as he watched Migor sift and scrape through the broken shards. A rapid jabber of language issued between shopkeeper and brother, which Baus construed as modern Hilgimic curses.

Migor's piercing yellow eyes fixed on Baus.

Baus uttered a dignified conciliation, to which was given snorts of hostility.

"You grin, swain," growled Migor, "but smashed are my two yuyuks in supplement to four expensive shellames at a cost of twenty-five cils!"

Uyu squeaked: "Do not neglect the chipped chertobyl valued at thirty-five cils."

"No matter," declared Baus. "It was terribly unwise to post artifacts so close to the booth walkway. Look at the grief that has come."

Uyu choked on his tongue and reiterated that recompense was due at one hundred and eighty-five cils.

Baus responded with an outraged croak. "A scandalous sum! I notice a definite lack of bonhomie in your words—particularly for an individual who has proven polite and discerning up till now."

Uyu laughed fondly. "That is the tally that you owe me, rogue, payable upon demand, which is right now!"

Baus held up an obstinate hand. "Technically, it was not I who fractured the articles, but Migor, who catapulted backwards in ignorant fashion."

Migor clamped his jaw with rancorous amazement. "Hardly! It was rather your oafish clumsiness which created such impetus, and hence, the ultimate aftermath!"

"Lay blame to the mud-baked demon in the birdcage who startled me. There you will find your only proper scapegoat."

Uyu grimaced. "Leave poor Bojor out of it. The manikin is a joke, nothing more than an eye grabber."

"Quite an expensive joke at that," Baus muttered.

Migor exploded: "Do not denigrate Bojor! He is part of a device triggered to lighten the mood when prospective buyers persist in wavering between browsing and buying!"

Baus raised a scornful forefinger. "So! The truth finally emerges! You would lull innocent bystanders into purchasing exorbitant wares through tricks!" Crossing arms on his chest, he glared at the shopkeepers. "Shame on you, sirs! I am at a loss for words. I remain wholly displeased at these crass tactics. Please sort out your complaints on your own time."

He turned to leave but the clamour had attracted several passers-by who were amused by the demonstrations and lingered at the entrance to compose jocular repartee. While the shopkeepers further engaged in grumbling dispute, Baus began to slowly backtrack out of the booth. The vendors remained preoccupied and Baus managed to slip past the gawkers and commence a rapid course down the nearest aisle.

The absence, however, was noted.

A cry of astonishment came lancing out of the booth before Baus was very far. Migor's balled fists comprised adequate testament that should he refuse to reimburse them, payment would be extracted on his flesh.

Knees pumping high, Baus ox-bowled his way down an intersecting aisle.

Not a moment to lose. He succeeded in losing himself in the brewing crowd, fumbling for safety, shoving and elbowing, cursing the need for such unseemly urgency. Darting between clusters of fairgoers, he reprehended the fact that he could neither sprint nor leap at sufficient speed. He could feel the hot reek of Uyu's breath on the back of his neck with Migor's cold strangling fingers almost ringed around his throat.

A slip on the wet grass had him crashing into a group of wagoners, toppling them and sending a sprawl of bodies to the ground. Crawling to safety, he slipped onto his belly. He turned, fought nausea, clawed his way through a sea of prickly knees where jumbled tent parts rolled every which way.

He was sure that he was about to be pounced upon any second, but he gained his feet, sprinting headlong into a human leg.

A hand politely parted a drape to a storage booth while a soft boot nudged him through. "Weavil?"

"At your service," came the poet's murmur.

The drape closed. Weavil remained hunched in the outer lane.

A harsh voice lunged forth from the aisle: "Where is the bumbling oaf?"

Weavil's clarion voice came through the drape to Baus's ears. "Do you mean the long-legged hoodlum wearing cheap hat and fake glasses?"

"That is him!"

"I thought to see a figure of similar nature fleeing on all fours that way."

The two pursuers dogged in the prescribed direction. After a time, Weavil hissed: "You can come out now."

Baus dragged himself to his feet.

"Must I always rescue you in this deplorable fashion? It is embarrassing."

Baus waved his hand. "The idea is more demeaning than the deed."

"Nevertheless, it is the reality."

Twenty yards away, a group of eccentric figures yammered away, engaged in antics in the public section of a demonstration booth: a green-haired ape capering in circles, a white-robed lizard-eyed man orating odes, a blue-nosed dwarf executing back flips atop a bear, three misfits wrapped in loose brown rags performing cartwheels. A grinning girl stood to the side with peaked, cat-like ears. She held up an evocative placard from her overhanging rabbit tooth that read:

Grolsner's Mini-Circus and Excellent Acrobats
Buy Tickets and Enjoy!

The grotesques capered about in their usual ways. If anything, there was a sprightliness to their steps, even derring-do. Now a juggler with a white dunce's cap tossed a bowling pin childishly close to one of the dwarfs. The playtoy bopped her on the crown; the dwarf gave a twittering chirp and began chasing after the juggler. The routine prompted howls from the audience, inspiring Baus to rub affectionately at his chin. It seemed that members of 'Grolsner's troupe' tended toward the harmless. Perhaps the entourage might comprise a legitimate substitute for his current predicament? The more he pondered, the more he warmed to the idea. If it were adventure he coveted, perhaps one of these ragtag bands could permit him to discover a bit of country, engage in some rendezvous with a few vivacious females, other worthwhile boons . . .

Various members swarmed around Baus. In his fascination, he had marched closer to the display than would be politic, leaving Weavil behind, griping at his lack of thanks.

He saw five exceptional persons: Hamma the Rabbit Waif, Larga the Strong-woman, Edulf the Dwarf Ape, Yipyob the Salamander Man, and Sandar the Nail Cleaver.

A white-furred bear with dwarf rider suddenly nuzzled up to him, scooting then after the sign holder in fun. As if on cue, the bear began skipping around in a two step strut with front paws paddling. The animal had no collar or leash, but was muzzled with wire cord and leather flaps. A well-fed middle-aged impresario seemed to be directing the whole farrago from a distance and when he came to see the interruption, stormed forward. "Here!" he called, adjusting his cape and orange star-studded top hat with brio. He marched purposefully. "Back to your capering, you indolent mongers! Am I to pay you for rubbernecking?—" The query was directed at Baus. "State your business, stranger, and desist from this rambling and distracting my staff."

"I have no intent of 'distracting'," responded Baus icily. "I am an experienced fisherman, the owner of a talented knowledge base among other skills. I toy with the idea of joining your minor ensemble, perhaps in an advisory capacity, for which Weavil, my esteemed colleague, will endorse me as a worthy candidate."

Grolsner looked for the person in reference but found no one. "A large thing you ask," he muttered. "Despite your self-professed qualifications, I know you not a whit from Darnar the jewel thief or Wistro the Mountebank. Your credentials are deficient. Begone! This is a tightly-run business—not one given to frivolity." He was interrupted by the two-stepping bear with the upside down dwarf. "Not now, Chancey!" he hissed. He shook the bear's brown-clawed paw off his shoulder, imploring the beast for peace. "Take little Ridfoo and give her some balls to play with."

The beast gave an endearing growl; it nose-bumped Ridfoo toward the circus chest overflowing with pins and balls.

"As I was saying," Grolsner continued pedantically, "I offer no sinecures in this business. The territory is much too fragile." He stroked his bearded chin and scratched at his goldy curls with annoyance, the varnished coils dancing with highlights. "That is, if I have a business left! That vainglorious magician Nuzbek across the way keeps stealing my clients! It was the same at Efoven, and the same before that at Loust. I simply cannot shake his presence from the circuit."

"Well, then, if Nuzbek is drawing more business than you," mused Baus, "perhaps I should direct my attention to—"

Grolsner made a noisy protest. "Improper logic! Nuzbek's 'Marvels and Miracula'—it is a complete sham!" The impresario hissed out an obscenity.

Baus raised an eyebrow. "A passionate exclamation for one describing a colleague's business. I suppose I shall have to witness this prestidigitator for myself."

"You may!" Grolsner grumbled. "But you'll forever be a traitor." Throwing hands in the air, the impresario battled to retain his composure. He finally grunted: "Ah! I suppose I must moderate my expectations of the common folk." With strained civility, he reached in his pockets and withdrew a roll of ruffled bills. "Here, take this—a complimentary two-ticket stub to the next show. Exhibitions occur on the hour. This is your chance to find out more about our outfit. You need only present the ticket to Darfa in the next wicket—Darfa the insect boy."

Baus accepted the bills; the circus master stalked off, chastising Denol the acrobat for a slipshod placement of left heel to right arm on his cartwheel.

Weavil, who had been watching from afar, chuckled and swaggered up to Baus, addressing him in a sardonic tone. "A fine speech, Baus. I didn't realize you were so keen to relinquish your tenure as a fisherman."

"A fancy only," admitted Baus coolly. The casual, indulgent smirk on Weavil's face remained brightly lit, irritating Baus. "Let me be away from these ragmops and appraise the magician. Grolsner seeks to denigrate him at every turn. After so much roughhousing, I feel a mild urge for some relaxing entertainment."

"An excellent suggestion. After you."

"No, I must insist." Baus bowed, offering his hand. "Far better that you create a shield from this barbaric swarm."

"How kind of you . . ." Weavil gave a dry hiss. Pausing to admire his new change of jerkin and tan breeches, he was surprised to find Baus gone when he glanced up.

III

Peering left, then right, Baus saw no sign of Weavil—nor the two skulking vendors. Only a knot of fairgoers amidst the clamour of boothkeepers proselytizing the worth of their wares. With bold strides, Baus continued down the aisle.

Sidling down the next lane, Baus kept his eyes roving for florid-faced shopkeepers or uncompromising constables. In an adjoining yard, he caught sight of a group of children apple-bobbing and rowdy teenagers digging their heels in a tug of war. A team of lumberjacks scurried up a set of greased poles. Horseshoes flew by the dozens; a group of elders absorbed themselves in checkers, cribbage and bingo.

The normalcy of the atmosphere reassured him. A warmer, less humid breeze tickled his sunburnt cheeks; pale sunlight slanted through cracks in the sky, letting dappled light fall on the grassy lanes. Booths were milling of folk, chattering and filing by in greater numbers.

Relaxed by the halcyon scene, Baus let down his guard. His manner was carefree, his knees loose; he felt an effortless leisure in his limbs as he strolled from exhibit to exhibit.

Several of the upcoming booths were cluttered and tawdry. He bypassed these kiosks with crinkled nose. After ditching a persistent saleswoman who persisted in 'donating' a vial of 'Xsalee's Herb of Best Desire' into his collection, he bumped into Weavil rather sooner than expected.

"I harbour no need for this stuff," Baus cried out indignantly, lobbing Xsalee's unwanted love potion at Weavil. "I bear a perfect physique and am owner of an ineffable charm. Further, I find it imposing that these vendors pitch their marketing ploys upon us. Pounce and leap! They hope one will get hooked on purchasing wares on a chance visit to their booth— such an irking nuisance."

Weavil thumped Baus on the shoulder. "Quite right! Are you not happy with your acquisition?" He cached the love potion in his pocket. He flashed Baus a contemptuous grin. "Where's your forbearance? The peddlers are only trying to turn out a profit. Xsalee, for instance, probably was only trying to offer you assistance. After all—" he sniffed "—your fragrance is not altogether what one might call 'socially just'. Perhaps a bit of Zizzazz, as Xsalee calls it, might dispel the fungi kelp I detect on you—or, is it gallfish? No— rockgobbler!... no offence to your 'ineffable' charm."

Baus drew away, rankled. "Are there other people to annoy, Weavil? Perhaps the few wishing to be alerted of Vrang's wrath or the possibility of drowning are in dire need of your skills."

Weavil ignored the comment and spoke with icy petulance, "I have forgone the act of monitoring in lieu of the fair and feast. And you? I'm sure Harky is little thrilled with your truancy; in fact, I thought to hear him shouting your name down at Knucklebone's Taproom."

"Do not overconcern yourself with Harky!" growled Baus. "He is a curmudgeon, a slave-driver. His idea of a Sunday picnic is to bring rod, tinder and shovel, and dig away to the centre of the earth for a few snails to roast."

Weavil was not easily dismissed; he shadowed Baus's heels like a stray and to Baus's further annoyance, he persisted in indulging in more, vapid commentary. At one point, after spying the pen and ink and oil studies of a Brimhaven artist, Nascar, he paused to linger by an engaging composition, infused in the Zan and Barbizan style.

"What of these works?" he inquired.

"What of them? They are on easels. Is that special?"

"The sweet maiden who wears threads of gossamer over her pearly-white loins pouts and pines with ever the look of desolation for a lover lost." Weavil gave a dreamy-eyed sigh. "It evokes a catharsis, which inspires me to compose an ode—which I will render on the fly."

Baus rolled up his eyes. He attempted a protest, but Weavil had already pinched his ears and drawn a sudden deep breath:

"Hearken and come ye in times of yore,

When a maiden's enthralled cry for August love,

Waxed in Wagwarth glade and was not, or would not be fulfilled,

Oh piteous amour! Fickle and sightless are your eyes!

Come to my side! Come to me, my dove!

Fly fleet-footed forever!

Thy ministrations of plangent affection shall not touch,

Thy young buck's noblest, doughtiest chords of—"

Baus interrupted with a peremptory wave. "Hardly are we concerned with your weepsy deliveries, Weavil. I think I detect the sneers of passer-bys."

Weavil gave a flutter of injured pride. They walked in silence.

By the time they had reached the end of the fair, the rain-heavy storm clouds had disappeared. Through the hasty wrapping of snow-fence the nearby seashore remained a ponderous plain of rising swells. Tangy air bit at their nostrils. Below, the tide had nearly washed over the mud isles, leaving behind a web of seaweed and shells. The beach was instantly full of clams and debris, and hopping gulls poking about for crab mites.

The crowd had grown to appreciable numbers and Baus and Weavil were alerted to animated sounds issuing from a nearby aisle. They exchanged critical glances. Through the throng they spied a commotion. The two elbowed their way forth and stood standing in a wide, populated alley. Yellow polka-dotted clowns drifted from booth to booth; they could see a stage of impressive proportions occupying a triple space at the end of the lane, backed with timber and gay terracloth. Above the platform a silver awning ballooned with ornate embroidery: fire dragons with fantastic sickle moons abounded, butterflies floated in cloud-mist, albatrosses soared in evocative poses. Front and centre stood a buxom woman aside a confidently-dressed gentleman garbed in a plush black gown. His costume was lustrously embellished with grey moon-sickles; a conical top hat, midnight black, perched on his crown. A wide belt of silver silk circled his waistline and was fitted with a star-shaped buckle. Feet were pressed into long silver shoes, curled at the toes.

Baus grimaced. A puff of green smoke wafted up the stage. The handkerchief in the magician's hand became a green-billed canary which flew off, shrilling banshee cries. The enchanter set two blue balls rolling across the stage. Upon a command, the balls became red spheres twice their size and burst into red plumes of confetti before bouncing off the edge of the stage. They lurched ten feet into the air and showered the first rows of spectators with liquid sprays, a scene which caused anguished grunts, at which the magician tendered smug apologies.

A gigantic toad suddenly limped its way across the stage. The entertainer gestured implausibly. The trick seemed to backfire. The toad did not seem to playact as required. The creature stared blinking at the magician before it was hastily shooed off.

The magician performed a triumphant bow, then wrapped a limb around the waist of his scantily-clad partner who swan-swooped on her back and looked out from behind moist, glistening eyes.

Not insubstantial hand-clapping spread through the crowd and Baus and Weavil were ill-impressed and flashed each other leery looks while hurrying to investigate.

On closer scrutiny, the line of snow-fence around the stage and grounds was of more elaborate design than what seemed evident at first glance. Inside the circle, no less than forty onlookers struggled to gain a better view: a mixture of upscale folk with their children, fishgutters, cartwrights, masons and dockworkers—all craned necks to behold the wonders that seemed to spring from Nuzbek's fingertips.

Baus looked left and right. A flag-poled entrance bisected the barrier, no wider than arm's reach. It allowed bystanders to pass into the enclosure. An unsmiling attendant wore a white tag on his breast writ '*Nolpin—stage hand*'. He planted feet to one side of the gate; hairy forearms were hooked belligerently across his chest. He wore a neatly ironed pair of orange breeches and leather-corded brown boots and glittering sleeves rolled up to the elbow while an opal earring dangled from his left ear.

Weavil and Baus attempted to bypass the attendant but the gatekeeper thrust out a knuckly fist: "The fee is three cils. Step back, or make your coins ready. Paying patrons wish to view the inestimable spectacle."

Baus wheezed: "Downright robbery! What vendor charges three cils for admission to his kiosk?"

"The great Nuzbek," the gatekeeper sneered.

"Nuzbek, shmusbek!" scoffed Weavil. "We wish to witness this so-called magician."

"You shall, provided you lay down your coin. Saunter up the next aisle if you wish gimcracks and curios. Here, you will find only the best entertainment, tendered by the great Nuzbek."

Weavil gestured to the snow fence in feigned panic.

The gatekeeper swivelled his neck. Weavil ducked under his arm and slipped through the gate—Baus no less nimbly. The gatekeeper could not react fast enough—the two had already merged into the crowd and were couched under a sea of shins.

Under Baus's advice, the two took up a cramped position on the far side of the gathering, where muttering was rampant. They seemed conveniently shielded by two tall heads and were pleased. Edging sidewise, they discerned a badger-like man mounting the stage now, garbed in a gaberdine, swallow-tailed suit. He stood beaming beside the magician's pretty aide. "Ladies and Gentlemen!" he cried jubilantly, spreading arms wide, wagging moustache and flaunting his oak-brown ruggedness. "You have witnessed the reputable 'dancing balloons of Bloom', Gomer's bereavement of magical rebirth, and the Carugiain nuptials! The Flight of the Yellow Canary was also admitted in the package. Now comes the pièce de résistance—Nuzbek's final act."

There came a barrage of applause. The announcer held up a hand. "It is time! May I remind you that the paragon known as Nuzbek, the same magician of Mosmornon—thaumaturge and miracle-worker, whose fame has spread throughout the lands from Loust to Owlen, will dare a feat of feats!"

More cheers ensued.

Baus hissed out a growl to Weavil. "Mosmornon? Where the devil is that?"

Weavil mustered a cheeky grin. "Who knows? A fable. The rogue has made it sound important."

Baus nodded. The announcer held up his hands, beckoned for silence. ". . . And now! During Nuzbek's following act, the great artist must make room for considerable concentration—a performance including stunning and near impossible thaumaturgics."

Hushed murmurs rang through the crowd. The announcer ceremoniously departed the stage. On brisk feet a twain of lightly-clad brunettes entered from the side, rolling out a large mirror on four wheels. Nuzbek's first assistant joined the train; the three halted beside the glass, flashing winning smiles before exiting offstage. Nuzbek adjusted the tilt of the mirror before dabbing a corner with his handkerchief. Satisfied at its congruity, he gave a pretentious bow and conducted three distinguished waves to the crowd.

Baus appraised the magician with sardonic disfavour. The man was tall, spare of figure, straight of leg, etched with tangly bluish-black brows. His round, amber eyes protruded from his rather austere face with a hollow-cheeked pomposity, but full of sly precociousness. The lips were immeasurably thin, like strips of wire, yet capable of a saturnine curl when necessary. Behind the look, Baus sensed a certain tension, a pulsing 'split personality' that was bound to erupt, not to mention, uncomfortable to behold.

The great Nuzbek cleared his throat, allowing the audience to settle down: "Friends! Fans! As my valuable aide, Boulm, has declaimed, I will endeavour to demonstrate a hazardous display of *dematerialization*, as Nuzbek the Magnificent."

Baus and Weavil indulged each other grimacing frowns. "What a hackneyed routine!" hissed Weavil. "Even the most jackleg magician knows the disappearing act."

Nuzbek accepted the crowd's approvals before he caught the flicker of a fractious response in the crowd.

"Mark well! The feat which I am about to attempt is extremely hazardous. Unpredictable. It is not an exercise to be attempted by the dilettante."

Weavil cupped his hands and booed. "The demonstration is jejune, 'Sir Nuzbek'. In fact, every half doodle knows it from here to Owlen."

Nuzbek craned his neck to see who had spoken. Catching sight of the rodent-like head, he contorted his expression into a sneer. "Opportunity strikes! What fortune! Perhaps we have a learned pundit in our midst—a savant who would trot up and explain the mechanics of dematerialization?"

A few jesting murmurs came from the front row.

Nuzbek nodded benevolently: "It has been so many years since I graduated from conjuror school—I'm sure we'll all have need for an *explanator.*"

Baus rose to attention. "A droll rejoinder, magician. Let us see your mettle. Give us a purely original spectacle—one never before witnessed!"

Nuzbek paused, pondering with care. "The challenge I must admit, is evocative, though certainly not impossible. Given my expertise, I suppose well within my capacity. Yes . . . a conception very exceptional—even flamboyant!" He gave his knee a jaunty slap. "Consider the dare met, young friend! I will entertain you this evening, at half past seven, with a feat upon feats with other of my fans. Is this adequate?"

"Very much!" called Baus.

"And your name—so that I may at least know who is my challenger?"

Baus peered about with discomfort. With a cough and a muffled exclamation, knowing that unwanted attention was unwise, given Uyu's and Migor's agitation, he declared that he was 'Baus, a fisherman of Heagram,', and that he was not given to any vanity by divulging any of his other skills.

"No vanity is implied," assured Nuzbek.

"And I," added Weavil importantly, "am a prestigious poet, Weavil of Heagram, who includes myself in the category of 'challenger'."

Nuzbek reached in his robe, jotted the names very carefully on a pad before tucking it back into his garment. "Very well, Baus and Weavil of Heagram. Consider the agreement sealed! I have a similar request to make of the two of you. To step forward as volunteers."

Baus and Weavil exchanged cold looks.

Craftiness bloomed on Nuzbek's face. "Normally I would intrude upon my associate, the vivacious Nadek, but for lack of a more impromptu test, I believe your services are apt."

Baus demurred. "I must decline, master Nuzbek. Perhaps my colleague would care to inject himself as a willing participant."

Weavil raised an angry cry but Baus urged him on. "Come, Weavil, it is only proper!"

"I am no more a toy than lab rat! Get me away from this charlatan."

"Charlatan, is it?" Nuzbek croaked. "Your words sting, Weavil! But alas, I suppose everyone has his hecklers." He addressed his audience with grave earnest. "Is there no soul venturesome enough to become part of my extraordinary experiment?"

An awkward silence gripped the gathering—followed by uneasy muttering.

Nuzbek paced back and forth. "I cannot wait till cockcrow to receive word from a single volunteer! Come forth! Where are all the brave souls? The redoubtable Baus and Weavil have elected to forgo a momentous opportunity. Why should stalwarts as these refuse my invitation? It is not known. How are matters to right themselves, faced with such abject torpor?"

Despite the appeal, no member of the audience came forth.

Nuzbek's snort was like a jackdaw's. "I see that I must sweeten the pot then. Alas! For Heaven's sake, you cravens and duffers! You test my patience! For the first man or woman, or even beast, who presents himself as a suitable candidate, I offer this winning prize of—ten cils."

There was a frantic movement upon the stage. Surly teens with expressions of zeal, tough old mariners with gap teeth, barefooted children with moony grins; blue-bonneted women with frills and lace, hunched-over dockworkers scrambling like wolves at feeding time. Nuzbek was amused by the unseemly rush. He leaped to the stage's edge to hold up a hindering hand. "Desist! I order all access barred!"

The participants ignored the decree.

Nuzbek, less amused, stomped on the fingers of stage-clamberers. "Let us exercise decorum here! Storming my stage like a bunch of ignorant urchins is foolhardy, especially on a platform as expensive as this."

The mob subsided; Nuzbek smoothed out the back of his gown. "That's better. Now, you!"—he pointed a bony finger at a dowdy frump who clung close to the stage. "What is your name?"

"Conikraul."

"How ladylike! Nadek, help Conikraul on stage. There's a lass. Ho-ha! No need to struggle! Mind her sun bonnet and froggish parka. Get Zlanda out to assist you, if her weight is too prodigious."

Conikraul resented the comment. With indecorous effort, Zlanda and Nadek hauled Conikraul up on stage. Propelling her over to stand beside Nuzbek in front of the mirror, they simpered.

Nuzbek addressed the audience with a patronizing glare: "First of all, it is of utmost necessity to—"

"What about my cils?" demanded Conikraul.

Nuzbek's eyes glittered. "First, never interrupt me; second, your stipend shall be forthcoming at the conclusion of this episode. Now, as I was saying, I shall prepare the requisite unguents . . ." He lifted a menacing finger, brought forth two tubes from air, rousing more murmurs of delight. "A bit of background," he explained, "these gels are to be smeared on the exposed areas of Conikraul's body, which as you notice, include shins, forearms, neck and visage. Then, as habitual, the incumbent is to be doused with wintergill, and a generous spray of gautz."

Conikraul raised a cry, at which someone suggested a jesting supplement.

Nuzbek arched a questioning ear to the audience. "What need I of unguents when my powers are all-encompassing? For this reason alone: the place where Conikraul is to go is fraught with danger and debasement! Do not doubt it! The place is one of abysms and abysses! Conikraul is to enter a world of Stygian rigour, a place devoid of kind thought, where she will be presented before a line of demonesses and dark dorlords and tested for the mettle of her essence. And here I fib not!—the spirits from the other side may decide her unworthy. Maybe they won't. But harbour no misgivings! I have administered the proper unguents, which are of nature too obscure to name, yet steeped in the ritual hours of litany. If Conikraul is to waver in the dusky weft of chaos, claimed by the demonesses—alas! With regret, she will not return. But, invested with the agents I subscribe and drenched with the goodness of my will and my puissant magics, she shall return to the world as we know it— unscathed from the claws of '*Ruthifara*', the vilest of demonesses!"

Never before had the crowd heard such necromantic prophecy and they roared a single note. Conikraul wailed and struggled to fight her way offstage. Nuzbek signalled Nadek. She and Zlanda scooted her back toward the mirror, positioned dead centre alongside the magician.

Accustomed to this quality of voice, Nuzbek shook his head in contempt. Weavil noted somewhat sourly how he had been barely spared such lampoon treatment, no thanks to Baus's jocular suggestions. While Conikraul thrashed about, she was subdued by Nuzbek's four assistants. Nuzbek applied more unguent with snaps of hand while Conikraul's exposed skin seemed to shrink with the application of gel. The magician proceeded on a rigid program of chanting while Conikraul's impassioned outbursts went unheard. They were met with the magician's casual withdrawal from his robe of a strange ebon rod which he tapped on her crown and which froze all her faculties to ice.

Baus eyed the device with fascination. The rod exuded a macabre flux which seemed genuine enough, and judging from its effect, an inestimable power, something which he would not resent tucked in his own pocket.

Anticipation ran rife in the air. Nuzbek's droning chant escalated to a ghastly cadence at which the crowd murmured in fright.

Weavil bared his teeth. Baus muttered oaths. Detecting a sudden unnatural disturbance to his left, Baus whirled. Not surprised was he to spy Uyu and Migor elbowing their way in his direction.

He tugged at Weavil's sleeve, grunting.

"Go, if you must," reproved Weavil, "I wish only to view the performance—as clownish as it appears."

Weavil shifted about, but was conferring to empty air. Baus had disappeared. A heavyset man with huge, punch-bowl face joggled him aside. Another massive individual kneed him in the thigh—not accidentally, and Weavil was not pleased as he was pitched to his knees. The two louts blundered on like sneak fighters. Weavil shouted for retribution. He was about to inject further outrage into the tumult, when Nuzbek raised his arms in frightful configuration and shouted a single, malign word:

Agarharunkujuhara!

A ghastly explosion ripped across the stage. Ghoulish plumes billowed outward from the place where Conikraul had been. All forms were obscured under a nacreous, mushroom cloud.

Suddenly the fog began to dissipate. Only Nuzbek's tall, wraith-like figure began to appear in the fumes, with an exultant leer writ on his face. Conikraul was nowhere to be seen.

"Kudos! Take note!" The magician touched a jubilant finger to his nose then thrust it at the quivering mirror. "Conikraul has vacated herself to the nesisphere—behind the magic mirror!"

Weavil gave a sour, helpless sigh. "This is no achievement, Nuzbek! It is the work of a tyro!" He began squeezing himself back through the gathering before pausing to thumb his nose at Nuzbek.

Baus was still nowhere to be seen; Weavil scratched his brow. The comic frown overshadowing his features suggested wonderment as to where his clam-happy fellow had disappeared. A new observation gripped him. Odd that the two foreigners who had bowled him over were tumbling their way through the crowd, attending a fleeing figure who much resembled Baus . . .

Several persons had developed a lingering dissatisfaction for the integrity of Nuzbek's spectacle as a result of Weavil's more pointed remarks and began to saunter off, grumbling over the implausibility of the act.

Pique swept across Nuzbek's face. With pompous outrage he ordered his audience to return. "Sceptics! What of my volunteer's return? Have you no curiosity in my work? The 'Resurrection' has not been completed—it involves an approved magic, of the third order!"

Weavil cupped hands and hurled a denouncement: "Enough bombast, Nuzbek! There are no demons, nor are there nesispheres—only a fakir with a gulling tongue and a wide lack of subtlety. The woman cached beneath the stage is testament to my accusation—that much at least is sure."

Nuzbek's face flushed a dangerous crimson. "Fibber! This is an impudent assumption!"

"Is it?" hooted Weavil. "Lift the trap and we shall see."

"Impossible!" cried Nuzbek. "The beobar holds the platform secure, tight as a carrack's deck—there is no trap."

"Ha! I find the notion absurd!" Pushing his way through the crowd, Weavil squirmed his way onstage. He jumped over a section of what he thought to be a suspicious panel and the magician, gaping slack-jawed, gave an inarticulate croak. Weavil scuffed his feet along the platform right before the mirror. Immediately, a tiny, perceptible lever presented itself. Now it was Weavil's turn to laugh.

"So! The trap of which I speak runs so and so. When the smoke engulfs the subject, it merely suffices to trip the valve, which involutes the door and renders the volunteer sliding helplessly down a hole. I stand vindicated." Nodding triumph, Weavil addressed the disgusted crowd. "This is the way a noble man snatches your coin and harps on about vapid things like 'nesispheres' and dark dorlords! Nuzbek! You are a barefaced phoney!"

Nuzbek's lips quivered. A malice like none ever seemed to enflame his crepuscular eyes. It surpassed any ethical essence of antipathy and he shouted a sinister challenge: "An outlandish fantasy! You are deranged, Weavil, even in your diseased imagination. I hereby denounce you as a simpleton and a clod. Nolpin! Apprehend this louse before I loose my toad-turning magic on him!"

Weavil ignored the threat. "I hear a familiar voice. Hark! Can it be Conikraul?" He tipped an ear, knelt on the beobar and implored the audience to silence. "Look, I spring the trap and what do we find? A chubby arm, a podgy shin, a milk-white visage."

"An illusion only!" shrilled Nuzbek. "I see only a varnished crossboard, appearing perhaps like a human limb in some form, owing to this afternoon sunlight. I brand you a blackguard and a lunatic, Weavil—not to mention an overweening pip!"

A shout rose from the audience. A rustling of flustered patrons and demonstrators rounded on the stage. "Here, you spider-tongued mountebank!" they cried. "It is Conikraul we see. Move aside so we can inspect this platform of yours."

"Yes, you hoaxing grifter—the profuseness of the smoke we saw earlier brings us to doubt. Let us climb your stage and have a look at your trap, the one that Weavil has exposed."

The magician tottered from foot to foot. "The requests are impossible! How can I permit so many hecklers to mount my stage? I prohibit plebeians to ascend!"

"An outrage!" shrieked a high-born woman dressed in a flowing green gown. "Weavil ascends the stage. Why not us?"

"Indeed!" stormed another patron. "Are you implying that we are plebeians and not Weavil?"

A group of men who were better cargo lifters than logicians accredited the declaration as an insult. The crowd was flung into pandemonium. A trio of indignant sailors leapt on stage brandishing fists and offering aggressive action. Nuzbek, Nolpin and Boulm, managed to pitch the instigators into the crowd, but several of the defenders regrouped and ploughed onstage, along with five rugged dockworkers. They slapped Nuzbek's attendants aside and seized the magician and began administering an incisive punishment.

Nuzbek's buxom helpers fled in panic. Conikraul was hauled up from the crawlspace. She was handed to safety. Nuzbek, horror-stricken, was ripped off the stage like a scarecrow. He watched in frozen dismay as a dozen members of the audience began pillaging his storehouse concealed underneath the slats. With moans of distress, he watched through sunken sockets as items of value were flung onto the lawn: fire-sticks, crystal gyros, runestones, ghost globes, bird cages, costumes, costly robes, polished horns, magic boots, gilded urns, assorted imploding, smog-ridden balloons, an ornate fume thrower engraved with the gyrfalcons of legendary Karsh. With the assistance of the seamen, they tore the awning down, dismantled the timbers and flung the segments about in disorderly ruin. Nolpin was forced to surrender his monies accepted for the show.

Persons old and young and rich and poor clambered amidst the wreckage to grab what they could, snatching at more than what they had paid for.

Weavil regarded the proceedings with irony. He scratched his chin, clicked his tongue in wonderment, pondering the cost of duplicity.

IV

In the meanwhile it was an enervated Baus who trudged up the mudflats, managing to evade the two bungling pursuers who were his bane, but only with cunning and a degree of subterfuge. In silence he stalked up the beach, avoiding the viscous mud that impeded his progress, contemplating his misfortunes with dark deliberation. Because of the unspeakable boorishness of a few oafs, he had suffered scuffs and abrasions and had failed to partake of the complimentary victual at Heagram's fair. An insufferable turn!

Slogging his way in deep deposits, Baus bent his mind on extracting a revenge upon the salesmen. The enterprise was not without its difficulties. Several plans floated in his mind but wilted in the hazy billows of pitfalls. Notions as these hinged on the fact that he must sneak up on the vendors unawares, an unlikely event.

Limbs creaking, Baus arrived at the seaweedy tract where his fair-going had begun. The wind picked up; grey ominous clouds had marched to plague the Heagram coastline. Nillard was nowhere to be seen: only a pile of ropy fishing nets, tangled with seaweed.

Baus frowned with disapproval. Where was Harky? The shoremaster was usually nosing his way around, skulking, barking rebukes and complaints.

Baus stumped away to a steeper, sandier portion of the beach where he was well out of range of the galling stench; there he set himself down to a proper snooze.

An hour later he was woken by a rude kick in the ribs that sent him flying down the shore...

* * *

It was a tetchy Baus who was guzzling grog at the Portman's pub alongside the Heagram docks in the early hours of evening. He had changed into warmer wear—a pair of cotton-grey breeches, a russet woollen overcoat. With brooding displeasure, he flung down his perogi and applied himself to thought. Harky and he had shared bitter words and blows—ones costing him his post. Ah, what of it? The world was a wide place for all who applied themselves . . . at least he tried to convince himself over his tepid brew.

Weavil arrived, helping Baus dispel his gloom. The two traded stories over mugs of ale and Baus eventually loosed a chuckle when his friend told him how he had exposed the magician.

"I wish I'd been there to see the look on that glibster's face. Instead, I was dodging those lummoxes from Hilgimi. What a farce!"

"I rather doubt we'll be hearing much of Nuzbek's pontificating too soon," Weavil pointed out confidently.

"Why's that?"

"He is in no condition to lift a magic finger at all—at least the last time I looked." He gave Baus a sly stare. "What of Iyuk and Gigor—those bumbling vendors?"

Baus flicked a glance out the window. "I shall deal with the goons on the morrow."

"Let us drink to that."

Baus lifted his cup, feeling the worse for wear. Slurring his words, he said, "A toast—yes, to who, or what? We have exhausted our supply of subjects."

Weavil chided him. "There is always a cause."

"You would know. Let us drink—to days and better health."

"To continuous flows of grog!"

The two clinked glasses.

* * *

Closer to midnight, the cronies found themselves doddering about the fairgrounds like a pair of hens. They were in much need of sleeping-off the ale, loaded with more liquor than was considered salubrious given their circumstance. The air was dank; smells of sea chill and rockgobbler drifted to their noses. An absence of comforting light confronted them, for a fog hugged their heels like a hound's wet muzzle. The restless energy of the night flitted in and around like waves from across the harbour. The forlorn croak of pelicans drifted eerily to their ears, with the creaking of masts and the flapping of furled sails.

Baus peered through his stupor. From either direction came the sounds of distant laughter, raucous shouts of convivial folk from the lighted pubs along the boardwalk. A grinning half moon cast a solemn glow over the trampled lawn where many tents stood amongst still, glistening aisles. Festoons of cloud scudded overhead like ancient birds. In the moon-washed alleys dogs foraged for scraps of oil cake, leftover eel, and whatever else could be obtained from careless fairgoers. The odd vendor roamed on stiff legs with lantern clutched in hand, packing up his wares or staying on guard to protect them from thieves. Some, having sealed their tents with tarps, lay down to rest inside for the morrow's trials: the pervasive thrill of festivity yet to come.

Absorbed in their mood of negligence, Baus and Weavil remained ignorant of dangers. Arm in arm, they skipped about like a pair of schoolgirls, down the lawn, singing a reel that Weavil had composed in his leisure, a chorus that went something like:

"Around the posy went the little red mosy,

A duck was in his hat, a feather was in his ear,

Hi, hi, ho and a bottle of rum!

Here we dance, here we strum,

On our zither and ziare, with minds very much numb!"

The two capered into tents, amongst the lanes, clapping hands and clinging to each other like jesters. Sleepy-headed vendors tripped out of their canopies to exhort them to silence. Baus egged Weavil on to more antics. A mettlesome weaver stormed out of his tent with a cane and a curse on his lips, which Weavil dealt with a cuff on the ear: "Our rhymes are important, garment-monger! Do you disparage our odes for pure mischief? We are not forcing you to listen to our refrains, so begone—they are too sublime for your provincial ears."

"Shut your maw! Sublime, you say? I call it doggerel."

"Your opinions are moot!" cried Weavil. "If you decide to endorse our prose, fine, else skedaddle. We have no need for belligerent critics."

And so it went. Baus nodded wisely, patting Weavil on the shoulder. "A poignant utterance, Weavil—which if Nascar our artist were present, he would have expressed an endorsement. For the nonce though, let us repair to a safe locale and essay a stanza or two of Hulcimer's lullaby, if only to appease the gentleman's complaint."

"By no means!" objected Weavil. "I am content with singing my unrivalled rhyme all night and day, if I must. I have titled it, *'A Seafarer's Symphonium'*."

Baus blinked his eyes. "Very astute! A profound title—but to bypass the euphoria of chanting our Hymn of the Philandering Mariner? A trifle silly, wouldn't you think?"

Weavil harrumphed. "Perhaps." Baus gave him a sobering look. Weavil brightened. "In mutual spirit, let us consider this our next project."

"An upstanding suggestion!" cried Baus. "To dual dactyl it is."

Arms joined, the two comrades embarked on a long ribald ode . . .

* * *

It was perhaps more blind fortune than kismet that had the two drifting near the late-night salvaging of an expensive rig where Nuzbek the dour, black-hatted magician, paced miserably about his wreckage, candle gripped in hand. He was more a whipped cur than a man, snatching here and there at certain pieces of detritus. His face was bruised. Irate words seemed to dribble from his mouth while bony fingers trembled on torn bits of props. Humiliated and chagrined, Nuzbek was not a kind sight. His suit was a battered affair. His fancy hat was stained with mud, squashed like a tomato. Neither of his henchmen, Nolpin nor Boulm, appeared in any circumstance of cheer; their movements were piqued, stilted and mechanical, like marionettes. As for the women of Nuzbek's troupe, there was not a sign.

Catching sight of the drunkards, Nuzbek rose up from the wreckage with delight. "Well! —what do we have here? A couple of birds!" He thrust the candle rudely in their faces. "If it's not our old chums—Baus and Weavil. What a fancy discovery!" His bloodshot eyes gleamed with a draconian pleasure.

Weavil squinted up at the magician with wry languor. "The connection is somewhat exceptional, Nuzbek—I would indeed prefer a more logical distancing from you and your squalor—like Tavilnook or Britobur, for example."

"Nevertheless, ample time has passed between our little interlude to merit reparations."

"True, and I hope you have considered your misdeeds. Secretly, I might make a bald observance—that the experience has proven somewhat soul-improving for you."

The magician gave an urbane laugh. "I have earned, so to say, a valuable understanding of plebeian caprice, as well as other poignant discoveries over the course of the last few hours." He paused as if in thought. "My ruminations have led me to certain impulses, including indemnification from injustice and revenge. From our last meeting, conditions seem to flow to better synchronicities, wouldn't you agree?"

The poet's lips pursed. Nuzbek trilled out an ululating call. Immediately his two lackeys emerged from the shadows. They made approving grunts, baboonish style. "These two stalwarts, Nolpin and Boulm, are what I call 'hired muscle'. 'Indispensable adjuncts', so to say. So then! Who shall proceed first engaging in sport-whipping our intoxicated scamps? Nolpin? Boulm?" Nuzbek prodded a thin finger into Boulm's chest, pinching playfully at his belly. "You are a niggler, Boulm! You first."

"A fine program, Nuzbek, indeed," he chortled.

Nolpin emitted a rankled cry: "What? Let it be me who has some play with these weasels."

Baus swallowed the clotting phlegm in his throat. "We have no quarrel with you or your dandies, Nuzbek. So desist! Move out of the way. Let us continue with our lyrics. Your presence intrudes upon our conviviality."

Nuzbek indulged himself in a dry chuckle. "An eloquent remark for one so vulgarly inebriated. Please bypass your plans for more appropriate programs." A casual sign to Nolpin had the attendant pouncing on Baus like a bison-dog. Baus parried double fists and landed a clean chop on the fleshy side of Nolpin's head. Weavil sidestepped Boulm's charge and flung out a foot, causing the oaf a nasty tumble and a hurtful grinding into some chipboard.

Weavil laughed. Nuzbek's cronies lay dazed. In a grim huddle they stared at their enemies with animosity. Lurching to his feet, Boulm made a feint; Nolpin prepared to retaliate with force. Wiser now, the two snatched up pieces of yew and hurled them without compunction.

Weavil and Baus ducked the projectiles. Pirouetting and prancing, they dodged left and right, eluding injuries with a grace belying their common state of inebriation.

Nonetheless, blows had their toll; the twain, while putting up a sturdy fight, were heavily outnumbered in brawn and were forced to succumb to unceremonious defeat.

Sprawled nose deep in dirt, Baus and Weavil looked sorry wrecks. Nolpin and Boulm tumbled ceremoniously on their backs. Perhaps a trouncing would not have been so bad had circumstances been different.

In a triumphant attitude, Nuzbek acknowledged the victory with philosophic deliberation. "It appears that a couple of comics have been denied their magic show. Tut! I had promised you an exhibition, and I shall deliver it!"

Nolpin uttered a plaintive cry: "The ingrates did not even come to witness your final act to its completion!"

"This is well true, Nolpin—something which I regard as unforgivable. Yet life moves on..." The magician stroked his angular chin with an aspect of reflection. "Despite Baus and Weavil's imprudent acts, it would smack of impropriety on my part to renege on upholding my part of the bargain and deny them an act. Nolpin—you and Boulm convey our guests to our tent. We shall have a proper chat with them and embark upon a program of restitution." He held up a hand. "No objections. But wait . . ." He stooped to search the two's pockets. "What have we here?—a couple of invitations to Grolsner's Circus? How grand!" He put a hand to his chin. "You shouldn't have! Donations of this sort are considered tokens of supererogatory nature. Yet—I shall consider them important benefactions upon our long road of amity!"

Unheeding of Baus and Weavil's cries, Nolpin and Boulm dragged them by the heels to the edge of the fairgrounds with blithe refrains humming on their lips.

Under the gloom of a stand of beobar trees, a dim structure took form: a tall canopy dressed with dragon vanes and buttresses of shattered planks. A single wegmor—half ox, half horse—lay tethered to the trunk; a wagon lay to the side. Partially hidden from sight was a queer glow masked in serpentine shadows; the structure was without doubt the hasty fabrication that Nuzbek and his cronies had erected after the destruction of their original stage.

Nuzbek's hirelings escorted the inebriates inside. The dark flaps rolled down. Nuzbek tied the canvas securely, then proceeded to light a series of candelabra tacked around the interior. Many treasures and marvels were cached in the confines: a petrified toad, a golden clock with hands swinging backwards, candles immersed in a foul liquid whose wicks seemed to burn purple, wrong-side up, an aquarium with fish, blowing luminous bubbles, creating explosions in the sediment.

Baus's eyes reeled. Boulm thrust Baus down beside a pile of crates and jumped forward to shake another strange lantern alive: a tall, creepy 'water lamp' which seemed to float in the center of the tent with dark purpose. It was the shape of a crescent moon, bathing the chamber in a weird sepia glow.

Baus looked despairingly up from his crouched position. He swatted away Boulm's ragged beard from his own face. The laughing, easy eyes had become badgerish orbs of menace. Now Nolpin worried Weavil with his boot while Nuzbek poised like a predatory eagle limned in the light with a triumphant gleam in his eyes. The emanation only confirmed Baus's suspicion that this travelling magician—sinister as he was—draped in his rags, was far more than just that.

Baus narrowed his eyes, taking in the surroundings with mounting dismay. The enclosure was stiflingly humid. It seemed to stretch to infinity, like some trick from a magician's nightmare. The constrained knot in his gut tightened to an unsprung coil. Cabinets and wood chests were piled off to the side, amongst which included a collection of obscure jars and rusty instruments, a tub of unknown elixirs. On a ledge, Baus discerned a collection of distraught figures. Puppets? All were bizarre enough to be indeterminable. The curious thing was that each 'puppet' was pickled in its own jar of what looked like brine. On further glances, Baus saw the figures appeared animated.

Hunching himself closer, Baus saw how queer it was that the figures seemed to kick and scratch at the glass as if seeking egress, yet standing no higher than two feet.

Baus made cursory note of the fact; with strained civility he addressed Nuzbek in wonder: "Clever, Nuzbek. Perhaps you are a greater magician than we had guessed."

The magician reacted favourably to the comment and reached out a hand, stroking casually the translucent curve of the nearest jar. "Allow me to introduce my four companions: Woisper the Wilful, Ulisa the Utilitarian, Salmeister the Saturnine, Trimestrius the Third. All are important beings in this universe, not to mention possessors of singular talents. Each soul comprises the only valued pieces of my collection, spared from molestation by the pernicious mob, as a result of my own foresight, which had them cached under the stoutest beobar timbers."

Weavil made an expansive compliment about the foresight which corroborated Nuzbek's claim.

Nuzbek ignored the token. Peering at the figures, he motioned toward the round, pot-bellied, grey-bearded homunculus—indubitably Woisper. Shoulders were stooped, his garb completely brown: brown hood, brown scarf, brown vest, hose, and brogues. The adjacent figure was yellow-bearded, of middle years—a man who wore a pair of voluminous tan and umber trousers. Owing to the sallow cheeks and bulbous face, Baus guessed this fellow to be Salmeister. Wearing a gold circlet atop his balding crown, the figure seemed hopelessly marooned. Dismal, if not moribund. Another silhouette was poised glowingly with an elfin, pleasing arrangement of breast, haunch and hip underneath an acolyte's violet robe. Under the liquidy tumble of tresses she upheld a most awful frown and looked out of her fish-bowl world through a pair of smouldering eyes. The last, but not least, looked a renegade-ish sort, a woodsman perhaps, who wore the green regalia of a 'hunter' with green cape and belled cap. A golden broadsword, now shrunken to the size of a gladius, hung belted at the hip.

Nuzbek motioned to the last jar which contained the weaponed swain. "This pretentious, foul-tongued varlet is Trimestrius the Third, schemer and misbehaver. He is a betrayer of most reprehensible proportions and I have kept him separate from the others. The brown-hooded reprobate is, as you can guess, Woisper the Wilful, a wretch and tyrant, but a prodigal in his hey-day. The robed beauty is of course Ulisa the Utilitarian—splendidly gorgeous, and puissant in her prime, but in many aspects an absolute harpy. Do not be deceived by the illustrious contours! They are illusory. The yellow-faced, cornflower-bearded buffoon standing so haughtily in his brine, is Salmeister the Saturnine, a repugnant oaf whose transgressions are too numerous to state."

"A daunting foursome," agreed Baus grimly. "But what have these wretches to do with us? Why the dark looks and sinister aspects on their visages? Even now, I think to hear opprobrious mutters issuing from Ulisa's vessel—the one who seems to project abuses toward yourself."

Nuzbek shifted in pretended amazement. He dropped to a knee, pressed his ear to the jar. "I suppose you are right, Baus." His gaze grew abstracted, as if trying to recall past times. "Ulisa can be a disparaging hoyden, if she wishes it. Once she was my tutor—a priggish pedagogue—a very long time ago. All these people form past liaisons with me. Either singly or in concert, they chose to betray me, and now they serve as decorations to my travelling chambers. Tokens of marvel, delighting me at times when my mood demands it." Focusing his glare on the disarray of broken bits of glass, bone, shell, metal and cloth in his trunks, he croaked: "These shards—they are all that remain of my last wondrous adjuncts! At times as these, I receive my greatest joys from these bottled bibelots. Look at their unique grace, amongst this ridiculous riot of ruin!"

Weavil let out a high chuckle: "Look on the bright side, Nuzbek. Even if you had tried to retrieve your adjuncts at an earlier time, they would have likely been demolished or purloined by the throng."

"Perhaps even shattered to oblivion," observed Baus.

"The fisherman does have a point," admitted Boulm.

"Silence!" thundered Nuzbek. "I'll not have baboons muttering jests about my condition. My commerce is set back an intolerable degree and wisecracks from banal minds do not appease the fact." He rested his gaze upon the treasured jars. "Perhaps all has not yet lost . . ."

Nolpin raised his brows.

Nuzbek gestured. "I believe Weavil shall prove a comic addition to my collections of homunculi."

"Now that you mention it—"

"Silence!" Nuzbek cried. "A better scheme evolves in my brain: the twain, Baus and Weavil, shall be cached as bibelots in a single jar!"

"The plan is myopic," spat Baus.

"Nonsense! Why carp over an innovation when an entire jar can be saved?"

"I am completely innocent in this affair," Baus protested. Recklessly, he writhed in Boulm's grip. "If you would so desperately seek a scapegoat, choose Weavil. Mystery does not abound as to the source of your ill fortune."

Nuzbek gave a shocked chuckle. "And how valorous and high-minded is that? You would sacrifice your only comrade to the wolves? A staggering concept, and frankly quite an implication of your character, Baus."

Baus scowled but Weavil agreed with fervour. "In truth, was it not you who was telling me earlier, 'how I would like to see the look on the glibster's face' when his exhibition was fouled?"

Baus gave his head a little jerk. "You have muddled your memories, Weavil—especially after much grog. It is a well known fact that you conduct your fibs at bedtime. Withal, was it not you who were pointing out to me earlier that 'we won't be hearing the labours of a certain huckster's pontificating too soon'?"

An inarticulate croak rose up in Weavil's throat. "What trash! Does Nuzbek care for all these specious yarns? Let us speak more germanely; for instance, of these miniatures stacked before us. I see an overflow of gewgaws. Why would our friend Nuzbek opt for more?"

"Indeed?" the magician cried, eyes glittering with malice. "This is the honest truth! I am always on the lookout for more bibelots. In fact, I am greedy for them!"

"Well, if it will make matters more agreeable," argued Weavil, "I would recite a ditty that will put everyone's minds at ease." He began humming a poem, which stated, *'How now, the dastard that has enchanted my magnificent mind?'* upon which Nuzbek uttered a sharp exclamation that forbade Weavil from communicating any more balladry.

The magician smoothed out his hat. "Now, if you don't mind, I shall progress to describing the embalming process which is presently to be enacted upon you. The transformation is unique! An exhilarating dip into an alternate world. In fact, we appropriate you to fit in a single half-jar."

Nolpin beamed appreciatively. "Nuzbek, you are always so definite in your plans!"

Nuzbek nodded. "First I will spread the talc-gum and unicorn-salve on this Kelshian slate blessed by Three Virgins of Krin; then I will mix the resultant mash into kalcyx—where? In this tub, of course! Filled with brine. Then, I must incant a dark ode to Lun, our modern day deity of the 2nd phase. Who is Lun in more precise terms? He, she, or it—is an unspeakable juggernaut who for purposes of safety, shall not be troubled to be called upon by true name, but I shall casually refer to as 'Dontz'."

Baus and Weavil both repudiated the invocation to 'Dontz'.

Nuzbek politely held up a hand. "The paste is pre-prepared and is somewhat delicate. So, I have pre-formulated the ointment for just such an occasion." He smilingly retrieved a salver of effluvium from a jewelled chest cached on a top shelf. Baus caught a glimpse of a crimson mixture, looking exactly like thickened blood of yantler, or some foul strain of snake. Quickly Baus offloaded the disregard he harboured to a more practical form of industry.

"Now then, Weavil," Nuzbek chided furiously, "the facts. As I see it, a certain number of prized appurtenances have been reduced to rubble as a result of your crass meddling."

Weavil brushed off the charge as a fluke of causality. Nuzbek, of course, would hear nothing of it. "The items number in the tens—or twenties: for instance, my balloon rockets, my flaring whipper sticks, sobospheres, polyglome toxomy, mystic fife, hurdy-gurdy, jumping shoes, ah dear, the list goes on . . ."

Nolpin addressed Nuzbek in a soft, consolatory tone. "You loved that hurdy-gurdy so! You polished and cared for that instrument for an age—also your flying puppets, which are now completely destroyed, having similarly come under fire of the perfidious villagers."

Nuzbek cried out in anguished fervour. "Ah, Nolpin, you are a cruel reminder of a past deed!" He clutched his ears with grave vengeance. "The point of contention is that, naturally I require recompense for these damaged articles. I dislike inequities in the universe of any kind! Now—I decree that a stasis be restored!"

"Naturally!" agreed Nolpin pleasantly. "But how, and under what conditions?"

"It is to be determined."

"How does this include me?" squeaked Weavil.

Nuzbek frowned: "An important query, Weavil, which will be answered in due time. But for now you should be concerned with other matters. Namely, being my premier 'test case'— in the new mode of embalming. Consider yourself favoured. First!—a swift reduction to the size of a centauro."

Weavil cried out in a hoarse gibber: "The procedure is precipitate. I find high aversion to it!"

"Nonsense! You shall feel only a prick. Hold him, Nolpin, whilst I apply the resin. Remember! As I administer the unguent, be advised to curb the squib's accursed squirming!"

Weavil swatted and cried. He voiced an unpleasant malediction, but Nolpin continued to jam his elbow into his larynx.

Weavil jerked; Nolpin ignored the inconvenience, whereupon Weavil chomped hard into Nolpin's ulna, prompting a cry of painful surprise. Baus struggled in Boulm's half nelson, but to no avail. He could not render Weavil any succour, or minister to his own needs.

Nuzbek clucked like a happy hen. "How I am fond of these play-times!" He clapped his hands. "Now, Nolpin, careful! Your blows are coming down hard upon Weavil. We must exercise decorum. I demand perfect specimens, for careful preparation of my expositions!"

Nolpin agreed; he conducted his exploits to abide by Nuzbek's wishes—yanking Weavil's ears, worrying his ribcage and cradling him fast between his knees while Nuzbek splashed the requisite noxious unguents over Weavil's entire upper body. Howls of pain and rage issued.

The air suddenly became thick with menace. The victim's eyes bulged; orbs popped with dread; Weavil's lips began to foam. For a brief second, he began to pulsate in a fish-scale blue, then a parrot orange while writhing like a serpent shedding its skin. The torso succumbed to an abrupt sort of jerking, then a shimmering of venomous green. To Baus's unadulterated amazement, Weavil's entire body, except his squirrelly head, compacted an entire inch.

Weavil stifled an outburst. Baus felt a limp cry rising in his throat. Before his very eyes, Baus watched Weavil shrink, inch by inch, to a knee-high homunculus. The trousers, vest, shoes and necklace seemed to diminish in accordance with the puppet that Weavil was becoming.

Something had gone amiss. Nuzbek's fey magic seemed tainted. Whether it was real or complemented with dark energies, the magic had been deprived of sufficient unction, for Weavil's crown remained clearly as large as before.

Nuzbek minded not in the least. Wielding a fist full of unguent, he gestured in an attitude of jest and judicial triumph. "Now, see who is a fraud and fakir!" Vainglory trebled, Nuzbek projected a leer into the candlelit murk.

Nuzbek reached for an empty cylinder. He called out a quip, gloating with trembling anticipation, "I shall presently prepare a canister of byke fusion. Let the ceremony commence!"

Weavil shook like a dog, slaked with salve and brine. "Release me! It is my right!" Weavil's howls were wretched and vindictive. Struggling to hold up his oversize head and squatting to snatch at his dragging coveralls, he wrapped up his privates, which he discovered to have shrunken to excessively tiny size. His wails were unseemly and to Baus's ears it seemed as if a knot of pub-crawlers, vendors and the like had gathered outside the tent.

Nuzbek, startled by the intruders, bounded over to obstruct the entrance. In the confused scramble, Weavil managed to elude Nolpin's grasp. Greased as he was, he darted between Nolpin's legs and whipped about the tent, groping like a zombie.

Nuzbek gave a brisk shriek: "Secure this obnoxious imp, Nolpin!"

The instruction was wasted.

"I said hold him, oaf—not be his hop-ball mate! Are you daft? Time does not demand mistakes; encapsulate our subject into a jar before the embalming! Be diligent!"

A rustling at the tent flaps alerted Nuzbek. He whirled in a crouch. Raising a quivering hand to the canvas, he shrieked out a command: "Whoever loiters, desist from joggling my canopy! The material is costly!"

The juddering continued. Shivering with annoyance, Nuzbek prepared to exert a more pernicious set of influences on the intruder, likely a spell, dismally wrought, but was interrupted by a long hunter's knife that snaked through the canvas and plunged dangerously close to his larynx.

The magician tottered back. Grief flooded his face. With a raw scratch across his pale throat, he subdued a rank cry as into the enclosure burst two uniformed men, gripping sharpened pales and long snapperwhips. Baus was beside himself with relief. Here was proof that he would not be subject to a molestation.

V

While Nuzbek frantically stashed away his precious formula in a trunk, Nolpin and Boulm were stuck frozen, like wild-eyed pigs. The two officers leapt into the light, snapping their leather whips. They announced their names: Captain Graves and Deputy Tilfgurd. Graves was of great physical presence, wrapped in a bubble of righteousness; Tilfgurd, a younger, mousier rendition of his superior, was a figure with boyish yellow curls and a frame of half the size. The two stared at the crazy imp Weavil zipping about the tent, whining and mewling. His arms were stretched out like a candy-grabber, gibberish oozed from his maw. Spectacle-hungry bystanders began pushing their way through the flap, looking for scandal. A pinch-faced Uyu and grim Migor fought for inclusion. Vapid-eyed booth-keepers poked through the gap while a bowlegged seaman and a dockscrubber squeezed through, whom Baus recognized as Gysod and Pisp.

Released from Boulm's vice-like grip, Baus dove into the shadows. He sank in behind one of Nuzbek's crates. He peered up over the iron-bound crate and saw Uyu's moustache perching like a snogmald. Migor's lips parted; an unctuous sweat pasted his hair like honey.

The Captain, balding, red-eyed and chubby, turned his attention upon Nuzbek, "Haven't you prompted enough violence for one day?"

Nuzbek pounced upon the Captain's misconception. "These two rogues, I caught intruding upon my domain. They are law-breachers and miscreants. I was in the process of salvaging my magic set when Boulm and Nolpin discovered these two lurkers and skulkers. Naturally, I assumed them to be malefactors. We implemented our own measures of order—enforcing spiritual requital and punishment."

A strangled cry came up from the darkness: "We have no interest in Nuzbek's property! We were only dragged here against our will. Grant no credence to this man's forked tongue!"

"Cease your bluster, Baus," growled Graves. "I see you skulking behind that crate. Why? I am a man of facts, not slapstick buffoonery!"

Baus cried, "I am disinclined to leave this crampy-hole. Dread prohibits it. I am collecting my wits so that I may outline the multiple infractions imposed on me and Weavil by this madman." Baus cleared his throat with effort. "It starts with the fact that Weavil and I were touring the fairgrounds when two swine, in the form of Nolpin and Boulm, waylaid us, beat us, and dragged us into this wretched tepee in order to inflict maximum damage. Nuzbek himself performed ungracious acts upon Weavil, which are self apparent."

Weavil sprang up midget-like to paw at Graves' thigh. The Captain swatted him away.

"As you can see—our poet has been thaumaturgized!"

Antagonism hung in the air; Graves' troubled scowl grew. "This is a serious affair! Nuzbek, what have you to say for yourself?"

The magician paced forward, mouthing a retort, "I shall put out a blunt reply, Captain. As sincere as this Baus appears in his rhetoric, he has a talent for distorting reality, to the effect of reducing this situation to bathos.”

“This is a fact beside the point,” snarled Graves. “Now be done with your pompous verbiage and transform Weavil back to his regular self. The sight of him disturbs me!”

A cunning humour sprang into Nuzbek’s eyes. “I regret to inform you that a reversal for Weavil is out of the question.”

“Why?”

“A collision of asteroids is not scheduled for an astrological-*ibit*, not to mention, a similar celestial conjunction in Cygnus X, necessary for transmogrification is not to occur for another 444 lunar ecliptics—if my mathematics is correct.”

Graves gave a sour grunt. “How long is a ‘lunar ecliptic’, Nuzbek, and what time period are we talking?”

Nuzbek scratched his brow with calculation. “I would guess, in the nature of fifty years.”

Weavil bounced forward to take a bite out of the magician’s shin.

The magician raised his foot and booted him aside, as easily as a pesky rat.

The sounds of cackling and rummaging alerted the officers to an infringement. Baus peered sideways. He saw two crones robbing Nuzbek of the contents of his fullest chest. The Captain jerked his bulk over to shoo the women away. Graves, in mid-step, caught a glimpse of one of the sinister-looking jars propped on the shelves and glared at Nuzbek in frigid consternation. “What is the meaning of those eldritch things?”

“Oddities only,” explained Nuzbek. “Please do not disturb them. Better to pay them no heed.”

Tilfgurd, closest to the glass-encased Ulisa, ignored the magician. He gaped at the finger of movement. Prodding gingerly at the foremost jar, he gasped. Nuzbek rasped out a warning. “The pursuit is dangerous!” The officer’s hand quickly retracted. The display seemed to excite a thrill in his blood. “How do you know these things are dead, Nuzbek?”

“They were certainly never alive,” said Nuzbek laconically.

Tilfgurd hesitated. “I thought I witnessed some macabre movement within.”

Nuzbek hurled a sardonic laugh. “Ordinarily puppets do not move of their own accord, Deputy. Now if one appears to fidget or jerk, then I would treat it as an anomaly of the eye, or at best, the brine’s movement—possibly a hint to stay away.”

“That is not what I heard,” Baus chimed. “In fact, Weavil was the next to become victim of your diseased jocularity!”

Graves started at another movement coming from Ulisa’s jar. His eyes fluttered. He saw the robed figure’s lips part, and the hair ripple.

“Nuzbek,” he growled impatiently, “I am beginning to lose all semblance of patience! Either you explain these weird conjurations or consider yourself under arrest!”

Weavil gave a rousing cry: “Bravo! Arrest the mutilator! His crimes are indefensible.”

“Do not forget the humiliations imposed upon my own being!” cried Baus.

Graves cracked down his whip. “Order, pips!”

A voice cried out from the sidelines: a whining, familiar bleat.

Baus peered. He saw an excited face, a squat form jumping out at him with vindictive intent—the same which had chased him half way to Sandsler’s pier. The oafish Uyu!—he now spoke with precise diction. "We are members of the grey guild. Honoured glassblowers and shellamists of Hilgimi."

"No need to announce yourself, Guyu," grumbled Graves. "Return to your tent. Police business is in order."

"It is not 'Guyu'," announced Uyu icily, "but Uyu. And you may call my colleague Migor."

"Yes, I know Migor!" muttered Graves. He stretched a hairy fist to haul Baus up from his lair. "Well, you claim that Baus destroyed your shellames or shellooks. He deserted the booth without furnishing you recompense. Is this correct?"

Baus put on a sulky frown. "In technical terms, yes—but more an issue of incompetent recounting."

"Then in probable words, 'yes, a crime'," snorted Graves. "The law being what it is, obliges you to reimburse these men's loss—after which, we deal with the magician and his deranged torturings upon Weavil."

Baus plodded forward. "Forget Weavil for a moment! How do you propose that it was not some other miscreant who damaged the glassblowers' artifacts? Where is the proof against me, Captain?"

Uyu called: "Perhaps these broken shards pulled from my pouch? Or these bystanders, Glysod and Pisp, who claim to recognize your rapscallion features from none other than those earlier during the deed?"

Baus threw up his hands. "The outlander drivels on. Can you be duped by his fatuous yarns?"

Graves gave his head a frowning shake. "I'm not sure. Having spoken to the alleged witnesses in question, I have verified their accounts. Unless you procure a settlement, which is your best option, I am compelled to charge you with a double count of vandalism, and a single count of fleeing the scene of a crime."

Baus swelled with rage. Hardly ten cils did he have to his name—and here he was terrorized with an obligatory visit to the 'Yard'.

How twisted affairs had run! He shook himself with wrath. The hidebound Graves and Tilfgurd demonstrated a mulish insistence on protocol. After giving vent to a loud series of complaints, he regretted the act for Graves began to snapplewhip him into submission.

"You are a mean, inebriated disgrace!" roared the Captain. "From what I hear of your conduct, you are in just dessert of a chastening. Your atrocious schemes are on a par here with Weavil."

"Do not mix me in with Baus's transgressions!" cried Weavil.

Graves wagged a didactic finger. "Baiting vendors, inciting mobs, promoting violence, incurring vandalism—it is not enough to desert your post and leave the townsfolk prey to a drake." Graves shook his head with disgust. "You ignored your watch, ill-protecting children's feet from razor clams, now you have rendered yourself culpable of a major misdemeanour."

"If I may kindly point out," hissed Weavil, "during the time of my leave, such 'tykes' were rollicking at the games tent. Maws were steadily chomping candy floss and youngsters were climbing poles and apple-bobbing. Thus, rendering my duty moot."

Graves shook his head with outrage. "The beach monitor knows no down time. If it were my decision, I would have you whipped, in spite of your despicable midgetness."

Weavil's cry morphed into a gurgling expostulation. Unable to master his emotion, he booted Graves in the heel, favouring contact with a special nerve. The blow gave Graves a spasm; he hopped on one foot. Weavil, for all his midgetness, seemed unable to avoid chuckling.

Nuzbek snorted. "You see what a peevish nuisance this weasel is? Perhaps now you are more empathetic, Captain, to my frustration born of these two brats."

Graves gave his head a jerking shake and mopped furiously at his brow. "Yes, perhaps . . . Tilfgurd, take this whole lot over to the yard."

"The task is menial," declared Tilfgurd, rising on his heels. "Nuzbek is fey—even a lout, and Weavil, is well, just a pest . . ."

"I don't care! Take them all!" Graves shouted. "Do you hear? Nuzbek, Weavil, Baus and all of Nuzbek's cronies are loons! Weavil is no more exempt from these crimes than Baus, having committed an act of aggression upon me. On the morrow we shall sort out this scandal, starting with an impromptu rendering of relevant particulars. Perhaps a day or two in the stocks shall teach all these rogues some manners—and humility. No less this starved owl of a magician Nuzbek."

Nuzbek took offence to the remark. He struggled to gain access to his tubs of adjuncts but the Captain gripped his arm and twisted it aside. A sallow gleam flickered in his eyes, which caught a surreptitious movement from the edge of vision, involving Boulm and Nolpin attempting a retreat in the midst of the commotion.

"Where do you think you're going?" Graves demanded.

Boulm gestured toward the foggy air. "A wee walk, Captain. The night air is fresh, can you not see? Too nice to not enjoy."

The Captain smiled. Nolpin tendered a similar response. "My foot is aching with all manner of gout, all the more needing of a good stretch."

Graves discharged another jovial laugh. "Remain in the tent, fobs, so as to clear up any extraneous mysteries."

Weavil attempted a sidelong sneaking of his own, but was curtailed by Tilfgurd who averted another important law-breaching.

Graves gazed wonderingly from Weavil to the contents of Nuzbek's bottles. "I am at a loss to explain this voodoo—or sorcery. It is best yet to determine how to handle your deviancies, Nuzbek. Your careless treatment of human life has reached an abysmal low." He fixed a disgruntled glance upon Baus. "And you! I expected more of you. Fisher-elder Harky is beside himself with wrath at your sloth and lack of dignity for the elders of this community." The Captain made a clipped motion. "Tilfgurd! Fetch Sergeants Madluck and Skarrow. We shall collect these rogues and be off."

"But sir, who shall watch the miscreants? I don't trust any of these hooligans, least of all the magician. If Nuzbek can wreak such devastation upon Weavil, I shudder to conceive what he might tender us."

Graves muttered a disparaging remark, swatting Tilfgurd on the ear. "The prestidigitator shall do nothing of the sort! Charlatans and hucksters as these are lummoxes. No more threat than a drowsy bumblebee in the forest. But"—he gnawed at his upper lip—"let us bind the villain's wrists, in case he elects to craft some escape."

Nuzbek choked on the idea and lifted back a black-draped arm. "As for my capabilities, Captain, you are in grave error. You would be likely to employ some respect." The saturnine face pinched; the amber eyes gleamed with a wickedness that made the gathering veer back with misgiving.

Graves made a brief inclination of head and motioned toward two brawny seamen who had recently elected to poke their heads in. "These are Leaster and Jubben, fine seamen, who I'm sure will keep an eye on your hides—capabilities or not."

The two men nodded jovially. "Nuzbek is indeed without his toys, Captain. Entertaining any cunning tricks while we are in charge is ill-advised." Frisking Nuzbek, they grunted assurance.

Graves mustered a gratified grin. "Very good. Fetch the others, Tilfgurd."

Tilfgurd strode off with discontent and returned shortly after, conveying three civilians and seven Constables, two of whom held fire lanterns and tallow-torches. By virtue of the white tags on their uniforms, Baus identified Officers Mulfax, Madluck, Smiss, Dunkin, Loops, Canjun and Burkothes. They were strapping, steely-framed individuals with well-built thews and biceps, yet their normally ruddy cheer was gone at being extradited from the pubs.

Mulfax, a lean wolf with a distrusting face, thrust a blazing torch upon the jars. "What are these sea krakens?" His eyes bulged like a frog's.

Graves spoke with irony, "Oddities only, eh Nuzbek?"

Nuzbek grimaced.

"I suppose we must lug the grotesques back with us," the Captain sighed. "Gather them up, lads, whatever they are—quick and clean."

The jars gleamed in the sepia light; even Baus had to suppress an involuntary shiver at the odd, unearthly interiors. Greenish in hue, they were equipped with four floating distorted countenances, cargoes nothing that any of the officers wished to hoist on their backs, Tilfgurd included, though a task of necessity. White-haired Skarrow was elected to be 'first' and he hauled a jar out onto the grass. So followed Mulfax, then Madluck, and Tilfgurd, though he handled his jar with finicky aversion, which Graves rewarded by jostling him with an impatient hand.

Officers Smiss and Dunkin secured Boulm and Nolpin while Jubben and Leaster helped control Nuzbek. Graves gave an order to Canjun and Loops and with Burkothes tackled Nuzbek's wooden trunks which they heaved forcibly onto Nuzbek's wagon. Graves lumped the bulk of the material into the category of 'spoils', though the term was loosely applied, undoubtedly a broader term for 'evidence'.

Nuzbek was appalled at the sight of his treasures being hoisted away. "Captain!" he cried. "This procedure grows more reprehensible by the second. Why preoccupy your valuable time carting away worthless gewgaws?"

"The procedure is self-evident," declared Graves. "To secure contraband, and collect possible case material."

Nuzbek rejected the rationale. "We have overstepped your laws, agreed. Nolpin, Boulm and I remain apologetic for this fact and are penitent. But arrest your tomfoolery! We shall be on our way and never take the law into our hands—you have our solemn pledge—indeed, you never shall see us again!"

Graves fixed the magician with a mirthless stare. "As desirable as this is, Nuzbek, I cannot comply." He faced the officers, giving a tired bellow, "Canjun, Burkothes! Hump it up! We wish to be in our sacks before dawn."

* * *

The hour was old; the moon, a blurry wedge in the sky. Clawish clouds obscured the growing moonlight glowing from the west like a sullen sconce. The troupe, illuminated under the ephemeral light, formed an odd procession, with several stooped figures struggling with their loads in the sticky fog, while Baus, jabbed along by Graves, muttered and cursed. Weavil bumped along by Burkothes, remained in joyless humour. Nuzbek and his cronies were herded roughly along by Smiss and Dunkin while the others hoisted the jars on their shoulders and struggled to keep up with Nuzbek's wagon.

An expected ragtag of gawkers tailed the troupe, pitching righteous stares and remarks. Amongst them were Uyu and Migor. Gysod and Pisp trotted behind: the Hilgimites appeared well pleased with their result, framing nods in the course of reparations being imposed.

The parade continued. The troupe traversed the lower fairgrounds. They reached the gate at Angler's Row and no sooner had they gained Heagram's boulevard when Mulfax stopped dead in his tracks. He let down his jar with a thud. "The brown-robed bibelot! It moved."

Skarrow thrust his nose in, extending Mulfax a critical look. "You must be infirm, Mulfy. It tends to happen when one guzzles hemp-grog like a fish at Leegrum's ale-house."

Mulfax gave him an angry swat. "Curb your guffaws! Look. The cock-eyed thing moved —an arm—scratching its ear. I saw it with my own eyes. The thing's trying to tell us something."

Tilfgurd framed an icy leer which was no kinder than a reed-snake's. "You heard what the magician said, Mulfy. The water moves, providing opportunity for displacement of limb or digit."

Mulfax remained doubtful of the theory. He lowered his ear to where Woisper seemed to stare back at him through the syrupy liquid and was even more perplexed.

Nuzbek clucked out an advisory note: "Old Woisper can hear your fear, Mulfy; he can whisper certain phrases to ear—ones that turn a person's brain to mash. In your case, this would be easier than most."

Mulfax missed the joke and withdrew in panic, brushing off his ear that had touched the glass. "If the little corncrake is that evil, why don't you just dig a hole and drop him in?"

Nuzbek uttered a croak. "A cack-brained idea! Have you no idea who the contents of this jar are? They are neomancers! Like me—I mean—" he coughed, trying to recover from the slip "—like methinks, Dark Archvungles— soul-stretchers, things of similar nature, partisans of omen! If some innocent were to stumble upon Woisper's burial ground, what would happen?"

"You tell me?"

Baus offered a stiff insight into the mystery. "Wasn't it earlier that you were describing the figure within, Nuzbek, as 'Woisper the Wilful', 'an absolute prodigal in his hey-day'?"

Nuzbek shot Baus a withering glare. "Where do you come up with all these fantasies? Heed my advice, Officers. Throw your bibelots down. They are poison! Be off! Else to your ultimate misfortune."

Such was the impassioned malignance of Nuzbek's remarks that the officers pitched their jars to the ground and griped amongst each other, berating Graves for involving them in such a perilous mission.

Graves, disgusted with such fickleness, denounced his troop. "Are you a bunch of lily-livered sissies? Nuzbek, you are a reckless obstruction to this investigation. Hold your tongue! or I will administer incendiary charges. I'm beginning to believe Baus was not far off in his vilifications."

"'Forked tongue' is actually an epithet that comes to mind," emphasized Baus.

Skarrow, Madluck, and Mulfax took up their jars. But they were not half way down the boulevard before Tilfgurd abandoned his load, frightened out of his wits at Salmeister's sallow-cheeked grimace which had begun to pop out at him every second. Smiss and Tilfgurd argued amongst themselves. Who was to carry the loads? Smiss suddenly refused to exchange jars with Tilfgurd.

Graves, weary of the vapidity, grabbed Tilfgurd by the ear and dragged him along the street, while the Captain turned his attention to a chuckling Nuzbek who glanced smugly back.

"This reminds me—where are those females attendants of yours?"

Nuzbek snorted, "They are capable women—they could be half-way to Owlen for all I know."

Loops put in: "I spied the tall lass playing up to old Calestum at the Fisherman's Pump earlier this evening."

"Eh?" grunted Graves. "Which one?"

"The one with the vampish smile—and vivacious swagger . . . Nadir, or something like that."

"That hardly narrows it down. All Nuzbek's dames are like that."

"Captain, you remember the spunky, raven-haired filly with whom we experienced the most funk . . . ? We were trying to control the mob turned on Nuzbek's crew."

"Yes, I remember."

"Come to think of it, her other lady cronies were striving to net Retrar and Douyou, and not making a bad go of it. They were all tucking it up, slogging four pots of ale when I left the pub—that was at half past nine."

Graves gave his knee a slap. "Well Nuzbek, your dames seem to know their business. How be it that you, Smiss, and Dunkin, leave our magician and his two thunderbrains to their ruminations and go gather the others up. I'm considering everybody in this train accomplices in this charade. Human-shrinking and bottle-caching! What degeneracy!—unless, of course the attendants can cajole their way out of a charge." He left the idea dangling, slipping a meaningful wink at his mates.

The front line of officers grinned.

Nuzbek bristled with outrage. "What kind of an operation are you running here, Graves?"

"A profitable one."

The officers voiced agreement, with the exception of Tilfgurd who was still peeved at having his ear pulled.

Nuzbek clamped his arms about his chest and sank into a dismal crouch. Baus could almost feel the hatred exuding from his pores.

Smiss and Dunkin departed. They went to fetch Nuzbek's aides. Three other civilians wearing grog-filled expressions stepped in to take charge of the magician and his two cronies.

Baus squinted in the gloom. Indistinct glimmers caught at the edges of the ragged fog. The lighted alleys shimmered in a floating haze and back to Baus's right he saw fingers of mist crawling their way between the black spaces, dragging over dismantled awnings and drawn-down canopies.

A vagrant gust ruffled a tent at the fairground's edge. Baus heard the restless flap of canvas over the wet moaning of the wind and thought he could be in one of those tents, just an ordinary vendor. What to do? He was not bound or tethered; no one roped him, outside of Graves' hard paw, herding him along like a wegmor.

Should he run?

Baus's eyes watered. Conceivably he could squeeze between the foggy tent-aisles and lose himself in the folds of darkness. He was in no condition to make a last scrambling run—grog-fogged as he was. Too many officers were in proximity; not even to say, thinking of the ploy, seemed to hurt his head. Matters could end up in darker waters than they already were.

Bleak anguish struck Baus and he rejected the plan. He snuck a dark look back at the Captain's face and was not pleased with what he saw. Weavil was plodding behind him, a miserable shrunken doll with a head like Dombhu the Clown. Nuzbek marched on with pig-headed obstinacy, a sagging back, drooping lips, eyes limpid fires, trained especially upon Weavil, who seemed in some ludicrous way to have gained an advantage on him. However, Baus was not aware that the magician was not as witless as he seemed. Before the officers had seized him, he had slid a finger onto a trunk, surreptitiously snatched at some very small articles positioned near the top—objects that the officers' attention had failed to recognize as items of potency.

A particular shape looked very much mismatched—a polished stick—a midnight-black shaft around nine inches long. It was the same rod that Nuzbek had grabbed and had rendered the volunteer Conikraul so limp during Nuzbek's exhibition. The other, a pinkish-golden pyramid, was no larger than an oversize marble, an item which wrought discomfit to the eye when it was seen from the side, vibrating and pulsing like a loathsome lantern. Pellucid coruscations gleamed deep in its interior. Nuzbek's face had been an emotionless mask during the act; so artful had been his sleight of hand that none, save Nolpin, had taken notice of the discrete transfer to a pouch within his loose-fitting robe.

Uyu and Migor hounded the company's heels with an irritating smugness, while Graves' crassly-disposed humour suggested that the vendors return in no less than a year to receive their final reimbursement, an act which provoked groans.

Through the still-animated streets of Heagram the procession wound its way, attracting gogglers whose faces, swarming in and out of the filigreed windows of inns, gaped in merriment. Lanterns swung high from the iron-traced lampposts. Muted custard-yellow glows penetrated the mist, revealing the glinting projections and cornices of domiciles and pubs.

Baus's neck burned with hot shame. The disgrace of being exposed like a common criminal was too much, but he staggered on. A vagabondish fierceness swelled in his heart. He winced to think of what Weavil must be going through at this instant.

The group threaded their way past the last line of pubs—the *Snogmald Tavern* whose fish caught by Baus, they served. They moved out to Maritimer's Square, past the town hall and on through the narrow gaps of the path through Grumboar forest. The pathway was root-riven and one of general unpleasantness, surely a disreputable corridor to gain the prison yard if there was one, but tread it they did, breasting the forsaken place of 'the Whispering Trees' also know as 'Watchwarth', the walled fort leaning on the western edge of hazel tree people nicknamed 'The Yard'.

The seaside fog hung in the air. Atop the cliffs, the sallow flame of Melgrum's lighthouse winked with a bloody undertone, barely illuminating the fog-rich gloom. Baus's spirits degenerated to an all-time low, drearier than ever, danker than the seaside's cloying chill.

What seemed to have been an impulsive gambit, had ended in a pervasive nightmare.

CHAPTER 2

SKULLDUGGERY

IN

HEAGRAM'S YARD

"While the criminal mind is a world unto itself, who is to say that a punishment is just for such a mind?—in the end, can any particular crime be given its 'due dessert'?

"Perhaps the superior criminal intellect is completely inscrutable to our means of examination, being imbued with a multi-layering of an incomprehensible depravity, not the least of which founds itself upon the basic pillar of artistic cunning . . ."

—From Alphonzo's Unabridged Almanac for Aesthetes, a controversial quote from 'Jargoon the Philosophist'.

I

Inauguration into prison life descended swiftly for the five new arrivals. Nuzbek's peevish airs had earned him diverse debasements amongst the inmates, as a result of three robust thugs, Zestes, Dighcan and Paltuik, who guarded penchants for brutishness and coercion. Zestes, with his duck feet and apish arms and long black bandanna wrapped round his balding scalp, loathed pompousness for which Nuzbek was famous. Dighcan, owner of the copper tangle of curls, deceptively calm face and flattened bovine nose, moved about on a pair of carboy-contoured legs. Paltuik, peculiar for his minatory curl to lip, had a foul temper and greased back his black lank hair with wax and boasted his indomitable prowess in brawling. All three ruffians were from birth committed to a callous course of crime in matters of head-bashing, wealth-seizing and respect-forcing from their peers.

Such was the way at Heagram prison.

The criminals who attended the compound were held on charges of larceny, banditry, rowdiness, piracy, extortion, kidnapping and murder—amongst other indictments, including bone-cracking and indecent exposure. Before Baus's first night had reached its conclusion, he and Weavil had been rough-housed, thrown into the latrines, chafed, bruised and pitched numerous insults and indignities. Nuzbek's troupe had been spared no more brutal handling; Dighcan had personally pulled Nuzbek's top hat over his ears and twirled him round like a top in the privy. Zestes spent a goodly time soaking him with cups of urine and hoofing him in the ribs with his hobnailed boots. There was a great deal more guffawing and knuckle-fluffing to follow. All pranks in good fun, naturally . . .

As was the uncanny way with the black-robed Nuzbek, circumstances had a means of achieving equipoise. On the following morning, as the first grainy rays spilled over the yard, watchguards Ausse and Germakk found Dighcan hanging upside down from his heels from a branch of one of the sprawling hazelwood trees standing in the center of the compound. His nose glowed a sullen fuchsia while Dighcan mustered no recollection of how he had arrived in that uncompromising posture. He pleaded ignorance of the affair, spouting a distorted tale of being bound, gagged and transported through shadows and mist.

By midmorning, Zestes was still missing; the constabulary began to grow alarmed, but Ausse discovered him a half hour later squatting dazed behind the 'hive' with his head gripped in his hands. By the solitary confinement adjacent the south wall of the compound, he had shared a similar experience to his muddled comrade. Instead of fuchsia, his nose glowed a sallow yellow. Altered humbly by the experience, Dighcan had gained a tolerable respect for Nuzbek—as had the rascals, Zestes and Paltuik, responsible for much of the mistreatment. When Graves witnessed the sorry state of Zestes and Dighcan, he wondered about the likes of Nuzbek and his shadow-doused magic. He scratched his head and looked narrowly at the leering magician who tottered arrogantly alongside the prisoners' barracks. The Captain ordered a search made upon his person, which revealed nothing—not a weapon, thaumaturgical adjunct or other industrious item, barring a handful of trinkets not worth their weight in sand. Graves had returned to the Warden's office to re-examine the disquieting mysteries tucked away in his cobwebbed storage closet. He studied the hollow and hopeless faces peering back at him with revulsion through the glass and could only evince an emotion of disdain. Twice he had resisted the urge to break open a jar and learn more about the freakish occupant cloistered within, but conventionality had prevailed; he had desisted—practiced wisdom had won out.

Baus and Weavil enjoyed perhaps an easier integration into prison life. Baus, as pugnacious as ever, decided that an altercation with the likes of Dighcan or Zestes, or even the red-bearded Valere, or sardonic, ferret-faced Lopze, would prove unproductive. For the most part, he remained aloof, humming sea chanteys to pass the time while alleviating his boredom with speculations on prison escape. He resided somewhere between midway to rock bottom in the pecking order of these rogues and so silently received his share of cuffs and abrasions from a new set of peers. But survival was critical and circumstance could not be altered. Weavil, in theory, caught the brunt of crude jokes, the majority of them accompanied by a swift hoof in the rear or a biff that sent him sailing through the air like a tamegendron. 'Ankle-nipper' or 'Globe-nogger' he was commonly called, as well as 'Poodle', a cognomen he had earned due to the comic nature of his head and height.

Heagram gaol consisted of thirteen inmates—a sordid collection of swindlers, thieves, kidnappers and ruffians—but now it boasted eighteen upon the arrival of Baus, Weavil, Nuzbek, Nolpin and Boulm. Overseeing the compound was the notable Captain Graves, who assumed the role of 'Primary Warden'—Heagram being too small and parsimonious a district to command a separate police chief and warden. While in an advisory capacity, Tilfgurd remained commander of the two prison deputies, Ausse and Germakk. On a part-time basis, Skarrow and Mulfax were their peers. The four were the two teams that patrolled the grounds by day and guarded the barracks by night, all wielding snapperwhips, poison daggers and a long-hooked bill to prod any disorderly convicts into obedience.

The compound consisted of a rectangular field: a waist-high barren of spongebush and tussock spread out on Heagram's northern quarter. About a mile from the sea, the turf had once kept the old keep of Lord Smitheron safe, well back in days of the region of northern Sarch when it enjoyed its brief but prosperous period of opulence. The blackstone of the turreted edifice had been razed by sea raiders a century ago, but the outer wall remained strong: an enclosure of limestone ramparts, a foot thick, fifteen feet high and weathered grey and white from salt and lichen. The barrier surrounded the entire grounds; the old court, roughly eight hundred feet by four hundred feet, a terrain which by some peculiarity of the architect's planning, ran on a slight downward tilt toward the sea. A replacement, a wooden watchtower, had been erected in the last half century: a twenty five foot high octagonal structure, itself part of the southern masonry and the gate that peered out over the beobar portcullis, fashioned of black-varnished, reinforced bars. A barbaric iron lantern overhung the portcullis and a crudely forged emblem depicting a man chained at the leg and striking a clam with a mallet instilled a memorable mental imprint. The watchtower, buttressed by slats of timber, was capped with an antique bronze cupola and stood upon a narrow portico, behind which sheltered the guards' quarters, the well-furnished Warden's office, and two dusty repositories, a lavatory and a refectory.

If Baus thought escaping the yard was to be easy, he was fooled. The inner-facing wall was sanded smooth of footholds and its summit was cemented with broken glass. Surrounding the rampart for a mile or more, spread a dense forest of hazel tree, beobar and rose spindlefax, whose tangly depths and murky pools were enough to deter even the most venturesome escapist. Limestone cliffs, sheer and forbidding, flanked the western wall which couched behind the guards' quarters and commanded an imposing sea view.

Upon the felons' arrival, Graves had confiscated all weapons and monies, a total of fourteen cils, razor, pocket knife and several soiled handkerchiefs. Five of these cils belonged to Weavil, nine to Baus, and none to Nuzbek or his cronies. The three 'emergency cils' taped inside the lining of Baus's right sock were not yet discovered, nor were the bizarre items concealed in the flaps of Nuzbek's black boots.

Graves had appeared the following morning to check on the new arrivals. A vicious cat scratch was raked along his left cheek. Nadek, who had been recovered by Skarrow and Madluck in the wee hours, apparently had proven to be a 'rather lively' house guest, and her spiritedness had earned her a charitable release. Now Graves, walking on stiff legs, had taken the newcomers aside, and with Tilfgurd hounding his heels like an eager lackhound, addressed them each in turn with a formal salute.

"Well, gentlemen, you are now official inmates of Heagram prison. Be proud, men, and stand to attention! No boorishness while I am in command." He sharpened his moustache.

"Normally I am not ruthless or a pettifogging man, merely a martinet for rules. Morals comprise the clear makings of law!—they must be adhered to with verve! Are we clear? Excellent! This brings about the most noteworthy portions of my speech. As Warden, I must cite certain regulations, which briefly, tally as follows:

"Item 1: Prisoners must maintain an appropriate level of bodily hygiene.

"2: Prisoners are expected to remain civil and attentive to prison officials. Politeness is considered a definite asset.

"3: Prisoners are required to perform proscribed duties day to day, to be determined at the commencement of each day.

"4: Curfew is strictly monitored and rigidly enforced—9PM—non-negotiable.

"5: Once lights are out, prisoners are prohibited to leave the barracks until 6AM.

"6: Prisoners caught trying to escape the compound are castigated with three weeks' solitary confinement in the flap-trap, or the hive, that stands by the south wall.

"7: No rows, combats, skirmishes or violent behaviours of any kind in the yard, barracks or work area are tolerated.

"8: Likewise, no offensive advances, abasements, molestations or vigours imposed upon fellow prisoners, are permitted."

Graves' lips parted and he paused to let the words sink in. "Are we clear?" He twirled his index finger toward the faded yellow notice pasted to the barracks' façade. "Here are the rules!" The newcomers gave no comment, only stared back with crab-like apathy. Baus's stomach lurched with hunger. The barracks were drab and unappealing. A long, low, green-lichened stone outbuilding sported an almost flat tin roof and two glumly-barred windows above a rickety veranda.

Graves persisted in his jovial discourse: "Here at Heagram, deeds are catalogued on the demerit system. Anyone caught contravening an injunction is awarded a penalty based on the severity of the crime. For example, the total demerits are posted, as you can see, next to each infraction. Is this illuminating? "

There were disruptive jeers, including one from Weavil, who blurted out a demand for an example.

"Yes! Here is an illustration for the purposes of clarification."

Graves centered on Nuzbek with a brave flourish. "Suppose our magician here was to omit a cleansing of himself after a toilet visit. Well, he would be assigned a demerit in violating Item 1. Having made two similar infractions, thereafter, Nuzbek would serve an entire day in the hive, having plunged his demerit tally in an excess or quantity of three points. Further, if Nuzbek were to neglect curfew and in wanton mood sneak an abasement or groping upon Nolpin, then he would earn himself an additional eight demerits. This totals eleven demerits, which earns him three days in solitary."

Boulm scratched his brow with polite inquiry. He raised a finger. "Sir, this scheme seems overtly convoluted. By happenstance, I have forgotten which rules apply to which detriments."

"Worry not, rascal." The Captain narrowed his eyes and spoke plainly, "In response to all further inquires of the nature, I shall defer to Deputy Tilfgurd at the time when an offence is perpetrated."

Boulm sputtered an objection. Graves intruded his voice. "On the general topic of escape: I advise you only to banish it from your minds! Each of you is allowed to roam independently throughout the grounds—provided you behave. Peer around! The walls are sheer, unscalable. Any attempt at transgressions pose hazards to health! Secondly, do not get any ideas of attempting to overpower my Constables. They have poison daggers in their belts. Tipped with prickle sap of the ollop-plant, one prod and you are as good as dead. So, Nolpin, I see your crafty scheming spidering toward the gate. May I remind you that master Oppet's canines guard the threshold." He turned to his deputy and urged him to do the honours.

Tilfgurd went to fetch the dog master. The portcullis bars came clanging up; into the yard trooped Oppet, a stocky, round-jowled man with a ribbon of gold hair. He had a benevolent face, a button nose, was of middle years, upon whose crown a bowl-shaped blue felt hat was strapped in place by leather chin guards. He was pulled along by two abominable hounds, all jowl, snouts, and rocketing tails—beasts which Baus guessed were the 'canines', ranging six feet in length from tail to snout.

Graves gave an appreciative grunt and motioned benignly to the two grey and black-furred yapping animals: "These are the snauzzerhounds, equipped with a kind of razor-sharp teeth. They harbour powerful hindquarters. Tapered snout easily works like a spear rammed into a man's guts."

Baus and Weavil's eyes met in a twisted grimace. The Captain, noticing the reaction, continued in a hearty tone: "A bit of history: Sir Oppet, our doyen gatemaster, raised the two as pups; bred them from far west Dharahdor, didn't you, Oppet?"

The hound master broke into an infectious laugh. "I did! A cross between a rockgrinder and a darpest, in fact . . . Captain, both are auspiciously intemperate and unforgiving breeds of steppe-wolf and Delasian hide-a-hound."

The Captain added an appreciative afterword: "To Oppet's command only do the hounds obey; he can induce them to yield only with the secret signal."

Tilfgurd who had been listening, added a sidebar. "Captain, Oppet's hounds do not actually cognize a command through ears alone. They sense the gist of a verbal command through an extremely sensitive olfactory network—"

Graves made a polite interjection: "Though informative, Tilfgurd, the matter is overdetailed. Outside of a basic awareness that the hounds are instruments of death, I think that our new recruits need no further prompting." He paused as the barks of the canines heightened. Signalling Tilfgurd to see Oppet and his pets to the gate, he demanded: "Any more questions?" He glanced about, eyes glittering.

Nuzbek dangled his offensive, bedraggled hat by two forefingers. "I demand recompense for this soiled property!"

Graves raised bushy brows in surprise but paid no heed.

"Well, when do we get breakfast?" inquired Baus.

Graves, waiting for the chuckles to subside, grinned. "A legitimate query, and certainly not as droll as some may think. The morning repast is served at 6AM and consists of gruel and leftover slops. Having missed breakfast, as we have taken too long to discuss Heagram compound basics, you shall do without." He motioned to the barracks in the rear. "These are your sleeping quarters. See them and love them! They are your asylum until such time as you are liberated. The structure is neither vain nor luxurious; in fact, it is rudely limited by clammy walls, foliated yimbir-wood rafters, mildewy dirt floor, a pair of barred windows that provide a questionable view over the yard. The edifice comprises an open dorm architecture—designed for a minimum of comfort and a maximum of space-saving. Yard labour commences at 6:15AM. It continues to 6PM when dinner is served. Tilfgurd shall be your liaison in these regards, at least until you are acclimatized to your new surroundings. Ho-hum! On the subject of particulars, since Tilfgurd exemplifies so eager-beaver an attitude, I promptly entrust him to advise you of your upcoming duties; in fact, he shall personally attend to the rest of the tour..."

* * *

Graves left the area, but before doing so, he had instructed Tilfgurd to outfit Nuzbek in a proper pair of boots to replace his foppish 'elf slippers'. His complaints received short shrift. The new boots pinched his feet. What of it? Tilfgurd promptly escorted the men to their quarters; he substantiated Graves' earlier description of decrepitude of the barracks, but in fact demonstrated a much more vivid clarity. There was a sour, ever-cloying stench of rancid clothes, unwashed bodies and dismal redolences. Around three of the four grimy walls ranged a collection of rudely-placed dormitory beds and a darkened hallway which Baus knew only too well led to the privy with the broken door.

Tilfgurd took them to a space roughly in the middle of the yard where a subset of the 'regulars' worked knee-deep in clam shells and reeking fish. Broken rock was strewn everywhere. The motley crew was one of such thatch-bearded ugliness that Baus fairly cringed. The muscle-bound, tattooed hooliganism of the lot was without equal; indeed, some of the same rogues Baus had briefly met the previous evening, exhibited their own unique assortment of broken teeth, eye patches, bandannas, leathers, chains and leers. The bulk was engaged in clam shucking, rock-grinding, with others in carting drays and cleaning tools.

Amongst the criminals stooped Dighcan, a florid-faced, sullen goliath. He still guarded his crooked smirk, and now shook his mass of shoulder-length blond hair and tweaked his golden moustache. His long lion's chin seemed ludicrously pointed in the light of day and his jewel-blue eyes turned inward a bit crazily. There was Zestes too, a short, thickset blackguard with an ever-present leer and loose blue overalls bagged at the knees. The criminal had a nonexistent neck and wore iron-studded wristlets and green dragon tattoos fleeing up his arms. Withal, two large looping iron earrings dangled heavily from either ear, largely suggestive of irascibility, rather than a preference for men. Valere was tall, purposeful and grey-eyed. His beard hung a flaming red, bright as his hair and he wore a sailor's orange- and blue-striped dungarees. A sun-browned face, and a scar breaching his left cheek near the corner of his lips made his satirical but jesting grin appear fulsome. Lopze was a middle-weight and wore baggy mauve pantaloons. His rat-sneaky face was latched with an orange eye patch and thin bartering lips and stubbly billy goat goatee. Paltuik was more of a hulking brute, bull-necked and young. He wore greasy, crow-black hair clipped in short bunches and an indigo kerchief wrapped too tightly around his brow. It was a feature which enhanced the bushy blackness of his threatening, down-curved brows. Vibellhanz was owl-like and wiry; he owned a bowed back and no visible teeth. His concept of hair was a collection of white wisps trailing down his back. Tustok sported a purple nose ring, a pair of sunken cheeks, hollow eyes, oily skin and the thin haggard look of his gangly frame showed the mark of the lowliest net-repairer. Leamoine had an annoyingly graceful manner, which his blue immaculate trousers, grey cape, right-ear bangle and shaved rounded chin, white face, delicate cheeks and placid grin seemed to accentuate.

Baus peered away to turn his attention from the oddball inmates to matters of survival and found the sky watermarked and grey. A sullen, oppressive atmosphere lurked about the earthen yard and its depressing spots of glum-shaped spongebush and gorse shrub peeked raggedly out of the corners like covens of hunched crones. The place was more like a livestock yard than a place for men. The mangy turf was trampled by a thousand feet—the feet of men who had worked for years on end. The watchtower loomed imperiously above the walls like some upright mantis with flanking buttresses and a dull copper cupola. Save for the drab sleeping quarters pressed against the lichen-rich west wall and the officers' hall hunkered down under the tower's shadow, there were no other outbuildings in the compound, except what might be called the hive, that dome-like sickly yellow construct off the south rampart.

The men stood up to re-assess their new inmates. Baus felt a singular chill crawl over his skin. Nuzbek was affected no less but for some perverse reason still chose to crown his head with his ridiculous black magic cap, and seemed to take exception to the attention. He threw a savage remark at the eye-winking Leamoine and got himself into another unsalutary involvement . . .

II

Baus and Weavil's adjustment to the daily duties in the yard proceeded infinitely slowly. Such activities granted rigor, and included fish-cleaning, clam-shucking, stone-chipping, wood-chopping and chores like lugging stones from one pile to another to build the sea wall and re-mortar the high stone bulwark surrounding the compound, which grew in disrepair every year. Every third or fourth day, a new group of convicts was summoned to work on the seawall project. Heagram's new construction scheme, brainchild of Prefect Barth, included the plan to protect the town's dwellings by the old port from killing breakers that raged during the winter months. Four to five inmates toiled away on the construction, hoisting stone upon stone, packing and sealing the cracks, while Voin the general contractor, watched on with critical attention, monitoring the work with a vulpine fervency, correcting the inmates when any one thing did not conform to his standards. While the free labour was a boon, they toiled and groused, and only a single guard was present, usually Ausse. An iron ball was affixed to each ankle, effectively negating any prospect of escape.

Being the fourth day of Baus's incarceration, today Valere, Zestes and Boulm were on seawall duty. Dighcan, Lopze, Nolpin and Nuzbek cleaned fish back in the compound. Baus and Weavil were assigned to clam-shucking along the seaward side, a task both despised and shunned. A neck high pile of clam shells reeked—the same fermenting reek with which Baus was altogether too familiar in his own vocation—or *former* vocation.

The land at this quarter dipped down to the sea and looking back toward the barracks, Baus could hardly see the tops of the gnarly hazel tree where the fish-gutters worked.

He stooped low, clapping a rock to a live clam on a flat chipping stone. The shell exploded with a gruesome crunch; he fingered the lukewarm meat, flinging it into one of the wicker baskets. So the morning had passed with a hundred other shell-crackings.

Baus loosed a sigh. From the frying pan into the fire!—Working free of charge on seafood-gutting to feed the ungrateful gullets of Smilly's taproom patrons or those at Snogmald's tavern. Something, somewhere had gone tremendously wrong.

Baus turned his attention to other more profitable thoughts—namely that of escape. Despite Graves' emphatic warning, he had bent his mind hastily on a plan of escape from the outset. Clearly the prison walls were too high to scale; they were too smooth to be breached by any conventional means; no less did Oppet's pike-nosed, flesh-champing monsters pose any helpful backdrop.

Weavil, dispirited by the glum turn of events, had sunk into a deeper mire of melancholy. He was less wont to joke, or join in on songs with Baus.

The behaviour disturbed Baus for the reason of pure philosophy. It had him arresting his clam-snapping and trying to cheer Weavil out of his doldrums. "You are flagging! We must all look on the brighter side. Where have gone all your infectious drolleries?"

"Flown away with the ekloons."

"Shameful, shameful!" Baus said. "Like all great men we must treat impediments as opportunities to excel beyond the modes of statute imposed upon us by casual circumstance."

Weavil's leer became a saurian grimace. "You can seek comfort in all the 'causalities' you want, Baus. I wish only my former stature—as a healthy, five foot, nine inch poet."

"And you will, Weavil!" thundered Baus in his cocksure voice. "We shall confront this gingerstamp Nuzbek and in due time we will compel the villain to comply with the whims of the universe. He shall reverse his foul deed! Even if we must move all the asteroids in Cygnus, we shall force him to do his duty!"

"A fine ambition." Weavil hunched desperately in the chill, face down and tapping his clams with a listless energy.

Baus paused, stroked his chin with a spark of reflection. "We must venture cautiously, Weavil. Any attempt to blunder on will doom us. Lawbreakers, lunatics, and maniacs are in our midst; they will make mincemeat of our persons. We must trust to our thinking caps, install cunning programs, concoct a suitable stratagem outwitting all the evil around us."

Weavil stared in contempt. "Where were these 'strategies' while I was being pickled like a common crab-apple in Nuzbek's jars? As I recall, you augmented your own blamelessness by enhancing my own guilt."

Baus gave a cry of resentment. "This is based on biased misconception! Chagrined and upset at the turn of events, I was forced to adopt desperate measures—an act with which you can empathize. You are my comrade, Weavil, and you should be able to understand!"

Weavil gave a chirp of cranky disgust. "Claptrap!"

Over the course of the disputation, there came a period of existentialist talk in which Weavil finally postulated that life was not simply a struggle for survival, but that every man and woman was out for himself, nothing more.

Baus shivered at the simplification and tended toward a more global, unified spectrum of thinking, based upon a view that the many beautiful things of the world were like art and literature and needed to be placed on a higher plane of order, beyond the crass hands of human conflicts. Ministered to and expressed with a fine tool of earnest need, they remained protected. To this ideology, Weavil voiced only a sneering refutal.

Baus thought the reaction overexaggerated. He peered at his friend with sidelong concern. Weavil looked far too small for the burdens he carried. What to do? The manikin, head bowed and tiny hands twitching, must glower and lick his wounds as he needed. Baus himself was not so easily discouraged by the limb-disfiguring acts. Somewhere there existed a solution to the problem of immediate escape—which meant that he would discover it . . .

Scanning the prison wall for the hundredth time, he found the rampart insurmountable; if anything, spiked in the remote quarter with higher and more jagged glass. Over the north-east junction, limbs of hazelwood and beobar sprang, but far out of reach, which was discouraging. A barely discernible murmur of distant waves swirled about the bluffs. The languid moan of the wind framed a backdrop. How it twinged Baus's heart to hear such plaintive sounds! To be free and roam the beaches once again! He had taken his pleasures for granted. But no longer!

He paused, frowning. Near a dip in the land, over on the wall . . . a large oblong crack outlined in the pale slate. A stone—maybe a foot in diameter—perhaps dislodged by age . . .

Baus stirred himself. He glanced both ways, and held his breath. To ensure Skarrow or Tilfgurd was not looking his way, he side-slipped over to the wall. Cramming his fingers into the crack, he attempted to jar the stone loose.

The impediment was immoveable. He could not displace the stone, but if he could, perhaps a small person like Weavil could slide through unhindered . . .

The hope was short-lived. It would take heavy tools and significant labour to dislodge the rock. Not impossible, but hardly a facile task.

Another disheartening concept: Weavil may squeeze through the crevice, but Heagram, far away, perhaps a mile or more, was accessible only by the grim woods, densely thicketed with crag-thistle and blisterweed. Doubtless this terrain would pose an indomitable difficulty to Weavil's mobility. How could his shrunken comrade hope to transport himself in a fashion before any of the guards discovered his absence?

The dilemma was real. Baus accepted the plight with solemnity. Escape seemed as lofty a target as instant riches, quite possibly as impossible as impossibility itself.

With a dull reminder of his misfortune, Baus returned to the monotony of his clams. Occasionally he mumbled curses or glanced at the wall, but these gestures did not help. A new line of reasoning entered his awareness. This evening, for example, could he bandy words with Graves to see what could be done about this cock-eyed sentence? What were a few miserable cils, after all?—The smallest bite on the Captain's foot was Weavil's crime only—a picayune prank. Were not Nuzbek's infractions all the more execrable?

After dinner, the prisoners took time to digest their cold onion pudding and stewed yams to reflect upon the day's labour. Leisure hours were few and Baus took opportunity to request an audience with Graves through his liaison, Tilfgurd. Baus received a brief consultation with the Captain and once he was inside the office, confronted him on the issue of his sentence, but here he found the Warden obdurate. "Graves, you are a stickler! How can I repay these ingrates from Hilgimi while I am in gaol and I can no more earn cils than court a damsel?"

Graves arranged his bearing in a dignified manner. "This is an evocative philosophical conundrum, which in all practicality raises profound issues. I advise you to forget it. I merely uphold the law, which in relation to you, states that people owing monies to other people are incarcerated until they can repay such funds."

Baus's mouth dropped. "This is a pleonastic logic. It admits nothing other than the presence of inept laws! I demand justice!"

"File your complaint to Judge Witherhum then," snapped Graves. "His Honour shall be free in about eight moons from now."

"Eight moons? I might contract a virulent disease by then."

"Possibly," admitted Graves, "but unlikely. Regard the facts: you tender no funds, you have no one to secure your bail. You are without employment and without sympathizers. It is a rather unfortunate situation, but what of it? If I were not such a seasoned law-enforcer, I might feel pity."

"Opinions!" snorted Baus. "Possibilities, facts!—they are all noise to my ears."

"You are entitled to your views."

The discussion was over. Graves summoned Tilfgurd and Baus was dragged away. Skarrow informed the Captain that an important errand was in hand in town, involving a missing bucket of hoarfish and two sick wegmors . . .

III

As was customary, at half past six, the convicts gathered at the barracks to engage in their evening game of 'Flanks'—a friendly competition that took pleasure at hurling projectiles at puppet-caricatures of inmates in order to profit on bets on razing them to the ground. The playing field was a worn track thirty yards long by ten yards wide, an area of pinkish sand cleared of grass, stones, tussocks and spongebush.

Tonight was the fourth evening of the incarceration of Baus and Weavil and Baus watched thoughtfully as the men drew their missiles and took practice shots. The list of objects to hurl included clams, molluscs, fish spines, pebbles, rocks, dead branches and beobar cones, anything a convict could find . . . Each man fabricated his golem: a creature from wood, shells, rock, weeds or mud. The size of each icon was strictly regulated—no golem could be any smaller than six inches high by two inches wide.

Baus leaned forward to better hear the boasts of Dighcan and Zestes. Paltuik and Valere were not far behind. In Baus's mind's eye, he saw the rules of engagement as an unabridged and slightly elaborate version of 'bowl-the-bottle', easily a town favourite. Each prisoner had with three attempts to knock over his adversary's icon: a knockover earned him six points, a slice, three, a dismemberment twenty. The last icon left standing was declared the victor. The loser not only forfeited his *bander*—the 'article wagered' on the bet—but agreed to play out a certain minimum number of rounds decided upon in advance. If a player were to forfeit all his bander after the requisite rounds, he would receive a debasement, or at least an embarrassing drubbing. The humiliations ranged from footling roughhousing to extenuating rigors, spanning the gamut from a single, jocular rump-boot, to a double-switching with strangle-weed, being stripped naked or forced to jog around the compound cane-whipped by hooting comrades. Rewards as these remained contingent upon the severity of the loss. Men acquired articles of bander while relieving themselves of stresses, a practice which Graves approved, owing to the health benefits and increased morale among the prisoners.

For the first three evenings, Baus and Weavil observed much of the play, and were now emboldened by their understanding of the game and decided to pitch in for a round—Baus at least. He approached the huddle of inmates with an easy confidence, mixing with their swaggering and posturing while presenting a flimsy icon of clam and withe. "I have come to join your sport, friends. Perhaps even a veteran gamester like Dighcan shall discover a thing or two about Flanks!"

Dighcan raised a pair of goldy eyebrows. "Shall we? You call that bit of brummagem an icon?" He sneered. "Ha! I see nothing more than baby clam shells trussed together with a bit of abalone meat. This is no good for outwitting my tosses." He pulled at his plump pink nose which still seemed tender from Nuzbek's experiments.

Valere with the fiery red beard shuffled up to Baus, sizing him up. "Why not, Dighcan? We shall have more prizes to divvy amongst the gang." He turned to Baus. "What have you to offer in the way of bander, boy?" His voice was daunting but his smile was high-hearted.

Baus searched his person with a feigned grimace. Unearthing a lint ball, used handkerchiefs, three dry moths and three cils he had transferred in advance from his sock to his pocket, he gave an unusually simpering grin. To risk his last coins seemed impulsive, and his attention naturally gravitated to the buttons on his coat. "These studs are silver-tinged and engraved with sea quail from the sunken isle of Aroo, now a land mass of mythic significance."

"Dainty!" heckled Lopze, fingering his eye-patch.

Baus elevated his voice above the jeers. "They are expensive and antique! At the very least—of equal or greater value than the glitzy gewgaws with which you wager."

"Here, we'll have none of that talk!" called Valere.

"Regard my colleague Weavil's timepiece," pressed Baus. "If that is not an acceptable item of wager then I must point out that it is at least an heirloom."

Weavil instantly lurched forward with an outburst of contempt. "I cordially refuse to gamble away my family property! Any who shall squander my trophy shall be me! Moreover, I insist on applying for the privilege to shoot at fifteen yards if I am to join this rag-taggle game. Thirty yards is too far given my diminutive size and damaged sensibilities which pose obvious disadvantages."

"Mayhap you have a point there, Poodle," Zestes cooed. He inspected Weavil's timepiece and noted its intricate shell detail and gold-worked craftsmanship. He evinced a note of admiration. "Very good! We shall accede to the midget's behest . . . only under the proviso that he tosses the wee clock into the potty."

Dighcan jousted Zestes aside. "By no means! Poodle has not produced his icon so Poodle won't play. As leading chair-member of the league, I render Weavil's application void."

Paltuik, somewhat sullen and ill-tempered with a head wrapped in black bandanna, lumbered forward with a growling complaint. "I like 'Ankle biter' better than 'Poodle'. Makes the tyke sound too sophisticated, too swanky to be called 'Poodle'."

Dighcan snorted, galled. "Who cares what you think, Pall-head? I'll call him as I like. Now move aside, as I have important functions to conduct." He carved his way to Weavil, jostling Paltuik aside with the rude force of his chain-studded hip.

Dighcan now loomed sulkingly over Weavil with glittering eyes. "Be off with you now, stoat, before I sit on you. Come back next week if you have crafted an icon of worth, at which time we shall reconsider your application."

Weavil glumly shuffled away and Baus was happy to see his friend occupied with some intermediate project.

At the barracks' steps Nuzbek sat unsociable and aloof. He watched the game disagreeably, reposing with quiet disdain while Nolpin and Boulm conversed in idle tones which grew to topics of heated debate.

Valere chanced to overhear a sour remark by Nuzbek and hailed the magician with resentment: "Here you, Nuzbek! Why not make yourself useful and gather up your lads and join the game?"

Nuzbek stared mistrustfully at the large inmate. Almost automatically he offered a negative response. "Not on your life! The day has been tasking. I wish to recuperate my energies for the morrow."

"How ladylike of you," crowed Lopze.

Nuzbek, irritated by the jibe, jumped to his feet and half parted his mouth in sinister insolence. "You think, one-eye? I shall join this puerile congregation, only to prove a point." Opening his palm, he manifested a thin ebon rod that seemed to come into existence as if by magic. The convicts stared at it with wax-eyed wonder. "I will wager this ganglestick. Its properties are mystical, and its origin emanates from faraway Fadnar."

Surveying the black rod, the men muttered appreciation and their expressions were ones of sombre reflection. Many grumbles later, Yullen called out in a derisive voice, "I could utilize this token for a hairpiece—what of you, Paltuik?"

"A teeth scrubber for me. Mine is caked with calcus."

Lopze gave a jeering laugh: "Because Vibellhanz's been using it as a butt cleaner!"

Nuzbek's eyes glowed with fury. "Silence! My ganglestick is not to be utilized for any of these disgusting activities!"

Lopze tried to reach out to make a grab for the stick but his fingers had barely closed on its silver tip when the criminal shrunk back with a panicky grimace. He suffered an expression of pure terror before an irritated Nuzbek swatted at the criminal's cheek, and Lopze's baboon's snarl released.

Instantly, Lopze shook the daze out of his head. He blinked his non-patched eye. "A fine butt-tickler indeed!"

"Keep your mangy paws off it!" Nuzbek warned.

Nolpin and Boulm ranged themselves around Nuzbek and demanded membership in the game.

Baus skidded forward with interest. "Already a bevy of players are enrolled. As it stands, the back line will be watered down with players whose skills are substandard, like Nuzbek and Nolpin, whose icons will be easy targets. In this mode, we are struck with an awkward choice and must reject Nuzbek and his cronies from the game to ensure ease and amity in our game."

"Nonsense!" protested Valere. He strode over to see what Nuzbek and his chums had to offer in the way of bander, inspecting their wares with curiosity. "So long as Nuzbek brings bander, he can play, as can all!"

Baus shook his head with exasperation. "Nuzbek is a sly trickster. You shall find out when he confounds you with magic! Look at the dull amber gleam in his eyes, the vicious twist to lip—it shows the insidiousness of a snake."

Valere guffawed at the simile. "So are Yullen's eyes and he's as harmless as a fly. I deny any magic. Go forth and fetch your icons, lads! We've got us a game tonight!"

Nuzbek nodded exultantly. Further remonstrations went unheard and Baus struggled to mask his displeasure. Disagreeably, he lapsed into silence. The prisoners bent their attention to the game and Nolpin and Boulm joined Weavil in the hunt for icons; as did Nuzbek who had slipped away and was nowhere to be found.

While the inmates practiced their tosses, many traded jests, several of them indelicate, and Baus elected to remain detached from the whole crew and their ribald talk, preferring instead to scrutinize the men's games with zealous interest. Zestes' throws were as flamboyant as his boasts—a style which Baus disapproved of and was convinced exhibited no great accuracy for a player who would prove at best a medium level contender. Dighcan, on the other hand, was a formidable adversary, a staunch thrower, and man of bravado, but the comparison ended here. Where Dighcan's tosses were calculated with force and precision, and had the uncanny ability of knocking targets off easily at will, Zestes' throws were mere passing vagaries. It was a skill belying the brutishness of Dighcan's character . . . forcing Baus to reconsider his tactics against him. Ordinarily Paltuik and Karlil's prowess reigned somewhere in the middle of Zestes and Dighcan's while Yullen and Valere fell short. Amongst the others—Tustok, Jorkoff, Vibellhanz, Zorez, Quintlo and Leamoine—it was a toss-up; Quintlo perhaps had the barest edge while Lopze's game, the most inscrutable of all, seemed unpredictable. At times, he threw exceptionally well, but more often he made jackleg throws barely above the dexterity of a child. He was left howling in outrage. After the last fractious tantrum, he had Valere in stitches and Dighcan twirling a didactic finger and expounding upon the basic principles of the game. Baus was prompted to believe that his paroxysms were linked to some psychological dysfunction, a repression crossing the boundaries of pure sportsmanship but Baus discarded further analysis. He assessed the emotional volatility of his peers to that of a weakness upon which one could prey. All in all, Baus estimated his chances good to fair against these rogues. To win, all he needed to do was avoid blunders and lull his opponents into an easy sense of victory.

Intruding upon his speculations came Vibellhanz's irritating voice. "Make haste! We are all keen to initiate the first round. We must pitch in our bander to the pot so that play might commence!"

Baus tossed one of his vest buttons onto the pile arranged at the throwing line. Appraising the small mountain of items, he scratched thoughtfully at his chin. An old black leather belt with silver buckle was piled top-wise in the clutter. There was also an old rusty toe clipper, a series of grotesquely-shaped pebbles of ochre pigments, a few broken flutes, five ear bangles, three dented nose rings, a soiled glove, homemade tilkweed cigars, two tins of red and brown wax, a bottle of green liquid and various other unpleasant essences . . .

What an uncommon mixture of trash! Zestes' belt and Lopze's toe clipper, however, could prove handy in chipping away at the rock on the eastern flank. The other items were subsidiary to the lower end gimcracks at the fair . . .

Play commenced. Along the thirty yard line the men deposited their golems: a pantheon of malformed shapes jutting creepily up in the rosy light of sunset. Baus noticed that icons placed at the outer precincts of the line seemed to be in better positions, being less likely to be knocked over from the back-spray of opponents' hits. Next to the bander heap rose a pile of projectiles: rocks, shells, wood chunks—all similar in size and weight so as to allow fair play.

The sun sank over the bluffs. The men drew sticks to decide who would throw first. Paltuik drew the shortest and so chose the order of play. Baus was picked to lead. Baus was new to the game, so the men agreed that he be allowed the grace of a two round minimum.

Valere announced: "Consider yourself fortunate in this regard, Baus. I've watched matches where men start as high as four rounds and turn swiftly unpleasant." He chuckled and wagged a finger.

Baus made a polite acknowledgment. He bent over to select his projectile and squinted wisely down the runway. The icons peered back at him with indifference. Glinting rose-gold in the light was Dighcan's, Lopze's, Zestes'... misshapen replicas, stamped with idiosyncratic signatures of their masters.

Baus threw—

Missed!

A bereaved collection of consolations hummed through the gathering.

Baus retreated to the back line with an expression of distaste. Paltuik drew next—a chunk of spindlefax which he hurled with confidence. Sideswiping Lopze's 'mud tower', it caused Lopze a fit of sneering. He retaliated two persons later to topple Paltuik's scarecrow, a mud-glazed spongebush to claim his opponent's bottle of yox, a potent homebrew of kitchen-variety, urine insect-repellent.

Cheers permeated the congregation. Dighcan threw, cast an expert pitch which proved him superior. He knocked the legs from underneath Jorkoff's jerry-built wegmor-icon and gave a chortle of satisfaction. Dighcan's competitor, normally a placid man, danced about on a foot, voicing obscenities. Dighcan's own icon, crafted of silver twig, wire and weed, was cleverly wrapped in black cloth and was padded with soft clay which seemed to spring back with repeated abuse. It magically evaded strikes which would normally have been mortal.

Yullen was up next. He took his time aiming but Zestes' crude skeleton icon remained standing and the prize of his black belt was denied. Surprisingly, Quintlo fared no better, who had his eye trained on Dighcan's famous knuckle-irons.

Baus made no improvements in the next round. His losses became heftier and his croak rang discordantly through the compound when he ended up forfeiting his precious silver button of sea quail. Pulling at his pony tail, he sat back brooding. Karlil had knocked over his effigy with ease.

Watching glumly, Baus witnessed Zestes and Valere unseat each other's icons. They concluded the match by trading a studded neckband for a tin of boot wax. No one suffered any ignominies—at least not yet in these preliminary rounds. Everyone harboured enough bander to pad losses and avoid the worst spectacles.

There was a break in the game. Before any convicts could get too comfortable, the stakes were raised—to a four round minimum. Hereupon, Baus peered nervously at his dwindling bander, which consisted of three buttons. No great comfort wafted from his limp form. Gloomily he chewed at his lip while the moments dragged, dithering on whether he should enter or forfeit. The other contenders voiced rebukes, insisting that Baus post his bander, but he ignored them; however, not wishing to be at risk of being branded a sissy, he gambled all three buttons at once.

The move was foolish. Dighcan and Lopze capitalized on the blunder and collected all of Baus's buttons. Baus was buttonless and the winners engaged in a free-for-all sing-along, skipping and dancing about the terrain arm in arm:

"Dighcan and Lopze have new buttons, fresh buttons, new buttons . . .,
Dighcan and Lopze have fresh buttons, nik, nak, no!"

Baus was beside himself with wrath. How could he have been so foolish to reduce himself to such humiliation? He had studied the game. Not diligently, but calculatingly. How was he to secure bander with Dighcan seizing his stash? Zestes' buckle was required to carve out the stone from the east wall!

Weavil, now trudging back from his search of an icon, had in his left hand a limp, child-size cuttlefish with dripping mollusc shells for arms and legs. Valere measured its girth and discovered it undersized a half inch. He returned the icon, denying the midget entry into the game on grounds of regulatory breaches.

"Yes, Weavil," chided Baus, "render the appropriate changes to the icon and then rejoin the game. The men haven't time to spend on unnecessary diversions. And, before you trundle off to make amendments, pass me your heirloom. Several gamesters, including Zestes, are interested in examining the piece for its worth as an item of bander before it is entered into play."

Weavil made a deprecatory remark, but in the end, reluctantly conceded the timepiece to Baus.

Baus waited patiently for Weavil to disappear before he quietly introduced the watch into the pile.

Karlil's eyes widened. "That is Weavil's bander. I abjure dishonesty in all forms!"

Baus dismissed the observation. "You are a criminal, Karlil, and should know that this is fair play. I can hardly see the profit in not accepting the gift. Besides, Weavil and I are comrades; close as clams. He would entrust me with his life!"

Yullen imparted Baus a look of marvel and respect. "You are indeed a fortunate man to have such committed support as Weavil."

"Agreed," grunted Dighcan. "I may have misjudged the peevish critter for an ingrate. He may yet be one who will prove to be one of those dying breed of contenders long missed in the line of Flanks!"

Valere danced about with impatience. "Enough chatter! On with the play! We must increase the rapidity of our throws, so that I may test out a new face cream which I shall surely win from the vapid Lopze here."

Paltuik sneered. "Less fanfaronade and more play!"

Lopze concurred.

Nuzbek was now returning with his effigy: a mass of pale spindlefax twigs which constituted neck and arms, and a thin torso of spongebush representing something akin to his own tadpole-like form. A slurry grin carved on his face seemed to contradict the fact that he was a newcomer to the game. Pug noses and slab-sided faces veered in from all directions to examine Nuzbek's icon.

The item was free of regulatory breaches. Grudgingly, the group unanimously voted Nuzbek into the game.

The magician remained unamazed at the judiciary ruling.

Dighcan called the next round to order.

Nuzbek threw first. He calculated, framed his toss, launched, astonishing all, blasting Karlil's effigy to bits. The magician accepted the double-twine of rope, which constituted the belt around Karlil's waist. Nuzbek transferred the item into his robe that seemed to gobble up everything that entered. There were grumbles, but nothing could be done. Karlil's luck had changed. Baus managed to elude annihilation in the next round, barely missing Dighcan's assault on the following and was exposed to a blistering toss from Zestes.

Baus emitted a disconsolate cry. Weavil's timepiece was transferred from the bander pile to Zestes' palm. With cheerful bows, Zestes stuffed the prize into his baggy breeches. His mood was filled with offhand delight. "On the morrow, I shall craft a sea-reed band with which I may wrap this lovely piece round my wrist!"

"A grand endeavour!" cried Jorkoff. "Tomorrow we will see who owns the timepiece, you or I."

"There is no question of who will own it!" blared Zestes. "I consider it bad luck to re-bet a newly-won item."

'How very endearing.' Valere smiled fondly. "These kind sentiments are not the characteristics of the Zestes of old—the same chap who threw bluffly and bravely for anything and all? You have grown balmy-mannered in your years at Heagram, you old goat!"

"Think twice, redbeard—at least I have not outgrown my acumen as these slack-wits have."

Baus threw up his hands with impatience. "All this badinage strains my nerves! Zestes, why snatch the timepiece when you could have purloined Paltuik's fine pewter poodle or Yullen's ear polish?"

Zestes' face crinkled. "What care I for Yullen's ear slimes or Paltuik's poodles? I care to annihilate their icons and dance a finger-snapping hornpipe to their lamentations."

"A cruel ambition!" roared Paltuik, "but watch! It is my turn to throw. Ho! A toss—a timble, a twist—" He pirouetted on his heels, pivoted while he whistled. The rock cracked Zestes' icon on the crown. The effigy teetered, wavered—fell like an old bole in the forest.

Paltuik injected a triumphant cry into the gathering. "Now, it is my turn to gloat and dance with a fine timepiece on my wrist! What say you of that, you bald butcher? Nothing? A pity! Hand over my fair trinket."

"By no means!" cried Zestes. "The round had come to a complete end before you tossed. We had not deemed the bander official yet."

"What is all this squawking about?" sneered Lopze, marching in.

"My toss was fair," cried Paltuik. "Play continues with bander carried over into the next round unless otherwise stated. Just because your womanish complaint was not heard before my throw, does not mean that I should suffer the penalties. Hand over my property, Zestes, or I shall be forced to acquire it by force."

Zestes blatantly refused, prompting Paltuik to lunge and tear at his breeches. Zestes twisted away and came to lose pieces of his baggy pantaloons. Grunting with indignation, he retaliated with a savage kick to Paltuik's thigh, coming painfully close to the groin and

Paltuik gave an outraged cry and stepped in to drag his knuckles across the bald ruffian's scalp. "There, you see what happens?" The action elicited a strangled bleat from Zestes.

Dighcan pushed his way through the figures and flung the two apart. "Six demerits for being caught rousting by Graves." He turned to glare at Paltuik with disdain. "Your manner is cretinous, Palsy. It was your turn to throw, and you observed, Zestes did not specifically forward bander into the next round, nor is he compelled to. I am the referee and I decree that Zestes guard his wins and that your toss be invalidated!"

"A cheap ruling!" roared Paltuik. "You are a favouritist!" With angry force, he lurched ahead, looking ready to fight.

"Your opinion is moot, and if you don't desist from these febrile quibbles, I shall be forced to disqualify you!"

"Go ahead!" exploded Paltuik. He plunged his weight on Dighcan. Fists were murderously clenched, muscles knotted and face cherry red. It became clear that blood was to come. Dighcan threw off the attack and the two stood eye to eye, nose to nose, blowing smoke down at each other's nostrils. The group fell silent; the blood could be heard thumping through the veins in both necks.

After a long while, Paltuik stepped back, glowering with contempt. He muttered caustic oaths.

Baus's eyes watered. How long had these bullies been at odds? Probably a lifetime. It was an important fact which he would use for future gain.

The next round got off to a shaky start as the men's speculative whispers came and went, but eventually play was resumed; humour gave way to comradely backslapping. Baus lost his last three cils, not surprisingly, and now observed the game from afar, tossing pebbles at the turf. Under no circumstance must his seaman's charm be put up so cheaply for grabs!

The third round opened with Yullen. Being caught off guard on a foot fault, he was forfeited a toss. Karlil did not win back his rope and now banderless, his effigy toppled, suffered the discomfiting shock of a risk-turned-bad.

The crew banded together, giving a great whoop-de-do. They ripped off his trousers and gave merry chase to him around the perimeter of the yard, hollering and swatting at his loins and bare legs with flail-cane. Nuzbek was not included in this play and sat back shivering with contempt.

Baus stroked his chin in similar wonder. He glanced around the yard, wishing he could snatch up some manner of bander with which to win bets. Tussocks, pebbles, weeds, all were useless. He was forced to accept his ineffectual situation and with dejected impotence, slumped to the ground, chin propped in hand.

The men returned to their game. Karlil, legs, arms and bare behind chafed, red and raw, accepted his fate. He limped over to sit out the next rounds where Baus and he exchanged glum, philosophical remarks.

Midway through the game Weavil jogged up, doubly enraged when he learned of how Baus had squandered his heirloom.

"Enough of your hypocritical platitudes, you impulsive traitor!"

Baus spread his hands in supplication; he moved back to avoid Weavil's furious but harmless blows. "There are some affordable risks we must take in order to ensure a dignified status in the game."

"Snake-tongued as a drake you are, Baus!" shouted Weavil.

"The judgment is harsh," muttered Baus through pursed lips, "but I accept your discomfort and its associated fervour—though with a certain, limited patience."

"You are a con artist and a clown! Win me back my heirloom!"

"As you wish."

Weavil snapped his head back. "And how?"

"With craft and energy!" Skipping away from Weavil's slaps, Baus constructed efforts to convince him that they must put their heads together if they were to win.

The sun had dipped well below the horizon, leaving a wan, purplish glow spilling over the trampled earth. High over the northern wall soared jade-coloured beobar, frowning with disfavour. They took on the guise of behemoths which in the fading afterglow, were eerie. Nuzbek strutted past the gamesters to spread his booty on the barrack's veranda before tallying his items: a stout length of rope, a hand-pumped oil lamp, a chert toenail cleaner, a brown tin of snuff: all items of mint condition.

The prisoners gazed on enviously, wondering how this tyro had procured these sudden treasures on his first foray, if not by thaumaturgy.

Grinning meaningfully, Nuzbek scooped up his spoils. He disappeared into the sleeping quarters. Ausse and Germakk arrived, wooden mallets raised, beating the bronze gong with purpose. Nine o'clock curfew was in order and Baus studied the guards with care. Ausse was immoderately tall, blond-haired, chubby around the edges and guarded a splayed nose; Germakk was pink-faced, stocky and harboured a lean to his ruffled, orange-haired head that did not mask the irritating habit of his scowling and muttering.

The sky's reach had deepened to purple-rose. The men trudged gloomily to their quarters. Many grumbled of how bedtime had arrived so early and yet each understood the reality that their ultimate purpose was to work, and to work, one must sleep.

Baus wrinkled his nose at the scent of unwashed bodies and the sweat-drenched garments. Slats of worm-gnawed wood were crammed together like dock planks. Each was equipped with a thin, brown moth-eaten blanket and a flea-infested pillow. Along four walls the hardboard beds were fixed, crafted such that the men's heads faced the wall and feet were extended outwards toward the center. To say that the sleeping berths were examples of torture was a euphemism: all slept crammed parallel to one another like sardines. The earthen ground was cold, flattened by untold years of booted feet. Cloaks, breeches, socks and rancid underwear hung on wooden pegs. The odour of clam meat and snogmald competed with the sweat and grime and years of accumulation of dusky odours and too-many unwashed bodies in a tiny space.

Baus was consigned to a narrow space beside Weavil along the north wall between Valere, Karlil. The taciturn Jorkoff lounged nearby, grumbling about being forced grudgingly to allot room. Nuzbek, Boulm and Nolpin crowded along the opposite wall, sandwiched in between sardonic Lopze, a boisterous Zestes and the rake-thin Yullen. A barred window poised on either side of the only door where Dighcan slept, on a wider bunk under the left window, while Paltuik reposed under the other.

The gas lanterns flared out. Germakk stepped outside to maintain guard by the door. A leather snapperwhip was held on the ready in his palm. Ausse climbed the watchtower to supervise the compound. The main gate was left to the snauzzerhounds. While Germakk called lights out, Baus pulled a grey woollen cover over his head and tried to ignore the lingering odours that oozed from the mildewy cracks.

Somehow the task proved impossible and he rolled over on his side and looked up at the silvery spanning webs lacing the rafters. He recalled how Weavil and Nuzbek had twice already gotten into fights. Weavil had smuggled in rocks to brain the magician's skull at night—attempts which had both failed and now the two had received demerit points from Mulfax.

If all went well, they would be out of this bull pen before any other calamity could strike, Baus mused . . .

IV

That night, as on the previous, Baus's thoughts were morose. They drifted into dreams in which his experience was visions of human-demon conflict. Driven on an unknown mission, he was compelled to battle some misanthropic forces, somewhat human-formed, with only a small dagger and his wits to protect himself. Under the glowering moon he fought a monstrous bird with man-like qualities and glowing eyes and unearthly limbs. A wide, black river flowed nearby with ominous stealth. Far over the forests mushroom-shaped towers abounded; farther still, the mouldering stone ruins of bygone ages. He felt his knees fall limp, his own desires well up within him: secret longings, impulses, passions, all dangling in his face like worms skewered on a hook. Weaknesses, banes—all his foibles—they were bared with purpose, all to undermine him. A dark presence hovered near his throat: something immutably dim, but all too real. The bite of knowingness gnawed at his being with cuts far worse than any blade or poison. He awoke, flushed with a cold sweat. He raked unhappily at his damp hair.

He was sitting erect on his bed—back at the barracks, chest heaving like a bellows. Pale silver moonlight crept in through the small windows like fairy breath. Weavil's regular exhalation played on his shoulder; the prisoners' muffled snores became palpable.

A sudden glimpse alerted him to a roving shape hunched peculiarly by the door.

He blinked, bared his teeth. What, another dream?

No! It was the black-robed Nuzbek hovering over Dighcan's snoring form with prejudice.

Baus leaned forward. He watched as Nuzbek flicked a thin baton out the barred window.

Baus rejected the scene before him. For a moment, he saw Germakk stiffen as if in stunned wonder. Then nothing.

Moments passed; the sentry made no movement. Baus watched in fascination as Nuzbek drew back from the window and began fiddling with the lock. The magician prodded the door open; he stepped past Germakk and out into the chillness of the night. He inclined his head in an arrogant way. Halting in a place behind the guard, he watched the watchman's stony, inflexible stance with a kind of malign satisfaction.

Germakk stood like a leaden effigy, snapperwhip held in midair, as if defying the laws of gravity.

Baus drew a confused breath. Bold of Nuzbek to attempt such a manoeuvre!

Baus extended his caution so as not to rouse Weavil or Karlil and he slipped out from under his blanket and stole around the bunk toward the door. Crouching at the threshold, he witnessed Nuzbek make a grand way past the guard and onto the Flanks' playing ground.

Soft lantern light spilled over the portcullis. The glistening bars were a stone's throw from where he crouched. The magician craned his neck, gazed up to the watchtower. He seemed comforted to spy Ausse dozing off on his stool; his back was set against a corner in a most indolent pose.

Nuzbek made a hurried dash across the moonlit turf. Ausse was looking elsewhere. He stood blinking in the blue black shadow of the watchtower, muttering deprecations while he began playing glove puppet tricks with his fingers in the shadows. Suddenly Germakk's chin began to bob, sagging in slumber.

Without warning, the lookout was benumbed. Baus stepped back in awe. Nuzbek disappeared into the shadows. The darkened interiors of the office remained quiet.

Puzzled by the act, Baus padded earnestly to Germakk's inert form and edged his way by the barracks' shadowed side. He crouched there like a lurking animal, waiting for something to happen. The indigo shadows continued to cast their bleak hues across the turf.

Moments later, Nuzbek emerged carrying two cylindrical objects in his arms. The objects were queer—the same canisters that he had so cordially coveted, conveyed to the yard by the constabulary.

Cargo secured, the magician stole his way back toward the barracks. As he passed, Baus plunged himself deeper in the shadows, and Nuzbek was so engrossed with his prizes that he failed to notice the tense form of Baus peering up at him like a snogmald; he continued toward the northern wall and Baus crept after him like a wraith, keeping hidden under the wallside shadows.

From a few stones' throw distance, Baus watched Nuzbek kneel before the north wall, snatch up a dead chunk of beobar. The magician committed himself to a furious digging upon the loose sandy soil.

Brief minutes passed; Nuzbek carefully dumped his jars in the pit and speedily covered them up. For a moment Baus's perplexity reached an apex.

Nuzbek scuttled back to the office to retrieve the last two of his trophies. Pausing on the way back to deliver Germakk another glancing blow with the ganglestick, he began digging again by the north wall: two similar holes where the last two jars were buried . . . here Nuzbek seemed troubled, in a manner which Baus could not readily define . . . fury? disdain? indecision?

Perhaps the sight of the encaged midgets evoked rancorous memories? . . . Baus rubbed his jaw in bewilderment.

His suspicion turned to doubt. He tried to imagine what use the jars would be to Nuzbek underground, but certainly it was for some sinister purpose. Obviously he coveted these jars; but why? Why bury them here when he could not escape?

Baus arrested the speculations. Nuzbek had completed his camouflaging and with a demure satisfaction, began retracing his steps back toward the barracks.

Baus was eager to be back himself. It was the height of careless impudence to loiter here while Nuzbek snuggled himself in bed. Fashioning hasty steps, Baus ducked under the shadows and scampered alongside the west wall. He gained the veranda, slipped by the immobile Germakk, and there he lay on his pallet feigning sleep.

Nuzbek no sooner had arrived than he calmly inspected the guard. He was in no great hurry and the magician wedged himself between Nolpin and Yullen while Baus watched with leery satisfaction. The magician tucked his baton neatly into a slit under his pillow. Squinting through hooded lids, Baus noted the hiding place.

Minutes later, Germakk chanced to sneeze. By force, the momentum dissipated the magic and snapped him into alertness. The guard seemed confused, disoriented, not completely his self, and he marched smartly up to the door. He thrust his face in between the bars, peering down upon the sleeping crew. His attitude was of suspicion. He seemed barely convinced that everything was as it should, yet he resumed his post, griping and grabbing whip and dagger and muttering curses.

Nuzbek shifted his position to better enjoy Germakk's befuddlement. Baus's mental functionings worked overtime. What skullduggery was Nuzbek up to? The power of the rod seemed miraculous, that it could freeze one indiscriminately. Apparently Nuzbek seemed to enjoy this kind of private joke; and yet, many of the inexplicable degradations cast upon Dighcan and Zestes became less ambiguous . . .

Baus directed himself to deeper musing. He ventured on speculations of marvel regarding the ganglestick. If a single prod could render a man incapacitated for several minutes, what vast potentialities might it have in his own palm?

The prospect was exhilarating.

* * *

The first glimmer of light patterned the dormitory floor with rich red and mahogany tones. Baus struggled awake to the sounds of groans, grunts and ill-mannered jests. Dighcan eased himself out of his bed, stooping as he did to habitually lace his battered workboots. He stared sleepily out and about and mumbled to himself about having to face another day, only a paltry six more years left in his sentence. He backslapped Lopze, a dazed and confused badger-creature, whose bleary raccoon eyes looked as if they hadn't slept a wink all night. Valere rolled himself over, grimacing, voicing a rude remark at Yullen, who had nestled himself into the crook of his neck, purring like an infant at his mother's breast. "Away, you foul-breathed hound!"

On his way to the latrine, Vibellhanz accidentally jostled Paltuik, framing a careless retort that earned him a buffet and a knife-draw. Paltuik lumbered over to converse with Karlil, who was himself on his way to the latrine and Tustok eased past and innocently belched in Quintlo's face without apologizing. Upon scenting the reek of last night's oilfish, Quintlo emitted a vile curse, at which point Tustok mumbled a belaboured objection. Nuzbek stood back by the window, with his rumpled hat in hand and was so engrossed in smoothing back his thinning hair, that when Leamoine sidled up and fondled his behind, he gave a sharp cry and whirled on him like a crane.

"Pay close attention, milkfingers! It is eight demerits to impose improprieties upon a fellow convict. Remember Graves' warnings?—or do I have to imprint it on your brow? Do you desire so badly the flap-trap?"

"No more than you, *Nuzbeka*," Leamoine purred, waving a delicate hand at him, "but, if no one tells, no one knows."

"Wrong!" railed Nuzbek. "If no one reports, no one is brave enough to initiate the act. I have tongue enough and I am brave, as are Zestes and Tustok here, who will vouch for my testimony."

Leamoine dimpled his cheeks with coquettishness. "They will surely not say a peep."

Nuzbek jerked forward to object but Leamoine began to fuss placidly with his right ear bangle. "Attend! As no witnesses are stepping forth, logic deems necessarily no complaint, therefore no demerits, no immurement in the flap-trap."

"Blind sophism!" cried Nuzbek. "Mark my words, you fluff, you are walking on eggshells."

Leamoine gave a fluting cluck as did many convicts raise jeering outcries which Nuzbek found entirely low-class. But he strode back to his bunk and discharged his angst upon Boulm, who was just rousing himself from his pallet.

* * *

After a cold unsatisfying breakfast of onion, hoarfish, and yams, Ausse and Germakk assigned the men to their day's duties. The dodgy meal went down heavily. It was Baus, Tustok, Valere, Quintlo, Zorez and Vibellhanz who were to report to the sea wall, while Weavil, Nuzbek, Nolpin, Boulm and others were consigned to various chores, including clam-shucking, fish-gutting and refuse-shovelling in the central yard. The wastes were to be loaded into barrows and dumped in the garbage pit at the forest's edge.

Baus fumed silently. As much as he despised this odious task of clam-cracking and its associated stenches, he secretly wished he was the one involved so that he could secretly scour the north wall and overhanging limbs for any possibilities of escape.

Oppet, Master of the snauzzerhounds, presently pulled at the chains of his dogs and drove Baus and the four convicts on, ball and chain clutched in hand, down the narrow pathway through Grumboar forest. The dogs were feral monsters, snapping at the prisoners' heels with slavering jowls. Six foot long masses of furred stealth, spiked ears and peaked snouts stabbed at the earth and made a formidable impression on the convicts. Oppet kept the guardians at bay, voicing several commands while tendering herbal sweetmeats which seemed to pacify the beasts in some way. Nevertheless, the dogs seemed to adore their master and obeyed him without question. They truckled to his requests with an almost religious devotion despite the intricate harness rigged up round their necks and torsos.

Although the journey through the woods was arduous, Baus had time to marvel at the great smoke-coloured boughs that vaulted over their heads. They were like magnificent rooftops reaching to the sky. Green-backed boles as old as time hemmed his path, through the gaps of which, Baus caught glimpses of salt-water pools, fallen logs, bull reeds and bog tracts which hid the wide-billed herons that stalked fish and frogs. Bristly weeds, spiky crag-bush coloured the rich and hundred-hued morass. All the time Baus heard faint murmuring amidst the trees: the sweet musk of old forest masked the oily exudations of fen, overshadowing its eeriness, but still remained a teasing reminder of the days when his father would entertain him as a lad with tales of the 'murmuring' forests of seaside Sarch. Too short were these carefree days that came back now . . .

Out of the shadows the company emerged, struggling alongside the mudflats toward Weavil's lookout, now a forlorn, black-blemished shanty shot against the folds of the sea. A short distance ahead, the half-finished teeth of the sea wall rose out of the sand like molars. Up to the wharf the rampart continued like a stony snake, continuing along the northern shore of the Flam.

A black-bearded figure greeted them with enthusiasm—Voin, who conveyed them with somewhat perfunctory authority down a shallow-bowled dune toward a section of wall that denoted the straggling terminus. There stood three piles of raw stone, a wheelbarrow and a beat-up bucket of cement powder. A grey tub of water was pushed back amongst the shovels and trowels.

The foreman rubbed his wrists, an officious fellow infused with a florid face and hawk features. He uttered curt instructions to the crew, whereupon trowels were thrust into Baus's and Vibellhanz's hands. Zorez and Quintlo were commanded to work the wheelbarrow and gather shells to add to the mortar. Tustok and Valere were handed shovels while Oppet went back with his dogs to tend the prison gate.

Trowel in hand, Baus caught a glimpse of the limitless Poesasian. It was lustreless, trembling in the damp, salty air like some untamed maiden. Today it was grey and bleak with the shadow of incoming clouds. The shoreline was dim, a flat and hazy swath—forming a languid blur with the waves that licked its face. A muted drone, merging with the nearby soporific creak of ships' rigging, set Baus to wistful reflection. The steeples of schooners of Heagram port felt somehow faraway, no more to Baus a home than a vague memory of the past. The seaside hamlet was lost to him. He felt no more attachment to Heagram than a wayfarer committing a fleeting stopover along the path of a long journey. What was more, outside of the sanctuary of his own mind, he fostered no hope of escape from this wretched prison. While remaining prepossessed with the murk of despair, he was jolted by Voin, who had noticed his break of industry.

"This is sluggardly work, Baus! Notice how Vibellhanz trowels with efficiency. Your handiwork is sloppy in comparison, and slapdash!"

Baus arrested his trowelling to peer at Voin with narrowed eyes. "And how might I attain this miracle?"

"Through diligence and passion."

Baus made efforts to comprehend the means, but the curl of his lip barely masked his sarcasm. "I have only pursued this line of work for a day now. Do you expect me to be a master?"

"In retrospect, no," responded Voin. "On their first essay, Lopze and Quintlo performed a grand job of mortaring, which was to be commended."

"Well then, let Lopze and Quintlo trowel and slave away, not I!

Voin gave a startled gasp. "You make demands then?"

Baus further growled through his teeth. "No, I merely ask, must we all be perfectionists in our first hour?"

"Essentially yes—and watch the timbre of your voice, you rogue. I am wise to your tricks and am generally lenient when it comes to inefficiencies, but as head of this operation, I am under pressure that the wall must be completed before the first winter gales. Prefect Barth has decreed the achievement! Do not forget I am chairman of the Bricklayer's Guild—now back to your work, ingrate, with speed! Adroitness must be augmented!"

Baus mumbled an epithet. Where had he heard those slave-mongering words before? Not too far up the beach, from the mouth of a certain Harky . . .

The day dragged on; rock piled upon rock. The barrow's wheels creaked, cement powder sloshed while shovels scraped and trowels clinked. The wall grew slowly in length. By five o'clock, ten more feet had been added to the crooked line.

Oppet came to relieve the exhausted convicts while Voin returned to the town, given to that self-satisfied strutting typical of his ilk. Baus trudged wearily through the darkening forest, knees bent under the weight of his ball and chain.

When the convicts reached the gate, Ausse received them with a peremptory wave, motioning them inside the yard. The bobbin released from the drum; a rattling of chains punctuated the stillness. The portcullis smashed down, causing Oppet's hounds a chorus of bays. At close range, Baus studied the beobar mesh with contempt: the grate was fifteen feet high, stout as shore pilings. It joined the ungainly watchtower that ran on through the low-lying, creepy beobar.

Ausse removed the anklets from the prisoners' legs. He returned the restraints to the repository; meanwhile Oppet leashed his snauzzerhounds with just enough slack to administer a deadly attack should any miscreants attempt escape through the gate. The houndmaster retired to the comfort of his small cottage deep beneath the plum-shadowed forest. To Baus, one thing was evident; there would be no escape by this quarter.

The prisoners supped that evening on boar stew mixed with overcooked perogi doused in cuttlefish oil. Fading damask light brought the evening ritual of Flanks, where Dighcan remained the undisputed champion. Nuzbek was too wary to be domineered by any sly play, and so he outwitted Tustok of his jade-coloured cape and Leamoine of his fine pair of ear clasps through means of magic. Throughout the rounds, Nuzbek forfeited only a few small items of bander. Such was his craft that he had only contributed tokens such as arrowhead, small flexible moon disk and boot lace which seemed to coil of its own volition. Other trifles he bid—which the winners and non-winners could not dispute. His tactics were sound: supplying multiple bander to the pot, he afforded himself the luxury of losing valueless items of which he seemed to have an endless supply in his black robe. His icon was crafted of thin and pliable withe which harboured an elasticity that seemed to spring back of its own accord and resist opponents' missiles with rubbery marvel.

Baus's lack of bander forced him to observe the proceedings from a distance. His scrutiny was imbued with certain distaste. He watched in offhand amusement as Weavil attempted a toss mid-way through the fifth round, but losing, thus deprived of two of his neck rings. Only very narrowly did the midget avoid a humiliating degradation. For their first time at hurling, Nolpin and Boulm stood eagerly at the throwing line and they proved contesters of poor quality—ones who also lost rounds beyond their supply of bander to replenish and suffered abasements: Boulm, a chicken whipping, and Nolpin, a vaulting up the old dead hazelwood, much to the amused jests of the gamesters.

The gong tolled. Curfew was signalled. Ausse and Germakk shuttled the prisoners off to the dormitory where they stood guard on deck with backs to the door. Ausse was first on patrol; Germakk assumed high post in the watchtower. Oppet and his hounds kept vigilance at the front gate.

The men engaged in a tradition of rude banter before retiring. Baus was unable to relax. He realized that he knew little of his bed-mates, and was prompted to inquire of his fellow colleagues' crimes.

"What interest would you have?" blurted Lopze. He was about to squeeze himself between Zestes and Karlil but heaved himself erect.

"Simple curiosity," said Baus. "You seem to be a decent fellow who poses some curiosity to me—for example—Valere, what sort of mischief have you committed to arrive in this thieves' den?"

Valere rubbed his chin. "Simple curiosity is one thing, friend, but malicious intent another." His frown softened and he raked his beefy fingers through his red mane. "A sad tale, though," he admitted, "but a good one. All the other lubbers in this warren have heard it a thousand times, so I shall not care for a repeat."

"Nonsense!" protested Zestes. "Let's hear it, seabeard, and we shall listen to it for all its usual clichés and embellishments!"

The big redhead shook his head with modest dignity. "Of embellishments you shall find none, Zestes. So pellucid are the images dug in my mind that they shimmer as clear as yesterday!" His voice took on a deep, resonant tone, at once melancholy. "I was a sea captain once—a happy one, with ne'er a sad thought to my name. But, I sailed the Poesasian in my little cog, '*the Illimmer*', named by my father's father and I knew woe after a time. We all lived on the Isle of Illim and loved the lonely, placid little isle with its soaring gulls, melodious winds and graven seas, with waves singing seaside chanteys fair as any minstrel to our ears. This was all at least this side of Brislin. I harboured a crew of six lackeys. Many contracts per month in haulage I gained before I fell afoul of the seductress, Rauseelia. Ah, she was a woman of visceral dexterity who would sunder a man's soul to tatters! I fell instantly in love with her; so stunning was her figure as to defy nature itself, as beautiful as any man could behold—tawny-locked, ruby-lipped, a body as lean as a tigress. She had the eyes of glistening marble, a bosom as full as two rising suns, a swagger that would tempt any man's resources ten times beyond the monks of Long Bight. Well, she came from a well-to-do family, in Britobur, of course, and thwarted my desire and after her hour of teasing would have nothing to do with me. She thrust away my advances like breakers that tossed surf on a desolate wind-racked shore. Into a knot of craving she had my heart pulsing! I could not sleep! By day I imagined her tawny-auburn thighs around mine, her sultry laugh, her inviting lips, her slender form emitting its warmth. Alas—by night she would have me lying awake in cold sweats. Even now, I can envisage her aura silhouetted in my porthole and cannot resist a tremble."

"Very poetic," muttered Lopze.

"Aye, more vivid than your previous anecdotes," commented Zestes.

"Do you want to hear the story or not?" Valere shot stern looks from left to right. "Well, one fine April eve, I heaved to at the docks of Britobur, that mightily proper town not ten leagues south of Heagram. She lived with her right ancestry and kin. I stole her stealthily back to my seacraft. Off to sea I sailed with the vixen and my jolly crew aboard my night-camouflaged vessel. She thrashed and bucked like a flounder—ah, true! I did have her for my own now, though I never would force myself on her—I was not that type of man. She was sly and cunning, this fiery-tempered Rauseelia, and one night in the weeks that followed, she slipped something into the drink of my mates while we were besotted. We slouched prone and she tied us up in our chairs. The next day she shouted to the open sea for succour and sailed alone as she could with her seaman's knowledge. Waited and waited we did for days with us trussed up like hares before a carrack bearing Arnin's flag detected our cog and fell on us like crakes. On a foray up the coast against the buccaneer triangle, Arnin's men so learned of Rauseelia's story, and with us tied up in our own squalor and unglorious shame, we were doomed. They rescued the girl and returned her to her precious Britobur, but they delivered me to Heagram, that being the closest jailhouse to my birthplace. Eight years ago that was, and I have been dealt a half life sentence since."

Baus stared misty-eyed. "A moving tale, Valere. It makes one wish to never plunge so deeply in swoon for a woman."

Valere uttered a laugh. "Cruel indeed. These are the twistings of heart which all men face at least once in their lifetime. Except maybe Leamoine. I have survived where others have not. Regard!—I haven't a better pack of rogues in which to keep company!"

"A touching confession!" crowed Dighcan.

"And what of you, Baus?" demanded Valere. "What shenanigans have you been up to, to get you in here? Something related to Nuzbek's magic show and his dim chums I gather?"

Baus pulled sorrowfully at his chin. "Something of the sort—though far less complex. In light of your own gloomy tale, I am almost embarrassed to admit—I broke a ledge-full of shellames at the fair. I bore not the funds to repay the insipid shop-owners, and so remain immured as you see."

Lopze roared. "What? For so trivial a crime? What does this world come to when men are gaoled for murder and sleep in the same bed as fledglings knocking over Mother Meegle's wee casserole bowl?"

"Don't mind Lopze," cautioned Zorez. "He used to reside in the old shanty overlooking the sea by the lighthouse, didn't you, Lopze?—until you murdered Klueshin's dachshund."

"The cur used to urinate in my yard."

Baus inquired, "And this is a crime to be incarcerated for?"

"It was not just on my lawn that the flea-hound pissed! It was on my precious bonsai— the one that I had grown for fifteen years. It was slowly being wasted away, poisoned by the bromidic bladder of that mongrel! Yes, I dispatched the mutt to purgatory. I also gave Klueshin, that jackleg barber, a proper thrashing when he came to complain of his dead dachshund. In fact, the lout put up such peevish resistance that I was forced to strangle him with my bare hands."

Baus nodded morosely, noting well the long span of years that Lopze had still to serve, hoping that more would be added.

Quintlo, squint-eyed and high-strung, jerked a thumb over at Weavil. "What about little Poodle here? He seems overly crabbed, like as if he had a beetle up his behind; at least he offers us a few words, but that's on a good day."

Baus offered a clarification: "Weavil is reticent, yes, but as a sensitive poet and scholar, he has suffered a mortification."

Paltuik exhaled a mocking grunt. "Mortification? And how is it any worse than what we have all suffered?"

Baus spoke gravely, "Acting in temper and inebriation, he committed a faux-pas upon Captain Graves, which necessitated an accounting."

Tustok snickered. "Certainly an error if I've ever heard one."

Softened by the sympathy, Weavil outlined in detail Nuzbek's insensitive, heavy-handed spell and how it had resulted in his despicable shrinking. Absorbing the story with uncharitable animosity, the prisoners rounded upon the magician. Yullen and Zestes reached up a hand and buffeted Nuzbek malevolently; others administered their own biffs and slaps in the form of jeering payback.

Nolpin and Boulm shrank back on their beds. They awaited their own abuse; however, Nuzbek tore himself off his cot and faced his foes with jerky defiance: "Imbeciles! I merely transmogrified Weavil into a pygmy to rid this town of one less pest and narcissist! Not leastly because of his own inexcusable, rabble-rousing which razed my set. Listen, jackdaws! I shall now provide an unabridged narrative of the facts!"

"Please do so!" urged Valere.

Nuzbek exhaled before his pink mouth gave vent to a pedantic spiel of the events at Heagram fair. He overstated his hopeless frustration and unrequited anguish with the heckling that had relieved him of his property, delivering his wealth to an absolute nadir. His address was conducted with alliteration, euphemisms and a more than usual amount of bombast.

Notwithstanding, many of the inmates regarded Nuzbek with a sallow wariness which they showed with attitudes of scepticism and unease.

Jorkoff offered a weighted comment: "If I didn't witness Weavil's own condition with my eyes, I would not believe a word of your tale, Nuzbag. How did you transmogrify him? The circumstance seems implausible!"

Nuzbek's expression turned grey. He spoke in an icy whisper. "In the face of rich thaumaturgy, nothing is impossible, oaf, for which I shall demonstrate."

Jorkoff quickly renounced the need for any substantiation. Zestes and Dighcan followed suit and rhymed off reasons also for such a bypassing.

"Very well," observed Nuzbek coolly. "I shall overlook this muckraking for once—but no more! My lenience is not infinite!"

Dighcan interposed a rendition of his own pathetic chronicle, explaining how he had forced indignities upon Madame Faul, the Snogmald Tavern owner's wife. She had taken great offence to the acts while he was in the throes of drunken debauchery. He went on to list other crimes, which the men laughed over and acknowledged with slab-sided grins.

Zestes spoke, revealing his presence as a notorious pirate of the sea who had been beached by his so-called comrades. They rode the black mast and black flag of the caravel 'Karkassus'. In an attempt to survive, he had 'borrowed' three wegmors from farmer Yahason to trade for sustenance. In time, the local Heagram constabulary had caught up with him; a week later, he was sentenced to fifty years for seaside pillagings and chicaneries numbering in the many. He was touted as the leader of the freebooter band, 'Mixtus', known by not just one of the sombre convicts.

Of his own accord, Paltuik admitted that murdering the blacksmith's brother, black-tongued Aingst of Heagram had been foolish. It was on a dark, beobar-shrouded section of the road between Heagram and Tavilnook that the two brigands, Aingst and Paltuik had lain in hiding, waylaying the moneylender Lapousis regularly known to travel the road at a certain hour by wegmor. They had leaped upon him, stolen his purse, bludgeoned him to death for his three hundred cils and his pouch of gold and then made off with his wegmor. The two robbers had argued viciously, with Aingst proving the loser. After hiding Aingst's body in a secluded glade after a vicious brawl, Paltuik had fled with bloody hands to Heagram, but had failed to consider the beast he rode which was easily recognized and he was seized by the Heagram constabulary.

Quintlo recounted his own glum chronicle which began almost as an anecdote a winter before last when he had stowed away in the hold of the cargo hauler, '*Sea Dancer*' sailing from Brislin. As the vessel lay docked under the new moon by the old pier at Heagram, Quintlo attempted to steal away with a double sack of jewels purloined from the captain, but was caught off-guard by wandering dock patrol. Seizing the gemstones, the watchmen dragged him to prison for accounting.

More tales were exchanged. Eventually, the men took to yawning and their beds—except Baus, who lay awake, remaining very alert to what nocturnal shenanigans Nuzbek would attempt next.

V

Nuzbek's gambit was not long in coming. The moon had risen to its zenith when Baus saw the magician sit upright in his bed. His gaze drifted out the window where Ausse shuffled about on the veranda like an old geyser. The magician roused his chums; they gathered toe clipper, twine and jade cape, and crept to the window.

Nuzbek reached past Dighcan's supine form. He ensorcelled Ausse. He ordered Nolpin to take the accessories and they snuck out into the night leaving Baus blinking in amazement.

Without a thought, Baus padded down to the Flanks field and established a clear avenue. He slunk into the darkness, stalking Nuzbek and his cronies with cunning. The night was cool—a silver moon shone high in the sky. The ramparts were lit in chiaroscuro. Keenly aware of mishap, Baus saw Nuzbek loitering amongst the dwarf-shrubs in the place where the jars lay buried.

Nolpin and the magician lay down cape, ropes and clipper and poked about, sizing four equidistant holes along the outside of the fabric. They managed to fit four equal-sized pieces of rope through each hole: Nuzbek gave a harrumph of satisfaction. Baus stared, fascinated. Nuzbek drew the rope tighter together to form a primitive grip of the four ends and pulled the cape up into the shape of a balloon. Germakk's largish head began to nod in his post up top the watchtower. Nuzbek hoisted the canopy up in the air. He studied it critically. From Baus's perspective, the invention looked like an upside down umbrella, or some vile parachute. Nuzbek drew forth a strange, amber-sheened pyramid from his cloak; he ignored Nolpin and Boulm's mewling remonstrations.

Baus frowned. The lurid luminescence of the pyramid was unsettling and he resisted the urge to creep up and gain a more compelling view. Nuzbek placed the adjunct carefully beside the other equipment and articulated more vocables. He gesticulated. The pyramid seemed to seethe with a malfeasant pulse, suddenly to vibrate very fulsomely with a low hum.

The device flickered suddenly hues of an eerie maroon, then changed to an eldritch, polychromatic flavour. A spray of light struck out at the umbrella. The fabrication blossomed to life, canvas bellying as if with invisible air. It righted itself up. Nuzbek grabbed at the ropes which he gripped with triumph. In the manner of a gangly balloon, the conveyance began to float up in a slow motion, hovering half way up the wall, leaving Nuzbek's boots dangling above the ground like magic ornaments.

Nolpin stumbled back on his heels. Boulm stood staring frigidly, crossing his fingers as if to ward off a curse.

Nuzbek rose a good two feet before the buoyancy of the device slackened and left him stranded. His muddy boots scraped against the stone. Muttering nonsensical words, the magician began to sink slowly. Finally his feet touched the turf and the spell was broken.

Baus crept back with profound wonder. So here was Nuzbek's plan! To elevate himself over the wall, treasures and cronies and all.

Nuzbek did not seem entirely satisfied with the manner events were proceeding in, evidenced by the way he slapped at Boulm, cursing him silently as the lackey tried to assist the magic device by lifting him up by the shins.

The pyramid refused to offer more magic.

Nuzbek kicked it.

The pyramid became vibrationless. Nuzbek's face grew dark with annoyance. His eyes lit suddenly with an idea, as if recalling some litany recessed in the back of his sinister memory. An arcane verse dredged from time fell forth from his lips:

Agowon Subra Satchwen!

The pyramid pulsed to life, sputtering an incongruous light. The magician expressed exultation and snatched at the parachute anew.

A shout lanced from the direction of the tower.

Baus jerked around in time to catch Germakk clomping down the stairwell. He was scrambling at a great rate. Baus dove back toward the dormitory.

Nuzbek uttered an expletive and snatched up his accessories. He seized Nolpin by the elbow and they both ran at a full tilt toward the barracks. Boulm trailed behind.

Baus whisked past Ausse, swiftly concealing himself in his bed, dragging the covers over his head as he busied himself with controlling his breathing. He was beside himself with wrath: through excessive risk, he could have compromised his plans.

Nuzbek, Nolpin and Boulm burst through the door. They scuttled to their pallets and pretended slumber, while Baus, glancing through the fold of the blanket, saw the magician fervently caching his parachute under his own blanket, with Germakk's silhouette sliding through the barred window like an eel. The guard pressed his square face against the bars of the window. His expression was of suspicious displeasure. He seemed unsatisfied that the rhythmic rising and falling of the men's chests was innocent.

Germakk returned to inspect his workmate with significant scepticism. Ausse appeared enmeshed in some sort of trance, frozen like an ice statue, unnaturally poised. Even the wave of a provoking hand seemed not to disturb him.

Germakk seemed further mystified by his partner's blue eyes which remained glassily open as a hoarfish's, and at the absence of any twitch of mouth or tremor of cheek. He circled round the back and gave his partner a slap on the face. Instantly the sentry jerked himself to attention, blinking like an owl.

"Never sneak up on me like that!" Ausse cried, white-eyed.

"Sneak up on you? What are you babbling about?" Germakk snatched at Ausse's weapon. "It's not healthy to be dozing standing up, is it? Especially when some villain can sneak up behind you and slit your throat."

Ausse growled, "You're one to talk! What are you doing down from your perch? Graves'll have your privates if he hears how you abandoned your watch."

Germakk blew hot air through his lips. "Graves is an overbearing oaf. I saw furtive movements in the yard and I went to investigate certain sinister peeps."

"Really? What kind of peeps?" jeered Ausse.

His colleague pointed toward the north wall where the clinging shadows hung eerily. "Gibberish, monosyllables, similar things—but I chanced to glimpse a large bat, or some kind of bulb. It was rising and falling, then suddenly it was motionless, as if suspended in the air—a most bizarre thing—given the circumstances—enough to give a man the heebies."

Ausse peered at him as if he were mad. "You're a ninny, Germakk. Perhaps you saw ghosts, or even coyotes masquerading as ghosts, gambolling up the wall like floating spectres."

"Now you're mocking me," groused Germakk.

"Smarten up! Too many late nights with no ale has made you hallucinating bulbs and bats and other floating phenomena."

"Shut up." Germakk grimaced. "You'd better watch your back, Ausse. If there's one thing I know, is that skullduggery's real. Take care! You'll be the first to die. Don't trust any of these hooligans. Especially Dighcan and his 'buddy' the magician. They're murderous wretches. If you get your mouth wagging to Graves, remember, he shall hear of your sleep-walking."

Ausse opened his mouth, but Germakk had already stalked off with a curse.

Digesting the information shrewdly, Baus gathered his wits. He did not wish to attempt any more excursions to the north wall, nor did he sleep any more that night.

* * *

At breakfast, Graves assembled the prisoners. He pulled Germakk and his crony aside and seemed discomfited by the news they had to offer.

The prisoners huddled in a sullen knot, conversing in desultory whispers. The three gaolers scoured the barracks: a rigorous inspection that revealed nothing of interest, save for Nuzbek's poke-holed cape and some frayed bits of rope which prompted Graves to pace ever the more fretfully before the group.

"Last night or the night before," he announced, "a remarkable incident took place, insofar as several articles, including my four bottled homunculi seem to have disappeared."

Dighcan put on a shocked expression. "A tragic loss, Captain, and I wholly sympathize with your loss wholeheartedly."

"Silence!" thundered Graves. "If the jars are not returned to me at once, you shall all receive punitive ministrations."

Dighcan stirred in anger. "This is not just! How can we be blamed?"

Graves waved a hand. "Easily. Unless the jars are returned, the edict stands. The canisters did not just walk off on their own accord—somebody appropriated them and hid them somewhere."

"An implausible deed!" objected Ausse. "We were on vigilant watch."

Graves grunted. "I have conversed with Oppet on this matter and he has concluded that none passed the gate—in fact, his testimony supports the theory that you solely are to blame for the theft perpetrated on your watch."

Germakk and Ausse stammered. The prisoners bantered; Nuzbek seemed to pick at his teeth in a most reflective manner.

"Well, Nuzbek," called Graves jeeringly. "What have you to say about this? You seem quite collected. The weird curios were yours, after all."

"The mystery is wholly perplexing. I would hazard a guess that the imp Trimestrius or the mountebank Woisper managed to escape. The spells of containment are not altogether infallible, or possibly, by sheer chance, one or more of them may have wrenched open a jar and returned to rescue his colleagues." He scratched at his chin with doubtful reflection. "A more apposite theory is that one of your prisoners stole them. If the miscreants are not apprehended, the risk upon us becomes insuperable! I advise you to take reparative action, Captain!"

"Do not counsel me!" snapped Graves.

Nuzbek made an insolent sound. "You have heard my opinion and now you know what is required."

Graves turned sharply to Baus and Weavil. "You troublemakers harbour more knowledge of Nuzbek than anyone here. Any theories?"

"None," cried Weavil, eyelids pinched. "Decipher your own conundrums. You shan't receive any beneficence from me."

Baus interceded a polite concession. "Weavil remains agitated for reasons of his midgetness. You must forgive him for his condition."

Graves gave a snort. "Weavil has dug his own hole."

Weavil chirped contempt. "Bilgewater! I could care less for your theories or Nuzbek's, regarding the collection of imps."

Graves spoke with easy irony. "Then who will save us when we are all murdered in our sleep by these fey creatures as Nuzbek alludes?"

"I don't know, maybe Santa Claus—or Buster the Bear," growled Weavil.

Baus, sensing ill effects to come, divulged what he knew of Nuzbek's chicanery. But while on the first sentence he desisted, judging that such disclosures would invariably hinder his cause—particularly in reference to his own curfew violations. He opted for a simpler, broader explanation: "Captain, these freakish individuals are alive!—warlocks or sorcerers I believe, of some insidious nature. From Nuzbek's disjointed hints, I believe they are invested with certain evil faculties. What do you say about that, Nuzbek?"

Nuzbek glared. "Not much."

"Psychokinesis? Teleportery?" Baus mused. "The possibilities are endless! Now, if the figures use the sum of their potencies upon us, we are all snake bait as Nuzbek has alluded! Hence in such wise, I urge you to surrender us for release—if only to forestall such a contingency, and our otherwise injurious malaise."

Germakk choked on his tongue. "You would suggest that we let you all walk scot-free from here? An unlikely occurrence!"

Lopze brought forward a galled outcry. "Enough of this raillery! Baus's words are sagacious! His argument is germane and it is imbued with a conviction that is compelling."

"True," announced Zestes. "Our lives are all in peril. Baus is our only invaluable comrade, a laudable spokesman who plays Flanks and augments our purses with bander."

Many agreements came supporting the cause. Valere locked arms with Zestes and they twirled arm in arm. Dighcan caught Quintlo in a clapping jig, and Zorez, Tustok and Karlil held up fingers and cat-called.

Baus moved to the front of the group and held up his hands. "Peace, brothers." Signalling for a space of silence, he entreated the men to quell their enthusiasm and allow the Captain to speak.

Graves gave a nod of a saturnine amusement at the courtesy. "Keep up the charade, Baus, for if any can do it, it is you. You have won excellent rapport with your bedfellows—bravo! Indeed you are a jocular fellow, bringing a merry cheer to this stark world of the yard. As for liberating the compass of your mongrel breed, that would be a breach of judiciousness—if not sanity. What would the innocent inhabitants of Heagram say when, tossed in the ditch, robbed of all chastity of their dulcet daughters, they lie broken and maimed? Would they come bloody-jowled to me crying, 'Captain, you permitted Dighcan and Zestes to foist atrocities on our persons? Why?'"

Dighcan made a small sign of resentment. "That is an offensive remark! Do you not know I am a reformed man?"

Graves gave a gesture of smiling compassion. "That may well be, Dighcan, but I am vexed by this unwarranted and perplexing theft of my stores. The mysteries shall be exposed! I shall await the moment with relish!" He turned to Deputies Ausse and Germakk. "Now summon Skarrow and Mulfax. Tell them to haul their carcasses over here pronto. I want them replacing Germakk and you."

Ausse's eyes widened with surprise. "A wise course, sir? When would you wish the order relayed?"

"Immediately!" he snapped. "Would I utter it only to have it ignored?"

"But after—? Where shall we—?"

"You," he cried frigidly, "are relegated to the scullery. I would have you first scouring the office for clues, and with a fine-toothed comb, if you weren't so inept! Nevertheless, give the space the best dusting ever! Then, after compiling the observations, report to me. Present yourself to Cemurk the cook and await your duties. As for the rest of you rabble, consume your regular slops. On the mark! I want three more volunteers chipping rock on the road to Tavilnook."

Dighcan thought to interject a complaint.

Graves interrupted. "Dighcan, Zestes, Valere! How quaint. You look like worthy candidates—with all that spry energy and capering about, you must be pining for a chance to employ it?"

"Me?" asked Zestes innocently.

"Yes, you."

"What of myself?" bawled Lopze morosely. "Do I not at least account for an honourable mention in this crew?"

Graves smoothed his cheeks. "How could I forget my favourite strangler?"

Lopze brightened with a cheerful grin. "A jewel, Captain—you are a jewel in the rough."

Graves murmured that he could understand the comparability. "Now!" he called sharply.

"Out to work! Cold weather is on the way. There remain numerous chores to be finished! Germakk! Ausse! To speed!"

Limping toward the office, Germakk gave a sour-lipped grumble. A dour Ausse followed on his heels to summon the replacements and gather the prisoners for the road gang.

VI

Two days passed. Then a week. Soon a fortnight had slipped by and the air grew chiller as the fall faithfully progressed. One bright sunny day Baus stood gazing reflectively up at the measureless sky. His mood was tinged with a melancholy of burden that he had never known. His cheeks were sunken; his brittle movements were dull and mechanical, but the hungry itch for liberation had never waned. His face had become a haggard mask. A sailor marooned on a island would have no better cast. During the interval he had grasped many things about the guards' regular movements, also he had learned much of the intricacies of the convicts' characters. No revelation was forthcoming on the nature of Nuzbek's magic. What was the source of his sorcery? The magician had made no excursions to the north wall, as if a decision had been made in his mind as to the unprofitability of jail-breaking. To lift the stun-wand from the magician would require a talent of scrupulousness.

The men had been rotated for their shifts; now Baus, Weavil and others remained fish-gutting in the compound by the handfuls. Quintlo, Yullen, and Zorez and Vibellhanz had been sent away with Nolpin and Karlil to chip stone for road repairs on the wind-worn route to seaside Tavilnook, eight miles away.

Drays of eelfish were arriving in the compound, along with sandcrabbers, golgonfish and rockgobblers. Speckled and varied, the fish were dumped into a heaving pile on which the men went instantly to work. Baus and company sorted the gobblers from the crabbers with fingers raw and bare; Dighcan and others cut, slashed and tossed the filleted flesh back into the drays. Zestes manhandled the barrows to and from the gate and to the town with Nuzbek and Boulm, while Oppet's minatory snauzzerhounds tagged along to ensure their fidelity. There remained no chance of escape by any impulsive means.

Stymied by the disappearance of the jars, Graves had not given up his search and elected to stay in the compound to supervise the work. From the office window, he watched as the prisoners went through motions of tedium. Baus spied him making gruff remarks to Ausse and Germakk who still were on part-time duty sweeping the office, but all the time the warden's eyes were cannily alert and on the lookout for peculiarity.

The morning passed.

When the lunch gong finally rang, the men convened to the refectory. The meal tables were set with plates. Many were draped in coarse, stained cloth, a colour which Baus disliked and guessed had once been white.

Steam drifted from the tin platters. Saucers, forks and spoons were strewn in random piles beside the smorgasbord.

Tustok and Jorkoff grabbed their plates and assumed a premier position. Leamoine crowded close in line, sidling uncomfortably near Jorkoff who, resenting the encroachment, nudged him away. The magician muttered a revilement at Leamoine's presence and steered clear, standing apart from the group with an obvious distaste for having to stand in line like a mule. Nuzbek waited for others to congregate, before falling in behind Dighcan whom he sensed shared an orthodox view on the matters of male intimacies.

Zestes, Valere, Boulm and Paltuik sniffed the air; they placed bets on who could deduce the character of the menu based on scent alone. Valere was successful: greased eel fillet, potato-leek, cold snail pasta and a smothering of smoluk-egg pâté.

One by one, the men received their dollops of victual and tried to guess which of the oleaginous helpings was which.

Three men behind Nuzbek was Baus, who watched Leamoine with shrewdness. The convict cast the magician a backward wink. The effect was mildly amusing if not entertaining, insofar as Nuzbek back-pedaled, deliberately blocked by Zestes who engaged in an animated debate with Valere.

Baus chuckled. How was Nuzbek to survive in this pack of rogues? He was disliked by all. Furthermore, he must be put to task before he could complete his savage revenge on himself or Weavil. There was no firm way of acquiring his baton outside of—

An interesting speculation gripped him . . . how efficient it would be if Nuzbek were out of the picture, unable to retrieve his wand hidden under his bedside pillow! A scheme began to form in Baus's mind . . .

The flash of insight was cut short as Skarrow passed, berating Lopze for an act of mischief. Baus whispered the idea to Weavil who put forth a cry of alarm: "The plan reeks of peril. Why put me at risk?"

"You are the tinier of us." He bunted Weavil ahead and put a mouth to his ear, "remember, this plan is sound. When Nuzbek is least prepared, you do your business!"

Dancing with reservation, Weavil pussyfooted down the lunch line. All was benign. Neither Nuzbek, Dighcan, Zestes or Valere were aware he was alive—he was so tiny as to be a leg ornament. The plan seemed intrinsic enough, but with the hint of a skull-bashing.

Charily, Weavil snuck under Valere's legs, then crept past Zestes' fish-smelling thighs. He eased over to Nuzbek to halt before Dighcan, grimacing as he inspected his backside. It was large and vulnerable. Straining for its tenderest cheek, Weavil bestowed Dighcan a jarring squeeze before flying back to his spot.

Dighcan whirled about with a face of a drake's. He glared at Nuzbek with rancour who was immediately behind, and roared, "You hypocritical dog! How dare you coddle my rump after berating Leamoine for similar activity?"

Nuzbek flashed Dighcan a scathing leer. "Speak in more understandable tones, not the gibberish of low-class folk."

"You insolent swine—" Dighcan flung himself forward and stung the magician a backhand blow to the teeth. Nuzbek reeled over in anguish. Dighcan was on him and crunched Nuzbek's top hat over his ears and began twirling him about while hoofing him in the butt and loins. The magician recalled a similar exercise from an earlier time, judging by the daft expression on his face.

Zestes staggered out of line, crying, "Hey, Dighcan, why hog all the fun? Little Nuzbeka needs a lift!" He upended his boot into Nuzbek's gut, lifting him a good two inches off the ground.

Dighcan chirped and repeated the process along lines of a slight variation. "You do have a flair, Zestes. But those workboots of yours are a tad harsh." He gave Nuzbek a laughing twirl.

Zestes cautioned Dighcan: "Careful does it! It smacks of inconvenience to block my angle while twirling Nuzbek!"

Nuzbek cursed, thrashing, unable to see anything in front of his nose. A lucky swipe caught Dighcan on the lips, prompting Dighcan to stab down his fist. Immediately Nuzbek fell to the ground whereby Dighcan plunged his entire weight on top of him like a barrel. There was a fierce rolling like two stray bullies from Angler's Row, each struggling for an advantage, while Nuzbek received the shorter end of the stick.

The convicts abandoned their meals, gathering around the fight, hollering and cheering for his favourite.

"You teach him, Diggy!" encouraged Valere.

"Yeah, teach him a thing or two about gropings!" implored Lopze.

Paltuik bent low, gripping his knees. "Ouch, that was a fine tummy tap, Nuzbag! Bully for you! Keep up the good spirit."

Cognizing a disturbance from the office, Graves came running forth with his snapperwhip cracking. He forced his way through the heated circle and whipped the grimacing prisoners to submission. "Enough of this tomfoolery! What goes on? You know I permit no hooliganery in my yard!"

Dighcan rose, puffing froth from his blood-smeared face. He expressed his concerns on woozy feet with a haughty attitude while he wiped his mouth of blood. "Nuzbek has instigated a gross indecency upon my person."

"Untrue!" Nuzbek rolled back, foaming at the mouth. "I thoroughly deny any such allegation!"

Graves lifted his eyes to the sky. He ignored Nuzbek's protests. "Oaf! What twisted pleasures have you been dipping into now?" He turned Nuzbek an intolerant sneer. "Your just dessert. Ten demerit points."

Nuzbek tottered to his feet. "What do you mean, ten?"

"You heard me."

"I am being penalized for unjust cause!"

"You are being penalized for instigating pugilism in my yard."

"Hogwash! Do you accuse me?" The rogue stamped a foot. "This blackguard tottering before you is a prevaricating liar. He fibs for no reason—outside of the pure joy of creating grief for me. Are you kid-blind to such duffers, Graves, to believe in his nonsensical poppycock!"

Graves grated his teeth unpleasantly. "An additional double demerit, Nuzbek, for vituperations, which pitches you to a three day confinement in the hive."

Nuzbek uttered an inhuman croak. "I hardly call 'kid-blind' a 'vituperation'."

Graves tapped a finger to his palm. "A repetition of slander. Another demerit. Your ears are indeed in need of a waxing. *Item 2: prisoners are expected to remain politely attentive to prison officials*—I would not adjudge 'kid-blind' as language outside this injunction."

Weavil piped up loudly: "I believe the exact wording is *'Prisoners are expected to remain civil and attentive to prison officials with politeness being an asset'*."

Graves nodded. "I suspect this is the exact wording."

Baus confirmed the rendering but then added that in no way did the Captain's briefer description undermine the dictate's fundamental essence.

"Curb the tiresome mewlings!" shrieked Nuzbek. "Can a man not expect a little justice when he is—"

Dighcan thumped him soundly on the crown.

Graves interrupted the crass exhibition. "Very good, Dighcan. You too are awarded ten demerits!"

"But—this is a gross overkill—"

"I agree!" Graves shrugged, waved an incriminating finger at Dighcan. "Save your energy for the beehive—with Nuzbek."

"Absolutely impossible!" cried Dighcan. "I'll not endure gropings and molestation in such close quarters." He leaned forward and jumped on the balls of his feet like an obstinate schoolboy. "The idea is deplorable! In the yard I have Zestes to watch my back, keeping an eye out for dandies like Nuzbek and Leamoine."

Zestes shoved his hatchet face into Dighcan's and gave a soothing belch of acknowledgment.

Dighcan roiled with disgust.

Graves justified his decision by adding additional mollifying communal qualms. "Nuzbek recognizes the penalties for various abasements, such as touchy-feelies and opportunistic groping and he shall have other tasks to absorb himself with while confined in the hive— such is my statement."

Paltuik rocked back with merriment. His round face showed a gratified grin as Skarrow and Mulfax hauled Dighcan and Nuzbek to the shade of the spindlefax overhanging the south wall. All eyes turned to the solitary confinement as the company watched in amazement. Baus noticed that the hive supported a small wooden door, a thick portal, a foot in diameter, fortified with iron straps. The construction was six feet high, a yellow mortared dome, like some giant beehive. It was set about mid way along the southern wall of the compound's wildest side. The interior was black, quiet as night. The guards thrust Dighcan and Nuzbek inside then drew back the bolts and left the two incarcerated until such time as their sentence was up.

The prisoners who had followed watched in morbid curiosity. Baus marvelled that a curious wegmor statue stood cryptically poised in the dome's shadow. It was fashioned of wood, painted in casque silver. Neither able to move nor rock, the saddle was a black brace of beobar, seating three men. Three men could sit with weights strapped to their legs—each seated for lengthy periods, learning humility with pain. Nuzbek, it seemed, was plunging very close to a saddling on the instrument, what with all the heavy yelling and blind cursing streaming through the door.

Satisfied with the outcome, Baus gave his shoulders a shrug and turned back to the refectory. Congratulating Weavil on the success of his exploits, he discovered his comrade quick to accept the praise.

At the lunch table, the two joined in merry song. A general enthusiasm infused their company. Weavil, enlivened for the first time in many days, went so far as to compose a small ode—of how a magician named 'Kosbag' caught with his hand in the honey pot, was sentenced to a tarring and feathering by king Gravioli, followed by an exile. Lopze took up the refrain with enthusiasm. He was so taken with the verse that he stood up on his chair, exhorting people to join in. Graves ordered the antic arrested—a sudden slippage on Lopze's part might entail one less spare hand to aid on the work program.

* * *

With the absence of Dighcan and Nuzbek from the gang, the yardwork resumed in full rigor and at a slightly more ponderous rate. Zestes and Boulm continued to haul drays to and from the compound without Nuzbek's assistance; Tustok and Leamoine fish-slitted and hacked without Dighcan, while Baus and Weavil sifted squirming fish with lighter hearts.

For the remainder of the day, Baus invested his faculties on a daring plan. Favourable opportunities existed in the cosmos as a result of Nuzbek's absence, particularly on his ability to recover his baton. There remained the displaced stone on the wall. The rock was an entity of stubbornness that would not budge despite his most aggressive thrusts. To pry such a rock from the wall would require a tool.

The hour of Flanks was approaching and Baus held no bander. He must win Zestes' belt buckle in order to dislodge the stone! The affair involved a circular logic that posed frustrating conundrums. He flung his fistful of golgonfish to the ground, leaving a rancorous taint in the air.

During the interlude, Weavil had happened to probe the depths of his pantaloons for a hankie and felt something warm to touch: a vial of Xalee's 'Zizzazz'—also known as 'Herb of Best Desire'. He chuckled and muttered smug surprise. When Baus learned of the vial, he demanded from Weavil the item immediately.

Weavil obdurately clamped the tiny vial to his chest. "Never! Find your own bander. Once I leave this filthy precinct, I plan to sequester myself with a comely woman to relax my jangled nerves. The maid must be given to considerable affection, and upon whom I can visit my affections without handicap, snags or wrinkles. It follows that I will require an elixir of strength to bridge this gap of reduced stature."

Baus nodded sympathetically. "I commend the logic, Weavil; however, the scheme is inept in all its phases. You are tediously whimsical! For all we know, we may be stuck here forever! What good is that?"

Weavil's fury became overstamped by Baus's ceremonial sweep of arm. "In the meantime, do you wish to look the fool, truckling to his ministrations, should he accidentally acquire the potion? He is a daisy, and one with no small imagination. An incidental point: the elixir was given to me, not you."

"The observation is taken out of context," observed Weavil curtly. "Recall that you rescinded ownership of the essence at the fair and under no circumstance shall I part with it as long as I remain lucid. Now, the answer to your demand is 'no' and I need not repeat how you forfeited my uncle's timepiece without my permission."

Baus made a gesture of impatience. "That was an isolated occurrence, governed by misguidance on my part."

"And so? What of the other losses you've incurred?"

"Ignore those. I have alternate plans for us—which include, escape and revenge. Now please, Weavil . . . tender me the elixir!"

Weavil tottered back in mulish hauteur, at which point Baus began grappling him in an awkward tussle. Zestes abandoned his barrow and pitched an irate yell. "Listen, you wiftbags! Sift slime or cut snogmald! Why should I toil while you jape about like Mug and Moe?"

Baus gave a conciliatory wave. Leamoine and Tustok lifted both their heads from their clam-gutting and voiced their own scorn. Baus and Weavil huddled guiltily around the fish pile while Tustok gave a flippant condemnation, "We've a job to do before six, or there'll be no dinner. Graves gets rubbernecked when his fish aren't cleaned!"

Weavil remained uncompliant; Baus tore the vial from Weavil's fingers. "You see what you've caused? Patience, Tustok! I was in the midst of repairing Weavil's button on his soiled vest. I have been hard-pressed to keep him properly attired in all this kerfuffle!"

Weavil choked on the pleasantry. Baus congratulated himself. He sang a stanza of '*How the Seaside shimmers when the new Year brings balm*' while Weavil fumed. The afternoon passed; Baus did not relinquish his hold on the item.

Skarrow prowled the yard a Flank's thrust away. Ever vigilant after the theft of the jars, he surveyed the prisoners' lethargic slime-sifting with suspicion. Twenty drays later of snogmald and eelfish, he came back merrily to collect the knives.

Dinner came; Flanks was next. With Dighcan omitted from play, there was a certain lack of flamboyance to the game: there was no referee, no formal rules of the play. The unconstrained atmosphere turned to a rampant crass fever. Baus took advantage of the mood, precipitating Zestes into losing his belt.

Baus took possession of the item but Zestes contested Baus's throw. He put forth appeals. Witnesses vouched for the legitimacy of the throw and Baus kept his prize despite Zestes' continued complaints that the toss had 'illegally been lodged'. Baus buckled on Zestes' belt and placidly sat out for the next three rounds. The behaviour caused a stir, but when the browbeating and upbraiding died, all were happy that Nuzbek's sabbatical was long enough to reduce their losses.

VII

That night, so keen was Baus on acquiring Nuzbek's wand that he almost gave himself away. At half past midnight, he stood grinning like a goat before Lopze and Zestes' dozing forms. The twain seemed to have absorbed Nuzbek's vacated space like hungry snogmald.

Finger to lip, he hitched himself closer. Groping carefully between the bedmates he obtained the talisman, finding it exactly where Nuzbek left it. Baus's lips parted in triumph: the baton slipped smooth as glass from Nuzbek's flea-infested pillow.

Exhaling softly, Baus stepped away from the slats, creeping back to his bed. Examining his prize, he found it ornately wrought, black as jet, comprised of a stiff shaft of wegmor horn tiled with inlays of silver near the tip, slightly tapered.

Valere and Weavil drowsed to either side of him. The seaman's mouth hung half open while Weavil grimaced on each breath. Baus debated whether to wake the poet, but decided not to—a better idea struck him.

He touched the tip of the wand to Weavil's nose and awaited results. Abruptly the large head lay frozen, while the chest neither heaved nor the mouth suspired. Weavil's lips looked like two cold strips of elastic, dull as spoons. The restless tossing had ceased, as if the poet were dead.

Baus gave a contented grunt, convinced now of the cogency of the baton. It seemed laughable that a fleeting fear had nagged him or that he would not be able to wield the curio.

At the other side of the room, Baus saw the prisoners dozing in synchrony. A fugitive thought crossed his mind: should he acquire Nuzbek's cape which lay underneath Zestes' hip?

The impulse faded. Of what use was a dysfunctional scrap of canvas without magic?

Baus peered carefully out of the barred window. Dighcan snored like a babe under the sill. Mulfax stood facing the door, grasping at his pike, ever on the alert.

Baus pulled himself back carefully from the window and reviewed his options. The barracks' lock had remained ever unrepaired since Nuzbek had jimmied it; perhaps that fact alone caused Mulfax consternation, and his suspicion.

A sturdy bolt had been drawn edgewise across the jamb, a situation which posed significant dilemmas to Baus's program. How could he exit? For a long while he crouched pensively in the gloom, waiting for an answer to come.

Suddenly as if by mischance, a figure emerged from the darkness—Vibellhanz, stumbling his way from bed to latrine. He was ambling toward the far side of the chamber. Baus became alert of the hazard of the situation, nor was he ignorant of the prospect of a lummox fouling his scheme. Four feet away, the convict passed obliviously, like a dazed sleepwalker. If the haggard convict had seen him crouching by the door, he did not show it.

Mulfax finally grew fatigued and plopped himself down on the veranda steps. The bolt was closest to Paltuik's cot. It could not be reached by Dighcan's sweat-smelling body.

Cautiously Baus crept onto the edges of Paltuik's bed. He balanced on his knees to poise on the window sill. He was pleased to note the fact that Mulfax's back was trained to the door. Reaching through the window, he could just grasp the iron bolt without disturbing the volatile Paltuik who lay comatose face down on his pallet.

With greatest care Baus lifted the bar from its hinge. A tiny scrape. He pulled himself back into the dark chamber and crept crab-like to the door, tugging it inward like a thief. Any louder sound would be a dead giveaway. He slipped through the gap like a wraith, creeping up behind Mulfax who remained unaware of his presence. A small, well-placed jab and the idiot would be standing immobile . . .

Baus gave him a light tap on the elbow. Oddly, the guard only swatted at his arm is if bitten by a mosquito.

Baus shrank back. Why was Mulfax still moving?

Baus became rigid. Moments ago, he had frozen Weavil with the merest tap—

He pitched his mouth into a grimace. Of course! The rod must apply itself to an exposed area of flesh. It could not work otherwise, namely through clothing.

Baus nipped forth, aiming the rod to the back of Mulfax's head.

The sentryman's flesh became one with stone—the totality of paralysis was complete, reduced him to a lifeless mannequin.

Baus resisted the urge to prod Mulfax. That mistake had already been committed by less thoughtful peers. A test could only prove unproductive, as only too vividly exemplified by Germakk who had awoken his fellow guardsman by pokes of surprise.

Baus stepped down from the veranda, pleased at his progress. The silver moon shone with force to detail withered shrubs, parched gorse, ghostly sand. He calculated that twenty minutes remained before a return visit was necessary to secure Mulfax—enough time to remove the dislocated stone from the east wall. Perhaps a foolish endeavour—only Weavil could squeeze through the orifice and escape. Yet was it worth a try? Still, a wandering guard might spy the loosened masonry and expose his plan.

No—escape by the eastern wall was an all or nothing affair.

Then how was he to escape?

Baus cursed himself for his vacillation. He had not meditated enough on this important fact. Where could he go? Reconnoitre the south wall? Scale the portcullis? Chancy! He daren't sidle too close to the watchtower for fear of Oppet's indomitable hounds or Skarrow's detection.

Baus sank to his haunches; his heart beat with frustration. The temperature had plummeted significantly, leaving the air dry and a frosty patina settling on the ground. Ruefully Baus put his attention on Nuzbek and his cursed umbrella-based conveyance. How convenient it would be to command that vehicle! But he had no magic by which to command. The pyramid remained cached somewhere on Nuzbek's person—in the murk where he traded jests with Dighcan.

Baus fidgeted. Perhaps a clue lay along the northern wall. The idea was evocative.

With a careless grunt, he scrambled to his feet and loped gingerly out in the frost-dusted terrain.

The plaintive call of a coyote drifted over the wall. Its effect was like a sharp lamentation on the lonely silence. Looking up into the star-jewelled sky, he saw the northern rampart rising intolerably high; the beobar loomed as a satin curtain; the foliage was monstrously frost-dusted in higher, swarthier ranks. No rope or ladder was long enough to access those twining boughs tucked in knots and clusters below the highest plumes. Aside from a few vagrant breezes, all was still.

Baus strained eyes upon the turf, the place where Nuzbek had buried the jars. Four equally-sized vessels were interred underfoot, each with its own eccentric and desperate occupant.

Baus caught himself wondering: why were they so dangerous? The creatures held allure —but did they house magic? If so, an idea flashed in his mind . . . would it hurt so much to unearth one of the inhabitants and check if he/she sheltered enchanted items? The risk was large, but the rewards were great.

Baus bit fretfully at his nail. Perhaps five minutes had elapsed since his last stunning. He must not waste time. The possibility of one of the unearthed things leaping at his throat in a bout of madness . . . it was not negligible . . . but then again, speculations of this sort were only presumptions.

Dropping to his knees, he began to claw furiously at the turf. One inch . . . two inches. His nails suddenly scratched at hard metal.

He spread away the sand. A tantalum-coloured lid gleamed in the moonlight. The metal was cold, hardly graspable, but it was inviting. Some effort would be required to dislodge the cylinder from the ground, but another thought: better to let the glass rest in the earth in the event he had to cover it up quickly.

Baus cranked the lid around. It erupted in a grating creak—an action which made him wince and required the use of his full force.

The lid snapped ajar. Tock! A strange pressurized pop like water gurgling from a snail's shell. Out came a hissing gloop of musty airs, like a preserve of ancient pickles.

Baus inched his way back, amazed. Bubbles formed on the liquid's surface, popping and breaking like sea spume. A green cap surfaced, plumed with white feathers. A small clothed head poked its way up and Baus heard a dolorous sigh. A set of hazel eyes blinked, twinkled like soft, glowing jewels. The mouth opened, showing a fine set of polished teeth. The figure rasped:

"Who are you? Why is it so dark?" The silky-beige locks were plastered wetly against the pale, raw-boned cheeks.

Baus scrambled back in shock. The figure had uttered words. Logically, this meant he or 'it' was still alive.

Baus finally found his voice: "Is it nightfall, or am I dreaming? You are in Heagram prison. A leprechaun? —a sprite? I am Baus of Heagram—alive, but how can you still be alive after so much internment?"

The figure arched his way forth with a fractured croak. He shook his head with contempt. "What do you mean, who am I, villain? Who in the devil are you? I am Trimestrius the Third... Third Descendant of the House of Witherwell of Desenion. Can you not see the pedigree embroidered on my vest?" He thrust out his chest, which displayed a faded, triple-ruffed, stylish green doublet on which he looked down in amazement to find himself plunged in a foul liquid that was half buried in sand.

His brows knitted in confusion. "What? I am soaked in brine and encircled in glass! This is unsatisfactory!—my own voice seems strange to my ears! As if I haven't talked in an age. Hellfire and damnation! Has it been that long since I harboured voice or memory?"

Green eyes flashed upon Baus with suspicion; the midget pinched his face into a dark mask, curling lips back in bewilderment. The realization of his own miniatureness had plunged him into a catalepsy. He flung out his rapier, gleaming sullenly in the moonlight.

"Heagram, you say, eh knave?" Flourishing his weapon, he stabbed out at Baus with reckless force. "Where in the name of Hellspot is that? No dissembling either, you uncouth rogue, or I tickle you with my bodkin, which is magical and as you see is plainly what I call Lolispar."

Baus forced himself a reply of friendly wonder: "Heagram is on the northern shores of Bindar—past Tavilnook and Brimhaven."

The figure did not seem to recognize the names. Idly, he frowned, pulling at his ear. "Are they far from Aurenham?"

Baus frowned. "Where is that?"

The newcomer ignored him. "Where is Voduspur, my valet, and why am I not at Desenion in my chamber?"

Baus shook his head in perplexity. "These names mean nothing to me."

"Do they?" The little green-garbed dwarf's astonishment was considerable. "You don't know Desenion—or Aurenham?. . . The emerald keep of the Magistrar? The three ancient turrets? Ridiculous!" The dwarf leaped out of his jar, stumbling toward Baus with awkward speed—an action conceivably remarkable for one who had been entombed for a great length. His drenched doublet was plastered to his skin, the hose no less tight; the figure underneath was sleek, and a well-shaped man of youthful bearing and impassioned temperament. The offensive liquid that dripped from his garments reeked of musselwort and vinegar, and not surprisingly, the frame he bore seemed to rock with a strange paroxysm threatening to twist him from inside out.

Baus hastened back. The incident smacked of weirdness. He could only conjecture what Nuzbek's spell had done to the poor creature.

"I remember!" shrilled the homunculus. "Oh, for the love of Galaspar!" His swollen face was ashen; he seemed stricken with a grief and loss beyond parallel. "My place of ancestry! Beloved Desenion!" He threw his hands over his eyes and emitted a plangent cry that flew into the night, distressing Baus to the extreme.

"It was on Saelsmir moor! In the light of the afternoon haze—on an ill fate set against me—in the form of the *Huarbane*."

Baus expressed perplexity but the little man persisted. "The crafty, murderous Huarbane —sent by Aurimag! A Lolarpian horror, hatched from a chicken egg of evil —a creature of myth; it would strike terror into anyone's heart, let alone the bravest knight!"

Baus expressed sympathy at the irregularity.

Trimestrius bristled at the condolence. "Picture it! Standing chest high, guarding four wood-block stumps of legs—a thing of ears, fangs and talons, a poison mat of dirty brown, furred and horrible to behold—and these, the best of its qualities!"

A quivering palsy had come over the little man. "Just to peer at the thing was an exercise of revulsion! It came to smite me, take my castle! Aurimag bred it himself!"

"Aurimag?"

"Dissolute Aurimag, yes! The neomancer from the dark cave, the Cave of Passions and Puissances—Aurimag who called himself, 'Gayire'—'The Golden One'—that, in the old Lengish tongue. What a joke that was—a blasphemy! 'Tis a sick sacrilege that the knave still lives! I had only to mount my wegmor and be taken away by the beast, but I chose to stay and fight—fight for my demesne! Weapon at hand, I slashed out, but the Huarbane bit into my wegmor's neck and blood corded in three directions. My brave steed fell while I was afoot only with my rapier and wits to guard against the fiend and the malevolence."

"Disturbing luck."

"Silence! The monster rushed at me on all fours—with hot breath upon my visage, its thorny bulk a mass of twisted muscle. I retreated, but it pounced, bringing talons from upon high. I ducked—and while the thing poised like death's nightmare, gleaming silver, I raked Lolispar across its guts in a moment of cold triumph. I spilled liver and organs and putrid things best not described across the glade. Ensorcelled from Loespring pool with Telulric magic it was by Faeta, the long dead Arch-Neon and wood nymph of the Nderian hills. I was about to deal the creature its demise when a mouldy net was strewn over my head; I was hemmed in from all sides, by cutthroats who beat me with cudgels and called me foppish names in crude, thuggish voices. They taunted my manliness. Lolispar slipped from my grasp; I could no more cut the strands that held me than cry for help. I would have carved that troupe of craven lilybellies from limb to limb but—" He paused to take in some air, and with grave disgust gathered his wits. "There were four of these vile foes in the brigand band and they seized my gladius and threatened my fair body—all an unspeakable nightmare. How I would dress them with agonies worse than Montgrainz, the Demon Crow if I could enact it all over again!"

The quivering figure gave a rueful exhalation; painful recollection debilitated him. "I realize that the beast was only a ruse posed by Aurimag to ensnare me as I was hauled into that mouldy net and back to the Brauvn forest. I was tormented by those grinning, leering faces—a drama which I shall never forget!"

Baus addressed Trimestrius with solemn concern: "A sorry predicament. Now, as to this business about the creature . . . alas, I jump . . . and yet you are alive, friend, which brings me to profess to puzzlement—how came you to be immured in this jar?"

Trimestrius's eyes flashed with bitter, insensate hate. "It was Aurimag—he performed his most depraved deed on my person to date. A mage, as I have adumbrated—but he was a mad mage—full of reptilian conceit and the most diseased of schemes. In exchange for auguries and divinations, I traded with him spices, wines, enchanted perfumes, even narcotics, incenses, essences and unguents acquired on my travels to the southern realms of Karsh and Sloe. I had come to gather some knowledge of the wretch, though I dreaded visiting his lair couched gloomily alongside the Lim river. Others were set against him—Sangdorn, head of the Mismerion Circle, now deceased, and his sympathizers: Ulisa the Utilitarian, Woisper the Wilful, Salmeister the Saturnine, Barbirius the Bellicose, Nojoar the Nourisher—to name a few. Aurimag was especially enraged when those of the Circle denied him entry into the Synode of 'Eleven'. Old Cascnus, the Theosopher, had died, leaving a small space for another amongst the neomancers. Aurimag believed he was the next in line to walk amongst their ranks.

"Yes! It is all coming back to me." Trimestrius's voice trailed off. A sad, empty hollowness played on his features; his expression mirrored memories of confusion and despair.

Baus considered the dwarf's animated monologue a threat to his fragile situation and made a sudden gesture.

Trimestrius skidded lugubriously away. Baus could not snatch him as he stabbed idly at the soft turf with his blade. "Alas—those days are all a blur in my mind—but as for the open position at Mismerion, I remember there were contenders present, and that Aurimag expected to win the round with ease with his newly acquired thaumaturgics. After his audition to the Circle at Mismerion—it was on the 11th of May—I was sent on a pressing errand, to pass a certain scroll to him. I was merely a peacekeeper, nothing more. I delivered the scroll, a deed which the Circle had invested upon me, abiding a trust which I was owing to them. Upon reading the parchment, Aurimag became stiff with resentment and so utterly dismayed that he seemed ready to commit murder upon me. It was evident he believed I was in cahoots with the Eleven—can you believe it? What could I have had to do with them?—fortunately I escaped the cave, for I knew the woods in all directions. All the mossy dells, the tanglewoods, brooks and brakes, spanglewoods and rills, all in the district of Desenion. When Aurimag's reason was compromised, he was pitched into a mood of rancour that aroused vengeance on any creature, living or dead. Too late he sent his spectral minions out to shadow me!—insectoid cynersyks, cautervosps, creatures with green and vermilion chitin, and their cousins—great blue bottleflies with pods and protrusions on their bodies that can scoop up a quarry like a mantis. They were huge and they passed my precarious hiding place tucked in the hollow of a maboar stump."

Baus glanced furtively toward the barracks. He gave his head a fretful shake. "This is growing interesting, but with each disclosure, Trimestrius, your tale grows ever more implausible. Who is Aurimag? How does any of this relate to your erstwhile entombment?"

"Ah! That is the question." A sad cluck came from the midget's mouth. He threw a backward glance to the site of his once prison and his eyes glowered with hate. "This glass cage—how the smiting memory of it brings me tears and to my tale's end! Somewhere, between the time of Aurimag's audition at the Hall and my confrontation with the Huarbane, some manner of treachery had been played on him. Something to do with his powers, something so dire to his spiritual essence and his dearest ambitions that he thought me his worst enemy. To this day I know not what brought the rogue to this conclusion, other than that perhaps I was the messenger of this untoward news. Only then do I remember, that in my three-day confinement in his forest cave by the Lim, racked by torture instruments—and interned in agonizing silence and ignorance, I felt a great rush of water, a sudden roaring in my ears—many queer sensations as nauseating as sulphur, as spell-ridden paste was splashed over my body."

Baus recalled the perfervid incident involving Weavil in Nuzbek's tent and wondered if it were similar. He only vocalized a smiling, offhand acknowledgment.

Trimestrius's ears perked at the comment and he agreed. "The final day Aurimag put to me a spate of questions about the 'Oblong', or some weird talisman, and its source—a thing of mindless unreason, a strange, fractured prism or pyramid that would strip men of their minds and mental powers—something that he seemed in the past to have come into contact with. I was totally without understanding as to the device or its perfidious nature and its relevance to my predicament. He claimed that I was a traitor, that with my associates of the Circle, I had spied on him, committed treachery so vile as to be punishable by death. To this, I could only claim ignorance. No solace could I offer this wicked blackguard on the subject of the 'Oblong' or the neomancer's wretched dark hate for the entirety of the Circle.

"Out of my mind's eye, I suddenly remember spying snatches of an ungainly apparatus cached in the backdrops of his cave. The grotto was hidden below the dark roots of the great phantom elm—tubes, luminous rods, dials, beakers, flasks, vials, funnels—a maze entwined and conjoined, bearing multiple fluids and arcane unguents and oils and bubbling slimes of greenish-brown filth. Vapours, stenches and miasmas—they all filled me with a great dread and contaminated that fetid space during the endless decanting and distilling, always frothing and bubbling alongside the unsettling whines of engines, gears and pulleys which spun and turned their power—all for some haunted purpose. A huge arcane disk pulsed luridly in the air, floating and twirling on high above all the pots and beakers—like a flattened saucer from hell, blindingly yellow. It marked the fuel and source of the great engine that was Aurimag's part alchemic, part mechanical apparatus, but whose soul seemed driven by litanies and forces born centuries earlier and that came whispering mystically from his bloodless lips. Of that oleaginous liquid that he spread on my skin, I knew nothing, except that when I was shrinking, I knew it would be some agent that promised midgetness for an eternity. My body oozed strength; my limbs slackened like dough. I felt like a water bladder that becomes suddenly deflated by the prick of a knife. My body sagged, it become an empty vessel! I felt my gladius thrust in my hand before me. I was imprisoned in one of Aurimag's ghastly spheres, entombed in a vile liquid in which I am still drenched, but which somehow kept me alive . . ."

Baus mused. "The yarn is most odd."

"Odd? You call it odd? I call it scandalous! Do not mock me, rascal!" His tone became sharply unpleasant.

"I do not mock you," Baus said in a voice of easy assurance. "It is merely *odd* you should mention the word 'neomancers' in your lengthy story."

"Why is it odd?" Trimestrius demanded, his thin-edged blade circling up to Baus's ribs.

"Enough of your pricks and barbs!" Baus cried, leaping back with rancour. "I only meant to say that there is a magician here who dwells on these premises who calls himself a 'neomancer', or something like it—so at least the slip came from his lips."

Trimestrius's eyes blazed. "Describe this magician!"

"A tall willowy man, skinny legs, a long back-sloping brow, narrow cheeks, black hair, a love for black hats . . ."

"It couldn't be . . ." The dwarf flourished his rapier close to Baus's privates. "The eyes! Describe the eyes!"

"Beady! Beady, like a snake's, set together craftily like a rodent's, amber not brown."

"And the nose?" urged Trimestrius.

"Pug and round!—like a small ape's. The lips are thin and white. The disposition is pompous as a wegmor in heat. What more do you want?" Baus cursed. "Shall I proceed to describe his toilette? Look, the hour is late!—I wish to return to my dormitory."

Trimestrius sank to the ground with moaning anguish. His face was a wet grey cloud and looked as if he had been struck a blow. "It is he!" He clutched at his hair as if seized with a vertigo. "I shall carve out his gizzard, feed it to him in cups of broth of his own urine!" He jumped up, poked the rapier's needle deeper into Baus's belly. "Where is this inhuman rogue?"

Baus blinked. "Yonder in the hive along the south wall. Is this all you wish of me? The rogue's name is Nuzbek."

"Nuzbek, eh? We shall go and visit this 'Nuzbek'." The dwarf crowed with delight.

Baus sniffed uncomfortably at the thought. "I don't advise the act. The villain is securely kept, but hardly the monster-mongering death-bringer you describe."

"We shall see!" Trimestrius cried with fury. Rubbing his damp locks with obsession, he demanded: "Can it be so easy to slay the louse who delivered me so much misery? Yes! If luck holds, then I must truly be a man blessed!"

"It is still an ill idea."

"Master Baus, hold your tongue."

"Snauzzerhounds haunt the hither side of the wall," persisted Baus. "They cognize intrusion at the drop of a pin and shall wake the entire compound." He motioned to the watchtower. "Look. Over there stands Skarrow guarding the tower as you see to the south. The sentry Mulfax stands aside the dormitory. Soon the lookout will rouse himself from his spell of immobilization and descend on us with snapperwhip and poison dagger. Better to climb back into the bottle where I can cache you and recover you at a later time."

Trimestrius laughed at the idea. "You are an amusing fellow, Baus. Suffice it to say that I shall not follow these instructions. So where does that leave us? Well! I suppose we must see about these rare hounds, won't we?" He piked a jewelled finger into the air. "Trimestrius, Prince of the Third Realm shall not to be deterred by a few mangy curs or drunken watchmen!"

Baus sought delicately to dampen the volume of the green-robed man's boasts. "Do not tempt me. Hush now! I shall leave you to your deeds whilst I repair to my pallet."

"Nothing doing!" railed the nobleman. "I have plans for you." He blocked the way and brandished his sword. "You are a likeable sort, Baus, so let us keep it that way. We have destinations in common—amongst other important missions. Speaking of which, what business have you in this bleak compound? I have prattled on for a fortnight while you have barely tweedled a note from time to time."

"I am currently on the lookout for means to escape this 'compound'. If you regard, we are surrounded by four very insurmountable walls."

"So what?"

"It seems that a mutual enemy has been responsible for our incarcerations and I point out that this 'enemy' is at least yours, and has buried more of your colleagues at our feet."

Trimestrius's eyes flashed on Baus with unpleasant emotion. "You say there are others like me interred under the earth?"

"I do. I thought to uncover at least one of them, namely you, and search for magical items or puissances that might be employed in securing an avenue for my freedom, but I was interrupted, as you can see. Modulate your tone! Skarrow guards with sharp ears."

"I grow weary of this 'Skarrow'." He skipped about with lips knitted in displeasure. "He can fly down from his perch if he likes, but I shall disembowel him if he annoys me. Now what about these 'others' in these jars?"

Baus refused to shed light on the mystery until Trimestrius had quieted down, at which point Trimestrius put two fingers in his mouth and loosed a loud whistle.

Wincing with exasperation, Baus snatched at the midget's fingers, but Trimestrius clicked his heels and strutted about in a very wide circle, smirking and hoisting his sword in time with his marching.

Baus fixed his lips into a distasteful grimace. It seemed matters were worsening. Skarrow was on the brink of sensing disturbance and Mulfax, of reviving from his stupor and delivering woe. His well-formed plans would be for naught.

Baus took a deep breath; he leaped backward toward Trimestrius's hole. Trimestrius came resentfully after him, the wandering blade questing for Baus's navel.

A sudden inflexible cry rang through the air.

Mulfax's! Almost as suspiciously, there followed a distant rumble of thunder drifting from the seaward direction.

Trimestrius spun short, surprised by the disparate sounds. Distracted as he seemed, he did not perceive Baus reach for Nuzbek's baton and touch his damp cheek.

The dagger tumbled from Trimestrius's grasp. The dwarf stood immobilized. His head was half turned in a perplexed grimace.

Quickly Baus hefted the irritant back into the jar. The touch released the spell and the dwarf began to squirm again in passion.

Baus ignored the dwarf's struggles and replied with blows. "Carefully there, pest! Into your shell." A fierce knock on the crown thrust the plumed troublemaker down into the foul brine. The lid clasped shut and Baus gave it a satisfied twirl.

The pounding of boots thundered nearby.

Baus flung himself to the ground. A visceral instinct told him to wait, that capture was impending, so he groped about in confusion in the sand, his fingers grasping a sizeable pebble which he hurled toward the barracks.

The stone smacked against the side face, creating a dull thud.

The footfall halted. Baus snatched another projectile and hurled it in the same direction. It found another trunk, of the lone hazel in the center grounds and produced further tumult as it plunked down onto a shell pile.

Baus snatched a look over his shoulder. Mulfax was speeding in the new direction. The guard raised a pike, ears cocked wildly as he bounded toward the pile of clams.

Wasting no time, Baus flung sand over the hole. He seized the midget's gladius and ran helter-skelter toward the barracks. The hilt was inlaid with moon sickles, the guard like a serpent's coil. The gleaming goldness of the instrument whispered of a magical presence, which he did not resent having on his person. It seemed gifted of a hue so brilliant as to enthral the eye.

Baus shook his head; he pitched the weapon into his pouch and had only just gained the front deck and lurched into the dormitory before Skarrow staggered on site. His whip was held high and he waved a guttering torch in front of the window. He had not seen Baus, but was ready to enforce a penalty on any skulker. Cognizing sudden commotion, Skarrow pre-empted his rush. He came dashing down to the hazel tree to join his partner. Mulfax was blindly spearing clams looking for hidden escapists, but there were none. He scratched at his ears in perplexity. "Come out, you villains! I shall skewer your black hearts."

Some of the prisoners were roused by the ruckus. Upon seeing Baus's entry, they raised outcries, but he hustled quietly to his bed and threw his head under the covers. Weavil noticed him and peered at him with distaste. Baus ignored the scrutiny—for it was an emotion of disgust with which he had become used to of late.

Moments later, Mulfax burst through the door. Skarrow was on his heels, rudely slapping whip, pike and torch. Mulfax's black-beard ran down his chin with oily disgrace; Skarrow's heavy chest puffed with annoyance.

"Who comes and who goes?" Mulfax cried. "It seems there's been a pack of miscreants skittering about our yard! Well, who owns up to the violation?"

Valere grunted up from behind a pair of blurry eyes, "Pester us with your drivel at a more appropriate hour, Mulfy. You and your girlfriend can plainly see we lie cached here as snug as maybugs. Count us if you like: Zestes, Paltuik, Lopze, Yullen—"

"And surely several angels more," ribbed Zestes.

"Cease the japery!" ordered Mulfax. "A serious circumstance presents itself."

Lopze looked up with concern. "An obnoxious dabchick, or just a killer tamegendron on the loose?"

"Quiet your tongue!" growled Mulfax. "I heard human voices, not a fowl."

Leamoine's eyes blinked dreamily under the glare of the brands. In his most captivating voice, he gave a sweet complaint: "Post your inquiries to Baus, Mulfy dear. Moments earlier, we saw him loitering by the door, attempting to hide his breach of curfew."

Baus scrambled erect with a throat thick of protest: "Careful with your declarations, Leamoine! Must I be designated a blackguard, monitored and judged while I simply rushed forth to investigate an uproar?"

"Enough of this inane disputation!" rasped Skarrow, cracking his whip. Turning coldly to Mulfax, he demanded: "These whispers of intruders—wouldn't be the same perceived coming from Nuzbek's bottles on the first night, would they, Mulfax?"

"They certainly are! But those were muffles only. These were actual voices. Recall, the fleeing figures I glimpsed under the beobar!"

Skarrow made a sullen noise. "Enough laughter, mugs." The whip came careening down. "You saw for yourself. There were no intruders there, Mulfy! Not even a little whelp like Weavil could be up to mischief."

Mulfax shook his head with stubbornness. "I know what I saw! Wizardry walks amongst us in tall shadows!"

Nolpin made a keen observation. "Nuzbek tried to warn you! Now look at the evil you have stirred upon yourself. Hauntings and phantasms!"

"Shut up, you cock-eyed loon." Skarrow slashed a stinging lash on Nolpin's throat.

Zestes, who feared none of the guards or their whips, put a hand of panic to his mouth. "Oh, Mulfy, please don't hurt us. Protect us from the big bad spirits who come to tickle us in the night!"

A ruckus of laughter broke out amongst the convicts, prompting a riot.

"Shut up, you gibbering mugs!" fumed Mulfax. "On the morrow there'll be an accounting. Oh yes, a substantial one! There's a full day's work on the Brimhaven road, which I know shall occur in the rain." He gave a satisfied leer. "The wind gathers and the stormclouds brew, so enjoy your little game while you can." He turned on his heel. "Come, Skarrow!" The lockless door slammed shut; Mulfax resumed his post.

Baus heard a battery of muttered curses. The retreating tramp of Skarrow's boots pitched on in weary disgust. Baus pulled the mildewy blanket over his head and breathed strangled relief. All could have gone terribly wrong, but it hadn't. Fortune had been kind; Trimestrius had not been dealt with kindly. The prince had failed miserably to undermine his sense of cunning—Baus's smile became wistful as he felt the new gladius press warmly against his thigh.

VIII

True to Mulfax's words, rain came hard that morning, a dull downpour that promised not to abate for days. Under the supervision of Mulfax, Voin and Skarrow, the bedraggled company was hauled out toward Brimhaven by wagons two leagues down the potholed, inland road. The men were issued chisels, hammers, mattocks and rakes and commenced chipping twelve boulders lying in the ditch quarried from the seaside bluffs. Another team, leg-bound with ball and chain, gathered road-ready chips into barrows and spread them on the track. The remaining convicts were enjoined to smooth the road, so that water could drain from the side.

Baus was a member of the raking team. Significant hours of labour ensued and he paused from his task only to peer drearily up into the rain. The umber-stained surroundings disappeared into grey wash of forest; the road wound raggedly away into brush. The sea spread to the east, barely a lime-blue mist. Huddles of cobweb spindlefax stood shivering northward in dispirited droves.

The wagon passed several country crofts: mostly hay, and wegmor-pasture. It had been a long journey and Baus had seen many byres pass, most with red paint peeling at the edges. Sagging roofs were set back amidst spindlefax bowed at the edges of their capacity. He had seen the rat-eaten track at perhaps its worst in this desolate quarter. Not a soul was in sight, save two sopping caravans mastered by drivers whose faces mirrored the afternoon dreariness.

The day dragged onwards. Cool rain thudded hard into the evening; Flanks was cancelled. The men huddled disconsolately around the lamplit table in the dormitory, trading grunts while the rain continued to drum morosely on the roof. Baus lay slouched in his pallet; nor was Weavil inclined to participate in the gaming. Half-bantering mutters remained all to be heard. Baus was concerned about how he was to effect an escape before Nuzbek's return from solitary. Trimestrius's gladius had been acquired—whose cutting power and golden effulgence was something of marvel, but the risk of using it against the guards outweighed any reward. With moody anguish, Baus abandoned schemes of unearthing the jars and dredging out more curios.

He humoured himself knowing that he had escaped Trimestrius's fate. Under no circumstances must he fall prey to such vicissitude as the little heir to Desenion had . . .

Baus's reverie was interrupted by shouts coming from the beehive. The prisoners swarmed to the window; they saw lambent flashes, flickers and glows—it seemed a remarkable battle was transpiring in the hive. As to who was winning or losing, it was difficult to determine, though someone had gained control of the environs—or more specifically—the glow pyramid.

* * *

The following day proceeded in fashion much similar to the last. Skarrow tramped to the hive to liberate Dighcan and Nuzbek, following which, the recently-released joined the road gang like the others. The inmates reacted tetchily to the rain; Dighcan and Nuzbek remained uncommunicative; neither was in the mood to offer anecdotes or memoirs about their incarceration; nor did anyone ply them for details. Dighcan seemed more frowningly taciturn, with his head a degree larger and redder, even rounder, to Baus's memory, while Nuzbek seemed pasty-faced and gaunt, guarding near-blackened eyes and bruises that were not unnoticeable. Dighcan had never achieved complete success in taming his cellmate's glow-pyramid antics.

Drizzle accompanied the workers on the extended labours. Graves surprised all by riding in on his fat, pointy-horned wegmor and came to oversee the operation. His primary purpose was to stimulate the prisoners to maximum industry, and secondly, to debrief Dighcan and Nuzbek about their return to prison activity.

That same afternoon, Nuzbek and Nolpin proved to be poor flake-haulers. They were demoted to rake-duty alongside Baus. Nuzbek remained cool, even discourteous, particularly when Baus queried him about the ferocity with which Dighcan had upbraided him a few days ago. "Imagine that Dighcan grousing about butt-fondling," chirped Baus. "He thought that you would grope his parts! What a concept! What could have come over the brute to think so extravagantly?"

Nuzbek made no effort to craft a civil reply. "Dighcan is that name whereby the word 'lout' becomes automatic."

Baus uttered an aspirated mutter. "Let us not disparage Dighcan, who has sharp ears."

Nuzbek ignored the counsel and pulled abstractedly at his sopping beard. "To boot, this whole scenario reeks of some peculiar insidiousness, as if treacherous forces were working behind my back."

Baus's eyes grew larger with wonder. "Skullduggery could never be at play here!"

"I would think not!" Nuzbek exclaimed.

Baus scrutinized him. The magician's rake-thin face and his spidery scowl were no easy things to witness. Baus tried to imagine Nuzbek as being the indomitable 'Aurimag'—the one whom Trimestrius kept vilifying, but for the life of him he could not absorb the concept. Proposing an experiment, he faked a cough and uttered the word 'Aurimag' under his breath.

Nuzbek twisted about with speed. "What was that?"

Baus's expression was ingenuous. "I was just in the process of clearing phlegm from my throat."

The magician's bloodshot eyes glimmered. "You uttered a name. What was it?"

Baus gave his head a doubtful shake. "You must be imagining things, Nuzbek. Is it odd that a man coughs while gripped in the crux of fever in the rain? You are a tiresome fellow!"

Nuzbek's lips peeled back, revealing a wolfish grin. "Well said, comrade." Rainwater had seeped through the gaps and had made him look ghoulish. "I thought that I had heard something I hadn't for years. I thought too that I had established myself as a man of serious nature." He reached meaningfully in his cloak as if to retrieve an object—possibly the glow pyramid.

A barrow came teetering out of the drizzle and nearly sideswiped him. Baus pulled him out of the way just as the barrow passed.

With cold dislike, Nuzbek shook off Baus's grasp and tottered over to the roadside.

"Careful there, Nuzbek! Jorkoff is a bear when it comes to stone-dumping."

Nuzbek struggled with his ball and chain like a bedraggled bird. He continued to cast Baus an evil glare.

Baus hoisted his own weight and moved off to tend to the other shoulder of the road.

Reviewing his findings, Baus found no solace. His intuition was bang on—it was far better to avoid this magician, Nuzbek. The notion of 'Aurimag the enchanter' had been imprinted in too sinister an ambience. Under the black-billowy robe, Nuzbek had stashed certain objects, including the glow pyramid. It was an adjunct whose puissances and dark emanations were of formidable mystery. Even at a conservative guess, he thought the accessory contained a breed of an elder magic that caused pain and woe. Nuzbek, or whoever he was, would likely not risk jeopardizing the use of this fey power in broad daylight—but then again, when confronted with desperate circumstances, a man could do anything . . .

* * *

What the prisoners did not know was that Graves had personally arranged a surprise that evening. The conflicting reports the Captain had heard from Skarrow and Mulfax regarding the disturbances of the past had made him more suspicious than ever before. Mischief was afoot in his yard, and he would find the culprit.

Nuzbek awoke fumbling with his pillow, discovering, to his dismay, that the absence of his ganglestick was real, a rummaging which roused both Baus and Weavil.

Watching shrewdly out of the corner of their eyes, they saw the magician elbow his colleagues awake and foist the sinister glow-pyramid in their faces before creeping over to the iron-barred window. Dighcan snored in peaceful exhaustion.

Boulm and Nolpin alighted, rubbing their bleary eyes. They followed Nuzbek dutifully on all fours, but on feet plainly ambivalent.

Baus continued to suppress his ironic conviction that Nuzbek was pushing his luck. He watched as the magician looked down malevolently on the fleshy face of Dighcan, whose lips fluttered with wheezing susurration. The coarse tangle of his yellow beard made him look like some abalone-sponge from the sea. Nuzbek seemed to desist the urge to perform some dastardly deed right there. But he thrust the pyramid gingerly between the bars and uttered some unearthly syllables that instantly had a maroon ray shafting out to strike Skarrow squarely on the back. The ray was calculated to inflict appreciable damage and here Baus cast Weavil a wry look.

Weavil withdrew an object of his own from his jacket. Before Baus could stop him, the midget had tossed a pebble at Dighcan's sleeping form. Baus cursed. The rock skidded off Nuzbek's outstretched arm and hit Dighcan's chest, causing the rogue to spring awake immediately. Sensing Nuzbek poised overtop him like a crane, he jerked himself upright and seized the magician by the neck and began striking him. The pyramid clattered to the floor.

Nuzbek, howling in dismay, reeled back in an attempt to snatch back the pyramid but could not hold his balance. Dighcan and he hopped back and forth in a shadowy bird dance. Nolpin acquired enough wits to lash out at Dighcan and send him staggering back, but

Dighcan kneed him in the groin. Nuzbek groaned but won temporarily free of the ruffian's grip and the offensive beating halted—but not before Dighcan had delivered Nuzbek a bully fist to the chest that had him scrambling for air.

The door burst open. Graves and Skarrow leapt in like stormcrows, cracking whips and waving torches. Dighcan was grimacing, rubbing his knuckles on Nuzbek's skull. Skarrow was efforting to shake the haze out of his eyes, likely the aftereffect of Nuzbek's eerie glow-ray.

Graves studied the scene with fervency. "Well, villains! What have we here? A dancing duo?"

Dighcan chattered on but the Captain silenced him. "Yes, Nuzbek has attempted an ignominy. Well, what else is new?"

Dighcan composed himself enough to speak with strain. "Captain, this molester reached for my chest. Perhaps to what? To tickle my privates? Whatever his lusty intention is, it is one of diseased quality and spurs me to actions of punishment. I abhor intimacies of this kind. As a prisoner of this institution. I demand instant protection. Assaults of this nature are insufferable. I shall sue if I my must!—I will ensure that my demands are met!"

Graves gave a series of sympathetic croaks. "In some respect, Dighcan, your claim is justified; however, other matters are of more urgency." Turning to the magician, he barked, "How do you explain this accusation, Nuzbek?"

"There is nothing to explain," Nuzbek muttered.

"Well, what is that weird curio you clutch in your hand?"

"A glow orb, no more," offered Nuzbek. "A bit of ornamentation which I won at the Killboar pub in Brislin. Nothing to worry about." He attempted to sidle away, but could not get far before Skarrow hip-checked him.

Nuzbek loosed a painful cough. "Careful, please. The orb is rare and has provided inspiration and luck during my trying days in the yard."

"I don't doubt it."

Dighcan protested: "Don't heed his words! The swine has attempted a perversion on me! I felt it with my own senses."

Nuzbek gave a low, dispirited protest. "The dolt is incurable. He is a paranoid hoodlum. Forget me, Captain—look to Leamoine for crimes of this kind . . ."

Nuzbek attempted to enhance his argument, but he was in pain. He fell back wincing. "As for the trifling knick-knack that glows, it is an item of luminescence which I was merely using to peer out the window."

"For what?"

"To gauge the upcoming storm and see how it will affect our labours on the morrow." Graves gave a distrustful snort.

Skarrow made a similar exclamation. "I have a hunch that Nuzbek is a liar and that this 'pyramid' is somehow responsible for the stinging of my back!"

"A vile imputation!" growled Nuzbek. "How could I be responsible for such mischief?"

Dighcan cut in with a sardonic retort: "Easily! In addition to your lascivious pussyfooting, you attempted to ram a Flank's stone down my gullet. Here is proof! Regard the missile that struck my left breast!" He pointed at the rock which Weavil had flung.

Nuzbek lifted an accusatory finger toward Baus and Weavil. "There are your culprits. Do not look to me!"

Graves swept his eyes to the ceiling and missed Baus's and Weavil's grinning smirks. "Nuzbek, these irrelevant statements are wearisome and become more feeble as time goes on. I am not far off in my convictions that you are a debaser, an incorrigible dandelion addicted to the fondling of Dighcan's body. No less, I am convinced you are a fabulist. I urge you to keep your hands to yourself! I award you a double demerit for disorderly conduct and prurient behaviour."

"Unfair!" raved Nuzbek. He gave a strangled murmur. "Even if I were this creature of baseness you describe, I enacted nothing of inappropriate nature."

"Only because you were interrupted from the process, which is why I am charging you with an 'intent of an ignominy'. Now let matters be! I shall suffer no more disruptions. Your gasbagging has made us all ill." He glared at the others in the gathering who gawked. "That applies to the lot of you lumpkins!"

The small diversion gave Nuzbek time to cache his glowing adjunct in his robe. Though Skarrow searched him, the device was never found. Nuzbek's thinly-veiled smile became ever more gloating. Peering about, Graves realized the object could be hidden amongst any of the convicts, and sourly he threw his hands in the air. The officers departed.

IX

It was in a dream that illumination dawned in Baus. Escape was so simple!

At half past three in the morning Baus slid out of his pallet, waking Weavil, infused with a rich, exalted plan.

Weavil sputtered an oath, deploring the callous treatment of being woken from his slumbers, but Baus quickly clamped fingers over the midget's lips. Weavil understood the momentousness of the scheme. Nuzbek's baton was gripped in Baus's fist and he crept after Baus without inquiry.

Cautiously Baus dislodged the bar holding the door. With a careful nudge, he took the handle and had the door shivering ajar. The two slipped through the darkness, disappearing on noiseless feet. There was no sign of Graves—only Skarrow hulking several feet away with boots planted on the edge of the veranda. His back was sagging, head nodding, mouth yawning. In such a state of torpor, Baus felt him an easy victim, and he was soon frozen fast to the slats. The two moved unhindered into the yard. Along the north wall they crept silently, mainly unaware that Nuzbek and his cronies had followed them moments after, creeping like vines under the high stone rampart.

Baus and Weavil skulked ever downward toward the east wall. The yard plunged dangerously into spikenard on a shallow angle, while Weavil tossed Baus ungrateful looks and remarks, which Baus ignored. In a petulant voice, Weavil complained that his comrade's urgency wasted on inexplicable preoccupation with 'ghostly treetops' and 'gigantic limbs' arching above them. Baus cocked his head, casting calculating glances at the beobar, as if his dreamy convictions were substantiated.

Five minutes later, the two came to the junction of the wall with the seaward side. Gloom hung rife: the yard's façade towered above them like slate. Cold bare flanks met their fingers, worn smooth and bathed in blue-black shadow. A brisk wind had picked up, swirling the enclosure with sea air, sending chills up their spines. Spongebush grew in clumps. Nevertheless, they stumbled under the looming trees, with Baus cursing and dragging Weavil along by the collar, subjugating him to his rigor as they fell victim to all kinds of scrapes, itches and abrasions from the prickly shrubbery.

They picked their way through the terrain and searched for the stone that Baus had marked and obsessed over for the last weeks.

A tedious fifty foot hike ended; finally, the two discovered the stone. The absence of light was a hindrance that was unavoidable; several times they had tripped to fall nose to nose with an ever more irking stench. There was all too much fermented clam meat here while the watchtower flickered with a buttery glow and the cupola lay pricked with viscid torchlight.

Gouging at the stone with Trimestrius's gladius, Baus hacked out a grim outline around the rock. It was a tense period, during which time Weavil's scepticism grew considerably. But when the deed was done, he gasped when he saw Baus's new blade hew a lip around the stone, mortar and chip rock flying off like sawdust, as if crafted of putty.

Baus stood back, exhilarated by the easy work. The stone finally gave way, revealing a head-sized opening for Weavil to crawl through. With the assistance of Nuzbek's baton and Trimestrius's blade, the exercise had become elementary—liberation seemed near at hand!

Weavil disputed the success of the escape. "How are you to win free, bright-eyes? I am only puny enough to pass through, not you."

Baus exhibited unconcern. "I have thought this out. I shall escape from another avenue." He motioned fervidly to the tangle of branches overhanging the north wall. The gently-swaying limbs were no more than ninety feet away.

Weavil issued a chuckling response: "And are you to leap up to those limbs or are they to suddenly bend over to your whim?"

Baus flourished gruffly. "With your help, Weavil, I shall breach those limbs—please, if you don't mind, get your torso through the hole."

Expressing irritation, Weavil refused to show cooperation and Baus was beside himself. Weavil persisted; Baus was compelled to divulge his means of escape. "Listen!" he hissed. "The outer wall is rough enough for footholds for a tiny person as yourself. Climb the outer wall, gain the parapet; crawl along the top to secure a bough pliable enough for me to swing down. If you can bend it for me I can loft myself up."

Weavil gave an absurd laugh. "Nothing doing! You think I can do all this? I shall trip and slash my skin on the glass which spikes the parapet!"

Baus's eyes gleamed with irritation. "Are you going to be touchy? Why be such an infant while I bust my neck? Try this: scale the trunks near the wall and from there ride a bough. There are many to choose from—rich with twigs and strong enough to support your weight. My height is only six feet; I have an additional two feet of arm's length. If I can grab on to a branch, then I am free!"

Weavil griped sullenly. "What of the snauzzerhounds?"

"Ignore them," Baus advised. "They sleep docilely at the southern entrance."

"The plan seems slipshod."

"And you have a better one? Do not fear, the scheme is solid! You have only to creep over the parapet. Do what I tell you!"

Weavil gave his jaw a snap. "A certain inadequate margin of outcome concerns me. Chances are I'll likely crack my skull on these rocks below."

"The risk exists, but life is a gamble. Now Weavil, hurry—as I see it, you have succumbed to sheer timorousness from fatalism. I have imparted my counsel and urge you to reconsider the fact that my freedom is at stake!"

Sensing no scope for argument, Weavil scrambled up on Baus's back. Awkwardly, he let himself joggle into the crevice, lying flat on his stomach then thrust feet through the hole, but discovered that his head was too large to fit through the hole.

Baus had foreseen this, and greedily stuffed clam guts from a nearby pile around Weavil's neck and ears to increase the slippage. Ignoring Weavil's rancorous tumult, he gave a hiss when a final push had Weavil worming his way through the wall and sliding down to the turf.

X

Baus's elation was short-lived—the moments fled by and the window of opportunity quickly closed. The wind gusted in fits, the drizzle began to die and the odd dripping of water spilled from the lower boughs, plunging the compound into an unnerving tick-tock murmur. It was too easy to be heard by the guards!

Baus shivered, knowing that he and Weavil would be tasked to navigate the bosky wilds beyond the yard without light and map. That is, if they managed to get beyond the walls.

As if to confirm the qualm, a plaintive coyote call drifted from the beobar forest.

Edging his way along the ground, Baus avoided clumps of blister brush and frog-hobbled to a place where he thought Weavil might emerge. Fog wisps hung in ghoulish trailers; damp, chill nonsensical shapes formed and dissolved like will-o'-the-wisps, tightening Baus's nerves. He craned his neck into the inky spaces, struggling to design news of Weavil's progress.

Not a stir. The beobar was almost bare of leaves and snaky twigs were glazed with a maroon patina formed from the cloud-wreathed half-moon.

Peering back toward the compound's heart, Baus saw the watchtower shining as before. On the veranda he could see Skarrow stiff and immobile. In minutes he would become mobile again.

Baus wracked his brains for a solution. Should he slink back and re-freeze him now?

No, he would surely miss Weavil's appearance!—the plan would be shot.

But where was the midget? He should be on a high limb now, dangling over the north wall, throwing down a limb. It seemed unlikely he had succeeded.

Mouthing curses, Baus paced up and down. But then he caught a glimpse of a quivering shape struggling perhaps eighteen feet above him. The hovering shadow was only a meagre three feet above the glass-spiked parapet and from the lower leafy tangle Baus discerned Weavil dangling like a possum.

Baus dashed under the shadow where Weavil hung. He cupped his hands round his mouth, he called up in a rich whisper.

"Curb your requests!" came the crass voice shafting down. "Can you not see that I am in trouble?"

Baus winced. Certainly Weavil's temperament was becoming taxing. The plan hinged on the poet's ability to sustain himself in the operation. If the long bough bent too much or snapped, they would be lost. As it stood, it had not bent enough. Even if six Weavils jumped on the bough, there would still remain six empty feet of air. Baus loosed an enraged sigh.

He was about to voice Weavil an encouragement when he heard muffled voices. He pressed himself low to the ground and strained his eyes in the gloom. He heard a strange whooshing, as of air being blown against a sail. Baus grimaced, knowing what that sound meant. In the dampness, he could just make out Nolpin and Boulm huddled fifty paces distant with Nuzbek floating several feet above four jars, which had obviously been disinterred.

Boulm handed the first jar up to Nuzbek. The magician tucked it under his arm and while essaying to control the bizarre parachute that ballooned unwieldily a foot over his head, he ordered another. The ropes were like ailerons. He used them to angle his weight alongside the wall with a strange wind-like murmur. The craft lofted him effortlessly higher in the air, over the parapet and into the trees where he passed between a gap and descended on the other side.

Baus hissed between his teeth. How could such a trickster perform these miraculous feats so easily? It was unnerving. What could he possibly want so desperately with those wretched jars?

Suppressing his displeasure, Baus felt a bursting urge to run over and brain the magician. He quelled the impulse.

Nuzbek returned to his high position, floating down over the wall. His face was chased with a pompous grin. He tucked the ropes in at his waist to control his speed. When his feet reached the ground, he motioned for Nolpin to take hold of one of the guy-lines.

The magician gave an order; all of the fantastic company, including Nuzbek, Nolpin and the second last jar, floated easily over the wall. Then it descended down the other side with Boulm watching wonderingly on the ground. The last two vessels lay exposed at his feet.

Deep in the shadows Baus wormed his way closer. Miserable thoughts fled through his brain but he crawled on. The answer to one of his questions was forthcoming. Nuzbek and company were about to rescue their own skins in a much more rapid manner than he or Weavil. The individuals in the jars meant more to him than he could imagine, but how this could disturb his own plans of escape still remained unknown.

The queasiness knitting Baus's stomach was testament that no good was to come of the evening's complexities.

Baus attempted to alert Weavil of the new circumstances but he could not. Weavil could not see him or easily grasp the meaning of his jiggery sign language and it would be easy for Nuzbek to float over and deal the two of them a blow with his glow pyramid before Baus could gain the branch.

Nuzbek was just returning on a final pass to transport Boulm when he ordered his lackey to straddle his legs. The two floated up, into the wreaths of mist, but just as they were gaining the parapet, a strange event took place.

Boulm's jar, clutched so fervently, seemed to shiver. The contents suddenly exploded. The lid, shooting off like a cork, geysered a spray of brine splashing into Boulm's eyes. Boulm squeezed his eyes shut and gave a hoarse trill. He thrashed about with one arm wrapped around his body. He was blind. In the process, he almost dropped the jar.

Trimestrius rocketed out from the canister. He dripped with unguent. A greenish froth oozed from around his mouth, cheeks and chin. His eyes were fierce pools of vehemence.

Nuzbek tried to navigate the parachute sideways, garbling a litany of imprecations, but having no free arms, he could do nothing to unseat the midget while Boulm clumsily strove to headbutt the troublemaker into oblivion.

The initiative failed. Trimestrius gnawed Boulm's nose. The lackey lost grip completely on Nuzbek's legs and the jar slipped from his grasp and thudded in the sandy turf.

Trimestrius sprang savagely upon Boulm just as he grabbed Nuzbek's ankles at the last instant. Straddling his shoulders, Trimestrius began to chew the convict's neck. Boulm wrenched his frame free and wretchedly tried to stop the homunculus's champing, but cramped and contorted as he was and fraught with terror, Boulm was thwarted. In a reckless Z movement, Nuzbek swatted madly at the dwarf, but the craft began to teeter sideways. Careening toward a thick trunk, the conveyance lashed wildly left and right, lurching in midair, then it knocked itself against prickly branches and jabbing twigs.

Boulm's left leg was pinned. He was slashed hard across a gleaming shard of parapet glass and howled in agony, and he could not restrain the impulse to clutch at his bleeding leg.

The urge was foolish! Boulm toppled, pinwheeling in midair, loosing a horrid shriek into the sky.

Nuzbek pulled up fiercely on the guy-lines. With the loss of weight, the buoyancy gained him several feet. Too fast! The damage was done. Boulm's shouts passed unheeded; the lackey's last outcry died in his throat as Nuzbek stared in stony perplexity at his comrade who lay inert in the fog wisps below. There was a sick twist to his neck; his knee was bent backward.

Nuzbek uttered a groan of despair; he twisted his face into a grimace and inspected his new lithe enemy who was clinging monkeylike on the upper stays. The illogic stunned the magician. Perhaps he believed his spells too indomitable to be breached; but here was a counterexample: surely beyond his knowledge was how the traitor could have freed himself from the jar—the lid was tamper-proof, no thanks to Baus's tampering.

A chance arrived and Trimestrius finally thrust a lethal strike at Nuzbek's throat.

The magician blocked the attack. The deflection momentarily unbalanced Trimestrius and the midget plunged five feet, sliding precariously onto a sprawling beobar. Twisting, turning, clawing his way back up, he only slid feet farther. The dwarf snatched quickly at the last branch. It held his weight and saved him from a twenty foot fall.

The conveyance started to buckle. Nuzbek, witnessing a new catastrophe, gasped. Boulm had landed on the last remaining jar, shattering it. Now the contents had gushed out on the sand, including the figure within: a sandy-haired, purple-robed woman rising woozily to her feet. She was amazingly beautiful, but no taller than knee-high. Stepping away from the corpse, she drew herself to her full height. Regal as a sorceress, her gaze rose upwards to scan Nuzbek, and with that, a cold wrath fixed icily upon a villain.

"Ulisa!" the magician suspired, completely overwhelmed. "How can this be possible?"

For a freakish second it appeared that Nuzbek was to become unsettled, but he kicked himself away from the tree and gained some air space.

The manoeuvre was swift—the parachute would have been ravaged by long, spiny branches if he hadn't angled himself precariously toward the parapet, kicking himself off from the ledge, avoiding the sharp glass that had undermined Boulm.

Shouts now arose from the barracks. The prisoners were awakening—as too the guards. Baus turned in time to spy Skarrow bounding across the sward like an ogre. Graves was on his heels. Farther afield, the prison's great portcullis rattled up. Oppet's hounds came leaping out panther-like, straining on their leashes as if they would snap them and maul the offender. They dug at the turf, jousted the air with their horned snouts and snorted evil symphonies of goring and gnawing to come.

Oppet loosed the chains. Like maddened fiends the hounds sprang out as one. Oppet rang the gong in quick succession—three chimes—a signal which Baus knew was the call for a town emergency.

Baus shouted up at Weavil. "Time is at an absolute minimum, Weavil! Hurry! Unfurl your branch!"

Cognizing the urgency of the predicament, Weavil struggled to propel himself along the prickly foliage. He was unsuccessful. Thrust upside down and with his face smothered in leaves, he could barely manoeuvre let alone perceive what was happening. But the midget understood the need for speed, and leapt out like a chimpanzee and earned an extra two feet.

The branch sagged six inches. Not enough! Weavil slid down the remaining length, but lost his grip; he began sliding down the bough at an alarming rate.

The bough curved over like a great bow. He rode the tip like a water drop.

The branch was within Baus's reach. With urgency he mustered an audacious leap. Fingers snagged at leaves; for an interminable second Baus seemed to float in ether then clutch at something more than air.

It allowed him time to capture a segment that supported his weight. Up, up he scrambled, tugging, grasping, grunting with all his force.

He gained six more inches . . . a foot . . . A new nest of horror emerged—what would happen if the snauzzerhounds jumped and tore at his ankles?

A strange shift in weight suddenly propelled him precariously upward another foot. He clung two feet below eye level to the wall's summit. He wrenched himself about in clumsy fashion and watched in horror as Weavil slid past him, down the clumps of leaves into a heap on the ground.

Baus cried out. What could stop Weavil from being gored by the hounds? The branch was too far way for him to grab. If he should leap down, he would perish too.

The dilemma was too obvious: two persons in the maws of the snauzzerhounds, or one?

The choice made him ashen and Baus watched in dismay as Nuzbek came floating down to a standstill, alighting nearby where Boulm lay dead.

The magician snatched up Trimestrius's jar and seized its lid with a rage before he gained the conveyance again.

Baus shook his head in confusion. What was the rogue up to? Did he not realize that claws, jaws and teeth were almost on him?

The answer was clear enough.

Nuzbek aimed straight for the dwarfed woman who stood with her hands tucked in her robe.

Baus yelled down at Ulisa in desperation: "Run! Run to the east wall!"

His cries were fierce enough to catch her attention. The sorceress turned. Baus pointed wildly to the wall. "To the far end of the compound! A breach exists in the wall. Hurry! An escape route is wide enough for you to crawl through. Run too, Weavil, you little wifter, run!

—or you're mincemeat!"

Weavil, reviving himself from the shock of his fall, hot-tailed it to the opening.

The shrunken sorceress did not waste any precious instants. Having grasped the essence of what Baus had cried, she fled, with her robe a billow of whirling Tyrian purple ballooning behind her.

Nuzbek dropped in behind, floating with a murderous intent. He gripped the pyramid in his free hand and unleashed a ray.

The brownish spray stung the air. It seemed corrupted with a sickly malevolence. As if guided by some inner premonition, the small figure ground to a halt, ducking.

The shaft careened wide, only inches away, blasting a spongebush to a crisp. The dwarf clamped her resolve, raised both arms over her head. A mysterious aureole enveloped her figure like a shroud: emerald and golden-red tinged on the fringes.

Nuzbek ululated tempestuous vocables. From the pyramid burst another ray, this one twice as wide, wracking maleficent colours through the air. The beam zigzagged and struck Ulisa, but miraculously it reflected harmlessly off her expanded glowing nimbus, causing Nuzbek to squawk in surprise and swing his parachute about.

He dropped in closer and came floating in, snatching carelessly at her robe only to lurch back in pain. He was struck with a forceful beam of her own wielded by her aura and he tumbled from the chute and struck the earth. He lay there face first for a time, moaning. Ulisa opened her eyes, ran fleet-footed to the wall where Baus had pointed. Such was Nuzbek's plight—he could not see her scrambling up, and through the hole she slid before it was possible to steel himself for action.

Weavil had taken hold of his senses. He fled in a terrible direction, the same as Ulisa, despite the slavering tumult of the snauzzerhounds two dozen yards away.

Weavil was too late. Nuzbek had shaken off his pain and had caught up with the midget on foot. He grabbed him by the collar and hefted him off the ground, his little legs spinning.

"So, my little rat!" he chuckled in irony. "Notice that we are at last face to face with each other—on terms less jubilant!"

Into the empty canister he shoved Weavil and clamped the defective lid shut with purpose. "That shall curtail your stink, you little meddler! Two of my long time foes have escaped, but no matter! For the nonce, you shall serve as collateral." He sprinted back to where he had left his chute and re-ignited the magic. Up into the air he climbed, clutching his trophy, with fiendish intent bristling on his gaunt face. The snauzzerhounds came snapping and yipping at his heels seconds too late.

Baus watched in helpless dissatisfaction. What could be done? Weavil had been kidnapped; he had been hopelessly trapped in a blue bottle. Nuzbek had fled off into the beobar on his bewitched conveyance.

Baus's spirits sunk; his resolve teetered on the brink of a breakdown. He could no more help Weavil than fly to the moon. Defeat loomed dark on his horizon; it smothered his sense of accomplishment.

The snauzzerhounds had forgotten their flying quarry and loped over to where Boulm lay mangled. After a brief sniff or two, they came charging away to the edge of the wall, snapping and snarling up at Baus with mad, opal eyes. If they harboured wings, they would fly and rend him ear to ear. Of Ulisa Baus knew naught, but if she gained the murk on the other side of the wall, perhaps she would be safe.

With no guard to contain the prisoners, the convicts scattered from the barracks. Baus could see them under the fog-shrouded lantern, a horde of madmen ploughing their way toward the open portcullis. It was a mass of thick, grasping bodies—Dighcan, Yullen, Zestes, Paltuik, Valere, Lopze, Jorkoff—all kicking and pressing each other with one obsessive motion.

There was a clank of weapons. The runaways had gained the portal and with no great decorum, bowled each other over and trampled Oppet and Mulfax who were no match for their blood-maddened lust.

They were rogues, true, but Baus wished them safe passage—at least for such time as to supply him with a diversion.

Two figures came bolting out the gloom—Graves and Skarrow. They stared up at Baus with disgusted rancour. Graves shook a grey fist; Skarrow flung a scathing oath.

Baus shrugged gamely.

The husky Captain issued a brusque order at Skarrow. The two raced back toward the gate while the snauzzerhounds, seething and shaking, on their heels.

Baus felt it time to depart. He leapt down from the parapet onto the gnarled beobar trunk and slid down in a heap of tired bones. A wet dampness of the forest struck him: of rich moss and decaying leaves.

It took him only a moment to shake the cobwebs from his head. He lurched off into the fog-haunted distance like a haunted spirit. It would not be prudent to linger. In time the Constables would be circling the wall, setting themselves out to organize a recapture . . .

CHAPTER 3
THE DAKKAW
OF
KRINTZ

"Solve his riddles, escape his plans,
Lest one remain, putty in his hands,
Fly from Bisiguth before a bride he taketh,
And so his vengeance he then maketh . . ."

—'Topical Fables of Sarch' from Xiver's New Contemporary Library.

I

Baus did not pause to belabour his predicament under Heagram prison's wall. He let his fingers claw free of the beobar's trunk then launched himself away double-time, thrashing through the maze of trees with no decorum.

His legs were limber; his lungs were strong. He took to the moonlit gaps with the swift instinct of an antelope. Through glassy eyes he noted the growing cloud muting the moonlight and illuminating his way through the tangle.

A mournful horn blasted from nearby.

He stopped short. Suspicious eyes he trained into the unfamiliar gloom. A sound echoed from farther away, implying reinforcements to rout him out. The position of the blare was inexact; but Baus guessed pursuers had reached the better part of the wall facing the sea.

He plunged deeper into the forest, preparing for attack. The idea was to elude the new threat, but a crisp snapping of twigs brought him spinning about, drawing his tiny blade. He strained to discern the source.

"No need to fear!" a pellucid voice called out from the darkness. "It is I, a friend."

The declaration prompted Baus to release his white grip on the hilt of his sword. The voice was richly melodic, a woman's soft voice, clear like a bell. Seconds passed; Baus discerned a robed figure, knee-high and subdued. A small hand and cowl partially covered the face—the same visage he had witnessed earlier in the yard, a face unfettered by malice or devilry. The figure appeared benign, trotting from behind a massive trunk, a small white hand tucked in a voluminous velvet sleeve and lifted in peaceful greeting.

"Ulisa?" He peered closer. His own murmur seemed muted in his ears.

She approached on calm feet. Dressed in a plain acolyte's robe, she was gorgeous, embossed with a pure presence difficult to describe. She exuded litheness; her figure was bathed with an emanation that captivated him. It was not for random that he took an instant like to this creature, despite her absurd size. Nor was the truthful innocence of her or sense of arbitrary power any diminishing quality. He scrutinized the figure more closely; he felt a keen stupefaction; the wet garments revealed her contours in evocative light, hardly vitiating his impression of her unsuspecting vulnerability. Even so, she shivered in the chillness of the night.

"Who are you?" she asked. "I am Ulisa—the Utilitarian."

"I am Baus of Heagram," Baus replied.

The rest of the distance she crossed with a graceful ease and appraised him with blinking eyes. "I am indebted to you, Baus. The like is not common in these backward regions. Let not some false judgment of character betray me, so please accept this token of thanks for warning me against the rogue. He was ready to dispatch me with prejudice. If you hadn't cried out, I might not have fared as well as I have." Her voice faltered, edged with a sense of tense memory.

Baus shook his head with good-natured affability. "I offered an avenue of escape, no more, as would any charitable citizen."

"You did," replied Ulisa frankly. Her smile revealed delight. "But I think you are more cavalier than your humility suggests."

"You saved yourself from the dissolute rascal."

Ulisa's face quivered from a painful memory. "The degenerate has created so much mischief for me! Dark days are upon us, Baus. Aurimag's ruthless deeds must come to an end; all creatures in the universe are in jeopardy."

Baus blinked with surprise. The absolute statement seemed melodramatic, but he controlled his judgment. "I hear that name, 'Aurimag' once again."

"The name is a mockery!" she spat.

"I know—it means '*Golden Mage*'."

Ulisa gave her sandal a stamp. "It is ironic that he has ruined any chances for all things 'golden' in this life."

"They are riddles to me," grunted Baus. He gestured to the sprawling forest. "I suppose we must fly from here. Ill fortune will have us if Captain Graves discovers us at this vulnerable setting."

Ulisa sighed, agreeing. She allowed Baus to escort her closer to the looming bog. He snatched her arm and half dragged her into the forest gloom before she could protest. A frosty sheen glazed the foliage, impelling her to jump and hop. Logs and stones proved cumbersome. She urged him to slow down.

Baus groaned: "Let us hasten! It bodes ill that Weavil has been seized by the lunatic you call 'Aurimag'. As you know, he is my friend and has been transformed into a wretched midget like yourself."

"Hold up, I am no hurdler." She cocked her head. "The small man who was fleeing next to me when I was dashed to the ground, he is Weavil?"

Baus nodded curtly.

Ulisa's lips showed a brief quiver. "He has been transformed into a homunculus by an arcane containment like myself. Weavil has fallen under the pall of Aurimag's sorcery—as many others. It happened for me in Lune's glade—not far from Mismerion castle. It passed likewise for Woisper and Salmeister—neomancers of the Mismerion Order. They were bewitched in the upper precincts of the Moon tower . . . I think. Lured by sly temptation, typical of Aurimag's skullduggery, they were fooled." She gave her neck a painful twist. "To remedy the situation is now where I hasten."

Baus's brows arched. "In what way?"

Ulisa peeled off her cowl and gave a sad smile. Baus saw hair golden as silk, enchanting to behold even when wet and tousled.

"To revive the Circle and repair myself to normal stature." She seemed careful not to stimulate Baus's interest in her. "Woisper, Salmeister, Adelyheim the Healer, Kazzasius the Projector, Ahrion the Astrologer—all shall collaborate in the pursuit of justice. We are neomancers!—Aurimag shall fall. We shall clip his wings—master him like the cur he is! Returning to Mismerion's Circle we will install ourselves as proper lords. We shall build our potency and create a new order, reviving the glory of old!"

Baus believed the presumption lofty but agreed that the quest was certainly noble. "If Aurimag is half as diabolical as you claim, then you will not succeed." He frowned at his own premonition and pulled at his beard. He felt it imprudent to relay the news that Weavil's transformation, which according to Nuzbek, could not occur for fifty years, if the magicker was telling the truth.

The wail of a horn sounded menacingly from nearby. It seemed as if their recent mobilization had not proven satisfactory.

Baus remarked, "I have just learned of the Circle from another source—a certain 'Trimestrius' of Desenion."

Ulisa's mouth hung agape. "What?" She rustled her gown in awe. "Trimestrius? He is alive?" A glint of hope shone in her eyes.

"'Twas he who loosed you from your jar."

Ulisa's face swelled with pride. "I don't doubt it. Were there others?"

Baus gave his head a dour shake. "They are bottled. They remain in Aurimag's custody."

Ulisa was crestfallen. "I must make haste!"

Baus looked about with uncertainty; the bramble and mossy roots formed a daunting barrier. The forest seemed a complex maze and the undergrowth a damp and dense mat, unruly as adders. "To where?" he croaked. "Grumboar is unforgiving. See for yourself. Your comrades remain captives of the malignant Nuzbek. This moment he flees by air, in his freakish parachute. He eludes those who are surely out to murder him. They will murder us too unless we are quick with our feet."

The pearly whites of Ulisa's eyes glittered with anxiety.

Baus pulled her along with speed. The two coursed grimly through the underbrush while

Baus dodged erratically away from yet another set of distant horns.

The bracken became obdurate, a choke of spine-weed, fern and fungus rock. The north wall had tumbled behind them faraway now, little more than a dim luminescence seen through the groping arms of an uncompromising forest. The going was tough yet Baus urged them on to new speed. With deliberate bounds, he hauled Ulisa beside him and the two plunged recklessly into the umber-stained trees.

Coils of unfriendly mist hung heavily on the ground. Sprawling branches oppressed them, groping their way to new spaces. They felt their way, eyeing the gnarled roots and aged trees without cheer. The trees seemed to wrap about them, to whisper, like human shades. Grumboar, 'the forest of murmurs', seemed a limp tangle of endless trunks, ever mossy and damp, forever splashed in deep shadow and buoyant fog.

Baus shrugged aside the thousand branches and plunged deeper into the hollows. Black shadows seemed to be stained a slightly plum colour. The moon's cool shimmer grazed bravely through the leaves.

There was no sign of Nuzbek. The spooky precincts grew only more disquieting: phantom shadows were mixed with deep murmurings of the forest and there was a closeness here and watchfulness that engulfed all thoughts and swallowed hopes.

Past a jade-tinted pool the two stumbled like ghosts. Various fauna lurked in the gaps: large pink birds with shimmering legs, horned frogs eager to croak and shine their glazed eyes. Ever did the trespassers search for signs of Nuzbek and Nolpin, but they found none. The villains had utterly disappeared.

Ulisa seemed worse for wear. She sensed the inevitable and staggered to a halt. "I exhort you to let up, Baus!" She dropped to her knees and gasped for breath. "The forest harbours mysteries of which we can't conceive." Her eyes showed tears, her hands shook slightly. The little neomancer drifted into a strange trance, unmarred by sorrow, but peaceful as if guided by an inner wisdom.

Time passed. In the interim, Baus's impatience grew to anxiety. On four fronts the tall beobar wrapped about him in an unnerving shroud.

Ulisa snapped alert; she urged them on toward an open space within the woodlands that promised respite from the closeness of Grumboar. A sizeable clearing with boundaries vague showed the ground soft and wet—an obvious swamp.

Baus was unsure of the neomancer's intent lingering here, but he was glad to be out of the stifling confines of the forest, able to breathe once more.

Ulisa set herself down on a moss-ridden log. In a queer voice, she uttered ominous words: "Our quarry eludes us for chilling reasons. Aurimag's cunning has grown; during the eternity I have been entombed as a doll, he has become ever depraved. Let us rest here—I need quiet, by this pool, by this glade . . ."

Baus complied. Overlooking the misty reach he sat with her, brooding on his misfortune, by the tussocked pool that dwindled into cattails in faint moonlight. The dark curtain of trees closed about the glade. Baus saw no solace in these frowning guardians. Deep within the pool, he saw a cluster of deadheads huddled in secret profusion: grey-mottled trunks with stumps half rotted. The water was inert. What could have been deemed olive-tourmaline in colour, the pool's thin gleam played beams on a frog which thrummed. Leaping from lily pad to pad, it spread ripples out upon the water's surface and submerged. The starry sky spread out its jewels, making Baus feel somewhat insignificant in the whole scheme of things, despite the profoundness of his thoughts.

The silence deepened. A plaintive-sounding horn split the darkness—swallowed in the night.

Baus broke the eeriness. "Something does not add up in all this talk about Aurimag. Yes, he is a rogue—but certainly not the despot you describe. Why do you seek him out, as if he were the deadliest villain on earth?"

Ulisa spoke in grim tones. "This 'Nuzbek' as you name him—he is a powerful enchanter—he and Aurimag are one and the same."

Baus scoffed, "It is hard to believe."

Ulisa murmured, "I suppose I must tell you."

"If you please."

Ulisa began thoughtfully, "Once he was a powerful sorcerer, though less now. When old Cascnus the Theosopher died, Aurimag applied for a position to the Synode—as did Llonon the Younger. This happened a long time ago, and I, being a senior member of the Circle, was present, along with others. Woisper, Salmeister and Barbirius granted the two contenders an audience. Ah, what an august assembly!" Her eyes misted, as if a glimpse of the memory long past was sorrowful. "It was at Mismerion, in our pillared Hall, the days of carefree and light temperament.

"Llonon, a budding neomancer, was first to launch his grand feat: a spectacle of dancing lights and flame. It was a breath of inspiration! The like had never been seen before in our keep. Such luminescences! Such incendiaries!—it was revolutionary for one so young and brimming with talent. Neither emitting heat nor harm, his forms made play, and yet were amazing vignettes of illusion with exploding rainbow showers of tones. How they filled the shadowy spaces of Mismerion with delight and wonder! I remember it as if it was yester-eve: Llonon, dressed all in his twill finery, mannerly, dapper and suave; he had the clever grace of hand of a veteran, twirling and snapping shapes, manufacturing faces and forms of the past: pilgrims, kings, martyrs, peons, tradesmen. All spoke in their own native voice, injecting a phrase of knowledge, a quotation, a witticism, a euphemism, even a tragic anecdote. Llonon's conjurations dwindled to motes, then suddenly rearranged themselves into the constellations, growing in size and wonder."

Ulisa's smile warmed in the moonlight. "It appeared as if we were moving toward a single star, a distant luminous orb that commanded the orbits of satellites. We fled on to encounter another star system. Finally we were whisked to the center of our own galaxy at incomprehensible speeds. Unquenchable fires shone there with a brilliance almost impairing to the eyes!

"There was a boom, a sudden wracking explosion—then a brief start—a juddering jar. We were flung back into the perplexity of our Hall! Llonon took a bow, his larkish eyes glistening like stars themselves."

"Impressive!" cried Baus.

Ulisa sighed contentedly. "But Aurimag became inflamed at the display. In a secret fury he flung a hex so wicked upon Llonon that the young illusionist ran to the fountain gulping water like a fish. Members of the Circle were at odds trying to figure out what happened. Our counterspell indicators indicated that Aurimag had cast a spell upon him. Barbirius the Bellicose opted for Aurimag's instant dismissal. Salmeister the Saturnine, Pizor the Polemicist, Dious the Philosopher and Maitor the Moralist, they were all in accord with the motion but Woisper disagreed and convinced his colleagues to let Aurimag off.

"I say with anything but praise that Aurimag's powers had grown since we had last known him as a fledgling aspirant. Ever since he had taken pilgrimage to the Nderian hills and had spoken to the wizened old shamans who roamed the misty reaches, he had changed —after that he retired to the stark quietude of his cave by the Lim. There he brooded and experimented with fey things. Years later, he came to demonstrate his magic of new thresholds, thought lost by all but our Elders. Aurimag's extravaganza was a demonstration of teleportation to another realm. With the help of an assistant of questionable repute, he arranged a giant rat on a podium, a creature of dishevelled and miserable appearance, caged in a metal mesh, over which he placed a mica shield. The rat was obviously under some spell. After spreading various potions and elixirs of pungency, he muttered an arcane canto which we could not interpret. He stepped aside, allowing us a view of that barbaric podium which showed that the rodent had disappeared. He voiced a cryptic saying and sung fragments of ghastly songs. Blasphemous and barbaric, these utterances exemplified all kinds of satiric buffoonery and arrogant bluster which included a flugelhorn performance and a hornpipe ditty and other melodies which were appallingly out of character for our distinguished company. As ridiculous as these exploits were, we endured them, perhaps from sheer etiquette. What more were we to endure? Only dogma and cryptic antics, rich with scandal. The gathering was not impressed, especially Salmeister, who held a particular hatred for Aurimag and challenged him to prove that he had enacted anything more than a dissembling of a disappearing rodent.

"Aurimag levelled his gaze upon Salmeister and shot a quivering finger in the air, tapping it down on his empty cage, thus imploring a single fell word—

"'Gloriglastonifix!'

"The rat returned, not as a harmless rodent, but as a black beast, fey beyond imagining, with a monstrous ten-foot high polyp-ridden hide and four gyrating heads. Its elephantine snout skidded around like a mallet, knocking out the lamps like thunder-blasts and snared Onzo in a trunk. Aurimag ignored the destruction even as it inflicted a near mortification upon poor Onzo. It was a demon, of course, drawn from the Zamariel netherworlds, of which I daren't name. Unmercifully it stomped about the chamber on rhinoceros legs. Aurimag stood there, cackling like a hyena, unintimidated by the devil he had conjured. Onzo would have died there had not Adelyheim the Healer administered curatives. Others in our company called forth protective spells and healing charms; at the very least we immobilized the demon before it could commit further damages.

"Aurimag laughed in a most disdainful voice: 'You cringing dawcocks! I have conveyed this thing from a dismal past to the present—a snapshot which you have witnessed and

abhorred. Perhaps this is what shall walk the earth an eon from now? Perhaps not. I defy you
to claim such a feat rivalled by any! Let Llonon and his tawdry feats drown in ineptitude
compared to my own!'

"Woisper spoke in the gravest voice: 'Aurimag, your pomp is deplorable! Your
neomancy has grown to capable effect, but in truth, you have raised nothing more than a
demon. A frightful abomination of evil!—of low standing even. You have transgressed
beyond the Code of Neomancer Ethics and must be punished!

"'Ethics?' Aurimag mocked. 'You, of all Neons[*], should know that hypocrisy is your gift.
What of all the failed experiments, and hushed accidents and disasters that you have wrought
upon innocent creatures of the forests while acquiring this knowledge of your craft? The
bestial experiments foisted on animals and birds in the forests not far from the Brauvn?—you
merged their life forces with others of lesser intelligence. Human too, if rumour is correct.
What of these artificial species you manufactured in your own tubs in the murky past? Do
you not know the walls you built in the Branx forest no longer hold the 'Wickles', and in the
darkest hours of the night, they slip through the cracks and haunt the forests of the Lim?
Your 'Sanctuary', your pretentious Synode call it, is slowly disintegrating! Even the crass
euphemism is risible. I call you the worst hypocrite, Woisper, and you can wallow in your
sanctimony! Fade and dwindle to mediocrity, be proud of your little rituals and pedagogies.
Your life shall pass as a mere fading vignette, while I shall be an icon of avant-garde wonder,
eulogized in the annals of history, honoured and adulated!'

"Aurimag whirled his black robe and sought to depart the hall, but not before hawking on
the floor like a peasant.

"Enraged beyond measure, Woisper roared: 'Return hither, pretender! On that
unpublishable account you are enormously wrong. It is precisely for these terrible reasons
that the Code was devised. You are a scourge! A bane! A disgrace to the proceedings! I
shall punish you with force for your forbidden reachings and your inexcusable, headstrong
diatribe, which is insufferable!'"

Ulisa paused in her narrative.

Baus twitched, frowning.

"But Aurimag had closed his ears to Woisper's sermon and then voiced a terrible curse
upon the assembly as he sauntered insolently from the hall. Woisper was forced to act on his
own judgement. He was not so noble as to be left untouched of anger or hubris. Reaching out
with his mind, he sent psychic intrusions to thrust Aurimag's limbs tightly against the wall.
Aurimag laughed. He pulled his hands free, but not before Barbirius had leaped and clamped
Aurimag's mouth from the progress of destructive evocations. Salmeister dragged Aurimag
to Woisper's secret chambers deep under the castle. They worked terrible spells on him,
stripped him of his rare powers, the ones he had toiled so arduously to achieve. Aurimag
fought like a demon in those clamps, irons and torques, under the fury of exorcisms and
purgations. He resisted the spells and counterspells and far-reaching assaults of body, mind
and spirit. It sickens me to recall the event. Though I was not personally involved in the

---

[*] The neomancers of old, precursors to the modern-day neomancers.

emasculating, the tumult of his cries and his stormings drifted up to the halls of Mismerion, reaching all corners of that keep for ears to hear. Still in my mind they remain as shivering memories . . ."

Baus paused to stroke his chin.

"After the ordeal, Aurimag wandered about the castle like a lost ghost. He was given a menial posting, an under-stewardship at the castle, but he disappeared less than a month later. Several neomancers too—including Woisper and Salmeister . . ."

Turning eyes to Baus, she laughed sadly; her face was dim, eyes welled with tears. "Alas, you know now why Aurimag has shrunken us to knee-high caricatures, encaging us forever. He thought us responsible for his skills being snatched away and the departure of his dream. He could only catch four of us though. I imagine after this harrowing purification, he became an amateur magician, grappling with whatever small spells and prestidigitations he could muster. It seems he has wandered far—to this out-of-the-way fishing port Heagram."

Baus stared pensively at the moon-beamed pool; Ulisa jabbed at the mud. The shady world of 'Neomancers', 'Circles', and enchantments brought a morose edge to his being. He stood up to leave. One thing was for certain: Nuzbek's acts were shameless and they began to make more sense now. The magician was out for blood and he had visited odious spells on his detractors, Woisper, Trimestrius, and now Weavil.

As if reading his thoughts, Ulisa demanded, "Where are you going?"

"To escape."

"Wait, there is more to the story you must hear."

"Later."

Ulisa caught up with him and grabbed his hand. "Aurimag and I worked in close association. I am sorry to say I was harsh with him, even as he was my apprentice. I made an example of him often in front of his peers. It was a mistake. His clever circumventions were so annoying! He took my teachings as pig-headed pedagogy and begrudged me for my meticulousness."

"It seems implausible . . . Though enough to ambush you, shrink you, and stuff you in a bottle?"

"Yes."

"But you are young, and he old in comparison. How could you possibly be his teacher?"

"Looks are deceiving," she replied gravely. "In fact, I am quite the senior; I am his superior in age, though you wouldn't know it. I will have passed ninety two years this winter."

Baus gave an astonished gasp. "How can this be—a youthful a creature like you, looking half his age?"

Ulisa beamed with frank modesty, "I studied the Arts of Longevity at the Conservatory."

"All is explained," muttered Baus. He could feel his own blood quicken with a bizarre attraction to Ulisa's exquisite body which he could not pinpoint. "I must confess, despite all the muskiness of this morass, I feel my own heart beating with an impulse of passion at your presence."

"That is very gracious of you to say," she said, pleasantly. "But, as circumstances have it,

I am many years your senior. The 'Auric Allure' is to blame for this. It pulsates with a rare flux, aggrandizing my emanation and playing havoc with your senses." The sorceress laughed ruefully. "A pity I was not cognizant of the spell while I was tutoring Aurimag." She trailed off, looking penitent now. "I shall have to de-vitalize the power—though a feat much easier said than done."

Baus maintained a sour expression. "This makes me feel so much better."

Ulisa offered a conciliatory rejoinder: "So—you will aid in this quest and ensure your friend's liberation?"

Baus grunted. He was irked at the quality of Ulisa's sing-song request. It smacked of utilitarianism. "It depends—what do you have in mind?"

"Aurimag has likely flown back to his lair of faraway secrecy, or seeking an equally distant place to hide. I require the aid of several colleagues to help me flush him out. You could be one of them. We will traipse to Mismerion and fetch these assistants—a journey of no small magnitude—eighty leagues or more. What do you say?"

Baus jumped back in amazement. "Eighty leagues? I consider myself a man of adventure, but no daredevil!"

Ulisa's mood became remote. "You are free to act as you wish. However you shall have to deal with the consequences." She stared off into the night, pondering weighty matters.

"Hearken! Others arrive . . . we had best don our wits."

She swung around. Crashing saplings and cries now filled the air. Baus unsheathed his dagger. There came a splashing from nearby, a swishing of underbrush and the approach of baying hounds. Tramping boots pounded the turf.

Baus licked his lips. He peered grimly about, hissing: "We have to fly! In an attempt not to seem repetitive, we—"

Baus's statement was cut short. While his back was turned, an irregular event occurred. An extraordinary glow permeated the surrounding trees.

Baus whirled in wonder to behold the pool, a pulsing luminescence, momentarily dimming. The water shimmered, with the same luminescence he had seen earlier effusing from Ulisa's aura when Nuzbek was ready to smite her in the gaolyard.

Baus strained to see into the fog. Only a marked glow dwindled, then became a small yellow zigzag, disappearing like a firefly, fleeing into the murk.

Ulisa was gone—so too was the luminescence.

A voice of encouragement spoke in his bewildered mind: *'Trust your intuition—we are only the true makers of our destinies, nothing else! . . .'*

The friendly mind-push was gone. Baus felt a sickening weariness that caused his heart to sink; his limbs felt empty and limp to the sense of the chill faraway. But he was left to his own devices, in a desolate glade, so crisp with dew and musk and its criss-crossing of tree shadows that he had to pinch himself to make sure that he was not dreaming. It took some convincing to accept that he was encircled with the same lonely beobar trunks that stood in the prison yard.

II

Baus had not liked the penetrating look in the neomancer's face before she had miraculously vanished. A brisk chill wind blew in his soul and infected him with doubt. He had never felt so fearsomely isolated; yet he was free! and on swift wings the emotion gave way.

The thrashing of boots and the yammerings of voices jolted his reverie. Over his shoulder, he saw torchlight glinting through the tree gaps, less than a bowshot away.

Baus wrenched himself to attention and approached the pool. He was no more than a few yards away before he ground to a baffled halt. Here was a new surprise: a set of separate yipping and yapping sounds. Trees blocked passage from the glade.

Baus shrank back. It appeared he was surrounded—by dogs and men.

Baus raced back to the pool and knew the fear of a cornered fugitive. He slumped down on the fallen log, hearing the thump of his silent heart. Defeat was ignominious, especially when he had made so much progress. Eyes fixed miserably into the mire and he saw a dull reflection: a mute and sardonic caricature of himself, with face fractured with angst. Why had Ulisa abandoned him? The vague, capricious firefly—could it have been her in some enchanted form escaping into the slough?

Baus felt a vagabond plan forming in the back of his mind. It was fight or flight. The pool, the dogs . . . perhaps all he needed to solve a dilemma. A healthy dose of the ganglestick too. Nuzbek's talisman must come to work to his advantage.

Almost instinctively, he wiped out the trace of his prints near the edge of the pool. He ran frantically back and heard, without warning, Oppet's two horrors burst in the glade. They snuffled and clawed, baying like wolves, ogling him with rare malice.

Baus wilted at the sight. Their rending claws and gimlet eyes and razor-sharp teeth—were all enough to strike terror into his heart.

The monsters bounded toward him without thought.

He was prepared. There was little chance he would outwit the whole gang of officers and the fierce dogs at once—but he would try and perhaps he might slay a few of them before he died.

Baus gripped his black baton. The first canine leaped, and he flung out the rod.

The rushing hulk fell in a sliding mass. Maw yawned agape and the thing croaked with its flapping tongue eventually stilling. Now its twin sister bounded from the side, snapping at Baus's legs, but not before Baus had brought the ganglestick down on its hoary snout. It sagged to the ground in frozen spellcraft. "There, you vile stabbing curs!" Baus hissed. "Lay down and die like the mongrels you are."

Baus wasted not a second, limping back to the pool at a running jump. His ankle had been gored and the cold water shocked him as he sank up to his knees. Slimy things twirled about his ankles, which he ignored, but the creeping pain from the snauzzer graze was a tough injury to reckon with. Out at the center of the mire he slogged his way deeper, wading neck deep, teeth chattering in the rank slough. The twin deadheads tottered, near enough to touch him.

He chose a place behind the nearest sagging trunk, tucked his body shiveringly close. Nose deep he sank into the mire—waiting.

The moments passed . . . the glade suddenly filled with pandemonium. Perspiring faces, shouts, wrath: all were his world.

Amongst the ragtag Baus recognized Mulfax, Oppet, Madluck and a grimy Tilfgurd. They were grim-faced with limbs and hands scored from a dozen cuts of bramble; the whole disciplinary troop flourished a host of weapons: swords, pikes, whips, and daggers. If anything, the posse wielded aspects of crazed rancour. From behind a crouching mass of spindlefax Skarrow lurched, then Canjun, Haimes and Burkothes. Their weapons hacked ruthlessly at the spine-shrub, slewing a path toward where Baus hid.

Baus thrust himself carefully deeper into the mire. He forced his limbs to arrest their cursed shaking, numbed as they were. He hoped that his time-sensitive plan would not be dumped by technicalities.

Oppet gained his pets and stood quivering when he saw them lying limp. "Kady! Zappy! What has happened?"

He gave a terrible moan, shrinking to his knees. He muttered endearments and discovered they were of no use and he bowed his head, weeping in turn as Skarrow and Haimes came struggling out of the woods. "Hoy Oppet, what transpires to bring such doom to your dogs?" sneered Skarrow.

The dogmaster shook his head erratically. He peered at the foremost hound and whimpered. Its front paws were splayed in an unnatural poise. Haimes, Burkothes and Canjun circled round the supine canines and gazed on Oppet in stunned silence. Kady's face was carved into a rictus; Zappy's eyes had rolled back like white pearls in their sockets, as if the creature had witnessed a devil.

Oppet reached out a trembling hand. Almost at once, the hound leapt to life with a mouth full of teeth. Zappy nearly chewed off his fingers before he bowled over Haimes. The two scrambled back, uttering dazed cries. The shaggy tail struck out at Kady, and with the breaking of the spell, she now struggled to her feet in a fit of confusion.

Tilfgurd rocked back on his heels. "Oi! Do dead dogs come back to life? Nuzbek has enchanted them with magic! Pay attention, men! Dire spells are in the air, the magician must be near."

The officers spun about, brandishing their swords. Mulfax and Skarrow stared about with half snarls, expecting the magician to come vaulting out of the air, pitching bolts of lighting at them. Burkothes's grave silence infected them with only a chill as the dark slick beobar hung about in brooding clots, watching them with dispassion. A faint blue mist huddled above their heads.

The dogs set up a wretched keening. They ranged back and forth along the pool's edge, seeming to detect an unlawful presence far out in the slough. They wagged their tails and lifted their snouts to the air.

Skarrow stood back, arms crossed bluffly on his chest. "It appears the enchanter is out there somewhere. Oppet, your hounds appear confounded, so that may well construe a good tiding. What do they see?"

"Who knows?" rumbled Mulfax.

Skarrow snapped back at him and addressed Madluck, "Any news from your squad?"

"None good," Madluck muttered. "We have rounded up Jorkoff and Zorez. Some other rogues were hiding in the spongebush by the old sea wall. The dogs flushed them out. Some of their cronies fled to the shore to fuddle the snauzzerhound's scent, but they headed north, to the shallows."

"Where's Graves?" demanded Tilfgurd.

Mulfax pointed toward the black-blue trees beyond the pool. "Somewhere west with Ausse and Germakk. They're searching for Nuzbek and his cronies—Nolpin, even Valere. The Captain dredged up a posse from Heagram to be headed by Jukeneb and Diangule. The last I heard they had caught up with Quintlo and Vibellhanz. The rest are still running."

Madluck shook his head with sad wonder. "What a farce! I can see only woe for us: an insufferable breakout, convicts running wild, two dogs playing dead. It doesn't add up. An uncanniness lurks in the air. For the flash of a breath I suspected the magician was playing us a foul trick. But now I wonder, with Mulfy harping on about Nuzbek flying up over the wall on some kind of shabby broomstick."

"It was a balloon, you idiot!" grunted Mulfax "—or some sort of floatation sphere, anyway. I saw it with my own eyes."

"I'll bet you did," mumbled Madluck facetiously. "What of the little green monkey from the jar who you say killed Boulm and fled into a tree?"

"Don't forget the little purple-hooded dame whom Nuzbek almost scooped up and bottled!" chimed Burkothes.

"Bah!" muttered Mulfax.

Burkothes shook his head with comic affection. "Balloons—little green men—I don't know what you two have been drinking, but those imps in the jars managed to escape and I know that we're in a mess of trouble unless we can round them all up."

"Here, here!" cried Canjun. "I commend the ambition." He jabbed his pike into the ground. "Let's get them—easy as pie."

Madluck glared. "Enough of your sarcasm."

"So why are we standing around then like a bunch of hens?"

Oppet raised a minatory finger. "Because the snauzzerhounds have led us to some thing —this glade, for instance, which is of some importance. Someone is out there—my dogs do not trouble themselves unnecessarily."

All eyes turned to the pool. "I'm not going in there, are you?" wheezed Madluck.

Skarrow rubbed his palms with grimacing annoyance. "Then let's get out of here."

Burkothes made a sour glottal noise. "Your pets are playing us for fools, scaring us half to death with their wanton terrors."

Madluck complained: "Oppet, can you not motivate your hounds to dispense with their whining and come up with convicts in their teeth? My ears are in withdrawal."

"By absolutely no means!" cried Oppet. "Kady has suffered a fright and Zappy has been smitten with some sort of thaumaturgy."

The animals affirmed the statement with snuffles and snorts.

Oppet brought out sweetmeats and fixed his eyes wryly on the deadheads. "Not likely, Zappy," whispered Oppet. "—But certainly not implausible . . . It is peculiar that we haven't crossed paths with those rogues Baus and Weavil. Their comic tricks have not assailed us over the course of our searches . . ."

Oppet knelt by the water's edge, noticing something pertinent. "The trail terminates here by this log, then it veers off toward the north end of the glade. The large footprints are a grown man's. These here are a smaller set, as one of those midgets that Mulfax rants on about."

Burkothes snorted, "We just came from that way and none of us discerned hide nor hair of any persons."

"We might have missed an important fact. I say we retrace our steps."

Mulfax cried out: "Weavil has been captured by the magician! I told you: I saw the villain stuff the wretch into a jar before he disappeared over the wall, floating into the beobar!"

"Well, what if Weavil escaped?" muttered Tilfgurd equably.

Madluck asserted himself with a chuckle. "And what if Nuzbek fell from his balloon and broke his neck while Weavil ran away?"

"And what if the night is actually the day, and we are all dream figures in an ancient mind?" offered Canjun.

"Curb your inanities!" growled Skarrow. "I say we resume the hunt. We scour Grumboar all the way back to the bluffs, then we make hay and cut off the rest of the refugees who are probably escaping by the mudflats."

Burkothes rubbed his chin. "It sounds reasonable. It would make tough going but I sense the rogues hope to reach Gooler's Point by dawn."

Haimes scowled. "Recall that the Captain instructed us to regard Nuzbek's capture as the highest priority."

Skarrow skipped forward with an obdurate whine. "Let the Captain deal with the magician. He is doing well busybodying on his own. I say we leg it to the shore, wash our hands of this fog-cursed woodland."

They grumbled assents and the others made motions to depart. Gathering weapons, the troop left Oppet behind still frowning at the deadheads. After a while, he dragged his hide away. The snauzzerhounds whimpered, but there was nothing to be done. Baus lay submerged in the murk behind the stumps and gave a relieved sigh.

The sounds of blundering retreat died in the gloom. Baus staggered out of the water, hauling his dripping form to the shore. He sat hunched in the reeds like a bedraggled crow. Plagued with racking shivers, he rubbed life back into his numb body, feeling terrible pins and needles, but no less, consolation. Lucky that he had taken steps to obfuscate his prints. It had saved him untold misery. It wouldn't have taken any genius to decipher someone had scrabbled into the pool and lay hidden in the marsh.

In brooding silence, Baus felt the brush of wind. A lonely fierceness ached his being. Odd! Now that he was a free man he felt so desperately alone. His situation had become more forlorn now that he was isolated. It was more daunting than that of being cooped up in any prison where at least he had his circle of 'friends'.

He realized he faced hardships on this long journey, possibly starving out in the hinterlands. Unimaginable privations loomed on his horizon, yet he was determined to see it through even if it meant being doomed to wander about, homeless and purposeless. Many mishaps were on the way—no less as a wolf's-head.

Baus squeezed the rankness out of his body. He felt the black tangle of hair fall in clumps as he shook his head. He peeled off more leeches from his skin and hastily summoned his wits. An almost spent brand lay in the grass. Smoking in the mist, it was discarded by one of the officers. He snatched it up and his frigid fingers shook and he began a hurried search for another brand at the glade's edge. He whittled a length of spindlelfax and urged the tip smouldering to life.

He returned his attention grimly to the rows of beobar extending north and east in the forest. He reviewed the facts: if he kept on, the forest would peter out, eventually leading him to the seashore as the harbour dipped like a hunter's bow to bear its breast of sun-blasted rocks. If he could summon his wits enough to surmount these rocks, perhaps he could take cover before Oppet's hounds caught up with him. He had a fighting chance . . .
With shaky confidence, Baus tackled Grumboar's trees. A dogged glint gleamed in his eyes.

III

In the black hours of flight, Baus faced the tender balance between capture and freedom. Disquieting murmurings and eerie hootings drifted to his ears. Grumboar forest lay wrapped about him like a grinning phantom.

He squinted in the gloom and caught unnerving glimpses of eyes—orbs quietly reaching out at him through the black folds and staring back like claret candles.

Bats? Night hawks? Coyotes? Baus's quick feet made short play of the miles. He passed no human company. He found his newly-acquired gladius making excellent work of the obstinacy of briar that created barriers in his path.

He might have ploughed two hours more through underbrush before he faced a misty hollow. Halting and listening, Baus perceived no sign of dogs or humans. A welcome relief! That his plan might succeed became even more than a fugitive hope in his mind.

A ruddy colour returned to his face. His coarse, black hair felt no longer a featureless tangle or ran like jellyfish ribbons down his raw-boned cheeks, but glistened wetly in the dew. His eyes gleamed with that single-mindedness which only the passing, glaring-eyed coyotes could appreciate. His thoughts strayed to Ulisa—and her disclosures of Aurimag— the neomancer.

His lips instantly compressed. The arcane faction to which Ulisa belonged was no more than a source of perplexing vexation to him.

The group was likely a squabbling club of pretentious intellectuals whom he would make efforts to steer clear of. As for this 'Aurimag', he would extract his justice at a time later. As for Ulisa, the dwarf sorceress was pulchritudinous enough, but a trifle too 'utilitarian' for his tastes. Quite a deal too miniature for the purpose of what premierly came to mind. Still—her adroit powers could come in handy, particularly at a time like this.

Baus threw his muscles into his plight. Onward lay his destiny. He edged his way with resolve seaward through the spikenard, down to the last ghost-fringes of the beach. He hooked his brand in a sapling's nook, crept wisely down to the foreshore. The surf pounded relentlessly there—like a soft mallet's drumming. Perhaps a half mile distant, he saw cloying mudflats whose smell rankled his seaman's nose, which he guessed sensed the sighing waters rising to mid-tide.

The gloom was not inconsiderable and Baus hovered in an almost numbing indecision. Dampness crept into his bones; he remained consoled that it at least screened him from prying eyes.

Up and down the beach Baus peered. No torchlight or human presence presented themselves. He acknowledged the fact that on this lonely tract of beach he was the only sapient occupant.

Baus bent his legs back to the wood; he gathered up his torch. A course north was the most optimal, but certain misgivings detained him. To jaunt amiably down this beach with glinting torch was not optimal.

He shielded his flame with his body and let his half-loping foray up the mud flats take him to his destination.

Perhaps two hours remained before dawn; he halted before a salt-rimed rock, neck high. He crouched grimly in the brooding shadow like some vagabond, squatting on his haunches, breathing laboriously under instinctive pressure. He marched around the hither side of the boulder, putting its bulk between himself and the town which was perhaps two miles distant. In broad daylight he would be a sitting duck: any party of foragers could see him.

Better to hide than be recaptured. It was too dark to effect an absolute cover. At best he might find a cave or some burrow up in the rocks by the sea.

Surely not impossible. Gooler's Point was within easy reach, perhaps the best maze of boulders and crannies in which to cache himself and make up his mind regarding an incisive plan.

Quietly, he set his sights on the upcoming bluffs. The cliffs were dim; they stood lined up against the darker backdrop of sky and the bluffs were the same buttressing the western wall of Heagram prison: lofty ramparts of grey, near sheer, that snaked their way around Grumboar and jutted upon the sea to form the rugged headland—Prisoner's Point. It was known to the fishermen of Heagram as 'The Hook'. For this reason no villages presented themselves—and yet for this reason the rockgobbler haunt would be the best hideaway where an escaped convict might find sanctuary—at least temporarily . . .

Baus put his feet before him, sidling along the headland's flank at a reasonable pace.

At last he scrambled up the first slippery steps. He was careful not to drop his torch or let himself slip down into water or mud.

He navigated the complex labyrinth of boulders, to clamber onto the low-terraced stones swept with seawater. Only feet below he could see the sea's awesome weight churning like a grist mill.

Such a secluded crevice was not late in coming. He swivelled his body down a narrower niche and bent his way through a wind-eaten nook, there to appraise a familiar sight: a sheltered alcove, fourteen feet high, sandwiched between two upright slabs. The rock was brine-darkened, scored by years of erosion.

Baus slid into the tunnel. Edging his way along a crabbed path, he cautiously merged into the darkness. The natural walkway included barely enough room for him to bend sideways, let alone breathe, but he felt the shoulders of the rock open, plunging him inside a small, domed cave.

He thrust his torch high, illuminating the surroundings. Two tidal pools lay at his feet, fed by sea waters. The ceiling vaulted up to twice his height, fashioned of a hundred russet streaks dipping down like creeping vines. The ceiling and walls were striated with primitive crystal; a dozen or so smaller stalactites twisted down into the pools. Around the cave's perimeter a rude terrace wound, extremely narrow and crumbly in parts, but sufficiently dry in others. The ridge, it seemed, promised a comfortable sleeping post as it careened around the pools' eerie waters like a promenade.

There were many such natural grottos in these bluffs, Baus knew. Finding them was the trick. He congratulated himself for this timely discovery. It had allowed him to arrive at a safe destination, which, if not for the providence of his brand, he would be totally bereft. Now he made play with the torch to ward off the bats nesting in the stalactite clusters.

He skirted the long narrow pools and moved toward the cave's deepest precinct. Here a raised shelf presented itself, less of a profusion of stalactites on which he might bash his skull. He stepped several paces closer, then slumped in exhaustion.

Time passed. Hours? Minutes? He rose, blinking with hunger. It seemed like an age since he had partaken of any food. He rounded his eyes on a half dozen or so eelfish moving about sluggishly in the pools.

Hungrily he withdrew Lolispar and skewered a fair-sized eelfish. He roasted it over the tip of his flame. In grunts and gulps he devoured the meat, lay down on his side, finally to sleep, overcome with exhaustion.

Hours passed. He awoke shivering, to find his torch spent and pale rays lancing down from the slits in the upper dome. His trousers were soaked; faint amber patterns played on his face; it reminded him of earlier times when he explored the hidden caves up this way. He snapped out of his reverie, finding the water rising to his ankles. Cursing, he found the brown overcoat soaked. The tide was intruding itself on his domain. Where ignorant slumber was bliss, he could not suppress a groan at the vile memory of last night's ordeal.

Baus wiped the fog out of his brain and staggered to the entrance, shaking sense into his mind.

The strength of his mental faculties was coming back. There came a series of pressing thoughts: the impulse of survival. To reside here, nibbling eelfish and shivering in the cold water was no sensible plan. He peered about, wondering how long he could survive before he drowned or caught a chill. A horrid hole—a dripping lair of a drake! Foul to be spending the prime of one's youth in such a gloomy den! It had served his purpose and he could only grumble gratitude at the forces which had allowed him to outwit Captain Graves.

On stiff limbs, Baus stumbled back through the passageway; he squeezed himself out of the cave. Instantly he was blinded by the daylight. White clouds scudded by; wind was a stern whip from the east—neither a good nor bad omen, yet his temples ached and he rubbed them with dispassion. Time and fresh air would be an excellent therapy. The familiar tang of sea brine was gladsome, yet the sound of crashing waves spraying rocky flanks of a headland was somewhat jarring to his headache. A thousand whitecaps furrowed the open sea; Illim Isle slumbered like a giant in the waves. The pale whalestone shelf on which he perched gave him a good view of the area and he brushed peacefully at the thought that the gendron and juniper that clung there would give him cover. The gull-haunted scarps farther north were lit up with a thousand scintillations spreading richly to swirling foam-flecked depths . . .

Baus raised his hands to shield his eyes. Following the mud flats to the empty stretch of sandy beach southward, he saw the first breakwaters of Heagram. A few lubberly scows rode the swells.

Baus knew that to surmount the boulders looming above him comprised an inevitable necessity. Pinched-lipped, he struggled to climb the sunlit rocks. The sea fell thirty yards down; the desolate tongue of exposed granite—Gooler's Point, swung out to sea.

Baus climbed and climbed. Through clumps of spinifex, salt-alder and gorse he climbed, noting the witch hazel that crossed his path, but he did not grouse.

By circuitous route, he gained the forepeak and the laughing cry of gulls greeted him as he rolled flat on his back to survey the sight below. Grumboar lay like a carpet sheltering in the fastness of beobar and birds. The prison was a small walled anomaly—a child's pit spread in an ocean of rippling jade. The old lighthouse occupied the high sward on the bluff and leaned out on an angle like an aged statue. Below, a maze of rooftops, corniced abutments and gables marked Heagram. All its matchstick people moved along the tidy narrow streets and the old wharf and caused him to scowl.

Baus's gaze wandered north. A straggling shoreline of boulders and pillared limestone shelves showed testament to eons of wind-torn waves. At onslaughts of white surf, the water created a flute-like graveyard of rock. A swath of rolling hills disappeared into goldy haze westward. Somewhere the dells halted, and beyond lay a welcome road.

He allowed himself a satisfied nod. Here was a sure route to take. The road, however, could only be freshly patrolled by constables, and so he must take caution.

Automatically, Baus traced his eyes along the faint path that breasted the ridgeline. He found it marked by generations of hooves of goats and ibexes.

Heagram remained a home to him no longer. He turned his back on his birthplace for the last time, and set sights on the seaside vistas.

He trudged upon the barren outcrops for hours and hours and felt a new sense of freedom high above the sea. With his gaze drifting longingly to the west, he let the faint fairy-blue gleam of the Tarnshorn Hills tempt his imagination—no less the graceful ease of the white peaks that floated luxuriously on the faraway horizon. It lulled his sense of desperation. He strode faster. At times he cognized human settlements below: steeples, quaint crofts, tidy granaries, silos, low-lying fences, byres, straw-filled sheds. These habitations were all that remained between the road and the hills.

Baus tramped on. Through the yellow furze and straggling shrub, up and down the bald plateaus of granite and glacial boulders, he saw wild and untamed countryside. And the sea! What an implacable, moving carpet of moody swells whose ripples shimmered with the softest aquamarine.

Baus reveled in his trek. This newfound sense of openness, peering lordly out over the sea, contented him. He was free, shed of responsibilities and duties!

By the end of the day, he was exhausted. The last clouds cast long shadows over the troughs of the land, yet little did it relieve him of fatigue. The afternoon's descent into rocky gullies had left him windburnt and woozy. Three leagues he calculated he had made, perhaps more—a lucky number, considering his notoriety as a jailbreaker, a distance which he attributed to his seaman's charm, which dangled ever so proudly about his neck. With no apparent shelter, Baus dared to sleep in the open—on a grassy outcrop, overlooking Longman's Bay while the stars wheeled above him, pricking the skies with their opalescence.

IV

Baus arose the next day to clear skies and high winds. His belly was hungry and the protests would know no surcease. Baus ignored the pangs and made considerable strides along the ridge. By mid-morning, he reached a less rugged patch where the foreshore had lost much of its look of menace.

He halted, musing, uncertain about the evolution of his pilgrimage. He peered away from the morning sun, taking reconnaissance of a shallow valley spreading before him. The main road was a mile to the west. He had studiously avoided it; it bent its way gradually toward his own path, now he had no choice. The crossroads was marked by a rickety sign with three arms angled respectively to routes south, west, and north:

Heagram	→	3 leagues
Hamhuzzle	→	4
Krintz	→	8

The sign's characters became easier to read as he trudged closer to investigate.

He touched a finger to his mouth. Better to head to Hamhuzzle? Or Krintz? The town Hamhuzzle was a well-known hub of trade, yet notably a near nucleus to Heagram for comfort. Of Krintz he knew nothing. What comforts it offered were unknown. The state of the crabbed, weather-beaten characters and the dilapidated condition of the road admitted to a definite lack of traffic in those parts.

Baus squinted up the ribbon of road. The rutted path continued to weave up a knoll northwards and disappear into a stand of cedar. Certainly the latter direction was of better consideration—particularly as an outlaw.

A twain of covered wagons came beetling their way from the Hamhuzzle direction.

Baus beat a hasty path up the slope. Warily he watched the two caravans roll themselves to a halt at the crossroads. The drivers, both bearded and unkempt, traded words before aiming their wegmors toward Heagram. The snorting beasts created a riot and showed traits of the local breed with dun-coloured flanks and upturned horns. A moment of settling, then the drivers whipped them off toward Heagram and soon disappeared in a cloud of dust.

Supply merchants, Baus guessed. Paid poorly likely—carrying wares of woollens, earthenwares and potatoes.

With the sudden reminder of food, Baus's stomach gave a croaking protest. It had been more than a day since he had last eaten—hopefully a deficiency he would remedy. With five cils in his shoe from his last wins at Flanks, the prospects seemed slim, particularly with Krintz two days' march away.

By noon, the trail dwindled to a straggling footpath. The larch thickened, closed in about him in unfriendly fashion—a hunger also, of depressing quality.

By afternoon he was overcome with exhaustion. He stumbled out of a copse to fling himself down at the edge of a wide clearing, licking his parched lips. Imposing larch ringed the glade. Lifting his head, he saw a rangy, grey-cloaked figure raising a mattock to a small tract of land. Three wegmors stood tethered to a fence a bowshot away. A dozen conical straw bales lay idly in the furze. The landtiller's cottage was mostly hidden by a crowd of larch, with cheery smoke rings curling from the chimney.

Baus felt optimism and approached the tiller. His demeanour was affable. The man was tall, middle-aged and wore an all-weather jerkin. His straw hat was perched over a thatch of peach-coloured hair and the rhythm of his hoeing denoted a sense of respectable innocence that was inviting to Baus, thus augmenting his confidence in his amiable approach.

The farmer caught sight of him and immediately stopped his hoeing.

Baus offered him a salute. The farmer squinted.

"I am a traveler from the south," said Baus, "and seek no harm upon your person or any creature of this land. What can you tell me, good man, of this trail which meanders into the wood?"

The farmer paused before replying. "None pass that way, stranger. The bridge is wrecked —the Saxe flows to the sea and is difficult to traverse."

Baus grimaced. "The disclosure brings melancholy to my heart."

"It is what it is." The man shrugged. "The bridge has been defunct for an age. "What brings you to these parts?"

Baus shrugged indifferently. "A regrettable incident in Heagram has left me bereft of practical options. All to say—I seek challenges in other locales other than that seaside rat-nest. My friends call me Baus."

The man nodded understanding. "When I was your age, I suffered such inconstancies." He gave his head a wry shake. "Life deals us strange turns. I am Rudik, a farmer, too old to travel now, but I'm contented to repose here in this peaceful grove between mountain and sea." He seemed warmed to Baus's practicality. "I fish where I may; I know secluded places up the coast of which many are ignorant. I farm, I exemplify good husbandry, I tend my crops and feed my animals and my two sons."

"An exciting life you lead," observed Baus.

"Ah, you think," laughed the man with charitable ease. "A simple life, yes, you might think, but not as shabby as others."

Baus acknowledged as much. "What of Krintz?"

The farmer leaned on his hoe with concern. "It is an old village, Krintz, as old as any along these remote sea bluffs. The folk have their queer ways, but none come from there now. The last time I remember a traveler coming from the north . . . well, let's just say that it does not come readily to mind."

A moody expression came over the farmer's face. "I am not certain, but rumour has it that some terror grips the area. Whether it be physical or spiritual, I do not know—but I've heard tales of bewitchment whispered in the glades, and the abandoned ruins of the settlements between here and Cant's Cove. Krintz is a far distance, and as I've mentioned, no sane person ever tracks this way to offer news."

Baus resumed a manner of easy camaraderie. Hunger tore at his guts, but he would not show it. He proceeded to casually cite maxims and pleasantries.

"I'll warn you, friend, there are no roads in those parts," said Rudik abruptly, "only old ghosts. The seaside is riddled with boulders, dizzying heights, chasms, gulfs. Do not underestimate them! They are as much hazard to the wayfarer as the bite of a tung snake! The region is far too perilous to fish, except by intrepids. Adepts like me who know the way are exempt . . ."

The darkness fell from the landtiller's face. "Well, if you mean to track all the way to Krintz—then I can only tender you this advice: follow the track and never stray from it. It starts behind my cottage. It is tended by the ibex which know better than men. Stray not a yard from their margin. There'll be little to aid you should you fall afoul of some unnaturality. The bridge may still be awash at the Saxe, in which case it will take you upstream. You'll come to Flander's mill; there you'll find a decent place to ford. In the meantime, I can offer you this bag of apples, a bit of bread, perhaps some good luck. By thunder, you look thin! You could use a bit of fat!"

"I could," agreed Baus with favour. The farmer went off to fetch the victual and the cottage door jangled open. Baus for the first time saw two boys, tossing hay nearby in a growing pile. The youths sported peach blond hair like their father and had eyes of matching blue. The wegmors munched happily away.

Rudik returned, thrusting three apples and an extra half loaf of bread into Baus's palms. "It's meagre fare—but better than nothing." He laughed fondly. "Good fortune to you, Baus!" With a hearty salute, he returned to his work.

Baus stuffed the items into his jerkin. *Yes, better than chawing wildgrass and blue furze wegmor-style in the wild.* Baus set off at a lope across the clearing, noting dourly that he would have starved if not for the capriciousness of his late fortune.

He gained the first silver-green patches of larch and took to the wegmor path like the old man had said, but was plagued with a flood of qualms. Could he acquire funds in Krintz? Funds which might allow him to buy back favour in Heagram? The idea caused him strain. He thrust the discouraging thought out of his mind. The earlier rumours of bewitchment spoken of were more pressing.

In more optimistic spirits, Baus confronted the sombre trees and the meandering trail facing him. He felt assured that no one would come looking for him in these parts.

Late afternoon passed slowly. The dusk straggled in and many times Baus lost sight of the path which seemed to stray in all directions at once. He came to ever lonelier and lonelier vistas: glades, carpets of yellow bay flowers, hawthorns, hollows. There was something incredibly eerie about the lie of the land here: the flora and fauna held an uncomfortable ambience—particularly the gaudy yellow flowers that stood out on their pale stalks and green leaves with tender white striations. The stems barely stirred despite the seaward gusts tousling his own matted hair.

Shadows scratched their way across the lands. Baus fought fatigue and found shelter in a cramped hollow, filled with ancient cedar, which to his dismay, brought uncomfortable dampness as the night progressed. Famishment had him awakening in the dark: he was accosted by foraging rodents. Twice by a claw-happy weasel, then a snuffling koot which harried him up a crooked tree. Hours later he crept down to fetch a bit of bread from the nook in a larch where he had left it judiciously high to avoid molestation in his sleep. Chewing through the tough fare, he listened wide-eared to the lonely coyote calls in the distance. It was answered by others, equally as estranged. Strange birdlike hoots stirred the silence; furtive shamblings of tiny feet, and soft eddies and suckings of the sea, churning not a few bowshots away, came to his ears.

Gradually Baus was lulled into a troubled slumber. He awoke racked with stiff limbs and fogged brain. He watched the horizon fill with low-scudding clouds. As Rudik had intimated, the Saxe was hidden by an alder grove a mile away. The waters were fordable only barely about a half mile upriver where the old grain mill sat and the windmill leaned on an angle, basking like an ancient tower in the sun. The water was coloured mahogany; the rocks were ochre-stained. The stream was wide, but shallow, and afforded a safe passage by means of limestone stepping stones, strategically laid out by previous pioneers.

Baus applied himself to thinking before crossing the river but spied through the screen of trees an abandoned wooden outbuilding. Why was the region so desolate?

For a day and half he trudged. No sign of folk or beast did he discover; gradually an ineffable loneliness crept over his being. Occasionally he emerged from tight knots of larch to stand upon a gusty promontory to stare bleakly out upon the sea. There were many such naked points, wind torn and eerie, like some wizard's perch. He spied a fearsome, three-masted barque, all black and wind-torn, lurching and bounding in the swells like some fabled menace—likely upon some dastardly voyage. The vessel slogged its way northward without flag, causing Baus to shiver, even though he was glad of its departure. He knew that ships of this size were manned by pirates. He recalled the horrid tales of mariners unfortunate enough to have crossed paths with those bloodthirsty rogues—killers who plundered the coast, despoiling their victims, and leaving only a tearful waste in their wake.

Baus moved on. Out of the knife-blade shadow, he ducked a flock of kite-thrush. Black beaks gave rise to raucous croaks which fought the wind's howl. Scavenging fowl as these were dangerous; they had down-turned beaks similar to wegmor horns and hollowed out yellow eyes. They were evil, all round evil cousins of the black-billed thrush.

Baus stood at the edge of a glade, taking in the barren remnants of a trio of old wind-eaten columns. He trooped closer, discerned a few toppled limestone busts of an unrecognizable statue, lying prone in the wind-blown grasses. Noses and ears had been shorn.

Discoveries as this were dispiriting and Baus took up the trail once again. The signs of what appeared 'grave-markers' began to appear in greater and greater numbers. Amongst patches of rubble and old stone, blackened cairns and fanes made themselves known. They were of skilled fabrication and of ancient quality: stone slabs and plaques and gravestones in the grassy emptiness inscribed with cryptic declamations like—

"Beware the remorselessness of the Dakkaw!"

    . . .

"Curse that which hoards—multiple maledictions to the Dakkaw!"

. . .

"On the way to Krintz may venturers beware! A hefty curse be laid on the Dakkaw's deeds. I, Druli, cousin of Falon, driven of hope and comfort, despair for his welfare!"

Baus frowned. The disclosures were queer. Who was this Dakkaw? What oblique nature inspired such frightful writing? A fanatic goes to the extent to inscribe such cryptic hints on his relative's tomb—? What was the world coming to?

Baus sought to attribute the significance as anything other than an omen, but was largely unsuccessful. An upsurge of superstition coloured his confidence. A malaise gnawed at his being—one similar to that which had afflicted him earlier upon the outset of the sightings.

The day progressed, but any attempt to decipher the nature of the queer avowals gave way to bleaker ruminations. At first thought, he decided to steer clear of this 'Dakkaw'. The person or creature referenced had indubitably perished a long time ago, along with the crumbling wretched fanes and the weathered markers. A speculative part of Baus's brain could not wholly dismiss the fact that the absence of wayfarers in this region was not entirely explained by the ruggedness of the landscape and the absence of roads. The terrain was meagrely salutary; it could support only shreds of barley, flaxhack, wheat, and doubtlessly a reasonable fishing or wegmor industry—if one ignored the unnerving ruins and the ambience that clouded the air.

Baus pressed himself to industry; he would take these noteworthy clues as counsel for caution and proceed with all speed.

V

The following day Baus felt himself in better spirits. He had managed to snare a rabbit and cook it over brambles and twigs fired with a flint chunk he had found. He bent his way northward, up the coast through the brightening wilderness. Passing an evening free from wandering koots had been advantageous; now he enjoyed fresh air that filled his lungs with invigorating ease. A taste of fall majesty was in the air; the vistas towering over the sea pleased him. High promontories formed such impressive eyries for studying the grandeur of the coral-blue and white-foamed Poesasian swells that much of Baus's apprehension began to diminish. Since he had put significant leagues between himself and Heagram, his muscles relaxed. He was in no mood to hurry to another cage—even if it meant possibly starving. Warm sunshine brushed his face; the landscapes shimmered in soporific warmness, a sultry haze enclosed the woods so untypical of the fall season. The larch had thinned to straggling clumps; now he stood atop a low hill looking through a screen of yellow gorse.

A gentle valley spread itself at his feet: majestic ruins, leaning towers, arches of stately synchrony. For a half league or more, he saw granite pillars, alabaster fountains, wind-carved obelisks, antique spires, low-domed repositories. He was further amazed to spy a jumble of dilapidated promenades stretching beyond the larger monuments. He had never witnessed such a ruined city—or heard of anything like it in these parts.

A large structure dominated the city. It was more massive than the other buildings and appeared a curious intrusion. It was in better condition than its brothers, glinting sharply in the distance, but even from this vantage, Baus saw a convoluted roof pitched on many angles and supporting two towering spheroids, bronze and crusted with verdigris, flanked by iron towers.

Baus descended the hill energetically. He set a course for the structure, bending gamely down into the ruins. He followed overgrown paths, flagstoned streets, narrow alleys, cobbled ways that threaded through the undisturbed city. He ventured past a domed amphitheatre, a shady vine-covered court, then some alcoves. He crossed a footbridge, and paused to marvel at a series of colonnades whose onyx entablatures seemed intact, but whose wooden rooftops had long since disintegrated. The intricacy of the ancient town was astounding! Snatches of murals caught his eye: majestic barques riding on blue seas whose pigments had almost faded... butterflies and sunflowers with slender wings and other items of craftsmanship. All offered some strange glimpse into the past, a hazy grandeur that made him wonder what had gone before. Had this city been deserted? Where had the denizens gone?

He trudged more cautiously under an archway and the hanging vines that led to more footbridges, where he paused to arrive at the forecourt heralding the singular edifice. The twin spheroids gaped down on him with frowning authority; a great sundial lay couched at his feet, weed-blurred in the shadows. A ruined peristyle stood forlornly while an overgrown garden reached fingers in from the right.

Baus stepped over the fallen blocks, marvelling at the quality of the massive masonry. He entered the courtyard. The edifice seemed to close in on him, shadow-hampering him like some great phantom. There was something odd about this structure, distinctly disturbing. As if the pretentious construction shouldn't be present, given the quality of the other buildings half gobbled and disintegrated. There was a peculiar impression of tight-lipped mystery wafting about this place, whispering of time-lost energies, secrets in the regal past when riches flowed in abundance.

Baus could not immediately appreciate the quality of the archaic spheroids. What was the purpose of the things? Why were they placed so obliquely? Could they be lightning rods? Decorations? Functional arches of unknown nature?

Baus rejected the surmises. He guessed the building to be some sort of fort, perhaps an abbey. The walls were limestone, with streaks of dun and olive-green clouding the exterior. A single brass door centered on the main façade; it had a moon-mossed lintel. No ordinary door was this, standing some nine feet tall and looming rivet-studded in the vivid daylight.

Baus stood closer to the doorknocker. He could not help but gaze on a coat-of-arms inlaid on either flank of the portal. To the left arched a roaring scorpion; to the right, a hooded falcon inclined with a piercing eye. Crenellated ramparts stretched to infinity at either side— only an illusion. The walls terminated into smaller, lower defensive outbuildings.

The spheroids dwarfed him. He frowned anew. There were no low-lying casements on this façade; only six diamond-paned oriels spreading equidistantly, high up near the roofline. They were plum-darkened, as if expressively covered from the inside.

Baus pitched himself forward, pausing before the door's wide, cracked steps. He edged warily into the deep shadow and halted mid-step. A slightly moribund sound impinged on his reverie, prickling the hairs on the back of his neck. The sound was not immediately comforting—a muted, vacant lament, exuding a waft of helplessness—this from the cracks of the stone, perhaps of some creature confined within.

Baus hurried back, feeling his skin crawl. Only silence greeted him. The rustle of weeds weaved in the wind, followed by the call of an ancient sea bird. The blood hammered in his ear. He twitched. Fatigue and anxiety had him jittering like a corncrake!

He turned to leave, but his eyes caught a glimpse of a small grate at ground level. The opening was perhaps a foot wide, twenty to the door's side and he could not help but investigate.

Baus moved toward it like a fascinated hound and found the portal no bigger than the roundness of his face, yet blacker than coffee. The mesh was tucked a foot beneath court level. Cool airs issued from the grate; the mouldy press of vapours caused him to shrink back. Something dwelled within—of what, he could not guess.

Baus back-pedaled his way out of the courtyard, stumbling over a trio of toppled stones. He picked himself up, cursing, and perhaps twenty paces later, felt a chill run up his spine as the appeal returned, filling his ears like a ratchet gong. The sound appeared remarkably human.

He contrived to bolt in the opposite direction. Far away did he leave that disturbing edifice and its eldritch ambience . . .

* * *

The miles drifted by.

Baus silently reprimanded himself for his graceless worry. What was there to it? If someone were trapped down there, then he too was not to be captured and trapped.

Provocations of this kind entailed perilous futures, and he was not ready to blunder into doom.

Baus could not dismiss the guilty feeling, reminiscent of Weavil's plight, of abandoning a potential soul in jeopardy. He had possibly left an innocent to a bleak fate and his display of callous unconcern would catch up to him sooner or later. He knew that perhaps his own self-fulfilling prophecy invited cataclysm and ill fortune.

Such rogue feelings he had known before. This one cast no less an unwholesome pall over his being.

He chose to ignore it.

Baus plodded on ever more grimly.

It was perhaps early in the afternoon when he came upon a large barn. It was the first so durably constructed in this area since Rudik's croft. Unlike the barns common to the region, this one was made of blue stone—in fact, it was cunningly constructed. Griffins decorated the eaves; remarkable gargoyles graced its polished exterior. A sharp, goblin-traced roof, tiled with red clay reflected the noonday sun. Baus saw the structure was minimally landscaped, but unnaturally large and seemed to betray a sense of unmitigated eccentricity and the amplitude of its owner, whoever that may be. Brown switch-vine grew along the seaward face. A massive pine door, stained from rich resins and age, leaned ajar.

Baus moderated his enthusiasm. He stared from a distance with a profound interest. The edifice seemed inviting enough, yet still slightly out of context with its goblin-like effigies and massive sturdiness. Perhaps the warmth of its interior could provide respite for his weary limbs?

Baus picked at his teeth. Was such a safe idea?

A long low wagon was thrust up casually against the north face. His ears detected the hollow lowing of a wegmor.

Edging his way around the side, he discovered a pair of untethered beasts. They were munching furze and inspected Baus with a prideful indifference. He was soon to discover a small iron plough, a tidy garden, a bed of corn-squash, carrots, arrowroot, leeks, and an annex erected to the barn's flank. An egg-laying hen-loft? A rabbit hutch?

Nothing seemed menacing here. Yet, something hovered on the edge of his perception, as invisible as thought. Baus suspiciously searched about for signs of human activity. None was evident. Puzzling! Only the sound of a hissing wind and the twitching of the wegmors' tails. The ripe scent of forest drifted from the nearby meadow. There was the whiff of aromatic cedar, musk, decomposing leaves, larkspur, asphodel.

Gaining conviction, Baus gave the door a tug and he entered the confines without fear.

A sawhorse and a long worktable dominated the foreground. A ball peen hammer, nails, screws, saws, and various instruments were arranged on hooks on the nearest wall. The instruments were ordinarily set lower down but they were irregularly large and demanded room. The facing wall supported a rack of rabbit skins hanging in tandem. Another massive table resided with stout legs. In the shadows stood numerous wood-carven effigies. They were of fantastic girth: foxes, antelopes, hares, geese, wild wegmors. A great mug and other edibles sat on the table, protected under a glass jar. All were enormous. Baus could sense the inordinately large aspect of all things—mug, tools, sawhorse, carvings, furniture. On the back of the high-backed chair hung a cloak of leather affixed with iron rivets. This, too, was suggestive of an overlarge being. What reasonable human being could fit in such a garment?

Baus's lips twitched with interest. Obviously the person, or persons, who claimed ownership of this well-kept barn were of an appreciable configuration. A cautious individual was wise not to cross such a person, in fact, such corollary reasoning severely hindered Baus's presence in the barn in the first place.

Casting furtive glances at the statues, he pulled at his lip. He could not detect any palpable evil, try as he might outside of a hobbyist's paranoia. Moreover, what was there to lose from a reconnaissance? He set forth to inspect the victual, with inquisitive care.

A wedge of oatcake, a tureen of brown mead, a slice of cold sausage—all were in plain sight, all well-laid out under a bell jar and appearing edible and fresh.

Baus licked his lips. To prolong any hunger for the sake of prudence seemed overkill. To indulge in food that was not one's own, however, suggested a flagrant act of trespass. Nothing under the table suggested any elaborate trap, or snare. Lures, deadfalls, or other discommoding deterrences seemed absent.

Convenient but odd! Why should an individual leave fresh sustenance for any wandering wayfarer to devour?

The question remained unanswered; the altruism of a theoretical figure appeared implausible outside of the scope of a normal lack of heed of one's own property and privacy.

Baus's temptation grew: the victual seemed untouched, harbouring a scent of appealing quality.

Baus glanced about in perplexity and thought that perhaps the owner had stepped out momentarily to complete an errand? Yes, that was it!

Baus congratulated himself on his deduction. Partaking of the sustenance, he would be off as quick as a weasel: the dweller, landlord, or occupant would be none the wiser.

Further vacillation continued, but he swiftly devoured the victual and departed the byre in satisfaction. Whoever had provided the lunch would be somewhat bewildered by the missing portions, but what of that? Would he not, in similar condition, offer sustenance to a downtrodden wayfarer? Gratified with the reasoning, he made excellent progress toward Krintz, along a route through rolling hills, flowering asphodel and fragrant heliotrope.

An hour passed. Then another. The lands sloped down toward the sea, rife with more strange, yellow, slightly acrid asphodel. More startling ruins came to view—chipped pedestals, crumbling birdbaths, porticos, weatherworn alabaster gates . . .

Around a small copse the path now took a downward turn and Baus halted before a glade of yellow brilliance. A wondering gasp hung on his lips. Flowers of such effulgence had never been his privilege! The field was sprawled with golden splendour: cornflower, saffron, lemon, zigzagged mixes of faint purplish cynoflex. Indeed, such a wonderful spectrum stung his eyes! A thin path wound its way through several hundred feet of swath and Baus moved forward like a spellbound child.

He had not reached the half-way point before he stopped, sharpening his ears. A sudden noise had disturbed him: a heavy wheezing—or perhaps a raspy, laboured murmuring. It was quite incongruous with the elegant grace of the wavering asphodel and caused him to frown.

Glancing quickly left and right, Baus put one foot in front of the other. He could not help but feel an unnatural awe at the urge to stagger off the path and wade knee-deep into the strange, yellow plants.

He ventured not twenty paces before the flowers seemed to stiffen and coil about his ankles as if alert for his escape.

Baus stamped a foot. Arrogant creatures! Was he mistaken, or were the flora rearing their heads at him, big as ham fists?

He uttered a carefree laugh, chiding himself for his alarm. Yet checking the rising of hairs on his back, he found there was something to his former spark of animosity. The flowers had reared up hauntingly, reminding him of those that he had seen on the path just outside of Rudik's farm. The petals had suddenly flared outward and spread: a lofty flower-giant emitted a soft sucking sound. A cloud of sulphurous air puffed forth. Baus coughed, almost gagging on the fumes. A strange low hum seemed to sicken the air with its vibration.

Baus began to back out of the glade. His trepidation only increased when he stumbled over a rigid object. He crawled to his feet in terror, and staggered back in amazement when he saw a bulky shape, one immediately recognizable. A red-beard wisped up—a rogue lying face up and arms slumped over his chest in some slovenly fashion. The figure was wet and soggy, obviously deposited there for some inexplicable reason. His blue dungarees were torn; his cheeks were scratched and his scarlet beard had gone miserably limp, drooping in a moist, dispirited way. A stout beobar limb lay partially hidden in the grasses. A club?

"Valere! Up, I say!" cried Baus in a frantic voice. "I am here, to fetch your bones to Flanks!"

The figure did not respond.

Baus nudged the sprawling frame with his boot.

No reaction.

The captain, or so he claimed, was obviously comatose, perhaps even dead and Baus become suffused with apprehension. He saw no mark or outward wound presented on the pasty skin. The circumstance brought him a ripple of dread. Surely the red-beard's foe, if such there was, remained lurking, somewhere, to spring on him.

Baus ducked low, trying to shield his figure from a prying figure in the undulating flowers. He peered left and right. He saw no one. Wrath and suspicion racked his brain. Escalated pleadings upon Valere's person made no difference.

How long had the captain lain here?

Baus tried to rouse his comrade, but to no avail. The rough-skinned inmate was damp, heavy as a brick, and under the influence of some evil reek that rose from his skin. His underside seemed almost cold as death, as if he had lain here for a day or more.

Baus fretted with indecision. Could he just leave him here? No! He must rouse the seafarer, get him to his feet or he would die. No longer would his conscience allow him to abandon another to an indeterminate fate. The clammy bulk refused to budge. The heavy form turned, the mouth slowly opened, offering a gibber or two, as if bewitched.

Baus reeled back in startlement. His mind strayed to Rudik's cryptic warnings—perhaps ghosts were not so farfetched . . .

Baus suddenly felt a curious and not so pleasant sensation crawling over his skin: something akin to insensate hunger—or a peculiar craving—for a sweet succulence. He thought the urge bizarre; he fought the ludicrous feeling. It was inconceivably peculiar, considering that he had just ingested a generous meal The fact that he was not normally enthused to such things of scent or taste began to rankle on his logic . . .

There was a tug again! How deliciously fragrant the asphodel smelled!

Reaching out a hand, he touched the petal of a particularly fragrant flower that had leaned forward and almost fondled the back of his hand.

Baus sniffed with interest. The flower bobbed in a tempting pose. Baus caressed the plant. He took a deep draft, and smelled the most wondrous fragrance pervading its petals—it was of a woman's scent, seductive and overbearing: lavender, anise, olive balm, spindleswoon. How had he missed these exalted essences? The mark of singular incompetency! Baus snapped his fingers with contempt.

He tore off the flower's petals and with an absurd delight began to devour them in gulps and smacks. Incomparable! Sweet as molasses and honey, and sweetbread, and candycake combined . . . His brain reeled with the grandness of it all. Such palatability! So flavoursome! His mad desire wailed siren song; it traveled across the gulfs of his mind and let him journey to a land unheard of.

VI

It could have been hours or days that passed, such was the torpor that Baus felt lying there like a bloated snogmald in the grass. Dusk was falling; it appeared as if there would be more lying around to do.

Such was not to pass. A gigantic figure, clothed in hunter's garb with a coarse leather hood, swung out of the furze and strode into the glade with imposing majesty. The gentleman, if such be, sensed something amiss within the patterns of the pernicious flora. There was an inconsistency that had him sniffing at the air and pulling at his sideburns. He looked this way and that, hooking a great knobnail of a nose with his finger, before he came restlessly heavy-footing it over to the two mounds that lay senseless in the garden of tangly enchantment.

As if from a dream, Baus remembered the figure stooping, peering into his eyes and blinking with ironic pity. Baus peered back into his dun-coloured face. He saw a loose, eel-like mouth, very greenish eyes, a hooked, hog snout. The vision was absurd—this monstrous, coarse visage, all gnarled and grinning with a head as bald and domed as an egg, with a nose as large as an old parsnip. But, Baus remembered the figure dipping down to inspect him with interest. The leather fit him well, the boots were tough, the jerkin and baggy brown pantaloons—well, what was there to say? Yellow belt and black buckles—they were all imprinted in his memory despite the dreary apathy.

How many fistfuls of flowers had he devoured?

Gods and demons! Baus winced. He felt exceptionally nauseated; it pained him sorely to think in such numbers.

He noticed further that the figure carried with him a long bow; three freshly killed hares were tied to his belt. A hunter he seemed . . .

A low-pitched rumbling suddenly filled the air, words which were not spoken unkindly, but which went unrecognizably unheard insofar as meaning was concerned.

The ogre picked up Valere's club and placed it in his teeth. He dragged the two of them through the glade by a leg each. He pulled them through the hazy hollows and fallow fields as if they were of no weight. Everything sheened—gold, yellow, mustard, flaxen to Baus's blurred eye; inchoate forms, absolutely dream-ridden, hazed in and out of his memory: golden blisterbush, yellow crackthistle, lemon asphodel, golden falling leaves. By the time he found himself laid down on his back, his skin was raw and edged with cuts and his cloak was stained from sliding. He was completely weary, but he was aware that he and Valere lay sprawled before the old byre where he had taken his lunch. Through filmy lids, he saw the giant retrieving the wagon and hitching his wegmors, thrusting his new catches onto the back like bags of flour.

The giant sang in a booming voice: an eerie song rendered in an archaic seaside dialect, while he hopped in the front and urged his wegmors on to speed.

Baus was not sure where they were headed; he only guessed they were heading in a southerly direction, back through the leagues to the old city. He grimaced. As the day drew to an end, the dreamy orange haze gave way to copper and grey. The incongruous party reached the stone ruins that stood forlornly as before, this time in the early light of evening. Baus's eyes adjusted and wandered over the rubble like sluggish marbles. He perceived a series of wind-worn skeletal slabs and vine-crawling alleys—the same as the forsaken city offered earlier.

The comprehension stirred a sense of ludicrous disbelief in his mind. He thrashed and heaved but could not react practically to the impulse that drove his limbs.

The cart rolled endlessly on—over broken stone pathways, through weedy plazas, under cracked archways. The wegmors wilfully tugged their load with earnest. In what seemed a never-ending odyssey over rubble and ruin, they arrived back at the fort-abbey containing the mysterious spheroids—not to Baus's surprise. The maze of black turrets lofted with ever more macabre authority in the waning light and had Baus struggling to thrash some more.

With a flourish, the giant alighted from the wagon and drew out a set of ringed keys from his inner sleeve. He plunged a mighty key into the fort's portal, set it heaving ajar with an excruciating creak. Such a door was no orthodox door—for it sagged too heavily on its bronze hinges, one of massive girth and fabricated with only the forethought of wizardry.

The ogre gathered up his charges and carried them into the gloom. He tossed them with indifference on the floor. They wallowed in litter spreading as wide across the dusty beobar planks as could be imagined. The giant set four wall sconces to light, then he closed the mammoth portal and barred it tightly with a stout brass beam. He scooped up Baus and Valere and slumped them into chairs alongside a monstrous table. The table spanned the greater part of his high, dark hall which seemed fabulously large. Baus remembered his paralysis, watching as his host repaired to a side chamber, gripping his slaughtered hares. There was a tumult: of pots and various cooking instruments, then a sizzling of frying meat along with idle jabber. The smells of stewed hare wafted in from the pantry, tantalizing Baus's tongue with aromas of promise.

Baus tried once more to jerk his limbs free but found them too feeble for motion. His brain was muddled—much too heavy, and signals could not be sent. He could barely speculate, let alone strive to stab out with his dirk at the foe. Valere was no exception and gaped vacuously at Baus from a round, pale, bedraggled face from across the table.

The giant returned a time later. He wore a curt expression, prompted likely from the listless droop of his guests which implied a disparagement of himself.

Muttering reproaches, he rummaged about a repository and emerged with a flask of amber liquid which he thrust forcefully down Valere's throat. Baus suffered no more gentle treatment. With revulsion he felt strong fingers drive the liquid down his gullet with no more scruples than an ailing pet might feel a worm pill being stuffed in its maw.

After ingestion, Valere's eyes grew waxy. His lips compressed into slits. Baus's nostrils flared out like a wegmor's and he plunged his fingers down his throat as if searching for a serpent that had tumbled within.

"There, that's better!" the giant sniffed. The knotty features of his aged face achieved an earlier joviality. "By Gladien's flowers, I believe you two jacks have been bewitched! Lucky that I happened along—else you would be part of the scenery by now. Welcome to Bisiguth!"

As completely awed as they were, their senses were alert. The potion had brought them vigour. Now they offered each his own ironical examination. Baus and Valere's eyes rolled to their surroundings where they discovered themselves in a spacious hall, darkened with cool shadows. They were at the extremities of a long table, with carven goblets of crystal placed immediately before them. Under the space of a vaulting, iron-filigreed ceiling diffuse maroon light filtered down from small diamond-shaped oriels to reveal a barbaric iron-grouted chandelier hanging from a chain over the table. The ancient staircase hunching to the side with its gargoyled banisters wandered up somewhere in the gloom to a second floor. Along the walls, three coats of armour hung with thick grime. Other artifacts made themselves known: bronze shields, medallions, brass gongs, garnet-mantled sceptres, musical instruments, fantastic oars, shelves, antique platters, porcelain cutlery.

Baus peered about with wonder. The floor lay littered with refuse: planks, pulleys, ropes, sacks of meal, bits of furniture, mouldering plaster, shards, glass, detritus and neglect. The place stank of mice. Dust and decay had had their way. Musty webs hung rankly from the corners; the wainscoting was something from the antique past. Despite Baus's preoccupation with getting far from this place, he could not suppress his revulsion.

From an ornate antique flagon came heady vapours; a huge figure pouring wine lavishly. The ogre's ministration was placid, a jocular smile twitched his lower lip. He stood monstrously over them like some great gnarled oak, casting an enormous shadow, stark and imperial. Despite the large potbelly dangling over his wide black belt, the bare forearms were thick and scabrous, built of not insignificant muscle. It was a feature Baus studied with care.

Bisiguth's lord plopped himself down at the table's head and gusted out a weary sigh: "Now that you are yourselves, swains, come drink my wine! It is of excellent vintage, pure and red, which I share with you. Secured from the finest wineries of New Krintz, when times were nobler, I must say—yet I offer it freely." He topped up their goblets with cordiality, then laced his own.

Valere uttered a poignant remark but the figure held up a hand. "Drink, my barrel-butt, drink! Let us conduct explanations later. I am the Dakkaw of Krintz—or more accurately, the Dakkaw of Old Krintz. Once I was a law-abiding grandee of the modern village, but since then I have given up that tendentious identity. I reign now as denizen and lord of 'Old Krintz', whose realm includes all that you see about you—ruined grandeur abounding in and behind this manse." The Dakkaw's eyelids drooped as if scrutinizing his guests for the first time. "And who might you rascals be? Do you have multiple lives? I have surely not rescued you from death for the first time?"

Valere creaked back his chair with force. "I am Valere—a renowned Illimer and Captain and expert seaman." He stared haughtily at the giant and Baus, who regarded him with an equally surprised concern. "If my eyes do not deceive me, here is Baus the shellames-stealer —vandal and conniver, and also my recent comrade at Heagram prison. Fancy this familiar rogue in a crypt of such dungeon-like quality! Light and Lords! Have a better torch will you, Dakkaw? We might all better scrutinize ourselves then!"

The Dakkaw twitched cheeks but the seaman would have no rest: "I am as much bewitched as bewildered! The last I remember, was trudging through a field of dazzling light —brilliant yellow, so rich of mischief that it blinded my senses! The dread flowers reached up at me; I could not help but become hypnotized by their allure. I inhaled their loathsome fragrance the like of which I have never smelled before. Now I find myself squatting dazed in this disorderly hovel!"

Baus bounded to his feet, apprising his friend of a similar fate. "I discovered you in a great glade of asphodel! You were lying wet as if dead. I tried to revive you, but only found myself eating of those same eldritch flowers, then tumbling into a moist, but incapacitated dream."

"Patience!" commanded the Dakkaw, holding up a hand. "I enjoin you to take your seats. After all, you are guests at Bisiguth and it is only polite. You have both raised matchless questions, which will be soon answered in due time."

Valere glared odiously at the giant and did not seat himself. His eyes wandered about the chamber seeking exits and egresses.

The Dakkaw clucked, "Ah! I see you gazing fervidly toward the front entrance, Valere. Understand that those doorways are brassbound and secured by deadbolt from within, the key to which I hold in my waist pouch. It is terribly difficult to retrieve, Captain. In so saying, while I am alive, none might take it. Likewise, below these floors exists nothing but a maze of repositories where I store my possessions, a place of no kind portent for visitors to wander about casually."

A low wail issued from below, a muffled and ragged sound, much as a gagged person might make struggling to break free from a bridled condition. Baus recognized the outcry instantly as one similar on his earlier trek to Bisiguth.

The Dakkaw reared back and roared, "Shush, Cedrek! This is no time for outbursts!"

Valere shook his head, with bitter understanding dawning. "So you wish to keep us here, Dakkaw—what do you want with us?"

The figure ignored the question; instead he appraised Baus, who had taken pains to inspect him carefully. "Mind that I have stowed your gladius yonder, Baus." The ogre lifted a thumb to a wicker basket tied well above the sconces out of reach. He gave a ludicrous smile and remarked, "It is a fine weapon—as fine as any of its size. And that buff club of yours, Valere. Really! You are quite the bone-cracker, aren't you? But of no import." He gestured up to the web-haunted heights as if lost in thought. "Where was I? Yes, your club! I have stashed it away in an unobtrusive place below in the tombs, lest it be discovered and end up causing mishap. The last, or rather, *second last* guest who sojourned at Bisiguth attempted a footling prank of comparable nature and met with a bitter fate which I care not to describe."

"And what was that?" inquired Baus hotly.

The Dakkaw brought up a large hand to dab thoughtfully at his chin. "Well, if you want to know, that would be 'Mearl'. The dandy came knocking at my door about this time last year. How avid the spice peddler was to pay a visit and perhaps scout out my valuables! How rambunctious! How avid I was that he could board with me for a time, but the cad simply refused!"

Baus put a hand of shocked surprise to his mouth. "Whatever for? Surely a brief visitation is not too much to ask?"

The Dakkaw nodded fulsomely. "Nine months ago and a day he spent with me. A passing trifle amongst friends."

Baus sucked in a breath of amazement. "You guard an astute memory, Dakkaw. On the contrary, the time you describe comprises an appreciable visit. Your magnetism clearly parallels your hospitality. What, pray tell, of 'Mearl'? Is the peddler no longer residing at Bisiguth?"

The Dakkaw narrowed his brows in melancholy. "I regret that Mearl has perished. Which brings us to another topic—vastly cheerier. It is of the love that I have for a bride whom I wish to take within the next fortnight. Forsooth, there are many complications in the endeavour! Capable maids are scarce in these parts, yet some few abound in the village of New Krintz—a hop and jog away—each with her characteristics somewhat more supple and inviting than her peers, though each competes with her colleagues on subtle counts. I daresay that I fear their reluctance to accept me as their suitor; nonetheless, I am not discouraged in this affair and believe I have reached my final decision!"

Valere's patience was wearing thin. "And who might this deciduous bride be?"

The Dakkaw dropped a mallet fist on the table. "I resent that allusion, Captain, and should others accompany it, I shall have no course but to resort to unpleasant deeds! The bride I have chosen is Delizra, the most beautiful and stunning example of artistry you have ever seen. She is an icon of pure rapture!—a maid so exemplary, so delicately configured as to be sublime, and notwithstanding her charm, the youngest daughter of the Lord Vulde, and indubitably, the fairest." His face had become a flushed mask of passion. "But it is best that I not speak of her."

"Why not?" called Baus, enthralled.

The ogre stared at him. "By the simple fact that I may jinx the occasion and betray our matrimony!"

Baus nodded with assent. "The possibility of jinxing another buxom maid who shall come knocking at your door to indulge in your sweet urgencies, is implicitly understood."

The Dakkaw eyed Baus with cold disfavour. "Careful with your remarks."

Valere tugged fitfully at his knot-ringed beard and voiced a vulgarity. "Never mind the brides, Dakkaw! Where do we fit into this scheme of yours?"

The Dakkaw tucked his head in reflection. "To answer that question, I must embark upon a long, morose tale—if you care to hear . . .?"

"It seems we have all night," muttered Valere.

"Then! Delizra—well, let us forget her for an instant—it was *I* who was considered the black sheep of the community. The villagers of Krintz cast me out, years ago, in light of my expansive corpus and my formidable appearance—branding me an 'ogre' and threatening me never to return. What audacity—what outrage! Because of my unmatched appearance, they chose to ignore the jewels hidden beneath, including my mettle, my expansive disposition and character. They shunned and persecuted me—not to mention, dismissed, my many singular habits and eccentricities."

"And what would these be?" inquired Baus.

"There remains only my insatiable desire to collect gimcracks . . . Not just regular 'gimcracks'," he added rather coyly, "anything of eye-catching appeal: diadems, oddments, trinkets, gewgaws, masonry, tools, scraps of wood, rope . . . even humans." He added the tag carelessly, as if hoping to gloss over a sore point.

"How outré!" said Baus.

"I thought so . . . but laugh if you like!" growled the ogre. "I have been exploited and abused by my compatriots and now I choose to extract a kind of vicarious revenge." He clacked his tongue in triumph. "Now arrest your condescending murmurs and sneers! Perhaps you might think me ghoulish, but I am what I am. I make no bones of it."

"Nor would we insist otherwise," assured Baus.

Another informal wail issued from the floorboards below. The Dakkaw stamped his foot and the planks juddered with the furious impact. "Cedrek—quell your vapid jabbering before I crush you! Can you not see that Sir Baus is speaking and I am entertaining?"

Cedrek reluctantly desisted and Baus's mouth dropped low. Toward the stairwell his gaze lingered. "Why is Cedrek so animated?"

The Dakkaw bit his lips morosely: "Comrade Cedrek, is—or rather was—a wandering bandit who thought to rifle my collection of gems one fine afternoon. The activity was definitely discourteous; now he spends his time reflecting upon his misdeeds."

"Life contrives ingenious opportunities for self-development," mused Baus.

The Dakkaw agreed.

Valere grumbled his confusion: "The act seems foolhardy. Considering the odds Cedrek was up against, the act seems more idiotic than bold."

"Agreed—as does Cedrek," replied the Dakkaw with frankness. "The burglar continues to lament his deeds . . . if only the wretch had agreed to become my house guest for a certain small period! Now he sits in disgrace, confined in darkness and solitude in filth. I managed to extract from him that his father was Halfhan the butcher, another uncouth character from Krintz, who, like other bullies before his time, had committed flagrant insolences upon my person. Now Halfhan is retired, and half blind, and I find it singular to note that Cedrek pays not only for his father's offence, but his own."

"A handy package," remarked Baus. "Now, let us speak of other matters. Do other guests repair at Bisiguth?"

"No."

"Then we are three in total at Bisiguth?

"Four, if you include Cedrek," answered the Dakkaw politely, "—then there is Rilben of course.

"Who is Rilben?"

"A very steadfast fellow! A very genial assistant too! But know it that I have had up to twenty visitors at a time at Bisiguth." The Dakkaw was pleased with the comment and for the first time, simpered. "The numbers have waned over the years, of course, for reasons that include the cunning of the New Krintz people who spite me by erecting sharp pales over their doors, which are otherwise capped with onions and garlic and shallot to ward off my nocturnal indulgences.”

“I gather you find these vegetables toxic?”

“Absolutely!”

“A most crassly cunning lot, these villagers!” fumed Baus.

“Neither do I season my meats, pastes and compotes or pâtés with onions. Which reminds me—I have invited you all to dinner! Swag back your beverages, lads, and partake of a glass or two more! Tonight we dine lavishly!—on fresh hare, roasted with pâté a l’orange and breadcrumb-stuffed pheasant!”

Baus clapped his hands with delight. “A splendid choice, Dakkaw! We shall sup and bathe, after which, my friend and I shall take our leave of you. We have urgent business to conduct in New Krintz and shall not wait for spoilings.”

“A project most unfeasible!” chided the Dakkaw. “You must lodge here with me tonight. Anything else is simply gauche and a disparagement of your honour!” He wattled his throat, an act which Baus found unnerving.

The Dakkaw proffered an affectionate smile. “Again these hasty words, and more simply voiced from an impassioned perspective. As salubrious as one night’s rest shall prove, another shall be better—”

“Another?” Valere roared.

The Dakkaw banged an impassioned fist down on the table. “Two nights! This is all I ask. A visit of this length is not inordinate! Three or four moons shall suffice and is more seemly a duration—much more of what I had in mind.”

Valere pitched a groan. He glided to his feet, staring poignantly at the ogre. “Are you off your crown, Dakkaw? You wish us to stay here for four months?”

“Yes, I do,” said the Dakkaw, spreading palms. His display of jubilance seemed more smote with greater incomprehension. “Where is the problem? I resent the insolence. Is there something ailing with my communication?”

Baus shook his head. “It is only that the Captain is stunned and thinks that things are happening so fast! Valere and I have plans to travel post haste to Krintz.”

“Then you must set aside these fly-by-night programs and abide by my new schedule! I have need of company—a thirst in fact which shall have no quenching—and what the Dakkaw wishes, the Dakkaw gets.” The pronouncement trailed off on an ominous note.

Valere was not thrilled. “And how shall we occupy our time in this gloomy warren of yours day after day?”

The Dakkaw fiddled his fingers. “This is your own worry.”

Baus offered a stout affirmation to Valere’s remarks. “We shall tire of our insipid solitude here, Dakkaw. Like Mearl, we shall languish in boredom!”

“Arrest these paltry fears. By day I hunt, garden and conduct my crafts, by night I boil rutabaga and radish, and together we shall feast upon wegmor meats and wild hares sizzling over slow fires. Dining amicably, we shall know only peace and exaltation—withal, for weeks on end. Such a splendid manner in which to pass one’s time!”

The Dakkaw paused to reminisce. “Warmth, care and comfort, ah! Nothing like it.

Withal, free from conflict and idle jabber. You shall have free rein of my abbey during this period in which to study my marvellous collection of folios, curios and artifacts. I harbour trophies, coins and collectibles that you cannot imagine! When I return from my hunting expeditions, you can oblige yourselves in amusing me with your tales—which I might add, neither of you jacks have shared but a single word."

"You speak in truth," observed Baus languidly, "but what if we wish to accompany you on these hunts? Shall we mope about Bisiguth's dreary and dismal fastnesses while you enjoy the thrill of the chase?"

The Dakkaw regarded them from under sullen, drooping lids. "Do you take me for a lunker? What would stop you from disappearing into the brake?"

Baus manufactured a croak. "That would constitute an impudence, disappearing before dinner. Wouldn't you think so?"

The Dakkaw frowned at the possibility. He pulled at his chin. "Perhaps! But I am not one for dichotomies." He grumbled under his breath and said that he would consider the matter. "In the meantime, dinnertime approaches; we must sup!" The ogre skipped happily to the scullery, from where he returned carrying heaping tureens of stewed rabbit and herbs. Baus and Valere reluctantly devoured their helpings.

VII

Over dinner, the Dakkaw went to fetch another bottle of wine, during which period Baus learned that only a handful of Heagramers had escaped the snauzzerhound jaws. The Constables, according to Valere, raced about scouring the wilderness like jackals, yet had failed to root out Dighcan, Zestes, Lopze, Karlil and himself, all of whom had fled north. Zestes had chosen to follow the road to Hamhuzzle, in hopes of escape. The others had fled south. Karlil, Lopze and Valere had been separated on the road to Hamhuzzle when a merchant had startled them, scattering their numbers with his wagon. Fearing discovery, all had bolted in opposite directions.

The Dakkaw returned with a mouth full of hare, urging the twain to continue with their interesting stories which he had only half heard from the kitchen. Baus plied the ogre from a different tack, questioning him on the origin of Bisiguth and the desolate ruins.

"Bisiguth is that manor erected by Baron Bisiguth," he said, "an eccentric visionary of Taven. In the early part of this age the estate was constructed by renowned architects, hence the hyperbole of the floating spheres. The city is in fact the site of *Old Krintz*, which is that settlement of quality which you see around you. Beyond the ruins lies the more modern village of New Krintz, a few leagues farther west—whose odious stench I deplore. The monuments, pillars and statues littered about Old Krintz were once the glorious possessions of our ruler barons—of that ancient realm of the south—Morveuntz, far beyond Owlen and Karsh. The forefathers sailed north by barque. They founded the capital of Kereuntz, which later was renamed 'Krintz'. Since then, it has dwindled to a straggling ruin, half forgotten. Bisiguth is that stronghold ruled by Noblore, and a succession of noblemen—the daring Estyon and Griffax whose armour and plates you see dressed on the wall, which give me great pleasure to display."

Valere deigned an intrusion: "I recall passing ruins myself on my way north while pondering the legends. I heard myths of similar nature—that the realm of 'Kereuntz' and its ancient brother 'Fereuntz' were still intact—at least the remnants of glory. But I never believed it to be this vast! I am baffled and humbled in the extreme. The enchantment that we suffered from those wretched flowers—it has something to do with the magic of those old days?"

"Right, Captain. Back when Kereuntz basked in all its glory, countless adepts roamed the regions, versed in the arts of sorcery, but it was not until Kereuntz's full days of waning that an alchemist named Murtle created an amazing potion—an elixir of such potent distillation that she let it sit in a quiet glade to temper, and cure it of its mettle. While she was away, a vicious storm blew from the sea. It brought howling winds and rain to plague the coast and cause her ewer to overflow, spilling out a putrid, yellow scum, blighting the land. Something had gone dreadfully wrong. Murtle's spell had backfired. Gorse, twitch, spikenard, furze—all such plants perished. Only asphodel, acacia and gardenia survived—flora yellow, for reasons only known to Murtle's understanding. The flowering seeds spread, drifting to other glades. They infected other flora with caustic blights. Whatever the original portent of the spell was, it was lost to record, but it remains only to eat or inhale of Murtle's asphodel, to become infected, then drowsing until such time as one is rescued from the peril."

Baus and Valere only framed solemn acknowledgements to the lore and the Dakkaw, while reclining in his chair, let his eyes pass glistening over their scruffy attire with a thoughtful intent. He motioned to the brass instruments affixed along the wall. "These gongs are the very same that the troubadours of old Kereuntz used to ring on the *hachylons*—those rowers of excellent quality who propelled the hefty vessels across the seas." His eyes grew rheumy. "How the dragon galleys, their prows carven with sea harpies and griffins, used to ply the routes between Kereuntz and Haikken! They fought dire foes and made trade in days of yore. Days of adventure those were—surely not to be revisited again in these torpid times today."

Valere grunted: "Haikken is the modern day port of Owlen?"

The Dakkaw nodded. "From where Prince Arnin now commands his fleet. I hear he makes his private war with the Poesasian buccaneers with avidity." The ogre turned his moody gaze on Valere. "Notice the poison nettles hanging from the oriels." He pointed a finger to the vaulted ceiling. "One touch, and the victim falls paralyzed to doom. Is this not frightful and ruinous?"

"It is an unnecessary precaution!" cried Valere.

Baus bit his lip. "Surely there is little chance of burglars entering from such heights?"

"Burglars, no!" the Dakkaw cried, laughing. "But guests? You would be surprised at the number of ingrates who would seek to strap ladders, ropes, stilts, mauls, lassoes, barbs and anything else to seek egress from my manse. They wish to cause me irreparable injury. Such tactlessness and cunning is without bound!"

"It hardly seems conceivable!" Baus cried adamantly. "What person would breach such a covenant of etiquette?" He motioned to the strange contraption beside Noblore's ancient armour. "What of this eldritch coat-rack and its coils? It seems a seven-foot high shaft, burnished of larch!"

"Aye, on it are attached many sizeable rings of various colours."

"Is it too a relic of long-perished Kereuntz? I see each ring affixed by mechanisms most peculiar."

"It is not a relic!" stormed the Dakkaw. "It is an invention: a game called 'Whig the rigs'—of my own innovation."

"Indeed! Is anyone eligible to play?"

"Naturally! 'Whig the rigs' is designed for two or more players. Shall we try?"

"Why not? I profess to interest," cried Baus.

The Dakkaw nodded, as if he did not seem to find the circumstance implausible. He explained that each player was to choose a poker, attempt dislodging a ring in such a way as to incommode its neighbour's opponent's ring—or at least halting its progress at midway. "But take note!" the Dakkaw cried fervently. "The rings harbour different weights and sizes. The lengths of each chain holding the rings are calculated to confound a player into committing faults. Attention is due to promote interesting play!"

Baus agreed.

The Dakkaw selected pokers; the ogre handed Baus a stout limb and a smaller one to Valere. He urged them to house their rings, but Baus lifted a hand, insisting that other noteworthy items were to be given attention along the farther wall, to which the Dakkaw agreed.

A short, squat, apish creature suddenly thrust itself out of the darkness. It had a plump, grinning face.

The Dakkaw clapped his hands. "Ah, Rilben. You arrive! Not getting into mischief, I hope?" He was pleased with the presence of the creature.

"Nothing of the sort, sir!" squeaked Rilben. "I was just cleaning up these ceremonial cymbals and antediluvian disks."

"What an excellent person you are! You are a nonpareil!"

"True."

Rilben, as Baus saw, stood no more than waist high to the Dakkaw. The ape was armed with a grey, goblin face and wore fancy shoes. A small leather skull-helmet with ear flaps was affixed to his skull. An embroidered gown over immaculate breast armour, and a set of tweed pantaloons which precisely matched his cornflower cravat covered the rest of his body. The creature harboured a parrot-like strut, which under the circumstances, and with its broad shoulders and matching lanky arms, seemed to smack of incongruity. Needless to say, it was not Baus's place to criticize.

The Dakkaw touched his cheeks with great fondness. "Right then! Smartly now! There are folks I'd like you to meet. Baus—meet Rilben! Valere—Rilben, and Rilben, Baus, a renowned wayfarer—as is Valere, a real life sea captain."

Rilben bowed and showed an admiring face. "Rilben the Bête, at your service. Many honours, sirs!

Valere acknowledged the salutation; Baus muffled a cough.

"Rilben is my 'associate'," explained the Dakkaw urbanely. "He is a creature, or rather pseudo-baboon, from descent in the Tarnshorn hills."

Baus narrowed his brows. "This is an appreciable distance."

The Dakkaw nodded vigorously. "I discovered Rilben in my travels across the Tarnshorns in a land called 'Bête'. It was in my youth," he exclaimed fondly. "Rilben was then only a pup, the breadth of my hand."

"Intriguing, if not beguiling," remarked Baus incredulously. "And what prompted such fortuity?"

"Ah . . . you ask. Who knows the ways of consequence more than Rilben? The imp was no bigger than my toe when I found him sprawled and abandoned in a lonely glade by his peers."

Baus clapped his hands in consternation. "Whatever becomes the world when one discovers travesties exposed in glaring condition?"

The Dakkaw agreed. "I had hidden Rilben in one of my pockets, whilst traversing the snow peaks of Tarnshorn, and then transported him to the Tevers pass, the stony gulches, and the windy swales of Sarch."

"An ingenious itinerary," complimented Baus.

The Dakkaw blushed. "I thought so." Fondness and nostalgia crept into his face. "Rilben had a pet, oh what was its name? I forget!"

"Moddly Middy!" Rilben sniffed sharply. "It died. Dear Moddly! How I pine for my vole-rat!" A tear dripped from the ghoul-ape's eye to splash on the floor.

Baus sought to ameliorate the mood. "Yes, Rilben, I bet there are others floating around Bisiguth—in some ratty hole or dusky corner." Baus chuckled at the notion.

Rilben brightened; he clenched his sagging shoulders erect. "I shall begin an immediate searching for such a creature." The ape turned to rummage but the Dakkaw called an order: "Rilben! Do not neglect your duties!—there are a hundred chores of maintenance around my mansion!"

The ape responded tartly: "I have automatically begun these tasks, sir." He swaddled off in a huff, engaging in his search.

The Dakkaw tsked affectionately. "Rilben! What an unassuming fellow—perhaps a trifle simple, but what of it? Where were we? Ah, yes! Whig the Rigs . . ." He gave a smirk and a processional flourish.

Baus made a polite correction. "Actually, we were on a tour of the *ceremonial* shields and associated regalia."

"Quite right! Baus, you are a sharp fellow; you shall go places!"

Baus acknowledged the acclaim, pointing to the tarnished cymbals and age-cracked oars pasted to the wall. The Dakkaw was pleased and began to launch into a lengthy oratory of the history of the oars when he clutched at his ears in anguish. "Dags! I have forgotten Cedrek again. The swain is likely at his end with hunger!" Grumbling grimly, he clopped to the trapdoor and set feet near the foot of the stairs. Almost apologetically, he chided them, "I have been so busy with you that I have neglected Cedrek's needs. It has been a full day—is it irresponsible? Nevertheless, time for his ablutions—a necessary though rough engagement."

Baus and Valere exchanged grimaces and the Dakkaw trooped down to the crypts with a lit torch. Slamming the trap shut, he paused to take his bearings, and they heard only the thud of his footsteps, and a creepy series of low-pitched howls. A ratchety sound suddenly came drifting up through the planks, then an ominous clank of chains and unyielding metal. Wails ensued, then a feeble moan, which Baus marked similar to one he had heard on his first stumbling upon Bisiguth.

Another oath filled the air, followed by a buffet, then a muffled groan, and the sound of a sloshing liquid—there was a terrible thrashing. Then, more ratchety commotion, superseded by blubbering and several complaisant sobs.

The Dakkaw emerged gamely from the basement. His face was flushed, his eyes were gleaming and he carried in his hand what looked like an immense glass-spice vial. "Lucky that I attended to that niggling task," he intoned bluffly. "On a side errand, this amber-root was my trophy; it will do well to season the pheasant I mean to trap for us on the morrow! Let us repair to bed! Tomorrow is to be a long day; I am fatigued with all this miscellany!" He clapped his hands, prompting them up the stairs.

Up the long flight of stairs Baus and Valere were nudged by the Dakkaw. Down a wide, disorderly hall the ogre marched, directing them to their chambers, rubbing wrists with contentment. Though sparse and somewhat austere, the chamber was perhaps less littered with refuse than the rest of the abode and contained at least a stout bed on which the two might flop.

Baus screwed up his face. "I need soft covers in order to sleep comfortably, Dakkaw. Not to mention a room less cluttered. This much you should at least provide your guests for politeness at least."

"Arrest your mischief!" The ogre showed Baus yellow teeth. "I have ears like a bloodhawk and I shall sleep close by!"

Two doors down he stalked and retired to his bedchamber. His tread was as heavy as gongs. He locked the black-plated door behind him.

Smitten with despair, Baus and Valere forewent an escape. Bypassing a listless argument over who would receive the better half of the bed, they slumped, groaned with exhaustion and sighed like two old beggars. No sooner had their heads touched the pillows, when they were fast asleep.

VIII

The next morning, Baus cried out imploring the Dakkaw to set them free from his hideous keep.

The ogre stood framed hugely in their bedroom doorway, like a gigantic breed of ox. Globe eyes glimmered like polished spoons; huge comic hands swung metallically as if plumb bobs on the end of iron-twined hawsers.

The giant seemed to consider the request with an air of affection. "A means exists. I will give you the option to solve one of my riddles, then you can walk free."

Baus clapped his hands in contentment.

Valere guffawed, "And if we fail to crack it?"

"Everything remains as before."

"Then we have nothing to lose," said Baus.

"Logic would dictate. Shall we begin?"

The two wagged their heads.

"To our first riddle! What is red, blue, and fits on the end of a shoe?"

Baus scratched his head with puzzlement. Valere peered cock-eyed up at the Dakkaw.

The Dakkaw bawled, "Too slow! Well, here is another! What lives on water and on land, and to date can nothing withstand?" Again Baus and Valere bit their lips.

"Dags, you two jacks are dim. You say you are riddle men? Poddycock!"

Baus gurgled out a boyish chuckle, "A dogfish, then."

The Dakkaw signalled failure.

Valere heaved himself up and announced, "Cuttleswipe, or a crake."

"Wrong on both counts." The Dakkaw flourished a ringed finger. "You two clowns are useless when it comes to riddles! Guess again!"

Baus and Valere consulted each other. They mumbled testy arguments. Trying several angles, they pooled their ideas with blurts, assertive taunts, maledictions, but nothing seemed to assist.

The Dakkaw began to grow impatient. "I haven't all day, swains. You call yourself seamen! Tach! Well, do you finally give up?"

"Never! Furnish us time," cried Baus. "We require concentration."

The Dakkaw gave an impudent snort. "Concentration is all well and good when it is administered with analytic skill. Not with vapid jabber. Now! Speak! I grow fatigued with all the fluff."

"Right, Dakkaw," agreed Baus. "Let us think. I ask for a very basic hint as to the nature of the riddle and you give us sneers. Is this too much to ask?"

"It is!—I simply refuse to supply any hints!"

Moonstruck with rancour, Baus shook his head. "Without a clue, we surely cannot answer."

The Dakkaw regarded him cheekily. "Then in that case I must cancel your chance at freedom. As an aside, not a single soul has guessed a single riddle of mine to date—not even proud Varanges the Wise, or Chanstros the Music-Maker. What do you think of that?"

Baus gestured to indicate that he thought little of it. "And now, Dakkaw, how are we to recognize that our answers are in fact inaccurate, if you do not at lest tender us the correct responses?"

"The query is inflammatory!" bristled the Dakkaw. "Now, if the answer is not quite obvious, there is none at all. It is neither fish, nor half mutants or birds, like you blindly spout, which never embark on land."

The brusque exclamation marked an end to the game and Baus and Valere were invariably obliged to forfeit their only chance at liberation.

* * *

Within a quarter of an hour the Dakkaw departed Bisiguth. He took with him his big willow hunting bow and a brace of small fowl. The skin of beer and extra snares were already strapped on his shoulders.

The bolts of the massive bronze door clanked shut; Baus and Valere were left brooding in the tomblike Bisiguth.

The twain exchanged rebellious glances and contemplated the grey gloom of their bedchamber. The surroundings were glum; dispiriting shadows hung everywhere; glazed black beobar trim and filigreed wainscoting gazed back without compassion.

The door was left unlocked—the ogre had kept his promise. In effect, they were imprisoned like rats in a big littered cage.

Up and about to work they scrambled, prowling the manse for a means of escape. The only notable discovery was a set of repositories and doorways favoured with huge brass knobs all along the living room walls. They branched into many corridors; the rooms beyond were filled with a ghastly assortment of junk—grimy relics and other bits of weird refuse that the Dakkaw had hoarded in his spare time.

A thin watery light filtered down from the casements, revealing significantly finer details of Bisiguth's interior than yesterday. An old marble staircase, rising to a black-plaited wooden balcony, engraved with nymphs and luscious mermaids in suggestive poses. The wood was cracked, pitched in frightening formations, but did little to enlighten them, nor did it lose its velvety splendour in the half gloom. The hallway which encircled the second storey appeared to house its own doorways which led to other archaically-designed rooms, which were in turn locked.

Bisiguth, as it turned out, was partisan to many strange marvels—like the old porcelain wall fountain, bubbling and soundlessly burbling with waters of purple luminosity. An elk head mounted over the armoire had black, authoritative eyes which followed them whichever way they turned; then there was the eerie stone paves, embedded into the planks at random intervals. Phosphorous, unsettling faces were embedded there, reminiscent of gargoyles and demons that glared back at them. Charms? Spell-blockers? The context was unclear and Baus shook his head. Additionally the staircase steps seemed to meld one step at a time in the opposite direction that the climber wished to go. Baus was at a loss to decipher its significance, or origin, sponsoring in him an odd, depressed flavour. He brooded that these were some magical mysteries that the Dakkaw had accumulated in his travels and that he would not speak of.

In their own bedchamber, a small diamond-shaped pane looked out upon the pale courtyard. Long shadows lay tucked in the dawn's sparse light. Toppled statues tickled with prickle weed and shrub-rot were in evidence below—a place they could not reach. The closet revealed a set of old jerkins with the smell of old leather, and other archaic bits of clothing: belts, hats, boots, trousers, all voluminous to the fit. A set of polished skulls were dyed blue, scattered on the floor under a stack of clothing. Baus thought the instance unorthodox. In idle reverie he manhandled the skulls like a court fool in a hand each. Valere dismissed the puppeteering as juvenile. Baus tossed the skulls in the closet, frowning, chiding Valere for his lack of imagination. Baus gave his time to other pursuits: the examination of furniture in the downstairs hall. Through grey murk sat the old table, its haggard collection of chairs, and barbaric, hanging chandelier giving it character. Various items littered the floor. Higher above rose the miniature oriels and the groined ceiling.

Baus shook his head in wonder. Where to start searching amidst all this rubble? As for Rilben, it appeared the ape had hidden himself again in a convenient location. At least there was no small lack of raw materials, and it was from these, that Baus and Valere began to fabricate the first legion of a plan: a battering ram made out of planks and meal sacks.

The scheme proved tedious. The front door was jammed and too heavy to crack open with even the best of their efforts. They endeavoured to craft a makeshift grapple—one manufactured of bent nails affixed to segments of rope. To loft the grapple on high was an option absurdly impractical. The windows were too high. Nor could they access any convenient place from the banister in which to lob the construction. Even the trap door under which 'Cedrek' lived, was barred heavily with brass and impossible to lever open.

Baus and Valere slumped heavily on the floor and attempted a discussion to clarify their escape. Rilben, rather unexpectedly turned up behind a suit of armour, surprising them with an oil brush and rag. He highly discouraged the prospect of escape with a wagging finger. The companions ignored the advice. They resumed their scheming. After several gambits they came to a dead end; Baus threw his hands in the air. The Dakkaw had pondered all the angles. Escape was futile. Midday had arrived, and they were no closer to liberation. Cedrek's moans and laments continued to fill the gloomy hall while Rilben's orthodox, pedantic instructions irked them to no end.

* * *

True to his word, the Dakkaw returned as daylight was fading. The ogre clutched new game: a white sea termagon, two small shrews, a brown-backed pheasant. His face was suntanned; he looked well-exercised and full of energy as the companions peered and could not help but feel jealous. Smelling of inviting scents: fall air, sycamores, beech, fallen leaves, fresh vistas—he afforded them stories of the day, voicing a polite inquiry into their own affairs. The companions had little to say, outside of a ribbing with Rilben. The ogre offered sympathetic remarks and set about preparing the evening's meal—a pheasant goulash and termagon pâté of quality. Baus fingered the thin ganglestick deep in his cloak. The Dakkaw served the hot dishes while Baus contrived a means to slide near his side, guarding Nuzbek's rod with a hopeful gleam in his eye. Somehow he sensed encouraging outcomes.

The intimation turned out to be misleading. The Dakkaw was quick to deduce chicanery and conveyed orders for Baus to keep a better distance. "Take your seat, skulker! I would think you harboured an ice pick in your pouch to plunge into my brain! Tell me of marvels, not prowl about my domain like an errant dog. I know little of you two swains—only that you are escapists from prison."

Valere gave a sullen twitch. "What of it?"

The Dakkaw's face congested. "Refusing to humour me, Captain, will result in your being thrust below with Cedrek. Together the two of you may review your obstinate streaks. For free room and board, I demand benevolence! Boons which number to the count of two! —first, a reception of capable company, second, an earful of salient news from the outside."

Sensing no alternative, Valere told a tale of how he had escaped the Constables, witnessing Tustok and Yullen being torn apart by snauzzerhounds. The Dakkaw's eyes gleamed at the news, especially about the violent capture. Valere affirmed that he had barely escaped the death-hounds by scrambling up the cliffside by the sea, hiding in clumps of furze where he could to stake out Gooler's Point. Baus related a much more optimistic tale, of how he had fooled the magician Nuzbek who had been sentenced to the flaptrap and had escaped the compound only after suffering days in the flaptrap and flown about the air on an occult-rigged parachute while clutching jars of miniaturized homunculi.

The Dakkaw laughed at the ludicrous visual and listened with fascination when Baus described of the magician's sentence to the 'hive' for a jocular misunderstanding. "Nuzbek seems an interesting fellow," remarked the ogre. "I would rather like to meet him one day as he has quite a summary of squalid little tricks up his sleeve."

Baus put on a sour face. "Perhaps you would not think Nuzbek so 'enchanting' if you really knew him. He is actually a rebel neomancer of Mismerion who applied to the Circle but was denied."

"Indeed!" The Dakkaw looked more interested. "Mismerion is in the far southern reaches of Sloe. I should have guessed. To anyone of learned disposition, he would know these places. Hardly are 'neomancers' a breed more than obscure sorcerers with strange ideas and inordinate abilities. They are of an ancient lineage, once known as the 'Neons'."

Valere pulled heavily on his beard. "You seem to know a lot about these people. Their history sounds ominous. I knew there was something sinister about that pretentious Nuzbek..."

The Dakkaw was only obliged to agree; he wanted to know more but Baus had become peevish and claimed that there was little that he could say other than Ulisa was a neomancer and Trimestrius a nobleman who had crossed the magician.

"What of Rilben?" inquired Valere, motioning to the meal plates. "Does he not eat?"

The Dakkaw set down his fork. "Rilben does not eat in the normal sense. I have not wholly discovered the method of his ingestion. Though the rats in the manor seem to avoid him. Here is the nub of the matter: he is a tragic substitute for dinner company!"

Baus nodded in sympathy.

Valere gave a grunt. "What does the ape's eating habits have to do with us?"

"Nothing. Let us speak of other matters."

The matter was dropped. The evening dragged on. The Dakkaw, pensive, mercurial, enjoyed their tales and exploits with polite courtesy and became ever drowsier with the wine. The twain secreted hopes that false conviviality may bring them an opportunity for acquiring his keys.

The opportunity did not arise. The ogre cleaned up the dishes and repaired below with a plate of bread and a wing of pheasant for Cedrek. The dim light flickered between the cracks of the trap. Muffled sounds similar to those of yester-eve drifted up to Baus's and Valere's ears. The Dakkaw tarried longer than usual, perhaps to tidy up the area and trade words with Cedrek, but then he returned, smiling under the dim sconces, requesting that his guests retire to their chambers.

* * *

Dawn came slowly: a soft maroon light filtered through the oriels and lit the manor in a somewhat eerier ambience of melancholy than normal. Left to their own devices, Baus and Valere were less industrious in their undertakings of escape than yesterday. Somehow they knew they were trapped and remained morosely resigned to their plight. They paced the floor, hectored one another, traded spiteful jibes and stale jests. Rilben was nowhere to be seen. What was he up to? They beat the walls, stamped their feet, made rude faces at each other and as a last resort, snatched at each other's noses, seeing who would object the loudest. They even played hide and seek, and 'Whig the Rings', (without Rilben of course, who was still not to be found)—anything to stave off the ineffable boredom.

Baus considered anew the ganglestick. Certainly it was an adjunct of puissance, likely the only appurtenance that could offer a chance at undermining the Dakkaw's supremacy. Baus had gained a more useful mastery of the adjunct, smiting Valere here and there when whim would have it. But to pad within proximity of the Dakkaw's presence and tap him definitively was a risk perilously fraught. The man's awesome bulk was deceiving; he was always on the lookout, a leap and bound away from pouncing on them like a panther. At night he slept behind locked doors; by day he was alert as a fox. At dinnertime he was shrewdly vigilant; he could read their minds like a yantler. After imbibing large quantities of spirit, the man was still indomitable! If Baus ever launched the baton wantonly, he must be sure of his idea—only striking with its tip, grazing an exposed part of the body. Only this would bring about a winning outcome, for to miss or blunder—the Dakkaw would confiscate the talisman, and all opportunity would be lost.

A week passed.

Sunlight deprived their skin of nourishment. Over-fed and under-exercised, Baus and Valere were becoming a pair of pasty-faced louts. They were bored, hot-tempered and apathetic in regards to the Dakkaw's forced conviviality. No number of rash endeavours seemed enough to secure their freedom. With sallow-eyed restraint Baus reviewed the fact— that they had run blindly into a trap, from one prison to another. They would have gladly exchanged this musty dim-lit manse for Heagram's non-comforts and mix of misfits.

On the eighth evening, the Dakkaw yawned after their story-telling and made motions that it was time to retire before tending to Cedrek's feeding in Bisiguth's crypts.

Perhaps it was with desperate exhaustion that Valere decided to take matters into his own hands. The ogre had no sooner disappeared into the crypts, when the seaman had gathered up a nail-studded plank primed for action. With eyes grim as a raven's, he sat crouched by the trapdoor, waiting. Baus pleaded with him to abandon whatever impulse he had, but the headstrong seaman would hear nothing of it. He called Baus a coward, an insufferable 'mamby-pamby'.

The trapdoor lifted. The Dakkaw's head popped up like a cork and Valere thrust his weapon down, sweating with the effort. The blow was curtailed. The ogre thrust up a shoulder, moving faster than a snake to Valere's vicious sweep, and deflected the blow, thwarting what might have been a fatal strike. The ogre burst up the steps with a fantastic speed, sending Valere flying back onto a meal sack. A backhand slap had the club skidding across the floor.

Baus gasped in dismay. The seaman sat there blinking like an owl. He rubbed his jaw dazedly and shook his head while Baus retrieved the plank and gained wits enough not to think of employing it. He witnessed the ogre rise up to his full stature glaring down at him with a chilling scrutiny, and he dropped the weapon penitently.

"So! You insolent puppy!" the Dakkaw roared. "Would you be so foolhardy as to raise wood against me?"

Baus spoke in deferential tone. "Nothing so vapid, Dakkaw! You misinterpret my intent. I was about to reprimand Valere for his insubordination." Slinking forward, he shook the plank in front of Valere's face and made motions to inflict punishment.

Valere shrank back, admonishing Baus for his contemptible treachery, "You lily-livered turncoat! Can you not see that the filthy ogre is the foe, not I?"

"Dispense with your insults, redbeard!" boomed Baus. "I fear you are addled with spite. I abhor deception, particularly breaches of etiquette upon a host. The Dakkaw is a man of honour—no less our host. Sit there and fume if you must! At some point in a man's life, he must come to terms with his lonely feelings and know he is in need of trusting company which is sadly lacking in this world."

The Dakkaw nodded agreeably. "Invariably this is true." He clacked his teeth.

Baus faced the Dakkaw with smiling courtesy. "As a token of respect for your extended hospitality, Dakkaw, I wish to tender you this gratuity." He offered him the ganglestick, tip first, and fabricated with a deep bow.

The Dakkaw's brows rose, then fell in quiet resentment when he studied the object. The item, though amiably presented, was a strangely impulsive benefaction, and by all means an item of suspicion. The ogre was overcome, however, with a glittery curiosity that would not be sidestepped. "A noble gesture, Baus—considering the fact that you know I am an avid collector. In truth, this ebon trinket you offer is not my real object of desire. Rather, the jade necklace around your throat. It has me enthralled, more than this scrubby piece of hornbow you hold."

"Nonsense!" cried Baus. "You speak of my seaman's charm, a legacy from my father, which never leaves my neck. Here—this ganglestick is much more of an endearing treasure, formerly the property of the neomancer Nuzbek."

"Is it?" the Dakkaw croaked, striking palms together with enthusiasm. "Why did you not tell me of this earlier? . . . let's have a look at the curio." With an eagerness born of a collector, he reached to examine the baton. The cold tip brushed against his fingers and Baus grinned as the Dakkaw's mewling cry filled the hall. The Dakkaw's mottled face prickled into an expression of stricken hatred—before he was frozen rock solid.

Taking a stately bow, Baus exhaled a sigh of triumph. "So, you ungrateful lubber," he blurted at Valere. "Am I so nefarious now?" He hurried over to help the seaman to his feet.

Valere let out a hoot of amazement. "You are a knave second to none, Baus! All the time I thought you for a pantywaist—now here you are the cleverest rogue of all!"

Baus ignored the compliment. "Swiftly now, redbeard! We must secure an exit from this squalor. Little more than a dozen minutes remain. Mind! We mustn't touch the Dakkaw. He will awaken and mash us to pulp."

Valere snorted. "No need to worry! Many more mysteries are now explained from back in Heagram's yard."

"Perhaps!" Baus muttered. "More mysteries than you would think . . . Let us make haste; much work is to be completed."

"What of our Dakkaw? He looks precariously poised and still more venomous than I like." He gazed at the glowering giant and put forth a questing finger.

"Stop!" Baus quickly slammed his hand away. "Do you not understand the danger? Touch the ogre and we die!"

Valere lumbered back, peeved. "The only way out is the portal." He jerked a thumb toward the brass bound door. "It is blocked, and the only way to open it is by the key in his belt." Unconsciously the seaman reached out to secure the item from the Dakkaw's waist but pulled it back. "We can't keep stunning him with the little magic stick."

Baus rubbed his chin in thought. "You are right. We would have to watchdog him from minute to minute. Not feasible. Should both of us doze . . ." He left that possibility dangling in the air. "Drakes! We must bind this loathsome brute, then secure his keys, and be away as quickly as possible."

"But how can we manifest all this legerdemain without touching him? We are not magicians! When the rascal awakes, we are doomed, as you point out."

Baus vented a frustrated sigh. "This is where we must use our brains, Valere. Let us gather rope at least; we can pre-loop it around his neck, and his feet. On my signal, the two of us shall ensnare him before he cognizes what it is all about."

Valere scratched at his brow. "The plan sounds risky. Much could go wrong, yet I suppose we have nothing better to do."

Baus turned him a peeled-back snarl, an indication that the quality of the plan was unquestionable.

Each set to work; Valere fetched coils of rope from the repositories in the living room. The seaman clambered onto the huge table and looped a generous coil over the chandelier. He twined its iron chain which dangled down from the gloom. Baus crafted a slip knot in wide circumference around the Dakkaw's legs so as not to touch the creature, and to enable him to hook the ogre's shins in an instant's yank.

Valere signalled that the task was finished. Baus peered upward, nodding in appraisal that Valere's lariat was sound. Any critical error would invite doom.

The Dakkaw stood immobile; his knotted visage still blazed in a most abominable fashion. It was almost as if some canny recognition lurked behind that piglet face, that he would suddenly come to life and crush them both yet. The evil glare continued, sparking a shiver down Baus's spine; either way, Valere and he were committed.

Baus told his friend one last time: "Remember, once I have the loop ready, I shall signal you to keep the ogre at bay. Do not shirk your duty. Secure the neck harness! I, in turn, shall pull my lasso taut and rear back to avoid his feet which must become bludgeoning instruments."

Valere proffered a reckless laugh, assuring Baus of his cogency in the plan.

Baus issued the signal. With celerity, the seaman hooked the loop about the Dakkaw's neck, pulling hard when the pale, flabby neck seemed most vulnerable.

The Dakkaw lurched to life. His eyes glowed with blue sparks of wrath. Maw gaping ferociously and yellow tongue lolling, he struggled like a trapped bear, with Baus yanking hard on the rope, causing a terrific force to coil about the Dakkaw's lower shins.

Baus ran at all speed to the opposite wall. Struggling to secure the rope, he bound it round the nearest doorknob.

The Dakkaw surged forth like a rabid beast. He snatched at Baus to crush his neck like a twig, but Valere had already leapt off the table and dragged the monster back in the opposite direction with his lariat.

The Dakkaw strained in a choking grimace. He clutched at his throat. Valere coiled the end of his rope around the inside doorknob of the nearest repository for security. Pulling it tight, he gave an exultant cry. Stumbling over the obnoxious clutter, Baus tied his end of the rope to other doorknobs along the opposite wall.

The Dakkaw uttered strangled roars. He was secured like a boar. To move forward meant a painful garrotting by Valere's loop; to move backward would have Baus's rope eating into his shins, causing him terrific pain to stumble forth and induce a gasping, strangling pressure from the noose around his neck. Now, sensing the hopelessness of his situation, the Dakkaw became a petulant captive. "Insolent puppies!" he bellowed hoarsely. Struggling with his massive hands at the loop digging into his wattled neck, he hissed, "Do you think you can subjugate me in my own home so easily?"

Valere reached indifferently for one of the bronze gongs. With mallet poised, he stepped within the Dakkaw's earshot to strike odiously.

The Dakkaw clamped hands over his ears, grimacing. Valere took great pleasure in striking the gong again.

Baus moved in as close as he dared and shot a faint smile at the Dakkaw. "Well, it seems as if matters have taken an ironic turn."

The ogre growled. It seemed he only wished for one of them to stray too closely and he would crush them to death. "Indeed—but can you maintain your edge? You shan't escape, grinning thief—not while my hands remain free and I guard the key opening the door in my belt."

Baus framed a tired sigh. "I had considered this before, Dakkaw, which is why I have another plan, don't I, Valere?"

Valere nodded. "How be I tug this rope a might smarter and constrict his knavish neck!"

"The idea has merit," agreed Baus.

"The gesture is rude!" the Dakkaw retorted. He allowed his tone to become notably earnest. "Let us return to an earlier state of amicability. You have me at odds, agreed, but perhaps we can work out a compromise. We are friends after all."

Valere gave a chirrup of laughter. "Friends? You would have us cluck over your infernal riddles? Nothing of the sort. We are bound for New Krintz . . . that is, after we dispose of you and possibly your valuables—" He bent to pick up the studded plank and contrive a means to brain the giant as was his intent earlier.

The Dakkaw's thoughts seemed to turn to the memory. "To Krintz, eh? Well, perhaps we would all benefit from a trip there."

"How's that?" sneered Valere.

"I am in need of a bride. You are in need of funds, particularly to advance this impoverished mission of yours as outlaws. I can provide access to Krintz's coffers—a stash more beautiful than you can imagine. With this, you can repay your sordid debts, purchase yourselves a vessel perhaps and gain safe passage to Owlen. All I ask in return is that you spare my life, and that you swear you will leave me and Bisiguth, once you get your treasure."

Baus pondered the information. "How are we to guarantee your good faith?"

"Bind my wrists," suggested the Dakkaw. "I offer this as a token of my good intentions."

Valere laughed jeeringly. "Do you think we are such simpletons? What prevents you from dashing out our brains at the merest instant we release you?"

"This is not in my best interests, considering you can easily freeze me on the spot."

"True," admitted Baus. "But what more do you wish of us in return? Easily you could have snatched up a hundred helpless wives without our help."

"As I have adumbrated," the Dakkaw grated frostily, "the villagers have spiked the town with shallots. I cannot stand them. You must chop them down or dispose of them as you can, otherwise I will not be able to pass through the streets and show you the way to the trove without suffering an adverse reaction to their poison. Such substances," he added sneeringly, "curb my amorous intentions and aura of appeal."

Baus nodded with reflection. "We can't have that. It seems a fair plan." He turned to Valere. "What have you to say of the proposal?"

Valere's humour was scant. "I say he's not to be trusted."

The Dakkaw was nettled. "Trusted? You, Captain, of all people, talk of trust. Have you forgotten who rescued your hides from the asphodel?"

"The point is well taken," admitted Baus, "though I question your altruism, Dakkaw."

"No matter! Deeds have their way of showing sincerity." He offered his wrists again. "Bind me, as you please."

Baus gathered a rope in which to tie the ogre tightly.

"Another condition," blurted out the Dakkaw.

"No conditions!" growled Valere.

The Dakkaw paid no heed. "Cedrek must not take the journey. He must stay below."

"What of Rilben?"

"He stays, as usual."

Valere shrugged. "I care not for either of them. Let's see those hands."

The Dakkaw produced his wrists and Valere lashed them together with tight, painful precision, paying particular attention to any movement or treachery which might constitute his own demise. Baus watched vigilantly a foot away, ganglestick on the ready. The Dakkaw meanwhile, eyed the magic rod with shrewd dismay. His lumpy eyes glittered with speculation. "There is something else."

"Nothing else!" remonstrated Baus. "I wish to view this 'Cedrek' and satiate this brewing curiosity of mine that has been eating away at me for a long while."

Valere expressed a similar, pressing interest. "Yes, this mystery of Cedrek has me bewildered too."

The Dakkaw gave an ill-mannered snort, but he had no choice in the matter and mustered a torpid shrug. "You must do as you must. But I warn you, considering the current stasis of affairs, I formally forbid tampering with the conditions as stated!"

"We shall do as we please, Dakkaw!" called Valere angrily. "Shut your maw. We are masters of this keep and you are hardly but a fly in a bottle. Do not make any demands."

The Dakkaw tempered his tone, for he knew the seaman was right. Valere finished binding the oak-tree wrists. He took from his belt the keys and proceeded to the trapdoor. Baus peered about the candlelit murk with uneasy foreboding. Rilben's absence was eerily discommoding, but nothing could be done. He retrieved his golden blade from the basket on high and helped Valere wrench open the trap. They snatched torches, and made cautious steps to investigate the crypts below Bisiguth.

IX

What greeted them in this dim sublevel was a dungeon-like undercroft ever dank and silent. Gloom was perpetuated by an absence of sconce-light and a noisome chill left them shivering. What comprised the mildewed spaces was supported only with mouldy crusted pillars and wooden beams from which cobwebs floated rottenly. Spiders clung in the darkness, like crabs, crouching steadily with grey abdomens and beady yellow eyes. Sensing the intruders, the creatures scuttled deeper into the shadows, spawning unwholesome scents and draughts with their spongy webs. Baus was mildly revulsed at the burrow. Eyes darting in all directions, he observed the floor hard-packed—perhaps twenty or thirty musty earthen rooms ranged off in the periphery.

For the moment the easy victory over the Dakkaw seemed cheaply won. The two new masters of Bisiguth took precarious steps away from the staircase, and now a torn trail of webs revealed the path where the Dakkaw had last forged his bulk. Baus set fire to the troublesome straggle which already was re-forming and the spiders snapped and hissed at the destruction to their homes, but foisted no further appeal. The two explorers gripped their resolve, fearful of traps that the Dakkaw had set. They searched vainly for any signs of Cedrek. No hint seemed to suggest the presence of any humans at all. Such could easily be a smoke-screen.

They passed several dim portals. Five subchambers down showed tarnished, brass doorways, each clamped shut.

One mouldering doorway still dangled open; Baus deigned to poke his head in and immediately he felt chill vapours sliding in and out. An intense odour hung in the air, like rat dung, or some stagnant water from an open cistern. The tightly-woven space was cramped with a criss-crossing of ledges and banisters, cabinets, compartments and components, in which, to his little surprise, a glut of packrat oddments resided: ibex skulls, wegmor horns, bison antlers, rabbit feet, ox teeth, mortars, pestles, flasks. There were belts, leathers, hides. In the chamber adjacent they discovered a catacomb jammed with an unlikely profusion of broken antiques, rakes, hews, mauls, pylons, chests, traps, bones, gnarls, whips, lures, nets, wire. What a packrat this Dakkaw was! Almost inaudibly they could hear his low-pitched grumbles wafting from the floorboards above as he stood trussed and seething. The sounds were pitched in casually triumphant cadences—which seemed to suggest the ogre knew into exactly which chamber they traveled.

Baus expunged his growing trepidations. The main passage branched right, then left, then he stopped short, holding his breath sharply. To lose oneself in the Dakkaw's maze would be foolhardy misfortune. Who knew what labyrinthine terrors lay in wait in Bisiguth's crypts? To stumble upon some unimaginable thing and save the Dakkaw the unpleasant task of disposing of the two of them, was unacceptable.

Baus edged his way toward the wall. He was about to urge Valere to do the same when all of a sudden they heard a faint mewling cry softly in the dimness.

It came in plaintive fits and starts, then a sound of low repetition and hopeless terror, which sent chills down their spines.

Baus flung himself into a crouch. The sound was real, coming from one of the larger spaces off the main corridor.

The moan lingered, past a rotting beam where clotted remnants of webs hung. From here issued a soft whooshing, which proved to be a procession of gimlet bats.

The call resumed itself: a piteous, wretched wail, devoid of any sane emotion.

Cautiously the two explorers crept forward. They ducked their heads. A low arch heralded a wide chamber. The entablature, as Baus noted, was ancient and marred with thick coats of dust and spider dung. Valere followed no more than a hair's breadth behind Baus, as if assured of a margin of safety by shadowing his peer. The two wedged themselves between the entranceway, plucking torches like ragbag thieves. The murk was illuminated to reveal a sizeable room held aloft by two round limestone pillars. A figure, hanging upside down from a chain was visible in the room's center.

The man, or what they perceived as a man, was hooked a mere few inches above an iron-strapped barrel. A matted tangle of curls fell low. The barrel was filled to the brim with an offensive liquid, rippling occasionally. Chains were wrapped around the figure's ankles, from which the frail limbs were strung up from the ceiling. The man's legs were pulled tight with his weight, his thin arms dangled loosely, slack as fishing wire. He twirled slowly—like some piece of cod on an odd string. He wore a pair of cut-off green dungarees, a soiled brown shirt, a tattered bandanna, all clinging to his emaciated frame like slimy rags. A complicated apparatus was connected to the chain—levers, ratchets, pulleys—the like of which was supported by a bizarre wooden scaffolding. The sudden light of torches seemed to hurt his eyes and he clamped them shut with all his waning strength, but he could not cover them completely because his hands were bound behind his back.

Valere fumbled along the nearest wall to light a rusty wall-sconce.

Baus moved in closer, afraid to peer into those strange eyes that surely must stare hollowly back at him. In the midst, he stumbled over a beat-up bucket. The gaunt, pinched face wrenched itself about, struggling to show a ghastly smear of welts, pimples and sucker marks edged from chin to brow.

The dry mouth wheezed—a ragged, phlegmy sound: "Come again so soon, Dakkaw? Well, do your mischief! Your poor wastrel is immune to your abuses!"

Baus discerned that the figure was not an old man, perhaps six years older than himself, though he was extraordinarily haggard and dishevelled of frame beyond his years. An ankle brace drilled into the back wall with a loop chain was from where he guessed the ogre played a hanging game with him. Game completed, the ogre was content to leave him shackled— with the spiders.

"Why don't you speak?" the figure croaked wretchedly.

"We are not the Dakkaw," came Baus's emotionless reply.

The prisoner struggled to peer up at his new visitors, but his eyes were mal-adjusted to the light and his attempts only brought him frustration.

Baus offered a commiserating shrug; he forwarded his credentials. "I am Baus of Heagram, an explorer—this is Valere, my seafaring associate. We visit Bisiguth only to drop in, courtesy of the ogre. Look at what we find! Cedrek, the butcher's son."

"I am he!" affirmed the hanging man with a thin snarl. "Cedrek, son of Halfhan, son of Golfan. But how is it that you attend me unescorted? The Dakkaw permits no one to roam about his underground lairs but he."

Baus responded in an affected voice, "Suffice it to say that the Dakkaw is currently 'indisposed'."

"Mollymuffins!" rasped Cedrek. "Do not lay fibs on me. The Dakkaw would boil your bones and suck its juice before he would let you walk here." The butcher's son tried to untwirl himself but was unable to do so. He became increasingly agitated. Meanwhile Valere was busy studying the mechanism of chains and gears. It was complex. He lifted a pawl. It sent the chain grinding down a few notches and Cedrek's nose plunged headily into the wine-coloured liquid, prompting a torrential gasp of sputters.

Valere hastily rewound the ratchet; Cedrek bobbed up to normal height, spewing water and cursing.

"Imbeciles!" he cursed. "You are as heedless as koots, no less the bully Dakkaw, who persists in dunking my head in this swiresucker vat for his own amusement!"

"Our sincerest apologies," mumbled Baus. "The mechanism is rusty, unreliably old."

"Apologies?" spat Cedrek. "Fine and nice! Let us see you dunk your head in this grape juice, then all these 'sorries' will be amended."

Baus held up a placating hand. "No need for such irritable remarks, Cedrek. The pawl is obviously flawed and easy for an unfamiliar hand to let slip."

Valere nodded and twirled a finger at the gearworks.

Baus studied the barrel with its viscous contents. A curious perplexity infused his expression. Alerted by the prospect of feeding, several fish-things swarmed to the surface in red and gold numbers. Baus thought it was an uncommon genus of 'porpsons'—or vicious 'swiresucker', a bottom feeder, whose leech-like orifice easily clamped onto anything for nourishment. Baus reflected: the avidity of the fish explained the rather shabby condition of Cedrek's face.

Sputtering rancour, Cedrek could not yet adequately discern the fantastic visitors that remained just out of visible view, a fact which seemed to unnerve him even more. The water stung his eyes, acrid from the defecation of the swiresuckers.

Baus surveyed the 'tank' with sombre-eyed scrutiny. He advanced to better study the 'hanging apparatus' which the Dakkaw had cleverly concocted. Instantly his eyes shot up in recognition. "What an ungainly appliance the Dakkaw has built for you, Cedrek! Your plight intrigues me! What deeds have brought you floating over a horrid barrel of porpsons? Truthfully, I am at a loss; I am in awe of the circumstance. The Dakkaw's tales are surely fulsome—but we would like to know the bare truth."

Cedrek's manner grew more unpleasantly terse. "It is an enthralling chronicle, with which I shall certainly entertain guests at a later time, however currently I am under duress. I would urge you to assist me! Currently I am unable to disengage myself from this apparatus."

"The fact speaks plainly enough," agreed Baus, scratching his chin.

"Well, I'm glad that we concur on at least one point. Now! Fetch me the Dakkaw's key, so that I may loose myself from these abominable chains. My legs creak with grievous aches and chills. Hastily, lagbags!"

Baus put on a grimacing frown: "Let us not become overeager, Cedrek. Gaps are still outstanding in regard to your histories and exploits. Since I am an individual who analyzes details before committing deeds, I must learn more about your predicament."

Cedrek considered Baus's line of reasoning fastidious, but Baus reiterated his concern of loosing a known felon into the world.

"The sentiment is irrelevant!" shrilled Cedrek. "Now unshackle me and you shall hear everything in its entirety!"

"That is a presumptuous demand!" Baus cried. "If this is how you wish to play it out, Cedrek, then—" He issued signals to Valere who, leading the way out of the chamber, chuckled consentingly. Cedrek, upon hearing the sounds of retreat, jerked his neck about with alarm and indignation.

"Where are you going?"

"To New Krintz," replied Baus. "My colleague and I have important business there."

"Business?" cried Cedrek in spite. "What kind of business?"

"Obligations and transactions, nothing more; they will brook no delay. The Dakkaw is an incisive fellow."

Cedrek gave a bray of sullen laughter. "Are you telling me you conduct deeds with the Dakkaw? He will boil your skulls, grind your femurs to meal. The day he lets you leave this warren is the day he lets you simmer in his stewpot."

"This may well be true," observed Baus. "But no doubt we have maintained an upper hand on the Dakkaw's roguery."

"Blather!" shrilled Cedrek.

Baus peered around, frowning. "I do not like that tone, Cedrek. Now, where is that cock-eyed key? I see it nowhere in this dog-kennel."

"Have you no eyes? It hangs on the wall, plain as a lily!"

Baus and Valere scoured the walls but they could spy no key or pin, prompting Baus to scratch at his chin with wonder. Perhaps Cedrek's extended sojourn had caused him hallucinations?

Cedrek's voice escalated to a peevish whine, which only affirmed Baus's suspicion. "Why tarry, hounds?" the prisoner yelled. "You only have to snag the key and bring it down from its perch, unclasp the rings binding my ankles and save me from falling. Surely you jest in regards to all this talk of transactions with the Dakkaw? Are you comics, or halfwits?"

Baus's tolerance reached a threshold. He demurred. "Not at all, Cedrek," he replied coldly. "Acts as this would conflict with our covenant with the Dakkaw, thus making us mean and dishonourable men—wouldn't it, Valere?"

"Very much so," remarked Valere gravely.

Cedrek howled: "Get me down from here, you rotten knaves! Retards is a better word!"

"Now you have gone and done it," rebuked Baus sternly. "Insults are an irrevocable breach. Shall you do the honours, Valere?"

"Gladly." The seaman took the ganglestick from his hand and issued Cedrek a stiff rap on the chest.

The ingrate refused to freeze. The chest was clothed of material, a circumstance which Baus explained as the source of the misfire.

Valere recognized the mistake; jocundly he stripped Cedrek of his shirt while reaching for his fish-white body, at which point, Cedrek burst into a tirade of invective.

Rapping Cedrek's bare throat with the ganglestick, Valere grunted as Cedrek finally became still, like a beast draining blood at the abattoir.

Satisfied with the work, Baus took back the baton and the two retraced their steps, pausing on the way back to gather up a length of chain and several shackles which they had found hid in a cobwebbed crate in one of the store rooms.

Valere showed a lukewarm grimace. "I do not like Cedrek's attitude; his manners are crass."

"He is an ill-mannered, pugnacious loon, agreed," said Baus. "I can see why the Dakkaw became irascible with him. Cedrek shall have the time he needs to reflect on his many slips of tongue."

Valere gave his head a knowing shake. "At least this chain should do the trick to bind the Dakkaw's limbs. I harbour little trust in the ropes we currently use. On the way to Krintz, chains of this sort will be of utility."

Baus nodded approval. "The Dakkaw is an artful creature. We must be prudent and wary."

"Absolutely."

"And intelligent, no less!" cried Baus, flourishing his bodkin.

* * *

The two gained Bisiguth's main floor and found Rilben unsuccessfully attempting to free the Dakkaw's knots and restraints. Valere shouted an oath and shooed him away. The grimacing creature disappeared into the gloom and was nowhere to be seen. The Dakkaw's wrists were still bound. He could not pull free, and Valere's rope-tightening earlier had proven fortuitous. Now he chain-shackled him double-tight for security before they herded him to the looming portal. Valere unlocked the ancient mechanism and stared for some time at the ogre's impudent posture. The seaman slid back the heavy bolts; Baus stood ever ready to administer a punitive measure with the ganglestick should the ogre attempt an indiscretion.

The sky was clear; the stars burned above like fireflies. A light breeze pushed down from the northerly skies, urging murmurs through the weeds in the rubbled court. Baus drew in a welcome draught. How glorious it was to be in the air, not cloistered in desolate Bisiguth!

"What of Rilben?" grumbled Valere.

Baus waved off the ape as if he mattered little. "Rilben will have to fend for himself."

Cedrek and Rilben were willingly and gratefully left behind.

With utmost wariness, Valere kept strict control over the Dakkaw, via the cord tied round his neck. Baus proposed it would be of better service to hitch the Dakkaw to his own wagon for transport. Valere enthusiastically endorsed the concept and before long, they were sitting up in the wagon like kings. They lit their torches, while the Dakkaw pulled the cart out of the courtyard and onto the main, north-south promenade. He seethed with annoyance. The rubbled path sheened in the moonlight, spectral cobbles glinting like bone. The thoroughfare meandered toward the shadows of the ruined plaza a hundred yards distant. Behind, Bisiguth spread like a blue-black mantle of faraway enchantment from an earlier time.

The dazzling stars tumbled away. The companions were well past the crumbling gates of Old Krintz when the last tottering statues of the old city fell behind. They were left with a barely-discernible flagstoned path. It too dwindled to a ghost-shadow and forced them out on a grassy sward where hedge and gorse loomed under the glare of brands.

"On, Dakkaw, on!" cried Baus impatiently. "To New Krintz."

"To New Krintz!" the Dakkaw muttered. He seemed equipped with more energy than would be imagined. "Drearily it is to Krintz I toil to win my bride!"

Baus gave a loud acclamation to the ambition.

Valere chuckled knowingly. "If this damsel you covet is as enchanting as you describe, then all your slogging will be worth it, eh, Dakkaw?"

"Your words are as insolent as you are, Captain. But they indicate truth. However, I urge you to minimize your sarcasm."

"If she is that haunting and spellbinding," Baus announced, "perhaps I will take her for my own."

The Dakkaw halted the cart and stared coldly at Baus for some time. He growled, "Over my dead body!"

"A jest only," assured Baus. "Do not become over-petulant, Dakkaw! At present we proceed to Krintz in amity!"

The Dakkaw snorted, disliking Baus's smiling insincerity. He gave his neck a jerk, took up the reins, bounded forward with Herculean force. The cart jolted ahead. They were bound for New Krintz.

X

The wind died and the air was very still, yet the long night was only beginning. Despite the jaunty songs that Valere and Baus sung from their perches, the oppressive memories of Bisiguth remained imprinted on their brains. Old Krintz was two leagues distant; they would not arrive before midnight—or so the Dakkaw forecasted in his glib, highbrow way.

Baus waved a showy hand. "The distance is irrelevant. We have important affairs to set in order regardless of the hour."

The journey continued. Except for some minor inconveniences, the journey passed uneventfully—barring a surprise confrontation with an unpredictable blue-eyed yantler which the Dakkaw recognized as a *Nosofix* breed.

The torches began to die. It was perhaps a few hours past midnight when the cart creaked its way to the outer peripheries of Krintz. Baus stared wordlessly at the stone pathway which weaved itself between the ragged mulberries like a tired snake. Two armless, ghostly, chalcedony statues jutted out from nowhere, grinning down on them without humour. Doubtless, they had been looted from Old Krintz, and were destined to spend their days keeping vigil at their gatepost. Glimmers of pallid light leaked through the mass of black baywolf trees, promising vistas of the town to come.

They gained the wooden gate, surrounded on each side by a low rampart. The gate was barred, as the Dakkaw had warned them—but the rampart was erected with sharp wooden pales from which the Dakkaw stepped away angrily, gesticulating to the large bulbs of shallot and cloves that were impaled over the parapet.

Valere climbed up on the mesh, impatiently discharging the bulbs, which Baus identified as old, dried up impotent bulbs—no cause for alarm.

The Dakkaw primly disagreed. "Age only increases the potency of these bulbs. They are nothing less than poison!"

Baus kicked gamely at the vegetables littering the ground. "Rotten things!" The Dakkaw, for the time being, was appeased with the contempt and failed to notice the two small perennials that Baus stuffed into his pocket.

Using his manacles as a sledge, the Dakkaw smashed a great hole in the gate; they all stood back with approving grins. The Dakkaw pulled the wagon off into the shrubbery while Valere, trailing him with the rope wound round his neck, discarded dead firebrands into the foliage. Baus wrapped his cloak tighter about him and the three passed within the precincts of the village.

Stealthily they proceeded down a trimmed lawn, filled with rich shadows cast by the tall hedgerows. The Dakkaw led the way circumspectly, but gained more confidence as he advanced. Valere shambled after, clutching the rope taut with the Dakkaw's neck. Baus followed at a more leisurely distance. The ganglestick was raised to forestall any contingencies the Dakkaw might incite.

A row of a dozen tall corniced buildings emerged into the dark foreground. Baus could discern high pitched gables set with shingle and ornate façades that stood silently in the grey moonlight. Text was engraved on the walls which none of the company could decipher. A few orange glimmers glinted through the casements in the upper chambers, but outside of a gleam or two, no glimpse or sound came from within. A large open plaza lay in the moonlight. Purling water, perhaps of a large fountain, trickled from this direction. Inching their way forward, they searched for the slightest sound of mishap, but Baus detected nothing, and caught only a downward glimpse of light, noting that the cobbles were waxed smooth by the passage of many feet. Toward the square's center stood a great obelisk, an alabaster fountain which also purled at its shadowy feet.

Despite the hour, ribaldry was about. Light spilled out from the plaza's pub where two tall oval casements waxed with movement. Undoubtedly popular, surmised Baus, judging from the clamour of clinking glasses and unmannerly jests.

The Dakkaw gave a sullen murmur, "Voydram's square is where we are—the louts drink ale like fish here. The coffers to which I allude are kept in the Vulde's private manor on the west side." He gestured at the edifice and remarked dully, "I've been there many times. Always I had no trouble gaining entry through the old post door near the root cellar."

"Very good," exclaimed Baus approvingly. "Show us the way, Dakkaw—and no tricks! The ganglestick is less forgiving than its last strike upon you." Baus gave the adjunct a meaningful tap.

The Dakkaw's gaze went stony. "Fear no chicanery, ingrate. The Vulde's own daughter, Delizra, slumbers in one of the luxurious wings on the main floor. After we secure your wealth, we will steal her, and you two jacks will help me escort her back to Bisiguth!"

Baus waved the ganglestick with cavalier license. "All in good time, Dakkaw. Let us acquire this 'mountain of gold' first, then we shall pursue loftier goals as time permits."

The Dakkaw flashed Baus a feral grin. "See that you do, swain." He lowered his head and stumped forward with frigid dignity.

Baus noticed more pales wedged in and around casements' sills, positioned above doorways and on the eaves of rooftops; some were even bunched in flower pots and gardens. How steadfast were the villagers of Krintz! The pales were more regular and stouter in shape than the gate and edged with three-tongued barbs that held up sacks of onions, shallots and cloves which Baus believed the villagers thought to ward off monsters.

Valere stood on the balls of his feet, gauging the sacks with a quipster's grin. "My, my, Dakkaw! You do appear to be the unpopular person! Yet it puzzles me as to why you have not already attempted to secure these barbs and sacks?"

The Dakkaw gave a disgusted grunt. "By the time I did, the villagers would have been all over me, with bills and snares."

"What of the cloves and the onions?" Baus asked.

"They burn my skin and wreak chaos on my senses! Even now I feel a leaden waxiness coming over my limbs; furthermore, my sense of smell is woolly; even my hearing is impaired; I feel a small chill down my spine, a burning in my throat. Some queer coincidence makes me feel the hated shallots within inches of my own vitals!" He gulped, peered loathingly. But he could find no sign of his scourge. His gaze swung heavily on Baus.

Baus moved away, not appreciating the scrutiny. Valere followed deeper into the back alley, tugging at the Dakkaw's rope with even more compelling force.

"I shall proceed, Captain, as soon as you allow my wretched neck some lenience," sneered the Dakkaw.

Valere loosed tension on the rope. Baus made eager motions to drag a pair of onion bags and shallot off to the alley's periphery. Valere watched with curiosity.

To their right a tall, smoke-blackened wall showed ragged smoke drifting from the two brick chimneys above. Baus craned his neck, spied a voluted roof rich with complex angles . . . a high balcony loitered, under which three darkened, filigreed window panes, were exposed.

He shivered, for the alley's narrow girth worried him; it plunged into chill shadow.

The Dakkaw requested Valere to dispose of the detestable sacks at the threshold of a nearby darkened doorway. Valere grumbled. The Dakkaw plodded to the door, a low affair it seemed, and sneered. The entrance was shut tightly and framed with grey baywolf posts with polished iron rings. A small oval window lay out of arm's reach to the left.

The Dakkaw grabbed the door-rings and twisted while heaving with his shoulder against the grains of beobar. The portal swung inward, bottom scraping noisily at the stone.

The intruders failed to notice a woman garbed in peasant's blouse peering at them from a distance up the alley, swaying tipsily. She put a hand to her mouth and uttered a cry. The warning was quickly stifled by Valere's deft hand clamping her mouth before she could wreak further damage. She caught a glimpse of the ogreish Dakkaw who was just whirling out the entranceway in menacing stealth.

"Careful, lass!" breathed Valere. "You haven't seen anything. Upon my soul, so long has it been since I kissed a pretty flower." He scooped her up and bestowed a sloppy kiss on her lips like a captured kitten. The thrusting of maw against maw had her struggling to escape. She pushed herself away, shrilling out a feverish cry. She slapped Valere hard on the cheek and tottered off back to the plaza.

Baus hissed: "Shouldn't we go after her? The wench may alert the authorities!"

Valere smacked his lips. "Gibbering out a story about a seven foot giant, a mad beggar and his drunken buddy? . . . I don't think so. The feint was deliberate, Baus. Ah, the wench's probably gotten over it even as we speak . . . some tavern hussy from one of the little ale holes. Ah, but did that embrace feel good!"

The Dakkaw sniffed disapproval. "You are an overbearing lout, Captain. Exhibitions of this kind would never win you a bride in Krintz."

Valere jeered. "What need I of a bride, ogre? I have already had my share of snakelegs and heartbreaks. It's a sham, Dakkaw, and I pity you for your mawkishness over marriage."

Baus grew restless. "Let us dispense with the philosophy and augment our stealth. Valere, I admire your veneration, but your ungentlemanliness surprises me. I seem to recall a certain Rauseelia from whom you seem not to have learned your lessons."

Valere's eyes flashed. "Never utter that unholy name. At least not in my presence." His eyes twitched, features knotted. "Let us get on with this deranged mission. I am ready to quit.

Notice, the night wears!"

The Dakkaw snorted agreement.

Baus curtly motioned the ogre into the cubbyhole; the giant ducked into the murk—albeit reluctantly. The two captors plunged in after him, but not before Baus had dragged back one of the shallot sacks and placed another inside to block the door. The action caused a flicker of annoyance to cross the Dakkaw's visage.

"What's all this?" he blared.

"To avoid detection by the locals," Baus replied candidly. "Also, should you attempt a cack-handed ambush of us in the corridor, you would invite your own doom. No one but us can displace the items."

"A foolish and unnecessary precaution!"

"A man must do what a man must do," answered Baus solemnly.

Valere chuckled, "A man who survives is also one who gets to take a bride, eh Dakkaw?"

Baus acknowledged the slogan with approval. Presently the two wedged the sack of onion tightly behind the door. The trio descended a low stairwell, hunched like beggars, unable to avoid stumbling over bins, barrels, jars and canisters. The gloomy place was rife with the smell of sour wine and fermented ale. A feeble watery light crept in through the casement to their left.

Not having the lie of the land, the two thieves stubbed their toes on iron-strapped barrels and old wooden crates left over from packaging. They probed here and there, muttering oaths until the two reached the far wall—real enough to grant them small comfort. Crude poles or staffs were mounted on the stone face. Valere expressed surprise and identified the objects as brands and hurried to wrench one off its hanger. On a nearby table lay flint and tinder which he took and had the brand firing to life.

"What luck!" Under the dull glare, Baus discovered the nature of the surroundings: a distillery, quite expansive, ornamented with high-vaulted ceiling and squared, heavy pillars. Dozens of holes were carved in the wall which were filled with bottles of antique design. Valere expressed an inclination to sample some of the liquor but Baus discouraged it. Rubbing chin, Baus thought it odd that the town's entire wealth would be stored in such a dim, out-of-the-way place.

As if reading the irony in his mind, the Dakkaw laughed when he told them that the Vulde kept the town's treasure down here knowing that no one would think of searching for it in so repulsive a place. "The distillery is an extension of his manse, which rises above us on three levels."

The proclamation was not entirely implausible and Baus found himself agreeing. They tramped on, up a metal-worked stair, and a platform, giving rise to a narrow walkway with wooden railing. Dimly they saw the expanse of brewery instruments below. The Dakkaw pointed to where a heavy bronze-strapped door stood with imposing dominance. "Beyond that portal lies the Vulde's wealth, and likely that of the town's. The entrance is locked, but when has that ever deterred me?" With an impertinent grin, he trooped down the corridor and gave the portal a jarring smack. The back of his fist had it creaking open and after some deft manoeuvring, he scraped the door ajar.

Valere edged past the ogre, keen to examine the wealth. He thrust out a torch, piercing the gloom to find a strongbox sitting on a plain dais propped along the far wall. He rushed over. The confines was a small stony vault, windowless, and the ceiling nearly brushed his skull.

The box was unlocked, and the lid was left ajar to reveal a heaping pile of gold coins, glistening seductively in the torchlight. Valere gaped and ran his fingers through the nuggets like a treasure-hunter. True to his word, the Dakkaw had delivered the goods and this time Baus gloated in celebration with his friend. They exchanged hoarse murmurs; here was a wealth greater than either had seen in a lifetime! Grinning like hounds, they sifted through the coins, scooping up as much as their pockets would hold. Baus suddenly stiffened, catching glimpse of the suggestive gleam in the ogre's eyes. Odd that the ogre was just leaning outside the entrance with a casual leg slung under the other without taking any wealth for himself.

"Well?" croaked the Dakkaw. "What is it now? Or are you all just ingrates? Here's enough glitter for you jacks to pass ten years. Glut yourselves plenty, filchers, but be quick about it, for other deeds await!"

Baus peered contemptibly at the ogre. He was eager to get out of this storeroom, having received a disturbing vision of the giant suddenly slamming the door shut on the two of them. "What about you? Aren't you going to gather silver? There is plenty for all." He thrust hands into the stash and let drop a handful of clinking gold.

The Dakkaw stepped back with scorn, eyes brimming with hauteur. "At Bisiguth I have treasures galore. My jewels would fill this repository a score of times over. As for myself, I desire only a bride."

Baus's thin grimace dwindled to a mocking sneer. "A bride, so you say! Well, let's make a deal; we shall visit these upper levels of yours if only you help us carry this box out."

The Dakkaw held up a mulish paw. "I have fulfilled my obligation, now loose these shackles and remove this wretched rope from my throat. I cannot be wheezing and jerking while my princess sees me court her like a common mongrel to be set out in the kennel."

Valere offered a thin, whining objection but the ogre rebutted the argument and Baus felt obliged to give him what he wanted. The shackles fell in a jangling heap.

"That's better!" sneered the ogre. Now, he flung down the noose, which lay in a discordant pile on the stone.

The Dakkaw held an advantage, checked only by the sack of shallots barring egress from the winery. But Baus tossed a shrug. What could he do? They would depart Krintz and leave this ogre to his repulsive lusts, at least this is what his wordless glance to Valere bespoke.

Barring the door, they retraced their steps, padding cautiously down the narrow walkway. They ascended another iron-grilled stair and before them stood a portal with a brass, hatchet-shaped handle. The winery swung below them like an abandoned tool shop.

The Dakkaw tested the brass handle. A quick jerk had the door parting with enough of a gap to let them through. Warm vapours graced them an air of assurance: fleeing smoke, odours of mutton and roast hare. Already at this hour, the household's woodstoves were at work.

"The lord sleeps upstairs," whispered the Dakkaw. "His daughters rest on the main floor.

In that, we are lucky.”

"Daughters?” questioned Valere. “I thought you said there was only one. Perhaps we shall tarry here a bit for a taste of fringe benefits? What do you say, Baus?”

"Absolutely nothing of the sort!” called Baus primly. “What do you think we are—opportunists?”

The Dakkaw gave an impertinent growl. “Shut up! Do you think there are others here who will not hear us? Slack fools! I doubt if the Vulde posts guards in the scullery, but I know he harbours servitors, so be alert!”

"A wise counsel, Dakkaw,” agreed Baus, “but what of these other daughters you talk about?”

"There would be only one,” the Dakkaw grumbled uneasily, “she who would be Griselda.”

"The next question is, who is Griselda? Is she as beautiful as her sister?” prompted Valere.

The Dakkaw’s vexation gave way to a cryptic smile. “You shall have to see for yourself, redbeard. I shall let you be the judge—that is, if chance will have it.”

Baus thought the reply ambiguous, but for the time he let it go.

They crept into the vestibule. The Dakkaw rotated his bull neck about with flair and proceeded with an air of authority toward the corridor. He flexed his wrists and swept thick, glabrous hands around his throat, glad to be free of his oppressive shackles. Of his intent, Baus could not be sure.

Valere held the torch aloft, beckoning with caution. Baus trailed dutifully behind at a hair’s breadth. They gained a small stairway—baywolf oak and spindlefax; noiselessly they slunk into a wide hall in the wake of the giant’s tread. They passed a small chamber of hanging pots, iron skillets and skewers and entered into a spacious chamber furnished with fur-padded benches and upholstered chairs. The last embers of the hearth glowered in an otherwise feeble glow and a pin-silent gloom. The walls were decorated with deep mahogany paneling; wall hangings depicted naval scenes of the legendary Boat Lords of Old Krintz. A tall set of antique stairs to their left rose in the shadows while a carpeted hallway ran to their right. Down the hallway marched the ogre with an altogether surprising speed. It seemed he knew the place well and as he strode, his mass rippled, causing Baus anxiety. Midway they encountered a room filled with crystal and rich furnishings, including a silk-robed table. Obviously the dining room. Glass vases were set with flowers; low end-tables lurked in the periphery.

Baus mused. Despite the austerity of the Vulde’s residence, there seemed a definite sense of opulence here. The lord was clearly a man of taste and wealth and likely power: one not to be crossed. The fluttery foreboding in Baus’s stomach began to grow.

The hall narrowed; two narrow rooms with closed doors lay to either side. The Dakkaw reached for the far doorknob, then smilingly, he reached for the other. Valere and Baus traded glances, wondering what this mirthful exchange meant.

The door opened soundlessly; into the murk they peered, spying nothing, but hearing only a soft, tangible breathing.

Valere raised his torch. Buttery light revealed a young woman reposed in a double bed surmounted with a silken canopy. The colour of her gown was pale robin's egg blue and Baus's brows raised at the damsel, for disposed even so carelessly in slumber, she was an incredible beauty in every respect. Fulsome brown locks tumbled exquisitely down immaculate cheeks. A sideways glimpse showed a visage moulded with ruby lips which purred sleepily like some gorgeous feline. Here was a pearly-white nape of neck, a seductive curve of breasts very neatly traced in silk beneath the covers . . .

The Dakkaw stared at the sight of her, murmuring a dreamy sigh. With little reservation, he struggled forward, ready to fling a hungry hand over her mouth and take her by surprise.

Baus flinched. The ogre was about to treat this innocent creature like a rough beast and he could not bear seeing such a flower coerced before his eyes. From his pocket, he withdrew two bulbs, which he had been saving for an urgent occasion. Boldly, he stalked forth.

His intrusion had no effect on the ogre who had already committed to his deed. Brazenly he reached to snatch at the girl, but twisted around like some slippery serpent when Baus attacked him from behind. With brutal disregard, he swatted Baus and flung him to the planks like a rag doll. The noise alerted Delizra, whose wide, stirring eyes turned into orbs of pure terror.

The notes of her scream hung frigidly in the air, echoing about the chamber like some ghost gibber before they raced down the adjoining hall. The next thing Baus knew the Dakkaw had her clamped in his arms, eyes gleaming. A madman's lust was in his face, his breath was a hot furnace upon her pale, trembling cheek. Swiftly he rolled her up in a ball and shambled away for the door.

Delizra struck at him with her fists, knocked him with her knees but her puny strength was of no avail. He only crushed her tighter to his foul body. Valere bravely blocked the ogre's way, but the Dakkaw swatted him aside as he had Baus, and now almost trampled the two underfoot.

Baus struggled to his knees. He flung the onion and shallot before the door. The bulbs fell rolling between the doorway and the place where the Dakkaw poised ready to exit. For a second the monster hesitated, then he hopscotched back, clutching one hand at his eyes, the other at the girl as if he were mesmerized.

Delizra clamped teeth hard on his knotty wrist. The Dakkaw howled; momentarily he lost his grip on her. The maid wriggled, scrambled off on her haunches toward the end of the room. The Dakkaw lunged but she was already skidding back to the bedside. A great ringing suddenly erupted from within the manor—an ominous gong. A furious motion came from the halls—scurrying feet, confused shouts. Steel slithered from scabbards. Baus saw a flicker of angry torches dimly in the hallway. The Dakkaw forced his eyes open. They glowed with icy purpose and sent daggers down Baus's spine.

The gong pounded on. The Dakkaw took hold of his senses and attempted to leap half madly over the two banes of shallot that obstructed his path.

The effort was dilatory. Valere thrust his torch into the ogre's face and singed an eyebrow.

A tall, ruddy-cheeked defender burst into the chamber. He had a wolfish countenance and was garbed in the grey-black robe of a servant. He brandished a single rapier which he used with fluid ease to slice at the Dakkaw. Without fear, he launched a vicious thrust. The stab was easily eluded, as was the next, which the Dakkaw repulsed with a quick duck-winging of elbows and caught the blade on his leather jerkin. Maddened beyond belief, the ogre thrust a fist to hammer back the fellow. The swordsman went flying to the wall, knocked out of breath. The blow had struck breastbone, and the avenger slumped dizzily down in a ragged heap.

The Dakkaw leapt out into the hall. His form was a lewd silhouette in the soft light. A triumphant howl formed on his lips.

He was not far in his escape before several adversaries were on the way, intercepting with prejudice. Garbed in overcloaks of red and green, the men wielded whips and long pointed swords. With glee, they snapped and hacked at the Dakkaw.

The Dakkaw danced and dodged the strikes with puppet dexterity. He fist-clubbed many, sending bruised and blackened watchmen to their knees. But by sheer numbers they overpowered him and weighed him down with chains and ropes.

It took thirteen men to control the fiend and quell the fierceness of his attack. Snarls and raging insults ripped out of his foaming mouth before his stupendous strength gave way to sagging impotence. The Dakkaw, humbled to a hunched beast, was dragged away to suffer whatever penalties the citizenry of Krintz had in mind.

Now Delizra stood weakly at the bedside. She hastened to console the tall, dark-haired stranger who was slowly reviving. The man was long-faced and thin-nosed and graced with keen brows, and not without a graceful air to his bearing. The girl noticed Baus for the first time. She hesitated. She seemed to harbour a curious affection for her protector, which Baus could not quite pinpoint.

A new figure abruptly emerged into the bedchamber. He was a hawk-faced individual standing thickly framed in the doorway: tall and confident, exuding an air of absolute authority. Lank, jet-black hair streamed down his flaring cheeks. Grey hair fringed his temples. His eyes were a flash of keen blue, writ with an imperturbable gaze. He wore a billowy chestnut night robe and soft slippers laced with purple ties. On his breast, the coat-of-arms of an eagle and a three-masted schooner was woven, obviously an emblem of distinction. He looked palely toward his daughter and tumbled in, with breath drawn like a plucked violin.

"Delizra!"

"Father!" she cried. The girl leaped, arched arms about the man. The Vulde, lord of the manor, clasped his kin with a thrill of discovery, knowing that she was safe from further molestation.

Baus and Valere attempted a half-smile. Their half-sidling retreat did not go far. Three scowling watchmen herded them back into a corner. Another attempt to slink away was thwarted with three swordtips aimed impolitely at their throats.

"Well, brigands!" cried the lord fiercely. He wasted no time making strides over to assess them. "What have you to say in your defence before I have you run through?"

Baus gave a laboured sigh. "Would you kill innocent men? We were as much the

Dakkaw's prisoners as was your daughter. If not for our impromptu plan, we would all be dead. Recall the shallot I lodged at the monster." He gestured importantly to the crushed bulbs that oozed on the polished wooden planks.

The Vulde lowered his glance and gave a soft grunt. He scanned the crushed items and his whimpering daughter, finally to settle his gaze on the two sullen-eyed intruders. "Well, what of it? " The intensity in the lord's eyes diminished.

"It is true, Father," the girl admitted. "The two intruders attempted to impede the creature by cunning force. The red-bearded man thrust a blazing torch in the ogre's eyes; the other fearlessly flung fresh shallots at his feet to beguile the ogre's lust."

The Vulde gave an incredulous frown. He declared in brusque tones, "Who are you and from where do you come? Speak candidly or I shall cut out your tongues like the Dakkaw."

"I am Baus of Heagram," answered Baus frankly. He bowed and made a small, reckless smile on his dry lips.

"I am Valere of Illim," offered Valere gallantly, "whose courtesy dips no less fulsomely than Baus's."

"Is that so?"

Baus hastened to explain: "The Dakkaw ensnared us in a glade near the Old Krintz ruins. In Bisiguth, he confined us, forcing us to obey his evil whims. Recently, he ordered us to remove the barriers you erect to commit acts of vandalism, which we were loath to enact, and were further obliged to guard the hallway under penalty of death while he was to champion your daughter."

The Vulde rubbed his eyes with anger, then he shook his head in ungovernable contempt. "This is what I know of the creature's depraved wish right from the outset!—as far back as the days when we exiled him from our community." The lord looked about the room appalled. Baus caught a glimpse of an anguished man and thought not to inject further fibs or requests.

"Well, if this is true, then you are heroes."

Baus and Valere accepted the presumption with humble bows.

Another man strode sullenly into the room. He had rounded cheeks, a baby nose, tiny blond ringlets pasted to narrow ears. His neck was thin, his mouth wide and he was dressed up in a pretentious gold and blue suit with silver lining, cufflinks, chain, tall black boots, the works. The features of the man's face seemed carved into an insincere rictus. From grey eyes he stole a look of almost condescending disapproval at the intruders and their relation with the girl who, frightened out her wits, was still trembling. He scooted over to her side like a shelduck, dropping to a knee and taking her hand. "Delizra, my sweet beloved! What has happened to your innocent daintiness? You are ruffled and distraught. Are you hurt?"

"Not at all," she replied coolly. She withdrew her hand and sniffed with ill-concealed contempt. "Brave Tulesio here, initiated the first feint upon the ogre, these two here finished the job—"

The newcomer glared about the room. "I shall have these rogues whipped and dragged through the briar before they are all hanged! Attend! These must be the louts themselves, grumbling while picking at their teeth like a pair of bawdy, low-life scruffballs and ragbeards, ne'er do wells, along with the monster Dakkaw, who we now have in our custody and is tethered to Woybur's obelisk."

The Vulde nodded curtly, "That's enough, Hysgode. You shall do no such thing. Little harm has come to Delizra, so we shall thank these men. In fact, I am not sure that the little scare hasn't done Delizra some good." He smiled affectionately. "On another note, I am glad you are here. I wish you to escort these 'ragbeards' to the guest chambers. They are to be spared no expense on our account."

The nobleman protested, eyes growing out of their sockets. "I find the courtesy overreaching. The task is menial and I am of title to renege such duties while these scandalous villains are—"

"Scandalous villains?" the Vulde cried. He lifted a quivering finger. "Summon my staff. See that the guests are given fresh linen and changes of costume and warm victual. Until further notice, they are to be considered in respect, with rank at Silsoor, and by you too. I shall suffer no further complaints or slanders upon their honour!"

Hysgode shook his head with confusion.

A guard held up a fistful of coins. "Look, Vulde! I have discovered these upon this redbeard—wealth obtained from our own coffers."

"How do you know they are our own?" barked the Vulde.

"Because it bears our seal, lord. You can see for yourself." He lifted a gold sequin to the light. The Vulde eyed the coin with scrutiny. The watchman's aides stepped eagerly aside as he frowned upon the pieces and emitted a cry of astonished acrimony. Snarling now, they laid hands on Baus and searched his person. They discovered a hefty pouch of more of the same, and briskly they secured Baus's arms. To Baus's distress, they discovered Lolispar and the ganglestick.

In response to the maltreatment, Baus flung off the invasive hands with disgust. "Fools!" he cried. "Are wayfarers suddenly forbidden to carry weapons or gold? As for the coins, they are easily explained."

"Do so if you please," growled the Vulde. He tapped his foot impatiently.

"My colleague and I were out returning them to your chest. It was all part of the Dakkaw's cunning plan. He is an instrument of greed and lust, this blackguard. He sneered at us, taunting us in a disparaging voice, 'If I am to have a bride, ' he guffawed, 'I demand a dowry as bountiful as her beauty!' Then he grinned at us meaningfully, 'And to what better source should I peer than the Vulde's own coffers?' He laughed with an uproarious delight.

"To this audacity, we replied, 'No, Dakkaw, we respect the Lord Vulde's property. The risks you describe are not for us, the deed is too precarious and recklessly exploitative for serious thought.' Once again he chortled and forced us on to the town so that we may raid your repository and carry his spoils."

Valere endorsed the statement with urgent gestures.

The Vulde scowled, leaped forward, peering from one to the other, as if they were lunatics.

Baus held up a reassuring palm. "Look Vulde, we delivered you the ogre. Is this not enough to show us our good faith, even if by mischance?"

The Vulde stroked his stony chin in ever shrewder precision. Searching for any tremor of a fib, he grew indecisive. "Perhaps you recount snatches of deeds of verity—but something in this business of 'cunning plans' and 'exploitative deeds' smacks of fallacy. Fancy this tall tale of yours being even minutely true . . ."

The lord approached the burglars, curious to examine Baus's weapon, which Tulesio, his chamberlain and bodyguard, now handed him with courteous regard. "A fine sword, Baus—a gladius if I'm not mistaken. The neomancer runes are inscribed uniquely on the tang. They are of peculiar interest. From one of the southern kingdoms, I suspect—Loust? Aurenham? It escapes my memory. Wherever did you acquire this rare piece?"

Baus bowed in stately deference. "A gift, my lord—from a deceased uncle who was well known for his exotic travels beyond Arnin's realm. I believe he mentioned, 'Desenion' at one time or other."

The Vulde seemed impressed by the reference. "Indeed, a marvellous gift."

"It is," Baus assured. "And the item which your underling grips so crassly, is nothing more than a knick-knack, a gaud which I carry on my person for sentimental reasons." He snatched for the ebon rod. The guard fingered the shaft of the ganglestick, pulling it away. Inadvertently his fingers touched the tip and he stood frozen like a stunned rabbit. Baus shot forward, snatched the wand away. The spell was broken. The watchman teetered back muttering and glaring about with perplexity.

With certain definite distaste, the nobleman Hysgode flourished pompously. "Vulde, I beseech you to seize these vagrants and confiscate their weapons. I sense their character is of low breed." He complained, "We know little of them—so it demands an investigation. At minimum they should be held for questioning, at least until we have analyzed the situation at length. The strange wand, for example—it harbours the marks of a macabre indication!"

Delizra cried out keenly: "Will you not let me have a moment to explain? These two men, as I have affirmed, protected me from the ogre. They may appear dishevelled, even uncouth, but they are saviours no less."

The Vulde addressed his daughter with keen courtesy. "There is something in what you say, Delizra. Forsooth, it would be a breach of etiquette to betray our trust of visitors without significant evidence of guilt. Our town of Krintz has always been hospice to wanderers, young and old." He turned a glance upon Baus. "You may keep your curio, Baus, but the golden gladius shall be withheld. I am entrusting it to Tulesio until I know more about the part you have played in this outlandish affair."

Hysgode whined, "I believe you speak too liberally for these vagabonds, Vulde."

The Vulde's lips parted with fury, prompting Hysgode to make a hasty alteration to his statement, "Of course, it is only my opinion. If ill comes of this though—"

"Ill shall not come of it, Hysgode, now curb your insufferable misgivings. I tolerate your sanctimony only because you are my daughter's spouse, or shall soon be."

Glowering, the nobleman lowered his gaze. His eyes flashed rancour on the intruders that was not missed by Baus or Valere. It appeared that to irritate the Vulde at this time was a foolish endeavour and Hysgode set his grimace into a fractious simper. At that moment, a young, corpulent woman waltzed into the room. She was a woman of dominant bearing and dressed flimsily in a white silk nightgown and pale brown moccasins that seemed out of character for her breeding. Disturbed by the tumult from across the hall, she had quickly learned that Delizra had been nearly kidnapped and Baus had heard the name Griselda mentioned—the Vulde's oldest daughter. Where Delizra was dazzling, Griselda was squat and plump and borderline obese, with a maturing harelip, and an indecorous mass of flesh gracing her abdomen; withal, a maid with qualities singular to her mother.

Griselda squared beefy hands on her hips and roared out a mighty declaration: "Thieves and monsters in the night! Glory told! No good has come of Mother's absence from this gloomy manse!"

"Nor any harm either," soothed the Vulde. "Now, Griselda, let us go back to bed."

Griselda paid no heed. She gave her sister a plump squeeze and appraised the two trespassers with a hint of carnal inquiry. Baus was stricken with revulsion at the attention, no less the seaman, and the two shrank back, clearing their throats and uttering meaningful objections.

Cognizing the nature of the lascivious hints, the Vulde grimaced and counselled his daughter, but the efforts seemed fraught with hostility.

Hysgode grudgingly escorted Baus and Valere out of the room, leading them down a narrow hall to the common room, while the lord stayed behind to see Delizra and Griselda to bed. When the nobleman was directing the intruders up a long steep stair, the butler Velnar intercepted them. Baus took opportunity to scan the lavish surroundings. Over the railing a knot of fifteen men clustered milling about the hearth, now roaring with flame. Amongst the figures, members of the town watch clanking about the salon with swords and bills: brusque, fastidious, loyal men with bright red- and green-liveried costumes. Baus saw the Vulde emerge from Griselda's room and heard snippets of information given to the watchmen to bind and secure the Dakkaw in the square with more cord.

Delaying no longer, Hysgode acquired the key from the butler and prompted them down the hallway to its end. Mahogany doors lay shaded under the yellow glow of lamps. The lanterns seemed carved into the walls themselves. At the far end of the hall, another stair wound to a third storey, on which Baus speculated other rooms existed. Silsoor was large, possibly even as capacious as Bisiguth. On the second floor they halted at a fourth doorway which bore a window graced with an opaque pane of glass. Baus paused to study Hysgode thoughtfully as he fussed about with key and lock. While engrossed, the nobleman was frozen stiff as Baus brushed the back of his neck with the ganglestick. The nobleman became a susceptible target for Baus's pranks while in stooped position, with Baus skipping about, miming various ludicrous acts.

Valere jigged about in equal jocularity. The seaman was ready to kick Hysgode soundly in the rump, when Velnar approached, carrying a silver salver laden with sweetcakes. The butler muttered disapproval. "I demand to know the meaning of this nonsense!"

Baus and Valere halted their antics. They stood amiably in their tracks, with Baus framing a low whistle which he extended to become part of a cheerful refrain. Valere arched his eyes, twiddling his thumbs and doing his best to hum along to Baus's melody.

The butler grumbled humourlessly and stuffed the platter into Valere's hands as he leaned over to shake Hysgode out of his torpor. "Sir? Why do you crouch like a mutt? Are you ill?" Evincing no response, the butler tapped him on the back. Hysgode immediately jumped to attention and rattled his head. Life flushed back to the nobleman's limbs and he peered at the intruders with intense dissatisfaction, as if disliking their all-too-seraphic looks. Velnar's vacant gaze was no less idiotic.

"Well, what are you looking at?" Hysgode shrilled. The butler shrank back while the nobleman thrust the guests' door open and beckoned them inside. The door slammed shut in their faces.

Baus loosed an easy breath. Regarding his new surroundings, Baus grinned. The ceilings were high, the furnishings posh. Indeed the chambers were as lavish as any he had seen, particularly compared to Heagram prison and Bisiguth. He felt his mood improving.

Three sizeable double beds were strung out with fresh linen; woollen covers were folded along the far wall. The beds were well-cushioned, raised to a comfortable level above a polished hardwood floor. Baus found it a tasteful touch that portraits hung on the walls. To left and right the House of Vulde and related figures appeared; behind floated a large tapestry stitched in fine embroidery; a green, winged serpent and a lone albatross were outlined with abstract floral design.

Stepping aside, Baus drew back the drapes. Two tall violet panes overlooked the court. Woybur's obelisk dominated the court below; a silvery tip reared another storey above. Baus saw the Dakkaw secured in the plaza. Arms and legs were secured with stout cord, manacling his torso to the obelisk. Around Voydram's fountain an indefinite number of sacks were spread—doubtless a second defence of onion and shallot should the ogre somehow miraculously break loose, though the prospect seemed remote.

The court was bathed in a sullen grey moonlight. The lurid torchlight winked off the taverners' weapons and the metal pales were hoisted everywhere. Villagers had come to gawk at the captive.

The Dakkaw took the abuse with rancour. Even from this height, his emotion was wrathful and made him seem all the more forbidding. Baus shivered. He saw the fleshy lips working with venomous energy, mirroring a mind full of retributive intentions.

Baus knew that these hale men tempted death.

Baus quietly closed the drapes. He turned his attention to the captain, who was now dragging himself onto the bed and giving himself a gust of thanks. "Shame that we lost the plunder, Baus. But if it's any consolation, it looks like we may have to settle for being mere heroes in the Lord Vulde's eyes, rather than rich lords that's all."

Baus offered a bland assent. "Our 'lord' doesn't trust us much, Valere—remember my confiscated sword?"

Valere grunted. "Would you? A couple of dirty fobs caught in his daughter's bedroom in the wee hours? I'd say not. We're doing quite well, Baus, considering the facts. You can relax—you've only lost a little bodkin in the Lord's hoity-toity mansion, what of it? You may never see the blade again. We should be lucky to be alive, thanks to your fancy bit of mummery back there."

Baus's response was one of more of reflective quality. "Nothing that couldn't have been done by any person given a healthy lust for life."

Valere gave a caw. "I hardly think so. Your prevaricating goes beyond any mere throes of expertise. The last stunt with Hysgode was a little rich."

Baus shrugged ponderously. "The clod had it coming; besides, what better way to practice my tapping than taking opportunities on an oaf?"

"True." Valere's smile was wry. "You seem to have everything packaged in a nice neat little box, don't you?" The big seaman's face wrinkled; he heaved himself erect. Feigning a yawn, he spread arms wide only to catch Baus unawares in a great bear hug. Wrestling him to the ground, he razzed his hair.

Baus was in no mood for roughhousing and he arched the ganglestick up toward Valere's neck. The seaman stiffened, then lay still.

Baus brushed himself off, smoothed down his ruffled cloak. He plopped himself on his bed and contented himself to munch on Velnar's sweetcakes, while Valere gaped hollowly up at him like a beached gobbler. Baus's mind had a way of drifting deliciously back to Delizra. Nor could he help but wonder what the beauty was doing and how he could maximize his stay at Silsoor.

XI

A tap-tapping on the door rang with obnoxious persistence. Valere twisted in his down-covered sheets, offering a yawn of indifference. Seela, the moon-faced servant, would not be shunned though. Through the small hatch in the window, she mouthed an insistent order for gathering for lunch.

Baus winced. Lunch? The quiet morning seemed to have gone by in a flurry. Groggily, he began to throw on some clothes, at which point he remembered he owned fresh garments to don: lacy hose and trimmings laid out on the sideboard, which were not as appealing as first glance might suggest, reminding him all too much of the effeminate garb worn by Hysgode, whom he abhorred. The awareness favoured a certain urge for keeping his own serviceable brown breeches intact and applying the mauve doublet laid out beside its peer, which he found rather abstractly committed with a taste of *haute-moderne*.

With an almost frugal flourish Baus outfitted himself—he donned his gold trimmed cravat, which he snugged loosely about his neck, and several complimentary ceremonial medallions which he pinned on his chest. Valere, who had drifted back into torpor, was summoned decisively to attention by Baus's sharp rap on the brow. The seaman jerked himself erect, wiped at his cheeks and smoothed his fox-beard. He blinked back the glow that streamed in from the casements. In his experience the task seemed simple; why wear pompous finery when one could wear the same old rags?

Baus deemed it prudent to set their stories straight prior to engaging in any formal discourse in the parlour. Valere concurred. For brief moments the two conversed, agreeing that any mention of Heagram and their prison scandal would run invariably counterproductive to their common aims. They nodded confidently at this conclusion and allowed the chambermaid Seela to escort them to the common room where Tulesio sat imperturbably on a comfortable couch next to Delizra by the fire.

The maid curtsied, and exited with polite efficiency.

Intrigued by the jocular buoyancy of the strangers, Delizra engaged her guests in an exacting period of questioning. Valere and Baus brushed off the enquiries with easy urbanity. In daylight and with proper attire and coiffure, the damsel was even more of a beauty than Baus imagined. Her face was slender, unassuming, slightly cherubic; yet her pale gold eyes were as sensuous as any queen's. She was garbed in a loose-fitting dress, a rebellious noblewoman's outfit, all pale orange with saucy sleeves and silken tassels that bounced seductively around the midriff. Thoroughly enjoying the moment of its impact, she blinked artlessly. The slit was open at the neck, so poised to casually reveal a furrow of shapely cleavage, amongst less importantly, youthful, pale ivory skin. Her wavy brown hair shone in the firelight, and her glistening tongue darted out in little clips and suggestive starts as she conversed in tones pitched to evoke a subtlety of ardour and flirtatiousness, rather than brazen presumption. A pair of rangy legs reached up to support a trim, pleasing haunch.

How long had Baus been ensconced in prison? It seemed like forever. Neither was Valere exempt from the maid's allure, but he remained controlled of his passions, and to his credit, a source of Baus's surprise.

After warming themselves, Tulesio took them to the refectory. The foursome dined on a light brunch of mealcakes and hot tea. Baus explained to her that he and Valere were not the rakehellish swashbucklers she thought them to be—merely ordinary, honest wayfarers looking for simple postings on the wharves, possibly even a small sea assignment. "Only recently did my colleague Valere and I even make each other's acquaintance," emphasized Baus carefully.

"A pity," remarked Delizra.

"In Krintz," Tulesio counselled, "'dock-workers' are unknown, and I fear you must travel to Nosoheath or even Pirate's Point to attract those types of contracts."

Baus shook his head with regret. "I suppose we must." He put on a doleful face as if they were accustomed to dealing with fearsome vicissitudes on a daily basis. Delizra's voice became edged. "You are all seemingly doughty men, but—" here she paused and Baus detected a strain to her coquettishness. Loneliness?

"At Krintz," Tulesio continued pedantically, "doughty men as yourselves would be better off tanning hides or apprenticing to Jeoulf the Smith. A wealth of shoe-tapping and bellow-work exists this time of year."

Baus nodded happily. "These are worthy enterprises. We are indebted to your advice, Tulesio, and shall consider the option with respect."

Delizra shot Baus a sharp glance. "You say you are seafarers from Heagram?"

"Yes, I believe that was what I mentioned."

"So, why did you leave so abruptly? Neither of you rovers barely seem to own the clothes on your back, no less luggage or any other possessions."

"True, but why should we?" Baus responded dryly. "Both of us are due for larger fish to fry and hence must make ourselves available to more universal modifications."

Delizra twirled her locks with sceptical thought. "That sounds serious. Hysgode is right—you two do have about you vagabondish airs." She shifted her eyes narrowly at Valere. "Are your goals as comparably ephemeral as Baus's, Captain?"

Valere combed at his beard with placid calm. "My plans remain inchoate. Having for many years commanded my own vessel, I have a mind to return to seafaring—at least when I secure the funds for an appropriate sailing vessel."

"Very ambitious!" cried Delizra, clapping her hands. "How large was your last seacraft?"

Valere's eyes lifted up to the ceiling. "Oh—fairly large. Perhaps 40 feet—even 50. The *Illimmer* boasted a fifteen foot beam, a fat belly, a main sail like a gull's breast singing her heart out. Ah! She was due for re-hauling in Brislin and taken off the water three winters ago. Sheer age had caught up to her, broadsided her from behind . . ." He trailed off glumly. The disclosure was not far from the truth and the seaman allowed himself a sigh to make any stretches seem more plausible.

"Then it appears," continued Delizra, "that like Baus, you are destined for a life on the sea?"

Baus nodded thoughtfully. "This is exactly Captain Valere's plan. He has been meditating on it for years, haven't you, Valere?"

Valere wagged his head.

"Delizra, you are an astute person and I must commend you for your intuitive grasp of our essence! Rare indeed is the charming and perceptive quality I observe in the likes of your youth."

The comment failed to achieve its flattery and the Vulde's daughter slipped into a deeper mood of melancholy.

The mystery was at last dispelled when Delizra herself revealed how insipid her life had become at Silsoor. "I hate this gloomy place. I shall miss you both when you take your leave! You saved me from a molester; furthermore, we don't receive often visitors in Krintz. Surely you will stay a bit longer, before embarking on these frightful journeys?"

Valere flushed with boyish excitement. "I believe we would consider extending our visit, particularly if it is to be in your company!"

Baus shifted uncomfortably. Though dubious of the circumstance, it was not his place to argue.

The foursome sipped tea, before Seela took further orders and removed the dishes.

Breakfast drew to a close; Tulesio offered his guests fresh towels. Summoning Velnar, he took it upon himself to collect a basin of hot water so that Baus and Valere could bathe and scrub themselves down in the sun room with white lye and cox-combed brush.

It was early in the afternoon. The two dried themselves off; feeling much refreshed, they returned to the parlour. Tulesio was instructed by the Vulde to be their escort: an excursion to the bazaar in order to seek out a respectable haberdasher.

An appropriate establishment showed itself two doors down from the main plaza, where they arrived to spy many narrow side alleys, busy with folk and trades-people of all ages. In the yellowing light, people went about their business hawking wares and hauling goods. The twain squinted awkwardly into the bustling throng, finding it difficult to keep up with Tulesio's strides. They disliked the irony of last night's escapades; they thought to keep a low profile.

A stir of commotion was forming around the obelisk where the Dakkaw was secured. It was an area which Tulesio strictly avoided, for the villagers buzzed in and about the square like crass gawkers, past the place of imprisonment, carrying baskets of turnips, bread, fresh cream, potatoes, shallots. Others commanded carts pitched full of geese, goats and meal sacks. The villagers stared at the newcomers almost inordinately. Seeing that they were accompanied by Tulesio of the Vulde's House, they reduced their squints, for it meant that they were under the Vulde's care—which could only mean that there was something special about these visitors. Snatches of conversation came to Baus's ears—that the two were indeed the *heroes* who had helped capture the famous 'Dakkaw', the fabulous menace which had been harassing their village for years. Youngsters crowded close to ogle and bait the ogre who stood roped against Woybur's obelisk snarling and spitting. Instigators appeared in small knots, but the pack grew to more profound numbers, committing reckless deeds upon the prisoner.

Some few came to pat the visitors on the back and offer them congratulations—ruddy-faced men, quaintly deferential, and the commendations Baus and Valere received were not readily fluffed off. The uncomfortable knowledge of the conflicting motives championing yester-eve's foray were imprinted in full memory.

Tulesio led them the long way around the plaza's north-east corner. Baus watched as smokes of a smithy curled in seashell rings out of the low lean-to. The tin roof slanted high to a vaulting soot-blackened wall. Hammer rings signalled the shaping of wegmor shoes; whishing air from bellows and roaring flames from furnaces implied cooling of instruments and farmers' tools. A tall peaked building crowded itself toward a stockyard, denoting what Baus guessed a hostelry. Adjacent were carpenters' shops while a small schoolhouse with a belled roof graced the square. Across the plaza loomed evidences of a bakery, winery, butchery, two pawn shops, three pubs—namely, the *Laughing Minstrel*, *Fanfare's Bane* and *Haggleman's Retreat*. The plaza was fringed by a stone-towered, aging courthouse, after which stretched more modest residences up the hill and thin bungalows with oddly domed roofs.

The tailor was able to see them immediately: a portly man with round face and paunchy midsection. He studied them for a while with bristling brows before humming and measuring them with tape. He scratched his high domed forehead and motioned his assistant to fetch the best fabrics.

Valere was outfitted in a costume of baggy-black pantaloons, also a neat white bow tie with snazzy, wine-coloured velour shirt and loose, flared sleeves. Baus was fit in a more ordinary green poncho decked with fine auburn woollen overcoat, grey-green breeches and brown designer boots. Tulesio endowed the tailor five silver pieces, a stipend no doubt compliments of the Vulde. The chamberlain took their old rags and wrapped them in an old sack to be fed to Silsoor's fires.

Pleased with their dashing new looks, Baus and Valere expressed regret at the demise of their old clothes but some interest in visiting one of the pubs before returning. Tulesio obliged. He took them to *Haggleman's*, ironically, the same not far from the fountain. The interior was pot-darkened. Quiet and panelled with red resin-stained larch covering the limestone walls, the pub showed cozy seats set in a wide circle along a chest-high slab of aged beobar. Cressets lit the opposite wall, where a warm fire crackled and a pair of polished wegmor antlers hung high from the wall.

Three tradesmen sipped dark-coloured ale. They could only have been carpenters or woodworkers for all the sawdust on their jerkins. On a signal from Tulesio, the bartender poured them all bouts of ale and shots of crimson liquor. He was a trim, bearded man with black oily eyes. Over a tittle of rank larch-whiskey, Baus complimented Tulesio on his choice of beverage and slipped in a compliment about Delizra and her impressive comportment.

"Comportment is the least thing I would attribute to her," Tulesio grunted, almost upsetting his beer. He upended his drink in swift order and clapped the shot glass down with speed.

"Perhaps, I was just essaying a jocular politeness," suggested Baus.

"Relax, friend," growled Tulesio. "I shan't tattle to our good lord Hysgode of your true feelings for our lovely princess. Yes, she is a dazzler, Delizra is; I even think her name was a calculated slip on her parents' part—*Desire*. I confess that ever since I was a lad I have been under her spell. Can you imagine? A noblewoman! The girl has every right to have the best. Yet she has suffered the scrutiny of every swain from all over the village, from lord to letch, from pubescent to geriatric. Now she can barely venture out of her home without being ogled. For seventeen years I have served the Vulde, and truth be told, I fear for his House."

"Why?" Baus mused.

Tulesio chugged another healthy draught before grumbling a complaint. "From a young age I have known her, as I have said. She is no paramour for that pompous pretender, Hysgode. She is a queen—an angel. He is a coxcomb, a prig with coin, a conceited ass! He invaded our House and the Vulde's mind with his oily promises of high family ties and wealth."

"We felt as much," related Baus.

"Well, it is more a threat than you think," mumbled Tulesio dully. He turned, rankled by the mild condescension writ on Baus's face. "Don't stare at me like that! I am more a brother to her than suitor. We have always been fond of each other, Delizra and I, in familial ways."

Valere lifted a hand. "Where is the illustrious Vulde now?"

"Taken a contingent of the town watch to Old Krintz. Why do you want to know?"

"No particular reason," he declared. "It seems it is odd that he's gone off with guests so early while his daughter is in such an unnerved state."

Tulesio sighed. "If you want to know, he's gone to search out plunder at Bisiguth—where else would he have gone?"

Baus almost choked on his ale. "That is quite unorthodox." He exchanged apprehensive looks with Valere and darted eyes to the pub's door.

"Ha, you obviously know not our Vulde!" laughed Tulesio. "He is no mooncalf! By the time news of the Dakkaw spreads around, every jackleg prospector will be parked at Bisiguth's court staking claims to the ogre's wealth. You see, besides the few statues tottering alongside the south gate, we are bereft of objects of our heritage—the obelisk of course, being an exception; but even its history is murky, outside of a vague tale of a troop of Kantmaclian slaves hauling it up from Sloe centuries ago."

Baus and Valere seemed hardly able to hear the historical lore. They finished their drinks and were eager to leave. Once out of doors, Baus swung on Valere and whispered: "If Cedrek is discovered, he may pose us a minor problem."

"What do you propose?"

Baus grimaced. "We did not part on amicable terms. The curmudgeon seemed to grasp more about our situation than I would have liked. He may alert the Vulde of certain *facts* of our callousness."

Valere clicked his tongue in abnegation. "Cedrek is a dolt. Hidden far below the main hall, he shall likely be missed."

"Let us hope so, for both our sakes—and also not. We can't let the oaf starve. It is no secret that the ogre has destined himself for a head-chopping and not likely to reclaim any governance of Bisiguth in the near future. We could not have protected Cedrek from that."

Valere stroked his beard musingly, "True—and I doubt if in practicality, we can rely on little Rilben to nourish the ingrate."

"Either way, one of us will be pressed to inform the Vulde that the butcher's son is kept in the cellars."

Valere stirred. "How can we do this? Do not suck me into your schemes!"

Baus ignored Valere's outburst and made a practical gesture. "In itself, the dilemma is tricky. We have woven not unsubstantial deceits. If the Vulde finds out and asks, 'why Baus did you not mention our good citizen, Cedrek, penned in the Dakkaw's dungeon? Is this not cruel-hearted?'—neither of us will have an answer. An event of this nature will force us to beat an ignoble retreat before Cedrek's tongue gets waggling."

Valere conceded a sigh. "I am no murderer, Baus—but certainly a few untimely fibs could work in our favour."

Baus added shrewdly, "Or make us nobler heroes . . ."

* * *

That afternoon, daylight views of the impressive geography showed the eastern hills separating the village from the sea. Ledges of forest were sparsely tiered, ranging low. A similar file of rounded, brooding knolls ran farther afield, dull bluish in colour, shadowed from the overcast. The three toured the village's cobbled paths. Tulesio picked up on the uneasiness etched on their faces and put forth a blunt query.

Baus grudgingly disclosed a brief rendition of Cedrek's plight—the lout's intractable behaviour which had prompted them to abandon him at Bisiguth.

"I don't blame you," mused Tulesio, frowning. "Remarkable, though, chancing on Cedrek, who has been missing for a year. Nothing can be done, at least until the lord's return."

Baus sighed. He hated the prospect of waiting. When they returned to the village square, he breathed more easily, for the cat was out of the bag. Yet he was still not wholly satisfied by the way affairs were proceeding. What other scheme could be put in motion to ensure an advantage?

Looking this way and that, a pang of annoyance seized him. It was a delicate situation. Surely there was a way to flee Krintz without alerting suspicion?

A diversion? A sudden flight? A promise to return to Silsoor at a later time?

No.

Neither he nor Valere could possibly range far before the Vulde unleashed a posse on their tail. There was the niggling matter of Lolispar too, which he was reluctant to discard. The gladius was an item which must be retrieved at all costs.

The three arrived back at Woybur's obelisk and Baus noted the Dakkaw suffering more unwanted attention. From a side view, the ogre's body was rubbed raw, his huge hands writhed at the ropes that bound him. His defiance sprang loudly in the air amidst the jeers. Tumult drowned the plaza. Despite the Dakkaw's unconventional size, the obelisk rose another twenty feet higher, with its age-black tip tapering to a pike, its exterior, a rich composite of grey, brown, and old green stone, glistening like some ancient talisman. Baus marvelled at the monolith. It was cleft with gashes and chipped in places as if it had suffered many ravages and attacks over the years.

The three edged around the obelisk's sunny side, pushing through the mob. A knot of common labourers was erecting a crude scaffolding by the fountain—a sweating and pinch-faced crew, taking pains not to tread too closely to the Dakkaw's flexing, rippling limbs. Other workers arrived, hefting rope and with arms full of branches and faggots for the burning to come. Obviously the Dakkaw was to be burnt or hanged, if not both.

Tulesio motioned brusquely to the rude gathering. "These roustabouts congregate because they know that it shall all be over at this time tomorrow. The ogre shall be dispatched, by as painful means as possible. The Krintz folk have suffered and planned this day for years. There is to be an early celebration alongside the coming of the fall feast. The Dakkaw's capture indicates an auspicious omen for our town."

Valere tipped his head in sober reflection; Baus wiped his mouth with dry irony. As the two walked within sight of the chained monster, the Dakkaw loosed a belligerent roar that had everyone's hair standing on end. The ogre rocked and heaved against his bonds, hating the sight of them. The scaffold workers tensed; they were ready for assault, but being accustomed to the gut-wrenching outbursts, they grabbed up hammers, saws and mauls in case the monster managed to escape. The thrice-coiled bonds held and the Dakkaw cried out once more: "So, traitors! You would arrive to spy out your handiwork? Well, look hard!" He grazed Baus a look of utter malice. "Does it please you to peer at me so? Study these dolts carefully!" he called to the crowd. "They pretend to be my friends, only to prove themselves perfidious turncoats. And you—fools!" He roared at the crowd. "You disassemble sacks of shallots, little staves bearing ineffectual fruit from sills and eaves. Ha! You think that by noon on the morrow you shall be rid of your fiend. Bah! What hope! If the inner evil of a man can be burnt or cut, then why all the fuss? Your spiritless hides shall see me rise again! You think me demented? Let the hours advance! We shall see!"

The Dakkaw blubbered on, spittle dribbling from his lips. With such vivid knowingness, he delivered his speech and Baus shivered. The Dakkaw was adamant, like an unhinged zealot, eyes bulging and neck distended, with veins pumping blood like rivers that looked as if they would burst.

Baus struggled to find sense in the predicament. The Dakkaw had been whipped beyond concept—the top of his crown was lacerated and his face was ruddy and blood-flecked; his pale tuft of sideburns could not even hide the merest wound. His brown tunic was filthy, torn with scabs running down his forearms. When the monster spoke, it was through mashed lips, swollen and red. His teeth were edged, peeled back like a shark's and seemingly almost sharpened like a vampire's. Such incisors were ready to champ on the flesh of insolent tormentors who happened to venture too close.

Baus felt an acute disgust. A fleeting sensation, sharply poignant. He wondered what complex stream of events had led the Dakkaw to this day of undoing.

His eyes blurred; he reminded himself of the Dakkaw's deeds.

Stealing a glance over his shoulder, he saw the giant quivering in fury. Two ragged teens had started pelting his hide with sour apples while others chucked a bucketful of turnip skins at his shins.

Baus hurriedly departed. Justice was remorseless, a stern mistress. Ah, well, such is life. Valere and Tulesio ran to catch up with him, flinching and muttering.

XII

It was late in the afternoon when the Vulde returned to Silsoor. Bisiguth seemed to have brought them good and bad results, judging from the modularity of the lord's movements, and his flushed features. Not surprisingly, the company escorted Cedrek into the manor's parlour. Several solemn members of the town watch carried six bins of jewels with an austere grace, also four antique fetishes and other items: bibelots, necklaces, sceptres, statuettes, clocks, spheres, rings, bells, various curios crafted of jade and onyx.

A squat, husky shape of familiar proportion was also present. The guards clutched the grey-faced, struggling creature with rancour. Its armour had been stripped; the loose ceremonial vest that hid the grey nakedness was soiled and bloodied.

Tulesio greeted his Lord with enthusiasm: "Good evening, Lord! I see that Bisiguth has favoured the House of Vulde with decent prizes."

"No outward contingencies at least; though this weird, wood-hybrid simian we found skulking about the manor's halls has me somewhat concerned. It was trying to brain Fisteo with some obnoxious oil brush—a ghoul, of some glandular dysfunction, I presume."

"Actually a ghoul-*ape*, sir. I recognize the creature as one of the extraordinary species from the lands west of the great, black Tarnshorn lake mountains."

The Vulde shuddered. "Whatever the case, the thing disturbs me."

"No less, I."

Rilben voiced a vigorous protest to the calumny. "You speak of things you do not know! I was merely protecting the property of my master, the Dakkaw."

"Silence, glib pup!" snarled one of the Vulde's chiefs. "Your master is no more—or soon shall be."

"Peace!" ordered the Vulde. I'll not have quips or jibes in my home."

Rilben was taken away, hauled to some unknown place. Baus stood erect with hopeful authority. "A clever deed, watchmen. The sight of this miserable creature is a burden to us all." However, the sight of Rilben's ragged condition had him wondering if his own fate would soon mimic it.

Meanwhile the Vulde's eyes flicked narrowly from the glittering riches to the burglars, Baus and Valere.

Baus deigned to scrutinize Cedrek with uncomfortable foreboding. The citizen's skin was pasty and pudding-ish, like the grizzled hide of a dead fish, not to mention coated with red welts. Baus squared himself in the periphery in an attempt to look as guileless as possible, but seemed to fail in the falling light.

"Well, what have we here?" called Cedrek jocularly, moving from toe to toe like an agitated stork.

Baus's voice rang fulsomely in the parlour's ambience. "So nice of you to drop in, Cedrek, after all this time. More pleasurably, I see, on your feet."

"Grand, isn't it?" chuckled Cedrek. "As I was outlining to the Vulde, who is a friend of my father's, it was under the most pressing emotional strain that I recently parted your company and I seem to recall a certain 'sucker fish' attached to my left cheek."

Baus expressed shock at the disclosure. "I was under the impression that the Dakkaw would dunk you in his vat for jokes. What of it? Were you that used to placating the ogre's whims with your usual obsequiousness to pretend an air of camaraderie?"

"From a superficial standpoint you might think so," admitted Cedrek, "but that was yesterday and today is today. Was it not your red-bearded bully here who tipped the lever to dunk me further in the Dakkaw's barrel?"

Baus frowned. "I know nothing of this. Nor my colleague. As memory recalls, it was Valere and I who tried to unbind your chains but you shouted at us so contumaciously that we were convinced that you were either mad, or you wished to be left alone with the Dakkaw, passing your time with his jocular airs and jests."

"A vicious lie!" Cedrek shouted. "I find this all humiliating! I was lucid even during my direst trials of torment!"

The Vulde, peering crosswise at Cedrek, did not miss the sound of his mewling and abusive whining and Baus began to detect a certain strain digging at the back of the Vulde's mind.

Baus continued with ease. "The Captain and I were beside ourselves with misgiving when we saw your volatile condition. We knew not what to think! For certain there was no hope that the Dakkaw would release you, though we pleaded with him to alter his plans. We had no choice but to abandon you! Hope for a rescue at a later time. If not for the Vulde's absence this morning, we would have immediately informed him of the news, but with the imbroglio and all, we were time-bound and distraught to learn that he had already departed on business to Bisiguth."

Cedrek's jaw dropped with fury.

The Vulde demanded, "Is this true, Cedrek?"

Cedrek slobbered out a strangled curse. "Absolutely not!"

Tulesio interrupted poignantly, "This man is obviously deranged, Vulde. I believe Baus's story to be true. He informed me earlier regarding Cedrek's captivity at Bisiguth; withal, how he and the seaman were ashamed to have not alluded to it earlier."

"Is this true?"

"Yes."

Sensing his advantage being taken away, Cedrek hopped like a mad bird and made a desperate claw for Baus's eyes. Members of the watch sought to avert the assault and dragged Cedrek back before the fire. Baus wiped at his poncho; dourly he extended his disappointment of how he had narrowly avoided an injury.

The Vulde clapped his hands in irritation. "Order! I'll not have oafish brawling in my manor!"

Studying Cedrek with new concern, the lord stood rooted, jaw clenched. An aspect of unsympathetic brooding split his face. Cedrek stamped and glared in the arms of the watchmen. Whatever brewed in the lout's mind was obviously deranged—at having been conned out of his simple vengeance. No less, the Vulde, for having believed Cedrek's lies, was looking like a fool. "We are all tired and confused here," muttered the Vulde. "Perhaps you most of all," he cried, glaring at Cedrek. "Certain facts remain obfuscated. In truth, there remains an abundance of issues to be clarified. But for the nonce, let us curb this insipid aggression and dine! I am famished; furthermore, I vow that we partake of our repast before we conduct any more disputations on these matters."

Baus exemplified approval of the plan. Shuffling and grumbling, the watch released Cedrek and the matter was dropped. By the Vulde's sole expression, Baus knew that his dissembling had gained him some credence in his eyes and that he suspected that Cedrek had gone almost certainly mad.

* * *

A short while later, Seela announced the coming of dinner. All repaired to the parlour. They found the table set—with yellow cloth, silver plates, jewelled cutlery and costly condiments. The chandelier was lit; a score of candles winked in the elegant surroundings, indicative of fine ivory, exquisite hangings and plush furnishings. There were spaces for eleven persons. Baus, Valere, Tulesio, Cedrek, Delizra and the Vulde were present; as for Cedrek's invitation, Baus thought it odd that the son of a lowly butcher would be cast amongst the likes of such a prestigious gathering. But then again, his father was the lord's friend. Obviously the Vulde was still dubious about the circumstances surrounding his imprisonment and the part his new guests played. He wished to observe their interactions, hoping to probe the mystery, searching for new subtle clues of guilt. Baus congratulated himself on his keen insight. Carefully, he thought to efface the singular suspicions from the Vulde's mind. It was nothing that his adroitness could not manifest.

Late arrivals were slow in coming: Hysgode, Griselda, Cedrek's parents and Sir Godol, a senior councillor of Krintz. The latter was short, mouse-haired, of upper years and a member of 'old guard' mentality. The Vulde's wife, 'Lady Boquk', was absent, delayed again on her healing sabbatical at Fickswith manor, though she was destined to return on the morrow.

Seela served her guests: red wine and hors d'oeuvres. Flambéed oyster, boiled leek and corkroot were forthcoming, tastefully grilled over slow fires and coals. Pleasantries were exchanged, introductions were afforded; however, laughs were short and tritely decorous. Velnar cleared the dishes; Seela distributed the viands: a reed basket of roasted bread, pork fillets, a rare shallot compote, potato gumbo, mutton goulash, a brace of roasted hares, all sizzling over long, gold-enamelled spits.

Baus savoured the victuals with relish, noting that Hysgode's appetite was not nearly as fulsome as his fine attire might suggest for such a privileged lord. He was decked in his finest hosiery—a prince's white, with hair duck-winged in a splash of fragrant oils and essences for good measure. For the time being Cedrek's frame sat draped in a dour baggy costume. He was hunched, pock-faced and cynical. Griselda wore a thin yellow blouse with woollen ruffs, absurdly tight at the haunch, which demonstrated her less than appealing boxy hips in meaner proportion than what ordinary light would offer. Delizra was attired in a pale green dress with rolled cuffs, remarkably fitted to show a maximum of beauty with a minimum of ostentation—a touch which Baus relished considerably. Sir Godol was garbed in a white bow tie, brown suit and ankle shoes; the Vulde was otherwise pleasant enough, attired in a respectably restrained but otherwise airy blue suit woven with red velour on thighs and forearms, which seemed to compete in austerity with his peremptory character.

The Vulde paused to assess Baus's and Valere's vestments and congratulated them on their choice of colours, as he did too the haberdasher's expertise in fitting them.

"Thanks to our tailor, Aeke, one of Krintz's finest," Tulesio announced, "our guests have been apparelled in the finest elegance and luxury."

The Vulde appeared happy with the treatment. "Let us enjoy this evening with a fine air of celebration. The Dakkaw is no more; Krintz is now free from the tyranny of his random attacks. I am pleased to announce that the acquisition of immoderate booty from Bisiguth is underway. Godol, can you imagine! Three chests of silver, two gold, and countless antiques and bibelots for the taking! By great king Henriok—it shall take men days to transfer the bulk of this stuff to Silsoor."

Godol raised his goblet in tribute.

Baus extended a sly suggestion: "Perhaps a token of the new wealth might find its way to me and Valere, Vulde. I don't imply this solely for reasons of altruism."

"Altruism? Where does the term enter the picture?"

"Nowhere. For purposes of advances to our continued education, I ask for your pledge for small services rendered. Recall, if not for our aid in the capture, the Dakkaw would be at large, plaguing your village with mischief."

The Vulde became instantly stony. "The observation is presumptuous. Furthermore, it is inexact. How can you suggest the proposal? The wealth is part of my grandfather's estate. To think of disbursing the legacy in so willy-nilly a fashion is to invite scandal and chaos of the highest order!"

Griselda tendered a snort. "Aye! Father is a fastidious sort. One who would rather see his lands and estate ruled by an outsider than share a portion of his booty—for that matter even secure a husband for me!" She cast a scornful look at Hysgode and Delizra, tinged with envy. "It is deplorable that Delizra, three years my junior, is to marry before I. It is too abominable to consider!"

"There, child," consoled Tulesio. "I'm sure your father is looking out for your best interests."

"Do not patronize me, you ingratiating whelp. You call me a child, well, think on it! I am a woman! What my father knows best is how to deal politics and placate weasels like old Godol here—a man who knows the fondling of young girls better than his own office."

Godol coughed. "Well, at least I do not include you amongst such lucky maidens."

Griselda hissed between her teeth.

The Vulde cracked his fist on the table. "Enough of this diatribe. Mind your manners, Griselda! We are nobles, not boors, and we reside at Silsoor demonstrating politic behaviour while entertaining guests, not flinging insults."

"Ha, so proper as usual!" Griselda whined impudently.

Delizra stifled an outcry; she perhaps thought better to impart peace than let matters escalate: "To be sure, Griselda—not so novel is it to be engaged. It has its insipid moments, for sure—in fact, many." She gave a curt glance to Hysgode as if to emphasize it.

Griselda glowered and turned Hysgode an unflattering scrutiny. Baus glimpsed the interplay with amusement: Griselda's churning upon the supercilious curl of the nobleman's lip, Hysgode's priggish gaze as he focused it on the swinish Griselda, Delizra's irritation at Hysgode's fawning and preening mannerisms. "Perhaps you are right in what you say, sister," Griselda croaked. "But, I shall not be domineered, or placated!"

There was a bitter silence; the hard words settled and the diners set upon their victual, albeit with a subdued zeal. Godol discharged a rather laconic inquiry to the Vulde regarding the Dakkaw, "Have we reached a final verdict on this dreadful murderer?"

The Vulde peered thinly up from his mutton. "Yes—the ogre is to be hanged while set afire; is this not fitting?"

"Very much, yet I condone a perhaps slower dealing of death."

Baus's brows lofted. "The penalty seems abruptly harsh. Wouldn't simple lifelong incarceration be punishment enough for this ogre's crimes?"

The Vulde stared at him as if he were a lunatic. "The creature has mauled, harried Krintzers and murdered its residents. What should we do? Have him over for dinner? Make a bed for him?"

"Alas, Vulde!" assured Baus politely. "I meant no disrespect. Only to plead my compassion for the lowlifes of the world like the Dakkaw." With deft rhetoric, Baus quickly redirected the conversation to other things. "Do many of these monsters haunt these localities?"

"None, thanks to providence. Why ask such a question?"

Cedrek, who sat on Baus's right, forwarded a sneer: "It seems that Baus's gormless humour lends itself to the odd knuckle-headed query."

Baus's eyes shafted indignation, but he calmly held his tongue.

The Vulde resumed his argument, now in more oblique tones. "It is for the protection of Krintz that we eradicate this menace once and for all, thus repairing a universal problem!"

Delizra countered her father's dogmatism, "Is it our duty to kill? Do we really have the authority to snuff out a life?"

Another uncomfortable silence ensued and Baus grinned. It seemed that confrontations were ubiquitous at Silsoor's table and Delizra was in no way any spring chicken at polemics.

A flurry of trenchant words flew across the table; Baus and Valere hurriedly nodded, listening politely, grunting from time to time with grave emphasis. On the Dakkaw's coming punishment it seemed that opinion was varied. Cedrek and his parents took the Vulde and Godol's side; Delizra, Griselda and Valere favoured Baus's. It gave Baus a noticeable pleasure to witness the support that he had and he smiled, giving himself time to casually draw a sizeable pinch of hot pepper and apply the mixture to Cedrek's mutton. Perhaps only Delizra noticed.

"I think what Baus and others fail to understand," interrupted Godol pompously, "is that the degree of depravity to which the Dakkaw is capable, is unrivalled, and is, by definition, punishable by death." He cast Baus a reprehensible look; he continued to blurt out in a clarion voice: "Several of our villagers have gone missing and are presumed dead because of the Dakkaw's depraved deeds, including Feistes the poet, Mearl the Spice-man, Salsha the Seamstress. The latter maid disappeared quite recently last spring. We all know of the Dakkaw's proclivities; his mistreatment of 'guests' is intolerable—" He paused, frowning. "Cedrek? Whatever is the problem?"

The butcher's son could utter no words. His face had swollen and grown blotched and ruddy with fire; his tongue flickered out like a snake's.

Baus rose to tap him several times on the back—to no avail. Cedrek gasped, flailing arms, and Baus deigned to display alarm.

Hysgode, who sat to Cedrek's right, offered him a decanter of wine, but the oaf swept it away. Glasses and tableware flew to the floor like worthless crystal. The Vulde ran fetching Velnar for smelling salts; others leapt from their seats. They were so busy that Baus took occasion to switch bowls with Cedrek's to allay any possible backlash, which again, Delizra only seemed to notice. With a shake of her head, she uttered a strangled chuckle. Baus attributed this to a person appreciating a good prank now and then. Little love did she have for Cedrek, who had been ogling her ever since he had stepped foot in Silsoor.

Cedrek was finally back to his seat shaken and subdued. After several glasses of water, he glowered at Baus. "You!" he cursed. "How dare you tamper with my goulash?"

Baus rejected the imputation. "The allegation approaches a pretence of absurd quality. Withal, it is in poor taste." To disprove the fantasy, Baus snatched up Cedrek's bowl and spooned a hefty portion into his mouth. Hysgode, for fun, tasted a spoonful too and shrugged as if nothing were untoward. The Vulde seemed more critically convinced of Cedrek's paranoia.

Cedrek, rising indignantly from his seat, beseeched the Vulde for justice, but was ordered to take his chair and curb his tongue. "You are a boor, Cedrek, and hereupon I bid you to control your outbursts!"

Cedrek's father shook his head. Godol looked on complacently at the shenanigans. "This is an unnecessary ruckus given the favourable turn of the Dakkaw's capture. As I was mentioning, the sight of Cedrek is enough to give us all insights. Even Cedrek's latter behaviour, I attribute to delusion, no more. But I drift; Baus and Valere, surely your own encounter at Bisiguth is not to be taken as lightly as Cedrek's?"

"An execrable experience," observed Valere, shaking his head distastefully.

"All of it is so discomposing!" said Baus.

Delizra shivered. "This Dakkaw—a murderer, and a monster—and chained hardly three stones' throws from our own dinner table, frightens me. He causes us grief in our own home! —It makes my skin crawl!"

Hysgode added his own view: "All true, but we must consider patterns down intellectual lines, distancing ourselves from profligate emotion and schmaltz and staying true to the pure and respectable logic of facts. We are at dinner, not a conference of war; withal, ladies are present, becoming overwrought with gloomy recollections." He cast Delizra a patronizing wink. "Never fear, pumpkin! We shall be together shortly. I know you are as eager as I to consummate our alliance, living together up the hill at Nausvere amongst the purple felfoons and the windle-larch. The wind blows freely as horns and will tousle our shiny locks with favour!"

Delizra rolled her eyes and clapped down her fork with contempt. "It is cold up there in Nausvere, Hysgode, and I am likely to fall sick. I quite like it here at Silsoor, and in fact, I think I shall stay. Your manse is distant. Who shall take care of mother? Her health is ailing, and if not for Tulesio's herbs which she imbibes twice a day, she may have already died!"

"Hush, my moffet!" soothed Hysgode, "we shall hire servants to take care of good Lady Boquk."

Griselda's voice rang with sarcasm. "And who will take care of you, Hysgode? Olefe, the magic elf? As it stands, an entire battery of servants can hardly keep up with your incessant demands, let alone the insistent wheedlings of mother."

Hysgode bared his teeth. "Indeed! But not half as many beauticians as it takes to minister to your own repulsiveness, which as your father hints, is 'insuperable'!"

Griselda opened her mouth, but only could utter febrile croaks. The Vulde seemed to have the last say in the matter and gave a brisk reprimand to Hysgode: "You are out of line, sir! I'll not have my daughter slandered in front of guests, even in light of her deficiencies."

Griselda muttered outrage. Hysgode held out a placating palm, "You misinterpret my remarks, Vulde. I was speaking merely—"

"Whatever—I shan't tolerate it!"

Stiff silence again pervaded the table, but it seemed easily managed by Vulde and Godol's businessy chatter. The conversation eventually resumed to topics of lighter nature, including Baus and Valere.

The Vulde inquired mannerly, "Are you not going to taste more of our goulash, Baus? I notice half a bowl which will go to waste."

"Your eye is keen, Vulde—but—" he grimaced down at Cedrek's erstwhile bowl "—I have imbibed too much wine and it hardly begets me a proper appetite—no offence to your cooks."

"None taken. But perhaps you shall indulge in some dessert? Seela has prepared some decadent little puffy-cream tortes and morfosia balls in blue-goose syrup."

"Titillating! You are so kind, Vulde. And this profusion of delectations makes my head swim!"

"Then," cried the Vulde, clapping his hands, "offer me a gift! Tell us more of your exploits, of which we know little."

Baus nodded graciously. "I shall." Forcing himself to assume an air of valedictorian skill, he reflected with care: to stray into matters too fanciful invited repercussions. His current successful pretence had emboldened him to advance upon a more exalted narrative than necessary. Dabbing daintily at his chin, he cast Delizra a courteous glance and sensed the spark of attraction, and challenge there; it impelled him to a flash of quixotry. He began to recite a perplexing mythology of his background, involving a tale of intrigue, adventure and altruism. Poetry and snippets were injected into the narrative, reminiscent of Weavil's finest, which added to the overall effect, as did the settings. The names and details dropped from anecdotes he had heard from Trimestrius and Ulisa did not hurt and succeeded in casting a better enigma of himself.

Valere listened with half-masked incredulity while Cedrek and Hysgode listened on with cold apathy. The Vulde, hearing enough, banged a mallet on a tine, signalling the time for games.

Delizra jumped to her feet. She smoothed her hands on her dress and prompted Baus to believe something was coming more enjoyable than mealtime pleasantries. Griselda, too, evinced some grunting interest.

They all repaired to the common room. The guests waited for the program to be announced as they embraced the fire's warmth. On the Vulde's signal, Tulesio explained the game of 'Sloops' to the Heagramers. It turned out that it was a match of skill and finesse involving teams alternately pushing coloured discs along the floor with ceremonial poles. "Discs are to land in 'zones' only," instructed Tulesio. "Points are allotted for discs landing in deeper zones—fifteen for a length thrust, ten for a mid, five for a shallow. Negative points are rewarded for throws that land outside the winning octagon."

Delizra positively insisted that she partner with Baus, to which the Vulde approved. Hysgode was livid. Valere teamed with Tulesio; Lord Vulde was paired with the butcher Halfhan. Griselda was paired with Halfhan's wife and Hysgode with Cedrek. Many rounds were played, of which victories were rendered in respectable count by the Vulde—Delizra and Baus taking the most. Hysgode was hampered by Cedrek's maladroitness and showed a keen frustration at being paired with the lout. He continued to suffer more embarrassing losses, much to Delizra's delight.

As the night flew on, the flask of larch whiskey dropped several inches. Laughter grew in force; tongues began to loosen in proportion to quantities imbibed. Even Cedrek, as vapid and cynical as he was, seemed lighter of spirit. All enjoyed the atmosphere—with the exception of Hysgode, who cast ever more loathing glances at Delizra and Baus, in whom his fiancée seemed to be taking an ever-popular interest.

On one particular pass, Delizra went so far as to sweep her breasts warmly across Baus's back, causing the hairs on the back of his neck to flutter. The touch of soft contours against his body was revivifying, if not arousing. To flirt with him was a way of making Hysgode jealous, he knew, but caution and appropriate reservation was a better foreplay than garish advances. Heedful of her every move, Hysgode became ever more inept at his own game. He was reprimanded twice for improper conduct. "Hysgode!" complained the Vulde, "your sportsmanship has achieved an abysmal low! Not only are your exceptions uncalled for but your drunken sulkiness stands you in poor stead. I shall not stand for repeated vulgarities or proprietorial rages in my domicile!"

Whether it was for pure fun or to make Hysgode dizzyingly spiteful, Baus fuelled the occasion, causing the hours to pass by in easy procession.

Seela served another round of dessert, an unctuous mash of shallot, goat cream and woffle-berries drowned in baywolf syrup. A new game was proposed: 'Spooks', a diversion entirely unique and more risqué than 'Sloops'. Straws were drawn, the loser blindfolded. The others were gathered round a circle and bidden to remain quiet. If the blindfold-ee could reach out, grab any one individual and name him or her on the first guess, then he or she would exchange places with the chosen and become the 'guesser'. The rules of the game were simple: the people around the ring were permitted to move at will; when each person had been named, the game was over.

Lord Vulde and Godol sat out this round, relaxed by the spirits; they busied themselves around the fire playing Sermaene, a game of ancient character, consisting of a board of a hundred pieces, inspiring each player to move his warriors alternately on a rectangular board, hoping to defeat the other's army. Cedrek's parents, not taken particularly with 'Spooks', watched the board game with glassy awe.

Valere was up first, immediately scouting out Baus. Baus confused Hysgode for Cedrek and deliberately was forced to guess another quarry, at which instant he spotted Delizra by means of her lavender perfume and husky giggling. Delizra keyed into Baus's flirting and purposely confused her fiancée with Griselda, an error which Hysgode deplored.

"Oh, you are such a prig, Hysgode—lighten up!" she cried.

Hysgode did not dignify the response; he ground his teeth into his gums.

At this juncture Griselda was up and very lustily groped Cedrek, whom she mistook for Baus. Cedrek, nonplussed, issued a venomous retort, bordering on affront. The slight nearly landed him into a fistfight with Griselda and in short he was up again, rather obtusely essaying a similar trick upon Delizra. When the Vulde's daughter dashed lightly out of his scab-pocked reach, Cedrek found himself gripped by Valere. Cedrek, clouded by spirits and the intensity of his lust, was soon convinced that Valere was Delizra, and his prurient reaches knew no bounds, to which effect Cedrek remained sprawled on the planks with an aching back and was forced to sit out the next rounds suffering pangs and contusions.

Hysgode was the 'Spook' next. Earlier reprimands had not discouraged his attempts to trip Baus while he was blindfolded. Delivered for maximum vengeance on his rival, Hysgode's lunge at Baus was miscalculated and he plunged headlong into the fire, sending the Vulde's and Sir Godol's game clattering to the floor. The elders were incensed. Hysgode singed his own eyebrows and pale forelocks. The result was a shambles, at which point the game was called off for reasons of fire hazard.

The evening drew to an end. The liquor was spent; the coals had burned down to dull embers. Lord Vulde, gentled by drink, employed Tulesio to return Baus his gladius, doubtlessly convinced of his genuineness.

The sisters took their leave; Cedrek and his parents were ushered to the guest quarters; Hysgode had already retired to nurse his scorched brow while the Vulde was quick to follow to bed. Baus and Valere repaired to their chambers alongside Cedrek's parents, in cheerful spirits.

XIII

In the quiet hours after midnight all were fast asleep—except Baus who awoke beaded in a hot sweat. He slipped out of his night covers and wrapped his limbs leanly about his chest. He sensed an unusual thumping of his heart. What coaxed such fervent drumfire from his regular self-possession?

Moving carefully across the floor, he remained heedful not to awaken Valere, who snored like a hound two arms' lengths away. Unlatching the door, he slipped out into the hallway, surprising himself at the daring of his indiscretion. What propelled such a foolish mission? Gratification? Puerile desire? Either way, fate was aiming a bloody arrow at a clear target.

Baus looked left and right. Not a soul. The incidence was not irregular at three in the morning. A single cresset only glowered in the hallway.

The fire's rich embers burned below, casting a navigable glow.

He tiptoed down the oaken stairs and felt his feet padding like cats' paws. He advanced through the parlour. Here in the hall of the two sisters, he contemplated an endeavour very risky when he caught a flash of movement. Atop the stairs crouched a figure—one garbed in an outlandish grey cloak and baggy breeches—which ducked awkwardly back into the shadows.

Cedrek! Baus's mind worked with increased speed. His enemy knew his whereabouts— the same who suffered a libidinous addiction to Delizra and who could merely bawl out his name and cry 'voyeur' or 'thief' or some such and have him put in irons.

Baus softly cursed. He was about to turn back and feign passage back to the pantry when a shrewder idea gripped him. Perhaps it was not so farfetched to include Cedrek in his scheme—better than claiming midnight hunger as a weak pretence.

Pretending not to have noticed Cedrek's presence, Baus sidled over to Griselda's door and made a clumsy show of trying to will himself to open the door. At last he could not go through with the deed, and knocked softly once, twice, and called out Delizra's name. He put an ear to the wood. Hearing a muted murmur, he withdrew while Cedrek slunk furtively down the steps with squirming curiosity. Baus heard a flutter of sheets. He riveted his eyes to the portal while Cedrek watched him with odious interest. Baus wrenched Griselda's door handle just as Cedrek wilfully advanced, cocking his head. The butcher's son crouched low, peered at Baus now from the edge of the common room. Baus, dramatizing caution, closed the door and ducked back, slipping down the hall toward the parlour, pretending to have lost interest in the affair.

Cedrek quivered with delight; noticeable glee showed on his sucker-marked face, which convinced Baus to disappear up the stairs.

Cedrek, now evidently pleased with his situation, advanced several steps and planted himself at Griselda's door. He quickly seized the knob and pushed the door ajar. Between the rungs of the balustrade, Baus saw a pair of swift arms reach out and pull Cedrek inside. The door clicked shut.

Baus tilted brows in interest.

Seconds passed. Twenty. He did not dare move. A minute later Cedrek still had not appeared. A wide grin split Baus's face. Griselda, living up to her reputation, likely would exhort Cedrek to various 'interesting activities'.

Baus congratulated himself. A most profitable outcome had transpired as a result of applied spontaneity!

With confidence Baus slipped down the hall. He advanced to Delizra's door, and knocked softly. He heard a stir of motion within. He deigned to enter. A tiny lamp flickered to life. In a trice he was over to her bedside.

The Vulde's daughter stirred, stretched arms languorously above her head, arching her back over her pillow with suggestive impact. "Baus!" she murmured languorously. "I thought you would never come! In fact, when I heard that tap-tapping on the door, I was given to despair, believing a robber had come to invade my home."

"A horrid thought, my dove!" Her inviting ease was a pleasant incongruence, perhaps too sublime to believe. Perhaps too many sips of brandy had made the noblewoman lose all pretence of inhibition. It was not worth the effort of analyzing. "Lady Delizra, it would be clearly impossible for me to avoid your illustrious pleasures!"

"I sense a small pandering in your words! Are you tipsy or just impaired? Let me guess. You are a confidence-man who has reached the limit of his narrative. What would my future husband think if he were to learn of your impulses, poised at my bedside here like a gypsy with a head full of ideas?"

Baus feigned injury at the imputation. "Would I be that crass?" He looked at the luxurious spread of Delizra's voluptuous figure. He wondered if luck were yet teasing him another time with an unobtainable trophy.

The misgivings were short-lived. He kissed her arm, her fingers, her cheek. His wandering eyes, hot with desire, ran over her ravishing body barely hid under the diaphanous satin nightwear.

Delizra cast him a coy look and pulled back her arm. "What of my fiancée? Surely you know we are to be married in a few weeks under the mistletoe at Banwar's estate?"

"Eh?" inquired Baus carelessly. "What's so troubling? I shall marry some day too—as impossible as that may sound." He surprised himself at this uttered notion.

"In twelve days it shall be I who is married!" she moaned. "Ugh! Now I feel a decided guilt that you are here—at my bedside, wooing me with your words, but I feel an incessant drumming in my bosom. It is all very queer!"

"Not really, my jade," Baus assured. "It is simply the ardent drum of true affection which has its way of compelling a person to recognize certain unalterable urges."

"And Hysgode? Would he ponder this phenomenon so philosophically?"

"Perhaps. What difference does it make? What distinction marks twelve days to marry— as twelve weeks—or twelve months?"

Delizra curled her arm about Baus's waist, prompting Baus to lie gingerly on the bed beside her, while he stroked her neck and kissed her lips with gentle passion.

Delizra laughed, a thrill in her voice. Baus had wasted no time in arranging himself in a more convenient position, the quickness which seemed to amuse her, yet Lady Delizra was already half naked, a fact which didn't seem to bother Baus. With a shrug and a bow, he started to peel off the rest of her garments as well as his own. The cloak and trousers seemed very cumbersome right now.

Delizra cried out in shock: "What haste! Wait—what is that noise?"

"I heard nothing."

"Silly! It strikes again. A kind of dull moaning, as if it is coming from across the hall."

Baus's expression took on a bland cast. "It could be any number of things."

Delizra frowned. "Like what? It sounds like a man's voice now—feverish and gruff, as if forced. There is a shrill cry!—Griselda's, I daresay!"

"Griselda is most notably having a bad dream."

"She suffers nightmares, but not with men's voices in them." Her voice was curdled with concern.

Baus proffered a cool glance. "I must confess that I cognized Cedrek sneaking earlier into her room."

"Cedrek?" Delizra jerked up in alarm. "What business would that lout have skulking there—" She gave a sudden cry. "Well, I never would have guessed! The two of them— Griselda! and Cedrek? It is better to have the butcher's son than none, I suppose. Bully for Griselda!—she has found a mate." She secretly confided to him: "As plain as she is, Griselda hasn't had luck with a man for some time now, hardly any in her life; she is terribly jealous of me, every moment of the day, in fact."

"I can't begin to guess why."

Delizra twisted his wrist playfully.

In order to arrest further chatter, Baus applied an enduring kiss; Delizra's warm thighs loosened. The gesture was propitious. Soon they were entwined in each other's arms in the throes of a very deep and interesting locomotion, when a sudden rap came at the door.

Delizra froze in loose-hipped pose. No lock was on the door...they were left unguarded... the knob began to slowly turn. Delizra shut her eyes as if painfully bracing herself for a scandal to bite.

A figure strode in.

Baus sprang alert, wondering what new surprise the evening would bring. Hysgode!—his eyes were cold, as insensitive as an eel's. With eyes adjusting to the blackness, the nobleman stared in dark fascination at the philanderer who was slowly unwrapping himself from his fiancé's body. He cognized the full extent of the lovers' engagement and his jaw hung slack for several amazed seconds.

The cry came late, gurgling from his throat in a merciless roar. "You! You conniving worm—filthy, licentious cur!"

Baus broke the silence. "A surprise, indeed, sir Hysgode—and a brusque spate of language for this time of night . . . nothing like our game of 'Spooks', but so good of you to drop in. In fact, Delizra and I were just discussing—or rather, philosophizing about your wedding."

Hysgode's teeth ground to the bone. "I'll bet!" His gasp came as a strident rasp that was horrendous from across the room. "Now prepare to die! A dead man at this point is far better than one alive!"

"Tut, tut," admonished Baus.

From his side, Hysgode drew a jewelled dagger. It was richly embossed with curled designs. He wasted no time and leaped up on the bed and made a downward strike. Baus twisted lynx-like, barely avoiding a bludgeoning to his chest. The blade nicked his thigh, drawing blood.

Delizra screamed. She thrust her plush nakedness off the bed and began snatching the covers to cover her pale breasts. Baus dove for his own clothes lying limp in a pile at the bedpost. He searched frantically for anything that could deter his opponent, spare him a demise. There seemed little time to grab anything. In berserk fury, Hysgode drew back the dagger for another strike, but Baus kneed him in the groin and he managed to ram the ganglestick up into his nose. Hysgode crouched there in the bed for half a second, with a look of frozen bewilderment crawling across his face.

Baus calmly snatched up his garments while Delizra stood trembling in the shadows.

"I trust, my lady," he whispered, "that you understand that I must leave."

Recovering her composure, she fumbled for words. "What have you done?" She clenched pale fists, reached for her nightgown. "Hysgode is slack."

Scudding across the bed, she made a grab for her fiancée's arm, but Baus caught the quivering wrist. "I caution you much against that action, Lady. Hysgode will waken from his torpidity in small time and I think it better that we leave. It is all better in fact that we be well away before that unhappy instant transpires. In about ten minutes, I guess."

Regaining a bit of her haughty demeanour, Delizra snapped, "I don't give a toss for that fussy little hare. But I warn you, conniver, if you leave this room without telling me what is going on, I shall surely scream!" Her hands were clasped imperially on her lovely hips.

Baus shrugged, feigning an uncaring grin. He spied the Vulde's daughter begin to fit a few pieces together and drew a deep breath. He reached out with the ganglestick and tapped her on the throat.

Transfixed like an angel or some sea nymph from fantastic Fandar, Delizra gazed sightlessly, like a tragic figure.

Critically Baus appraised the two figures hunched on the bed. He made a regretful sound. It was not a placid scene—bloody sheets, strewn covers, naked Delizra and her chosen popinjay poised with eager dagger clasped for the kill . . . No, the Vulde would not like this diorama at all.

Baus paused to depart. He scooped up Lolispar, the ganglestick and his wits and took egress from Delizra's boudoir with haste.

Just as he was about to close the door, he looked up to see Tulesio and the Vulde striding ominously down the hall.

Baus jammed the door shut, jerking into the corridor with apprehension. The predicament was delicate—glib responses would not earn him a pass. What to do? Curse his luck! Had the two seen him ducking out of Delizra's bedchamber? He was not sure, yet, the inimical way that Delizra's sire now stared at him did not inspire any great hope.

Baus forced himself to act; he cried out in pained relief: "Lord Vulde—how reassured I am to see you!"

"Why?" grated the Vulde sardonically. The demand was gruff and the Vulde's blazing eyes were wrathful. He gazed from daughter's door to Baus.

"There is a certain matter which I must take up with you," Baus insisted. He draped his arm familiarly around the Vulde's shoulders and essayed to propel him away from Delizra's door toward that of Griselda's.

The Vulde studied him with displeasure. "What are you doing? Why are you loitering around my daughters' chambers?" His gaze fixed on the bloody patch oozing from Baus's left thigh. He seemed to automatically guess the nature of the wound as he glanced inimically back to Delizra's door.

Baus addressed the gruffness of the query with carefully-placed words: "I was making sure that your daughters were safe. It is a love story—I mean a long story!—" he laughed at the slip "—but before you draw inappropriate conclusions, listen to what I have to say. I detected sounds. Upon waking, I emerged out in the hall, spying Cedrek sneaking into Griselda's bedchamber."

"Cedrek?" snorted Tulesio. "What would that cretin be skulking about her room for?"

Baus opened his palms in perplexity. "I can hardly hazard a guess—outside of what would seem indelicate."

"What of the blood on your garments?" demanded the Vulde sternly. "It has stained your costly outfit."

Baus pointed downward. "Cedrek has gone mad. He inflicted this wound upon me when he saw me ready to expose his private ploy."

"Private ploy? What ploy?" fumed the Vulde. Quaking with fury, he turned to Tulesio, "We shall have to investigate this matter and the churl Cedrek's involvement, shan't we?"

"Yes, my Lord. The plebe has been a constant source of agitation ever since he arrived at Krintz."

Jaw clenched, the Vulde burst into Griselda's room. Stalking inside, he was determined for an answer; however, his expression turned into dumbstruck wonder when he saw Griselda, hips on top of Cedrek, interlocked in what could only be construed as an intimate embrace. The bedcovers were disarranged, in a tumble of sweaty folds, and the maid was making vulgar sounds in similitude to a wegmor. Baus, poking his head in from behind, marvelled at the scene. The Vulde instantly raised his voice to a strangled roar. "Dawcocks! Miscreants! Unprise your scandalous flesh from my daughter this instant!"

There was a thump and a bang. A spent, withdrawn figure released itself from beneath Griselda and rolled off the bed, landing in an untidy heap on the floor. The butcher's son, much paler than he was in the Dakkaw's vat, gasped with an apathetic shudder. He lolled his eyes under black heavy lids and held forth palms in a wretched appeal. "Sir, I can explain. It was Baus. He tried to—"

"Baus, is it?" the Vulde blared. "You are a liar, a salacious villain—a sorrowful scoundrel —not to mention a blackguard. Not Baus, but 'tis you who I see wrapped in indelicate embrace with my daughter."

Griselda now stood with massive hips squared. "Father, you are a prude. You bore me with your sanctimony. Be off and leave us to our sport! Cedrek is a fine lamb, but a newborn babe just the same, but beginning to warm to his potential, aren't you Cedrey?"

Cedrek made a nebulous, mewling sound.

"I must say," she quipped, "his talent for entertainment is budding, yet at the moment his endurance is substandard, but what of that? Everyone is in need of a good teacher, is he not?"

The Vulde's throat congested with rage. "Silence, wench! I shall not tolerate this damnable foolishness. You are an impudent slattern!"

As was his original project, Baus retreated with alacrity. He took to his heels down the hall, leaving an enraged Vulde in dispute with Cedrek while his daughter screeched at him as he frog-marched Cedrek to the wall for punishment. Baus skipped straight on through the parlour. He beetled to the heavy door which was heaved open with a brief flurry.

Slipping out into the moonless night, Baus felt a moderate relief. Good to be out of that snakes' pen, he thought. But time did not avail itself to confirm safety. What of Valere? He could only hope that the sea captain, being trouble-wise, would escape in time.

The cobbles were slick, dusted with a patina of frost. Inopportune for sprinting, Baus thought, but sprint he must!

He had gained no more than fifty yards, when the massive front door of the manor crashed open. A huddle of figures burst out, followed by a peal of furious orders. Over his shoulder Baus spied Tulesio and Hysgode, and three of the red- and green-liveried watch-members pounding pell-mell after him. From the threshold came the Vulde's foul shrieks.

Baus winced as he skidded across Voydram's square. His heart beat in his ears. "Fly, Baus, fly!" He urged his feet on to new speeds. How such a pleasant evening had evolved into sour fortune! It seemed likely that he would not outdistance five frenzied attackers at once, but how else could he outwit these oafs? Now the obelisk shone like an ominous spire in his path. He hurtled closer to its pale, worn face and could discern the fateful grin on the Dakkaw's visage, carved into a rictus.

A hurtful lump wedged in Baus's throat. He bore defeat, and despair, knowing that it would be beside this sorrowful wretch that he too would burn.

With disconsolate thoughts pouring through his mind, Baus's spirits started to ebb. He could feel himself giving in to apathy, yet an unalterable plan germinated at the back of his mind. The captive perhaps could be used, rather than a bane . . .

With a grim grin, Baus groped for Lolispar. He ran around the other side of the obelisk. Quickly he slashed at the Dakkaw's bonds. Loosening his legs, his arms, he knew it was a death wish, but only desperate men can commit themselves to desperate deeds.

"There, Dakkaw!" cried out Baus fiercely. "Never criticize my methods, or say that I did you no favours. You have your freedom—use it to your advantage for both our sakes!"

Bonds stripped, the monster reared alive. He tore at the ropes and ripped off his shredded cloak and flexed muscles with fury. Revealed was the oak-knotted nakedness of an upper torso. Graphic clarity showed corded limbs flexing like serpents. From sheer mass alone, the Dakkaw proved himself a formidable adversary, still enormous and powerful. He pulled his legs to motion, freed himself of the prison spire and stood facing Baus with a hateful glare that knew no comparison. Baus expected the worst, but did not flinch. The ogre could easily have crushed him like a hunter's bird in his palm, but he hesitated. The shouts of the villagers echoed in the ogre's mind. It seemed to remind him of something deep in the past, hurts committed—injustices far too numerous to give a free pass. Baus gave a fateful wave. Beyond his hopes remained a glimmer of thought that he would pass on to the afterlife with a mauling.

The Dakkaw flashed a grin—a crisp idiotic smile, no chuckle even, but a vitriolic bellow that was to turn men's bowels to ice as he hurtled toward the manor to meet Baus's pursuers.

With no staves or sacks of shallots and onions to hinder him, the ogre became an invincible thing—a thing not even human, but even that was not a fair assessment. He was something that men could not be. A thing of fable, an aberration of nature that would rise in its hour. Hysgode backtracked to Silsoor's threshold on viewing the leviathan. He gaped over his shoulder with terror. Turning tail between legs, he scuttled back into Silsoor like a powdered waif, despite the Vulde's vindictive persuasions to engage the menace. Tulesio was marginally braver; he drew his sword, uttered a battle cry, but was fast on Hysgode's heels, as other members of the town watch imitated.

The Dakkaw ripped after them. Howling with rancorous glee, he snatched a brand off the lintel and set fire to the stray sacks of shallot and onion strewn about the plaza.

The bakery began to burn. So too went Gwaent the carpenter's thatched roof. Soon the whole village was catching in flames. The monster staved in doors, smashed windows, pulled down flags and banderols that celebrated the hanging on the morrow. Nothing could stop the ogre in his moments of madness. He smashed the unfortunates he caught—and without remorse, dashed their brains to the cobbles like dolls or stamped their legs to pulp with tramps of his elephantine feet.

Panic swept through the village. Like an infectious disease terror spread. It was one thing to subdue the Dakkaw in close quarters, but to lay him low on open ground—it was impossible, especially with an unorganized resistance pitted against a foe whose blood was afire.

The pandemonium gave way to discordance. It was well past midnight; lights were ablaze in the old manors, and now Krintz's gongs pounded with a relentless fury. But their vehemence could do nothing to stop the unbridled wrath kindled in the Dakkaw's spirit.

Baus did not pause to critique the slaughter. He grabbed a torch and ran pell-mell to *Haggleman's* toward the north end of the square. Ale-sotted patrons staggered out from the open door and rushed out to intercept him. They were alerted by the unruly disturbance.

Baus howled: "The Dakkaw has escaped! Run for your lives! Are you fools?"

"What say you? You call us fools?" they demanded in ever swaying numbers.

"Yes—fools!" Baus shrilled. "The ogre is on the loose! Flee, or perish—it is up to you!"

Many followed the advice; others snatched up weapons and stumbled toward the center of the square, taking up arms against the ogre. Baus was spared a lengthy argument; he tore himself away from the throng the first opportunity that arose. Fleeing as if he never had, he scuttled down the back alley, stumbling over bales and rain barrels as if half blind, shaking the miserable, cobwebby haze out of his head. How foolish were the fools of Krintz!

Fleeing harum-scarum, Baus passed through another darkened alley, then cramped spaces between stanchions, sacks and iron gate. Weaving a path at intervals, he swerved, leaping, ever upward toward the hills that must give him succour. He passed the town's extremities, stumbling through sheds, sties, gardens, other shadowy places where no one was about. He looked into the chill night. He still luckily possessed his brand, otherwise he would have been lost.

Reaching the outer palisade, he stopped, puffing before what he believed to be the northern gate. He tossed his torch up over the wall and began a hasty clawing up the wooden pales that defended Krintz from its enemies before jumping down the other side. The fall made his ankles throb. He rolled off, coddling the stabbing pain and cursing himself like a child as he clutched at his heels. He picked himself up, and snatched at his torch and limped into the darkness. Even as he hobbled down the cobbled path angling toward the larchwood forest, he looked back to see orange pillars of flame roaring skyward. The fireworks lit the black sky in ruinous wreaths. Baus knew that this grim outset had in part been spurred by his own doing—and that the Dakkaw's grisly work had only just begun . . .

FREEBOOTER

BOOK II

CHAPTER 1

PIRATES OF THE POESASIAN

"Old Ridgar and his mates made merry on the seas,
To put to port with a hold full of gold,
But little did they know, of seeds sown,
On a blustery day when legend was made,
When old Ridgar lost his precious Eye!"

—Sea chantey, bands of the Poesasian.

I

Baus, an impulsive, rebellious young man, seemed destined to become an outlaw. He had escaped guillotining by the Vulde, Lord of Silsoor manor, but only by a hair; now he ran, all through the night on blundering legs of worm-knotted wood and flashing scenes came to his mind—of light and colour—creaking with resonances of fiery death and anguished dream. He remembered the cobbled path, weaving its way from New Krintz's palisades. . . dwindling to disappear into dry earth and leaves. He remembered scrambling away from the trail on a frantic tack through uncharted woods, fearful of wrathful villagers . . .

Now he emerged from the wood like a wolf, discerning silver larch clustered in bulky knots. They hemmed his path like a cabal of ghosts. Prickly and old, battered by the harshest winds from the sea—only his torch kept him clear of their brambly fingers, but he squeezed on, down whatever zigzagging paths his intuition picked. But unknown qualms had him bending on a course toward the sea to rejoin the trail he had quit.

No pursuit followed in those darkest hours before dawn. Whether because of clever manoeuvring, he was not sure. Likely, such men as who could net and drag him back to the ogre's home town of Krintz, were in worse predicament than his own.

Where to flee? Baus allowed himself a harried croak of misery. North to a port and seek haven?

He was not entirely certain; the blithe ease of recent days had utterly abandoned him; they had ill prepared him for this fiasco. What had Tulesio of Krintz told him? Nosewreath? Neseheth? He had heard of the place before—some nondescript redneck town dropped uncordially by old mariners on weathered docks. Heagramers never ventured up the coast that far—too rough and uncouth for their likes.

Legs aching, Baus shambled his way through dense shadows. He could not gripe, for he had experienced tender moments wrapped in the Vulde's daughter's hot-blooded thighs. Yet what short-lived pleasure! It brought a nagging cloud of melancholy to his haggard, hollow-eyed face.

A handsome youth with sea green eyes and long sable hair, Baus felt no great exhilaration for his past deeds. By extraordinary means he had managed to gull the Vulde, lord of Silsoor manor, into believing his cock-eyed yarn that he was innocent of collusion with the ogreish Dakkaw and not involved in a cunning scheme to pillage his stores and steal off with his daughter. What a loon! Valere, the sea Captain of Illim, and his crony, had been part of this impulsive escapade—more from necessity than choice. But deception had had its shortcomings, and a grand bungling had him now fleeing for his life.

Baus glowered down regret. Glimmering dawn forced its ruddy fingers upon the knotted trunks. Through cracks in the trees, he cognized a dull red glow bent over the horizon: a purple drape of sky smothering the sea, arching to the firmament, rounding on the fastnesses of the west.

He had seen such skies as these before: brutal, swollen canopies—the inauspicious omens of a sailor.

A chill lump formed in Baus's throat. Dropping to his knees, he felt the pit in his stomach grow. He saw the sea swell the colour of old wine. Squinting once more, he saw the maroon light gone.

Crisscrossing again the path he had left hours earlier, Baus felt a dismal twitch. Once more he tread the familiar patches of mulberry, larch and aspen and the season's colours had demoted themselves to a dull waxy auburn, yet overshadowed by an impending sense of doom.

The path faded, one badly tended by townsfolk. Now twin ruts of pikeweed and guar-thistle struggled forward through the brake—a source of sprained ankles and scratched palms for the weary wayfarer such as himself . . .

* * *

The first travellers came at midmorning: a woman and three swains. They bustled toward him with purpose. Baus did not pause to conduct pleasantries; he immediately dove off into the woods, peering out somewhat dolefully from his hiding spot, to await their passage.

The wayfarers looked like pilgrims of sorts, garbed in the drab brown dress of merchants. They wore rounded cowls, high-ankle boots, and carried with them the demeanour of entrepreneurs. Baskets of dried fruit and preserve jars were strapped to their backs. Home-brewed pots of wine peeked from the sacks, causing Baus to salivate and prompt a savvy guess that they were itinerant merchants en route to the town of Krintz.

Not very carefree would they be when they arrived at their destination . . .

Baus grinned to himself ghoulishly. Any sane individual would turn tail at the signs of flame and terror of Krintz. But, at least these peddlers would not betray news of having seen him—one lone bedraggled vagabond hunching in the gloom like some rat, struggling a passage north.

Baus's heart sank. The thought of his seafaring comrade Valere was disturbing. How had the sea captain fared at the hands of the Vulde?

Baus could not suppress a pinched sigh. The redbeard risked danger, but what of it? . . . If the captain had followed his lead . . . Yes, he was wily enough to take care of himself—perhaps the captain had fled the manor at the first sign of trouble . . .

* * *

By noon, Baus had succeeded in locating some edible berries from a ragged billberry bush. He managed to survive the brunt of hunger's undignified constrictions.

But soon it returned in double force. He had made no more than three leagues from Krintz before he stood panting beside a rank copse of cedar at a bend in the road. He debated whether to ingest the stubby white mushroom at the base of a gnarled tree or bypass it. Eyeing the umbrella-like vegetable, he realized its bulbous, meaty shape, despite his hunger, did not appeal. The thought of him lying convulsing here in the lonely hinterlands was abhorrent.

His hunger overcame caution. He fried it over his brand—the tough spongy pith tasting fleshy and peculiar. He glopped it down his throat with a wriggling struggle and did not give it much thought.

The price was a spinning headache. It struck him like a ton of bricks. For the next three hours Baus stumbled, bedevilled like a demon through woods and glades. Cedars swayed like enormous toads floating above the ferns; angels exploded from the sky, feathers dropped like bombs. There came a period of dream-hallucination—of beautiful mermaids dancing in the mist with flowing manes of carven gold and crimson jewels hanging in their braids and sporting wonderfully large breasts. As far as the outlaw could tell, the apparitions were psychedelic; the forest and sky was a fantastic playground of delight and terror! But feral or not, he was terrified of them, and filled with a stunned marvel at the same time.

As far away from the trail as he could, he crawled. In a wonderful land of pink light and faery ether he floated, dancing first into one spinney, then another, but the psychedelic bursts refused to depart. The fantastic, sliding-doors of his mind persisted in opening and closing . . .

* * *

Hours passed. Baus finally jerked himself to sitting position. He was armed with a splitting headache. He had no idea where he was. He slouched beside a rotting stump in a dank copse. At his side burned his brand, still smoking, yet nearly expired.

He cursed. Somehow he had crawled his way to this eerie burrow. Somewhere came the dawning realization that he would have to crawl out again. An unpleasant suspicion gripped him. In this light, he estimated that the miserable scramble would allow him significant time to regain the path—yes, but it could take him days. Would it take him to Nosoheath?

Baus shook off the lingering misgivings. Dusting his breeches, he saw everywhere fleece aspen and blue sycax billowing like ghosts. Still—warm spirals of jelly dripped from the trunks.

He clenched his fists with unhappy frustration. Wobbling on, he found his toes barely touching the ground as he struggled to get his bearings. Fearfully, he clutched his brand, forcing his rogue feet through the thickening brush. He became aware that it was getting late in the afternoon. He would have to be on guard. In the coming of darkness everything would be more difficult . . . a situation which incited his imagination . . .

He stumbled on. He had appeared upon an open area on higher ground. He could detect the sounds of crashing waves, a monotony of soughing wind, mournful seabirds. Through a patch of aspen his curiosity was piqued. A single dead oak stood strangely off toward the edge of the clearing. On its hooked branches jangled nondescript black and white pieces of fabric, banners of some sort.

Baus half staggered over to investigate. The grass was dead and grey; knobbly vines coated with mould infested the immediate foreground. They were all too reminiscent of a place of danger. He sensed this glade was some rare place not visited for many years.

Further reconnaissance exhibited a trace of truth to the latter conjecture. A skeleton hung nimbly in the tree—perhaps the gauntest and gangliest set of bones Baus had ever seen. A crazy jigger coursed through his frame. The fluttering material denoted cloth—an old costume, undoubtedly hemp, manufactured from old cunning—the unfortunate corpse was wearing his last garment. The figure was poised in an angle of ghastly dignity. The head was pitched with a black peaked hat and green beret. Outstretched limbs had been nailed to the branches, by some fastidious caretaker, undoubtedly as some token of skulduggerish enterprise. The bones were parched, long pecked by scavengers. A crusty dagger sat clenched in the outthrust hand. It was gummed with a dull paste which Baus assumed to be ancient blood, dried by years of wind and sun. In the other fist, a rattling set of digits clutched a fantastic green jewel, worn smooth by age—completely lustreless in the grey overcast.

Baus's eyes darted about, first to the small skull—an ovoid which was corroded, ghoulish, and a horrid pumpkin shape. It grinned at him as if knowing that all rogues were despicably cursed.

Corsairs' country, Baus hissed to himself. His mind focussed on the reality that he had entered the zone and he efforted to take a step backward.

He tripped. Here, leagues upon leagues was no man's land—the haunt of thieves, rogues, killers and cutthroats. What little of it he knew, made his flesh crawl. Dimly he recalled the fearful tales of sea robbers, chanteys of butchery and pillaging. He remembered the black, pennon-less ship he spied earlier on his travels—tossing its jaunty arrogance in carefree superiority. Perhaps days had been kinder in times when these lands had been peaceful and civilized by benevolent lords. But now? Tracts of barren wastes—lawless leagues, hospices to outlaws, outcasts, and a breeding ground for ruffians, cutthroats, scoundrels. For whatever reasons this unfortunate man had been left nailed to the scrub-oak, perhaps a hundred more of his kind lay secreted elsewhere. But, as Baus reasoned—at least he would garner himself a souvenir.

The compact jewel he emptied from the eroded fist. Segments of bone clattered to the turf, causing him to shiver. No matter—it was all one. Death was another form of the ultimate reality. The corpse's skull yet seemed to throb recklessly, scrutinizing him with a brooding cynicism. An evil memory fluttered in the eyes, causing Baus to shrink back. He tipped his head back in a bland salute. Superstition was hardly his foible at this moment.

He appraised the dull jewel with rare scrutiny but when he stuffed it in his pocket, he felt an odd feeling of premonition.

Turning away, Baus felt his wits begin to catch up with him. Was this the way out of the trees? How could he be sure? Logically, the route back to the path was behind the vine-covered copse—but it appeared unfamiliar. Was it through the sea beech, then a sharp left through the dank thicket?—was it a gentle rise through the marsh marigolds then into the eldritch tangle of sycax?

Baus chided himself. How could he be so careless? A dire screech drifted out of the treetops. His eyes lifted: he saw a rude flock of sea thrush.

Bloodthirsty, raucous birds these were—with yellow eyes and stone black wings. Their hooked beaks came harrying after him with greedy anticipation.

Baus ducked and bolted. The birds squawked and lifted their beaks to the sky. They hewed at his limbs, thrusting cruel claws down at his face and eyes.

Baus pitched back in anguish. No reminder did he need that these birds were some of the worst winged scavengers one could encounter on a lonely path through the woods. The birds could easily fly down, peck one to death, gouge out an eye or a segment of flesh then rise with meats clutched in beaks, gnawing and tearing while their peers fought over the spoils.

The squawking rose to a crescendo. Baus pitched himself into a loping run. The eyes of the birds' prey were always the first. Once a victim was deprived of these precious organs, the prey was finished! Any limb would soon be pecked to the bone.

Baus sprinted back through the underbrush. He hastened toward a cluster of gnarled beech—then realized he had a weapon—his brand! He slashed it left and right, whirling it like a club. He vented whooping cries—bird upon bird careened, singed with flame.

More unlucky fowl followed. Baus harried them with more violence, jabbing and hacking at them, fending the gnawing beaks away from his face and eyes.

He had half scrambled to the fringe of the copse before he dog-hopped for cover of a balk-cedar. The birds flew unluckily after him. They swarmed in clusters, forcing him to assume an undignified position. He squatted and hunched like a frog. Worse yet, the weather began to shift; rain fell in thick torrents from the sky and Baus's flame was now sizzling.

He flung out a new set of imprecations. The clouds and the birds were not abating. The fowl crowed with delight, clucking between saw-edged beaks.

Renewing their fury, they turned Baus's half hobble into a loping run. What appeared to be a grove of dank cedars could be a safe respite, brooding aside a brook.

The rain splashed harder; Baus was pelted with drops, but at the same time, they seemed to deter the birds' horrid flight.

The flock lost interest. Nettled by the rain, they seemed to hate the rank-sweet scent of the balk cedar. The avian horrors disbanded and Baus's groans became palpable as he watched the offenders recede over the grey-brown wetlands—a sodden swarm of triangles, keen on scavenging other victims.

He took up his journey, clenching fists, raising curses.

II

By the time night was falling, the fugitive peered upon clouds thick and furrowed on the horizon. The innocuous grey columns had turned from tufts of wheat into ominous purple flagships. At last, the wan light was fleeing from the heavens and a drab stillness descended over the forest.

Baus shivered. The night had to be spent in cold wilds and without shelter. Luckily, the rain had abated and the drizzle would carry its absence into the evening and then he would have to worry his way through the forest like a bumpkin, looking for some drier mode of habitation.

Reflecting on the prospect, he gave his shoulders a sullen shake. More so, it seemed coincidental that the pecking birds had flung themselves on his person not minutes after stealing the skeleton's bauble . . . it was no singular occurrence . . .

To Baus's good fortune he managed to stumble across a path in short time. The trail wound glumly left and right, puddle-ridden and straddled by flanks of gloomy scrub-oak. Immediately the path forked; a branch continued north along the scarp, another down to the seaside toward rusty-grey cedar. He was reluctant to risk taking any path at night, not knowing these lands in any capacity. But devils! When was he any ordinary adventurer?

He took the lower trail, hoping there would be fish or eel that he could spear in the shallows. Likewise, where he could take shelter from the wind.

The downward path proved precipitous and he pitched headlong amongst rocks and giant boulders. Fallen trees and mossy logs thrust themselves in his path, causing him sneers of irritation. Stumps and pale stone showed through the riven moss and sea bramble. One slip and a turned ankle would spell the end of an adventure. Caution was the key. He was no fool to the pitfalls of haste and he clutched his brand as a staff of gold—a useful weapon, should any surreptitious enemy present itself.

He did not see the vessel at first. It was a willowy ghost, a barque of some sorts, some menacing mirage of imagination dredged from an earlier time. It lay at anchor not a thousand yards up the beach, bobbing placidly in the swells in an eerie fashion. Could this minatory apparition, bannerless and lanternless riding in the thin mists be a corsair ship?

Baus did not doubt the suspicion. The outlaw had to blink to be sure. No amount of depredation could fabricate that grim, despotic hull staring back at him with glaring challenge! It was infernally black—pot dark, cave umber—with broad masts, creepy yards, lateen sails and square-rigged sails, spars, figurehead, winches, rigging, after-cabin—all basking in a dim sultry light. The three spires reached for the moon; the furled sails and spidery spars were all parts of some dire skeleton, listing grotesquely in its glory in the tranquil water.

Baus paused to collect his thoughts. Beached in the sand were a pair of high-bowed longboats. Oars were tilted over the barnacled gunwales; rank garments also. Obviously the vessels were pirate-manned; but whose crew had piloted them? Baus frowned. What had brought these lurking freebooters to this lonely place beyond settlement and civilization?

His first instincts were to turn tail up the hill and scramble away from these villains, but indecision gnawed at him. What could be the harm in taking a small search for a spot of food? The smells were tantalizing: cooked fish sprinkled with salt. He had no weapons to hunt down small game. How far away was Nosoheath? It could be a league as well as ten!

He squinted gloomily in the greying twilight. The pirates' elfin fires winked two stones' throws up the beach. Lazy, slinking trails of smoke rose from a generous cookfire, sheltered fast in the scrub. A forested hill rose sombrely to his left—a thick shield of command for the reavers. He had to compliment the seamen for their hiding place—it seemed a perfect hideaway.

Baus ruminated anew: what wrongdoing was there to have a look-see, to learn what they were up to?

The argument lost momentum as he crept closer. He might have filched a weapon, or at most abducted some food, but then only if boldness were stretched to a maximum. Perhaps he would even be blessed to overhear some useful information—or perhaps a location of plunder.

Such reassuring convictions were key points in his final decision. He inched down the incline.

Skulking down amongst the scrubby line of cedar, he carefully plodded along the first rubbled sands gracing the darkening beach. The sea spread to his right, a dark blue-grey cape, a warden watchful of his anxious approach. The first stars were grazing the heavens when he saw ragged clouds scudding by on the wind. He crept closer, catching smells of fried gallfish and clam fritters now. Sniffing at the air, he heard only a low bout of laughter, like the caw of an injured crow. He crouched on his hands and knees. The aromas were tantalizing—a man half famished could only crawl on . . .

He wormed his way behind a ledge of tussocks and gingerly peered upon the unsuspecting group. Perhaps sixteen men were gathered around a crackling fire, lounging on crates and hogsheads of spirit. They jostled about, laughing and jeering at the same time, rioting with their mugs of ale in their hands. Amongst a collection of sagging reeds sat a great sea chest, against which leaned a half score of cutlasses, rapiers and dirks.

Baus winced. He saw they were well-dented, oiled and looking efficiently-used and demonstrating a healthy degree of blood and stains. Two smaller chests were arranged tidily up the weedy slope with a host of other crates packed with foodstuffs and plunder—a barrel of pickled eels, a box of mackerel, two tubs of jewels, various jugs, rum and a trio of kegs of ale.

A barrel-shaped rogue suddenly pointed to a skillet of fried gallfish as he tossed the fish. His mate who cooked eelfish in a similar manner, laughed and pointed over a makeshift brazier—a very lean-jowled fellow with a ruffian-ready bandanna. A beady-eyed lout managed a black cauldron to his side which boiled and frothed some odious liquid. Another wore blood-spattered dungarees and sported a blue tooth in his maw; this man halted before one of the cheerful cooks and made a comic show of brown jug which he tipped over the barrel and splashed within. Snatching up a hogskin, he upended the spirits into the cauldron. Sensing the gesture making an impression on his colleagues, he cracked open another and repeated the process with a circus-master's flair, draining the vessel into the main cauldron.

The antic raised guffaws. A commanding individual suddenly stepped up, dressed in silver cloak, black hose and white stockings. He seemed youthful, even though he wore a grey mane and looked as if he wore a wig about his gleaming brow, which he did not. He rapped the gleaming cutlass on one of the barrels and demanded attention. To his left he pulled up a young man from the barrel-stool. The youth had been sitting uncomfortably at his side, whose shoulder he put his arm about and gestured to him in a teasing way. The other seemed rankled by the gesture, possibly abashed by the attention, but it was unclear. The group made gracious praises, raised mugs and tossed bawdy benedictions. All seemed unaffected by the jocular formalities, save a pair of villains who sat wordlessly aloof at the back of the gathering. The leader, or whom Baus suspected to be the leader of the twosome, was an evil-looking, sullen-faced lout garbed in a green bandanna. He cast his roguish colleague a meaningful, cock-eyed look.

Now the chief of the pirate band spoke more allaying words on behalf of the younger man and pointed to a handful of men, who voiced their obedience at a summoning up the beach, though their bloodshot eyes swam with rum. Four stayed behind, including the two delinquents who seemed exhibitive of wayward behaviour.

The grey-maned leader departed for his jaunt. The others followed, shambling with crudities on their lips. Baus heard laughs and quips. The group swayed in tandem, pirouetting up the beach. Obviously they had drunk a considerable amount of rum despite the hour not yet midnight. The four that were left behind exhibited not the smallest stitch of revelry and seemed not worried in the least that the task of guarding the plunder could be compromised. Folly for them to think that any enemy would come unbidden into their camp, commandeering their trove—or their food!

It was a cue for Baus to creep forward with wolfish interest. His rueful grin was a toothy sneer in the dim light. His hope lay in the fact that such unsuspecting rogues would soon be soothed into a state of languor, that he would take proper advantage of their apathy to secure sustenance, perhaps acquire a decent torch, and be back in the scrub without anyone the wiser!

Ah, such providence!

A harsh call interrupted such fantasy. Two of the pirate fellows, thin-bearded and sour-faced, didn't look as if they would be retiring too soon. One was a tall, blond brute with squinty-eyes, the other was shorter, broader, and a curlier rendition of his chum with black oily sideburns looking like fresh soot squeezed under a green bandanna. Tweedledee and Tweedledum, thought Baus sardonically. The others were still far up the beach and the two casually took up shovels. As to the procurement of the instruments, their comrades seemed unaware. Baffled, the peacekeepers formed sounds of inquiry. In answer, the advancing pair tossed them jests and pranced about with hopping skips, ham-fisting their weapons like jester's toys. The defenders drew back, cautioning them with speculative hisses. Something bloody was in motion and the men were not about to stand around for a beating.

Baus braced himself for a confrontation. A certain bully whacking was in order. Though ready to bolt, his own morbid fixation stayed his flight and he watched with fascination as the two moved in with their shovels. The two, sensing that their comrades were not in the least bit affected to jocularity, lofted drunken bodies to defensive positions, snatching for weapons.

Too late! The shorter of the two stumbled over a crate. The taller bravo was instantly on him, jabbing and hacking. The fallen man crabbed back on his elbows and shouts and pleas became gushy gibberings of mercy.

The blond man slashed down. A cry and a death rattle wheezed from his lifeless throat. The man slumped. The attacker rejoined his grinning comrade and they both plodded comically after the remaining defender who was swiftly bludgeoned to death. No hasty scrambling could alert his fellows up the beach.

The assassins licked their lips. They wiped brows and grinned, plopped themselves down on the crates before rewarding themselves with strong swigs of ale.

Baus squirmed back in the shadows. What grisly work! A twain dead! All in the time that it had taken him to swallow his terror.

The murderers strapped shovels to their sides and slung cutlasses to their belts. Hoisting a small chest each onto their backs, they drew away from the fire, bantering jests at their slain comrades and sweating like royal pack-beasts.

Baus plunged his head down into the weeds. The cutthroats were approaching. This was no time to die, sprinting away headlong to be cut down in shreds. The killers were not in the least affected by their bloody deeds, nor were they addled enough to qualify as easy foes. Baus reckoned they had only feigned their own drunkenness, pretending to tip liquor to their lips, in order to preserve a semblance of bibulousness.

The intruder's eyes remained locked on his enemies. His knees knocked, a deft prayer arched on his dry lips. The pair grunted on by like hogs, not noticing him in the least.

Baus summoned courage to peer after them. Their heaving industry followed a rougher route that wound up the hill. Of course, the villains wished to flee!—a mile up the beach a medley of torchlights flickered like fireflies—a misfortune that it should return prematurely.

Baus thought it better to quit this place before the mariners returned. He scrambled toward the dying fire to snatch up a hank of gallfish which he hastily stuffed in his mouth and was off down the beach before a kingfisher could chirp.

Grimacing, he fairly retched on the meat. It was vilely undercooked and bit at his taste buds like liver. Hunger stayed his impulse though; he swallowed the mash.

The two villains were not far ahead. He noticed they were plying their way up toward the cliffside path. The trail was rocky and wooded; yet, it was easy for him to climb. The brutes had a heavy cargo while he was packless and expert at skulking amongst bramble in the gloom.

Many schemes formed in the back of Baus's mind. They were all checked by the fact that there were two of them and only one of him. He had no doubt that they would break his bones and crush his skull should it come to hand-to-hand combat.

The rogues began to climb with lewd songs on their lips; now they dwindled to a faint humming as the steepness of the incline took its toll.

The conniver followed, at a healthy distance with dogged stealth. He remained vigilant to stay out of scrutiny of the cutthroats, marvelling at the two's strength—thus, ever more the reason to avoid their fists and sharp swords. The shorter, sallow, scar-faced thug almost had a nasty spill on a patch of loose scree, but he recovered before tumbling headfirst chest and jewels to the bottom of the scarp, jesting to his colleague at his hasty save.

The pair reached the brow of the hill. They set down their heavy loads and heaved gusty sighs. They were crouched between a pair of rounded, windworn boulders. Perhaps half an hour had elapsed since they had last slaughtered their peers. Overhead, the sky reared a purplish black and cloud patterns reached like distended claws. Below, the sea spread like a lamprey's mouth whose tang of salt and seaweed only betrayed its mockingly languid prostration. Somewhere in the moody pool of sea the marauders' ship lay berthed. Baus thought the pirates would return to their fellows' bloody sprawls and trails of blood and find a pair of precious chests missing. The discovery would make them ever giddy with rage, provoking a wrath sufficient to seek uninhibited revenge. The presence of shovels only indicated that the traitors had planned this heist from the outset and meant to bury their spoils. Where, Baus could not guess, but he would soon find out. It would be information he would covet with care . . .

Heartened by the thought, Baus grinned, while the villains, comforted by their victory over their peers, quickened their paces so as not to be discovered.

They met up at last with the forest track from where Baus had descended. The pirates knew the area like the back of their hands, it seemed; they would be off toward Nosoheath in a flash. Likely it was even a favourite haunt of theirs . . .

Craftily, weasel-like, Baus pattered behind covertly, wondering what the skulkers would attempt next.

The wind gusted, carved mournful sighs through the breeze-battered larch. The path was crowded with trunks whose lower shins swept out like dried seaweed.

Moving closer, Baus hunched like a grinning gnome, yet careful of any clumsy tread. One false move and the twain would be on him. The two continued to guffaw and make loud, moronic boasts over their clever manoeuvring, which for the most part had been clumsily carried out. Their names were Kribby and Saul—a pair of bravos who had been planning their heist for some time, as evident in the quality of their braggartly talk. Ever did Kribby, the curly, black-haired rogue of their lot, urge his partner on to scrambling haste. "What's on with you, you dull sot? Are you an ungracious laggard?"

"Mind your tongue," called Saul, the blond bravo. He voiced a complaint regarding his partner's fatiguing jocularity. "Captain Zoren and his halfwits are far off, Krib, so relax! We shall take our time and do the job the proper way—stealthily and skilfully."

"Aye, stealthily and skilfully, my bumbling little lame gull! 'Twas you who nearly bumped me tripping to my doom, while I had the brains to mastermind this enterprise in the first place. What a bevy of loose-hipped wenches we shall have roosting in our beds before cockcrow once we get these blasted chests off our backs. They must be hauled to the safety they deserve!"

Saul pinched his face into a scowl. "Myself, Krib, I shall acquire a mansion, somewheres safe and sound away from these wretched seacoasts! It sickens me that Zoren and his goats have been on my back for so long. The crow should never have led us on that last venture—gads! We lost Takken and Leske, good men, Kribby. Good men. Thrail's bite!"

"Aye, Saul, what a senseless waste! Taking the long way about Kantmacle in blind mist and fog—'twas an imbecilic blunder—on our captain's part, his worst. Ever do I curse that do-gooder Arnin and his busybodying patrols. Bah! But I detract from your disclosure! What of this pretty mansion of yours?"

"In this domicile of mine," continued Saul with dignity, "I shall harbour not a bed, but a whole suite of beds: couches and divans for kings of the sea, in which wise I can hastily multiply my brood! I shall take my bare-breasted beauties to dreamland, all day and night! I shall—"

Kribby acknowledged the innovation with critical impatience. "Yes, Saully, yes." His wet eyes gleamed under the rich torchlight and his sweat glistened from his bare forearms. "A worthwhile vision. But we have to secure these items of luxury. Confirm our pact!—we shall not rest until we have these boons cached to safety."

"Confirmed, Kribby. What of it?"

Krib laughed blithely; they heaved on with their loads, made lighter by the comfort of crude banter.

They had perhaps marshalled a half mile along the scarp when events began to go awry. Unlike Baus's presumption, the two broke into a foxglove glade populated with a phalanx of feathery sycax. With grunts and snarls, the traitors lumbered toward the glade's far end where they struggled down the forest path in a southerly, not northerly direction.

Baus set up a frown. Why south? He drew a halting breath.

Puzzled and not a little suspicious, he trailed back a little. Where were they going? Was it prudent to follow the rogues at a close distance, especially in a direction toward Krintz?

Baus scowled. In the midst of his indecision, he inopportunely stumbled on a root.

The thieves halted, stiffened like jackals. "What's that?"

Krib sniffed the air like a hound. "Nothing—just a sea wolf."

Saul twisted in his boots, listening. "That's no sea wolf!"

It was not Baus's tumult on which he concentrated now, but the faraway shouts of men hacking their way through the underbrush from the cliffside path.

Saul muttered a foul oath. "Curse the blood moon! How did the lads come on us so soon?" He turned just as Baus glimpsed a flicker through the undergrowth: Saul's head was ducking low as if to fend off a detection in the shadowy gloom.

"How should I know?" whined Krib. "'Twasn't to be an hour before Zoren and his cretins were to return from that pansy Guor's initiation."

Saul shook his head with fidgeting dissatisfaction. "Well, looks like you were wrong, sod! Nothing to be done, Kribby. Let's haul tail off of this path before the brethren make a broth of our privates!"

With groans of perturbation the two shuffled off the trail. They plunged eastward through the wedge in a beech stand like bears.

Baus crouched warily, overhearing all. He strained his ears in the gloom like a cat. Now he was caught in quandary! The sounds of enraged shouts were struggling up through the underbrush only a bowshot away, and he was vulnerable. The two oafs were much closer. What to do? Flee or follow? To be caught between these two packs of rogues was not an option.

Licking lips, Baus waited for an opportunity. He cursed his indecision, but the harsh voices intensified—all too nearby. He could make out various forms swatting at the underbrush with sharp cutlasses.

The miserable echoes grew. Conditions demanded action. Yet the situation was full of an unpredictability . . . No answer could solve the dilemma. Great rewards were to be made—for one who could command a semblance of calm at a dire time . . .

Baus picked grimly through the weeds; he sprinted after his quarry.

Seconds or minutes passed. Baus could hear Saul and Krib's scrambling through the dark trees, blundering on like tasked wegmors. They struggled, heaving under the duress of their loads. He could pursue them by sound, but it was a crude method of pursuit. Its only advantage would be that unknowingly, the two would think it perhaps part of their own band who now raced after their company like wolves—not Baus.

The thieves struck off through the underbrush. They took different directions, and yet seemed loath to abandon their precious chests, and so they teamed up again, but soon abandoned their loads when panic mastered cupidity. The act of leaving one chest behind and keeping the other gained them some time. Sharing the weight of the remaining chest became superior to having a bloody dirk thrust down one's throat . . .

Over the abandoned brass-ringed chest, Baus almost tripped, but he caught himself on his run, jerking sideways at the last instant.

The chest was crusted with a faint verdigris. It shone faintly with a dull waxy gleam, like something out of a storybook legend. The fickle moonlight continued to paint the unlikely hoard in hues of silver and blue. The heavy lock was sealed, festooned with rings of brass, but Baus knew better—the chest's weight and the fervid manner in which the pirates had lugged it, suggested that it must contain a kingly treasure!

Baus hauled the trunk off to the side, jamming it between two stout birches. Tugging at its latch, he wondered what to do. Bury it? Abandon it? Hide it? Rifle the contents? Surely there sat enough wealth under this one coffer to cure himself of any debt, while simultaneously allowing him to live like a monarch!

Baus tensed. Life was never that simple. The volley of curses behind him grew to discouraging proportions. He caught more glints of torchlight winking through the spidery cracks in the trees.

The pirates had gained the path and were on their way to carve him to pieces!

Well, what to do? Follow the set of footprints that had quit the path? The pursuers had done it shrewdly—those who had sniffed out the traitors were certainly in better stead.

Baus shook his head in dissatisfaction. How was it possible? Did the rogues have a tracker amongst their lot? Surely the cutthroats harboured some kind of diviner amongst them. Who else could have stumbled on the trail that easily?

No answer to the queries. Baus took to his heels, leaving the treasure behind. To bury such a burden or even rifle it was a task born of stupidity.

Yards behind, Baus heard glad cries. Despite his attempts to slide the chest off the trail, the pirates had found it quickly, and now they engaged in revelry.

Baus's heart sank; he sprinted faster through the scrub, stumbling over saplings and up-turned roots. He felt his equanimity dissolving to shreds. His only chance was to catch up with his quarry, get within audible distance.

Once, twice, he landed face down in the leaf mould; barely was he up in time to unfurl the twist out of his ankle and temper his headlong rush over the mossy rocks hidden deep in the humus.

No disturbance issued from those ghost-indigo spaces behind. The leafy tangle was unmoved, unstressed by thrusts or brute entry. The main pirate band was somewhat appeased with the reunion of half of their loot—perhaps they were awaiting orders to regroup and storm the thieves by force?

Unlikely. Baus stopped to convince himself that shrewd play was not in order.

Nothing of peculiarity was in evidence. Neither sound nor sight nor curse nor call presented itself and he resumed his reckless pursuit.

Baus began gulling Saul and Krib into believing that they enjoyed a healthy margin of safety by dropping back a distance. Perhaps a quarter of a mile he tracked them: over mossy dells, ferns, shallow black pools, sucking bogs. His arms were fiercely scored by bramble; his face a pin-board of piercings, but the two fools did not seem to lessen their pace. Signs or signals of pursuit were non-existent. A half moon hung sullenly in the air; a cloud passed the moon and the forest became a shrouded mask of darkness, a thick veneer of silence.

Exhausted from their hasty scramble, the two bandits halted in a shelter of alders. They dropped their load, venting gusty sighs. Baus waited now, crouching gamely out of sight while Saul struck up a torch and motioned urgently to his henchman. Krib had posted a torch in the soft soil, gathered up flint and tinder while his partner hoed and raked with the blunt end of his shovel under the dim waver of torchlight. It was obvious that the two meant to bury their trove and scramble off like woodlarks to retrieve the stash at a later time. Saul had broken open the chest and had shoved fistfuls of jewels into his pockets. Baus caught glimpses of gleaming necklaces, diadems and rubies luscious as any maid's lips. Coins also —golden and silver; sparkling emeralds, green as apples, garnets large as acorns, pearls as pristine as pigeon eggs.

Baus pondered the stash carefully . . . it was doubtful that the main band would allow such a fortune to go to waste, or dismiss the prospect of revenge . . . Yet, the two filchpurses' fevered faces were drained of life. They were jittery. Their vapid greed was progressing to volatility and their fate seemed sealed. Baus thought to catch the look of doom in those eyes. If he could but lure them away, gain an advantage, he could double back, acquire some of the wealth, and secure a better hiding spot.

A sly, indulgent smile flicked across his face. The wry admission alarmed him, for he too was covetous of the wealth. Perhaps he was craftier than his ape-armed colleagues. To elude the pirates was not an easy task. To save his skin and to be grandly rewarded in the process, were both goals to outmatch any he had so far concocted.

Gingerly Baus edged his way back through the brake. Testing his way with toes and fingertips, he took care not to alert the bandits in any fashion. They crouched a stone's throw away, rummaging fractiously. Perhaps forty paces, he began a program of making calls: "Scallywags! Dawcocks! This way, lads! We shall rive these craven rapscallions limb from limb!" Baus cupped his palms together and strove to keep his voice low, raucous like the pirates.

Kicking and slashing at the underbrush, he adjusted the timbre of his appeals to create an illusion that many foes were about. To create such a ruckus and stay out of sight was perilously risky, but like all worthwhile endeavours, certain risks were to be implemented to bring about reward.

Baus peered. Through cracks in the trees, he caught sight of the treasure buriers knuckling their shovels. Gnarly, sunburnt hands shook in fright; they argued furiously amongst themselves. The two came to blows. Baus heard a brief spate of scuffles and livid curses. There came a strained silence. All the while the treasure gleamed like a hallowed boon. The conspirers went undoubtedly ballistic, unsure over whether to wrap up their desperate wealth or extinguish the flame and flee. Both were clearly appalled. The danger they faced was real. Baus saw the pair jamming jewels and gold and coins into their pockets before jerking themselves out of the clearing. Their miserable plight seemed doomed now and caused them all imaginary hysteria.

Baus grinned; his provocations had caused a stir. He resumed his harrying to a cadence of terror.

Panic ran rife amongst the rogues. The alarm had them lurching through trees, abandoning precious treasure and torch.

Baus quickly loped up out of hiding to snatch at the brand and peer at the jewels. He caught a closer glimpse of the chest and experienced an awe and ache of speculation. Hardly could he believe his eyes. A hoard of fabulous hoards—the key to his liberation!

A torch snapped; Baus whirled in confusion.

'Twas only his own flame guttering in his hand. The ponderous glare flickered off alders and ruffled birch, casting strange, malformed shapes about the glade.

He scooped up handfuls of coins from the bottom of the chest. He left the larger jewels behind. The coins were old and warm to touch and worn perhaps by a hundred years of handling. Some were exquisitely moulded by gifted craftsmen, others bore the insignia of King Rygard the IV, many years the predecessor of Prince Arnin. All were valuable pieces.

He was about to douse his light, when a better idea struck him. The flicker of torch would draw the main band of pirates closer . . .

Baus shook with the very thought of this daring scheme, but the reward was grand— grand enough not be dismissed. The blood pounded in his ears but he hunkered down to the task at hand.

He tossed all but a few of the coins back in the chest before he closed the cover. Loosening his belt, he hooked a shovel through the loops by the buckle and hefted the chest on his shoulders. Struggling under the ungodly weight, he managed to stumble a few steps out, though his legs shook. He pushed his way through the gaps in the trees and he could hear Saul and Krib's painful progress through the woods. Fools! They must be drawing the cutthroats away from the road north to Nosoheath. Good! At this juncture, he could not be more elated. The louts in their panic were heading on a blundering course. They were not pausing to cover their tracks—the first thing that would undermine them!

Baus forged his way back along his original path. The chest ground on his neck and caused him to wince with the exertion. But the thought of capture, and the fruits of success kept him staggering on. Taking risks and following his intuition would lead him to the adventure of his life . . . indeed Baus's tale would hardly be the one it was had he not been following his gutmost instincts. If he took too many steps, he would come face to face with his bane, or at least a party of them, so he banked left from the setting moon.

It was a fortunate foresight. Shouts had not gone unheard. A band of cutthroats hurtled its way toward the glade, six of them, attracted by the dim glare that sheened in the secluded glade. Another small band was lumbering on an angle south of him, though the underbrush only slightly masked trace of the fleeing traitors.

The pursuers carried torches, cutlasses and murderous moods. In the flickering light, beards were like birds' nests; faces like greasy, grim-taut platters. Ruthless men with cold-blooded desires and goals roamed everywhere . . .

Stifling a bleak croak, Baus halted before a gangly, feather-leaved birch. He knelt unceremoniously on the bed of damp leaves where he set down his loot shakily, pushing himself flat to the ground. He gripped his shovel, conscious that each slightly, rattling wheeze could betray him.

The band of six rogues thundered by like beasts. They were no less than twenty paces away when he swore he could smell the rum on their breaths. They hadn't seen him or the traitors; but they were bent on discovering him, and the cause of the yellow glow wavering in the alders.

There was no time to lose. Baus unhitched his shovel and with frenetic speed, began hacking his way through the leaves. The ground was soft—to his gladness. Ages of fallen leaves had created a mat of humus. One inch, two inches, three inches . . .

He scrabbled deeper.

Shrill echoes rang through the forest like bird wails. Cries of pain, distress, torment filled the quiet spaces. A series of piercing yells and curses stabbed the air.

Baus winced. Everything was proceeding too fast. If his guess was correct, Krib and Saul were now undergoing a most gruelling and necessary requital.

No time for remorse—or for a proper job. He thrust the chest deep into his shallow hole and jammed earth around the edges. He spread leaves overtop with speed. He ran twenty paces back; sweeping eyes out, looking, dashing twenty paces to a place conveniently close to the scene where the awful sounds were being perpetrated in the night.

Baus scabbed at the earth with tremendous force. Plunging six or seven coins in the hasty hole, he hardly bothered to cover them, or take care that his concealing was unobvious.

There was a method to the madness. The pirates were returning in numbers. An angry band just came scrambling dizzyingly close, eight figures, one by one—silent stalkers, each searching for an item lost.

Baus risked a look back. More figures were appearing, perhaps six, including the two traitors. Their heads lolled on swollen necks like pumpkins and slumped on naked, blood-streaked chests. They were being beaten and herded closer, like slaughter beasts . . . questioning was taking place with prejudice.

Baus unsheathed Lolispar, that magic dagger appropriated from the shrunken nobleman Trimestrius; noiselessly he notched a nearby birch with a criss-cross at its base. He hobbled away, ducked into the moonlight with the golden blade bared.

Not a moment too soon.

The scouts had come back this way and were sniffing about, perhaps no more than thirty paces away. Baus discerned grim silhouettes in the dark, lurking indiscriminately as if wondering what would be their next move. They wandered about like a pack of hungry wolves and under the patchy torchlight, Baus heard truculent grunts and cold-hearted sneers. They were looking for the same missing chest which undoubtedly Krib and Saul had proclaimed to have lost.

If they discovered the chest . . . Despair fell over Baus. The pirates were too near for him to flee. His life hung on a silver thread. Any sounds of a hasty retreat would be recognized—the result, death.

Four villains edged their way near to the place where Baus crouched. He realized that sooner or later they would spy him and he would be cut down.

Desperation rose to terror. He desperately squinted into the gloom. The forest floor lay flat at his feet: a fine spread of larch needles offering numerous corridors into the daunting tangle. Hope seemed faraway. Darkness fell in deeper pools. The moon slipped beneath silver clouds and once more cast ghostly sheens. Another giant birch could be barely made out in the distance poised to his right. There, a small creek gurgled somewhere in the dimness just beyond. Ahead, huddled a stand of larch, perhaps the same he had passed when pursuing the traitors.

Baus grimaced: if he could make for the copse without being noticed, even get within range, at least it would mask sounds of his retreat . . .

Baus bent to his task, inspired by a fugitive hope. If only he *could* follow the grove upstream and beyond the range of the pirates' view . . . ?

Risking a look back, he saw two of the eight disbanding. They were spreading out in insidious numbers from the main group; a pair was coming straight his way, poking their swords into the shrubs, prodding at the ground. Baus realized with hopeless anguish that escape seemed impossible. The least he could do was make for the cover of the birch!

Crouching like a cornered cat, he skittered from his hiding spot. Hands and knees shook; with his back crabbed to the tree, he slid noiselessly to the ground, trying to mask the bursting flood of panic assailing his lungs. He knew that he would be soon discovered if he did not act quickly!

Involuntarily he turned, grasping the gnarly trunk. He jumped. Nails clawed into the bark. He inched his way laboriously up the shaggy bole. The tree between them shielded him from his enemies. It was fortunate, else he would have died there. The trunk was miraculously wide, marked with knots and fingerholds which allowed him to climb the base and mask the sounds of scraping and slithering. The grandfather birch, deep in this sheltered lee of unknown forest, still guarded the bulk of its withered leaves—and for this, Baus kissed its lower branches with a gratefulness to which he now owed his life.

As high as he dared, Baus climbed the boughs and clung there like a rueful opossum. The stout branch fanned out over the grove. It had bent slightly down toward the rill. Far to the right he could spy his quarry moving like hornets. There were three black figures now probing about the tree and glancing suspiciously toward the gurgling water.

To his dismay one long-haired, frog-faced buccaneer was poking near the base of the birch where he had last buried the chest. If the loot were discovered, his efforts would be in vain. Eyes pinched, Baus steeled himself for failure. But a sudden crisp cry of exultation rang from the opposite direction. A pirate had discovered a handful of coins and fortuitously had prompted all to abandon their current searching. The brief hole that he had dug earlier had been found. The encroaching mangy-haired brigand whirled; with eyes gleaming, the mariner whisked away. Crowding around the newfound hole, several corsairs scrabbled and slashed at the turf with dirks and cutlasses. Neither chest nor gold did they find, and soon they were all churlishly annoyed.

Other men arrived, including the grey pirate and his ear-bangled comrade. The two beaten traitors, long-stripped of their loot and weapons, tottered in helpless misery before the leader. They were dragged forward again by four swaggering buccaneers. More rogues arrived in numbers. From Baus's vantage he saw a grisly gang dwarfed the two unfortunates. The thugs wore cutlasses, peaked hats and leather jerkins: a club-fisted, scowling and vengeful lot.

The ear-bangled pirate blurted out a deprecation. "A bad business, Zoren. Guor killed— and now Gully and Darmester. We'll need to replace these goons—and another lad for good luck." The brigand whipped back his loose, oily clumps of hair that comprised his long, stringy mop.

The grey-maned pirate did not reply. He stood implacably, narrow frame casting a leaden shadow over the leaf mould.

"Hear that, Kribby?" cooed one of the captors. Thrusting a sweating turnip-like face close to the other whose countenance was crushed and bloody beyond recognition, he barked, "Where's the loot? You can tell us, we're all pals here!"

Krib whined nasally: "I told you, Onde, we forsook it back in the copse, by the fire torch."

"Well, it's not there, is it, Kribby? You saw for yourself. It means you must be fibbing to us!"

A gigantically tall, curly-haired brute gripping a wicked sword, sneered. "Answer us, Krib, or it will be the worse for you."

"No, Fuurdhal, I swear! The chest has to be there; we were just burying it for a spell and a look-see after!"

"Look-see, eh?"

Zoren, the grey pirate, appraised the character cowering before him. He appeared to gauge the response with placid disgust. Extending a soothing hand to the cringing lout under the shadow of his calm face, he emitted a soft exhalation. The eyes were small, grey, absent of any warmth or affection. The movements were unhurried, almost unconsciously automated.

Saul's face remained bloody and terror-stricken. An obscene, pitiable helplessness seemed to ooze from his pores. One eye was swollen, the other blurred to a ghastly purple. His right arm hung limp like a broken sandgull's wing.

Zoren spoke for the first time: "It was unkind of you to despatch Darmester and Gully back there. Fuurdhal and Onde have taken well care of your skulkishness! I compliment them! They were my dutiful friends—Gully and Darmy were, and deserved better. Who were you to grant them such demise? Eh? Speak up, you poltroons! Nothing to say? Well, shame! Perhaps you shall learn a similar inconstancy—and horror."

Saul scrambled crab-wise, squirming back against the bulk of his captors. Chest sunken and quivering, he gibbered out a moan under the cold, fish-like gaze of his captain. It was enough to have him wetting his pants.

Zoren pushed his bland face closer to the captive's. "Just how did you do it? How painfully you will die, Saul, is a matter of your own choosing. Where did you hide the loot?"

Saul's head lolled back like a rag doll, as he mouthed pathetic pleas like a child.

Zoren's cutlass slithered forward; he shore off two of Saul's fingers.

A whimpering gasp escaped the pirate's maw; Saul reached for his bloody fingers lying in the leaves, but he could not grab them as Fuurdhal held him back.

Zoren, unperturbed by the carnage and hellish gibbering, advanced with ruby-stained blade and waited politely for an answer. None came. The pulsing blood and the palsying in Saul's arm somewhat stabilized. "Tach! Tragedy in the woods, Saul!—Obviously you attempted to bury the treasure either in one hole or the other. Then you heard us coming. The facts remain written in your fiendish eyes. So, you hid the chest. Hoo-hoo! What a pedestrian idea! But common or fancy, the mystery remains, without clue or answer outside of a last minute rogue's temptation, or perhaps cowardice. Now . . . where is the loot?—for the final time . . ." Zoren spoke the words ominously, like a father whispering to a delinquent son before punishment, and Saul shook his head as if it would wobble off. The villain began to sob babyishly, pleading for his life, harangued with the knowledge that he would die soon— and in excruciating pain.

Zoren ran him through. The cutlass cleaved clean through chest to backbone, not too close to the heart so that the traitor's suffering would be the worst. Now exhaling, Zoren advanced on Krib who watched in horror as his expiring comrade twitched and frothed in his own blood.

Baus watched appalled from the branches above. Dread fear dripped in his heart. Intellectually, he knew these men deserved their fates and would be executed either way, but the question was the manner in which they were to die, and he knew that Krib and Saul had been played perhaps a crueller fate by his own hand.

Krib, gibbering like an infant, knew that he had seconds to live. Abasing himself before Zoren, he demonstrated no less gracelessness than Saul, knowing nothing more about the treasure—a fact that somewhere Zoren loosely acknowledged. He motioned to his ear-bangled aide to slash twice. A third time and Krib fell, croaking on his own blood. The expiring was inelegant and the pirates grimaced, leaving the two there bleeding, gurgling their last breaths.

"Scour the area!" snarled Zoren. "We'll have a last look around this rat hole—then we depart."

Some objected to the task; the prospect of departing empty-handed was abhorrent, but they all joined hands in a rigorous search. Scouring the area, they searched high and low but found no clue of the missing coffer. Tensions escalated; curses gave way to brawls. The scuffles ought to have ended in more bloody affairs had Zoren not interceded and put a stop to their juvenile quibbling. The art of his cutlass play and the inimitable control he wielded over his crew were inestimable tools in pacifying the restless condition of his henchmen. Denied a portion of the spoils, they still burned for vengeance. The cutthroats made half-hearted attempts at foraging for more clues and jabbing at the underbrush but a great many of them were thrusting torches about the shrubbery in vain while others pushed their weight around like surly adolescents hoping that rowdy displays would suddenly produce miraculous wealth. In such dispirit, the pirates never did return to Baus's hiding place, nor did they turn their eyes upward . . .

Zoren expressed disdain at the aftermath, "I can't explain this, Oresno, but Kribby and Saul—the nummies they were—could not have done all this digging and played games with us like this. They haven't the brains for it." Zoren's keen eyes roved about the glade with an incomprehension; a flicker of distrust remained etched there. "It is as if a third accomplice lurks somewhere about."

"An accomplice?" Oresno perked up ears. "Where?" He stared about in wolfish suspicion. "I see none. We haven't seen hide nor hair of anyone but the traitors."

The comment brought a scowl to Zoren's lips. "It irks me. I like not a rogue more cunning than I. But alas! Perhaps we shall never know. The missing element has come and gone . . ."

"Perhaps the rogue sleeps right under our noses then?" suggested Oresno scowlingly.

"Certainly not implausible."

The captain rubbed his beardless chin. He bent a thoughtful gaze upward and not far from where Baus perched precariously in his sprawl of branches. Baus ducked back. The captain's eyes dipped to a more leisurely place on the soil below. The captain grunted out a complaint, clapped a hand over his felt cap and put on a cheery face while addressing the giant Fuurdhal, "Well, there are mysteries superior to one misplaced chest." He gathered the crew. "Listen, you pack of rat-ears! The other half of our hoard is lost. So? We shall regain our loss, by claiming another of Arnin's milksop ships and recount our booty—in double time!"

Ribald cheers rang forth and Baus watched as the last of the ragged crew disappeared into the trees, and with them their glimmering brands.

III

Baus waited a goodly length before he crawled down from the tree. The memory of murder and death was still heavy in the air and he was not eager to bump into stray pirates. His breath came out as steams in the chill air. Silence pervaded; the moon was a sinking galleon in the west. Baus limped over to the nearby birch, while at the same time scuffing at the earth covering the treasure. Without ceremony, he began to claw at the leaves which covered the disputed chest. The soft, slightly mossy earth gave way to hard wood. The treasure was still intact—jewel-studded and dense with brass rings. Wasting no time, he hoisted the battered trunk on his back and began a clumsy struggle toward the road. The journey saw him crossing a small stream, struggling through briar and stumps. While there were as many slips as curses, he felt some comfort in knowing that when he regained the trail, he would be well north of the perilous place where the pirates had doubtlessly been foraging their way.

Baus forced his apprehension aside and plunged through the undergrowth. He thanked the skies that they had been clear and not swallowed traces of the moon. Rejoining the path, he let down his load with a sigh. The moon was a pale disc; the air wet with a chill of seaside damp. Dawn was but a few hours away and he was famished!

Baus withdrew a handful of gold coins and stuffed them in his pouch. He busied himself with reburying the loot and he chose a spot about forty paces off the trail—behind a dark patch of thick ferns where tall brooding trees flanked his stiff crouch, rooted like statues. Dead leaves rattled in the boughs; stray gusts made lonely play in the dimness. On the opposite side of the road he notched an old bearsbottom tree—with the hope that the sign would pinpoint exactly where he had hid the loot for future days.

Haggard and crink-lipped, Baus teetered up the path.

The trail wound on. Exhausted and dazed Baus plodded, hardly noticing the path. Deep mud puddles potted the root-torn way and the fact that the corridor was grooved proved that carts frequented the area, knowledge which in itself was comforting.

No passer-bys showed themselves. With smug satisfaction, Baus noted during these early hours of the night that he was a man significantly richer—and one alive to enjoy the lifestyle he deserved!

* * *

Somewhere in the pale hour before dawn, Baus forced himself to drink from a small stream. It was hardly midday before he came tottering out of a stretch of wind-larch—to behold a settlement.

Baus paused, chin upthrust, glancing down upon a graceless slope from where a cluster of drab outbuildings huddled near the water's edge. A tumble of boulders brooded unhappily. A high hill reared to his left, bearing stunted cedar and he knew it was Nosoheath that lay in front of him, for the sea spread its pale and lustreless flanks about a mile away at the edge of the slope.

A rickety sign stood posted dubiously, pinched with an arrow on top of a boulder, pointing the way to the town.

With the journey at its end, Baus found his legs yearning to complete the last steps. His throat was as dry as sawdust. A wispy grey sky showed wan shafts of lemony light. Putting his misgivings aside, he was glad to be where he was, though the sentiment was loosely conceived. The village was nothing more than a scar of drab rock lining a darkwater inlet. A cluster of ramshackle buildings huddled along the shore and across the narrow harbour stood another shelf of houses before which a host of boathouses and squalid docks hunched, white and grey. Punts and grubby vessels were moored in the comb of weather-beaten wood, shadowing the weatherworn harbour side.

Baus descended the slope, his weary legs crooked and strained. The only decent ship was a schooner named *Macy's Reach*, sporting two high-squared masts, a trim bow, a broad hull painted white and cornflower yellow. The port flank was freshly wiped of salt and sea-lichen. He wished no more than to take this craft out and be away from the unspeakable tribulations of the last weeks! While other decrepit sailing ships brooded in the bay, gulls circled, screeching their open-beaked shouts while a gentle offshore breeze rattled cleats and tugged at furled sails.

A dozen sailors worked, loading cargo in and out of several vessels along the pier. The several docks were padded with oiled bark. Over slow fires, dock hands boiled pitch and bantered, staining the underbellies of the flat-bottomed punts so that they would weather the years, a ceremony with which Baus was familiar—due to the many monotonous hours shucking clams on Heagram's shore. Also they coated the ragged nets of the fishermen that were hauled in from the boats. Further inland, a knot of timber-cutters chopped stunted cedar up the hill.

Baus curled his lips into a frown. Nosoheath's comforts would be scant, her pleasures simple; nonetheless, he would engage her character in the best possible humour.

Baus broached the main road and spied two inns on either side: the *Hungry Mariner* and the *Whistling Maiden*. A series of seedy dwellings hung caked in robin-egg blue, goblin green and grease-yellow nearby. The residences bore battered shutters, shallow gables. Bric-a-brac siding and sagging eaves were much in disrepair—also crumbling chimney pots. Tired-looking wegmors lounged off in the alleys; puddles and mud ruts abounded.

Liking less of what he saw, Baus passed a wooden stanchion, which served as the village 'street lamp': perhaps serviceable item in old days, but not today. An old crone sat huddled on the muddy curb flicking onion peels into the running water. She muttered miseries to herself, ramblings which Baus could barely make sense of. Her brown face was sea-lined and she looked up at him with an apathetic curiosity. Baus's expression showed critical reminiscence. Perhaps this woman had once been a beautiful damsel, but now her charms had fled and she remained unkempt and alone.

He moved on. The yard behind the first inn wafted the stink of goats. He caught a similar glimpse of hogs rutting in the mud.

Doubt started to prick at the edge of Baus's convictions. He thrust the feelings aside and approached a group of stevedores tugging ropes and dragging bales on cargo-hooks by the nearby wharf.

"Here, stalwarts! What is in the making? Where may I find decent lodging?"

The workers afforded him grunts of disinterest. Baus muttered an inquiry about a good meal. Thumbs jerked in the direction of the *Hungry Mariner*. Baus looked critically at the tavern, with its surmounting steeples of crooked masts and broadly tacked mainstays. They were mounted under pretext of a 'tourist attraction' which was perhaps some official landmark. Elsewhere, the street terminated in a sprawl of lich-grass, dropping off to mingled black shingle where wandering gulls fought over decayed crab legs.

It was an understatement to say that the town Nosoheath had nothing of the charms of Krintz. But Baus wished only an undisturbed sleep in a dry place, so he plodded on. He could not dispute the panorama's desolate raw reality. On the opposing street, he appraised the first reputable inn: the *Whistling Maiden*. Front windows were grimed white with salt and pale timbers were lashed by sea winds. A skipper's wheel bore a cracked oar that hung in between two windows. In the centre window hung a crude effigy carved of a mermaid playing a flute —the maid was engaged in singing to what appeared, a gang of rascally seamen.

Nodding wisely, Baus picked the closest of the lodgings, avoiding the ramshackle pub on the other side of the street with the warped ship's masts. Pushing his way through the timber-framed doors, he paused to squint at their rudely inscribed characters '*Whistling Maiden*'.

The place was dimly-kept and smelling untidily of burnt cooking. Accumulated dust and sour ale hung in the secretive spaces of the taproom. Three wall sconces burned on battered pillars, adding their own goat-tallow reek to the mix. A half score of patrons faced the counter on stools, or lounged about at crudely-hewn tables while finishing their midday gruel.

The innkeeper stood aside, polishing his glasses behind a knife-notched bar ledge. He was a rotund man, bearing a stiff jaw and lank hair the colour of sea oats. Several buxom bottles of brown homespun racked the rickety shelves.

A door swung open; a matron paused before retreating into the kitchen.

The innkeeper regarded Baus without sympathy and Baus indifferently approached the counter with dog-eared fatigue. A few of the locals paused to examine him but they turned their heads, discharging low mutters before eye contact could be made.

"A bed and a hot meal," Baus demanded without verve. "I am spent of energy and wish only a decent meal." The lordly tone did not improve the innkeeper's mood.

Raising a pair of heavy, hooded brows, he regarded Baus with stern attention: "And how many days, will you be staying, sir?" The courtesy was sardonic with a flavour that Baus did not appreciate. Several of the patrons turned about with mirth.

"One at least," declared Baus. "Perhaps two, if I can submit to such rigour."

The innkeeper seemed displeased. He looked ready to bark out a retort, but Baus tossed one of his pirates' gold pieces on the countertop. "Attention, master, with speed!"

The innkeeper cried with reluctant enthusiasm. "Vittles, Molly, vittles!" He snatched up the coin. He went to fetch the woman from the back with a ridiculous sweep of hand.

"Gallfish with silver slay balls! That'll be all for now, Molly, thanks." Baus heard the nasal tenor of the voice echoing in the stuffy gloom.

Baus raised a hand of reproach. "I require a platter of fine food, innkeeper, not gallfish. The very least of my requests."

The landlord returned with his mood growing surlier. He gave Baus a sour shake of head. "As you like, stranger! Scratch that, Molly. Make it skewfish with warm silver balls for this coxcomb. Will that be all now?"

"It shall," Baus answered with icy dignity.

Muttering grievances, the innkeeper poured out for Baus a mug of mead. Grudgingly, he performed the same for himself. "I don't like your attitude, stranger. In Nosoheath it is no ordinary occurrence for a ragged wayfarer to come waltzing in on a lazy afternoon making demands. Still, I can put this aside, given your rapport with wealth, and I'll have you know that I like the colour of anybody's gold! This beverage, for example—it's the best clam mead this side of the Poesasian."

Baus offered the beverage a courteous scrutiny. "That is a pleasant observance."

The innkeeper peered at him with frowning disfavour. "You haven't much zest in you today, have you, sailor?"

Baus spoke timidly: "Brio is the last thing which I would describe befitting my present mood."

"Well," the innkeeper grunted. "Who are you anyway? Your garments are of low quality and you smell of forest dung."

"My name is Baus," the outlaw replied curtly, "and my itinerary is none of your concern." He followed up with a yawn which was rudely received by the innkeeper.

"Drifter, eh?" the landlord muttered. "Well, they don't call me old Kruthgar for nothing. I'm master of the *Maiden* here—and if you desire services in Nosoheath, you'd best go through me and have a civil tongue."

Baus yawned at the idea. The innkeeper's wife emerged from the scullery. She held a tray of gravy-smeared skewfish in her work-worn hands and her grey hair was tied back with a red polka dot sash.

Baus looked eagerly upon the viands. Kruthgar took the plate and plopped it down in front of him. On second appraisal, Baus regarded the spread with minimal interest. He wolfed down the victual. "Hold the 'slay balls' if you like, Kruthgar." He ordered another.

The follow-up meal went down no less heavily.

Striking a quick bargain with the innkeeper, Baus rented one of the small dusty rooms on the second floor for a reasonable price. Sleep came quickly—though invaded by disturbing dreams: of soused buccaneers singing raucous songs and twirling bloody-tipped daggers.

* * *

In the early evening Baus awoke to a fogged skull. The reek of oil fish irritated Baus and clung damply in the room. From the small bedside casement, he could see the harbour's sheen rippling under the jungle of masts. The stench of tar and drying fish drifted in the window, along with the smell of sea kelp and smoke. Baus had insisted a lock be put on his door, but he found it somewhat irking to note that claw-hammer marks on the outside metal indicated that filchpurses had been at work. Nevertheless, pranksters would be pranksters. It was comforting to note that as a result of his wise forethought, his pouch and coins remained safe.

Baus returned leisurely to the taproom where he found the local folk livening up, guzzling from square cups of mead, indulging in jokes, story-swaps and gossip. The fire roared heartily. Laughs and quips rang animatedly in the sweaty hall; men were eyeing the handful of buxom ladies who served mugs of local mead. The maids, better known as 'mead stewardesses', comprised the colour that made up the *Whistling Maiden.*

Baus took an unobtrusive seat somewhere off in the back shadows, lounging on a beat-up stool. He ordered another plate of food—bicorn ribs flanked with potato fritters. Baus felt at ease and an urge for greater excitement; he wished to forget this recent disagreeable experience trudging aimlessly in the wild. The pretext prompted him to wash down tonight's repast with a more abundant portion of liquor—a few flagons of bitterwort ale and eggcup shots of rum, which he unarguably ordained vastly superior to the overly syrupy clam mead that was akin to molasses.

Kruthgar, dressed in his white pajama and brown boots, served Baus's meal with promptness and panache and eyed another of his gold pieces greedily which Baus produced so easily from his pouch. He could read the innkeeper's mind; he set himself upon a plan of avoiding thievery throughout the night.

Kruthgar regarded Baus with an oily inspection. The outlaw had ingested three more tall bitterwort ale tankards! The innkeeper showed no great enthusiasm in the fact that Baus had cozied up to one of his livelier 'mead stewardess', Yola, a mousy blonde who had taken an instant liking to Baus's largesse in the matters of gold. The wench had served him his last three tipples with augmented amorousness.

The coquette now sat in his lap, gracing him with a spate of kisses while whispering huskily in his ear.

"Back to work, minx!" Kruthgar growled with vexation. "There are other pumpkinheads in the *Whistling Maiden* to be watered aside from this jay!"

Yola, who sat perched saucily on Baus's lap, jerked around and simpered. "Not nearly as rich or handsome!"

Baus emphasized the declaration: "Yola speaks candidly. Rich and handsome. Run along now, Toothgar, lest you become a door-block in others' affairs." He reached into his pouch, tossed another coin on the table. Without looking up, he waved the publican away. Teeth gritted, Kruthgar snatched up the coin, striding away furiously.

Emboldened by his suave handling of the innkeeper, Baus allowed indulgences to pass a threshold. His guard was perhaps a tad lower than usual by the effects of the ale and his high confidence in himself. Incautious conduct for one who has committed a rash deed against villains of unscrupulousness ran rampant, and so he failed to notice the four seamen drifting into the tavern like meerkats. Three of their lot were garbed in dirty dungarees, two wore capes and jerkins, and the last ordered stiff cups of rum and took up a healthy questioning of Kruthgar.

The innkeeper was hauled up, arms, pajama and boots over the counter in a very disagreeable way. He was emptied of his pockets and showed a remarkable courtesy when he displayed the single gold coin given to him by Baus. Baus who was now reeling on his feet in a new fling with his honey in an attitude of excited sophistication, was oblivious to the interplay.

The young, clean-shaven man with prematurely greying hair and placid face who had ordered the rum now approached the pirouetting Baus. His face was unsmiling, his garb immaculate, his rapier gleaming. Three of his rough-clad brutes wore bandannas and blue-toothed faces and dread-locked coiffures. They were stationed very powerfully behind their master, muttering a crude endorsement to his observations. They were heavily armed, cutlasses swinging at their hips. Green and black hats framed their brows, up-curled brims and uncouth plumes flared up in the middle.

The leader spoke a brief command. "I assume I am graced with the presence of a certain 'Baus'?"

Baus growled, without looking. "Most certainly." Almost up-ending his cocktail, Baus became frantically unsettled when he did catch sight of the sea wolf squared before him. The newcomer was decked all in silver and grey, with cloak and breeches and baggy black patches at the knee. His trailing cronies leered at Baus through comic maws. Oresno, the hooligan with the green bangle dangling from an ear, croaked out a quip. Bargil, with the short, greasy black hair and a single black and blue fore-tooth gave a crooked grin, and Calley, with a blond pinch of a mop and yellow, ragged beard, muttered obscene hints.

The grey leader continued companionably, "It seems that a certain peacock has entered the lion's den. "Woo, how droll. And a bizarre coincidence! With a fortuitous stash of gold even! Eye-alert for such stashes, my mates and I might have ordinarily thought to take a look-see of our haunts for gold."

"Aye, Zoren. You are wise," croaked his nearest crony.

Zoren nodded. "The quandary: a series of bizarre thefts has us amazed—also puzzled as to how our coins end up in your grubby hands." The pirate framed a menacing move, held up a gleaming coin.

At the mention of pilfered coins, Yola scooted off on tender feet. Despite the immoderate strain of inebriation Baus was facing, he was quick to dispose of any unseemly hesitations. "Much gold exists in the world, swain, like the piece you hold in your hand. Claiming ownership of everything in the world seems a trifle overweening to me." The airy tone served only to irritate the pirate.

"Perhaps!" he grunted. "But let us not get ahead of ourselves, peacock. For example, this coin is engraved with the mark of Rygard IV. *The Rygard*, 18th king of Owlen. Such pieces are not ordinary! Attend!" He made a jaunty gesture with fist. Baus's pouch was the target. The rapier, thin and lean, caught the edge of Baus's leather pouch and unravelled its string. "You seem to be possessed of a wallet of outstanding girth—the jingle of which, any toothless sot could hear from nigh across the harbour. Well—such a waste! You must be a man of some talent!"

Baus attempted a diffident shrug. "Perhaps." The ribaldry in the tavern had suddenly dimmed to a dull roar; now the air hung heavy with stillness like a line of wet sheets.

"I am a man of means; so what, is that a crime?" complained Baus. "Why launch so ignoble an attack upon my person?"

"Nothing is furthest from my mind," exclaimed Zoren amiably. "I merely emphasize the fact that a transgression has taken place—and at my expense. Now! Enough of this dawdling. Enlighten me as to the source of your wealth."

Baus took moderate pains to explain the coins. "Relax, pilgrim. I will explain the particulars regarding the character of this purse."

"Please do so."

"I discovered it on the roadside somewhere between Krintz and Nosoheath. A twain of wayfarers, hastily striding away in unison, flung it down at me in the ditch, as if I were some beggar and as if it were an abhorrent thing—in fact, they were garbed in vestments similar to yourselves: black hose, green hats, black buckles and garish bandannas. These fellows were remarkably distraught!"

"I bet they were!" marvelled Zoren.

Bargil the boatswain twirled his cutlass. "This tone of yours, pip, smacks of insolence. I rather advise against it."

"You read too much from too little, fellow," objected Baus. "Alas, I listen and grow more perplexed by your incivility, but if you would care to let me explain—"

"By all means!" exclaimed Zoren urbanely.

Baus fashioned a polite bow. "Thank you." Smoothing out his poncho, he attempted a reconciliation. He lifted his chin to a more impressive angle. "After struggling to catch up to these two gentlemen, I became desirous of a return of their purse, being an altruistic soul, but they fled deeper into the brake. With such fervid haste that I was unable to keep abreast! Now, I merely reside at the inestimable *Whistling Maiden,* only at the behest of certain landlord, Kruthgar, and a loss also to discover the reason why the braves exhibited such peculiar behaviour. True! I spent a niggardly amount of their wealth—what of it? For that you might consider me a dastard, but I am not. Who would not spend a coin or two given a chance, knowing that one was unlikely to meet up with such unhappy fellows at any time soon?"

Zoren appraised Baus with a chillin, sardonic sneer. Baus could not help but notice that the sea rover seemed to see everything around the edges, retaining a placid knowledge of everything that set his nerves on edge.

Hands clapped lightly behind his back, the grey pirate skipped forward with verve. He was nimble as a deer, eyes wide with clarity. "Quite impressive, master Baus! I can't imagine why Saul or Kribby, rest their cravenly souls, would flee from such a drowsy proclamation to return without their money when they could have as easily slit your throat. Can you not see my puzzlement? I see you are a complex liar—as well as a poor drinker." He motioned to the serving girl who trembled but yards away. His face remained cheerful, despite the cold discernment framed in that clear-cut visage. His three comrades grinned like snogmalds and Baus smelled the fermented rum on their breaths.

Oresno uttered a low growl: "Perhaps, I shall repossess these coins which Saul the traitor stole."

Baus responded with formal politeness, "As you wish, but I warn you that Lolispar lays bare even the sliest tricks!" With surprising speed, Baus drew his compact bodkin from its sheath and pointed its quivering tip at Oresno.

The pirate skulked back in pretended horror. "Is this how you would treat a new comrade?" He grinned in mocking delight; his mates began to snicker. "That little matchstick, do you think it can do aught to tickle my hide? Bargil? Calley? Am I dreaming? Shall I cut off this oaf's privates and drag him along the dust after I cut out his heart and stuff it with breadcrumbs?"

The challenge was met; Baus scoffed at the pirate's rudeness and the shimmer of his cutlass lashed out at him like a snake. One hand was fitted in the small of his back, the other played graceful strokes before Baus's nose, tempting to pluck ears and lips as a lutist plucks strings.

Baus leaped back. Lolispar was swift to block. The blade was magical, forged from early days of smithing by craftsmen invested with clear vision. For every thrust Oresno plied, it seemed the golden shaft spoiled his impetus and parried with an air of its own unpredictability—It was like some canny weapon double its size. Baus was amazed at the dexterity of the miniature and he could not help but laugh.

He shuffled inside and out, back again like a dancer, parrying, lunging, stabbing, spurred by the mead, gauging the surprised flicker edging across Oresno's paling face.

Patrons young and old crowded close. They goaded the duellers on to stormy bluster and greater flamboyant heights of sport and marvel.

Baus moved upon a thrust. He gained tempo and fumbled for his ganglestick which luckily he had managed to cache up his sleeve. The ganglestick was a talisman that could freeze its incumbent touched to immobility—albeit for a brief interlude—no longer than ten minutes, and Baus recalled saturninely how he had ironically lifted it from the magician Aurimag in Heagram prison.

The artifice went unnoticed; Baus adjusted with a series of long artistic lunges.

His advance was matched by Oresno's dog-cruel riposte; instantly the pirate charged. His insistent belief that he was the better swordsman pervaded the fight. Now Lolispar's elegant ease cut through the pretext and the rogue watched helplessly as his groundless advantage soon fled.

Baus's anxiety had dispelled itself; Oresno sallied forth to attack him from a new angle for which the outlaw seemed to have no answer.

Forced backward onto the next table, Baus felt his calves pinched against the grainy legs. He pitched sideways, clambering under the table, ducking out by the other exit. Oresno crouched, cursing at him to emerge and fight, but Baus scrambled up on the tabletop laughing, wearing a clown-like grimace. He kicked mugs, toe-tapped ale everywhere. Oresno jerked his head up—but the sword was too late to draw. Baus leaped to the floor, pushing his face impudently close to the pirate's and swiping his ganglestick along the exposed cheek.

For a helpless second, Oresno remained floating in a kind of astonished limbo. He was poised in midair when Baus pivoted, slashed back and knocked the weapon out of his grip.

Blood oozed to the planks; Oresno's sword clattered to the floor. He had the stunned expression of a hare being ravishing by an eagle. Gasps of amazement came from the audience. Oresno stared stupidly at his cut wrist.

Laughter came with pride; the crowd cheered. It was no lie that they loved an underdog.

Zoren's baffled cry came as one of admiring praise. "Excellent, Baus! Capable work! Your swordplay poses a unique surprise, and yet it demonstrates another of your remarkable talents!" Slipping forward, the rogue flicked his blade and quick as a cat, caught Baus's golden gladius from under his grip and whisked it clear from his grasp. The blade left Lolispar swirling in midair, glinting under the sconce light with mystical wonder.

Baus's eyes went blank. Zoren reached out, grabbed the blade by the hilt and clutched it between his eyes.

Pinch-eyed, Baus exhaled defeat. The grey-haired victor retracted the weapon and inspected it; he shook his head with a keen disfavour. "A marvellous weapon, Baus, but much too mysterious for this arena. No matter. You have the spunk of a badger, or a muskrat, I'll give you—or some sort of mental disease taking on my mates like that."

A medley of guffaws reached his ears. Baus sought to disclose a suitable rejoinder but Zoren cut him short, "What nerve! I should call you 'Baus the Bold', for if any title is more fitting, it is that. You are an unblooded fledgling taking on my band of rogues! What gall!—a proud pretender, someone who can't hold onto a single opportunistic wench. I could almost dance with merriment! Reminding me of my earlier days!" Zoren's colleagues grinned, but eyes followed Baus with queer distrust. "The makings of a pirate you have in you, Baus. Think about it." Zoren's teeth showed sharklike stripes in the harsh sconce light. "Obviously you've not an idea who we are. Calley! Bargil! Shall you do the honours?"

"If I must," whined Calley. "We the rogues of Zoren's wee band be, wiliest, roughest villains ever to sail the sea!"

"Quaint, very quaint . . ." uttered Zoren. "That being said—" he gave a jaunty flourish. "Search the coxcomb."

Bargil lunged forward and laid hands on Baus.

Baus took exception to the rough mistreatment and lashed out.

The gesture was inefficacious.

The boatswain and his dirty-haired cronies boxed Baus's ears and frisked him with the earnestness of scavenging coots.

Baus's back creaked bowed over Calley's knee, inducing him to cry out in outrage. Calley ripped the seamen's charm from his neck and ran the coins through his knuckly fingers. "Twenty pieces all, Zoren! Not a piece less."

Bargil revealed the small bauble that Baus had recently seized from the hanging corpse by the sea. The mariner's faculties began to register the nature of the jewel, and his eyes grew pink with terror.

He almost tripped backward, dropping the gem as if it were a hot coal.

Zoren made a savage bark, "What in Draul's name has gone wrong with you, fool? Can you not see that the bauble is worth money?"

"It is the Eye, Captain! 'The Eye'!"

"What eye?" Zoren sneered.

The boatswain blabbered: "Deadman Ridgar's talisman—the Eye if I ever saw it!"

"Let me see it!"

He snatched the gem away from the lout and Zoren inspected it with the liveliest of attention. His gaze swooped down upon Baus, amazed now, as if seeing him for the first time.

"Captain," blubbered Bargil, "You know what the legends say . . ."

"What exactly now do they say—scholar?" charged Zoren with a sardonic tang.

"They say," explained Bargil pedagogically, 'that whoever holds the Eye has endowed with him the luck and curse of the sea'."

Zoren guffawed. "Is that so? Well, perhaps you are becoming ship historian? Maybe it says that 'whichever simpleton chooses to believe in a pack of wives' tales is fool enough to suffer a wallop'—" and he cuffed Bargil soundly on the crown. But his voice was edged with a quiet sobriety. "I'll keep what I want, Bargil—when I want."

Oresno sat at a nearby table nursed his hand malevolently. "What a dimwitted thing to say, Zoren! Do you wish to bring the sky down upon our heads?"

"Mind your tone, Oresno."

Calley, sensing Oresno's disquiet, endorsed the first mate's opinion and raked his hand through his blond curls. "Captain, we all sail under one mast!—if the legend speaks true—"

"Fools!" Zoren banged his fist on a table. "What of the legend? You dopes sail on the sea marauding, murdering for years, and then all of a sudden, you're all a pack of sissies when some little jadey gem pops up! How despicable." He turned away with snorting displeasure. He thrust his anger back upon Baus. "Now you, rogue! Start talking. You wouldn't happen to be hiding a chestful of golden nuggets up in your little hidey hole, would you?"

Baus nobly struggled free from Calley's grip and brushed himself off with dignity. "What do you think I am? A thief?"

Zoren's expression remained bland. "I'm sure you are just a model citizen. There's a tale to be told, squib, and by the teats of Dagar, I'll hear it! Old Ridgar's Eye didn't just happen to pop up from his grave and place itself in your pocket." He gave Bargil another smack on the shoulder and gave a bitter knuckle-whack to Calley. Without a glimmer of hesitation, the two bounded up the stairs to search Baus's room. Oresno cast Baus a glare of hatred. He muttered foul promises of atonement to come. The buccaneer slipped off to the scullery with the innkeeper's wife ostensibly to fetch a bandage for his cut.

Baus and Zoren were alone now. The patrons gawked, but Zoren was oblivious to their presence. Strutting closer, he hissed in Baus's ear. "Where did you steal the jewel?"

Baus reflected that it was pointless to lie. He explained that about three leagues from here in the forest between the path and the sea, a skeleton was tied to a tree. Dabbing fastidiously at the blood on his lip, he added, "All the bones were picked dry and the skin withered and in such dilapidation that—well, you could imagine—it was hardly a man. The skeleton's hand held a gem; the other held an old blood-caked dagger."

"So?" The grimace tugged at the corners of Zoren's lips. "What of the grounds around the corpse? Was there a treasure?"

"None. Bones only, and some rotten bits of clothing. A wind-beaten hat with a bird's feather in it and the cry of more than a single carrion fowl in the air, irking me to no end. I was attacked by the flock—thrush, the like of which I'd never seen before. I believed them to be possessed of evil spirits, guarding the corpse."

Zoren's voice hissed out a soft warning, "Old Ridgar knew magic in his day. I don't doubt the buzzards were commanded by him to protect his ghost from predators, beyond the grave."

Baus frowned. "Such magic could not be so far-reaching."

The grey pirate's gaze grew misty. ""How do you know? You say the corpse was outfitted with a hat? What colour?"

Baus searched his memory. "It was dark, late in the day. My mind was jumbled, due to an indiscretion regarding certain noxious mushrooms."

Zoren pricked forth his rapier.

"And yet, I seem to recall certain details," Baus muttered sullenly.

"That is good."

"The cap was black, high-peaked, with the mark of a faded logo on the brim. A femur, if I remember—crossed with a pale yellow sword to the left of the logo."

Zoren grumbled in corroboration. He seemed convinced of Baus's account and a dire truth dawned on him and from his mouth came a tired, defeated sigh. "Ridgar was my great uncle, pilgrim. He used to sail the seas and harry King Viluven's seaway for fun and plunder. Viluven was the king before Arnin—you know—the prince's ailing father."

Baus professed familiarity with the fact.

"One day Ridgar just up and disappeared. His crew with him. I reckon they were ambushed in some coup and killed by Viluven's mercenaries—for stealing from Owlen in a disguised vessel. I expect some of Ridgar's mates survived, but they never lived long enough to tell a tale. Expressing fealty to the last, these hardy souls managed to recover the body and to string old Ridgar's bones somewhere up there on the cliffs—overlooking Draisma's Bay." Zoren became quiet, looking away moodily. "He always had a great flair for the macabre, Ridgar did—also a fear of mouldering in the earth, having his soul stripped by worms. He wanted to be perched high and dry away from the darkness of graveyards, to feel the salty tang on his withered cheeks, to feel the sun on his brow! I guess he got it."

Zoren grimaced. "Superstitious fool! The tomb-picking would have been well-secret, for sure! My mates and I combed those waters for a year looking for wreckage but saw aught of any gutted vessel. We did not waste time to scour the land. Yet you seemed to have stumbled on his final resting place. Of all the rascals! Very pretty."

Zoren's gaze pricked Baus like a thistle and Baus saw the pirate's eyes were very grey and gold, touched with the purest honey tinges, sparkling around the edges with a savviness he daren't fathom. The lips were drawn, pale like azaleas; the cheekbones were high, the face narrow; the hair was prematurely grey, neatly combed. Zoren was not an unprepossessing man—he was lean, handsome, even roguishly charming in some battered sense. He was youngish, enthusiastic, commanding a certain unpredictable flair and an outward portrayal of preternatural calm that was disarming. Now he bored holes into Baus's skull as if looking for deeper truths. Perhaps the ability of laying bare the truth of his adversaries was how the seasoned captain became the leader of these rogues—penetrating men's darker layers and fleeting hearts for richer insights.

The pirate mused absently: "You took something from a sacred grove which didn't belong to you. For that, kinder men have died . . ." He laid a hand gently on Baus's shoulder. "Relax, swain. Had you not done what you did, my great uncle's demise would not be for me to hear today. His resting place—his fate—they would have never reached my attention. So it would have remained a secret for eternity. I would have continued believing that the *Kalikan* was lost and in some sense, I pardon you, Baus. But only very tenuously . . ."

Discourse was interrupted; shouts came from across the tavern. Bargil and Calley came booting down the stairwell and their looks were glum, their hands empty.

Zoren's smile was stiff. "So, it appears you didn't find my chest."

Baus nodded vigorously at the truth. The reaver tossed him his sea charm, the one given as a good-luck keepsake from his father, a reminder of less adventuresome days in Heagram harbour. He handed him back also his gleaming blade. His comrades hissed consternation.

Bargil tugged at the captain's arm. "Why give the villain back his sword? You're keeping the talisman? The Eye is an evil omen."

Zoren shook off the boatswain's grip. Fixing his mates with a sepulchral glare, he barked, "'Twas my intuition that we come to this stinking port, was it not? And look what we have to show!—evidence of gold, and information of Ridgar's grave."

Bargil allowed himself a haughty laugh. "Who cares about Ridgar?" Calley's eyes were dimly slitted. They dropped sullenly to the ale-stained floor.

"Do not speak insolence. Now let it stand!" snarled Zoren. "Nothing is by chance!" He swept his gaze back to Baus. "Now, I reckon we shall guard this rascal close to our company. The depth of his chicanery is not yet clear. The treasure has been stolen, that is obvious, and I find this an insufferable act. If what this rascal says is true about Saul and Kribby, then he is our best and last link to the treasure. We don't have time to quibble and go back to Cant's Cove searching for gold, but we must rendezvous at Devil's Isle come the new moon. By then we shall resume our search. When it does, we'll be ready!" He turned a baleful look upon Bargil. "Tomorrow, boatswain, we sail for Devil's Isle—and our friend, 'Baus the Bold' will be joining us!"

Baus maintained a tight, purse-lipped equanimity. "The plan is supererogatory, Zoren, considering we will find no gold there; besides, I will catch my death of the croup when I am out at sea."

The pirate interrupted churlishly. "Quiet your lame chatter, you oily-tongued rogue."

What was there to be gained by quibbling? Baus could feel his control slipping away. The fact that a chest full of valuables was at liberty for the taking not far distant, was irrelevant.

The rogues would take him to a faraway place and he would never see it again. More important was keeping himself alive.

Zoren addressed his crew in sombre tones. "Gather that popsy Oresno up and let's be off! The crybaby gets a little scratch on his finger and he's off to the infirmary crying for swabs."

Bargil nodded his agreement. "Yeah, Oresno's off getting a bit of nooky, I'll bet."

Calley guffawed: "Aye, Oresy always enjoys his dames portly and grey."

The jocularity was wasted on Zoren. He shook his head in disgust. "I don't care a whit for Oresy's preferences. Get on with it. The night's a-wasting and we require three more brain bashers for our crew. Good men, Bargil! Not dandies or pips. Ruffians! Strapping fighters. Killers! We want bone beaters and head-bashers—not puppy dogs. Hardy hooligans, ready for a brawl. Men ready to cash in their souls for a catch of silver. The more cutthroat these braves are, the better—not like those yellow-bellied cowards whose gullets we slit yester-eve!"

"I hear you, Captain," Bargil intoned. "We shan't find such bravos in this pussy pen. Better the *Hungry Mariner* across the way. That's where we'll find our mates."

"Why are we standing here then?"

Calley fetched Oresno from the kitchen. The innkeeper's wife came truckling out of the scullery. Her face was slightly flushed. Hair out of place denoted a sign which Baus believed coincided with Calley's guess. He turned unhappily to the seamen.

Without interference from locals, Zoren and Calley and Bargil dragged Baus out of the pub into the ink-stained street . . . it smelled all too rankly of goat urine and sour vegetables for Baus's tastes.

IV

The night was clear and the stars rode in the heavens like pearly baubles. The moon had not yet risen, keeping the harbour doused in a murky stillness. Baus could see neither hide nor hair of the tall, bannerless ship that he remembered so clearly tucked in the black cove. Even if such a craft were hidden out in that black vastness, it seemed that the uncaring townsfolk would pose no objection to its presence, or to his being kidnapped.

Across the street came a guttering torch's hiss, above the *Hungry Mariner*. The door showed an emblem carved with an unhappy wegmor being slowly roasted over a fire. On the logo Bargil deftly tapped his cutlass; he politely suggested that they enter the establishment.

At the surety of his manner, Zoren obliged, even as a flutter of wings took them by surprise. Sad-looking pigeons swooped down from the gables to defecate on them. Oresno gave a grunt of revulsion; he thrust a heavy shoulder into the door. The five figures tumbled into the taproom where they stood blinking under the harsh glare of sconce-lights.

Baus inspected the scene with mixed amusement and resentment: it was a smoke den crowded with sweaty bodies; a pit loitered off to the side and fermented ale, fried fish and goat fat odours exuded from every cranny. Gallfish was never so repulsive as at this instant. The tavern was a converted barn: a low roof was shored by square baulks and punctuated with rusty nails. Loops of gnarled hemp tied the ancient beams together to keep the roof from falling down. The floor was covered with rank straw rendering Baus's nose defunct and his sensibilities ruffled. He learned that the straw was used to obfuscate the blood and vomit left over from feuds and 'sports' in the tavern. Of the hard-nosed, heavy-bearded rowdies present, only a handful took time to notice the newcomers; they peered up from their ale horns and sordid dice games with disinterest. Half of them gathered about a pair of troublemakers who gesticulated, baiting cockerels in the sand pit. Wagers were thrown on which fowl would claw the other; men rolled skew-faced dice hoping to outwit opponents. Bluff boasts and rude jests rode the air with a style and vigour that was incisive and the high tumult of insults and jeers was ever present.

To say that the pub was seedier than the *Whistling Maiden* was an understatement. Blue smoke billowed up the walls from the grease grill, but it was somehow not altogether as intoxicating as the *canak weed* burning headily from the braziers to the other side. There was no hearth here—nor any fine polished larchwood counter like that of the *Whistling Maiden*. But of this, Zoren hardly cared for he guarded only a mission to fetch himself three replacements.

Brusquely, he motioned Oresno to spread out. His men scoured the dive for prospects.

The pirates disbanded. Zoren watched Baus scrupulously, searching for any sign of recognition from any of the shabby louts milling about. Possibly they were accomplices in the conniver's treasure-stealing.

Oresno sauntered to the ale-stained bar stand to accost the bartender; Bargil and Calley flanked the grill. Baus thought to spy a familiar face in the throng—it was somewhere in the back of the tavern, but he could not be sure. He blinked back his most tearful hope and thrust up hands in surprise and astonishment. Could it be? Yes! The smoke was raw, thick—but surely! It was Valere, nestled up to a twain of lean, quiet-lipped sailors, guzzling ale over a low stained table. From the ragbeard's appearance, it looked as if the captain had been through a war. His hair was scorched, the top of his crown was black and the sides of his curly head charred as was also his beard and moustache. Baggy breeches rode low on his hips; they were torn, soiled and ragged. His right forearm held a nasty cut just below the elbow; his left cheek was scratched and his gentle grin seemed somewhat lopsided.

Baus broke loose, struggling to carve his way over to his comrade, but the impulsive motion had Zoren tumbling after him. Baus's spirits would not be denied his chance: he would not miss the opportunity to befriend a familiar face in this wolves' den.

Zoren arrived first and Baus stared in bewilderment as Valere gaped from Zoren to Baus. In mute surprise, the two captain's mouths dropped in awkward recognition on sight of each other.

"Zoren, Grey-chopper?" Valere ventured. He lurched haltingly to his feet. "What miracle is this? Can it be?"

"He and only he," announced Zoren with crisp acknowledgement. "You've lost some weight, I see, Captain. Though it hasn't done you much good. Your semblance is ghastly, but when has that ever been new?"

Valere grunted. "When did we last meet? Seven years? Times were happier then."

"Yes, I recall," mused Zoren.

Valere tossed a frosty greeting to Baus. "I see you are familiar with this dabchick." He motioned to the outlaw brazenly. "Hopefully, you haven't gotten yourself into the habit of keeping dissolute company?"

"Generally not," remarked Zoren. "But new habits are always easy to break. Baus and I met but hours ago—we are like old comrades! In fact, the pilgrim has recently elected to join our band."

"Has he now?" Valere crowed. "Even as a dabchick, Baus has shown a remarkable talent for being daringly obscure."

"Too true, too true. And would you know the pip well?"

"I would. We were—until recently, prison mates in Heagram."

"A singular occurrence."

"Our paths, of course, took divergent courses. Now we endure the label of outlaws."

"Outlaws! How ironic! Life plays us such rude vicissitudes!"

Valere grimaced. "True." His fateful shrug was frail.

"And what of yourself, old sea dog?" plied Zoren. "Perhaps you would care to join our reputable band? We have need of another fighter, a robust scrapper like yourself . . . we might essay to indulge our altruism on the high seas."

"Really?"

"Aye, why should others carry so much coin, when there are good Samaritans like us to divvy up the burden?"

Valere gave a soft laugh. "The truth of your slogan goes well, Zoren."

The cutthroat tipped his hat. "Seriously, Captain, we are searching for the likes of a worthy mate—a replacement for a batch of perfidious imbeciles whose services have proven substandard."

Valere quickly sized up the situation. "Well, no surprise. What emoluments are you offering?"

"Fair to good," replied Zoren casually. "Spoils are split generously. Expenses divided. Hardships shared. Nothing less than the usual."

Valere indicated comprehension. The scowl on Baus's face tightened; Valere's familiarity seemed to tell him many things.

Zoren took this as a cue for acceptance and he clapped his hands with enthusiasm. "Well, then it is settled!" He looked around to appraise the sweating rogues about the *Hungry Mariner*. "Who else would you recommend amongst this sloppy collection of dogs? It is all such a collection of ragbeards, roughnecks and oafs. What of these strapping lads here at your side, whom you have yet to introduce?"

Valere grunted. "This here's Jama. The other is Sruk, a reputed swindler. The men are patricians of the art—choice sailors, if not able-bodied mariners of excellent vintages."

An inquiring glance from Zoren prompted Valere to add an endorsement, "They can each lift a wegmor if necessary. And for each, I can vouch, if references need be made: neither would blanch at the slightest sign of blood."

Zoren nodded absently. "These are the beginnings of a good resume."

Sruk seemed to appraise Zoren with a barely insolent interest: his jaw clenched, he seemed to hold back his private thoughts. Jama was more cautious in his body language and remained hopefully expectant of a posting.

Calley and Oresno sauntered over to the table and fixed eyes on the crew. Scrutinizing Jama first—dark-skinned, curly-haired and heavily built—their eyes wandered to Sruk who was blondish, sloe-eyed and seeming significantly slower of movement. He stood no less muscled or baggy-breeched, as he clucked his disapproval.

Valere raised his voice over the sounds of the cock fight. "These two bullies were about to fetch me a ship to commandeer."

"Really?" complimented Zoren. "Where would that be?"

"Out of Nosoheath."

Sruk jerked a thumb toward the casement which had fogged up with the men's breath. "Up in Sarby's wharf—there is a mean cutter named *Lynxlight*. It'll do our captain well." He frowned at the newcomers. "What exactly is it that you reavers are looking for?"

Zoren ignored the impropriety with arched brows. "It is as I've said—recruits."

"Ha! Since when do merciless freebooters and bluebeards ask for anything nicely?"

Jama took opportunity to excuse Sruk's behaviour. "Sruk is an old gull, Zoren—frank and earnest, but he knows his seafaring as well. I cannot mend breeches or perform laundries, but I can surely heave an oar, bail a boat, rig a sheet and turn a rapier into a man's belly, if that's what you are looking for."

Zoren seemed not unmoved by the skills. "A decent beginning . . . Though your chicken-faced comrade, Sluck or Cluck, seems less polite in his address."

Sruk writhed, shifting forward to grope for a weapon.

It was a mistake. In a flash, leather and steel whirled and Oresno skipped forward, dealing Sruk a simple, decisive chop. The result left the attacker lying headlong on the wicklewood floor, landing filthily at the feet of a brood of laughing, grog-heavy dockhands. Valere opened his mouth to complain but was stayed of tongue as Sruk came charging angrily to his feet, a flesh wound on his face.

Out of nowhere came Oresno's boot heel catching the rascal in the teeth.

Sruk did not rise. Valere's cawing censure was cut short.

Zoren looked on approvingly. A patch-eyed bouncer came to pick up Sruk's body and drag it out of the tavern and drop it in the street.

Meanwhile, the cock fight was achieving a level of fervour. Blood and feathers flew up like dust in a stampede. Calley took opportunity to slip around Jama's flank and foist a keelhauling blow to the back of his head. The sailor was savvy; he caught the wrist and turned the knife cleanly out of Calley's grip. Now Jama flubbed his fingers on the tip of Calley's nose and caused Zoren a laughing chirp. The grey pirate casually brought forth a spiked ball. He lofted it in the air.

Eyes lifted to the orb in fascination. No bigger than a pullet's egg the ball was, yet it floated soundlessly and caught the fleeting sconce light with an energy of marvel; it twirled about like a lazy toy. Instinctively Valere hunched, narrowly missing Bargil's sword as it grazed his cheek. The ruffian sought to bludgeon him while the egg-like 'toy' was being hurled in midair: an old sailor's trick called the 'Spinning Jack'. But Valere was no greenhorn to tricks and he easily sidestepped Bargil's blade with the ease of a practiced fighter. This dangerous ruse would normally have a common dockhand contending with a razor-sharp blade slicing through his neck but not Valere. The two captains faced each other down. A tension bordering on malign filled the air.

"A nasty prank," growled Valere. "Especially to play on an old friend."

Bargil stepped in between the two rivals and patted Valere's belly. "No hard feelings, old timer. We was just testing your reflexes. The same the thrush do to the gulls when they swoop down to peck out their eyes."

"Is that a fact?" murmured Valere noncommittally. He turned Zoren a meaningful look, then almost imperceptibly, a rangy arm slid around Bargil's neck and his knee caught the boatswain on the chin. Knocked forward, Bargil was propelled squarely into the edge of a knotted table and disrupted an important dice-throwing game of brawny gamblers. Bargil suffered grief in the forms of a skull-whumping and foot-stomping and a blue-tooth cracked.

Valere jerked a thumb at the mêlée. "Would you really have old blue-tooth here plough iron into my gullet?"

Zoren spread his hands. "Well, you know how it is, Valere; it's all part of the game."

Baus grimly noted the interchanges between rogue and captain while Oresno and Calley took stock of the situation, exercising measures to excise Bargil from his bloody predicament. The incident brought cuts and abrasions to them all and Baus tsked sourly on the pitfalls of violence. It seemed that Zoren had only one more lackey to add to his troupe of cronies. The desperados would then be off to sea . . .

Baus made a grimacing snort. Zoren was just setting about the matter with ruthless purpose, when two more likely prospects failed and a strapping, flaxen-haired youngster, Poli, not a day past nineteen, became the object of Zoren's attention. The youth was pawing at a half-naked, powder-faced strumpet who was in the act of posing herself expertly on a rude table, dancing to the giddy jests of a bunch of red-faced stevedores. Though Poli lacked the sophistication of Jama, he was not missing the unquenchable spirit of passion—and his sledgehammer fists proved it. So much was evident; upon seeing the juvenile fervour pumping in his veins while clasping and pawing in excitement at the trollop dancing thigh-and-butt-naked, Calley had underestimated the dexterity of the besotted youth and attempted to yank his head back from the table and box his ears. Had the brainless fledgling not been so loaded with ale, perhaps Calley would be a ghost and not able to talk of the tale. But matters stood, and Zoren's rogue managed to unhinge himself and hook his fingers into Poli's nostrils to rip softly the cartilage, prompting the lad to yield from his murderous advantage.

Zoren enjoyed the sport. "Lads, be proud! The hour is not yet ten and we have acquired our batch of buccaneers! We'll take this headstrong bully with us. To boot, such business done, I suggest that we repair to my vessel and quit this miserable dive."

Valere put forth an objection: "So soon? And you call this a dive? Do not forget that you insult my lodging! No less, you'll set me trolling lines and hooking barrels while trimming sheets just after arriving from my weary trek. I'll have a keg in my belly for starters—then at least a lithesome wench soothing my jangled nerves! This, my Captain, is a minimum wage." He cracked a fist down on the table and turned to the others. "Oresno? Calley? How can you tolerate this wolf's servitude?"

Oresno gave a discordant laugh. "We shall get along admirably in the days ahead, Captain."

"I daresay," replied Valere. "But for how long?"

Zoren frowned. "I suppose the gluttonous desire coursing through men's loins will have no surcease."

"They are necessary and important functions of male physiology," asserted Oresno. "And more to the point, Zoren, we must engage in a rare fleshy celebration to commemorate our success before sallying back to our ship."

Bargil cheered the motion: "And how did you get so witty, Oresy? Club a man to death and he lets it go to his head!"

Baus did not appreciate the humour. The whole egregious affair was beyond him, and he could only sigh with dismay.

V

The 'festivities' hinted at by Valere included fist-whacking, roughhousing, boozing and ribaldry. Then they devolved into a tuneless song-singing and harping, accompanied by lascivious and licentious pursuits that continued well into the night. There were brawls and incessant whoring, in which Baus was forced to participate in his own inglorious share. When the deeds were done, he was not rather disposed to spurn the quality of the three bar maids whom Zoren, after some haranguing with the podgy-faced landlord, had managed to arrange for the crew.

In the fetid dark of the back room, the pirates lay sprawled in sottish heaps. Calley and Bargil were slumped over broken chairs, torn and bloody, moth-faced and incoherent. Through some miraculous means, Zoren had managed to retain some sense of dignity and chimed out a command:

"Mugs! Up now! You've had your bit of brain-bashing and touchy-feelies. Get your lazy hides moving! There's work to be done. Hurry up, you bunch of bantlings!"

There being no general response to the command, Zoren hoofed Bargil in the ribs. Calley groused at his rude awakening and earned a painful heel in the ribs. Another jarring hip-check swept him off his feet and out of his thick stupor. Responses were varied, but fraught invariably with upchucking groans.

Baus staggered woozily off his hard-backed chair, finding himself squinting about with painful scrutiny. How could he have gotten so throbbingly head-sick? His brain reeled, feeling inundated with one of those endless nightmares, filled with terrible loops—loops that experience the same execrable image over and over again. How had he forgotten the many horns of mead he had quaffed, the many fists he had thrown or had been thrown at him? He had surely almost forgotten the goose-hipped lady, straddling his loins like a heat-filled mare for half the night while he casually retched to the side. Curses and maledictions! How his muscles ached! Now he was going to sea . . .

Valere was in no better condition. Though having more meat on his bones, he at least could stomach the abuse and hold his liquor with a flair. Poli whimpered after cognizing his powdered wench had long since abandoned him with all his cils. An ambitious, ever-smiling Jama sent up a long, dolorous refrain intended to console Poli, but Oresno, dry-heaving in the back, disturbed the chorus. Calley attempted to gain his feet but somehow stumbled over Oresno and sent him headlong into a pile of his own vomit, an act which the pirate took personally. Oresno staggered upright and pin-wheeled to attempt to stab at the perpetrator with his rapier, but missed, losing his balance on one of those quasi-rotations, collapsing headlong to the floor.

Zoren was poorly impressed and lashed out with the tip of his boot. "Enough, you idiot! To your feet! All of you dull sots! We have voyages to make and shan't be dawdling." The grey captain had drunk his share of liquor and contributed to whatever recreations were in order, but when it came to command, he was ever bullheaded, and his common dominion shone with a cold cruel light.

The seven shipmates staggered out of the *Hungry Mariner's* taproom into the crisp air. A welcome relief after the grease-vomit pit of the after-chamber. The moon wound itself up in the eastern reaches, floating limned like a fairy crescent in cloud-mist over the sea.

A dog howled up in the drab hills. The call was answered by a reproachful bay; boats shifted and creaked in the harbour's waters. They were like dark phantoms. Baus heard the thump of rigging, the bump of old wooden hulls jostling against their moorings. He tried to navigate a straight path down the dock, but Zoren herded him back in with the pack. The captain, sensing efforts being wasted to steer the lot in straight lines, snatched a bucket and drenched his troop with sheets of water.

More buckets were on their way and the salty frigidity caught up with the company and had them all shivering like a pack of curs.

"Up, you snivelling bandits!" cursed Zoren. "Up or I'll salt your weenies! I shan't call it out again! Drag you by the teeth, I'll do, by Daga's tit, if I must."

Calley showed a dunce-like lethargy. It earned him another hoof—a beating which the chortling mariners acknowledged with merriment, if not complaisance, a fact further aggrieving Baus's sensibilities. What servile cause joined this pack of villains to their grey master?

The troop's stultified senses began to improve as they staggered down a more or less cohesive path—off the dock and down onto the seagrass where Zoren conveyed them up the shingled beach. With sea birds calling in spite, lewd ramblings murmured from the men's lips. Baus saw fifty paces out a small pinnace trembling in the water. It was fore- and aft-rigged with a slim hull and low freeboard. Quietly it was anchored, floating peaceably like some lost soul, shipping four good oars for manual transport. Under the stars a land mass loomed out of the water—a steep headland, mostly bare, crowned with ghost-like shrubbery. Baus guessed it to be sea cedar. Now his dim brain asked him where the pirates' black barque was tethered.

In the hidden cove far south?

Baus's surmises were vague. Still, Zoren and his small entourage had sailed this small vessel to Nosoheath. Why? To collect men, of course—but the pirate had also hinted that he entertained an intuition that the missing treasure was nearby. He obviously didn't want to rile up the villagers, advertising the fact of a flagless ship, so he had opted to sail on a shorter-range craft.

Zoren stood unsmiling, contemplating the glossy waters like a seahawk. His men's boots crunched quietly on the gravely rock. Laggard postures from his peers would not dull his ebullience; he bunted them into submission into the cold waters. Baus felt the sharp chill lapping up to his neck. The alcoholic acidity of his stomach began to lurch and did not abate as he dogpaddled the distance over to the craft.

Oresno was to first gain the ship's ladder. He hauled himself up the ropes before sliding over the glistening gunwales like a glistening seal. Now it was Jama's turn. The seaman scrambled up gerbil-like, then Bargil, Calley, Poli and finally Baus. Valere appeared with Zoren last on a ratty punt hidden behind the bushes.

The yawl teetered; the deck was shifting. The uneven weight of the mariners made it yaw more. Baus's nagging vertigo blossomed. Calley brushed the excess water off his person and began hoisting the anchor. Bargil unfurled the old crinkled foresail and Oresno fumbled with the main sail while Zoren stabbed moodily at the bow, motioning Valere, Baus, Poli and Jama to take up the oars.

Little wind stirred in this dark cubbyhole; the absence of breeze implied that a long haul would be necessary to reach the mother craft. "Row, you mutts, row!" growled Zoren. "Get the mead out of your heads before we get to the barque!"

Poli whined: "But Captain, we should have conveyed our wenches with us."

Zoren sent him a cracking buffet. "What is worse than having a fool woman aboard a ship? Oaf! Look at Valere. Ask what the red-haired vixen did for him in terms of luck when he took her out to sea?"

Poli, of course, had no answer. Valere, sour-lipped, bit his tongue. Baus thought to see a flicker of smoke oozing from his nostrils.

The mariners towelled themselves dry and sluggishly the mild wind pushed the craft out to sea while the gentle lampblack swells sliced against the lightly tarred hull.

The sails flapped; the oars dipped into the oily swells. The men heaved upon waters which seemed carved of liquid glass; as their liquors sloshed about their abdomens, each wisely prayed he was not the first to upchuck.

The headland waned to their right and round its murky outline, the company steered south, by which time a quantity of wind had arrived to favour gusts, inspiring Calley and Bargil to tighten the sheets and tack out to sea.

The pirates rode without lantern. Cold spray flecked across the rowers' faces, but the toil seemed less rigorous in these dark waters around the breezy Nasler's Point and Baus loosed a grateful sigh, relieved as he was to be able to let up on his rowing.

A darker shoreline peered out toward starboard bow. The dim blur was set against a wilder, lighter sky pitched against a backdrop of stars.

The hours passed and the ghostly coastline slid by in dreamlike stealth. Now these were hours in which Baus gained no opportunity to query Valere on how he had escaped New Krintz and the dreaded Dakkaw. Baus daren't speak of the chicaneries with unfriendly ears about.

In the midst of his newfound company, he felt an increasing lack of companionability. A disturbing foreboding warned him of worse things to come. With disquiet, he felt the raw anxiety whittling away at his confidence. He felt his fate hung by a thread. If these cutthroats even suspected remotely what he knew about their treasure . . .

He hunched dourly by the vessel's foredeck. His apprehension grew to sharp, dagger fervour—if he could only somehow stun the four of these ruffians with the ganglestick, smote their sneering, bandanna-browed faces! But no, the four held their weapons in check; each was positioned strategically around the deck, always on guard, always on the alert for any sword prick or sapper's lunge. With new recruits like Poli and Jama keen and eager to make a good impression on their captain they would hardly care for an incapacitation of their new master. . .

The pirates mumbled for the most part about being pre-empted from the revelries at Nosoheath and the complaints received short shrift from Zoren who cuffed them and berated them. Finally they dropped into a drowsy sullenness. The wind began to gust to greater ardency. It took them on their speedy course south and Zoren stood alone at the bow, peering grimly into the darkness.

Baus thought to inject a complaint: "The voyage is frightful! Already I feel a croup coming over my lungs. Is it at all fair?"

Zoren gave Baus a harsh chuckle and ordered him to tend the wegmor hides strapped to the port rail whose wretched slatting had become irksome.

Baus complied. To do anything else invited doom.

Straining eyes into the gloom, Zoren sharpened his ears. It seemed he was ever vigilant, steeling for any manner of mishap despite the freakish improbability of it. In the dark before dawn, anything was possible in these ungoverned territories and he stabbed a knuckly finger out to shore. "There!"

Baus peered out but could not see. Black waves rippled across ranks of the slightly moon-greased crests. A sense of familiarity tugged at his instincts. A velvety sky tinted maroon reared low, twisting with black-grey clouds. Zoren harboured excellent eyesight, for there in the gloom loomed the pirate's great warcraft: a cadaverous hulk, an unmissable blemish plunked on the waterline. Its piked main-mast and profusion of scallop-shaped, square-rigged sails rose eerily out of the water like some obscene sea creature. The two boats jostled silently alongside each other and Baus saw the larger ship dwarf its cousin by twentyfold and sprawl overhead like some quiet, unsuspecting monster.

A heavy hemped ladder was tossed down and Zoren clambered up to the slick stern rail. Calley and Bargil stayed behind, tending the yawl while Oresno prodded the others up the ladder with prickly haste. At last, the first mate himself followed while Valere and Poli jigged up the rope like monkeys.

Baus climbed in front of Valere, but despite the seaman's mutters he could hear the chortling echo of water gurgling in the muffled spaces between the two craft. Gazing up, he spied two huge elk-like antlers and old cones of wegmor horn tied to the gunwales. These were not the only anomalies. Skull upon skull of beasts were attached to the spaces between rail and davits. Horn and antlers angling down on him in toothless, gaping horror. An iron-chased windlass eased off the stern—obviously an instrument for hauling sizeable cargos aboard. On deck a score of skulduggerish, sleep-deprived deckhands stood with blinking faces and sharp-slitted eyes. The gunwales were full of rogues—an army of them, patch-eyed sallow faces which Baus found distinctly disturbing and recognized as the killers from the beach.

"Welcome to the *Last Laugh*, boys!" came Zoren's jaunty cheer. Poli was dragged on board and his features lost some of their rugged flush and turned to those of astonishment when he hooked glances left to right. "Last laugh? What's so funny here?"

"The name of the vessel, you imbecile!" snarled Zoren, jabbing him in the ribs with the blunt edge of his rapier. The blow had Poli doubling over and Zoren beckoned for his band of reavers to gather round. A tall, goateed man lit the lantern. He stepped back and grinned, wearing a green musketeer's hat and a black wavy moustache. Magretir, swordsman and swashbuckler, was next in command after Oresno and with the glittering broadsword and cutlass looped at hip, he looked it.

The deck was bathed in a pale glow and Baus could divine more wegmor and ox horns piling up the masts. Huge, curled antlers abounded. The skulls plied grotesque shadows across the deck under the ghostly lantern light and more bones and horns were twined in X-shapes, posted as talismans upon the forecastle. Beyond the quarterdeck stood a small stateroom, upon which an emblem was placed: the insignia of a pale femur crossed with sword.

Baus recognized this symbol. An emblem of doom and death. In the gloom, the vistas were becoming forbidding and he shivered with bleakness. Such an environment was none of comfort. He counted eleven rogues: grim-eyed, brass-necked ruffians, with cold, defiant faces, hardened veterans—cutthroats, robbers, villains and murderers—all with itchy fingers clamped on curved cutlasses—weapons which would carve out flesh at an instant's notice. The other portion of the villains was very much a-grog with the lean authority of their kind and the pinched and hollow grimaces continued to glance back at Baus with every motley arrangement of eye patch, scar, ear bangle and piercing.

Zoren called out another cheer: "Fuurdhal! Hoist the light! March it up. Magretir has tipped the lantern too low, curse his sorry hide! Onde! Juuliq! On the deck, the lot of you. We have work to do—get to it, you bumpkins! And acquaint ourselves with this medley of new pups in training. The swart chum looking so glum is Jama, and his pubescent pal is Poli. They were a couple of pips we snatched from Assrag, or Nosoheath, whatever the people call it. Also in attendance is the famous Captain Valere of Illim, whom we all know as the erstwhile master of the *Illimmer*."

Murmured 'here heres' filled the gathering. "Aye, mates, surprisingly enough, captain Valere exchanged the look of Royal red for his pirate's black—Drakes' teeth, praise his soul!" Zoren looked around happily. "And not leastly, we have with us here—a very bold and engaging fellow—Baus—a remarkable trickster invested with style and sophistication."

Fuurdhal, the giant mariner, all piggy-tailed and mangy-shaven, strode forth on a pair of bowed legs. His eyes were black and his brows bushy. He inspected Baus with a mirthful demeanour, casting Valere a respectful look and the other two he logged doubtful glances but generally companionable grins. "Well Zoren, it seems you've had a bit of luck in that smoke hole. I wouldn't have believed it—bagging all these braves, had I not seen it with my own eyes." Fuurdhal stood a head over Baus and stared down at him with a peculiar, smiling affection. "This one's very bold, you say?"

"Yes, bold, indeed!" assured Zoren. "I have given him the specific title '*Baus the Bold*'—a signification of respect."

Baus protested vigorously to the claim. "I do not wish to seem larger than life."

"No worry of that!" sneered Onde. "You'll wear a shirt smaller by the time we've had our ways with you."

Zoren snuffled out an amused chuckle. "Now, now. Seems the blighter was fool enough to try and take us all on with his pippy little knife! What a lark! Oresno's finger got messed up. So? I'll confess, Bausie knows something of swordplay; better yet, the rascal seems to harbour some information of our little treasure."

The light framing Fuurdhal's face suddenly turned a dark hue. Others of the crew crowded around the outlaw in unfriendlier numbers. Fuurdhal growled, "He does, does he? Well—we shall have to keep our eye trained on him, won't we, mates?"

"Of course it seems logical," admitted Zoren. "But the dabchick is not to be mauled!— you hear that, you ugly mutts? Neither maimed, nor roughed-up or pinched! Under strict pain of my punishment. Is that clear?"

The buccaneers muttered oaths. Zoren cast them feral looks and threw a particularly trenchant leer toward Oresno who seemed least likely to obey such a ridiculous command.

Calley cupped both hands to his mouth and yelled up from the yawl. "Baus had squirreled away in his pouch Ridgar's 'Eye'. Bargil and I found the gem ourselves. So, our Captain Zoren says 'let's keep our memento' and guard ourselves a little souvenir for luck—or better yet a gift from my old grandpappy."

Zoren leapt over to the rail and spat down at him. "Shut up, you little pip! If I want your tongue, I'll roll down my drawers."

A short bald pirate stomped forward with a face looking as if it had been screwed on over a blacksmith's anvil. "Ridgar's eye? What in Drakes' teeth would the pip be doing with it?"

"He had it on him, that's all I know, Juuliq," growled Zoren.

A squint-eyed, skinny rogue turned a curious glare on Poli. "And who's this smiley urchin? Looks like he's still got his baby fat on him."

Fuurdhal clicked his tongue in reproachful amusement. "This here's Poli. Did you not hear our captain introduce him?"

"Nay, I did not! Poli, you say?" The other gave a nasal sneer. "That's a girl's name! But I like the sound of it anyway; I reckon '*Polly*' has a better ring to it. Like *Polly* want a cracker." With riotous hoots, he began strutting about like a parrot, croaking bird-like squawks from the sides of his mouth.

The remark earned Onde a buffet from Poli. After sour interchanges of insults and rebukes, a fight broke out between the two and had Oresno not been on hand, a significant amount of blood would have been shed.

"You morons!" Zoren crowed sorrowfully. "Is that all you can do, fight?" He cackled at his joke. He slapped Onde on the back until he was blinking senselessly. He peered out to sea with eyes as lucid as a falcon's. His mirthful rage expired, even before his long grey hair whipped about in the wind under the advance of dawn.

Oresno, Fuurdhal and Valere subdued Poli who still fought like a demon.

The achievement was bootless. "Enough!" Oresno cursed. "There'll be enough brawling for you to come in the days ahead. Save your puny strength while you have it—unless you wish to have your head sawed off."

The giant Fuurdhal approached. "I knew your brother, Valere, rest his soul. Cailro was a carpenter aboard our ship, before he left for the deeps when we boarded *Mimers Peep* and laid those pips of Arnin to rest in pools of their own blood."

Valere gave a solemn nod. The memory of his brother seemed painful—one that he would rather avoid.

Bargil and Calley left with the yawl. By the time they had returned after hiding it in a sheltered lee on the mainland, they were rowing stertorously out from the dark folds. Baus noticed that the two navigated one of the low wooden boats which he had witnessed on the bloody beach two evenings ago.

The first pale rays of dawn began creeping over the gull-flecked horizon. The rowboat was pulled on deck. The pirates tipped it over on its side and strapped it down with hemp and covered it with canvas.

Zoren snapped orders. Sails were hoisted. Rigging was tugged. Fuurdhal and Onde cranked the capstan. Masts were climbed. The ugly iron anchor came ratcheting up out of the inky depths and lay dripping on deck like some black octopus. There was little ceremony in the departure of the *Last Laugh* and from the patch of lonely coastline, she turned her beast-ridden prow south, edging her way brazenly into the waves and ploughing through the swells like a behemoth.

Baus, Poli and Jama were herded down to the hold. There was a cluttered and dingy mess hall where they were fed a cold broth laced with wegmor haunch and rum. The smell of sweat and stale oil caused Baus almost to gag. A few chairs were scattered, also scarred remnants of a table and meal sacks. The space was cramped, littered with rags, broken furniture and scraps of food where apparently the sailors slept after imbibing copious quantities of ale. A pot-bellied stove, positioned in the centre of the room, served as warmth and cooking—as was a small stone tabouret. The blackened chimney wandered its way up through a disc-shaped hole in the ceiling to the upper deck.

Baus caught a faint glimpse of the outlines of previous raids: spices, boxes, dyes, trunks, linen, hides, fabrics, sacks of ivory, other treasures, all wrapped in wool and hemp to protect against the dampness of the sea. Despite the stench and the shabbiness of the hold, Baus wished no more than to curl up on the planks and snore his miseries away, but no sooner had his eyes fluttered shut when a boot came flying out at him, lifting him up off the floor. "This is not your bed, ingrate!" called a rogue.

So much for leisurely sojourns at sea . . .

VI

With the coming of dawn, the newcomers' tasks hit hard and heavy. With the exception of Valere—Baus, Jama and Poli were stationed at strategic points around the deck to begin their swabbing. The function caused some stir in the recruits; they commenced their duties, nonetheless, with brisk efficiency, forced on their hands and knees at knife point to put as much elbow grease into the job as possible. Grubby rags and blocks of lye were their tools. While engaged in such labour, Baus noticed there were no nets or rigging to haul in fish. Odd —how did the pirates manage for food?

Well, why fish when one could steal? A grimace pinched Baus's haggard face. He paused to peer up from his scraping and caught only a placid plane of shimmering water reaching in all directions. The coast had slipped away; now long leagues wandered between the spaces from shore to ship where he was as much a slave as a prisoner on a floating island.

Baus drew a deep breath. Valere had it easy, being fetched on deck to aid in the navigation. Obviously the captain considered him a superior crewman and held above their lot.

The sky remained a cold and sterile blanket. Its distant blue measured endlessly to the zenith. The sea, a sparkling azure, rippled and stirred to the tune of breezes and spread its plush radiance toward the place where land once was.

Zoren retired aft to the captain's cabin. He consulted his charts and instruments; now his eyes focussed on the antique glass pelorus mounted on a small portside window. Bargil, Calley and Oresno retired in the hold to catch up on some rest.

As the hours passed, events seemed to float by in dreamy succession. Scudding cumuli drifted through the boundless sky; light scintillated off the myriad waves. Zoren's barque tacked gently in the swells like some creaking manor while billowing sails bellied to the wind like balloons. Skull-masked timbers groaned while the crew chattered bawdy banter. Already Baus grew accustomed to the heavy-footed clop of their booted feet and their rude address while bullying. Deck-scrubbing was an inexorable task; it went on and on without relief until the day closed. Any chance at escape was dashed—not that deliverance would mean anything here in the middle of this ocean with the dark scrutiny of Fuurdhal and Magretir lurking.

It was late in the afternoon; thin-faced Danop, the crow's nest pilot, jerked his spyglass away from one eye. Making a gleeful report, he did a jig, shouting that a one-masted sloop was listing, lumbering off to port.

Ever and always the reavers were on the lookout for ripe plunder. The current vessel was no enemy, simply a victim—some small fishing sloop bearing south a league from the barque and sauntering at a respectable pace on her unsuspecting tack westward.

The *Last Laugh* heaved to intercept. Bristling in the chop like some mechanical drake, she plunged, with Zoren rousing every man on deck. Mercilessly the barque bore down on the sloop. The crew of the *Sander* had gained an awareness of the pirate vessel long before she could make any headway and started a desperate saltarello to shore in an attempt to outdistance her pursuer. She was no match for the unchecked power of the *Last Laugh* who broached her victim's gleaming hull with wrath. Baus caught glimpse of the knot of frantic sailors scrambling to her store-hatches for weapons and charms.

They ground the wheel to port, set up a daring tack—but could gain no advantage.

The crew attempted to veer into heavier waves, but the larger ship threatened to ram her and sink her. The defenders cut hard to port again, slowing themselves to near irons, but the feint gave Zoren opportunity to order his men howling over the taffrail like predators. It was easy slaughter—only seven crewmen were required to slide down from the rigging onto the victims' decks. They howled with lust between their teeth clenched on knives. Of the four sloop crewmen three were bludgeoned to death. A swift melee ensued. The last man lifted his maul in a feeble attempt to protect himself, but was overwhelmed by sheer numbers.

The pirates stripped the mariners of their garments—boots, jerkins, caps—also of any coins they carried. The bodies were pitched overboard, dumped in the sea. The vessel's fresh catches were hauled on deck: two gallfish nets, a barnacle-crusted cache of snogmald. The nets were temporarily appropriated, shorn of their cleats.

Baus looked down at the wash of blood painting the deck. The rest of the ship was thoroughly plundered—a stash which totalled two rum barrels, a mead cask, three lanterns and two maps, fifteen ells of rope, five old hardbread loaves and enough wegmor to last for days.

The pirates threw pitch on the masts and splattered the deck with oil. The bow was set afire. Baus recoiled at the column of smoke rearing blackly into the sky, which soon became an inferno and sank out of sight.

Baus shuddered. The fates of the men on board the *Sander* were ghastly; to those gutted, their ravished and vanished vessel was no more. There were no laments for these deaths. Oblivion had taken less than a dozen minutes and now Baus trembled, wiping his brow and swabbing at the midship deck, appalled and uncomprehending the ruthless manner in which the plundering was perpetrated. His previous wish for some quiet adventure seemed ridiculous now after having sat through so much horror!

Fuurdhal and Magretir sharpened their swords. Zoren congratulated his men on their brute efficiency. He stroked off points of improvement for the next round. Exig, Jispir and Onde beamed, tending to the barrels of spirit and plunder, while others gave the occasional nod. All seemed in order: regular business continued on the high seas amongst roguish slayers.

Baus shook his head with disgust; he swallowed the dry lump in his throat and experienced an eerie unease. When and where would come his time to face a reckoning? He doubted these sea wolves would keep their promise and let him live for long, knowing that sooner or later they would find him expendable and see through his chicanery and garrotte him. Baus shuddered. Everything seemed so supremely unreal under the harsh sunlight of Zoren's nightmare. The captain conversed with his second mate, Magretir, and Baus yearned to know what was being spoken. Valere advised Zoren on course corrections. Calley and

Oresno made busy motions at the quarterdeck while Bargil whistled out some sour tune and twirled ropes by the ship's wheel. Jispir and Juuliq wiped down the captain's gig and the jolly boats were re-tarred and the one longboat hanging from the davits was checked for rot; they pitched gallfish scales in the sea and laughed at the terrible scrubbers' dull work. Deneo and Zanzibar lengthened the sails; Danop tended the crow's nest. The moods were ones of relaxed alertness.

Late afternoon came in pink effulgence. New ships had not been sighted—'twas an absence of which Baus remained grateful. The barque was far out to sea, a fact which further puzzled him. If these rogues' mission were solely for plunder, why the distance? Surely the fattest ships were always apt to potter close up the coast?

Baus continued to mull over the substantial puzzle and whatever answer came to him late that afternoon was distressing.

Poli and Jama became fast friends, swabbing companionably in the sun near the midship davits and ladder. Valere had been in counsel with Zoren for some time and emerged from the cabin, flushed, staring westward over the wind-chopped waves. The Illimer scratched his head as a man riddled with doubt. He seemed to read Baus's thoughts and wandered up to the bow to pay his respects.

Kneeling by the hatch, he lit his pipe and puffed somewhat lugubriously, waiting for Baus to speak.

Baus did not oblige.

Valere offered a casual laugh, "Well, rascal. What have you gotten yourself into?"

"Thieving, whoring, becoming an idiotic member of a black-hearted crew. What of you?" rasped Baus sardonically. The response was more than a bit high-handed, but Baus lowered his volume so as not to alert Bargil who swung the great wheel not far away. "Why don't you get me out of this jam, Valere? You seem to know these cuthroats better than me, who is only a 'dabchick' in their minds."

"True, but what would you have me do? Land you a post as a first mate?"

"Nothing so ornate." The remark was cynical, and Baus resented it. The ship tacked to port; the great rigging creaked. On his knees, bucket to side, Baus rounded small circles on the planks. He set his features into a determined knot and whispered, "How do you know this sea wolf Zoren anyway?"

"My son knew him," grumbled Valere. "Zoren had him sail on his last ship, the *Wastrel*, as had my brother, Cailro, though that was many years before."

Baus stopped his scrubbing. "I didn't know you had a son."

"Either did I, until a long time after . . . Rauseelia never told me. I don't want a lot of people knowing that."

Baus nodded. He stared out to the sea where gulls cried and circled in long loops. "No hard feelings, redbeard. I tried to warn you that last evening in Krintz—at least, after I went to attend to some pressing affairs. But you know—the die was already cast. To scramble back up to your bedchambers during the Vulde's fireworks and fetch you was an act of the impossible."

Valere waved his hand peremptorily. "Relax. We had both our own agendas. It wouldn't have mattered anyway."

"Why?"

"When I heard you make your 'amorous' exit for the parlour, I thought I had had about enough of lords and ogres. So I slipped out the back before you even considered romancing your sweetheart."

Baus made a heavy snorting sound. "So, my concern was for naught."

"I saw you sneaking down the stairs toward her boudoir. You thought I was asleep, but I gathered what was on your mind. While you were so absorbed in your mission, it was *you* who did not see me in the bigger picture."

Baus stirred. "So you spied Cedrek, before I did?"

"Aye, the loon was practically breaking down Griselda's door when I elected to make my exit. She was rough on him, I take it? What a lark." The burly mariner squeezed out a laugh. "That was a mean trick to play—but I suppose the lout deserved it. I expect your crude chicaneries are for some higher purpose." He shook his head with perplexity. "Anyway a prankster's sport is a fool's undoing. No wonder you're in this fix with Zoren. I have a mind to let you sink on your own merit."

Baus gave an apathetic grunt. "You are harsh, Valere. Peculiar how doings work out, eh? —we never shall quite understand the caprice of the universe."

"Maybe not." Valere's squint revealed much, bristling across the sunburst swells. The waves were mounting; the whitecaps were brewing and only golden shimmers met the arching sky.

"We must take care of ourselves," warned Valere, "—we must watch our backs and our tongues. Zoren is a sly fellow; you can never really know what is going on in his mind, and it's a nasty one, with his troupe of mangy curs. Listen, they are as cold-hearted a bunch as you'll ever cross this side of the Poesasian! Listen, have your wits about you; don't go letting your guard down!—no one's perfect, but at least discard these temptations of yours with that devilish little magic stick. The Dakkaw and the Heagram guards are small fry compared to these felons. They'll not think twice to chop off your arm or a few fingernails and toss you into the deeps."

Baus managed an unconvincing smile. Valere looked at him with scepticism and lowered his voice. "Well, let's speak of other matters. What's this rumour about a treasure you're hiding?"

Baus swivelled his frame about. "Zoren's delusional. A couple of nights ago I was scrambling off for Nosoheath. What of it? I came upon two of the traitors he's been babbling about. They were hauling hide west with a chest full of riches deep into the woods. Feverish men—desperate men—who knew they were about to die and they dropped some of their coins. So what? I managed to scoop up a few and continue on my way toward Nosoheath. Zoren, the suspicious lout, thinks I know where his whole chest is. Valere, I ask you—what would I want getting mixed up with this bunch of thugs?"

Valere gave his head a plaintive shake. "You tell me? It seems kind of incredible."

"Zoren and his lackeys are buffoons; they caught up with me at the *Whistling Maiden.* Unlucky for me that the rogues saw me spending a couple of their fool coins on wine and women. Dotard! He thinks I know where the traitors made off before his men took swords to them—all on account of a bit of money I was spending."

Valere looked hard at Baus. "A foolish gambit. And do you?"

Baus gave a mournful sigh. "The dead men could have hidden it anywhere. There are miles of scrub there."

Valere seemed to accept the information. "True." He puffed at his pipe wistfully. "Zoren's a good ally, Baus, but a bad enemy. I advise you not to lie to him." He rose to his knees, looked about with wariness. "I wouldn't give him any reason to believe you're involved with this imbroglio or have him think you crossed them with your double-tonguing."

"No worry of that!" declared Baus confidently.

"It is for this reason that I do."

* * *

An hour later, the wax-moustached Magretir jumped to the bow-side to order Baus up to Zoren's cabin. Baus threw down his rag and brush and walked with fascination alongside the proud buccaneer who, in his immaculate garb, swung lithely across the deck. He wore a knotted scarf, black knee-high boots and an embroidered waistcoat and a green and red tricorn hat with parrot feather in it. He was going to fetch weapons—staves, poleaxes, halberds and mauls, all wicked looking—and even a few, twenty seven-inch blades of tempered steel when he paused to squint dubiously at a particularly blood-caked item. He brought a host of killing instruments from the fore-cabin and Baus, scrutinizing the mariner, saw a cunning gleam barely masked in his cobalt-blue eyes.

Baus could not guess what the impulsiveness of the occasion was; Valere had long ago vacated the scene, leaving the outlaw to his schemes, and was not at liberty to shed illumination. Meanwhile the black ship sliced through the whitecaps torn by ragged gusts of wind. A twain of small crags lay to the north. Danop cawed down to the mariners to steer clear of the obstacles. Where there were unknown islands, inevitably existed treacherous shoals. Nearby impedances like this could grind the bowels of a fast-running ship such as the *Last Laugh.*

Zoren lifted his spyglass. He peered eastward for a long time. Setting his jaw in a tight knit he curled lips into a sanguine smile. Another efficient and economic signal—Magretir relieved the rest of the deck-swabbers of their tasks and all were summoned for weapons' practice—Jama, Poli, Baus and Valere and a half dozen other pirates. They were brought forward onto the maindeck and under the lengthening shadows, Zoren came to address them, eyes filled with critical distaste.

"Listen up, mother hens!" he called out. One leg was slung on a cask, his black cap had blown to the side and his long grey hair flapped wildly in the wind. Aside were stacked a heap of Magretir's weapons.

"Not true members of my band are you—until you exhibit certain prowess. Fuurdhal, Juuliq and Magretir are my most gifted fighters; they are about to teach you some important lessons. Hand-to-hand combat. Fuurdhal, master of the staff, is benignity impersonated; Juuliq, a knife virtuoso, enjoys quaint dialogue. Magretir, on the left, is wizard of the sword and knows no scruples. These veterans will teach you manners and precision—also humility, that you might become better men." The grey pirate bowed his head, showing a magnanimous grin. The disconsolate crew listened sullenly, fighting to hear Zoren's words over the wind and the rippling sails. "My friend, Magretir of the mass of oiled curls, shall acquaint you with the grimmer techniques of the Sulki, that rare lineage of swordsmen far west of Owlen in the forests of Drasla. Oresno shall be your overseer, Bargil the amender, who shall from time to time pass polite corrections. Is this clear? Each will offer his own unique wisdom on the subject. Be mindful of their tricks! These rogues are fiercely unpredictable! I give my counsel freely."

Zoren left the words hanging before he climbed up the mainmast to view the spectacle.

Juuliq clopped forward with his bald pate glistening. A head lower than Baus, he smiled brightly like a cherub. "The weapons," he pointed out cordially, "are stacked by the mead cask. Take one and attack me."

Poli frowned. Running eyes over the ragged assortment of weapons, he jerked a thumb dubiously at the weapon stash. Cutlasses, small round willow-board shields, daggers, swords, knives, poleaxes abounded—even a few halberds loitering in the skewed mess.

Poli cast a perplexed look at the shorter, stouter man and shrugged with curiosity. "You wish us to attack you all at once?"

"That is what I said," replied the knife master casually. The pirate inspected his younger adversary with kindly tolerance. "Is there something wrong, Polly? A situation posing too much of a handicap for you?" The disarming gleam showed red in his eye.

"Well, I don't condone mindless slaughter—but, if you insist."

Bright guffaws gusted from the other pirates.

"What's so funny?" barked Poli.

"What weapon are you to use?" demanded Baus, who seemed no less puzzled by the distinct advantage. Perhaps he was a little wiser in his scepticism than his blond crony, Poli.

"For the nonce, none," murmured Juuliq cheerily.

Poli laughed, wagging his hand with confidence. "Very well, 'knife virtuoso', if that's what you call yourself. If you truly wish to stick to absolute imperishability, then why argue?" He ignored the small bossed shields and snatched up a long metal poleaxe, gleaming somewhat desultorily with blood-gobbed dollop at its tip. Ever eager, the bully capered forward without plan or program. Juuliq stood his ground, hands strung implacably across his chest. Poli aimed a strike in a hissing loop. The blow would have lopped off a major limb if Juuliq's statuesque form had been any less solid.

The pirate jigged sideways; the axe raked through clean air. For a clear instant, Poli's right side was left exposed. Juuliq skipped forward in a deliberate attack to deliver an urgent knee tap under the youth's armpit. Poli staggered like a drunken doll and ploughed nose first to the planks. He was forced to release his weapon, while squawking in irking fashion and Juuliq tightly pinned his shoulders to the ground and held him there sprawled in a painful neck hold, to the amusement of his peers. The younger bully very ignominiously resented the humiliation.

Jama, sensing a beneficial cue, charged the swashbuckler Magretir with a halberd. But the pirate easily cut left this unscripted attack and slapped the axe-blade away with the back of his broadsword.

Jama was stunned that a man could move that quickly. He stood with his grin fading. Magretir's weapon had materialized from nowhere—magic was in the air!

The swashbuckler hawked within hitting distance of Jama. Jama knew he was beaten and folded his palms in defeat. The tall buccaneer feigned an accepting nod. Jama fell for the ploy. The pirate kicked him down to his knees. Baus was bewildered by the sudden fury of the attacks and stood frozen. Fuurdhal drew a quarterstaff. Baus snatched at the first weapon he could find: a short light stick of beobar.

It was a wise decision—anything else would have had him brained.

Fuurdhal smashed down on Baus's tough whittled pole, forcing the weapon to jiggle out of his grasp. The horrible stinging surged up Baus's arms and he almost gasped. The weapon crashed to the deck. Oresno charged him from the side. The assault brought him plunging to the planks, knocking every bit of wind out of his lungs.

The trainees were pinned down helplessly in various demeaning poses. They were picked up and tossed like scarecrows onto a sorry pile.

"You retarded oafs!" called out Oresno in contemptuous manner. He landed Baus a cruel kick in the abdomen, roaring, "First lesson in combat—there is no such thing as chivalry. It is every man for himself! A tussle is a tussle. A brawl is a brawl. Any unfair fray is one that you walk away from alive. Ignoring a defensive weapon is a stupid attitude. You all chose weapons of offence, but ignored the shields and plates, which could have easily saved your hides from a beating. To underestimate your opponent, is to court death. Beguiled by your opponent, is a *call for* death. To underestimate your opponent's cunning, is to *scream* for death. These rules are simple."

The overseers did not wait for the words to sink in. Fuurdhal lifted Poli up by the scruff of his neck and hauled him into the circle of combat. "Up now, you sullen-tongued cockerel! Attack me. No, not you, long hair—just you two!"

Baus backed away. He could not see the result of this clash for Magretir and Juuliq had jerked him to his feet and were goading him to attack them.

Baus gulped air back into his pinched lungs. He made a clumsy advance for Magretir. Without knowing what next to implement, he fumbled. The pliancy cost him precious moments and he was met with a concerted attack. He was felled again like a rotted oak and lay on the deck half gasping, hardly believing that two fighters were piling on top of him, jabbing fists and elbows into his ribs, thighs and several sensitive places.

Throbbing bruises plied Baus's limbs and everywhere he stung with aches. Somewhere his mentors lifted themselves clear of his squashed body and he heard Oresno's voice cooing in his ear. "When you are given an order, pip, obey! On your feet, Baus the Bold! What a lackwit! Baus the *Bumpkin*, is more like it!"

Baus lay dazed there and Magretir and Juuliq had to yank him up and shake him as a hound would a rabbit in its teeth.

With odd detachment, Baus felt himself thinking that life could be worse. He saw out of the corner of his eye Poli, then Jama rounding on Fuurdhal. The grinning giant cast them woodpeckers' glares before reaching down with brawny fists to dash their skulls together. Baus was sawtoothed by a double-elbowed rush from Oresno. He scrambled aside just in time to deflect the bunting assault but was not deft enough to dodge Juuliq's swinging leg that felled him on his hindquarters. Baus lay there groaning, fighting for air.

He felt the return of pain shooting up his spine. The fight was over. It was horribly skewed, deliberately staged. Oresno had promised it . . . Bruised and beaten, Baus grit his teeth, bit down his frustration.

Watching the fight from the bow, Bargil and Calley, wandered closer to nearly double over in laughter. Valere was not as mirthful; he watched from afar the skirmish with eyes of keen disfavour. "Not to worry," Zoren shouted down at him from half way up the mizzen. "It's only to toughen up our lilies a bit. We can't have them dashing about like dachshunds in battle. We need good men! Hard-nosed ruffians with iron hides! Not pousties." He clambered higher for a better view.

Baus came to his senses. He overheard Oresno's derisive taunt and scrambled aside, "Lesson two! Inexperienced fighters are rewarded pangs of pain, only if they are left standing —or crawling, that is."

Baus struggled to his feet. His calves ached; his arms shook. He had a strong urge to retch. He was not able to hold back his insides and from the depths of his gullet came a dozen colours of discharge on the recently-scrubbed planks.

The pirates howled in uproar—Calley went ape and jocularly went to fetch a bucket and mop. He danced around like a milkmaid offering his wares. Baus hated the mocking laughter ringing in his ears, but he could do nothing about it, especially Oresno's taunts, for he knew the devilish rogue was enjoying his cat and mouse game. It felt good to relieve himself of the midday slops at least—but it was a poor side effect, degrading and without argument. *Payback for the humiliation dealt out at the Whistling Maiden*, Baus thought. The jocularity came at a cheap price; he forced himself to maintain his equipoise. He humped it over to where his miserable, rat-eyed comrades Poli and Jama huddled disconsolately. They gave him a slow, dazed look but Baus paid them no heed and shook them to attention. "Listen, you lubbers! We can't be mauled by these brutes and expect any respect from them. They think we're a bunch of milksops—but it's not true! Let us beat them at their own game. Start with the overweening pip Oresno!" Even before Baus had framed the idea, the two trainees were scrambling to their feet, eager to execute some of Baus's plan. They tackled Oresno and beat him down to the deck with the rain of their fists.

Baus joined in with ruthless zeal. "Lesson three!" he croaked in Oresno's ear. "Sack the leader and you're likely to create a terror in the ranks. From *Baus the Bold*." The triumph in Baus's eye unnerved the pirate and he fought to deflect the fists plying down on his seaman's hide. The free-for-all beating felt insanely invigorating, and Baus felt the necessary relief to revel in more last-minute revenge.

Fuurdhal and Magretir jumped in to haul off the attackers. Their faces gleamed with surprise; they examined the offenders with merriment. Oresno lay on his back groaning; he held his heaving gut with chagrin. Since he was a bully, the cutthroat shook the mist out of his eyes and wrenched himself upright to face the recruits with a mask of pure hatred. He snatched a saw-edged cleaver and lurched over to where the three stood complacently grinning. He would not have spared an inch of their flesh had not Valere scrambled to the maindeck and snatched up a sword. He caught Oresno's cleaver in the down thrust just nearly mutilating Baus's shoulder.

Zoren croaked out a stabbing cry. "Stand down, Oresno!"

Oresno chose not to listen. He backpedalled, rained another merciless blow down at Baus's throat. Baus watched amazed as the blade was caught again on Valere's sword.

"Oresno, damn you!" shouted Zoren. He was furious now. He jumped down from the mizzenmast and hurled his full weight across the deck. He looked a daunting sight, rapier slashing and veins pumping out on his forehead. He locked weapons with Oresno and the two villains stood eye to eye glaring.

"It was simple collusion, Zoren," sneered Oresno. "The rogues'll pay for it shamefully!"

"The move was fair enough!" Zoren growled. "If you kill any one of my pups, I'll carve out your gizzard. Do you hear me?"

Oresno bared his teeth. "That's a cock-eyed attitude, Zoren." He pushed away from his captain and pointed his ugly weapon at Valere. "This scum of a redbeard deserves exactly no less punishment—just like the rest of his mollycoddled rabble. Trying to gang up on me— it's worth a keelhauling."

"That's what they're supposed to do!" roared Zoren. "Fight dirty. Is it not the whole lesson of the exercise? Or are we on different sides?"

Baus, whose arms were pinned in Fuurdhal's grip, pointed out a much more cogent disparity: "Ta, ta, Oresno! Perhaps the next lesson will become a more relevant disclosure for your fragile sensibilities."

The taunt was unwise. Oresno whirled on Baus vindictively. Cleaver whirling, the pirate reined in for the kill. Fuurdhal hastily pulled Baus out of the way before Lolispar's blade caught the strike. Zoren intervened, crying out in savage glee, "That's it! Now you've got it, you rogues! An eye for an eye! An ear for an ear." His grey-gold eyes blazed on Baus with admiration. You're finally getting the gist of this! Fight! Kill! Maim! Destroy! Goad your enemy. Drive his heart down to his belly, spur and hack what's left to ribbons! The true path of the pirate. By Drake's teeth, only death and no mercy."

Fuurdhal released Baus. He flung himself away and stalked off toward the weapons' pile to seize up an axe. He hefted it high. The haft was notched, browned the length of his forearm with old blood. Baus liked not being a pawn in this circus or made fun of and a fire burned in his heart. The lust for battle boiled in his chest like molten lead. Fuurdhal saw the dark passion mirrored there and acknowledged the shock of adrenalin. "A spunky attitude, sir swain; but watch where your fire burns and what it catches."

"I'll watch what I want!" Baus spat.

Poli and Jama cheered. They scrambled over to the cask like badgers and snatched up weapons of their choice.

Zoren smiled grimly at the zeal of his new dogs and looked on with pleasure at the spirit being incited. He remained wholly unconvinced of Oresno's half-muttered promise not to despatch the lot and he discharged him on the spot, replacing him with Bargil.

Oresno saw red ruin. Being released from duty was an insult, but he had no say. He received only some satisfaction in watching Bargil take up the goading with a similar violence to his own. Zoren seemed worried for the most part of this heavy-handed dealing and appointed Valere to act as 'arbitrator'. Happily, Valere's added protection allowed the three to survive that day.

VII

Baus did not know how many hours dragged by into the early evening, but under the remorseless sun and the bitter, howling winds sweeping the deck, he knew chagrin. The fighting, lunging, panting and cursing continued and he knew himself to be a pincushion of cuts, welts, aches, and eyes swollen half shut and with a nose half flattened and blood-caked. His ribs felt like pith; one was perhaps cracked, for it seemed to hurt just to breathe. Jama was no exception; he was invested with the only advantage of having a swarthy complexion, hiding the rude mass of bruises and contusions. Poli, who endured the worst of all, became known as, '*Polly the Imperishable*'. From this afternoon on the pirates looked on him as more than a juvenile bully boy.

Valere received his rough share of handlings too, even acting in his limited capacity as 'advisor', but as a veteran fighter he was able to curtail the majority of batterings upon his fellows. Perhaps his wards would have been mauled to greater extent had he not interfered in their favour.

Early evening saw the sky splashed with a plush pink. Glowering wetly was a haloed crescent moon on the horizon. Everywhere the sea remained a viscous red. Before the first stars flicked on, the winds had died and the ship's progress became a snail's gait. The few buccaneers who still ranged the foredeck stood drawing rum pottles to their lips; but no lantern winked in that sombre light nor any banner flew from the mainmast.

Below-ships, the mates sang chanteys into the evening. They were helped along by dirty flagons and gritty mead and warm beer. Rude slogans and cheers waxed loud. On a stone slab the iron brazier burned with a vengeance, warming a pot of thick stew and mulling mead. The crude chimney siphoned the smoke up the hole onto the deck; back and forth the men rocked, draping arms about one another like boyhood mates, gibing out tuneless rhymes:

"We are rascals of Zoren's crew!
This is our life, this is what we do!
We steal, we burn, murder and pillage,
Casting terror into every village,
We wreak wrath and mayhem,
On friend and foe alike,
Yo, ho, ho, a bottle of rum!
Under the sun, we partake of fun!
Under the moon, we sing our tunes,
What is it like, a pirate to be?
To sail off and beyond the sea!"

Such refrains buoyed the rogues' spirits. The men threw dice and coloured chips over a low wicklewood table. They fought over the spoils and many were content on accusing the other of cheating. Baus noted the 'games' seemed more baiting than playing. Insults and jokes became parodies as the hours rolled by and challenges were flung and fists were hurled. At one time Magretir became irked and threw down the cocksure braggadocio exuding from Oresno's lips. He lifted blade to tickle the other's cheek in challenge.

The defender bared his sword, struck up an aggrandizing strut. In seconds a strapping duel was in play. Silver sparked against iron; the two rivals danced about like a bunch of drunken dancers to the claps, jeers and hoots of their crew members.

Zoren allowed the sport, enjoining each to keep the other sharp, but he put a stop to the fanfaronade when friendly rivalry turned into something of a gore-carving. "Arrest your maulings, you stupid dogs. Magretir, you know better than that. Mind your demeanours while we sup!"

Magretir grunted rankly and sat down at the table.

Inspired by the conflict, Jispir and Juuliq flung themselves into a sultry wrestling match which Jispir predictably lost. Danop was pitted next against the brawny Exig who received the brunt of the mistreatment. Exig reviled Danop's repeated flagrantly-unfair tactics, but was silenced by slaps and jeers. Baus could not help but guffaw, but not when he was forced to wrestle Jama. The swarthy mariner toppled him and the outlaw was forced to stomach his loss with unceremonious defeat. Poli was pitted next against Valere who not only got the better of the lad and had the youth on his face with one arm twisted cruelly behind his back, but indulged in a little toe-tap. The pirates laughed and watched the sport with high spirits while eyes watered and mouths continued to swill more fetid ale until it seemed that the very air was a brewery. The hold became a hot tub of distillery fumes and Baus marvelled at the capacity of Zoren's cutthroats to hold their liquor . . .

An odd regrettable incident occurred when a drunken sailor ejected his mutton, prompting Zoren to force the man to clean up his miasma. Like all hardy sots, boozers as these just kept on guzzling ale, mug after mug . . .

The moon was sinking. Poli, thoroughly sotted and sore, staggered off to a cramped cubbyhole beneath the foredeck. He was kicked for his leave-taking and rolled back to the 'common room' like a swine should amongst his peers. The newcomers were all considered fledglings and un-blooded in battle, so were not allowed favours. With the exception of Valere such was the rule—it had the newlings sleeping in the straw cubbyholes in the refectory. Poli finally began to foam at the mouth and moan from his numerous aches and pains and overzealous drinking but the seasickness sat like lead weight in his gut.

Baus too, had tumbled into a vile dream. A sloshing stomach-full of apple mead now sloshed in his gut and urged him on to penitence with the heaving of the hull over the not so insignificant swells.

* * *

The next morning Baus was stirred awake by an irksome stench in his nostrils. The miasma turned out to be Exig's dank breath intruding in his face. Jispir's bearded face also jutted close to his own, crowding his comfort zone. Exig, lanky, skew-eyed and bow-legged, wore a pair of rank red dungarees low on his hips. He favoured a black bandanna strung tightly across his temple. An open vest showed a tanned chest thick with a mat of greying hair. Jispir was moon-faced and sullen and held an elderly stoop while chewing on a red root which made his teeth look like muddy stumps when he uttered a laconic laugh.

The crewmen boxed Baus's ears and delighted in ordering him up on deck. "The day's a wasting, lambchop! Quick, now! Be on your toes!"

Baus swayed to his feet, plummeting light-headed into a soft swoon. A yielding body cushioned his fall—Poli's. The seaman's sides were soft and ale-full and served well to shield him from a contusion. Meanwhile his own back ached from the harsh treatments of yesterday and was he assuaged little by lying on hard-planks all night.

Jispir hollered at him and gave him another boot. Baus could not focus. His nose was flat-pressed and had gotten used to the fetid smell of the oily bilge: vomit, rum, sweet mead, various other scums ranked heavily from the nearby casks. Perhaps the urine of mice and nighttime rats had also entered into Baus's memory.

He lifted his weight gingerly onto a cask. His head felt ready to swim in a sea of sighs. Exig carefully kicked the barrel away. Baus's sensitive brain went a-tumble into shock. "Now, lubbar! Did you not hear me?" cried Exig. "The Captain desires you on deck. Not cat-lounging on a cask. Up! All of you filthy mutts!"

Baus, Poli, and Jama were forced up the rickety ladder into the sun-dappled deck. The pirates guffawed, catcalling when they came up and goaded the newbies up through the hatch into the watery daylight with purpose and delight.

The harsh glare turned Baus's swollen eyes to wax. The full force of the disarming light and the west wind were enough to have him swooning.

The *Last Laugh* bent a powerful course east. The open sea was never more troubled— never more devoid of human life. The black sails bellied like great scallops; they rattled like cleats at their slightly-frayed cuffs. The sea was a mass of blue glass, over which a carpet of sunflower glimmers rode. The eastern sky shimmered a frightful yellow between pocks of grey where cloud dotted the horizon. They would make good time today, announced Zoren. Baus could see the captain wearing Ridgar's Eye ostentatiously in the form of a gaudy amulet hung round his neck. The sight did not please the crew.

Baus and his companions were spared another cruel term of deck-swabbing. Today they were shown methods of how to maintain the rigging, check the davits and splice the ropes and oil the winch.

It was midmorning and Danop sighted another vessel, a small ketch which was a half league to the west. The craft was the *Sea Hare*—a fast runner bounding away after sighting the pirate vessel looming to port. Needless to say, her crew had embarked on a lengthy course of outmanoeuvring her stalker. Zoren's men scoffed at the tactic and boarded her and ransacked her goods without mercy.

The sailors found only dissatisfaction. A single lamp, a few wicks, some paltry jars of wine and three tawdry bolts of wool. Of the four crew members all were dead except one; the one taken prisoner was a flint-faced, tousle-haired dandy who called himself 'Ifetin'. The captive pleaded for his life and Zoren kept him alive just for the pure amusement of it. When the prisoner saw that the egg timer of his life was fast draining, he divulged a singular secret —which harboured intriguing possibilities for the buccaneers who seemed intent on squeezing the yarn out him. The cringing captive knew of a keep, three and a half leagues up the river Rhuon near the iron-mine of Sliss. A blacksmith's apprentice had told him about it: that an old ship master had kept his loot hidden in the castle's crypts. Apparently, it would be easy to infiltrate such a stronghold. The fortress was manned laxly and when the watchmen were softened with ale, it proved a perfect time to acquire old Kigsten's wealth.

"Is that so?" snapped Zoren sourly. "Well, what's to stop us from voyaging to this castle ourselves, seizing the treasure and ridding ourselves of a snivelling toad of a homunculus?"

"You'll need me!" Ifetin protested. "I can inform you where the guards are stationed. To navigate the cellars is a risky endeavour, lord."

"*Lord*, is it now?" chuckled Zoren softly. "What kind of a treasure are we talking about here, Ifetease?"

"Gold and silver," Ifetin clucked. "Three brass-bound trunks of it each, with at least five hundred coins. The coins, your Excellency, are—"

"Five hundred coins?" Zoren interrupted. He brandished his rapier and stalked forward. "A sizeable treasure for a mere ship master."

"Yes it is, my lord," fretted Ifetin nervously. "Kigsten hasn't always been a shipmaster. He cheated Prince Arnin of his taxes and robbed whoever he could—ploughmen, wayfarers, merchants, you name it. He entertained no distinction. For this reason, the crooked lord amassed considerable wealth."

Zoren screwed his face into a pumpkiny smile. "Something I can relate to. But how would you know all of this? Why haven't you taken the loot yourself, instead of hobnobbing here on this shabby ship?"

The captive explained in a hurry: "My nephew, Tinsi, worked on Kigsten's staff three years ago. We agreed to make it a joint effort. One day he came to me suggesting that the both of us attempt a heist, sneak into Gestilwil, secure the treasure and divide the loot. I was still waiting for the lad's return. For such information, I'm asking only my life."

Zoren fingered his weapon. A scowl crept over his face. He looked ready to run the seaman through and Baus felt sorry for the wretch, aside from a dislike for his crass, feeblish mumblings.

"It's amazing the stories," guffawed Fuurdhal, "that a man threatened with his life can fabricate."

Zoren grunted in accord. "The situation is not uncommon, Fuurdhal." He conferred with Oresno for a while, then the blackguard reminded him of their upcoming engagement at sea. Doubtless such a hostage would allow some leverage amongst the peers. Weighing such counsel, Zoren finally allowed the wretch to live, ordering the others to tie him down in the hold.

* * *

Training resumed at midday and Baus could see his cronies bending to the rigours of the situation, perhaps more discriminately in their deployments of offence over defence. The recruits did, in fact, protect their flanks with more decorum and half way through the battle, they were outfitted with heavy leather chest pads and shank guards. Today would be real weapons' training, they were told. Fuurdhal, Magretir and Juuliq offered their unique advice —parry with backward stance, balance like the crane, lunge like a lion, browbeat your opponent with prejudice, feint him like the wind with nothing less to lose than the cunning of a white wolf, dodging the jackdaw who pecks the snake . . .

Baus was disbarred use of Lolispar. "Use real weapons," advised Juuliq. For the first time, Baus fended off two attackers at once—Bargil and Deneo who were startled and caught off guard. With a real halberd and cutlass in his hand, Baus even staved off Magretir's attack for a half minute and Juuliq watched on with surprise as he clucked softly when Jama and Poli were forced to engage each other with knives.

The training continued . . .

* * *

The slugs, slashes, parries and thrusts were awful to witness; the battering that resulted in bruises and welts was not to be spoken of lightly. At the end of the day, the companions shared not the end-game bloody spurts that would normally have killed off lesser men. Protective leather outergear had been worn.

The afternoon was dying. Zoren retired to his sterncabin, consulting certain key mariners and his charts, a period during which trouble festered amongst the crew . . .

Incited by gasps and heaving men, Onde and a couple of rascals had snuck below decks to harass the prisoner. Jealous that they were not participating in the newlings' 'training', they had decided to have their sport with the captive. They tied him to the foremast extending below and used the victim as a pincushion for target practice. A spray of daggers quivered mere inches from his mousy locks. Pleadings were useless; the prisoner struggled against his ropes with such an abandon that one of the knives actually sheared off the bottom of his ear.

Ifetin's anguished cry alerted the captain. Zoren came racing down the stairs and discovered the deplorable state of his prisoner and dragged Onde across the mouse-turded planks and half way to the bow and near throttled him to death. The other delinquents, Jispir and Exig, were kicked in the teeth and sent reeling to clean the bilges. "You stupid, insubordinate dung mites! Any more of this sordid trickery and I'll have you all walking the plank!"

In the protracted period of hush, Baus finally learned from whispered snatches that the pirates were on a course for Dwiterin, otherwise known as 'Devil's Isle'. The rogues were to congregate with certain kindred marauders: Borath the Butcher, Urseth the Ugly, and their entourage, both ringleaders of fear and rapine, forbidding pirate chiefs in their own right.

Borath, Urseth and Zoren comprised the 'Buccaneer Triangle'. It was called this for right reasons—easily they were the Poesasian's most feared criminality prowling the seas. The portent of such a tryst remained shrouded in gloom. Even Zoren seemed slightly on edge.

The pirates drew closer to the island. A sea chest of jewels was missing and comprised no insignificant cause for alarm. Though his men showed nothing of the anxiety of their master, they spoke in whispers and muted praises of his exploits and his place amongst the leaders at Dwiterin isle. A general cheer rang out in his favour.

Baus learned that Urseth was a veteran of sea piracy, a very old and wise leader, as sea chieftains go. Valere guffawed when he heard Baus's story and claimed: "These old sea dogs will say anything for an audience. They'll end their bloody days in a heap of bloody flesh. One must perish or the other in the attempt to vanquish his enemy."

"So, what are you doing here then?" demanded Baus.

"To save your skin," Valere growled. "You delivered me from Heagram and ultimately the Dakkaw, so I merely am returning the favour. I saw you in Zoren's clutches in Nosoheath and knew that you were a dead man before a jester could chirp his quip."

Baus quieted his tone. "I'm flattered at the gesture, Valere, but I'm not a milksop; I can take care of myself."

"Let's hope so," scoffed the seaman. His age-lined visage was creased a shade of worry. His newly reddening beard rippled in the wind in a way that Baus thought was peculiar. "Between you and me, Baus, I'm sure you can. You are a capable trickster, anybody can see —more capable than the pack of louts I've come into contact with in my day. Perhaps you'll even succeed in this insane scheme of yours, with this cursed ganglestick, but there's a chance that—"

"A price is to be paid?" injected Baus.

"Something like that."

* * *

By mid afternoon of the next day, Danop sighted a lone albatross. Another bird was spotted, and finally the crow's nest master yelled down that land was in sight. A half hour passed and the first rocks of Dwiterin appeared—jagged rusty stumps rising up out of a backwash of foam. Danop warned the helmsman to veer sharply to starboard to avoid the devil's teeth.

The ship veered, creaking on a list in the side-slamming waves. Baus peered vertiginously over the railing; he saw a flash of white foam piling up on sides of the rocks. Gurgling hisses and whirlpools met his eyes. Puzzled, he gazed further afield, saw the brownish-green waves. The surging swells were more than dark menace hidden beneath—jagged boulders and doom-riders of outcrops.

Jispir and Onde trimmed the sheets. The macabre underwater crags gave way: the craft shuddered and groaned to heavy seas and wind, cantering its way to gentler tacks in calmer waters. Baus marvelled at the unbridled lust of the *Last Laugh*. The pirates had chosen their craft well. This place, too, deliberately remote, was specially secluded because of the very danger of rocks presented to intruders. The narrow channels were treacherous to explore without incurring tragedy. Only careful and experienced seamen could navigate the islands with a ship of this size.

Danop whooped. Peering mistrustfully down into the waves, Baus spied two rocky hulks rising dimly out of the chop. The foremost was a slick finger of volcanic rock; the other, a featureless slab on which flocks of gulls perched. Behind and farther south, loomed a large domelike shape—a green and broad island rearing up out of the sea. One face was plied rich with plush woodland, the other fronted by a tract of sandy, shimmering beach.

Dwiterin came to sight: a long sickle-shaped land mass bending outward, like a bow, watching the sun's early rising.

The ship circumnavigated the southern edge of the rock, ploughing through the swells like a knife between the two standing pillars. Flocks of tamegendron and thrush came down to wheel and chatter. The mountains grew; the ship passed away from the treacherous false channels and outlying rocks. The barque came abreast of the island's enchanting southern quarter and lush forest loomed up from pale seashore, edging into the water. About two leagues away a narrow headland gave way to a tongue of rose-grey granite upon which coral-coloured waves beat their froth.

The ship passed along the shoreline. They sheltered in a calm bay. Zoren ordered the sails furled. Baus caught a glimpse of two other great barques no less gaudily attired with similar skulls and regalia. Anchored side by side, the first vessel proved a square and fore-and aft-rigged, sporting a thick mainmast of blood-red adorned with myriad wegmor skulls. Rows of antlers were hammered onto her gunwales. On its prow, a ghastly effigy was carved: a bearded merman grasping an iron ball which he was about to hurl out to sea. The bow strakes were plated with metal and littered with a hundred bronze morningstars, ideal for ramming ships. The other ship rose high out of the water and was plastered with a green gummy substance, enough to drown a drake. A pale green banner drooped from her mainmast, an indelible insignia, hidden due to lack of wind in the lee. The prow consisted of a huge carven devil with long slender white wegmor horns, caked with the same mysterious green slime which Baus was later to learn was maulwood gum, protecting the wood from salt spray and tendering her a more menacing look. Beyond the two ships a sickle-shaped beach lay basking in the late afternoon sun. Green maulwood dominated the foreshore. Baus could see a clearing cut into the woods where a crowd of milling men waved. Bowl-topped, flower-like trees bunched in ever thicker masses. A half dozen hauled a heavy longboat into the water, then ran pell-mell back into the forest to carry out another landing boat.

The beach shimmered; Zoren ordered the *Last Laugh*'s anchor dropped.

The men applauded wildly.

They had reached Dwiterin.

VIII

Zoren was first to arrive on shore; ten of his seamen were in tow, including Baus and Valere. Two gigantic warriors came striding out to greet them—men of importance. Others tagged at their heels. The latter remained deferential in tone to the two elders. The first was Borath, leader of the Pirate band *Losloriath* and captain of green-gummed *Windbane*. He stood straight-backed, black-haired and blue-bearded in his outlandish silver mail and greaves, yet sleekly handsome aside from a grim face and a set of bad teeth. Urseth, captain of the skull-bedizened *Sea Warlock*, had brown skin and was significantly older, also less prepossessing with his warted bulging right cheek and ragged eye-patch. Shaggy grey dreadlocks were pitched over a fearsome face and he was armed to the teeth with a wicked-looking sabre and two daggers that thrust out of his belt, quick to draw should the need arise. The man himself sported a rare mirth that showed as the moments passed. The older pirate stood barefoot, in a pair of nicked rust-coloured bagged-at-the-knee dungarees while Borath's chest plate was of real, light-weight silver in need of a good polishing. Several rings were missing from the breast-piece and his morion was dented on its shadowy side.

Urseth strode ceremoniously to embrace Zoren. He clutched him in a great badger hug. Borath and Zoren gave each other wary glances; barely a perfunctory nod passed between the two.

The longboats herded the last of Zoren's men ashore and the mariners joined their leaders in a procession up the beach. There must have been two-score buccaneers amongst those who laughed and joked. Baus, Poli and Jama felt awkward climbing up the hillock into the woods in such a grand company, and straggled behind on clumsy feet. Valere fell back a pace to offer the recruits some advice—"Make yourselves known, avoid exhibiting any 'overweening presence'."

The ragtag company cut through the greenwood and were now faced with a space of pleasant shade on either side. They reached an open glade; a shallow pit was mixed with red soil and white sand. A sizeable hearth had been dug, around which makeshift wooden tables were arranged. Baus saw a series of huts and thatched roofs peeking out from the shady tangle. Smouldering in the fire was a huge log and a circle of rounded, charred rocks. Down the path lurked the lagoon and Baus saw the day's final ruby rays ebbing in its mirror. The placid silhouettes of the three tall ships wavered in the gloaming; yet the calm bay appeared not so calm in their presence.

The fire was stoked up. A deer and a boar had been speared that afternoon, now, skinned and flayed, hung hooves up on sharpened stakes aside the fire, ready for roasting. By the time the hearth was roaring, the buccaneers began to assemble. The sun was sinking low and the three chiefs took their respective places by the fire in large wicker thrones crafted after the image of the royal seats of the kings of Owlen.

A gesture of mockery? Baus was wryly unsure.

The wind had died to an acrid puff; cool vapours crept out of the forest. The pirates were just settling into their easy banter when Zoren's prisoner was hauled forth. The hostage was dragged before the three 'kings' where four of Borath's men rolled a keg each over to the high tables. A half score of pirates sat with mugs in their hands, waiting for the judgement to begin.

Baus, Poli and Jama watched the ceremonies with wary unease. Soon they were commanded to sit closer and join the gathering. "Come closer, you batch of cringing knaves! What do you think we have, scabies?"

"It is good to see you back again, Zoren!" boomed Urseth fulsomely. He held out a strong hand and slapped the pirate's back. Borath sat stiffly to his side. "My mates and I have been away for a long while looting the fog coves of Kantmacle. Aye, and those credulous fools! They still believe that sea drakes appeared and were the cause of their split heads, and broken vessel. They think they stole their gold and glided off to Long Bight like sylphs of nightmare. Well, we secured a hoard of plunder, didn't we, Borath?"

"In yonder storehouse all manner of gold lies, silver, flaxhack, silk bundles, rare essences, casks of spirit and oil."

Urseth pointed a gnarled forefinger to the shadow of a barred hut some twenty paces off. "The Butcher arrived just yesterday. Many successes Borath boasts of, which, I believe, he is eager to relate."

Murmurs of approval arose from the gathering.

The silver-mailed pirate Borath spoke again. "Our forays to the south went very much to our liking. We shed much blood and our swords were wet with flesh; cleavers saw much play. The *Grandis* of Aurenham is still wondering what ravaged him."

Jests and crude murmurs rumbled out from the company.

Urseth harrumphed. "Borath is modest in his accounts. The rogue managed to secure rare rubies, and the emerald of the Arch-Grandis's own aunt. I see you have some new men amongst you, Zoren." He gestured to Poli and the other ragbeards, who sat staring waxily at the company's leaders.

"We do," confessed Zoren. "However—" his voice betrayed a sense of misgiving. "Good men who have survived their first bouts of initiation."

"Excellent! And what of the trove of the other Arch-Grandis? What is that pretender's name, Kellasion, or Kasaparion or some fool thing? The treasure is well hidden, I trust?"

Zoren hesitated, bit at his lip. Looking toward his mates for support, he found none. Urseth foisted a frown which had a twitching shiver disturbing the hazel of his one bulging eye.

"Speak!"

Zoren muttered curiously, "Two of the three chests have been buried, which I'm happy to announce. The third—" and here he broke off with unpleasant hesitation, wincing as expectation began to knit in Borath's sardonic visage "—It is missing."

"Missing! By Krakus's doom! What do you mean? Foppery, if not ineptitude!" He slapped Zoren soundly on the crown. He raked his cutlass hard on the polished maulwood arm of Zoren's chair. "We've worked months to secure the treasure. Explain, if you would!" His voice was struck with a foul warning; the tone fell like ice crags on all.

"Treachery, Chief," growled Zoren. "Kribby and Saul stole our loot while we were up celebrating at Cant's Cove. We were initiating young Guor's coming of age." Zoren's voice was low and furious. "The youth was unfortunate to have been killed the same evening in the skirmish when we caught up with the two ruffians. We retrieved the first chest thankfully, but the other was lost. We don't know where it got to. We figured Kribby and Saul buried it somewhere—at least before they died."

Urseth shivered. "And you stupid fools killed the louts before they told you everything?"

"Aye, we slew them—but they knew nothing about the treasure, other than what they told us. We tortured poor Saul until his broken body was a bloodless pulp and Kribby received no better handling. In the long run, the two appeared as surprised as we did, knowing that their second trunk was nowhere to be found, particularly not where they left it, plotting to bury it in some forsaken glade."

Magretir confirmed Zoren's story. "Zoren speaks cogently. Nowhere could the two have fled to displace the loot. There is one, however, who claims knowledge of this affair."

"Who is this one?" demanded Urseth, fingers itching at his sabre.

Zoren made a curt motion. Lame-faced, bared before the chiefs, Baus was fetched and plopped before the assembly. He lifted a hand in placid salute. The pirates remained mute and unsympathetic. With the fire snapping behind him, Baus felt like the proverbial lamb before the slaughter. Borath and Urseth inspected him with a rare malevolence. Borath even hunched forward and pulled at his teeth while Urseth picked at his cheek with a twig and spat out the remains at Baus's feet.

Feeling the press of hostile eyes, Baus did his best to look both cheerful and ingenuous. "Hail, sea people and denizens! What Magretir and Zoren have disclosed is in verity, but with the exception of some flippant suggestions about inside knowledge of a treasure I categorically disavow—"

"Shut it and cut the flower talk!" bawled Urseth abruptly. "Get to the point."

"Yes, weasel," grumbled Zoren. "We nabbed this glamour boy in Nosoheath," Zoren explained to Urseth "—in the *Whistling Maiden*, with a dozen gold pieces in his hands of Prince Arnin's coinage stamped with Rygard's mark."

Urseth became peculiarly moribund. "What a surprising coincidence." He jeered at Baus. "Well, who are you, coxcomb?—and what do you know of our treasure?" His face exhibited no beams of cordiality.

Baus licked his lips. Staring from one pirate to the other, he could only think they were all demons. "Well, being Baus the Bold, from Heagram—a small town up the coast—"

"I know where Heagram is!" barked Urseth. "Get to it!"

Baus cleared his throat. "Of course—well, being a wayfarer bound for Nosoheath, I discovered a pouch lying on a path in the woods. One of Zoren's colleagues seemed to have dropped it before fleeing with a curious chest bound in brass. As for the contents of the trunk, I cannot say for sure as I did not follow the twain who were swift as weasels in the dark and impolitely ignored my beseeches to halt. Naturally, I took the pouch, which turned out to contain gold, continued on to Nosoheath in the hopes of completing my pilgrimage. Zoren and his master impolitely seized me in the rude light of the *Whistling Maiden* and were very unmannerly in their handling of me, insisting that I accompany them on some dismal journey to this forsaken place you call 'Dwiterin'. Now here I am, abiding your service, and with greatest humility." He gave a courteous bow and settled himself in a seat beside Fuurdhal.

"What a pleasant story!" grunted Borath with disgust. "Now why should we believe it?"

"Because there's nothing else to believe?" suggested Baus.

"No!" jeered Borath. "Because there's a jackleg liar in every grifter I know hiding behind a bush! Now, if there's one thing I am familiar with is a villain—and you are everything closest." He tossed an ophidian look at Baus while examining him under hooded lids. "What say we don't spit you now? You could have dug up Zoren's scums' treasure for yourself. That'd be a dainty package, wouldn't it?"

"If I did, I'd have more coins on me then, wouldn't I?"

The logic brought sneers from the group and Urseth brought a heavy hand down on his throne arm. "Peace, jackals! Only a fool would be daft enough to carry that amount of stash —especially in a town like Nosoheath. You, my long-haired glibster, are as clever as a beaver—I believe Borath is right, and a bit closer to the truth than we think. You knew where those dogs buried the treasure—stashing it somewhere, and now you venture to hide the truth."

Zoren intervened, "Very possible, Urseth, which is why we are keeping tabs on this dabchick. The rascal shows signs of becoming a good fighter at least, which explains why we haven't tortured him to death since he may be a trickster. We could always 'initiate' him completely into our band. If what you say is true, then at least we'll have a finger on him and can squeeze him for information when the time comes. We'll return to Nosoheath as soon as we can."

"You had better, Zoren,!" boomed Urseth in desperate fury. "By the moon, I want the rest of that gold back in our hands before the winter storms. Drake's beards! Half a year's work!" He quaffed the rest of his mead, levelled Baus a rancorous glance. "You, my silver-tongued villain—shall be well guarded. Attend! We'd best broach another matter, lads, before our heads get too addled with ale. Thrice a year do we meet at Dwiterin to conduct business."

A black-kerchiefed bravo bawled happily from the back, "We plan our raids with precision!"

Borath clicked his tongue. "So what, Hasselbuf? This is common knowledge."

"Our final is due," declared Urseth huskily. "Now is as good a time to formulate a plan."

Zoren piped in: "Perhaps you will be gratified to hear some news from our quarter, Chief. We have secured a prisoner, a certain Ifetin of Sliss—captured from a cog bound on a southerly voyage to Maena's realm. His news may bring you comfort—at least minimally."

Urseth waved a tolerant hand. "Bring the swain closer."

Ifetin was hauled forth, struggling and frothing at the mouth; Zoren had to bash him several times to keep him quiet. The pirate explained the background behind the captive's existence and the gist of the celebrated 'news'. Baus pretended disinterest in the hopes of evading attention from himself.

Inspecting the prisoner, Borath projected an intimidating leer. "Well—" The blue-bearded knave leaned forward and cruelly stroked his cutlass. "Ifetin, you seem a bit nervous! Whatever for?" He caressed the wretch's neck with the sharp edge of his blade. "We are all friends here. Swallowed a lizard or two?—or had the unlucky fortune of crossing paths with our grey devil here?"

Ifetin nodded prodigiously. His formally pink face was now banded a seashell white. "I've told this 'grey devil' all I know, master Borath. Sir Kigsten, the shipwright, shall be away from home, up the Rhuon for a moon or more. He'll probably be a deal heavier of coin than when my cousin last reported."

"I thought he was your nephew?" Zoren blurted out coldly.

Ifetin stammered. "I mean—my nephew," he asserted. "Nerves are a little rattled, that's all." His voice harboured that harried quality to it which Zoren recognized immediately and was not fooled. The prisoner seemed worried at the possibility of being caught in a lie and was endeavouring to choose his words carefully. "As I alluded to earlier, Dinsi has connections, as you can rightly imagine."

"I thought he was Tinsi?"

"Land sakes, did I say Dinsi? I meant—"

"Details! We need details, you filthy lubber," growled Borath. "Times, numbers, distances."

The prisoner gulped. "I don't see the point of any particulars at this point—"

"Shut your gobbet! I'll decide what should be said and when."

Words seemed to have abandoned Ifetin's vocality; Borath the pirate sprang forth with cutlass gleaming.

"Give him a slug of rum!" piped up a red-nosed buccaneer from the back. "They always have more to tell then."

"What he needs, Jarrit, is a pike down the old throat," cried Mambert the Murderer.

"Bah! What a waste of excellent ale on a fructuous liar."

"Shut your mouths, you filthy cocks!" thundered Urseth fiercely. "Why would we wish to hear your dull roars when we can hear the pickings of this mutt's tale? Now let the dabchick speak!"

Ifetin seemed to have nothing more to say. A cutlass was jabbed near his throat, another carefully placed in the fire. Slowly the blade was heated up to a soft glow. Upon sight of the red blade the prisoner began blubbering out a yarn in a chaos of words—essentially repeating the exact things he had told Zoren and the others, outside of the fact that he had been heading south to see his son-in-law, Kirkste, to be married at Taven: a detail seemingly trivial and not worth mentioning.

For a time, Urseth listened to his pleadings, then rubbed his jaw with malicious scepticism. He stared off into the darkening trees. He seemed to be brooding upon the prisoner's words, with poor consequences. "I think," he intoned at last, "that you have been feeding us a tub of fibs, Ifetin, and we shouldn't have been wasting our time listening to your crapwagon of wishful thinking. Now, if you don't mind, we have other business to attend to —so nice knowing you. Deal with him, Zoren! Get him out of my sight!"

Jispir and Juuliq dragged the cringing captive off into the bushes where he was run through. There came only an oily squealing ending in a sharp howl, which was all the signs that Ifetin was no more.

The two pirates lumbered back to dispose of the body while Urseth called out to them in a jauntier voice: "A shallow grave for the fabulist! Seems the best news and the beginnings of a plan belong to me. Hugar! Ponce! Fetch me the boy!"

A hardened twain of Urseth's rogues disappeared into gloom and returned dragging a struggling, golden-haired, well-fed brat by the collar from a nearby shed. Propelled forward unceremoniously, the lad was not a day older than ten. He looked a youth of good upbringing, though perhaps of noble heritage. He was proud of carriage, disdainful of poise but clearly frightened. The blues of his eyes burned brightly, the cheeks were plump, the golden hair straight as larch needles. His fine woollen breeches were dirt-stained and his new doublet, slightly crumpled, had lost its original lustre.

"This here is Adrik," informed Urseth sardonically. "He's a perverse brat of an urchin if I've ever seen one." He flicked a leathery finger at the fox-faced youth. "His father was aboard the schooner *Ismalde*—with a message."

"What message?" inquired Zoren.

Urseth held up a hand. "Listen!" All eyes turned to the old chief and the boy stared sullenly.

"The *Sea Warlock* ground abreast of the *Ismalde* a week ago. 'Twas my judgement that we spot an opportunity and not put the lubberly piece of dung to fire. His father was a *Sir Dunkar* of some sort, some envoy to prince Arnin, but when we read his parchment, it was none other than an invitation to the ball from Queen Maena herself!"

"Maena? That seems impossible," cried Zoren.

"Aye, a parchment from Maena to Prince Arnin to attend her daughter Solstress's wedding. The idiot was trying to eat the paper before we yanked it from his mouth."

"Is this the truth? And who is the sultry Solstress to wed?" crowed Zoren incredulously.

"Clavius of Cleauch."

"Karsh's prince?" Zoren almost choked in amusement. "He's nothing but a powdered fop —some dandy. Fancy the robust little wench being taken by those wambly-pambly bones?"

"I can't," grunted Urseth. "And wouldn't want to."

Borath balled a fist. "So what does this have to do with us?"

Urseth's face creased with annoyance. "Borath, your lack of imagination sometimes causes me chagrin. You banter too much and cogitate too little. It has everything to do with us, fool! The invitation for the princess's marriage is scheduled the *17th of December*—at Sloe palace. Guests are to arrive within no less than two days of the wedding. That being true, and several weeks from now, gives us an opportunity. This means that we know the date, location and particulars when our good Prince will be sailing—and his general itinerary. The information is extremely valuable—remember—these are the same dung heaps who've never lifted a royal finger to do an honest day's work, and who persist in defaming us as the lawless hounds!"

"No doubt," added Zoren with unrestrained pride. "Prince Arnin will have an ample supply of expensive gifts on board to pass on to the royal family."

Borath made a soft chortle. "So—we ambush *him* before the precious ceremony—then what? We won't have his filthy ships tagging our behinds. Yes. He won't be expecting us to be out trolling for raids that far south and so close to the mainland." Borath paused, fingering his cutlass with shrewd intention. "So, how will we set the trap?"

"The details are to be ironed out," muttered Urseth quietly. "I keep the boy as guarantee that Sir Dunkar will uphold his part of the bargain and deliver the message as promised. I assured him that if the Prince is not near Sloe on the 15th of December, he will never see his wicked brat again."

The boy's cheeks swelled with tears. "You are a foul villain; my father will shave off your ears. You'll see!"

"He can try," laughed Urseth.

Adrik shrieked: "He'll come with a thousand soldiers. He'll cut off your ears, pickle your toes and feed your deranged hide to the squids!"

There were whoops of laughter. The men guffawed at the boy's tall imagination.

"Your spirit is to be admired, boy," approved Urseth soberly, "but—and here I emphasize —I rather much doubt that your father has that much clout."

The youngster grew unruly and began biting his captors. Adrik managed to wriggle free of Ponce's grip and heel-stomped Urseth on the foot and spat in his face and fled away through the ranks, dodging brawny arms, ducking under toes, and leaping dangerously close to the fire.

Urseth was livid with rage. "Get the little cock back here!" he cried, seething.

Adrik was half way through the assemblage before he was finally dragged back. Three of Borath's rogues lifted him in the air. Had the lad been a tad swifter he might have cleared the camp and escaped into the night. As it was though, the boy's useless scrapping was in vain. He hollered and scratched at the men's eyes but was finally brought back to where the three thrones ringed the fire and forced to look Urseth in the eye.

"You little weasel, you've got courage!" boomed Urseth. But he was not as angry as he seemed. "I respect courage in this den of rogues—where men are only judged on their deeds alone. But don't cross me again. If you value that little perfumed hide of yours, behave. Drakes and devils! I swear this mite has a streak of the killer in him. Under happier circumstances I'd train him myself, take him under my wing and mould into a killer. Put good steel in Arnin's gullet and his royal swine."

Gig, one of Urseth's ginger-haired bravos, cried: "Gadsen knows where the little tyke got it, after a look at his father."

Zoren pointed a finger, "Perhaps he's not Dinkar's own, but a bastard whelped on his mother."

"That's not true!" cried the boy.

Borath laughed. It seemed that aside from a healthy dislike of the brat, he could at least favour one of Zoren's jokes. "Well, only Krok knows. To the Twin Rocks of Hamshead we go! Three leagues offshore from Sloe and not a league more. *Two Silkie's Rock.* We can slumber in those rocks and await the dandies' coming."

"A plan as such entered into my own thinking," observed Urseth.

Onde blurted from the back: "What of the legend of Lestra and Baian? Those two mermaids haunt *Silkie's Rock* and do not like visitors."

"Aye, they cajole sailors to their doom," cried another.

Urseth gave a disparaging grunt. "Those are ghosts of legend. The phantoms are mere boys' banter—simpletons' fiction."

Guffaws endorsed the fact. Opal of Borath's crew cried out with a lewd overtone: "If we find maids on that scarhill, we'll surely have us a romp and roil and much more."

"Quell your remarks, mutt," whispered Urseth sternly. "It's evil to talk of spirits like that. Chaffing at the lore is known to irk the gods and feed the legends more power."

Zoren turned about to face his chief with sardonic wonder. "And I thought you said this legend was pure fiction?"

"Maybe it is, maybe it isn't," grunted Urseth impatiently. "What do you care? Why take chances?"

Borath gave his chief a dull swat. "Enough! What do we do in the meantime? A fortnight's left to twiddle thumbs. The men'll be restless—"

"Listen!" interrupted Urseth severely. "We train, Borath! We train like we've never before. Arnin will have an escort, yes, but the fight will be short-lived, provided the prince doesn't get whiff of our trap. Why should he, if old Dunkar keeps his mouth shut?"

Borath nodded proudly. "The prince will not suspect an attack so close to royal shores. Like lambs to the slaughter—they'll all come sailing to their doom!" With a cheerful laugh, Borath cut deft arcs in the air with his blade.

Zoren shook his head in doubt. "It's all too easy, Borath, you muttonhead. Arnin won't fall for it. It's too predictable." He fingered Ridgar's gem with an unease as if ugly premonitions crept up his spine.

"And why should it, Zoren?" asked Urseth. "Are you turning yellow on us?"

"No! I've just come to apply a generous degree of caution in my old age."

Urseth gave a mirthful hoot. "You're one to talk. Is this all so distasteful to you, Zoren, Grey-Chopper, to say we are all not men deserving of great victory and spoils?"

"No—I mean," faltered Zoren, "I just have a bad feeling about it. Ifetin's proposal could have guaranteed us good plunder; now you overrode him and shafted him to Krok. What's the advantage in that? There's still a chance we may have followed his alleged route up the Rhuon and saved us a deal of trouble. Conceivably, some dangerous double-dealing with this Dinkar fellow could have—"

Urseth reached out a hand and shook Zoren on the shoulder. "Think, man! You know our best course lies south—deposing of Arnin's royal brigade!"

Zoren did not appear convinced, but Urseth was not one to be swayed. The grey pirate was forced to abandon the argument.

Urseth and Borath rose to their feet. The buccaneers conducted a last toast to their spoils and drained their mead-filled horns with relish.

After the fact, Baus saw Zoren looking away into the bushes, as if his features were flooded with misgiving . . .

IX

Sometime in the early morning while the pirates snored off their stupors, Baus went to relieve himself in the bushes. Squinting dazedly, he discovered a small shrine hidden behind the shadow of a woolly maulwood copse just beyond the last of the huts. So unobtrusive was the structure that it looked almost invisible—a tissel-framed construction half-covered with green-yellow alpadacus fronds. With blithe interest, Baus stumbled over to investigate. He found a rustic interior graced with a wooden altar on which a ship's wheel was mounted, warped and weathered, engraved with the feeblest but unmistakable markings of 'Kalikan'.

Baus pinched his face into a frown. 'Kalikan?'—was that not the same name of Ridgar's last ship? It was purportedly piloted to doom off the coast of Nosoheath?

Baus fretted. Zoren had said the wreckage had not been found—yet the relic looked as if it could be as old as that of the original.

A scarred copy? A sentimental token?

Baus could not decide.

An ancient reliquary reposed before the wheel, around which a dozen candles glowed. They tainted the air with a musky redolence. Stooping low, Baus discovered several antique rusty blades leaning haphazardly around the fetish. Pinching his chin, he grimaced absurdly. Holly leaves and winterwash hung in streamers on all walls. An ashen fire pit smouldered before the reliquary, in which he discovered a residual heat of recent use.

Baus contemplated the possibilities of the setting. Significant innovations stirred, yet not without directly proportional consequences. Baus did not wish to incur the irascibility of the seamen. He decided to withdraw with wisdom. Other discoveries were at hand, particularly certain jewels and old coins, but they were better left for another visit. The pirates continued to sleep off their torpor and now as any time appeared as propitious as ever to reconnoitre the island.

Gazing into the forest, Baus discovered a log fence barring a small footpath running up into the maulwoods. He strayed forth on it, finding it barely used as he wandered on to the rugged spine of the ridge.

Baus skirted the barrier and found the path rising sharply into blue, cool heathland. A team of ballou birds made their nests; their morning squawks resounded, nestled in crooks of the ancient trees. The birds arched their wings, opened beaks, hoping to intimidate him. But in truth, Baus was more startled by the reptilian aardvark that burst its way out of the foliage and caused him a frantic rushing up a tree, barely evading not insignificant claws.

From that point on Baus exercised more caution in his excursioning.

A half hour's brisk march had him gaining the summit of Faylor's ridge, where looking out over the treeline, he observed the lagoon glistening in a half circle of brilliant aquamarine. The three barques lay berthed not too distant, like prickly insects. Another small island rose to the east winking in the afternoon mist.

Fissures in the crumbling rock exuded warm gases, a sign which caused Baus to guess Dwiterin island to be of volcanic origin, relatively recently formed. The pirates had chosen the island well. The thick ruggedness of the landscape barred ships from sea and was a perfect shield against foraging parties. Baus recalled how Borath had bragged about how he had lured Arnin's spies onto several false trails near the 'Pirate Isles' far north—to keep their royal noses away from Dwiterin.

Baus climbed higher. The island view was impressive from this vantage. A sinuous buckle of verdure spanned north and south and showed an area heavily wooded, save a thin band of beach straggling along the isle's eastern end. The western shore stood clogged with boulders, behind which jade deodar and dry spanflax abounded. These were the same flora which comprised the majority of driftwood idling gently along the shore's beach.

The southern tip of the island rose higher. Pasted with deodar, the vista showed bands of olive-coloured maulwood. A towering hill rose from above the drowsy forest, offering an even more possibly awe-inspiring view. Baus thought it was far too out of reach to climb, and he bypassed the urge. The island seemed untroubled, surrounded by its blue sea, and with no other land mass in vicinity, except for the treacherous boulders guarding the northern and western channels in the froth of relentless waves, it seemed untouchable.

Baus stretched out his stiff frame on a flat rock, feeling the pleasant, soothing warmth of sunshine massaging his battle-worn face. While cumuli drifted across the firmament, gentle breeze continued to caress his features.

He fingered the stone about his neck. There must be a means by which he could utilize this resource to better advantage!

He dropped his fingers in his pocket and felt for the ganglestick. Aye, it was there, but how to use this little bane-bringer? Was he to sail a crewless barque single-handedly to the mainland? The pirates would be wary; their ale-drenched bellies would be rousing soon and their moods likely fractious at his absence. Best he be back.

Clicking his tongue in irritable reflection, he began his tired way down the rugged cliff.

As Urseth had ordained, more rigorous training was planned for the earlier part of the day. By noon, hand-to-hand combat was in force. Baus found it not only challenging but brow-breaking. The agenda was a punishing program of block, lunge and spear by the lagoon beach. Baus, Poli and Jama faced a host of new adversaries—Urseth's and Borath's combined bands, comprising opponents not as discerning as those of Zoren's. While the sun blazed upon high, the recruits found themselves heaving scythe-reapers while struggling to stay alive. The beach was a swarm of activity. The tranquility of the woods was disordered by groans, screeches, appeals and yowls. Heavy bodies, knuckled fists and iron-tipped boots met faces and combatants fell blood-shaking to their knees. Everywhere pirate fell on adversary in order to incite the mewling of his enemy.

By mid afternoon, Urseth called a halt to the madness, after which the training resumed once again—aboard the three anchored ships.

Borath the Butcher suggested the idea that light weaponry be used, a suggestion which Urseth favoured.

As chance would have it, Zoren was paired with Borath. The two chiefs paired off, faced knife to knife on the stern deck of the *Last Laugh*. They had donned padded jerkins and horned helms to provide scope for more interesting conflict. Almost at once, Zoren slipped on a freak patch of oil and Borath took advantage of the blunder, clobbering heavily Zoren across the chest. The grey pirate howled with surprise. Borath brushed off the injury as 'one of those vagaries of battle'. "Lucky you were, Grey Mane, not to break a tooth, or to suffer worse against a veteran like me. Easily you could have been choking in your own blood!"

The thesis left Zoren unsatisfied and further investigation proved that the oil had been purposely spilled. Zoren was brought to rage, and the chiefs progressed in a face-off in the form of a heated knife fight, with crew gathered on either side cheering their leaders on. As grandly unsurpassed as Zoren was with the rapier, Borath seemed the better scrapper and events would have gone less happily for Zoren had Borath not been the worse for ale. The villain was driven back, grunting and snarling as the sun slanted on his body armour and highlighted the sweat staining his face and glistening off his mail like drops of wine.

Knives locked over both the combatants' heads . . . a jerk, snap, and flick! . . . now Zoren used the full weight of his upper body to undermine Borath's advantage, drawing weapon and the arm down on the winch.

Borath uttered a yelp of discomfort and dismay. It was either yield or be pinched mercilessly against the cuticles of machinery.

Borath let out a rancid curse and growled for mercy. Zoren expressed triumph, announcing that his injustice had been assuaged. Borath took the loss with poor spirit; he tossed insults at Zoren and took refuge in the chattering of his peers.

That evening around the fire Baus discovered the reason for the two villains' bitter enmity...

Magretir disclosed that ever since Urseth had appointed Zoren a chief, Borath had become insanely jealous of him. To the small group, he admitted that Zoren's closeness to Urseth was a position Borath resented and did not share one iota.

"It was many years ago that the five leaders: Wisthal, Urseth, Borath, Zoren and Heoglo had successfully raided the coast of the Poesasian—before Wisthal had died from a sword wound to the chest. He had passed on his chiefdom to Urseth, who was next in line. Heoglo and Zoren were *friends*."

Laclil, one of Urseth's seaman, interrupted sagely: "Aye, I remember. It was the following winter of Wisthal's death: two ships chosen by the remaining chiefs to sail round the southern hook of Karsh, raid the exotic kingdoms beyond. The journey took over a moon; 'twas over two hundred leagues along the line of the Drakes—long even for a pirate . . . The region was unexplored and legend had it that sultry territories were rich with fine ores, grains and harvests. There was a belly-rich cornucopia of plunder! Heoglo and Borath had won the honour of the voyage, through trials of steel. On a squally afternoon, blue-masted *Stormchaser* and green-gummed *Windbane* set sail in the chop, destined to return on a unified mission, with enough gold and bounty to inflate any mariner's dreams."

Magretir reflected. "It was to be a three-month mission?"

"Aye, whoever returned would be rich. But when four months elapsed and no ship returned, Urseth feared that the two of his chiefs had met with demise. He called a conference and discussed the impending possibility at Dwiterin that should they be killed, there should be someone to rule from among the remaining chiefs."

Magretir confirmed the incident.

"A month later, Borath's ship limped back to Dwiterin, battered and scarred, scorched and fire-wracked. Her hull was warped, her masts were knocked with strange metal bolts. Her green sails were full of ghastly holes and only twelve of her eighteen crew had survived. Four of whom were critically injured. The survivors claimed to have been besieged by horrible foes with square sails of orange emblems and decks manned with heavy-cheeked men wielding darts with the ability to project at great speed. Only had they outwitted their pursuers at the last instant by hiding in the squalls and sailing by night. Bad weather had hit hard, plaguing the reavers all the journey back to Dwiterin. Borath affirmed Heoglo's ship, *Stormchaser*, had been caught in line of fire by enemies and her men butchered and her hulk burned and sunken off the coast of Karsh. *Windbane* had fought off her attackers well; no small steel and savagery and luck had privileged her to return crippled but alive."

Magretir showed a mouth of grinning teeth. "I remember back on Devil's Isle, Zoren had questioned the Butcher's men in an attempt to discover the truth of Borath's conspiracy against Heoglo. A dying man painfully admitted dissent amongst the two captains. He saw treachery had been afoot when Borath was in command. With forces divided and Heoglo's sheets torn and rigging slashed by skulduggerish means of Borath's own men, what but disunity could be the reason behind Heoglo's fate? The bloodshed, carnage and ambush on the high seas were unwarranted. Zoren learned of the tale and shook his head with fury. He confronted Borath, but the Butcher denied the accusation, laughing at Yarath the dying man and calling him an idiot, half spiked on rum most of his days for the pain he was in. The next morning Zoren found Yarath dead in his straw pallet. A knife stuck in his throat. Zoren and I knew that his fevered disclosures were not a product of delirium, but that his death was a warning to all, to consider carefully before wagging one's tongue."

A silence gripped the small group. Only a few men were awake at this time around the fire pit.

Magretir sighed; he was wont to take up another story with quiet reserve, but with a sombre shake of the head, he held back and Fuurdhal growled, "Aye, Zoren held his tongue, but he didn't forget. Our captain probed the whispers and investigated Borath's chicanery when his men were pigheaded and drunk. Zoren looked deep into his bluster. He was convinced that Heoglo had been murdered, over plunder, women, and command. It was all the same—this fight which Heoglo could never win, was only because he had never been given the chance."

Laclil sneered: "Either way, the Butcher will repent—or Zoren will be bludgeoned. It all amounts to the same thing. I believe the Grey Pirate will have his way—if his convictions are right, then revenge shall be his!"

X

The days were long and the weather fair. Lengthy sunny afternoons turned into nighttimes of mead, song and drunken ribaldry. Sufficient food was stocked in the store-huts to last for moons: salt kippers, pickles, figs, banyan flour, flaxhack and what game to be hunted. A large part of Baus's imagination could empathize with the rogues, getting used to this kind of life: bantering, bullying, filching, brawling; but not perhaps the murdering, and the lack of women.

Throughout the next weeks, the pirates trained. It seemed there was nothing but training. The chiefs formed teams, some leaping from trees on ropes and others, in the sands waiting for ambush. Some wielded weapons, others lay in wait, fighting bare-handed. When evening came, the fighters returned to their ships, anchored hulls side by side, so that men could throw practice hooks down on an opponent's deck and leap from the rigging. The freebooters struck each other, with dulled staves, padded daggers, blunt-edged mattocks, employing as much skill and skulduggery as possible. The players wore leather pads to protect themselves from mishaps—and flights of ebullience. Combatants were forbidden to engage a charge's throat or head. Any disobedience was punished severely, a man bound by the ankles and hung upside down, paraded about the beach for his breach of authority. The universal command, 'I yield!' was agreed upon as the tagword by which an enemy could declare his defeat. That, or an obvious unparried thrust to vitals. Then he was promised no further suffering. For every ten men a man 'despatched', the hero was awarded a 'Red Star'. It was a badge pinned on the chest, marking a warrior of prowess. It was a further incentive for the seamen to fight and conquer as many enemies as possible.

Over the course of the next two weeks Baus had not yet earned a Red Star, but was significantly more steeled in the guiles of battle. In comparison to the might that faced him, he had no great brawn, but he harboured a wily and intelligent mind which put him in good stead around the mates and kept him alive. His unexpected moves were the talk of the reavers; they placed him in a position of respect. During the mock skirmishes, Baus could count the times he was captured or 'killed' by no less than five. Poli had earned himself a Red Star, so had Jama—Valere two. Borath boasted four, the same as Zoren, while Urseth had tallied five.

The commanders knew that their men needed real action to keep them sharp, so Urseth devised a competition to promote enhanced freshness for the upcoming ambush. The captains encouraged their men to take his ship, crew and weapons out to sea and search for plunder. The five-day foray would include a two days' sail hard west toward the sea lanes, a day of despoliation, then two days to return. It was a race to see which ship could return with the most spoils, and yet not exceed a five-day ceiling.

At the first light, Urseth bore the *Sea Warlock* out of Dwiterin's harbour while Zoren drove his black-shrouded ship after. Borath's green-tarred barque followed in similar ceremony.

A day passed; then another. The isle of Dwiterin lay empty. Borath and her crew were first to return—on the late afternoon of the fifth day. The crew carried with them a trio of superb roans gelded and caparisoned and arriving straight from Maena's Royal stables. On board were several bronze and iron ingots, stolen from the freighter *Wisgal* out of Sloe. The pirates boasted a score of barrels, spiced wine, pine-flavoured rum. Urseth returned a half day later, triumphant with an ingot of gold, five barrels of salted mackerel, three bundles of wool and five hackets of flaxhack. Zoren's head hung low. He had returned empty-handed, his horde encountering only a near miss with a sea drake whose mustard yellow hide and looping coils and glistening scales had scared the wits out of them as it clacked in the sallow light of morn, causing them no end of fear of damage to the *Last Laugh's* hull. But no ships, carracks, cogs or yawls had they sighted. The beast was fortunately rendered sea blind from the easterly sunrise and did not attack. Amongst the mates mutters wafted. Their luck had turned ominously grim. The blame was put to Zoren's wretched amulet, and so, the crew took to fierce mumbling and obloquy. Borath and his cronies gave cheery rejoinders. They were declared the champions of the contest by reason of the excellent bounty and the rare prize of horses they had brought with them and a fine pine rum with which the Butcher's pirates celebrated well into the night, singing ribald songs and mind-numbing chants.

Baus recalled the event with wry vividness after the encounter with the drake: Zoren had suffered more than a simple blow to his pride. He had returned one man short, facing serious dissent amongst his crew. A grisly affair with Exig, but it was his own fault—

Late on the third evening, the *Last Laugh* had tacked back toward Dwiterin and Exig had made a footling attempt to skulk into Zoren's cabin. His aim was to seize the Eye from round Zoren's neck and plunge it into the sea.

The poor fool had been caught, lashed, bound and entreated to walk the plank. In the early hours of morn his hoarse appeals were melancholy and had been heard in the glimmering light as the men—sullen and withdrawn, watched their peer wallow on the open sea.

The gulls had cried and the winds howled. Magretir had reflected on Exig's demise with a disturbing fatalism that such a man might last an hour in those frigid waters and rolling swells before he was taken under by a monstrosity or sucked down by a tentacled gornflorn, or a sea drake or some hammerhead billfish.

* * *

Certain likeable qualities had marked Baus as a tempting target amongst the rogues. Certain other jealous pilgrims amongst the band had not failed to notice his rising status. During the hard morning's training on-ships, Onde and Jispir had tackled him unawares and had dragged him onto the midship deck of the *Last Laugh* where no one was in sight. They rough-housed him up and badly maligned him behind some casks and barrels while he lay muttering and groaning on his back. The outlaw heard snatches of Onde and Jispir chuckling in the background. Out of the corner of his eye, he caught sight of Oresno slip up the midship ladder and grant the two approving slaps on the back. Obviously the black-hearted knave had been the instigator behind it all. The two had taken unfair advantage of his trust and even now they laughed at his helpless nature for even hinting at revenge.

A lunch of roasted eelfish followed; the sailors repaired to the beach to prepare for another mock skirmish on-ships.

Limping back to the lunch tables, Baus contemplated his situation with black humour. Prior to the last engagement, Oresno had taken the opportunity to relieve himself and Baus, floridly seething, did not fail to notice the activity back of the huts, nor the confident swagger in which the brigand moved up the foreshore.

Baus ruminated ever hostilely over his options, while brooding on the dying ashes of the fire. How could restitution be effected regarding this indecent humiliation? To waylay Oresno would only broadcast a guilt and result in his own punishment. A general rough treatment should he be caught that he wished to avoid. Subtlety was necessary.

Oresno's pig-headed attitude must be altered!

At last the bandanna-ed villain emerged from the brush, buttoning his pants, opting to bypass the outhouse. He had stood to relieve himself arrogantly at the edge of the wood not a score of paces from Ridgar's secret shrine.

Secret shrine. A sudden idea brought Baus somewhat vengeful satisfaction. A gleaming shine struck his leering visage. At a safe distance, he crouched, waiting for the blackguard to return to the beach.

The shrine reposed in a shady bower of gendron tangle. Peering about, Baus thought that the position was advantageous—a vantage capable of stifling shouts and suspicion. To lure Oresno into such an enclosure and play tricks could constitute a not abnormal setting for a piece of daring. But how? A curious medley of pleasing sounds? A trail of coins?

Baus gave an amused grin. Why not all?

Oresno turned to wander up the path and Baus half trotted behind him around the side of the shrine, being careful to avoid discovery. He pitched two coins onto the lawn by the shrine's door, pushed the door gently ajar. The coins he had won from certain gamblers' pockets, Magretir's and Jispir's and others, would prove useful for this purpose.

Around back of the shrine Baus scrambled. Within seconds he heard Oresno's heavy tread coming his way.

The footfall subsided; the villain was about to pass him by. The bait was set. Baus's glee escalated. He started to fabricate sinister sounds as if a god were speaking: "Come one, come all! He who hears this counsel has ears for the ancient Ridgar! Attend! The spirit of mighty Ridgar is alive and well! Feel his glory! Feel his fibre! Come one, come all—listen to his sagelike counsel. The deceased Ridgar shall reward any with great boons, including wine, women and song, who heeds his counsel!" Baus spoke in a garbled tone, distorting his voice in a low monotony, which he accentuated by cupping hands round lips pinched in a clam's grin.

Oresno was predictably attracted; he paused at the door, expecting some kind of ruse from his peers. He gave his head a comic shake, then stooped to snatch up one of the coins from the trail. Sauntering, he grabbed up the others. A morose grin lifted off his face. He seemed to guess that one of his mates had pitched a prank and was looking for a good-humour moment.

"I come, O Ridgar!" Oresno chimed in mockery. "To hear thy counsel and accept the perfect opportunity to attain fortune!"

Baus heard a cutlass scrape. Instinctively he dropped behind the bush. He arrested his chanting while circling back to the entrance where he saw Oresno poking amongst the swords by the altar. The villain was probing for more coins—definitely he was not amused. Quiet as a mouse Baus tiptoed up from behind and struck him a resounding blow with his fist to the back of the head. Without hesitation he rapped the ganglestick neatly on the back of his neck. The hairs pricked on the exposed area; the pirate stood frozen like an icicle. His cutlass was drawn; his knees were slightly out of whack with the rest of his body and his legs faced the ship's wheel on the altar.

Baus allowed himself a genteel smile. Such moments deserved full savour. Triumph had never been so rich. The pirate hadn't seen or heard his approach, a condition which instilled Baus with the awful opportunity for vengeance.

Quickly he defiled the shrine. He pulled down Ridgar's wheel and tipped the reliquary, stripped the walls of hallowed herbs and vines and uncompromisingly urinated on everything and anything he could find. The sour ale consumed at lunch was useful for this task.

Six minutes passed. Not much time remained as a whole to destroy the tabernacle in its entirety, but enough to rouse considerable angst from the worshippers.

Baus inspected his handiwork with relish and reclaimed his coins, ensuring that none were left behind accidentally.

He left the door hanging ajar in glaring juxtaposition, which he thought a decorative touch.

He skipped back to the beach in a gleeful mood, choosing a circuitous route designed to thwart all suspicion. He mingled innocuously with the gang that was engaged in pleasant conversation with Jama, Valere and Poli. Most of the fighting hooligans were gathered about the sandy shore, grunting and discoursing at length in breezy dialogue. Many were wholly refreshed from mead and the anticipation of more battling. They were about to take the punts and longboats out to the tall ships when Baus felt a troubled twinge pinch the ease of his confidence. He did not wish to inadvertently draw attention to himself, or the shrine, yet all were assembling for battle, and Oresno's blood would be missed.

Baus counted mentally five minutes pass. The next part of his plan was crucial! If no one discovered Oresno in this interim and the damage before the scoundrel roused from his stupor, his bold scheme would fail. The rogue would scramble off into the woods, drawing no ties to his vandalism.

It was Zoren who brought salvation to the day.

"Where is that grubby fool, Oresno anyway?"

"Probably out pleasuring himself," jibed Fuurdhal.

"Yes, I suppose this is his regular hour for that," griped Zoren. "But no reason to hold up the entire clan!"

"True," grunted Magretir with a concurring nod.

Baus offered an explanation: "I thought I saw the wretch earlier up by the fire."

"What's he doing up there?" demanded Zoren.

"I think he was heading for the latrine."

"Don't think—get him!" snapped Zoren. "We can't be dawdling around taking leisurely pisses. We are fighting men! Not dames with captious bladders. The longboats are ready to launch."

"I know they are!" sneered Onde. "But who is to go?"

Zoren stabbed a finger at the three closest. "You, Juuliq, and Baus."

The three left to fetch Oresno. Borath had two of his dogsbodies join in the search for another of his own crew members. The five jogged up the sandy trail just as the first longboat was being hauled out of the maulwood. The group had just passed the shrine when Borath's missing man, Halgar, emerged from the latrine. "What are you girls up to?"

Onde and Juuliq stopped short.

The sounds of a creaking and banging came from the wind-lashed door of the shrine. They peered past the doorway, spied Oresno crouched bent-kneed in an inglorious pose. Frowning and hissing, Onde rushed in to discover the deplorable state of the fane and his fellow exposed in all guilt in the middle with urine splashed up to the crotch of his dungarees.

Onde uttered a strangled cry. Baus and Juuliq came rushing in on his heels. Juuliq gave a quarrelsome howl; they bent low to shout an imprecation in Oresno's ear. Gaining no reply, Juuliq seized him by his sword arm and suddenly the dazed pirate stumbled sideways, gasping, as if waking from an anguished dream.

For the first time Oresno seemed to notice the damage about him and he fell back on his heels.

"What the devil—"

"What the devil are you thinking?" cried Onde, slapping him hard on the gullet. "It's one thing to miss the outhouse, but another to micturate over Ridgar's sacred relics! You're a filthy disgrace, Oresno. You must have had some batch of wild canak to do this kind of vandalism."

"What are you talking about?" Oresno sneered. "I didn't micturate on Ridgar's relics!" Instinctively he reached for his cutlass, but Onde danced aside and pulled out his own blade. Borath's men were arriving in numbers. Peering about with outraged wonder, the crew members gave Oresno steely glances and hostile reprimands, and sped off back the beach to alert Urseth.

There came a seething argument over who would catch up with the news-bringers and stop them. Onde quibbled with Juuliq. Who was to subdue Oresno? Halting Borath's men and their wagging tongues seemed too onerous a task.

Juuliq hauled Oresno back to the fire pit. He tried to protect him from the mob—but to no avail. The reckoning was swift. Unforgiving hands laid hold of Oresno. Urseth saw the wreckage for himself and ordered the pirate beaten and strung up on one of the deer spits and left there for the day, particularly when he smelt the tang of the urine on the sacred swords and the debased vulgarity of vandalism. The evening after the training was over, Oresno was hauled up and paraded round the campground like a prized wegmor, posted by the crackling fire to endure the indiscriminative jeers of his colleagues. Later on, when the fire was in embers, Baus overheard Zoren speak solemnly to the shipmate.

"You have gone too far this time, you idiot. I don't know if I can help you."

Oresno's swollen eyes fluttered to life. The response, hardly intelligible, seemed to hint at a lack of knowledge of the event.

Zoren frowned. Most of the others were passed out in drunken heaps by the fire and they could not hear his rattling hiss. Oresno dribbled out a half-baked story of some salt-grimed misfortune, upon hearing a voice, spying a trail of coins, entering Ridgar's shrine; he discovered it empty, then blankness hit him and he thought to hear a noise behind him, with Onde shaking him awake and accusing him of inhuman vandalism.

Zoren bent down to stare at him with pity. "Silly pip! You think any'd believe such a yarn? You think Urseth won't skewer you first? There were no alleged 'coins' in the shrine of which you speak. This pitches you in even more delinquent light."

"I know it sounds cack-brained, Zoren! but it must be sprites or devils or something visiting wrath on old Ridgar," Oresno howled miserably. An old manner of thick arrogance was in Oresno's tone. "You must believe me. Even though Ridgar's twice dead in the grave, I swear it was his devils. It was your star-cursed gem that did this. You should have hurled the bane into the sea long ago—like Exig told you—now look at the mess we're in!"

Zoren gave a harsh hoot of laughter. "We're? Mischievous elves? Ghosts of Ridgar's spirit?" Zoren shook his head with wonder. "Oresno, you're a dreamer. If there's anything I know, there's nothing I can do for you—you're on your own. Urseth may cut off your genitals or he may let you off with just a proper whipping, in which case you should praise your fortune. A word of warning, though, breathe a word of Ridgar's Eye at the heart of this nonsense and I'll geld you."

Zoren left his assistant hanging there to join the stragglers in a last round of 'Rousts'— the uncomplicated drinking game.

Oresno endured the punishment. All throughout the next evening hogsheads of rum were being dragged from the huts and passed about like sugar cubes and he was thrice whipped by Urseth's chosen pirates and dressed like a frump and ordered to lick off the urine-crusted relics. Forced to abase himself before the shrine, he begged for Ridgar's forgiveness—this was the most generous punishment. Exhibiting a forbearing nod, Baus watched on with satisfied concern.

Soon after the revelry began to moderate itself, Baus felt himself relaxed and at ease, remarking to himself that one tiny wrong in the world had been rectified.

The meat sizzled; the smokes swelled. The men who had fallen to their ankles sotted were kicked awake with the smell of roasting venison and boar wafting through the common area. The boy Adrik was hauled out of captivity and given a slab of boar and mead to wash away his misery. He dunked his mug into the sand and was returned roughly to his thatched prison.

The business of the day being done, members of Urseth's band brought out hornpipe, large drums, tin whistles and zithers. A gang of drummers beat elkhorn mallets on the round leather-strapped kegs. The result was a lively rhythm which left pairs of ribaldish sailors twirling about arm-in-arm like barroom maids. Some fell backward over tables, others jostled liquor onto fellow comrades; others whirled into the fire and singed their hair, catching clothes on fire.

Zoren called harshly, "Careful, you lax mugs! You mightn't have the sense to live, but I do. I need your muscle for tomorrow's pillaging—and slaughter!"

"Leave them be," advised Fuurdhal. "The mead helps them relax—gets the lead out of their bones. So, we have a few less ninnies to babysit, what of it?"

Zoren shook his head. "Bloody fools is what they are!"

Urseth peered at him with amused concern. "What's wrong with you? You've been edgy all evening."

Onde who slouched nearby, sneered: "It's that blasted charm of his. He's got it wrapped round his pig-proud neck. It's been hexing us since he commandeered it! I don't care if it's his bleeding uncle's or his great uncle's or godfather's—it'll be the death of us all! Death at sea!"

Zoren raised his arm and backhanded Onde. "Shut up, you grubby little whore! It's my great uncle's talisman—The 'Sea Wench'. 'Tis Ridgar's eye and legacy. A family heirloom."

Onde cried out with spite: "I couldn't care if it's Villea's tit or Uncle Agar's foot corn. It's an ill omen to us and shall smite us with misery before long!"

Borath reached out to strip the stone from Zoren's neck but Zoren caught the fist and stopped the motion. Between Borath's grimace and his own curled leer, Zoren jerked a providential fist, digging nails into Borath's flesh. Borath reacted and retracted the limb painfully.

"Keep your ugly mitts away from my property," muttered the grey devil. Glaring at his counterpart, Borath was the first to turn away.

"You don't care, but you should," Borath growled dangerously. "The curse is on us, and it's real."

Zoren spat at his compatriot's feet. "What curse? I've not seen any."

Urseth scowled; he ordered his two chiefs to let up. "The fact is that we're bickering here like a pack of tomcats, Zoren. We haven't formalized any set plan of action. The legend of Ridgar's talisman is two-fold: the luck and the curse of the sea, so it's said, and so I believe it. 'Twas the curse that caught up to old Ridgar in the beginning when he was butchered near Nosoheath."

Zoren stubbornly refused to endorse the concept. "When the geezer was fifty years old, he told me as a boy hardly four that the Eye would be mine. Ridgar instructed me to ignore all the banal superstitions, that one day I might know of its origin and wield it with honour. The bunk and mysticism surrounding this talisman is spread by old women and harridans with phlegmy throats. This, Ridgar told me laughingly. He said I would wear it on my breast proudly and guard it for the rest of my days."

Zoren's eyes misted; he blinked in some faraway direction. "Old Ridgar knew some magic; whether he had the foresight to use it, I am not privy, for he died not a handful of years after I came of age to hold my sword. Now, his prophecy has come to fruition . . . 'Tis I who hold The Eye!"

Zoren thrust himself erect and bared the talisman before all.

Urseth shook his shaggy head. "You're an incorrigible fool, Grey Mane!" Borath threw down his hands with disgust. From Baus's perspective, Borath looked a man resenting much that his own neck was on the line by some fanatical reaver parading a cursed gem. Borath was more a brute to await an opportunity to seek vengeance when circumstances demanded it. As for the legend, superstitions abounded this side of the Poesasian. Nary a rhyme had ever been proven false—at least by this bunch of cutthroats . . .

XI

It was the thirty sixth day since the recruits' descent into pirate hell. The pirates were ready to strike out on their mission of ambuscade with lean crews, confident and high-spirited pillagers; so confident in fact, that Urseth bade Zoren and Borath create symbolic banners to fly on their masts.

Dressed in such regalia, the three ships scintillated in the harsh noon light. The ships were tarred, re-gummed and provisioned with enough food for two weeks.

The following dawn's departure was heralded with the rattling of chains and the shouting of ruffians as anchors were drawn and sails were unfurled. Seamen from all ships took up raucous cheers and engaged in boisterous song:

"Off to sea we blow!
To where, nobody knows,
To plunder, to burn,
From bow to stern,
Those ships of woe,
Which devil-wind blow,
Hi, ho, ho, a bottle of rum!
A fistful of cheer, and a long kettle drum,
What is that which the devil most needs?
The Poesasian buccaneers to fulfil her deeds!"

Throats rumbled; tongues shrilled out the coarse stanzas. Baus did not doubt the words to these uncouth songs meant something deeper than what it seemed but he could only find them eerily chilling. The harbour seemed to cringe at the sound of the harsh laughter and the incongruous soughing of gulls gliding in low arcs against the flash of morning red.

Three ships—a black mammoth destroyer, a red leviathan, a green goliath—slowly pushed their way out to sea. Dwiterin was left in a shimmering haze of rose.

A three-quarter moon lifted its face. The new year was almost upon them and so the days became shorter and colder. On this brave voyage, the morning wind blew steady from the south, keeping the temperatures above average. Perhaps a few degrees higher than what Baus would expect in Heagram. The pattern of clear skies and halcyon warmth was not enough to guarantee fair weather. Baus believed the mariners were faintly worried that too many fair days in a row would bring only foul weather. Urseth envisaged his pivotal battle in foul weather, also his rise and the downfall of Prince Arnin and the greatest enemies of his craft with the keenest of anticipation. He became deaf to anyone's hint of foreboding. The stupendous victory to come over the next few days would be the only thing worth obsessing over. He would be heralded as the de facto leader of the Poesasian!—Slaying his nemesis, stamping his claim on the Buccaneer Triangle's dominion once and for all, he would be remembered through all time.

The winds blew in flurries and gusts. The sea greened about the pirates as powder-puff clouds raced about a sky so low as to be almost touched. The tempo was slower than what the confident captain would have preferred. He paced the deck, his toes almost leaping. Many leagues were to be covered—perhaps a hundred or so to the southwest as the crow flies—yet, the base of the freebooters' ambush was the twin isles of *Two Silkie's Rock*, far away amongst brooding seas and curtains of cloud wrack.

The ships sliced proudly through the ocean in wide V-formation and Urseth's barque ran first, flushing the viridian swells with rude merman's prow and iron and ram-rod morningstars. Borath's green barque followed at a temperate pace, three hundred yards back to the right; Zoren's black barque plunged on in somewhat more ponderous gait to Urseth's left. A crew seeing those ships from a distance, might be stung with numbness and terror. The mariners who had the foresight to veer away from them, were fortunate; others, of course, were not so favoured.

As it stood, the buccaneers were leagues away from any major shipping lanes and were not surprisingly short of prey.

For the duration of the afternoon the recruits trained on deck with Zoren and his sea reavers. Magretir, Juuliq, Jispir and Bargil proved worthy sparring partners. Oresno was in mediocre shape after his roughing-up and was disbarred from teaching. The ill mood between himself and Baus had only escalated: fights, feuds, vulgarities, trickery—all were abundantly reciprocated. The trainees worked with cutlasses, staves and knives—proving leaner, much-improved opponents than weeks prior. Once they were used as bean bags, now bodies were hardened parcels of lead. Eyes were lamps of strength. Nerves were steeled against the first sign of attack or treachery from a grinning foe.

"Watch the eyes, always their eyes!" Magretir had warned with much repetition. The last weeks had given Baus a feral, wind-beaten aura and he remained anaesthetized to the violence that was becoming part of his daily regime. A guise only, he knew; indubitably, the veneer of roguery would be a life-saver in the times to come. But whether or not he could sustain such grim service in keeping with Zoren, Magretir and the others' expectations . . . was a thing to be seen. Hopes of escape seemed slim. The cutthroats were ever ruthless, paranoid, and no opportunity unfolded. One wrong move could spell the end, an instant garrotting and Baus rued the day he had ever crossed paths with this gang—and only after slapping a few cursed coins on Kruthgar's grime-stained table . . .

Throughout the night Baus tossed and the ship rode the midnight swells with ease. The glistening stars helped the sailors navigate; they took turns keeping lively watch on deck. These hardened criminals were not immune to Arnin's roving patrols . . . neither did they face resistance, nor any vessels of plunder.

Not until daybreak—two days hence.

Sailing low in the water, a stout freighter *Villunder* built in Kantmacle more than a half century ago, caught the crests, carrying a fine cargo of hides and ingots from Brislin to Alcax. Perhaps she came as faraway as the sea ports of Karsh, none knew and hence her awkward lean to deeper, meaner seas. Her varnished fore and aft masts were straight as arrows. Her bronze rigging and gay new white sails gave her a fresh look of aspiration. Yet so heavily laden was her hold that she could not slow or turn about. Sure prey was she for the plunder-ships marauding the sea, slashing through the gilt water like vultures on the prowl.

It was evident from the morose scowl on Urseth's face that he wished to move on and not engage marks in unknown waters, especially when there were bigger fish to fry. Borath drew up alongside the *Sea Warlock* and confronted the captain. With mordant shouts and goads he urged the old pirate to attack. Baus saw Urseth shaking his fist in answer.

Windbane began to draw away, gaining speed, aching for a fight with the freighter. Zoren kept his position, refusing to yield to Borath's impetuousness or threats. "It's his brainchild," Zoren spat to Magretir. "Let the fool laden himself with the heavy cargo, not us. He'll draw water and slowly drown."

"It'll keep him and his mad pips in check," observed Magretir.

"A grand hope," mused Zoren.

Borath's freshly-trained sailors were eager for an exercise. They were itching for blood and hurled abuse over the gleaming gunwales. They cut alongside the doomed craft and five sailors threw grapple irons which went high over the railing and tore across the freighter's deck, snagging teak gunwales and hooking men, dragging them to their deaths. Men pulled at lines in synchrony, expecting sword and plunder. Baus shuddered at the terror the mariners must be experiencing aboard the *Villunder*. The wegmor-skulled gunwales sliding up and down, the macabre regalia adorning her attacking vessel . . . all were a demon's nightmare bringing only anguish with no bound. With the creak of straining ropes, Baus watched the boats inch closer. Borath's killers screeched their plunder oaths; they flung their bodies onto the victims' deck. Bearded faces were a-swim with lust and weapons clanked; steel whirled, shimmering blood sprayed. Shrieks stung the air, as twenty rogues clambered aboard the freighter, massacring the defenders the instant their black boots touched the gleaming planks.

The freighter's crewmen, by no means, were cowards: they simply were unprepared. The defenders drew swords and notched scimitars, and the opposing parties parried and hacked and slashed, but dodging and screaming was no defence for the *Villunders* and they were brutally chopped down. Expert killers made professional work of them; yet one brave man, a tall, muscle-bounded, ginger-haired hero, ran amok swinging his axe in all directions. He pitted one of Borath's men clean, scalp and skull and all and the man lay thrashing in his death throes before his life drained away. He lay still, but the killer was finally pinned down and cudgelled without compunction. Borath personally saw to the dismemberment of the man, raising his headless corpse like a trophy on his shoulders while the head was pitched savagely into the sea. Predators made short work of the member, swirling in the soft eddies.

Despite the poetic ritual, Borath was definitely displeased with the loss of his good sailing hand, but he was somewhat mollified by the swiftness of the death of the lionheart and the quick victory. *Windbane* and the *Villunder* locked gunwales. Borath ordered the gangplank lowered so that heaps of the freshly-cured hides could be dragged onto his ship and secured in her hold. Three of Borath's men were still soaking the *Villunder*'s deck with pitch. The ship's departure to the deeps was fast in coming. Urseth's voice rose commandingly over the wind.

Baus could see Borath's face flinch at being countermanded. The order was to curtail the destruction—which was surely a waste of life and needless slaughter. Good iron would sink to the bottom of the sea. Pirates normally spared ships of this kind and kept survivors aboard so that the same large freighters might ply the routes again to be robbed. Borath was not a man of logic. His primal instinct was to butchery, hence his name, and he would never let up. Baus detected more in Zoren's pinched visage than simple contempt for the murderer. It was the same blackguard who had disposed of Heoglo, the warrior chief.

Borath ordered a net dropped astern. The defender's skull was recovered. Four sea predators had already greedily gnawed out its eyes. But Borath wanted it for other purposes. The flesh was flabbily flayed and somewhat gleaming to the bone. The net retrieved a grisly talc-whitened skull, the same of the man who had received his final pittance. Borath had the head skewered on the demon horns at prow to serve as an example for all to see who resist *Windbane*'s will.

Berly the dead mariner was given a proper burial and was stripped of weapons and bandanna and thrown off to starboard. The men sang a low threnody, bordering on a dirge.

Soon the ships were put solemnly out to sea. They rode the swells like kings.

The hours passed. The three lone marauders rode timeless crests, skimming the leaden swells. Mastheads glinted in gold and the mauve rays of afternoon were fleeting, as sullen clouds drifted eastward and scraped the skies with pale yellow and grey. A diffuse light permeated the languor of the air and infused it with a wistful foreboding. The seas were bottle-darkened and leaden purple. Patches of sea dropped thirty fathoms causing Baus to shiver, wondering what ships had found their way to the deeps below.

It was mid-afternoon and it felt like early evening. The sailors sensed the premonition, some whisper of death which sent silent sibilances amongst their depraved ranks. Omens hissed from the men's lips; weather-lore murmured in the dark cubbyholes of their minds. The sailors became silent, watching from all sides, searching the tides—hoping for some indicator to show better signals. The Sloeian coast became a visible, hazy ribbon, perhaps three leagues distant. A thinly-poised blue-green band showed soft shadows and more ethereal contours in the afternoon mist. Small fishing boats had tucked tail, beetled toward their safe wharfs.

Danop's cry rang lustily from the crows' nest: "*Two Silkie's Rock* is two leagues off starboard!"

Zoren squinted over the moody swells. He saw from the distance the twin fangs of rock barely rearing up from the slightly leprous sea. The wind faded; the enormous ships were kept almost in irons. Now an ever more snail-slow pace seemed real as they creaked along. The seas were placid; yet the incoming tide hedged them forth like kittenish children drawn by mothers.

The coast became darker. A few fledgling lights seemed to glint back at them like fireflies. There was a resentful quality to the habitations, and even Baus, squirming like a toad, could barely discern some higher stone dwellings rising behind the quays of small fishing villages like mantles. Sloe was perhaps five leagues south, and impossible to distinguish.

Slowly, the mysterious fanged mass became more distinct. *Two Silkie's Rock* was a bulge of sinister islands separated by a U-shaped span which arched over a narrow strait. The leftmost isle was a long, fog-carven mass draped with tall gendrons. A rugged cliff sat aside with boulders at its feet crowded close to the inlet side. The adjoining island was a quarter of its partner's length, harbouring a more inviting presence. However, the beach was set back from tall gorse and a bullshrub hill shouldering the land bridge.

The ships drew nearer. Danop's cry came loud again over the wind. Baus tilted his head, to see what had aroused the knave so fervently. A small ship with triangular white sails bellied itself toward the smaller island.

At first Urseth called pursuit, intrigued by the fugitive. The three vessels closed in. No competitions would there be, or last minute 'bungles' on this excursion.

The pirate ships passed the shoal, buried now under millions of tons of water. The fleeing ketch, a slender two-master, berthed herself in the narrow straits at high tide under the land bridge between the two islands. A strange place to anchor, Baus thought. He glimpsed three or more crewmen disposing of their landing supplies with quiet unconcern. Most bewildering was the way in which the sailors raised their cocky challenges while their ship rocked in the gentle chop. The water was less scalloped by wind, though her bow reflected the two facing shorelines. The pirates were amazed at the flagrant insults drifting to their ears from the landers and joined back in boisterous defiance. The men on the ketch were unmoved. They had barely thrown down their anchor when they tossed back a last challenge and dove over the side to swim to the sandy beach perhaps forty yards away.

"To speed, Borath!" Urseth called authoritatively. "Dispose of the coxcombs, before they complicate our mission. There's room for only one group of scallywags."

Borath growled. He watched the four caitiffs run up the beach and mount the bracken forming the lower half of the hillside.

Urseth kept the *Sea Warlock* aloof. Borath ordered his ship creaking into the narrow channel. Zoren moved into position to anchor the *Last Laugh* at a distance. He contemplated landing a team on the beach but hesitation gripped him. Something was out of place. Borath navigated slowly with grim intent toward the ketch and noted that the water depth here seemed to lessen. Further, it took only one missed boulder, a single unnoticed straggling rock to tear a hole in the ship's bottom. With such trepidation and danger of scuppering, Borath urged his men to scour the gloomy shallows.

The enemy ketch was anchored directly beyond the land bridge. *Windbane*'s mast barely cleared the arch at present tide. The distance turned out to be a few scant yards, but a margin which was placed ominously, and would lengthen as the tide withdrew.

Grapples were flung. The ketch's deck saw white-knuckled fingers gripping; the boarding planks were dropped. A medley of bearded reavers swarmed the decks, weapons cocked with red eyes trained for plunder. No vanguard erupted from the hold; they expected a horde to come flailing out.

The invaders scratched their chins in surprise. Where were the foes?

Borath ordered five sailors to drop a jolly boat in the water and go ashore to hunt down the fugitives. The Butcher stayed aboard to oversee the plundering of the vessel.

The *Last Laugh* anchored nearby and Baus could see the ketch in full light, painted a fresh silver sheen. Why? No insignia was carved on her hull and her masts were bare.

Unusual. Such chicanery comprised a pirate's trick, thought Baus. The craft's girth was somewhat narrower than other ships of her ilk and it was almost as if the paint on her timbers had been freshly coated.

Again, for what purpose?

Baus was at a loss. There was no one on board the vessel, nor any sign of other inhabitants on the island—a fact which further complicated the issue and raised uncomfortable questions in regard to the motives of the people of the vessel.

The cowardly display was irregular. Why taunt the pirates and lose their ship at the same time?

Baus could not approve of the glaring contradictions and turned his head to the beach, perhaps to seek out some pressing detail missed.

Something was amiss with the whole scene. A small smoke wisp began to curl up from the brink of the foreshore. Baus froze. Men had been camped here earlier. They had taken pains to stamp out a recent fire.

Borath's pirates continued to search the vessel but found nothing: only a small lantern, some musty old blankets, a pair of rusty chains, loops of oily rope.

Ripe with disbelief, Borath cursed the failure. He returned on deck, made an exaggerated show of beckoning Urseth who waited impatiently for news.

Urseth was startled by the discovery. Everything seemed to be too unnatural. The gloomy skies began to weigh oppressively on him and the dampening of the day began to generally rankle his men's temperaments. The air became sinisterly still; the sea remained inscrutable, as if her winds were caged for some dastardly purpose.

From a deck side vantage, Baus saw Urseth growing more irked and pulling at his chin. Something was afoot. The ship should have supplies or cargo aboard—food at the very least. Her hull was all too freshly painted . . .

All became suddenly clear . . .

Urseth's cry came too late. By the time he caught the flash of moving figures on top of the spanning bridge, events were already in motion. A throng of twenty armed men came bolting out along the sides of the archway heaving cauldrons of oil and tubs of steaming tar.

A dozen more warriors assembled on the flanks; all were quick to start upending the cauldrons.

The tubs upended one by one, raining hot tar down on *Windbane's* crew, scorching her deckhands and sending her sails and rigging a-smoulder. Stones and wood were plastered on top of men's skulls. The onslaught lasted barely a minute but was too agonizing to not cause harm. Men died with split skulls and palsying, broken limbs. Some had their eyes singed out. Hot washes of pitch came next tearing down on the unsuspecting faces.

Borath had time to barely dodge a spiked missile, aimed ruthlessly for his throat. He leaped aside into the forecastle's shadow. Men were shouting and cursing and dying all around him. He yelled at his crew to man the helm, drag up the anchor, cut the grapples!—but they were all too preoccupied with the predicament of both flailing their weapons and scrambling for cover that they could not focus on long range tactics. The rain of debris and oil continued with prejudice. Borath tried to get his ship moving, but was impeded by ravaged bodies. Slippery oil, clinging smoke permeated the wreckage. The pirate managed to cut loose the last grapple attached to the decoy vessel, but had barely enough time to pull *Windbane* through the strait and avert complete destruction before the treacherous liquids hurled from the ledge killed them all.

A greycoat tossed down a torch and suddenly a great patch of the bow went up in searing flames. Ruddy tongues raged across the planks like lightning. The foremast caught, soon was a column of drake's breath, searing, howling and roaring. The jib was suddenly ablaze and jagged banderoles of scarlet mayhem ruled.

Baus heard curses from Borath as he tried to gather his men together, but all was a chaos of fire, and ruin of tortured screams. The ship was foundering!

Urseth knew his chief's ship was lost. He hissed at his crew with disgusted fury. He exhorted men to put out to the island and despatch the men-at-arms.

The longboat was lowered. Oars dug into the placid waves. Perhaps ten of Borath's surviving pirates dove into the strait, but Borath was last to jump. *Windbane*, crackling with fire, assumed a tragic stance, hissing and sputtering with flumes of guttering flames that skated higher. Fingers of fire blew dangerously close to the ketch, now still miraculously avoiding their greedy reach.

The assailants shouted triumph on the rock bridge. They rushed down the nearest side to cut off their enemies' escape. Some headed to sleek longboats hidden in the reeds behind the sheltered lee. Baus caught the detail on their grey and maroon surcoats—the telltale golden arm stripes and breast crests of the star and the stag draped burnished armour, unmistakeably Owlen's insignia.

Zoren ordered the assault on land. The majority of pirates were already distributed on the high-hulled jolly boats and the longboat which was heading for shore but Urseth yelled down at them. "Get out of the water, you fools! Prepare for battle on-ships!"

Zoren seemed confused. But then he gaped, awe-stricken as Fuurdhal pointed to two enemy carracks miraculously circling from out behind the smaller isle.

The pirate cursed. The *Last Laugh*'s crew wheeled about, only to spy a fluttering mass of great white sails bellied on tall, teak masts. They were huge ships, attacking with square-rigged sails and extra topgallant flying from the mainmast. The men-of-wars shared features in similitude to the *Last Laugh,* but were larger. Rippling with blue-black banners of the Stag and the Stars, the icons of law and order had been hidden behind the shoreward island all the time!

With good reason—for in hidden water lying in wait they were a deciding force and prompted Zoren to snatch up a halberd and stare up at them with morbid apprehension. He came to full understanding, as did Urseth, that their man, Dunkar, had betrayed them . . .

Instead of hunters, the pirates were now the hunted, and Baus observed with strange fascination the pirates' dumbfounded sense of defeat. The attitudes changed from antagonism to terror. Urseth knew wire-edged peril when he saw it. The threat of doom was on their doorstep. Two more eagle-prowed ships had emerged from the opposite curve of the island and were now converging on them at an alarming rate.

Normally it would have been a fight or flight—but four foes against two? Baus winced. It was suicide. The likelihood of survival, despite the opportunity of weakening one of the ships, grew ever dimmer. The first sighted vessel was fast rounding on them. Retreat was the wish of death: too late to think about escape . . .

Urseth banked his barque to the open sea and bent a hard tack into the blustering wind. Being the farthest away from the strait, he saw the sky grow sallower, with more ominous threat of storm. The old sea wolf grimaced; the falling darkness and the progress of his ship were bad omens. With cunning and anticipation, he hurled a small screeching figure into the abyss. Adrik! The wily buccaneer had kept him alive—to offer the brat as bait should enemies pose threat. Predictably, the foremost of the two Royal vessels slowed to a crawl, dropping a small rescue crew to save the drowning boy.

The feint proved of little utility. Baus and the *Last Laugh*'s crew could see the grimly triumphant looks on the liveried soldiers. The floating chimaera, a great flaxen-coloured carrack, haunted them like a drake. The prince himself was aboard, standing head high on a jewelled dais looking proudly alert from the helm. He wore a silver-gold jupon, a mauve casque; silver sword and chain buckled to his side. His hair shone fair and coved down to his neck to merge with the epaulettes while black boots hiked up to the knee. His orders came crisp and clean with a commanding trumpet-song: "Attack the filth and destroy! Forthwith, warriors!"

The crew stood to attention, ready with weapons. Rather than risk grapples, the crew wielded catapults that were arranged bow and stern. A handful of engineers were instructed to adjust the tension of the first stones and fire test rounds at will. Thunderous claps of power found two fiendish balls hurtling through the air.

One of the stones dropped short of the *Last Laugh*. It plunged deep into the glowering water midships; the other was thrown wide off its target.

Zoren's men jeered. The soldiers' abortive attempt had been bungled; it brought whooping laughter to their lips. The sailors rapped their cutlasses lustily on the gunwales. However—even as the din faded—Arnin ordered his engineers to reload . . .

The second volley was launched—with the proper angle and pressure—the screeching howl of stone cannon raced over the tumult of the wind.

Zoren knew what was about to happen. He shouted hoarsely at his mates: "Prepare for battle—watch to port, mates!" Arnin's second vessel was now slithering dangerously close to the *Last Laugh*. A formidable slayer, if not combated. Calmly Zoren ordered Bargil to whip the stern rudder. The great sails flapped; canvas caught noisily at the wind. Baus ducked low; he sensed another cannon shot whistling through the midship rigging. His heart missed a beat. He gripped the pommel of his cutlass. The *Last Laugh* whirled away from the certain gap reduced by the enemy. It came to an almost stop, within range of the catapults—an inevitable ploy that Arnin had calculated, and now the tactician surveyed his battle scene with grim aplomb.

The first missile went awry, sliding wide off to stern. But the second, a lighter, rounder projectile, sailed far into the boat's breast and the black warship ploughed unheedingly through the choppy swells. The stone found its mark, caught the back starboard flank and stove a jagged hole in the stern.

A deluge of water began gurgling into the *Last Laugh*'s bilge.

The ovation was so loud that rose on the decks of Arnin's warship, that it drowned the wind. The enemy had been lucky; Zoren knew it—and he cursed. He cursed the sea; he cursed Arnin's mother, Arnin's mother's mother, every mother before that, and he cursed Urseth for deserting them at this desperate time. The old chief had fled to sea, leaving them alone on a lone crusade against a rampaging foe.

The *Last Laugh* lurched as it caught an obstreperous swell. Minutes remained to live; yet not two minutes before she could have fled like Urseth and avoided such an impending disaster. Now Arnin's escort sighted her prey—some wounded gull—and gained her starboard flank and presently a host of greycoats hurled snaffle rods upon Zoren's gunwales.

Armoured men snatched up their swords. The shields were scooped and men were seconds away from hacking across the enemy craft and cleaving buccaneers' skulls. The defenders had barely snatched shields and maces of their own before they were shrieking battle cries. They had the wise sense to don their jerkins, knowing armour would not stop a direct sword thrust but would at least allow minimal protection against glancing blows.

Zoren rallied his men. "To me, men! To me! We shall force this Royal rabble to their knees—Oceans of blood shall flow!" Baus could discern the ruddy turmoil boiling in his cold grey eyes.

Enemy planks were heaved on deck; a score of Arnin's soldiers rushed to the *Last Laugh*'s rails. The phalanx was four rows deep and they wielded scimitars, shields, morningstars and broad-bladed halberds. The fighters were dressed in grey, open-faced casques, tactically sloped on low brims. Grey and maroon jupons pinned thin body armour. The first jet of soldiers met instant ruin. Magretir's sword and Juuliq's whirling knives saw to the slaughter. Juuliq's dirks were pitched from close, lethal range, catching the most earnest of warriors in their unprotected eyes. The second wave was recipient to a punishing sword-slashing by Zoren's flank—Fuurdhal and Onde, Calley and Bargil, whose lifelong training in the arts had not deserted them. The grey and maroon-coated men of Arnin's troops died noisily, amidst chopping sounds of flesh-hewing gurgling, clawing at the air and stretching silver gauntlets, with limbs cleaved.

Eight of the enemy were despatched in less than a minute. Onde was left dangling from the taff rail with a sword pierced through his guts; Juuliq was badly injured and losing blood every second. Oresno had deflected a morningstar away from Zoren and had loyally saved his captain from certain death but had inopportunely walked into a spiked ball and gazed vacantly as his life dripped away.

The *Last Laugh* was listing. The bow tilted and the stern fell away. It was low in the water; presently more of the enemy were trooping over the side.

A greycoat saw an opening; he leaped over the rail to accost Baus. The sight of an up-raised cleaver was enough to make Baus wince. He was driven back to the aft mast with force. The warrior laughed at Baus's puny effort. He gripped his sword, guffawing at the golden weapon Baus clutched. Two greycoats clambered over the gunwales to engage Poli and Jama.

Baus parried, striking out at the man's weapon, a flimsy thrust that his attacker could easily brush aside. He chirped back a pleasantry with a grin, sword raised double-handed over his head.

Despite Baus's inexperience, he was no fool. Deliberately he had undermined his opponent's impression of him by feinting, just as Magretir had taught him. The soldier heaved sloppily, emboldened with the whiff of success. Baus sidestepped the rush, ducked to his knees and slashed out harshly across his body. The greycoat fell face first, without knowing what had skewered him. A glassy eye rolled up to stare at Baus.

The outlaw whirled to catch Valere out of the corner of his eye. The captain struggled with a huge brute of a soldier now thrashing at his left flank.

Baus ran forward. Though the ship was teetering, he swung a low arc that caught the man's ankles, piercing greaves and slashing tendons to the bone.

The attacker lurched, fell howling and crippled to his knees. Valere rammed the sword into his gullet. The seaman bowed, bellowing a shout of gratitude.

Fuurdhal's axe smashed a gory wedge into Jama's attacker relieving Jama from a hasty exit from life. At the edge of the foredeck Zoren fought two greycoats in a desperate hack and slash game. He stepped over the first body, blood staining his beard, and ran the other through the breast. The blade was stuck deep in the opponent and a vicious tug-of-war ensued with boots digging and the dying man sliding off his sword and rolling into the sea.

Poli was in grave predicament. Two attackers held him further sternward. The deck was slippery and wet with blood and he was sliding perilously into cold water. An enemy was armed with a wickedly-outfitted chained morningstar whose three spiked balls were raining mercilessly on the smaller man's shield. Poli's other aggressor wielded a scimitar which he used to undermine his lower shanks. Despite the youth's ferocity, the bully was being slowly propelled closer to the swirling water and survived only by frog-dodging the scimitar sweeps to his legs. Desperately he umbrella-ed his warped wooden shield and blocked the hammer blows of the spiked balls. But he had neither the training nor experience to contest two frontal attacks at once and with his shield being shredded to bits, things would have gone sorely for him had not Magretir stepped in and hacked off the man's arm at the elbow while the man was still clutching his morningstar for a killing strike. Poli gasped at his luck. He finished off the other fighter with the help of the swashbuckler who was bleeding at the thigh and forearm.

Valere scrambled for a weapon. He acquired a sword from a soldier staring up at him with sad, fish-hungry eyes. The blade was notched in the middle but true.

Bargil was facing his turn to be worried from behind. Calley rushed to his succour but was cut down in a flash of crimson. Bargil narrowly escaped a bludgeoning but was forced to scuttle underfoot of a blood-drenched greycoat and was mashed with a boot heel to the upper shoulder.

A swarm of enemies gathered on deck. They were ten strong, lunging, frothing, stabbing, hacking, nearly trampling each other to death. A dazed Bargil whom they thought was dead, was almost crushed. Some tripped over his body and others, while men lurched on pools of blood flowing like tankards of ale. Jispir was down with a sword through his eye. Deneo and Zanzibar were pitched headlong into the sea. Danop was mortally wounded with double injuries to midsection and staggered with a bleeding right hand holding his abdomen before he was run through by two greycoats, who clambered on top and chopped him out of his misery.

Zoren jumped down from the bow with dismay. He hacked a path to the remainder of his men. "Amidships, lads! To me! We must finish it now or we die! Let's send these devils to their graves!"

With a belligerent roar, Zoren and the survivors charged with disoriented fury. The bemused greycoats were stupefied. In a crush of heaving bodies, Baus met his man head on. He was narrowly divided in two by a sword flying through to his right shoulder. He delivered the lethal blow to put his attacker out of his misery. The face sagged; Baus ran the blade through a small rent in his mail. Zoren was locked in tooth and nail skirmishing with a twain of axe-wielding brutes who fought like demons. Fuurdhal and Magretir met three soldiers in their front and Jama and Poli and Valere battled three on three.

The sheer energy of the pirates' attack unhinged the scattered soldiers. The remaining men-at-arms fell back in huddles by the rail. The defenders rushed ruthlessly forward; they hacked and slashed in one galvanized sweep. A blood-mad brigade swarmed the deck. Nothing to lose, these men, nothing to regret or cry over on the grisly day except blood and death—now a few men stood against many, on a sinking, dying ship. Under the incomprehensible fury, the soldiers faltered. In the wake of non-idyllic mayhem, the ship listed. The men staggered. Bashing against one another, they slid back over bodies of their comrades. The attackers gave way to gusty shrieks. Blood dripped in the pirates' eyes. Ears rang from sword blows to casques. A group of four greycoats were hacked back on the planks; three fell screaming overboard while the sky reared a bulging mass of yellow hollowness like some great, yawning rictus. It was the greycoats' death, and the attackers were joyous.

The Royal carrack's ship captain, a hatchet-faced man with fiery yellow beard and blazing blue eyes, watched in sullen awe as his men were cut down before him. Despite their initial advantage, the troops were about to lose this fight. The pirate ship was sinking. Now the score of grapples that gave his men access to the ship was actually plunging his side of the vessel down into the deeps.

The captain barked out orders. Rather than risk his own ship foundering, he ordered the grappling lines cut.

One snapped before a sailor could get out of the way and it sprang back, lashing out an eye. Zoren, sensing the opportunity, slipped away from his last attacker and rallied his crew: "Tar, men! Tar! We need these burnished clowns leaping to their watery graves!"

In a frenzy, the men ran headlong into Fuurdhal and the two side-slipped down the pitching deck after containers of pitch and tar. Some casks had been upended and were rolling feebly toward the sea. Others of his tottering band struggled to grab the containers before they rolled into oblivion.

Zoren screeched out a maniacal cry. Magretir and Fuurdhal carried a huge bucket of the tar right up to the enemy's stern gunwales. They heaved it with all their might. The gummy oil slushed at the edge of the enemy's rail and dripped down the hull. Zoren snatched up the lantern and with crow-clawed fingers, lit it; he flung it at the vessel.

The retreating hull was not retreating with enough alacrity. Flames sprouted on the exposed flank. Zoren sank to his knee. A harsh dribble of a laugh rumbled from his crooked mouth. "Now you know, mates, why I call my ship the *Last Laugh*!"

The lower part of the enemy's hull began crackling at stern. Hot flames fled across the aft cabin. Water was piling round Zoren's knees. Desperately the remaining sailors fought to douse the orange menace, but the dirty pitch was formidable and could not at this late time be quenched.

Arnin's ancillary vessel lurched. The captain clawed at his hair, bawling orders at the helmsman who could barely hear him: "Open the sails! Bend on a beam reach. Tip the craft larboard to the water! Quench the flames!"

But the damage had already been done. The ship was sinking beyond repair. Foundering in flames off *Two Silkie's Rock*, the carrack descended in swirls and eddies into the olive-black water. The eight or so crew members dropped their longboat into the frothing waves and paddled away from the dying ship. They pulled like madmen toward Arnin's craft which lay two hundred yards away.

The prince surveyed the destruction with outrage. Flames leaped over his escort, consuming it like a scourge, but it had no effect on his visage. The stern bubbled. A hideous mud-sucking sound erupted from the waves as the ship was dragged under.

For a moment the air seemed frozen. Arnin raised his voice in such shrill remorse that he ordered a boat despatched to kill the survivors and torch the fleeing jolly boat.

Zoren's fighters managed to cut loose the captain's gig and escape the sinking *Last Laugh*. But now eight sailors crammed themselves in the trembling hull: Bargil, Magretir, Fuurdhal, Poli, Jama, Valere, Baus, Zoren—sweating, grimed, cut, blooded, bruised and battered, the desperados tugged at the larchwood oars. No sea birds cried or screeched on this dour day. The craft rode the cat-pawed swells like a black-winged crow. She was deeply weighted—her gunwales sank almost below the water line, but they pushed on with grim hope, desperate for life. The faces of the crew were delirious; their losses had been inordinate. Dark bands of jade rode on the brooding seawater bespeaking of omens to come. A daytime half moon hung low in the east where piles of slick, yellow cloud came racing in to obscure it.

The wind howled, a low, contemptuous moaning. It presaged a dire fortune which could prove the company's undoing.

Despite the odds at survival, Zoren and his crew paddled on with fury toward the smaller isle. Baus could see Borath and his few staggering seamen fighting a last stand on the beach. A half score of the greycoats had them besieged between the land bridge and the sea. It was easy to see from this vantage the pirates would be cut down in rags despite their savagery and cunning. A dozen more armed soldiers had scrambled down from the hillock to swarm Borath's buccaneers. The pirates bore only knives and daggers and what other weapons they could strap on the trainees' persons before abandoning their sinking vessel. The water was not deep here, but enough to claim Borath's ship, for its submerged hull lay on a forty degree list. Mast, sprits and rigging hung in ragged tatters, blackened high above the water line. Baus looked at it and shook his head, thinking it looked more like a shredded skeleton than a barque of power.

The prince's longboats were already in the water, eager to intercept Zoren's gig. A cry came up from a watchman on deck. He was hanging from the masthead, gesticulating to the north.

Heads turned. From a far way off, the lurid balefire burned redly in the sea. Urseth's barque was returning from the ruin! Like some mythical hero, a rufous slit wide with open ragged sails, the pirate had miraculously survived the attack of its twin foes.

A great crow-cawing came from Arnin's crewmen.

Zoren laughed aloud. As experienced as he was, his face looked a shocked mask. A great purple gash ran diagonally across his right cheek; crows' claws parted corners of his eyes. He looked frightfully old, ashen, as if he had aged ten years in the last hour. But his gleeful cry championed to cheer his spiteful men to fervour. "By the moon and the sun, bless Urseth and his ugly goat hide!"

Fuurdhal loosed a cheer of his own. "We should have known the old dog wasn't deserting us! He was luring them out to sea so that he could work his magic—let them catch up, and turn and ram them. What mastery! The old trick of the sea buccaneer."

Magretir coughed up a bout of blood. "Judging from the flames, I would guess the other was roughed up the old-fashioned way. Urseth probably managed to ram one of the ships and sink it."

"Whatever—board, slaughter and burn!" laughed Fuurdhal crazily.

"Aye, we shall not forget this turn or lose this fight after all, Zoren!" cried Valere. "Let's keep our heads and chins up."

The grey pirate croaked out a rude agreement. He wiped at his own bloody cheek. "If Urseth does fall against Arnin, we might not be able to get Borath back to speed . . ." His own ghastly face seemed to show measured truth in the statement. "Who knows how many men died out there on *Sea Warlock*?"

"We can only hope that many did not . . . Row, lads, row!" cried Fuurdhal.

XII

Perceiving the distant flames, prince Arnin revamped an order to send his men-at-arms onto his two longboats after the pirates. It appeared the prince needed all his men to salvage the defence. From the expression on his sallow, pinch-lipped face, it was inferred that two of his warships had been overwhelmed, and one of the pirate chiefs was bearing down on him with dispassion.

The odds were evened; one vessel was pitted against another. Arnin's hand was forced; Baus watched as the prince's flagship drew a slow arc out to engage Urseth in the darkening wake.

With a gleeful howl, Zoren's men paddled to shore, joining Borath and his butchers in the hope of defeating the remaining opposition.

Even before the gig reached the beachhead, Borath's men were falling like flies. Magretir and Fuurdhal piled out of the craft, waist deep in foam, sloshing with all their might and rude battle threats on their lips. The clink of metal on metal was the first thing Baus heard as the heaving of grunts and howls of fighting men fast-flying to oblivion increased in tempo. Borath and his men were pushed back to the water's edge. Only four warriors were left in his company—three of his best men were left dead, bloody stalks reddening the near white sands. The attacking greycoats had lost many more in the skirmish and lay on their bellies, face up or eyes distended and bodies skewed at unnatural angles.

Baus and Valere struggled to haul the boat ashore. Zoren raised a hopeful shout—but Borath was singly engaged in hand-to-hand combat with a lanky man-at-arms dabbed in mail with snail-brown hair creeping round his ears under an iron cap.

Zoren's boat slid gratingly onto the unyielding sand. Even as Borath lost precious ground, the grey pirate ordered his blood-smeared fellows to grab extra weapons and join the outnumbered crew. Bargil, Poli and Jama tossed weapons at the grateful defenders—cutlasses, halberds, a notched broadsword. They all hurried to raise their own weapons.

The half score of Royal defenders met their new attackers with ophidian fury. The air was thick with strident clangs, axe-grinding, blade-thrusts and jeers of anguished battle. Cutlasses were drawn, axes were hefted, shields were belled.

Baus and Valere seized the initiative; they drew back. Neither wished to fight a battle against these fearsome fighters, especially in war that was not theirs. Four more bodies had gone to the underworld, leaving Jama pierced and torn through the gut by a surprise jab from a grinning, vindictive greycoat. Three other soldiers too, hacked to their knees, begged for quarter but were slashed, dying in crimson sprays as Borath and his men cut them down in dark retribution. Ruby ichor stained the beach; bodies piled up and joined the ranks of the dead by the minute.

The two captains, Zoren and Borath, fought side by side—a rare sight.

Borath swirled his halberd; Zoren carved slashing loops with his cutlass. The twain scythed together a Stygian corridor through the invaders as farmers cut flaxhack. The soldiers were losing men, but it looked as if reinforcements were struggling with broadswords and axes up the hillock . . . soldiers who were ungraced of armour and thinking twice about engaging these new, blood-crazed avengers.

On the edge of his vision, Baus saw a sudden flash—a disturbing vision, an aureole, limned under jagged white flash-lightning. He could hear a low wailing coming from the direction of the ridge.

The sound stopped, then repeated itself again—in mournful abandon—the cry of a maiden perhaps, rising above a grinding howl of the wind.

Baus squinted into the darkening fog. He glimpsed a bewitching image that completely unnerved his senses of reality: a fraily beautiful creature—a lost ghostly profile, somewhat slender and young, like some waif or maid of lovely proportions. The figure was rising above the gorse between the boulders of the ancient rock, floating like some mysterious ghost with mystical effervescence. Then, another figure appeared—a spectral maid, a shadow of green luminous cloak and fishy scales glimmering on thighs.

Baus's blood curdled. Silkies! Lestra and Baian—each wearing an egg-white garland of hewn fish heads!

A moribund marvel—and now old Ridgar rising between the twain, dripping seawater from lank locks and draped in wet, billowy rags as if he had just crawled up from the sea. Baus gaped. Others too. The dead buccaneer's face was ghostly white and wastingly withered. He flourished a crooked hand that clutched out feebly for the 'Eye', pointing a distended, wrinkled finger toward Zoren.

Zoren gasped aloud, groping for his amulet. He found it nowhere. The grey pirate crowed out a strange, hollow cry. Refusing to believe the awful truth he faced, he gulped—and only a leather cord was where once had hung his precious talisman.

The trio of spectres drifted behind the greycoats. They surrounded one and more of the soldiers. Lestra wrapped her fishy figure about a burly brute of an axe-man who had his weapon raised at Bargil.

The touch was like ice and the brute fell, blue as a winter gillfish. Craal, one of Borath's men, bulled his way through the throng and was next to fall. Bargil narrowly escaped the lethal toxic embrace of Lestra as he dog-hopped a ridiculous path away from the harpy, barely out of reach of those cold, fiendish fingers.

Baus could see very plainly that every slimy detail of those beautiful skins was evil. The garlandy gruesome wreaths, the dull blue eyes, the twitching visages, and no less the pulsing fish-scaled thighs . . . All details hinted of a hostile, impudent presence—but no more insolent than they, who had invaded their home upon which the Silkies meant to exhort justice. Ridgar's Eye was holding up to its name . . . at least in relation to the Eye's curse.

Apparitions? Hallucinations?

Baus could not explain. It would be easy for a sinister trick of the fog to conduct such nightmare. Other men descried the fiends: greycoats, pirates, who fled by the dozen in all directions, raving berserkly while old Ridgar swatted uselessly at the air where the Eye had been snatched from his grasp. One of the green-glowing maiden's restless hands had seen to that.

Baus quavered. He tried to flee but his legs would not budge. Many of the pirates had stayed their ground, captured by a superstitious numbness that had fixed them to immobility. Watching horrified, they were reduced to stupor as Ridgar pawed for his bauble in vain, then crumpled to his knees as if part of his spirit had been siphoned away . . . his body shimmered, then crumbled out of time and mind.

The Silkies, for all their lust for Ridgar's Eye, seemed to wither and waver too in abandon. Later they flickered like glow moths, then dissolved into nothingness.

Everything had changed. Baus found himself left speechless. The apparitions had vanished, yet the pirates were left in hunching humility, not sure whether to believe their eyes or not. Fewer enemies stood before them, true, but this was a limited boon. Baus swivelled his head in dream-like apathy—seeing the ketch rocking in the strait as if defying demise.

To engage a beachside enemy was not his wish. Yet somehow he liked it better—to be faced with the slow, unreal death of the dream players. The brooding sultriness in the air reminded him of some gallow's dream which unnerved him to pieces as the sallow sky deepened its shade of menacing yellow. The gendrons on the hillock seemed grouped in conspiratorial clumps. The onset of a new vagrant gust caused witch-like shrubs to bend in sinister supplication. A storm brewed from afar, prompting vultures, sea thrush and other scavengers to throng and enjoy the taste of blood and the bodies floating in the strait. Soon these predators would be the ones feeding on those up the beach.

Everywhere death . . .

Baus tasted the melancholy of ruin with a fulsomeness that he had never known. Reflecting on this useless slaughter was an exercise in sorrow, so he abandoned it.

His reverie was pre-empted. A sword blade came angling out from the thicket of steel, slicing a perilous curve hair-breadths from his chin.

He recoiled. A burly, fleshy-faced soldier cut his way past Bargil and aimed a mortal thrust at his neck.

Baus cringed with horror. Two quick leaps and Valere deflected the near fatal stroke. The attacker's weapon clubbed Baus heavily on the side of head—and he crumpled with a gash above the ear.

Bells tolled in Baus's head. The pain was astronomical. Parried by Valere's saving thrust, his life had been magically saved, but as time dimmed to candle-flickers, he perceived the soundless void of the unreal world. It was lonely here—a cavernous afterlife, frozen in some miserable time and space—a cove of death. His life ebbed out on the bleached sand, and a coming storm washed away all memory of his blood and grief. A new twist suddenly emerged into his weary silence: Valere engaged an enemy who was his killer and Baus saw a vicious struggle of sword in minute by minute detail. Fatal lunges, brutal heaves, cutthroat feints . . . all were boarish tricks—all coming from some dreamlike vantage, in slow life. As if a hundred years had passed, dimly tempests moved and suns and moons rose and died . . .

Poli rushed back to the throng. On sight of Jama skewered, he hefted his halberd and in one running leap carved it heavily along the length of Valere's opponent's back, thus searing through mail, skin and spine. The greycoat crumpled without passionate cry.

Raindrops fell. Like cold, indifferent pricks, they soothed Baus's hallucination and calmed steel around him. How many minutes passed, Baus could not know. The last strike had laid him within a hair's edge of death. The memory stirred in his consciousness, somewhere in the ether of awareness, tugging at his subtle body, telling him that he was already dead, but that only his spirit floated over his body, infused with some bleak knowledge.

Baus struggled to rise. But he was unable. Valere and Poli helped him gain his feet. With head swimming, the first things he saw were the beach and the ketch. Toppling again, he realized with painful cognizance it was their only chance. The same sleek and unassuming craft bobbing so innocently in the murky strait—it was a hundred yards off and was a saviour. He saw also Zoren's gig slapping at the growling waves. The two craft gave Baus cause for a grand idea. With heart booming, he heard his own voice echoing in his brain like some distant drum.

"Valere!" He motioned toward the ketch, uttering a croak.

"What?" Valere's brows knitted. "The boat is a fair way's off."

"I can push off the gig; you take the ketch."

Valere shook his head grimly. "The rogues'll slay us. We are deserters to them, nose-pickers."

"Not if we're fast . . ."

"We'd have to be awfully quick."

Poli instantly realized the plot. He pushed himself forward and growled, "Do not exempt me from your ploy!"

"As you like," Baus muttered. He felt the blood returning to his limbs and was thankful. "Time ebbs as we bicker." He staggered to his haunches. Pushing up from his knees, he began to lope off toward the gig. The boat was beached precariously in the slapping waves and to any who saw the craft, it looked like a lone, desperate longshot, not worthy of worry.

Valere grabbed him by the arm. "Not you! Poli and I'll take care of the gig, you make for the ketch. We'll meet you there—and if we don't, please tell everyone it was a great ride and to have a pot of tea boiling for our ghosts."

Baus missed the grin on the redbeard's face. The captain and Poli tore away from the pack and began a half-hobbling lope toward the waterside.

Zoren and Borath thinned out the attackers. With Magretir and Fuurdhal still fighting at their flanks, they were now chasing a half dozen soldiers up the fallen boulders shouldering the land bridge. The greycoats, suddenly realizing that their luck was not infallible, staggered on in helpless formation. They understood that winning this fight meant commanding the higher ground—and outmatched by the brigands, they were not so eager to expose themselves and be clubbed and gored down the beach, while exhausting themselves unnecessarily.

The fugitives reached the summit's drab pale outcrops. They huddled amongst the clustering rockthorn and stringy crowswheat growing amidst the low hedges of gorse. Here, patches of goat trails marked the upper slopes—though what sensible animal would inhabit the barren crags, Baus was not privy.

Poli and Valere grabbed the gig. They were grimly running it out into the water and as it floated into the open sea, they chuckled at its effectiveness in sabotaging the pirates' attempts at escape. Baus was cheered, recovering some of his backbone as he shambled down the beach toward the strait where the ketch lay anchored. A figure lagged behind, one who had been trailing him for a while, blood oozing from his tattooed forearm. This ruffian and villain had spied Baus fleeing gracelessly with cutlass dangling from his slack arm. He believed him a coward, and rushed to intercept, knife gripped on the ready.

Baus heard the yell from behind not moments too soon and he turned to see Bargil. Sizing up his mettle, the outlaw realized he had two practical choices: the boatswain was still a formidable enemy, wounded as he was and without prime weapon, and Baus had no doubt who would be the victor should the pirate be obliged to skewer him with his dirk.

Baus swiftly dropped back a pace. Fingers scrambled for the ganglestick. Bargil bared his bloody-smeared blade, hesitating upon seeing the feeble talisman. Baus could read the boatswain's mind—slay or be slain by another vermin—the choices were clear. No matter, Baus laughed. He ignored Bargil's mirthful chortle and lifted the talisman. "What humbug contrivance is this pin you clutch?" cried Bargil.

It was the whisper of the boatswain's undoing. Baus cut down with a rigid sweep, slashing an exposed part of Bargil's unprepared wrist. It clutched the dagger and in midstep Bargil teetered and fell paralyzed. An expression of reptilian disbelief strained his face: a horrid grin changing from victory to an astonished grimace.

Baus carefully scrambled toward the ketch, leaving Bargil to his ruminations. Baus's own skull throbbed with the force of his recent head blow. The shortest route to the ketch was through rocks and mats of gorse. Baus flinched. Certainly not the most pleasurable venture, but the most practical. Reaching the battered shore, he crossed the slippery rocks with no few erratic steps as he struggled amongst the reeds with awkward urgency. Murky slimes had him grappling for footholds in the knee-deep water.

The waves were cold; Baus's skin instantly broke out into hives. But he plunked one arm in front of another, looking back over a shoulder to spy Valere and his crony sprinting for the rocks and hop-scotching their way amongst the reeds like clowns as he himself had done before plunging into the icy water.

Baus cringed at the oily feel of the water. It contaminated him with its sloppy spillage from *Windbane*. Zoren heard the splash behind him, perhaps even Bargil's cry and seeing his gig floating free on the water and the tide skewing it toward the mainland, he called out an anguished roar. He raked bloody fingers through his hair. Shimmying back to the shore, he cocked his sword. Furious at seeing his boat bobbing so foolishly out of reach in a rain-dappled sea, he seemed half-puzzled to spy Bargil frozen there like some lazy bumpkin. But he was less mystified to spy the three retreating deserters flailing arms through the water like tasked pumpmills toward the ketch.

Zoren roared out a blasphemy. Borath turned in his felling stroke, caught the gist of what was happening and pulled his man Yalleor out of the fray. The two abandoned their axe play, raced toward the ketch.

"Zoren, Seacrow!" Borath thundered. "This is all your doing!" He bared a scorched fist at his enemy. "My ship, your ship, now these bloody scum bugging off with the only good boat left on this turd of an island. You're an idiot, Grey Mane. It's the Eye's curse!"

Zoren shouted an obscenity, but he dared linger no longer with Borath to receive his effects. Zoren's new recruits were bellying up fast to the ketch.

Borath pulled at Yalleor to hurry. They sucked in anguished breaths before diving into the murk. They scrabbled after the fleeing traitors. Magretir, Fuurdhal and Mrik and Quinsad were the last remaining pirates of Borath's crew who hurried over to swim.

Baus was halfway to the ketch when he heard troubled shouts ringing from behind him. Valere and Poli struggled less than a stone's throw away.

Baus urged his arms to swifter momentum, but was puzzled to hear the crunch of timber to his left. He jerked his neck around and listened. The grinding was followed by a sudden splashing, as of some great body thwacking itself against the water.

Baus treaded water, ears perked with amazement. His back shivered from the chill. He saw yards away, the ruins of *Windbane* swaying in the glowering mist like a lost derelict. Such remnants were cast in portentous shadow under the towering cliff dominating the foreshore. Perhaps a spar or joist of burnt timber had fallen? But why the precarious crunch? The tumult seemed more like a set of gripping fangs ripping into wood than of falling debris.

Large drops came down from the sky. Wind hurled itself into Baus's face and forced him to squint. He swam on. Valere caught up to him, and Poli, not the greatest swimmer, dogpaddled far to the rear. The oily water was strewn with chunks of flotsam—bits of planks, bales, ropes, rigging, scorched sails and blood. The latter was of grave concern. Over his shoulder, Baus caught sight of three thin, triangular fins jutting out of the water near the murk of crippled *Windbane*. Ten inches high, the appendages were the counterparts of a gaping face set three feet from the fins. The visage housed a set of great white, brown-flecked teeth veering out of the inky stain like menacing sawblades. The creature seemed engaged in some facile procedure of devouring a floating bale as if it were a sugar cube.

Baus's teeth nearly chewed off his tongue. He began a paroxysmal dogpaddling. The monster now submerged in a foaming rush. With a livid energy, it plunged toward Baus who now scrambled like a fiend through the filthy water. "Get out!" he cried to Poli. "Hurry, you fools! Extract yourself from these vile waters! It's hammerfish that lurk!"

The blood and bodies of the dying had attracted the predators—cold-blooded monsters, armed with three-inch spiked teeth easily snapping through a plank. The devourers' white, three-foot long nose-bills tapered like giant's spears were easily equipped to gouge out their prey's vitals and drag them underwater to feed on. In relation to the wounds inflicted by a man's sword, these prongs were terrors incarnate.

With frantic haste, Baus thrashed and flailed. He realized that his wounds and those of others were attracting the vile monsters.

Valere and Poli back-clawed their way toward the ketch. They were in a state of panic. Aware that he was farthest out, Poli shortened the gap in one frog-kicking spurt. It appeared that Borath and Yalleor were a bit slow in cognizing their danger, and the grotesque, rubbery body was frogging itself ever closer to their cluster. They ploughed frantically toward the shore.

With alacrity Baus hauled himself up, straddling the ketch's ladder and beaching himself on the deck. He choked back his fright, lying there like a terrorized fish on his back, forcing air into his lungs. His head swam like an eel; Valere clambered up almost on top of him.

Poli was next. Valere hauled up the anchor and Poli manned the stern. The three managed to unship the sails.

The ketch rocked in a lash of winds. The sails were like wet board; the vessel was moving, but in a slow, maddening, snail-like crawl.

Borath and his mate were just clawing their way out of the rubbish-littered water when the snapping teeth came clacking inches from their heels. Zoren and Magretir hauled them out of the water. The remaining crew breathed relief and joined the party. They watched the ketch depart.

Zoren, Magretir, Fuurdhal and Borath stood bleakly on the shore, gazing at the ketch as it slowly pushed its way away from the arch and inched toward the island's shadow side. The pirates were stranded on Silkie island. Appalled and furious—they realized their escape avenues were gone or destroyed and the cunning of the deserters had left them high and dry. Siege or skirmish was what they faced by whatever garrisons of greycoats came after them. As to the success or non-success of Urseth's campaign against the Prince of Owlen, none knew. Low-lying clouds had obstructed all vision.

The pirates bawled at each other. They hurled insults, threw fists in the air and at each other. The ketch's crewmen accepted the abuses while they waved briefly to them on deck, ashen-faced and sopping, but they were alive and grateful for the timing of their exploit.

A feud had erupted on shore. Borath lashed out at Zoren. Zoren retaliated with a brisk sweep of his rapier. Borath's left arm was sliced in a sickle curve. Borath let out a great howl which became a painful, rancorous gasp. The villain uttered his own battle cry. Prospects did not look good for the Butcher—or his mates—as Magretir and Fuurdhal rounded on them. It was a fight long overdue, and Mrik and Quinsad, Borath's men, did not defy Zoren in his final moments of retribution.

The weather was turning fast. Out of the shelter came the ketch, biting into the high, rebellious waves which shook the vessel. Out in the northerly sea, two blurred forms circled each other in perilous sweeps. One stalked the other, the other dodged like a prowling drake. It was impossible to see which vessel was to better advantage, for visibility was dimmed to obscurity. Only streamers of lightning took centre stage, flashing from all directions while black clouds brewed and billowed on the horizon.

Dark folds unfurled in the sky. The cumuli were devoid of any pity. Thunder clapped in men's ears like the beat of war cantos. The wind pushed the cold beads of rain in the fugitives' eyes; the vicious storm drew close: perhaps ten, maybe fifteen minutes would have them caught in its full wrath.

The sailors returned to the narrow task of their navigation and flushed with exhilaration, they realized that their efforts expended now would be those that saved or sunk them. Squalls began to stir the ketch's sails, making the canvas ripple like fury. The willowy craft, bent over at an impossible angle, seemed to steer a clumsy path toward the phantom mainland.

The vessel rolled up and over the looping swells like some plumb bob. The water—greased with black pitch—seemed an unreal boiling cauldron. The storm had grown to grey quavering squalls that squashed funnels down on them like giants' wrath. The fragile vessel was too vulnerable, too much wanting to capsize.

Valere spun hard to port. The captain veered round the south tip of the island showing nothing but a grey-green blur. The tide would not help them, but the unrelenting lash of the wind might—if it did not capsize the boat before they could steer further north, or catapult themselves closer to Sloe, home to Maena who had little love for freebooters . . .

Baus clung feverishly to his mast. His nerve-frayed fingers reached for the sea charm. He felt a tiny ghost of hope there—he could feel a near palpable warmth, moving from the favoured talisman to his breast.

CHAPTER 2

SLOE

"From the gates of Slaen came the hue and cry,*
The portcullis was lifted, the helmed warriors died,
Hefting axes, lifting spears,
Towers gleaming, gongs a-toll,
The armies fell on Slaen's foes . . .
Journeyed from around the world on square-sailed brigs,
Her thousand, sapphire-hued ramparts kept distinct,
From blood of all minions to come,
But who now pines for days when glory lies undone?"

—From 'Ballads of Old Slaen'.

I

The ketch was a mass of splinters. Brine gushed over her gunwales while scraps of sail and fore-spar were driven into the hungry sea like chaff.

The craft's life was ebbing. Slippery crags of foam half as high as the foremast poured across the hull like mountains of ale. Now forked lightning crawled across the sky like glistening webs. Thunder boomed in the outlaws' ears: Baus could hear the whistling of wind as he clung frantically to the fractured stern rail and watched the last of the mainmast sag and her main-stays disappear forever into an oily deluge. Soaked and windswept, Baus gave a great howl and fell several fathomless feet as the breaking waves wrenched his grip . . .

The outlaws were driven into the tumultuous waters like half-flogged hederpest. Through dark swirls they pawed their way, drowning like dogs, aimlessly swirling, grappling, snatching, clutching, groping for safety, finally grabbing a haft of the mainmast . . .

Valere beached himself on a sandy crest. He pulled his comrades to safety, dragging them by the scruffs of their necks. They slapped themselves out of their terror and coughed out seawater from stinging lungs. Obviously the gooey shelf of beach that spread in either direction was nearer than they thought and they squinted hopelessly into the rain like

---

* *Slaen*: Sloe, as it was known of old; also known as *Slevan* and *Smaerna*.

drowned rats. Valere, half spent, clutched his cutlass for strength and the sodden, nearly-spent mariners lay on their backs, pumping for air.

Lifting themselves to wobbly attention, they found only a stabbing downpour and hard wind pressing at their frames. It tore at the walls of their resolve. Gimlets of light peeked from a ridge to their right.

A promise of shelter?

A miserable trickster of a mirage?

Baus could not say; but the glinting appeared a double bowshot up a long slope . . .

He limped a few steps, gripping his aching head. Poli wrestled with the contents of a sea-sick gut. Valere escorted the two of them under his armpits with unsympathetic authority. The unique passage of the company was unnoticed as they trudged the dark, slippery foreshore like beleaguered beggars . . .

A settlement appeared to the right under the bright glare of lightning. Baus saw a twain of old barnacled dories beached up the shore. Poli suggested they drag a wreck over and crawl underneath to wait out the storm.

"A pedestrian idea," coughed Baus. "'Twas I who chanced upon the glow, shall be I who investigates first."

Poli mumbled an oath. Somewhere off in the rain-washed distances tall wooden buildings loomed, along with deserted cobbled streets, a bell tower, flickering with lamp light.

After a decent quarrel, the three struggled up to the *Rambling Mariner Inn*, a timber-framed tavern crafted of antique quality. It leaned off a wooden-planked boulevard called *Windlass Way* which they perceived as the main avenue of the fishing settlement called 'Alcax', owing to the large sign swinging under the lantern's light.

The trio staggered into the foyer, shook off the water and took stock of their surroundings. They had entered into a cozy, low-key establishment where low-ceilings showed smoke-blackened beams and decorated pillars, indicating a progressive harmony mixed with air smelling of beeswax, aged pinewood, roasted pheasant and boiled fish—a place where men clenched ale-tankards and talked in the philosophical tones of men of the world. Still there were enough mutters and grumbles of the havoc being wreaked on their sailing boats and residences.

In the soft amber light, a fire crackled in an open seashell hearth. Baus scrutinized his companions critically, ill-liking Poli and the lurid bash over his eye and the odd feral look gleaming in his face. His arms dangled at his sides with what could have been construed as the stance of a sea thug. Valere sported no small raffishness of his own: a number of horridly disfigured welts decorated his brow. The seaman's face was clamped in a mirthless grin. His jerkin, slashed, was tar-blackened and noisome, and his aspect was more than slovenly; yet, the water had at least washed away the excess blood from his garment and thankfully his weapon did not peek out too obtrusively from his dripping belt.

Under the squinting inspection, the three saluted the patrons who grunted in convivial acknowledgement. When asked of what misfortune made them look like a bunch of war-torn soldiers, the outlaws left out such details as wrecked ketches and blood-wracked duels with unsavoury rogues. Fibs and confabulations slipped from Baus's lips. He managed to convince Huske, the innkeeper, that they were antiquity dealers and spice merchants, businessmen who had encountered footpads on the way south from Aurenham, despite their best intentions to remain inconspicuous, though no small number of animated gestures and forthright confessions portrayed this image. The long and short of it—Huske hired them out a room, ordering fresh linen and whistling reassurances at his mates while the landlord graciously served them hot food: boiled scallops, ox-tongue soup, braised black olives. The outlaws were grateful, though exposed to too much small talk, and consumed their dinners with sullen, wolfen grimaces.

The storm let up and after some bawdy interchanges and clinking mugs, the companions retired to their room, with no wistful longings about staying overlong, to impair their shared exhaustion.

* * *

The mariners did not wake the following morning—or the next. They could have slept a week, but such was not to be.

By noon of the third day their slumbers were interrupted by Aefta, the innkeeper's daughter who was carrying a salver of tea and bath oils. She had come to tidy up their room.

Perhaps it had been too long on ship—but Poli's eyes were agape and becoming large saucers at the sight of such a comely woman after so long a hole-up in a stinking ship and a rude hut. He jerked his head to attention and put on a cordial manner as such to engage the girl with his charm.

Valere was unimpressed with the juvenile urgency and pushed Poli out of the way. He sported a grin much broader and smoothed out his ragged beard and garments, jocularly suggesting that the two dip in the tub in the back for a small oil massaging or scrubdown-trade.

The girl, of course, was offended by such a proposal and splashed hot tea in Valere's eyes. The seaman cried out in anguish, hopping from one foot to the other in blind dismay and confusion.

Quietly Baus herded the charwoman out of the room before more improprieties could be perpetrated.

Puffy-eyed and heavy-lidded, Valere muttered oaths while Baus staggered to the window. He felt his muscles racked by tongs; his bones felt like death had claimed them. Disregarding Valere's tumult, he assessed the scene below in the street. The village road wound down to the harbour where daylight showed thinly. The road, awash with mud, was a mat of wobbly planks fitted over runnels of dark water. The storm had washed away most of the harbour-side soil and storehouse roofs sagged; the lighthouse looked a jarred pylon. No lamp shone. The old basalt pier looked grey and ancient. Northward the bleak and sandy shore ran, the same one on which they had landed, now swept clear of boats and nets. North winds blew canvas and scraps of wood about the narrow alleys.

Baus looked up to a clear and cold sky suffused with pale gold. He felt a sombre melancholy. Tattered cloud moved swiftly out to sea. Top-heavy wagons rolled noisily on the clapboard, bringing with it the clop of wegmor hooves.

Baus inhaled the smells of fresh-baked rye bread, nevertheless, from the casement.

Across the road a chandlery reposed while a candle-maker's shop was shuttered beside a bakery and barber shop. A silver-tasselled shoe shiner vied with a fishmonger to attract business to his drying racks of meagre saltfish and hederpest.

The scene charmed Baus and he lost some of his sober mood. The sea took on a particularly bland sight in Baus's opinion, though. Past the crumbling, tumbledown shipyard, slow, methodical waves rocked the pylons where a few stalwart dory-men poked for wreckage amongst the scraps and any cast-up seamen. Overturned ketches and half sunken sloops were listed on distinct angles. How many had lost their lives? Baus did not care to surmise. Lean-skinned sailors dug fingers into mooring lines, shaking heads in melancholy at the deplorable damage inflicted upon their fishing vessels.

Yet life continued. Fat barges plied the routes between Sloe and the Quelion reach and Aurenham to the north. The tar-glistening hulls were laden with timber, fleece, flaxhack, olives, raisins and oils. *Two Silkie's Rock* was seen less as a menace from the distance and shimmered in the early light, no more than a faint luminescence on the horizon.

The sight registered poignantly on Baus's memory. He drew back from the window, tendering a prosaic grunt.

The ganglestick, after its rude sea-voyage of two nights ago, proved still operative, insofar as its demonstration proved efficacious in quelling Poli's obnoxious snores of yester-eve.

Combing back the dark clot of his matted locks, Baus peered dourly at himself in the mirror. He gargled his mouth out with cold water and sat with an aching slowness, donning his garments, feeling stiff and rank from salt and grime. He upbraided Poli for his tardiness and roused Valere to do something with his loutish hair.

The trio finally descended to the tap room.

"What? No breakfast?" squawked the innkeeper. His grease-stained apron was yellow with age.

Baus held up a reassuring hand. "Our company is on a fast."

"A fast! All of you? For two days? 'Tis not too expensive at the *Rambling Mariner*."

"I'm sure it isn't," commented Baus dryly.

"What of the indelicacies posed upon my daughter?"

"A brash incident, nothing of concern."

The landlord grunted but could not argue with the logic and he and the patrons gave each other respectful waves. Tipping their heads, the companions quit the inn, trooped southward upon the waterlogged lanes. Past fish stalls and the wine merchants, the water wells and the plazas, the three shuffled like glum peddlers. All were entertaining moods of mixed apathy. Valere maintained his stiff crouch in regard to the tenuous destination of the city of 'Sloe'.

"What of our presence as freebooters?" he complained. "Have you forgotten that we are outlaws, wanted criminals?"

Baus tapped his cheek wisely. "Pirates are not on anyone's mind here, Valere. The mugs in the *Rambling Mariner* inquired no further of who we were, or whence we came."

"So what? This is only a small sample of the vapid burglars about these shores I bet—"

Poli offered support of Baus's argument. "The wretches were only too glad to avail themselves of our few coins while we drank. Perhaps we can hire ourselves out as fishermen —or stevedores."

Valere shook his head mulishly. "I don't reckon myself spending months on end here in this cesspool. I think the rainy season is here. I yearn for a stiff north wind, a pint of honest brew!"

Baus brushed off this nostalgia. "As do we all. We are safer here, seabeard. The farther we head north, the more dear will be our heads, particularly in Heagram, much less Owlen—owing to a toxic familiarity with Zoren and his rogues."

Valere winced, smoothing his moustache. "True, while this may seem to be the best course, there is always the distinct possibility that we'll be discovered as sea wolves and hanged. Which would you rather have?"

Baus shook his head indulgently. "Neither—if we remain hidden."

II

The air was surprisingly warm for the season and away from the town's centre, ateliers and Spartan domiciles, the travellers came upon a coastal road, drifting south, weathered and assaulted with fitful sea breezes. From afar, they spied the gilded mountains of the Aldevean reaches, stretching to the south, rich with snow tips white as candles. The Tholsian Sea spread to their left: an aquamarine blanket of brooding eternity. Greyish gold meadows swept inland, fixed with winter wheat and barley, drifting off to olive-grey woodlands.

The road turned from gravel to pavestones. Now a fine granite path met their feet and thrust a pleasant route amongst boulders and sea-larch where bright spume receded in scintillating inlets. Gulls gathered in force to harry the travellers in the search of food.

Valere swatted at the scavengers. "Fiends! Nothing more than opportunistic freeloaders."

"Hmph! Are we anything less?" inquired Baus.

Valere had nothing to comment.

"A trio of vagabond exiles bumbling their way to Sloe without a groat," sighed Poli. "We've got scavenging to do if we want to eat."

"Aye, but hardly reason to cite the obvious," grumbled Valere.

"What's eating you anyways?" Baus muttered. "You seem tetchy."

"I am," he responded. "Recall, you interrupted me from a lucrative morning sport."

"'Twas not me who failed. Remind me again never to save your hide from a beating by a wench or a landlord."

"Bah! That fop and his milksops couldn't fight their way out of grain bags."

Baus calmly rectified Valere's flaw, "A dozen of his dockside friends might have given you a go if they had wanted."

Valere grew silent. By luck, or circumstance, the conversation ended in silence, and they managed to purchase a ride in the back of a goose cart. The farmer, on his way to a place west of the city, claimed it was a journey which would take them half an hour and somewhat closer to Sloe. "The rest of the distance you can manage on foot."

Of course, they were happy with the news. Perhaps they had covered two leagues to this goal when the sights of glinting masonry appeared on a gently-rising slope abreast the sea.

The three augmented their pace. They peered curiously upon one of the bluest sets of walls they had seen. No less palatial were the dozen skyward-reaching towers of an ancient city. The minarets surrounded the citadel with the majesty of a sorcerer's garland. Along its leviathan ramparts huddled teams of turrets, battlements—and archaic cannons and catapults. They all glowed with an uncanny luminescence—all of which seemed to be crafted of magical material, cast in a hundred shades of blue. The wind caught the resplendent flags and they saw polished stone quarried from the precious sodalite and gypsum mines of the nearby mountains. The city was architected from aquamarine to ultramarine—and all exalted hues between.

The walls encircled the city and wrapped around it like some great ox's tongue. Baus's heart was struck with marvel. The citadel blazed, the towers glinted: huge, onion-shaped cupolas rose on high and great hanging copper bells and bronze clock arms dangled low. They whispered many untold secrets to the new wayfarer. Meanwhile the highway meandered its way through manicured copses and old yellow dondar trees where the roadside met the old golden bridge to the north. Seven fantastic arches stretched over the Lix river. Wooded hills struggled down from the old road where great birds, arion-condors, soared. Tucked in behind the city, Baus saw brooding, serpentine-shaded forests; they all seemed to contrast with the opulent towers, resonating more harmoniously with the river's stealth. The ocean bloomed a carpet of jade to their left; her moody caps spread massively, dwindling onto a horizon of pale grey.

From the southern tip of the known world to her auspicious harbours, the Sloeian empire extended with its monarchs and suzerains of old and rich heritage. Now her reach was small, withering to only the still viable capital under the humble smattering of towns stretching not a score of leagues across the countryside and up the Tholsian sea.

It was said that, Kaung, the roving sea monster, half tortoise and manticore, had dredged out the famous horseshoe bay still extant along ancient Slaen's wharves. It would need be, thought Baus, for the quay was enormous! It made a prodigious shelter to huge numbers of barges, galleons, warcraft, sloops, luggers and cogs that lurked in her brackish waters. The old basaltic pylons were now dim ribs set in low tide. Fresh timber slats and oiled baulks made her present-day pier serviceable.

The spellbinding dissipated and the adventurers approached the north gate. They hunched their way across the bridge before gaining entrance to the city proper. It was another two furlongs through pleasant gardens and trimmed hedges before they reached the city's inner passage. Another paved road, much wider than the last, invested with a richer smaltish texture, wound down from the outer wall to the harbour where folk drove wagons, drays and cargo to the ships along the pier. Baus spied pulleys, chains, gantries, and low-roofed storage warehouses with silos of fused brick . . .

His awe only intensified, for sloops, schooners, ketches and barges filled the crescent-shaped harbour in plenitude, but pennons hung at half mast, indicating casualties that had occurred at sea. Baus frowned at the sight. A gigantic, haggard warcraft lay berthed in the northern jetty. Its resemblance to Arnin's formidable vessel became an eerie misgiving. The mainsail was rolled-up, yet her drooping billows lay in shreds while her jib yard hung lame and her battered hull listed severely amongst other damaged vessels.

Baus took himself to instant rumination. What terrible significance could the ship portend?

Ahead rose two barbicans housing uniformed gatewardens. The soldiers seemed to peer dispassionately upon the throng and the gatewardens were strapping fellows.

However, they were lax. Everyone today was admitted, excepting those most suspicious of characters, of whom Baus and his company were now exempted.

Passing the North Gate unchallenged, the three stamped ahead with the teeming hordes to file through the gap into the city. Citizens were stockier and swarthier than their northern neighbours yet their hair was flaxen-coloured and their complexion dark, Baus noticed—from ash-brown to oak-brown. The people were a mixture of carters, smiths, wheelwrights, shipwrights, grassherders, swineherds, merchants and musicians. All seemed rather loose-legged and inclined to wearing baggy clothing. Caftans were in vogue, and muslin jerkins, tall bottle-like hats, cloth boots, wegmor-sandals and goat-leather slippers.

The north-south road opened into a great plaza. Stone pillars tapered to spires, wooden stalls were bunched everywhere while daises spread with hawkers. There was a flurry of open-backed carts and broad columns carved everywhere today with signs and charms. The space was cramped, clotted with mud and chaos: overall, a confusion of pack-beasts and strident sounds. Teams of beasts huddled in the wet, shadowy corridors: wegmors, oxen, mules, shaggy marbacks and goats abounded.

The blue walls closed about them. They heard the throbbing of hawkers' voices, the keen tumult of commerce, the clatter of wares, the creaking of carts, animal grunts, squeals, bellows of contempt, hoof-clopping, shouts of palace waysmen. Beard-shavers sat in the muddy aisles or on greasy daises or low stools. There were shoe shiners with coiled topknots, foot-massagers with dragging shawls and linen cleaners with suave tongues, along with medleys of beasts which roamed the alleys where dirt-flecked urchins ran bare-footed and amok. Clambering carts of dung were hauled by bow-backed wegmors—all a profusion of noise, mud and stench.

All was not business, however. Dartboards were pitched against plaster backdrops—toy-clowns, bottle jugs, puppets, urns and other articles were the small targets, at which any member of the crowd could throw pebbles for money. To the side, bright-caped jugglers tossed lighted cubes; tambour and pipe players hawked for coins thrown into felt caps; caped merchants nodded, grinning behind their counters, each hoping to induce new citizens to purchase their wares.

Baus, Valere and Poli surged on through the milling crowd without interest.

Shoulder-bumping gave way to irritation; the outlaws evaded certain accostings by bards and cheerful eye contact with bumptious vendors. Yet all was overwhelming and no description could be accurately given for what they perceived, nor for which would define their usual habits in the secluded villages of the north.

A gong tolled from one of the towers. A melancholic knell shook the city like a thousand instruments. Two more gongs replied, prompting Baus to peer up in surprise. Three o'clock already! Nary a one of them had gained an extra cil, a condition of misfortune.

Baus gripped his ganglestick. Valere and Poli stopped short.

Ahead a shrill voice rang out. In the bustle appeared a man was arguing with a merchant over the tally on a weigh table of confections. A sprinkling of sweetmeats and assorted freshly-scrubbed vegetables gleamed with other comestibles to the side. The fellow was tall and his mien serious and he wore a great golden hat with fleecy layers wound up into meticulous coils like a beehive. Baus thought the orderly headgear indicative of a like inflexibility of character—but his opinion was secondary. The customer was inherently well-padded, wrinkled of skin and sported a small pinched nose.

"Ho, Rustas!" this man called out. "You would cheat me with this vicious scale."

"Never!" cried the vendor. "Such a device cannot lie."

"Ha! I'll be the judge of that. What is this plumb bob and suspicious little lever I see adjoining the hidden side?"

"An ornament only. Do not be concerned. Must you beset me with queries?"

A mule-faced woman hobbled up to the display and grabbed hold of her pawky man's arm. "Give him not an ounce more of his quack, Rustas! My Dartinet is a stuffer—a stuffer for tobacs!"

Dartinet grimaced down at the hag with dirty brown teeth. "Away, filthy crone! What know you of my gentlemanly habits?"

"Much!—and as like as everything, no more do I wish being bedded with you the last nineteen years of my life—or have you not noticed?"

"It is best forgotten."

The woman waved a meaty, raw fish in her husband's face. "On your way, cabbage-eater, before I swat you with my snogmald! There'll be no tobacs today."

Dartinet pinched his face into a grimace.

Baus turned his attention to the great forum that spread hugely in the marketplace. Queen's men marched in formation through the gathering, whether peacekeepers or heralds, holding aloft the ceremonial pikes of Sloe hung with feathery green and white pennons. The palace's blue walls glittered with tradition, interlocked sodalite that rose steeply to the eyes. To the casual onlooker, the ramparts seemed completely seamless, inscribed with coats of arms and glyphs of extravagance throughout the ages, but beyond the palace, the citadel's ramparts showed mystical, jewel-crusted spires and private apartments. The inner city revealed a gigantic conglomerate of elegant villas, gabled homes and exotic pubs that rested comfortably along the courthouse and baths. Past the bazaar, Baus could see great grey-blue blocks adjoining the East Gate. The wall itself rose thirty feet high; atop, pure Prussian-blue merlons perched proudly like turtle's teeth. Baus marvelled that each block was hand-carved and remained engraved with a mysterious emblem. More of breathtaking notice, were the ranks of lapis lazuli heads protruding from the high walls over the marketplace. They were monstrous and cut portentous grey shadows over the milling crowd. A bust even of the great tortoise Kaung hung with ponderous care, with its eyes carved of ancient opal. In shape and colour the effigy seemed several degrees older than the surrounding constructions.

Not a score of yards farther on, the palace wall was cut short by an entrance garrisoned by palace guards in buffed armour. Baus had to glance away at the great gilt portal, for the carved lintel and the daunting phalanx of columns soaring above his own small figure, awed him. Two columns spread to the right to flank a magnificent arch featuring six gonfalons of the Royal House. A red eagle was mounted on a green background; white clouds and haloes ran above and, through a small peep hole in the city's wall, Baus spied the Tholsian waves with grey-green swells glinting silver in the afternoon's light.

Forward, always forward. Baus sighed. The crowd surged. Valere and Poli moved with it —a sinuous rhythm, ancient and subtle—as was the way with old Sloe.

Baus looked wistfully back upon Rusta's table filled with its gamut of exotic fruits, cheeses and vegetables. How best could he strike a bargain for some victual? . . .

An idea brewed, giving way to Baus's husky whisper in Valere's ear.

Poli overheard the remark. "This would constitute common theft."

Baus gave Poli a slap. "You are a tiresome bore, even when you are not so jejune."

"And you are exploitative," countered the bully.

"Quiet down, you gulls!" griped Valere. "We've just slaughtered men. What's a few pilfered rutabagas? They won't be missed."

"How would we cook them?" asked Poli.

Valere cuffed him also on the head. "That's the least of our concerns, you dolt. Now we have to acquire the rutabaga first. Listen! You and me'll run interference on our friend Rustas while Baus will work his usual charms at the victual counter. Hoy, Rustas!" he cried jauntily. "We are in need of some excellent snuff, also some of this green, nasty powder which resides over here near your candles and your sweetmeats."

The kiosk-keeper's brows peaked into a frown. "Is that so? My powders are nonpareil, but the stock is very low, hereupon I must caution you to—" he scowled at the sight of their ungainly costumes and hesitated before waving them into his stall. Rustas went on to describe the benefits of his snuff, a dialogue which grew tiresome and waxing, owing to Valere's unending questions regarding its every associated minutiae.

While Rustas remained occupied, Baus shambled close to the display and used the crowd to shield him from scrutiny. He reached for a rutabaga then withdrew his hand. Numerous items were to choose from: legumes, beets, confections, spices, day wares. The question was, which item should he acquire first? A parsnip? Onion? Rutabaga?

The onion became Baus's premier choice. He snatched up a healthy specimen and tucked it in his pocket while leaning against the counter pretending to peruse other items, whereby he nonchalantly nicked a parsnip or two and two radish. He was about to foray for a carrot when up jumped a thin, glinty-eyed woman—she was long of face, sharp of chin and wore a light grey robe and tight hood. "Onions are out of season these days, sir, and a trifle expensive, if I say so, six sequals each."

"Outlandish!" cried Baus.

"You are not the only one to think so. Please put them back. The radishes you stuffed in your pocket are two sequals apiece. "

"These specimens—" warned Baus in a critical tone, "were acquired for a mere half sequal from the vegetable monger, Barbak, yonder."

The vendor seemed to marvel at the disclosure. "Really? Well, you are a magician then, to induce me to believe such bilge! Begone, you flutterbug. You seem to know all the vendors by their first name. Let us put an end to this nonsense and make Barbak's acquaintance. He shall surely put us all straight."

Baus dismissed such a plan. "I would not trouble to consume so much of Barbak's time."

"Poppycock! Doubtless he is an accommodating fellow."

By this time Rustas had escaped Valere's grip and was marching belligerently to his wife with whom Baus stood haranguing.

Baus felt his innards plummet. It would be easy to be seen as a common thief in such circumstance. Several of the royal guard were nearby, pinning banners and banderols along the walls of the palace. Very inopportune. It would take no moron to recognize a single call or calculated outburst from the vendors to have them plodding over with staves and dealing with the vendors' wrath.

Plucking the ganglestick from his cloak, Baus waved it about in an important way in the woman's face as if it were a thaumaturgical scourge. The woman allowed herself a comic snort. "What means this bit of dandycock you wave under my nose? Shall I use it to curl my hair—or swat at a fly?"

"Take heed!" Baus thundered authoritatively. "I shall introduce myself as a magician. Should this wand touch your person anywhere, you shall instantly become a decade younger! Watch the exposed area on the back of your wrist, for example."

No sooner had the remark been uttered than the vendor was left stiff as a zombie and her husband was standing gaping at her side in slack-jawed wonder.

Baus whispered admonitorily: "Take heed, merchant! You too are at risk. Your spouse has been ensorcelled. Regard! A poisonous blue bottle fly descending on your neck." The man peered. "Allow me to shoo it away, free of charge."

Rustas shrank back, shrugging off the imaginary fly. Baus was given time to lean over and touch the wand to the nape of his neck . . . Frozen to the core, the vendor stood mute like his spouse.

Baus moved back, sighing, admiring his handiwork, nodding with satisfaction at the problem solved. Rustas, quelled of peevishness, stood with chin bent and wearing a fractious look. His woman was not two paces away, with a half grimace on her lips. Baus, so absorbed with his finesse, failed to notice the shrewd rodent-faced figure inspecting him who was wrapped in a wine-coloured cloak, loitering in the shadows near the palace wall.

Baus was instantly on his feet, merging into the crowd, before any discovery of his deed could manifest. While the vendors were left behind, Valere and Poli had drifted off in casual wonder. They were now separated in a clot of people. Baus deigned to look for them but the same eavesdropper from the marketplace came sliding up to him in oily interest. "Listen, friend, I need only call out a few utterances, like 'thief' or 'swindler' and you, my fine vagabond, shall be serving the last of your days in a dungeon, a very dank and disreputable one—that or a hangman's noose." His announcement was ornamented with a hiss and a gripping of wrist.

Baus shot up brows in cool amusement and disengaged the grip. "This is a colourful threat. Refrain from the jokes, sir! They do not become you." He gained time to appreciate his opponent and sought to buy advantage with his idle blather.

The conniver however, grinned mirthlessly and side-stepped the banter. He moved about with restless energy. He was a slight man, wiry and secretive, wearing a dark, saturnine face and seemed an untypical person of Sloe in that his hair was rat-black and tied back in clots of curls instead of flaxen and hung loosely. He wore a thin oily cloak, a black skull cap and grey buskins whose tread made suspicious imprints on the muddy court. A thatch of disreputable beard swung unmannerly down to his chest. Black, ferret-like eyes were set close together, like some vulpine wanderer and his nose was a curious example of mismatched creation and artistry.

A subtle, dangerous fellow, thought Baus cannily—not to be trusted, so he did not underestimate him, and such remained his final, definitive assessment.

Despite the unpleasant development, the outlaw decided that to approach the situation with amity was the best course. "Let us converse together in private discourse, friend!—to a place out of sight of opportunists and sly rogues."

The other prodded him with blithe sarcasm, "Do not take me for a fool! You would herd me into a convenient alley and club me to death."

"Not at all. You misjudge my personality!"

"Now! Quickly! Tender me your funds—or I call out to the waysmen, and denounce you like the filchpurse you are."

"Now, now." Baus curled lips into an aspect of friendly familiarity. "That is an unwise act. Two of my brawny colleagues prowl a stone's throw away ready to pounce on any extortionist. They would beat you silly, not to mention cordially resent the fact that I had given up our communal gold on a mere whim. The men of whom I speak are impeccable fighters—bone-crushers, persons not to be given maudlin shrift. So, hear me when I say that altruism would not enter into any argument for your defence."

"Silence, you glibster!" the rat-man hissed. "I shall not subject myself to quips or badinage!"

Baus peered placidly past the blackmailer's loosely-cloaked frame. What on odd fellow! Poli was seen already well ahead in the crowd along with Valere and could not be accessed at this time. Nonplussed, the outlaw feigned a discouraged yawn. A look of worry flicked across his adversary's face. "Ah, what a jokester I am!" Baus cried. "I was just ribbing you. The other day I was telling my friend Poli how poor I am. As you note, I was trolling for rutabaga, not the sign of any rich man."

"The stick then!" ordered the opportunist. "Give me the magic stick and I'll go my way."

Baus crossed arms in obstinate hauteur. "Never! It is an heirloom."

"I don't care. Pass it over or I shall denounce you!"

"Go ahead!"

The stranger's fury reached an apex and wiry fingers suddenly dug into Baus's torso. Clawing for the ganglestick, he raked Baus's throat but Baus twisted aside, thrusting an elbow into the thief's throat. The man gurgled, but did not desist in his belligerence. So unexpected was his fierceness that Baus was left stymied and pitched backward, slipping on the muddy paves.

The thief pressed forward, one fist latching onto Baus's talisman. "Tender me the magic stick or hang!" The voice was like a guillemot's descent.

Baus fell; he pulled the thief with him. His hands were at an end of the ganglestick and the rogue and he tugged and rolled end over end. Baus had the silvery, nocuous end and was careful not to let its tip stun him into oblivion.

Tumbling shoulder to shoulder, the two sloshed in puddles, struggled amongst the curious, mocking crowd, rolling, dodging, feeling hobnailed heels, boots, knees, carts' wheels, and goose-bills catching their limbs. Baus could have easily clubbed the thief to death, but was wary of his talisman being damaged in the process and so opted to avert calamity.

A modest crowd had predictably gathered and were eager to leer at the tussle. No different was this crowd than any mob of the cities that hosted a conglomerate of uneducated peasants and lowlifes who come to enjoy such spectacles for the pure entertainment of it. Several had already wagered bets and were egging on Baus and the thief to toss assaults and aggressions and defamations which would escalate the conflict. Baus was disinclined to such crass sport; he struck out a blow without restraint. Suddenly the thief found himself congealed in a web of bodies and Baus gasped as he felt a ghastly snap in his hand.

The ganglestick wilted in his grip. Baus caught a puff of translucent smoke rising thinly into the air.

He looked down frozenly at his baton. It showed a jagged splinter running centre-wise. The device hung ever more spiritlessly in his hand like some sun-warmed mist—the shaft of a weapon shedding its last breath.

A livid curse sprayed from Baus's lips. He beat the rapscallion silly with his fists and knees.

The crowd hollered and whooped.

Baus gained his feet, snatching at the ganglestick. He took scrambling strides away from the circle, but was pushed back into the fray by members of the crowd. Further attempts at flight proved useless. They were forced to fight on. Now three uniformed guards thrust pikes into the mob and carved a way toward the fighters.

"What's all this ballyhoo about?" cried the lead watchman. "Jeracles! Kotax! Seize these oafish mischief-makers!" The uniformed men wore iron helms and nose-cheek guards. Gleaming dirks lurked in their broad belts; pikes were gripped in white-knuckled fists that showed ugly fishhooks at the end, an axe blade on the other. The deputies groped down with gloved hands, hauled up Baus and the opportunist. Crouched thickly in the mud, Baus gave a trenchant cry and the guards stared laxly while his oppressor remained sprawled supine. The soldiers pulled the scrappers up. They were blond-bearded, soot-faced and rude men with violent eyes and hard expressions ruling their blunt, uncompromising faces.

"What is your business accosting this citizen?"

"He is a robber, nothing more," explained Baus hotly.

"A robber, you say?"

"Aye, a robber!" declared Baus in more pompous language. "That is what I said! Do I need to shout it out? The rogue pick-pocketed me of my baton, which as you see is ruined." He offered the ganglestick, once-sleek, now sagging in fragile and forlorn flavour.

The watch leader remained impassive. "So what? What's so special about a stick of cheap glass and wood, fragmented at one end. Is this so much cross reason for inordinate kerfuffle?"

"It is an heirloom," cried Baus indignantly. "As I have said before, passed down from my great uncle to my cousin, and is dear to my family. The stoutness of its haft has never deserved such shameful demise."

"Well, such stoutness has proved surely lacking today," the sergeant laughed. The comment earned mild guffaws from his peers.

Baus suspired outrage at the lack of respect and flourished the baton. The blackmailer took effort to reject his juvenile theories. "Sheer malarkey! The 'heirloom' was frail and snapped of its own accord. Is that a crime? Search the storyteller's pockets for onions and radishes and you shall see who is the real thief."

Jeracles, Baus's captor, glanced down at the squashed vegetables and drew Baus a contemptuous glare. "Is what Sansix says true?"

Baus shook a flailing fist. "The man is daft. I harbour neither knowledge of vegetables nor contraband." The soldiers turned evil eyes on Sansix. Baus entertained the urge to bolt, but knew it would only confirm his own guilt. He stared down at the waysmen haughtily, feeling no small need to embellish the explanation. "Several vegetables appeared while we rolled. What of it? The bulbs came from this cullion's garments, not mine. Look," Baus cried adamantly, pointing at the throng, "even a crew of grim peasants fight over a single radish in question."

The lead watchman grunted to the truth of Baus's remark. He ordered Jeracles to seize the persons. The peasants fled and were seen no more when they saw signs of the waysmen.

The rat-eyed hustler exhorted Jeracles to pursue their justice. "Why do you delay in having this cur whipped? It is insufferable. If you notice, Merla and Rustas, the two vegetable mongers yonder—shall corroborate this jackal's misdeed!"

"An impossible fiction!" expostulated Baus.

Valere and Poli, by this time, had managed to ply their way closer to the scene. They stood gaping at the suspects. "Baus speaks the truth," boomed Valere over the din.

"And who are you?" grunted the lead watchman.

"I am Valere," asserted the seaman proudly. He pushed his way forward and offered an explanation, "This here is Poli, my comrade. Baus is my associate. The three of us are travelling minstrels—balladeers, if you like. We have turned easy prey for hoodlums like this skew-nosed sharper whom you clutch in your hands."

The lead waysman grunted. "This I can believe. It has been brought to our attention before of Sansix's villainy on many an occasion."

"Guard your tongue, Heruldatrix!" cried the thief warningly. "The blackguard, Baus, is a bluffer—a competent but dangerous one. He touches a person with this alleged 'heirloom' and the victim falls befuddled. Am I not right? Rigid as a corpse!"

"What blather is this?"

Baus called out a furious protest: "This declaration is both fantastic and deranged!"

"Intriguing," muttered the watchman. Rubbing his chin, he scowled. "And I suppose that the wand will render a pot of dabchick dung into golden nuggets?"

"It might, it might." Sansix's eyes blinked and when Kotax's thick-browed, skullish face came bearing in close with hostile intent, he gulped. "What—you pretend not to believe me? Watch then!" Sansix briefly tore the ganglestick out of Baus's hand and touched the tip to Heruldatrix's hand.

The guard remained whole. His beady, ironic frown deepened into that of a sneer. Sansix's smirk faded.

"So now, *Sansix*, what will it be—the truth or the stocks?"

"Neither!" cried the thief. "I see my altruism has come to mere mocking."

"As it always shall," chided Heruldatrix. He proceeded to slap Sansix in jocular fashion. "There, now! A small lesson on the ignobility of fibbing . . . Witnesses! Are there any witnesses? Please come forth!"

The crowd shuffled about in distrust. A pair of ragged-cloaked youths pushed through the throng. They bore mops for hair and pegs for teeth. They wore smug looks and were keen for reward. "We saw it all, Excellency!" they cried. Each wiped phlegm from their noses in sniggering fashion. "They were fighting one another, these louts, arm in arm, rolling about like a pair of hogs."

"A brilliant observation," jeered Heruldatrix, "which tells us nothing more than what we already know. Any sot could have seen what you saw—now move back, you greasy fools!" He turned to the rest of the gathering. "Any more deadbeats have something else to add?"

No one else offered any incriminating remarks. Heruldatrix surveyed the stony-eyed group with rancour.

Baus peered left and right. Frustration vied with panic. It seemed both flight and continued exchanges with certain cretins were of equal risk. A feeling of foreboding filled his chest and somewhat heartbroken pangs at the same time of losing his talisman. It was fractured! "You see, watchmen, the mendacious cunning of this robber's words? My heirloom remains broken. I use it merely to entice my trained chimps to sing."

"Trained chimps?" Kotax barked with incredulity. "What's all this?"

"My chimps have fallen sick and I have quarantined them at home in their pens."

"Really, now?" Heruldatrix smoothed out his greying moustache. He pondered the truth of the statement. He pushed his nose helm forward with interest. "You say you are performers—balladeers of some sort, ragbeard . . . with trained chimps?"

"Yes, exactly like that," responded Valere guardedly, "what of it?"

"We are in need of certain 'entertainers' for the upcoming festivities," grunted the waysman. "You might have an in—" He handed the seaman a poster. Over his shoulder, Poli peered with curiosity while Baus snatched a leery glance back to where Rustas and Merla were reviving and making strides in his direction.

Poli read from the stylish calligraphy:

"Performers! Entertainment in imminent need!

Acrobats preferred—troubadours, mimes, jesters, dancers, jongleurs, songsters, minstrels and any other comic outfits.

Mark well! Accepted acts are paid well in advance!

Auditions commence immediately! Please be expeditious! Interested parties are asked to report to the Palace's Eastern Gate . . ."

A crowd of citizens had swarmed about the waysmen to read the proclamation with excitement. Now a thin, owl-faced carter stepped back with an expression of amazement. "Why the sudden demand for entertainment, Heruldatrix? It has been known that Princess Solstress of Sloe and Clavius of Cleauch are to wed. Surely there has been plenty of time to gather performers for the nuptials?"

Jeracles gave a sarcastic answer: "Have you forgotten the storm, idiot? The Royal House has had all its jugglers, acrobats, dancing waifs, along with leaping toads and yodelling baboons for a long time. In fact, they were scheduled to arrive by ship from Karsh. But the bulk must have sunk somewhere south off the coast. Now we have only 'Jasmeer's Powder Puffs' and 'Jamoon's Flounders' to cover the festivities—surely a pathetic bunch if I've ever seen any!"

Baus eyes narrowed with concern. "On the basis of Jeracles' remarks, it would appear an exiguous number of acts."

Heruldatrix gave a snuffling grunt. "Troubadours, from Owlen arrived badly injured and in no proper state to perform ballads, or solos or slogans. Zithers cracked, flutes were marred, and nerves were shot. We've heard news that Prince Arnin has limped sorely into port last night, battered and bruised by ornery pirates waging war upon his galleon *Arfast*. Many deaths are in his wake. Arnin barely escaped with light wounds. To add to his miseries, it seemed that he and his troops suffered a bout with the idiot corsairs on their way down from Sarch."

"You don't say?" Valere raised a brow.

"Aye, the infamous Urseth, Zoren and Borath too," blurted the carter. "The Buccaneer Triangle is what they call themselves. Three shipfulls of the meanest, lowliest bunch of butchers afloat with all their dog droppings."

The crowd plied the carter for more information, but he had no more to add.

"Do these pirates live still?" inquired Valere.

"Naught is known of their fate," asserted the watchman.

Baus put on an awful face. "How dreadful that cutthroats commit such atrocities so close to Royal soil!"

"It is true."

"It angers me that villains of this ilk remain unscathed and sail unhindered on the open seas!"

"'Tis a grievous thing." The watchman nodded grimly, giving Baus a queer look. "Indeed —this world is full of scoundrels and scapegraces who would murder and steal as easily as drink wine or carve bread."

"It is utterly unthinkable!" stormed Baus. "Now, if I had my way—I would rive—"

Valere gave Baus's wrist a painful squeeze and he pre-empted his narrative. "Let us leave our law enforcers to their duties."

"Yes, very wise," chirped Baus.

Heruldatrix nodded and turned Valere a brief scrutiny. "You are a savvy sort, minstrel. Now, as to the possibility of a simple processing?" He peered narrowly at Baus. "Do you wish to mete out charges against this villain Sansix, or shall I rescind them?"

"I should think mete them out!" cried Baus indignantly. "The criminal has damaged an irreplaceable object."

"As you have emphasized." A scowl of deep irritation hardened Heruldatrix's features. "Very well. We shall see to it that the scoundrel is punished, clapped in irons, and that your petition is properly lodged at the judicial office."

"Wait!" cried Sansix bleakly. Striking momentarily free from his captor, he hissed out hasty words into Baus's ear. Baus frowned and peered at him with an expression of loathing before finally giving into a glowering compromise. "Very well, I will renounce my charges against this scoundrel—but only on the proviso he repent his evil ways!"

"Excellent! You are an exemplar of true benevolence." Heruldatrix tipped his helm. "What is more, this is a sensible decision. I shall leave you to your amusements. Now, Sansix! You are free to go. But, on no condition continue this petty knavery of yours. On your ways, the lot of you! Exercise prudence in the future! The streets of Sloe are no place for antics!"

"An entirely accurate remark!" exclaimed Baus heartily, "and I thank you, sire, for your high-hearted attitude."

Heruldatrix glared at him. "Do not call me 'sire' and now, off with you, scum! All of you!" He turned to foist glares at the gathering. "You rabble, no less! There is nothing to be seen here!" He turned to march on his heel when something of the ironic tendency in Baus's face caused him to swing about with suspicion. "You say you are performers? Why the brassy contusion across your forehead?"

"A small flesh wound caused by a misbehaving monkey, no more. Please do not alarm yourself unduly."

Heruldatrix's jaw dropped. "Bah!" he cried cynically. "What of the fellows in your company who seem no less battered with their own battalion of bruises and scuffs?"

"Occupational hazards," waved off Valere with ease. "We hold titles of 'troubadour', but harbour also something of the titles of stuntmen—'amateur acrobats', if you wish, who perform dangerous acts, which at times incur occupational hazards as that you see."

"A convenient explanation," growled the watchman.

A great brass bell gonged from across the city. The eerie ringing was left signalling half past the hour.

Heruldatrix frowned. Cognizing nothing amiss, he turned and merged into the crowd. His two burly, heavily-armed fellows followed him.

When they were all out of sight, Baus grabbed the blackmailer by the throat and pulled his muggish face close. "Now listen, you miserable rogue! What of this alleged 'plan' of yours? Quickly!—else I lose patience and tickle your ear with Lolispar here." Suspicion and hatred flared in his breast.

"Boasts and braggadocio will derive no quarter with me," sulked the thief.

Valere unsheathed his sword. "And this?"

Sansix gulped. "Listen!" he squeaked. "You hounds recall that I mentioned the Palace of Sloe?"

"Yes, what of it? How are we to gain ingress to 'Her Royal Majesty's chambers'?"

"The means is elementary," muttered Sansix fancifully. "Being adept at surreptitious tracking and a fellow swindler, we should have our ways."

"Get on with it! Why would you assume us to be swindlers?"

Sansix turned Baus a moony look. "Your appearance suggests nothing less. You are strangers to Sloe, any halfwit can see that. A more perspicuous man might peg you as cons, crude vagabonds, or likely slimy outlaws, though the incident with your 'heirloom' has me baffled."

Valere's mallet fist shot up and Sansix was held aloft against the palace wall, attempting to thwart a major thrashing.

Sansix squeaked through compressed lips, "Your fib of being troubadours has merit, and I retract my earlier statements." Valere slightly loosened his grip. "I would add that your pretence lacks all expert direction. Let me expand on my convictions! A definite effort is to be made to ensure a lucrative foray!"

"Dispense with the frippery!" called Baus.

"Alright! We need money, agreed? Our good Queen Maena is desperate for genuine entertainment. With a simple application of ingenuity we can all supply such diversions to her Highness. Ah! I see you doubt. Well, abandon it, and visualize! This snaffle-faced puffboy, Poli, if I get his name right, I doff with gowns and laces. He becomes—instantly, paff!—a girl, the beautiful *Rayuzel*—a doll, of graceful singing proportion, if not an instantly likeable heroine!"

Poli calmly emphasized that such enactment was foolishly out of the question.

"Hush now!" reprimanded Sansix. "I hardly sense a sanguine sentiment there. The redbeard here can be our choirboy, or an acrobat if he likes—or at most some kind of comic blunderer. Naturally, I shall be induced to hold the post of 'conductor'. And you, my long-haired hothead, can be harnessed as an instrumentalist or a page boy, if you like. This is the simple gist of my program: brilliant but efficacious. Does it not sound excellent?"

Baus scratched at his chin. "Your ideas—though farfetched, have some modicum of merit."

Sansix rolled his eyes. "They are absolutely fantastic!—now curb your qualms!"

"The idea is daft!" called Valere without sympathy. "Such an idiot's scheme is likely to get our heads chopped off. Performers? Bah! I utterly repudiate the idea. I doubt Maena or her retinue wishes to be made a laughingstock of the kingdoms in front of her guests by fools like us."

"Speak for yourself, redbeard," growled Sansix. "I intend to keep my part of the bargain, and my fertile brain."

Valere surged forward to apply injury to Sansix's 'fertile brain' but Baus forestalled the aggression. "Valere, let us put emotions aside and employ logic. We must focus our energies in favour of profit over angst. Our bellies remain empty, true, and yet we continue to languish. According to the literature, the auditions continue until eight tonight, which gives us ample time to practice a dress rehearsal and tighten our act."

Valere made small grunting sounds which were frustratingly caustic. Baus went on: "We have a chance to make an impression before the court. Before other pretenders acquire the same idea and afford us unwelcome competition, we must act."

Sansix smiled approval. "Baus, you are a genuine genius, and I happily apply my endorsement to such reasoning."

Valere threw up his hands. In defeat he moved off toward the market, mouthing cynicisms.

III

In short order, Baus, Poli and Sansix caught up to the seaman. His stony stride was a sulking reaction to the earlier words. "Where are you going, Captain?" said Baus mockingly, blocking his path.

"Looking for a way to acquire sustenance, if you don't mind. It is of important concern." He looked about the group with contempt. "It kills me to see that there's no place for an honest seafarer to obtain a mouthful of hamshot in this crowded community!"

"We are all stomach-light here," pointed out Baus.

Poli flourished a finger. "What if Rustas the vegetable monger chances to see us? Our immediate plan is to acquire funds by entering the Royal audition, not get nabbed for vegetable filching."

Valere gave a sardonic laugh. "*Our* plan? I think it is a scheme cooked up by none other than Baus and this weasel-faced scoundrel. My opinion pegs the 'scheme' retarded. We harbour no skills, stagecraft or otherwise, and yet you insist on committing to this ludicrous program. We don't even know where the cursed audition hall is."

Sansix spoke with an edge of annoyance. "First, redbeard, let it be known that you are somewhat ornery, and we simply must get you out of these rags and into a proper costume!"

Valere reached meaningfully for his sword.

"Props. We also require props," Sansix mused, ignoring the weapon. "Have you no other bludgeoning tools amongst you?"

Baus and Poli shrugged; Sansix fumbled through Poli's vest. "Here—!" He uncovered a cutlass with a blade nicked in three places.

"Good! Very good. Now we have a dented cutlass, a twain of daggers, a fine golden short sword . . ." He rubbed his wrists with calculation. "Follow me, people; we shall repair to my abode. It's on the southern side of the city. There we will assemble our ensemble."

Valere refused to assent. He ordered the villain to promise a tangible prospect of victual.

"I'll not have much in my larder," responded Sansix primly, "truly, barely enough to keep your own belly from collapsing."

"Good for now," growled Valere.

The foursome ploughed through the mobs of carters and cobblers, down the narrow, tar-stained alleyways branching south of the city. Baus kept a keen grip on Sansix's arm lest the opportunist bolt or try to contrive some cunning scheme leading them to catastrophe.

Over Sloe's massive blue-gleaming walls Baus saw fleeting glimpses of gilded mountaintops rearing like ancient fairy castles. Sansix, believing himself immune to harm, hummed a carefree melody while he led them on through the brick-paved backways and obscure dark alleys with vague twisting walkways here and there where less and less people seemed to be lingering, and from where high eaves seemed altogether too dark and dripping with the latest rains. Framed in old weathered stone, the alleys were grimed and salt-scarred.

Sansix at last beckoned them meaningfully through a narrow dim archway.

Reluctantly, the three companions edged cautiously along the puddled alley. Instantly, a gang of brown-cloaked footpads came barging out at them.

Sansix broke away with satisfaction and tucked himself in a safe niche. The brigands were shadowy foxes, short, stumpy creatures who had bolted from the curtained-off alley, and for a moment the companions were caught in an abrupt quandary. Three of the attackers carried moon daggers; two swung short, balsimar clubs clenched confidently in gloved grips.

Despite the odds, the fight was shockingly brief. Overconfidence and crass stupidity had undermined the gangsters. Armed to the hilt with lean weapons and very recent training, the pirates stretched themselves to maximum offence—swinging and striking with vengeance. Valere took two of his foes in the ribs. They fell in howling, gasping heaps. Poli egged his opponent on with more taunts, forcing a presumptuous lunge, which had the villain whirling before a great swinging club. Poli backhanded his charge with the pommel of his sword. He wrenched the club cleanly from the killer's grasp and struck him down in military precision. Baus caught the sly arm aimed for his face and saw the oily features diving for his torso. Not a second too late. A quick stab to the shoulder and the rogue was tumbling in the throes of agony. Savagely, Baus twisted aside, vetoing two more attackers who nearly slit his insides before they stumbled into peril, striking each other and hitting the dripping wall. Slipping in the mud, one foe caught Baus's knee in the groin before collapsing to his stomach. The other managed to discover Lolispar jammed to the hilt in his upper thigh. Loosing a squeal, the marauder hobbled back shrieking into the hole from whence he had come.

The companions eyed each other grimly. Slowly they fixed their malignant attention on Sansix, whose purposeful grin had suddenly faded.

"What?" The thief gasped. "Do you think me responsible for this tomfoolery?"

"Who else?"

"Impossible! I claim no allegiance to thugs or their profligacy!"

"Shut up! Why did they not attack you?" Baus demanded. "Perhaps I shall rouse this brown-bagged bravo at my feet and give him a proper thrashing." He plucked up the blunt end of Lolispar and knocked it against the man's skull.

"I give it three to one odds," growled Valere, "that this sorry rogue is a hired thug."

Sansix loosed a beseeching groan. "Come now! We have no time for this puerile talk." Pawing at Baus's upraised arm, the opportunist exhorted a plea for restraint. He gestured, "Into the leftmost alley! We must scoot before the gendarmes arrive. Certain recent activity of screams and violence will have them lumbering after us any second."

With scowling enmity, Poli and Valere stepped over the quivering bodies. They allowed themselves to be ushered into the gloom of another narrow alley. Here Sansix claimed he made his abode which was but a crow's fly away.

More of a tunnel than an alley, the path gave way to coppery gloom. A definite lack of sound here unnerved Baus—there was a veritable hollowness imbued with a vague sense of disquietude. Higher up, certain dim balconies could be seen against a backdrop of traceries allowing streamers of light to trickle through the dirty cracks in the planks. A small stream of sewage coursed through the gutter. It was choked with filth—affirming only not just the squalor of the district, but the miasma of poor plumbing. Through such dismal corridors, Sansix led the companions with surprising stealth. It made Baus suspicious. Surreptitious as the thief was, he hid worried glances at them over his shoulder—all very neat and tidy and only further confirmed Baus's conviction that the thief was a master double-dealer.

Down an adjoining alley, Baus caught glimpses of white oily eyes gleaming in between the half-draped windows. He caught a whiff of incenses, the stream of foreign perfumes: spices, exotic oils. Rogues were watching in all corridors of this place. Though footfall was masked, the sounds of depravity seemed to echo in Sansix's mind; every shadow seemed pitched with lurking cutpurses.

At the alley's end, the thief pulled aside a hanging. There was a dark door which he shakily opened with a small key.

Inside, the room showed a low-ceilinged, cramped and dingy space. Nothing more than a hovel, holding the permanent reek of onion and kerosene. The drapes were pulled back—loose, dusty and soiled. A pair of wooden chairs sat askew a rude table whose one leg was tottering. A lopsided picture of a peacock hung on a wall; in a dim corner stood a chipped statue of a nude maiden.

"Very pretty, Sansix," observed Baus.

"True—I am neither fastidious nor scrupulous in regard to orderliness and hygiene."

"I can see that."

The conniver lit a wick. Rusty gleams from the oil lamp showed a miscellany of objects: a jade flower pot, a dusty pillow, a worn settee, two rancid sets of garments hanging on a wire, a bookcase on which reposed wilted plants in cracked earthenware pots. All about seemed to cling the odour of sickly cunning schemes and oily bachelor—attributes which Baus found off-putting.

Sansix reached for a folio jammed in the top shelf of his bookcase. Spreading a dog-eared manuscript on the table under the lamp's eerie light, the thief exclaimed, "A play, written in three acts. My own production, though in essence, a pastiche only, of which we shall indulge in the first act."

"Says who?" crowed Poli.

The rogue paid no heed to Poli's outburst. "The play is entitled, *"How high the clouds circle round the dastard that my heart is."*

Valere gave a nauseated croak. "More like 'How sappy can a man's heart get'?"

"What of our emoluments?" barked Baus.

"Simple. A fifty-fifty split, which includes all wealth tendered by Queen Maena's accountants."

There was a pregnant pause, in which Valere, Poli and Baus turned sepulchral stares at their host. Baus's sardonic grunt became heavy when he ventured an inquiry. "There being four of us, how does that compute?"

"A matter of simple mathematics," announced Sansix sagely. His crooked teeth split into a petulant leer. "Fifty percent is paid for myself; the remaining fifty is for you drifters. How you split your share is your business. I, on reflection, wouldn't doubt that the final monies would be any less than fifty silver sequals."

Valere's eyes betrayed a casual quiver. "A generous distribution."

"I think so."

Faster than a snake, Valere whipped out his cutlass and bared it tightly against the villain's pale throat. Sansix gulped with a frog's swallow with each caress of cold, hard-forged steel.

Valere pushed the blade closer: "So—fifty percent is for you and fifty percent is for us? How about ten percent for you; the rest is for us?"

"Marvellous!" chirped Sansix. "I couldn't have suggested a better amendment." He gulped a cautious breath under the jutting metal on his larynx. "Blaze though you shall in the Witch Seldra's cauldron, redbeard, for harbouring such sad, puerile avarice!"

Valere laughed, showing grinning teeth. "I suppose 'Seldra' shall be the judge."

Baus and Poli hunkered down in Sansix's gloomy kitchen hunting for spoils. The larder showed various victuals slung in a high cupboard—foodstuffs which more or less fulfilled their basic need—their humour was improved in vast quota. Baus munched on a mix of chick peas and zalfa fruit. He returned Valere a chunk of gruel-bread and a battered tin of goatmeal. Poli gnawed on a half gorse-onion. All foods were poor combinations, but general ravenousness outweighed any indigestion issues.

When Sansix saw what little remained of his larder, he emitted a strangled yelp: "Your greed has emptied my stores and now left me bereft!"

Baus called out commiseratingly, "but of relative unconcern: one must train, not eat."

Sansix went on with icy precision: "The victual must be deducted from your pay when the Royal accountants consign us our sequals!"

"The details will be ironed out later," declared Baus, mouth full of goatmeal, though his conviction seemed scant.

The sounds of various feet came pounding along the ceiling, followed by a scream and a slap—obviously the tenants in the upper quarters included a young family.

"Careless rodents," grumbled Sansix ungraciously. "They breed like fiends. Now they come crawling and bumbling about on all fours day and night."

Baus outlined patiently the benefits of supporting young families as tenants. "They enchance the district's reputation."

Sansix ignored the philosophy. "I am usually a man of agreeable temperament, but when screams abound, I tend to lose my forbearance—but on the other hand I suppose you louts wouldn't know anything of that, killers and brutes that you are!"

Baus swung about, smilingly flourishing Lolispar. "That is an unkind remark, Sansix, which I urge you to retract. You discredit us—we are kind, hypersensitive, compassionate men—as spiritually driven as any."

Sansix gave a wild sneer. "The factuality of that comment remains ever to be seen. I've seen less ethically-minded rogues kill with less facility than you. Never mind! We have tasks at hand. Let us begin our rehearsals. Time is not to be wasted!"

Baus couldn't agree more. An hour later, after some energetic coaching on the thief's part, Valere and Baus demonstrated a convincing swordplay with cutlass and gladius. In their respective roles as 'Vandebul' and 'Bardek', the two filial adversaries in Sansix's production, they hyperbolized a rousing scene—dressed in mock doublet and loose hose that Sansix had dug out from the closet, they practiced feints and lunges demonstrating the high point of Sansix's drama. In the meantime Sansix fussed over the pinning up of Poli's white dress about the haunch. Poli was required invariably to play the part of 'Mistress Rayuzel', a voluptuous blonde, or melodramatic, teary-eyed damsel of Utropa, a role which he little liked, but into which he had been plunged in the face of Valere's rationalization and Sansix's honey-coated appeals: "Who is better off to play the glum, golden-haired hussy than you? Baus? Valere? I doubt it! With your fair hair and blue eyes as catching as gems, you are perfect! Not to mention your wonderful, youthful flaxen complexion!"

"Careful with your compliments, you slime. The idea is inept in all its implications," croaked Poli.

Baus and Valere took a break from their duelling and Baus tried to soothe the agitated Poli, to whom he expressed congratulations and muttered at length about the state of his damaged ganglestick. The talisman was noticeably bent and fearfully out of true, pervaded with a lustreless ambience. It was effaced of all its magical abilities, half cracked up the middle. With resigned melancholy, Baus set about to deal with his loss with practical wisdom and was about to toss it aside when struck by a whim, he stayed his hand, noticing a portion of Poli's backside exposed. Baus crept forth and gave the buttocks a luxurious tap.

Poli ceased to sigh or fidget. Baus's eyebrows arched. At first, he thought the bully bluffing, but the reaction was genuine and astonishment gripped him. He tapped again and Poli came out of his spell, grinning like a fish. Baus jabbed once more, just to assuage his sense of sureness. Poli remained as before, shuffling about, complaining at will of his overtight gown.

So, how was it possible that the stick was so unpredictable?

The seaman snatched up the wand and Valere exchanged with Baus a meaningful side glance. Slapping the wand at Poli's backside perhaps a dozen times, he experienced failure. Sansix continued his ministrations upon Poli.

The magic was tainted, wholly unreliable.

Poli jerked around to peer at them with rancorous disgust. "What do you two clods think you're doing, swatting at a naked behind with the heirloom? Does it excite you?"

Baus grinned appreciatively.

Poli grabbed the tip of the ganglestick and instantly became rendered immobile like a stalking stork.

Baus's face glowed. He surveyed Poli's mute form with a bland elation.

"The curio," Valere remarked, "seems to be something of a fickle mistress. In light of not wishing to sound too critical, Baus, I advise you to jettison it. It will fail us—again and again —at inopportune moments."

Baus bit his lip. He gestured with stubborn emphasis. "The baton is my saviour; it has promise yet; I feel it. It may save our hides yet from a calamity."

"The condition is remote," opined Valere. "Nevertheless, heed my warning! Abandon the devil stick before it causes us ruin."

Baus obdurately tucked the wand into his cloak. "Absolutely not! I must sadly disagree with your dogmatism and shall pursue my own programs."

Valere groaned.

Sansix scolded Baus for distracting Poli and bent low, tucking up Poli's silver-laced hems. Poli's squirming had reached an intolerable apex and was of some annoyance to Sansix. For all outward appearances, the rat-faced grifter seemed oblivious to the fatuous attention that Baus placed on the impaired talisman, but was perhaps not so naïve as to show his canniness.

Clapping hands for attention, he called, "First we must travel to *Gutters Alley* to fetch our instruments, then props and devices from Myla, my fellow associate. We shall return to practice our moves before donning make up!"

"Sounds like a scrumptious plan!" cried Baus, clapping his hands.

Valere returned an impatient flourish. "So be it, rogue; but let's make it snappy!"

IV

Three hours later, the 'performers' were trudging down *Alycon Way*, past Hog Market and on toward the Royal East Gate. Baus's stride was brisk. He followed Sansix wielding a truncated leash. The latter wore a prim black suit with underlying trailing white blouse. His coarse, soot-black hair was greased back and heavily spiked; a fake mole ran to the left and below his nose. An artistic touch, Sansix claimed. An orchestrator's baton was tucked at his side, nothing more than a yellow willow sharply whittled at an end. His pleas for the privilege of Baus's ganglestick as a conducting instrument was denied.

Baus was dressed smartly in a pair of green slacks and olive doublet. He felt remarkably at ease. Touching his grey felt hat and red feather pitched jauntily on an impressive angle, he sighed with pleasant satisfaction. A yellow-speckled scarf was wrapped about his neck; he gripped a two-stringed zither under an arm. He had recently managed to perfect a two-line child's rhyme, adequately capable for their crude pantomime. Poli was obliged to accompany them by voice—as before, he was decked out in a white and silver gown but with the addition of fake breasts, high heels, and a smear of red lipstick and lime eye shadow. He carried with him a battered flute with which he could pipe out a raw-boned melody. Valere cringed at the discordance but he had no say in the matter. He donned what most resembled woodsman's attire, looking confidently dapper in his brown and red-checkered jacket, black pantaloons and black, knee-length boots. The seaman had forfeited the lute impressed upon him by Sansix in favour of a sword, due to its sense of dominion and his otherwise noticeable lack of musicality. Valere—aka Vandebul—had surprisingly astonished the group with a nimble display of toe-tapping and a natural ability to dance which Sansix had incorporated on the fly into his musical melodrama. Now the troupe was well prepared, practiced and pumped to dazzle the Queen's adjudicators with an endearing performance, original and entertaining.

The troupe arrived at the East gate in good time. A long line-up of candidates greeted them. The aspirants stood disgruntled under twin marble arches, Sansix much in distress, chewing on a woolly tongue. Like themselves, the candidates dressed in a variety of finery, eccentric and outlandish, and they carried themselves with the hopeful hauteur of glamour-stars.

Pushing himself into line, Sansix dismissed the contenders with a wave of hand as if they were nothing more than dilettantes. "Peasants and simpletons!" he muttered under his breath. Baus thought the appraisal arrogant, but he had doubts that the competition would be as simple as Sansix suggested. Nevertheless, he abided his time. A regiment of attendants in ultramarine uniforms ushered the next contenders through the gate and into the palace's common area.

An hour passed. The troupe was finally admitted into the common room where they sat on hard-backed wooden benches. Sandwiched amongst four other hopefuls, they were pressed between an urn and a ladle and some small pewter cups. A trencher of pear and olive compotes and scallop pastes nestled upon a low table but the refreshments went untouched; none of the troupe members dared accept the offer so as not to offend sensibilities or mar their chances of entry.

The minutes passed; the soft orange rays glinted down from the louvres and cut long stripes on the stones. Muted echoes drifted from the adjoining chamber—sounds at once semi-tuneful and melodic, rich with trills, glissandos, cadenzas, codas, refrains, fortissimos. They were expressed in a variety of sentiments on instruments of fashion: lutes, banjos, guitars, clarinets, bongos and bungos.

Slogans accompanied such music. Baus envisaged ale-laved lips muttering refrains and soliloquies. He curled his lips. Otherwise, melodious laughter struck the corridor, drifting with boasts, groans and disgusts—the province of drama. The companions saw as many disgruntled entrants as prospective applicants drag their heels past the waiting room—each clenching instruments and props in an expression of abject woe. Perhaps these people were rejected from auditions or demonstrated lack of talent?

Baus scowled. There seemed to be an awfully high number of rejects.

Another hour passed. With an impatience bordering on exasperation, finally their troupe was admitted to the adjudicator's chambers. It was an intolerable wait, during which period Poli proved nervously inept, squirming like some schoolboy in his seat. Two footmen dressed in the indigo and navy-toned garb of palace stewards, directed the foursome down the wide, gilded pillared hall inlaid with smalt-marble floors. Their silver-belled caps tinkled with authority as they marched. Baus could barely resist a guffaw. Sansix urged the actor to prudence, whispering to him to not show disrespect while proceeding to the adjudication hall.

The first glimpses of the palace grounds were impressive—whispering fountains, manicured gardens, spiralled columns, beautiful bowers dressed with glittering gems. The troupe passed an open garden carved with cinnabar and complete with a shimmering pool, afloat with indigo flowers. The cool waters were those of rainwater, where a pair of colourful koi swam contentedly. A servant girl was busy chasing a butterfly by the pool's edge. Baus saw her hair was hazel and face the dreamy pink of diverting innocence.

When the servant saw them, she doffed an orange feather-duster and set upon a vigorous brushing of the surrounding masonry to pretend she was busy. Initially flustered, she skipped through the garden, sandaled feet echoing on the polished stone. She pretended a great interest in her work, but really was more interested in snatching curious glances at Baus. She ducked behind a pillar, across the hedges, flowering shrubs and elegant blue-tiled patios. She seemed particularly enamoured with his gallant costume. His confident, raffish air of authority was no less an allure. She cast shy glances at him, but when Baus turned to look, she was gone.

Dismissing the servant's behaviour as that of a coy underling seeking the callow fruits of a daydream, Baus marched ahead. However, he remembered her button-bright eyes were full of promise, and her alluring expanse of hip and haunch did nothing to dull his imagination, as did other vigorous fantasies.

Baus did not give dignity to the feelings. He thrust aside these idle musings as the chatter of adolescents. To investigate the charms of one garden nymph in more exacting detail in this bower required significant investment and resources, none of which he had.

The two footmen motioned the performers along the patio—their manner was abrupt.

The company finally reached a large studio full of bright light and air. Inside the jewelled entrance, sat a bald, thin-set man hunched over a cluttered table. He looked neither distressed or enthused at his task. His aspect was peremptory, almost glacial and aloof. A pince-nez dangled from the end of his pinched nose; his stylus remained officiously busy, striking text into a dusty ledger.

The footmen left them there standing puzzled.

Baus studied his surroundings. Crystal lamps hung high upon chains from a lofty, domed ceiling. No less than a score of copper casements surrounded the upper perimeters, allowing the last gilded rays to grace the windlewood floor with splatters of light, waxed shiny as white sand. The walls were frescoed a dignified orange, set at irregular intervals with various octagonal pillars. The chamber was wild and rococo, at the same time, as disappointedly sparse and unadorned with plants, refreshments and sweetmeats as could be.

Baus saw a bulb-shaped contrivance stood to the adjudicator's left on which a bell and tine were geared with hardy spring. The adjudicator had only to pull back the tine, and impact the gong which would produce a shrill resonance. Baus rightly guessed the signal to indicate an act in progress a definite 'no'.

Cognizing the gist of the speculative admissions, the adjudicator fixed them an all-appraising stare. "Well! Welcome, contestants! My name is Reptolodus—the appointed judge of talent to appear in Princess Solstress's upcoming nuptials. Should any of you desire to entertain a posting in this event, it is through me that this function shall occur. Now! To business. Be good enough to answer my questions, which will allow us to be underway. Are we clear? What are your names?"

"Valere, Poli, Baus and Sansix," chimed Baus.

Reptolodus scrawled the names in his ledger.

"Place of origin?"

"Sloe!" answered Sansix unctuously, interrupting Baus's pre-planned response.

"Name of production?"

Sansix spouted off the long, presumptuous title. The adjudicator paused to glance up at Sansix from his writing with critical impatience.

Feeling uncomfortable, Sansix asserted a more forthright announcement of the act: "'Tis a humorous pastiche involving true events related with the second dynasty of Xatoon of East Karsh."

"This is well and good," came Reptolodus's dry response. "But—I should warn you, Sansix. I discourage dithyrambs, buffoonery, toilet antics, waggling of rumps or similar boorish practices which are all too common amongst the citizens that I have interviewed. I am particularly loath to limericks, crooned in bogus dialects—yet, any topical ballad sung in the alto tenor shall be favoured, accompanied by something indicative of quiet, bucolic drama."

"This is sensible and I laud your tastes," Sansix murmured.

"Attend!" stated Reptolodus crisply. "You may proceed with your act. If any of you feel sudden remorse after my adjudication, there are plenty of handkerchiefs on this tabouret."

"That is kind of you," responded Sansix, "but there is little possibility of that, as we are seasoned artists, hardened to the uncouth critiques of our trade."

"Very encouraging." The adjudicator beamed icily. "Please proceed with your ensemble."

Sansix held up his conductor's baton. Poli, in the guise of 'Mistress Rayuzel', tiptoed softly across the polished wood and began her lament in the voice of a plaintive, mating thrush. She spoke a few poetic words—of dew-dappled meadows, golden cornfields, rainbows after an early May rain. Arms crossed on fake bosom, she bore an imploring look of rapture and spoke as if to no one but the dimming light dipping down from the casements, expressing her love for an inamorato who was not one, but two! Of whom she could not decide whose ardours worked the heaviest on her. Bardek came skipping on scene, extending his palms in simple, extravagant luxury. The swain dipped back on his toes to play a simple ballad on his zither while dancing lightly on all toes. The scene, though maudlin, set the tone of realism for such a period of time where gallantry, passion and etiquette played their prospective roles. Never before had any such eloquence been portrayed in this hall—or so Sansix believed. As Bardek disappeared offstage, Vandebul came blundering on stage with a most lummoxy tread, rolling his lover in his arms. He played no strings or sang no mawkish song, but only danced a raucous reel in time to Poli's hoarse, high-pitched flute and Sansix's broad beating of hands upon flanks. Vandebul tired of the dancing; he grabbed his mate by the haunch and made a desperate play for passions. Bardek again reappeared primly, spying the lovers dimly entwined and so indecently in congress that he bared his golden weapon with indignation, and ordered the bear to cease his maulings upon his betrothed lest he run him through. The declaration went unheard. The perpetrator, who either pretended fatigue or ignored the command, had possibly missed his cue and continued to frolic, at which juncture, Bardek was obliged to stab him in the shoulder.

Bardek had yet not realized that it was his own brother who was his rival so disguised he was, as some woodland troubadour. The feint was perhaps more real than fiction and Vandebul jerked from his sport and gave a cursing shriek, perhaps filled with more angst than deemed necessary. The woodsman unsheathed the cutlass at his hip and ran at Bardek with a rage in his eyes. Bardek fell back, recuperating from the surprise attack. Reptolodus stared in rapt attention, seemingly absorbed in the drama. From his expression it looked as if the troupe had hooked an admirer, impressing him with their generous amount of real-life training.

The sword duel persisted, unfolding with ever more verve and vengeance and Bardek and Vandebul lunged, parried, playing villain for buffoon, dodging back and forth across the floor like heroes, feinting, grappling, blocking, while each traded insults and jeers and promises of one-upmanship and sophistries with rival, chivalric repartee. Their cries rang out into the next hall. All blended to become a euphonious melody sung by Sansix. Mistress Rayuzel swooped and swooned, trying to stop her lovers from dismembering themselves.

To no avail. They each spitted the other in the breast and fell to their knees on the floor in pools of their own blood, brought about by jars of beet juice cleverly distributed in their undergarments.

Sansix's eyes grew wide with affectedness. His face grew hot with sentimentality. Flourishing baton, he urged his performers on to a more fervid, keener and more vibrant cadence of death. The two wormed their way about the floor, contorting in dying spasms. Mistress Rayuzel danced and shrieked with heart-torn laments.

Bardek, suddenly annoyed by Sansix's over-extended urge for drama, augmented the tenor of his gyrating to clownish effect and in a totally unprecedented change of script, reared himself erect to thus jilt Sansix out of his saccharine fervour.

Baus grinned at Sansix's flushed glare. Each awaited the horrid sound of the gong . . . which never came. Sansix flourished the signal of closing. The cadenza trilled. Now Rayuzel and Bardek held themselves with extended earnestness on zither and flute. Sansix's baton descended in a brave, indulgent flourish. The performance ended. The performers fell to their knees, hands outstretched, chins jutted skyward.

A stunned silence fell over the hall. A pin's drop could be heard. Almost palpably an expression of austere respect settled across Reptolodus' face. In three purposeful strides, he bounded forth, clapping his hands. In a slow, unbiased approval, he gave a rapid series of nods, speaking with hands tipped to lips, "Normally I would dismiss such acts as jejune, but —" here he coughed "—there was a remarkable spirit to this conception—as buffoonish as it was achieved. Ha! Well, so goes entertainment . . . You are dilettantes, no doubt—perhaps the worst in the business. And yet, tyros. But you have dared an original number, and when all is fared and the fat lady sings, is this not the stuff of poetry? Yes, I say! Bravo! You have my sentiments and qualified approval!"

Sansix slapped his thighs with enthusiasm. "Excellent news, judge!"

Reptolodus frowned. "On the contrary this sudden need for last minute entertainment has turned out to be somewhat of a shambles. You are lucky, all of you. With this mishmash of low-end talent and juvenile monologues, I have become worried of contriving a proper program for Her Highness's nuptials. It is so late in the auditions!"

Baus announced, "I would not assume that our competition has been anything less than expert."

Reptolodus gave a barely-concealed chuckle. "My impatience is evident in such nondescripts as you have seen in the waiting room—'Goscar's Flying Fish', 'Petrospios' Gondos and Gambies', the 'Dancing Bear Deluxe Trio'—absolutely ghastly numbers."

Baus affirmed his agreement. "This would be my own opinion."

"No less mine!" stormed Sansix, casting Baus a competitive glare.

Reptolodus wrote briskly on a blue sheet of paper and ripped off the segment which he handed to Sansix. "Present this ticket to Vodel who waits in the adjoining room. The steward will issue you a voucher of acceptance into tomorrow's nuptials. The ticket can be presented to any bursar for funds immediately owing."

Sansix studied the blue fragment with pleased dignity. After a moment's scrutiny he scrunched it into a wad and set his face into a grimace of resentment. "The voucher is writ for only ten sequals! I was under the impression that we were entitled to fifty—all paid out in advance."

"The assumption speaks only half truth," replied Reptolodus. "To honour our contract, monies are paid not until the afternoon *after* the entertainment. Why? You would be amazed at the number of scapegraces and grifters who would hoodwink us out of a good performance. They simply don't show up. Our system circumvents such scandal. Only a lack wit would choose to be absent and miss his receiving share."

Sansix crafted a clever snort. "Sly subterfuge! If I understand you correctly, then the agency devolves on us to—"

"Carefully, now," cried Reptolodus. "You test my patience. These are trying times and further instructions await which I would listen to."

The same blue-eyed maiden Baus had observed ogling him earlier, gave an inopportune peek from behind a column.

Reptolodus saw the flutter and snapped, "Have you no chores, child? Get you gone! Let's have no more of this skulking about."

Flustered, the servant scurried out. Reptolodus, at last, turned his chill attention back to Sansix. "Now, present yourself at this same place no later than two o'clock. You will be received, admittedly, prepped for performance that will occur no later than three o'clock sharp tomorrow. A word of warning! Do not tarry. You will be disqualified and incur severe penalties, including floggings and an incarceration by the Royal guard. At Sloe we are a fastidious folk. We consider our royal affairs of extreme importance, and shall brook no frivolities."

Baus bowed deferentially to the edict. Reptolodus returned to his ledger, apparently a signal of dismissal.

Sansix haughtily padded his way toward the arched exit with Baus, Poli and Valere departing on lighter feet. All felt their own emotions of satisfaction.

V

The extra sequals proved pleasantly efficacious in mitigating the recent misfortunes suffered at sea. In such attitude, Baus, Valere and Poli bypassed the option of sleeping at Sansix's hovel amongst the dustballs, mouldy cheese and rank odours; instead they took up residence at the *Laughing Gull* on the far East side of town. The pub was situated near the docks, a stone's throw from the famous *Trilby Fountains*.

Mourning doves and sea pigeons sang noisily amongst the trickling runways. The alabaster figurines and gargoyles were fulsomely carved, decorated with garlands, banderols, wedding wreaths and bunting. The choice of relocation allowed the companions a modicum of comfort—an opportunity that encouraged Valere to settle for nothing less than the inn's most stylish room where he ended up dropping half their earnings on it. It was a room with a view, three beds, a stylish table and scrubbed commode placed overtop the kitchen where all was relatively quiet and away from the din of patrons rollicking in the taproom. The sea captain took the opportunity to increase the joviality of the situation by slugging back a few tankards—the region's dusky 'boar brew'—and Poli followed suit, enjoying the thick, tarry beverage.

Baus did not share in his comrades' bibulous proclivities. He remained aloof and taciturn, sensing something awry regarding the performance to occur on the morrow.

Baus answered noncommittally when asked about the morose turn of mood. "The risks are not immoderate that we undertake."

Valere reassured him with a laughing slap on the back. "We are sixty more silver pieces to the rich! ere we finish this mawkish farce, then we flee this horrid little town."

Baus sighed. He efforted to think over the tambour and drunken din. "Hardly a little town —a city." He looked past the seafarer's bulk and felt the tug at his solar plexus. It reminded him of all sorts of potentialities that could go wrong. "I cannot shake this sinister feeling roiling in my guts."

Valere wiped foam from his beard. "Ah, go on! I am not one to cater to spirits being dampened by stray forebodings."

Baus cast him a flavourless look. "Speak for yourself, ratbeard. Was it not a series of hours ago you were averse to this whole idea of auditioning?"

Valere gave a grinning shrug. "That was then, this is now." He raised his mug, drained it and Poli proposed a toast to the ultimate success of their deeds to come—wine, women, wealth—in that order.

Baus turned away with distaste. The urge to remove himself from this crass scene was overwhelming. He pushed past the knot of patrons and bumped his way along with a gang of toothless, smiling ship-carpenters, and a motley band of black-bearded iron-workers. He ascended to their shared bedchamber on troubled feet and even as his head hit the fleecy pillows, he was asleep and barely did he hear the clunky return of his comrades, carrying two drunken bimbos slung over their shoulders—idly, remembering cataloguing many noisy grunts and heaves that followed.

VI

After the two wenches had been ejected from the room it was early afternoon and Valere and Poli had commenced their sobering up, which included slapping at each other's faces, gargling with vinegar, hopping from one foot to the other while singing praise to *Oma's Three Sea Seraphims*. Baus deemed the two cronies fit for public and he sourly negotiated them down the dim back stairwell into the back alley and out onto the sunny, dockside streets.

The winds blew fair; the sky shone a bright gold-azure. It was flecked with powder-puffed clouds. From the city's magnificent walls, flags and pennons hung jauntily. Royal blue and indigo bunting was raised on staves and hefted onto every vendor's stall, flapping in the breeze. As was customary, the citizens were expected to flaunt themselves with a blue duck feather tucked into their hat, or a blue pomander on their feet—symbols of auspicious occasion.

Baus and his company neared the palace's Eastern Gate—just in time to observe the massive door being thrown open and a double line of waysmen riding out on decorated steeds, hoisting the age-old coat-of-arms of Smaerna. The procession comprised two warring drakes encircled by stars and clouds. A set of silver trumpets blared forth plangent flourishes.

The three actors surged against the flow of the gathering crowd and they hoped to head deeper into the city—but *hope* was a tenuous word. They bypassed many sotted jesters, painted clowns, clattering carts, rustic wagons filled with wares of all kinds and bibelots aplenty while hawkers' cries filled the air, besieging men and women from all quarters: "Care for a wedding fig? A rose-kiss? No—I see . . . well, then! Perhaps a sheckled roundel?"

It was only with obdurate force that they brushed off the leech-like vendors and negotiated a safe passage through the throngs of peddlers and solicitors in the direction of Sansix's den cast in the southern district.

The alleys narrowed, darkening with the overhang of canopies which tended to shut out the light. They met Sansix in his residence, though somewhat later than expected.

The conniver regarded them with measured exasperation. "Regard! It is half past two. What of the rehearsal I had ordained before noon?"

"Shut your maw! What of it?" grunted Valere.

"You could have informed me you would be late."

Valere loosed a churlish bark. "Who are we to report to you? Are we pubescent children, indentured by your curfew? No! 'Tis you who are indentured to us. Besides—we needed to catch up on some sleep after some convivial company."

Sansix peered with disapproving eyes. "How very nice to hear. You could have at least informed me of your place of residence." Disgusted, but sensing an unsympathetic vibration, Sansix bypassed the argument. The four gathered props and perfected their costumes, adjusted instruments and set a pace toward the palace. At an extension along the palace wall, they arrived before a tall maulwood door embedded with blue-green herring-bone stone slightly open. The access point was attended by four guards, who wore silver-blue regalia and wielded daunting halberds.

Baus produced his voucher. The guards stepped aside, admitting the actors—albeit the courtesy was performed in grudging mood. Sansix led the troupe along the esplanade, through a thick, lush topiary and past a marble colonnade, through which they caught provocative glimpses of luxuriant gardens, groomed to perfection, pools gleaming and cleansed of all lily pads. An elaborate stage was decorated with balloons on which the artists were to perform. The three nearby blue fish statues were adorned with silver cloaks and dressed in silver circlets on polished crowns. They must have been sea goddesses, Baus surmised.

The marble steps led down to the terrace, bedizened with white lilies, golden daffodils and coloured stones: carnelian, lime, orange. In every tree, flags were pinned. Wreaths and decorative origami figures abounded.

Baus looked upon Sloe's inner palace with unconcealed amazement. The cornucopia of domes, spires and turrets were dazzling to the eye. Banners and regalia of moment seemed to grace the skyline. Wondrous terraces blazed in the foreground; walkways and gardens shimmered in luxury, enclosed by frescoed loggias, shell-adorned pilasters and magnificent galleries.

The outlaws' late arrival was greeted with chill gruffness from the palace officials. Reptolodus strode on short legs, urging the latecomers to proper etiquette. He wore a thick green-gold smock with smalt blue jewels around his neck and a fake cowlick affixed to his brow.

"I trust you have tightened up your performance?"

"Absolutely!" assured Sansix.

Reptolodus's hauteur was obvious. "Wait here with the others then. You are scheduled to appear after 'Masolin's Fascinating Fishes'—no less illustrious than 'Kruger's Lolling Dolls' and the 'Infamous Flying Rascal'. We have endured other spectacles at length." The adjudicator paused to listen to the sound of lutes while voices came tittering from beyond the doors. "Normally we mix our more abstract numbers with the more outlandish, like that of yours, but we allowed for a certain pause of congratulatory activity to prevail between."

"Only fitting," acknowledged Sansix.

Reptolodus fixed Sansix a cool gaze. "In this endeavour, Sansix, my advice is this—do not bungle up your number. My associate, Cargax, shall be your overseer. Should he provide you with precise and accurate clues as to when and where you are to enter the stage, be sure to follow them. It is only extended for your own benefit."

Sansix began to frame a complaint but Reptolodus interrupted him vehemently. "Listen! You are not to miss, bungle or misdiagnose any entry signal. Appearing late, or early, for the record, is culpable of a punishment. Do you understand?"

Poli raised a hand of disclaimer but Valere quickly pulled the fingers down.

Reptolodus continued icily: "Be aware that your voucher has been signed and the monies have been accepted, so you are committed to the affair."

"As for the monies," Sansix declared irritably, "we still have yet not received our outstanding quota—"

The adjudicator reached in his pretentious smock and tossed out forty sequals. "Here you are!"

Sansix collected the wealth but Baus snatched up the coins on his own and deposited them in his tunic.

Reptolodus gesticulated sharply, "As to a breach of contract, it incurs penalties and no leading hints need be discharged."

Sansix put on a face of sobriety. "Do we look like a bunch of amateurs to you?"

Reptolodus crinkled his face and proffered no reply. Beckoning to Cargax, he led them brusquely to the waiting room.

Cargax was a lean, elderly man with wisps of yellow hair. His chin was crooked and his jowls sagged. He loped forward with a noticeable limp and led the entertainers into the vestibule, which expanded into a sizeable hall that adjoined the garden.

A large group had been gathered—the members shifted in nervous anticipation of the performances and conversed in clipped whispers. An arbitrary silence was enforced by the single monitor whose grey-tipped beard and chapped, grave face showed nothing of invitation. This goliath straddled the front of the gathering in important ceremony—a *Squand*, one of the Queen's loyal aides—an inside circle of lieutenants who wore light, blue crustacean-mail and a plumed morion. Pike and halberd were clutched inimically at his side. Ham fists clenched and unclenched the haft. As for the gathering, it comprised a motley group of singers, dancers, acrobats and musicians, some jesters other jongleurs, all dressed in various garb—capes, gowns, overcoats, blouses, regalia and flowers. Many held instruments of value and exhibited keen faces, a few of which Baus recognized prior from the audition.

Four female acrobats huddled close to the door. These nubile creatures were dressed in grey tights and pomanders; lean-figured and nimble specimens, which Baus took care to notice. A juggler and fool approached him. They whirled on blue and red foot wheels, on which they danced sprightly, entertaining coloured balls in hand. The fool cried 'ha!' with every fourth step and caused Poli some awe. Standing in the midst of the gathering was a giant garbed from head to toe in green leaves and twigs. He wore a white cummerbund about his waist and he clutched an excited midget about the armpits—an imp who was dressed in red and wore a cardigan and cap and fretted with a small banjo.

Baus paused to identify the nature of the groups. Ventriloquist acts? Cheap masquerades? Comic burlesques? All guesses could be as easily inaccurate as the other. Baus let his eyes droop over two lumpy shapes draped under a blue blanket, vaguely reminiscent of steeds. The horse head was affixed to the front person, a frayed rope at the back indicative of a tail. Baus guessed a jousting steed. An arm was stuck out of the left side of the animal's torso, holding aloft a long stripped branch, evidently a lance.

Baus's attention was tasked. He moved away, trying to shadowbox the horse into a playfight, but evoked only rancorous murmurs. He bumped into a copper-haired minstrel who was wrapped ear to ear in a coil of brassy tubes and pipes of an alto-tuba.

The musician bawled: "Watch where you're going, pilgrim." He swivelled toward the doorway. "Hoy Reptolodus! Bring us our beer! You have backwatered on your promise!"

Reptolodus brushed the musician with an idle glance. "Mind the volume, Harbsep. What promise is this?"

"The beer you promised us, yester-eve!—while we waited in the preparatory chamber—remember? Repair this deficiency at once! We are thirsty and our needs are immediate and of priority. Your behaviour has been lax to the point of irresponsibility!"

Reptolodus allowed himself a dignified chuckle. "Shush! Libations have been bypassed for the nonce due to new policy."

"Bah! What care we for your protocol? Fetch us our beer!"

"All in due time, Harbsep. I would advise you to devote your last moments to reviewing your cues, lest your fingerings lapse—and you suffer a punitive mortification."

Harbsep gulped. Others amongst the musician quarters quietly endorsed the adjudicator's opinion, amongst them the green giant and his indentured midget. Now Reptolodus's voice rose a degree higher as he ticked off points on his hand. "As I enunciated! Beverages will be supplied at the appropriate interludes! Now quiet and be attentive! In the meantime Zazenis the Barber is in process of completing his inestimable performance. Her Majesty does not wish any disruptions!"

Through a small slit in the drapes, Baus saw 'Zazenis' delivering his final pious soliloquy. He peered further out upon the lush garden and saw to the left a screen of fabulous rippling proportion. The waterfall of stone ran sheets of shimmering waters. Past the three standing fish stood a great purple velvet canopy. Members of the nobility reposed on their high-backed chairs in a mini-amphitheatre. As many as twenty sat on the padded benches in the most expensive silks: complete with hats, jewellery and robes. The lords were garbed in crimped doublets, vests, woven slacks and twilled breeches; the ladies in residence showed varieties of gossamer gowns, velvet dresses, silken robes, and assorted stockings.

A dozen waiters hastened about the fountains to deliver silver teapots and salvers of assorted victual to the elegant tables. Poached quail, roast duck and boiled hederpest were the delicacies included today. The air floated with an air of festivity—confetti and essences filled the spaces. An attendant camped out in an olive tree, blowing small bugle notes to signal the end of each performance. The announcer threw handfuls of confetti from a small bucket. Present as always, were the Squands. A double pair now stood at attention at either end of the exquisite amphitheatre—legs straddled, arms crossed, weapons hefted in austere majesty.

In the middlemost tier of the amphitheatre sat Queen Maena herself on a jewelled throne fitted with a high silver back. She was decked out in a resplendent white topical gown cuffed with brown ferret fur. The queen showed a serious countenance—intense, artlessly logical, though not unlovely. Her hair was coiled up in a complex silver topknot and both sets of her long lean fingers were cast with large topaz rings and rested on her sea drake-carven arm posts with sybaritic purpose. Neither joyous nor ecstatic, the monarch reviewed the performance which comprised a more serious enactment of *Xosostes'* last tragedy—*Farfellion*, as played by the portly Zazenis.

The scene was familiar. Four nude women, pigmented in alternating monochrome bands, danced with mournful abandon. A cloudy-eyed, bearded recluse was the centre of attention—Zazenis—who was pigmented in black and tied to a gnarled torturer's post. The women sang hysterically about his punishment—consequences of infidelities and intrusions visited upon the royal blood of Utiken long ago during the vagaries of youth. The executioner suddenly clomped onstage holding a fake axe. He hefted the weapon, flourished it with the grace of a blacksmith. He wished to lop off the prisoner's head and the dancers flew about like Maenads and whisked the prisoner off to safety. Glumly, the executioner lowered his weapon, sang a brief philosophical verse before exiting the stage.

The act was over. Desultory applause drifted from the audience. The bugle blew a mournful note; steward Cargax briskly signalled the next number.

The Princess Solstress, Maena's daughter, sat beside her mother with a look of pinch-lipped boredom. There was a mixture of other basic instincts mirrored there, of which resentfulness and rancour were high contenders. The princess was a lady of exquisite loveliness, endowed with a delicate chin, wonderful gleaming golden-brown eyes, a restless smirk of rebelliousness. Her jet hair was beaded with ruby cabochons and braided to contrast with her rouge-powdered cheeks. Around the nape of her neck was hung a light flounce of fleece, almost carelessly donned. Her aspect was neither supercilious nor purposeful; her constitution was neither overweight nor pencil thin. In no way did the princess resemble her mother except in a hierarchical formality and that was only incidental. The disinterested demeanour she showed did not diminish her inarguable refinement; it augmented her allure to gain that kind of subtle advantage for which most women pine. She seemed to radiate a healthy girlish aura of appeal, and to waft that sense of authority which exudes an altogether invigorating air of petulance.

In the tier below sat Lady Bala of Galania, Sir Gustach of Flem, the Count and Countess of Pixbury—all grandees of repute from Sloe and districts of Karsh. Sitting to the princess's left was Duke Narm of Titzen and the Seneschal of Robar, and her suitor, Clavius of Cleauch, reposed in such prim ceremonial position, wearing an exultant pride, a golden wig, a small false cornice beard and curled mustachio below his ample jowl, that he seemed only a caricature. He was the senior of the three, perhaps twice Solstress's age. His eyes were fixed close together, like a mantis's; his nose was contracted, his pink ears were elongated. He dabbed at his mouth with an immaculate napkin while picking at a small plate of pepper pickle. Baus marvelled: here was a new contingency! Could it be Arnin, sombre Prince of Owlen? He was seated two tiers below.

It was! Baus stared agape. The very same foe whom they had warred against no less than four days earlier. The prince's cheekbones and beardless chin were haggard; his pale eyes burnt with injury and a half dozen of his men-at-arms sat slouched at his elbows like hounds. They were hollow-faced men, not much impressed with the quality of entertainment put before them. The prince wore a crimson surcoat, embroidered with yellow drakes and raised black epaulettes.

Baus mused with amazement. So! it was true that the prince had survived the ordeal. How utterly astonishing . . .

Unsettling thoughts began to course through Baus's mind. Could this pose a dour dilemma? If the prince were to recognize him, what then? What could they do?

Baus churned on the prospect. Doubtful thoughts began to rage in his mind—the prince had only caught a glimpse of Zoren's rogues upon the *Last Laugh's* deck—and for that, from a distance in the midst of battle—so what was there to fear?

Further misgiving pinched Baus's throat. Could this be Adrik too, the little brat whom Urseth had captured, and whom Arnin had saved at sea?

Baus's sinking heart realized it was.

His muscles twitched; now his glistening eyes trembled with uneasiness for here was a figure who could readily recognize them all for what they were.

The thought of battling a horde of Squands before him brought an abrupt revulsion to Baus's spirit. He pulled away from the peephole; he stood numbly facing the streamlined acrobats nudging him, crowding him with little smirks and cool giggles. Ignoring the flirting ministrations, he took Valere aside and Poli thrust himself forward, keen to be included in the conversation. Valere attentively listened; while swatting Poli away, he agreed that disconcerting news was in hand and that at best, they were fraught with danger.

They could no more abandon their obligations though, than rob the palace's treasury! Valere and Baus exchanged glances.

Sansix tugged pettishly at Valere's sleeve: "Quiet, seabeard! You are disturbing the performance! We are bid to quietude and will earn the disrespect of the Squands."

"Who cares? I don't give a rat's ass for the Squands!" growled Valere. "Sidle away! You annoy us! We are about to forgo the performance anyway."

Sansix gave a gasp of outrage. "You can't! I forbid it and will not allow a breach. I will instantly summon a monitor—look, I am heading that direction now. Yiol approaches!"

Valere grabbed Sansix by the ear and dragged him down to the marble floor without compunction. Poli proceeded to slap his ears. The two jocularly roughhoused him, while knock-kneeing him with bunts. Cargax hobbled his way over wagging a admonitory finger. "Stop this hooliganery! Your number is up soon! Heed my cue, rogues. Yiol will impose detriment upon you ruffians if you attempt to scamp procedure!"

Yiol, shortening the distance between himself and the companions, cut a halberd sweep in the open air, commanding an efficient silence. Poli took a backward step, without weapon and feeling naked, outfitted only in his girlish costume.

The current act came to a conclusion. Cargax's frail fingers motioned them to make their debut onstage.

Baus looked to Valere with apathetic uncertainty. What could they do? The monitor advanced, sensing hesitation. He flourished his halberd.

Valere softly cursed. Shielding brow with whatever subterfuge his cowl could afford, he shuffled to the entranceway. Baus mimicked the procedure. They tried frantically to apply more resin to their ears and cheeks for better disguise. Poli could do no more to his face or costume except perhaps squeeze a bit more rotundity into his breasts. The action appeared impossible under the circumstance. Glumly he trod behind Sansix who strutted on stage with an easy aplomb, eager to address the new fans.

Taking the podium, Sansix exuded an urbane confidence. "I am a writer!" he exclaimed, "of the unprecedented drama which you are about to witness. Its inaugural portrayal is a brainchild of mine, born of an afflatus sprouted in the early days of May seven years ago. Blossoms were ripe and birdsong was rich in the orchards of Rhoom, whence my bosom yearned for an expression of ardour as any young paramour would, in the prime of his youth. Yearnings such as these—"

"Quiet the backstory!" called an imperious voice from offstage.

Sansix muttered, "I will now allow you, O illustrious spectators, to judge my most spectacular creation for yourselves . . ."

Spreading arms, Sansix made way. On cue, Rayuzel appeared on ginger toes. She commenced the opening scene, dancing in small circles, looking up to the clouds, creating small mewling sounds in her throat. After a pause, she withdrew her instrument and began to play an even shriller resonance than in practice. Sansix approved. The melody wavered over the audible spectrum. Baus was compelled to shield his ears, but his cue was quick in coming, and he blundered to his position with an imprecision that had him tripping over his lines and asking for prompts which frustrated Sansix. He mouthed words to the outlaw. Baus's monologue went overlong, prompting little amusement from the crowd. Done with his deed, he trotted out foolishly. Valere's grand entrance followed with no greater encomium. In executing his overbearing lines, he fared two noticeable blunders, exchanging adjectives which made Rayuzel seem more like a market whore than a lover, but, as chance had it, Adrik had not recognized the two comics yet—a happenstance which afforded them a new level of confidence.

Acting as Muse, Sansix now sang his water-lily lullaby and skipped onstage urging Rayuzel to greater romantic sentiment for her lovers. Rayuzel blinked teary-eyed and held her instrument to her lips—a small yellow daisy clutched to her bosom. Bardek and Vandebul stormed closer. Finally cognizing each other as authentic competitors, they engaged in a duel. Full metal-on-metal contact was part of their program but Baus and Valere deliberately down-played their skills. They did not want a repeat of the last time—or to advertise the fact that they were sword-masters. They even went so far as to sabotage the strength of their attacks to avoid being cited as cutthroats. The manoeuvre went on to infuriate Sansix who was hoping for a display of topnotch, impressive realism. Instead he got banal sword-tapping.

While Baus feinted and bluffed, he stole glances toward Adrik. The spectators now became visibly concerned with the actor's interest in the boy. Turning and peering, they saw Adrik fidgeting and frowning upon the stage. Baus's eyes momentarily caught the princess's glance and his heart gave a sudden leap. How could she be so beautiful? Alas, what was the ardent emotion she sheltered in her fair face? Disenchantment? Caged despair? Smothered innocence? Baus was not privileged of answer. Bound into a marriage of which she had no love?

There seemed many mixed emotions, and Baus had to drag his attention away from the scene. Amongst the potpourri, a vague interest in himself.

In a sudden fury Adrik shot to his feet and began pawing at Arnin's arm. The signals were clear; Baus acted on impulse. He veered away from the path of Valere's lukewarm wrath and directed his golden weapon to the sky. Crying out to the audience in the heat of the moment, he beat his breast:

"Bardek and Vandebul—they are no more! Fair people of Sloe and Karsh. The old Bardek and Vandebul are finished, gone, kaput, expired! They are dead, deceased, expunged again and again in this trite drama."

Baus held up a hand. "A spoiler I know, but hear me out! Before the twain should commit to their shedding of blood—brother Vandebul, let us call on an arbiter to assuage the dispute."

Valere blinked dumbly.

Baus pointed up ceremoniously to the stands. "You fair maid—princess Solstress! You are to be wed and are known as delicious and fresh! Who is fairer than yourself in these lands? I beseech you to join us on this humble stage—the stage of 'life'. You may aid us in this sorting-out of bloody peccadilloes between Vandebul and Bardek, so that our fortune may be fair and our future brethren may be free from strife and sorrow!"

There was a hushed silence. Valere looked at Baus as if he had gone mad. Sansix was speechless; tears of frantic humiliation dripped from his powdered cheeks.

Events hung on a thread. Sharp eyes turned to Solstress, who in turn, climbed calmly her way down the tiers, over the heads of the noble spectators, pressing the toes of gentlemen and fleecing the tails of her silver dress over ladies' bodices. Heedless of her marred gown, she came onstage, standing beside Baus, her breath a-flutter.

"Fair Bardek!" she cried. "What is it of me that you would ask?"

"I ask only this," beseeched Baus grandly. "Who is the more qualified to wed the fair Lady Rayuzel—I or Vandebul?"

Solstress's voice rang clear and singsong. "Neither—you are both superior handsome swains, of which fair Rayuzel is not worthy; she is a frivolous tart who cannot make up her mind for her man, and is so typical of her kin. She is not an exemplar of authentic love or genuine matrimony."

"Then . . . what pray should Rayuzel do?"

Solstress croaked: "She should clean up her act. When a man and woman are enamoured, they see none other but themselves. That is grounds for marriage—none other."

"All is illuminated!" Baus agreed importantly. An impish glint shone in his eye and he encouraged the princess: "It must be something akin to the passion you foster for your own fiancé?"

An awkward silence ensued as the princess opened her mouth and nothing came out. Her eyes swam with confusion; her features were flushed; yet still, they bore a haughty, resentful look and glared back at Bardek for his leading statement.

Baus chided her. "Surely your imminent betrothal is the case of a perfect partnership?"

Solstress's eyes jumped. She seemed to show a sick fear shadowing her conscience. "Not the case, Bardek; I cannot tell a lie. Sadly, and by my own truth, I must profess my lack of love for my fiancé, and I do not condone this wedding of mine to my suitor, Clavius of Cleauch, as dearly as my mother wishes it."

Shocked whispers rang out from the gathering.

A croak of dismay erupted from Queen Maena's throat. She hissed and sputtered and a reprimand bit her lip.

Prince Clavius stood up to challenge the declaration. He was held back by his squire.

"Bardek, you callous louse!" moaned the prince. "Why do you instil such dissension amongst my betrothed and cause shame? You camouflage your jackalishness with easy convenience while you incite libel. You stultify your features behind grease, powder, and paint, and yet you seek to escape our recognition. Take off this infernal mask and show your true face!"

"Never!" cried Baus. "My hat, pigment and cowl are integral adjuncts to my role as Bardek—noble liegeman of Nardook and lover of Rayuzel."

A loud clangour indicated Queen Maena's displeasure. She rang her staff on her chair. "Enough of this fanfaronade! Solstress, back to your seat! Let's have no more of this unseemly charade!"

Solstress ignored the command. "No, Mother! I shan't." She stood with arms pressed to her chest, grumbling in a momentous huff.

Arnin who had been enjoying the drama, suddenly leapt to his feet from his cushioned chair. He unsheathed his broadsword. "Your Excellency! I have just learned news from our boy, Adrik, that Bardek and Vandebul are nothing but imposters, villains from the Urseth's criminal band. They are masquerading as mummers! For what purpose I cannot imagine. They plotted to ambush me before Sloe, and I order them seized and taken to an appropriate dungeon!"

The Queen, perplexed and galled, voiced a sharp query. "Speak, boy! Is this true?"

Adrik's voice filled the garden. "It is, O Queen! These actors are two of the band of pirates who kidnapped me and danced about the nightfires of Devil's isle."

There were shocked mutters. Maena stood ablaze before her throne, signalling to her Squands.

Baus hastily backstepped. Solstress's face was lit with a flushed thrill at the promise of escaping this betrothal. Listening from backstage, Reptolodus waved Yiol to action. The monitor rushed forth to intercept the fugitives.

Arnin had just leapt down from the stands with a circle of his peers to instil their own plans of justice. The audience erupted into mayhem; shrieks and defamations ran amok through the garden.

A servant sounded the alarm. Gongs echoed mournfully through all four corridors of the great inner courts.

With all its glorious foliage, the great olive garden seemed a beehive of turmoil. Baus grabbed the princess by her wrist and propelled her along with heat. His gait was reckless and her gown-cumbered legs stumbled and lucklessly, she fell. Baus abandoned her and scrabbled back to the vestibule. It was every man for himself. Valere and Poli knew likewise and tumbled at his heels.

They were met by Yiol—halberd raised and face latched into a malevolent grin.

Valere charged on past Sansix, swinging his cutlass on a definitive trajectory to the Squand's clavicle. The guard blocked the assault. The two met headlong, teeth gritted, weapons locked. Poli leapt in behind the warrior and rammed his flute up into his groin. It found a soft place under the shell armour not too fortified.

The Squand murmured an ineffectual plea; the massive warrior jerked back. Baus scrambled close to plunge Lolispar in his ribs. The Squand slumped quavering to his knees. Valere chopped down mercilessly. The Squand collapsed in a bloody heap, his life draining away. Feverishly, Baus and Valere scrambled to safety under the arch and down the terrace. They looked here and there, beheld only a brood of enemies no more than a dozen paces behind them.

The guards swept up the princess. Several rushed headlong at the pirates; already more palace men-at-arms were raging at their heels, swarming onto the stage with hostile intentions.

Baus, Poli and Valere wasted no time. They pushed past Reptolodus and fled out into the waiting room to face the stunned performers. Pell-mell they bowled through the ranks, staggering on through the colonnade and out into a greater hall within. They knew not where their feet took them, only away from the death that awaited. They felt the prickling of fate that capture would give.

Onstage Sansix sought to take advantage of the situation. He called out with authority to save his own skin. "Catch the miscreants, guards. They are pirates!"

Arnin's response was a palpable, feral snarl. "Woe to you, you ferret-faced mountebank! To the hounds for you!" His grim sword blazed high and snapped down to deal Sansix a mortal blow.

Sansix blanched, scrambled away like a rabbit. "You err, lord! I was only stringing the villains along before lawful forces could—" But his words were cut off; he was suddenly fleeing for his own life, in the wake of Baus, Valere and Poli.

With no more desire to see their fellow play-actors captured, the musicians formed a rude barricade against Arnin and his men.

The prince broke through the clot and roared orders back to his men. "Take none of them alive, you hounds!" His men-at-arms broke through the knot and gave chase to the fugitives. Several Royal Squands trod their heels, hurling acrobats and dancers this way and that. Baus caught a glimpse of hurtling bodies thrust helter skelter. Shivering at the carnage, Baus knew that he and his troupe would be next if he did not do something quickly.

Grimacing, he stumbled to a halt. Drawing the ganglestick, he faced his team of aggressors. It was a profound, bootless act, but nothing else could be done.

The prince was first to skid before him. Panting, he assessed the strange confidence of his new enemy. Here was no more than a youth—hardly a pirate. At first glance the prince saw a haggard-eyed, quixotic rebel, but he grew uneasy in discovering that his enemy stared him back face to face with no compunction.

Arnin raised his grey-silver sword to deal death, but Baus caught the prince's shining weapon on his own golden dagger.

Weapons were held magically in sway, almost surreal in their play. Faces remained pressed only inches apart . . .

Arnin loosed a gasp: "I would know your name, you cockerel, before I cut out your gizzard, like any common dunghill mite and feed it to you."

"A proud boast, Prince, but you may call me *Baus the Bold*, as I was christened by my tutor, Zoren the reaver. I was once, however, 'Baus of Heagram'."

"Baus of Heagram?" The prince blinked incredulously, for he could hardly believe his ears, and his true wonder only unnerved him the more.

It gave time for Baus's weapon to slide free of its cincture.

The prince's sword stung out in a faint hissing loop . . . it was like a whipping whirl that would have slashed off anyone's head, but it did not. Baus's training had been rigorous.

Baus ducked the sweep, looped his arm underneath Arnin's armpit and touched him a glancing blow to the side of his neck. The ganglestick made playful contact. Yet the feint did nothing. Arnin remained a coiled ball of steel. Baus's hopes died. In the seconds that remained he would be cut to shreds. Frantically he poked again. The ganglestick brushed Arnin's fair cheek. The prince failed to deflect the thrust and was ready to chuckle out a fruitless snort, but he was already as stiff as a slab of curing pork. A fractious grimace caught the prince's pallid visage. Behind him, his men came charging, but they skidded to a halt, perplexed at the aspect of their lord so weirdly immobilized. The prince was inert as a carving; silver sword gripped aloft; ultimately, at the behest of Baus's magic.

Baus did not linger to ponder the soldiers' reaction. He fled down the dappled hall, calling curses back at the prince's colleagues not to pursue him. So dankly and darkly riven were his warnings "that his wizardry would send them to the hells of *Dagar the Dismal*" that they paused to quail.

It was Baus's saving grace, for with those precious instants he was allowed time to disappear around the bend and merge into the shadows of a pillared hall.

Through the archway Baus fled and into the next foyer, noticing that his new surroundings were hugely high-ceilinged. Two guards lay torn and skewered at Valere and Poli's feet. Poli was wresting a silver halberd from one of the nerveless fingers, claiming his jerkin, but a slender maiden with long hazel curls ran out, pulling vehemently at his arm.

"No time for that! Quick!" she ordered. It was the same pale, blue-eyed creature who had taken a fancy to Baus the other day. "We must hide—before the others appear!"

Baus scanned his surroundings. They were in a large oval chamber filled with high stone pillars and carved of ancient green rock. The pillars rose high above to a domed roof. Orange light flooded through the high slits and did brilliant justice to the circlets of gems woven there: green, gold and silver. Baus's eyes, however, were only for an avenue of escape. The chambermaid led them across the tessellated floor, so brilliantly dappled with the afternoon's light from the high louvres that it stung the eyes. The girl was demure, yet yielding, and capturing all the same attention as before and she slipped down a side chamber, motioning them to a cramped alcove and broom closet whose door she had jarred open and beckoned them inside.

Sansix drew back, claiming an aversion to claustrophobic spaces. Valere stuffed him roughly in the gloom and hissed at him to be silent.

Not a moment too soon. Heavy footfall issued from the corridor. The servant girl remained outside to redirect them. Baus and Poli took fleeing counsel in the closet. An angry voice stabbed out of the stony dimness: "You! Slave girl! Where did the villains go?"

The girl motioned down the hall. "To the left, Lord, toward the Septarium!"

"Septarium, eh?" There came an excited chorus of grunts.

"That is where the Queen and noble ladies bathe in the seven emerald pools filled with essential oils."

"I know the pools and their foolish uses, wench, so don't talk back to me! Well, the rogues had better hope they have not defiled her precious sanctum." There was a scraping of boots, a jangling of swords and a whoosh of halberds as scowling men cursed and grunted and made their way to the exit with weapons.

Booted heels rang rancorously over the marble floors. The tramping receded; now only muffled voices filled the spaces and the dull thuds of feet.

Feverishly the servant girl pulled open the closet door and whispered to Baus: "The only safe place for you is in my mistress's chamber. Come! I am Uella. I know a way to her boudoir. The guards'll never think to look there."

Baus scratched at his chin in amazement. "There comes a time when a man is thoroughly amazed with providence. A small chance that we met you. Away then!"

VII

The palace was a beehive of activity. Guards, Squands, servitors and the odd, intrepid nobleman poked behind pillars, searching for fugitives; others engaged in wrathful discussions. Prospects did not look good for the felons. But fortunately Uella knew the palace like the back of her hand. She led the party through many back corridors, crossing foyers, entering portals and skidding through alcoves with unerring haste. Baus lost track of the chill atriums and stale-aired antechambers, lonely with disuse and gloomy, but relievedly unpopulated by questing eyes and sword-bearing Squands. Uella led them up a series of winding staircases, through a triple-tiered door and on past several quiet, empty rooms—she bounded up yet another ponderous flight of steps and through a jewelled arcade.

She muffled a hiss at them and tensed, for at the top of the stairs, one of her fellow maids came running on furtive feet. Grimly, the handmaid rose to greet her co-worker. "Murdering marauders, Lietza! Many have infiltrated the palace! It is not safe to roam the halls. Return to your quarters! Lock the doors!"

In seconds, her colleague was fleeing down the corridor out of pure fright.

Uella scooted back the hall and gestured her charges to retreat onto the landing. Through a brass-tiled door they crept—up another long flight of stairs and desperately down a dim-lit hall.

The corridor was carpeted with velour with small woven beasts tasselled at the gleaming gilt edges. Splendid paintings dominated the walls and exuded an ambience of stately grandeur. Tapestries lurked at the far end, depicting scenes of noblemen and women clad in their hunting gear and portraits of royal family members on elegantly-garbed mounts.

Baus thought the décor pretentious but then he was no connoisseur privileged to criticize. The upper floor was barren. The bulk of the commotion raged below where the palace security focused on intruders' probable paths. Baus laughed. The fugitives they would neither find—nor dare to enter the Royal private apartments.

Uella halted, taking scant notice of the hubbub below. Her keen senses were heightened and she emitted a small sound and a sharp exclamation into Baus's ear. Hunching gravely, she put a pale finger to her lips aside a narrow, jewel-engraved door and rummaged in her gown for a key. Deftly she unlocked the door and swung inside. Safely within, she latched the door after beckoning the others inside. Baus praised the depths of this charwoman's courage. She blushed, perceiving the affection as something demanding a passionate embrace, but she did not for she quickly realized the act would be improper. Demurely, she smoothed back her hazel-cream curls.

The princess's chamber was long and wide and invested of impressive quality. A high shell-embroidered ceiling rose to plush heights, pressed with crystal chandeliers and a few candles burning in the sconces. The interior was cast in a not disagreeable, soft plum light. Below the window a pair of upholstered settees reposed, dressed with the finest cottons and silks. A large oval, jewel-bound mirror surmounted an intricately carved maulwood desk. To the right appeared a queen sized bed, with white blankets and fluffy white pillows. Baus scrutinized the luxury with appreciation.

Uella led them across the carpeted floor and she ushered them to the closet, only slightly larger and dimmer than the last.

Sansix balked at the sight. Valere elbowed his way past the thief and hunkered himself down into the cramped space. He pushed aside dresses redolent of perfume and expressive essences and Valere climbed in between boxes and perfumes, grinning gamely in the wake of making himself more comfortable in the unlikely hiding spot. Poli's eyes gleamed in the soft light.

Baus paused before the closet. The corner of his eye caught a view through the brass-enamelled window—of shrubbery and a gazebo shading a group who congregated by the dinner tables. Servants, men-at-arms and Squands were talking animatedly and stalking about like insects. The tables were set with viands. Two ruby-coloured spires pitted the sky beyond; a line of pale battlements appeared farther away—the placid sea a distant slash of reflected light.

So much for a halcyon wedding, thought Baus.

Uella interrupted Baus's trance. She urged him to snug himself in the closet. "I shall return—with foodstuffs!" she promised happily. "Until then, do not make so much as a peep during my absence!—" She blew Baus a kiss which prompted disgruntled sneers from Sansix and the others when Baus returned the affection.

The key turned in the lock. The four fugitives were left in the complete darkness with nothing to contemplate but the quietude of the stone and their dim predicament. "Well, what are we to do now?" Poli asked.

Baus's shrugged. "What else?—follow the maid's advice, wait here until she returns, then enjoy the treats she brings."

Sansix uttered a contemptuous bark. "I'm not one to sit about while others fabricate schemes to apprehend us. I feel like a gnat."

"Then go and be thrashed if you like," grumbled Valere. "Don't drag us into your dooms! Sit here without complaining or feel the bite of my blade."

Sansix sank back into a glum silence.

The hours passed. Nothing but the direness of the situation and the bloodiness of their weapons kept them company. There remained an awful edginess amongst the outlaws. A plan of action was not forthcoming. Suddenly a rattling sounded at the door, a clopping of boots. The four stiffened, daring not to breathe.

The sounds moved on—likely guards doing their usual rounds.

Baus poured over in his mind the strange events of the day, but could find no logical synchrony to the thread. Uella did not seem any more reassuring an asset. She did not return and the group began to become anxious. Arguing in spurts, they refuted and confided in plans and programs to effect an escape. Baus had the idea of tying the mistress's dresses together to make some kind of a rope ladder or a 'kite' and leaping through the window. The idea was rejected. Each ploy seemed more preposterous than the last. They abandoned their schemes. Sneaking out of the bedchambers and negotiating a maze of halls and stairways seemed equally dubious, capturing some guards and impersonating them no less. Indeed the successes of all plans depended on several circumstances which were for the most part impractical, hinging on the presumption that the palace grounds not be littered with Squands.

The companions sank into bitter gloom. Twice they ventured forth to peer from the casement, only to find the sun sinking and the mournful gongs tolling even louder. The grounds teemed with guards. Those that skulked were eager for reward—apprehending the intruders and deriving glory from the twenty sequals Maena had offered.

Perhaps nine o'clock came round and a small rustling came at the door. A key slid soundlessly in the lock; a candlelight peered in. The portal swung inwards, shutting noiselessly again.

Baus perked up his ears with anticipation. Huddled in the closet, the company were of belief that it was Uella returning. The tread, however, was more assured, with the scent of anise and lavender—also fresh azalea, rosemary.

Through a crack, Baus peered out; he was dumfounded when he saw Princess Solstress. She was brushing back her hair and sighing wistfully before her maquillage desk. She had turned to walk right past their hiding spot, head held high, back straight, with an air of distinct aristocracy. She wore a dazzling white gown, dragging low at the hems and rustling like feathers in the wind, but her hair was tousled and an air of exhaustion seemed to overcome her bearing. An elfin smirk yet crinkled her lower lip. For whatever reason? She was husbandless, and her kingdom was plunged in turmoil. Baus caught in her demeanour the whiff of temporary respite from matrimony nevertheless.

At the make-up table she examined her flushed face in a mirror, dipping daintily at her chin in inward glee, puckering ruby lips and fluffing up her hair. She began to remove the costly gems adorning her dark locks and naked throat. She undid the buttons at the back of her neck, at which point Baus began to take a lively interest. His cronies too, sensing something remarkable about the peering of Baus, fought to sneak peeks through the peep-hole.

Baus was loath to the action. He struggled to retain control of the crack. The price was an inordinate amount of scuffling, which the princess could not help notice. She marched indignantly to the closet and flung open the door.

Seeing the four sullen-eyed men huddled in the shadows like badgers caused her no immoderate shock. She leapt sideways, clamping a stunned hand to her pink mouth. "What in the devil are you doing here, villains?" Her cry was a raucous squeal. "Brutes! Beasts! Voyeurs!" She whirled in anger, stupefied, covering her half-naked breasts and reaching for her jumper. "Why do you sit there like monkeys and watch my Royal bosom while I am undressing? How flagrantly unmannerly!"

Baus jerked to his feet with judicious appeasement. "The complaint is unsubstantiated, your Grace. At best perhaps partially true, but I voice a cordial offence to the imputation!"

Valere agreed, "You have confused us gentlemen for a batch of ruffians and louts—the kind who loiter about the fish market."

Solstress scoffed, flinging on her shawl. "You are callous cullions! Looking rougher than rough, half mauled by panthers at the city menagerie than men. I shall call the watch! You shall be flogged and beaten, and jailed!"

"That is a harsh option. I urge you not, Princess," pleaded Baus.

"And why?"

"We are not your enemies. In fact, we hope to gain your trust."

"Really?" Solstress shrieked in hysteria. "Not likely. How did you get in here?" Her royal hauteur was razor-edged.

"Your charming handmaid, Uella. She unlocked the door and brought us here."

"Did she now? The little minx! I shall have her whipped, and scolded—perhaps slapped, if I am of mind!"

"Again, I bid not, Princess," enjoined Baus. "The maid trusted us with her confidence and she had no wish for you or us to come to harm. Such is the goodness of her heart that she demands my respect. She knew you would harbour sympathies. Listen! As a result of our good intentions, we have allowed you to escape an unwanted betrothal—is this not a service? I believe you owe us a debt."

The princess demurred, reached again for her shawl. She readied herself for an outraged objection but her shoulders sagged and her chin dropped. "It is true! You have guessed well," she sighed. "Clavius is my bane; I have been forced to accept him as my spouse. He and his 'barons' control the affluent kingdoms of northern Karsh; so what? My mother wishes to cement strong relations with our neighbours. Between our House and the House of Cleauch there will be commercial advantage! My espousal is a fait accompli. The Queen will never let me escape. Our date for matrimony has been postponed—only a fortnight hence. In the meantime, royal face must be saved and I am to be its martyr!" She gazed stonily off through the casement, hope and vivacity lost to the wind.

"How is this to be carried out?" inquired Valere. "Surely you can protest the marriage?"

Solstress could not restrain a bitter croak. "Fat good that will do. I am to repent before the Lords and Ladies of Sloe, to make a public announcement to the effect that my words of this afternoon were spoken in haste and under the influence of drink!—what a joke!—boar mead to be exact—though I have never swallowed a swill of the stuff in all my life!"

Baus nodded with approval. "My condolences, Princess. This is a sorry state."

Solstress squeezed back her tears. "What else could I have done? In any case, I cannot house felons in my bedchamber."

"Nor would we broadcast it," conceded Baus. "I ask only that you house us for a little longer—until the Royal guard lapses. If the Squands believe that we have escaped, or have hid ourselves elsewhere in the city, they will loosen their leash, and we shall be on our way."

Valere voiced another suggestion, "If Your Highness could think of alternate means of escape—?"

Solstress voiced a rancorous chuckle. "Me? What do I know of escape-tactics and villainy? I have heard of no end to the horror of your depraved deeds! Murder, rapine, piracy —the list goes on. I find you now ironically concealed in my apartments; I can still hear my mother's morbid threat: "'Never fear, dearest Prince Arnin! If we discover any of these foul brigands in our palace, then we shall have them executed by any unpleasant means. Hanging is too elegant for these rogues!'

"'Very good, Queen,' Arnin says. 'At least your words are comforting to my ears. In the meantime, your Graciousness is generous in offering us a courtesy galleon for the lengthy trip back to Owlen.'

"''Tis nothing! Our kingdoms and families have been long friends—for sixteen generations! But of this we shall speak no more! The wedding is to be delayed as a result of the meddlesome pranks of a few insufferable mountebanks. If you find these men, kill them and bring them to justice!' and so away flew the prince with his minions. He is out to scour the fair halls of ruffians and corsairs."

Baus's expression remained imperturbable. "Perhaps you would wish to comfort our feelings with more positive disclosures?"

"Hardly—I merely pass on the information." Catching sight of Poli's costume, she gave a chuckle of laughter. "Your mate here has need of a cleaner dress, I think. Perhaps I can oblige."

"Choose one as you like," declared Baus blithely. "Poli's garment is soiled beyond repair —I see blood, saliva and even some noisome urine spread upon the front."

Poli's face showed a trenchant look that did not justify the degree of antagonism he felt.

"Such a strange name, 'Poli'," the princess mused carelessly. "What kind of a name is it?"

"A northern one," snapped Poli. "No weirder than Baus's or this skew-nosed jackal, Sansix's."

Sansix interpreted the words as those of reproach but the princess's gaze swept about with reflection. "Perhaps there is a way for you brigands to get out of here after all . . ."

Valere jerked himself erect. "How?"

"It would be dangerous."

Baus croaked. "We have some experience in this department."

Solstress hissed in a soft whisper, "There are chambers below the palace—they are said to connect to the boulevards of the northern city. Yet—the tunnels are reputedly haunted by ghouls—or some abominations no less ghastly. They are dank and miserable, these tunnels . . . . so it is rumoured." She looked at each of them with imploring apprehension. "Are you so sure you wish to proceed? Any who have ventured beyond have never returned to relay their discoveries."

Sansix's eyes bulged. "And why would they? How can you expect us to navigate these fell sewers and gain our freedom?"

Valere raked his knuckles across Sansix's scalp. "Quiet, hound! While one is in the presence of a princess, a citizen is expected to be humble to the point of penitence."

Solstress agreed with the injunction. With bland forbearance, everyone ignored Sansix's moans.

Sansix, gloomy and frustrated, mouthed several follow-up maledictions which earned him more knuckle raps from Valere. Baus pushed the distractions aside. He was in favour of more pleasurable views, including the princess's waistline and figure, which were all too noticeably trim in spite of the dimness of the light. "Do you harbour any knowledge of the points of ingress to these alleged tunnels?"

Solstress narrowed her brows. "There is a trap door somewhere hidden in the scullery. I believe it proceeds to the depths below. Whether it is a tube or a ladder, or a well or a stair, I cannot guess. I have never been there personally. There is a corridor similar to that rumoured to reside in the stables off the West Court."

Poli gave a miserable snort. "How can we hope to gain access to these burrows? They sound very far away. You saw—the palace is a-crawl with minions—out for blood. It is hardly a jaunt in the park to reach the access points you describe—let alone with the threat of ghouls and other inimical creatures of the night."

"Pessimism will get us nowhere," called Valere. "Poli, we must maintain optimism in the midst of adversity."

Sansix gave a strangled laugh. "Optimism, redbeard, I attribute to a crude boyish infatuation with derring-do. I agree with Poli. The plan is specious, not to mention impulsive. Even if we could escape the city, what then? South lies the Aldevean mountains—unpassable even in the summer's height. Westward lies the Waun forest, gloomy and unpredictable, and thick with spectral bandits."

"The answer is toward Owlen then," Baus answered wisely.

"The roads will be patrolled by Royal waysmen," Sansix argued.

"Then we will disguise ourselves as wandering minstrels or cobblers, or some-such, take your pick," said Baus impatiently. "We can hide ourselves until our absence is old and our trail is cold. There are always solutions."

"So you say!" muttered Sansix. "But how can you be sure?"

"By definite logic! Now curb your insatiable misgivings—"

At this time, another knock came to the door, causing a ripple of alarm.

Solstress hissed: "Who is it?"

"'Tis Uella—come to bring you your evening snack, my Lady."

A tension fell from the company. Solstress jerked open the door. The maidservant emerged with a buoyant mien carrying a salver of heaping sweetmeats: banyan fruit, gellerfish cutlets, leeks. The maid blushed when she saw Baus, and her fond glance was not one that Solstress appreciated.

"So much victual for a skinny little princess like me!" Solstress laughed with forced surprise. "Either Hardouk the cook is spoiling me or I am pregnant."

"Neither mistress, I—"

Solstress held up her hand. "No need to explain. I am not distraught with you, Uella, only amazed. How could you let strangers into my private boudoir? I have come to discover your friends in new wonderment though. We have discussed a grand plan, of which you shall play an important part."

The news seemed to reassure the maidservant; she vaulted over to give Baus a playful hug.

Baus sidestepped the affection and looked down at her haunch with helpless affection. As charming as the maid was, she was no equal of Solstress. Standing nearby was the princess, from whom Baus could almost feel a lithe attraction. She vibrated, pulsed with a vivacious excitement of her own.

Baus kicked himself. The daydream was foolhardy. "Then—you have a plan, wise Princess?"

"Very much so! Uella and I shall guide you and your friends to the scullery. But we must foil Juru and Pepit first—they are my two watchmen. They reside at the landing of the lower hall and practically all of our guests are mustered in the ballroom, dancing and chittering like larks. My mother flits about attempting to keep them all reassured. To maintain royal face in her house is her main concern. She must endeavour to keep all guests cheery and convivial. What policy! I should be present during these formalities, of course, but I am feigning exhaustion, which I like much better."

Solstress took them aside. "The overnight guests reside mostly in the south wing. We shall not travel there directly—instead, I suggest a course along the outer hallway to the east and north wings, then we sidle our way along the arcades secluded amongst the eastern pilasters. In the loggias there are places to conceal ourselves, also escape public scrutiny of the Squands. Once we are back in the palace we can take steps down to the baths and then go the route of the game rooms and the astrotarium where astroloegiacs and learned people sit to study the stars and interpret their enigmatic meanings."

"Very intriguing!" Baus smiled appreciatively at the princess. Sansix spoke in a guarded tone. "What possibility is there that we will bump into these Squands—or astroloegiacs?"

"The likelihood is small."

Valere prodded Sansix in the ribs. "What is it to you? We proceed, regardless of your concern."

"It is like you say, red dog!" howled Sansix bitterly. "There is no need to become bigoted!" He sank down onto the settee, brooding in fearful silence.

Baus clapped everyone to attention. "I deem the Princess's idea sound! Who is for employing it?"

Poli's hand shot up, to which Valere seconded the motion. Sansix refused to vote, at which point Valere raised his hand for him.

"Very well!" concluded Baus happily. "It appears that the vote is four to none. Unanimously, I decree that we follow the Princess's program. Solstress! I appoint you deputy director of this improvised exploit. Now—in what capacity are we to enact phase one, which includes bypassing Juru and his compatriot Pepit?"

"Uella shall lure them out with her female wiles."

"A scheme of unparalleled excellence! In what precise manner shall she do it?"

"With charm and coquetry."

Baus nodded, considering the response cogent and looked to Uella for support. Uella humbly smoothed her petticoat. "The arousal of masculine impulses are not all of my skill set."

Baus nodded approvingly. "I don't doubt. Any objections? Valere? Have you any supplements to add to said program?"

Valere shook his head bluntly.

"Then I ordain the case closed. Let us repair to the corridor."

Solstress grabbed Baus by the arm. "Not so fast, gypsy! Is your mind such a whirlwind that we must bob and swirl in confusion while you march sword-waving?"

Baus modestly explained that the inference had been corroborated on several occasions.

"No matter. Uella and I must don proper garments. As ladies, we cannot be gliding about corridors on perilous missions with only flimsy frocks and high heels to support us."

"I never would suggest any such condition," declared Baus frostily.

Solstress ordered the men to turn faces away from the dressing table. She discreetly changed into more appropriate attire, which included green trousers, grey flax jumper, knit knee socks and scuffed boatshoes. Uella, being of similar girth, availed herself of Solstress's baggy blue pants, a flannel slip gown and soft walking shoes.

Baus stared with approval at the women. Both were comely, of good stature, address and well-fitted. Bosom and haunch were well stocked and tasteful even in the simple and somewhat rudely assumed garments. Raven-haired Solstress stood blinking in the candlelight, her chin raised grandly and an ever haughtiness of demeanour showing; Uella, coquettish and almond-haired, thrust out a hip and demonstrated a confident feminine swagger which met general approval.

Several more ministrations ensued, which occupied valuable time and Baus tapped his foot with impatience.

The princess began searching within her armoire for a dagger. It was a weapon equipped with green jewels and gilt-edged pommel which she tucked assuredly into her waist belt. Baus performed a quick inventory of other weapons. Poli harboured a bloody halberd; Sansix, a sleek knife and dented cutlass. Valere guarded a cutlass and halberd, and he himself wielded Lolispar and the ganglestick which were kept hidden in the deepest folds of his breeches. If it came to a skirmish, they may be outnumbered, but certainly not weaponless.

Solstress peeked out of the doorway, down the gloomy hall. Behind her Baus saw that the way was clear. Two cressets bathed the hall in a dim, sultry light. The trio of paintings hung austerely as before. Underneath those, sat the antique rosewood settee.

On furtive feet, the gang advanced; the princess directed Uella down the hall then stealthily followed herself. She paused past the sitting room at the top of the stair, biding her time before confronting the two watchmen. On Solstress's signal, the servant slipped brazenly down the steps to engage the two. In a lively program of furtive little pats on shoulder, sultry glances, hip and body movements she captured eye and attention. So doing, she coaxed them easily from their positions and gently swayed from the landing, using her body as a provocative instrument to gull the night watchmen. Indeed her skills were incisive and Baus gave a ceremonious smirk. He and Poli crept ever closer, weapons clenched. Should they be discovered, they would be invested to fight their way to freedom.

There was no need for such solicitude. Even when Uella had lured the guards toward the end of the corridor, Baus beckoned Solstress to accompany them and they slipped noiselessly into the gloom of the lower hall.

Uella became coy with the men, realizing that her duty was done and she slipped safely away with her friends. Puzzled, Juru and Pepit clambered after her, boots and weapons clanking about the stone.

"Uella! Come hither!" Pepit cried. "Why do you tease us so cruelly when moments before you imparted such promise? Is this a way to treat men who patrol the corridor day and night? It is lonely in these halls—for which we are given little thanks!"

Solstress strode out of the shadows. "Juru! Pepit! What are you yapping about? Why are you not at your post?"

Juru thrust himself to tense attention. "Your Highness? How did you—? Never mind. We were out striding after Uella, sensing it strange for the maid to be lurking about these corridors while rogues are at large. We became concerned."

"Indeed! Uella has been acting strangely and I shall have a talk with her. Now, please, back to the stairs! Do you wish my chambers to be breached? The palace has been compromised by villains!"

"Yes, I know, my Lady!" they chorused. "That is exactly what concerns us! Why are you not yourself in your bedchambers?"

Solstress explained in a cross manner, "While you earnest people were so busy with my handmaid, I descended for a bite of sweetmeats in the parlour. Is this so remarkable? Now, please! Back to your post—or shall I call you to the major guard keeper, Boyko?"

Juru hurriedly repudiated such an action. The two hustled back to their post.

Solstress turned on her heel. She signalled her friends out of hiding. They filed off, Sansix grumbling aloud about being forced into a hazardous situation. The complaints were ignored.

The group traversed the suite of darkened halls on noiseless feet. They arrived at the eastern pilasters which Solstress had mentioned and with assurance, she led them out on an interconnected balcony that boasted a grand view over the gardens. She padded her way like a regal tigress, silently aware that the liveliness and aura that was hers was her birthright. The city slumbered under rising stars and Baus and Valere stared out through the gold-plated balusters: a jumble of distant rooftops glistening beyond the wall. Within the inner court, shafts of pale moonlight reflected upon the fantastically twined forms of the elaborate garden: shrubbery, pleasances, carved bushes, hedges, topiaries, ornamental trees. The sounds of crickets, frogs and purling water wafted from faceless pool after pool. Sublime music drifted from far places. Here Baus thought to detect a glint of a weapon or a hulking figure twitching in the gloom. The six proceeded cautiously, feeling their way along banister and rail between dew-dropped columns.

Despite the dangers, the inner courts were good hiding places, and Baus noted a shadowed conglomerate of terraces, cloistered alcoves and apses held aloft by massive, jewelled columns and fluted buttresses.

About midway along the façade, Solstress led them back to the heart of the compound—through a narrow hall and down a wide corridor spanned with many wings. Soft golden light spilled from the hall's end. They heard the faint trickle of voices and whispered sibilances.

Sidling away from the sounds of human presence, Baus noticed a chamber of small chessboards also set up in a remote wing. He saw a gigantic marble chessboard with man-sized marble pieces; in another, an elegant dining salon, outfitted with onyx tables and fine cutlery. In another, a room full of canvases and easels filled with long windows affording a supply of natural light during daytime hours.

The group huddled close, passed more rooms than imaginable and Baus caught glimpses of ancient armour, bossed shields, tarnished pikes.

Hurrying, he heard a faint humming, possibly a chanting. At last he knew they had reached the astrotarium. The door to the auditorium was ajar. Baus risked a peek inside, seeing twenty scholars perched on high stools and armed with optical devices of all sizes. They gazed up solemnly at him where before they had been peering through a low, open domed portal bared to the night sky. The humming came from the lips of acolytes who sat hunched in a tight knot on the marble floor. The acolytes waited for the scholars to impart their knowledge as they saw it writ in the sky. One such happened to scrutinize Baus, and he invited him to join the team of devotees.

"Perhaps another time," Baus responded politely, "as I am due for pot scrubbing in the scullery."

"You shall miss a glimpse of destinies and worlds colliding!" the acolyte explained. "Here, pilgrim, take heed! Revise your itinerary. Attend the course of the Planets as they traverse the Houses!"

Again Baus courteously declined; withdrawing, he blinked his eyes dubiously: the scene, though wondrously esoteric, was much too highbrow for his tastes.

The princess had led them down another side passage away from the lights and voices. The corridor was neither wide nor narrow and silvered with puddled moonlight creeping in from the row of high, slitted windows. In a hushed voice, she explained: "The kitchens range directly below this floor but we must take the long way around to ensure our passage unnoticed. If we launch headstrong toward the voices and lights, we must pass Boyko and his fastidious under servants. We would be sure to suffer discovery. But wait! I thought to hear a clink of armour . . ." She drew back with anxiety. "We cannot pass here! The way is guarded! I know of only one other side passage past the drawing room, but likely it too will be guarded!"

Baus gave the grimmest nod. Solstress's disclosure was disquieting. Gripped with a sudden idea, he ripped off two of Uella's buttons and tossed them down the corridor.

Uella gave a sour squeal of contempt. "What do you do? You rip my buttons? Are you unaware that these buttons hold shut my gown and prevent my breasts from dangling out on a sudden run?"

Baus pointed out a cogent fact. "The Squands will know otherwise. They will come to engage us."

"Perhaps in your dream but not mine!" cried Uella.

Baus pointed didactically into the gloom. "Look! The guards clamber forth. The enterprise has not been in vain."

Valere and Poli rushed forward to sandbag the two sentries. They were not leviathans but came blundering blindly as if eager for requital. The twosome clutched their halberds with wrath and their eyes blinked in the sudden change from dimness to black as if they were sea fish washed up in a gloomy lake. It was easy to crumple them into sorry heaps and swift sword pummels soon proceeded to level them. Injuries turned to more mortal assaults when the guards fought back. Baus, Valere and Poli were obliged to use lethal force. Blood sprayed and cries waned. Dragging the corpses out of sight into the blue black shadows, they wiped their weapons of blood and turned to face the women.

Solstress gave a croak of terror. "You kill men like livestock. I cannot abide by this cruelty! It is wanton butchery!"

"It is reality," declared Baus testily. "Now listen, their clamour was outrageous."

"But—"

"Onwards!" cried Baus. "There is not an instant to lose!"

Solstress scuttled ahead, casting a horrified glance back at the carnage. Shivering at the sight of Baus's bloody doublet, she dropped a hand to her mouth and covered a whimper. Baus had closed in a hair's width behind her backside and could not help but notice the features of her curvaceous body. Indeed such slender contours of hip, breast and waist were not lost in such loose-fitting garments. Certainly he would envisage her in more engaging attire, or lack of attire—but under happier circumstances, facilitated in the comfort and privacy of a proper, cushioned love nest, such could be accommodated.

Carnal fancies were hard to conceal in this closed space and were not missed by Uella who swaggered in to Baus and whispered darkly in his ear: "Solstress is of Royal blood, dear, quite out of your league. But, I on the other hand, am of suitable birth, warm and amorous, and if not exotic, and necessarily, available."

Baus proffered the maid a look of surprise. For all her buoyant, quaint, schoolgirly manners, she was attractively convincing.

Uella was about to expand upon her sultry qualities when Solstress gave them a shove and a low wail. Almost before any could react, three hefty patrolmen loomed out of the darkness, flourishing pikes and axes. One was a harsh-featured Squand, alarmingly quick, and blessed with a protruding fleshy jowl. A blue tabard rippled over his copper-studded mail. He swung forward to engage. The defender made a grasping lunge for the princess who gave a high squeal. The Squand grunted. Solstress slid eel-like out of his grasp. The other two leapt for Baus and Poli and their gleeful bellows were loud enough to wake the entire palace.

Poli, Baus and Valere winced at the ruckus. "Quick! Silence is essential!" hissed Baus.

Poli and Valere engaged the Squand. Sansix and Baus awkwardly wrestled with his henchmen. Baus created a diversion. He leapt aside while Poli hewed at the monstrous guard. A horrid outcry pierced the air. The Squand pitched forward, half his calf ripped open. Valere heaved himself aside only in time to avoid being bludgeoned by the patrolman's axe.

There was a long moment of ruthless hacking where grinding halberds, cutting cutlasses and fishhook poleaxes hissed through the air.

In a flash, three guards lay slumped lifeless on the cold stone. Throats were cut and life's liquids draining. The women swayed in shock. Instantly they shrank away from the upturned bodies, sickened that such bloodshed could occur in the sanctuary of their home. It prompted Baus to console them. His forearm was cut; Valere's face was scratched and Poli's left leg wobbled but was otherwise undamaged. Sansix had escaped a rueful demise with superficial wounds, but perhaps remained the most shaken of them all.

Muted shouts and challenges issued from the corridor behind. Baus jerked aside.

"Let us be away! Now!" he cried.

Valere whistled between his teeth. The cringing women hustled to their feet and Baus's lack of compassion was justified. The bodies would be discovered and more Squands would be hot on their trail, harbouring little mercy.

"This way then!" Solstress cried, gesticulating to a side passage. "The wine cellars."

"Nay!" protested Uella. "The entranceways have been sealed off. They are guarded by Squands. We must take the left corridor—to the kitchens!" She waved furiously to a place where a dark double archway loomed out of silver moon shadows.

Valere snorted: "Well, let's make up our minds, ladies. We cannot take all day, especially if we are dead!"

Under the forbidding arch they fled, racing into a wide domed hall that was filled with endless passageways with little light. Side-chambers ranged everywhere, decorated with antique furniture, statues and bibelots. The rooms were austere, cold and sterile, harbouring few windows. The company's gasps seemed like windy hisses in the muted dimness. Their hurried footsteps echoed like hollow thuds on aged, cold stone. Twice the ceiling unfurled to show feeble starlight and Poli and Sansix plunged into one of the pools from where rainwater fell, cursing wet ankles and sopping boots.

Keeping to the left, the haggard group gradually discovered the naked hallway narrowing to three abreast. The passage was unlit. Neither moonlight, cresset nor flambeau was in evidence; ultimately it ground their progress to a snail's pace and feeling their way with hands and feet along the mortared walls, they felt themselves clutched in a lower, narrower space. Uella could not imagine the place from memory.

The voices and shouts receded behind them. Now Uella hesitated; she seemed lost.

Baus's sense of direction was utterly forsaken and he foraged about with bleak gropes. Twists and turns left all hopelessly disoriented. The palace was huge, populated with endless corridors, mazes, interconnected wings—enough to beguile even the savviest of rodents seeking only the smallest crumbs of kitchen droppings.

There was more light now, owing to certain louvres etched in the upper reaches.

The six descended a short flight of steps, only to round a bend where the feeblest of cresset light shone from a crooked T junction.

Uella brightened and pointed a finger. "We are on the ground floor! I know this place!" She clung excitedly off Baus. "Scullions transport wheat, water and daikon to the kitchens along the back walkways. We are close! I feel it. Only a few paces. The stables are near at hand!"

Baus mumbled a quick acknowledgement. The troop fled on through the dim murk.

VIII

The stone was more crudely wrought in this section of the palace, a circumstance which prompted Baus to believe that they were broaching the deepest and most ancient part of the stronghold. Large angled flags comprised the floorstones, filmed with salt and iron dust from labourers' sandals.

The group rounded a narrow corner and tripped into a stuffy hallway. It was thick with ribbed columns. They froze. The heavy tread of boots clomped on the stone ahead.

Solstress hissed at the outlaws to slide back into the shadows. She stood with Uella to face the detail while Baus hustled behind one of the fluted pillars running near the back of the chamber. Valere and Poli found columns of their own to hide behind. Sansix scrambled trembling behind Poli.

Baus dared not breathe; the heaviness of his breath could give him away. The menacing cadence of the approaching feet only portended doom—possibly Squands, fierce for revenge and order.

Baus scrunched down in a ball to make himself as unobtrusive as possible. Risking a glance ahead, he caught a glimpse of a face emerging from the shadows. Arnin! He almost gasped with dismay. The prince was striding abreast of his two men-at-arms: one a trim lean fighter gripping a broadsword, and the other a short, stocky knight holding a firebrand. The prince wore his nut-gold locks dangling to his epaulettes and beneath that a peaked silver morion. The blue of his eyes blazed with such an intensity that Baus could only gape. A furor seemed to consume the compassion of his office and made him a force to be reckoned with. His spirit had been possessed—curdled with the prospect of hunting down a rogue who had slighted him, and particularly one who was a part in causing him so much grief in the recent past. Slim and garbed in his crimson tunic slung overtop silver mail scudded with silver sea scales, he hastened to intercept the two figures whom he had not quite recognized in the chill dimness.

The prince uttered a terse challenge. Solstress returned a deliberate reply. The prince nearly jumped out of his armour. "Solstress! My Lady! What brings you to such sombre precincts?"

"A restless caprice—my lord, grief over a fouled marriage."

Etiquette won over unmannerliness and the prince promptly crafted a deep bow and doffed his morion. "An unexpected pleasure!"

Solstress gave him a sober look; Uella curtsied. Arnin's two taciturn men-at-arms gave small, mechanical smiles. The prince added ceremonially, "It grieves me to find you traversing these dark halls unattended, Princess. Do you know not that felons are at large?"

Solstress blinked, pretending shock. "This comes as a complete surprise! I assumed that you had rooted them out by now?"

"Alas no!" Arnin sighed. "The uncouth thugs work mischief in the dark, hiding in secret places, possibly flirting with magic, and with red blood on their hands! Forsooth, I must impress on your grace to return to your chamber; these cold corridors are no place for a Royal descendant to be lurking at will."

Solstress compressed her lips into ribbons and she spoke with measured patience. "I daresay, Prince, that this my home and I shall do what I like."

"Of course! No offence. But these are troubled times, my Lady. We must launch efforts to flush out these murderous reprobates who haunt our castle keeps. The men of whom I speak are savages—bullies, thieves and slayers—who would not in an instant think to work unspeakable malice on your person."

"Do you think?"

"Aye! I have fought against such men."

"Where?"

"At sea! Recently . . ." he spoke gravely, "and it is by sheer providence, that I arrived safely at your palace without grave injury."

"How fortunate," Solstress replied in silky condescension. "Savage and uncouth, you say, these knaves are? The description fills me with dread—and some excitement!" she added mischievously.

Arnin's eyes grew resentful. "That is hardly a term I would employ on these rogues. If such scoundrels were to leap out of the dark, say behind this pillar—" the prince leapt sideways and clanked his sword loudly against the stone "—what would you do?" He laid a gloved hand about her fair neck and attempted a squeezing which Solstress adroitly evaded. "Would that be an 'exciting adventure' for you?" Sarcasm was echoed in the tone.

Solstress was neither impressed nor intimidated by the prince's bluster. She drew herself up and whipped out her dagger and drew it close to his pelvis. "If such a villain were to come at me, Prince, I would launch this instrument at his personals, thus eliminating every problem which drove him to such absurdity."

"A wise tactic."

She strutted closer and flashed the weapon dangerously close to Arnin's throat. "The gullet is also an equally effective target too, though less merciful."

"How very impressive!" The prince weakly recovered. "If I only knew that you were so expertly-outfitted with your dagger and your rejoinders! Ho-ha. Earlier I duelled with a certain villain who called himself 'Baus'—'Baus the Bold' if I remember. I was about to run him through and he employed some foul wizard's magic upon me, bewitching my limbs into the state of torpor."

"How dreadful!" Solstress cried. "You seem quite unscathed, Prince. Did this 'Baus' harm you in any way?"

"None physically," admitted the prince ruefully. "He failed in his attempts, thanks to the providence of Krutu, greatest of sea witches, to damage me. Of course, the steadfastness of my own personal resolve to assaults, was largely to credit. My men saw the scoundrel flee like a banshee before he could complete his perfidious task which would have wounded me spiritually."

Solstress nodded with comprehension. "That was certainly cowardly of the pirate to flee in the face of being cut to pieces."

Arnin frowned, not knowing whether sarcasm lurked beneath the princess's words. He looked at her sidelong before attempting another tack. "You are an exquisite May flower, my Princess—if you excuse the forwardness and I apologize for my presumption, your Highness. But you are of utterly pristine presence. How long have we known each other? Since we were children?" He grasped the princess's hands. "There is a great matter which tests my spirit, which I must broach."

Solstress listened with interest. She disengaged the prince's hands though with purpose.

The prince smoothed his cheeks and patted his thighs. "I hope that it would not be indelicate of me to say, that I am completely enamoured with you. I always have been and always will!" He gave an urbane sigh as if it were difficult for him to relate the next part of his delivery.

Solstress could not stifle a laugh. "What a surprise! How artfully expressed, Prince—and so perfectly droll! Imagine us as a happy couple! Two peas in a pod. Pity our interests are not shared in mutuality. Now, if you will excuse me, Prince, I have pressing business to attend to which warrants no delay."

Arnin's jaw dropped. His face seemed to cloud to the pitch of old tar. "Yes, of course! Rowin, Hilleus, if you please! Accompany 'Her Holiness' to her destination, which interestingly enough she has still not divulged."

Solstress expressed shock at the idea. "While murderers roam my halls? Never! Your best duty would be to collect the degenerates yourself—rather than focussing on me."

Arnin began to argue the point but Solstress shook her head. "You are a maudlin fool, Prince! On your way," she laughed, "and with your two bullies. Your utilitarian chivalry and pleasant manners do nothing for me—except maybe to leave me feeling somewhat limp and shivering."

The jab stung; perhaps Solstress had pushed frankness too far. The prince reddened at the rejection and a visible hot anger came streaming from his body. Grabbing Solstress by the waist, he exercised his authority and yanked her roughly. The princess resisted, but was propelled down the hall in unceremonious fashion like a reluctant mule. She gave a soft cry. Upon his signal, Rowin and Hilleus clamped a paw onto Uella and began towing her along, like some goat at the market.

From behind his pillar, Baus gnashed his teeth. He bit back his tongue and urge to rush out and extract apology from the coxcombs. All his well-wrought plans . . . all were slowly disintegrating before his eyes! If Arnin were allowed to take the women—

Out from behind the column he leapt, brandishing Lolispar. He cried out a spiteful call in an orotund voice.

The prince whirled, amazed at the visitor who so audaciously rushed to engage him.

"You again!"

"'Tis I, indeed!" came Baus's stentorian cry. "Now step aside, you graceless cur. Unhand the princess, who appears displeased with the manner in which she is being conducted."

Arnin laughed rudely. "Whilst I command strength in my limbs, coxcomb, not likely! 'Tis you, peacock, who should step forth and admit to surrender." He shook his head in indulgent wonder. "Aren't you a pompous rogue? And what are you? A simple cockerel— from Heagram. One against three? How could you possibly hope to win against my warriors, with or without your pathetic magic?"

"With competent allies!" cried Valere, who had suddenly vaulted from behind a pillar and had knocked the brand from the nearest man-at-arm's hand.

Poli rushed the other soldier. Seizing the moment, Baus engaged Arnin in a running stab. The prince unsheathed his weapon barely in time to combat the lunge, so stunned was he with the sudden turn of events. He pushed Solstress aside. A well-rehearsed oath reached his lips as he began hacking his way toward Baus.

Poli slung his man backward. He slashed left with his whistling halberd. Sansix shied back in the gloom, whimpering with distaste. He was loath to enter this arena of death. He was rewarded for his lack of valour with a hissing sword slice, which the soldier next to him (whom Poli had head-butted and flung off balance), had slashed out awkwardly and diced off Sansix's left finger. Sansix gaped at his bloody stump where the pinky had last been. He slumped to the ground, crying heavily out in woe. Clamping hold of his hand, he tried to staunch the flow of blood—but was unsuccessful.

Valere pounded his charge to the ground and shouted at Sansix to stop his whining. "Ingrate! It's only a flesh wound."

"Easy for you to say!" howled Sansix. "Your digits are intact!"

"As they shall stay," grunted Valere. "Now stop your grousing." He tossed a fragment of tunic from his stunned charge's light mail coat. "Here," he called gruffly. "Wrap this round your finger, fool."

Poli was battered against the wall. Arnin's stocky henchman took him with his superior weight. Using a trick he learned from Juuliq, he squirmed free, laid a crippling stroke to his attacker's thigh. Uella cringed with distaste at the carnage and delicate meat-chopping she heard as Poli's bronze blade ripped into flesh. The axehead squelched home. She sagged sobbing to her knees. Meanwhile Baus danced back and forth with Arnin in a cat and mouse game. They duelled between the hexagon of columns like pirates. Arnin slapped his sword angrily against a pillar. He shouted for Baus to come out and fight like a man.

"Stop this instant!" Solstress cried, appalled at the amount of blood and fury she witnessed. Baus emerged, lunging toward Arnin's left unprotected flank. Sword cracked on gladius and the clash threw hollow echoes around the chamber like queer giants fighting with magical staves. Baus did not fear his attacker or the risk to his own flesh, rather he reviled the sinking feeling that a new patrol would come clambering by and make the odds unbalanceable.

Valere stood grimly away from the scene, awaiting a fair opportunity to sandbag the prince.

Solstress impulsively seized the initiative and dashed up behind the prince to stab her dagger into his shin. The blade did not completely penetrate the heavy leather greaves but was deep enough to joggle the prince to unmaskable fury. With a baleful groan, he kicked her aside and Solstress flew back, jarring her knee. A cry of pain jarred the tomblike space which only infuriated Baus the more. He attacked Arnin without compunction. The prince's lack of gallantry was insufferable, prompting Lolispar to fly in wilder circles. The blade was magic, imbued with a rare violence when needed, and crafted from times of yore, handed down to Trimestrius from his sire. The present eerie and gleaming fire unnerved Arnin, who had never seen its like. He was instantly on the defensive—unedged, awed by this fantastic weapon which traced arcs of savagery in the air.

Teeth clenched, grasping, Baus ploughed into the fray and dealt Arnin a wicked blow that his light armour at the midriff could not arrest.

The prince sagged sideways, wheezing out a gasp. He staggered to the wall holding a pierced left rib. Baus veered in, pulled the Prince's arm painfully behind his back and jerked him down like a maimed crow. Valere and Poli jumped in, tackling the prince to the ground. They ripped off his surcoat and used the bloody fabric to bind his legs and arms.

Baus dragged Lolispar across the prince's face, drawing an edge of blood. "Now, Prince, would you wish your fair visage marred more permanently? I pity you, for you could neither vex nor woo pretty maids like Solstress against their will."

"Begone, you cursed hexer! Let me never see again your blithe, ugly little face. If you mar me, you'll only make your death more painful."

Valere looked down at the prince with pity. "I reckon the coxcomb's right, Baus. We can't send him to his wench Krutu. His cronies yes, but not this one. He is a special prince, after all. We are not butchers, only misguided wretches, isn't that right, *Prince*?" Valere laughed at his own joke which became quiet as the brand nearly flared out. "'Tis pity that we can't ransom this jade for a million. What a bounty he'd make!."

"Wrap the wound," ordered Baus. "We don't want our prince bleeding out."

Arnin glared at the two brigands. His eyes took on the look of pure hatred. "You are the gutless milksops who escaped *Two Silkie's Rock*, aren't you? On my white ketch? The mystery is explained."

Baus crouched, face inches from Arnin's blanched, blood-dripping cheek. "Aye, though you haven't all the facts, Prince. Further, your low opinion of us is unwarranted. Explain a thing or two. How exactly did you get to the island so quickly, and what was all that chicanery back at *Two Silkie's Rock*?"

Arnin masticated to spit in Baus's face, but thought better of it. Turning, he refused to speak, but Baus ground his elbow deep into his wound and the prince gasped and reeled.

"Mercy!" Arnin cried.

"Mercy!" Baus mocked. "You are defeated. Your life hangs on a thread—remember, when I ask you again."

The prince hissed out in bursts then folded: "Alright . . . Our ship began taking on water. We followed . . . the gutless, cursed *Sea Warlock*. For a heartbeat it seemed the right thing to do—but then the storm raged. We lost sight of her. She lumbered back toward the cursed island, shaking and creaking like a haunted castle. We knew that she must founder and all her men die. We followed to finish her off and the lot of her scum and clear a blight from the sea once and for all. But we were swept sideways—away from the island toward Sloe. Our sails were beyond salvage. We struck north of Sloe's piers, but barely escaped, rescued by cityfolk who saw us foundering. The next morning, we took three of Maena's warships out to search for survivors on the island, but found none—humans, no life of any kind. We combed every inch of that bleak, blasted rock and still the mystery remained. Naught of Zoren, Urseth, Borath or any of their bedevilled crews. There you have it! The sea swallowed them up . . . like ghosts, or they sailed off on their drowning ship like silkies or drowned under the fury of the storm . . ."

The disclosure brought an unearthly silence to the outlaws.

"A mystery then," mused Baus. Even as he contemplated the puzzle, an image of a score of pirates floating fish white on the sea's bottom came to mind. Perhaps the pirates' fear of the cursed Ridgar's eye had been their bane, despite Zoren's brave conviction to the contrary.

Valere muttered with his head, shaking disbelief, "I think the rogues survived—good old Arnin just does not want to admit their victory."

Arnin cursed. "You are entitled to your opinion, low breed."

Poli stabbed his halberd hard down on the floor. "How do we know the prince's jabber is not just a bunch of lies?"

"Why would he lie in such a position?" chuckled Valere. Lifting his boot, he hoofed Arnin in the ribs. The prince gave another shuddering gasp and writhed until the throbbing of his wound lessened.

"You filthy lot!" Arnin cried in between gasps. "You have no concept what I will do to you. I don't know what you are up to, skulking about these corridors like a team of ghouls, but you should know it that you'll be caught, and hanged." He sneered at Baus from his blood-disfigured eye, "Baus the Bold! What an absurdity! You have hoodwinked dear miss Solstress into playacting in some league with your wickedness, but there it ends! You'll pay handsomely for your crimes—all of you, you depraved villains! Even you—my faithless harlot," he sneered at Solstress. "You shall one day rue you ever flouted me, strayed into the realms of darkness."

"Let's go," moaned Solstress, not liking the fatalistic truth of the prince's remark. She pleaded, tugging at Baus's arm, whose fingers now trembled to employ a regrettable strike upon the prince. Solstress picked up the weeping Uella and drew her down the hall. Baus retrieved the prince's firebrand. He blew it to flaring health and beckoned to Poli. Hauling Sansix to his feet, Valere clamped a hand over his lips and quelled his irksome moans. Arnin was left bound and gagged at the foot of the midmost pillar, struggling with his bonds and croaking curses under the duress of his wounds. The bodyguards remained groaning or twitching, in no state to help.

Baus turned to regard the disreputable scene with a shiver of distaste. What cock up had he committed? Treason beyond treason! To leave the prince here in such a condition—it was not an act to go unpunished. But what other choice did he have? Options were slim and time was rapidly running out.

IX

From the wretched gloom the company hastened, fleeing down a narrow hallway lit by cressets guttering in the cool draught. Solstress pointed anxiously—to a junction blocking further progress.

Baus halted, crouching. Warily, he perceived the presence of fresh air, and hope wafting from the leftmost branch of the corridor. Jumping to his feet, he flourished his brand.

He moved swiftly toward that which appeared a low brick wall. Moonlit columns reached out from where a pair of crudely-cut windows gazed across a cobbled esplanade. The low rampart was stationed solemnly at the end of the courtyard—incongruously graced with a zigzagging stairwell. Elsewhere the plaza dropped off to murky shadow; muffled sounds of men's voices drifted somewhere in the distance.

To cross the open courtyard entailed risk and Baus was not about to jeopardize his life for a wanton purpose. He stared broodingly; while the cobblestones glistened in eerie moonlight, blurred movement of figures indicated a deadlock—in the direction of the wooden gate. The adjacent wall was affixed with iron rings and chains and judging from the strong odour of dung, Baus surmised that stabled mounts had recently taken residence. The gateway, no more than sixty yards distant, was like a palace exit or some sort of route to a service yard.

Cautiously, he and the other seamen urged the women on toward the rampart. They crept on all fours, across the cobbles, wary of every breath. Baus felt a judicious urge to leave behind the torch, which could only give away their presence.

They reached the stairs safely. At the foot of the wall, they climbed the crumbly steps, up to the parapet where they lay breathless on their stomachs. Pitted brick formed the platform's floor, wide enough for a pair of guards to walk abreast. Baus was the first to peer out over the crenellations and saw below that a moonlit pasture spread, slick with dew. Between embrasures Uella motioned to a low timber outbuilding, cemented with stucco and clay. It lurked at the edge of the pasture perhaps a few stone throws away from where they crouched. The structure housed a team of wegmors, steers with hooked horns and riding steeds. All were of assorted ages and possible escape agents, but the compound was heavily guarded. Squands of imperious temperament were dressed in blue and gold, patrolling the area in groups, likely a command centre.

Solstress's gloomy whisper fractured the stillness: "The Squands are out for revenge: they seek retribution for their brothers who have been murdered. Mercy will not be quick in coming."

Baus gave a dour grunt. There was scant chance of their gaining the stables without detection. It meant they would have to forgo that avenue in favour of another possibility. To linger on the parapet was a perilous risk—any sentry patrolling the rampart could easily spot them.

Baus risked a last look back.

Past the outbuilding he saw the Tower of Peace rising in the thin mist. Adjoining the palace's outer west wall, its cone-shaped summit showed two lone sentries pulling ropes to brass gongs. North and west, beyond the palace, nested the low-sloping gables of the city and dusky hills brooded in the distance, at whose feet the Waun forest nestled.

Every so often, a light would turn off from one of the honeycombed streets—from here Baus hoped to gain access . . .

With fastidious care, he motioned them down the cramped stairwell. They snuck out alongside the rampart, running across the moonlit court like rabbits. Away from the guards and the service yard, they slunk blinking and ducking back into the palace colonnade where Baus knelt and retrieved the firebrand. Down a narrow brick corridor they passed, under a high, scalloped roof before they struck south, to a place where Uella and Solstress indicated, granting avenue to the kitchens.

Underneath the archway, they stopped and continued along a flag-stoned alley bronzed with age. They fled toward another low wall where yellow lights glinted from a pair of circular windows.

Solstress urged the outlaws to caution. To scout out the kitchen and rout out any workers was their mission prior to entering.

Baus directed his mates to hide behind a cluster of wine barrels while he directed Solstress to step within. Sansix, who was in a bad way, was hopping from foot to foot and Valere restricted his cussing and moans to dull murmurs.

Solstress filed out minutes later. A troupe of adolescents came with her: pot boys, skillet scrubbers, potato peelers, on night duty. The youths dragged their heels: surly and disobedient wretches. Unsure of the princess's intent in dismissing them, they knew only that her wishes were not to be disobeyed. Solstress advised an early retirement for the crew and warned them not to send replacements.

Gingerly the companions entered the kitchen. The chamber comprised a long, low-ceilinged affair cluttered with pots, pans, skillets and potato sacks. Rounded day-old loaves lay in a jumbled heap on the counter, a bevy of half-peeled turnips, potatoes and onions reposed on cutting boards. Tubs of dirty water hugged the back wall. A crude drain slowly seeped its clotted contents to the chamber's unlit end.

Wasting no time, Baus searched the enclosure for tunnels. Uella, who knew the kitchen best, pinpointed the access point, directing Valere to the dingy corner where he and Poli pulled back sacks of grain and potato barrels to reveal a rounded wooden grate.

From without came the clank of weapons.

Baus dropped to his knees. One or more of the bodies had been discovered! "A posse is out to hunt us down," he exhaled between his teeth. Men's voices murmured raucously in the dim recesses between rampart and inner court. "Either we go down, or we die in an unwinnable situation."

Valere pried open the grate. Instantly, cool fetid airs wafted from the depths, stinging their nostrils. Baus felt down into the orifice, discovering a wooden ladder trailing down into the gloom.

Dipping his firebrand, he saw twenty feet below lurked a dank, earthen pit. Scattered pools of what looked like brackish water glinted in the meagre torchlight—hence the source of the sickly smell.

Baus stood up heavily, heaving Solstress a bow. "It is time now to make our adieus, Princess. It has been a pleasure knowing you!" He gave her a lengthy and salubrious embrace and stood back ready to depart at which she tossed her haughty head. "How dare you affront me with such informal dismissal? Shall I fend off my own guards on my own? Are you meaner than a snake, Baus?"

"Quite the contrary," Baus explained heartily. "Neither myself nor Valere can condone —"

"I cannot go back to the palace!" she wailed. "I shudder to think of what my mother would do should she learn of my involvement in this affair. To return to that prison is . . . to endure the punishment of disgrace and shame."

Baus addressed the princess with sympathy. "Where guilt reins, trouble gains. Were I in your shoes, Princess, I would think likewise; but consider! The way is dangerous—fraught with peril and mishap, not to mention stenches."

"I don't care." Solstress's sultry mouth writhed in mocking disfavour. "I have made my decision. Uella may go as she pleases, but I shall continue on this adventure of yours."

Uella let loose a reproachful howl. "And I! We are all in this fix together. Both are accomplices, fair Princess. I accept the consequences—great or small."

Solstress looked at Uella with misty eyes. She gave her servant an appreciative hug.

"Then, it is agreed," called Valere. "Hurry, we shall descend. Haste is of essence."

The women proffered nods.

"Very well, who shall go first?"

Eyes drifted to Poli.

"Not I," croaked the bully indignantly. "Choose Sansix!"

Eyes levelled on the thief, who uttered a denigrating, wolfish howl. "I utterly object! I insist that the 'Princess' be nominated for the excursion as it is her idea!"

Valere ignored the outburst. He forced Sansix down the ladder. The conniver's cries were lost as he was pushed down into the hole and prodded forcibly to navigate the rickety ladder with a maimed hand, for which nobody felt pity.

Valere cried out warningly, "No need to be dramatic, Sansix. You are an unvalorous rogue! Somebody has to reconnoitre the pit."

They heard the thud of Sansix's feet; a surge of noxious sloshing came up as he plummeted the rest of the way. The ominous clank of weapons and iron-shod boots in the adjoining alley pierced the silence. The fugitives crouched low. A low wail came from the murk where Sansix had disappeared.

The sounds of passer-bys faded. Baus descended into the hole himself and berated Sansix for his uproar. He held the torch high, eased himself down the ladder into the water. His senses became acclimatized to the gloom, and also desensitized to Sansix's obnoxious moaning. Poli followed, then Uella and finally Solstress.

Valere clapped the grate shut; he dropped down with a thud. Wolfishly, he pulled the ladder away.

They huddled in a grim press, gathering wits. Striving for any sense of direction, which was difficult in this impenetrable gloom, they struggled to make sense of their surroundings. Aside from Sansix's whimpering, all was preternaturally quiet. Breathing cold damp airs, they felt the atmosphere around them thick and mysterious, in some strange underground place.

In the eerie bronze-lit distance, they discerned a steady drip-drop of water and Baus surmised they must be in some vast cistern. Distances deceived; sounds and sights fell short of the mark and took on surreal proportions. Baus could feel his resolve sag. He felt himself plunged in a chamber of giants, some crazy, forgotten place lost out of time. A sentiment of estrangement crept over and gave him the shivers, as if he had been plunged into some enormous dungeon, or some great fish tank stretching to infinity. So far, that the light lanced out but could do nothing to penetrate the fastness.

The group clutched each other's arms, groping about in the darkness. Step by step they made their way through the amphitheatre, north toward the outer city where rumours said that the tunnels led under the palace and connected to the lamplit streets beyond.

Baus gripped the quavering torch with new respect. He mumbled imprecations. What an awful leap of faith to have agreed to come down here!

The monstrous weight of the masonry veered around him, supported by ancient stone posts, twenty feet high and hewn three feet in diameter. The stoneworks seemed to appear in and out of the gloom like giant boles of an ancient tree. The baulks, however portentous, comforted him, etched with the knowledge that man-made things still persisted in this crypt of darkness.

Careful plodding allowed Baus to avoid many of the slime puddles scattered about randomly. However, accidents were inevitable and Solstress was soon to discover one. Stumbling sideways, she slid into a malodorous pool and was quickly found voicing an unladylike curse. She quieted down, naturally, and they took up their trek. All noticed that the floor dipped down on a peculiar angle. The air grew steadily noticeably cooler. The surface had turned from packed mud to smooth olive-coloured stone.

"These are the signs of the old builders of Sloe," stated Solstress solemnly. "It is said that the palace was built on top of the old citadel—more than ten centuries ago. It sunk after the first Sisorian floods."

Baus noted the facts with half open ear. The sound of rushing water came to them—from somewhere up ahead—perhaps an old stone bridge spread across a rivulet. The signs of more pronounced stoneworks made themselves known—pillars, arch-works, steps, trestles. A dolomite-flagged causeway wound like a snake, arching like a cat's back over the running water. Baus shone his torch down and spied a chute of dark, turbid liquid churning its way eastward, under the city and toward the sea. The furtive rapids had doubtlessly originated from the western-crouching hills of the Waun.

They crossed the bridge and discovered a set of rounded, aged stairs at their service, which took them naturally downward into another stone-haunted bowl of mystery. The pillars holding up the roof grew more massive in girth; higher and higher they vaulted, and more frequent in number. Baus was not surprised at these constructions; he could only assume that there should be nothing else present. The strange thing was that the architecture began to make him anxious, taking on a more labyrinthine quality as the minutes passed.

They took to a direction that they hoped was still 'north' and finally arrived at the foot of a clammy wall, blocking their way.

Valere stopped short. The maze seemed to end in abrupt fashion. The ceiling had long since been pushed down upon their heads to rise perhaps twenty feet up to a smooth limestone-like dome. Without map or guide, the companions felt cheated—helpless, feeling their wretched way along the wall, and in what they believed was roughly a westerly direction.

Another barrier presented itself: a massive wall as high as the last, but more aged and marred than the previous. Chisel-marks infected the face as if some being had hewn mortar with sinister efficiency. They perceived themselves enclosed in some kind of malignant maze. The dripping water had disappeared. Sounds included those of the huff of their laboured breathing and the anxious thud of heart beats, beyond which, they sensed that they were utterly alone.

Baus performed a superficial investigation. He discovered that the cul-de-sac in fact, sheltered a bizarre ambience, a panel of volutes and stone levers marked with looping scrawls. He was about to utter a theory when all of a sudden, a faint hooting sound drifted from the dim corridor in the inner stone behind them.

"Goblins!" cried Sansix hoarsely.

Valere reached for his cutlass and Poli looked about with wonder. "What do you mean, 'goblins'?"

Sansix croaked out another nervous disclosure: "As I have intimated, redbeard, ghouls live below these palace walls—owl-like creatures, hooting and peering at will, but like moths they fly about on powdered wings of green and yellow. The old Squands knew them as the 'mothseiks'—so did their mentors."

"Utter claptrap!" barked Valere. "Control your wives' tales. *Ghouls!*" he mocked. "And you call yourself a man? What would creatures eat down here?" But even Valere's surety did not seem to carry great conviction.

Uella sobbed with the thought of being eaten alive.

Solstress pointed out that they must retrace their steps, or stand here gaping like fools.

Baus rubbed his chin. "Perhaps not entirely. Regard this arrow above the main lever on this contraption or panel. Perhaps if I grip its adjoining dial!"

Sansix made a fevered grab for Baus's hand. "I strongly discourage the act! You do not know what peril lies in wait! Some ancient minion could jump out at us, dead or alive, and drag us to ruin."

Baus frowned. "I highly doubt the possibility. Now, Sansix, if you will step back, I will prod a lever."

Sansix recoiled.

The strange hooting struck up again, now terminating in a long, low wail.

Sansix warned urgently, "Whatever it is, it is coming for us! Do not underestimate its mournful abandon!"

Baus clicked his tongue with peevish wrath: "Let the beings come! I shall rive them limb from limb with my gladius!" He pulled out the sword and turned then to catch an unsettling glimpse of a webbed, flapping shape—entirely green and waspish, scrabbling back into the corridor with appendages striking needlessly against the stone walls. It created an eerie, thudding reverberation and uttered unwholesome chitters.

Baus took up a lever and fumbled it clockwise. A sudden rumbling of inner gears wrenched itself from within the stone.

Baus instinctively stepped back. The slab slid aside, revealing a dark passage.

Speaking in a tone of certainty, the outlaw motioned them inside. "My indiscretion has proven worth the risk—now into the crevice! The passage likely leads in a northerly direction."

Valere agreed. They all hurried within. Sansix scrabbled first, but was pulled back by Valere while Poli did his best to urge the women forth and console their trembling.

After moments of blankness the companions came out to another impasse: a sheer wall writ with no sign of egress, cracks or holes. To either side, the corridor gaped. Three huge skulls wrought of pressed dolomite hung lugubriously. They were half mythical in depiction, carved with protruding rams' horns and bear snouts and bicorn crowns.

With nowhere else to flee, Sansix devolved into a fit of gloomy misery. Underneath one of the massive heads stood a block of masonry, chest high, equipped with a complicated panel on which Baus noted similar symbols, arrows, levers and knobs. The switches, dials, rotaries, pegs and protrusions were peculiar to him and seemed more tailor-made to this section and not the other.

Baus gave the apparatus a buffet. "Ha!" he cried. "Another device of mystery whose levers and latches I shall turn, punch and flip to appropriate an efficient exit!"

Baus engaged the apparatus with confidence and found nothing of import to occur. The wall remained as rigid as before. Tugging with abandon, he achieved nothing of significance, only the primitive panel's queer toggle switches seemed to glow with a peevish aura. Baus's leer grew more morose as the seconds passed.

Solstress grew fatigued. She flashed Baus a look of exasperation. Baus sought to remedy the situation. He clasped the slim warmth of the princess's waist and consoled her with courteous regard, taking care to draw her near to him most intimately. Suddenly from out in the gloom, came a great slithering and grating of stone on stone.

Baus swept the princess aside. The great door remained fixed but the portal that had once opened for them earlier, had slid shut tightly behind them. A stifling silence gripped the company. The quietude was immense, infused with suffocating force, interrupted only by a strange repetition of the hooting, which caused Uella a fit of insufferable sobbing, "The door has closed on us forever! We will be engulfed in here groping about in the dark for eternity! Suffocating—quivering like mice, consumed by slavering mothseiks!"

"Do not be disheartened!" Sansix appealed abjectly. "We are doomed, fair girl, trapped insularly with moth-beasts, but we have each other!"

Baus rolled his eyes, Valere bared teeth at the thief, Uella moaned.

The hooting only escalated.

Baus attempted a casuistic explanation of the phenomenon but failed to console the girl. "With the passage obstructed, enemies from above can no longer assail us."

"The mothseiks are similarly barred," Valere grunted wisely.

"Squands may drag us back in chains," observed Sansix.

Solstress plugged her ears. "Enough of your drivel! I wish to hear no more vapid speculations!"

A stone panel suddenly slid ajar. Two of the carved heads parted and revealed an opening. From within, as if from nowhere, a gigantic figure appeared. Looming in their path, its aspect was both intimidating and grotesque. Like some unorthodox non-creation, the ungainly outerbody was composed of blocks and bricks of stone. Its legs—grey, blue and black—were composed of thick bundles of masonry, as too, its torso, head and arms. The stone seemed to exude some weird, translucent glow—entirely unearthly and grey-green. From within, the disturbing figure housed a vaporous, almost human-like body, sporting neither nose nor ears nor chin, but only a round wattle of mouth which slobbed forth below two greenish eyes, seeming not to blink. The neck was a nest of mummified skin, looking somewhat vulnerable in comparison to the rest of its body, which seemed to balance strangely on magical supports.

The figure spoke in a robotic monotone: "I am Daemroid—Keeper of the subsection. I block this passage—You cannot pass—I must eat your skulls."

Uella fell in behind Baus; Solstress was quick to follow.

Baus blinked at his colleagues, staring up at the mountainous slag of stone. He wondered if his perplexity was as profound as those of the others. He found his courage, "Sir, the options you cite are clearly impossible. Please advise us of any substitutes."

"Silence! I am Daemroid—Skulleater." The voice continued with neither inflection nor emotion. "For a thousand years I have stalked these dark halls. Failing to utter the secret watchword, you have ventured to these precincts as infidels, nor did you flute the consecrated pleasantry. Such intransigence comprises blasphemies tantamount to affront!" The creature beckoned Baus closer with probing fingers. Come here, little creature, to your annihilation. It is better not to struggle—death comes less gruesomely to one who is willing."

"Absolutely not!" protested Baus.

"What is this lummox thing?" cried Poli, shuddering.

"A rock ghoul!" Sansix wailed. He turned to flee but Valere blocked his passage. "Stand and fight! Is everything a 'ghoul' to you?"

Reason seemed to be beyond the creature and Baus hastily thrust the torch into its face. A blocky limb reached forth, grabbed the end of the brand and crushed it to bits. Only smouldering fragments fell to the floor.

Baus frowned with displeasure. The creature was obviously tetchy. The passage and its mouldering walls dimmed to fuscous amber.

Baus slashed out with the ganglestick. The aggression caused the creature no visible harm. It stood on its stilts unhindered. Baus mumbled an oath. Repeated slashes of the ganglestick proved useless. The lithic armature seemed impermeable. Whether it was the inefficacy of the baton or the opposing puissance of the robotic enchantment, all was not clear and when the creature took two clunky steps toward Baus, the company quailed.

A bizarre thing happened. The Daemroid suddenly shuddered, halted, revolved its block-like head in succession, then peered left and right, but gave only a groan so hideous that it stood quivering like some tortured leaf, as if its spirit had been abruptly snatched from an unfathomable bondage.

The green eyes blinked in the ghastly light. The shiny, ghoulish face relaxed into an aquiline semblance, sprouting nose, cheeks, dimples, also a pair of sage-like ears.

Baus and Valere exchanged doubtful glances. What had caused the creature's sudden transformation? The ganglestick's dwindling puissance had created some kind of fabulous flux. Did the thing actually metamorphosize sensory organs as to better hear their shrieks when it ate their skulls?

The question was better not answered. Baus shrank back with loathing while Sansix hung off Poli in abject fright.

"What now, Daemroid Skulleater?" called Baus in brave tones.

"Daemroid?" The name seemed to quiver in the creature's ears. It cocked its head on a puzzled angle. "Skulleater?" The tone seemed less harsh of metallic twang and sounded now prodigiously more human.

"Once I was Kaelinon," the half-man thing said. "There were two keepers of the city. Ewlen and myself—the designetrix and the maker. Once I was a man, one of the greatest, original architects of Slaen! I was commissioned by the three Wizards—Thoum, Buzol and Glyspon—to build this ancient city!"

The stone ghoul seemed to recall something, during which period it coughed out a profound commandment, like some haunting echo of the past.

The creature spoke in a peculiar tone: "I remember now! The Wizards were Muses . . . commissioning wise Ewlen and myself to build the great palace as we know it—the greatest edifice in all the three lands! The Palace of Smaerna! How I loved that palace! Forgive me, friends, my memory comes in only bursts and waves. 'Twas I who commissioned the first blocks of celispar and blue alapite cleaved from the mines of Aldevean. 'Twas I who laid the initial foundation and instructed the bricklayers, lathers and masons to carve the first rotunda of the original citadel. I fortified it—with fluted gold and the finest smalt ores of basolomite and malachite." The being paused, proudly angling his head on a majestic tilt. "But my memory has grown dim over the ages, guarding this silent fastness with dark solitude."

The figure pushed awkwardly on a nearby figurine. From a dial on the panel, the creature caused another door to slide open to reveal a musty chamber full of old stone bookcases.

Beckoning them forward, he cautioned them to mind their heads. "The rams' heads are uncompromising. They are guardians of Slaen—Kor, Nor and Slor—all dead, like myself; this chamber too—once ancient Slaen's most prized conglomerate of knowledge. It includes wisdom of all Seven of the known Philosophies. But now, as you see, the scrolls, tomes and pandects have mouldered to dust."

Baus and the others gazed at the treasures of the past, stacks upon stacks of old, unreadable books. The cramped interior began to unnerve Baus and suffuse him with an eerie chill. It was flushed with a lambent glow held alive by some inner light of the stone—which glowed weaker and weaker.

"You say you were a man," repeated Baus with wonder. "But who or what enslaved you into this block-like bodywork of yours?"

Daemroid sighed and paused as if memories were painful. "My craft was formidable in the years of my youth. I was accosted by rulers of all the faraway lands, including Gazoff of Ceulurian, Beniad the Seneschal. When the king, Coyrus, learned that my talents were to be used by other rulers, he ensorcelled me. He and his wizards held council in the Antique Tower by the South Domino, and on Grand Wizard Buzol's advice they opted to terminate Ewlen and imprison me in the body of a stone gargantuan to forever watch the lower halls. So it was. I was to be their slavish guardian! Wicked deed! The wizards plotted, to summon me to architect more splendours and annexes to the palace, and simply to gloat at my powerlessness to create more copies of my art. They damned me as the 'Daemroid', which means *the spirit that rules*. They told me that to repeat the name over and over, that I would forget my heritage, and my real self, which was Kaelinon—and eventually I did.

"Almost. They told me to keep vigil over the old city, with all the alertness and loyalty of a sea kraken. So great was the enchantment wrought on me that I still watch over the old city to this day. All the powders, mirklewaters and other fey puissances that blighted my soul could not save me! But you have touched a soft spot in my memory. When flowers bloomed and I felt real sunshine on my skin, I was happy. Yet, I sense a magic in your midst, something murky which has raked my cold stone armature, liberating me from a singular curse—or plunging me into another—my mind at least, not my soul. Lucky for our mutual cause, it happened otherwise, lest I would be Daemroid forever and you would be ones with your skulls ripped out." The creature left that hanging and attempted a laugh but only arrived at a hiccup. "Enough of me! What of you? The world above? Afford me news!"

Baus glanced around the chamber with hopeful urgency. "It is ever the same, Daemroid," Baus ventured. "Men vie with their enemies, for better trade and better rule. Women are fickle; sea beasts rule the oceans and reavers pillage the coasts with impunity."

"A pity!" commiserated Daemroid. "And I thought there would be progress in the long years I have slept. Obviously not—and a wishful hope. What noble professions have you taken up to guard against these ravagings?"

Baus gave his head an ambiguous shake. "Currently, my status is inchoate; my philosophies are somewhat overlapping. I, who call myself, Baus—Baus the Bold—present my colleagues, Poli and Valere, who are wanderers of similar disposition. They are in-between métiers, which include mixed talent: seamen, fishermen, reavers, entertainers, bodyguards and others. My female peers, Uella and Solstress, recently accompany me as we applied to the entertainment board at Sloe, specifically to a certain adjudicator, whose audition turned out to be rigorous and we were largely awarded success at the afternoon's wedding festivities."

"What delightful news!" cried Daemroid, clapping his granite hands in succession. "Tell me more."

"We sang, we danced—we duelled," bantered Baus facilely, "what more to say?—to a tragic drama written by a dour fellow named Sansix here who used our efforts for his own gain, our belated leader and choreographer, but with whom we have now fallen out of favour."

The Daemroid frowned. "This explains the lack of a digit?"

Baus nodded. "The stump is a direct cause of a tragic and philosophical misfortune."

Daemroid sighed. "Certain causes bring about effects which are not only incongruous, but inscrutable."

"On that topic, Daemroid—Solstress here, daughter to Maena, is also propelled to your realm on business of her own. She is a princess of Sloe!"

"A timely synchronicity!" Daemroid exclaimed delightedly. "The joy is all mine and stupendous!" The blocky knees started to loosen their lock, and the crystalline fingers twitched in pleasant concern. "What is it about her predicament that involves the likes of you rogues congregating within my dark chamber?"

"That you should ask, shoulders important philosophical consideration," exclaimed Baus. "The princess is escaping a marriage, a very insidious one. She is absolutely entrancing, as you can see—so is her assistant, Uella, who is of no small beauty likewise"—this added Baus with speedy emphasis, after detecting Uella's painful glare. "In fact, our entire fellowship is bent on an enterprise of escaping this palace. Can you help? In assisting the princess take flight, and in the hope of mutual self preservation, I would inquire if you could supply us with the necessary information which might assist us in this emprise."

"You must elucidate your needs to better exactitude, Baus! You skip and dart like a puff owl in your discourse. I am of mind to think you somewhat eccentric!"

Baus bowed and agreed with the assessment, mumbling out a solemn apology. "Your words are of course judicious, Daemroid, and I bid you to forbearance. In point of fact, Solstress and I began harbouring misgivings of her betrothal to a certain Clavius of Cleauch, a lank-toothed dawcock who would use her for political ends, which leads us to the conclusion of my little anecdote, that, in a nutshell states that the princess committed rash deeds—and here we are as your testament."

Daemroid pondered the information with care. "Ho hum. Am I to understand that you are fleeing from a higher authority?"

"In less roundabout terms, yes."

"And are you in need of directions to a safe haven that does not include the modern day palace of Sloe?"

"Precisely the point!"

The Daemroid nodded thoughtfully. "Then—in retrospect, I might be able to offer some service, for I have long reflected on certain gnawing crises of injustice."

Solstress voiced an animated cry. "Daemroid, we would be immensely grateful!"

The Daemroid jiggered happily, "Simply pass down yon corridor, foist a right at several hundred paces, then a crafty left. You have no more than a skip and jog up a stone tube and out into the light. You are free! It may become a trifle cramped and rank at this juncture, but ho! such is to be expected when citizens pitch refuse, offal and excrements down the sewers. Normally even this route would be impassable, as I would crush and split your skulls like walnuts and eat your brains for hors d'oeuvres. But thankfully, this danger has been averted."

Baus expressed thanks for the information and voiced a curious interest in the enchantment which had resulted in the Daemroid's thrallish servitude.

The creature's mood shifted in sudden vanity. "They are horrid machinations! A task, bestowed upon me on the malicious whims of the pompous wizard Glyspon! Ah Glyspon! If I could pull out his ragged beard and make him eat his own curls, it would give me a tenth pleasure of vindication. But he is dead! For centuries I remain only half alive by his vicious spell!"

Baus attempted to assuage the Daemroid's animation and looked to his peers for support. "One is indeed forced to contemplate similar vicissitudes."

Several uneasy mutters accompanied the declaration, with Poli offering a formal curse upon Glyspon and Sansix adding his own repudiation upon Glyspon. Valere propounded similar epithets. Perhaps the thrice named curses upon Glyspon invoked a certain concord of supernormal forces latent in the air, for Baus found himself staggering back when he heard groaning creaks issuing from the stone. Eldritch crackles of light appeared in the gloom, like intoxicated starbursts.

Glyspon perhaps was not yet dead? Or did the wizard simply employ silent, ethereal monitors in the dark recesses of time to enforce his decrees? Such facts were not known, and the Daemroid abruptly stiffened and reared erect in a very ghastly way. It gave a gruesome convulsion, racked the passage with an epilepsy and threatened to bring the ceiling crashing down on their skulls.

The Daemroid's eyes glazed over, his voice became an irrevocable glottal, monotone shriek. "Eat skulls! I must eat skulls. Daemroid is my destiny! Daemroid eats skulls. Blasphemous entry is not permitted!"

Baus blithely bypassed the avowals and spoke in an amiable voice, "Daemroid! You are addled. Remember, you are our comrade!"

"I recall nothing! Skulls are mine—to eat and enjoy!"

"This is ludicrous!" came Baus's emphatic cry.

The observation did not please the creature and it reverted back to its earlier mode of primitiveness. Baus slashed out with Lolispar. The creature dodged. Baus tried the ganglestick.

To no effect. A blocky limb reached forth to crush Baus's skull.

Baus eluded the machination.

Valere let loose a livid howl, launching himself at the creature with his cutlass. Off came the creature's head with a scraping tumult that had the mummified, bloodless flesh tumbling askew to land upside down on the floor.

The green lambent eyes glowed as before; the Daemroid spoke no more. The thing raised its arms in anthropomorphic fury and fingers twitched like scissors, levelling out an outward portent, and the body began walking toward them in a zombie-like creep.

Baus, Poli and Valere backpedalled, hacking at its limbs, but all such efforts proved inefficacious and they were impelled to backtrack around its obtrusive mass or suffer annihilation.

The way was blocked by a solid wall. Fleeing seemed a non-option.

Baus, Poli, Valere and the others scrunched down on their haunches, managed to slither under the creature's legs, then past its grasping members, running pell-mell up the passageway.

Without so much as torch, the blackness enfolded them. Baus struggled to recall the Daemroid's advice: Was it to the left or right that they must scurry to gain the nauseous tube?

The din was deafening. Baus clicked his tongue in exasperation. The discomfort of it all was frustrating. Deprived of his sight, the Daemroid ran amok behind them, blundering into walls, capsizing columns, smashing its inordinate weight about like a sack of stones.

Baus scowled. He knew not how far they ran before Sansix slammed into a rocky wall. He fell backward into a dazed heap. Baus crawled his way overtop the trickster and could not help but ponder the remarkable truth: while maintaining a position farthest from the menace, the opportunist had unwittingly plunged himself into the maximum peril. The significance was profound, and Baus would have stopped longer to ponder had he not been so absorbed in defending his life, and he bolted with Solstress in tow.

Along the walls Baus and Valere fled in tandem. Uella and Solstress latched on to the men's resilient bodies and scrambled helter-skelter along with them. They could hear the creature scratching, clawing, scraping, clanking behind them. But the Daemroid's progress grew fainter. They edged their way closer to the surface and as luck would have it, the creature could not easily track them. In any case, to flee as far from the menace was of paramount priority. They did, owing to the fact that the creature's mobility was hindered by sightlessness and its speed was somewhat more so by the loss of a head.

There appeared a series of twists and turns in the passage. Sansix was lucky to recover from his stupor and skipped to his feet, stumbled idly, lucky not to become brain food for the Daemroid.

The labyrinth grew in proportion. The only signals the fugitives had of a means of escape was an upward sloping floor heading in a direction of which Kaelinon had hinted. With eager relish they scrambled up the last length of the passage.

The tunnel narrowed to tube-like constriction as the Daemroid had described. The smell of sewage and raw, organic gases was poignant. They crawled as fast as they could—up the fleeting tunnel gasping for breath. Hands and knees negotiated the filth with ill grace—upward on a small, slimy angle toward a sliver of light.

They gulped a whiff of clean air. A sudden freshening of space and light graced them; they all began to feel pangs of hope. The tunnel's end showed an oval grate; bronze ribs rose a foot above their heads, leaking cool light.

Valere, Poli and Baus gripped the rungs and pressed up with all their might. The lid flopped over, rolled away.

They were liberated!

X

Valere hauled Baus, Poli and the women the rest of the way out of the cramped tunnel. Sansix was left behind until last. The company stood in the dark, contemplating their plight, breathing ragged gasps. A cobblestone street lay clutched with emptiness, permeated with a damp chill before them. They all shivered spasmodically, yet were relieved to take leave of the foul tunnel that comprised their catacomb prison.

Dropping dazedly on their backs, they stared up into the black sky with the moon blazing full, illuminating ghostly clouds.

The palace gongs tolled their dirge. At half past midnight, somewhere in the eerie distance a dog barked. Up loomed a tall silhouette—the *Crier's Tower*: a long tapered cone with a surmounting cupola obtruding at its base. The palace's old north wall flanked the portentous sentinel and the dark sawtooth edge was lit against a blacker sky. Many singular shadow-edges and curves, cones and spires ranged beyond the wall, denoting the ancient citadel of Sloe, complex and mysterious in its clasp of night. Baus knew that those sights signalled they had successfully passed under the outer battlements of the palace into the residential streets, and were now plunged somewhere along the northern lip of the city.

Low brick homes ran on either side of the street. Windows were dark and devoid of movement. Rooftops gleamed sullenly in the moonlight like fools' caps, but a faint odour of melting candle wax and boiled onions wafted from a nearby window.

Baus's eyes naturally drifted to the lower floor. He wondered what comforts lay beyond this particular window. His eyes wandered lower down—saw a drowsing dog lying at the foot of a hedgerow. He also noticed the street was bowed with purpose to allow rainwater into the gutter and down the sewer—hence explaining the stench they had endured.

Another dog growled in the distance. Cold sea airs tousled Baus's hair and he tugged at his soiled garments as it brought him a prickling chill. A wisp of smoke curled from a blue brick chimney. At the same time, Sansix gesticulated and called, "Grand luck! I now know exactly where we are, friends. This is my goodbye. This domicile marks the residence of my compeer, Alfodel, to whom I shall apply for lodging. Good night! Best of success!"

Valere grabbed the thief's shoulder and swung him round. "Not so fast, twitterbug! What do you think we are, second-rate citizens? Why leave us that easily? Do you deny us lodging?"

"Alfodel's invitation is surely not universal. You can not expect me to extend the hospitality to you?"

Baus's face was pressed with injury. "Your words smart, Sansix. And I thought we were friends. But your concern is not without some modicum of truth."

"I fulfilled my obligations to you, that is all," he hissed.

"I would grant you release," murmured Baus. "Yet I ask myself: what would stop a blackguard from appealing to certain royal persons of being 'forced' into our company and dragooned into pursuing unlawful deeds?"

Sansix's face showed saturnine amusement. "It hurts me, Baus, that you would believe that I, of all people, would dislodge information of such nature to our enemies."

Baus stirred. "Let me cite facts, Sansix: you are aware of the princess's condition, and of our situation. The information could be supplied of her Highness's whereabouts and our deeds which would earn you a significant purse and useful rapport. Do you not agree, Valere? Valuable enough to get your head off a chopping block?"

Solstress studied Sansix's rippling features with contempt. "In this wise you are correct, Baus. Guard this fink with our lives."

"The concept is deplorable!" objected Sansix. "I am six days overdue in my business as it is and I am of one less finger!" He waved the bloody bandage as if inducing a flag of sympathy.

No sympathies were forthcoming.

"No great worry," declared Valere. "Time is in abundance, Sansix. I wish your commerce all the best, but I suggest you keep to our company for a while longer."

Sansix's groans were ignored.

Baus made an imperial suggestion: "I bid that we flee this city. To approach the problem we must pool our energies. Sansix, you claim to harbour knowledge of the area and comrades living in yon residence—does this fellow possess a sizeable wagon, or at least some useful cart which we might use? Quickly now, the matter is of utmost importance!"

Sansix made no effort to respond politely. "Alfodel no—but Jacosiah, perhaps. Predominately a swineherd, my peer maintains a smallholding near Quelion and has been made somewhat of a carter on the side. I would harbour a suspicion that he possesses such a vehicle as you require."

"Very good! Where does Jacosiah reside?"

Sansix showed his palms in dismay. "To transact such a proposal at this hour, is impossible. He is likely indisposed."

"It's a risk which we must take. Lead on."

Sansix cringed at the sight of Valere's weapon sliding out of its sheath.

Creeping westward they took to a shadowed path down *Sakesin Lane*, then turned onto a dark backstreet. They ducked north on *Candlestine Way* where only chill vapours rolled about their ankles.

No one was about. Cramped and sore, Baus shook out his legs, more rubber than flesh, and they passed a darkened smithy whose forges still radiated warmth. A water well ranged nearby, also a mat of loose straw set out for mounts. Down a narrow flagstoned street they crept, and beyond a battered arch held in such sagging disrepair that Baus thought to question the venture. He caught a glimpse of a dimly lit square. Sansix motioned them up another dubious lane curving slightly westward housing many cheerless side ways. The sight caused Solstress and Uella unease. A dingy pub, known as the *Fat Lamprey*, lounged somewhat disreputably off the way between a row of shared units and darkened glassworks. The units were low and had sloping roofs and decrepit gables. Frayed shingle and eavestroughs were ubiquitous. The pub was open at this hour and the patrons seemed largely involved in bibulous affairs—a circumstance which Baus deduced from the raffish laughter and jeers issuing behind yellow lamps glowing through the windows.

A heap of iron-ringed barrels lay aside the pub's iron signpost, amongst square straw bales and casks of mead, all which blocked a darkened dirty alley running up the back.

Sansix carelessly flung a bandaged finger down the street. "Jacosiah lives in yonder residence with the gingerbread siding. He is usually incapacitated at this hour in the *Fat Lamprey*."

Baus made a curt acknowledgement. "In that case, Sansix, it saves us the trouble of waking him. Be so good as to fetch him."

Sansix refused the errand, whereupon Valere roughly accompanied Sansix inside the pub. The swindler might not, this way, easily signal any allies or sympathizers or organize any team efforts to commit atrocities against them.

Valere and the rogue disappeared into the pub while Baus whistled a sad tune in the evening's chill. Poli, draped in his mud-stained dress, gripped his halberd balefully. On Baus's recommendation, the bully led the women behind the barrels into the alley.

Three dark forms presently emerged. Valere, Sansix and a newcomer. The latter, tall and spare, graced with turtleish eyes, had a leathery face which seemed patched with orange-ruffed beard. Grease and ale were smeared on his coveralls and his flushed cheeks and onerous gait seemed to suggest a person of surly disposition. On cursory inspection the patron could have been any alehound in the street, but he was much more vigilant than would be seen at first glance. He was wary of the sight of Baus and the other foreigner, before whom he planted himself erect.

"You are Jacosiah?" Baus inquired.

"I am. What of it?" The tall figure squinted. "Who are you?"

"I am Baus—but that is of no concern. My colleagues require a large cart or suitable wagon, for which they will pay good silver. Do you have one?"

The newcomer rubbed his chin. "Perhaps. But how much silver would you be willing to pay for such a vehicle?"

"Depends. We require several blankets, a pair of scissors, many ells of rope, and also at least three changes of clothes. Possibly some unguents too, preferably neutral in odour."

The man gave Baus a mirthful sneer. "What are you up to? Sheep shearing and hog tying? A lot of requests for so late an hour. It strikes me that a person who cannot wait for business until morning risks higher cost."

"That is a definite possibility. But supply the goods, wine-drinker, or we have nothing to talk about."

Jacosiah thought about the proposal for a moment. "Okay—come on then." He motioned them down the street. In a half-soused gait he paused at the foot of the gingerbread-looking house, while inspecting the sloping roof with disdain. Upended shingles seemed to suggest a leaking roof and Baus and Valere followed the lanky man, grinning impatiently, while Baus motioned to Uella and Solstress who crouched in the alley, urging them to stay out of sight.

From outside, all appeared quiet. Two darkened windows stared from the patchboard like lidless eyes. The siding was weathered; the paint was peeled and nails protruded askew. On the right side, a narrow, puddled lane stretched, down which Jacosiah led them into his back yard.

The cramped space was rank with weeds and dark shapes grew everywhere. Presently, they took on more meaning. The place was a veritable junkyard, littered with lathes, broken wheels, tools, horseshoes, crates, wheelbarrows, and old farm instruments. Astride a small overgrown garden a rickety cart reposed, and a two-wheeled, open-backed wagon.

Baus trained his attention on the wagon. For a fact, the vehicle was in better condition than he imagined, and to this he was given to hope.

The junk dealer signalled to the wagon.

Baus gave an unimportant gesture. "The vehicle suits our needs."

Jacosiah noted the surety of the assertion and took record of any lack of urgency. He demanded proof of funds before he would relinquish any control of the vehicle or even allow a brief inspection. Baus curtly produced a fistful of coins—the sum of their wealth and the spoils of their last balance of the palace drama which had drawn them so much infamy.

Jacosiah eyes widened at the size of the booty. Instantly he became alert. "You'll be needing a nag then too, I guess? I can throw one in for an extra five silver bits. The clothes are more—" He spoke with a fluent, entrepreneur's ease. "I would reckon a fair price of four silvers as being modest."

Baus barked out, "We are in informal discourse here, not bartering at the Royal Auctions. I will say this—for cart, nag, clothes and accoutrements, I can offer a generous eight silver pieces, no more."

Jacosiah's throat trembled with an incoherent gurgle. "Not in a century of booze-guzzling!"

A window frame slid back. "Jaco! Is that you?" The dark, curly head protruding out grunted. "Come to bed this instant! This is no time for marketing. I formally forbid you to auction off our possessions! You are an incorrigible drunk. For all I know, you'll sell our house for a peanut and a pint!"

Jacosiah snarled up at the gables. "Quell your tongue, woman! I'm no more drunk than you are a ravishing lioness. Can you not see I'm engaged in the middle of an important transaction?"

"Perform the transaction in more favourable hours! Someone has to catch a few winks around here to do some work!" She gave rise to more bitter words before the window was slammed shut.

Jacosiah cringed. "Intractable wench. Sows like this have no concept of the degree of toil I do around here to support a household."

"I daresay," said Valere.

Baus turned his attention to the wagon. A brief examination revealed several facts: the understruts were sound, the wooden wheels were sturdy and more or less round, though the back rim seemed a few degrees out of true. The side slats were a foot high and ridged with uncorroded iron. The back wimble-slats were greying with age, but otherwise not rotten. The frame was wholly sturdy—enough to support five or more persons lying concealed under a large blanket or tarp. The driver's bench could easily seat four more persons and a cargo, if required.

Baus nodded with satisfaction. He nosed around the yard for brief moments and gathered up four or five stout leather straps and an adequate coil of rope. Valere discovered a tarpaulin, a canteen and more rope while Jacosiah mustered up a pair of rusty horse-hair clippers and two dry blankets.

Sansix stood about blank-faced, absorbed in his glum rumination while Jacosiah frowned and ogled the foreigners' tally as if trying to cognize the nature of their errand. He bent his efforts upon a mental computation. "Forty silver pieces, that's quite a total."

The sum was flagrantly well in excess of Baus's expectation and he growled. After a degree of haggling, he and Jacosiah finally agreed on a price—twelve silver pieces, no more. "Provided the nag is adjudged in proper condition!" warned Baus.

"You shall find Nellie of certain mettle!" declared Jacosiah wryly.

Baus was wont to harbour doubts. The word 'nag' had him troubled. "I do not desire an animal with the dropsy or suffering any bovine endemics."

Jacosiah spoke with a caution bordering on conceit. "I'm a trader and you know it. I've only a single wegmor for sale. She's no beauty, or in her prime, but if you desire her for travel she's a dependable one and'll go leagues and leagues with little fare." The latter feature was added with confident assurance.

"The qualities sound promising," admitted Baus. "However, I promise no more until I see the 'nag'."

"As you wish." Jacosiah led them through the 'garden', past a weed-covered picket fence and into an adjoining property where a small stable was lodged. The premises reeked of flies and dung and Jacosiah's knees knocked together as he strode, causing Baus and Valere to wince. Would he actually make it?

The junk dealer managed to jerk open the ramshackle door and peered into the moonlit gloom where they beheld a grey-roan nag grazing dejectedly by a tower of hay. On round, stubby legs the nag wobbled. Her head was pitched rather sharply and her eyes glued shut. She sported a grey mane, brownish forelocks, and was missing a horn. Her back bowed, though, as Jacosiah had alluded, the beast appeared stolid enough and capable of a journey of length.

Baus was dubious and stooped to examine the wegmor's teeth. Valere checked the hooves. All seemed in good order. The wegmor blinked at them in complacence. Though spiritless the outer bearing, 'Nellie' seemed no more wayward than any other animal, and Baus declared her sound and 'its mother-of-pearl eyes demonstrated a hale disposition much inclined to loyal forbearance.'

"An admirable observation!" called Jacosiah. Ale-slicked eyes gleamed at the comment. "Your eye is sharper than most. The majority of the lumpkins who come here accosting me to rent out my mare would see not half of the animal's exalted qualities!"

"I am happy to hear that. Note that my auditory sense is keener than my visual."

"Another pleasant discovery! Now—here, I must bring forth Nellie."

Valere snatched up an armful of hay. After pocketing some flaccid carrots, he let Jacosiah lead him back to the yard with the mare and Baus helped him hitch her up. They piled clothes, blankets, rope and grease into the wagon. Valere sat in the driver's seat, hefting reins and urging Nellie down the side-alley. Out into the street they clopped where Baus followed, nodding with approval.

Jacosiah tripped at Baus's heels, snorting for his coins. Baus, disliking the ale wafting in his face, snapped his fingers under Jacosiah's nose. "More garments, please! A selection of brown, blue, green and grey of unobtrusive hues would be preferable!"

Jacosiah's greedy features slobbered irritation. "The cost expands with each garment I must fetch from my residence."

"Then so it must!" Baus waved the junkdealer to speed. "Hurry, we are not impecunious men. Nor are we in favour of snorts or leers."

Jacosiah peevishly trooped back to his domicile. He returned moments later armed with a pair of corded breeches, brimstone gaiters and old-style hats. Also jumpers of high quality. So eager was Poli to rid himself of his ridiculous white gown, that he jumped out of his hiding place and stripped himself naked and donned what clothes he could. He was heedless of his exposure in front of the women peeking out from behind the barrels sniggering.

After recovering from his brief shock, Jacosiah gestured at the stash of articles piled into the back of the wagon. "A strange load of goods you have, strangers. I trust the articles are to your satisfaction?"

Valere gave an agreeable nod.

"Surely you do not require all these tins of bear grease?"

"What if an axle were to seize up?" declared Baus tersely.

"A small possibility," said Jacosiah.

Baus stirred. "Were we without lubricant our position would be intolerable, stuck in the hinterlands."

Jacosiah gave a gruff sniff. "You cark over obscure improbabilities! My wagon is intact."

"As you vouchsafe, but I am a man who makes caution his watchword and a backup plan his habit."

"Do as you wish! As long as you hand over my pittance! My time is valuable!"

"Ours no less!" Baus flung over the coins. Jacosiah ticked off the exact count with fastidious exactitude. Content with his evening's work, he put forth a cordial wave and departed. Sansix, skulking in the shadows, attempted an escape, signalling a covert gesture to his comrade, but was debarred by Valere who grabbed hold of the thief's stump and squeezed, to the definite dismay of the thief who pitched over in almost a double faint.

Jacosiah peered down at Sansix in alarm. "You look miserable, Sansix. What's the problem? Perhaps you should get that hand looked after?"

Sansix opened his mouth to speak, but nothing issued forth and Baus waved the junk dealer to reassurance. "Your friend has endured several misfortunes recently which have affected him in an adverse way. Not to be concerned! We will take care of him. He is a hardy soul—Sansix—made of material that most normal men are lacking! Isn't that right?"

Sansix uttered a tight-lipped squeal which prompted Baus to add a further remark, "A good night's sleep shall have Sansix's hand up and ready again in no time!"

Jacosiah beamed. "A kind sentiment. You speak with the confidence of a man of the world and I can only rest assured! Something which many youths of today are spiritlessly lacking."

"True, and your remarks inspire a similar gratitude of my own," Baus declared, proffering the junk-dealer a warm-hearted salute, to which Sansix responded with a gurgling whimper.

The junk dealer returned to the confines of the *Fat Lamprey* and Uella snuck out from behind her barrels. She and Solstress stood blinking in the moonlight with the women giving the wagon and its worn-out old wegmor a critical gaze.

"Can the beast ply our combined weight?"

"For brief periods, I would imagine," intimated Valere. "We only need her to cart our weight in certain instances: like passing a patrol booth or a checkpoint—which shall become our first real test."

Baus gave a half-hearted nod. "Right, Valere. It's a trial for which we are not going to be ill-prepared." He motioned authoritatively to the princess to advance a step closer. Curious at the summoning, Solstress did, prompting Baus to grab her in his arms. He scooped up the wegmor shears and proceeded to trim her hair above the ear. With the greatest possible inconvenience, Solstress resisted—but to no avail.

"Arrest your squirming!" called Baus fractiously. "The precautions are obligatory—for subterfuge—unless you wish to return to your dour old mom?"

Solstress quickly shrank back at the possibility. Nor was Uella spared any partisan treatment. While Valere held her down, her hair was hacked short as a hound's and Poli helped smear mud from the gutter on her cheeks thus camouflaging her pretty appearance and the odour of any perfume which may have leaked over, surviving any squeezing through the sewers.

Baus stood back with approval. A look of contentment crawled over his visage. "Now, for our own disguises!" he exclaimed heartily. He commandeered Uella's kitchen knife, proceeded to shave his beard, a process which was urged upon Poli. Valere and Sansix repeated the same exercise with solicitude. With the pastes collected from the shed, Baus began to grease his hair with a wholesome nut brown while Valere waxed his gold with beeswax, thus masking the conspicuous red. Poli refused to resort to such measures and sank back groggily in the shadows while regarding Baus and Valere with cold sneers as they rubbed pastes and unguents into Sansix's scalp.

Valere appropriated one of Jacosiah's cornflower yellow hats which suited his costume quite nicely. Baus removed his own skullcap, a remnant from the wedding skit, and replaced it with a green, high peaked hunter's cap drawn from Jaco's stores complete with black side flaps. Baus unfurled his ponytail, greased the hair, rank and raw and shoved it up, pinning it in place, making his disguise complete. Solstress and Uella selected trousers and jerkins which were not too masculine or overlarge.

Solstress waspishly pointed out that Baus was a hypocrite. "Why don't you cut your own hair?"

"Silence! The process would be supererogatory. With the help of this cap my long locks are completely obscured—and no need for alteration."

Solstress's tone grew sour. "Why couldn't I have greased my own hair and hid it underneath a cap also?"

"Because." Baus's sigh became petulant. "You argue to no purpose. To allay suspicion we must not copy each other like chip-larks. Each of us must propel himself to his own unique style, to which mine includes the full benefit of my hair."

Solstress remained dissatisfied with the explanation; her derisive comment was riddled with impertinence. "I dislike mummery which seems to abound from your maw."

Baus obdurately ignored the jibe. "No matter. The action has been completed. Now, quickly, back up into the wagon."

Unenthusiastically, Solstress, Uella, Sansix and Poli climbed up in the wain and hid underneath blankets—save Valere, whom Baus quietly delegated to the front to steer them toward the North Gate.

Down *Whaleskin Way* they trundled to the quiet clop of Nellie's hooves and the chirp of crickets in the hedges.

All was quiet; the moon dipped low in the sky. The horizon showed signs of maroon awakening and drops of rain falling momentarily caused some sinking foreboding in Baus's heart. The residents of Sloe would be soon waking. The realization brought Baus a panged fervour.

Tossing off his blankets, he sat up peering about. He ordered the caravan to an immediate halt, and Valere voiced a surly complaint: "What is it now?"

"I fell a fey feeling tugging at my innards. Something inexplicable."

"Like?"

"A premonition—no more."

Valere maintained his stubborn crouch at the driver's post.

"Simply this," murmured Baus, "what if members of the watch check under the covers and discover our contraband cargo?"

Valere turned to regard Sansix with a frown. "The worry has merit. Our conniver cannot ride out back nor up in front being known as a felon and likely to get us nabbed."

"In that case, let's strap the rogue to the bottom of the wagon, as we must too the princess and Uella."

The women vigorously protested the suggestion but Baus insisted on the gravity of the approach. "Like as not, no soldier will ever expect the hideout. He will not trouble himself to look underneath. While we can only assume that the princess's absence has not been detected —to not assume it, is foolhardy! Know that the waysmen will be looking for us! Particularly you, Solstress, so we must cache you in a fashion most cunning."

"And if they find us?" the princess inquired shrilly.

"Only spontaneous action will decide our course."

Displeasure boiled on the princess's visage. "This does not sound like a hopeful prospect to me."

"It is not intended. Now quickly! Underneath the cart. You too, you club-handed jackal! Do not attempt to skulk away like a slippery sheldrake. Valere and I are keeping our eyes on you! We will strap you and rope you all face down, backs flush to the wimble-board."

"This is not at all comfortable!" cried Uella, nearly sobbing with the idea of it. "What if the strap breaks, or one of us tumbles to the cobbles and is trampled by beasts?"

Baus gave a hysterical laugh. "That is a foolish and senseless concern! Now quickly, underneath the vehicle!"

Uella, Solstress, Sansix and Poli were all secured underneath the main carriage and Baus hurriedly inspected his labours. From a standing position, the extended outer slats seemed to obscure the persons below. The deep underbelly was a bonus—a propitious arrangement. Grunting with satisfaction, Baus jumped back in the wagon and motioned Valere to proceed.

"Wait!" cried Poli. "Who is to strap you in?"

Baus blinked. "The precaution is unnecessary."

Poli put forth an outraged exclamation: "What am I to do? Why do I need to be strapped in, when you could be in my place and I could ride in the front?"

Baus answered with flat brevity. "In terms of simplicity you are not equipped to supply words and suggestions of cunning import. Who is to aid Valere should he slip or muff his cue and cause a scene of suspicion? Me! Now dampen your impetus, Poli and cache yourself out of sight."

Poli continued to fume, but Valere slapped the reins. The beast rocketed off. The cart jerked ahead, creaking toward a marketplace of silhouettes.

XI

The towers of the palace loomed behind them: many eerie outlines set against a waxen sky. The ancient gongs droned in synchrony, announcing the dolour of the missing princess. Shadows crept about the bazaar. Few pedestrians were about, mostly early birds toiling assiduously away, cleaning stalls, clutching cloaks and shaking sleepy bodies to ward off the chill. Beyond the section of sea wall, waves crashed and Baus caught momentary glimpses of swaying masts, furled sails, moon-gleaming stays, cargo holds, drays, spyholes in the hulls. The foamy harbour was mottled with slow breakers glazed over in ghostlike precision. Familiar odours wafted in the breezes: washed-up kelp, decayed brine, tarred hulls, old pitch. From the city's interior, a few torches glittered from the eastern wall. The gritty cobbled way was bathed in dim luminescence.

The moon was sinking fast; the sky was yet to show a veil of plum-purple by the time Valere veered the cart in, clattering past the marketplace's last grimy stone stalls. The wagon groaned its way past two old men who sat on stools reaching into buckets of slimy fish. A woman wrapped in shawl and wimple cleaned off their stall's canvas while a young boy was busy scraping off snogmald scales.

Eager to escape the lingering smells and general decay, Baus urged Valere to greater haste. They approached the Northern Gate with urgency, where there was a better than good chance that they would be challenged by sentries and confronted. Either boldness, or weapon's play might be necessary, but better than cringing in slinking cowardice, thought Baus.

The two outlaws fingered weapons that were stuffed under their cloaks. Hurriedly they instructed the women to action should events come to a skirmish.

"Do not try to face the sentries," advised Baus. "Grab your weapons, run, do not look back!"

Uella's sob came trilling up through the slats. "Why such deviancy?"

"The guards will not recognize you for who you are. Thinking you are accomplices, they will slit your throats."

Solstress wailed. "I disparage such dreadful guesswork!"

"Believe it you had better," Valere emphasized. "Heed Baus's guidelines! If all goes according to plan, nothing shall come of it; if not, we shall but be fading memories in the grand gamut of the universe."

"Once we are past the gates," snorted Poli up from the undercarriage, ". . . otherwise, we are as good as free. Certainly we are in dire straits—especially after roughing up the prince and bringing death to so many waysmen."

A mounted patrol suddenly came clopping out of the gloom. Baus jumped aside, hiding grimly on the hither side of the wagon. None of the three lightly-mailed soldiers on their marback roans seemed to notice.

The lead rider reined in close and waved a torch and issued a flat challenge at Valere. "You there, lout! Halt this crapwagon! Announce yourself and report your mission!"

Valere looked up into a face with an expression of inquiry. "I am on a legitimate mission, patrolman. Varlor is my name—keeper of this cart. I am bound for Furfong's Farm. It is a small eight miles to the west of Quelion. We intend to return with hens, hogs and geese. As you can see, we harbour no funds and only enough hay to make the round trip."

"So you say," grunted the captain surlily. Baus, crouching under the wagon, wished Valere success and hugged the spokes of the front wheel with anxiety. He saw a long broadsword sheathed on the patrolman's mount's saddle. Daggers were looped at his comrades' waist belts like marlin spikes; likewise, the waysmen entertained looks of gross suspicion.

The captain peered past Valere down into the cart, which for all intents and purposes appeared empty. He heaved about at a sound which alerted the riders to attention: a woman's high-pitched cough.

"What was that?"

"It appears to come from underneath the wagon."

Baus shifted from foot to toe with uncomfortable alarm. He was just about to bolt and create a diversion when, hidden within barely the limits of caution, he desisted. After consoling the terrified women, he snuck out from behind the wheels and pitched himself forward, jumping toward the three mounted men like a clown. Valere, blinking under the torchlight, glared at the outlaw and foisted a moony challenge at the lead rider. His fingers were not far from the sword hidden underneath the seat.

"Haroo!" Baus cried, vaulting up and bobbing. "Bauken the bumpkin—at your service!"

The riders reared back with apprehension. Instinctively they reached for weapons. "Who are you? Why are you lurking in the dark?"

Bauken replied with a glassy-eyed look. "I tend to my master's wheel. What do you think? It has become slightly out of true. Can you not see? I am in need of grease! Here is some in my hand." He held forth his dirty palm and crossed his eyes with loony urgency. "Haroo! Isn't that wonderful?"

The riders looked at him with queer revulsion. Baus held up a tin of unction acquired from Jacosiah's shed. "Would you care for some unguent, gentlemen—on your boots, perhaps your saddles? No? How about your Deputy? On your cheeks? Some peredrin paste then? Your stirrups perhaps?"

"Stand back, you filthy imbecile!" warned one of the deputies. He raised his sword to strike.

"Bauken, you rube!" cried Valere reproachfully. "Be good enough to leave these fine gentlemen alone." He reached over to tug at Bauken's ear. "These are serious people!" He winked at the foremost rider and drew him aside. "He is a bit of a half wit, my Bauken. I forget he is with me sometimes when he becomes so quiet—like a temple mouse creeping about the altar!"

"Well, keep him away from me!" the rider grunted with disgust. The simpleton continued to paw at his shins, but sensing some underlying weirdness, he cried, "You seem an odd pair, you two—almost conniving, as if you conceal nefarious motives. Ironic buffoonery?" His face showed troubled wonder. "Don't peer up at me like that, you fool! It's disturbing! Why, for instance, does your jackleg halfwit sidle a-spry of your vehicle when he could be sitting up front with you?"

Valere attempted a polite appeasement. "A good idea, but sir, the answer lies in a direction less complex than you think: old Nellie is not what she used to be and Bauken is out to re-shimmy the wheel and to re-grease the bearings and make the ride easier."

"Who is this 'Nellie'?" interrupted the watchman impatiently.

"The nag, of course, who else?"

"Do all your beasts have names?"

"Of course! Nestor, Esta and Nellie. Why have Nellie's old bones tow the sum of our bulk when one of us can walk?"

The rider shook his head with contempt. "Why not both of you get down and lead your nag by the reins and thus absolve the quandary of human cargo?"

Varlor scratched his head with amazement. "Master, you are very wise! I had not considered that up till now."

"Rotten bumpkin!" the rider roared. "On your way!" Reigning in, he dealt Valere a kick in the chops. "And for your sakes, let us not see the likes of you again."

Bowing, Valere intoned, "That is very large of you, sir."

The three riders clopped away, likely to harass some other unfortunate party.

When they were well out of sight, Valere reached down for his weapon, quivering with rage. "That oaf was fortunate! I was just ready to spear-hook him before he could say 'Jack chop'."

"That would have been immensely foolish," said Baus.

"Well, no need. I earned the kick in the lips. Good thinking, Baus. From now on I am 'Varlor' and you are 'Bauken'; let's get it straight before we land in another sticky situation that nearly gets us killed!"

Baus sighed with resignation.

The sea captain wiped a trickle of blood from his mouth and pointed to the twin dark shapes of windlewood gates looming up in the shadows ahead. "The North Gate is not far. I can catch glimpses of it already past these moonlit fountains. Remember, we are simple farmers—nothing more—simpletons—"

Sure enough the great portal was within range: clapped shut by two mailed sentries who stood atop the seaward barbican and did not look easily pliable. Hastily, Baus wiped more of the noxious bear grease on his cheeks. Valere clumped some into his hair, and they stuffed the pot out of sight under the blanket.

At once the gatemaster marched up to the cart and banged pike on the cobbles. "Where are you mutts off to at this hour?" he demanded.

"Duty calls," replied Valere. "Jacosiah demands his wagon in Alcax before sunrise so we'll be picking up his gaggle of geese and his herd of swine before the market opens at noon."

The gatemaster's features crinkled into mirthful disbelief. Raw-boned and wearing full mail and morion, he looked ill-disposed to small talk. "Market or not, my uppity bag-bottom, my orders are to search all wagons going in and out of the city."

Valere groaned a protest. "Again? We were just accosted by waysmen but five minutes ago."

The gatemaster thrust a pike at Valere's midsection in malignant jocularity. "So what? In case you haven't heard, the princess has gone missing. Possibly abducted—news is not known. At large are four felons, believed responsible for the deed, of which three of the villains are wanted buccaneers."

"Buccaneers? Is that really true?" quipped Valere. "I had heard something of the devilry back at the *Fat Lamprey*, but I laughed it off as rumour only. That the princess is gone is shocking—isn't it, Bauken?"

"Too true, Varlor."

The gatemaster sneered. "Well, it is hardly rumour, and none of us are laughing. So watch your tongue, oaf. Citizens of Sloe are on the lookout for four rogues who match certain descriptions and may have infiltrated the palace. One is known as a mischief-maker, *Sansix* of *Gutter Lane*. The villain is of moderate height, wears a cunning jowl, sports a rodent-like nose, and a pair of weasely eyes and a crooked, rapscallion grin."

Valere peaked his brows in mirth. "It's no mystery that we have so many diseased chicaneries running rampant in our city. A man of such quality should be put behind bars, captain, if you ask me. But, to answer your question, 'no'—no such persons have we seen. Isn't that right, Bauken?"

Baus shook his head in blatant emphasis. "Nor would we wish it, Varlor. We are simple folk, having not the meanest bone in our bodies. Why loiter in the midst of sordid persons when we can choose honest, upright citizenry? What of these other rogues, these buccaneers?"

"Less is known of them," muttered the sentry sternly. "Sly, unpredictable fellows travelling incognito. One of the freebooters is a barrel-shaped thug, somewhat akin to a Draslian bear with a reddish beard who carves his men like Bish the butcher his stags. Another wears his hair unconventionally long and is owner of a lean physique and looks almost gentle if it were not for the immoderately loutish, roguish and slippery tongue he guards."

"Absolutely impudent!" piped up Baus.

"Agreed. The other is of juvenile disposition, predominately blondish and fair in complexion, though is believed to harbour no great intelligence."

Valere gave a squawking laugh. "What a lumpish sounding lot of mooncalves you describe, gateman! You would say you have not caught these yobs yet?"

"Indeed not, or why would I be describing them? What are you—on par with your halfwit? The felons were last seen wearing bizarre costumes, of mountebanks and mummers —escaped from the princess's nuptials."

Valere announced a purposeful program: "Then, we shall be on our way, and on the lookout for these knaves and scapegraces!"

The gatekeeper gave a curt acknowledgement. "See to it then. Normally, I would let none pass at this ungodly hour, but I see no cause for alarm with your lot." Biting deep into his apple, he stabbed a pike down into the back of the wagon. The blade passed clean through a set of dirty blankets and a mound of Nellie's stale straw.

"There's nothing here. Nargo! Open the gate!"

A hatchet-faced man in a brown uniform cranked the wheel in the upper barbican. An iron crankshaft rotated which leveraged a heavy box of machinery. Through a complicated set of physics, the necessary torsion applied the pull-chains with enough impetus to give the great windlewood gates a heave and to draw themselves apart.

Valere urged the wegmor forward. The gatemaster gave a cry. He was alarmed by the bow in the wagon's back slats. He held up a restraining hand.

Mirgo, his compatriot, was ordered to arrest the progress of the gate. With sweating belligerence, the engineer reversed the crankshaft and called down an impertinent shout, "Make up your mind, Drago! I am not your she-thrall!"

Nargo, the dartman, peered down with somewhat rueful interest. Baus noted the heavy weapon slung on his shoulder. An iron stem and wooden beam-sight installed in the transom suggested it could spray a bronze bolt at deadly speed into one's leg or spine.

Drago addressed Valere in sober tones. "Why does your cart carry so much weight, bumpkin? It creaks and groans as if tormented by ghosts."

Valere gave a polite laugh. "Tormented by ghosts—that's a good one. The wheels are, well—" Valere trailed off, floundering, muffing his role. Baus quickly took up the thread: "The wheels are ungreased, is what they are. The entire frame is a thorough mess, gatekeeper —antique, old bicklebark, waterlogged to death, as heavy as mallow stone."

Valere nodded foolishly. "Aye, Bauken is right! He is not such a fool as he seems. I keep after that miser Jacosiah to have this contraption fixed and re-panelled but we just can't get him to spare a few coins! He refuses to grease the wheels—he dodges his duty in providing us new basil wood! Can you believe it? Jaco likes his beer too much!"

The gatekeeper waved a disgusted hand. "I don't care about Jaco! You farmrats still have not answered my question." He curled up his nose with a grimace. "Ah, forget it! You two reek of the plague! Like a couple of bears in rut. I doubt either of you clowns have the brains to be murdering Squands or infiltrating the Royal Palace, let alone smuggling your way out. Off with you now! Mirgo! Haul up!"

Valere gave a smart salute. "It shall be as you say, captain."

"Don't call me 'captain'. And next time," he growled, "pick a proper time to roll by our gates!"

"We shall do our utmost to accommodate you, sir," answered Valere politely.

Mirgo struggled above; the chains and gears rattled to life. The great windlewood gate creaked open and revealed an open path.

Valere aimed the vehicle. Baus, hoping to be of assistance, walked to the other side to conceal any arms or limbs that may have been dangling out.

Drago made a curt signal; Mirgo let the gate creak shut with a great clangourous clap.

Baus risked a look back. Nargo, the dartman inspected him with wary distrust.

They were well away and round a swerve in the road and Valere gave a syrupy guffaw.

"Idiots! A bit testy on the nerves, Baus, I'll say, but not so bad."

He halted the wagon and the seaman alighted and with Baus's aid, he liberated the others from below.

Solstress and Uella, pasty faced and anxious, brushed cobwebs and tar off their garments. The jolting of the wagon had not comforted their tempers in the least.

Poli blinked in the moonlight. He gave a yawn of indolent exhaustion. Sansix sagged with lethargic defeat. Nursing his swelling hand, he stared at them with glowering contempt.

On Baus's suggestion, Valere brought out the water pot which they used to alleviate their thirst. For fear of discovery, Baus motioned the women back into the cart. Before he had time to sling the blankets overtop of them, Uella was eliciting a series of bubbling complaints.

"I abhor being treated like a meal sack! What is to become of us, covered hither with tarps of smell-ridden barnyard and goose? I thought we were as good as free when you said we were past the city gates?"

Baus explained to her: "In a sense Poli's remark was only figuratively spoken. Insofar as caution is concerned, our group must remain cached under the tarps to promote least likelihood of discovery." He glared at Poli and pushed Uella's head under the tarp, grinning pleasantly, and joined her under the rank coverings.

Too disheartened to argue, Solstress and the others fell back under the covers, groaning in enervated heaps.

XII

The companions left the city and the sprawling advance of the Waun far behind. The fading moonlight swept over the forest fringes and cast long, tiresome shadows over the gravel patches of dusty road.

Hours passed. The sea did not wander far from their sight, a reassuring presence with its murmur of surf on rocks and moon-speckled sand. The highway wound inexorably through the boulders, scree, and ragged gnolewoods that stole from the last frayed edges of the Waun and toed close to the roadside.

The road sometimes tilted above the water and the travellers could see precarious gull-haunted cliffs. Valere steered clear of these drops. The comrades passed no other vehicles or travellers—it was too early for wayfarers. The forest seemed to languish, the lands spread ghostly swaths: byres, hilly crofts, fields of winter hay. Fields were demarcated by old fence posts, stumps, and the occasional grazing wegmor munching on wild flaxhack.

The moon sank lower. Phantom waistbands of cloud appeared, under which the light dimmed with a plum glimmer beginning to show seaward.

Lulled by the motion of the wagon, Solstress began to dream. Twitching beside Baus, she felt his warm body impel her to caprice. It caused her to twist one way and the other. She squirmed with her head into the nook of Baus's shoulder and made small mewing sounds.

Baus was not averse to the attention. With Solstress to his left, and Uella to his right, he was aware of an arrangement with which he felt pleasantly contented.

The princess sat bolt upright, stretching, cooing, refreshed and warmed by her drowsy languor. Solstress seemed to be mildly intoxicated by her rest and further, incommoded by Poli and Sansix who lay elbow to jowl in inconvenient proximity. She deigned to ask them to create a distance: "It is almost daybreak and I require some space to myself with Baus—to convey important thoughts."

Poli regarded the princess with stony amusement.

She ignored the stare and beseeched, "Uella, you may ride up front with Valere too, and Sansix and Poli, for that matter."

Uella and Sansix made efforts to comply, but Poli maintained his rigid crouch. Solstress posted a stern address: "Poli, I am the Royal Princess! You must heed my orders since you ride in my domain."

Poli gave a strangled grumble. Baus urged him to scoot forward as per the princess's wishes. Poli growled, resentful of the overruling, but he did clamber up to the driver's bench, muttering curses.

While the others decamped, Solstress took time to sling a less offensive blanket overtop her and Baus. She pressed a finger to his lip, urging him to silence. "I am free of Clavius now," she hissed, "and my mother's failure has left me light-headed and giddy! I feel almost enthralled! It is a sentiment that comes not often, Baus. You should be grateful! I owe you much, yet I do not know how to repay you."

Baus could think of several ways. In fact, he suggested a more recreational pattern of activity that might prove satisfactory under the present conditions. The princess did not seem averse to the proposal and Baus, with all his genteel kindness, clambered up on top of her and lavished her with all sorts of kisses and caresses, with his sharp eyes glinting in the moonlight.

"I have another divine idea," she whispered, returning Baus's affection with fervour.

"Really?" inquired Baus. "They seem to abound from your agile mind."

"'Tis an idea which shall liberate me from Clavius! Should on the large chance I be discovered in this shabby wagon—we shall consummate a joining."

Baus immediately was attentive of the proposal.

Solstress felt her belly and in between her legs. "Yes, it is time."

"Time for what?" Baus demanded, perplexed. Solstress slid her luxuriant waistline close to his. Feeling her pleasant warmth soothing his stiff joints, Baus felt compelled to reciprocate, and his own body stirred in natural response.

Solstress's advances seemed whimsical, almost comically wrought, even in spite of the rude setting and the royal rank she held, but Baus, being the tolerant soul he was, did not care to argue, nor was he in any hurry for intellectualizing.

Solstress kissed his arm and hooked her fingers underneath his tunic and began slipping it off. Baus felt obliged to return the favour. Soon the princess was struggling under the blanket, peeling off her mud-stained jerkin—an action which Baus followed with almost automatic celerity.

Many thoughts coursed through Baus's mind, the least of which included the perceptions of his peers crammed like glum owls in the driver's seat.

In due time, Solstress gave a trill of ecstasy and she rolled back lustily on the planks. Her fiery eyes stared forward in wolfish need. Baus hunched in a side-crouch, feeling almost instantly vainglorious, though about as instantly shallow . . . a prickling dread crept over him.

He half attempted to identify the perception. A rogue presentiment? A subtle, far-reaching psychometry? The feeling of post-coital melancholy? It was not obvious and a feeling permeated him with the dread of repercussions beyond his control that would set future calamities in motion.

Solstress pressed the contours of her body close to his and her face was aglow with flaming warmth, and yet she seemed almost detached. Baus felt soft fingers on his ribs underneath the rude blanket. "Poor Baus!" she cried. "Such a woeful face for one squire who enjoys the charms of a princess."

Baus gave a poignant laugh. "'Tis true, my Lady; I should be joyous to the extreme! Kings and princes should be envious of my luck!"

"They should!" Baus threw off the blankets and sat peering up. He pulled on his breeches and while the under-servant Uella eyed his naked body with envy, he hitched up his trousers and buttoned his tunic with dignified simplicity while the handmaid stared past him. "What?" he blustered. "Must I become the dastard for taking a nasty little sliver out of the princess's back?"

Uella was snorting a haughty tune and her mood was scorn mixed with cold jealousy. "Oh? Is that what you were doing?" she cried. "There seemed to be a lot of sliver-pulling going about back there—but we hardly noticed that."

Baus shed light on the situation: "The road was bumpy, Uella, amidst pits and potholes, and the two of us had to shift positions innumerable times."

"Oh, really? And the cry?" she pressed.

Baus explained curtly: "A small release from the barb's pressure and pang upon the princess's spine, nothing more."

Uella snorted her disbelief.

Solstress drew back in surprise. "Uella!—I believe you are spiteful. Even begrudging a lady's moment of fun!" Her servant's face, round and pink, was flushed painfully; Solstress seemed at loss to explain her distress.

Clambering over the driver's post, Sansix took up a corner under the tarp like an old dog. Uella followed, chillingly aloof and Poli stepped over her, squatting beside Solstress with a tone mildly ironic, "I would not deign to intrude upon the privacy of her Highness's carriage."

"Mind your tone, Poli. I am not insensitive to sarcasm."

Baus climbed up and took a seat beside Valere. With bravado he fluttered his fingers but Valere flashed him a warning smile. "Always pushing the limits, aren't you, conniver?" He flicked off Baus's foppish cap.

Baus remained nobly benign. "A life not yet lived, Valere, is one pursued in the dark."

Valere laughed at the maxim. "A life pushed to folly's brink, is one coming to a bitter end."

Baus deigned no response. Daybreak was upon them. The sea's lapping blanket drifted lazily across the tracts of black sand and the barnacled pinnacles of rock limned like fairy castles in the early light. Cordons of salmon pink and rose reflected off the water. Gulls circled in the maundering breeze while thrush and sea heron fought for scraps pushed on the high tide. Other pedestrians plied down from the north to make slow, dusty routes into the city. Behind, set far against Sloe, rose the Aldevean peaks, snow-capped, domed and magical, slick with ghost-silver-purple light.

Within the hour, the troupe snatched the first glimpses of thatched byres and the tin roofs of Alcax. No patrols were in town. Through the winding streets the wagon trundled indifferently past the *Rambling Mariner* and the fish stalls and the leather kiosks and wine shops, familiar to memory. Baus's memory of their landing here a week hence brought heavy emotions to his heart. Sloops, sailboats, and dories trawled the naked shoreline for blow bass and whelks while some of the larger yawls conveyed supplies to Sloe and more southerly ports. Baus spied shivering men crouched on the decks of their smaller vessels hauling in nets of fish. He felt no urge to return to that line of work; indeed, he was cheerfully encouraged to guard his current lifestyle, which was progressing in a surprisingly decent fashion. His knowledge of the substantial stash hidden away in faraway Nosoheath made his undignified mode of travel seem all the more palatable.

A sudden yelp issued from the back of the wagon: Poli, perhaps in the spirit of a copycat, attempted an impulsive foray upon Uella's anatomy.

The gambit had gone awry. Now the blond pirate flew up like a crab, alerting Baus to the circumstance that he was no longer welcome in the back of the wagon.

Baus gave Poli a wan glance. "One man's means is not the other's ace in the hole—so the saying goes."

Poli uttered an unflattering remark and gave Baus a swat in the ear, which Baus patently endured.

Valere reacted unkindly to the roughhousing. "Fix up your costume, Poli, if you dare ride in front. We are hardly a morning out of Sloe and patrols will be eye-alert for irregularities."

At Alcax's market the seamen stopped to gather fresh hay and discarded apple peels for Nellie. Baus and Poli disappeared to wander up the aisles and haggle over a bundle of smoked eels, a jar of olives and a sourdough loaf.

An offshore breeze lifted the smells of the market and brought a clear chillness to the air. Glimpses of sea caught through arches and gangways caused Baus a hollow pang.

According to the last weather-beaten sign, the next village, Dohon, was four miles away.

Baus sighed. Between the members of their company, they retained only twelve silver sequals—a paltry sum considering the number of leagues to travel.

Nellie gave a wistful bray; the wagon lurched ahead.

XIII

While the women slept in the wagon, Sansix crouched listlessly at a respectable distance, almost comatose. The sun shone brightly through wispy clouds, granting the company more cheer. Past Dohon, the community of Mieney poised on a low hill beside a marshy bay. The wagon took a wide bend around the town and broached the edge of a low rise that peered out over the countryside. The road wound along the top of a broken coastline, disappearing in golden haze. Fields spread like flat mantles, cut sharply by distant dense hogback trees. Glancing back on a whim, Baus spied a billow of dust and a cloud rising in the mist.

Baus's cheeks twitched.

Such a cloud could only foreshadow trouble.

Baus braced himself, flashed a tense glance at Valere. Presently the pounding of hooves brought misgivings that were real.

Heedless of any delineations of the road, Valere veered the wain off onto the grass and hopped out on the sward. Baus scrambled after him, getting the women strapped back underneath the carriage.

The team of riders was fast approaching. None looked terribly disposed to any compassion.

The outlaws finished tying Poli and Sansix under the wagon and hopped back just in time. No sooner had they stuck their feet up on the slats, feigning sleep with hats pulled over their eyes, when the riders bounded up the knoll as if on some unpleasant business. They poured past the wain, a whirlwind, a thunder of hooves and flashing tabards—four helmed men garbed in the blue and green garb of Sloe, with mounts spewing black gravel at them. Galloping two abreast, the Squands rode with the standard of twin golden gonfalons lanced with a silver ram. There was no doubt that these grim messengers were out on a pilgrimage, alerting residents to watch out for knaves matching the four's description.

The event cast a worrisome cloud over the company's mood. For some minutes Valere and he huddled near Nellie's shanks absorbed in a hasty discussion.

"Perhaps we should head inland?" Baus croaked. "Our snitches seem bent on patrolling the narrowest corridor along the coast."

Poli rejected such reasoning. "Why not hire a boat and commission passage to Kantmacle? Plenty of skippers this time of year for hire in these villages with what little coin of ours remains." He cast doubt with his mutters up through the slats.

"'Little' is the key word here," argued Valere. "Our enemies have spread the word; any captain is thickheaded as sin to smuggle outlaws out of the area. Worse yet, 'Her Majesty' will have offered them a supernal reward for betraying us on the flick of a sequal."

Baus sat back in glum silence. With heavy thoughts, the troupe resumed their habit of old, tying the weary women back in their harness, heedless of the bitter revilement.

The morning passed; the winding cobblestones grew barely wide enough for two carts to pass abreast. Baus's uneasiness grew. The looks of passer-bys and their calculating, reward-hungry scrutinies remained ever a worry in his mind. Baus feared their disguise would be discovered, and they would be set upon like animals and that he would never see his treasure again. With every passing hour, the outlaw grew ever less optimistic of the possibility of seeing reward or freedom . . .

At a fork in the road he advised Valere to turn off so that they might escape the main traffic.

The road wound inland. Rich farmland pocked with piles of stone and deodar-thicket reigned. The sun glowed dully over the land and the wind was like a feather's tickle, leaving only a warm ambience on their faces as it wafted asp flower and honeydew across the fields.

Halting at a T junction, the company remained hidden from sight, crouching behind a dense copse. Baus advised Valere to unstrap the women and Solstress and Uella groaned, spitting out dust, rubbing their aching limbs and blinking in the hazy light like bunny rabbits. In order to dispel suspicions of favouritism, Baus tossed them each a handkerchief, with which they each wiped their runny noses and teary eyes. Heedless of laments, Baus plied them for information of the lands.

In their distraught state, the women could only confer disjointed information. Neither had ventured far from the palace—Uella, for instance, had been an under-servant all her life. Sansix grudgingly revealed that he knew something of the geography of the area. "To the east lies the seaside village Yesimar known for its silver lodes and coffee and is the place where mendicant friars make their yearly pilgrimages. The people of the Triburne Faith journey to the sacred groves by the rustling waterfalls to pray and scourge themselves. Northward are the settlements Quelion and Fauche, labourers' towns full of rednecks. Both populations are tied closely to Sloe and contain garrisons that will surely cause us woe. To the west lie less travelled paths, of course: forests of the region of Farling's Wall, beyond which I know little. Unsettling tales—the reputation of the denizens is at best questionable. Yet if I were a fugitive vagabond, there is where I would head."

"Why?" clipped Solstress harshly, drawing herself up to her full height. "So we can all be mauled by hillbillies and thrown in snares?"

"No," Sansix replied blandly, "to cache ourselves conveniently and stay out of the sight of the maximum of patrols. What I spoke of earlier are mere wives' tales."

Baus pursed his lips in annoyance. "Let's have no squabbles, Sansix. Yet—there's something in what you say."

Valere blurted out: "How shall we finance this journey? It smacks of toilsome leagues and more. *Sarch* is our true destination—the northlands! our homeland. The purchase of this wain has sorely depleted our reserves." Valere's tone had taken on an aggrieved flavour.

Solstress offered news of more noteworthy aspiration. "Perhaps there is hope yet, Valere." She produced a small, lace-knit pouch under the hem of her trousers that gave a merry clink. Ears perked. The cord's untwining displayed a glitter of gold, enough to finance many ventures, scrupulous or not.

Sansix gave a foxish yip, ogling the wealth with disquieting savour. The princess shivered. Baus, however, found himself scrutinizing Solstress's wealth with no lesser lack of zeal. This trove could purchase pardon back in Heagram, finance a steed, or hasten away from this miserable condition and enjoy boons of fairer countrysides—and possibly the pleasure of a few fair maids.

Solstress's voice intruded upon Baus's musings. "Naught is there to worry. With these resources we can hire a whole suite of chambers at my expense! We can stay hidden away from my mother—which is the best part."

Valere laughed at such naivety. "Every landlord from Sloe to Owlen will be on the eye-alert for our eccentricities, Princess. A quartet of armed vagabonds and two ladies of quality. Ha! Tongues will wag. In the long and short, we'll be forced to camp it in the rough."

Solstress's eyes glittered with revulsion. "We shall do no such thing. We'll give these landlords gold to stay their tongues!"

"Ha!" Valere gave a sarcastic laugh. "You draw too much credit to your influence, Princess. Any landlord I know would take the information and receive reward from the highest bidder—which would always be your mother."

"Crassness at its worst!" cried Uella, dismayed. "I had no idea this venture would be so offensive. I hope to take a warm bath somewhere along the journey."

"Guess again," Baus muttered. "Rivers are there for the taking."

"You are no help at all!" cried Uella, overcome with distress.

"Take my advice—head west," affirmed Sansix.

Baus was for once in concord with the thief. Valere entertained his own doubt. "An inland jaunt is strenuously unnecessary."

"I am bent on a heading due north like Valere," said Poli. "I believe it's the fastest route back to Nosoheath.

Solstress and Uella could argue no further. They were apathetic, listless; hearing of Nosoheath's and Heagram's dismal charms, made them even more torpid. They hunched underneath the wagon like glum robins and hissed. Here the company was split: a camp to head north up the coast, the other to plod inland contending with Farling's wall and the horror of dubious creatures—even sorcerers. Baus, being the pivotal party, sought to maintain an equable relation amongst the companions and yielded to Valere and Poli's wish, despite his qualms. The company retraced their path to the main thoroughfare, resuming their dreary trek up the coast.

Moments into their journey Uella complained of choking dust and the excessive noise of the road. Valere reluctantly agreed to allow her topside if only for the condition that she curb her callow sulks.

"Who shall keep me company?" griped Solstress. "Must I endure the wagon's undercarriage all by myself like a pariah?"

Baus and Poli cast awkward glances at each other. A cold gleam slipped into Sansix's eye. Grudgingly the thief offered to trade places with the handmaid if only to keep the peace amongst the fellowship. "My only proviso is that the princess must be allowed a bandanna to cover her nose from the dust—likewise my own."

Valere was happy to consent to the suggestion. He was fatigued with all the quibbling and instructed Baus to wrap the twain's mouths with cloths and tender Sansix's snug straps for tightness and safety.

Sansix thanked Baus for the care. Baus gave the opportunist a sour look. The rogue was always up to some scheme . . . nevertheless, the journey proceeded as before.

Before long, Solstress's piercing cry rang over the drumming of the wheels.

The vehicle halted. Baus, Valere and Poli dismounted to investigate.

It turned out that Sansix's alleged altruism had been for naught. While Solstress had dozed, the scoundrel had taken liberties to probe her figure, lulled as she was by the monotonous movements of the wagon. In a fearful fright, Solstress had jerked to attention, feeling cold, spidery fingers groping about her waist and clamping on her purse.

The matter was efficiently amended with Valere beating Sansix to a pulp and ordering Uella back to her previous position. Glowering in hate and nursing a few new blue bruises, Sansix was hurled back into the driver's seat, kitty-cornered between Baus and Poli who held weapons to either side curtailing so much as a grouse's stir from the conniver.

XIV

One day passed and then another. Whenever dusk struck, the travellers would seek out havens to retire for the evening, avoiding towns and villages like the plague. The refuges included dry haylofts and small ivy-ridden fanes set at intervals in out-of-the way crofts or secluded glades. In such situations, Valere suggested that each of their trusted members stand on watch for encroachers. Poli went even so far as to propose that Sansix's hands and legs be bound at night so that he not sidle away, or betray them while they slept—a plan which Baus condoned. All remained immune to Sansix's accusations of ignoble treatment.

During rotations, Baus preoccupied himself with important activities, which included the soothing of Solstress's distress over sufferances of dust and tumult below the wagon. Invariably the stressful privations of Uella's misfortunes too. At alternate times throughout the night, including double, two-hour shifts, Baus's personal ministrations affected each woman, all the better to address their individual, idiosyncratic needs. In terms of locale, a place was selected conveniently far from the sleepers' positions so that Baus and his nude partner could enjoy therapeutic connections and intimate embraces without disturbing the other woman's important rest. Baus marvelled at the simplicity of the arrangement. In itself, it was an expression of his own genius. Also, convenient to the point of perfection in relation to his own personal pleasure. During the mornings, neither Uella or Solstress remained inclined to speak of the matter to each other. Naturally each other's nocturnal proclivities were her own affairs. This was an arrangement upon which Baus congratulated himself and beamed with approval on his wise tactics. He remained armed with the knowledge that during the day there would be no unpleasant confrontation over a shared custody of the 'therapeutic assistant' while on the road.

On the fourth day of the sojourn, arid plains drifted left and right. The trek dragged on with a cadence best known as 'plodding'. The sun arched, the winds blew; the wheels of the wain rolled on in inexorable fashion. Nellie's hooves clopped; the passenger's heads nodded. A general sluggishness descended over the company, in sombre languor.

Traffic, however, was not so slight as to be negligible, and the varieties of peddlers, shoe shiners, saddlers, cobblers, carters, fishwives, ploughmen, drinkers, tinkers and masons made for interesting spectacle. The way was a funnel of noise; confusion lay everywhere: clopping carts, honking geese, braying nags, bleating goats. The lowing of marbacks and the squawking of children was sometimes tasking. Despite the tumult, the company's unique camaraderie remained intact—if such could be said—and they were not on the whole perceived as anything out of the ordinary—just a few dusty wayfarers of the many of nameless faces plying the north road.

The highway slanted to the sea, allowing persons of leisure to ford a small freshet that swung lazily out from the plains. Over a wide wooden bridge the company passed and down onto a green sward where reposed a small rest area, milling with folk. Nearby an olive grove offered shade and rocks to sit on. The setting was agreeable and Valere swung the cart about to refill his canteen.

Baus remained dozing on the driver's bench, head slumped on his lap. Undoubtedly he was fatigued from his nocturnal exertions. Poli did likewise, growling from time to time as Sansix rubbed his chin next to him in dozing stupor, and who now sat staring woodenly off into space like an abused doll. Amongst the travellers gathered were a dozen itinerant monks —a clan from the temple of Serat in the hallowed section of old Aurenham. Each clutched his own white yew stick and wore his threadbare tunic of blue-black wool as if he were a divine prince. A circlet of woven laurel remained clasped intimately round his short cropped, shaven crown as if he were a lord, while each coenobite wandered about in unhurried fashion, reciting praises, psalms and pedantic glorifications, to Zon—god of gods. Some bent to wash their hands, pausing to sip frugal little sips of water from the river.

An important individual sat on one of the flat stones drinking spirits from a silver teacup: he was a short, plump comically-attired minstrel with a tanned hearty face. His forehead was peaked, his chin tapered to a fine V and his head crowned with red hair curlicuing a philosopher's brow. Atop his skullcap, a flap of orange fool's hose stuck up like a cock's comb and his breast was outfitted with a green doublet. Feet were pressed snugly in a pair of fresh brogues whose toes curled up at the ends in grey green balls. On his lap a miniature concertina was strapped whose yellow pipes and ivory keys were extraordinary in the sense that they were tiny enough to appear as bird's teeth. In fact, the instrument's bellows pumped and wheezed with enthusiasm while the minstrel squirmed and shifted on his sizeable buttocks.

Catching sight of Valere, the musician called out an affable greeting. Valere did not take time to bend from his task at the water, cupping cool liquid in his mouth over a beardy chin.

The minstrel learned that Valere and his colleagues were bound for Owlen on a very important mission and he became instantly attentive. "Ho so! For so extended an expedition, what better opportunity to harbour a capable musician on board? What say you, squire? I am a convivial compadre! I may aid you in some sport and revelry. Pezla's my name—most illustrious minstrel and esteemed bard of Loust!"

Valere scratched his cheek, showed concern. "I am ignorant of your repute as a bard, sir Pezla."

The minstrel frowned, searching for words. "Ignorant of Pezla the bard?—the same swain whose fame as storyteller, toetapper and fine musical orator is known throughout the lands?"

Valere conveyed no further enlightenment to the declaration and Pezla was soon given to distress. "No great worry, squire! Not uncommon is it that people here are poorly informed of my repute. As an aside, I'll let you know I have lowered my fees for daily entertainment to a paltry sequal."

Valere raised his eyebrows and peered at Pezla queerly. "I am even sorrier, Pezla, that in terms of funds, I find myself at an impecunious low."

Pezla sought to hide disappointment. He plunged hands into his pockets and shrugged. "Well—then perhaps I may perform a small ballad or a canticle, for a copper or two?"

Valere smilingly shook his head. "I must bypass the offer."

Pezla bowed low and attempted to grasp how he might effect another entrepreneurial angle, but he was struggling. "The crime of parsimony rests on your head, cartmaster! Offering me no other choice but to play for free!"

"Then so it must."

Pezla harrumphed; he jumped down from the rock and without further ado, began to strut about on nimble toes, raising two fingers to his button pad, giving his instrument a lusty squeeze.

The gatherers remained indifferent to the fruity notes.

The minstrel paused, slightly miffed, voiced an all-round inquiry as to whether there were other musicians in the audience.

"For one, I am tone deaf," Valere admitted. "But Sansix here harbours a fair vocal range —and our lad Poli plays a half-decent flute."

Pezla gasped. "What? Where is the lad? Bring out the instrument so that together we might ply a rousing duet!"

Poli perked ears, muttering, "My instrument has been misplaced, minstrel—as has my spirit."

"A dreadful pity! But we shan't give up yet." Pezla glanced craftily out of the corner of his eye. "Tirra lirra lirra lee, what next will red robin see?" He giggled at his rhyme and beat out a lively jig with melodic glissandos and exuberant refrains.

He suddenly stopped . . . drumming fingers on the keypad and looking about in the hope of appealing to others: "Any requests? There is no end to my repertoire of melodies!"

People were disinterested. The monks paid him no heed. Pretending ignorance, they kept to their quarter by the stream, as if Pezla's notes were an embarrassment to their ears and the sweetness of the air.

A rankled Poli loosed a fretful yawn and asked if Pezla's interlude was soon over.

The minstrel piped up: "Not at all, sleepy-eyes! I am only beginning."

"Pity. My colleague Baus drowses in bouts and starts and is sensitive to noise. As for myself, I am hardly inclined to revelry."

Pezla called out in a brassy voice: "Be off! Your opinion is moot, young scoundrel. Considering you are a twain and there are many fine folk gathered here in this grove, I would ask you to hold back your pronouncements."

Pezla drew Valere aside: "Your blond bully seems irked. What is the matter? His mates seem a trifle dazed, if not apathetic."

Valere gave a regretful sigh. "'Tis true. My colleagues are sluggish. Truthfully, I do nothing to interfere with their way of being."

Pezla crinkled his lips. "This lassitude speaks of the gravest malady. Attend! I would recommend a slice of bitterroot or a wedge of pikehastle to infuse them with brio—the more astringent the better."

Valere chuckled out a fond reminiscence. "I would recommend a cup of grog."

"Better even!" laughed Pezla. "You are a smart soul, cartmaster!" He foisted Valere a quick side glance. "You don't happen to have you any liquors to offer?"

"Not at this moment, Pezla; however I shall keep you apprised."

"That is kind."

Uella had managed to unbundle herself from the straps and slipped down to join the men by the river.

Pezla raised his brows at the pleasing contours of the woman. "Do you keep all your nice beauties hidden underneath the vehicle?"

"Not usually," came Valere's sardonic response. The seaman cast Uella a moist frown. "Only the ones who get themselves into the most trouble."

Uella gave an indulgent grunt. She curtsied. The seaman allowed the transgression to pass but restricted the maidservant to drinking water from the stream and eating her black olives. The handmaid slouched lazily in the grass, hugging her knees to her chest while listening to Pezla's snippets. Her gaze was one of fascination. She seemed hopeful to catch a whiff of the musicianship, judging from the few stray snatches of melodies she had heard already.

"Ah, fair lady!—perhaps you are the most worthy of my attention of all gathered!"

Uella beamed. "Perhaps! The journey has been taxing for me. I pine for some tranquil melodies to comfort my troubled spirit."

"No sooner said than done!" Pezla cried. With an inward grin, he launched into a ribald tune, which quickly devolved into a more suggestively lewd refrain which Uella could stand no longer and stalked back haughtily to the wagon. Pezla halted his ode, shrugged and loosed a humorous cackle. Women! Shaking his head, he muttered about the inscrutability of the female species.

Meanwhile, the minstrel had chanced to notice a thin, wiry scoundrel creeping along the grass, searching for Valere's belt. The chin was hooked, the nose crafty and showed an inclination to knavery.

The lips under Pezla's dandyish moustache moved in an indignant ripple. "What do you do, common thief!?" he cried. "Yes, you, quick-sneaker, the one with the cross-eyed look and the bold fingers touching my comrade and sporting very straggling beard."

Valere wheeled, caught the hand of the mischief-maker and pulled the figure into the river. "What's this?" he cried. "Are you a poufty? Itchy fingers? Drown you I ought, you snivelling grifter, for sticking your thumbs down my backside!"

The thief, recovering from his shock, embarrassed and dismayed, embarked on a gibbering explanation: "Please, Honourable Sir! Pity a poor beggar only out to touch your person. I need only bread."

"Silence, cajoling knave!" rumbled Valere. "I'll be deciding what is worth pitying." He hauled the rascal out of the water and seized him by the throat, dragging the cutpurse to standing position. The seaman's formidable sword tickled in his hand.

The thief gasped, trembling with parboiled eyes. "Please do not be slicing off my beard, sir! It is true and pure yellow, a golden wonder. My only legacy. You may punish me with anything, but not my precious hair! I've suffered worse woes!"

The seaman bared his teeth in disgust. "So, it is your beard you covet, eh, blackheart? Well then, why do you mean to keep it?" He grabbed a tuft of the goatish, smelly beard, chopped down so that it splayed on the grass like a clump of flaxen seaweed.

The thief gasped, raked at his naked chin and grovelled about Valere's feet with horror before the stricken member. "Look at what you have done, my beautiful lord!"

Valere laughed. "More of that shall be coming, groveller. Now up, on your knees! Your due is not yet done."

Arresting his song, Pezla stared austerely at the craven who slouched and abased before Valere. He rhymed off a jaunty ode—of a thief from Efoven who had tempted to pilfer Sir Osgald's pithy swain of his wage earnings.

With the penitent criminal contemplating bleak prayers, the arrival of yet another figure predicted conflict. It was an elder monk, a taller and broader sort than the rest. He was solemnly-poised, entertaining keen eyes of authority. He approached now on soft feet, speaking in a pious tone to Valere: "Release this miscreant at once! I command it in the name of Zon! The wretch is undeserving of any foul punishments that you would prescribe, cartmaster."

Valere grunted with amusement and squinted at the man.

"The wretch knows not what he does," continued the elder monk benignly, "only misdeeds, which will be his undoing before Zon in the end."

Valere peered comically at the balding newcomer. "So—who might you be, pompous mountebank?"

"I am Sakoon, Hierophant of the Order of Serat." The monk wiped his robe with austere dignity. "I am leader of the small, unpresuming party you see congregating before the river. "I have come to administer order and reconcile men to their proper station."

The criminal moved child-like on his knees toward the monk with pleading sincerity. "Many wondrous thanks to you, sir! You are a saint, a martyr of excellence, and justness and grace. Were there more of your kind in this heartless world then—"

"Silence!" the monk hissed. "Spare me your rhetoric, black beggar. I have no coins for you, nor am I a dupe for your treadling fingers."

For a second, the thief's lips curled. Then he shrank back with a snarl. The monk's pious face appeared deeply inimical. The hooded eyes narrowed, as if to take in the entire gamut of the vices present.

Scrutinizing Valere, he spoke with sanctimonious deliberation. "And you—beard-cutter, kindly refrain from violence with the sword. It is against the teachings of Zon."

His critical eyes shifted to Pezla. "Now, hearken!" he addressed Pezla with cold rigour. "Forgive—but I could not help balking over the lubricious lyrics spewing from your maw earlier. Please refrain from the improprieties while decent people congregate at yon water pool."

Pezla gave a bald flourish. "I'll treat that as a compliment, fair friar, but I shall fare as I please—" He twirled his finger and launched forth on an obnoxious yodelling and a series of plangent chords.

Sakoon's ears held to the tumult and he began an argument with the minstrel. The quarrel escalated into eschatological matters and bystanders gathered, thinking it might come to blows, but the Hierophant retained his aplomb and re-emphasized the fact that the minstrel's music was scandalous and that its blasphemy must cease.

"I am Pezla of Loust!" roared Pezla vaingloriously. "I sing and speak as I will! Once I was a rich bard—renowned of grandees of Loust. I would crush your smug airs with the merest sweep of my cashmere glove. But alas, the days of grandeur have gone, as all things must."

"A highly philosophical anecdote—but highly irrelevant!"

"To you perhaps. But I? Nay! Ah, the life of a humble bard!" Pezla jumped back, crooning like a bird in heat. Dejection had slipped from his voice with tenors of dignity. "For me, it is now the life of unknowable bondage!" His fluting discord rose to an endearing timbre. "Shall I describe my life? Yes—I will. From the goodness of my heart, I will grant you this glimpse into my vast, poetic memory!—First: to participate in the carnival of Loust! To ride the fabulous balloons floating on wings of heated air, to taste the excellent pink cotton candy, to suck the whipple sticks, to drink the rum and the excellent bonker, to hear the riddles, the fiddlers, the clowns, the cries of jubilant children, the guffaws of jesters and buffoons! To view the giants, the beasts, the games, the prizes, the tears, laughter and cascading frenzy of fanfares! Ah, the tin whistles—careening off the hills—the bushpipes, the fabulous flutes, the rebecs, zithers, pitchpipes, drones, bassoons, masoons, and fasoons!" With that Pezla let rip another chord which startled the Hierophant into a chaotic half-skip. "Do not forget the fall fair at Efoven with its pumpkin-riding scarecrows, its menageries, its ribboned foxes, its hounds, its games of tug-of-war, its climb-the-beanstalk game and its horrors of bait-the-bear. Ah, what sights have I seen, my sheltered, pious anchorite! What sounds have I heard! All to the various heights and delights of my imagination—which is profound." Pezla rolled his eyes in rapture.

"Sheltered anchorite?" Sakoon bawled. "You cannot conceive of the towering vistas I have witnessed through my moonlight meditations upon metaphysical rapture atop Mount Aron by Long Bight!"

"These are not germane to my knowledge," stated Pezla peevishly.

Sakoon purpled. "To study the infinities of Zon would be a better alternative to your bawdy prattling, sir! and it is to these everlasting harmonies that I calmly redirect your attention."

"A conceited hope!" growled Pezla. "Zon seems more an abstract pressboard in the field of ephemerals and the vapours of conjectural existence than any."

"Untrue!" an excited undermonk cried who had come running up to the Hierophant's defence. A white claw-hand clutched a coil of prayer beads. "Zon is everything! And nothing —and all gamuts in between!"

"A convenient generalization," Pezla wheezed. "What of Kron, Boton and Plopon? Are these not enviable deities in the important admixture of metaphysical pseudology that defines the modern age?"

Sakoon did not dignify the comment. He raked helplessly at his circlet. Sputtering a dismayed cry, he gathered up his followers and implored Pezla to calm his outbursts, but the minstrel had long since abandoned any idea of logical discourse.

Sakoon held up his sacred nonagram in an attempt to exorcise Pezla's intractability but Pezla bypassed the charm with a resounding guffaw. The monks of Serat crowded about him, rattling their snapple rings and beaded nets, warning him to take refuge in Zon's blessedness.

Pezla was far too clever for such charades, and escaped the trap, laughing in glee. Skipping about in wide circles, he sounded obnoxious little diapasons on his instrument, tweaking the zealots' ears which they covered with consternation. After several rounds of concertina bumping and grinding, he did a pirouette; his coxcomb went flapping, then he lapsed into another bawdy flight that had the monks mooning about in mortification, pitching pebbles.

Valere did not wish to be party to such commotion and turned and stalked away. Clambering up on the driver's seat, he drove smartly out of sight.

XV

About three furlongs up the road, Valere stopped to pick up an old woman and her two nieces who had earlier been in attendance at the water hole. The maids wore bowl caps and yellow knee socks and clutched satchels of hand-knit caftans. The matron was wrapped in a maroon cloak and a felt burnoose.

It was good cover; Baus secretly nodded his approval. Helping the three up front, Valere relegated Baus and Poli to places in the back under the tarp and Uella was compelled back to her halters, much to her chagrin.

"It is a very kind gesture, sir!" announced the matron gladly.

Valere waved a courteous hand. "My daughter, Uella, as you see, is hardly incommoded. As for our nag, Nellie, well, she is a stout beast if there is any. She shall not mind the extra haulage—not to be critical in any way."

The woman dismissed Valere's fear with a polite laugh.

Nellie would beg to differ and Uella no less. The road swerved and banked and they left the folk straggling behind at the watering hole.

A vast salt bog stretched opposite the sea; now low sand dunes spread seaward dotted with white quince, blocking sight of the grumbling water. Baobab and swamp olive were in plenitude. Dim, huddling shapes of jackdaws flapped and cawed in the depths of the quagmire, while crests of sand drifted over the road in portions causing minor inconvenience.

The matron chattered on through her crooked teeth and gabbed on about the unforgiving countryside, the terrible tilling, the knitting she had to finish, her cousins, her nephews and various other bucolic bothers. "Ah, Paot is a poor town for an old woman such as me; the countryside is nothing but a scrub land, a ghost territory of what it used to be! When I was a lass how times were kinder! Wealth now trickles to Sloe's maw. She is like a suckerfish! How the culture, architecture and history becomes forgotten. Like our old traditions, our fanes, our legends—as the Sea Walkers which only an elder like me remembers . . ."

"A sad scenario," agreed Valere. "I was unaware of the legend." His response was pre-empted—for three golden-haired geldings bore down upon their wain with fabulous fury.

Valere gripped the reins, reached for his sword. The mailed riders fled on—a patrol likely from Quelion.

Valere saw a square-jawed captain—a slim Squand, riding in his stirrups, with steely eyes drawn out somewhere ahead. Others of the cavalcade held dull helms angled on arrogant tilts. But seeing the woman and the youths, the storm thundered by without hiccup, and Valere congratulated himself for his foresight in picking up the old woman.

Unscathed, the company arrived at Paot, which proved to be a small hovel. Crooked, puddled paths led from the market to the nearly empty stalls. A huddle of huts offered no port and very little of the rustic antiquity of Alcax. Valere bid the women good day; likewise she wished them all well and gave them a wistful smile, perhaps wishing to be part of the entourage.

* * *

The time was about mid afternoon. Baus and Poli were fully awake, staring about the brooding landscapes with dim apathy. All felt somewhat humbled by the sights around them: rugged cypress, haunting headlands, bare outcrops, dipping cliffs falling to sheer drops over jade-foamy water.

Besides that there existed somewhat of a distance between them and Sloe's main garrison. Valere allowed Sansix to ride up in front. The thief made no display of what he had suffered so far, beaten and strapped under the wagon. Uella and Solstress were perhaps no less disgruntled to have to remain below-wagons, enduring the endlessly rolling wheels and thick fumes of dust, but at least they had the rude bandannas to protect them from their heaves of nausea. Yet the lack of padding to their bosoms was becoming tiring, and Baus sagely counselled them that it was folly to have them back up in the cart and discovered by any patrol that may happen to trundle by, of which there seemed to be no uncommon number.

The leagues passed—for the most, lonely ones. Seaward, patches of cypress showed, and the travellers caught glimpses of battered ruins, pillars, breakwaters, remnants of bygone days when great kingdoms ruled. Ragged blackhorn sheep roamed the steppes shepherdless amongst the ubiquitous pegmatite statues; elsewhere curious rhodochrosite blocks and sawtooth slabs loomed against the leaden sky. All expressed a delicate fragility that was both tender and moving. Alone on a hill overlooking the sea's waves stood an old trio of columns, wistfully blackened and deprived of any magnificence of paintings, or contoured roofs that were long collapsed. A flock of guillemots soared over the nearby cliffs and met the sea in a headlong rush.

Windmills and vine-covered fanes appeared and disappeared; stone villas and tumbled manors came and went, so too, crumbling cupolas and cenotaphs, columns, memorials and obelisks. It was a graveyard of stone, which struck marvel and melancholy in everyone's hearts. Over the course of the lonely miles, one such monument stuck out in Baus's memory, a raised bust sporting a knowing face mantled by an arched ring of red rodomite. A tribute to Skalkor—so Sansix reported—the legendary explorer and adventurer of Sloe who had set the first woven flag on Slaen hill and crossed the rugged Aldevean mountains and founded the kingdom of Karsh long ago.

The old road switched at times from plain dirt to wagon ruts of ill repute, finally to a fine pave-stoned highway, ancient and pitched straight and wide with deep, masterfully-lain octagonal flags. These, Sansix proudly attributed to the original blocks of the 'Trae-way' built by the Tuskon clan of mythic Fraesia. "They were a race of master craftsmen! Even before the time of King Keolin and Coyrus of Sloe."

Valere mocked Sansix's adulation. "No such race ever existed. The granite roads were well established before any mythos was propagated. All the ancient monuments and ruins were crafted by scattered clans with penchants for stone and lithics and whose greatest skills were tall imaginations."

Sansix gave an indifferent shrug. "So you say, seadog—if you're the expert." He turned to Baus. "What do you think?"

"The southern realms boast a rich and complex archaeology," Baus temporized, "which, fairly said, requires further analysis. I can make no further comment. Such is my wisdom."

Valere clapped Baus proudly on the back. "An admirable viewpoint, outlaw, never let yourself get pinned down."

* * *

So drifted the somniferous afternoon. Untoward effect was unfelt. The sea deepened to an azure and the fields became smaller and rockier as the hills became rounder and paler with their spoon-like shapes. The trees tended to maulwood, but some were more frequently stunted and pearly grey with gnarled limbs dragging low. They spied roe deer, wandering about the unkempt fields and meadows, like stray hounds, tanned bodies becoming hazy shadows in the thickets. Other times they spotted squint-eyed locals clearing the land of old stumps and rosebush, or a team of wegmors being whipped along to drag a boulder or two toward the fence line along with a large log.

Sansix bluntly asserted that Owlen lay no less than fifty leagues away, and that having bypassed Quelion, Fauche was still a league or more to go. All food, including buttered eels, rampwort and flatbread had been devoured long ago and all were hungry. Baus frowned at the circumstance. He kicked himself that he had not purchased more victual back at the last settlement. Again their stomachs growled and tempers were short.

By dinnertime, the sun was sinking in a haze of misty maulwoods. Golden bands cast up upon the glades. The company was ravenous; they were forced to stop at Fauche which itself proved a sizeable, busy town. Across from a baulked wharf, a patch of greenwood presented comforts, squat ollomberry shaded and freshened the interior with fountains of jets of water offsetting the industrial utility of warehouses and tool sheds lining themselves up the main road.

Four major arteries threaded their way back from the dusty intersection. Baus spied a glazed brick schoolhouse, a trading post, a two-storey inn, some market stalls and dingy loading platforms. Purple spires showed in the hazy distances, possibly a temple or two of some prolific ruin.

The town's deteriorating shipyard showed general dinginess too. At the north end of the town, a port lay just beyond a plain of dolmen-like boulders. Wind pressed from the sea, tugging at the sails of small ketches and sloops, yellow, white and red. A slew of dories, punts and luggers piled up in the waters, or were upturned amongst the rocks. A multitude of dockhands worked the pier, staining weathered hulls and setting new yards out to dry on logs. On the open sea, Baus caught a Sloeian galleon gracefully plying the emerald swells.

Valere halted under the shade of a baobab. A walled plaza was set brilliantly against a copper-coloured archway leading to various areas of the town. Sansix had assured them that the garrison was well west of here, that they would be safe. Baus was dubious of the thief's counsel. For the nonce he would have to take him on face favlue. A group of fieldworkers returned from their rocky pastures, hoes and rakes rattling on their backs. Weary and footsore they hoisted baskets of field radish, gingerroot, rutabaga and eggplant and under a shaded awning, a group of their wives fussed with a homespun wooden press, grinding olives to a thick paste to be drained into red ochre pots and amphorae. A variety of animals roamed about the square: goats, low-limbed marbacks, wegmors, all munching hay littering the plaza's brick flags.

Valere was craving for liquor. He was not faring well at hiding the fact either. While Baus was off looking for sturdy fare to eat, the brawny seaman went lumbering off to glut his need, which could only be fulfilled at the local alehouses or bordellos along the main boulevard. Poli and Sansix stayed behind to guard the wagon and see that the women remained safely cached below.

Alone with Sansix, Poli seemed to sense a rare insidiousness in the thief's countenance. With beady eyes roving with vengeance, Sansix plotted his mischief. A long due requital was seething in his pores; he was soon swinging into action. While Baus had been dozing in the olive grove, Sansix had used his special skills to acquire his ganglestick, a theft of which Baus was still ignorant.

Creeping unpleasantly up behind the blond bully, the thief jabbed the wand into his neck. Poli stood stunned senseless, hunched like a crone, causing some amusement amongst the bystanders.

Sansix was not at all interested in the result of his play. He skipped down under the cart, probing Solstress with indelicate purpose. He hurtled down the plaza with her valuables, shouldering the townsfolk aside after he had gained the purse. Baus returned to the square only chancing to spy the weasel scurrying away past the oil presses and beasts, stifling jubilation. He rushed to intercept the thief.

Sansix, sensing nothing to lose, augmented his haste. He forced his feet through the crowd.

Then he halted. Jumping up, he jabbed with the baton, threatening Baus's wrath, but the weapon was in a flux and seemed only to stun under a cloud of its own caprice.

Baus lunged like a viper. He snatched the villain in between his arms and the two struggled like bears, rolling across the paves with Baus exercising a maximum of choke holding from which Sansix could little escape.

The outlaw ripped the wand from the conniver's grasp. Sansix gnashed and fumed, but his scheme was foiled and he lay slumped down in apathetic defeat. Baus dragged him back to the wagon and upbraided his luck. He slapped Sansix with merciless energy. Kicking Poli back to life, he rallied the seaman to help fling the thief back into the back of the wagon.

Almost immediately a red-faced bravo came strutting up, threatening the outlaws with a crooked hoe, "Here now, you bullies," he cried, "what's all this fuss about? If there's any roughing up to do, it'll be done by me! I'm Ionset, chief of this here crop-layers' guild!" The man's face was sketched with an angry brown and his brown buskins and dirt-stained tunic matched his breeches which were dun-coloured from toil.

Baus drew Lolispar in an ugly flash and the villager staggered back, striking out with his hoe but Poli caught the implement on his halberd, and grinned.

The lout tottered. He drew his breath with indecision and seemed spooked by the sudden unwavering precision of the seasoned foes. He lunged haltingly. Poli snapped the weapon out of his grasp and muttered meaningful threats. He had the offender slinking away in a humble-toed strut.

Ducking under the wagon, Baus returned Solstress her pouch and peered around with Poli. Both were appalled at the undue attention they had created. A gang of the fieldworkers gathered and spoke in hushed murmurs, casting forbidding glances at the outlaws.

Baus danced sourly from foot to foot; he berated Poli's carelessness. He cursed Sansix's cupidity, which had started this whole affair. Valere's truancy was of no lesser fault and he looked about with rancour for the seaman, but he saw no sign.

Baus was about to pack up and go, but then demurred. Valere would be an indispensable adjunct in the days ahead—but what to do? A familiar anxiety came over his body. There was the redbeard now, striding carelessly up without hat or grease shielding his beard or hair. A shoulder was braced with a moderate wineskin, the other a keg of spirit.

Baus pulled the seaman's greasy hat out of his pocket and slapped it on his head.

Valere tried to brush off the gesture with a chuckling rejoinder but Baus was in no mood for camaraderie.

"Where have you been?" he remarked huskily.

"A pub, where else?—the *Peddler's Rest*, if you want to know."

"It was a reckless venture!" Baus hissed. "Do you know how easy it would be for the queen's emissaries to find you? You were lucky."

Valere gave an offhand shrug. "Maybe. But a man cannot live on smoked eel alone, Baus —besides the ale they sell in these marketplaces—Listen, I'm sorry if these two guppies gave you trouble, but—" he pointed irritably at Poli and Sansix "—I learned several things back in the pub: the Sloeians are up in arms about the princess's disappearance and Arnin's botch-job has earned him many demerit points. Now to redeem himself, the prince has added another fifty gold pieces to anyone who brings in our heads alive. Fancy that! Maena's up in arms; she's put an unheard of trophy on all our heads and the safe return of her daughter. The town's out for blood—it amazes me! The townsfolk won't suspect a meek old carter, by the name of Varlor."

With pained care, Baus explained the obvious fallacy of the seaman's argument. "Do you think the lackwits back at that pub won't figure it out? A stranger from out of town, garbed in greasy garb and carrying a barrel of ale and posing as 'Varlor'. What do you think? This bodes ill for us, dolt! With Sansix's treachery and our cover blown, we're in a heap of trouble."

"Ah, I wouldn't be such a worrywart."

Sansix objected to the vilification: "My only motive to your 'treachery', Baus, was to safeguard your baton in the event that it was seized. As it was by me. Am I remiss in this beneficence? I shall relegate myself to whatever fate Krutu has in store for me!"

"Shut your maw, you two-faced grifter!" called Poli, slapping him in the mouth. He pointed meaningfully to the harbour. "The yellow-bellied schooner over there looks promising. Sound enough for us to sail away at a moment's notice."

"We have discarded any such an idea of seafaring," reminded Baus.

"Says who? If we cannot hire a boat, let us commandeer one! What are we—a bunch of day lilies? We used to be the most infamous buccaneer band in the Poesasian! Now we are skulking vagabonds." Poli's voice had risen to a boastful frustration.

Solstress would hear nothing of it. She called up in a loud voice. "Forget the plan. Let's move on."

"The plan stands," grunted Valere. He rolled eyes to the sky. "Let us keep to the north—and on land."

"Agreed—" but Poli threw up hands in exasperation.

Baus brushed the plaza with another suspicious gaze. On a wooden bench off to the side lounged a thin man with a disturbing, vulture-like face. He was in cahoots with the red-nosed lout with the hoe, for they seemed to be scrutinizing the wagon with sinister interest.

The former redneck, catching Baus's scrutiny, was on his feet in a flash, beetling under an archway by a team of marbacks and scampering back off to the heart of the town.

Baus grimaced. He did not like the look of the motion. Such a character would betray them in a trice. Well—he trusted this pulsing figure of knavery less than Sansix himself. Ah well! Nothing to be done. Back into the wagon . . .

The outlaws jostled off in a clattering cloud. Down the northward cobbles they flew, under the archway.

XVI

The road veered inland. The sea was a dull roar. The light was fading fast and the tree shadows were long and sombre and the proud blue streamers stretched across the lazy fields of bronze and gold like ribbons. A rustwater stream purled alongside the roadway and here Valere halted the caravan in hope of striking up a camp before night could catch them.

From the stream's hither bank rose a loom of dark trees flecked with purple and amber boughs in the sun's dying glare.

They had not progressed a league when certain indications suggested that their place of repose was not the wisest chosen. Flanking them from behind was a motley crew of rednecks and bravos, mounted on steeds and on foot, brandishing mattocks, pitchforks and rakes. They were no less than blood-hungry and a mere hundred paces away.

Seeing their quarry so easily outnumbered, the mob was on the edge of an unrehearsed attack. They forged their way on buskined feet like bulls. The mounted men heeled their beasts. Baus and Valere now stood helpless, rooted by the wagon, feeling agonizing chills creeping up their spines. Poli crouched low, readied for attack. The women remained strapped under the wagon, oblivious to the threat.

More unsettling was the sight of the four gaunt cavalrymen riding in from the side behind the throng. The Squands seemed to not be part of the ranks of the mob. They thundered through.

Baus grimaced; he thought to see the same men who had ridden past them earlier from Paot.

Baus unsheathed Lolispar and reeled in, struck with the tragic significance of the misfortune. How had the riders doubled back and stumbled upon them so inopportunely?

A peasant with a black beard cried out a bawdy challenge atop his black marback. "Fifty gold crowns, mates! Get the traitors there! He who brings the buccaneers to their knees, dead or alive is the one who claims the reward!"

The mob's rumbling grew to a fearful crescendo. Baus's limbs sagged. Forward the enemies coursed, eager to massacre the caravan's members and bring the outlaws to their knees.

Baus, Valere and Poli steeled themselves for attack. They gripped their weapons, braced their feet, but were smacked back by the sudden surge of a vanguard, helpless to defend themselves.

A quailing squeal suddenly alerted the attackers to persons cached underneath the wagon.

There was no time to rescue the women. The villagers overturned the vehicle and were uttering whistles and cat calls at the pure joy of their discovery. Uella and Solstress were plucked from the straps, gripped like eels. Baus and Valere struggled to get to the women but were instantly flung back by ham-handed peasants. The women struggled, kicked and scratched at a dozen dirty hands that groped for them, but they were hoisted over their heads like trophies.

The women lofted horrified screams in the air. Baus watched in dismay. Uella was carted aloft by rude labourers, then just as quickly, Solstress.

The four horsemen came reining in, pulling the women to safety with amazing suddenness. They dragged them up and away from the growling mob and several ploughmen tried to take back their prizes but were rewarded with shafts of steel through the gullets. To the mob's further anger, the crew was mowed down by flying hooves and the peasants shrank back with snarls on their lips, turning their attention to the outnumbered outlaws.

On swift feet, Baus, Poli and Valere scrambled down the stream's slope. The marbacks would have a hard time charging at them at a full speed here.

The outlaws formed a tight bow, backs facing the water. The villagers raced gleefully after them and proceeded to lustily beat down their ranks. Sansix owed his present company no allegiance and was ready to run, but a crude understanding crept over his cunning visage: his own head was lopped if he rushed off on a solo venture. He squirmed like an errant fool into the huddle and Valere flung him a rapier which he snatched up eagerly. Baring the weapon, the thief slashed and tore with his good right hand. Poli backslashed his halberd, pedalling up to deliver a meaty stab on a cockerel who rushed impulsively close. Poli danced back into formation with the assassin staggering back gripping a bloody belly. Baus goaded others into committing errors. The brash, blood-gurgling rush continued.

Despite the exhaustion, Sansix hacked and parried. His thin rapier cut bloody ribbons of a bumpkin—one who had no inkling how to fight.

The back end of a hoe caught Valere smartly in the ear. He was maddened and grabbed his assailant by the shoulder, and shoved his own cutlass through his ear, spilling blood on the turf. The seaman's crazy shout hovered above the din. Clashing blades and the cursing din of fighting, dying men raged everywhere.

A stave aimed at Valere's head flew wide.

Baus's save had deflected its bounty. The sea captain caught a mattock with the edge of his cutlass and flung the mattock aside to chip off his charge's upraised hand in a jet of gore. Baus jumped in earnest, avoiding a singing quarterstaff aimed at his knees. He lunged, digging Lolispar talon-deep into his attacker's chest. The oaf howled, fell to the turf, clutching a punctured lung.

Despite the depressing numbers of the dying, the mob pressed on. They snarled, spat, spun curses and jabs of weapons, lunged and hacked, and the reek of their grog-ridden breath was appalling; yet closer they struggled, and more it became obvious to them that the companions' hopes of remaining on their feet were short-lived. A peasant sensed the opportunity and sought to overpower the outlaws by sheer force, but lay in a pool of his own blood when Baus gutted him.

"Across the stream! Into the forest!"

None of the party needed prompting. Across the water the fighters drove: first Valere, then Poli, followed by Baus and Sansix at their heels. Once across the turbid froth, the outlaws swung a desperate arc up the weedy slope and into the forest. A reckless posse was hard on their heels, splashing waist-deep in the water, but others hesitated, daunted at the sight of the ruin of a half dozen of their comrades sprawled askew in the grass.

Fourteen of the lynch mob remained. Ten hardy souls took flight after the outlaws into the forest.

The riders stood by the roadside. They did not rage after the townsfolk like their impetuous allies, but watched from afar, like silent, calculating wraiths. Two of the company held Solstress and Uella in check. They gripped the women like trussed swine and spoke words to them of imperial nature. Though the captives struggled with all their strength, they were cowed to silence.

Through cracks in the cypress, Baus caught despairing glimpses of the women—captives of the same horsemen who cantered back down the road and disappeared into the afternoon's dwindling shadows. Baus knew the outcome of the silent retreat. The women would be forced back to Sloe; the princess, her gold, and her winsome maid would be the trophies returned.

A variety of emotions clutched Baus: emptiness, hollowness, sheer despair, sentiments of acute desolation. Grief and frustration overcame him like a pall.

True, he had not known Solstress for long or Uella, but he could not wonder that his seed was inside both of them—and that their fates were inextricably linked. Fondness and remorse erupted in a single surge of fury, particularly for the stunning Solstress who was to be used as a pawn in the hands of the wheedling nobility like the dandyish Clavius or some fop in a lifetime of patriarchal servitude.

The idea was so repugnant that Baus felt a whimper catch in his throat. A swell of new fury sliced him almost sick with rebelliousness. The emotions were too poignant to stand— no less were they futile and he steeled himself to the matter at hand. His duty was to vanquish the immediate foes: aye, to stay alive! Whirling around with blood-maddened wrath, he turned to face the remaining apple-knockers who stumbled blindly after him, through leaf mould and dead leaves, itching for a share of gold.

Sir 'Red Nose'—the bravo from the plaza—was first to die. With one gruesome slice, Baus disembowelled the hoe-wielding brute from crotch to sternum.

Shivering from the expiry, Baus gathered his compatriots. He bid them to take up hiding places in the forest. The woodland was of tissel and maulwoods, and here, enough dark cover lingered amongst the few sunlit gaps to provide proper resources for an ambush. Moss and fallen logs became ideal places. A trained, ruthless fighter could hide behind such clumps and leap upon the back of an aggressor and rain down a dozen bloody blows before the attacker knew what hit him. It was with such remorselessness that Baus and his peers took up their plight: wreaking ghoulish havoc and macabre vengeance, stabbing, slashing, pitting and carving.

Ambush and slaughter! What grisly work! The three staved in skulls as if they were pumpkins.

Resistance ebbed. Poli cried out as two more fell to their knees amongst clumps of yellow bogwort. They gurgled out death rattles from carefully slit throats. Sansix was almost spitted in two by a three-pronged pitchfork, but was saved at the last instant by Baus's gladius, hamstringing the perpetrator.

Two foes remained. The terrified weasels bolted back to the mounts across the stream. Baus and Valere harried them all the way.

The last vigilantes took up the best mounts, and with the handful of other cowards refused to enter the bush. They fled pell-mell back to Fauche, licking their wounds and howling back at the buccaneers. There was no sign of the mounted cavaliers. They were gone.

Baus expressed untold dissatisfaction. The women were taken. All that was left of the mounts were a few dusty nags and two-toothed wegmors. He flung out his sword in disgust. "How dare they? How the day has gone foul!"

"The animals are useless to us," Valere raged. "Slow and unreliable. We can no more take them to the open roads as run after Uella and Solstress on bare feet."

Poli stared back at the forest. A countenance of sorrow showed in the dying sun. Blood dripped from his open cheek, also a connecting scalp wound. "Let us be away from this cursed glade then." The battle lust dimmed from his eyes; his fist slowly unfurled from its tight knot. "I'm sorry, Baus. We did not heed your advice and quit this road when we should."

"What is done is done," Baus growled. A harsh shadow had stained his expression but not masked the sorrow writ there. "At least we are alive, and together."

"Let us remain that way," grumbled Valere. "Other reprobates'll be searching us out before long. They'll fill their paws full of warm gold if they have the chance."

The wolf's-heads agreed; they wiped blood from their weapons and rescued what food remained of their stash before standing hunched by the broken wain, contemplating their options.

There were not many.

Baus deemed the ale keg too heavy to carry. They drained whatever of it they could, knowing that little of that would come in the days ahead.

Valere released Nellie's tethers; he let the faithful beast wander across the road into the gilt field away from the toppled vehicle. They too crept back into the forest, now a glum, cool and misty fastness, permeated with dolour and watchfulness.

Night was approaching. Farling's wall was closer than they thought—and nothing that they could ever imagine . . .

They steeled themselves for the grim hike ahead.

REDEEMER

BOOK III

CHAPTER 1

MISMERION

"Mismerion, o Mismerion!
Why do you weep?
In days of battle,
You were once stronghold of the West,
Graced with a thousand lanterns and royal banners,
But then you became a den of sorcerers,
A place of shadows and sly experiments . . .
O Mismerion!
How the people of the forest pine for your elegant halls!
Your fabulous regalia, your festive pageants,
Your ambience of old!"

—Poet and Lyric-weaver, Pezla of Loust.

I

Invested with wondrous powers of flight, Ulisa the Utilitarian, shape-shifter and neomancer of Mismerion, floated on powder-puff wings of white gossamer. Her firefly form rose through the mossy cracks of limb and bramble on through the night, drifting silently through woodlands and copses each wilder than the last. In such guise she fled, with a faint luminescence emanating from her thorax, displaying her a clear path. Over fern and brimbleberry her miniature wings carried her—over trickling creek and bubbling bog, away from the urgent eyes of sinister things, away from the prison walls of Heagram Yard and the hoarse cries of the Heagram constabulary.

A bleak feeling clutched her thorax. Aurimag, her nemesis, was fast fading from her innate radar. How could she locate her sworn enemy?

The woods were thinning. At the edge of a hollow she caught the restless outline of a familiar figure: a little green-cloaked dwarf with thoughtful but suspicious eyes. The figure had a distinguished nose, a small round chin, a peaked, white-feathered cap. Leaves were stuck on his cloak; his head, a thin mat of beige curls, was curiously regal. He was not miniature for natural reasons—he had been shrunken to knee-high height by the same Aurimag for reasons of vengeance. The figure sat a-sprawl in a bed of humus aside a fallen log. He was snapping fingers to a sour tune, cursing his unfavourable luck. He was a nobleman and seemed to be in the vilest of humour, debating whether or not he should quit his journey or tramp deeper into the gloomy forest.

Ulisa blinked. She gave her head a luminous twitch. Slowly, she began to descend. She effervesced back to her original form as a golden-haired woman. She was about to speak, but was only two feet high (shrunken too—in similar fashion by the rebel neomancer Aurimag), and was still surrounded by her pale yellow nimbus. A luxurious figure she struck, garbed in her purple silken robe with swallow-feather belt. Her clear eyes shone with the radiance of most innocent daring, defying any quality of guile or malice. Quartz earrings shimmered in her ears; the moonlight flung glints of luminescence on her lustrous golden tresses falling slantwise on her finely-contoured shoulders.

The little man leaped abreast. "What luck!—or what clever trick?—I spy a lovely face in all this muck!" He paused to assess his visitor with appreciation and surprise.

"Trimestrius!" cried Ulisa with joyous accord. "I would offer you the same term 'dashing' in view of 'lovely', but the moment has passed." She gave a polite curtsy.

The nobleman responded with a gallant bow. "A kindly thing to say, Lady, yet I am not worthy of your company. I fear we are not liberated, though we may be out of Aurimag's cursed jars. Wretched midgets we are, but lost children in the woods we remain."

The Utilitarian sighed. "Better than suspended in brine, Trimestrius."

The nobleman embarked on a bit of grumbling and chin-wagging. "Well, did you discover the whereabouts of our black-hearted tormentor then?"

Ulisa hunched her head with sorrow. "No, Aurimag has departed—on his magic airborne conveyance, with our peers Woisper and Salmeister. They too, are entombed in some ghastly liquid not dissimilar to our own."

Trimestrius compressed his lips. "Dirty, very dirty! The scoundrel has always been something of a blackguard to us—and having a way of disappearing at the last minute." He lifted a finger high. "What of the fishmonger who plunged me back in my jar when the moon shone high in the prison yard? The rogue is nothing more than a lank-haired weasel."

Ulisa offered Trimestrius a sidewise stare. "That would be Baus—a very resourceful fellow."

"A resourceful fellow—you think so?—what of the word 'scapegrace'? I have bones to pick with this person."

Ulisa spoke in a very reproving manner. "Remember, Trimestrius, you have this saviour to thank for your freedom."

Trimestrius choked on the word and his whole frame shook with outrage. "To me he is a dog, like Aurimag. No more than a thieving, backbiting vagabond who stole my blade Lolispar, and as I recall, offended my honour. The mannerisms of this oaf are insufferable, like that of a common ale steward. The acquisition of my blade has no doubt something to do with his miraculous fortune . . ." The midget turned seething eyes upon the wood. "Well, I shall take no rest until I avenge myself upon this cullion and reclaim my talisman!"

"No doubt you shall," Ulisa murmured the words with some doubt and she gripped the little man's wrist and gave it a meaningful twist. "But first you must learn to cope with the circumstance. For now, Baus is our ally. Let us return to our respective castles to the south. We shall gather wits and courage to rally the other neomancers of our order. The sum of our numbers will be the ones to confront this bully Aurimag!"

Trimestrius's face congested with a clot of amused mockery. "Gather wits, you say? My keep Desenion is cold. What is more, I am puny and destitute."

Ulisa stamped her foot. "Even if this is true, you must refrain from negativistic thinking. You must perform this bidding of mine without question. To extend spite upon Aurimag at this time in haste is folly. You shall jeopardize our mission. Now—our hope lies in aligning our might against the traitor single-mindedly."

Trimestrius's lips pinched in a sulky pout and he projected a thin ironic leer. "I have seen what this 'might' has accomplished, Ulisa. Nothing. It left Aurimag so bereft of dignity that he rose up against us and committed terrible things upon our persons."

The shape-shifter soothed the woodsman's qualms. "I can only stress, Trimestrius," she said with a little smile, "that we must strictly avoid *mistakes* of the past."

Trimestrius scoffed. Shaking head in dour fashion, he set his cap on a jaunty angle. "I suppose we must act as dignified as possible."

"We must," Ulisa averred. "Now, we are forced to travel to Mismerion and summon the council. You cannot keep up with me you who have no wings; therefore, I urge you to hasten to Desenion directly and await me there."

Trimestrius was crestfallen. "Your ideas are fatiguing. I don't even know where I am."

"You are far north of Drasla, near the seaport called Heagram. You must fare south—to Owlen—then to Aurenham and finally Loust and Desenion. 'Tis your home."

Trimestrius's eyes burned with frustration. "I know 'tis my home, but 'tis a huge distance! What will people think when they see a puny man striding down the leafy lanes?—'*Here now, come see the pithy homunculus with his green cap and merry walking stick. Let us sneak up on him and give him a little pinch!*'"

"That's a paranoid and sardonic attitude to take," scoffed Ulisa.

"A real one, though."

Ulisa had no more to say. The nobleman had no choice but to lope away, tipping his cap rather ungentlemanly and ducking under a mossy log. He was gone into the gloom of the night, knowing as well as anyone, that 'twas folly to argue with the shape-shifter.

The hollow of weeping thickets was peaceful again and Ulisa the Utilitarian lifted her hands high in the air and uttered a strange sibilance. She shimmered out of ordinary sight and into the ether of her shape-shifting magic. She receded, only to assume the form of a yellow-backed hummingbird. She flew up, high . . . bending into the night, out of the hollow to dip gracefully to the darker bands of forests.

How exhilarating it was to be free of the ground! She soared, she swooped, like some glorious denizen of the air. Over lakes, moonlit meres, trickling streams and purling creeks . . . she hummed and buzzed, swept through forest and fen, and dales and woodland.

The spell-weaver thought many thoughts; she concocted many plans. She was a natural initiator amongst her brethren of the magic-wielders at

Mismerion and now that she was freed from the tyranny of Aurimag, she felt an uncommon urge to make amends for the wrongs he had committed.

The neomancer's trail was cold. To where the villain had fled was anybody's guess.

She projected her powers of clairvoyance upon his form. But her inner sight glimpsed only murkiness—a twisted, swirling void, around which spiralled the faintest, almost corrupted corona. It was as if the rascal's destiny were not to be read—as if the sorcerer had blocked his passage intentionally by some unscrupulous means.

Ulisa frowned, felt her heart sagging . . . she flew on. She grew clearer in her conviction. Her waxy wings were near translucent, but as the days turned into nights, her wings at the point of aching, she switched from one favoured bird to another. First, a hummingbird—then a chickadee of soft brown feathers, then to a firefly of night's pride, of such lurid brilliance as to pave the way in the thick night air and the dusky shroud of forest. Her transformations alleviated any weariness and strain on her wings—it cast light only when she needed it. The birds of the night were her friends— mostly . . . the magpies, the finches, the rock doves, the dabchicks, the starlings, the swallows. But more carnal were the thrush, who spied her advance and brewed malevolent schemes from atop their crooked twitch-oak and phantom elm branches. On the second night out of Brimhaven, she had been sighted by a particularly hideous thrush that had flown down from its goblinish perch and in a trice it gobbled her whole . . . But at once the bird suffered a ghastly spasm which had caused it to regurgitate her whole body. She burrowed into a hole to hide.

Sickened, she remained ever vigilant of airborne marauders. Yet large cornflower wasps were her next concern . . .

The little firefly meandered her way through warm breezes. Her halcyon thoughts drifted to the fisherman Baus. Despite her mixed impressions of him, she faltered in mid-flight. The thought of the lanky youth and his unassuming confidence flashed like a brand in her mind. The fearless way in which he had provided aid at a time when 'twas needed, still made an impression on her. True, the youth had called out to her in Heagram's yard and alerted her to the danger of Aurimag's floating form nearby . . . and yet? He was but a rogue, a common outlaw, a chronic young opportunist, if not a strikingly handsome one, and a gallant one in some vainglorious way. But he was also a resource of utility, which she must admit could be made use of—

an enterprising fellow such as he was a gift, despite Trimestrius's foul opinion of him.

Could the fisherman be the one holding the balance of power of the fate of the neomancers?

Unlikely!

But yet not impossible . . . And here Ulisa brooded. Baus's skill in foiling Aurimag's powers had proven formidable. The scales had turned—despite the outlaw's desperate odds, and yet he had managed to prevail under the most harrowing circumstances.

The thought was both comforting and disturbing. Ulisa considered the fragility of the Neomancer Circle and was forced to accept that, faced with an enemy as unsavoury as Aurimag, it was prudent to guard oneself against these menaces of high order.

She flew over the nearby wood-trestled bridge which carried a team of villagers and a wegmor-driven caravan. The neomancer gave them wide berth, for companies of this sort were a danger to her. Well across the river, she impressed her clairvoyant power upon the presence of the outlaw Baus's physical form.

Her attention melded onto his past and future, onto his current motions of mind. There she let her imagination rove, become one with her filmy visions of second sight.

The projection faded into mists, mists of the future . . .

Her clairvoyant powers allowed her to swirl and ebb in reverie like surf on sand. She felt her mind's eye drift, then motes like transparent sparkles fled before her eyes. Then, as suddenly, she cognized all sorts of blackguards and thieves, rogues and pirates and plunderers. She wrinkled her nose in distaste. A trio of sailing ships surfaced. They were huge craft and bewildering. All were skull-ridden vessels, floundering on a leaden sea. A blue palace suddenly materialized, sumptuous and opulent beyond imagining, then a raven-haired princess—stormy and passionate, both at once. Dusty roads and rickety signs and many fatal flights, passed in profusion, followed by fury, sharp words, death! All materialized like shadowy snatches of dream memory upon her mental plate . . .

She staggered in her glide. Somehow none of these visions seemed real! She inferred all these images contained a canny synopsis of the outlaw's life —knowledge that her destiny and those of the neomancers were twined with the fisherman—though it was ludicrously presumptuous.

Late in the evening, Ulisa felt a darkness crowd over her. The lands were sinking in twilight. She floated down on her diaphanous wings and crossed a black rill that gleamed softly in the starshine. She settled on a cluster of drooping hollyhocks and began sipping gladly of the night dew with her firefly lips. Corncockles, daisies and cloudberries—all trembled to gentle winds. How she wished to regain her self as a real woman! To take lithe steps, not those of some ensorcelled pygmy. But—the prospect was not in her power. She was vexed, a fated wretch, if not a shape-shifter whose power was hedged by unknowable forces. She gave an exasperated shudder. By means unknown, Aurimag the neomancer had caused the enchantment of shrinking via his 'Charm of Miniaturization'. The spell permeated the nexus of her aura and swept around her body. Adept at the arts of transformation, she could normally countervail such magic and send corpuscles streaming through her body, but here, alas, there had been a complex twist developed in the spell, creating a barrier against her ability to deflect. But, if she could liberate the neomancer Woisper, perhaps the two of them might nullify the effect of the spell . . .

'Twas a wistful hope.

As for Salmeister the Saturnine, the sallow-faced comrade of Woisper, he could wait a year or more for his liberation. She remembered all too well how the watery-eyed, paunchy conjurer had tried to trick her into one of Mismerion's gardens two summers ago, seduce her with his flaring-cubes and blazing Alpion torch. He had desired esoteric knowledge, withal, a whisper under the breath of unnatural healing practices and forbidden spellcraft. Wisely she had kept them hidden from him even while under duress.

She felt her wings jarred back to reality. A soft rustling in the reeds warned her of a visitor. She floated, suspended like a pod in air, two inches up from her flower pod to stare across the river. Only a tense, moonlit blackness lay in waiting.

A sudden movement caught her eye. At the edge of the clearing a shape appeared . . .

She flew up instantly and away, her tiny wings aching with the effort. Wariness dispelled danger—with delight she beheld an exceptional thing of beauty. 'Twas a rare unicorn, a coral-coloured and regal creature, poised at the clearing's brink: one of those graceful stray beasts wandered from the wolds west of the Shadehue mountains. A single voluted horn protruded from its crown. The horn sparkled, both coral and gold and the creature's back and long mane were crusted silver and pink. Ruddy strands of silken hair ran down its slender legs.

The creature moved without haste—its tail swished as it ambled with an elegant ease that defined the enchanted things from an elder time.

The mystery of the beast fascinated her. How she loved creatures of this kind! She altered back to her female form and stepped out of the mist, whistling a graceful tune beyond audible range.

The creature did not immediately sense the music but then perked up its ears. 'Twas full of timid wonder now, and without fear treaded closer through the mist and dew to stand towering over her like a silver bastion limned with fairy light. She struggled to understand the reason for the creature's presence. Here, so far away in lands remote. The light continued to glimmer between snatches of switchwillows and ghost-dondar. Adept with animals of the forest, Ulisa led the creature to the water's cool edge and fed it grasses and scented cones of aromatic juniper. She gazed into its azure eyes, when she sensed the creature dip a horn in a way that she could grab hold of it. It tossed her aloft, and there she fell straddling its mane which glistened brilliantly under the moonlight. Off into the night the creature thundered, while she rode her messenger, clasping its neck like a wild jockey and the mist swirled about her legs and the beast's flanks. Secret instructions she gave to the steed—to seek out the hallowed halls of Mismerion!

For the most part, unicorn and neomancer rode untamed—they traversed untrodden paths, dense copses and gloomy niches, giving the roads wide berth. Residences and smoke rings were seen through the trees. To ford a river meant to cross a bridge and pass near a human habitation. The villagers of Toulasibar of that smoke-hazed hamlet, were no exception to this rule and were brightly intrigued at the sight of this rare unicorn deep in Drasla! The forest was no place for a child-rider cantering along the banks of the Ul river! Eagerly, they sought means to capture the rare beast, which was surely an auspicious prize. But the unicorn was too savvy for such ploys and far too swift to allow any such herder's lasso or arrow to snare it.

Ulisa and her new ally struck through the mukklewood trees far past Toulasibar. The rider was wise enough to know that there would be no kingdoms in Drasla—only thatch-roofed hamlets in long corridors of silent jade and a thousand unseen textures. The whisper of lore lay etched in the ages of her mossy trunks. Her majestic boughs told secrets never to be told.

Two days of solid riding had the unicorn feeding at the brink of the confluence of two sluggish rivers, the Lim and the Ul that framed a grassy vale. Shape-shifter and steed glistened from a recent light rain. Ulisa urged her mount on through several dripping arbours to pause at the site of a half hidden view where looming crenellations stood. Wondrous Mismerion! Disposed in a hundred shades of grey, rose-amber and ultramarine, the castle rose, resolute and tall: a sprawling mass of shell-inlaid domes, mushroom-topped towers and spires, dipping and leaping parapets and ancient stone. The nearest village, a league away was old Mismerion, strategically placed across the Ul river. The local wood-landers gave the castle respectful berth —also its queer inhabitants who were a mixture of conjurers and oddballs. To them, the neomancer jinxes[*] were rarely humorous or healthy; more often than not they were highly life-inhibitory. (Footnote: [*]Jinx: Spell, enchantment, rigour or blight. The most commonly known imposition by invocation, or the flux of a magic riddle.)

Ulisa's heart skipped a beat. She approached the castle's barbican. Caution tempered her steps, for it had been a long time since she had last resided at the castle. She saw the mortared sea shells which defined its crown. It lay unmanned—a tattered black banner rippled restlessly in the wind which stirred a nostalgia and unease in the shape-shifter . . .

Two huge iron ravens cawed raucously, mounted on either gatepost.

She winked thrice at the larger bird. The grand creature gave her a candid glare, then after her one gracious salute, the door creaked magically ajar—so were the opening signals effected.

Ulisa approached with ginger heed; rusty hinges groaning as the unicorn nudged its way between the grates and plodded its way up the central aisle. Its steps were tentative. Rows of ragged junipers lay to either side, and verily the unicorn seemed a small toy in a great court, with hooves fashioning dull echoes about the cold grey stone.

The unicorn halted; it looked astutely this way and that. The creature was a knowledgeable one and Ulisa honoured its shrewdness. The high double doors of the ancient keep loomed old and weary before her and it was all she could do to hold her breath. The shadow of Mancer Hall loomed a stone's throw away . . .

442

Redeemer

She dismounted and stood appraising the castle's portal with reservation. All was silent. Soft clay-coloured shadows played on the flagstones and about the massive courtyard. On its fringes stood a ring of seven towers— basalt and marmor, toadstool in shape, eccentric in formation. Three constituted the most antique structures on the grounds. Each commanded their own presence—flagstoned terraces, weathered statues, figurines, pools and shrubbery much populated with growth and debris, ungroomed for many seasons. Ulisa was dismayed. Several of the effigies were left unwashed, streaked with dirty grey. There was a coolness here about present-day Mismerion that she did not like. It was insufferable that the flagstones were damp, cracked with weeds. A cold wind gripped the air. Here, a loneliness and despair clutched her heart, in a place she had last known as prisoner in one of Aurimag's stifling bottles.

Shivering, Ulisa reached up and extended a hand of gratitude to the unicorn. The creature bowed its head with ancient respect as it remained slightly bent on its knees. It shook its glistening mane and gave a buoyant whinny and was off, into the mists on swift hooves, racing through the gates and around the earthworks to disappear in a flash into the green forests of Mismerion.

Ulisa stared up at the antique portal before her. Weathered pallid blue pilasters enclosed the façade.

She reached for the woodcock and saw an odd iron-shaped handle. But intuition had her pausing with reflection. Such was the way of common louts seeking access to the gilded doors of Mismerion!

She gave the one secret signal—'twas a complex flourish known only to the eldest neomancers.

From inside the entranceway came a strange musical note. Dull echoes trilled on stone. A long period elapsed, then the haunting sound of chimes which seemed to drift through the lonely court on wings, but suddenly a small oaken panel slid open and an old man popped out an eye—a figure bald save for a brown ruff of looping curls twined around his ears. Squinting in the fading light, he scratched at his pate. Doubt gripped his grizzled face which he turned to surprise when he heard Ulisa's familiar sniff of disdain. He gave a joyous cry when he recognized who it was standing below:

"Ulisa? You have come back from the dead! But you are no higher than a mastiff!"

"Indeed, I am, Dious," she muttered Ulisa. "Grant me entrance to Mismerion before I fetch my death of cold!"

Dious apologized; immediately he ushered his colleague into the vestibule. He studied her new stature with an expression of astonishment, then he gave a formal bow. Here was a man of debonair airs, exquisite punctilio, and a small spark of charm. In the foremost corridor lanterns hung heavily on iron chains and infused the hall with rich melancholy. Shadows played everywhere. An ermine rug covered the fore-chamber. Walls of glossy stone surrounded all sides, blue and mauve. The presence of lost grandeur and antiquity hung indelibly in the air. The chamber was stuffy, like a crypt and yet exuded an ambience of neglect.

Ulisa saw that the only two members who remained in residence were Dious and Helaar, philosopher and historian. Dious, the chief steward, was master of records while Helaar was keeper of the old library and the resident chronicler. He was a man of no great stature with widely-spaced eyes, with small hands and an ornate set of spectacles. His face was pinched; rather pallid looking—and one known to exhibit a facetious acerbity. He shuffled forth to greet Ulisa, though without undue enthusiasm. He was dressed in a customary grey-brown singlet and seemed to exhibit as much surprise as Dious at the presence of their guest. Both men gave Ulisa queer looks. They were men of books and letters and would never stray far from the castle. The library and the sanctitude of high-vaulting studies were sacrosanct. Apparently both men had grown accustomed to their diminutive roles as stewards, yet each had once been an affluent-practicing magician. Imprinted in their auras was a bustling, officious industry, to say the least, which had, for the most part, kept Mismerion's halls alive and clear of rodents and clutter, also wandering vandals who would hanker to rifle the place.

Ulisa skipped by Dious and marched along down the high hall. 'Twas a corridor of polished marmor so familiar to her memory, yet so melancholy in its memory. With craned-neck, the shape-shifter eagerly marvelled at the vastness of the hall. 'Twas as if she hadn't been away for a day! The place was like a giant auditorium—the neomancers would conduct their group jinxes here and conduct oratories with great effect.

At the hall's end rose a lofty granite archway which towered above both windows and lanterns. It was inscribed with proud Lengish script:

'Mancer hall, circa 453, home to the multifarious masteries

of the wise and worthy!"

In the wall behind was fixed a six-foot high astrolabe. On the central disc swivelled a series of needles pointing to arcane Lengish mnemonics.

The establishment was just as Ulisa had left it—time-worn, antique and pitched with a procession of fluted pillars that rose to soft, gloomy heights. Mismerion's alcoves were grand, her apses elegant. Ancient were her walkways and austere her inner courts. In the arched recesses lurked several formal galleries and gloomy wings. Long narrow casements peered down from high amongst rows of carved gargoyles and scrolled lanterns, casting pale beams on her mosaic flags with insignias of drakes and flashes of lightning of power and fantasy. A few of the lanterns had burned low—it had the effect of setting the hall in an unearthly hue of mothy, earthy tone. Added layers of dust, and a few newfound bats clung on high . . .

In the uncomfortable gloom, Dious and Helaar set themselves stiffly on ornate pews. They recalled the old times when the neomancers were a happier crew and several pleasant interchanges took place. But the three did not seem to relax their restless moods.

Ulisa told them of how Trimestrius had fallen afoul of Aurimag, how he too was encased in a jar of brine. Aurimag's plan had backfired and Trimestrius had escaped by a hair, thanks to a certain mysterious outlaw's tampering with the jar. In fact, the nobleman was on his way this moment to Desenion and awaited Ulisa there. "Nevertheless, Aurimag is at large," exclaimed Ulisa, "and now he must be set to task!"

"Alas, some happy news at least!" murmured Dious sonorously. "Fie, but our might has waned!" He shook his head gravely. "'Twas to be expected when Woisper, our Hierarch went missing. You and Aurimag had vanished too and we knew not where to find you. Salmeister had also been mysteriously snatched. We lost hope. Our once-mighty Circle became corrupted, infected by greed and ideals of power!" The steward's voice trailed off, becoming an echo fading in the lingering shadows.

Helaar took up the tale: "What Dious means to says is that from a purely historical point of view, events remain consistent with the Arch-Neon's own record. We all bickered and quarrelled and fought like factious courtiers in a hall of wolves. We proposed divergent plans and conflicting schemes, and imposed penalties for those who would not comply with our dictates. Ultimately, we were split part, polarized by the schisms of our own design.

We were swept under the wing of ambition, and many of our more dissentient members were tempted by the propaganda of Barbirius the Bellicose."

"Barbirius! What happened to that lout and what would he trumpet so loudly?" demanded Ulisa.

"Much! He revelled in talk about starting a *new* clique—in the mountains of Nderian, in his Mansion of War," came Helaar's dry reply. "Others retreated to their own domains, to cogitate and dwell—Aksila, Roso the Recluse, Slaene the Sardonist, Diophenes the Dour."

Ulisa ingested the news with dismay. "This is completely upsetting! What inspired such nonsense? Mismerion is our home! What has Barbirius gone and done?"

Dious shook his head dully.

"Where is my niece, Adelyheim the healer?" Ulisa cried. "And what of Bithuma the Pragmatist? –And my friend and confidant, Alvius the Alchemist?"

Dious murmured in gentle tones: "The latter have departed. Scattered to regions remote, I gather. Perhaps if you were to find Adelyheim, or even Maitor, they would lead you to Bithuma."

Ulisa forced back a sorrowful sigh. "I shall sally forth and seek these colleagues! The most brittle quarry of them all is first on the list— Barbirius!"

Helaar's voice rose in warning. "Perhaps, Ulisa, but you would think twice about the mission. Barbirius is fey. And what of Moto the Motivator and Palono the Philologist? Are you forgetting these worthy souls?"

Ulisa waved a brisk hand. "I will leave the task to you."

Helaar gave a disheartened croak. "Never! I shall not tread from Mismerion. Persons on your list could be anywhere in the realm—from Drasla to Karsh!"

"Perhaps—but gentlemen, I bid your leave! Not to mention, your leg bars my way, Helaar, please lift it."

The historian grunted. "As you like!" He moved out of the way, rising with a chill grace.

Ulisa departed to her chambers, her lips murmuring as she climbed the ancient stairs: "*Apathetic lumps. Tomorrow is to be a new day . . .*"

Redeemer

II

It had taken Aurimag the neomancer, aka Nuzbek the magician, rather longer than he expected to reach Thresbane, his lair. The trials had been rough, the distances expansive. Losses entailed two of his precious charges, Ulisa and Trimestrius, who had been wakened of their spell from his magic jars and passed out of his clutches.

Now the magician stood before his Imine-reflector[*] in his Cave of Passions and Puissances at the edge of the Brauvn forest. Thresbane was seven leagues from Desenion and the glass before him emitted a rudimentary glow. Bathed in an eerie light, the magician took on an even more macabre cast. The grotto, hollowed out through ages of erosion, was an enclave of dankness visited with little surprises or sounds, but was otherwise a safe haven. The burrow sported five caverns—tailored individually with the help of elm-sprites and hop-loblins. The magician could move from section to section, ponder his fortunes, chant, dreamwalk, chime out arpeggios, meditate, drone on his dopek, practice his woodcock imitations, read aloud of the Lengish scripts, apply himself to cogent work or study . . . he was in a salutary environment! Anything he wanted was at his fingertips. Such was his privilege. (Footnote: [*]Imine-reflector: Once an antique possession of the Arch-Neon, Guaski, the mirror had come into Aurimag's possession in a game of chance pitted between himself and two drunken relic traders, who caroused at Loust's famous, *Green Bull Tavern*. The 'mirror', if such name could be applied, was purportedly possessed of singular ability to transfer the power of youth and revivification. Those looking upon its magical expanse beheld his own image and were graced with the power of youth, but as of yet, Aurimag had not yet penetrated its mystical secrets. The failure thus ignited his frustration and desire to curb his own rapid aging. The Neons were the precursors to the modern day 'neomancers', a breed of magickers who later appended the suffix 'mancer' to their titles, which indicated 'manipulators'.)

Aurimag assessed his thin bony figure. The reflection did not appease his image of himself. In fact, it showed a certain inimical contempt. His moon cowl, unadorned and ruffled, replaced his black magician's cap of a previous life. A villainish moodiness was etched in the hooded, unblinking eyes. The neomancer's cheeks were shrunken, scornful pockets, only accentuating the upthrust lip which twitched from time to time and revealed a lofty jowl, teeth to chin. Aurimag's purple caftan fell down over his black breeches, lustreless and threadbare. His face, normally fuller, was now pallid from lack of light, cooped up in his cave. His crown, supporting a high, back-sloping forehead, was weighed down with a fringe goatee, now a freak wisp of mouse grey and rat brown. Black brows crowned oily amber eyes, which emphasized a peculair, owlish disdain. He was curiously possessed of an economy of motion, like some parrot or marionette. High ankle boots graced long feet, remarkable only for their pale green tassels that were sewn from toe to shank.

Disliking his current situation, the magician shifted from toe to toe. He remained greatly aged over the past moons. The transformation was mirrored by the thinning hair and its speckled grey cast as a result of brooding stress. He was holed up in his domain like a vole. He was the first to admit to personal failure.

For an unknown period, Aurimag gazed into the pale serpentine glass. He could not help but wonder how the escape of his precious charges had left him stunned, defying all form of reason.

Retribution and revenge! That is what he would have! Now, his enemies would repay him for their transgression. First, the scattered spell-casters of the Synode; then, the new irritants who had added themselves to his list of reprobates. Weavil, of course, was one of these irritants, who under his authority, presently shrunken to the size of a centauro, stared out from his home of glass. The poet would make a pleasant new addition to his collection. But of Baus?—the conniving, egotistical rascal? There was an exceptional balance of retribution to be extracted upon him, the source of his pain, who had caused him much grief, especially at the prison ward.

The magician applied his thumb—to an enigmatic, scarlet ermine-coated rod strapped at his waist.

The reaction was automatic. An orange puff of vapour instantly gusted out from the ferrule and engulfed him in cloud of smog. He sucked in the intoxicating airs, inhaling them like an addict would. After a time, he gazed about somewhat glassily.

Aurimag's sigh was of palpable relief as he discharged a cough and snuffed in another gust.

The flood of soporific assailed him; instantly he stumbled backward, relaxed, feeling almost whole, as his fingers trembled, releasing their hawk-like grip on his rod. The malt-gas fumes were a form of hypnotiate which he used frequently to soothe his jangled nerves.

Aurimag's lips parted in a cryptic smile. Somewhat assuaged, he slapped his knees with sinister relish. One of his particular recreations included narcosomatics—the branch of somno-therapy, which, during the course of his hibernation from Mismerion, had brought him the solace he required to stay focused on the important tasks ahead.

He recalled events since Heagram prison. Escaping the yard, he had flown airborne with his accomplice Nolpin and the three captives, Salmeister, Woisper and Weavil on his makeshift device. They had flown over the Ulbone forest, drifting over russet treetops and making steady progress toward Sliss, a mining town of small repute on the river Rhuon. The conveyance had more or less petered out, not far from Hoarwich, a village even less memorable than Viseldown. The source of the umbrella's magic, the 'glow pyramid', had been depleted as a result of grievous attacks at the prison—a memory which still rankled on his nerves. The demise of Boulm, his assistant, had been tragic, yet not overly calamitous. New minions could always be hired. The troublemakers—Ulisa and Trimestrius —posed more of a threat and would be dealt with soon enough. Already he had instituted preparations through some rudimentary divination which had provided him knowledge that his enemies would march to his lair to confront him. How opportune! The shape-shifter had always been foolhardy and much against him, ever since he had quit her moralizing tutelage at castle Mismerion. She had done nothing to help him at the time he was so vulnerable against the heavy-handed persecutions of the Mismerion neomancers. And Trimestrius was nothing more than a grandiose pretender, a Desenion spy, posing as an occasional messenger and a hobbyist merchant peddling some odd spice or rare somatic gathered from the woods or faraway lands. The nobleman had scouted out his cave only for the purposes of tattling his secrets to the hated Circle.

Aurimag recalled recent grievances—of being stranded in the dankness of certain fens, while his uncooperative assistant, Nolpin, had refused to carry Salmeister and called him, a 'keeper of creepshow entities'. What insolence! The remark had urged Aurimag to discharge the 'Spell of Hot Feet', which had the lout dancing on his toes. The spell and warning had failed, insofar as further insults by Nolpin had galled Aurimag into dashing him with three pinches of Gusmaye's ghost powder, a magical elixir that caused Nolpin's face to bulge a ghastly green, then he had sprouted ears like a rabbit's. Aurimag had laughed, and off into the woods Nolpin had fled shrieking like a hound.

Aurimag pursed lips. Freed of Nolpin's pompous predilections, he had addressed the manner of cargo transportation with that silent inward inquiry of a notary. There were three bulky canisters. How could one man move three? Southward, Aurimag had plodded for less than a day before resolving the quandary. With ease and proficiency the magician had passed the remainder of leagues with the help of a new hireling—a deaf lack-wit, Jaymar, whom he had coaxed from the nearby village of Loamere by means of hypnotic suggestion.

Along the feet of the Crown mountains the two had trudged with the jars containing Salmeister and Woisper, over the green swales of Aranhale, through the rocky gulches of Glist, the wild copses and glades, crossing dazzling fords of the enchanted Rhuon River and through the sombre forests of Drasla and the Ul. Mishaps had been few, the weather tolerable. Few villagers dwelled in these parts, and here Aurimag had been forced to hunt small game by means of magical conjuration. He created sparkles that beguiled, and snares that snapped. Sections of the Ul and Drasla had proven gloomy—a source of inconvenience. Aurimag had inscribed a Three Hex-Sigil in the soil around the campsite which had shielded him and his ward from the lust of night prowlers. By luck and craft, the two had survived. The unbroken fastness of Drasla continued, and ever across the banks of the Ul River, they finally stood, peering past stony terraces, and the fallen gates of Mismerion. Acting on impulse, Aurimag had crouched to brood, agonizing over the familiar surroundings, the ghost of feelings of injustice shrouding . His mind engulfed in fervid concentration, he stood not far from the Ul's umber water, peering at the grey, haunted castle—a thing of massive masonry and awesome configuration. A large part of him wished to penetrate the ancient keep and send its dwellers into swirling oblivion!

But no . . . His powers were debilitated. Failure in such a mission was high. Biting back his frustration, he had plodded onward.

Nearing his cave overlooking the south banks of the Lim, he had ordered the mute to discharge his cargo. The servant, hypnotized, was instructed to forget everything he had seen and done, and was despatched back to his kin. A risk—of course, Aurimag realized. The simpleton might tell of his servitude, but Aurimag had thought the dullard incapable of betrayal and he laughed . . . laughing further at the prospect of administering a dose of Gusmaye's powder. ''Twould be an overly heavy-handed gesture. Without light or sustenance the mute would either starve or perish in the dark. Food to the jowls of night prowlers . . .

Aurimag had not always been so heartless. Once he had been a well-disciplined, eager pupil, apprenticed years before to Ulisa and Woisper. Being somewhat benevolent of inclination, the aspiring acolyte had done their bidding, yet naively full of artlessness. The grimoires, the finicky spells, each pulsing node of light . . . the inter-dimensional marvels took on sparks of their own significance! They had impinged their sense of mystery and marvel on his mind. Over the course of several years, he had come to understand the sense of the nature of things through his unorthodox schooling. The inherent truth of illusion versus the reality of manifestation was a somewhat humbling realization—particularly, the hypocrisies of Mismerion's own instructors and their vain grasp of the basic tenets of good and evil. Aurimag's own mouth curved in a sardonic leer. Coupled with the disappointments of his own experience, the unsatisfying spell-wielding, and the toilings and the useless experiments of his tutors and peers—all had broken some fragile cord in him... driven him upon this path of subversion.

Finally he had confronted Woisper the Hierarch himself while applying for entry into the Synode. Llonon the Illusionist had been his rival for the single new opening as 'junior neomancer' at Mancer Hall. While his summoned demon had raised a fuss and the display of his new sorcery was a little over the top, he had unanimously been voted down. True, the demon had committed untold damage to the hall's pillars and had almost killed Onzo. Likewise, his numerous insults upon the senior members of the Circle had been a trifle excessive, but what to say for a little expressive licence? Bah! It was all one. The act had incited Woisper to fling him into the dungeon, with the help of several allies. The trials endured at the behest of those rude people . . . they had tied the knot of hate and revenge in Aurimag's soul, and twisted every bit of morality out of him. Mercurial glimpses flashed across his mind—the indelicate prodding of Woisper's gastro-calipers, Salmeister's cryptic leers and hyena-like howls while he launched charm after charm on his person . . . Barbirius's cruel gropings to the accompaniment of crass incantations in the gloom . . . his own half-lucid tumult while he lay pinned helplessly upon Woisper's traction board. These scenes he remembered, too well . . . and his own powers lying stripped, bared. Here was a newborn cub, offered to the gods as an unjust sacrifice . . .

All came to him in his darkest memory. Then the image was gone—the past left in a flurry of searing scars.

Only the yellow-fumed hypnotiate allowed Aurimag a brief repose from his hate for the Mismerion Circle.

Incompetence! Insolence! He vented a curse. His enemies would pay! Once his magic had been formidable—a dozen spells committed to memory which could blast a tower to bits—now he was relegated to a few tawdry illusions, dull deceptions of ordinary prestidigitator's magic—a few tricks, powders, shabby potions, and one single, singular spell of miniaturization. Everywhere he looked about him he seemed surrounded by imbeciles and thwarted by hypocrites and lummoxes!

Aurimag tore himself away from the mirror. He marched darkly to the vestuary, standing before his prized cache of possessions. All were intact, including three magic viols from Gargimest, a magical pottery set, a book of old poems, twenty odd riddles from ancient Desenion, a twain of antique vats, a handful of tortoiseshells, vials of calcx-syrup, a hypnotiate pot . . . all stashed in a dank cranny on the right-facing wall.

The magician's mouth moved in a disturbing leer. Sitting isolated from the pottery reposed the brine-filled encasements of Salmeister and Woisper, and Weavil—indeed, his most famed treasures. To ensure that these deviants would entertain no 'surprise' escapes, he had replaced the ancient glass seals with omonium adhesives and set latches upon their lids. He landed an impudent kick upon Woisper's jug and the brown-faced geriatric experienced a sense of vertigo. The canister rolled away, bashing against the wall.

The magician gave an affectionate laugh: Woisper seemed not appreciative of his moments of discomfort. The Hierarch's lips moved in the flows of magical brine, with a rhythm of no small consternation.

Amusement at its drollest! Aurimag made a point of conducting some ancillary research into how a black-toothed suckerfish could be injected into Woisper's liquid matrix. Such a creature would comprise a joke of novelty. As for the yellow-bellied Salmeister, a miniaturized leprolizard or a blue schasm[*] of the most inquisitive variety would constitute a worthy addition to the mix. Such a creature befitted his old comrade. It would keep the geezer's wits sharp. As for Barbirius, the barbaric oaf of a warmonger who had

452

participated in his tortures, he had proven a quarry too elusive for capturing and so had evaded his net—but doom was on its way for the warmonger . . . (Footnote: *Schasm: An underwater predatory anemone.)

Aurimag's feet echoed about the cave's stony walls. Polished white marmor stretched everywhere. The rock was smooth as bone, polished by ages of rushing water.

The magician ducked his frame between twin rows of crystallized stalactites in the Mantle Room. Many ornaments hung there—crystal gongs, amethysts, cabochons—all reflecting the carmine colours of the many candelabra hanging from vine and cord. Brackish pools lurked in the periphery, mirroring eerie light. On waters quivering to the thrusts of submerged creatures, ghostly shapes reflected—stalactites, black crevices, hanging moss. Aurimag thought this a pleasing place for his labours.

In a distant pool, ripples broke over the smooth surface.

Aurimag smiled. 'Twas a froglike creature that leaped. Soon after, a red-striped serpent lunged with three, fanged tentacles. A flicking yellow tongue shot out to swallow the smaller prey.

Aurimag gave a soft chuckle. The frolic was another source of his amusement. He strode purposefully into the Bronze Hall where a few dozen ancient shields and bucklers hung. Bronze plates and plaques were bordered with brass filigrees. Blood globes and similar, luminary devices bathed the rich confines of the cavern in mid-tone colour. On the southern wall hung a collection of silver emblems and golden horns. The horns trumpeted forth magical notes of their own accord while spelling warnings or advance indications of psychic invasion—a necessary adjunct in times of trouble. The doctrine of the Arch-Neons spoke of the many psychic energies of brass, gold, bronze and silver as being indispensable for warding off creatures of nth order* malice—'spitfires', 'spirit probes', 'bright-crakes', 'fulomones' and other such lesser demonitia, to be specific. (Footnote: *N^{th} order and its various modifications, N+1, N-1, N+2, N-2, refer to a classification of finite subspaces from the tangible to the intangible to the hypo-probable. The reference, taken from a treatise on 'n^{th} order' entities and phenomena, describes the classification below: "'N^{th} order' alludes to the soulless, less soluble spirit world, including ghosts, changelings, chameleons, poltergeists, sprites, woolly-woolies and other phantasmagorical existences; $N+1^{th}$ order includes the realm of angels and demons; N+2, currently unknown, is in need of further study. At the other end of the spectrum, $N\text{-}1^{th}$ order refers to the gross manifestation of existence and its neutral containing field. $N\text{-}2^{th}$ is at a level lower still, subhuman in nature and deals with those forces of lower volition including primal motility, basic amorality and ingestion. Examples of such creatures of $N\text{-}2^{th}$ order are igomorphs, valules, leprolizards, and protoleeches." So it has been written by Zasist, Arch-Neon, 531 years deceased.)

The thought left Aurimag somewhat hollow. His sacred chamber was known only to a few and remained impervious to intrusions of mischief and to many persons who had known of his existence prior and had perished in various unpleasant ways, burning in boiling pits, scorched in oily rain, deadly conflagrations, or pitched into roiling chasms of nth order oblivion.

Aurimag sported a pinched mouth. Access was forbidden to his cave, granted only to himself by means of a steep descent at the northern edge of the Brauvn forest, over which the gnarled roots of a single phantom elm leaned. A triune of boulders marked the entrance to his cave which was cleverly concealed—a dark hole, blacker than black, guarded by a brotherhood of forbidding elm-sprites held in check by an invisible, but not insignificant spell. Below, the river Lim cut its placid course where the forest spread its phalanx of jade, russet and sable.

Aurimag reflected on his defences. Upon breasting the workchamber, he slowed his pace, but he felt something gnawing at the edges of his comfort. Many questions remained spinning in his mind: who would suffer the most for his implacable outrages—Woisper? Salmeister? Perhaps the arrogant Weavil?—The magic-less stripling had, after all, sought to disrupt his essentially basic, if not flawed plan to secure anonymity in assuming the role of a travelling magician.

The arguments ran long in Aurimag's mind. To the forefront came the poet Weavil . . .

The neomancer harrumphed. To recall how the little pest had galled him so long time ago at Heagram fair! The act was risible. What unflattering times those were! How he had assumed the role of the 'Magician Nuzbek' so naively and ingenuously and sought to raise funds to finance his campaign against the Circle. 'Twas almost comical. Gulled by Marb the Maug, a peripatetic soothsayer, he had been convinced that upon hearing the auger's psychic readings he, Aurimag, would travel 'far distances with small entourages' and 'reclaim a sense of old power and wisdom'. Folly! "You shall take on a new name, Aurimag!" came the soothsayer's voice. "A name of choice to go with your luck, to singular places and manifest substantial deeds! This is destiny of reverence and much bespeaking honour and dignity!"

Marb had advised him in an ingratiating tone of promise.

What mummery! A sneer escaped Aurimag's teeth. Still, he could not judge Marb unfairly for his effrontery—his own inculcation by the soothsayer's dogma was only to blame. Marb had laid claim to the Jade of Masleria, a symbol of accomplishment, and Aurimag, at the time a wretch struggling at an absolute nadir in his life, had been compelled to believe any yarn to boost his self esteem. Bereft of his powers and reduced to a wandering vagabond, he had been duped by a flimflammer, for a patch of foot ointment, the last of his healing possessions, in exchange for the enlightenment of Marb!

Folly! But not all had been unfavourable. He had visited many exotic locales and discovered several interesting local customs, and made significant cils, even enjoyed some private pranks at the expense of certain lack-witted bystanders while called upon as volunteers for his thaumaturgical lampoons...

Aurimag gave a soft chortle. But not nearly enough to merit the energy expended given his misfortunes—or enough convivial female companionship to merit the rigours he had endured . . .

Fists clenched into balls, Aurimag vowed to recuperate these energies and devise superior strategies! Litanies and programs would flow in rivers! —Enemies would be vanquished in maximum manners!

As for the other meddler, Baus—many vengeful schemes played themselves. A swarm of Hunter bees? A spell of purulence? A sudden thrust into an inescapable maze? Aurimag chortled. An audience with the mad death demon, Varial? No, all too lenient, if not anticlimactic for the fisherman. Perhaps the creation of a sinister golem as an ultimate agent of destruction?

Aurimag paused. He tapped his brow with interest. He felt a tingle of inspiration. A fine plan!—a savage sprite, so to speak, properly crafted and conditioned—it would fetch the fisherman here, and he might then inflict a certain long overdue punishment. Baus and Weavil, as a twain could entertain him in a small burlesque, or perhaps some cabaret on a puppet stage.

Aurimag drummed his fingers with growing exhilaration. Currently he maintained five mannequins. Lifeless hulks—but injected with a certain amount of animal magnetism, they could give him spectacle. The magician began to clap and laugh.

Bony fingers spun crazy patterns in the air. With eyes ablaze, he felt a tensile smirk spring across his pale lips.

Such emotion stirred, Aurimag gave himself to caprice. He arrived at a definite decision. To construct a golem. He descended the series of stone ledges to his workroom and in the central candle-lit gloom, spread puissant scrolls on his worktable. A massive brass crucible lay some five stalagmites down, framed by twin descending stalactites under which smouldered a glowering fire. Fumes from the crucible wafted high—invested with a heady steam to be swallowed in bird-like crevices where the gas escaped above. The cave glowed rose and amber under the fire's glimmer. Drakeish candles dripped thick wax and trailed cords heavy as rope. Embedded upon the far wall was a *Bitomoth*, a glass octagonal device, four feet tall and five wide. A bone-ringed compass sat on its face and bore significant magno-needles which switched on and off at various speeds. As for the purpose of the device, Aurimag was at a loss, convinced that its use lay somewhere between an agent of destruction and grief—such was writ in the annals by Narx the Nog-lodder, reputable Arch-Neon and necromancer of the 14th dynasty. The castle Mismerion would be a tempting target for the device!

Aurimag went to his workbench which was littered with scrolls, compendia and manuscripts, also a miscellany of bronze medallions. A puppet lay somewhat dissected with various moveable limbs and glowing bones, along with some small magical rotating imps and shape-shifting toys with elements of iridescent colours. Experimental pieces, thought Aurimag whimsically. Elsewhere stood an old loom, a bundle of wool, a crate of gyros, boxes, balls of wire, a hundred or so translucent shells, various potions, herbs, substances of weird organic nature . . .

The incandescence of the crucible remained potent. The heat wafted up to brush Aurimag's face and he squinted, grimacing. The heat was necessary in fending off the cloying dankness that would otherwise impair his sanctuary.

The magician swept closer to the crucible to better observe the condition of his brew. Smoking elixirs stirred: the mix exuded a scent of vile purpose. Stripped of its marmoric calcification, the floor had been loosely fitted with bull-rush mats. Other parts showed reddish clay and tar reeds. A trapdoor led to subterranean depths, very cramped and chill. Even he had not yet explored that tunnel for reason of frights and stenches.

A decade earlier—seemingly a lifetime ago—the catacombs of Thresbane had been carved by a team of hop-loblins contrived from a two-day-in-the-making spell he had wrought, a complicated and dangerous incantation.

He stoked the fire under his crucible and his teeth showed a white glint of relish. Twigs and bracken whispered underfoot. Quietly Aurimag hopped back over to his workbench—there to make the necessary preparations . . .

III

Dawn of the next morning arrived, heralding Ulisa flying west behind Mismerion on wings of a blue-bottletailed butterfly. She was rested and ready. Her destination: a secluded place in the misty uplands of Mys, where she would pass through the greenwood of Wayheal. Not long into her journey she spied the nearby foothills of Nderian, dull copper mounds draped with copses of velvet tissel and soon, a grey mansion appeared at the summit, of not insignificant proportion. The edifice was oval in shape, three-stories high and fixed with nine, onyx-glass pyramids. The structures seemed to reflect the thrust of daylight in a very gloomy way. War flags and emblems of every manner hung on the edges of the mansion's projections. Conic flares ranged the battlements, with sling-pults, javelin piercers, cannon bolts and stone bangers.

Ulisa let her wings relax. Over the outer palisade she flew, taking care not to brush her white wings against the pulsating ghost crystals set high at intervals along the parapets.

The shape-shifter reached the doorstep, metamorphosed back to her regular self. Before her a massive portal loomed, set between two eight-foot high hammers. The onyx was poised high like a bell, to strike at a carved anvil, comprising the portal's guardians.

Ulisa thought the architecture odd if not menacing. On tiptoe she crept out and reached to grip the brass knocker. But she found it lay four feet above the stony threshold on the scarred gnolewood portal which she couldn't quite reach. Chilled by the anvil's shadow, she fussed. Surprise hit her when a pair of half-ape, half-sylvan bellhops appeared at the door.

Ulisa stepped back in astonishment. The creatures granted her entrance to the mansion. Whether illusion or real, the neomancer was not sure.

Into a dim parlour she was conveyed, almost enthralled by the grandeur she witnessed—gigantic warrior statues of warlord heroes cached in and along the shadows about the far wall. She shivered in the gloom, for chill airs wafted through the old spaces and invested the statues with macabre possibilities. Amidst the quiet, antique stone depictions of battle, ranged from frenzied, iron-clad armies to single combats with human and animal foes. Racks of weapons adorned the walls: maces, daggers, sabres, axes and hammers. Closer to the salon's end hundreds more weapons hung—pikes, knouts, mauls, nets, toebusters and tridents.

Ulisa's porters ushered her into another hall. They wound up an ancient staircase into gloom. To the left a stairwell ran down to draughty depths—likely a basement.

The hall adjoining the corridor was enormous and Ulisa felt the little dwarf that she was. Weighty pillars ran up the central corridor into umber darkness. But that was not what struck her most. She was appalled to see two half-man, half-fish knights duelling to the death in a liquid tank. In another exposition, an angry horde of gnats, cordoned off by tinted glass, battled an army of locusts over a field of flaxhack. In a section barred off by iron pales ranged three pygmies battling to the death with knives and tridents. In an aqueous sub-enclosure swam a dozen blue hammerfish chomping on the fins of smaller creatures; elsewhere, humans fought against shades, knights against warriors, slaves against their masters, various reptiles and $n\text{-}1^{th}$ order entities against other unthinkable things . . .

Shuddering, she tripped to the exit, pushing her ushers out of the way. She was eager to get out of this place, this museum of horror, as fast as she could.

Yet the 'butlers' herded her to another chamber whose ceiling was lost in shadow and whose dusky walls were carved of black limestone. The hall seemed altogether too close for Ulisa's liking.

The shape-shifter trembled appalled. For here, she witnessed Barbirius himself and his coterie activating some sinister charm etched grimly on the floor. A set of transparent polyhedrons of unknown derivation rotated about two feet above many interleaved phosphorescent triangles that were carved in the floor. Disturbing faces of fanged beings swirled in the midsts. The shapes rotated, twirled, moved in strange orbits. Ulisa saw slab-sided cheeks, forked snouts, hooded eyes.

She loosed a gasp. Four light, onion-shaped lamps dangled from sets of corded beanstalks in the periphery. The room glowed in an eerie ambience and the strange beanstalk sported vines which themselves seemed to grow out of the floor to rise to the ceiling.

Of those in the cabal, five men participated in the ritual. Ulisa recognized Llonon the Lipreader, Pizor the Polemicist, Aanab the Anarchist. Two new members bore faces that she did not recognize.

Barbirius's eyes shone duskily in the half light, glowering like a fiend. He was dressed in a heavy iron helm, leather greaves and a menacing coat of bronze mail. The warmonger never ventured far without his enchanted adze which he seemed to clench at all times proprietarily in a fist. He was tall and known to scalp his enemies with such a tool. Llonon was at his side—lanky, fair-haired, handsome, a man of much younger years dressed in a beige swallowtail jacket and knee-high boots. Pizor was a dark-faced and spare man, bent over his triangles, impatient to insert a key or some device to open a trapdoor in the stone. Aanab, his counterpart, crouched gamely in the shadows, bobbing like some rankled gnome, rattling a handful of twenty-sided dice. Ulisa twitched in wonder. The wretch tossed them gleefully in the midst of the triangles. All eyes peered to discover the result. Ulisa saw the dice were carved of human bone, obviously invested with power to cast manipulations of chaos into the human universe upon each throw.

She could not repress a shiver. Aanab's bones rolled, creating harsh sounds in the air like rattlesnake tails. He wore a peasant's smock and clenched in his other hand an old gnarled cane. The dice assumed strange positions in upright postures—all amidst the arcane triangles, some near the keyhole where Pizor was fidgeting.

Aanab stuck his nose down to inspect the markings. "Ha, Barbirius! My domino varlets reign victorious over your six ghouls of oxblood!"

"Quell your vainglory, Aanab!" came Barbirius's rumbling cry. "This spells doom for my helpless harpy. But you must now wallow in my hexahedron's wrath! I laugh at your vile ghosts. I shall gall your lords of chaos with my minion, even as I toss my next hallowed runestones!" He hoofed Aanab's dice to oblivion and Aanab gave a squeal of outrage. The dice scattered in all directions. Aanab jacked about like a frog, jabbering nonsense and scrambling about the beanstalks to retrieve his devices of entropy.

Barbirius laughed, but disturbed by the evil display, Ulisa suspired a note of apprehension and unintentionally alerted the warmonger. He whirled, grunting. "Who is this little woodcock?" At first sight, he let his adze sag with an air of confusion. "Who let you in? My little ghosts?" he called. "I shall have to chastise them." He could only peer down in resentment; a furious frown flickered across his lips. "What is your business here, Utilitarian?" he demanded.

Ulisa spoke in a drawn voice: "I have been released from Aurimag's jar. I voyaged fortuitously league upon league to return to fabled Mismerion." She wasted not a breath to embark on a terse account of her mission and its purpose to recover the Hierarch Woisper and to spark action against Aurimag, their true enemy. She spoke in such earnest that the others seemed to stop to listen. But not for long and for a while the little shape-shifter began to feel immoderately foolish.

Aanab recovered the last of his precious dice and leapt forward with obvious contempt. "Hoy there, bird-fly! What care we of Woisper of Mismerion?"

"He is our Hierarch."

Barbirius gestured rudely. "What does that mean now? Woisper has passed on to the dogs. The jackal has proven himself incapable as a leader. Woisper the Wilful! Ha!" He spat. "Aurimag—and what is he, but a washed-up has-been—a scarecrow of a warlock? He is a misguided rebel and can rot. We stripped him of his powers long ago."

Ulisa gave her head a reproachful shake. "Not so, Barbirius. The wretch gathers puissance even as we speak. He plots malice and retribution against the Order. Have you not felt it? I have no doubt on the matter."

Aanab cawed like a hyena. "You are an overweening little busybody, you know that, Ulisa? Bah—the Circle is dead. It has no credence or standing here! Can you not accept it? The beginnings of new import are in order!"

Pizor affirmed Aanab's convictions. "Yes, Ulisa—the cycle ebbs; the neomancers are gone, the *automancers* begin a new club."

"Automancers? You are wrong!" Ulisa turned wildly to Llonon. "What's your opinion, Llonon? Do you believe all this? Or are you as steadfastly opposed as your peers?"

"My life is different now," the Lipreader admitted quietly. "The winds of change do not blow in the same directions. During my inauguration at Mismerion, I felt green, fanciful, disillusioned; now, wisdom has been imparted—though subtle and inscrutable."

Ulisa twitched. "Very pretty, Llonon." She felt a stab of dismay. "Your illusionist's flair has transferred itself to your tongue, I see." Llonon's grandiose tone had rankled her and she could not help but feel a bit betrayed. The admission of his doubt about the Circle only confirmed her conviction. Yet her lips sagged. A new quandary!—a man of such percipient intellect as

Llonon, gulled by the lofty mantras of Barbirius! What had Llonon given up to allow the warlord to inject him with such dogma? She could not guess. Llonon's too obvious complicity with the rogues had her shoulders slumping.

The warmonger's lips curled. "So, flowerfly! Even your pretty boy agrees with my judiciousness. A disclosure which pleases me!" He fluttered a hand. His new supporters grunted and he urged the rotating shapes at his shoulders to new intensities.

The objects glowed—pulsed. A sudden vibrant maliciousness seemed to overcome them. Without warning, each object spawned a creature of new horror—as if to instil some paralysis in the shape-shifter . . . First a three-horned bull, then a two-headed harpy, then an orange griffin with sucker-pocked limbs . . .

For a second, Ulisa caught her breath, then the images became blazing, rainbowish colours—cinnabar, serpentine, taupe. The sounds of distraught voices became audible, perhaps *languages*, perceived only in snatches or whispers.

Barbirius blazed to his full height. "See here! Behold, our new order! These are but a few of our new n^{th} order minions. Love them and worship them! They are creatures of the night, fantastic horrors of breadth and resource! Can you imagine anything more divine? They are capable warriors of the most wondrous evil!" From the war-master's lips came an otherworldly rasp. "Ah, and be apprised—they are not corporeal yet—just models. But, alas, soon will be . . ."

Ulisa quailed. She strove to back-pedal to the exit but found her way blocked by the 'ushers'.

Barbirius sensed her distress and gave a grim little chuckle. "Ah, your repugnance shows! Tsk. Do you wish to join us here at *Furnath*, my War Mansion or flee to your windworn Mismerion? Here you can lend aid to our manipulations? Decide now!"

"Never!" Ulisa felt a shudder of revulsion run up her spine. "The arts of the neomancers were never meant for evil, Barbirius."

The warlord guffawed, a low growl; he performed a saturnine jig. "So, our little angel-face has puritanical ideals! What else should I have designed from your fastidious habits? When great Sangdorn, our revered preceptor rendered you your title, he was certainly drunk: 'Ulisa the Utilitarian' should have been 'Ulisa the Hidebound' or 'Ulisa the Unartful'."

Ulisa ignored the insult. "On the contrary, your title was even less well, Barbirius, although I would have proposed 'Barbirius the Brainless' or 'Barbirius the Brutish'."

Barbirius gave her a coarse leer. "Ha! I applaud your rejoinders, Ulisa, as feeble as they are. Even I lay claim to 'the Brutish', having some ring to it— but if you will not come and join me, then begone! Never darken my doorsteps again with your puritanical dogma!"

"With all pleasure!" cried Ulisa haughtily. She turned to face the warmonger and the ushers parted and moved away. "But before I depart, let me ask you this—do you know where Maitor or Bithuma are?"

Barbirius raised his adze in fury. "Flee, little chit, before I send you a scourge! What care I of these feckless lackwits, or the others of such feeble capacity?"

Llonon called out in a clear voice, not as stubbornly set in his animosity toward the neomancers of the Circle. "Ulisa, scout out Marmere's meadow, and then Shadow Bay on Lake Loese. These are likely trails to Maitor, and Alvius. They were always fond of each other and were last seen here. Before you went missing, they were still confidantes."

"Thank you, Llonon," whispered Ulisa.

The disclosure brought Barbirius to rage. He chopped down with his adze, rending a great rift in the floor, and with a mouth rippling full of expletives, he launched a double-handed jinx upon the illusionist.

Llonon cognized the multivariates. He managed to deflect the full force of Barbirius's rigour before it was set in motion. Llonon's lip-reading[*] skill was legendary amongst the neomancers and being weakened only fractionally by the jinx, he countered with his quick and famous illusion— the 'One for All', a gigantic transparent bubble which floated up in such high blue horror as to engulf the seething Barbirius aloft. (Footnote: [*]Llonon was an accomplished lipreader as well as a talented illusionist. He had gained widespread popularity across the lands for his jocular applications of light, colour and auditory showmanship.)

Barbirius stumbled back on his heels. But he was inside the dome, so compelled by the illusion that he lost his grip on his adze.

The bubble pressed and moulded around him like glue, surrounding him with a filmy gauze. Blue jellyfish film engulfed his mailed frame. Now he plunged headlong through the mesh, amazed and helpless as a child. He huddled inside the film without his magic weapon—somewhat like a small bug caught in a spider's web.

The bubble lifted. The warmonger was lofted soaring up to the upper extents of the chamber and over the spinning polyhedrons. He banged fists and scratched nails against the filmy exterior—to no avail.

The neomancers marvelled at the feat and applauded Llonon. They looked up, choking in delight.

Lunges and heaves on Barbirius's part proved ineffective. His heavy frame bounced dutifully off his globe's walls. Suspended like a circus animal, he bumbled aimlessly from bubble wall to bubble wall at the behest of higher magics.

The neomancers voiced unique cheers and offered shouts of amusement and praise. Pizor even went so far as to cry out, 'Hoy, Barbirius, we never knew you were the circus type! Tally-ho!' and he added his own embellishment—of sending the three monsters growling below suddenly to float inside the bubble and offer their own bout of confusion. They at first annoyed Barbirius with their gusts, snorts, and stenches. But Barbirius spoke a single word and the images in the polyhedron burst apart in livid gouts of fire.

The bubble snapped like a toy, liquefying the exterior. Barbirius fell to the paves, landing on his feet, scooped up his adze and glared at the neomancers with a terrible vengeance. His nostrils heaved like a bull. All around, the empty polyhedrons floated about his shoulders, in baleful synchrony. Everyone stood to attention—no one dared breathe.

Ulisa gulped; carefully she exited the chamber.

She fled through the weapons' hall and pushed past the discomfiting porters to burst through the doors of the mansion. Up to the palisade she sped and looked back only in time to see flashes of ominous purple streaking from the windows. Demonic calls and cachinnations reverberated from the castle like cannon blasts. Thuds, booms and hisses whipped about the air like storms. Pizor attempted to escape through the garden window but was hauled back in by a great green hairy arm. Ulisa recognized the member as belonging to Barbirius's harpy. Almost as swiftly, a double-headed pterodactyl crashed out of the upper gallery and circled around the mansion before plunging back in through the window.

Obviously the members of Barbirius's 'cabal' had some working out to do before they would become true *automancers*.

Redeemer

Ulisa smoothed out her flushed face. She transmuted herself back to a hummingbird and took to the skies.

* * *

Recovering some of her dignity, Ulisa whished effortlessly along the shores of the Ul. Heading north toward Bayrune's forest, she found the water blue and brilliant. The breeze was fair which propelled her ever onward toward the brown boles of the Bayrune reaches.

The time was midday. All frights were forgotten. She was a carefree fairy creature in hummingbird form speeding over the green spanglemoss and the dried mukkle-cone. She flit here and there between airy gaps in the trees, finally to arrive at a large, pleasant glade full of birdsong and warm sunshine. A tall figure knelt knee-deep in the weeds. The person looked vaguely familiar and to her eye, a trifle older and sadder. Ulisa gave an endearing sigh. She changed back to her regular self just as the figure looked up and wiped her fingers on her coveralls. With surprise she staggered back from the garden herbs, brushed back her mop of daffodil curls and on skinny bare-shinned legs ran to her visitor, tripping with excitement. The two embraced—awkwardly, for Ulisa was only two feet high while Adelyheim, her niece, was several heads taller, strong and gangly and somewhat tomboyish. She clutched her in a strong grip. Ulisa looked up at the youth, who had tiny tears in the corners of her eyes. The healer was dressed in eccentric polka-dot coveralls, pink scarf and black leather boots. Her small round cottage stood at the glade's edge into which she conveyed her aunt. Over cups of mulberry tea, the two exchanged pleasantries. Long-in-waiting tales were rich, and somewhat overdue.

Adelyheim learned of her aunt's ordeal and she was aghast. She strode into the pantry, fetched herbs and roots, which she recommended her aunt drink instantly as a poignant tisane. Adelyheim liberally applied herbal salves to her limbs, hoping to combat her shrunken appearance, but Ulisa experienced no alteration in height. If anything, the little shape-shifter felt more nauseous and dwarfed.

Adelyheim expressed her bewilderment. "I feel that we must overlook our expectations and look to higher sources to reverse this foul enchantment. Aurimag has done his nastiest to you! The blight you suffer requires a magic greater than ours, Ulisa—possibly Woisper's. So far, my ministrations have been ineffective."

"Your efforts have been laudable, Adelyheim," asserted Ulisa soothingly. "Asters to oilflowers you've done your best! I must report this anomaly to the Circle, and then rally Alvius the Alchemist and Maitor the Moralist!"

The healer pinched her face into a frown. "I have heard of Maitor. He has been sighted near the lake and rumour spreads that he is trapped somewhere on the shores. Beware, Ulisa!—I fear a doom has befallen him. Fly farther, Ulisa—to Dol village. Learn of Bithuma. The Pragmatist has renounced her neomancers' vows—and teaches her own doctrines in the style of Magwen."

Ulisa was shocked to learn of the news and reconsidered her mission to Lake Loese. In the meantime she learned many changes had taken place during her entombment. Adelyheim had been cast out of the Circle for practice of dubious magics, bordering on witchery, (according to Barbirius), and Onzo had almost had his head cut off for disrupting a certain 'flue orb' of Aanab's. Ulisa shook her head. Adelyheim agreed to make haste to Mismerion. "After your disappearance, I was given to wandering Bayrune woods, looking for clues to your whereabouts. I stumbled upon this clearing, not far from the castle, very quaint and agreeable and I initiated construction of a cottage. I tended my garden; I continued my studies of herbal lore. Now, I feel as if my craft is slipping—perhaps it is time to move on, explore greater goals . . ."

Ulisa was touched by the story. She gave her niece a gift of silent blessing. With farewells, she flew north to Lake Loese in the guise of a familiar robin. Sure enough, she discovered a small grass hut, lonely and forsaken hidden on the western fringe of the lake. The construction was positioned in the centre of a long strip of green meadow populated with a thousand golden dragon flowers of eerie variety. The crooked petals and prickly leaves fluttered in the wind with a sinister purpose. The heads and pistils looked ever so much like grinning bestial faces, the leaves monsters' wings, which troubled Ulisa.

Ulisa paused in mid-flight, reflecting. For some inscrutable reason, the single hut remained alone and untended, as if wrapped in a neglect or avoidance.

Driven by a sudden intuition, she resisted the urge to fly right to the hut; instead she flew to the forest's perimeter and perched on a tall mukklewood. From high up she watched. She preened her feathers, hopping from limb to limb, pretending innocence. For all appearances, nothing untoward appeared. Satisfied that all was not evil, she alighted to the mossy ground. She poked about on twigish feet. Suddenly she discerned a movement and changed back to her human form. She called out a strained welcome—a very melodious one on an unassuming note—to the owners of the hut.

Time passed. Not a stir came from within. Suddenly, the door burst ajar. Under the sagging lintel emerged a stocky figure whose head was wrapped in a bandanna which held his dirty brown dreadlocks. His dress was rich with rags and tatters. He was a man, peering this way and that toward the edge of the forest where he seemed to put on a wry face.

"Carefully there, schoolgirl!" the man cried with some animation. He raised a hand in meek warning. "Do not venture within! All who enter this forsaken glade experience only sorrow and woe."

Ulisa pressed her hands to hips and called out a crisp protest, "I am no schoolgirl, Maitor—I am a Ulisa the Utilitarian! Don't you remember me? Furthermore, I resent the condescension. What nonsense is this?"

The figure paused; a pair of sad eyes pinched tightly together as if pained by the coppery fringes of light that filtered by the mukklewoods. "No nonsense at all. This curse is germane and not at all a joke." He drew back. "Well, so you are! Ulisa! You have returned from the grave—or from a never-ending pilgrimage? Your magic must be potent to have escaped whatever foul turn you were dealt!"

Ulisa blushed, but frowned. "In several respects, Maitor, yes, my magic has been challenged."

The proud admission offered Maitor no comfort. "Well, let us dispense with all the dithering. Alvius, did you hear that? Hope is not all dead! Ulisa is alive—" he turned to Ulisa "—Our dear Alchemist cogitates now upon a scheme to release us from this diabolical prison . . ."

"Indeed!" chortled Ulisa.

Presently a spare, red-headed man with long cheekbones and pale drooping eyes appeared hesitantly at the door. His thick spectacles seemed to dwarf his face and his eyes were hoisted above a coin-shaped nose and like his peer's very round and bright. His clothing looked moth-eaten and stained with oils and grime. "Aye!" he croaked. "The adze-wielding brute has inflicted us all with one of his swinish tricks! Look! When we refused to join his cabal, he deposited us here in this wretched meadow, without weapon or magic, and with only the barest of information to keep us alive!"

"This is all so discomforting," emphasized Ulisa.

"Indeed it is!" Maitor moaned. He turned to his companion and gave a wretched groan. "How goes it, Alvius—any luck with your caustic solutions?"

The alchemist grumbled. "None whatsoever! I have attempted an encoding upon the air, but the mission becomes ever more farcical. I lack the proper materials. My elixirs and potions are back at Mismerion! Barbirius has ensured this and sealed our doom!—as witnessed, the depths of my frustration know no bounds! I am making progress, nonetheless, if it were not for the little rain that I collect from the eaves, but which is not yet enough to kickstart my experiments. I cannot disarm a jinx of immutable quality that contaminates the glade, which prevents us from moving beyond the fringes of this floral nightmare."

Ulisa stood sceptically aloof. She assessed the cabin with new eyes and peered distrustfully at the meadow. "What makes this meadow so jinx-ridden then? The lawn appears reasonably normal." Other than the two inhabitants and the weird array of flowers, the place seemed relatively benign. No sign of birds or squirrels, or any other foraging denizen—which in itself was odd—nor was there any frolic of creature near the dragon flowers.

Ulisa drew closer, sensing the flowers collecting their stems in thicker bunches. So innocent . . . and yet so peculiar and unnatural . . .

Ulisa bent to sniff the grass. The flowers herded together in a menacing line. She loosed a small gasp. They tilted away from the sun, gave off an acrid stench—this toward the direction of Barbirius's war mansion. What was this unearthly sign? Ulisa tipped her brows. Toward the glade's fringe, the flowers seemed to inject the air with a thin film of sporadic, unnerving mist.

Ulisa pinched her mouth into an 'o' of disgust. "What was this spell? A purulence? A way to self-watering?

She stood considering the facts. Only a spiteful suspicion remained in her mind. It was just like Barbirius to cloak his neomancies with some vulgar conspiracy . . .

Maitor uttered an anxious cry. "Venture no farther! I reiterate, Ulisa. Once you tread into Marmere's meadow, you will not be able to return. Be wary! All three of us henceforth must be trapped like prisoners on a barren isle!"

Ulisa cocked her head to the side and uttered a note of rejection. "Do you think I am of ilk that foolish?"

Maitor made a dignified sound. On unsteady feet he trotted out toward the place where the glade met the forest. Carefully, so as not to crush the dragon flowers, he made a ginger, springing leap. The sudden movement across the threshold from meadow to forest caused the flowers to jerk. They whirled on him instantly, propelling him about several paces and Maitor landed in a heap on his haunches. "You see?" He was subjected to groans and grumbles and angered squirts of the flowers. Lips clenched, he hustled away down to the waterfront where he made a show of wading out in the reeds.

A great wave suddenly crested from the water and bore him back in one splashing leap.

Maitor rolled doddering to his feet. "Now do you understand?" He shook a dripping fist. "Immoral! All very immoral!—Barbirius, I name you a bane!"

Ulisa compressed her lips. Wonder warred with distaste. "Why not uproot the flowers then?"

"See for yourself. Every time we try to uproot one, three more spring up in good time."

Ulisa scratched her cheek thoughtfully. If she were to concoct a blight to disrupt the flowers . . . perhaps it would be enough to liberate them from the spell? Ulisa remained unsure. It would be only through an agency of years of experimentation at best . . . So how had the warmonger effected the charm? Surely there were antidotes?

The shape-shifter peered left and right. A miniature garden of pumpkins and brittle-pods grew innocently against Alvius and Maitor's hut's side facing the sun. The vegetables were benign. It seemed that the twain had survived on this fare alone . . .

With a gesture and a shrug, Ulisa returned to her form as a yellow flutter-moth. Dreamily she flew back out of the glade into the aisles of the wood. The sunlit places allowed many visits to the elder beasts. Whispering sibilances and woodland dialects, she was pleased to witness the denizens emerge from their hiding places. 'Twas a grand summoning of a singular horde of animals—all to Marmere's glade. From the corners of the forest came the balk-wegmors, wild fringe-elk, swamp bear, horned forest rams. They all came to avail themselves of the sinister dragon flowers' pith and stalks and feed their hunger heartily. In one great storm, they all champed and fed.

The flowers trembled like mice. They were cut to shreds, ingested and torn like carrion. Those that were not immediately devoured started to wither; stalks crumbled and roots upturned. Other flowers fluttered like birds in a hope to project themselves in the air and escape the champing teeth. But the dragon flowers were rooted too deep; a myriad moribund voices cried out all at once in abject despair. The tumult was deafening. Alvius and Maitor lay cupping their hands over their ears. The spell was broken; by the time it was all over, the animals crept away, melting into the forest as if they had never been.

The dragon-flower stench gradually washed itself away by the winds off the lake.

Inspired by the casual ease in which the flowers had met their demise and the beasts had made their exit, the neomancers wondered if they could follow a similar path. Creeping from their hut, they made mincing steps. At first they made timorous shows of advancing beyond the boundary along the half-chewed path—but no resistance came and they danced arm in arm, congratulating themselves. Liberty was theirs! After so long a period of deprivation, they shouted and danced with glee.

Ulisa turned to them, somewhat put out by a lack of thanks.

The two arrested their reverie.

"In reward for my service, I ask that you return post-haste to Mismerion," she asserted. Her lips were pursed and she put forth a further request: "I will call an assembly of the neomancers, of which you shall be part."

Alvius objected, scowling. "Absolutely not. The Circle is no more. The same is true for all of our colleagues. The castle Mismerion marks the origin and place of our unspeakable imprisonment!"

Ulisa replied tolerantly: "I have important disclosures to convey, which you must hear. It is important that we all pool our knowledge."

Maitor and Alvius made loud grumbling objections. Through means of compelling arguments, the two were persuaded to join the assembly. They revelled in their newfound freedom and accepted the task and set out for the old castle, carrying on in high tones like schoolboys.

One by one, Ulisa gathered the neomancers from their various locales: Kazzasius the Projector, Onzo the Optimist, Ahrion the Astrologer. Of the neomancers, Kazzasius had been convinced of his much-needed presence at Mismerion from his green-glassed belvedere that overlooked the river Ul. Onzo had been plucked unawares from his mushroom-picking and weasel-trapping along the forest paths of Wayheal. Ahrion, persuaded from his three-turreted observatory high up on the summit of Billup's hill, though he gave vent to several surly disclaimers.

There were failures, of course. Ulisa could not tempt Roso the Recluse or Dista the Dissenter, or Diophenes the Dour, no less Sordess the Sunshine Swallower. One or more had passed away to oblivion; others she could not locate in any quarter, including Arkus the Adventurer and Solusa the Shepherdess. She feared that the two had met unfavourable ends at the behest of Barbirius.

Ulisa flew the last sleepy leagues to the village of Dol, where, from a band of woodcutters, she heard further bad tidings. That Bithuma the Pragmatist had been here but was nowhere to be found. Many of the villagers—weavers and haymakers included—claimed that Bithuma had wandered off—west, east? None knew. A few speculated that she had met with mishap.

Ulisa glumly retraced her path—back to the waters of Lake Loese, from whence she made her way on to Great Hall.

IV

Over a period of several days Aurimag bent to the task at hand. During this stint of intense labour, he had augmented his necromantic work in progress and felt a certain flash of thaumaturgical excellence returning. A feeling of pride and exhilaration swept over him after so many moons of impotent lassitude.

On his workbench sat a dark, malevolent shape. Bulging in aspect no larger than a man, the shape stood maladroitly—like some thing of half-dried mud stained dark amber. The thing was vaguely anthropomorphic—incorporating a set of knotted limbs, a pancake crown, two thumb holes rich with green pigment and litch-pod which comprised eyes. The upper portion of the hulk was supported somewhat precariously by a teetering set of scaffolding. Two roundish pebbles served for nostrils and two dollops of marsh scum formed ears, a down-turned grimace and knife-edge gash suggested a wattled mouth. Evidently the 'creature' was something more grossly symbolic of andropod or andromorph. Notably, Aurimag's latest brainchild, this *golem*, was an incomparable feat. Nothing of its like had ever been crafted in all of Bindar!—or at least so the magician thought . . . Aside from the ghoulish features and the slinky limbs, the thing remained completely inscrutable, an icon of complete ambiguity.

Casually, the magician raised a hand to stroke the head of his bench top ghoul. Strange whisperings issued from the nether-corners of the room; they caused the magician to twitch distressfully. He glared about. Perhaps the play of underworld sprites?

Imaginative folly! He thrust the notion from his mind. He bent closer to his golem. Pulling nodes and cords attached to the lower temples, he could not help but wonder at the evil genius of his scheme and radiate a gleeful smile. Amorphous wonder! When the creature was unleashed—ah! but how it would shock certain odious persons!

Aurimag idled his fingers. Not just another dull featureless glob or strengthless suppository to add to his mock show of freakish inventions. But one of superior strength, agility, and intelligence to be used as a sharp instrument of vengeance.

Aurimag ran his fingers through his dry scalp. Five yellowed scrolls written in Lengish sat on his workbench—the arcane text which had been consulted in earnest in its fabrication.

He grinned with an unpleasant confidence. The question remained: on whom would he test the golem first?

Trimestrius? Ulisa? Baus? Perhaps any of the above, including the three, Woisper, Salmeister or Weavil in captivity.

The answer came to him almost immediately: Baus of Heagram!

Aurimag allowed himself a bawdy chuckle. Once the golem brought the conniver back to his abode, he would minister him with torments, use him as a pin-cushion, thrust him into n^{th} order evil, or any endless variety of dooms. The golem would wreak damage upon the remainder of his enemies—the Circle of Mismerion for starters. The neomancers remained scattered about the realm, somewhat to his annoyance. A few candidates came to mind: Barbirius—who with his pompous pugilistic airs reigned top of the list, Bithuma the bowlegged Pragmatist, Dious the Dolt, Maitor the Manic, Alvius the Autocrat, Slaene the Slipshod, Llonon the Lip-servicer. The idea of sweet revenge on these persons brought flickering glee to his eyes and a dampness to his brow.

Aurimag peered down at his glass sand timer. In another three, or possibly four days, the first inaugural test would be scheduled . . . Tears of delight dribbled from Aurimag's cheeks; he hastened back to his work.

* * *

Four days passed. Still, the neomancer had not achieved success. He glared upon his creation with an air of disapproval. The creature lacked substance, a certain vitality, or 'stimulus' that would render its life essence beyond a mere twitch of sentience.

Aurimag reviewed his situation with glaze-eyed apathy. What to do? The golem had started off as an unorganized lump, now it remained a slightly less unorganized lump. A discordant truth struck him: that the creature had acquired an unexceptional promise but despite his cajoles, invocations and spell-weavings, the dark swamp hybrid was no more than a dull piece of earth. The blue torque affixed round its neck contained a red nexus, which was supposed to infuse it with life. The gem remained dull and inert. Such a dullness exposed the totality of this failure. Designed to become an 'animatrix', the torque had shown little sign of singular pulsation, a necessary quality for the creation of a living being. The eight-sensored Potent-Meter, a round, clock-like adjunct of utility, lay dangling motionless about the creature's dry-baked chest with no sign of impetus.

Aurimag suppressed a croak. The situation seemed hopeless. The needles on the device's sensor remained devoid of the minutest spike of consciousness.

Failure!

Aurimag groaned. His mind drew back in outrage, seeing only black and failures by the dozens.

The neomancer flung down the nexus in disgust. He kicked at the Potent-Meter and sent it to the 'off' position. He turned his back on his creation and strode into the Bronze Hall, mollifying his frustration with a plan to meditate on forbearance or conduct anger-management affirmations. He left the Potent-Meter dangling uselessly around the golem's neck.

* * *

Four more days passed. During this disconsolate period Aurimag could not so much as excite a jerk from his golem. What a despicable predicament! He clutched his hair. To climb to the stars on a ladder of faery crystal would be easier. He hopped disagreeably about his workroom from workbench to crucible.

How then to animate the creature?

He cogitated. Certain breakthroughs required leaps of faith, not through conventional means . . .

Spells and elixirs and sprinklings of puissances were useless. Sacrificing a wild newt to the Geminix twins had proven ineffectual; invoking Kron, Boton and Plopon, questionable deities, had advanced the project no further. Only a whoosh of joyless airs, moans, gnawing terror and morose oscillations and as many laments filled the gloomy spaces from the nth order dimensions to echo hollowly about his grotto.

Aurimag essayed a summoning of the half demon, Kansx. All in the hope that the behemoth would populate the mud husk and assume the guise of the golem . . .

The venture was ill thought out. Here Aurimag's conceit caused him almost certain woe. Invoking entities of such kinds was fraught with perils, particularly when one valued his life. To become a demon's plaything was not something to take lightly. . . In the greater picture, what respectable demon would emerge from the nether regions to play such a piddling role?

The magician gave his head a solemn shake. He re-read his journals and paced back and forth in his workroom. Time seemed to stand still. With the cool fixation of a man impelled to obsession, Aurimag likened his cause to the quintessential outcast, struggling against unfathomable odds to achieve a sense of excellence in an obscure field. Finding such musings unproductive, Aurimag returned to a more traditional path of investigation.

His mind jogged to a sudden passage—a poem written many years ago by a certain 'Jargoon the Philosophist', a piece from a larger work entitled the *'The Metaphysical Importance and Invariance of Verity'*. Jargoon spoke of an obscure wisdom realized through his aged character, 'Osaron', in the form of a monumental revelation:

". . . all inanimate objects, once 'living husks', have only lost their 'liveliness' because of a change of form. As animate beings change to the inanimate through death, the cycle must repeat itself . . ."

Provocative—but of what value? Aurimag clenched his teeth. The dim memory stirred something within. He discovered, while digging through his mountain of tubs, a mouldering tome covered with frayed jacket. It read: *'Index of Ineffable Marvels'*, a controversial title. Sure enough, his bloodshot eyes passed over a cryptic entry that expressed the validity of his recollections:

" . . . inanimate objects are motionless because of the cause and effect of decaying nature, or PROTO PHASE . . . In light of the vastness of life, considering death's phenomenon, the two contradistinctions are considered identities of the other, reprints of some small thesis, an archetypal synthesis of a larger, polar reality. To re-animate the objects back to their former 'aliveness' requires the stealth and skill of an 'obductrix', a truth-being allowing such matter to 'witness' the image of its former life. The feat is no facile undertaking; it involves the singular coaxing of the animus back into the inanimate husk—or more exactly, an isolation of the flux of REO-GENESIS . . ."

Aurimag mused. His face became flushed with excitement. *An isolation of the flux of REO-GENESIS . . .* Underneath was writ an archaic, near-indecipherable passage:

"REO-GENESIS—a process to be conducted with extreme caution! . . . an obscure system of necromancy known only to the few philosopher-scientists of the Barvish Ideology. It includes the matter of displacing life with non-life and non-life with life. Intrinsically, it is a delicate science involving a pooling of a variety of ingredients into a substratum of alchemic potpourri. Applying a suitable energy charge of nefro-crystallinic energy, with, of course, various magical ores, it shall infuse the core to sufficient impetus, or at least thrust a comparable infusion of talismanic energy. Warning! A sublime understanding of the Higher Manifestations is recommended in order to succeed—i.e. an obeisance to a strict rule-set. Note: a catalogue of procedures as described by the Philosopher-scientists in length below . . .

Addendum! Any rare adherent who seeks to triumph in this direction, must sustain the 'warp' of PROTO-PHASE. There is risk of adverse effects on the body. Nose bleeds, hernia, heart palpitations, coronary failure, death —all are possible aftermaths to be expected upon the initial experiment . . ."

The last footnote caused Aurimag a bleak uncertainty. He read and re-read the final instructions. Confidently he tossed the reference aside. He released the elm-sprites of their duty, they who guarded the antechamber, taking notice of the time it took to get them in their 'safe' zones. He left his cave to collect the requisite ingredients from the forest.

Out of doors, Aurimag squinted painfully under the naked sunshine. He adjusted his sight to the pale rays, and felt his own skin warming to the light. The experience felt almost alien to him after subsisting so long underground. Small trails became known to his eye—the strangest of forests beckoned; he navigated the woods behind his cave like a shambling gnome, stealing over soft mallorn leaves, through copses of ruffled ghost oak, phantom elm and twitch yew rooted amongst mossy dips and inclines. Aurimag's destination was a special hollow, located not far from the river Lim where it snaked its curvaceous breadth deeper into the plunging wilderness.

Redeemer

The path became denser, glummer. Gingerly Aurimag stepped between folds of fungus and toadstool. He carefully took pains to avoid insect-asms which clung to the undersides of the giant mushrooms whose fulsome stings could prove injurious to a person of lesser prudence.

At last he came to a place deep within the forest, a rich and damp recess permeated with musks and salamander ferns twice as high as himself. The glen was replete with limy ledges of rock salted with yellow husswort. There was much to be avoided here, as in most of the mysterious outcrops along the Lim.

Bottle in hand, Aurimag gingerly collected several samples. It was fecund stuff: spores, spanglemoss, witch-fungi—all scraped from the crumbling crevices and dank niches with finicky little pokes and dabs of his stick. To touch the stuff with a naked hand would be unheard of. Substances as these contained the most primitive atoms of insurgence—a necessary flux to spark the REO-GENESIS process—at least so Aurimag understood from the limited lore of the tomes.

The time was nearing dusk and Aurimag detected melancholy glimmers of light peeking through the arching creepers. The gnarled branches of ghost oak seemed to reach down and touch him. He shivered despite his experience. Shadows brewed in the hollows; a portentous weight of moss and stumps brought leery feelings to his breast.

He hastened to his task. The forest became home to many marauders after dark, whose philosophies were in direct contrast to his own.

Feeling less confident, the magician capped his bottle and began retracing his steps back through the darkening glades. Forcing himself to make do with his meagre collection, he mentally prepared himself for the meditations involved in his final exposition.

* * *

Such meditations proved unilluminating. In the subject of REO-GENESIS he remained wholly unversed, even a tyro. Leeriness was his only real emotion, inspired by hints of dangers outlined in the old documents. Aurimag's mouth dropped in a cool scowl. So what? Nevertheless, he prepared himself for the inevitable letdown. Due discipline had him expulsing spectral qualms from his mind and channelling himself into a ritual of empowerment. He launched himself on a mission of purpose!

Chanting, humming and droning he chimed off spells accompanied by notes on his two-stringed dopek. He plunged powders and liquids at his anthropoid creation until the thing was drenched with elixirs. He was fatigued, but continued on, muttering hoarse-voiced. By the end of the ritual, the neomancer had managed to break through certain ghost-haunted thresholds—though with a nose a bloody mass and a heart skipping about at an abnormal rate. The process of REO-GENESIS was not for the weak of heart. The trial had taken a turn for the rigorous and tasked his resistance to dangerous levels. After a week of fasts and gasparon-root, he felt only a modicum of potency returning.

Standing back in awe, the magician thought to detect a glimmer of life in his golem. His eyes widened in hope. Mud muscles bulged, ropy mouth quivered. The green eyes of his golem glinted—with an awareness that he had never before seen, eyes that never knew the likes of concepts of good and evil. The minion surveyed Aurimag with a wary dispassion. For reasons as these, Aurimag kept the creature restrained with double loops of strept-vine. The cord that wrapped the golem round a stalagmite was secure—he had ensured this before he had committed himself to the final phases of REO-GENESIS. The precaution was an act of survival following his earlier murky attempts at infusing life into 'inanimates' through means of higher n^{th} order entities. The memory was better left unstirred. Now, the golem was straining the vines like a hound on leash. It would not, in a trice, hesitate to inflict a mortal strike if released.

Aurimag pressed the Potent-Meter to the creature's chest. The golem instantly bridled, as if seeking to resist the flux of the device. The magician plunged it more forcefully on its mud-baked chest. The vines twitched. The creature curiously pressed on with desperate hope, but the calliper swung significantly to the left and Aurimag's mouth curled in a twisted leer. The device was functioning! Such were grounds of celebration. The magician accurately concluded that 'Phase 1' of his golem experiment was a success!

He studied his 'golem' with new dispassion. Not arbitrarily could he help balking over a new quandary. What good was a beast savage enough to tear him to pieces released without tethers?

The magician rubbed his chin. A dilemma. To subdue this thing within a comfortable perimeter was no small hitch. Certain of his own powers of hypnotism could only marginally be expected to win over such a servant of nth order.

Aurimag again consulted his compendia of inducements. A certain treatise, the 'Spell of Ulterior Volition' (SUV), remained his most compelling option. He wasted no time in submitting the golem to a series of rigours—blasts of piercing lights, claps of cymbal, gongs in the ears, threats of chastisement in three of the four nether-languages.

To no avail. The inducements remained below the creature's threshold of sublimation. The thing remained undaunted. Aurimag groaned. He was compelled to try an ingestion of soporifics—dry rookweed, barbicon stalk, mevviavelian tonics. At least these might prove efficacious. The combination of rigours triggered an alteration in its psychic chemistry and the golem eventually succumbed to the tonics and elixirs. It remained submissive. The creature was so docile in fact, that Aurimag acquired his viol and began to play it a lovely sonata. The sounds seemed to dull the creature's senses into a state of heightened languor.

Pleased, Aurimag set down his instrument and began to engineer tasks for which the minion might be put. Such was the beginning of a most harmonious relationship between the golem and the sorcerer. "You," Aurimag rasped in a cunning voice, "will be my new 'Warlock vassal'!"

The creature showed no enthusiasm.

* * *

Further impedances brought Aurimag's scheme to a grinding halt.

How was his golem ever to discover its quarry? Was it to hop randomly about Bindar looking for the dastard, Baus? The fisherman could be anywhere in the lands—the chance of his re-capture by the Heagram deputies was not remote and he probably still skulked about the Heagram compound. But how could Aurimag be certain? How long would it take for his golem to locate the fisherman by unmethodical means?

The queries were endlessly disturbing. If he were to dispatch a multitude of golems on the hunt, perhaps the acceleration of the venture would be augmented. But Aurimag frowned deeply at this scheme. He inspected the creature's vacuous face. No great intelligence was mirrored there. Even a large number of creatures would find the task daunting of locating a single target. These golems were anything but detectives . . .

Aurimag became infected with despair. The hours dragged by. The Bitomoth made a fluting chime. He knew he was in need of a whiff of hypnotiate. Grimacing vacantly, he ached for his saffron drug. He gave himself a blast. Almost at once a glimmering scheme came fluttering to his mind. Digging through his tubs of journals, he found a reference: Appendix B, Paragraph 4, '*Spells and Jinxes for Novitiate and Acolytes to Detect Magic*' (SJNADM)' . . . apparently this was the universal antidote for plateaus and blocks!

Reviewing his facts, Aurimag reasoned that the conniver Baus likely guarded the ganglestick—a magical wand stolen from him that could help his case. As long as the fisherman still retained the talisman, it was possible to track its emanation. What fortune that the fisherman had in fact filched it! With the SJNADM spell, the ganglestick could be detected via the waft of its magical flux—provided there were no other devices in the vicinity. 'Twas a poignant scheme!

Aurimag re-traced his fingers along Paragraph 4's particulars. His tongue lolled. Continuing in unhurried fashion, he discarded the literature and acquired a virgin moolstone of $n\text{-}1^{th}$ order. He set an invocation of magical cantos upon the pearl, so as to induce a vibration of significance.

Aurimag pitched it with dry morels, walnut husks and dry zinzabar.

He laughed aloud. The cantos reached a cadence of indulgent proportions.

Aurimag rendered the text with a crude portraiture of Baus. Into the mix he incorporated an auxiliary flux by tapping pearl and nexus with his whip-stick[*], a variation of the ganglestick. (Footnote: [*]Whip-stick: A magical wand which stuns for shorter duration than the ganglestick—one minute or less, after which the individual becomes immune to the spell for a period of one hour. The whip-stick is much similar to the ganglestick, though smaller and less puissant, and carved of red muttleglass.)

Shades of rose-purple glimmered upon the moolstone! The colour settled into an opaque blend of rather odd-looking daffodil-yellow.

Aurimag loosed a breath. He waited for the pearl to glow back to its original colour—a rose-purple vermilion.

It did not.

Aurimag combed his beard with disgruntled perplexity. The daffodil colour indicated that a quarry matching Baus's description was less than seven leagues away.

Seven leagues? Aurimag's eyes widened. How could this be so? Surely the fisherman could not be that close? Had he bungled the spell?

He rejected doubts. The cantos was not wrong nor was it falsely scribed. Roaming about his workroom, he rechecked the journal's appendices and encountered a cross-indexed entry entitled *'Detect Magic Table'* (DMT). No error! Neither did the nether-magics lie. The blight was cast. The pearl was infused with flux. The magician had imprinted it himself. Everything was exact!

Aurimag stood up, unfazed. He seemed almost removed of expectation—then, an insight struck him. Perhaps the golem's search would turn up respectable fruits. Could he dare hope?

He made a terse gesture. No matter; so long as the object was affixed to the golem's physiology, it would feel a sting in direct proportion to the distance between quarry and itself. The phenomenon comprised an incentive for the golem to be honest in the affair of acquiring the quarry.

Aurimag mused aloud. So long as the beast was rational and somewhat moderately cognizant, it could locate its charge. He rested assured that the golem would complete its task—the moolstone was his win-card and would act as a beacon guiding the creature to its quarry . . .

Aurimag whispered into its ear incisive instructions. "Bring the fisherman! Do not delay." He described Baus, taking pains to outline the flagrant vanity of his appearance and the depths of his chicanery and braggadocio. The creature seemed to evince no great level of understanding.

With a sharp pair of tongs, Aurimag snatched the moolstone from the glowering coals in which it had been cached and stabbed it deep into the dry muck of the golem's upper shoulder.

The golem quavered, almost falling to its knees. Its mud-flesh body sizzled; the torso reeked of horrible fetid earth and rotten toadstools. Meanwhile the object glowed with a maleficent yellow. The golem rocked about on its heels, committing no further aggressions or outcries upon Aurimag, nor did it inflict any display of treachery. It could neither speak nor communicate, such was the limit of its powers given by REO-GENESIS, as too the power of the SUV spell.

* * *

The following morning Aurimag suited his minion in a baggy costume of leaf-twined trousers and a gown of green-gangorn leaves. On its lumpy head the magician affixed a brown peasant's domino. The golem was armed with neither weapon nor sustenance—it needed neither. To the Vestuary he led his brainchild, then down to the two entrance pillars. It was an impassive, forbidding portal, casting disquiet and fear into the heart of an observer. The golem was a sullen mass of earth shrouded with amber-mottled face. Long twiglike fingers graced its spatulate arms; on flat, bare feet it padded. Giving the secret incantation, Aurimag ordered the elm-sprites to release their hold and step back into their meshes and commit no molestation upon his servant. The meshes drew down upon touch of a hidden valve in the stone and Aurimag repeated the instructions to the hulk: "Capture the human; do not impose any unnecessary ministrations upon his person. Bring the prisoner alive to this location! I repeat, 'alive'!—and here Aurimag's icy glare hit home. "Do not disobey me, fiend, else malfeasances will be mirrored upon your own existence! Are we in accord?"

The golem signalled its understanding with an awkward nod.

The golem was dispatched. Over boulders it scrambled; up valley and over turf it flew like the wind on earth-rich legs in a rustle of green and brown fabric to disappear through the dank underbrush and into the ferns and bracken beyond.

* * *

Over the next few days, the neomancer ministered to his basic research into the manufacture of golems. 'Twas tedious work! But with the help of a nose-mask and a protectorate sprite, he conjured up another minion of unique quality, thus sparing himself the tedium and negative effects of REO-GENESIS. Seeking to improve upon his last creation, he produced a simulacrum of himself, of clever engineering, which was organically sound. From purely organic materials it had come into being, unlike the predecessor of gross soil and stone. In such wise, the creature became marginally superior at least—it could experience human-like emotions and apprehend some basic sense of humanness. Aurimag had engineered it such, though he had mixed vials of his own blood and inadvertently injected its mud essence with increased cognitive power. Limbs and visage had been sculpted to the apex of perfection, painting skin and body ochres of flesh pink. Now Aurimag stood back staring admiringly at his new creation—a marionette of flawless proportions so much like himself, yet so less in spirit. It gazed back at him with a certain blank indifference. A tableau sat on his workbench—

one fixed in a series of lightly-pulsing, platelike nodes. The neomancer merely placed his hand on an indigo knob. He could witness the sights that his simulacrum saw. A huge practical advantage! Why sweat and toil when one could delegate a minion to do all one's inconvenient work for him?

Aurimag congratulated himself.

To augment his brilliance, he had only to peer into the tableau's ruby alter-sphere of seven vortexes to periodically inquire upon the progress of his minion. What a rare fortune! He could craft other zombies of similitude and put them to more incisive use—one disguised as a troubadour garbed in scarlet robes and a grey domino, to play beguiling music on a bassomo and lull into languor any of the youthful maidens of Vishire and Lillenvir, the nearby hamlets. Such pretties! They could be quietly herded back to his cave and thus entertain him throughout the night when his toil might become unbearable.

Another example excited Aurimag's imagination. He would recapture Ulisa—the alluring minx, and add her to his private collection. For what better purpose could her youthful vigour be employed than in his personal nymphosium? Of course, the shapely body would have to be re-augmented to proper size first, as he disliked midgets of any kind, particularly in any forms of recreation.

Aurimag daubed affectionately at his beard. Bits of bread and meat had got caught there and made him look a little hillbilly-ish. Ulisa's transfiguration would certainly be a non-trivial one, perhaps even impossible —but what of it? The prospect entailed new research, and provided a certain provocative inspiration . . .

On the affairs of golems, Aurimag's imagination knew no end. He plunged himself into a deep pondering and creative brainstorming. A simulacrum to pour over Tibatius's scrolls, a simulacrum to probe Auscolias's formularies, another to forage for rare herbs and leeks in the Brauvn forests bordering Farling's Wall . . . Such comprised a complete, singular application to important tasks, thus discovering purposes and programs for slaves to accomplish life's menial tasks while one devoted himself to more meaningful pursuits! So much to do . . .

V

Within three days of Ulisa's liberation of Alvius and Maitor, an assembly of familiar faces stared out from the archaic pews at Mancer Hall at Mismerion. All who promised to appear were present—except Vyo the Validator, Adelyheim, (who was never a fast traveller), and Sisler the Sceptic who by her very nature, was a most defeatist person and refused to be swayed to Ulisa's cause.

Sitting away from his peers was Ahrion, a man of fiery disposition, pale bland eyes and flaming orange beard beaded of tasselled jewels. A long ultramarine fustian trailed from his neck to his toes. Onzo the Optimist twiddled his thumbs in a central seat. He grinned cheerily as was his wont. Here was a man of idealistic temperaments, boyish charm, sunken cheeks and long red fingers wont to fiddle with the thin ruff of waxen hair coiled into a peacock bun. His white caftan was labelled with four distinct crests of the House of Hoton, all outlined in green. Kazzasius the Projector sat moodily aside, imbued with a sense of importance and consequence. He was a lean and fox-limbered magician with a thin jowl and weasel-brown hair varnished neatly over peaked ears. A cape was draped about his neck and over his thin shoulders.

Maitor and Alvius cleaned themselves up, wearing new double-breasted top-jackets, matching ties, pressed and starched, polished black shoes, all which accentuated their frames. Both men had shorn their ragged beards. Maitor had even gone so far as to taper his sideburns and coif the hairs over his upper lip into a semblance of twin mustachios.

The afternoon was growing older. Wan light stretched down from the ancient casements, shedding a penumbral luminescence on the stone mosaic floor. The remaining grand hall was lit with candelabra, placed somewhat strategically around the pillars of the hall to afford more cheer. But what little light remained cast soft terracotta shadows and barely punctuated the gloom.

Dressed in her finest, Ulisa stood on a jewelled dais before a lectern to face the group. "As you know," she announced in a distinguished voice, "several moons ago I was abducted by Aurimag, our detestable enemy. Unlike Woisper the Wilful and Salmeister the Saturnine, I managed to escape by extraordinary means . . . with little machinations to my person, outside of this oppressive shrinking. I am not fully healed yet as you can see, but 'tis of no import. I will not belabour my misfortunes; forsooth, I will broach a more pressing topic. Namely, the miraculous hero who aided me in my escape—a certain fisherman of Heagram who resides in a faraway village to the north—Baus."

"What of him?" cried a voice from the back.

"Patience—the village is the same where the villain passed on his mission of wealth-gaining while in the guise of a travelling magician. He went under the name of a certain 'Nuzbek' then. To allay the tedium of this lengthy tale, I will only say that I harbour categorical conviction that this commoner can help us in our plight against the villain Aurimag, whose powers, I fear, grow to the point of danger and concern."

A hoot came from the audience. "What possible aid can this 'fisherman' provide us?"

"All will be explained," counselled Ulisa. Her face remained a serene mask. "I attempted to convince Baus to join our band and lobby against our enemy, but he demurred. My attempt was met with flippant reserve. Two moons later, I wish I had compelled the man with more persuasion—as we all might have, and if had been in a better position."

Ahrion gave a sceptical grunt. "This seems a farfetched assumption. Why is he so special and what can he do? What possible magic can the stripling yield?"

"None—as far as I can observe, and this is precisely the point," emphasized the shape-shifter. "He has none. So remains a perfect foil against Aurimag. Perhaps Baus's greatest skill lies in his ridiculous presuming airs, notwithstanding a capacity for quick-thinking and duplicity. It seems to foil villains and abusers of power. Not only did he outwit Aurimag without the slightest aid of any higher magics, he emancipated Trimestrius and myself from our jars. Now I ask you—who amongst you could have done that?"

There were grumbles and mutters but there was no claim to the feat.

Ulisa continued: "I would point out that these events are not random—nor are they trivial or lucky. They occurred in tandem, where we failed."

Maitor gestured with an implicit smile: "So—these are certainly singular observations, but I still remain unconvinced."

"As is expected," Ulisa said. "For that matter, I shall say that I am highly convinced that he is our key in countering this treachery of Aurimag's. He can bring the blackguard to justice."

"A bold assertion," muttered Alvius peevishly. "Aurimag is a sinister specimen. Likely he will rend this fisherman limb from limb. Then we will be graced one less hero. The cunning of the louse's tricks is not limited to macabre punishments which will make short work of your poster-boy."

Ulisa acknowledged as much. "We must explore all the avenues. First, we must liberate Woisper, our Hierarch, then we must confront Aurimag. He has cached himself in his cave. At least I feel it strongly. I hazard that Woisper is a shrunken bug—much like Salmeister, trapped in their jars. I foresee a strong flux around Aurimag's cave, even though it lies five leagues to the south by the heart of the Brauvn. I sense too, a flux of doom around Baus and his colleagues, for which I fear, and the same about our own Circle . . ."

Murmurs came from the gathering.

"The fisherman is somehow linked to our Order's successful preservation," continued Ulisa authoritatively, "though my abilities as Divinatrix remain limited. My clairvoyance has waned under the rigour imposed by Aurimag's brine." She sighed, turned disgruntled eyes upon a sleepy figure in the audience. "Kazzasius! Say alert! Can you not set up a reading on your xenophone?"

The fox-eared man blinked in dazed surprise. "I can try."

"You will have to do more than that," grumbled Ulisa. "We have a serious issue on our hands."

Kazzasius gave a long, appeasing bow. From a side chamber, he dragged a queer contraption with Alvius's help out to the front of the hall. The machine was no more than a scarred, wooden crate mounted with a mesh of cogs and a great gear attached to a small hand crank. A glass scope projected from the metallic crown and emitted some kind of mystical glow, mustard yellow in colour and alternating with moss green.

"This is 'The Causal Projector'," Kazzasius announced proudly. Positioning his fingers to adjust the pitch of the scope so as to focus the glare upon a patch of the wall, he motioned instructively for all to gather and look.

Eyes trained on the screen. The neomancer busied himself pinning it on the wall.

Ulisa watched the Projector paste an image of each member of the council onto the scope. Then, he superimposed a depiction of Baus, hand-drawn by Ulisa. The resulting kaleidoscope was a functional, but weird display. It showed members of the Circle as pale cut-outs; then, as Kazzasius cranked the wheel, familiar forms began to take shape on the screen: oddly distorted figures, neomancers, laymen, Alvius, Ahrion, Kazzasius, Onzo, all neomancers of the Circle dressed in postures of abject regard: crying, pulling at their hair, lying prone on the paves, pale and fish-like corpses strewn about the unkempt lawn.

The members were appalled. "What nonsense is this?" blustered Ahrion.

Kazzasius adjusted the magnification. Cranking the wheel, he produced a more horrid configuration. "The image," he explained sombrely, "is projected obversely proportional to the axis of time. Time is an upside down bubble, if you like, which by means of a reflection lens through an inner 'convexus', remains inverted. The device sets itself 'right side up' and allows for a temporal shift and a lenticular displacement. In such wise, the mechanical gyros effectively can distinguish a visual ordinate which can safely track the causal implications of the superimposed images."

Onzo blinked. "If the machine can do half of what you say, it certainly is a miracle machine."

Kazzasius remained grateful for the remark. There came a brief period of irregular blasts from the machine and a spurting of a geyser-like light. Suddenly a blip appeared on the scope. All eyes turned to the screen. The castle at Mismerion shimmered into existence. The castle loomed resolute, a grey, preternaturally still stronghold—several weathered towers and marble-flagged courts stood as silent as monoliths in a chiaroscuro of opaque shadows. The keep began to fade; now an oasis of cloudscape appeared.

The light wavered; a new image appeared: a lone human tottering on his feet in a midnight glade, struggling for his life against an unpleasant half bat, half man.

"Here is our 'unknown' factor!" cried Ahrion with fervour.

"Yes, regard the 'fisherman' engaged in a fiendish skirmish with a manlike creature," observed Ulisa. "His face is contorted into a twisted grimace."

Onzo frowned, hitched himself closer. "Here now! What are all these long fangs and talons on the beast? The creature displays appendages with an audacious ease! Hoy! It seems as if our hero is about to be gutted!"

"We can all see that, Onzo," cried Ahrion irritably.

Ulisa snatched at Kazzasius's arm. "Why is the screen so dark?"

Kazzasius's tone became edged with doubt. "The implication is profound. The future of the Circle at Mismerion is at stake—and skewed by the fisherman's plight. It is a projection that bodes ill for us!—the fisherman's future is our own!"

Ulisa gave a bleak cry. "The youth is an important link to our future. How can we fabricate a counterpoise? We must act now!"

"Agreed—but how?" snorted Kazzasius. He held up a hand in helpless annoyance. "I am a Projectionist, not a manipulator of destiny."

"We must interfere with causal manipulations," called Dious. "Causal manipulation is not beyond our means."

"But the fates will not tolerate our meddling with their cosmic justice!" cried Ahrion. He alighted from his seat with a fanatical urgency. "The heavenly bodies are not playthings to be used. Conjunctions are all cast in proper alignment, including the moons of Siros and Dilonos!"

"This cannot be contested," agreed Ulisa, "—but not all heavenly bodies are equal, Ahrion. If we but intrude a single juxtaposition to the projected equation, the heavenly bodies will bend to our bidding."

Dious digested the information with sombre care. "Or at least look the other way."

"Difficulties present themselves," pointed out Maitor. He rubbed his chin doubtfully.

"As they always do," stated Ulisa gravely. Looking from face to face, she loosed a sharp breath. "Aurimag is not exempt from manipulation, though he has achieved a greater extrapolation than we have. We cannot penetrate his flux around his cave and I harbour suspicion that he has blocked entry with psychic alarms—perhaps even through physical projection." The shape-shifter's voice dropped a few tones.

The first glimmers of understanding began to dawn in Dious's mind. He reared himself erect and spoke sonorously, "If I may present a suggestion— our only means to affect Aurimag's impetus is via indirect channels— through his weakest link, which, is Baus."

Ulisa signalled her agreement. "I hate to introduce alien figures into the picture, but it seems necessary. We must inculcate dissenters—like Barbirius."

Alvius and Maitor protested strongly against the insertion of Barbirius.

"I despise the methods of their ilk as much as you, Maitor, but we are up against more than we think."

Helaar ignored the mewlings. "Barbirius is bellicose—a true war-monger and bully—but perhaps he is our last resource and hope for the future."

"Heresy of an insufferable sort!" stormed Alvius.

Maitor made a mutual blasphemous sign.

Helaar shook his head with indulgent disregard. "Not entirely! Barbirius could certainly effect a change in the causal fabric. His magic is fervid."

"What, and Llonon's is not?" cried Onzo. He lifted an accusing finger. "Is he some pipe-singer?"

"We have neither of these rebels on our side!" Maitor pointed out irritably. "To effect a resolution rests entirely upon our crew of 'vigilantes', which would be as effective as a hound against a rabid mouse set loose in the forest. Aurimag caches himself too protectively—we cannot easily penetrate his stronghold!"

"There is something in what you say . . ." Ulisa mused, "nevertheless, there is something in what Helaar says also. Kazzasius can pinpoint Baus's location to an accurate degree."

"Possibly, possibly," complained Kazzasius, flicking hands onto his apparatus as if it were a toy.

Ahrion called out a disdainful reproach, "The images confined in this 'xenophone', while edifying, seem of little practical utility. All are based on nebulous conjecture, and bombastic extrapolation."

Kazzasius disagreed with the judgement. He put on a dark face. Rotating the xenophone's gear with impatience, he peeled off the image depicting Mismerion. The lens then left a crude chalk drawing of Baus on the glass piece. Again, adjusting the luminous lens, he tweaked a node, cranked the wheel, and instantly a new image flashed in view—of four blurry forms walking in a huddle beside an immensely high wall. The wall seemed something of an anomaly, a tree-trunked goliath. The figures seemed all to be backing away from the rampart and casting fearful glances in the wall's direction and the nearby river.

Ulisa fretted with annoyance. "This looks to be Farling's Wall . . . The company's apprehension is merited. The Lim River is the only one that size to be so forbidding, which sets them—" she made a rough calculation "—approximately twelve leagues east from the castle—somewhere before the

Lim takes a sudden jog south to Farfus. Is the time, the future, or past, Kazzasius?"

Kazzasius consulted his glass scope. "It would appear the future."

"Then time still remains!" breathed the shape-shifter. "This is an encouraging sight!" She turned upon Kazzasius with gleaming eyes: "Can we pinpoint Aurimag's location in any capacity?"

Kazzasius gave his head a dour shake. "The dastard will probably have set up a negative projection which thwarts our detection by causal probes."

Ulisa made a wry face. "Well—" She brightened. With a lively inspiration, she entreated Dious to draw up from memory a depiction of the exterior of Aurimag's cave. Dious's sketch comprised a single phantom elm, roots dangling over gaunt boulders. Kazzasius replaced the scope with Dious's rendition.

Black fuzzy motes suddenly began to play across the screen. A lantern mysteriously went dark. The auditorium was plunged into darkness.

The neomancers quailed. When the candles flared up again, all glanced about the hall with a nervous apprehension. Perhaps Aurimag's psychic probes were more potent than the xenophone's causality?

Kazzasius raised his voice, "I am receiving no pattern at all."

"It indicates that my theory is sound," mused Ulisa. "Aurimag is cached in his cave."

"How do you deduce that?" Maitor demanded.

"Only a specific protect-charm could ward off a direct probe to a location that specific."

Kazzasius gave his head a wistful shake. "It would take a constant force and physical projection to employ such defence indefinitely. There are some grounds to your theory, Ulisa."

Ulisa addressed the assembly: "All points to a plan of action. I will launch a campaign east along the Lim to search out Baus and shed some light on this mysterious linkage. A team of you shall prepare an assault upon Aurimag's cave."

Alvius's eyes glazed over with trepidation. "Surely you cannot suggest that we—?"

"I do and no joke whatsoever," Ulisa intoned. "When I have fully completed my mission, I will double back and lend you aid; hopefully we will infiltrate Aurimag's abode as a group. Punitive measures shall be dealt out upon any laggards! We shall see how Aurimag fares!" The shape-shifter turned fiercely upon the company. "Who then is to accompany me on this mission?"

Members of the assembly gaped in sheepish unease. Ulisa's earnest appeal was met with blank faces. A somewhat slack-jawed shifting ensued, and a mumbling and whispering, and neomancers and steward alike engaged in much ear-scratching.

Ulisa swept critical eyes across the gathering. "So—are you all a bunch of pusillanimous fuddy-duddies?"

Dious narrowed his owlish lids. "These are gruff words, Ulisa. Perhaps for more unsophisticated ears than the spell-casters and honoured bachelors of Mismerion?"

Ulisa waved off the aggrandisement with contempt. "I think that sterner words are needed." She turned a deprecating glace to the Philosopher. "What of it?"

Dious cringed. "Surely you cannot expect me at my age to embark on such an outlandish venture? I am currently entrenched in important research involving the analytic comparison of Fesbians's 2nd lemma to Cosmia's 4th dichotomy, formulated in the earlier part of the century. The study, though somewhat abstract, is open to interpretation, for which I, as a dedicated scholar, am uniquely qualified."

"No doubt you are, so I take this as a no?"

Helaar assumed an exuberance that bordered on hauteur. "Dious's remarks are based on pure veracity! Although he is my colleague, he fails to mention that his co-colleague in this project, is me, who demands a singular historical expert to be available on site; hence, I must remain exempt from the recruitment."

"As is only just," remarked Ulisa sarcastically. "Well, Onzo, what of you?"

The normally mild-mannered bachelor spoke in a haughty tone. "By all means, Ulisa, I suffer periods of stigma which shall certainly mar the operation and my effectiveness during the foray."

"Well then, Kazzasius, what of you?"

Kazzasius fluttered his fingers. With a morose simper he said diplomatically, "The honour is supreme, Ulisa, though my availability is invariably limited. As a field agent my experience is scant. Never could I hope to win over such stalwarts as Ahrion or Dious, nor keep up with you people on foot, while you fly like the wind as a phoenix in the air! In terms of my moral efficacy on this project, I must defer to Maitor, our Moralist, whose skill at roughing it out in the wilds, is greatly in excess of my own."

Maitor gave a half barking croak of consternation. "Do not entangle me in your webs, Kazzassius!"

Ulisa moved to break up the argument with a flourish of rancour. "You buffoons." What a bunch of fancy, overdressed charlatans!" Nonetheless, there were other means to attempt a reconciliation, but sadly, at the moment, there was no great choice. With judicial tolerance, she modulated her tone and spoke with a diffident hope. "Let us calm our emotions, gentlemen, and approach this matter with impartiality. Kazzasius, your diction is impeccable, and while I respect your deference in terms of affairs of espionage, I find your squeamish justifications implausible, and invariably unproductive. Amongst our more distinguished members, like Dious and Helaar, you are the official 'Projector', a title bearing aptitude, which will prove itself cogent in the days ahead. With the help of Alvius and myself, we will reduce Aurimag to a maybug—by reducing you to the size of an elliptical 'eye'. This transformation allows you to be crafted of wings to keep up with my mobility and have the power to fly back and forth, thus tracking Baus's movements."

Kazzasius instantly objected to the idea. "I only uttered the remark in jest. Besides the idea is foolishly outrageous! Intellectually plausible perhaps, but dangerous. What, you depict me flittering about like a drunken magpie with no trace of dignity?" He groaned in mock remorse. "How an 'elliptical eye' is supposed to draw on the power of the xenophone is beyond me!" He swung his arm about the device. "Shall I drag the contraption behind my tailcoat like a kite on a string?"

"By no means," responded Ulisa with annoyance. "The device can be integrated into your anatomy by the simple means of an electrical power surge placed resourcefully upon your upper back, which after reduction to a hypothetical size, of course, shall be quite within the realm of possibility."

Alvius, eager to have escaped the possibility of 'field agent', rubbed his hands with eager speculation. "This comprises a definite breakthrough, Ulisa. With a co-mingling of byke-crystal and fluid-conetrics, the xenophone and Kazzasius' body can be fused together into one synchronous entity, thus enabling a new order to exist within Kazzasius's physiology."

Even Dious had to admit that the idea was marginally plausible. Linking a causal device with human flesh seemed promising, but if success were likely . . . as it was, certainly there was a fair to good cost-benefit ratio to be had, as he pointed out decidedly to the group.

There were scattered hoots of approval and Helaar commended Dious on the cogency of his remark. The Historian blushed and went on to further ratify several remarks regarding his own thesis. "You are forgetting that the scheme, while hinting of abstract conceptuality in all its forms, hinges on the improbable assumption that the 'device' you speak of, and its various apparatuses, are still functioning to perfect order."

"I claim no such assumption," asserted Dious.

Kazzasius pushed himself closer in half-wincing outrage. "Dious, I find your attitude hypocritical and your compliance as outrageous as even Ulisa's, or Alvius's."

Ulisa held up an appeasing hand. "Gentlemen! Let us not waste breath arguing over conceptual probables."

"A fine idea!" sputtered Kazzasius. "You are not the one being transmuted and implanted."

"Silence!" cried Onzo. "Ulisa, your voice resounds with the best reason of all!"

"Excellent then!" called Alvius. "It is settled! Let us begin the procedure at once."

The shape-shifter slapped her podium with approval. "With pleasure. Alvius! Retrieve your didometer. Assist Kazzasius in hefting the instrument over to the courtyard. The three of us will march to Woisper's tower. There is workspace and suitable equipage for the taking, including ziziofluxogram, flux-screen and momometers!"

Kazzasius's face dropped in sullen bewilderment.

"What of me?" blurted Maitor like a foghorn. "Do you exclude my presence from this auspicious undertaking? I am morally-minded, you will recall, and I find the idea reprehensible."

Ulisa blinked peevishly. She cried out a high note of strained patience. "All may view the apparatus, Maitor, though I find your recent lack of involvement in the affair somewhat two-faced."

Maitor gave a wolfish laugh. "So? A man must act in the way he feels moved in the moment. Withal, I find your argument out of context, and your attitude representing a hidebound mode of thinking."

Ulisa frowned darkly but chose to ignore the remarks.

Alvius gestured with impatience. "Everyone is entitled to his or her own opinions. Now! Let us not dawdle here. For whatever reasons, we are only interested in the success of this undertaking."

"Here, here!"

Griping insincerities, Maitor and his colleagues repaired to Woisper's tower.

Alvius drew Ulisa aside. "The plan seems somewhat slapdash, Ulisa, don't you think?—not to mention, what of the pizofield fluxogram? Do you believe that the antique device is still usable? After all—you remember the scandal it caused when Woisper, while not entirely lucid, almost blew up half of Mismerion."

Ulisa narrowed brows. "I do—and of that we will see, Alvius. In the meantime, not a word!"

VI

The time was mid afternoon. Only tattered bits of sky showed beneath a grey overcast. The company plodded its way to Mismerion's northern court and the octagonal flags seemed pale and worn from their many years of pre-eminence. Woisper's abode took centre stage, overlooking the court and forming a portentous cone of black basalt. Flaring to an umbrella, the summit hulked like a toadstool. Several brass-gilt effigies were surmounted on the cupola—minor deities, bright crakes, gargoyles, centaurs.

Despite the imposing exterior, Woisper's tower remained as enigmatic as ever. It was a lofty cylinder filled to the brim with dry air and emptiness—and neglect. The innermost nexus comprised a dim space, hollowed out of chalky grey marmor. A ring of steps radiated about the shaft, ascending to dizzying heights. A pair of rusty old chains hung from upon high to attach itself to a monster pulley and a weird oblong bell rising far in the dimness.

Ulisa swallowed the chill in her throat. A sudden flapping of pigeon wings startled the newcomers. On the topmost tier Woisper's workroom lurked—a mysterious chamber filled with the memory of magical rituals. Alvius and Kazzasius tackled the first steps, dragging their cumbersome device step by step on its small rolling wheels. Ulisa followed, heeled by the others, who paused at the top of each landing, catching their breaths.

Up the company tramped. The stairwell wheeled and the crumbling steps crunched underfoot. As they gained height, a pungent odour made itself known: Ulisa thought bat dung mixed with pigeon droppings. Maitor frowned and the sudden hoot of a tower owl almost plunged him to his doom. The stairwell, as fate would have it, remained dangerously devoid of guard or balustrade.

The company eventually reached the last landing, barring frights and mishaps. Each cast indecisive looks at his new surroundings.

The chamber was as Woisper had left it months ago—crude, basaltish, a vague semicircle of ruin. A side wall was streaked with black cinders, the result of a failed experiment. The other wall was crowded with objects from the old blast. Elsewhere stood a great gnarled table, a scattering of old books, some broken beakers, archaic bottles, pastes, specimens, punch panels, gourds, copper kettles, overturned tureens, a ragged mesh of chicken wire, gadgets, gears, boxes, wires, an old broken pillar and grinning gargoyle hunkering off to the left with a facsimile of a lightning bolt gripped in its bronze claw-shaped paw.

There was no evidence of any attempt at cleanup—all disorder appeared as it had—up to the time that Woisper had gone missing.

The xenophone was immediately brought forth and taken off its trolley. It was assembled in a prominent position at the edge of the table from which the Alchemist Alvius selected several half intact beakers and carboys and mixed dubious chemicals into a smoky mixture. All gathered poked noses into the admixture. They recoiled at the vapours. The red-headed Alchemist picked up an old yellow gourd, cut it slantwise (apparently as some sort of power source) and hastened to top it up with a healthy dose of electrolytes. He infused a half quantity of vinegar and a crusty block of salt from some of Woisper's intact bottles and looped a pair of copper wires from gourd to the mesh of upright chicken wire, apparently to act as a ziziofluxogram, or 'shield'. The Alchemist's plan was to surround the incumbent with enough plausible means of protection in case of mischance when the electrical flux was applied. Ebon rods and multicoloured crystals were hung from the shield—in order to create a field defence, where copper-coloured chimes and canes jangled in the draught from one of the higher windows.

In the presence of Kazzassius's desultory complaints, Alvius extended a cautionary hand regarding the apparatus and its associated 'extensions'. "When the pitch and crystal-mix mutates a half octave above the accepted range, I insert the tongs or 'forks' into the gourd. The adjuncts constitute low access-keys to the causal-pyscho plane of existence—the same in which Kazzasius will be plunged. Watch—as I add a third wire!" Alvius's eyes gleamed afire. "Now, watch again!—I apply a multi-ground patch from gourd to table . . . connecting from gourd to crystal, inducting a stream of energy from incumbent to mesh—mesh to gourd—and then we back to crystal! Is it not ingenious?"

Ahrion shook his head with annoyed confusion. "This neo-science of yours is galling." Peering crosswise, he emitted a rancorous grunt. "Speak in common terms, Alvius, so that everyone might hear."

The Alchemist gave a brief, conciliatory sigh. "Alright already, Ahrion —I will strive to accommodate you. Attend! . . ." He conveyed Kazzasius inside the shield. After a time he affixed several nodes of metallic composition to the Projector's cranium and assessed the linkage from temple

496

to mesh, mesh to crystal, and ebon rod back to the sensitive upper reaches of his skull.

Kazzasius stirred with the liveliest of apprehension. Ulisa demanded that Maitor lift her up to the workbench so that she could inspect the methodology. Certain immediate flaws came to mind, in which she voiced a dubious appraisal of the procedure. "Are you certain, Alvius, that the subject is properly installed in his harness? I simply cannot condone the possibility of mishap."

Alvius lifted a finger of competency. "Stand back, Ulisa, while I douse the incumbent with more balsolo."

The neomancers looked on with more anxiety; Alvius began a studious appraisal of the interconnectory meters and nodes and crystals. The diodes and plate-meshes seemed work-worthy. The analysis was complete. Alvius muttered a phrase about the presence of a small, tolerably low flux-to-meter ratio, which could prove deleterious if certain critical steps were not applied.

The Alchemist cautioned the group to move back several paces in the event that acid might splatter! After repairing the anomaly with a tweak of sound chime to fork, he addressed the company with exuberant forbearance: "All is well! Please allay your fears. The experiment will proceed as planned!" He beckoned Helaar and Ulisa forward. "You are to be my witnesses. Others may assist—but please resist the urge to tread between gourd or shield or make contact with shield or pizo-fluxogram. I need not mention the folly of such an endeavour."

"Why no touch?" bellowed Ahrion.

"Doing so deactivates the flux," responded Alvius. "Withal, it invites chaos, if not disaster to the health of Kazzasius."

"Hold on!" called Dious with disbelief. "Where does the xenophone come in to play?"

Alvius spoke coldly as if explaining the birds and bees to a child. "The xenophone shall be inserted in the shield, but only *after* a preliminary checkpoint has been reached."

"Meaning," added Maitor, "that Kazzasius has assumed the form of this elliptical eye?"

"In a nutshell, yes," explained Alvius.

"What of Kazzasius's 'wings'?" blurted Onzo. "When do these miraculous appendages appear?"

"When the requisite time has arrived."

Helaar could not repress a sardonic snort. "You exhibit a remarkable confidence, Alvius. When is the requisite time 'ripe'? When the flux implodes and sends us all to n^{th} order oblivion? Perhaps when the field creates an interlull of causality that will instantly confound poor Kazzasius and us into sprouting protuberances?"

Kazzasius could only call out a nasal complaint at the cynicism. "I shall not have jokes or calumny injected at this crucial time, nor will I slob off the fact that these apparatuses revolve upon a sensitive part of my anatomy which dangles on a thread!"

The declaration brought a hushed mutter from the group and also muted snickers and hoots. Ulisa stamped her foot. "Gentlemen! Please spare your pre-pubescent repartee until *after* the procedure. Alvius's task is important and obviously nerve-racking—and I'm sure he'll appreciate a space of silence."

Alvius gave a gesture of polite endorsement. "In all respects, quietude is greatly appreciated, Ulisa."

Ulisa gave a curt inclination of head.

"Incidentally," inquired Kazzasius with a mocking overtone, "how are we to reverse this procedure once the mission is complete?"

"The method," explained Alvius, "is somewhat in its infancy." He gave a distracted look. "Although I hope it to be partially documented in Woisper's "Volume of Reformation Jinxes'—or perhaps in one of his personal diaries."

"What?" Kazzasius roared. He squeezed through his restraints and ripped nodes from the back of his skull. "I will not have neophytes and amateurs operating on my cranium!" He directed a series of abusive insults at Alvius.

Alvius gripped himself stolidly and flashed several small white teeth at Kazzasius. "Please moderate your invective, Kazzasius. Before you erupt into diatribe, be advised that we are in the middle of a sensitive experiment here, in which a breach of continuity can only result in your disfigurement."

Kazzasius raised a finger to lip in derision. He opened his mouth to turn Ulisa a threatening gasp but could only croak. "Should mishaps occur in this freakish surgery, I shall hold you personally responsible!"

"Nothing to fear, Kazzasius," assured Ulisa. Keeping her tone judicious, she gave a flourish. "Proceed with the unification, Alvius."

The nodes were reapplied; Alvius flicked a dram of chemo-boxo through the mesh and Kazzasius's fox-brown hair stood on end.

A sound chime bonged out a sullen note. The mesh vibrated in unison while Alvius stabbed a fork into the gourd's liquid. Several lurid frequencies of higher tone tinkled the chime.

Alvius cocked an ear. He measured the induction rate with didometer and witnessed the needle rise. He pointed to an acceptable gradient.

"The flux is operating at a moderate to high level of congruity," he affirmed. "The hydro-static condition of the gourd-electrolyte has come as a worrisome irregularity, but as foresight has won out, the anomaly has been stabilized in a hyper-balance between ground crystal and mesh. I am thus impressed to say that a solution is at hand, absolving any hint of error."

Alvius's voice had taken on a heady, didactic tone which many were given to treat with annoyance. "Very informative!" called out Helaar caustically. "Your on-the-spot techno-babble is very entertaining. Can you not channel this lively energy of yours into something useful which involves results at high speed? Our knees quaver and our backs buckle—meanwhile our dinner awaits in the refectory!"

Alvius fixed cold eyes upon Helaar. "Kazzasius's transmutation cannot be so vulgarly precipitated. As I have outlined, if you wish to aid in this experiment, please do so by maintaining a respectful distance from the work area, and remaining silent."

Helaar's voice cracked in displeasure and he began to utter a repudiation, but Ulisa interceded to stave off a quarrel.

Eyes were suddenly turned upon Kazzasius who had begun to glow a disturbing luminous green. His face pulsed orange, then indigo. His mouth popped open, eyes puckered, nose twitched. Then his limbs went slack as he felt his senses beginning to topple into a bottomless pit, but he could not physically fall being strapped into the saddle.

The Projector reached out a hand . . . a trembling fist clenched at the mesh . . . in order to circumvent vertigo, he bared his knuckles and seemed to suddenly want to explode. There came a horrendous crack . . . A speckle of phosphorescence burst about his head and flashing motes flew everywhere: a hundred infusions of pulsing colour, ripped from the realms of chaos and discharged throughout the workroom . . .

The neomancers were thrown into bedlam. Eyes were shielded, but all were rendered dumbstruck, crabbing back in confusion. The detonation was over but they cast about, searching for Kazzasius but he could nowhere be found. Almost as spontaneously, the projectionist was reborn—as a great crimson eye with enormous wings, the eye the size of a huge rutabaga, rolling on the cold stone like the toy of a child.

All leapt back in confusion. The eye continued to roll—absurdly—a mismatched orb, switchbacking back and forth with veins and arteries and long black lashes on its convex, and making ironic twitches in an effort to maintain focus. The wings seemed to tremble with anticipation, and had attached themselves underneath the awkward, egg-shaped eye-body in a most peculiar way.

The orb became stationary. Blinking and pulsing, it cast a glow of variegated colours, only to achieve a peculiar stasis.

A voice broke out in the stillness. "I can see! I can view the world!" The eye's shrill syllables hung in the air. "Ha, ha! You are all woozlebrains—can you not see how comical you look? I can't decide whether I am in the midst of a crew of walking insects or a batch of stilted homungojugs! Descriptions are meaningless." The eye split into a bout of cacophonic laughter.

Helaar cautiously hedged forward, fixing Kazzasius—(or the eye)—with an indignant inspection, "It seems that the procedure has addled Kazzasius's perceptions."

"Not at all!" the eye chortled. "I see all quite rather clearly!"

"He sees all!" declared Alvius, flinging up his arms in triumph. He turned to assure the gathering of his success. "Kazzasius is alive; now, people—that includes you, Maitor! Onzo! Assist me in rolling out the xenophone, so as to plunge it into the shield."

No one hopped to comply. Alvius reiterated his request in greater force. Grudging hands eventually helped. A wire was pulled from the gourd. The eye chirped on about various experiential remarks and the mesh was unfurled; the xenophone clattered inside overtop the eye.

Kazzasius cried out in a fearful voice, "Caution! Do not crush me! My eye-body is a new place. I see only through lids full of allure and wonder! The xenophone crowds my horizon!"

"Calm yourself, Kazzasius," soothed Ulisa. "We know you are exhilarated, but promise that we shall exercise utmost diligence in transporting the xenophone near your person."

Kazzasius was little appeased.

Alvius reinserted wires into the gourd. A safety ground was affixed to the eye's lid then the Alchemist turned to all and explained this would avert damage to Kazzasius's synapses in the case of misometromical spikes.

Onzo and Dious conferred agreement. Kazzasius was about to object, but the flux was reinitiated.

Rods attached the gourd. The xenophone pulsed in mad colour—eggplant jade, plum, flaming crimson. Kazzasius, a small quivering shadow, remained hidden underneath the xenophone, remaining strangely shielded, protected from impairments of flux.

The xenophone hazed over. In an amazing explosion of light it was recast.

The neomancers sprang back, rubbing the sting out of their eyes. They coughed, harrumphed, mumbled about the exudation of gases and inconvenience, and the great eye remained shut in the midst of the miraculous pressure wave.

The Alchemist pushed back his fogged spectacles. He blinked wonderingly in the cloudy light. And yet there was a grimace on his face—of flushed confusion. He removed the chicken-wire, carried the eye onto Woisper's workbench and the spectators crept closer to inspect the new Projector. No perceptible transformation had come over his 'eye-form'—Kazzassius only seemed somehow different.

The time was entering the third phase. Ulisa hastened to Alvius's side where he was preparing a miniature version of the xenophone, Woisper's *novo-xenosphere*. Ulisa scanned the bookshelf for a particular volume, '*Weird Flying Things—Past and Present*'.

The shape-shifter found it on a lower shelf. She selected a yellowed drawing from the compendium—an elder griffo-falcon apparently, depicting a pair of hoary outspread wings. Carefully she tore out the page and handed it to Alvius who circled one of the wings and carefully cut around its edges with a paring knife. Following the procedure, Alvius inserted the drawing over the lens of Woisper's novo-xenosphere. He filled the gourd and affixed five wires from gourd to machine and set the machine cranking in motion.

Rays were projected onto the eye.

The space surrounding the orb became leaden. Almost at once the field was warped in all directions by incalculable forces. The image of the griffo-falcon struggled to remain extant, projecting a bold chiaroscuro onto the 'Eye'. Now Alvius faltered, sensing that something was amiss. He thought to pre-empt the experiment, but Ulisa stayed his hand. The wings on either side of the eye grew to magnificent length, forming appendages, a foot in length, then two, and three—all in similitude to the actual size of the griffo-falcon's!

The neomancers stood back, appalled and amazed. Kazzasius hovered a foot above the table—a central eyelike monstrosity. The Projector flapped about; dust and papers flew every which way.

The ocular globe swung, swivelled closer, assessed the neomancers with a quick, suspicious glance.

Alvius jerked himself back, clutching at his brow. "Kazzasius, control your displeasure. We must reverse the experiment! Quickly now, we must start anew!"

"No!" Ulisa advised. "A reversal entails re-projecting the eye with non-wing! Time does not permit."

"Kazzasius has no legs! How will he land?"

"An oversight," asserted Ulisa. "Do not be alarmed. Let us consider the larger picture: the wing span and lack of talons is a practical boon."

Alvius repudiated the speculation. Further arguments and vindications proved unproductive. Onzo and Ahrion each seized a wing and essayed to convey the creature down to the court. They shuttled the transmuted form down the stairs, wings and body, all in folded quality. Kazzasius was in a daze. Ulisa transformed herself into a moth and flew out of the window. She dove down to the courtyard and resumed her position as overseer.

Under the greying light, the neomancers assembled in the courtyard. All were grave and affected. Conferring in low whispers, they shuffled about on restless feet. They peered here and there, struck with hesitant conviction. Ahrion looked to the sky. He saw a wrack of gloomy clouds and squinted past the floating eye, perhaps searching for some hope of portent, but saw none.

Ulisa spoke with a forced fondness. "Kazzasius's guiding eye will help lead us to Baus." The mutant eye, recently released by its porters, bobbed in halting flight at Ulisa's shoulder. "Either way, we require a new leader for the operation." She glanced about the group and motioned sternly to the magic-makers. "Maitor! I appoint you leader of this brigade. Fare forth! Kazzasius and I shall converge with you at an appropriate time at Aurimag's cave a week hence."

Maitor shook his head in anguish. "'Tis beyond my scope, Ulisa, nonetheless, a commendable appointment. Dious is more   suited to the occasion. He is venerable and wise. His experience, not to mention rectitude, is far beyond my own."

"By no means!" sputtered Dious angrily. "In the absence of Barbirius and Salmeister, Woisper had appointed *you* as superior officer. Ulisa is second in command, so it shall be she who decides!"

"Dious speaks to the mark," agreed Ulisa. "Heed my words—Maitor, you shall lead the group, else I am forced to impose paragraph six, subsection three of neomancer law."

"What is that?" inquired Maitor mockingly.

"The clause is explicit; I shall not recite stanzas verbatim in this formal company; either way, the particulars are self evident."

Maitor pursued this new line of thought. "You appoint me as your leader of this brash expedition, and now browbeat me for making inquiries. It smacks of immorality. Yet if my peers fail to recognize me as leader, you have no tongue!"

Ulisa spoke with a gruff voice of impatience. "Where torpor exists, a true leader must muster morale."

"Yes, Maitor," jibed Dious, "you are a Moralist, aren't you?"

"I am, Dious, so quell your snide hypocrisy. What is so stupid here is that you all have entirely confused your understanding of the term 'moralist'."

"Nevertheless, my mandate stands!" Ulisa called out sharply. "Now cease your squabbling. We must stand back and allow room for Kazzasius to navigate!"

"Here, here!" commended Helaar.

Maitor shafted Helaar an acerbic glare. The two agents departed the castle: Ulisa, as a yellow-backed hummingbird and Kazzasius, as a red-eyed potato with great grey wings flapping formidably to either side. The pseudo-projector-bird was last seen zigzagging toward the serpentine waters of the Lim while the neomancers gazed wonderingly after them.

CHAPTER 2

FARLING'S WALL

"Farling's Wall, built strong and tall,
In days of yore, before stories were told,
Should the wall crack or crumble,
Or eventually tumble,
Who will grin?
For the people of the Lim . . ."

—Old children's rhyme from Gumthorn's *'Tales of Spooks and Faeries'*.

I

The Bastol forest, dank and gloomy, stretched ever more ponderously with the absence of day. Ruby light flickered down from the brooding sky, outlining tall hazel flower and the woodland flora in a tint that was magical, but unnerving. Through the mossy spaces, the four outlaws staggered. The glow was fast dimming. Charcoal-rose silhouettes stretched over the woodland: moths fluttering in and about the trees, weaving paths and traceries, gracing the silky branches with an expression of dreaminess. Spider vines stretched from trunk to trunk with orange twinkles-firefly moths and luminescent insects, also enigmatic scurryings which set Baus's nerves on edge.

The forest seemed to forge in all directions—each offering its own possibility of mishap which led Baus to increased anxiety.

A flutter of movement—a flash of a bushy tail, the heady gleam of watchful eyes.

Baus loosed a quick breath. Relaxing his grip on his sword, he realized it was only a roving coyote . . .

Mustering his composure, he shouldered his comrades on and they plunged into the gloom.

Scrambling bent-kneed through the underbrush, the outlaws found the brambles were claw-tipped and ripped clothes and skin. All semblance of trails had been left behind. Bounty hunters, if anything, would be sorely taxed in pursuing this trail, at least Baus thought. He was prepared for pursuit, yet he was inclined to believe that safety was only ensured by long leagues between them and the vigilantes from Fauche who had almost killed them. He urged his feet on to haste. Queen Maena had put a large price on their heads. Only a fool would think that any lank-toothed opportunist wouldn't cut them down for 50 sequals of silver.

His colleagues were raw-faced from grim flight: Valere, a brawny red-bearded adventurer, effectively a seasoned mariner, was the oldest, forty years at least, once captain of the sunken *Illimmer*, and an experienced fighter. He harboured unique skill in sizing up his enemy which was an asset they could not do without. His sword had indeed carved them a safe path many a time. Being former prisoner of Heagram's prison, many moons ago, he was Baus's longest running friend. *Former* prisoner, in light of thanks to Baus's ingenuity in liberating the two from Heagram Yard. Poli, the youngest recruit was a handy, blond-haired brain-basher of twenty years, a proficient addition to the crew with his quick sword and proficient knife. His mettle was renowned in the pirate circle of Poesasian raiders. He had contributed to many a skirmish in their brief time together, with many bloody, bad ends to their credit. Sansix, street thief and opportunist, was the most controversial scoundrel of their lot. He was of great guileful mettle, a dreadlocked rascal who they had picked up on the way in the gutters of Sloe —more by necessity than choice . . . a wiry rogue, dark curly-headed, with a ruff of black goatee and sideburns. His rodent-like face and vulpine eyes spoke of a person not to be trusted in their ranks. Needless to say, he was a degenerate double-dealer; and yet, he was the only one who had any inkling of the region.

Baus—with title 'Baus the Bold', was a natural leader amongst these outlaws. His subtle skills of sword-wielding, situation-handling, and suave-talking were not to be underestimated. He had been given his cognomen by the sea-wolf Zoren himself, captain of the now sunken *Last Laugh*. A lady's man, he was the only one of the group grounded in some basic experience of magic, listing two items of potency to his name—an ebon rod which rendered its victim immobile upon touch for ten minutes (when it was working)—and a golden gladius invested with the power to conduct swordplay in passion and excellence in proportion with that which ran deep in the wielder's heart. 'Twas a talisman appropriated from the shrunken nobleman Trimestrius, in conditions of misery at Heagram Yard. The other item was thieved from Aurimag the neomancer, Baus's proclaimed enemy, who had resided in Heagram prison so many moons ago.

So went the complicated history . . .

Valere and Poli covered their tracks swiftly, doubling back across the streams and rills in an effort to befuddle trained foxhounds.

A brief time later, they halted, out of breath. They grasped their weapons as they surveyed their surroundings. To either side crowded numerous lichened trunks and mossy stumps hunched like fur-clad dwarfs. A lavish pool nearby swam with green algae and was thick with chokes of muskog-reed.

Shivering, Baus muscled his way forward and sniffed the air. He recoiled with distaste at the pool. He was eager to plunge farther into the woods, not sit here sniffing at pools—but he liked little the risks and consequences involved in scrambling impulsively on. He knew that travelling by night would gain them scant profit running afoul of beasts in the dark.

"We must employ our heads," he muttered.

Valere was convinced of halting too. "Sansix is a bumbling oaf. Our fink stumbles about with noisy plods and clumps."

"True, so what to do?" grumbled Baus.

Sansix held no tongue on the matter. He was too stiff from fatigue and battle-wounds to argue.

"At least, let us move away from this odious pool!" Poli advised.

Valere waved a hand. "Let us move on then—there is little light that remains."

A hasty reconnaissance uncovered no more favoured grounds for camping.

Pinch-lipped, the troupe convened in a sour huddle away from the gloomy pool. In the end, they elected to camp in the vicinity under a sprawling maulwood near a series of woolly thickets. They shambled as far away from the noisome pool as they dared . . .

Sansix and Baus gathered dry leaves for a bed while Valere searched the neighbouring woods for fallen branches. Poli kept watch for bounty hunters. At the brink of a mossy bank Baus halted, peering over the stream. Its trickling coolness provided fresh water and a less prickly clot of tisselwood. He swatted at blue luminous moths that drifted by, contemplating the weaving playful path on plush, waxy wings. If only he were a flower fly, he mused . . .

They made camp. The night was long, filled with furtive scamperings and animal-like roars. The companions awoke beaded with sweat, recalling the snatches of horror of their last engagement with the Fauche villagers: Baus saw the maniacal rictus of the villagers, raised mauls and bloody axes champing hard onto a shin—also the fleeting glimpse of the princess being snatched away from their hands by ruffians and horsemen who took her away. If only he could have done something sooner, he might have saved the fair damsel! . . .

Water under the bridge.

He flung off the dream images, rolled on his side, face away from the ill-smelling Sansix. The blunt edge of roots dug into his hip.

Before dawn, Poli woke the others. Baus essayed to shake the cobwebs out of his head. The moss-covered trees seemed more brooding in the morning light and offered little solace. The moths had departed. Like mystic giants, the maulwoods loomed on all sides, huddling guard over their camp, grinning omnisciently upon their company, a high rooftop over the age-old carpet of humus, strept-vine and spanglemoss.

Sansix stretched his limbs idly, complaining of a slight ache in his left thigh. He yawningly wished that he had more time to reflect on the seriousness of their plight. "All this early birding around hinders my morning meditations."

Valere put on a kindly face. "Well . . . that is really a shameful circumstance. Perhaps you would require some room service?" He reached for his blood-caked sword, at which point Sansix quickly bolstered himself to attention. The thief at once sat upright, grimacing at Valere's blade.

The abduction of princess Solstress and her handmaid Uella had left Baus heavy with melancholy. They had taken great efforts to smuggle the princess out of Sloe city, according to her wishes to escape her unwanted marriage to the powder-puff Clavius, but also arousing Queen Maena's outrage in the process. The night's passing had hardly released any of his pent-up angst, yet more pressing concerns were to stay alive. He steeled himself for the long flight ahead.

The four of them shuffled uneasily through the predawn gloom, gathering what little items they had, stealing like weasels through the shadow-draped foliage. With little clemency Valere employed his sword to hack through vine and creeper, while Baus cut swaths through fern with his little golden blade. Sansix trundled gloomily behind, ever an unknown entity in this group. Poli, with his stony smirk and restless hands, straggled back as a capable rearguard. Never once did he lift his gaze from the murky passages, nor Sansix's wavering gaze to a potential path of freedom.

Gradually the blue mist began to lift and the fog to dissipate. Doggedly the companions crept on with spirits rekindled. They saw an apricot luminescence begin to warm the lands and suffuse the air with cheer.

Sansix identified the segment of bush as the 'Bastol' forest, known for its conspicuous clusters of sorrel and pikeweed. "The pikeweed comprises an irritant to skin and limb," Sansix warned, "which will burn like the devil if touched, but I shall make use of this woodland clover for our meal—best in a soup or even a goulash."

Poli gave a grim chitter of glee. "Hurray! We can all eat, sing and be merry around the campfire, with neither pots nor utensils to cook it with."

Valere noted the fact and slapped Sansix on the head. They shoved him grumblingly along.

The troop stumbled upon some sorrel, which they soon washed off and ate ravenously with raw chestnuts and juniper cones. The fare was poor, but nobody could complain.

A gnawing ravenousness began to take hold of the company's spirits before long. Hunger pangs grew to crankiness. Bickering grew to quarrelling and scuffles and plans soon dissolved. None had slept well and all were heedlessly exempt from a good bath.

All day long they trudged, and on into the night, alert for unexpected wayfarers and menaces. Sylvan depths swarmed around them. Within the innermost reaches of the tissel and maulwoods they crept, and they once accidentally broached the fringes of the forest to catch a wistful glimpse of arable land. A thatched hut came into view, near a small twist in a crude road that straggled along the line of the forest.

Quickly they ducked back into the trees. Little did they wish to encounter posses or vigilantes that would tear them to pieces over a few silver coins.

The journey brought them in a huddle together, murmuring and grumbling and peering distrustfully at each other. Several tongue-lolling coyotes had loped after them with looks of hunger and violence in their eye, though at a comfortable distance. Creatures as these were only haggard mongrels with russet pelts, though their large panther-like paws and black grinning jowls could make short work of them if they wanted.

Sansix gestured grimly at the creatures that glared out of the bangle-thicket at them. "Perhaps these wolves are the least of our concern as we head toward the Branx."

"And why's that?" Valere raised an eyebrow. "What's the 'Branx'?"

"'Tis the forest beyond the wall—old beyond reckoning, and somewhat eldritch."

"This tells us little," announced Baus peevishly. "Elucidate, Sansix." A dark green frond had slapped him on the cheek. Now he cut it to ribbons irritably with his weapon.

The swindler was quick to voice a comment: "The woods beyond the wall are populated with misfits and misanthropes." Sansix's voice had taken on an eerie edge and it complemented the vindictive gleam glowing in his eyes.

"What are you mumbling about?" growled Valere. None had taken comfort in his remark.

"Farling's Wall, the great barrier—as I have mentioned."

Baus and Poli pressed the thief for details, but he would divulge nothing more. As he had claimed, he guarded an intrinsic ignorance of the local lore.

* * *

'Twas early evening and simple hunger had taken its toll. All in all, the outlaws were desperate for sustenance. Each looked about with ravenous purpose. An eerie gloaming had spread upon the lands, casting the maulwoods into mauve, leaden pillar-plumes of mystery.

Baus halted, holding high a firm hand. From a distance came the lowing of wegmors and the bleating of sheep. Sounds as these could only portend human habitation.

In a bent-kneed crouch, he thrust himself closer, all the better to hear the nature of the bucolic beasts.

Several minutes passed. Presently the smell of burning hay and tanning goat-hide became known. Smoke rings hung in ivory circles, floating up through the gaps in the thinning trees. They squinted into the moonlight, saw a village—perhaps eighty paces away, with the roofing and mud-sod sides shrouded in mist.

"Sarfil!" Sansix muttered under his breath.

"What?" grunted Valere.

"The name of the village."

Baus swivelled his gaze to a place beyond the settlement, where a trio of crude huts stretched before another swath of grim woods. Cradled within the black smear hulked grey bastions—Farling's Wall! Now the barrier was revealed as a high, crude palisade. It almost burst with the pressure of the foliage behind it.

Valere loosed a distrustful growl. "What's so special about 'Sarfil'?" he demanded.

The thief replied, "The last outpost before Farling's Wall. Look! You can see for yourselves. The rampart was built by hands who wielded magic —in days beyond our reckoning."

"Very poetic, Sansix, but we will hear no folklore," chided Valere. "We want facts, not mysticism. We must forage for food."

"It's a dangerous and necessary risk," Baus hissed. "Let us accost the villagers, though our dishevelled appearance may prove our undoing." He cocked an ear. From nearby came an unmistakable cluck of a fowl. Likely of egg-laying variety, Baus thought.

He set his mouth in a wry line and motioned to a series of outbuildings near the rude huts. They were fashioned of grey weatherboard with roofs sagging heavily with sod. "There we may find our rabbits and chickens, lads —you, Poli, go stand guard. As I despise thievery, I am loath to commit to a criminal proceeding. I believe I will belie that distinction at this juncture. An outlaw is entitled to one small indiscretion at one time or another. . ."

Sansix showed a cynical smirk. "Even in your hypocrisy, Baus, you can be eloquent. Nor do you fail to neglect the pragmatic side of the recidivist's life. Perhaps if life were not so capricious—"

Valere swatted him to silence.

Baus disliked the assessment and likewise urged the thief to refrain from tagging personal convictions to his remarks. Valere stumbled past the two. He snatched up a handful of stalks from last year's dead leaves and breathed, "Here, let us draw lots. Someone must reconnoitre the village terrain. As volunteers are scarce, we'll see who is to perform the lucky deed. Whoever gets the smallest twig advances to obtain our dinner, the others stay behind and keep lookout."

"An excellent plan!" croaked Baus.

From Valere's grip the men drew stalks. Examining their pickings, some grinned, others moaned. Valere collected the shafts and peered down to notice that Poli, of course, had pulled the shortest stick. The bully-boy was elected to head the expedition.

He threw himself into a sulk, refusing to carry out the mission, citing dangers and mishap to be gained along the way, and a thorough embellishment of the risks.

Baus chided Poli for his irrational fears. "You are the man of initiative! Move along! If we think you are only the pea-brained pirate, prove us wrong!"

Valere likewise congratulated Poli on his lucky opportunity. Sansix half chuckled from the corner of his mouth.

"What are you sniggering at, thief?" grated Poli unpleasantly. Sansix shied away from the youth's upraised fist. Poli paused, wry musing framing his lips. Accepting his fate, he crept along the wegmor-trampled turf to the murky hutch.

Dogging at his heels came Valere. His blue-grey shadow became a crowding influence. On hands and knees, the two crept closer to the shed with Baus taking up the rear—ten paces—twenty paces—now Baus edged along the cool mist like a prowling cat.

They arrested their crawl. From around the corner of the byre, a team of wegmors shuffled restlessly. Each was tethered to a large wooden post. Fortunately, as well as could be determined, they were docile. A wedge of moon rose from beneath the patch of cloud, illuminating the plain ahead in a ghostly silver. Under the moonshine, Baus could discern three mud huts whose possible use included smoking meat or tanning hides. The rising of fumes and the wegmor hides indicated human presence.

Within the enclosure dwelled an old covered well. Baus discerned shapes of an open kiln, a battered rain barrel, several wooden posts. He was further amazed to see a curious fane whose core rose from the middle of the small tract of raised land. The shrine consisted of grey timber buttressing the midsection, and leafless branches and chopped logs piled on top of each other, with a set of antlers and skulls mounted on its crest.

A thrum of voices suddenly burst from the barn: a team of farmhands tramping closer.

The voices wavered; a local dialect—one of the sod-layer patois.

Emerging from the poorly-hinged doorway clomped a figure.

Poli had just unlatched the hatch and had slipped inside when suddenly —a squeak and a rattle alerted the locals to his presence.

Baus winced. There came a flurry of wings, and a clamour of angry shouts. Surely the denizens of Sarfil would be ill of humour!

Out from the hatch burst Poli. He clutched his startled hen in a red fist. A stable boy bolted out of the byre, just in time to catch sight of him. He uttered a livid screech, tossed his bucket away and ran back into the barn.

Poli now bolted. Another muscular figure came forging out of the byre— obviously the stable boy's master. Raising his pitchfork, he came charging after Poli. The stable boy sped after him, rake and a lantern clutched grimly in hand.

Poli took a wrong turn. He got himself entangled in the three horned wegmors hidden around the backside of the barn and backtracking, swung madly about, stumbling into the irate farmer. Pitchfork met halberd, a strike which Poli caught expertly. Luckily the blow had not been fatal, but the stable boy, springing after him, jabbed him with his rake in the ribs.

Poli mouthed a shriek; he loosed his hen. He raised his weapon, but was not so angered as to spill innocent blood on a mere boy's behalf. He landed a boot in his gut and sent him flying. The other turned racing across the moonlit swath. The oil from the boy's lantern dripped on the loose hay and suddenly the mound was on fire. Pink flames shot everywhere.

With desperate strokes, the farmer efforted to extinguish the conflagration while Valere had rushed forth to scoop up the hen. The clucking beast was squashed inside his cloak and he essayed a mad dash out of sight.

"Stop, you thief!" the farmer cried. "That's my hen!"

Valere ignored the command. Brandishing his sword, he stood nose to nose with the farmer.

The farmer seemed to edge away from the grim features of Valere. The seaman was a formidable sight and the great tangly flaming beard and the gleaming sword had him cowed.

A baulky woman suddenly dogged out of a doorway, raising a poignant cry: "Kaghardt! Get your mangy bones together, you oaf! I see two more vagrants are skulking in the shadows! Wait! There are three. They are scampering off into the shadows. Grab them! Thrash them within an inch of their lives! They can't be stealing our hens. 'Tis the same brigands for which we were warned to be on the lookout!"

The woman turned her shrill attention to the other yokels poking their heads out of the adjacent byre. "Bobbleteek, you fiddly old fuddle-dub! Gnash them with your hoe! Crack them with your rake! Why do you sit there like a lame gopher and fumble about with your milk pail? They mean us harm, these bandits—but for us they could be easy sequals!"

Baus sprinted forward, grabbing hold of Valere by the shoulder and yanked him back in the direction of the trees.

Valere shook off the hint. The two shot after Poli—across the pasture toward the blue black forest broaching upon the mysterious wall. Sansix they left glumly behind. With a yelp, he trotted grimly to catch up.

Now the villagers came rushing out from all quarters armed with fury. They gathered courage and swept out into the pasture, gesticulating and cursing. Baus counted a half-score of them: rough, leathery-faced men and women with straw in their hair and chaff on their cheeks. Some wore coverall hides and fur hats; others stumped about in big elkhorn boots. They wiped beefy hands on baggy breeches and tossed imprecations in the air and words of bravado. They took up chase, waving rakes, hoes and firewood blocks snatched from their fane. Before any could act, Baus and his crew were herded into the gaunt trees, ducking beyond fern and bramble and properly shielded.

The companions drove themselves deeper into the scrub. They sensed no pursuit, but their chests heaved and they stopped, sucking air into their lungs.

Baus strained ears in the gloom. The sounds of villagers had died down. Noiselessly they crept on hands and knees closer to the edge of the trees, peering through the gourd-shaped fronds.

Baus could see a handful of labourers, clad in baggy smocks, slapping rakes and hoes against the brake, trying to flush out their quarry. They cast gap-toothed grimaces into the night and made sounds of disgust and frustration.

Sansix gave a triumphant hiss. "We are safe, for now. The cowards! Sops! They won't step a pace nearer for fear of devils and horrors in the forest." He waved a four-fingered hand, his pinkie sliced from Prince Arnin's sword in a melee at the palace. "All their fanes and cairns can't save them from the menace beyond the wall."

Valere stared at him gloweringly. "What do you mean by that?"

Sansix grunted innocently. "Merely a figure of speech."

Valere growled. "Are these farm rats such milksops then?"

"They are pantywaists!" announced Sansix. "They could drown themselves in a glass of water!"

Baus brooded thoughtfully. "'Tis true the people from Sarfil do not seem much given to swordplay, nor are they inclined to stray into the forest—but this disclosure from a man who blanched at a certain cry of a mothman under Sloe palace?

Sansix objected cordially.

Valere gave a mocking grunt. "Sansix tends to easily forget his womanly frights."

The thief spread his palms in offended innocence. "The example you cite is hardly worth a comparison, considering my mutilated finger by Arnin's sword."

Valere made motions to negate Sansix's grievances. "How about two fingers then?" The hen gave an excited croak. On continued flapping and tumult Valere was obliged to snap its neck. He showed a jovial face to Sansix, muttering, "This is what happens to creatures of lower order. Witness? Come! Let us quit this damp burrow. I grow chilled. We cannot stay here all night. Light us a fire, then we'll have us some smoked pullet!"

Through the lichen-path the rebels crept crook-kneed. They negotiated the path through stumps and fungused trunks with care despite their fatigue. Perhaps a mile they hacked their way, swords and halberds scything, before the undergrowth became so thick that they were forced to turn in a different direction. Far behind the village they heard disgruntled cries. The spaces between the trees had became roomier, easier to navigate at least in this direction. Great gamgkos towered above them like flowering umbrellas. A gentle breeze now rustled the treetops, sighing through the night airs, instilling a sense of warmth in their hearts. An owl hooted in the distance, offering a hollow, sage-like counsel. Somewhere to their left loomed the great wall called Farling's, the one that seemed to be their sentinel—and bane. Hidden from view, its awesome presence remained an ominous enigma, inscrutable as a legend lost in time out of mind.

They discovered a small glade in short order whose grasses were full of fallen gamgko and seedlings. Bending, they gathered the seeds and nuts so as to dress their hen.

They decided to make camp here for the night. Soon they had a capable fire going aside a gnarled twitch oak which rooted off toward the edge of the forest. The sky was approaching plum lavender and the warm flames, brought to roaring heights, roasted them their pullet and brought them contented sighs.

They sat with backs against the wizened oak after dinner. Despite their harrowing experience, they digested their victual with a feeling of satisfaction. Each etched future plans, most of these knavish, for none had a clue as to where they were heading, or what was to come next. Quibbling in low whispers, they tossed ideas back and forth like quarrelling bandits. They heard hoots and slurs in the distance, followed by haunting chirps from the forest.

Baus sat back with an attitude of misgiving. The sounds originated from the black woods where flickering flames from the campfire did not penetrate. Amongst the disturbances included monosyllables and intonations of speech vaguely human.

The implications were disquieting and urged Baus to practical action. Under the dying fire's light, he encouraged his companions to initiate construction of a crude lean-to in which they could pass the night. They braced it by the double trunk of the twitch oak.

Holding their weapons close, they huddled under the shelter, nursing uneasy feelings. The fear of any unknown assailant or menace striking at an inopportune moment was not all that absurd. Under the canopy they each lay, taking turns at guarding the fort while peat-rich fumes filled their nostrils and the thoughts of nocturnal surprises weighed heavily on their minds. Ambush seemed yet a reality . . .

II

Drenched in dew, Baus snatched himself awake. He looked left and right, ears trained for deviltry. Nothing. Soft light filtered through cracks of the maulwood. 'Twas morning. A fine mist lurked at the edge of the glade. He frowned. Why was he feeling violated? The emotion was sinister, like a spider's caress.

Brushing off the sensation, he peered about the glade, spying three forms dozing next to him. He also half expected Sansix to come vaulting at his throat. But the villain was ironically tucked between Valere's and Poli's shoulders, snoring like a baby.

Baus twitched, struck with a suspicion. He hitched himself forward, scrutinizing the dozing rogues. Strange. From the rascal's forehead dangled a tattered red hunter's cap; also a peculiar mark was etched in red dye at the base of his neck, something in the manner of an upside down triangle.

Baus scowled, thinking it peculiar that a hat should be draped on the thief's crown. He shook the swindler awake. Sansix snapped open his eyes, sputtering a protest. He professed no memory of the cap nor sign of anything on the last watch.

Poli murmured, "I recall only a fragment of a dream—a vague, rodent-like shape, a woman perhaps, pawing at Sansix's chest. I thought it was a nightmare, and I went back to sleep, too dazed to reply, hallucinating perhaps . . . and yet, the creature that was sniggering at Sansix, was hissing."

Sansix shafted him a look of vile outrage. "You have now proven yourself a complete imbecile! I have been branded for a sacrifice and you do nothing. What doom is upon me!" The thief flung down the cap, stamped it into the ground, amidst the leaves and roots, with hate.

Valere interrupted. "We don't know that, Sansix."

Sansix grumbled. "Surely we do!"

Baus ignored the outburst. He knelt down to study the ground where the villain kicked and spat. Coyotes had foraged for last night's chicken bones and had gnawed the remains clean. Something was perhaps sinister about the coyotes, as evidenced by the mysterious prank committed on Sansix.

Baus, hand to chin, noticed there were several disturbances in the area altogether queer: strange, claw-like scratchings in the soil made by no animal he had ever seen. Was it even coyotes? A strange mini-turret of rocks was steepled ten paces distant.

"The coincidence is irregular," he mumbled to himself. "Nevertheless, we must ply forward, taking advantage of our wits."

"Easy for you to say!" croaked Sansix. "Had you been marked, perhaps you would be singing another tune."

"Curb your yapping!" grumbled Valere. "We are all in this together."

"But you weren't marked," persisted Sansix.

Baus turned the villain a suspicious glare. The knave was an anomaly that defied understanding. 'Twas a wonder that he remained even in their company. Clearly he despised them all . . .

With a thoughtful grunt, Baus motioned them into the woods to gather twigs and leaves to build a fire.

The time was early morning. The last of the three pullet eggs were devoured—the ones Poli managed to snatch—and Baus, at some distance, peered about the misty enclosure, looking for any hopeful clues as to the mysterious visitors of the night.

None were forthcoming. A small clearing was poised at the base of the wooded knoll. Through the trees a glimpse of Farling's Wall caused him an intake of sharp breath: he saw a tight mesh of upright posts, bone-grey, perhaps five times the height of a man. Somehow the barrier was fused with a queer synchrony as if each tree trunk had been hewn or grown together too closely. The boles were crumbling with age. Baus wondered if it meant really a sign of age or some magical construction.

He squinted up at the bleached blue baulks and saw a dull shimmer in the golden sunlight.

He frowned. A riot of crimson clambered over the wall's top. Green-yellow vines and ragged foliage of texture almost alien, a sight most eerily composed and which disquieted Baus. Was it from here that the mischief-maker had come to brand Sansix?

The outlaw returned gloomily to his comrades. They lay sprawled in heaps, masticating the last of their small gulps by the fire. He noted that Sansix seemed wryly out of favour with his last mood and to have forgotten his earlier woes. He bantered on to Poli, growing less interested in his branding, than boasting of his knowledge of the folklore of the area. As for the knave's braggadocio, it had prompted Poli to trot off to make his toilet, during which period, Baus asked Sansix of the legend of the lands: "So what is it about this wretched wall that makes it so daunting to the villagers?"

Sansix fluttered his four-fingered hand. "Superstition. They are all a pack of credulous hounds; morbidly petrified of its grisly aspect—the lore is real in their minds yet the wall shelters unnatural things beyond it."

"Hmph! Specifically what are these 'unnatural things'?"

Sansix let his jowl loosen a bit. His rat-like cheeks showed dimples. "Who knows? As I've already mentioned—harmless aberrations, probably nothing more."

"Indeed?" Baus scoffed. "What about the cairn back in the village? I saw stone squares laden with skulls and barbs. Is this not grisly enough to what you call natural?"

"'Tis only local ceremony."

Baus hooted, "What is the purpose of the fetish?" He reached for his dagger.

"That depends on your degree of open-mindedness."

"Grace us with what you know!" bawled Valere. "Quickly now! Or else I will carve it out of you." He brandished his blade.

Sansix let out a peevish howl. "If you insist. The fanes harbour gateways to elder gods, icons to which the villagers sacrifice their votive offerings. Backward hillbillies they are—like those in Sarfil—the local folk are known for their rude practices: bloodletting, chanting to ward off evil. Once, not long ago, more of the fanes were hidden along the river, and the presence of more vulgar fetishes, but I shall not dwell on those. They have waned since the wall came into being, which I consider a good portent. Common fact attests that the folk even welcome the barrier . . ."

Baus frowned, pulling at his chin.

After a pregnant pause, the rodent-faced villain's cockiness seemed to return and convinced Baus that he was being deliberately played. Baus casually reached for his blade and Sansix gripped himself to attention. "Like I say, you are a prickly sort! The dimwits make offerings to the wall—what of it? The subhumans that exist beyond, if they exist at all, are of nature unknown to me. They do not molest the villagers, if they make their offerings. That is the extent of my knowledge. So please, allow me to eat my victual in peace!"

Poli, who had been scouting the neighbourhood, emerged with an air of excitement. "A river!" he called. "A large one. 'Tis a bowshot from here, just down the slope. I saw a covered punt and the craft was making its way downstream, with two passengers."

Sansix nodded in decisive fashion: "They are fishermen probably—come from the nearby villages, likely Farfus. They ride down the Lim quite frequently."

"Well—" Valere made a brisk gesture "—let us follow this river folk and see where our happy fish friends are going. Perhaps we may be able to share a ride."

Baus commended the idea. "You are man of deeds, Valere."

The seaman bowed; they hacked their way through the underbrush with stands of gaunt wortbush and gillnut gorse posing the most inconvenience. It made difficult going but the four eventually stood at the edge of the river's embankment, where, gazing down upon the Lim, they saw a great ox bow river inching its way ponderously through forest and fen toward the sea. The banks were shallow and muddy; occasional marrow thistle shot up from the water to complement the green, yellow gendrons that hugged the shoreline at various intervals, drooping out over the lustreless water like canopies.

Baus trained his eyes but could see only dim forms huddled in the craft. The persons whom Poli had described seemed young and to gesture to one another as if in familiar discourse.

The boat approached the bank. With an air of ease it bobbed: a low-bellied flatboat which veered toward a small landing and berthed on the river's nearest shore.

The companions skulked their way through the yellow gorse to stand more or less directly opposite the newcomers, hidden from sight. An elbow in the river cast a dull limb to the east and the watercourse swung a sluggish curve toward the sea. Baus saw it disappear beyond a fork in the path. He saw also a weathered claw pointing the way to the village 'Devestok'. Another claw ran north, upstream, in the direction of the landing where the fishermen began eagerly to beach their craft.

Calculating swiftly, Baus instructed his comrades to make haste to the place of landing. On all fours they crept amongst the sedge so as not to alert the fishermen. In the sharp shadows they saw the craft rock in the shallows, long and flat-bottomed, shaped like an odd, rectangular box, bobbing in the murky waters like a fantastic toy. Its outer hull was laced with brown wickerthorn and spiked with three-inch prongs. A canvas canopy protected the bow while several weird two-pronged forks rose a yard from each corner. What were these? Baus wondered. A low bench was crafted of winewood and curved round a comfortable cooking area, seating four, from where a black chimney reached skyward through stretched canvas.

Two youths stood aboard the craft each of indeterminate age. They worked away with their rods and reels. One, a bare shinned adolescent, wearing coveralls hiked up to the knees, sported a thick swath of flaxen hair. The other guarded long, shoulder-length chestnut-black hair and a face like a cherub's, impishly composed. He seemed somewhat older than his peer and more of a domineering personality by reason of the brisk commands he gave to his friend while the other sought to comply in tolerant fashion. Both wielded corkscrew-like daggers belted at their waists, which Baus thought overkill. Cloaks were fitted with leather cords to inseams, and buckles for quick access.

Baus gave a silent signal. The band crept into offensive positions and watched with expectant attentiveness. After beaching the craft, the youths tested the waters with grapples before they broached the shallows. Obviously something lurked in these waters that was hostile and they were not about to take chances. Satisfied that nothing untoward threatened the proximity of their craft, the youths jumped down onto land and secured their boat with ropes to the nearby gendron.

At close range the fishermen seemed harmless, also unaware that they were being watched. The pair continued to laugh, retort, remarked on their own jokes, removed bait, planted two long rods loosely in the mud and sat in easy postures aside their fishing gear.

Baus pulled Valere aside. "Now—let's make this clean: this is not a blood sport, gentlemen. The youth's weapons, agreed, comprise a singular nuisance. The items are to be confiscated swiftly, with a maximum of elegance and skill."

The three crept closer. Baus pinched index and forefinger in an 'o'. The three leapt out of the brush, disarming the youths in a trice. Poli gripped the dark-haired youth's corkscrew dagger in a palm and Sansix sat back in the shadows, watching the drama played out with impersonal distaste.

The younger, flaxen-haired youth cried out belligerently, "Why do you grapple us?" He scrambled to his feet amazed and irked. "You have seized our spit-blades, now you affix them to your own belts!"

"The observation is sound," remarked Valere.

The dark-haired youth growled and Valere did not care for the manner of his tone. Baus skipped forward to meet the older fisherman who vented more brazen retorts. "Patience, stripling. We have only come for food and to gather information."

"That is our flatboat you seize, entrusted to us by our elders."

"A pretty fact," noted Baus. "But we require the craft to transit us upriver."

"And what of us?" the youth complained. "You filch our means of transportation and demean us with your rejoinders. Now you confiscate our fishing gear. What else is next?"

"On the contrary," reasoned Baus, "we are thieves liberal in our dealings. You could have iron thrust in your gullets. Be thankful. Now, of the terrain—what do you know?—" There came an ugly silence. Baus pursed his lips wryly. "So, not going to say anything? Well, I will emphasize that you know the terrain, of which we are ignorant. Who is then in better need of a boat?"

The flaxen-haired youth snorted out his disgust. "I am Gueppe, fish-spearer, and this is my brother Vorlo. We are Fisherfolk of Farfus, hardly four leagues away. We are on a fishing venture five leagues from upriver. We are scheduled to return to our kin with our decks full of bucklers and roustagouts before four days have gone by!"

"This is a happy announcement," agreed Baus.

The youth continued unabashed: "When we do not return, our elders will be worried. They will come hunting for us with grapple-rods and grip-sticks. What will you do then?" His face was hitched in an impudent sneer.

Valere blinked. "Say that you perhaps dallied with maids from Sarfil?"

The dark-haired youth choked with fury. "No, not with any of those harelips! My kindred will retaliate with force."

"If so, when?" murmured Baus. "Either way, 'tis a risk to be embraced. I emphasize that your youth and vigour lie before you, whereas we have less days left in our lives. I urge you to cherish these moments while you have them. Who better to guard your boat and tackle than us? Remember! Goodwill makes a person noble."

Gueppe gave a chirrup of contempt. "I could care less for noble."

His brother whined intolerably: "We will be forced to hump it back to Farfus on thistle-scratched legs."

"What of it?" laughed Baus. "Consider it a means to build character. As I have hinted, we will return your craft in due time. You are able-bodied youths, as I've intimated, and we are in need of haste. You have your rods and reels and wits about you. Capture bucklers as you need and slake your thirst with waters from the river."

"Bah! And have wire worms scourging our livers?"

"That is a pessimistic thought."

"But true."

Poli stepped forward. "I sense a tone of insolence in these pips. Perhaps I should right it. There's a discontinuity in this alleged story of theirs. What need they of daggers if they are just fisherboys?"

Gueppe gave a sullen croak: "To deter the wild women of the forest, what else, you halfwit? Don't you know that it's prudent to beware of their fiendish tricks in the night?"

Valere gave a laugh of wolfish merriness. "Fiendish tricks, is it? Well, do we look like a pack of namby-pambies to you? Who are these 'wild women' you talk of? And who is scared of a few muck-faced viragos?"

Vorlo assumed a lofty air. "They are neither 'muck-rakers' nor viragos. They are Wickles! Creatures that beguile the eyes, seduce the ears, cloud a man's reason. Beware! Their deceits are known far and wide. All of the river folk erect fanes and cairns to ward them off. They are mantled with skulls and bones of the same creatures who have stolen our blood-brothers and sisters."

"We have some experience with these fanes," Baus mused. But the statement stirred him and he gave a deep frown. He thrust his attention upon Sansix, at whom he hurled a question. "So, rogue! Why are you skulking away and what is this demise that you were planning for us? Cannibalistic death? Slow roasting upon torture?"

Sansix's bleak face showed injury. "Not at all! Why do you confound your ears with the mirthless drivel of these urchins?"

Baus locked eyes with the villain in distaste. "So, there was more to these cairns than you would allude?"

"Not in the least," argued Sansix. "These boys' fears are fuelled by imagination!"

Baus was not gulled by the conniver and turned to the newcomers. "How are we to elude these 'Wickles', as you call them, and maintain our equipoise from imminent machinations and charms?"

Vorlo retorted, "With scepticism and sagacity! Trust nothing that you would not otherwise spy with your own eyes."

"That is an over-generalization," Poli grumbled.

Valere rolled his eyes. "It seems we have no dearth of advice in our company."

Vorlo addressed the seaman through pinched lips, "Your blond bullyrag is right, Redbeard. It may be well for you to thwart these Wickles as soon as possible before you are entirely at your wit's edge—neither frazzled by thieves nor ambushed by louts."

"Mind your impudence," warned Valere. "You have a wagging tongue that I'll soon soak in bog water."

Vorlo scoffed. "So, it seems we are at an impasse."

Baus gestured to the slow-moving river. "Matters will resolve themselves in good time. We will board your vessel, then gain your village before nightfall. After that we will acquire our fill of victual. Then, we will make plans to continue our pilgrimage."

Vorlo uttered a plangent groan. "You think you can outwit my kinsmen and accomplish all this without incurring retaliation? You are loonier than a Wickle! My kin will set upon you, hunt you down and spear your gizzards before you make one step! What do you think they will do when they see you with our boat, for starters?"

"A good question, but you assume that we will be that stupid?" quipped Poli.

"And what of us?" thundered Gueppe. "It's neither safe nor wise for us to wander these sordid paths while Wickles abound! Have you no compassion? The fiends creep from the woods well before nightfall, they ooze through cracks in the wall, creating mischief and terror with mind and body!"

Valere advanced with short patience. "Wickles again?"

Vorlo positioned himself in defence. He snatched an opportunity to plunge the sharp, corkscrew-edged knife dangling at Valere's belt into his belly.

The seaman caught the wrist and squeezed hard as the youth made a run for safety. Gueppe, in similar style, attempted a grab and stab on Poli, but the bully grabbed his arm and impacted him with no less ruthlessness.

The youths sagged to their knees, wailing in unison.

"Enough!" trumpeted Baus. "Release these youths!"

Vorlo, moaning in agony, shook out his limb: "Vile oafs! Gueppe and I will be prey to the Auk king without our weapons!"

"Auk king, is it now?" Valere laughed. "Another of your ill—formed Wickles? Or perhaps a Wickle's Wickle?" He chortled at his joke, grabbing hold of Vorlo's wrist and gave it another crushing squeeze. Vorlo sank to the ground, howling.

Baus intervened. "I say, enough—"

The seaman grudgingly released his grip. "Well, if you wish . . ." Waving a scarred fist, he scoffed, "Away with you, you batch of insolent sissies. Wickles! Has your imagination gone daft?"

"You laugh, grandfather," seethed Vorlo, "but not for long. You'll see."

The ominous threat hung in the air and the seamen looked about the forest with uncertainty. The fisherboy's grin was like a sinister snake and he shook the blood back into his hand. "'Tis a dread thing, this Auk—a monster, which swoops down from high and snatches folk for its pleasures."

Poli scanned the sky. "I see no such 'Auk'."

"You will."

Valere clicked his tongue. "Enough! There never was any 'Auk'. Faugh! Do you forget that we have travelled leagues without molestation? So why should we be mauled now?"

Sansix made a mournful bark, "You are forgetting the prank imposed on my person last night!"

Valere grunted. "That was no Auk. It was an act well deserved."

"The Auk is real!" sobbed Gueppe. "You would be wise to take our warnings to heart." He sank into a whimper, gaping at the red-beard who wandered over in unhurried fashion to grab the sacks of bucklers from the boat.

"What are you doing now, barrel-butt?" cried Gueppe.

"Taking your red-bucklers and marsh-mullet for lunch, what does it look like?"

Vorlo choked back his fury. "An entirely unnecessary procedure! What shall my soul brother and I eat for lunch?"

"Whatever you like. You will be left to your own devices. You have your lures and your tackle," explained Baus equably. "We are not the callous filchers you think. You may troll for more bucklers, or mullet—as you wish."

"How shall we cook them then?" demanded Vorlo sullenly. "Fry them in the sun?"

Valere pushed past the youth; his face reddened with annoyance: "A man is given brains—to think—to overcome his dilemmas and problems with savvy, not to whine and grouse."

"Pah! I care not for savvy," complained Vorlo. "I curse your redbeard hide. I hope that the Auk pecks out your eyes and hauls you off to Thrallsmoor to eat piece by piece!"

"Tut!" protested Baus. "That is not language to harp at an old man about."

"Such tone leads to perdition likewise," added Poli.

"My curse stands!" cried Vorlo.

"As you like," intoned Baus. Bowing stiffly, he moved off toward the boat. "Masters Vorlo and Gueppe, I bid you good day."

Striding with decision, he lifted a foot to the gunwales. Then, in sudden recollection of how the youths had tested the waters prior to alighting, he snatched one of the nearby poles and probed the water with brief care. Sure enough, a three foot, black-banded suckerfish leapt out of the murk at the grapple's prod, biting and gnashing at the rod like a demon spitting fire. Baus leapt back, blinking, killing the toothy menace with prejudice.

"Clever, swains," muttered Baus. "Contriving to bypass a warning, you would hope one of us hopped to our doom."

The fisherboys grinned malignantly.

Baus embarked on the vessel unscathed, congratulating himself on his insight. "Very well," he muttered. Gripping the wheel, he gave it a carefree twist and then began to search for contrivances to control the craft's functioning.

Valere and Poli shoved the vessel off from the shore. The seamen almost jocularly left Sansix behind, but the squabbling villain could find no humour in the act. The two youths stared at the outlaws as if they were mad. The craft receded before their eyes. They pitched rocks and fumed, but nothing could be done and soon they sat down in defeat, stranded on the shore.

Baus chewed on his lip. Was it wise to leave the youths in the wild untended? Perhaps they could serve a greater purpose aboard? Hardly. Baus's inward grimace gave him comfort. They would certainly jab a dagger in his ribs upon the first chance. Again, he congratulated himself on his reasoning.

After settling his resolve, Baus assessed the control panel and felt another niggling doubt. The flatboat contained some means of interior locomotion, of which he was ignorant. How was the paddle wheel possessed of motion so pitched under the bilge?

He shifted a lever in the bow. A thrumming transpired and Baus grinned.

Selecting the 'High' lever position, he saw that the craft propelled itself forward as if by magic, coursing across the river with an air of authority. To Baus's satisfaction, another lever controlled a basic rudder system affixed to the stern's lower housing. A flap of maulwood shaped like a shark's fin caused the craft to speed upriver, or to move to port or starboard at will.

Regardless of rights or wrongs, the foursome was underway and they soon gained significant speed.

A strict course upstream due north was Baus's choice, slightly to the west. He dipped up the middle of the river which jogged left like a mongoose's tail. The craft shot over the greasy water with surprising agility. The two-pronged poles posed at each corner proposed something of a mystery—no less the craft's mysterious propulsion.

"The forks are perhaps lightning rods," suggested Poli.

"'Twould be an overkill," grumbled Valere. "The practical utility is so small to be neglible."

"They are weapons for some assault," observed Baus. He tugged at his chin. "Perhaps the 'Wickles' attack from the water—and so a handy pike would come in necessary."

Sansix, who had been listening to all, offered no comment. The villain seemed to grasp something of the implication of the forks and began to peer cautiously about the nearby forests, with no small amount of wariness and unease.

Talk was abandoned. The four bent their attention to the water ahead and the affairs at Farfus.

Baus reduced his speed by two degrees. To be caught unawares around another bow in the river on a hijacked vessel was a foolish happening.

Poli lit the fire under the stove and soon the companions were enjoying fried bucklers and muskey fillets dosed with chiliberry juice which the youths had thoughtfully stashed in the hamper below.

The foursome ate with a staid reserve, feet pitched on the table. Baus reflected that life on the river could never be grander. A gentle headwind flowed past to warm his skin; the green waters floated by in effortless ease; tissel and gendron laced past like fairy reeds, a pleasant, gliding backdrop complemented their quiet sojourn. There was nothing untoward in this environs. No Wickles, no Auks, no ghouls . . . only suppositions crafted from fear-ridden folklore of questionable heritage. A soothing insect whine lulled them to somnolence.

The companions broached an islet of chirping bazelles. There, they caught glimpses of ruined chateaus, vine-covered terra-cotta masonry, and toppled pillars peeking out of the dense forest.

Darting eyes westward, Baus perceived hillocks tumbling in the distance. Hucklethorn and bottlegums rose from the shore, rich with brown-furred maks and gasklets. Baus's imagination soared to the kingdoms that had once ruled these lands. For a time, Farling's Wall had lost all its menace—seen from afar as a distant knife's edge but then popping up again, glinting palely atop slate-coloured bluffs and plunging out of sight amidst hollows of creeper and mangleroot. Unpleasant aspects were not wholly absent in these quarters: long green water snakes stalked the shallows and long silver-backed gariali equipped with carbuncled snouts roved undetected. With a single white eye, a long flat-backed garialis surfaced, gazing at a river flamingo. A minute later it snatched an unsuspecting waterfowl, dragging it under in a gush of feathers and blood.

Baus swallowed. Later in the afternoon, the outlaws were alerted to a more macabre presence. Downriver, in the hazy mist, an enormous condor-like creature flapped up into the yellow sky. It clutched aloft a single scraggly figure. The cargo appeared the size and configuration of Gueppe perhaps, or Vorlo. Baus inhaled a sharp gasp. The companions felt an undercurrent of terror course through their veins.

They flung themselves under the pronged canopy, murmuring as the great moon-coloured thing flapped directly overhead in three ear-piercing sweeps. Three times it circled them, close to the vessel—once gurgling out a torturous lament—a coarse, primal wheeze and a bellow. The thing raised a dihedral anthropoid head and stared directly at them. It fled westward over the forest, clutching a human prize. High over Farling's Wall it soared to become a distant speck in the sky.

Baus murmured aghast: "This is what happens when one fixates on a negative concept."

"Fools," muttered Poli sadly. "They should have stayed hidden. In all their cockiness and stupid clamour, they must have baited the beast."

Valere grumbled. "Possibly, but we'll never know. Let us hope that we too do not fall afoul of the thing, or 'fixate' on a negative concept as Baus has suggested."

Baus scowled. "'Twas not our fault if one of the fisher-lads got snatched. Every resource was at their disposal.

"I suppose . . . " But the thick sound in Valere's throat lacked conviction.

III

Mist on the river turned a scintillating gold. The day drew to the end; a last loop of the river revealed itself. Several dim pillared shapes swung into sight: stone projections rising from the water which proved archaic ruins, possibly a bridge. The pylons had rotted away. At one time they had supported a mortared causeway likely, linked with timber baulks, spanning the Lim in all its glory, thought Baus. Now the platform had disintegrated to a patch of submerged rubble. The pylons were time-eaten. They looked upon the passing ages with wise sorrow; yet the clever people of Farfus had obviously constructed a rope walkway between markers of the ruin, stretching wide across the river. The villagers had anchored it with two great gamgkos at its endpoints and the ropeway allowed boats a clear vertical clearance under its span by both shorelines.

The river's western shore wallowed in sand. Nestled by a driftwood dock a pair of flatboats lay moored. Baus studied the landing thoughtfully, for he could see the brown hulls glinting dully amidst beds of feather-reeds, wild and untamed. Behind the foliage loomed a tract of cleared land where rising smoke showed evidence of a small village.

Baus swung hard on the wheel. The craft banked gracefully into the cover, concealing itself under a fan of overhanging gendrons. To continue upstream was folly. Everyone knew it. Surely there was a correct way to approach these villagers?

To abandon the craft and bypass the village was the wisest course. In this way, they avoided the uncomfortable irony of stealing the fisherfolk's boat and inadvertently prompting controversy regarding the demise of a family's son. But even as Baus approached the gunwales, a cloying unease warned him—any surefire plan was flawed. As long as there were unknowns, there would always remain need of an 'on-demand' plan.

The keel scraped against a bed of crooked roots. Valere and Poli jumped ashore and hacked out gendron fronds and shrubbery to hide the presence of the craft.

Sansix stood frowning to the side, staunchly averse to helping. Water lapped at the hull and birds chirped in the boughs. Valere's methods proved crude and Baus scolded him.

Up the slippery bank they heard voices drifting—a band of youths? Baus stifled their clamour. He urged the four to scramble parallel to the shore and they gained the river road. 'Twas nothing more than a rude runnel of wegmor hooves. High yellow daedilias flanked the path; the green forest showed heavy limbs beyond. Evening was drawing close and the hum of insects and marsh fowl grew once again in numbers.

The adventurers hastened up the path. With caution they approached the ropeway's junction. They did not need to tread this path so warily, for abreast the river ran a great gamgko anchor whose white trunk was hidden by orange-blossoms and where 'twas only a gang of children who roistered about the tree's foot. Its trunk was easily eighty feet high, punctuated with ladder-step planks, nailed every foot. Thirty feet up, the ropeway swung down to the first river-drowned pylon. The rope stretched across the water, binding the twined slats and tissel guards that formed the precarious walkway. The companions' eyes turned to the youths with curiosity. Engrossed in a flag-whirling, ball-tossing game, the children did not immediately see them, but a young girl spied Sansix's red garment and came rushing forth to stare at them with awe. She was graced with sandy hair and a tomboyish smile which contrasted with her candy-coloured smock. Her fearlessness became obvious when she approached to touch Sansix to see if he were real and inquire of their names; soon others were joining. Cognizing that stealth was now redundant, Baus announced that his troupe was from a faraway land and would trudge peaceably to the village with the youngsters —on condition that they could spare them food and water.

Instantly there was a chatter of superiority amongst the crew. Who would escort the newcomers to the village? Who was to divvy out their small supply of dried fruit and sweet cones? There came a sudden army of knives pointed up at the travellers' bellies. Valere and Poli stumbled back, blinking.

The four were herded with prolonged ceremony up the tree ladder and across the roped plankway toward the village—all part of the ritual. Sansix objected to the treatment, professing to vertigo at the top of the landing, but he was ignored. The youths ushered him along with pokes and prods. They were impertinent youngsters and at pains to demonstrate their boisterous authority. Ropes swayed, planks creaked. The group swung the last ten feet over the foaming waters and climbed down to the other shore by means of the rickety tree ladder.

The companions were met by an elder dressed in a grass skirt. Her expression was solemn; her vest was knit with orange and red shells and

530

decorated with blue flowers and tissel cones. Her hands were pressed smartly to hips; from her discerning face were a pair of widely-spaced bovine eyes and pale lashes; limp cornflower hair framed her aristocratic cheeks that bespoke of tradition and propriety. She identified herself as Arla —Matron of Farfus village, and neither did her action or speech suggest anything of threat to Baus or his colleagues.

Baus breathed a sigh of relief. He made a gesture of peace implying he would be honoured to accompany her. It seemed that news of dangerous outlaws had not yet reached these environs . . .

Others were soon joining the gathering. The forest folk seemed genteel and posed congenial remarks and the companions returned warm greetings. A gentleman with long jaw and shiny pelt of black hair announced himself as Nartholeme, village Scout and Elder of Farfus.

Baus, Poli, Valere and Sansix politely introduced themselves. They were in need of shelter and sustenance—casual wayfarers, just passing through, Baus emphasized. Ifra, Brefus, Cogiste and Raagerie—important villagers, presented themselves as persons of reputation. The older folk were dressed in costumes of green weave with matching bell slippers and gazed at them with awe. Here were strangers come to visit their out-of-the-way hamlet! Baus gave happy acknowledgement of the fact. The Farfus folk seemed friendlier than those of Sarfil, but then again, circumstances had been different. All carried a dagger or a small sword at hip, even a gleaming knife or some miniature hatchet. Baus grew amazed at this fact. The youngest too —for reasons extraordinary, other than the appearance of the grim flying creature.

Several quick glances later, Baus took in the panorama of the village and concluded that it was somewhat agreeable, owing to the dwellings crafted of green roofs and outer yellow sod patched over bickerwood. The most distinguished residences ranged in a respectable circle a distance from a central pavilion facing the river.

The children accompanied Baus and his companions before they gave over to the side of boredom. Many insistent cries later, the elders instructed the youths to gather their acorns into baskets, which were to form the grist of the villagers' beer.

The Farfusers conveyed the newcomers to a grand pavilion. All took seats on wire-wood benches around an ancient stone well. Walnut-coloured boughs swayed in the breeze.

The time was early evening and the two leaders, Arla and Nartholeme, indicated two open fields by the pavilion. "These are our gardens. Bird baths, trellises and walkways are groomed and well-maintained. Our niches are pure playgrounds!—for the children, of course, for pleasure and leisure."

"A halcyon atmosphere of unmatched grandeur," Baus agreed. "Were the cities of Sloe and Owlen so picturesque in their old world tradition in relation to the masses they support, we would be in a far better world."

"Were they indeed!" exclaimed Nartholeme heartily. "Baus, you are a man after my own heart." He laughed. "I for one, have never visited the capital—though I have heard much in its favour. Apparently, it is a wondrous place."

"Surely, at the very least," declared Sansix wisely.

Baus gave an automatic scowl. The swindler proceeded to absorb the villagers' attention with his tales of Sloe and Baus was not sure this was a good thing. The outlaw took occasion to peer toward the river anxiously. Gendron and gamgko were in abundance, but cleared back from the water. At either side of the last rope ladder, shrubbery most manicured was glossed with shellac and resin. The horrid stone and twig mishmash of a dreaded village fane loomed just visibly behind the mulberry bushes. Baus, shivering, noticed the tree ladder was varnished too, polished and strengthened with sizeable buttresses. Other flatboats plied the river, of various designs, some of which were barely recognizable as boats, yet able to negotiate their way with ease under the low-spanning ropeway.

Baus's eyes wandered to a line of wooded hills behind the pavilion. Farling's Wall ran in a high blue palisade. The barrier had been clothed somehow with sombre foliage of brooding shadow, crumbling in sections and hatched with notches; yet at Farfus, the parapet was affixed with tall rods and spikes like those of the flatboats.

A curious anomaly. Four box-like tree forts were arranged at heights of twenty feet off the ground. These structures were purposely stationed around the perimeter of the pavilion in the trees . . . Baus's puzzlement only grew. Children's hideaways? Storage depots? Lookouts? The forts seemed all too suspicious, as if guarding a macabre element. Again the boxes were set with two-pronged forks at each corner, a design similar to those obtruding from Gueppe and Vorlo's boat.

Baus puzzled over the enigma. A foghorn heron hooted morosely from the river. As evening deepened the first stars began to flicker. Noiselessly the river purled no more than a few stones' throws away from the companions' seats while they continued to discourse and mists curled about their legs and up the pavilion.

Moon crystals glinted in the treetops. A trio of maids extended long lighted poles to light the soft tallow wicks set high. The crystals were contained in vari-coloured panes—setting a soft maroon glow sweeping through the glade and bringing cheer and song.

Fireflies began to dance. The air grew fresh and cool; everywhere the atmosphere seemed filled with the dreamy aromatic scent of gendron— evoking a pungent longing in Baus who pined for kinder days from the long stint of privation and hostility on the road. The hum of insects formed a background soporific and if not for the omnipresent wall and the mysterious iron stakes, all might have been idyllic in this out-of-the-way Farfus . . .

Two of the lantern lighters, the fairest damsels of the village in fact, approached the group to serve refreshments. Their selection consisted of mir ale and tissel juice served in high-topped pewter mugs. Baus took an automatic fancy to Emo, the tallest, who with her stunning beauty, stooped low with a rather full bosom and a saucy air to fill his mug. The maid retreated, with small, provocative steps and a whimsical gesture which Baus thought presented intriguing possibilities. A brief but heated conjoining in a private night-lit bower would not be inconvenient. However Emo shied away, under the weight of his overlong gaze.

Baus's attention was wrenched back to the table. "Emo!" cried Arla. "Please repair to the kitchens! Your mate, Vorlo, shall be returning and would be aghast at the manner at which you moon over our new friends!" Arla turned Baus an indecorous gaze. "You seem a decent fellow, sir Baus. But mind your eyes. Do you recall having seen Gueppe and Vorlo—our two blood sons? Gueppe is my own and Vorlo is Nartholeme's. The youths exchanged the covenant of everlasting comradeship of blood-brothership when they took their river walk at only two!"

"Land sakes!" cried Baus, struggling to show exuberance.

"Aye, what precociousness! Ah, the youth! The twain are likely to have been aboard a wicker-rigged flatboat riding downstream, conducting their fishing expedition. Did you see them?"

Baus swallowed his tongue. Reluctantly, he admitted having seen more or less a vehicle matching that description.

Valere added a grudging nod. "I believe a similar boat was speeding fast down the Lim—or was it upstream?—to conduct trade with the villagers of Sarfil perhaps? The passengers appeared to be entertaining a longer voyage somewhere. We do not know. We were not privy to their itinerary."

Nartholeme gave a jovial laugh. "Sarfil waxes a few leagues past the jog in the river. It makes an elbow with the Juan forest, before it heads toward the Tholsian Sea by way of Devestok then Evelstine. Our youngsters would not venture that far—at least if they did not wish their rudders snared!"

"Or the tree sponge swamping them," pointed out Brefus. "Their craft would have been impeded with wig-serpents falling from the tissel."

"All too true," affirmed Raagerie.

Arla put her hands to her cheeks. "Oh—I hope the children are safe. Such good boys they are! Not a mean or saucy bone in their bodies!" She gazed at Baus with inquisitory eagerness. "Were their barrels full? 'Tis the season for bucklers and musselgill, you know."

Baus gave a dim murmur. "Undoubtedly. My memory seems to be inexact on this point, yet I recall the barrels being well stocked, were they not, Valere?"

"I believe so."

Baus pointed out that being forced to slog it by circuitous route abreast the river, their perceptions remained muddled.

"Undoubtedly," exclaimed Arla apologetically. "You must be greatly fatigued from your day?"

Baus admitted the truth of it with a laugh. He lifted a leg showing a slight weariness of joint.

"Goodness! I shall set you all out plates of glotton heaped with toad trimmings and heron—leg while Derla and Emo arrange fresh clothes and a bed in our homes!"

"This is most kind," exclaimed Baus.

The meal was served and Emo made a point of lingering longer than perhaps necessary to dispense Baus's dish and provide him hot napkins for wiping up, during which task, some suggestive winks and signals were indicative of interesting possibilities to come. Baus did not shrug off the promising vagueness or the courteous attention. More folk were to gather in the pavilion. All residents wore a variety of gowns and festive costumes. Apparently there was to be much drinking and dancing this evening by local custom.

Baus turned to admire Farfus for the craftsmanship it presented—the elegant gardens, pathways, domiciles and river rope crossings. No less the flatboats which now huddled hull to hull in the harbour. The river vessels remained lantern-lit from bow to stern in the small harbour.

"Your boats are magnificent!" Baus commended. "But Nartholeme, how do you manage to send them gliding so effortlessly on the water without fuel or beast to tow?"

The village elder gave a profound sigh. "Our ships are sources of marvel. The secret to their locomotion lies in their meshed paddlewheel. A trundle underneath the lower housing connects to a wheel which contains certain breeds of energetic fish. When the treadle is set in motion, a spray of feed is released into the bin, enticing the fish to swim with animated fervour. The paddlewheel enables the watercraft to glide as efficaciously as you see, like water over glass!"

"Ingenious!" cried Baus. "An invention of daedal proportion. Surely you have not taken the occasion to market your technology? Such invention smacks of a reservation beyond reason."

"It does," remarked Nartholeme perhaps a touch sadly. "We do not wish to share our inventions, insofar as neighbouring villages may hold an advantage over us."

Baus blinked. "A bit hidebound, but perhaps wise."

"More shrewd than wise," grunted Nartholeme. "Certain clans amongst us are at odds with each other. Denying our neighbours the means is the first to cause us convenience. So we stubbornly cling to our ideals with an air of caution. The outlying villagers consider our stance niggardly, to which we have no argument. But, we mustn't grouse over particulars! We don't get on admirably with our Sarfil cousins anyway." He swished a brave mouthful of ale in his mouth. "What brings you to these realms?"

Valere and Poli scratched their beards. "We are spice entrepreneurs—come from the city," Baus broke in. "Looking for new redolences—tastes, innovations, 'piquantes', if you like. We delight in stimulating palate and sensibilities."

"'Tis a lofty ambition!" marvelled Nartholeme.

"It is. The markets are hardly glutted with the wares of which I speak. We are in the process of discovering new product lines in fact."

Sansix gusted a hilarious snort and Valere buffeted him harshly on the ear.

Nartholeme raised brows, missing the undercurrent of the roughhousing.

Nevertheless, he continued. "A long way you have come to Farfus. I'm afraid that our little hamlet has little to offer in the way of condiments. Gruels, pastas, goulashes perhaps—but these are not the delicacies you speak of."

"I'm sure you are only being humble!" Baus cried with good-natured charm. "The leeks, for example, they have every bit of succulence as would a master chef season them! Charged cleverly with mange pepper and a derivative of sparro-root, if I'm not mistaken. I must have the recipe! And this okra pudding!" Baus smacked his lips with delight. "The sweetener is exquisite. The cream evokes a provocative sentimentality in my taste buds which my stewards shall readily analyze. Eh—Valere?—Poli? Look—both move to procure a sample for their own satchels." He brushed Valere a dry wink then turned to Arla. "Is it honey-gall?"

Arla gave him a cool nod. "I notice that your comrades carry neither pouches nor packs replete with these 'tantalizing' arrays of yours." She peered sceptically at the 'supposed' satchels—rude sacks which were either quite empty or non-existent.

Baus smiled. "Only empty to the extent that we have not yet discovered suitable spices befitting of the subtlety as our ambition requires. We discarded many 'possibles'—jilt-weed, bangthorn, manglestitch, mokki—the sum of which burns our palettes and stifles our appetite." Baus gave a rueful sigh. "An old crone from Sarfil tried to peddle us some bilkerstut, but we cringed at its texture! The price was exorbitant, no less."

Nartholeme gave a laughing cry. "Those rascals at Sarfil will try anything! They are clearly unified in their avarice."

Valere agreed. He offered an echo of Nartholeme's mirth. With jovial affection, but disliking the irony, the captain essayed to change the subject: "What of these sinister fowl that haunt your skies? They seem to cast a worrisome cloud over your halcyon settlement."

Arla cried out in fervent angst: "What do you know of our Auk king?"

Valere twisted and an uncomfortable silence gripped the table.

Poli gestured. "Too little, in fact, we saw—"

Valere ground his heel hard on Poli's toe.

"In fact, you saw what?" cried Ifra. He gained his feet and stared hard at the blond pirate.

Poli shrugged back in a tight-lipped silence. His mood seemed black at the moment, being subdued by Valere.

Arla's face showed a green despair. "Surely you did not see the winged one?" Her voice rose and trailed off in a hoarse, pitiful whimper. Ifra's long heavy jaw hung sinisterly low.

Baus raised hands in an effort to assuage alarm. "The truth of the matter is that my colleague waffles on with his elaborate imagination. Right, Poli? You should know better than to exaggerate! I shall dispel your qualms: earlier we spied an extremely out-of-place, beguiling creature that I'd never seen before. It hovered in the air with malice, clutching a nondescript quarry while we journeyed upriver—I mean, footed it upriver."

"What kind of creature?" demanded Brefus harshly.

"Oh, nothing of singular substance," confessed Baus. "Some kind of Alcidae, or perhaps a Podicipedidae."

"Are you then a student of ornithology?" cried Brefus angrily.

"Peace!" insisted Arla. "Enough of these word games. Be specific, outlander!"

"In terms that are definite, if not precise," declared Baus sullenly, "it was an 'auk'. However, if you would prefer a more detailed exposition—I would say the thing was unruly, harboured scaled legs, a bony spine, feathered torso and some weird appendages akin to wings. Its back stood erect while it flew with a kind of morbid zeal. Something of a bird-man? Who knows? It soared in the air like something from another world. We heard squawks and appeals of exultation. The creature was large, harbouring a live being gripped in its talons. We could not distinguish who or what, surmising only that the aggressor may have been your 'Auk king'. Overhearing casual slurs of rumour in the village, one tends to be prone to speculations."

Arla began wringing her wrists with dismay. "It could not have snatched Gueppe or Vorlo, could it?" she asked fiercely. Pinching eyes shut in misery, she seemed not to convince any of her assertion. "They had their vessel to protect them—their sharpened prongs!"

Nartholeme consoled his blood sister: "You are right, Arla—not to worry. I feel that Vorlo would have taken all precautions."

The village elder's effort was strained; Poli cast awkward looks about the company. Those who stared back did so with animosity. Poli opened his mouth but Baus intervened with a jab and the topic was abandoned.

IV

The airs of anxiety gave way to a heartier atmosphere soon enough. The Auk king's mention became a distant murmur in the minds of all. Villagers gradually began to arrive in numbers, mingling, piping practice notes on a variety of instruments about the glade. Farfus, as all were to discover, was renowned for its pavilion and its colourful moon lamps perched on high. The beer garden was perfect for dancing and entertainment. The trimmed lawn and wooden tables were quaint additions to the ambience. The moon, hanging low, cast a mystical shroud over the pavilion. The purl of the river lulled the villagers to merriment; folk were in favour of the celebration to come.

The children were put to bed and the locals set about dancing in pairs. Baus watched the capers from his bench with a sense of restrained enthusiasm. The high-kicking tarantellas and lively rumbas were a tad ebullient for his tastes. He employed most of his energy ogling the spirited mayflowers who graced the dance floor, particularly Emo and her friend. Emo's brown curls and glistening features, slender legs and buxom figure, were more than enough to snap him out of his wearied torpor. In return, the girl was not so impermeable to the amorous scrutiny he supplied; she turned him the occasional sultry glance just enough to provoke fantasy.

Valere participated in the festivities too, though he had not marked out any particular maid. Poli drank tankard after tankard, hoping to encounter a village maid and gather the nerve to approach—perhaps Skotcha or Derla. But he became ever more loutishly garrulous as time passed, the result of liquor which he imbibed—so the little charm he had was destroyed. Sansix withdrew to a moody corner and remained unresponsive. An invisible shield seemed drawn around him although the villagers attempted to get him up on the dance floor.

Around the sacred well, the village folk capered. The light of the moon waxed and the lanterns with their ever varying tints, displaying a crowd of animated forms swaying to the rhythm of castanets. Other catchy melodies looped about the glade.

Emo contrived to casually set herself down beside Baus and attempt a luxurious arching of arms behind her shoulders. Her face was a flush of crimson and her lips glistened in the slick lantern light. A respectable mist of cocoa-coloured hair sheened in the moonlight. Baus did not fail to be aroused by her deep-nested eyes and flaming warmth. She squirmed closer, tempting him with her vibrant heat as she twisted in ever more suggestive poses.

The flirtations were not uncalculated. By no means was Baus immune to such impulses and he felt his limits strained regarding etiquette. Was it proper to make advances so early on a maid of Farfus? The outlaw hoped to impel the situation into a more profitable manner over time—also above the general banality of comradely conversation. However, the tactic was fruitless, insofar as several compliments on her anatomy were met with coy shrug-offs from Emo, as too, suggestions of a more revivifying nocturnal itinerary. A prompt inclination for her return to the dance floor came unexpectedly.

What a tease! Baus thought with disgust. He earnestly urged the girl to reside longer under the tissel but Emo pulled away. "Vorlo is absent. My worry grows for him and I fear he may have suffered a bad fate. By your hints, I fear that you would have me drifting into areas of languor, even scandal."

Baus laughed at the allusion of scandal. "Hardly." He attempted a snaking of arm around her waist, but she wriggled away, whereupon Baus assumed a more dignified position.

A disturbing image fled across his mind: a youth being snatched up, lifted skyward by some bird-god with golden-tipped wings.

"Vorlo may be absent for a while," muttered Baus, "but we are here, so let us enjoy the moment."

Emo sniffed. "Many fear that Vorlo or Gueppe has been snatched by the 'Auk' you described earlier."

Baus's eyes grew wide. "The probability is not insubstantial. What exactly is this 'Auk' anyway?"

Emo stiffened; a hesitant hand groped her mouth. "The legend is old. You would not wish to hear it. The lore has been passed out of time out of mind, thus onto our folk for generations past."

Baus made an uneasy gesture. "On the contrary, I am a scholar and am particularly interested in domestic folklore."

Emo snorted. "Is that so?" She spoke in a low tone. "The elders swear to the legend of the 'Auk', but I do not know if it is credible. 'Tis an unearthly story born from regions dark and depraved."

Baus refused to endorse such a view. Flustered, Emo clicked her tongue and began to recite events as she knew them. "The legend is well known to our kind. When the sea rose nearly as far as the Lim today, the king was Oulder, a feisty and paunchy old goat with walrus-whiskers and a shaggy mane of hair. Oulder experienced many joys in his hall carved of marl and oak with its many fanes and gardens, celebrating, drinking and feasting into all hours of the night. His closest cronies indulged no less luxuriously while he took many brides to bed. The folk loved their fish—as do the fisherfolk here at Farfus. They relished them in their meals at any time of day. The people of Oulder's time fished and flourished. They trawled the sea dry and their platters were heaped with fish on the coming of the next ceremonial banquet. However, the sea did not like them, Oulder's clan, nor the birds, including the great auks, ivory and almond-feathered creatures who had no provender after the rapine by the clansmen. They all withered and died. Only a collection of the most studious stock took flight to the great forests of Drasla and then the Brauvn abreast the headlands of Shadehue. Ever more did the auks become carnal. They devoured worms and grubs and centipedes and beetles of all kinds, anything they could get into their beaks.

"So time passed; the great birds were forced to ingest more loathsome creatures: gnoles, brown-devilled koots, cave vermin. Raised on the blood of vermin, the auks became deformed. They survived, coping with hunger through the blustery winters. But at huge cost to their frames and their spirits. Nightmarish things they became—they took up diabolical acts and depraved habits, poisoned by the flesh of their feeding—centipedes, crawly things of the earth. So befouled were they that they plotted revenge on Oulder's kind who had destroyed their food supply, especially the king himself, who was not well and past his prime. A hundred more of the warp-winged things swooped out of the sky, grabbing hold of Oulder and taking a limb each and dragged him airborne away from the Feast of Garangeti. Far over the forest they took him by a leg each in their ravaged beaks—to a place for what purpose, none knew. Only the people remained aghast at Oulder's kidnapping, suggesting that the king had at once been conveyed to a great eyrie where he was subjected to violations and unimaginable punishments. Oulder became a great, solitary grey-golden auk himself, so fed with the awful fare that the birds had been forced to eat themselves."

The Farfus maid paused, took a deep breath. She licked her lips and flashed Baus a mournful look. "The king's folk tried to save themselves, live

540

out their lives, but any king they appointed was dragged by the Auks back into the forest. The marauders grew in numbers. They recruited an infamous ghoul as their leader—the 'Auk king', a fiend closely resembling Oulder, the first king, though a marauder with wings and horns. He had a black cape for terror, a conical domino for status, a foreboding of the horror to come when the beast troubled to swoop on them and claim whole persons at a time."

"That's terrifying!" Baus croaked.

"Aye, the new ghoul, this 'Auk king' was a *terror*. The thing was surmised by the king's advisors to be Oulder himself! The citizenry were dreadfully afraid. They jumped at their own shadows. They became cravens, hardly daring to show their faces to the light of day! . . ." Emo gazed unhappily at the dance couples, now moody and taciturn. Perhaps she had spoken too much? A lone tear grazed her flushed cheek.

Baus took her in his arms. He was wholly entranced by the beauty of this girl. Other villagers had arrived, including Brefus, Ifra, Nartholeme and Raagerie; they too had overheard snatches of Emo's tale and listened with sorrowful attention.

Ifra took a seat beside Baus and consoled the distressed girl. "Alas," he said, taking up the tale, "the people of Oulder fled in complete terror. So the kingdom fell to ruin. Villagers can still observe the memories of Oulder's Hall—its once grandeur, now a degenerate crumbling shrine! 'Tis a mile from Old Farfus, on the other side of the Lim." He lifted a gnarled finger, which traced a circle toward the forest, where the sky was the darkest.

Raagerie took up the tale: "It has now been an age since the first Auk came. Wise folk have said the birds fought amongst their numbers. They tore themselves to bits—in the name of dominion and terror. Their beaks were filthy with flesh. All except one—"

"Aye, all except one—" observed Nartholeme. "Either Auk, or ghoul, we know not. The spirit withdrew to its eyrie, mayhap to sleep, but the marauder still keeps vigil. Its memory is long."

"A touching anecdote," remarked Baus.

Nartholeme grunted solemnly. "'Tis no anecdote! 'Tis the shocking truth. Several of the Elders have watched the Auk's patterns, made note of the fiend's debauchery. They have divided the 'King's' movements into 'Night' and 'Day'. In the guise of 'Butu', it prowls by night, with grey and gold body and a wild mane like a unicorn's with horns of bone and spikes of seashell on its hide and a powerful chest. By day, the beast hunts as a 'Raksoi', the god-bird you saw earlier—russet-maned, hook-winged and clothed in silver and fur hides, flying haphazardly with its foot-talons dangling low and a back pitched unnaturally straight."

"The description matches what I saw," admitted Baus.

A strained silence was capped by a clearing of throats.

"The legend has become our gospel."

"Folklore, I would guess in part though," mused Baus idly. "I feel a reservation regarding this legend's validity."

Nartholeme slapped an angry fist on the table. "What do you know?"

Baus hastened to explain: "Why would such a creature snatch humans in plain sight when it could just as easily nab some animal inhabiting the forest? It is illogical. Why fly all the way over Farling's Wall to risk your axes and pikes?" Stroking Emo's hand, he made a casual observation: "I would think there is superstition here. But how I could listen to your tales all evening, Emo, so receptive and sweet your tender words are!"

"Do not mock us!" cried Nartholeme angrily. He rose to his feet. "My uncle, Babuur, was snatched by the sky rogue three years ago. Do you mock that? Call his disappearance a superstition, but, by Butu, 'twas by a Raksoi he was snatched, and a most sorrowful deed indeed! You witnessed your own proof today of the menace. Did you not? The creature exists!"

"It does."

Sansix, overhearing all, voiced a quiet remark. "It may well be that your horror is nothing more than the spell-craft of the neomancers. They came from Mismerion and constructed monsters, confining them in the woods beyond Farling's Wall. 'Tis the purpose of the Wall, is it not? Your 'Auk' may simply be a descendant of one of these creatures, and nothing other than one of the neomancers' fiendish fabrications."

"The argument is a joke," Brefus repudiated. "Only women were given as tests to the so-called 'neomancer's' experiments, 'tis said."

Sansix's eyes flashed moodily. "Perhaps. But the record is imprecise. The women may have given birth to male imps."

Brefus gave his head a vigorous shake. "The Wickles are known to drown their male newborns in the Lim."

"And what if an imp survived?" posed Sansix.

"And how would you know? How could this happen?"

"By holding its breath?"

Nartholeme strangled out an impatient curse. "You may dispute it all you like, rat-face! But the facts remain." He clapped a fist loudly on the tabletop again. "The legend stands true!"

Sansix tilted his head. "So you say, so it must be true."

Nartholeme did not like the condescension in the swindler's voice. "Careful with your tongue, rogue." More revellers had wandered over to see what the squabble was about, Valere and Poli included.

"Why not take arms against the fiend then?" demanded Valere. "You hesitant villagers harbour enough manpower in your numbers—also weaponry."

Brefus made a sour sound in his throat. "And have the Auk ghoul descend upon us in ire? Never! We are helpless against its power! It's possible that you can't conceive of its deviltry, spice-peddler, or that we tolerate the occasional tragedy, if only to appease the beast's gluttony."

"In that case," guffawed Valere humorously, "why not throw all your hatchets and stakes in the river and let fate have its way?"

Nartholeme was pitched to wrath by the statement and his mouth pinched into a savage grimace. "Such foolishness—it invites only apathy."

Emo changed the subject. "Enough! Are we to argue all night like bears? Let us dance!" She dragged Baus to his feet and pulled him onto the terrace.

Relieved to be spared of the interrogations, Baus allowed himself to be towed. The two dalliers swayed to the sounds of nonexistent flute and lyre. Gradually the music returned, but only tenuously. Musicians put tentative fingers to their instruments. Castanets invariably clicked. Men drank, women bustled about, finally many paired to take part in the celebration. Once more the pavilion resumed a semblance of its former gaiety.

Valere and Poli gained confidence to invite two spirited maidens to join them in some spirited jigs. With joy they came bouncing up and grabbed the men by the arms. The maids' eyes were wild; they each wore costumes of shimmering silk and lips were arched in playful giggles. Sansix was obliged to join in the merry-making, but he demurred, feeling somewhat disinclined to revelry, due to the misery of his cleft finger and the coarseness of the drunken urgings. A particularly moon-faced lass attempted to wrest him onto the dance terrace, but he objected to her muscular arms and rotated his body out of arm's reach. "Easy, girl! I profess to lassitude, and I must retire early to meditate!"

The maid who was the fishgutter's daughter arched her brows with sullen distaste. "Really? That sounds hardly romantic. What do you see in all this meditation?"

A flicker of doubt passed the swindler's eyes. "Bright lights, halcyon glows, imprints from the past, a merging into a quieter place."

The girl remained suitably unimpressed. "For what purpose?"

Sansix frowned. "A vacuity of senses, an expression of solitude, a release from despair—what is my opinion? If you are interested, try it out. Let us retire to a candlelit room where we may chant monosyllables and sit in silent unison. I find that contracting the muscles of the lower chakra for a significant period gives rise to a certain euphoria, also an equipoise and purpose. Come! We must practice together, visiting such thresholds of pleasure and exaltedness as felt never before!"

Jansa gave a withering glare. "I defer." Pleading fatigue, she moved back a pace, even as Sansix hurried to disclose more perfervid details of his experience. "No? Then I must hop and skip solo amongst the garden paths like a waif-faery!" With a milk-watery simper, he flung himself down the lower path, flitting like an elf, slapping thighs in time with the castanets. He fled away from the houses of Farfus, glad to leave his hectoring friends and the cozy domiciles of Farfus far behind. Immediately he disappeared, weaving a path along the line of Farling's Wall, unbeknownst to the outlaws, and to where none knew . . .

* * *

Under the climbing moon the hours passed. Laughter was heard from all quarters deep in the mists surrounding the village. Lulled by the potency of the mir mead, the Farfusers, engulfed in passions of music and two step tangos and tarantellas, achieved a restive release from the insularity of their day and the terror of their legend. Baus cavorted with his new found Emo and reflected that perhaps all this jigging and side-stepping about was an attempt to contend with the horror of the Auk.

His conclusions were not far off. Lights were lit in the tree forts should they be needed as a refuge or place of defence. More captivating was the entrancement of Emo swaying in his arms. She was a heated bundle, filled with the pink pleasure of tomorrow's promise, and untold excitements to come.

The hour was late; finally the music came to an end. The moon waxed.

High in the clear night sky it rode like a beacon. The air was chill and sobered up the effects of mead. The space about the pavilion was infected by indulgence. The villagers of Farfus urged Baus and his companions to retire for the evening. The companions were hard put to reject the offer of lodging and softened by drink and vigorous exercises of dancing, they graciously accepted. They were happy for a warm bed and a hospitable environment.

Nartholeme agreed with Baus that to take up their journey in the middle of the night was farce. He gave Baus a playful slap on the back and invited them to his own home. Much to Baus's regret, for Emo was sleeping over at Derla's, so the two were out of reach. Meanwhile the companions were restricted to requisitioning cushions and blankets by Nartholeme's fire. Baus attempted to avoid a possible overcrowding at Nartholeme's bungalow, by suggesting that he bunk over at Arla's. Arla, however, was quite adamant that Emo and her daughter reside alone. Baus's presumption led to a strained silence and after a tight-lipped discussion, Arla remained fixed in her opinion that Baus was a man of sly intents.

Trudging disconsolately to Nartholeme's home, Baus thought to judge the village elder not a man disposed to much risk. His bungalow was surmounted with thirty sharp-pointed stakes and many weapons were cached within. Sansix was nowhere to be seen. The village scout's age-lined face took on a worried cast. "Perhaps the Auk king has taken your friend?"

Baus affectionately rejected Nartholeme's theory. "If I know Sansix, the gadabout'll be skulking about the shadows, up to no good." Yet an unwanted worry did grip the outlaw. What if Gueppe or Vorlo should return by chance, expose them as bandits?

He brushed off the anxiety. 'Twas a risk to be taken—a smaller one than trooping in the black of night right now, prey to airborne assaults by the Auk. In the future he would have to limit his imagination he told himself.

V

The next day Baus, Poli and Valere did not rouse themselves until noon. They drowsed in their snug couches and remained curled under the warm blankets, soaking up the comfort of Nartholeme's insulated hut. The weather was warm and breezes played soft patterns on the green-shadowed river. Such tranquility left little desire for Baus, or his cronies, to vacate the pleasant haven of Farfus. But vacate it they must at some time. Baus donned a dapper brown vest, a pair of willowy trousers and a yellow-feathered cap, all courtesy of his hosts. He did not trade his black boots for the cheesy, bell-topped slippers the villagers supplied. Valere and Poli donned smart aquamarine pantaloons and dun jerkins. During the afternoon he and the companions relaxed, taking much-needed baths in the hot springs behind Nartholeme's residence. They indulged in sizeable meals while stretching their legs in the shady pleasances behind the pavilion. Baus took time to flirt with Emo, while sipping teas and discoursing. They engaged in strolls arm-in-arm up the river.

Nartholeme managed to unlatch the two from each other and took Baus out to a place up the river where many of the villagers fashioned traps for their famous 'golden fish' that fuelled their watercraft.

Baus stepped down to the shoreline, peering sharply at the water. Only a few feet out, a half dozen ill-looking weirs hung suspended under the bubbles of the current like angled-ironed spikes. He began to make an inquiry when without warning, a fanged grey face sloshed out of the water, lurching with a vengeance, teeth flashing at him.

Baus leapt back, unleashing a mournful cry.

"Mind the gariali!" laughed Nartholeme. "Their dog-incisors make short work of an unaware soul. Man is as easily devoured as a fowl."

The remark did not amuse Baus. He stalked back to the village in foul humour. Seeking out Emo's comforts, he soon was appeased. However, the newly-found equilibrium between the two was becoming a trifle strained. Would they achieve the physical union that was building between them? A pleasurable thought, but it was not Baus's primary focus—more to circumvent one of the fisher-youths returning at an awkward moment.

Baus's worry seemed unwarranted. He and his companions would be long gone—with none the wiser.

The hours passed. Baus's qualms were not wholly assuaged; Emo's suggestive hints of warmer pleasures to come, were blossoming. Valere and Poli had absorbed themselves in gluttony and their own flirtations with their recent dance partners had kept them busy. Worries and qualms were far from those outlaws' minds. As for Sansix, none knew; he had disappeared. Yet it was a relief to be finally rid of the villain. The condescension and pompous dissembling that had come from his maw was intolerable.

The night passed. Much dancing and revelry ensued, with the difference that Emo, in light of her early admission of betrothal to Vorlo, seemed to have become more affected by Baus's charm. At some later hours of the night he felt his petite swoon in his arms—a situation precipitating events in a definite direction. Yet the outlaw, feeling a presentiment, quietly professed that he and his friends would have to be departing soon and that they could not be tempted to overstay their welcome.

Emo was rankled. She slapped Baus soundly on the cheek. "What are you saying, you vagabond! You flirt with me and dare tell me this now? After fondling my anatomy so privately?" She hitched herself closer, play-biting at his neck. Baus found it difficult not to yield. The lemon-scent of her intoxicated him; the moonlit air infused his imagination with caprice. Emo's nubile body slid against his, with ginger and other sublime sweetnesses, and with an urgent passion that roused him.

Nevertheless, pangs of guilt and misgiving thwarted Baus's languor and he reiterated his plan to depart.

Emo fixed him an accusatory gaze. "So, you do not love me?"

"Of course I do!" Baus held his arms wide. "My ardour is all for you, my dove. Is it not palpable?"

Emo's conviction was not conveyed in the furrows of her pinched brow.

"Do not doubt, my Emo! My passion has never been more formidable! In fact, your sweet aura—"

She pushed Baus away and wrapped her arms disconsolately about her shoulders and sat down and pouted. Baus attempted a soft reconciliation which was met with shoves and sobs. His kisses, supplications, embraces did nothing to mollify the depths of her rancour.

Out of the lower dewy river grasses came a sudden distraught figure. He had blue eyes, a sullen face and an inflexible frame, with whom Baus was familiar.

The outlaw gave the youth a disquieting stare. "How goes it, pilgrim? I see that you have found Farfus—to enjoy the fancy pirouetting under the glows of the night lanterns?"

The youth ignored the jocularity. He reached out, staggering, to pull himself past the tall bull reeds. Crying out in a husky murmur, he gave an evil flourish. "What have we here, a rogue? A surprising sight!" Jealousy and anger flared in one hateful gush. Emo did not recognize the figure at once, but then stepped back with a gasp. The youth's chestnut-black hair was unmistakable, piled back with matted disorder and dripping with twigs and water flies. The cherubic, almost delicate face was pocked with sores, and Baus winced, noting the insect bites and privation.

"Is a ruffian I spy trifling with my Emo? Regarding the swoonish way you hang off this blackguard's arm, I would guess you have found a new confidant!" He thrashed forward with a hostile heat.

Baus raised brows with an affectionate bewilderment. "Well—perhaps you have mistaken me for another of your riverside cronies?"

"Unlikely!" Vorlo hissed venomously. "You are no more than a tawdry knave, a licentious cullion—a crook who be likely to confuse *Emo* and double-tongue my kinsmen."

Emo, recognizing who it was, detached herself from Baus with an air of stony dismay.

Baus sprang sideways. He realized things were going sour and he must act fast. "Behold, varlet! We are all peaceable here. We are honoured guests in fact, and I oblige you to conduct a more politic tone!"

Meanwhile the village elder had stepped closer to see what the ruckus was about, squinting at the newcomer. "My son! Vorlo." He stopped dead in his tracks. "You have returned from your expedition. What has befallen you? Why the sores, and what is this hullabaloo?"

Vorlo choked. "Perhaps you would ask this thief and varlet yourself, father! Any of his dastardly schemes come to question. Where's the fourth rat—that rat-eyed grifter, or should I say cross between half jackal and vagrant?"

Baus made a disapproving sound. "You must be referring to Sansix. That kind of talk never wins friends. Our peer has gone missing like yourself. But 'tis hardly reason to conduct vulgar gossip behind his back."

"Cease your chatter! You have much to answer for."

Nartholeme waved his cap in peace. "Enough, Vorlo. 'Tis truly glad we have you in our company. Now let's have a truce. This halcyon atmosphere we have created in our garden is not to be polluted. We observe the appropriate rituals of hospitality and we must speak concisely if we wish to make rousing accusations!"

"'Tis a wise proclamation!" cried Baus adamantly. Hopping forward, he hoped to gain some room for reconciliation. "Skipping about and uttering slander is intolerable." Darting between father and son, he hoped to forestall an inevitable scandal. "Nartholeme, I find your son's behaviour laced with disrespect!"

"The accusation is just, but perhaps we should hear the boy out first—"

"Inadvisable!" cried Baus. "Your son is subjected to some sort of jungle fever, I think."

"What?"

With a great restraint, Vorlo rasped: "I have jogged, trotted, and scampered for two days, through jungle and fens. I have eluded Wickles, gariali, unkind creatures, snakes, fiends, and other sick and repulsive things —all in the name of justice—and now, here, returning to my village, I find this filthy, sleazy rascal amongst us! What trickery! With news of theft and death, I speak only of woe."

"What woe is this?" Nartholeme cried out, startled.

The First Matron had trotted over to investigate and demanded, "Where is Gueppe, my son and your blood brother?"

"This is what I mean to say. He is deceased!" blurted out Vorlo. "Carried off by the Auk ghoul. And no thanks to these jackals! Two days ago they hijacked us before the fork to Devestok. They commandeered our vessel and used it to convey their sorry hides upriver. Now they are here, gulping our food and dancing with our maids"

Arla let out a grievous wail. "You brutes! What an ill!" The news of Gueppe, her son's fatal kidnapping was too much for her to handle. She pounded fists into Valere's chest.

Nartholeme rushed over to console her, but the Elder whirled about in fury upon Baus and Poli. "Explain yourself, you two-faced rogues. Devestok is leagues from here. Vorlo! How could you have arrived here so fast by foot?"

"I hot-footed it to the bay where Yurmi had hid a flatboat in Snaker's Lee. Navigating to Farfus at full speed, I lucklessly ran out of fuel—well, fish feed, if you call it, and was forced to abandon my craft and leg it the last three leagues, which is why I suffer these worm bites and pangs."

"Mere measly afflictions," chided Baus. "A trifling scourge which yamroot and congstock should remedy."

"Silence!" thundered Nartholeme. "I'll not have your jests here."

A breathless voice called out from the grasses: "Knavery is on us!" cried a voice beyond the pavilion. "We have discovered Vorlo's flatboat. Abandoned a furlong downstream."

"Is it indeed?" Nartholeme purpled under the collar, hardly able to believe his ears. He glared at the newcomers with an inexpressible loathing. Valere and Poli shrank back in the shadows, ready for battle. Baus looked askance, as if trying to let his eyes wander from the approaching villagers to the safety of the river.

Raagerie strode up, clutching a tapered sabre, which he pointed to the black stalks of fernbanks. "The flatboat was concealed amidst the shelter of cloudfern draped with flaps of gendron."

"You see?" Vorlo gloated. Whirling on Baus, he showed a set of teeth. "So, vermin, do you think me confused now?"

Baus peered awkwardly upon Vorlo's obvious distress. Poli and Valere remained numb. Matters were progressing along courses of disaster.

Nartholeme's face congested. "Now facts spring to greater attention!" He swung a quivering finger upon Baus. "All of you connivers—are to be locked in the detention hall, until further inquiry can be made. A tribunal will be brought on the morrow to draw final punishments!"

"This is unreasonable!" objected Baus. "The gesture is ill-wrought and I sense a discourtesy to what began as civil hospitality."

"Take that and burn it!" bellowed Nartholeme. "I will brook no mischief! Come along, you despicable villains, before I enjoin Brefus, Raagerie and Ifra to drag you to the detention hall!"

Ten brown-faced villagers circled Baus. Valere and Poli were outflanked. Several of the host raised knives and hatchets. Instinctively, Baus reached for his blade. Not a second too soon. It would be a fight to the death, one which would be fought with passion and blood.

On a signal to his friends, Baus scrambled aside. Valere and Poli dodged in concert, striking with sword and halberd.

Poli shouldered Raagerie out of the way. Baus made a lightning fast thrust with Lolispar. Raagerie's wrist dangled limp. He cried out in pain. Members of the Farfus dance crew erupted in mayhem. Bodies crowded in from all angles. Heaving and thrusting and flashing of weapons erupted all at once. Grunting, Huiste the boat-maker, set up a running block. Valere raised the butt of his sword and sent the boat-master reeling. Vorlo flew at Baus. In a last minute rush, he twisted sideways and Baus ducked his strike and ran for the cover of the forest. "No bloodshed!" he cried. "Fly to the woods!"

Though full of ale, Baus's companions were not so out of sorts to close their ears to his good advice. Incarceration loomed like a mummy's tomb; only teamwork would prevent them from getting bludgeoned.

He was unfortunate enough to be caught in the middle of a strangled web of attackers. Three fighters, now armed with sabres, began a feral game of slice and dice. Baus ripped out his ganglestick. He tagged his first attacker, but the device refused to operate. It sputtered in a despondent hiss.

Baus cried out in disgust.

He was rewarded with another buckled boot to his gut that had him gasping for breath. Stumbling back, with no other recourse, he began hacking his way through the throng, employing a mode of brute force as necessary. Smashed sideways, he blundered into the rose bushes but with grimacing, impressive bravado he recovered and cut and slashed.

Lolispar looped and menaced. A fuzz-faced villager fell suddenly bleeding to the turf. Two snarling defenders rushed to finish him, but Baus rolled sharply to the side and laid a body check to the first who frog-hopped his way into the pavilion's flowerbeds. Baus jabbed without remorse. He felt a knife rake across his upper arm, leaving a spasm of anguish stinging his left elbow.

In the midst of all the blows, a wan shape slid across the moon. The pavilion changed from moonlit radiance to sombre terror.

Baus peered up in alarm. A flapping monstrous thing pounded above his head. He felt the whoosh of devil-drawn airs. An instant glimpse showed a great auk's beak, superimposed upon a manlike countenance.

He swayed back in giddiness. The pavilion wheeled, turned to utter chaos. Cries ricocheted like banshee wrath, the vengeful turned to whimpers. A whorl of panic turned to choking madness and folk scattered in all directions—to the flower gardens and the nearby woods, many trembling under the shelters mounted with pikes. Villagers and defenders alike frantically clawed their way up the ladders to their secure forts.

Sure enough the winged demon re-appeared. In all its glory and guise it was 'Butu', the night Auk, magnified a hundred times over in its most grotesque clarity. The creature dipped low, sending a flap of bulging wings dimming the moonlight. Now a crescent of blackness covered the sky. The monster snatched at the hair of a fleeing maid, pulled her up along its swooping arc like a plucked carnation.

An axe sang through the air, that thrown by an intrepid villager. The metal chopped into the beast's spine. Almost at once, three arrows loosed from a nearby tree shelter. The projectiles ran through the Auk king's leftmost wing and the beast uttered a hideous squawk, releasing its cargo. Prying axe and darts out of its barely-impaired member, the fiend hopped riverward where several more men came out frantically scrambling for a better shot. The assailants were encouraged but the assaults had hardly hindered the vitality of the beast.

Vorlo was a protector now. He grabbed Emo's wrist and made efforts to drag her to safety up the nearest ladder.

The act was unsuccessful. The beast swept Vorlo aside like a bag of chaff. A single brush of the powerful wing had the youth rolling like a hound down the hill into the river. The Auk king's talons grabbed hold of Emo and lifted her by the waist in a cruel scissor lock. Twisted sideways, she knew horror. She dangled six feet off the ground.

Baus sprang to her defence. Grabbing hold of her legs, he tried to pull her down, but she was like a ton of bricks, burdened with the weight of the Auk.

The Auk's grip was unbreakable. It beat its scaly wings against the air, lifting the girl higher off the ground—and Baus too, dangling, cursing and clinging to Emo's slender legs with panic.

The maid fought, struggling, faring worse for her efforts. The Auk king's talon-grip was abysmally tight. The monster slowly began choking the wind out of her.

Baus gritted his teeth. He searched for a new means to pry the girl away from the ghoul's noxious grasp. Quixotic as the hope was, he realized he was no match for this terror.

He clamped his eyes shut, hoping for the nightmare to end.

It didn't. He glimpsed in his mind's eye a monster with limned horned helm, a primitive bone-carved beak, a wretched human face. What was the thing? Its white glazed eyes glared back devoid of all mercy of understanding. Leathern wings bit the air like demon's teeth. The thrash of claw on iron was like a tempest in his ears as another axe raked the beast's talon.

The monster glided higher. Vociferous caws shattered the air. Emo and Baus were carried high above the ground—twenty, thirty, now forty feet. Soon the ghoul would clear the treetops and begin its macabre descent toward Farling's Wall and whatever foul lair it called home.

Baus peered at the claws clamped mercilessly onto Emo's waist just above the beltline. The beast's progress was impaired—by injuries; not quick was it in covering the ground it needed.

Emo loosed a painful scream. In his haste Baus caught a glimpse of the receding village. He could not discern her agonized expression, but heard her plead with all her might, to whatever gods she knew for release. Hacking with her knife against the creature's horn-scaled legs was valiant but limited. She walked a path of death and wailed and thrashed. Again, the beast loosed its abominable screech and did not flinch or relinquish its grip.

Her defence seemed only to amuse the devil; in fact, it dropped its enormous head and knocked the weapon out of her hand. Struggling up upon her torso, Baus let his free hand windmill. He made desperate play with Lolispar in the hopes of undermining talon and foreclaw.

The act was late in coming. By magic alone, the weapon seemed to make a dent, and the Auk king emitted an absurd screech. Twenty feet the bird plummeted and Nartholeme and Brefus took courage. They bolted forth to attack the beast with their axes and grapple-irons.

Brefus grabbed hold of Baus's legs. He tried to drag down both of them; meanwhile Nartholeme threw his hatchet straight at the Auk's face.

The bird blinked, gnashed, hovered a foot over the terrace, faltering. The additional weight had tasked it, but its supernatural strength prevailed and it lifted again. Nartholeme grabbed Brefus's legs. With grimacing effort they heaved, gushing clan cries. The extra weight stopped Brefus from likewise floating away with the others.

Mercifully, the load reached a limit and the god-bird ascended no more.

A volley of arrows hissed forth. Wings deflected the assault and it lifted beak to catch many of the projectiles in its maw, snapping them like twigs. Its mournful bellow blasted upon the night. Almost in irony, the creature perversely decided to drop its prey.

Emo fell, crumpling in a swoon, with Baus landing on his feet beside her.

Leathern wings twitched. A paroxysm of rage erupted from the beast's throat. At capricious speeds it catapulted straight for the shelter, the one that had loosed the hail of shafts that had pricked its hide.

A keratin-crusted beak slammed hard into the fort, crushing its timbers. Wood and beams went flying everywhere.

The tree-box's platform gave way. Fifteen villagers fell down the side of the ancient tissel like stones. Arla and three young children lay dazed on the turf in a bed of ferns. Flustered but luckily unharmed, the defenders picked themselves up and made desperate scrambles for the woods. Vorlo was amongst them, cringing in his thicket, sopping wet, holding his blade aloft with shaky fingers.

The Auk king was suspended in mid-air like some gleaming ghoul. In upright posture, it scrutinized its prey one by one with alien dispassion. Oddly, it seemed a creature disinterested in easy victims.

Its vulpine eyes swivelled, trained on the rebels below crouched on the grass like mice: Brefus, Nartholeme, Emo, Baus, Valere and Poli. Poli and Valere had just scrambled up the garden path to face the horror themselves. In a wide crazy circle, the Auk spun fretfully. With three golden flaps, it flopped down on a wicked trajectory in front of Baus, gnashing its beak like a thing possessed. For an instant it stopped, arrested its frenzied hopping and seemed to look Baus in the face with a corpse-like knowing . . . a look of utter malignancy—and death.

Transfixed, Baus felt the blood in his veins run cold. Never before had he seen such a primitive visage. The rictus was almost prehistoric—a mask of pure brutality: grey, gaunt and ghoulish. Bat-like ears flowed from a sallow, beaked face. Three protruding rhino horns hedged the brow—and all the appendages swam in a tangled memory, soul-stripping and evil. The Auk was something which he suspected had once been human, though was too devil-spawned to be grouped in that category now . . .

Flapping three strides up in the air, it poised in menace to descend upon Baus. The outlaw made a frantic play with Lolispar, but slashing at its talons and wing tips seemed useless. The umbrella-like weight bore the assaults and weighed down on him with remorseless strength, pressing him flat to the ground.

He fought and slashed, but fetid wings closed in on him, like some evil, man-eating flower petals blotting out the sky. Immediately odours most obscene made him almost gag and lose consciousness that instant.

Despite the injuries, the menace seemed impervious to pain. Driven by mad impulses rather than logic, it seemed immortal.

Valere and Poli high-tailed it forth, cursing and hacking at the creature's spiny exoskeleton. It flared its noxious wings.

An edge of wing caught Valere thick in his woollen outercoat and slashed a great gash across his bicep. The thing opened its wings, at last flapping upward, leaving an impaired Baus gasping and choking for breath on the dank turf. Crow-mad with fury, the monster hopped away, hissing and spitting like a cat.

Valere and Poli scrambled to safety, pulling Baus with them. Across the lawn they raced, sickened by the creature's putrescence. Near the old well, they prepared to defend themselves, weapons raised—Brefus, Ifra and Nartholeme drew grapples, gasping for breath.

Brefus emitted a strangled yell. He and the others twirled weapons and goaded the beast in their direction.

The creature seemed to tire of the game. In a last convulsive leap, it flapped ten yards toward the edge of the pavilion, limping on what appeared a damaged leg.

Brefus stooped breathless. Unprotected, he was vulnerable for a fatal instant. The Auk lunged with lightning speed and its talons stretched, raking Brefus's ankle and dragging him across the green.

The villager loosed a dismal howl. He hacked with his hatchet, but the feeble strike was of no use against its brawn. The creature swept the weapon out of his grasp. It flew against the side of the well striking with a clang.

Mighty wings lifted airborne. Brefus was towed upward in the black wash; he uttered a heart-wrenching squeal. Before any avenger could reach the defender, the monster had launched itself into the air, beak first into the dark sky with a thrashing cargo in tow.

The silhouette blotted out the moon. Soon the Auk fled west out over Farling's Wall and toward the brooding fastness of the Branx forest.

Nartholeme clutched the air with anguish. Brefus was lost. Ifra fell to his knees. Others covered their faces, with sobs thick in their throats. All grew quiet. The folk of Farfus glade crept forth from their hiding spots; all watched appalled as the Auk king's shadow grew smaller and Brefus's shrieks dwindled in the darkness.

Valere and Poli pulled themselves into the shrubbery, half-dragging Baus along the perimeter of the pavilion. They coursed through the garden and off into the forest.

VI

The villagers did not give chase to the outlaws. Perhaps they were appeased that their guests had made singular efforts to thwart the Auk king and his fiendish lusts. For back at Farfus, many waxen figures scrambled about their hollow grove, searching for tools and cords to repair their collapsed fort and to refortify their pavilion before the menace returned.

There was a sorrowful mourning about the loss of Brefus and Gueppe.

A mile away, Valere and Poli snatched air into their lungs. Baus was flagged with cuts and bruises. They hustled him through the dense ferns as if their lives depended on it. The earthy wetness kept him conscious, but they constantly slapped him to keep him conscious. Probing the bracken, Valere and Poli slogged deeper into the underbrush, following the shine of the sallow moon. All agreed it was expedient to put as many leagues between themselves and the doomed village as they could.

The forest grew dense, and increasingly rank. Fronds grew like creeper vines in their midst. Never had they seen such dire tangle. They dragged their hides forward with new speed, plagued with a crippling worry that beyond a bend a sudden swoop from a taloned beast would render them death.

Beyond Farling's Wall came a gut-shivering chattering: ululations, hoots and bewitching laughter—the same that they had heard earlier on their pilgrimage west. From all corners of the forest came exudations dripping with danger and casting clammy fingers over their spines.

Valere dispensed many critical curses. It had not been possible to cross the Farfus ropeway prior to fleeing the village . . . now they were hopelessly sentenced to the west bank of the river, the one closest to the cursed wall.

In a drowse of exhaustion, the three could go on no longer.

They stumbled to their knees, into a dank mat of ferns. They rolled on their bellies groaning, while Valere cursed his predicament and swatted at Poli who had thrust his boots into his face. Valere bade him to spread damp leaves on his lacerated back; Baus remained immune to the tumult, nursing his own wounds. Under the evanescent moon, they could see disquieting shapes standing silhouetted by the wall. Baus struggled to stay alert. They took their watches, but none could forget the sad memories of Farfus stirring in their minds, of fair maidens swinging off an arm, in a blaze of fantasy wonder, rose and sapphire light . . .

* * *

Dawn came in swirls of mist. The countryside was blotted out with grey and dun fog. Only the incessant cricketsong gave backdrop to the river's nearby purl, fostering them any hope or sense of location.

Gradually the company's perceptions sharpened. Gathering resolve, Valere shouldered his companions aside. They bent to their task, plodding on through the veiled hinterland with bellies bursting with hunger. They saw the river weave, contort in a bow. To their left, Farling's Wall stretched, a tall, knitted wooden rampart of mysterious origin. Various tiers of hucklethorn posed significant barriers, but its accompanying gimp briar and elf-shrub were less hardy, yet no less menacing. Many black-shadowed water-stumps protruded from the inky water.

By midmorning, the mist had dissipated, revealing certain eldritch terrain: spinifex, blue bottlegum cedar, hedgerot, yamroot, moss-log. Across the river stood a tantalizing wold—awash with golden flaxhack, ancient magnolias and sunshine.

Baus sighed. The sights and sounds were too much for him. He realized maddeningly that he and his colleagues were trapped on this sinister side of the river, between river and wall. To sprout wings and fly across was but pure fantasy. The strip of unkempt bush that stretched a half mile, narrowed in width to a few uncomfortable hundred yards at times. To sneak back to the village Farfus, cross the ropeway was a foolhardy wish . . .

The future remained in the hands of Butu—the Auk-god, and the comrades' spirits sunk to new lows. A swarm of migrating bees assailed them, then a cloudburst, a lone wandering garialis, then a brief interchange with a gang of bandits eager for coins and their boots, but nothing could be done. Perhaps it was the outlaws' draconian training by Zoren the pirate that saved them from the latter attack of thieves. So unnerved were the raiders that a heated resistance against blade and halberd had the attackers dashing, stumbling headlong into the muddy shallows where they perished.

Two bloodied brigands were pulled under by lurking gariali; another was torn at the shins by green vipers and suffered a demise of horror and astonishment. The only survivor was favoured to find the far shore, but was seized while scrambling away by a swift-spreading shadow that descended from the sky—a familiar Raksoi—the *Auk King*.

Taller than a man, the winged nightmare hauled its prey aloft, flapping back safely beyond the Farling's Wall to glut its need.

Baus shivered. He stared appalled. The companions immediately snatched themselves to defence. A brief sprint had them dashing under a sumac cluster, terror beating in their hearts. They crouched like gnomes, glaring at the retreating god-bird with its grey and gold feathers. Its bicorn crown gleamed under the mid-morning sun like a blazing jewel. In a hoarse falsetto, Baus croaked out a lament on the impermanency of life.

Valere agreed, though he was not much of a metaphysicist.

"I suggest picking a course that obscures our passage from view from the sky," said Baus shakily. "This simultaneously allows us to defend ourselves from attack behind and in fore."

"And how can we do this?" growled Valere. "We have no clue as to when the next fiend may attack us—from above, below or some other horrid direction."

"Trust nothing but our own eyes!" Baus thundered. "Not even our own shadows, for that matter as they are semblances of deception! In this wise, one should not even breathe!"

Poli retained a critical frown. "And how is de-oxygenating our blood going to assist us?"

Baus cried out in exasperation: "If something comes at you, Poli, you stab it with the pointy end of your sword. You strike, you spear, you menace —everything else is ancillary!"

"A statement of overkill," announced Poli dryly, "but at least it's something I can understand."

"Very good! Now let us be in agreement. We advance with stealth. If we detect enemies then we stab first, alert others second. Furthermore, if we spot the robbers' boat, which is likely tucked away in a dark nook along the shore, we may yet survive this ordeal."

The outlaws devoured the only sack of flaxmeal left behind by the thieves. They laid out a search perimeter but discovered nothing. The robbers likely had never had a boat and Baus felt a mild resentment at the fact, as he rubbed hands to stave off the marrow-thistle itches he had received. He flexed his palms, gritted his teeth.

The day passed . . . trepidation mounted. 'Twas not unlikely that another Auk would soon come lancing out of the sky . . .

A creature, however, made no further appearance. By the end of the day the fugitives begun to foster dim hopes that they had outdistanced their bane, perhaps progressed beyond its hunting ground, in which case there would be no sudden conclusion to their lives.

A disquieting presence was the imposing wall itself. The rampart hovered above them fifty feet above the river. 'Twas crafted of woven trunks of an odd bluish hue. Each bole was marked with a sinister endless graffiti. In some places, the trunks were dangerously cracked or splintered. 'Cracks' even looked like odd peepholes from where denizens behind could glare at passer-bys. For whatever reason, Baus could not be sympathetic to the situation . . . especially when enemies could scope out advantages on them.

A gap suddenly appeared in the thickets.

Baus strolled over to inspect the station of wall that towered unnervingly before them. To the touch the outlaw found the wall chalky and old, like some punky barn-wood that infested the Sarch backwoods of his homeland. At certain places fungus grew, along the wall's foot with a variety of moulds and blights.

The outlaw wrinkled his nose. He test-banged his fist on a weathered section. A hollow thud came to his ears and he felt curiously some resistance —or resonance, as if the trunks were hollowed out or eerily composed.

Valere and Poli joined Baus in their astonishment. All rubbed their chins, assessing the graffiti with scepticism. There were several crayon markings scrawled on various slats, with notations like *'Hoodoo was here'* and *'Waste no wood'* and *'Think fast before the pasts collapse'*.

'Twas nonsense, but who had written it?

Baus could discover no answer. Poli read further along, a lengthier stanza:

"How do you fool an old Wickle?
Do you stuff her in your pocket, or do you plunge her in your red locket?
Or do you toss her into a pot?
Whatever way, don't let her spy with her peepy little eye,
The likes of your hide or your fabulous bride,
Betwixt river and wall where the wisest must fall!
To drift and wither, as all things thither."

He frowned, reading yet another:

"Fool your Wickle!
Or end in a pickle.
Give me a nickel,
For every wretch snared by a Wickle,
And I'd be rich in a stitch!
There's no doubt of that, dear lout,
So be wary! not scary,
And don't tarry,
By the gloom of Farling's Wall . . ."

Baus stared at the verse with somewhat bewildered disapproval. He remarked how ill-composed the verse was, and how somebody's property had been crassly defaced, exposing neither art nor subtlety.

Valere blew out a sour grunt. "I despise this place, Baus—this poesy reads most ridiculously."

Poli managed an impish smile: "I think the verse is actually witty."

Valere clipped him in the ear. "Keep quiet!"

Poli leapt at him and the two were soon tussling on the ground like curs.

Baus pulled them apart with annoyance. "Listen, you imbeciles! 'Tis paramount that we pool our heads and remain vigilant. Mischievousness abounds in this evil precinct, and possibly misanthropic forces." He flourished his dagger in a flamboyant twirl. "Even Lolispar gleams a baleful green. We harbour no solace of belly, or plan. To stay here is a death wish made real—perhaps we shall survive the day if we keep on."

* * *

A day passed and then another. Soon the Lim cut an eerie path ever closer to Farling's Wall. The brooding forest seemed to hem them in like a noblewoman's girdle, winding them in ever more tightly. Disturbing tumult issued from beyond the mysterious wall that towered over them. Now cool skies seemed teemed with weird unsettling fowl which haunted the altitudes: elfin nightjars, jackdaws, condors, some with discomfiting horns, others with upturned beaks, many with gangly snouts and stubbed wings, strangely indicative of human qualities.

The birds swooped low and dove, fighting over scraps of meat that one of them had stolen and they gnashed their beaks like predatory scavengers. They became ever more diverting concerns.

Baus loosed a strangled grunt. Rising above the wall loomed clumps of spinifex, jade-green creepers, serpentine leaves and umbrella-shaped fronds. Another dozen varieties of flora likewise became worrisome.

The river purled ever fainter to their right. With more subtle currents the water dragged its sinuous mass across the lands. A leaden glint winked eerily through the twitchwort. Water-stumps crowded the foreshore with feathery reeds swaying farther out. Steadily the murky waters slid by with surreptitious stealth, carving musk clumps and sod in its wake. On the opposite shore, hills huddled, blocking the pastures and cut the company off from any signs of human habitation. Bridges and boats were nonexistent, likewise ropeways or human trails—indeed villages were not to be found in these parts.

The outcasts slogged onward, with the sodden slush of boots squishing in their ears; often they found themselves gazing toward the Lim's far shore where ever more rank water-stumps and sedge stood rooted in fiendish clumps. Slit-like vents opened and closed like gills of evil blowfish on the stumps. The river's uncanny movements caressed their fears like feather wraiths.

More than once they thought of building a raft to gain the far side.

The plan was abandoned, despite Baus, in exacting detail, visualizing a construction of a rack of bottlegum cedar, whittled branches, bound with tight loops of wire-vine . . .

The river was too wide, and the thought of rogue gariali lurking below-waters remained an ongoing horror. The pilgrims gazed gaunt-faced at the sodden heathland ahead of them. The strangely-forested valley was ancient—alien, as if it would never alter its course.

With the early light of evening growing dim, the three stood parch-mouthed at the brink of a festering bog. The mire joined the river in a soggy wetlands. An anaemic sky stretched languidly overhead. Lowlands spread far and wide—an oily mass of lily pads, pimpled stumps, drowned bottlegums and bogwort, reflecting the solemn emptiness of the sky.

With difficulty, the comrades skirted the morass, then too they saw certain half-sunken ruins arching out of the waters.

Baus voiced a speculative murmur. He gazed upon a half toppled ziggurat. Several lichen-eaten slabs eroded beyond measure may have been statues of kings at one time. The whole drowned scene brought Baus to a sudden melancholy. He imagined an opulent civilization with ancient rotundas and pergolas of the finest splendour—this, after recalling the ruins on the river islands spied before Farfus. He could only guess that this region had once supported an ancient culture—lands, eerily disposed and invested with a memory of a lost population yet guarding wiser ways.

Beyond the dolour he had ever known while sailing on Zoren's ship across the endless leagues of the Poesasian, Baus felt a sorrow in his heart.

Heaving a sigh, he urged his companions to new speed. They struggled over the moss-covered mounds and left the mist-clothed ruins behind.

In a wash of silver mist night came. In programmed rhythm, the sounds began again and the three hunkered down in the greenery for defence, hearing the familiar hootings and bewitchments drifting from Farling's Wall. The urgings were accompanied by the harsh thrash of some sordid viper slithering across the Lim.

Baus wormed his way deeper in his rude protective cradle. Tucked between lichened boulders and a bottlegum cedar, he braced himself for the night with his peers, exposed to the elements and danger, now a familiar mistress.

VII

Morning arrived and besieged with hunger, Baus discovered a yellow feather plunked in his cap. A buckler spine cleaned of meat had been placed on Poli's rising and falling chest.

The two leaped to attention. The implication was chilling. Sansix's 'marking' had occurred immediately after they had first encountered the mysterious wall—before the scoundrel had gone missing. Two more of their company were now marked.

The sign indicated foul things in play and Baus offset the portent by shucking off his cap with a grimace.

By noon of the third day Valere managed to discover some mushrooms. Poli loosed a cry, for some innocuous-looking bottle-berries lay in a hidden hollow. Hunger was their world; the travellers wolfed down their scant fare with rude nips and smacks.

They broached a wild crab apple grove, parch-lipped and sore. Twitch elm ran in clusters down toward the eldritch wall and a faint coyote trail forged ahead, now forking in opposite directions—one bending eastward running parallel to the line of the disquieting river and away from the wall. The other continued dead ahead, ominously near to the ponderous wall's shadow.

The junction was disturbed by a peculiar presence of a frail figure—one looking very similar to their missing comrade, Sansix.

The companions halted, perplexed.

The figure seemed exceptionally haggard; Sansix, if it were, was not the Sansix they remembered. The villain stooped, persisted in an inner dialogue of a queer flavour, pointing fingers up to the sky, as if cursing all things natural. He seemed to be pondering a pathetic choice of paths, with no small animosity.

Baus pulled at his nose, frowning deeply. Indeed, a peculiar sight . . . prudence was necessary. Surprise being his first reaction, he felt a strong sense of distrust grow. What had caused the villain to exude such a play of dementia, and no less, why in this particular unearthly locale?

Baus had no answers. Oddly, it seemed as if he were heading back in their direction. There was no reason for it—outside of a lunacy, especially when there were only swamps, shivers and disgusts in these quarters.

Catching sight of the three, Sansix raised a glad cry. He came trotting over on dogged legs. Nursing his left calf, perhaps from an injury, he seemed somehow bent and out of shape, possibly smitten by a blight. Baus, Poli and Valere retreated instinctively, all wearing expressions of bewilderment. He continued to shamble toward them, mumbling in a very foolish way; his unkempt hair skewed in all directions and his wiry physique looking very much undernourished. The gaunt person they once knew as 'Sansix' was invested with a curious diamond-shaped wound on his lower neck, by the bridge of the collarbone.

He rendered them an awkward greeting.

Baus gave a guarded reply. Sansix's eyes, he noticed, were glazed and out of kilter and his face was flushed. Small beads of perspiration trickled down his brow as if he were running a fever, or prodded or stung.

"So, here then, who do we have?" Valere wheezed gruffly. "What brings our fink creeping out of the brake?"

Sansix gave a mournful grunt. "I never thought I'd be glad to see you thugs—truly a sight for sore eyes!"

"The same cannot be said by us," grunted Poli.

Sansix did not respond; he seemed only to notice that Baus paid an inordinate attention to the lower path straggling toward the river. "I've been down that way," he grunted, "there's no good to come of it. Unless, of course, you have a penchant for quagmires, bogwort or gariali." He drew them aside, his hand slightly shaking.

"Indeed," mused Baus icily. "So why are you coming back this way?"

Sansix seemed to hold his breath. He regained some of his composure. "I am vulnerable to isolation and opted to adjust my situation—I allowed you three some time to catch up—that way we could amalgamate forces. Of course we are an effectual team and I pine for the days of old!" He reached out a comradely hand to pat Baus but Baus drew back. "I am eager to explore the path which minimizes prospective jeopardy and maximizes our collective interests. We must search together for practical solutions in these bleak wilds."

Poli gave a sardonic growl, "What is that sick red mark on your neck?"

"A bite only," explained Sansix. "A gnat or some insect has taken a crack at me. No more." He smiled extravagantly which aroused further doubt. "It seems that I have been stung more than once, perhaps a few times. What of it? Another testament to the bleakness of these lands." He waved a shaky hand. "Shall we depart? I grow fatigued and am eager to discover sustenance, not to mention clean drinking water."

Baus grunted suspiciously. He stroked his chin with displeasure. "I am of mind to attempt the lower path, with the intent to put as much distance between myself and the wall as possible."

The swindler sprang back with disapproval. "Are you oblivious to the dangers I have cited? Taking the lower route entails gariali and bogwort. Strike the upper path so as to come hastily to the benevolent, if not kindly uplands! The forest is diminished there! The path follows a pleasing route— look!—the trail meanders along a lawn of fresh promise through adjoining bowers of twitch oak—at least this is what my eyes see from this vantage."

Valere, frowning, confirmed the fact with a grumbling glance. "Sansix speaks truth. If our fink should be fibbing though—we can always double back and feed him to the gariali. We could always try the other fork—we are free men, after all . . . and have excellent means of dealing with treachery."

Baus was taken with the thought. After some strained negotiation, they all agreed to take the upper route.

Striking out with new resolve, they kept wary eyes on the trail: it spread along the interminable wall where the green lawn widened. 'Twas perhaps no more than a few stones' throws later that less and less graffiti began to be observed upon the façade. To Baus's eye it seemed almost as if the scrawlings had been hastily effaced.

Why? The terrain seemed unusually cultivated, as if water stumps had been removed. Thicket, marrow, gimp briar and thistle seemed to have been wholly clipped away. Instead of the unruly foliage, pleasant ox-eyed flowers shone in brilliant swaths.

The four stopped at the brink of a white- and pink-flowered knoll, wide-eyed, gazing upon the scene with a mixture of uneasy reflections. To the left loomed the implacable wall. To the right a manicured slope dotted with cherry-blossoms, azaleas and the languid, brooding river. The wall imposed a sense of serenity upon the hillock's summit. Farther afield the charming sight of the azaleas faded to grey, to the tune of bangle thicket and purple phantom elm dotting the river.

Curiously, a child's skip from the wall, a low table was set, upon which baskets of fruit and fresh bread had been placed.

Baus frowned with amazement. The tablefront was designed with decorative motifs and a lurid sign written in bold red crayon:

"Come one, come all! Eat plenty of this fine, famous goat-bread. 'Tis baked fresh today this Wednesday and comes as a remarkable treat to whomever, wayfarer or pilgrim, stumbles across it first—without covenant or price!"

Underneath the text 'Wednesday', the word 'Tuesday' had been effaced. Underneath that, the word 'Monday' evidently had been scrawled. A comparable situation existed at the adjacent table which advertised a similar quality of grapes found in an exquisite copper urn with antique script. The placard on the table announced in ever grander and larger lettering:

"Come sample these grapes! FREE— Absolutely FREE! Dip handful, fingerful or fistful when or as desired! Single fruits may be acquired at a moment's notice, at a beck and call. Quantities have no limits! Supplies are unmonitored, and absolutely free!"

Next, stood a third table with a heaping bickboard bowl full of walnuts and acorns spread with fresh cinnamon buns and apple honey. The placard simply read:

"If nuts are your fetish, then gather with relish!
All victuals are absolutely free!"

Baus stared with dumbfounded reservation. He paused, peering past the tables. The wall seemed to gleam with a cheery sterility and as clean a slate blue as he had ever seen. The aged wood seemed carefully scrubbed— devoid of moulds, fungi, spores and other noxious elements which might cause one misgiving.

His trepidations only deepened. He looked about the knoll with a studious suspicion. Pleasant vistas abounded.

Baus mused: a person would not sponsor such benefactions, at least for altruistic purposes, without some kickback. There must be some exchange of goods or a compact at least, of service required for free offerings—even a minimum of diffident praise or token of philanthropy. Was the display simply an elaborate ruse designed to ensnare a gullible traveller?

Baus's face curdled into a grimace. The latter seemed the most plausible.

He scratched his head and sighed. Bright puffy clouds plied across the sky; the wind was nonexistent, only halcyon views presented themselves. . .

Baus peered back at the wall. In itself, the barrier seemed more innocuous than ever, somewhat largely swept of maudlin graffiti and surprisingly devoid of hedgerot.

Humming a sour note, he tapped his foot while Valere picked his beard and ground his teeth. Squinting at each other, the two could offer each other no explanation. They became even more given to unease. Baus took liberty to address Poli and Sansix of his qualms.

Sansix brushed off the misgivings as overcaution.

Valere forwarded his vigorous disagreement. "Temptations of this sort smack of selfless charity strung to cunning advantage. We should steer clear!"

"Agreed!"

"By no means!" cried Poli. "My hunger remains unrelieved. You may do what you like, but I am here to eat!"

"A heroic attitude!" called Sansix, slapping Poli on the back.

Baus regarded the swindler with resentment. "Indeed, you rascal? Do you not remember the warnings the villagers gave us against Wickles?"

Sansix gave a derisive snort. "Wickles? What are they? Surely you do not believe in such infamous wives' tales? Not the other day I came across naught a soul, while strolling by here freely eating of these comestibles. No less, in ease and comfort!"

"That is a consoling admission," Baus remarked sarcastically. "So why are you so keen to retrace your steps? You failed to mention the presence of 'foodstuff' anywhere in your maundering."

The swindler gave a spiteful hoot. "'Twas a suppression launched in the intent of forestalling emotions of disappointment should viands not be forthcoming upon my return. Is that so bizarre?"

Baus grunted his disbelief. "So you say! This cleanliness of the terrain and the eeriness of the flora seem suspicious. I, for one, remain cynical. I thought you said you hadn't taken this route before?"

Sansix attempted a grudging explanation. "You have simply arrived at an erroneous conclusion."

"Ha! Shall we clarify matters? I shall plant myself between you and a possible escape route while I eat, in the event that you bolt."

"Do as you like!" cried Sansix with exasperation. "Before we met at this junction, I succeeded in rerouting myself through the tissel and managed to recapture the path north to double back by the wall. Is this so bizarre? Or is it one of my many 'criminal acts'?"

"More conveniently, a lie," snorted Valere.

"Balderdash! Consider!" cried Sansix. "Watch as I trudge, stoop and acquire grapes without harm or remorse, as indicated on the placard!"

The swindler tramped up the slope and halted at a defensive position. Before the last table he stood cunningly poised to assess the nuts which Baus noticed he appeared to scrutinize in a very calm way. Also a very intent eye was drawn on the lawn before the table prior to taking a protracted step toward the middle podium. He approached with a smug grin as if harbouring some secret information regarding the setting.

Baus stepped back with the utmost suspicion. Sansix clutched two grapes in his hand and plunged them into his maw with a flamboyant flourish.

The seamen smacked their lips. Flashing teeth, they shot each other hungry glances. Each tipped eyes toward the bread basket; inevitably they took steps toward urn and tub.

Poli stole forward, reaching into one of the bread baskets. He extracted a chunk of bread without harm or hindrance. Swallowing his fare with satisfaction, he helped himself to another.

Baus padded five paces closer. He thought to detect an odd slur of motion.

A movement, a flicker? From a knothole behind the table there seemed to be a stir.

He peered slant-eyed at the hole in the wall. He laughed a private joke. Were his eyes playing tricks?

No, wait! Another movement—a very sinister flicker, like the flash of a white, oleaginous eye darting slantwise through the crack.

Baus scowled. A trap? A seemingly innocent one then—a deadfall?— and yet, both Poli and Sansix inarguably had tasted the food without penalty . . .

Fatigued, he sauntered brazenly up to the bread table with Valere trotting at his heels. They stood to inspect the baskets and saw nothing of menace. The residing loaf sat with a crust of maltberry seeds; likewise, Valere's fruits were ripe for picking. The baskets were elegant—brown wicker wrapped in quality straw ties and laden with fine white cheesecloth. A jug of clean water stood aside. The tables themselves were covered with a stylish, green terra-cloth embroidered with white-gold trim: an overall design which pleased Baus and with which neither he nor Valere could find fault.

Moistening lips, Baus gave a murmur, "Curses to all diseases of misgiving!"

Poli moved back to tackle his urn, shovelling nuts into his mouth like a bear in spring. Valere busied himself with the grapes and scooped dollops of cinnamon onto each mouthful.

Sansix stood aloof, wearing an unctuous smile.

Baus eyed the conniver with steadfast attention and beckoned him harshly.

Sansix mutely acknowledged the call. "Why do you vex me? I cogitate on what I shall eat! Is that prohibited?" He stamped his foot.

Baus nodded sourly. "Your remarks seem innocent, Sansix, yet perhaps they would be more convincing if you were less glib."

Sansix gave his head a fanciful shake. "The tone of your remark stings. I simply want to forestall a semblance of rudeness should I gorge all the victual prior to your feasting."

Baus grunted in annoyance; he took several steps forward and recognizing the largest bread basket as finest, dropped a hand to acquire a small sample of bread. Something squashed under his foot—a hidden hibiscus? A sodden lever? A misshapen bulb? A treadle of unknown design? The nature of the object eluded Baus.

With appalling swiftness however, the grass under his feet began to bulge—in an altogether peculiar fashion. Buckling left then right came earth and grass, then certain thin, wiry tubes protracted themselves from the ground like whipping wire.

The outlaw stood rigid in amazement.

Poli hot-potatoed himself away from the table.

Valere stabbed down a blade at the moving turf.

Too late! The ground erupted like a forest of exploding bombs. All three were thrown helplessly into the air like dolls. A jinx!—everyone except Sansix was plunged into bedlam. The opportunist had nimbly hopped aside in convenient time and appeared to have dodged a fatal tensile drag of snare with easy anticipation.

Baus, Poli and Valere crashed heavily to the ground. All were covered with a mucilaginous film. They thrashed and rolled. The black gauze restricted their movements and their surprise and disgust went unparalleled.

Poli struggled to his feet, scowling and thrusting against the spidery strands of reeking withe that held them. To no avail. Valere had no chance to draw weapon. He could not cut the threads fast tightening about his knees. Now his torso was puckered into a tight ball, knees clenched so tautly to chest that he gasped, bound in a fearsome grip. Elsewhere the dinner tables were strewn; food lay littered about the green like barnyard fodder.

Within moments the three sat clasped in tightly woven black balls, groaning and quivering.

Sansix surveyed the scene with judicial dispassion. He stood back a healthy distance and gave his head a dour shake. To assess the sorriness of the scene was an exercise in ministerial forbearance. He offered condolences where he could and embarked on a lengthy treatise castigating the evils of gluttony.

Completing his sermon, he spoke in a voice of high wonder. "Friends, rogues and dullards. Attend! Events and programs now proceed in a singularly new manner of distinction! Do you recall the indecent mistreatments—the abuse, the diatribe, the cheerless vagaries, the deprecations that I have endured over the past weeks? No? How amusing! Where are all the boasts now, you sorry oafs? The crass taunts, the infamous blows and pokes, scares and clouts so quick to spill from your rude hands?" The swindler pranced forward with spritely humour and plucked Valere's ear. He swatted the captain on the brow that peeked through the fine black gauze. He poured himself a glass of water from a half overturned jug and dumped it unceremoniously on Baus's head, as if to declare a coup d'état.

Almost at once, a near invisible crack opened in the lower half of the wall. Very expertly, the crevice swiftly widened. The outlaws blinked in stupefaction. It showed a modest round door by the knothole. Out bumbled three oafish, stocky grotesques. To Baus's amazement the monstrosities appeared somewhat female, but this was only in a marginal sense. Capering behind came a slender waif with peculiar aspects of physiology that Baus was not at liberty to diagnose in his cramped position.

The three largest hulks stomped heavy-footed up to the disaster scene and inspected the offenders with austere gazes. The foremost, a tall, broad-bellied mass of flesh with ratty, rose-coloured hair had the hoofs of a goat and a pig's snout. She cried out in a voice of graceless contempt, "Look, Paiesmy! We have here a cadre of braves . . ! Hoy, Loeitch! Briskly now, get the snips! How I love those spider bombs of yours! Don't forget the shears! We have a bit of pruning to do!"

Paiesmy, the tall gangly one of their lot, elbowed her porcine, pork-haunched colleague aside and thrust an upturned shark's nose upon the three neatly knit balls. She mouthed a fulsome retort. "This is a fair fetch, Graeitch!—which does you well, considering 'tis so early in the season." She snorted out a happy conviction. Morose-jowled and inordinately tall, the creature was all knees, elbows, skin and bones.

She ambled sideways with a shuffle, but otherwise appeared to suffer no animal-like deformities like her sister, barring an eyebrowless forehead and an unmistakable androgynous aura.

Loeitch, a pear-shaped and green-eyed goliath with a mop of yellow curls, shaggy arms and long splayed feet, now hurried forward to bunt Esling, the smaller, daintier of their group out of her way, bending to pat Baus's head and give a strident call, as if he were her pet hound. "Right you are, sister!—the fates have shone well on we Wickles. 'Tis a remarkable boon!"

"Aye, 'tis, Loeitch!"

The last slender creature, Esling, fair-cheeked and slight, comely too—if one were to ignore the brown and white doe's tail and the two small black horns budding from her temples, came delicately and quick-footed to select a grape from the ground and plop it into her mouth. The creature sighed; she seemed contentedly disinterested in the black bundles at her feet, more intrigued by the birdsong and the buzzing of bees around her. She skipped harmlessly a short distance away, proffering a teasing flourish to the captives and showing off her dexterity to her peers with careless regard.

Poli cursed the grip of his unspeakable bonds. He bit at the organic wire that stuck so tightly upon his face. Valere rocked back and forth, trying to roll himself down the hill.

All worthless endeavours.

Loeitch, eyes a-glitter, latched onto Valere's bulk and gave him a laughing tug. Baus fought against the sticky mesh, but the strands were too resilient. Lolispar—his loyal weapon—was flattened against his thigh, useless. He pitched back and forth in an attempt to jiggle his head upright, but lucklessly he could only peer slantwise, examining the grotesques in better detail.

Graeitch, lumbersome and intimidating, was double his own size and wore a greasy red and black-checkered hunter's jacket with short knee breeches. Her shins were unpleasantly exposed, like old wood overly scabbed and hairy. Paiesmy was ostrich-tall and wore a mauve outer girdle with grey pantaloons and long ribbed shindrifts while Loeitch, dumpy-shaped and ever fixed with a grebe's grin on her face, wore a dowdy, robin-egg blue apron covering the extent of her upper body and her three trailing swallowtails. She appeared without trousers, only wearing a ridiculous pair of high-heeled fur boots, allowing her nether portions to remain unexceptionably exposed. Baus took offense to the posture and curled his nose. Esling was garbed in an unmistakably coral-crimson jumpsuit, very boyish in fashion, outfitted with an emblem of a lizard, a lion and other animals which Baus could not recognize.

Baus bit back his distaste. The contemptible creatures were plainly Wickles, that the Farfus villagers had warned them against. What an abominable fate!

Sansix loitered uneasily from a distance, pulling at his chin and calling forth a cocksure remark: "Well, Graeitch! That's three oafs to my tally!"

The Wickles returned a frown. They pretended not to hear and returned to inspecting their catch, causing Sansix to shimmy forth with a wretched caw.

Graeitch seemed not to notice and finally thrust out her pig-like snout in his direction. "Here, you rat groom! Come closer, so I might get a better glimpse of you."

Sansix turned a hasty step away. "Nay, wood-witch! I bid you stay your ground! I have not fallen prey to your vile deceits for no reason at all. I have fulfilled your obligation—now consider my indenture discharged!"

Graeitch looked to her sisters with quiet amusement. "I seem to keep hearing a little tit-bird chirping."

"Don't dither about, you swinish hag!" roared Sansix. "You heard me well enough. Remove this blight from my neck so that I may be on my way to Bickerwell, which is less than a league away, if memory serves."

"I seem to have heard a naughty bird chirping again!" called Graeitch jauntily. "Sansix, is it not? Off with you, villain!"

"What? You dare deal me such nonsense?"

"My sisters and I have important business to conduct. Why should we waste time on a jackal?"

Her sisters gave chittering laughs.

"You are neglecting your maxim—*Three grooms for one*'," called

Sansix. "I have delivered you your 'three' to my 'one'."

Graeitch blinked; she made an expository sign at her sisters.

Baus took the opportunity to interject a complaint. "Here now, Wights! I trust that you have heard enough from this oily-tongued rascal?"

"Correct," answered Graeitch with indifference. "What of it?"

"Then I trust you are a Wickle?"

"That seems evident."

"Then, I beseech you to release us. We have no quarrel with you. My colleagues and I are in collaboration with powerful allies, whose number does not include that pansy-faced Sansix. Our friends are remorseless. They shall rend you limb from limb for your infractions!"

"Indeed, and who are these 'allies' of yours?" jeered Graeitch.

Baus gave a steamy laugh. "Do you think I would reveal them at this tender time?"

Graeitch rubbed her cheeks with disdain. "This poses an unpleasant dilemma for all of us. You have imbibed certain viands which belong to our guild, and I believe that comprises an infringement."

Valere bellowed, "The victual was free—as was overtly proclaimed!"

"'Free' is a relative term," countered Paiesmy with hauteur. "It need be interpreted in its own particular context; for example, not considered equivalent are 'free advice' and 'free will'. One entails a transfer of words without contractual obligation, the other is merely a philospher's dream."

Graeitch endorsed the disclosure with a high snort.

Loeitch added: "Even the word 'freedom' is an absolute description on its own, which allows scope for ambiguity and misconception, as we call to judge."

"Well said, Loeitch! 'Freedom' never ascribes to what it actually means," laughed Paiesmy.

"I do not care a whit for your vagaries!" sneered Valere.

Paiesmy hitched herself forward with animated spite. "That is no way to talk to us, Redbeard. Aye, you are a feisty one! The basis of reasoning ideology is never to be fluffed off!"

"Silence, Paiesmy! You'd do better to save your breath!" panted Graeitch. "Obviously these grooms have no head for philosophy. They are simply illiterates."

"What do you fiends want?" cried Baus. "A beast slayed? A treasure retrieved? We can do that and more. Loosen our bonds and you will see!"

The Wickles stared at each other with whimsical amazement. "Such an amusing proposal!"

"Amusing or not," growled Baus, "what do you say to a few hours of drudgery in your swamp garden, shovelling out say one of the hoghouses?—perhaps a narration of a lewd yarn?—or the propounding of a philosophical maxim, or an aggrandizement of ego?" The hope seemed to grow in Baus's throat.

"Nothing so banal!" called Graeitch with decision. "What else can you provide us with? Our desires dance only to the tune of *magic*."

The disclosure set Baus's spine a-tingle. He searched for a means that would end his thraldom and avert the possibility of unsavoury outcomes.

Sansix was averse to the program—he hopped forward with an impatient fervour that puzzled Baus. His knife was brandished to strike Graietch and a rock was balled in the other fist. "One moment, you hogs! You have neglected to supply a reply to *my* earlier query."

The Wickles seemed oblivious to the request.

"You know well what I demand, you pompous hags! Recall: in exchange for my life, you offered me a chance to shepherd you more grooms."

"Exactly so!" Graeitch stormed. "More grooms! Now we have them." Arching her head high, she gave a humorous grunt. "So then—what is the problem? You have secured us our grooms. Now be off. Go catch salamanders or whatever you eat on this side of the river."

"Very amusing." Sansix danced with fury. "Is your memory so lax that you cannot remember your promise? What of my neck? You spared me a day to procure two 'grooms'. I have brought you three, now pass me the antidote. Time is of an essence!"

"Hush!" called Graeitch. "I'll not have you pipsqueaking about my turf like a common bumblebee."

Sansix yelled an oath, "I'll not be daunted! Your greedy existence and thuggish attitude brings me to the edge. Your lack of attention to my health has me completely irked! Now, you have received your boons—so be happy and return me my due before this afternoon wanes and this festering wound causes me to swell up and die!"

Graeitch brushed Sansix an indifferent leer. "The possibility is not remote. In fact, the antidote is before your eyes—'tis in my possession; ha, hum . . . let us return to my lair where the administration will be more painlessly effected."

Sansix loosed a clucking howl. "Do you take me for a simpleton? In fact, I despise your gulling chicanery. 'Tis insulting. The distance I must travel is farther than I would care to attempt and I suffer plantar's warts."

"The ailment can be easily remedied," the hag muttered. She dug nimbly in her grubby jacket to impatiently toss a wet sack at Sansix's feet. "There! Don't say I didn't do anything for you, ingrate. Take the antidote or leave it. Be happy!"

Sansix distrustfully eyed the satchel. The sack apparently contained a healing potion though it dripped a vile white ooze, or paste most peculiar to smell and sight.

Graeitch turned prudently to her sisters. "Let us take our prizes with us and be off! Sansix is puzzled. Take the ointment, dear Sansix. Smear it on your wound, if you like."

Loeitch and Paiesmy giggled and Graeitch spoke in a rich tone, "The application must be applied liberally, Sansix. Seize it like so and squeeze! You eye and scrutinize it like some wet nimp!"

The swindler demurred and Graeitch cawed out in a jocular voice, "I advise you to smear it on your skin—slather it! Let the paste become a foil for grief! Fret not, little dabchick—the unction does not invoke fatality."

With fear and loathing Sansix extracted the satchel, lifting high the dripping ooze with a sense of distaste. Fearing the worst, he pinched his eyes shut and grit his teeth. With an awful moan, thumb and forefinger pinched, he let the paste drip over his neck and shoulder.

The villain's fears were not unfounded. Croaking and vomiting, he bent over nearly double. A three-inch centipede sprang out from the wound at his neck. The worm lay writhing on the grass, a thing of pale blue, pus-ridden and noisome and full of dilating pustules. In seconds, Sansix nearly fell in a swoon and the afternoon light had the thing smoking, withering to a crisp as if it had never been.

Sansix's wound had nearly faded, but almost at once he felt invigorated, as the worm evaporated into the air like water on a heated rock.

He wrenched open his eyes. He appeared remarkably better.

Now a satisfied grin crept over his face. He skipped and cavorted down the hill, remarking on his newfound freedom. Arresting celebration, he flung Graeitch a malign look. "A nasty token, Graeitch. You and your putrid means! But from you, I would expect nothing less—neither from your hobgoblins." He thrashed out a finger of warning. Take care! I am not the mooncalf you think, but a remorseless enemy!"

Graeitch paid no heed. She trotted over dutifully with her peers and Sansix deigned to hop back an equal distance.

"That last remark was insensitive," called Loeitch, shaking a knotty fist. "Such impudence; it imposes a blemish upon our trust!"

"Nevertheless—" croaked Sansix, "the damage is done and I must be recompensed. Take this as a study of ingratitude and a farewell malediction. Good riddance and good luck!" He cast a last scornful look at Baus and Valere. Each lay hopelessly bundled in balls of tough spider-withe. "Farewell to you—rogues."

Loeitch fiddled with her weed-twined braids and cried, "What are the grooms' names? We must know their names—if we are to perform our magic!"

Sansix gave his neck a pliant jerk. "Find them out yourselves. Ah, what does it matter? The first, black-haired knave, is Baus. The lout with the malodorous red hair and hirsute body is Valere. His blond sidekick is 'Poli'."

"Excellent!" Loeitch snickered gleefully. "This comprises a useful triad. So we have, Baus"—she touched his damp head—"and Poli,"—she ruffled his curls with affection—"and Valere!" She straddled the captain barelegged like a pony and caused him to roar in revulsion.

Sansix winced, but gave his head an approving shake.

Baus thrust a virulent glare upon Sansix. To express his utter contempt required a lexicon of language with which he was not equipped. So, the swindler had been leading them to this insidious trap all along—ever since their parting at Farfus's beer garden—and, as he suspected, possibly before, when the vigilantes had forced them to abandon their road up the coast. Undoubtedly the opportunist in him had not counted on his own ensnarement by the Wickles . . .

Sansix crafted a genteel bow. He turned on his heel and marched away, tossing his head at the grove of phantom elms and hedging his way purposefully away from Farling's Wall.

Graeitch gazed after the villain thoughtfully. An inquiring glance crept over her grizzled features and before long she was calling out his name in a somewhat lewd manner: "Watch your step, manling! Old Dorty loiters where crafty eyes cannot see her. I suggest you stick close to the wall. Avoid the river like a plague. 'Tis a place where shadows breed, and where a man's luck may run out."

Sansix gave back a harsh guffaw. "Hush your maw, hag. If you think I am that credulous, you are mistaken. Most definitely I will not stay near the wall. I will steer clear of it! In fact, I will plant my feet wherever I wish— particularly closer to the river and farther away from your reeking hides!"

The Wickles tittered and Sansix trotted down the slope at a more presumptuous pace. He took deliberate strides toward the phantom elm that teetered ominously near the river.

Graeitch and the Wickles watched him with an expectant leer; each casting the other knowing glances.

No sooner had Sansix stumbled into the small copse when he came bounding out in frightful hops. A great grey-green moth, the size of a barrel, fluttered out after him on bisected wings. The creature had legs of a heron and the head of a baldish baby. The creature mewled, bobbed and gnashed above the villain's shoulder like some balloonish ghoul. Sansix was terrified out of his wits. The creature showered him with weird, scintillating green flakes that no one could decipher. Sansix yelled. He rubbed at his eyes, which became instantly clogged with foul dust from the flakes.

The Wickles saw great irony in the situation. They gave titillating guffaws.

"You have hoodwinked me again, Graeitch!" cried Sansix, shaking a fist, rubbing his eyes with wrath. "We had formalized our indenture! Why did you have to let me fall into another booby trap? Now, call off your floating spook!"

"By no means!" A look of sulky hauteur passed across Graeitch's grey face. "Now you plead for succour when I expressly warned you to steer clear of the phantom elms. What audacity! No, you are solely responsible for your own fate!"

Sansix frantically tried to dog-skip away from the baby heron moth, but he barely avoided begin bashed about like a bowling pin as he attempted to evade the attack.

Sansix forced a surly cry from his lips, "I stand victimized, Graeitch! Call off your spook!"

Loeitch gave a spiteful croak: "The ingrate accuses you of foisting the baby heron moth upon him. What sauce!"

Paiesmy cried: "The accusation reeks of gall!"

More of the baby heron moths emerged from the woods to harass Sansix.

From what Baus could intuit (though his perspective was limited in this situation), the creatures appeared to be a colony of insects—monsters, if you will, hanging or clinging from one branch to the other like opportunistic bats. Now they clustered above Sansix's head in a brainless ring, dumping more of the hateful green speckles upon him. They had paralyzed the villain's sight. What were the misfits? A weird assortment of proto-lepidoptera of unresearched genus? Bizarre pseudo-homino-papilionaceons of a transfigured order?

Baus was at a loss. Certainly elder omophibians could not be discarded from the mix, as would it be presumptuous to gloss over the possibility of 'honophibian' didantrixes.

He marvelled at the basic implication of the creatures' existence— diseased genera walking the lands to accost innocent wayfarers.

In swift order Sansix could not see three feet in front of him. Thrashing about like a bird in blind terror, he flailed his knife, kicked and spat at the baby heron moths.

But they did not grant him an ounce of quarter and came at last in more reckless numbers, bumping and grinding against him by means of their woolly-wisped wings.

Sansix cursed in glottal bursts. But twenty paces away, a flap suddenly unfurled in the earth.

Out jumped a squat, bowl-shaped Wickle—decorated with a fan of peacock feathers surrounding her rude shoulders. A black ruff of tangled fur fell from her crown. A buzzard's beak framed the darting white eyes and instead of hands, the creature harboured raccoon-like paws which clutched a rusty pail filled to the brim with some sort of caustic liquid.

Swiftly the Wickle plied through the army of moths and upended the bucket onto Sansix before he could defend himself. Sansix uttered a painful cry. Evidently the contents of the bucket was a viscous green slime of dire quality.

With rage and horror, he lunged forward—but the movement yielded no advantage. The defence seemed only to land him in further doom.

A cracking and creaking filled the air. The adhesive solidified instantly and Sansix was rendered motionless like a statue. He was fixed on the spot, arms laying outstretched like a ghoul, digits clasped tightly on his dagger in some outraged hunter's stance. A snarl of incommensurate hate remained fixed on his lips.

The baby heron moths seemed to cognize some of this emotion and arrested their hectoring. They hung back, surprised that their quarry didn't move. The pack flew about like curious wasps. Now others hovered close to Sansix like hummingbirds, peering into his eyes, sensing no further life there and returned to their forest, disappointed at what seemed an amusing game gone dull.

Graietch tsked. Now the waddling Wickle who had tossed the liquid croaked a greeting to her.

The kindred offered desultory acknowledgements.

The newcomer extended further pleasantries to the trio. But Paiesmy intervened, fist held high. "Dorty! Do not cajole us with your happy salutations. This is what we call 'opportunistic scheming'. You capitalize on our turf!"

"Touché, Paiesmy!" called Dorty with a laugh. "'Tis a good day to you too, Graeitch. I trust that your broths have brewed favourably, Loeitch, and your bowels have voided regularly?"

"Not nearly as often as they might," intoned Loeitch coolly.

Pleasantries hung stiff in the air. From somewhere in the sky came a terrible squawking. Eyes peered up—a fluttering and flapping caused Baus's skin to crawl. A golden form suddenly dominated the sky, a shape of mighty ancient origin, like some sun-swallowing leviathan.

The Wickles twitched. The form dropped a dozen paces from Sansix's frigidized body. Twice as tall as a man the thing landed with a dull thud. Only the terrified's lips were free to move, which mouthed a mixture of horror and disbelief. The creature had perhaps been attracted by the moths' busy mischief-making?

None were to say. The incidence was altogether unaccountable.

Dorty initiated a complex system of flourishes which the moths construed as an attacking command. All at once, they descended upon the Auk-man, crowding it with prejudice. The creature buffed the swarm away like bottleflies. It stood towering like an avatar, gleaming a face of ominous and grievous wrath. Gnashing its beak, it snapped off baby head after baby head like ripe apples. The moths clustered in more hideous numbers, swarming about the menace from the purple-leaved phantom elms.

The Auk king paused in its assaults. Thrusting out an enormous, jagged beak, it uttered a bellow of rage. Dorty was cast a brooding, hateful gaze— the same small, smug, dry-faced creature that had caused Sansix such woe.

Cognizing malice, the Wickle lifted her pail. No more quick-drying reagent was there to throw on the Raksoi and it caught handle and pail and sent it spinning to the river.

Dorty stared bemused. Clamping talons onto her ears, the Auk king plucked her high off the ground.

Dorty's shrieks were bitter and abrasive. The slander slipping from her mouth came in bursts and rasps as she was hurtled higher. She tried to disentangle herself from the mangling constriction, but found the action was futile.

Pumping with vigour, the Raksoi launched upright like a jet of water. Soaring out over the forest, it disappeared in a haze of light with its wriggling prize, leaving Sansix alone with the moon-struck baby heron moths spinning about him like aimless automatons.

The Wickles gave rise to a series of laughs. With tripled haste, they stuffed as much food in their pockets as could be plunged there and set about fussing with the grooms. They appeared undecided at first—should Paiesmy and Graeitch roll the catches toward the aperture in the wall, or turn tail as quickly as time would allow them?

Paiesmy took the initiative. She began heaving Valere toward the wall— even going so far as to cast a longing glance at Sansix by the river.

"Forget it!" Graeitch barked. "That gamble shall get us all killed! Now into the forest! The ghoul rides in spleen."

"Common reason suggests that we salvage—"

"Avaunt!" Graeitch roared. "There is no time to second guess!"

Wincing at the quality of Graeitch's breath, Paiesmy helped her sister wheel the companions toward the small round door.

With no gentle persuasion the three hip-checked their charges within. Esling the doe-waif followed. The door snapped tightly shut. Only a ghastly groan was heard in the silence.

VIII

On the hither side of Farling's Wall, all was densely obscured. A wood-brown glow permeated the niches like a harvest gloaming; the air was thick and sultry, pervaded by a dozen earthy composites: toadstool, ryttle-hemp, humus, mugwort, moxa, beetlekin.

The Wickles took up each a bundle and hefted their quarries through the forest, rolling them like balloons. They plied the rooty path, as would monks, leading their charges dead ahead through the shadows.

Trees taller than Baus had ever seen, clustered about both sides of the path. Row on row of taupe-tinted trunks, smooth and branchless, reached silently a hundred feet into the air. They arched into dark green plumes deflecting all sunlight.

Mushrooms abounded in these fastnesses—as large as thrones. The forest floor was a thickly woven carpet of melodious colour: dusky reds, malt-ochres, greys, blacks, browns. Ages of fallen leaves had covered the mosaic, ones that never had decomposed and gigantic roots, as thick as a man's thigh, snaked outward from the hollows in random shoots. Faery shrubbery lurked in the distances: multi-tiered, bronzed castles moulded by ages of rain, fog and mist. At their toes, flower-weeds stood out outlandishly, rising in thin stalks with sting ray bulbs mantling their crowns. Puffballs grew in clumps near the elder trees.

Not a wind stirred in this quiet corridor, not a branch creaked, nor did a cricket chirp—and yet—large butterflies drifted by in droves with solemn grandeur through the narrow gaps in the trees.

The Wickles plodded on, unhindered by any fear. They watched the insects ride on their blue and yellow wings with no more fuss than seeds in the wind.

The air remained fused with that melancholy and mystery subtly suffused with the ancient wisdom of the forest.

Baus stared numbly from his webbed constraints. He rolled and banged. The restraining net had him clutched horridly; incessant motion distorted his horizon. Somehow, under the presence of the wall, the flora had merged into an odious sub-reality, progressing to fantastic states of evolution. The eerie beauty of the setting had failed to mitigate Baus's insane misgiving. How could he win his freedom from this ludicrous development?

Graeitch pushed Baus through the shrubbery. Her grunts were happy and the gathering murk only thickened, pressing down on him like a sheet of iron. Baus's skin constricted to more violent oppression, causing him an ache of frustration. The ugly Paiesmy grunted under the exertion of Valere's bulk while Loeitch fought with Poli's cargo. The delicate, more benign creature, Esling, pranced about at their heels like a carefree fawn, murmuring nonsensical phrases.

Ahead the path veered. Lichen and spongerot spread like mildew. Valere blurted out an oath. Loeitch responded in kind, chiding the seaman. The Wickles struggled to roll their charges around a monstrous obstruction but presently two sylph-like creatures popped up from behind the rock—one was an angular-looking female with a rabbit's head, another a woman in the fashion of a tailless dachshund, with human limbs waddling on all fours.

Baus stared, nausea-ridden. The two creatures joined the procession, casting purposeful glances at the 'grooms'.

Baus's astonishment grew to dizzy horror. Paiesmy halted, complaining that the rabbit creature was treading on her heels: "Ah, Tootsy, how inopportune of you to come! Mind your step! Would I had the power to wish for less weight from these fresh catches."

"Does this one look heavy!" remarked Tootsy with a wincing grin. "All the more flavourful, I suppose?"

"Speak for yourself!" cried the four-legged Wickle who hopped from side to side like a spider. "I like my grooms alive and kicking."

"Enough of this nonsense!" reproved Graeitch. "You know the drill, ladies—the grooms roll to their futures!"

Valere cried out with hostility. "Let's trade positions, you hag, you for I —then we shall gladly 'roll' to any destination of your choice."

Graeitch hissed out a reprimand. "Silence! 'Tis an amusing suggestion, but entirely unfeasible."

"Carefully now!" barked Baus. "I spy more rocks up ahead and I am already on the verge of vertigo."

"No less I!" cried Poli with fury. "Nausea has set in with all force!"

"Hush, mules!" cried Graeitch. She clapped her hands with authority. "We are soon at our destination."

"Which is?"

"You shall see!"

Muted light seeped down from the gaps to illuminate a small lawn up ahead. Bathed in rich colour, the glade shimmered ochre and gold. Encircling the clearing loomed a sullen rank of crooked ghost oaks, and zizasters whose dead leaves clung to their haggard limbs. Off to the edge loomed a curious dome. The dwelling—if such could be said—could only be described as a gigantic beehive of yellow jasmine, eccentrically constructed. A crooked sign hung from a rope above the door. '*The Honey Home*' was what it said. Twelve or more portentous myrtle saplings were bent over double and pinned with large wooden stakes to the ground—this formed the infrastructure. Sheets of wood-wax had been tacked over the saplings to create a semblance of a 'honey-comb'. A system of clever eaves had been posted, collecting rainwater which fed into an egg-shaped barrel of wood and brass. Aside grew a shaggy garden of vines and a gaggle of morose-looking poppies with star-shaped petals.

Baus caught a glimpse of the various domes and slab-sided huts that ran deeper in the forest. He grunted.

Paiesmy took up her rolling and tossed a merry call: "Hurry, Esling! Do not gawk! You cavort around like a dawdling poodle. 'Tis like you have not a thought in your head!"

Esling twitched, perhaps her way of sending a message to her associates of displeasure. Despondently she drew closer to the pack.

By and by, more of the denizens of the glade dogged along at a studious pace. Baus caught unsettling glimpses of all—an indescribable potpourri of creatures shed in a terrifying light. Notably, feminine beings—of which stood a huge three-footed stalking goose, a parrot-headed woman with foot-long arms and gangly legs, three eagle-faced bipeds, a womanish creature with fox-furred cheeks and coyote snout, several medium sized fliers with banded torsos, two beautiful ghostlike sylphs wearing gossamer gowns and white slippers . . . Others congregated at the fringes of equal marvel. The entire assemblage was at last bustling with all company of half-human prodigies!

Baus peered sideways from his ball—he took in the scene with an emotion that brought confused distaste and bile bubbling to his throat. Obviously a colony of Wickles! But how many lived here? Twenty? Fifty? He could not guess. How many more communities existed in these sinister forests?

Climbing upon a mossy stone, the goliath Graeitch raised her hands and cleared her wattled throat. "Friends! Wickles, Elderbeasts! Today marks a most auspicious day! Several grooms have fallen into our possession, as can be seen—they are with us today— and have graciously volunteered for 'experimental initiation'. For what purpose? None other than to nullify the servitude applied to our own citizenry years ago. Many dark and dim years ago that was, and it was decreed that all would be liberated. Recall the blight of Farling's Wall!—the inscrutable barrier constructed by the evil wizards of known proximity. All to keep us concealed from the world. At last, we will receive guidance from the 'Beyond'—to shed light on our bleak future, being imprisoned in this matrix like rats in a cage. Not forever shall we skulk and cower in our hidey-holes invisible to the world. No! Herein lies the hope for all Wickles to be emancipated for generations to come. Rendered whole again!—not freakish hybrids of female and animal."

A crescendo of murmurs rose from the gathering. Baus glared with odium. He heard a tumult of grunts, hopeful barks and mewling cries amongst the menagerie.

Graeitch held up a hand for quiet. "Citizens!—Hear me out. History indicates that the plight of our race was foisted upon us by the neomancers of old, the Mismerion manipulators, those duplicitous mages of malice and arrogance, known to us first as 'The Neons', and who subjected us to their depraved experiments. Some call their breed 'pretentious buffoons'. I call them patriarchal swine. Old Faëngraver proposed his mechomistic arts on us from the 'Neomancer Cabal of the Chosen'. He passed his dogma on to Daëndowser, who ultimately, in collusion with his evil apprentice, whispered in the ear of Woisper, who in his final impudence, struck us with the unlawful spells which you see today."

There ensued a keen flurry of hisses and exclamations. Retribution and reprisal burned earnest in the minds of the Wickles. The mob surged closer. Baus shivered. Graeitch stood in gesticulating authority. They inspected the grooms with an anticipatory flavour and possibly thought to commit physical molestation upon them. Graeitch launched herself off her podium and kicked hooves at the few contraveners, who included a hirsute, bear-snouted woman with crabbish claws, also a fish-eyed sylph who fought slavering over whether she should drag Baus into the bush and commit outrageous acts upon him, or indulge in just plain lustful day-to-day fancies.

Baus gaped appalled. Graeitch summoned her two sisters to act as monitors. "I charge you to guard our grooms, Paiesmy. All must keep their filthy digits, tongues and appendages away from the catches!"

A rabbit-footed creature with a fox-face and a woman's furred body raised an outraged paw. "And when can we expect this proposed 'miracle' of yours to take place?"

"In due course!" Graeitch intoned. The expostulation gave way to a rash and impulsive chittering. The audience grumbled on in bitter dispute. Graeitch strictly eschewed enforced conviction: "The question is obtuse and displeasing to my ear, Gladdus. Now, go; please employ yourself in better stead, rather than bullying my charges and busybodying."

"True!" shrilled Paiesmy. "Gladdus's manners are frightful; they lack all decorum. As far as propriety goes, she is bereft. As for her question . . . well, when will it next rain? How is one to know?"

Graeitch set her mouth in prim loop. Gladdus the fox-woman, bridled. A Wickle with a bulbous nose and a toad-like torso with girlish face suddenly leaped up on her hind feet and gave a vicious croak. "Now that spring is on its way, certain 'urges' make themselves known in our group. We require grooms to satiate those urges and continue our species. They are undisciplined and distracting but we deserve appeasement, and a strict set of rules regarding a solution. My question is—when shall we be able to palliate our 'impulses', and who shall be the first to engage the grooms?"

The import of the query infected Graeitch with a sharp annoyance. "I know of your hungers more than any, Banaga. Though you are a sensible and renowned member of our clan, your remarks are emotionally charged and pose risk of provoking unsound behaviour. So quell your qualms. All shall be endowed proper sport in due time. Our priority, of course, is to abide by the 'experiment ritual' with which we are all familiar. The credo supersedes any formal teaming of man with Wickle, or Wickle with man. Serving only as a platform to yield useful clues as to the future of our Wickle race."

A salamander and half badger creature blurted out a rasping ultimatum: "A bunch of fat lies, hog! This does not answer our question. Proceed to outline a cogent plan! I am unclear as to what prompts your prolixity. We are all busy with hectic lives here, and have no time for your incessant word-smithing!"

Graeitch ignored the outburst. In a cadence of dignified rectitude, she continued with her important remarks. "Since my sisters are the official captors of the grooms, they shall be given first couplings. A trifling sacrifice —considering the prodigious efforts in procuring these samples. It has taken significant ingenuity and risk on our part to ensure their capture!"

The same Wickle pushed paws to hips arrogantly. "This comprises favouritism, Graeitch. The grooms, while appearing robust and hale, may not be able to withstand the thrust of our lusts for too long, which are fulsome in Rastule glade."

Graeitch gave a stoic nod. "Quite possibly, Banaga; but should our grooms remain living beyond mere wretched husks after the ordeal, they will each be yielded to the general public-likewise, on an official trial-by-lot basis."

Birdlike caws flew out from the gathering. A set of glaring eyes on tall neck stared and a mouth blurted out in appeal, "What of the Wickles who are beyond child-bearing years? Are they to be vouchsafed access to the grooms?"

Graeitch considered the request germane. "Wickles of this category shall be allowed lowest priority, for practical reasons."

Muted squeals and hysterics came in force. Older Wickles strove amongst the younger to raise paws, limbs, wings, fingers and digits to have their arguments announced.

Baus, Valere and Poli looked on with frozen horror. While their innards curdled, they struggled against their bonds—with futile result—actions which led Loeitch and Paiesmy to pay stricter attention to their charges, while Graeitch mollified the gathering with nods and grand gestures.

Finally, physically exhausted, the Wickle called out an end to the proceedings. The grooms were rolled through the crowd like a pack of hedgehogs and nudged toward the honeycomb dome. Graeitch and her sisters dragged the three inside and staved off the brunt of miscellaneous gropings and clawings from the gathering. The door was clamped shut.

Baus remembered rolling to a halt and banging his head against a giant leg of a ghost oak table. He ground his teeth and sucked in a breath. Who to revile more—Sansix or the execrable Wickles? It was a toss-up. The opportunist's treachery had led them to this hell; nonetheless, Baus smugly recalled the ironic fate to which Sansix had been relegated. Vengeance and vicissitude were not constructive at this time. The outlaw essayed to divert the roots of his misery to a more practical action.

The rank, earthy aroma of the dome assailed his nostrils. A cluster of burlap sacks filled the area, chock full of roots and stalks near his head, the cause of the unpleasant stench. To his left, a small round casement poured forth a rich glow of oily light. Beehive panels shone from the ceiling—an uncanny luminescence lighting the dim confines and giving the captives little cheer. Elsewhere ranged a high flat table with three high-backed chairs. A workbench and hearth with a crooked chimney ran to the roof, and a black cauldron hung from the braces of an iron tripod. There was a grill, several pots, pans, cutlery and knives. A series of cots stuffed with weeds were arranged around the beehive's perimeter; a small kitchen equipped with wash basin and tub.

A cluster of staves leaned against the cupboard, surmounted with white fish skulls of unknown variety. Protruding eel teeth were plain to sight—assists which Baus was to learn, were instrumental in promoting punishment to recalcitrant guests.

Curiously, a small swarm of bees hovered in the dome's apex. They fabricated their hives, which comprised the source of the Wickles' honey.

In the immediate foreground, the floor had been hollowed out and Baus saw the depth to be about eight feet. A clay-plastered drum of impressive configuration lurked below. To what purpose? The outlaw could not immediately fathom the implication. More baffling was the presence of the four large posts sprawled before the cylinder. Ropes and halters were wrapped at their bases.

Graeitch barked out a series of orders which Paiesmy and Loeitch carried out, force-feeding the men a vile liquid which stung their palates. All went limp. The three Wickles took shears and cut the men loose from their sticky mesh. They rolled dazed. Esling divested them of their weapons. Paiesmy, Graeitch and Loeitch continued to move about the compound with a sinister briskness, dragging the companions to an upright post and binding their wrists tightly behind.

Graeitch hung the most notable weapons on a peg where several utensils in the kitchen also hung.

The Wickles' concoction wore off and Baus discerned a blurred version of Lolispar pinned far on the opposite wall. His impaired ganglestick hung not too distant.

Graeitch pointed to the drum's side. "Who shall appeal for indenture? Baus, or is it Poli? Sansix the groom-bringer was first to rise to the challenge—now he squats like a statue."

The companions stirred but remained huddled in their slack heaps. The rank worm springing from Sansix's wound suddenly came to Baus's mind and he framed no eager response.

"Come now!" jibed Graeitch. "There must be one amongst you who is brave enough to vie for his freedom."

Baus glared at Graeitch. He fought the haziness of the soporific that kneaded his guts. "I shall do the deed, Wickle! Just release me and tell me what you need. Go, inflict your blight; I will stride back and forth and track down these grooms of yours—bandits, recidivists, robbers, reprobates, then I will gull them to partake of your foul banquet!"

Graeitch gave a reckless chuckle. "Sorry—a joke only. Our household harbours enough subjects at present." She turned to the others. "Carry on, sisters."

Loeitch and Paiesmy unhooked Baus from the post and hauled him to his knees. Graeitch lifted a podgy finger. She spoke with an almost unnerving precision: "At least I know who amongst you is the most valiant—very well, you shall be first to endeavour upon our *wheel*, Baus. Up, into the hub! Bear the groom hither! Quickly now! Before I become irked." She clapped her hands.

Resisting with all fervour, Baus was unable to break his bonds or exact any type of escape from the Wickles. He was too weakened by hunger and fatigue.

Paiesmy warned Baus to cease his floundering: "If you continue with this rebelliousness, we shall be forced to utilize goads." She tested one of the eel-pronged staves out on Baus's right knee, which caused him a frightful paroxysm. He clucked an uncontrollable moan, then experienced a throbbing spasmodic pain shooting up his spine.

Poli and Valere grimaced, both appalled at what was unfolding.

"Now! View the hub!" Graeitch called out in military tones. Dangling near the rim of the odious circular pit, Baus saw what appeared a gigantic spool of wood and withe. The hub was affixed with zizaster ladder extending down to the interior. Five zinc braces and canvas straps were bolted to the spool's edge where a person might be confined, though standing upright. A complex rotary of chains, pulleys and gears huddled to the side. They were obscured in the dimness, but whose basic intention was self-evident when Loeitch hopped down to crank a dark lever.

"Regard the hub's 'drum'," boasted Graeitch with arrogance. "As our first groom, Baus must ride the drum in order to achieve an equipoise of vertigo. I warn you, the rigours will be unpleasant. While rotating at supra-speeds, you will be prodded with frightful objects—ostrich feathers, astrid polyps, finger rods, wands-plexuses and nodes of energetic import beyond your understanding. Some objects may sting more smartly than others, such as this nimbu-claw, or canker-blight, eel-tooth, or goad. But let this not be a deterrent. The materials, latter and former, will be calculated to induce an impetus of knowledge flowing from your mouth—from the force of 'Beyond'."

Baus's eyes blazed with terror. "I know nothing of the 'Beyond'. This is an entirely infeasible curriculum!"

"Perhaps, but things will unfold as they will."

Valere called out for a clarification, "Why not clamp your own limbs and subject yourself to these rigours from 'Beyond'?"

The Wickles laughed. "That is an absurd notion. We are Wickles."

Baus was forced to accept the predicament. He bravely lowered his gaze upon the rotating device, to which he applied a more circumspect scrutiny. The drum was ponderously placed, easily twelve feet in diameter. The ladder and the holsters were fixed to the drum's inner wall which revolved around a certain central axis at a significant speed. The central core—a wooden platform—was packed with earth and root, appearing stationary, but apparently extended to within a foot of the drum's outer edge for purposes not immediately apparent.

Baus invested himself with a bleak hope. *Perhaps* . . . he mused with morose conviction: obviously, a crude and cumbersome device of torture—nothing less, a project spanning several years' work . . . There must be a weak link . . .

In an attempt to appear knowledgeable, he uttered an erudite cry: "The invention and its signature are admirable, Graeitch, but exhibit a risible rudimentary foundation. For one, these speeds, make no sense at all—why not manually spin the incumbent with enough force to induce vertigo, *before* administering feathers and polyp at requisite frequencies?"

Loeitch and Paiesmy both glanced uneasily at Graeitch. "The groom has a point."

"Silence!" Graeitch hissed.

Paiesmy teetered precariously at the hub's edge with peevish annoyance. "The groom's remarks are relevant!"

"Not at all! Nuncupative transmission of knowledge is next to useless until scribed on paper and attempted in a full capacity of formal trials. For the sake of fairness, the groom's idea might contribute to a minor modification of the system. Particularly, if promise is demonstrated, I will allow for a small adjustment to the prospective hub and the stag rotor."

Loeitch nodded her approval.

Graeitch above the hub, acted as 'supervisor'. Paiesmy and Loeitch were 'assistants'. They herded Baus down the ladder and into the requisite cylinder. They hustled the captive with graceless hops to reach the inner periphery where they strapped him in the drum with eyes facing centre and limbs hooked into braces. Baus was thrust and jerked this way and that and could not help but notice the pelt of duck down glistening on the back of Paiesmy's hands.

Shivering, the outlaw thought again of Woisper and his infamous spells which the neomancer Ulisa had alluded to. Paiesmy could in fact, be a composite grebe, a result of the wizard's machinations.

From a cache below, the Wickles stooped to gather a series of instruments. Paiesmy turned to face the outlaw, now pale with glowering wrath. The creature planted herself on a non-moving section of the platform's centre and gripping all manner of materials—goads, crystals, feathers, fossilized teeth, polyps.

The redoubtable Loeitch yanked the crank. The rotor started—a horrid whirring which clutched the air—the hub began a brief, slow circle. Baus gritted his teeth, steeled himself for the rigour to come.

Loeitch twisted the crank faster. The cylinder revolved in speeds proportional to the thrusting. Baus swung round—each time, Paiesmy jabbed a wad of some despicable thing at him from a rod, to which he felt utterly vulnerable: first feathers, then ux-claw, then raven-beak. Paiesmy called him by a name he did not understand, summoning the forces of 'Beyond'.

Graeitch stood above like an enigmatic ghoul, exhorting the outlaw to utter truths from the 'Beyond'. The Wickle made further demands—that all Baus's phrases be voiced in language indicative of the survival and existence of the Wickle race.

Baus put on a defiant stance. Diverse objects pummelled sensitive members of his anatomy. He attempted to thwart Graeitch's obnoxious whims but he revolved a dozen times more with Paiesmy alternatively prodding heart, throat, navel, brow, loins and through his plexuses, he felt an unwholesome electrical charge pricking at him and a sudden urge to utter some inanity, nothing more.

The exercise proceeded for several minutes. Essentially the spell did not precipitate any momentous effect and the Wickles seemed irked. Cranking the lever faster, Loeitch slapped her thigh, whooping in delight like a bronco-rider.

Graeitch gave a final, dismissive grunt. She ordered Baus unstrapped from the harness and Poli was dragged down next.

Being returned to his post, Baus saw Poli whirled about at ever faster paces. The bully disgorged his breakfast of nuts, whortle-berries and cack-mushroom—a sudden flying eruption, at which Graeitch became excited and ordered Esling to scoop up the effluvia on a plate for analysis. Graeitch admitted proudly: "The ejection marks a singular breakthrough, supporting the fact that the apparatus is functioning properly!"

Loeitch surveyed the mash sceptically. "Evidence, Graeitch?—or simple vomit?"

Graeitch responded in a feverish voice, "Silence! Vertigo was our first priority! Now, an unquestionable symptom of emotive force arises. The immediate conclusion—as primitive and repugnant as it seems, the effluvia harbours simple proof that words, messages, and even 'spirit signals', are embedded within the exudations."

Loeitch listened with a reserved frown.

Baus blinked back his disbelief. Obviously the Wickles were unhinged and on the verge of losing all grip on reality.

Poli was enforced another rigour, while he was constantly pricked with elk tooth and boar hoof, next tickled with bat hair and bear droppings, also bandoo wings. His knees began to jerk, his lips convulsed. He seemed a straw man pulled from all directions. His eyes flung open in wide terror, then some dry rapture, a darting tongue lolled and flashed in and out of his maw like a snake. He muttered, moaned, sent forth a strange glottal sound like groans from an unknown force.

Graeitch, less excited than before, gave a grimace. She scratched at her hoof in vexation. "Not exactly profound, Loeitch, but certainly steps guided in the right direction." She turned a didactic glare upon Paiesmy. "Now, see to it that this groom is kept in the drum for two more hours until regular symptoms can be observed. You may decrease the revolutions after every second stage. Alter the frequencies and valences as you like to what the subject can manage. Thus will promote the 'spirit-listening'."

Paiesmy acknowledged the demand with obedience.

"And Loeitch, you lazy cowbird! Get your hide in order. Whirl the drum at a faster speed! The task is singularly unique in its urgency. The rate must not fall below sixty rotors per minute. And—if we require more servo-gears, get that minx Finxsta to install the new machinery!"

"As you wish, sister," grumbled Loeitch half-heartedly.

Baus regarded the Wickles with revulsion. He wondered what esoteric torments lay in wait for him next.

The anagogic experiments continued . . .

* * *

The time was early evening. The bees had quieted down in the midst of their upper precincts and the Wickles had exhausted their repertoire of tricks; so, a break was called and it was time to warm up some dinner. About seven, the Wickles hunched over their hot bowls of spider soup and chattered around the cluttered table, slurping here, slurping there, smacking at their meals, which came as loud swillings to the grooms' ears. Everyone except Esling, who sat quietly on her cot, immersed in cogitation. The grooms had been returned to their posts and Loeitch shook a long, tube-lantern to life. The glowmoths, entombed within, fluttered chalky wings to animation, emitting all colours of the rainbow. The muted afterglow revealed familiar shapes in the Honey Home—ghostly reminisces, unsettling shapes.

The companions sagged in apathetic defeat on their posts. Their backs were bowed. They slumped back in lethargic heaps. Each was the worst for wear after receiving his turn in the 'hub'.

Baus pressed Poli for details, but now the bully merely shook his head at the mention of any alleged 'trance'. His features showed utter blankness. The pirate seemed listless and zombie-like. He guarded no memory of the experience at all.

The response struck Baus with a chord of desperation. He sank back into gloom. What to do? The Wickles were conceited despots. They were demented monomaniacs. Abusive slobs too. He had just recently learned that they never washed their hands before a meal, or, after ministering to a bodily discharge. 'Twas something of acute concern considering his own feeding, which had thus far, been substandard. If the revolting spider soup they were fed with gasps and grimaces was a promise of what was to come, then they were doomed.

Worming fingers about the post, Baus discovered a small protuberance behind his back ringed with an edge. He gave a grunt of hope. Awkward fumbling revealed a more substantial knot which led to an attempt to saw through his constraining cords.

The essay was unavailing. Loeitch cognized the motion and leaped forward like a ghoul, projecting an outcry.

Baus put on an innocent face. "What is it now, miss goody two shoes? Must I huddle here in the dark like some possum, while bearing witness to your disgusting eating habits, hunching in filth and suffering abominable itches?"

"Silence your tongue!" Paiesmy thundered. "I will not listen to your hypochondria over dinner!" Gulping down the last of her soup, she galloped over to frisk Baus and uncover his shenanigans, quite possibly a misdemeanour worthy of punishment. She rifled about his bruised shoulder and discovered a sharp knot in the post underneath and several blatant abrasions to his wrist cords. "Ha! What's this? An attempt at escape?"

"An old, possibly frayed piece of hemp."

"A cunning scheme!" retorted Paiesmy. "You would loosen your bonds and on quiet feet murder us in the night! Loeitch, procure the file! Grab the scratch-paper . . ."

Loeitch complied. Paiesmy took the file and began to smooth down the post to near baldness. "No protuberance, no knot." The Wickle applied a final polishing with the scratch-paper and left Baus seething with dismay.

The companions, later, set to a nervous whispering, involving a plotting of an escape, but the undertones were heard by Graeitch and she quelled them to silence.

That same evening, a pair of luminous eyes peered forth from the rim outside the window. Amidst humming and growling could be heard certain inquisitive mewlings—barks, whimpers, groans, retorts, gurgles and lewd sniggers.

Baus cringed. Fatuous Wickles! he thought with disgust.

An hour passed and amidst the tumult of Graeitch's hog-loud snores, Valere attempted a similar scheme to Baus's sawing, though the seaman extended more care in the chaffing of his bonds.

Baus grinned in delight. Valere had managed to lift himself to standing position, even with back astride the post. Flipping his corded wrists back over his head, he lowered his knees and managed to discover a protuberance on the post where an abrasion might be attempted.

Sorrowful luck! . . . An untimely slip of ankle and Loeitch came bounding awake, blinking with wrathful suspicion. She leaped over and shook the glowmoth lantern alive. The insects fluttered to life.

The wash of ghost light roused Graeitch. The hag, peering virulently in the grooms' direction, identified the guilty culprit and ordered Valere strapped to a chair with his back bound to the post. There would be no escape this time—'sleepwalking' or 'exercising', were excuses that met with short shrift.

"A goad for your trouble!" Graeitch barked and she slashed out at the seaman. The punitive strike had Valere moaning; she retired to her bed. A dark cotton rag was thrust over the moth lantern.

The interior of the Honey Home was plunged once again into darkness.

IX

Baus breathed the haggard gasps of a man stressed. He jerked himself awake. A blinding yellow sunshine warmed his cheek. Exhaustion was his world. Piquant smells wafted from the kitchen and a babel of Wickle chatter came drifting to his ears. The outlaw discerned the chopping and mashing of various foods. The raw bruises of abuse on wrists, chest and ankles offered proof that the nightmare was not just some hazy fabrication of imagination.

He stared woodenly at Valere who sagged off his post. The outlaw found him in worse condition than yesterday. Poli was in no better state. He slumped on the floor, muttering curses to himself.

The Wickles hovered and moved about with industry. They seemed engrossed in their cooking, their ladling and tasting. The shadow of Paiesmy's bird-like figure hung heavily in the dim light, a shape of epicene fright.

The Wickle's syrupy voice whined: "Our supply of goat-bread is diminishing, Graeitch. You know how invaluable the loaves are when we cook for our grooms!"

Graeitch shot her sister an indignant look. "Then procure the requisite ingredients! Must I do everything? Bones and meal! That is what we grind to make our johnnycakes!"

Paiesmy frowned and cast a dubious frown at Baus. Marring his normal blithe disposition was a dark despair. He peered past Graeitch, focussed on a patch of the sloping honey-coloured wall behind.

His eyes betrayed surprise. The ganglestick was gone! He had seen it yesterday. 'Twas dangling on high, a tempting target. Lolispar was still hooked, along with Valere's sword and Poli's dented halberd. Both gleamed ever so dimly on the wall in the clear morning light. Where had the ganglestick gone?

A canny glancing about proved that Esling had managed to purloin Baus's wand, sneaking into the kitchen and by some means of trickery reviving its potency. In a shadowy corner she waited a long time until all the cooking was done. She sprang to action from behind a bed, extending the ganglestick in a loop upon Paiesmy.

Loeitch fell to her high jinks next. The two stood like absurd statues out of a midnight hallucination.

Esling giggled and circled about the two like a rakish fawn, crooning in a waggish voice:

"Boo-hoo and tiddle dee,
How does it feel to be?
Frozen and woven,
In a spell so potent!
With a twinkle and a brew,
I'll sit you in my morning stew,
Where you'll not be able to spy,
My magic stick or I!"

"Quiet, little chit!" Graeitch cried, stamping her hoof from somewhere in the kitchen. Her eyes remained glued on her recipe book, which involved a certain sinister means for creating a procreative stimulant for the grooms.

Cognizing no movement from her sisters, she became suspicious and bawled out in a booming voice: "What are you up to, you little brat? More mischief? Well, I'll tan your hide. Dispense with your impishness! Ah, my wand! Where is it?" Before the hulking creature could blunder to snatch it, Esling had scampered off behind her cot.

Graeitch was beside herself. She leaped from her cooking station and moved side to side to corner the miscreant. But the grey pig-Wickle could only trap her between Baus's post and the wall. She was wise to Esling's tricks and would brook no foolishness.

She snatched at the adjunct and cached it deep in her hunter's jacket. "Well, that'll teach you to play jiggery-pokery with me. These are items that don't belong to you!"

Esling pouted. "The wand is mine, Graeitch. You know it! I discovered it long ago on Baus when we first lay hold of him."

Graeitch's meaty shadow loomed ever monstrously over the little Wickle. A self-absorbed sneer stuck from her fat face. "While that may be true, I alone, as eldest, harbour the sagest wisdom—so only I can foster its utility!"

"A fib, no more!"

"Silence!" stormed the hag. "I'll have no more of your backtalk." She stamped her hoof with a vengeance. "One more outburst and it's the back shed for you. The stick is mine—an item of potency." She swung her hefty torso around and whirled the ganglestick with an imperial motion. "Such technique is what I use to wield the magic—not in a manner of frivolous little loops like your child-like ways!"

Esling slunk to a corner. She was cowed, but she huddled behind her strawberry-coloured cot with a thoughtful appraisal. After several jarring shoves, Graeitch revived her two sisters. Each snorted bewilderment and struggled to attention, with neither the wiser of their immobilization.

Baus shook his head with disgust. A scenario of woe clouded his world. Esling, the creature of guile and whimsy, had a curious breed of sprite and wilful energy in her, which could just possibly help them in the future.

The afternoon waned. It was a time of trials as Poli was the next pilot in the 'drum'. Baus gave himself to poignant reflection.

The experience was unsatisfactory. The Wickles would not abate in their experiments—until success was breached. One of the feverish beasts must achieve success in the emprise, or decide that it was time to enforce an odious union with the men.

Baus gave a miserable shudder. Coupling with any of these grotesque figures was a heinous prospect. A further frantic urgency overcame Baus as he strove to refine his agenda along lines of an escape.

He felt beads of perspiration coursing down his cheek. A cunning scheme was in order, but it was yet to come to fruition in his brain.

Baus closed his ears. For he could not stand Poli's miserable howls.

Judging from the magnitude of the clamour, Poli's trial had yielded results little better than yesterday. Not without unpleasant authority did Graeitch and Paiesmy goad Baus down into the hub.

They braced him into a zinc holster and Paiesmy paced about with sneering contempt. She ordered the outlaw to arrest his foul squirming and his sharp imprecations. From the centre of the wheel Graeitch stood ghoulishly squared, a force of unbounded malice with a dour grin carved upon her porcine jowl. Loeitch skipped forward, with a polite offering of her services while Paiesmy gimped about, haunting the drum's epicentre like a tall, egg-headed owl.

The device began to whirl. Baus felt a familiar experience of vertigo.

Graeitch and Paiesmy pointed objects at him, in sharper, ruder frequency. Paiesmy prodded areas of his anatomy at which he found great offence. The outlaw bridled at the pokes and prods. He almost vomited in the midst of objections and complaints, but the Wickles ignored him. He fought with a compulsion to lash out at them, but, prompted by an inner voice, he returned to a state of early cunning and let his eyes roll up and assumed an air of deadness. In a high-flung voice, he clucked out several brave words: "Wickles! Your enterprise is decisively depraved! The drum is sordid! From 'Beyond' I bid you to release these upstanding grooms and feed them only fried buckler and bread of the highest quality. This is my command! Send them on their way! They are innocent and virtuous. You have heard my counsel—now pay heed! This comes from 'Beyond'! Offer the grooms a dozen freshly-baked mallow-tarts or sweet, baked mushrooms if you like, but do not expect any forgiveness from them regarding your obscene deeds!"

Loeitch stood back in perspiring heatand placed a clammy palm to her cheek. Paiesmy, likewise, tugged the hook of her nose with critical doubt. Graeitch remained subdued, abstracted in her own breed of cynicism. Baus's zombie-like act had presented more lamb-like jabber than anything and the pig-Wickle became suspicious. She wielded her goad and blasted Baus a horrid jolt on the navel. The hagwipple tip caused Baus a convulsion and he keeled over, snorting out a moan of anguish.

"So!" Graeitch shrilled. "You would deliver us a cheap jest!"

Loeitch put a hand to her mouth. "Blasphemy! How did you know it, Graeitch? The pilgrim was in the throes of ecstasy, I think!"

Graeitch ground her teeth with annoyance. "Shut your gobs." She displayed Loeitch a vitriolic smile. "A true medium under the trance of 'Beyond' would never suffer from such a trifling paroxysm. The fit was induced by guile, nothing more—a stimulo-reflex."

"So ho!" Loeitch gave several decisive nods and Graeitch ordered the outlaw dragged back to his post, where he was tendered a half dozen goads for his duplicity.

Valere, who sat back watching the chicanery, was next conveyed below with jerks and shoves. He attempted a variation of Baus's scheme, but it too was met with harsh measures and resulted in his rotating at higher speed with pitch-gong thrust at his groin. "Speak, groom, speak! The 'Beyond' calls! We must learn what the 'Beyond' has to tell us!"

Next a monster—ant thorax was aimed at his solar plexus.

Valere struggled, wheezing with rigour. No great profit was to be made. He clamped his tongue in teeth and grimaced with most horrible anguish while his face remained rictus-stricken.

The Wickles returned the seaman to his post where he was made prey to goads. "Now learn our discomfit—you perfidious mountebank. Never hoodwink a Wickle!"

Graeitch's displeasure seeped into the pores of the Honey Home. "I cordially despise buffoonery and deceit of all kinds! Now—let us move on. Should pranks persist, they will give rise to only more severe punishments!"

Poli was pitched in the hub. The cycle continued . . .

Graeitch subjected the recipients with shots of waizelwilk to reduce risk of lampoon—a worm juice afflicted intravenously by penetrative jabs of goad prior to whirl, likely a mild derivative of what had been injected into Sansix. Thereafter, Baus displayed a heightened cordiality in accord with the Wickles' wishes—as did Valere. In situ the rebels demonstrated little results, but with greater obeisance.

* * *

Now it was late in the afternoon and the Honey Home was bathed in a soft plum-coloured glow. Sounds of the forest were pitched in muted whispers. A sudden rain injected the air with dankness which the wind pushed gently through the casement. The bees buzzed in agitation. The lack of sunlight had the insects spooked. The small smokestack the Wickles had constructed offered no solace, either in exit or entry, whenever rain or wind hindered them.

Baus was plopped on the Honey Home's earthen floor and fidgeted. A dry nausea coursed through his body like poison. He assessed his companions with a helpless grimace. Their contusions and abrasions were insufferable. He reckoned his wounds were as rudely placed as Poli's when he was worked over by Zoren's pirate cabal so many months ago; however, his mood had lost none of its teeth-gritting vengefulness. His wrist bonds itched. Not possibly could he raise himself high enough to standing position without alerting the monitors—Paiesmy and the execrable Loeitch. Several schemes coursed through his mind. Not the least of which included the Auk king and how its power could wreak havoc on these grotesques! But how could the ghoul's power be harnessed in some perverse manner to throw bedlam upon the fiends?

Improbable, if not impossible.

Baus pinched his eyes with frustration. Brainstorming a stratagem seemed hopeless, yet if he wanted to escape, he must persevere! The presence of failure and triumph existed in the same breath, with results equally as unpredictable.

His eyes strayed to the swords and weapons hanging above the sink. What if they could be used as instruments of coercion? But they were far out of reach; no less the ganglestick which seemed placed on a higher peg to thwart Esling's mischievousness. Even if one of them could snatch the wand and arouse it into working order, how long would it last before Graeitch the wretch noticed and tormented them with goads?

Upon the worktable dwelled a projectorate of brown fluid. Baus gave an involuntary shudder . . . 'twas the one Paiesmy often used to launch at certain offensive bat dryads that were wont to creep about at night in the Wickles' garden. If he could impose the projectorate on the bees above, perhaps impel the insects to—?

Baus shook his head in wry futility.

His only hope lay with the rebel, Esling. There were certain agreeable aspects to her character, also a general artlessness which was certainly pliable. He was struck with her naivety. An intuitive conviction arose that the creature could possibly aid them . . .

Baus peered at her with reflection; the Wickle was crouching down over the lip of the hub, watching Poli whirling and listening to his moaning with a kind of distracted fascination. The experiment involved balroon-hoof and nimbu-claw this time. Yes, the Wickle was an odd duck, but what of it?— transfixed by the curious sounds and the sinister movements, not to mention wholly perplexed by the day-to-day horrors, she seemed given to entertaining an air of pathos.

Baus ruminated. What if the Wickle were further compelled to rebel against her masters? Many times he had heard Paiesmy and Loeitch crooning to Esling softly in the evening hours: "Esling dear! Bring us our wash brush", or "Esling, scratch our backs" or "Esling, be a good little Wickle and fetch us our night slippers!"

Ordered about and goaded like an unwanted pet, the poor Wickle was not like her housemates—she was neither mean-spirited nor crabby, like the wart hogs in heat—and hereupon, Baus bit his lip in surmise. How to entice the Wickle onto his side? A tender word? A sound word of sympathy? A warm shoulder to cry on?

The Wickle, so maltreated, might tender favour to them.

Redeemer

Baus's grin cut into his reverie. She was not that ingenuous, yet, she appeared to fancy his presence and often he had seen her flashing him sidelong looks whenever she thought his head turned or he was sleeping. Looks of sly quality, appraisal, even affection . . .

Baus set himself to a crafty plan . . .

* * *

As darkness crept over the Branx, the Honey Home began to slip into an eerie, nocturnal somnolence. The bees had returned in force, buzzing busily about their hives. The glowmoth lanterns had been shaken, causing a slinking light to spread over the cluttered spaces of the Wickles' abode. The Wickles' failure to retrieve the secret information they coveted had pitched them into a sour mood. Their usual banter was filled with a heated bickering, overtones of obnoxious punitive slaps and kicks. Scratching and hissing, they spat insults at each other . . . watching with interest, Baus hoped to gain an advantage over their visible acrimony.

* * *

All was now quiet in the Honey Home and the companions were herded back to their posts. The Wickles were ready to retire to their cots and Baus surveyed them with wry dispassion. Rude, loathsome beasts, they were. Each eyed him with distrust and took their turns in the rude bathtub. The sisters sloshed about, like vain, ungainly pubescents of the most vile kind. Unconscious of their offensive nudity, the two were only more smuttily rendered in the soft chestnut light. Graeitch's obscene, lubberly form was directly propped in front of Baus's line of sight, a view which became ever more heavily repugnant to his eyes. He was forced to turn his head away— moreover, on a stressful angle. Esling was last to bathe, being somewhat demure in her habits and thankfully of comelier condition. She ordered the grooms' heads turned before she would even doff her jumpsuit.

Nightgowns were donned and the Wickles slept.

* * *

During the wee hours, Baus awoke to the sounds of scratching at the door. Amidst a buzzing and humming could be heard a sinister clicking of paws from the outside. The rustling grew in potency—'twas an insistent clawing heralding forces at work. Familiar luminous scarlet eyes stared in from the window and hereupon, Baus's upper lip twitched. The weirdness had caused him several missed heartbeats. Two sly forms managed to jimmy the door. They stole silently in, past the burlap sacks and into the Honey Home's interior. The portal was shut and the two silhouettes eased themselves in, pausing in reflection. They swayed gently in the pale moonlight like two unnameable wraiths.

The door was relocked—only a barely perceptible click was heard in the gloom. The first figure was a fox-eared silhouette, set against the lightness of the window pane. The other crouched at the door, bobbing, a bulky and amphibian form, reminiscent of a calculating blob. Lewd, gleaming eyes peered forth, blazing like some weird abomination of nature. Both creatures seemed to search for signs of human vulnerability and the presence of traps or deadfalls.

Graeitch and her sisters remained undisturbed in their slumber. The rhythmic sounds of their breathing rose and fell with loud wind fall.

The intruders relaxed, sidling in with a confident stealth. A curious fascination came over Baus. He remained fixed, frozen to immobility; his tongue cleaved to the top of his mouth.

The stealth of the first figure was so practiced that it managed to inch within grasping distance of him before he knew what was happening.

A damp paw clamped over his mouth. Before he could squawk out an adjuration, his trousers were quickly peeled down. A furry abdomen negotiated itself onto his lap and began a halting industry—habile ministry pitched in the pretence of arousal.

Baus careened back against his post with an emotion hardly recognizable. He grunted out a thick disgustful wail.

An alarm trilled suddenly. The end of an imminent coupling with an elderbeast! Graeitch came leaping forth from her cot in heroic anger. Her sisters were on her heels. Esling gaped, running this way and that. Loeitch ignited the lantern. Paiesmy was hard upon the heels of the intruders. They huddled, quivering, scratching at their flanks. One hissed an admonitory croak and crouched in the shadows, looked like a ghastly ghoul.

The lights came flaring on. 'Twas plain that the culprits were none other than Banaga and Gladdus.

The purplish-black froglike form was Banaga who squatted on all fours, with a back bowed and a half amphibian, human face. Gladdus smirked with insufferable cunning, a slinky half-woman, half-fox with body red-furred all over that sidled back and forth like a trapped animal.

Graeitch demanded an instant explanation.

The intruders muttered glib words, pretending that they had perceived soft, melancholy hoots around the Honey Home. Being worried about the grooms, they were prompted to check on their safety with an altruism to boot.

Graeitch sneered. "A brazen lie!" In unison, she and her two ugly sisters beat the interlopers within an inch of their lives with goads. Out into the night they shooed the opportunists with heavy brooms and kicks. In the midst of the screeching and caterwauling, the perpetrators attempted retaliatory blows.

To no avail. They were chased away. The three Wickles returned triumphant. Graeitch ordered Loeitch to fashion lassos as anti-intruder mechanisms which they quickly assembled near the front door.

Hand to mouth in cogitation, Graeitch began a planning of an effective deadfall for subsequent invasions. Fuming, she chastised Loeitch for being remiss in not installing one earlier and alerting her in time.

Loeitch framed a haughty objection but couldn't help but be doubly annoyed by the criminal intrusion. Peeved at being ignored for the ignominy, Baus called out in a brassy tone: "The security of this domicile is abysmal, Graeitch! I find these cloak-and-dagger assaults on my person disgusting and immoral! Please remedy them at once!"

"Silence! How dare you speak to me in that tone of voice?"

Esling sprang to Baus's defence, hoisting his pants back up to his waist.

Graeitch smoothed out her polka dot nightgown and pursed her lips in amusement. "And yet, the situation is more serious than I cognized. As you witness, dire measures are being taken to prevent future assaults."

"These admissions are unsatisfactory!" thundered Baus. He was glad of having his pants on again. "In point of fact, your peers have overslept, and have failed to thwart an outrageous act. Furthermore, others in the village are obviously incorrigible and culpable of unimaginable mischief. You cannot protect us from these clandestine infringements and I demand our instant on-the-spot release!"

Graeitch smiled with an offhand gesture. "Some of your complaints are merited, true. We Wickles are merely in oestrus and our female receptivity cannot help but be aroused, so you must bear with our impulsive behaviour and move on."

Baus puffed out his cheeks in fury. "This is an unacceptable conciliation! I quiver at the concept. We cannot be mauled like chipmunks in the dark."

"Baus has hit hard to the mark!" croaked Valere in piqued fury. "I for one am only glad you were its recipient, not me." Poli was quick to agree.

Baus took no comfort in the remark. Graeitch let her eyes rove about, glittering upon Valere's physique. "My thinking is along similar lines, Captain, and my convictions have been wisely confirmed."

"What do you mean by that?" the seaman bawled. "Release us, you vile pig. If you are so prodigal with your promises, let us have no more of these rough-and-tumble surprises!"

Graeitch ignored the demand. She turned deaf ears to the outlaws' protestations and insults. She assisted Loeitch in fashioning a sturdy lasso to ensnare emboldened interlopers. "As I hinted," she added grandiloquently, "we Wickles are broaching singular periods in our cycle. Loeitch hankers for a robust groom—Valere would not be a bad match here—Paiesmy lusts for Poli and his vigour. I, on the other hand, am biased to no one in particular and so shall indulge in the passion of whomever I choose at the appropriate time. My belly shall conceive hardy imps."

Baus recoiled at the thought.

Paiesmy gave a blushing cry, "Graeitch! You speak in indelicate terms of our Wickle-ness!"

"Silence, owl! Though your thoughts are immature, I come to tolerate them. Nay, the facts have been exposed, Paiesmy. I insist on a mutual co-existence in this domicile and harmonious rapport!"

Loeitch and Paiesmy shifted back to their labours, frowning at Graeitch's imperiousness. They were clearly resentful of the work put out for them and not for Graeitch, and they plotted dark retribution.

Graeitch, missing the nuance, nodded with approval. Each of her sisters toiled with care to complete her portion of the snares—including rock-rig, mop-bucket and tripwire.

X

The following morning, Graeitch was out for her morning stroll. Aurimag's golem swept swiftly on bare feet through the forest. A thing of wraithlike terror, it seemed hardly a discrete entity of its own in its guise of earth, mud and slime.

The pulsing node embedded in its right shoulder gave the creature a clear path—'twas like an antenna which drew it toward a beacon, pulled mightily to the psycho-magno exudations of Baus's ganglestick.

The golem won past the fastness of Desenion and encountered a fearsome obstacle in its mission—a massive wall, towering fifty feet high, which loomed ever imperiously over thorn and thicket. To its newly-developed brain, the barrier was of daunting significance. Hours before, the overgrown ruin of Desenion had become a formidable obstruction, an enigma for it to ponder in the dripping stillness. Desenion's dark, jutting halls and shadowy courts and crumbling parapets had lurked ominously in the mist. The creature had run parallel to the castle a mile south then plunged deep in the forest. It had discovered a breach in the mammoth wall, known only to a few denizens, then it proceeded beyond the compromised obstruction into a territory most remarkable.

The golem leaped and bounded—over waist-high pumpkin mushrooms, championing mossy logs and sprawling roots, fording fantastic brooks and fungi-haunted forest and tortured stumps. Its legs, singularly bog-water fed, knew no fatigue. Through copses of grey ghost oak, it skirted hidden glades of the Branx, enchanted pools and meres of the fairest blue, twitchgrass, haunt-flower, careening past ruins of ancient stone, fanes and crumbling old villages choked with weed and creepers and phantom elm, as if from a forgotten time. Off through the silent ruins it passed. . . broaching tracts that had never been disturbed in a hundred years . . .

The enchanted moolstone's pulsing came at last to a grinding halt. The golem ducked low under a lichened bough, peering this way and that. Festoons of creeper framed its brow. It paused at the edge of some secluded glade and for the first time in its thraldom, appeared unstressed by the moolstone's pulsation.

The golem looked around with wry impartiality. At the edge of a small bubbling pool perched its quarry. Buttocks raised high in the air, the figure slurped leisurely at waters a hundred shades of green, surrounded by dour mukklewoods and mukkleshrub. The figure was obese and lumpish, and yet it did not jog the golem's brain that this was not its charge after all. Training googly eyes in the after-dawn, it found the pool fed by a rich waterfall and the burbling rills which ran softly over mossy boulders and roots.

Graeitch continued to drink. She sensed a presence hovering nearby; immediately a faint dismay crossed her mind. The golem meanwhile fought its impulse to leap out and seize her.

The twinge was fleeting.

Having the element of surprise, the golem rushed out with stealthy strides; it pushed through the fronds with purpose, and without complex plans or intents, extended its crooked arms and twiglike fingers in a zombie-like grasp.

Graeitch pulled her snout fast out of the water.

The action was dilatory . . .

In a second, the golem had ape-like arms clasped around her hulking frame. It had no trouble lifting her impressive weigh, so strong it was. Snorting and cursing, the Wickle dangled helplessly above the ground, kicking and bucking, but to no avail. Not a league from the Honey Home, Graeitch was trapped like a fish in a net.

North through the sticky dampness the golem bounded with the Wickle in its grip. Graeitch was unable to tear herself free or reach the ganglestick that she had so jealously guarded—'twas pinned tightly to her bosom, crushed hard against the golem's bare breast.

She could only wonder as to the creature's intentions as she bobbed up and down with the golem's rhythm. The golem fled indefatigably through the fens and forests, toward the outer regions of Farling's Wall, back to Aurimag's lair.

XI

Loeitch and Paiesmy were in a funk. Since Graeitch had gone missing, they had become fidgety and fretful. Yet their eldest sister was wont to engage in long morning walks and search out the best insects and vermin for her infamous stews.

Noon had arrived and Loeitch still exhibited signs of distress. "Most odd!" she cried in a complaining tone. "Even our impertinent sibling is never this occupied or impolite! She tends the grooms and feeds them their broths and monitors their experiment schedule. Where has the she-pork gotten herself to?"

Paiesmy let out a staccato chortle. "Graeitch's always been a laggard, Loeitch. Hardly like her to be tardy for noonday repast though, or even away from the Honey Home for so long." She let out a belch and flung out a haft of eel-fish. "Likely she's playing us for a scare—or a jest. We shall see!"

Loeitch dipped her daikon into the afternoon stew. Stirring the cauldron with a looping spoon, she shook her head with glumness. "Perhaps the Auk's nabbed her. Graeitch has always been a sort to take some awful risks on her sojourns."

"By no means!" Paiesmy cried. "Graeitch has always been an impulsive harridan, but never naïve."

Loeitch twitched with unease. "That's just what old Dorty said—before she was taken off by the Raksoi. Where is the justice in that? Plucked away to some foul eyrie! Ack! Ground down to jelly in the belly of a little auk or worm!"

Paiesmy gave a snide chuckle. "Your imagination runs wild with you, Loeitch. Though, I must beg to disagree. Dorty has always been a gosling too full of her own britches. She got her just desserts. Imagine! Thinking herself a rival to us, thrusting her lewd fanny into our jurisdiction and laughing it up at us. Good riddance! The years we put up with her snivelling audacity. What has her petty prattle done for her?—Nothing!" Paiesmy waved a truculent palm.

Loeitch nursed a dark scowl. "Well, it's a niggling mystery, Paiesmy." Sniffing, she scratched her behind. "Would you please pass me my cagilgrass? I wish to finish this stew early, thus to christen it as good luck for our grooms . . . ah, to incite the raw passion of our charges for the union which will be soon coming!"

Paiesmy's words were a pedagogic drone. "Don't get ahead of yourself, you warthog!" She dunked index finger and thumb into Loeitch's stew and winced. "The preparation lacks sublimity, Loeitch—prickle prills and milkseed pods, I think—pooh! I shall compel Esling to fetch the requisite ingredients. Esling! Esling! Where are you? Oh, where is that miserable runt? Too often I need her and she's not around." Paiesmy surged about, snuffling and swabbling. "Ah, there you are, you fur-tailed wight! Run and fetch us some prill and pod. We desire our grooms fat and sated before their next performance."

"Aye, Paiesmy." Esling curtsied without any noticeable sense of sincerity. The fawn-girl bustled off and Baus, sitting trussed like a rabbit, struck up some polite conversation with the Wickles. "If you add a bit of rice wipple and some vinegar to your stew for just five minutes, you'll have yourself a combination of excellence!"

The Wickles swung about in full circle. Baus reassured them that his intentions were only pure. "Try my recipe," he urged. He shook the black hair out of his eyes. "You've nothing to lose—you harbour only my fondest convictions."

Instantly suspicious, the Wickles narrowed eyes upon Baus, but complied out of curiosity.

They were pleasantly surprised with the results. Baus was allowed another recommendation which involved a smattering of hare's jowl and beetlewort—mash sprinkled with river-kelp flakes. It proffered the Wickles no lesser delight and Baus could not restrain a smile. The first step on a long series of winnings-over had begun . . .

* * *

Graeitch's absence persisted but the two sisters remained industrious. They swept floors, dusted the table, collected honey from the hives, boiled frogs, fried apples, sautéed astrids. Pickled gritchswill and hog's hoof, and other unearthly items were on the to-pick list while the duo remained modestly cheery in their attending of the grooms' feeding. Eel-stew, locust croquettes, spider-soup and mugwort pie were all delicacies that were presented. Hors d'oeuvres were served with precision and punctuality.

In the midst of these devoirs, many other residents of the Wickle community had come to call on the Honey Home—naturally to inquire of their progress. Paiesmy coldly brushed off such intrusions; yet reluctantly she acknowledged to two old Wickles that headway had been made in a marginal sense. She kicked herself for admitting the two crones into the Honey Home—'Eelrid' and 'Beargrie' they were, nosy and prickly old goats. Eelrid maintained a set of salamander eyes and a thin green tongue which Beargrie loved to see flicker. The bearish Beargrie harboured a woolly-toothed bear snout and a set of four crooked, waddling legs. Both were conveyed forth and offered nods of approval on seeing the grooms. Well past their child-bearing years, it seemed they were put up as clever spies to discover the state of the 'experiment ritual'.

"Where is Graeitch?" shrilled Eelrid in her banshee-like voice.

"She is off on a pressing errand," informed Loeitch coolly.

"Oh, is that so? Well—she owes me a house call!" snapped Eelrid. "I wish to confer with her on a matter of three electric eels which have mysteriously fouled my aquarium. I feel they have been exposed to too much blight!"

"A highly plausible theory," Paiesmy agreed. "And I shall be sure to pass on the message to Graeitch as soon as she returns."

"Bah! Be sure that you do, and do not mock me, Paiesmy! My pets are of high value!"

"I would not dare think otherwise," insisted Paiesmy.

With a darting of eyes, the eelish Eelrid slipped to the back of the dome where the fumes of the cauldron were thickest and offered an authoritative view of the Honey Home's interior. She glanced toward the grooms, eying each of the sullen-eyed captives with a barely-concealed insolence.

Beargrie was no exception. Both of the Wickles, though beyond child-bearing years, contrived a sophisticated artifice and lengthy pleasantries which, upon being exhausted, were abandoned in favour of a more extravagant ogling of the grooms. A salacious inspection followed, involving carnal darting of eyes and tongues, before the two went their way. Paiesmy and Loeitch were pleased at their departure and set about to bolting the door, and once again went on with their work.

No sooner had the door slid shut, when new knocks came at the door. Loeitch stomped over to repel the invaders, but Baus noticed two pairs of glittering eyes poised outside the window—two familiar sylph-like forms shifted ghostlike, as they glimpsed ripe grooms in the half gloom.

With sharp brevity, Loeitch posed an objection, "What is your business here, Mralti? We need no visitors."

"We have come to offer benefactions," responded the sylph in a dark murmur.

"What benefactions would these be?"

"Unicorn's tail and an elk horn."

"Very good." With oily interest, Loeitch opened the door and stuck out neck to snatch at the gifts. The two sylphs slipped briskly past. They glided in on barely visible feet, robes nearly touching the floor. Loeitch latched the door shut and came scurrying over to repudiate the presence of unwanted newcomers. Loeitch condescended that their robes were of purest white and gauzy chiffon-like quality, and that the gifts, while ornamental, seemed paltry in offering.

The maidens did not reply, only continued to shift about the home on invisible feet.

Without comment, Paiesmy inspected the horn and the tail and gave a disdainful sniff. She noted the former was half-petrified. "Hey!"

Not a moment had elapsed before another barrage of knocks came pounding at the door.

Paiesmy gave a frustrated snort. "The knocking persists without hope of surcease, Loeitch! Would you please answer the door?"

"Why don't you?" Loeitch bawled. She snatched herself to the portal, flinging down her marrowroot and slugs. Calling out a bluff challenge, she asserted a disincentive through the door crack—that the Wickles at the Honey Home would be taking no more visitors for the day.

The remark was ignored. New knocks arrived in numbers.

The sylphs' inspection of the Honey Home became indefensible and began to vex the grooms. The conversation had slipped into obloquy and now laconic half whispers had escalated to shrill taunts and Paiesmy and Loeitch were hard put to respond. The new arrivals afforded Baus and Valere additional queer and calculating looks. A shiver ran through Baus's spine, for he felt a fear for his innocence. The two sylphs swept by with an impetuousness that cast an unnerving disquiet over their beings. On superficial examination, the creatures seemed somewhat normal, but as each brushed by, Baus noticed fetlocks on the back of their heels and tiny protrusions jutting out from the small of Mreelta's back.

Horns? Carapaces? Baus was at a loss. The rest of Mralti's anatomy

610

showed through the near diaphanous robe and was not necessarily to his disrelish.

Mreelta began to brush hips against Valere, and Paiesmy seemed to lose all decorum. She bunted the intruders out of the house, squared herself with a kickboxer's stance. She breathed a sigh of disgust and locked the door. Flustered beyond measure, she and Loeitch ducked below to minister to Poli.

* * *

Graeitch did not return that day, or the next. The sisters began to worry. Each guessed that she had met up with some unfortunate doom. In truth they had been tendered unpopular favour amongst the clans—Wickles, due to certain 'advantages' intrinsic to their position, so it was not beyond doubt that Graeitch had been ambushed by the Wickles themselves.

Paiesmy and Loeitch shivered at the concept. The topic was a sensitive one and they bickered long about it. Who would be next to fall on the vigilantes' list? The only point they seemed to agree upon was that an arming of the deadfall was absolutely necessary.

So they did with grunts and snorts. During this time, Esling was free to roam the house, a victim no longer of the terrorizations of Graeitch. She became increasingly emboldened and was not frightened like the fluffy kitten of old. Paiesmy, being absorbed in her unguents and arguments and cooking, gave the little Wickle every opportunity to wander about, to speak frank words to Baus as he hunched dourly at his post. Esling professed in shy fashion that she admired Baus. He had a handsome frame and his hair was long. She intimated that his figure cut a respectful fancy to her eye. He agreed smilingly. He let the Wickle know that he was more genuinely concerned with the treatment conferred upon her by her sisters.

Esling let out a sigh and confided wistfully that her mother had been taken by a wandering tasm when she was only six—that her sisters had been snatched by rival Wickles and that Graeitch and the matrons had taken her as their ward, in return for a rendering of household services.

Baus nodded with understanding and addressed the Wickle in a sympathetic tone. "The circumstance is evident, Esling, though tragic, and effective action must be taken! To achieve any justice, you and I must work in tandem."

Influenced by Baus's words, Esling landed him a friendly kiss. Baus arched brows, thinking it a bold act. Esling, conscious of the threshold she had crossed, twisted away awkwardly. She let her pink, flushed face turn in a self-conscious way. "I have never kissed a groom before!" she giggled, placing palms to her cheeks in plush embarrassment.

"I too have never before kissed a Wickle," Baus confessed. With rueful gallantry, he fluttered his fingers, "though I am still slightly stunned by the frank advances of a Wickle I had thought so demure as to be chaste. I am wholeheartedly pleased that your feelings are out in the open."

Esling was taken back by the remark. Reviewing the experience, Baus thought the kiss not so terrible. Aside from harbouring a fragrance like an animal and the deer-like cock of head, the Wickle was actually quite a charming creature indeed. Her lips were sweet as milk, her eyes as wide and bright as a doe's.

Esling composed an admission of artless quality, "There are good Wickles and there are bad Wickles."

"And you must be a good Wickle, I presume?"

Esling blushed; she hooked hands to her jumpsuit. Somewhat awkwardly, she could not get herself to scamper away. "No, a bad Wickle, I daresay—at least this is what my sisters think of me."

"Shush—they are imbeciles."

A peevish voice rang from the kitchen: "Arrest your chatter, Esling! You know it is forbidden to prattle with the grooms. Your fatuous amusements with the man-groom and your flirting can only bring ill luck upon our ceremony! Now scoot! Scat!"

On nimble feet Esling skittered away, even as Paiesmy came beetling around the corner with a fresh eel-goad.

XII

In the dank obscurity of Aurimag's cave, two brass bugles blew. Three dismal discordances echoed in the hollow dimness.

Aurimag paused. He was annoyed to be distracted from his travails. The dissonance indicated a minor psychical flux; instantly he bounded from his workroom to the security of the Bronze Hall. He glared about. Behind limpid pools tooth-like stalagmites gleamed, growing up in clusters to dusky heights. The magician had already surmised that his elm-sprites would have committed several outrages upon intruders, so he was not about to leap in with sword in hand to hack and jab idly, yet he intoned a spray of fey words and was instantly aghast to see his warlock golem emerging from the darkness with purpose. The automaton staggered, dragging some pugilistic-looking figure behind him which seemed to gaze at him with a very heavy-lidded quality.

"What do we have here?" quipped Aurimag. "A boar-or a swine?" He strode over to tap the hulk on the head. "Obviously neither." The monstrosity had enthralled him enough to voice a theory, and the recently-arrived, pig-snouted figure had left him baffled. "What need for this prize?" He turned critical eyes upon the golem. "What have you to say for yourself, oaf? Where is my fisherman, you slime-eyed ghoul?"

The golem remained mute.

The captive screeched an outrage: "Ghoul? Fisherman? You jabber, little man. Instruct your minion to release me. I shall unleash a pestilence upon you!"

"Hold your tongue, witch!" ordered Aurimag. He turned a set of disapproving eyes upon the golem. "Is this is all you have procured?"

The creature nodded, slightly taken aback. The blinking of an eye reflected an intelligence under the blood lamps.

"Dolt! Diddle-tit!" Aurimag cried furiously. He slapped its crown. The force had it quivering and Aurimag jogged back with contempt. "What am I to do with you? . . . Ah, well, never mind. This is what I incur for contracting the help of a snivelling simpleton."

The golem stood impassively. It bore the abuse as one who is eventually out to get his revenge.

Graeitch addressed Aurimag with a brash vulgarity: "Pipe down, little man! I demand my liberty, and if not given, I will deal you a blight."

Aurimag glared at the Wickle with wonder. "Such a droll threat—I would guess you are something of a female, though this remains debatable."

The creature spoke with dignity: "I am Graeitch—senior Wickle and Herbalist of Farling's Wall. Who might you be?"

"I am Aurimag, Neomancer of the New Order, as can be seen by my badge." He montioned a bony finger to the seal of his demi-metrix medallion on his right breast. "You have entered my abode."

Graeitch hissed with venom. "I despise all neomancers—even the word *neomancer* sickens me."

"That is pleasant to know, but otherwise irrelevant. Your erudite opinion means nothing to me. Now, I exhort you to answer my questions, 'Graeitch', or whatever your name is. My new Order is an avant-garde mode of spiritual discipline—drawn from a superior mind—my own—I shall lead this sect to utter dominion! Antagonizing an overlord will neither help you nor extend sympathy on your most meagre lease of life!

Graeitch was unimpressed with the threat. She fixed the neomancer an appraising glare and grimaced evilly. "These boasts do not ruffle me."

"The world is changing, Graeitch," came Aurimag's dull voice. Clasping hands behind his back, he marched back and forth. "Certain 'old-world' savants have proven themselves inept, not to mention foolish. Not only in the eyes of the Arch-Neons but the Emmi-Lords themselves!"

Graeitch gave a shrill squeal: "What do I care for this? You cite petty concepts, but your witless minion has dragged me forth to this dank hall—for what purpose?"

"All will be explained—but first—" He snatched the ganglestick from Graeitch's fur-smelling person. "Ah, my talisman! So good to get it back. So, you would steal this property of mine and know of my fisherman then?"

Graeitch gave a short sniff. "I know not to whom you refer."

Aurimag turned Graeitch a chill grin. "Come now, hobgoblin! Do not be so coy. My golem is not as daft as he looks—though that is something for debate. I supplied him with the stuff of life—REOGENESIS—even impinged on his animo-cortex specific magics that might guide him to return me my fisherman—a tall, egocentric-looking villain—lank-haired, a swaggering bravo. These qualities are bared before you, hag—now where is he?"

Graeitch let out a rich snigger. "This comprises a unique stand-off between us. You have something which I want and I have something that you want. Who will win out?" Squirming sidewise, she cast Aurimag a rancorous look.

Aurimag bellowed, "If you know where my fisherman is, you will tell me, or suffer horrible vicissitude!"

"By no means! The groom is sequestered in my Honey Home, currently a guest of my 'sisters'."

"Bah! Sisters! Your quirky references mean nothing to me. Where is this 'Honey Home' of yours—and where are these sisters of yours?"

"They are hardy souls, though a trifle simple," Graietch confided. "My abode is three leagues west of Farfus—and your fisherman is friend of these siblings of mine. He fell prey to our ward trap, as was simply set. Artless buffoons!—felled by an innocent basket of bread and an urn of grapes! Can you imagine? Ah, how the grooms are foiled by carnal desires in the end! I shall twist and bake this bandy-legged frame of yours from ear to ear, I shall —"

"These maunderings are doubtless fascinating, Graeitch," Aurimag interrupted, raising his voice, "but I warn you—this fisherman is mine and will suffer penalties by my hand and none other. Those penalties will be in exact amplitude to my wrath!"

Graeitch gave a luxurious laugh. "And so? What about me? I paid for the wretch as an indenture owing me from a certain swindler, 'Sansix'."

"Another petty rogue of yours?"

"Worse. He is a swindler who fell into a similar trap of mine a day or two earlier and for hours on end, I played with him, enticing him to extract the *Secret of the Seven Convocations* . . . He did not! The varlet simply would neither speak nor yammer anything of import. Feathers, wire, flank, bone bristle, phlanx—we fired all at him. Not even the simplest plexical epiphany came forth. Now as for Baus—"

Aurimag listened with growing vexation, while Graeitch chattered on: "Baus's blond-haired crony, Poli, has shown promise though. Currently he was faring better from the ritual in terms of four test inputs clamped to his navel probed by nimbu-claw for illumination. At the second pass, my sisters put forth a rigour." Graeitch laughed. "It has proved most—interesting." The sound of her cachinnation echoed through the stony, dripping darkness like a fox's bark.

Aurimag curled his lips into a white-toothed grimace. "Is my fisherman to be mauled under the orders of these obscene 'rigours'?"

"Undoubtedly. The groom shall be treated no better than his compeers. In fact, worse. His failures in our dousing experiment have set us back many days. Being a man after all, he must be put to the test, and pay the very chaos of his existence for the fate of his birth and his impertinence upon all the Wickles. If death must be his reward, then so be it!" Graietch's cheeks puffed out with spite.

Aurimag's face struggled to control its anger. "If the fisherman is damaged in any way—" He lifted a provocative finger.

"If you think that my sisters are more lenient than I—you are mistaken."

Aurimag hopped from one foot to the other. He advanced menacingly toward the Wickle. "Perhaps, hag, you shall pay for the damages inflicted upon his person, when I find him."

"Away, crowbeard! Your feathers moult. If you value your prize so fervently, dispatch your golem—retrieve the lout, if you would!"

Aurimag chewed on his lip. There was a certain truth to the Wickle's insolence. He knew little of the Honey Home and its probable jinxes. The Wickle was of no use to him. Perhaps with an appropriate elixir, he might transmogrify the ropy flab and repulsive warts into something more agreeable—like some manner of appealing human to benefit his collection of night-time concubines.

Aurimag gave a ghastly shudder. An absurd idea! The mere mention of the repugnant creature's flesh against his would erase any quality of the illusion.

"The request is impossible," announced Aurimag priggishly. "I sense an overall inequity in the ontological fabric." He frowned on the lewd odours, doughy limbs, graceless hips and hog-snout of Graeitch's person. "Had it not been for your infernal meddling, I would now be foisting grievances upon Baus this instant—in form of a 'human-puppet' at a comic-ballet. Instead, I am bandying words with a miserable half mutant, for no useful purpose whatsoever."

The rejoinder brought a galled silence over Graeitch.

"You could have been a worthy item in my collection of nymphs—aye, a pleasing doll or some such ornament for moments of small pleasure." He shivered at the absurdity. "But I am left bereft, muttering, 'Ah Aurimag, such a quixotic dreamer you are!' Perform this last service for me—" he grinned, bowing "—step over to this singular pool."

The neomancer motioned to a gap twenty paces away past some stalagmites. It prompted Graeitch to pitch herself left and right in unease.

The Wickle perceived a sudden movement in the adjacent pool. A sizeable shape flashed in the area toward which Aurimag motioned. Beyond a row of voluted stalactites, leaden waters glinted in the gloom like a baleful fire-moth's light. The golem enforced a more rigorous restriction on her fleshy hide in response to the Wickle's retaliations.

Aurimag beckoned his golem forth; the creature transported Graeitch between a cage of stalagmites and boulders rounded with age. They passed over a small shelf, a ridged abutment, almost mirror smooth. The group struggled over to the edge of a pair of greenish pools. Up from the rightmost, wafted a sour stench of indescribable potency. It curled about the feet of the stalagmites with fog-like intensity.

With little cooperation, Graeitch shrank back, discerning in those tepid waters a rousing steam and many evil-smelling liquids. They included a composite of aliphatics, slime and unguents. Cursing hatefully, she gnashed and bucked.

"Come now, Graeitch!" crowed Aurimag jocularly. "Are you afraid? You of all creatures, should be accustomed to the stenches and rigours of a natatorium. Ah—you hesitate!" Aurimag made a small smile of mirth. "This mixture, a product of diophanine is . . . well, perhaps more than a nib of frog's egg, and mullock dung, and stag faeces. Nothing untoward! The melange is particularly critical for tenderizing. Before the distillation procedure and soaking of the subject, he/she is left rather white and doughy. A side effect, for which I apologize. This is explained by the diophanine which harbours an effect of shrinking the victim, and which in turn, acts as a painless reagent—at least in theory."

Graeitch struggled with all force; just as the magician raised a finger to speak again, she caught sight of a gummy, globular eye jerking itself up out of the nearest waters. She recoiled. The orb on the cork-like stalk quivered and revolved in a most peculiar way.

Aurimag flourished a hand with negligent regard. "Never fear, Wickle! Fang is actually more of a creature of curiosity than a fiend; in fact, she is quite peaceful, provided she is not provoked to excess." The magician made a slow show of stirring up the water in a spirit of 'show-and-tell'.

The snake or serpent started to bob and twist.

Graeitch gave a violent shriek. The creature hissed and with spectacular speed, Graeitch heaved her weight back against the golem. Her bulk struck with force and the minion reared back. It lost its balance. Suddenly the golem was losing its grip on her and teetering back on its heels, slipping on the slimy stone.

Graeitch loosed a triumphant roar. She jerked herself free. Her head slammed against Aurimag's chest.

Aurimag flipped backward into the pool. He did a comic somersault, only quick enough to slosh about in the water with a thick shock, blubbering briefly in the greenish water stirred by his plunging. Instantly he was beset upon by Fang, his four-tentacled monster . . . Undoubtedly the lepro-serpent appeared to resent the breach of her territory and seized her master by an arm and leg and hauled him under.

A battle ensued—a very heated and lugubrious one in the ochre-stained gloom, endowing Aurimag with shrieks, howls, painful gasps, sucker-welts, constrictions, stings and abrasions.

A tentacle reared, wrapped unceremoniously around Aurimag's left limb. Then another latched to his right leg. Two coils twirled about his waist, then another about a sensitive generative member and remained anchored there.

Aurimag blubbered. The battle raged—with tempestuous strength upon which Graeitch watched with glowing interest.

Aurimag resisted with superhuman strength. The ill-fate of the magician remained in the hands of Krutu, the witch of chance, as he was abraded and plunged up and down in the water, rolled about and tumbled like an octopus's prey. His skin was mashed against the rocks; his senses were rendered numb. His head struck the bottom and he became giddy. Vaguely he attempted to disengage himself from the horrid creature's grip, but the privilege was denied him.

The golem watched with dispassion. Not a twitch of emotion stirred in his mud-mottled visage. Lacking all supervision, the golem stood detached while Graeitch was free to wander about the cave, whistling to herself, humming a whimsical tune:

> *"Hopety-popety bumpetee!*
> *What shall I gather for me?*
> *Riches, spells, lore, or rings of gold?*
> *Anything that Graeitch wishes—fine or old!"*

Peering critically at Aurimag's ornamental horror of bronze shields and horns, she hauled them down from the walls with acrimony. The Wickle smashed his brass horns and de-strung his precious viols while pushing unlucky frogs into their sound holes. After taking care to avoid Fang's wrath, she fouled his Bronze Hall pools with her pent up wastes. She tired of vandal's sport and seized a collection of Aurimag's adjuncts and stuffed them in her own sopping pockets. These included bliton-medallions, proto-meters, n^{th} order sobo-spheres, glow spots, visual accessories from Aurimag's workroom. She retraced her steps back to the Vestuary. There she paused to gaze up in rapt wonder at the gaping, fishlike expressions of three jar-encased prisoners. Woisper's and Weavil's countenances seemed to stare back at her from some kind of brownish-green slime; Salmeister's, no less comical.

Graeitch fixed her jowl in a grimace and tapped on the glass; to her surprise she drew back with a gasp. The freakish jerk of knee and toe had startled her. No less the bewildered blinking of Woisper's eye and the rude opening of his mouth.

Graeitch fluttered fingers in interest. She traced a line of delight across the cool glass, thinking how she must have these bibelots! Let her abandon her whole array of spoils, only to transport these three wonderful curios back to her home!

The plan was marred.

The haulage would require extra exertion and Graeitch knew, with no minion to transport them, it would be an impossible task.

Pausing for only a second, she studied the lizard-leathered visage of Woisper with disturbing intensity. How it reminded her of a despised tyrant responsible for her Wicklehood, a figure whom she had glimpsed in a faraway cave on some mouldered document discovered in a fane along the Lim. And so? The jar was impregnable—as was the other which contained the sallow-jawed figure with the saturnine visage. Who could this be? The seal on the boy-dwarf's canister appeared slightly askew.

Improperly screwed? Carelessly manufactured? The Wickle gave a perplexed shrug. The reason was not evident.

Graeitch allowed temptation to win out and she pried off the lid of the dwarf-boy's.

An incredible marvel transpired—a pale-faced homunculus slid out of the brine with comic abruptness! Brine spewed every which way, also other unsavoury substances. The boy's roundish mouth gushed fluid. The figure, disoriented, looking cold and shivering, was somewhat bleak. His memory seemed tainted with a catalepsy.

Graeitch prodded the shape.

The homunculus did not respond. His body slumped back on the limestone like a sack of jelly.

Graeitch touched the figure's hair. It was slick, black and greased with an oily substance—the mousy chin seemed to pull back in air of a complaint, as if one lip peeled back to accentuate the overbite. The teeth chattered with a foul release; the moon-grey eyes shone with a dull apathy defying the ruddy chill of the dim blood lamps.

"I am alive!" gasped the homunculus.

Graeitch replied with asperity, "Kiss my hoof, boy, as an exchange for your release. You are a squirrel-eared manikin, you know that!"

The tiny figure recoiled at the sight of the hog-like creature before him, "By no means! Lick your own heel, hag, if you wish it." Old memories warred with a horror as Weavil struggled to resolve the commemorative patterns of his cruellest nightmares.

Graeitch bridled. Raising her hoof, she bent to apply a blow. "Brat! Pay heed, 'twas me who liberated you. Now would you like to revisit your tube?"

"Nothing doing. Who are you?"

"I am Graeitch—Matron of Rastule glade."

"Very impressive. And I am Weavil, Poet Laureate of Heagram School of Arts and Affinity. It seems I have been encased in brine. Ho, ho. Well, stranger things have happened. It has been an edifying experience chatting with you, but I must return to my homeland." He turned awkwardly to limp off.

"Not so fast! Declare obeisance to me, squib, or I must punish you and throw you back into your tube!"

Weavil assumed an overbearing tone. "In that case"—he pretended horror and submission—"Let me know what foot to caress!" He scrunched down in a guise of genuflection and unmercifully clamped teeth into the flesh above Graeitch's left hoof.

Graeitch danced and cavorted. She held aloft her throbbing heel while rotating about on the other like a wheel.

Weavil laughed. He took care to scamper away from this horrid locale, tripping over rocks and cave moss through the upper precincts of Aurimag's dark cave. He gave eerie pools and niches wide berth, breathing relief when he had finally hidden himself behind a pair of weathered barrels that were bundled in the back of the Bronze Hall. Over his left shoulder he spied a long macabre mirror—Aurimag's Imine-reflector now cracked by Graeitch's despotic vandalism.

Tiring at last of searching for the midget, Graeitch hesitated. She listened —her hairy ears caught whiff of sounds and crabbed voices. Her ears perked in perplexity—taking two striding hoof-steps forward, she heard not those of Aurimag who sloshed miserably in his drowning pool, but faint female voices. What were these? A slimy maze presented itself, rearing with taunting cave formations. No bloodlamps were in sight. The voices appeared to be coming from a shadowy, out-of-the-way corridor—tucked in darker recesses.

Graeitch clacked forward. She halted before a tightly-shut portal crafted of ghost oak. Cautiously she creaked open the door and in mid-step, suspired at the sight of two slender maids cached in a fine-cut cubicle of white buffed marmor. They duo sat on the bed, young and supple, sloe-eyed and sleepy, garbed in rich silks and fostering fearful looks and darting glances of dismay and urgency.

Graeitch peered about the interior with indignant regard. A divan of plush silk ranged off to the side. Here, a shelled chest sat amongst racks of garments; there, perfumes, incenses, redolences, lamps, flaghorn nectars and flowers. Ha!—a nymph-nest, concluded the hag spitefully. She was irked by the sumptuous beauty of the occupants and their dress and slender physique compared to her own half-animal ugliness. She slid out from the darkness and shooed them out of the chamber, taking delight in chasing them into the chamber of horrors, frightening them with loud belches and n-1th order blasts on Aurimag's horns. Graeitch played them a hide and seek game, rewarding the losers with manic disgusts. Rolling back on her hooves, she guffawed in an attitude of triumph.

Weavil cringed, remaining hidden as far as he was behind his wine casks. Given time, he could perhaps wet-nurse his loathing, but he remained steadfast in his conviction that Graeitch was the most repulsively odious creature he had ever witnessed.

Graeitch halted, convinced now that misdeeds were conclusive. She trooped back to the Bronze Hall and satisfaction burning in her visage, she checked for any outstanding treasures that might have missed her eye. None were evident. Amidst Aurimag's frenzied and despaired calls, a head would occasionally resurface from the pool to be sucked down under again.

Hand pressed to jaw, Graeitch found the situation edifying, though not entirely gratifying. What if her oppressor managed to stay alive by repeatedly springing up from the pool's bottom to grab life-giving oxygen before being dunked again by his opponent? Was there a way to somewhat expedite the demise that must surely come?

Graeitch discarded the idea. To endanger herself unnecessarily was a foolish risk.

She gave a wise grunt. The turn of events was somewhat gratifying. She sauntered out of the Bronze Hall and realized that Aurimag's ploy of survival could not last for very much longer . . .

The Wickle came abreast the cave's vestibule—a dark, dank hole flanked with twin columns three feet in diameter. She ducked head into the gap blacker than black. Pressing her cloddish frame within, she tendered Aurimag a final salute, while pausing to reflect upon a caress of the most cloying sensation imaginable.

Instantly she was jerked back with suspended astonishment. She found that her lower limbs were not at liberty to move. She gave a mewling cry, struck with a nameless fear. She gave a kick, a livid shriek . . .

Indeed the Wickle would have enjoyed a merry joke at Aurimag's expense—had she been able to outwit the guardians which flanked the exit point. Such was not the reality. Entities of the order of elm-sprites were minions beyond her match and they took mordant delight in tossing her into an $n+1^{th}$ roil.

Graeitch disappeared from sight—her spirit buckled, warped to the press of fields and fluxes too formidable for understanding. Yet only the occasional bewildered squeal echoed hollowly throughout the cavern, at intervals at last to subside in a dusky silence.

Weavil stared back dumbly from behind his wine cask. He had witnessed the horrid unfolding with dread and terror. Riddled with disquiet, he scurried about the Bronze Hall, searching for means of escape.

Weavil found none.

He felt only a vague memory lurking in the back of his brain—somehow, he had been shrunken by a magician named Nuzbek . . .

Nuzbek! Of course! That uncouth, scandalous phoney, of the nature of a loutish magician, who was now nowhere in sight—and yet here he was, confined to this clammy cheerless cave without exit or entrance.

Weavil gave a wretched grimace. The sound of blubbering curses and sobs came from a pool beset with dank horrors on the hither side of the cavern. Weavil cognized the thrashing and frenzied tumult as something singular but could not set himself to venture near the water lest he too become ensnared by doom.

Gripping the surrounding rock, Weavil compelled himself to cache himself somewhere in the cave's blackness. He finally found such a cranny, in Nuzbek's workroom, though not without significant knee-bashing. From workbench to stalactite, he leaped up, climbed the meshes of calcified stone, rodent-like. Carefully he managed to squeeze himself into a high cranny. Peering with fragility from the ceiling, he cringed like a dawcock, shaking from the detestable perch. He looked down from the ceiling out upon the magician's cluttered worktable. His goggling eyes took in the import of the newly-constructed brood of vacant-eyed golems . . .

* * *

An hour later Aurimag was granted reprieve of his desperate plight. By chance or fate, Fang had committed an atrocious error and dove too deep dashing its head on an underwater ledge. And so from Fang's jaws, he emerged—or more accurately, *crawled*. His breath was a rasping rustle, a pathetic wheeze of blood and spume. He clawed himself away from what *was* Fang's pool. His goatee dripped with a rank spanglemoss. His limbs were a bedraggled mess, his body a mass of scrapes and contusions.

His ordeal was an exceedingly narrow victory over the forces of $n\text{-}2^{th}$ depravity.

Staggering to trembling feet, he knew himself for the half-drowned shambles he was—a tooth-chattering martyr, teeth dripping greenish serpent blood as he had been forced to clamp his jaws deep into that fetid neck at the last instant to avoid being dragged under and suffer the heinous constriction to ignoble death.

Aurimag's senses were not yet fully lucid, stripped to that thin fabric of sensibility that only a dying man could know. He had endured disgusts of this nature in his rise to a neomancer, but Fang's rigour topped most—Fang, the lepro-horror—thankfully, it was no more; nor would it ever be again . . .

Aurimag made grim note of de-populating his n-2th pools of lower order creatures. It was only sensible.

Hobbling over to the Bronze Hall on numbed limbs, he paused to inspect the damage wreaked by the vandalistic ghoul, Graeitch. His favoured horns, bugles, shields, puppets lay twisted and turned—How had he allowed such an inconceivable maelstrom to run loose in his abode? Nevertheless, the damage was done. Biting back stone-faced fury, he reviled Graeitch, and all her kind. Where was the hag anyway? He peered about through outraged eyes, craning his head this way and that like a stork gone loony. At various junctures he sniffed in wrath and discovered a lone bugle or horn, shattered at the foot of a stalagmite where many of his books were torn away and strewn about the floor with disregard. The abasis horn was crushed, as was one of his 'specials', an invaluable flugo-tenor gifted with four spiralling volutes and two chrome sound bells. His concubines had fled shivering at his approach and he stalked toward the nymphosium with a fury. He waved a hand at their cringing, snivelling forms. Their mischief was nothing compared to the fate that the fiend Graeitch would endure.

He ordered his golem to collect his mistresses—where had they all fled to?

The golem! Restraining his outrage he studied his impenitent cretin with a glowering distaste that was hard to match. The automaton waddled about on mud feet. An air of slow understanding fell upon Aurimag. His last command had been nebulous to the point of uselessness. Giving it a wicked slap, he ordered the creature with sad resignation to ignore his last order.

The golem dutifully obeyed and followed its master to the vestibule. The magician grabbed hold of one of the twin pillars for support. He gazed into the black abyss that looked between the columns. Framing a mudra with knuckles clenched, he intoned a sub-auditory chant.

The tones alerted his elm-sprites to obeisance who lurked beyond. They assumed their true forms as wood-sprites-with no glee whatsoever—weird, lanky, ghost-limbed trunkish-shapes. Each sprouted a pair of abominable gorgon heads, wrapped in filth and a myriad tree limbs, floating and writhing like a sea-witch's hair. Oyster white, gold, nankeen yellow, black. Loath to tempt their master, the minions desisted from their branch-tossing and let the green-faced Graeitch roll heavily to the floor.

Aurimag called a sharp order. The Wickle was released from the mesh spell and the neomancer had his golem drag the near dead thing back into the Bronze Hall.

Aurimag chugged a tonic to help revive his strength. Zombie-bitten and horror-stricken, the Wickle blenched in the murky light. She was afraid of what fate faced her. On sight of Aurimag, she gasped a quailing cry and grimaced. She bit, hoof-kicked, crawled on all fours—No success. With eyes glued to Aurimag's reaching hand, she hissed when she saw him take one of his sobospheres out of her jacket pocket, and now he rubbed the object on her crown and struck her a stinging blow.

A strange orangey cloud appeared over Graietch's head. A single tone rang out in the air—something reminiscent of striking a brass bell. Graeitch's head seemed to swell like a balloon. Her crown remained suffused with a lurid orange before it began to pulse. Flitting helplessly, Graeitch attacked the golem's grip. Nails grated on marmor; the captive's expostulations became feral, but the clamour quickly died, and Aurimag had the golem drag the Wickle back to his workshop for a final reckoning.

Aurimag grew fatigued with the tumult and tapped Graeitch's kneecaps with the sobosphere. Instantly, she grew rigid with only a grievous wail ensuing. He clothes-pinned her lips and, back in the closed comfort of his workroom, nodded phlegmatically at her whimpers and appeals. He jocularly promised punishments of colourful order and an itemized list of her crimes, which he ticked off with fastidious precision: ". . . trespass, vandalism, violence, theft, vilification, impedance of an important order, disturbance of a psychical peace, maligning of a peaceful habitation, inducement of hysteria upon members of a private nymphosium, an allegation of general nuisance upon an otherwise upright and ethical homestead—and so on—" The tally terminated with Aurimag's bald comment on his despising her beyond reason of imagination. In fact, he hated her perhaps only a figment less than Woisper who had thrust him into this squalor-ful condition in the first place; also, that an ensuing program of retribution would be quickly underway—this, in brevity, was Aurimag's rant, and an elementary tutorial in the consequences of cause and effect . . .

* * *

Two days passed and Aurimag found himself moderately relieved. Back in his workroom, he gritted teeth, making note of the fact that Weavil had not yet been recovered. Where was the miscreant? Time would be a benefaction in this drama, he told himself. Woisper had been tendered a gift —a new and novel home rendered with a slightly indigo tint. 'Twas a canister double the volume of his old confines. Cramped in the intimate glass container, there resided a playmate of superior quality, a rival beyond any blue schasm, and with whom Woisper could enjoy freakish hours of entertainment! In fact, the last time Aurimag had peered, Graeitch had looped her large, muscular thighs about Woisper's neck and flubbed at his nose with a recklessness approaching whimsy. Aurimag laughed. All the time she constricted him first with her thighs for failing to succumb to her domination, then her rude charms.

How droll! Aurimag thought with another dry laugh. His scientist's interest was stirred. How compelling to see neomancer and Wickle co-joined in blithe and fresh refrain!

In the days that followed, Aurimag secluded himself in his workroom. Many of his meditations progressed toward the unnatural and with a rare sublimity. He had been graced with a humbling experience—true, perhaps 'twas the one experience that had prompted the synergy of his next epiphany —a merging of his consciousness into an $n+1^{th}$ substratum—for several seconds!—and in total harmony with his most exalted vision. A singular feat, if he did not say so himself!

Aurimag congratulated himself on this illumination. He ambled ever so thoughtfully back to his workroom where he brooded on his two new simulacra. They were erect in their harnesses of wood and iron and gazed back at him without interest. Braced by stone slabs, the vacant expressions they cast at him seemed only tinted with enmity. Aurimag frowned. The replicas were perfect imitations of himself; for the nonce, forms of superbly manifested craftsmanship!

He left the creatures 'unanimated' for the time being, should they decide to turn against him. There was always a chance that these things could wander dreadfully astray. If ever the need for backup should arise . . . well, at least, he would have an escape route. He gave a bland chuckle . . .

Reviewing his successes of the last eventful days, Aurimag sent a 'test scout' golem to Lillenvir, the nearest village—on a 'maiden gathering mission'. Currently the most competent was a minion whose talents produced a nymphosium that had never seen greater numbers.

Aurimag heaved a contented sigh. He strode up before his original golem, the one which had brought him so much misery in the form of

626

Graeitch, and touched it gamely on the skull.

The magician issued a barking command: "Make speed to the Wickle haven!—Go to Rastule's glade. Recover my quarry, spare no expense, or life, not even your own!"

Thereafter, Aurimag bent to his task, employing prodigious energies to capture a certain mischievous inconvenience named Weavil . . .

XIII

For six days and six nights Loeitch and Paiesmy took up their experiments with driven zeal. It was a period during which Baus, Poli and Valere were forced to endure stenches, rigours, assaults and affronts beyond their ability to protect against. Indeed, the Wickles' rituals reached all pinnacles of infamy! Day and night the hub ran, spool to spool at unsustainable speeds. Poli's whimpers indeed reached pathetic and unbearable pitches.

Baus writhed in his bonds. The sounds were stretched with a wretchedness even more than he could remember and he wrenched futilely at his bonds. The act was useless—Poli was always their favourite and remained the Wickles' guinea pig to most painful effect. His results always outdid those of his peers . . .

On the ninth day of their rigor the pirate bully disgorged an ancient truth . . . the ominous words piped in a long-dead tongue, in concert with his being poked and prodded with mugfish bone and elfwort chips:

"Fiend-hoar speaks! Wickles of the Branx—Harken! Afford thyselves grooms on the eve of the new moon of Springshaven. The firstborn imp of each Wickle shall fight in a battle in an army against the neomancers who defy your autonomy. The imps shall be the minions of the future! Love them! Cherish them! They thwart the age-old debasements and defilements you once suffered. . . This is my last homily! . . . Now I depart, confined to the eternal realm of the 'Shadow', my spectral haunt! . . ."

Poli's droning voice became ever more threateningly grim over the rattles of the gears and the weary echoes of un-oiled machinery that still resounded in the hub's interior.

Paiesmy clacked her teeth; Loeitch offered words of reasoning. Paiesmy's eyes peeled back with dogmatic fire. She cried out, "Now it is ordained by the spirit *Fiend-hoar* that the Wickles should raise a troop of incubi to avenge their forebears!"

Loeitch caught the expression of fanaticism mirrored in her sister's face and gave a dismissive flick of finger. "I opt that we pursue a path of more practical use, Paiesmy, not your pagan rhetoric."

Paiesmy's eyes swam with egg-like lunacy. "What could be the use of that? And what is more useful than an army?"

Loeitch corrected her sister's logic, "I see that I must be less ambiguous. Seeing to our own needs and making use of the grooms we have is of more essence than tramping through the hinterlands with an alleged army, making war with wizards."

"So you say, Loeitch! You are a witless oaf!" Paiesmy hopped over to the crankwheel, hissing. "Your feeble mind will corrupt our sense of purpose and dilute the pure intent of our ritual!"

"Nothing of the kind," scoffed Loeitch. "I merely suggest that we redefine our goals, executing a more pragmatic approach."

Paiesmy's wrath dimmed pruriently upon Poli. "There is your pragmatism!" She gave a throaty roar. "And yet there's something in what you say—" She brought out a stiff kerchief and daubed frugally at her brow which was sweating profusely. "We must procure ourselves more grooms!"

Loeitch snuffled,"How are we to secure more of these 'grooms' for this 'army' when it is tasking enough just to manage the few we have?"

Paiesmy had grunted and stopped listening—already she was scooting up the ladder with thoughts ravelling on a new scheme. She emerged from the hub, grabbing a hypodermic from the kitchen. Injecting it with trailing drip of blue effluvia, she crowed loudly while Loeitch trailed after with somewhat stupefied annoyance as her sister advanced upon the lank-haired Baus. "Here, groom!" she called, "I activate your indenture! Go forth, bring a twain of grooms—no, a foursome, to feed our hub. If you fetch four, I shall exempt you from this blue epidemic!"

Baus vehemently objected to the hypodermic but Paiesmy held up the needle in front of Baus's face. "Three days!—not an hour more. Procure me my hosts before the blue worm has its way with you and hatches inside, feeding on your vitality!"

Paiesmy brought forth the bone-tip and bent forward to puncture Baus's neck but Baus veered away in loathing. "Before you install this odious doom, Paiesmy, hear me out. Aye, I shall ply forth to the forest and seek what you require! But no hypodermic. I need only your pledge, of no harm to my person, and thus the covenant restraining you from feeding my veins with this vile, trailing drip."

Paiesmy flashed Baus a menacing glare. "Do not seek to hoodwink me with your rhetoric! Your double talk gulls perhaps lesser intellects than mine

—so prepare for a sting!"

"Wait!" Baus roared. He grimaced, recoiling from the syringe. "Dusk falls in but two hours. Without any light, I shall be prey to wandering Auks, then you won't have a vassal to fetch your grooms. Call off your blight, Paiesmy—at least until first light."

Paiesmy hesitated. Loeitch gave a concurring murmur, "Dawn, sister— then we shall loose our fisherman. He will secure us more grooms."

Paiesmy huffed: "I suppose the concept cannot be refuted. Loeitch, for once you are right"

Loeitch made a sour face but made no attempt to quarrel.

For the remainder of the day, the Wickles worked with meticulous vigour and Loeitch brooded unpleasantly, much frustration pinned on her sister's puritanical attitude. She fretted and schemed; all the while a tangible heat had begun to gather in her loins. Perhaps it was the presence of the grooms. Yet the discomfort caused her ever more pangs of urgency and she peered often and meaningfully upon Valere with a nymphomaniac's interest, crafting her own programs and plans to bypass her sister's authority and satiate her own desires.

Esling had managed to snatch more time with Baus, taking care not to scratch his brow with her horns as she gave him kisses. Baus felt a growing affection for the Wickle and a confidence that he could inveigle her into offering aid at the appropriate time. When and how this miracle might transpire remained largely a question of chance and necessity. Paiesmy and Loeitch's reach was long-as monitors, they maintained vigil on the grooms' activities, hardly allowing the companions to speak a single word amongst themselves without a sharp reprimand. Loeitch was especially a nuisance, habitually outfitted in her boar-fur boots, remaining an oppressive presence to Valere. She strutted up to him pompously, frequently foisting him hip butts and endearing tugs of cheek. All such affections goaded Valere to wrath.

* * *

A heavy silence gripped the dome. It was in the wee hours of morn when Loeitch awoke in a semi-lascivious sweat from an evocative dream, rustling about and blinking languorously. She felt a heightened tautness in her loins. Reaching down, she felt a damp heat. Galvanized by instinctual pressures, she felt compelled by forces beyond her control.

Baus and Poli dozed perhaps a dozen paces away, heads lowered in torpor, muttering grim resentments in dream. Valere snored in his prison chair, with head tipped to one side, mouth agape.

Acting on impulse, Loeitch disabled the precious alarm of tin pots and trip wires around Valere's post.

Creeping softly to his chair, she drew herself up impressively to feel the warmth of his legs. The Wickle loosed a jubilant sigh. Letting loose her black gown, in one deft motion she had mounted herself on the seaman's lap and had jammed a foul dishrag in his mouth, thus smothering his powers of speech before he could jerk himself awake.

She plied back his breeches and groped and writhed upon his brawny body. She was half way through a libidinous act before she was pre-empted by Paiesmy, who had been alerted by the discord and efforted to instil a halt to the lubricious recklessness ensuing before her eyes.

She grabbed Loeitch by the hair and dragged her away from the seaman with rude force. "Witch! . . . Tramp!"

Loeitch lay a-sprawl, pale lips glistening in the soft lamplight. Valere gave a muffled roar, impeded by the rag. Paiesmy wrenched the foul garment out. Valere bucked and thrashed, lifting himself an inch off his chair. His face remained the colour of a red beet, but Loeitch ignored his invective and donned her black robe and gave Valere a tender caress on the cheek. "My hero!" she crooned, turning to stare at Paiesmy in sultry displeasure. "Your motives are crass, Paiesmy. I had almost completed a congress. Simple female spite! Jealousy—the bane of all Wickles."

Paiesmy stood hands pressed to her hips, her flat bosom heaving. "Your sluttish behaviour, Loeitch, does no one favour! I stand here exasperated and embarrassed."

"Hush your priggish tongue!" Loeitch clucked. "You are a prude eagle. Should a groom fall on top of you, you wouldn't know what to do with him."

Paiesmy advanced with a goad. "I warn you, Loeitch. No more of your cheesy jibes. Graeitch has warned me about your juvenile side and your wenchish lust and of your potential to contaminate our wards. Look what your disgraceful behaviour has brought about!"

Loeitch gave a rancorous laugh. "And what is that? My feisty redbeard is unlikely to dole out any 'whisperings' at this late hour. Settle down, o pious

Paiesmy. Poli-poo is a better guinea pig."

"Arrest the endearments on our grooms!"

"I will not!" roared Loeitch. "Graeitch is absent; And I shall do what I wish. No longer shall I be bullied!"

Trenchant exchanges were hurled back and forth and finally the two returned grudgingly to their cots, clenching goads, each eyeing the other with mutual mistrust. Esling sank back into her pillow, drifting back into sleep.

* * *

When morning arrived, Baus felt a sickness to his heart. Recent developments had taken a turn for the worse. Not only were their honours in jeopardy but they would soon be violated and sullied like beasts for breeding. In such wise, they would be injected with the Wickles' worm juice, and there was no plan to counteract it.

Baus grimaced in frustration; he caught sight of Loeitch strutting about in her foul heat. Poli was a useless accomplice in the effecting of a plan. He was exhausted to the point of coma, on being tortured in the hub. Paiesmy marched to the pantry to fill her hypodermic. Baus kept his cool and was surprised when Paiesmy's howl of annoyance reached his ears. "The projectorate is strangely diminished!" she moaned. "I could have sworn it was half full yesterday—Loeitch! What did you do with my fluid?"

Loeitch growled. "'Twas not I who fooled with it."

"Then who was it?" muttered Paiesmy. "I will require a full day to replenish my supply." Her furry cheeks became puffed with ruddy displeasure. "Something is afoot!" Frowning, she studied Baus with fervour who looked to and fro with an innocent bewilderment as if he were as astonished as she. Esling had slunk into a corner, shoulders hunched with an unease and wearing a sly look. What had the little Wickle done?

Baus showed his teeth in ironic annoyance. Matters were becoming rosier. His luck, as chance had it, was turning. The bond between the Wickles was strained to the point of breaking, and showed promise of capsizing.

A lively smile played across his lips.

He darted a shrewd glance at Paiesmy—a moment was all he needed . . . as such, when Loeitch was out of the Honey Home answering a call of nature. He addressed her in a voice of silky importance.

"Here, Loeitch. Listen to my counsel!"

"What do you want, groom?" sighed Paiesmy. "Can you not see I am busy? Or do you seek the hub so badly?"

"Nothing of the sort," cried Baus with dignity. "I wish only to apprise you of certain truths."

"And what would they be?"

Baus ticked off several points. "Loeitch seeks to undermine your authority. Being a jealous sort, she covets your leadership and becomes ever embroiled in schemes to advance her own habits. Be warned! Her schemes are of the utmost cunning! Even on the instant, she gathers secret puissances in the forest to direct spells against you."

"Such spite is notorious of the witch, but how could the ingrate stoop that low? It is indefensible!"

Baus gave several indulgent nods. "I know for a fact that she mumbles thoughts while strutting about foisting lewd insinuations at myself and Valere. Is this not right, Valere?"

Valere gave his head a conspiring wag. "The implication is as Baus states."

Baus continued with bold confidence. "Mostly, she speaks in riddles and rhymes while she works away at the chopping board. Cutting daikon and salamander, she mumbles thinking no one hears . . . but to the ear sensitive as mine, the meaning becomes apparent."

"And what meaning may that be?" Paiesmy grunted. She thrust a hawk-owl face into Baus's, but before hearing the answer, she pranced back to the kitchen with fury, steeling her anger while grinding certain cankerweed, roots and other ingredients into a mash.

Baus silently congratulated Valere upon his input.

Loeitch returned a jot later, smiley-faced and fresh. Paiesmy, more suspicious than ever, made a casual pretext to go out and gather bottleroot and listen to the mourning doves.

Loeitch lifted brows in suspicion. "What prompts such whimsy, Paiesmy? Esling can collect such ingredients at this early hour."

Paiesmy pursed her lips with grim disfavour. "Must I always defer to your counsel? 'Tis splendid weather! What is so peculiar about that? I want to enjoy the spring in the Branx, as I seek leeks and dillowasp, as would any nature-loving Wickle. Seeing that I work incessantly here in this sweaty kitchen, doing drudge-work and pitching endless objects at these intractable grooms, I believe I am entitled to a little leisure!"

"Perhaps, but be back soon!" barked Loeitch. "There is an abundance of housework to be completed, and Esling is useless at it."

Paiesmy scoffed at the remark and gobbed out a snobby retort, "I shall return to the Honey Home when I am good and ready, Loeitch. Likely before tea time."

"See that you do!"

Paiesmy was about to dole out a satirical rejoinder but refrained.

Baus called out a sage remark: "Yes, hurry home, Paiesmy! You know how querulous the grooms get when you are gone!"

Paiesmy inspected Baus with rancour. She delayed a punishment and attended to her otherwise pressing engagement.

When she departed, Baus called Loeitch over in a hushed whisper. "Quickly, Loeitch, I must have words with you!"

Loeitch sneered but cocked her head in curiosity.

Peering left and right, Baus put forth words describing her sibling Paiesmy and Loeitch clicked her tongue with contempt. "What about that rude owl? Must we always talk about her?"

"Yes, this time we do! She seeks to inflict malice upon your person. Just recently, while you were out, she muttered inflammatory schemes about mixing bottleroot and guar gum together to plop in your morning tea. 'Tis an arsenic, I fear. Fortunately—you have yet to sip the elixir."

Loeitch planted hands on hips and sniffed at the tea suspiciously. "It does have an odd smell." The Wickle reared back, quite pale. "Why would the virago consummate such a malicious plan?"

Baus answered with astonished concern: "I don't know. I only know she sees you as a rival. She wishes you out of the way so she may garner sole time with the grooms. For example, she grunted in her bragging tone—'*with Graeitch gone and Loeitch no longer to question my decisions and authority, there will be no impedance to my role as absolute mistress of the Honey Home!*'"

"Did she now?" cried Loeitch, flushed.

Valere called out an endorsement. "Baus speaks sensibly on this issue— you are wise to take action! After sampling your charms, I do not wish to lie with Paiesmy."

Loeitch huffed, "As it should be. Well, let her seek her ambition! I shall have no more to do with her. In fact, I shall thwart her ghoulishness once and for all!"

"That exemplifies unique spirit!" called Baus.

In vindictive humour Loeitch slogged her way to the kitchen and began working on a counter-elixir. She cut insects, chopped bogwort, daikon and thistledown with visible indignation. When Paiesmy returned, Loeitch immediately confronted her. She hurled an accusation. Paiesmy laughed in her face, denying treachery and whistled an oath through her teeth. She disclaimed all ownership of Loeitch's imaginative charges as farce, emphasizing that she had been gulled by an overactive imagination. Loeitch gave over to fury. Paiesmy accused her sister of paranoia and called her a filthy hypocrite. The retort stung. Loeitch launched into an acerbic rejoinder that rankled Paiesmy's sensibilities. In seconds the sisters were at each other's throats. Grappling each other to the floor, they bit, clawed and scratched each other. Nails dug, teeth flew. The battle, heated and indecent, was perhaps shorter than would be expected and Baus had hardly hissed a hurried suggestion at Esling to loose his bonds when Paiesmy jerked herself to attention, crying out in a rude tone: "I thought you were picking bottleroot and caustic billowflower in Gadmere's Glade to poison me?"

"By no means!" protested Loeitch. "Whatever gave you that idiot's idea?"

"The same that gave you the juvenile notion that I was setting up a hidden deadfall in the hub!"

"Well then, that means—" Both glared meaningfully at Baus.

Baus looked away innocently.

Loeitch addressed Paiesmy in a conversational tone, "Perhaps our groom would care for some 'refried' spider soup?"

Paiesmy nodded vigorously. "Of course. Pinched with an extra handful of millipede?"

"A notable embellishment!" Loeitch grated. "Paiesmy, you are a genius."

"My adornments are unique."

Baus licked his lips with disapproval. "These suggestions, while droll, comprise a rather early start for a smorgasbord."

"Yes, very early!" the two laughed, sniggering.

Baus put on a face of disapprobation; he tried several helpful gambits to ameliorate the Wickles' mood, but all were ineffectual.

Loeitch stirred the cauldron, ladling out a heaping bowlful of steaming soup which Paiesmy heartily and laughingly sprinkled with squirming wigglies.

Baus let out a miserable howl.

Esling stamped her foot, addressing the Wickles with displeasure: "Leave poor Baus alone! He is innocent, as you know, and you are bullies. You can quite see he is clearly not hungry."

"Stay out of this, pea-brain!" roared Loeitch. "We know you've a fancy for him, and we'll not tolerate your squeaks and coos!"

Baus vented a series of expostulations but Paiesmy ignored them and held a goad to his throat, pried open his jaw while Loeitch spoon-fed him the steaming spider soup. Baus gurgled in sick heaves, imbibing the spider-millipede broth in reviling slurps. With lip-smacking disgust, he gulped and spat like a dog given a despicable medicine. It was too much and he vomited —the Wickles retaliated by declaring that for the greater good their groom must be given the best nutrition—in the form of another bowl.

Baus's cries went unheeded. A splash of liquid tumbled down his gagging throat.

Time passed, so did the night. Baus spent the evening contending with pressures, cramps, eructations and fitful nightmares. He could only attribute his disgust to the insufferable Wickles and gain any sense of solace from the retribution he would inflict upon them, when the opportunity arose.

XIV

That same afternoon, Aurimag's golem, padding on pale bare feet, halted some paces before the Honey Home. It put a hand to its frowning chin. Garbed in a loosely-wrapped domino, it was perhaps one of the least conspicuous creatures gracing the glade.

None took notice of the surreptitious creature; in its splattered pair of trousers and a vest of green leaves, it watched the clearing from a distance with a murky guile-moving covertly through spaces between the tall zizasters and mucklewoods with wraithlike stealth.

A grey overcast shrouded the meadow. A smudgy grey shade draped the scene.

The golem knew this place. On its last excursion several days earlier, it had passed near Graeitch's dome. What it was not aware of, was that the sisters had doubled their guard on the door and had installed new traps in the dark corners, including near infallible deadfalls.

For several seconds, the creature stood amazed, blinking with bewilderment. The many passers-by with their strange wings and claws and snouts and slab-sided faces were of curious quality. The golem did not stumble upon the matter of its own incongruities or the apparent oddness of its own manufacture; it lacked such percipience.

When the way was clear, it bounded over to the Wickles' dome, carefully testing the knob on the door. It put an ear to the shell-glossed wood; feeling confident of its enterprise, it forced its way through with a brief splintering of wood.

Almost immediately, an alarm was tripped. A tripwire pulled taut. Down crashed a hail of stones and pointed debris on the golem's pancake skull. The upended bucket fell and conked it on the crown. Dislodged of its domino, the bald, black-amber head was exposed to further crushes of rocks. The creature stumbled in a cloud of dust, tripping over fallen rock like some kind of somnambulant zombie. In and out of shock it drifted, gazing unblinkingly with an attitude of shock. What had caused the detritus to fall?

Loeitch caught sight of the fiend floundering in the dust. She flew up out of the hub with a vulture's spite, scrambling for her goad. She struck, once, twice.

The creature groaned, fell with a stream of electric pulses shivering through its body.

The golem shook off the electrification. It lunged with instinctive violence at its aggressor. Spying the upright posts wrapped with the lank-haired Baus, it sought to rip the fisherman off and be away. The Wickles prevented such a seizure.

Esling bravely stepped in to obstruct a kidnapping. She caught a glimpse of the zombie-like visage and fled back cringing to Baus's post.

Paiesmy, now vengefully roused, bounded up from the hub and quietly snatched a lasso. She snuck behind the golem and arched a loop. While Poli whirled away in the hub, she tossed the loop around the golem's neck and worked with adder-like efficiency.

The golem sprang back, arms twisted in orang-utan menace. Loeitch pitched herself into the fray, tripping the golem with her goad and making a grab for the table with its half-finished bowl of spider soup.

The golem whirled, swatted at Loeitch's midsection.

She flung the spider soup in its eyes.

The golem thrashed about and Paiesmy rammed the goad into its face. The thing toppled to the ground. She heaved her spindly frame onto its back while Loeitch pulled hard on the lasso round its neck.

The creature groaned, twitched limbs in anguish. It made a gurgling sound and stung Paiesmy a smarting blow to the chest. The owlish Wickle only tightened her grip on the lasso while she also wound loops round its baked clay legs.

Huffing and puffing, the Wickles now rocked back and forth like ranch hands, sneering at their abominable catch. The golem stared back at them like a black buckler in a net. The Wickles regarded it with clinical interest. Its gaze of inhuman enmity was not unlike an incarnate demon, certainly one not lacking a certain primal intelligence.

"What is the thing?" Loeitch hissed.

"Some ghoul intent on bringing us harm," growled Paiesmy. "We have outwitted it."

Loeitch opened her eyes with appalled disgust. "Look—a pulsing node throbs in its shoulder. It exudes a flux. I feel my own mind being tugged by it, as if some sheer exotic horror beckons me to comply to its will."

Paiesmy gave a sombre agreement.

With the help of Poli's halberd, the two pried out the moolstone and the golem twisted, grimacing and yowling with an almost inhuman desolation. It could do nothing to prevent the extraction. Almost at once it underwent a macabre change—the brooding mass became an entity of rippling excitation —a primal, ancient unpredictability, filled with demented turmoil, as if the powers of evil and good lay concentrated in that husk.

The Wickles remained surprised but unmoved. Forces of conflicting nature warred in the creature. Instantly it became a sterile hulk, a thing of bleak otherworldliness, one that could feel no emotion or pang of warmth or compassion as a living creature could.

Baus and Valere were stricken with revulsion. Sagging astride their posts, they assessed the situation with almost psychotic despair. The golem's head was outlandishly oversized, its torso was blasted with sand and rippled with mud; a pair of slimy, goggling eyes bulged out of its sockets, and a worm ribbon of lips dominated the ugly face. While the creature writhed, each motion seemed to unravel as part of a larger dream. Baus marvelled upon the monster's strength and freakish resilience. Yet the Wickles had won the battle against its lunatic fortitude, defeated the undefeatable with their own ingenuity. Better yet, how could the outlaws use the situation to their advantage?

Loeitch waved the moolstone in front of its sand-blasted face. "What is this, ghoul?"

The golem's expression remained implacable. "It won't tell us anything," Loeitch mumbled.

"Then we must induce it."

"How?"

"Chain the miscreant in the hub and enforce rigour. Secrets will be dislodged!—as in the case of Poli."

Loeitch put a hand of doubt to her lips. "Only grooms are permitted in the hub—not creatures of weird obscene nature like this hobgoblin."

Paiesmy controlled her irritation. "Loeitch, sometimes you are a bore. We have occasion to bend the rules sometime."

"Save your denigrations for other uncouth saps!" growled Loeitch. "If Graeitch returns without warning—she might catch us in this state of chaos —"

Paiesmy gave her lips an insolent curl. "Graeitch is not here. Likely she will never return. We have no better idea how our sibling met her fate, other than that this miscreant has likely dragged her away somewhere. If we probe the creature's knowledge, perhaps we will find an answer."

"Perhaps," grumbled Loeitch. She looked sceptically upon the captive. A new understanding gleamed in her eyes.

Paiesmy began to show a familiar zealotish glint in the whites of her own. "Indecent forces have been unleashed upon our persons, Loeitch. From nether-realms comes a beast hindering our purpose. Take note! The 'Beyond' has given us a signal! From Poli's lips came a rare insight into an interdimensional mission—a hint that we had never thought possible. Now we must entertain a path of wisdom and plod along without fear! We must hold fast like sailors on unfriendly tides, assuming the principles of martyrs and soldiers on a greater vision of battle!"

Loeitch blew out her cheeks with contempt. "Enough of your bombast, Paiesmy! I shall not be drowned in your pedagogy."

"Take care, Loeitch!" Paiesmy looked frowningly upon her mocking face and lack of faith. "How you continually enjoy belittling my ardour and my creed is beyond me!"

Loeitch ignored her. The two stitched the golem up in chicken wire and Loeitch went to fetch more from the shed, also a net with which to wrap the golem tightly. It took both their efforts to drag the creature down to the pit, but once they did, they began levering the monster to a standing position, affixing the shape in the slot opposite Poli.

Poli stared amazed. The Wickles set to a course of industry, pitching the wheel into a frenzied motion.

"By the order of 'Beyond', I bid you speak!" thundered Paiesmy. "Cretin! Make penitent your centres to the higher orders! We are watchful, take heed!" The golem glared; it's ferret-like eyes shot straight ahead. Paiesmy spoke in a loud, lugubrious voice. "Who sent you? For what purpose?"

The creature deigned no reply.

Disgusted with its reticence, Paiesmy pitched a blight upon its knees. It howled. Loeitch wound the crank to multiple tensions. The drum rotated with a fiendish intensity; Paiesmy stabbed out at its plexuses with a goat hoof, goblin root and witch-flax.

Nothing occurred.

Paiesmy ordered her sister to fetch the node that they had extracted from its shoulder.

Loeitch returned, bearing the medallion. The object glittered with strange hues—maroon, macaroon, lead pink. Paiesmy grabbed the disc and began stuffing it into the creature's maw.

The creature bent nearly over double. It became a cruel caricature of paroxysm and anguish. Out spat the node; it uttered a chittering guttural in coughing, jerking spasms. Several nether tongues spilled from its mouth. Organs not meant for speech, suddenly framed unearthly phonemes.

The voice was clear, dry, filled with a sylphian dread, perhaps a dryad's voice, then at times a caterwauling tomcat's, then at once a low, garbled menace, muffled in its delivery like that of a crazed, other-worldly omen. From 'Beyond' came the golem speaking with a chilling conviction:

"The future is everlasting! I speak through the voice of Nlion—the Spirit of Sighs and Sorrows! Fear now, Wickles! You must destroy my husk if you wish to live, but I shall remain aware of your presence for eternity. I dwell in planes above your intellects. 'Destiny' precedes all that which can be witnessed. You cannot hinder me. Of my form's master and designer, 'tis one of the neomancers of the New Order, who created my husk from scratch —from magic marsh clay through the physicochemical vitalism of REO-GENESIS. The intrepid has sent me on a mission to retrieve the black-haired man of the sea, to escort the stick-wielder to the neomancer's Cave under the single phantom elm betwixt Desenion and Mismerion !..."

Baus gave his neck a startled shudder. Black haired man of the sea? Who could that be but him? Neomancer of the New Order? None other than *Aurimag*!

So . . . it had been Aurimag's golem after all! thought Baus with a sinister chill. An awful dread came over him. The monster had been sent to procure *him*—to root him out!

A dozen dissonant memories floated back to his mind.

An eerie reverie enveloped him, interrupted by Paiesmy's snuffling grunt ringing out in the air: "Fiend! How did you find our sanctuary?"

The golem answered without protest: *"East and south I fled, guided by the moolstone, which you clutch in your hand. You removed the talisman from my flesh and thus have released me from my master's covenant. I thank you. But be wary!—lest I break free and commit acts of horror on your persons, which you would not care to imagine..."*

Baus shook himself out of his uneasy trance. While Loeitch and Paiesmy remained intent on interrogation of the golem, he took occasion to whisper several instructions at Esling who hovered nearby. With a quick nod, she hopped to the kitchen. From its wall brace she acquired Lolispar and made not a sound; hastily she cut Baus free.

Loose at last, he rubbed his wrists with satisfaction and took Lolispar. He stroked the smooth edge with a fiendish anticipation and hobbled over to the post to free Valere. With relish, he cut the seaman loose who likewise furtively retrieved his own sword from the kitchen wall; he clutched it with an insidious rapture.

Baus motioned the seaman toward the cauldron. The two stood grimacing with meaning. The broth was bubbling with a barbarous intensity. It was topped with fresh spider soup and the pungent odours permeated the dome. A perfect medium, thought Baus malevolently. Grinning, he helped Valere lift the vessel over to the lip of the hub and they carried it awkwardly by its handle. They efforted not to spill the contents lest they scald themselves and alert the grotesques.

The Wickles remained engrossed in their interrogation, hooting and gnashing.

". . . *Graeitch is now the plaything of my master!*" came the golem's awful caterwaul. "*The witch dwells in a small glass tube while not otherwise occupied with performing on my master's puppet stage. The spectacle is paralleled only by the fates of his other neomancer prisoners.*"

"This erstwhile 'master' of yours—" croaked Loeitch disgustedly "—why is he so given to droll and cruel punishments? Describe the wretch!"

The golem proceeded to describe an unflattering version of Aurimag, as he was last seen ravaged by Fang. When Poli was farthest from the edge, Baus gave a tiny signal. With a mighty heave, he and Valere upended the cauldron into the pit. There was a splash and singeing of flesh. The residents, other than Poli, jerked and thrashed, engulfed by a gush of hot steam and liquid.

The Wickles lurched sideways, uttering such screeches that had never been heard in the Honey Home.

The din did not pass unheeded. The Wickles treading in Rastule glade became alerted and at once thought of mishap and pounded on the door.

Esling bounded over on nimble feet to barricade the door from possible intrusion. Through the small window, a babble of voices inquired of the wellness of the grooms. Esling hastily assured everyone that all was well.

Baus nodded approval and took Valere aside; together they descended into the hub, wielding their goads and swords. Poli was still harnessed. He was a dazed and tongue-lolling mess. Soon he was loosed from his braces and fell limp to the ground. Thoughts of vengeance raged thickly on the outlaws' minds. The Wickles cowered and gulped, quivering in their heaps of scalded flesh.

The golem, black as goblin's shadow, sat erect in its brace. The hot spider soup had caused it no mishap. Its small green eyes gleamed and now its long brow glistened. To the Wickles' right, without its domino, it had an odd feral look with its back-sloping brow and bulging mud body. It strained at its braces and Baus guessed it would not hesitate to crack their skulls if given the chance.

Valere gave a disapproving frown. "'Tis an ugly spook, if I've ever seen one."

"I could hardly agree more," said Baus. "We must act swiftly before the fiend breaks loose itself and the other Wickles discover us."

Valere grunted. Slapping Poli to attention, they dragged him to the centre of the drum well away from the Wickles who sagged in wracked piles of vileness.

Baus returned topside; he began searching for items of utility. Gradually, Poli came to and upon scrutinizing the two cringing grotesques, he recognized them for what they were and strove to wreak havoc on their persons.

Valere pulled him back. While the Wickles burbled and moaned in agony, with skin seared and popping of bubbles, Poli shouted imprecations of what he would do to them. Exercising a minimum of delicacy, Valere helped him heave Paiesmy into the brace he had just vacated. They manacled her tight and applied a similar lashing of Loeitch to the adjacent brace.

The two Wickles gave hoarse shrieks which were ignored. The pain-ridden howls gave smiling pleasure to Valere. He gagged them with articles of their own clothing, and the two freemen took turns applying goads to various sections of the Wickles' bodies, while the other laughingly twirled the crank.

The drum whirled with an intensity of hostility.

Baus, who had been ransacking the place for weapons, finally hissed down at the two to curb their sports. "We must prepare for departure!" The outlaws, though disappointed, halted their amusements.

Baus whistled down impatiently. He had only acquired a few dry crusts of bread, a kitchen knife, and a small hand-held moth-lamp and was in foul mood.

Poli and Valere reluctantly climbed out of the hub. They found Baus and Esling peering intently out the window.

Esling gave a dry hiss: "I can spy only Gladdus and Eelrid loitering about the glade. The two will drift off to their domes soon enough. It will be possible then for me to lead you past Farling's Wall."

Baus returned her a grim nod. "Very good, Esling. None of us are in moods for awkward explanations from your Wickle friends."

"They're no friends of mine," she retorted.

The time was clearly early evening and few Wickles remained roaming the glade. Only a dusky light glimmered between the plumes of high clouds. The tallest zizasters cast a melancholy shadow over the meadow.

On Esling's signal, the foursome stole across the communal ground. Silently they loped off into the woods. The little Wickle led them on a twisting trail along secret routes, away from the Wickle residences. Through carpets of bullbush and tongue-thistle, they skulked, on through waist-high mushroom and ostrich-stalk. Fairy castles of fungi clung to the elder trees like fantastic bladders. Only Galta, the screech owl, could possibly notice their passage but she sat immobile on her tall zizaster. She was a half drowsy white-faced creature that did not recognize the incongruence of their passage in the twilight.

On ginger feet the fugitives crept around the back of her perch. They cautiously edged their way past her trunk through a drooping cluster of huge blue mushrooms.

The passage went not unnoticed. With a cantankerous hoot, Galta suddenly reared herself erect and squawked an objection and hopped from branch to branch, ruffling feathers.

Baus looked up into the glinting malice of those blue hooded eyes. On wide silver wings, the owl-girl scudded back through the gaps like a phantom shadow. Darting between eerie, green-leafed limbs, she fled back to the glade where the Wickles lived.

Within moments, sounds of near-distant commotion came to everyone's ears.

"They're coming!" cried Esling fearfully.

Baus stopped short; he cocked his head. His grimace was rich with alarm and dread. There was the quiet thrum of gathering bodies and also thudding feet, the snapping of twigs, squawks, retorts, and rattling threats.

Baus gazed back through the dusky spaces with tense reflection. There were numerous fates which could befall them, none good.

He put his feet to good use, and the others followed suit. He saw glimpses of half human faces and macabre appendages through the trees- bird, elk, parakeet, bat, bear, frog, fox.

He shouldered Valere on. "Fly, if you wish to live!"

In a dog-tailed run they fled deeper into the forest. Their sweat ran full and took them grim distances.

Esling was quickest, as fleet-footed as a doe, vaulting between mushrooms and over creeks.

Over mossy-covered stones, fallen trunks and burbling brooks they scrambled and Baus and Valere helped drag Poli along, who was suffering still groggy health from his hub nightmare. The Wickles were hard on their tail and galloped furiously, mowing over toadstools and yellow spindle-rod. It seemed the whole clan was out to capture them!

The three outlaws loped after Esling with desperation rich in their eyes.

Esling slipped over the leaves like a sylph; humus and blackroot kicked up in her wake while the others stumbled on near legs of straw.

The path weaved, then parted; Esling took a sudden turn. The low ground was marked with stumps and tussocks. The Wickle herded the fugitives closer to Farling's Wall. The way was damp and slippery and great roots piled up in their path. Baus and Valere found the way impossible, almost absurdly so, and stumbled often. They loped after the Wickle as best they could, dragging Poli along with force.

Esling veered aside and disappeared into a hollow filled with bosky, bottle-green mist. Farling's Wall was still a great distance ahead. All could see the upper flanks of the rampart floating in the mist—great greasy smears of wood taunting them in the sylvan gloom.

Baus's blood ran cold. The thought of being caught in these dank lowlands made his flesh crawl. The Wickles, gripped in various phases of oestrus, were capable of horrendous acts at this time. Guided by the image, Baus urged his feet to new speed. Gladdus, swiftest of the Wickles, was on his heels. She snapped and howled; he could feel her fox-like breath lusting after him and her paws pounding with fervid and lusty enthusiasm.

Baus jerked around, hoofed her in the jowl. The fox-creature spun in a circle, landing on her haunch.

Esling re-discovered the forest path soon enough and the men struck after her. She arrived at Farling's Wall, clawing her way to the low squat door drowned in the weeds.

The door wrenched open. With a grunt, the companions burst through.

Not a moment too soon.

The Wickle army surged against the wall like a ton of battering rams. Milling and pressing, the onslaught struck, stabbing and jabbing with beaks, tongues, talons and claws menacing the wall. The elderbeasts struck at one another, trying to oust their peers and squeeze through the orifice.

Their tactics were limited.

Delay was inevitable as access was restricted to one at a time.

The companions hurtled down the slope with small hope. The river loomed darkly to their right. They were out of the Branx forest but the oily waters of the Lim gurgled unnervingly, cutting off escape. Reeds of rust-colour and sombre grey patched the surface. They surged along its shore. Phantom elms shivered in the chill vapours.

Baus herded the group closer to the first boles of phantom elm. He stared up at the purple leaves with fright and unease. The thick gloom appeared more unpleasant than that which he had left behind.

He hesitated. In his memory flashed the troupe of gigantic moths floating out to harass Sansix. A dry brittle wind had grown, rustling from the boughs, bringing a rare mist curling around the roots up from the river.

He peered back toward the sinister wall. Wickles were now streaming out of the trap door in numbers, up and down the slope like mice . . . hesitation would prove disastrous . . .

Baus quashed his trepidations. He bunted them into the mad darkness of the copse, gazing frantically through the gloomy aisles. Each aisle was a fractured glimpse of something more terrible than the last. The pursuing Wickles raged behind. The hillock's white flowers wilted with their cherry blossoms sagging from frost-bite. A chill breeze rustled through the treetops —the dry leaves crackled overhead in the amber gloaming. Despite the little chance they had, Baus felt as if it had been a hundred years since he had last left this glade and his heart missed a beat; his own presence seemed almost unreal . . .

He edged on past the place where Sansix had last met his fate. Of the villain there was no sign—only a heap of brittle white flakes where his feet had once been confined.

Baus frowned, tripped over a root; cursingly he looked up through an opening in the trees. He saw a patch of indigo sky . . . Scrambling up, he pulled his colleagues with him and they edged back closer to the wall. Out of the grove they stumbled, seemed safe. Snatching a hasty look over his shoulder, he saw a headstrong host of Wickles almost filling the air. Others straggled along to form an indomitable cluster along the knoll. From Farling's Wall to the edge of the water came Wickles of all dimensions: fat, thin, snarly, prickly, wide, base, squat. None—however—would stray past the first rank of the phantom elms. Even the furious monstrosities forming the first great line of flying foes would not proceed—though they stomped, gnashed and yammered like an explosion of angry gnats. Baus recognized the creatures as Banaga, Beargrie, Eelrid, Gladdus, Guezzela and Drizli, the elk woman.

Valere stared with eyes of vacuity. "Why do the freaks not advance on us?"

Esling croaked: "The Wickles dare venture close to the Lim only at night."

"Why? What about you?" prodded Baus.

"I am least bound by Farling's Wall," she explained, "—more human than animal. The spell does not affect me so."

"Very fortunate, but we have to leg it," moaned Poli.

"Aye! There remains less than an hour before dusk!" insisted Valere.

Esling demurred. "You must go—not I. This is where I leave you." Her expression was blank. "The way is clear—the Wickles shall not pursue you until darkness is here. Make haste! Go now! I shall lead the clan away from you, into the bushes on a false trail."

"A true martyr you are, Esling," praised Baus, studying her with new admiration, "but you cannot possibly sacrifice yourself for us. Come! Returning to the Honey Home is not an option—the Wickles will kill you. I bid you come with us."

A tear came to Esling's eye. "I—I would like very much—but—"

"But what?"

"You are men—and I am Wickle, herein lies the essential difference."

"And what of it?" Baus cried. "Is being a Wickle so singular? Poli is a bully, Valere a pirate, I am a rockgobbler hunter, so what of it?"

Esling squinted back her tears. Warm tears coursed quickly down her pale cheeks. Her shoulders trembled; her fine coral hair seemed to cling damply to her brow. "All my life I have been told that men are my enemies .

. . now—after knowing you, I can hardly believe it to be true. My heart tells me that the truth is faraway, yet it feels like such a lead weight. The tug of the forest—the wall, they all beckon me—I am not so immune to the spell after all . . . I must return to my kin, perpetuate the life of an ill-fated Wickle."

"Nonsense!" scoffed Baus. "This is complete fiction. Your sentiments betray you. Consider yourself liberated from your indenture! You are now part of our band!"

Thick emotion caught in Esling's throat. She embraced Baus with a force he was not prepared for. She pressed him a delicate kiss.

Poli made a restless movement: "Listen, lovebirds. Time is of an essence and we cannot be canoodling. Now that we have mutually included a Wickle in our company, can we now cross the river? 'Tis now or never."

Baus looked dubiously to the sky. "The river is not our friend, Poli. Aurimag is testing us. He, too, has set a zombie on our tail and will not let up until another seizes us."

Poli gave a wild cry. "It seems he has sent a zombie after *you*, not me."

"Whatever the case," grumbled Baus vexedly, "we cannot counteract Aurimag's assaults by sitting here. I am as good as dead—does that not mean anything to you?"

Poli stared lame-faced.

"Aurimag is a remorseless cur," continued Baus. "He will continue to hunt me until he catches me."

Poli screwed up his eyes. "I don't know who this Aurimag lout is, but he smacks of a pigheaded—"

"He is that and more!" cried Baus fitfully. "Do not underestimate the depths of his skullduggery! He is a manipulator, an evil-minded petty machinator. He has shrunken my friend, Weavil, to the size of a pygmy and caches him in a glass jar while he plots further depraved schemes."

Baus turned grimly to Valere. "The gibberish the zombie spoke earlier . . . I have heard of this place 'Desenion'. Perhaps we can reach it and discover clues to the whereabouts of Weavil—'tis a cave at the edge of the forest the golem said—below the phantom elm by the great river. Here is the river. We can deal with the villain and his lair when we get there."

"A tall order!" growled Valere. "Are you so certain that we could traipse all the way there through these eldritch wilds?"

"We've nothing better to do," suggested Baus.

Valere gave his head a wistful shake. "Surely . . . in your imagination at least. Well, Poli—no more of your quibbling! As I see, you are lucky to be alive—thanks to us."

Poli gave a dispirited groan. "Valere—has he duped you too? Why? For what?" But they had stopped listening. The companions scrambled deep into the shadows—shadows lengthening by the minute. In desperate hops and bounds the four left the Wickle haven far behind.

CHAPTER 3
DESENION

Says the cat to the rat:

"Is it too much, to be in touch,
With disreputable habits as these?
For this, I shall take you in my teeth and make you meat,
For what will you say, my little rodent, so sweet and fey?"

To the cat said the rat hunching on the castle steps:

"Who are you to make me shoo?
Frighten me as your vilest prey?
Are you so vain that you cannot ascertain?
Censure of the most vile conceit!?"

Says the cat to the rat on the castle steps:

"Do not be so polite, my impertinent little vermin!
For I see you verily squirming,
Under my furry paw I shall put you in my drooling maw!
So take a look and see that you've lost,
In this fine gullet before you are tossed!"

And while the white old feline was greatly entertained,
The crafty young rodent gnawed her maim,
She poked her spiny tail in his one rheumy eye,
So that she could scamper swiftly away to lie
In a dark and stony hole where rainwater seep,
While hearty young rodent did not weep,
While a mean cat stood shrilly blinking,

Redeemer

Taking fright in a rat's sneaking . . ."

—From '*Four Sad Cats*', the oldest known rhyme of Desenion.

I

Dusk was deeper than a reaper's cloak in the wilderness shrouding the river in a soft blanket. The companions struggled. Outdistancing the Wickles was no easy chore, but they feared that their efforts would be in vain if they did not maximize every precious second. Baus only hoped that they would escape a harrowing doom.

With a tenacity born of schooled survival, he propelled himself and the group into a shambling run. They hugged the river which was rich with water stump, in an intimate embrace. The lopsided moon rose in the sky, showering enough glum luminosity to show them a way. Straggly shapes hung in the dimness: ghostly gendron, peaked bottlegums, yamroot, gimp briar, hedgerot. Scratched and torn, the fugitives slogged footsore along thorny shoreline, breath rasping, legs burning. Poli finally collapsed in a heap, unable to plod another step.

His collapse was not something that could be fixed in any short time. They were all sorely in need of a rest. To carry the battle-worn Poli like a wet sack through the hinterland was not an option.

The moon bent its grinning face below the black cape of the horizon. With a pinch of dismay, the companions camped under an old yellow yew.

"I hope this is far enough away from the Wickles," murmured Baus.

Esling had no answer.

The gurgle of the river continued in the heavy, humid darkness. Little chance that the spell binding the Wickles to Farling's wall remained intact at this late hour.

Baus perked his ears. No Wickles . . . Had the brutes abandoned pursuit?

A vain hope. Baus withdrew into a brooding huddle; his lips formed a cold, cynical scowl. The hare-lipped hags more likely loitered in the dimness, waiting for the right moment to attack.

At this, the hairs on the back of Baus's neck stood on end.

A tangle of moss-covered roots offered the companions a somewhat rude shelter. They slumped themselves between roots and stumps, making crude mangers of the natural habitat while Esling clung to Baus with a passion. A long, frantic scramble through the bush had made her heated.

Baus fumbled with her damp tuft of tail and became deadened to the steamy wrigglings of her embrace—not able to bring himself to carnal course with the Wickle.

The night passed. The Wickles made no appearance. That they had eluded their scent was almost too much to hope for. Before the first glimmers of dawn, the foursome took up their flight into the growing mists, following a line of grim bottlegums that delineated the river.

The morning grew cold and wild tracts of open heath lay before them. Weeping-tussock and brindle-grasses formed the tawny-coloured mat that trembled in the wan sunlight.

The long cramped night had not revitalized anyone's spirits. All were stiff and sore and desperately famished. Poli was still enervated and pale. Accustomed to the raw things of the lands, Esling happily chewed her roots and yellow fungus and small round wilter-berries of questionable quality. A habitual ravenousness began to gnaw at the companions. Baus stopped to rub his belly; he blinked, yawned in the sullen dawn, but could find no sustenance in quick time—at least of superior quality to Esling's fungus root and bitter bottlestalk.

Farling's Wall was behind them many miles—only empty lands greeted them, all swept with a loneliness and chill of which none had experienced— only the whispers of wind and the wild patters of rain. The leagues left the mysterious wall a shivering memory in their minds. Across the Lim a silent crimson-coned forest spread. Yew and white tarn-larch grew wildly—a scene, wholly similar, to that on the opposite side of the river. Esling explained that the Branx was deserted, barren of human settlements, and the next village was much farther than guessed. Sansix had obviously miscalculated the distance between Rastule glade and 'Bickerwell'—that settlement was more like several leagues away.

Mid-afternoon brought the travellers the first signs of human habitation.

They spied a large tree bridge that cradled the river where the rapids narrowed to a rocky defile. Shoreward mallorns straddled the chasm, forming a natural bridge over the rushing water. The crafty villagers had manicured a bridge out of the trees!

Ladders and planked walkways were contructed for human convenience. On the river's farther side glimpses of log homes supporting tall peaked roofs could be seen. Through the trees came the sounds of distant music.

Baus drew his companions to colloquy. He noted that Valere and Poli were inefficiently garbed in their light blue vests from Farfus. Passable, but not for their purposes, if they did not wish to look like bargemen or chimney-sweepers. Esling's garish orange jumping costume was likewise unacceptable. They would think her a loon—or some evil cherub. Baus winced at Esling's tiny horns too; the bulging tail from her small rump—all would betray them in the end.

Frowning, he tore strips from his sleeves and wrapped them about the Wickle's hair. A crude bonnet replaced her coral-coloured mop of hair, which was in disarray. The Wickle twirled her slim frame about with coyness.

Baus bade the outlaws tear off strips from their own clothing and he stuffed them in Esling's rearquarters. The act concealed the bulging hint of tail and made her backside appear a little more normal, if that were possible. The job was tasking. Bickerwell would hopefully supply food and shelter. Hospitality and a bath would be a bonus—but without sequals, the likelihood seemed remote.

Baus sighed. How better to convey a sense of unobtrusiveness than to skip the village altogether? The answer was not forthcoming.

Baus admitted, grimacing, that they had the look of rogues about them. Neither sequals nor etiquette could allay the fact.

He recalled Zoren's fast-fading treasure, dim in his memory long moons ago across the Poesasian. His physique was bony, gaunt after days of privation; indeed, incidents as harrowing as those of the recent past would be the death of him.

Baus tucked feet up the rickety ladder. Up the boughs and high into the yew he crawled.

The others followed, hopping from tree top to tree and Esling plied gingerly at his heels.

The planks zigzagged from branch to branch and soon the river swooned below them in a roaring foam. Through the branches, the companions glimpsed a village caught precariously in a snapshot out of time. The common glade was festooned in regalia and sported pillars of yew lined in stately procession.

Odd, thought Baus. Many posts were lit up with moonlamps, and the pillars were cut of four sides and carven of eccentric faces.

Fetishes? Gods? Baus could not guess. The whole architecture seemed eerily out of place.

Two score people milled about the lawn conversing in their jaunty dialect. They danced about the glade to mazurkas and reels, dressed in leather caps and high-buckled boots. Some wore brown burnooses and rich caftans while others wore rustic jerkins of dyed leather. The glade's music began to grow in intensity and captivate the wanderers and together they drew closer, eager to join the laughter and merrymaking below, and feasting. Reconnaissance proved that tables were set about the grass with woodwork and stoneware. Pergolas adorned the flanks, many traced with white flowers and bowers sectioned off. Upscale houses and cottages seemed quaintly visible in the background—like gingerbread houses. While lamps glowed richly from the windows, Esling, who had never witnessed human settlements before, began a hasty, saucer-eyed retreat down the ladder.

Baus caught hold of her arm. Soothing her with wise words, he chuckled. "Hold tight, have courage. 'Tis not as bad as you think." The Wickle hung trance-like off his arms.

The company, hunkering possum-like in the boughs, were sighted, yet no great worry. Following Baus's lead, they dropped several notches down the ladder and began mingling with the arriving throng. Baus emanated a casual ambience that created a disarming effect on the locals. He noticed several houses of distinction in the periphery that cut deeper into the forest. A sign of a large inn—*The Lucky Wolf*—was in evidence.

Baus thought the prospects good. The village was Buskerfield, not 'Bickerwell' as Sansix had proclaimed, so a plaque announced. There were all sorts of buskers jigging about and crafting clever melodies on their zithers, lute and lyres, some antique. Reed fife, pipe, tabor, castanets and bells were not unknown, as well as banjos and two-valved cornets. Jugglers and mimes framed posturing antics to the bystanders.

Baus scratched his chin. The village seemed a more jovial district than he would have expected; larger than Farfus, and by and large, a community amiable to its artists.

Baus saw couples strolling arm in arm. Laughing and cavorting, they radiated merriness, stirring in him a pang of loneliness. Troubadours sang spirited songs. An excessive gaiety followed this place, a vigour which accompanied the most ordinary of movements—side-sweeps and high-kicks, the laughing strides and amicability. A particularly golden-whiskered troubadour stumbled forward and sang a bright ode to 'Oust', an old, wise blacksmith of Buskerfield—a tale of a hero who once had captured a trolling cabal of Wickles. The villagers were pleased with the legend and his voice rose in sonorous bursts, above the pitch of the tumult, while open-aired pavilions wafted softer music—dulcimer tones to which the folk listened with serene faces: a scene not altogether dissimilar to Farfus.

"Here you!" cried a voice from the crowd.

Baus turned, politely addressed the hailer—a rotund woman somewhat of his own age who had deigned to snatch at his arm. He pulled back with dignity. She clutched her long dangling scarf and whirled in a costume of green cowl and black boots. "Come, ye wayfarer! Grab your instrument! Do not waffle. Dance, if you will—show us your gumption. Here—take some toots on my reed fife!"

Baus respectfully declined. He deferred to Poli's expertise on the fife— need he not mention his own lack of musicianship.

The woman turned sternly to the leg—weary Poli, as did others in the group who had come to gather and scrutinize the newcomers with an expectant curiosity.

Poli grinned, though unpleasantly. Snatching up the fife and turning a sharp flash of teeth at Baus, he put fingers to stem and blew a fanciful gust that whooshed out a discordant note.

The villagers laughed with glee. "Is this all you can blow there—big blondy?"

Poli growled. True, 'twas his first essay, dry and harsh as it was but he managed to bluster out more notes, unfazed by the criticism and the sea of sniggers. He sucked in a breath and trilled out a sequence of rich notes which captivated the throng and gradually they warmed to his skill as he formed stanzas much remembered from the long-ago audition at Sloe.

The villagers stood back with interest and Baus swayed to the phrases, jerking neck like a river stork. Poli gathered wits, played faster, while the villagers swarmed about, warming to his melody, slapping their thighs in rhythm. Poli became inspired by the attention. Esling grabbed hold of Valere's arms and pulled him up to dance with her. She had never been exposed to such revelry and was ecstatic, swaying fancifully with eyes wide as saucers. Round and round she spun and Valere whirled about Poli in a high-bound fling. Poli smirked, playing on, exotically framing glissandos and flourishes, rich with parenthetical leaps which looped in the air while

Baus praised the seaman for his flamboyance.

More and more the villagers gathered to witness the astounding music. Dancers continued their manic performance. Soon there was a clapping of hands and a whooping of voices, and much dancing in syncopation. Others joined in on other instruments and Esling began to lose her cowl, a circumstance which Baus remedied by hobbledehoying over to tightly wrap it.

The outlaw marvelled at the folk of Buskerfield. They were so ingenuously festive! Odd! Could their brewed spirits be so potent?

He grabbed up a dropped hat, inspired by a new idea. He tipped the rim upside down and jigged about to the music, gesturing foolishly at it, as if it were impolite for people not to toss in a coin or two.

The gesture was not as ill-crafted as it seemed. Within an hour, he had accumulated eight sequals, a miracle of no small proportions. Buskers stared, glaring at their near empty baskets bearing not half as many coins.

Baus ignored the mutters of disparagement. Satisfied that his return should at least earn them a meal, he waved Poli to a halt.

Poli stepped back, returned the bystander her fife. He was left pale-faced from his blowing and looked ready to fall over in a swoon from a lack of nourishment.

Baus herded the troupe down the lawn toward the inn. Fortune favoured them in that the villagers, like the Farfus folk, appeared not to harbour any knowledge of outlaws . . .

Along the mallorn-flanked grassy avenue, the *Lucky Wolf Inn* showed itself as a sturdy stucco façade framed with black timbers and purple casements. The roof was steeply-sloped, showing a bric-a-brac shingling. A bakery adjoined the inn with a fish house standing next to the rear of the butchery. The inn's iron-framed door bore a tasteful plaque carved in stylish characters. Older residences showed themselves in the wooded periphery, outfitted with casements and chimney pots, contrasting in the soft plum light of the street moonlamps.

Baus's nose followed the smells of wild boar. In the taproom he discovered a cozy environment of celebratory and light-hearted patronage. The companions took a table near the back and each took turns admiring the smoke-blackened beams and the iron-decked lanterns. The smell of varnished wood and waxed floors mixed with the heady pungency of homemade mead. A half score of tables ranged around the edges where dozens of patrons clinked mugs and laughed uproariously. Many instruments hung on the walls—reed fife, bugles, shriek-horns, banjos, dosalas and shrill whistles.

Baus ordered sizeable meals of buckler, roast boar and yam soup with their new coin. The men pounced on their meal, washing it down with hearty mugs of river mead.

An unresolved feeling remained amonst their company. Esling was not accustomed to the heavy fare and she ate in mincy gulps. She would imbibe no mead and she sniffed suspiciously at the waft of Baus's froth-topped cup. None of the outlaws tendered enough coin for lodging—only two sequals remained to their name.

They traded grumbles and bent to discuss a plan of action. Esling caught curious sight of the landlord when he came for their coins, a new custom, money exchanging hands obviously meant a return for the meal. She pondered the concept with an intense curiosity and announced that she would pay for her share of food with wealth of her own.

Baus fought not to emit a chuckle. The landlord, a short, brawny, bronze-faced man, smiled with lively interest. He beckoned to Coyod the baker—a heavy-cheeked, balding man who had chanced to emerge from the back of the smoky room that shared a door with the inn.

The landlord gestured and explained Esling's desire. Coyod laughed. With a flourish of beefy hands, he spoke in a tone of sardonic condescension. His ruddy face showed a wanton goatishness that Baus did not like, nor the unctuous grin floating on his face. Like many of his peers, the baker seemed somewhat large-hearted but of false sincerity. "One or two of you vagabonds may work," he declared. "The feast of Marsipal is scheduled in three days. Folk from all parts will congregate and will require bread, fruit tarts, sugar-coated bangles and more."

"What is the pay for our services?" demanded Valere.

"Three sequals per head per night."

Poli guffawed. "You can count me out! A fare like that prompts one to rather starve."

Coyod shrugged.

Valere growled, "I'll not work for free either!"

Baus asserted his own priggish counsel. "We earned a triple wage entertaining a dozen of your villagers just an hour ago. We harbour plans to accumulate more wealth in upcoming days."

"Then do that," grunted Coyod. "A laudable ambition. I leave you to it. Take my offer or leave it."

Esling, having no aversion for money, wagged her head with fledgling exuberance. "I like work! I did it all the time for free for Paiesmy and Graietch!"

The baker nodded fondly. He seemed to understand the Wickle's nature. "A lively little lass you have here! A bit doe-faced, but toss off her turban and tuck in her behind and you've got yourself a respectable mistress." His belly wriggled at his joke and his oily speculation spilled from his coarse maw. He looked down appraisingly at Esling's dumpy haunch. "Well—not to be too critical, easy to trim down those straw buttocks!"

Baus fixed the baker a venomous look. "I'll not hear such vulgar talk directed at one of my friends."

"No need for prickliness, pilgrim!" he chuckled. "I have my own lassies on the go—and new ones too."

"That is good to know," remarked Baus coldly. "Now, kindly take your leave and return to the kitchen. Prepare your 'fruity tarts' or sugar-bangles, whatever you do. We have important affairs to set in motion; Esling included."

"Esling, eh? We shall have to see what 'Esling' decides."

Much to Baus's dismay, the Wickle seemed obstinately determined to work for the baker and pay her own way.

"Well," croaked Baus, nonplussed, "if you are so determined, go ahead!" He offered her an open arm.

Esling turned Baus a phlegmatic look. She trotted off with Coyod and they disappeared next door. Baus was not happy with the development and now the companions settled into a dim crouch around the fire, swallowing memories of the chill nights and the disgusts they had endured. All looked hungrily to the kitchen.

Villagers had arrived in numbers—farmers, labourers, fishermen, musicians.

Baus rolled up his sleeves. He thought to engage the villagers in grand talk.

A thin-boned man garbed in a rough cloak peered sharply at the outlaw. "I remember you!" he drawled. "You are one of those buskers-newly arrived from across the river—on the treeway."

"That's correct," said Baus, noncommittedly. "We came from Farfus."

He made a sweep of arm with dignity.

The man gave him an admiring stare. "Farfus? That's a fair ways. Did you come across any Wickles?"

"That we did; what do you think?" Valere showed a rim of mirthful teeth. "Several hags wished to infect us with their cursed blights, but we showed them the folly of their ways, didn't we Poli?"

"Nothing less!" growled Poli. "'Tis the penance we inflict on freaks who attempt to subjugate us."

"Impressive!" cried the man. "You are truly a trio of stout souls!"

Another fellow with salt and pepper beard moved closer with an air of brio. He had a thick-curled moustache and a leathery face, sunburnt lines speaking of much outdoor toil. "Do you think," he inquired, "—to hump it back to Farfus in one piece?"

"The Wickles have long memories," rumbled Baus solemnly.

"You have risked a blight already, why not another?" His watery eyes showed a teasing mischievousness which prompted a fretful grimace from Baus. "The challenge is poignant, but hardly practical. Why tempt fate when a foolhardy impulse might lead one to riding a Wickle hub?"

"Wise words. I see you are no greenhorn."

Baus nodded. "We guard more ambitious projects at hand. What can you tell us about the lands to the north—or are they just mythical unknowns?"

The white beard chuckled. "If it's trade you seek, go to Loust. There's the Busker's capital of the world!—Not a league more than five up the northway. You'll find everything you need—women, wine, festivity, or my name's not Coistax."

Baus frowned with cultivated care. "We shall not skip off to regions unfamiliar to become dalliers—despite the tempting prospect of maids. We seek Desenion."

A hushed silence descended over the gathering. The patrons seemed to arch their brows, to stare at the outlaw with stiff discomfort. A splayed-nostrilled labourer leaned forward, offering a croak, "That's a foolish wish!"

"What do you mean by that?"

Distrust warred with his hostility. "'Tis a long way to Desenion, a ghostly long way . . ."

"Call it a whim—a healthy curiosity," declared Baus heartily.

"Well, if it's your destination," piped up Coistax, "perhaps I can offer you some insight: the castle's cursed and spurned by those of decent mind.

Old Viluven, the last of Owlen's kings, was rejected by Mirkana, Desenion's loveliest princess, and laid waste the area. The fair hair's hand was promised in marriage by her father, king Tirimes, to Viluven—but the harlot backpedalled on her duty—ran away with her lover, Rioulk the busker, to the Nderian hills. He laughed. "Meanwhile Viluven wreaked his wrath. Now there are only two villages across the Lim—Xes and Tolnun. Desenion was reduced to near ruin and remains a ghost town."

"What of Mismerion?" inquired Baus.

The bespectacled man, Elergin shook his head with a hint of repugnance. "Mismerion! 'Twas once the capital of the western provinces—now a home to a coven of mages and neomancers. It was once run by pious rich lords as would oppress the peaceful labourers."

"Aye," croaked Coistax, "the magickers of Mismerion are wont to inflict spells on people and work their mischief than put their magic to good use. Fie! Hundreds of years ago, I heard that Lord Kreo was resident—one of the Arch-Neons. He had given up the keys to the castle to grant the rest of his entourage an 'inheritance'."

Elergin pinched his face into a frown. "What a lot of humbuggery, Coistax. My advice is to stay clear of Mismerion—and Desenion too; they are both places of evil, full of desolation."

Baus gave his head a fretful shake. "We are on a mission of scholarly import. We brook no delay!"

Baus saw that the white beard's expression remained questioning, an indication he thought the remark artless.

"Then have it your way! Jequ, serve these braves a round of mead on me! Where are my blasted tankards? Undoubtedly our new friends are thirsty!"

Valere dipped his head in grinning salute.

The landlord appeared and cheers arose. Elergin motioned to the publican to replenish all their mugs. A smile trickled out of the corner of his mouth. "We Buskerfielders are always welcoming of new folk," he said generously. "We would invite you to join us in a small round, of 'Spin the Cones', say—at least before you go gallivanting around the countryside, losing all your coins to vandals and the bellies of tasms."

Baus's eyes glowed with disapproval. "I begrudge the prediction—all things considered we are quite hardy when it comes to prowling the wilds. I imagine your intent was only to evoke a spirit of jest, was it not? What game is this 'Spin the Cones'?"

"'Tis 'Fool's Gambit'—or 'The Ruse of the Roustabouts' as it's popularly called in these parts."

Baus raised brows with wonder. "Drakes alive! Sounds likes an intricate game. And yet the game seems familiar—"

Elergin gave his head an easy shake. "The fact is secondary. A diversion, no less; 'tis like dice, but not."

Baus feigned a last moment's indecision. "Very well, but you must counsel us as to rules of play. This is the least courtesy."

The gamester nodded urbanely. "Not at all. Yes, yes, no worries, pilgrim. We will teach you finer points of the game—won't we, Coistax?"

"Surely we will! If I'm not Coistax, Councillor of Buskerfield! Come, Simperstoy! Bardo! Gather your lard butts around. You've heard our friends! A tournament is in order! Four is the minimum number of players!"

A iron-grey bearded man clapped a staff on the floorboards. "What about me? Am I Chief Dung-gatherer around here?" The gentleman sprang limberly to his feet and peered crossly on his peers.

"An oversight," consoled Elergin.

The goatherder Ingerstand was not mollified.

The gamesters moved over to an unoccupied table near the window and each wrestled with his own satchel of painted cones to drop them on the table.

Baus detected a waft of chicanery and voiced an impassioned outcry: "Why the flurry of peculiar odd-carved cones? I warn you! We are not mooncalfs. I will tolerate no duplicity. Our combined wealth consists of only a few sequals."

Black-bearded Bardo clicked his dark tongue with friendly assurance. "'Tis a paltry sum, pilgrim, but let us not bat heads over trifles; one sequal is as good as any—eh, Elergin?"

"Exactly so, Bardo! You are a clever fellow and I am glad of your company!" Coistax congratulated his peer, slapping him hard on the back. "I bid we commence our enterprise—with merriness and ease!"

"A favourable plan!" called Coistax. "Come, let us play."

The Councillor produced a leather satchel full of oddly-planed mallorn cones. They were faceted with multi-coloured symbols—face on face, the tokens were unconventional and Baus and Valere looked upon them with expressions of confused wonder.

"Regard the symbols," Coistax exhorted. "Skulls, Sticks, Crosses and Hatchets. These sigils are important! Study them with care! Insofar as the motifs are concerned, they impart suggestions—pastiches, glimpses, of hierarchy and value, more noteworthy than elegant. Here! A fact of note— we work in pairs. Each team attempts to foil the other. Two men only per team. Skulls defeat Sticks. Crosses defeat Skulls. Hatchets defeat Crosses. Sticks defeat Hatchets. Are we clear?"

The outlaws framed hesitant nods.

"Good! Each representation has an edge and a bane. The team that affords the minimum losses is declared victor and procures the spoils. Is this not easy?"

Valere nodded a curt affirmation. "The assertion is over-placating but I will allow it. Clearly the game is plain perhaps to those who have had years of practice."

"Come now, Redbeard! Do not trumpet whimperings in this arena. 'Tis well known that grousing betokens the mark of an ingrate."

Valere gritted teeth and bent to voice sharp words, but Ingerstand the goat-herder jumped in and voiced his endorsement, "Yes, redbeard! We'll have no morose banter around here!"

Baus and Valere accepted the attitudes. They teamed together, while new players joined the scene in numbers: Flugo, a yellow-haired flutist; Tofax, a beefy miner; Elergin and Coistax were paired as partners on the right who sat craftily across the table wearing indulgent smiles. Simperstoy and Bardo hunched opposite with no less surety.

Baus felt a vague uneasiness about the game.

Grimy hands were rubbed and oily grins were traded. Flugo and Tofax sat glittery-eyed across from him like bailiffs. Papus and Gomglo sat between Poli and Baus, obviously muscular village smiths.

Cones loosed from hands; dice were set spinning dizzyingly across the table. The first round won Baus and Valere a single sequal and they congratulated themselves. On the next round, they lost the pot and each made a great display of gnashing teeth under warm lamplight when their pledged coins were forfeited by the Coistax's superb tosses and Elergin's valiant *Crosses* which made havoc with Valere's *Skulls* and Baus's *Sticks*.

Elergin extended his sympathy. "My peers' tosses were only lucky gambits, pilgrims. Perhaps owing to an ebullient spirit perhaps heightened by mead. Take no heed. They are agile people and eager to throw, but will not likely win again."

Baus nodded tersely. He conceded their last sequal to the pot, which Coistax very much accepted, ogling the losers and cautioning them upon the merits of persistence when the chips were down, especially when stakes were invariably as modest as that in the company of easy fellowship.

Bardo wagged his head with cheery agreement. Coistax was congratulated on the broadness of his doctrine, and here too, Baus had to admit that his own philosophy seemed at least sanguine. When the next cones were drawn, Baus aimed his projectile on a side-winding loop that had numerous eyes spinning.

Baus chuckled. The flamboyance of his toss was not purely original. He had watched Zoren many times perform the same dexterity a hundred times over against the more savvy cutthroats on his ship. Pinching face into a frown, Baus pulled ever so delicately on the projectile with third and index finger to spin the cone with marvel while Valere grinned on like a fish. The Buskerfield gamblers smacked their foreheads and grumbled oaths, crying out when their wager was lost and jingling coins changed hands.

More rounds were played—a tense period ensued which gained Baus and Valere substantial coinage. Simperstoy the shoemaker called out a bald threat regarding thamauturgy at play. He claimed that the cadence of the game was too slow; he bade fair play to be upheld.

Baus objected to the oversimplification. The shoemaker's ploy to undermine their winning streak failed. Baus and Valere won rounds with more agility. Nuggets clinked in their pockets, rattled in fists.

The Buskerfielders suspected trickery; they began searching the foreigners' pockets for signs of knavery.

No false cones or questionable articles could be discovered.

Elergin loosed a wheezy sigh.

Simperstoy and Coistax accused Baus and Valere of being sinister magicians. Perhaps they should never have been admitted to the game. Baus and Valere repudiated the suspicion. The outlaws offered their condolences and pitched more conservative throws which earned them ties or at worst losses. With a modicum of suspicion allayed, they escalated their tactics to winning strategies.

Hours passed and mugs were filled and refilled. Ornery accusations and belches resounded from the mouths of round-bellied tradesmen and hatchet-faced labourers. There were loud boasts, japing threats and coarse bluster.

Quips reigned too, with lewd overtones and blowhard displays involving knives and swords.

The passage of more coins continued from the pockets of the Buskerfielders to the outlaws Baus, Valere and Poli who continued to swig ale and offer shrugs of amazement when the villagers finally begged them to relinquish their wealth in exchange for gifts.

"Gifts?" inquired Baus. "What gifts are you talking about?"

Coistax gave them a terse flourish. "Nothing ornate, or bearing any over-description. View these!" He offered his wegmor whip, his flap cap and brand new bootlaces and a wedge of melted chocolate which Bardo offered along with a pocket knife and a double-ringed compass. Flugo pitched in a reed pipe and an old dog whistle. Tofax brought forth a ferrule of explosive and another of varying size which he clutched greedily in his coal-sooted hand.

Baus and Valere exhibited casual interest in the devices, but nothing too apparent. The miner explained that through the use of explosives, he and his workmates quarried the smalt-stone hollowed deep in Fargull forest. "A ring of the little destructos removes all burden of obstruction." With flashing teeth he presented palms in proud format. "With this—the orneriest of barriers is obviated with the mere lighting of a single wick."

Baus exhibited a peculiar wonder. "A marvel, indeed! But why the second capsule so grey and limp compared to its peer, all bright red?"

Tofax indicated the ferrule with smiling urgency. "The exchange of colour is a misconception. The colour switch means a composite only of a 'flare disc', while the other is a singular blunderbust of potency. When fired, the flare brightens, see? It illuminates a miner's tunnel in case of mishap."

"An excellent innovation."

Valere gave his head a brief wag. "Such items—" he motioned carelessly "—particularly the blunderbust—could prove useful in days ahead."

The outlaws relinquished their pile of sequals and swung back into the game, only to win back most of their losses in a single round.

By the end of the game, exhaustion finally won out and the Buskerfielders could no longer keep afloat. All, including Baus, Poli and Valere lay slumped in chairs with fellow gamblers, faces pressed to the table, snoring and wheezing, comatose. The pot boy came to collect the mugs—the dues, surprisingly, came to an amount just exactly matching the outlaws' earnings . . .

* * *

Hours passed. The fire dwindled. Cool embers winked from the fireplace. The lamps dimmed to slits of luminescence.

Suddenly a muted howl issued from the bakery—'twas a hound's hop away from where the gamesters' sprawled.

Baus jerked immediately to his feet. The cry had been forced—a low whine, wailing and pleading, unmistakeably Esling's.

Baus was beside himself. He looked about. He was flushed with mead. A mounting anxiety had him muttering and cursing. The Wickle should never have gone off! he told himself. She should have returned long ago.

He hauled himself to the kitchen, closer to the dismaying sound. Valere and Poli snored happily away at the table, noses pressed in their pools of ale. Baus cursed himself for not rousing them. He propelled his feet to the battened door near the side-kitchen, only to find it locked.

Rotten luck! Baus kicked open the door in a fury.

The chamber beyond was empty. The smell of burning wood permeated the air. The dim light revealed a tub of dough, piled high on the table, lumped in heaps. Two barrels of flour were propped up against the nearby wall along with a stack of bread shovels.

The space was rich with the scent of baked goods, which sickened Baus at the moment, but devoid of activity. Where was Coyod? Odd! Coals glowered redly in the bread oven. From where had the cry originated?

Baus marched further within. Suddenly he caught sight of Coyod. The baker was hunched behind one of the dough tubs, cozied up to Esling in an oafish posture. He was in the process of attempting a deeper familiarity, to which Esling was not amenable, pinned down in so shameful a sprawl over the table, and hoping to avert an eager act. She efforted to elude the portly baker's greasy clutches with her bonnet and jumpsuit peeled back. Now, the lecherous face of Coyod showed a greasy grin. Oily hands groped down to her bare skin in a manner of rude handling. But before Esling could react, the lout had suddenly cognized the horns on her brow and gave a strangled cry.

Outrage mastered his disgust. He grabbed the Wickle by the hair and dragged her across the floor. "Wretch! Demon! So you would hoodwink me with some freakish spell of yours. You pose amidst our persons as a decent dame, only to be a cursed Wickle? Well—we shall see about that!"

He raised his bread shovel over his head and Baus vaulted over with a thundering rush. He landed the baker a painful kick in the abdomen. The man did not crumple—or even bend over. He lurched with sinister speed and feinted at Baus's lower limbs. The outlaw was ready to draw his sword, but the fat man was faster. Elbowing Baus in the ribs, Coyod hefted the bread shovel and smashed it down hard between Baus's shoulder blades.

Dazed, Baus fell and shook the haze out of his skull. He was deprived of breath. Stars winked. In the mist he saw a lecherous shape abandoning Esling and shuffling for the door. The Wickle was crawling on her hands and knees over to the far end of the room.

Spooked and outraged, the baker stumbled back. He was out into the common room and many stony words spewed from his mouth: "Awake, you bibulous imbeciles! Get your ropes and your knives! We have with us here a Wickle. A lynching is in order!"

Staggering, Esling hunched back in fright. Baus consoled her. He looked first one way and the other. No way out of the bakery. Only the door to the taproom looked accessible. An iron-studded portal fronted the pastry room.

Limping over, he tried to claw back the heavy bar. No luck. The thick wood was locked—no doubt Coyod's doing should anyone try to discover his clandestine activities.

A small dark window showed a high spot above, but 'twas too high for reaching.

Frantically Baus looked about for an avenue of escape. There seemed no accessible alternative. With wild understanding, it dawned in him that he had no choice but to pull Esling out into the taproom.

Coyod was in the process of slapping palms upon Bardo. With others, he was jolted out of his stupor and lights flamed from the kitchen. Bannik the innkeeper's sleepy growls rose and now the tavern was alive with motion. Valere and Poli raised heads in perplexity.

Hands moved to weapons. Baus staggered on his heels, clutching at his blade.

Valere and Poli scrambled to their feet amidst a sea of benches and tables. Understanding that Esling's cover had been blown, they upset stools, trying to secure a line of exit.

Tofax lurched to his feet, venting an open-mouthed threat. A mad dash to the door had him plunging a leg between Valere and Poli. Valere belted him in the teeth and the bumpkin went flying over the bench.

Esling, whose horns were bared in plain sight, had the men growling and cursing.

"She means you no harm!" Baus cried out in disgust. "Are you all a bunch of lily-livered cravens? Look—would you let your mutton-headed superstition bully you into wrong conclusions?"

Coyod essayed to rally his supporters. "Hurry men. Stab them! Slash!"

Coistax hesitated. "Here now, Coyod! The outlander speaks sensibly. Leave the poor dame alone. Krakens! You must have looked the maroon groping her, but enough of your spleen—this Wickle's as harmless as a bunny."

"Shut your mouth, you foolish politician! I don't care if she's a crooning dabchick. You know our laws—it's a lynching for all of them if we catch them—*no exceptions*. Remember—who is it that steals our sons whom we never chance to see again?"

Stares of hostility fixed on Esling. A phalanx of mingled hatred stared back at them.

Baus reacted before it was too late. He knew there would be no appeal. For all their jocularity, these oafs had the hardbitten edges of bigotry bred into their bones.

They converged on the companions who took up a circle around Esling. Knives flashed; swords clinked. Amongst the rabble was black-toothed Bardo and slab-jawed Coyod. A loose-limbed Simperstoy thrust out a fist.

Valere slashed out at Bardo. The lout fell with a thud. Poli stabbed down at Simperstoy; the lackwit crumpled to his knees.

Frightened out of her wits, Esling ran between the men and the fire, brimming with haunted terror. Baus leaped over to save her from Elergin's outstretched hand. He missed her narrowly and the knife jab in the ribs. Coyod leaped in to pull Esling to her doom, but Baus plunged Lolispar up to its haft in his thigh. The baker let out a shriek and froghopped about the taproom, clutching the fast reddening smear about his upper thigh.

Teeth-clenched, Baus, chivalrous to the end, held a penchant for righting injustices committed against women, even a Wickle.

He snatched at Esling and hurtled her toward the door. Poli and Valere were on their heels. The three burst out of the tavern and with Esling fled down the grassy boulevard toward the main road.

The Wickle was faster, far in the lead, but to Baus's dismay, she was swiftly disappearing into the darkness. "Esling!" he cried with alarm. "Not that way. We'll be caught. It's worse to fight it out in the open—into the trees! The river is not far!"

Heeding the advice, she cut down a back alley and sped between the shadow-drenched smithy and the smoke-stained shadows which marked the tannery.

Baus and his cronies made a final dash through the blackness and the narrow confine of manicured mallorns. Overhead yew spanned and ghostly walkways looming thickly against the pale, moon-washed sky. To their right a break in the shrubs. The silver-stained Buskerfield glade lay open for flight.

All fled to the forest. Cries of dismay flared behind them. The copse was filled with raging shouts. None looked back.

Redeemer

II

Contrary to Ulisa's counsel, Trimestrius had not struck out directly for his forsaken homeland. He had carved his way along several surreptitious corridors overland through hushed forests, untamed glades, brooding copses, avoiding towns and villages, travelling by narrow, root-riven trails at night. He had managed to avoid perilous beasts and dangers to his credit—and ridicule—so dwarfly configured was he to the size of a young toddler by Aurimag's thaumaturgy. His quiet woodsman's feet knew no fatigue—he was driven with an impulse to reach his destination. Never had his thirst left him for revenge on his enemy!

The dirk clinked at his side; his boots tramped through the ferns. The blade was 'borrowed' from the back of a robber's packbeast, acquired when the foursome of 'peasant bandits' or what looked like them, had paused to drink from a creek when their wagon was parked abreast a knoll. With an uncomplicated skill, the little nobleman had managed to snare wood pigeons, grouse and squirrels by means of his woodcraft taught by his sire's squire and so did he survive. Fried meat on spears of whittled wood were adequate to his needs.

The nobleman rocked on his haunches. He reckoned he had passed some thirty nine days on the road since the last northland meeting with Ulisa. Now, five leagues west of Desenion nestled in a hollow abreast the eerie river Lim, he felt the weird sensation of fatigue and anticipation prickling at his scalp, while sitting wetly and entirely bedraggled amongst clumps of dripping ferns.

He studied the dank crevice that intruded upon the hill that granted entrance to a very large cave. The nobleman's gaze was attentive—also scowling with an innate scepticism. A sombre pall permeated the hillside to shroud it in cloying mist. Marmor calcification hung out in rope—like configurations and roots and mossy clumps clung to the edges of the hole like outlandish bangs.

The small man resisted the urge to breach the cave. 'Twas not an environs to be taken lightly. Prior knowledge told him that the presence of certain 'sprites' were employed as guardians by his enemy. Those seeking to enter Aurimag's lair prepared for death. Many years earlier the nobleman had witnessed such a pair of foolhardy wayfarers make the specific mistake of entering Aurimag's abode. Their screams were hideous, their howls ear-jarring as their souls were wrenched from their bodies, pulled into a blinding blur of nth order anarchy . . .

The nobleman shivered. He did not want that fate. The seconds seemed to pass like hours. Lavender gloom quickly lapped against the hidden crannies of the hill while he tipped his cap over his eyes. He lay down in the cool foliage, allowing himself a nap.

He awoke in the wee hours, disturbed by a sudden shuffling in the undergrowth.

He started up, eyes glued to the crevice where he was startled to see a moving shape—a dim form edging itself obliquely amongst the boulders.

Trimestrius almost fell back down the hill he was so surprised. Who was this? Aurimag was known to venture little from his cave. The rocks were dimly illumined: grey and mauve under the nacreous moonlight. Out of the black shadows, a chill figure crept unseen.

He clamped his mouth; he did not trust his lips. Aurimag? Why was the figure shambling so weirdly? The villain seemed to emerge from the dark as some gawky puppet—as if he were rudely hewn, or out of sorts . . .

Trimestrius frowned. Had the blackguard been imbibing ale? Such was unlikely, the fastidious fellow he was. He chided himself, for his imagination was not usually this wanton, but the figure's motions were jerky, as if his frame were maimed or had been delivered some insidious blight.

Trimestrius failed to recognize the meaning of the movements and stifled a grunt. He thrust the questions out of his mind. He knew to blunder forth was an act bound for destruction. Revenge was his only bitter desire—yet better served in brine . . .

No, weapons and snares were useless against Aurimag's magic. Necessary acquisitions, however, if he were to capture the wretch unawares.

Fast disappearing into the shadows was the graceless shape which stumbled down the wooded slope toward the river. The river's lisps were faint and Trimestrius followed not half way down before he heard an unseemly sliding, as of some craft being dragged down upon the water.

His muscles knotted into coils. The shuffling subsided; the little nobleman crept back to his hiding place, taking care not to alert the figure in the small craft.

His quarry was escaping! A discouraging emotion gripped him. What now? None the wiser was he of his mark's purpose, or the conniving furtiveness he perceived, outside of an urge to paddle downward toward the village of Lillenvir.

Sadly Trimestrius poked his way toward Desenion. He followed the faint wolf's trail etched along the outer feet of the steep slope. He avoided virulent herbs—bottle stalk, canyon root, witch hazel. Yet a vindictive spark burned in his eyes, fuelled of a fever lit of passion to avenge himself on his tormentor.

Into the cloying shadows Trimestrius passed from sight—a small pygmy in a big world of bleak shapes.

* * *

Three leagues south and east, Baus, Poli, Valere and Esling trooped speedily down a root-jutted path adjacent the river. The way was narrow and dim. 'Twas no more than a reckless plunge to nowhere. For the meantime, the path meandered, staving off pursuit by the Buskerfielders, yet was likely to peter out soon.

They dogged on, tripping over vines and roots, keeping to the shadows, cautious of roving beasts and predators.

The forest became denser. Soon moonlit limbs loomed overhead like thick ropes: 'twas a tapestry woven of disquieting shapes, forming an almost sinister canopy.

For a time Baus and his companions remained unmolested, but the condition could not be guaranteed and, biting back apprehension, Baus recalled the angry curses of the Buskerfielders. So much abhorrence and fear over these Wickles! Over a creature so timid! The scenario seemed laughable, yet it had almost got them killed.

So life went.

Mist wreaths hovered over the river. Chill fog rose and fell from the hollows, obscuring the moon glowing like a galleon on the horizon of darkness.

Baus reflected: the futile mad-scrambles of the villagers and their own frantic flight . . . what a wretched way to live!

Baus gave himself a disconsolate swat on the crown. The so-called 'gallant' life of the outlaw was a ridiculous wives' tale! Certainly his own sardonic chuckle caught in his ears—a hollow and cruel sound born of mockery.

Poli sensed Baus's thoughts and uttered a hoarse croak. "I can hardly believe that there was a time when I was a free man—perhaps back in Nosoheath, or that grease-pit, the *Hungry Mariner*. I traded all that—for this!" He spread his hands in a laughing spite.

Valere gave an apathetic murmur. "Perhaps not the best comparison, Poli."

Poli flapped his arms in irony. "Then what? Even if we survive this ordeal and make it to this Desenion, what then?"

Baus did not answer. He had a certain vision of how it would all end; indeed had developed a sense of detachment to the whole affair. Yet ever since his companions had fled Fauche near the coastal road, things had gone steadily downhill—Wickles, pitch-forks, privation, fear and terror. How could he blame his friends? After all, he was the instigator of it all.

Poli raised an irate protest. "You heard what that golem said: '*A cave under the single phantom elm*'. Do you think that we are actually going to find such a cave amongst the hundred hidey-holes along the river?"

Baus held forth hands. "It doesn't hurt to try."

The blond bully thrust a heavy palm to jerk Baus around. "Let's say you confront this mage. What then? If he's as powerful as you say, what chance do we have against him?—we are a piddly rag-tag of dilettantes!"

Baus flashed his Poli a reproving glance. "Much, if we're clever, Poli— quieten down."

"I'll not quieten down!" Poli growled. "Can you knock some sense into his skull, Valere? Better we scramble to Loust like the Buskerfielder said, than march against a loutish sorcerer and his army of ghouls."

Valere frowned. "I for the most part, am in accord with that plan. Though, Aurimag, I think, is in need of a dressing-down. Perhaps a reckoning. He is not that invulnerable. He must have a weakness."

"What then?" quipped Poli. "Are we to trundle a hundred leagues to perform this service and risk our skins?"

"Enough of the grousing!" warned the seaman.

"As I told you, Poli," appeased Baus, "This rogue Aurimag will stop at no ends to exact his vengeance on me. The fact that you are my company, puts you in the line of fire too. Like it or not, you are as involved as I—do not doubt it."

Poli suppressed his bitterness.

"Who is this Aurimag anyway?" asked Esling speaking for the first time.

"He's a detestable magician," grunted Baus. "'Twas he who despatched the golem that assaulted your Honey Home."

The Wickle's eyes grew round. "Why would he do that?"

"'He is somewhat of an evil baboon, and has a somewhat vested interest in me," muttered Baus. "I've rubbed him the wrong way, or something like that."

"What he means to say," grumbled Valere, "is that he sabotaged one of his magic tricks back in Heagram and got himself on the bad side of the magician. He was thrown in jail—a very foolish error, which has had us running ever since."

"A slight exaggeration—but essentially true," admitted Baus.

"How can the golem find us?" Esling asked wide-eyed.

"It can't," replied Valere. "The thing is strapped in Graeitch's hub, don't you remember?"

"What happens if it escapes the thaumaturgy?" mused Poli grimly.

Baus flourished a hand. "Aurimag's power is waning. I'd rather face him head on now than have him sneak up on me unawares while I sleep."

"A wise idea," said Valere.

All fell silent.

The path strayed ahead into darkness. Damp mist and coiled fog brought them to a near halt. Earthy odours floated about eerily. Sinister fronds dripped with a cold dew and a few blue stingrays hummed by in twos and threes.

The first rays of dawn gradually edged through the miserable gaps in the trees and the ancient trunks glowed with a soft luminescence. The foliage remained limned in the first radiant hues of morn: amber and mauve.

The company lengthened their strides. Mid-morning brought the river to their left, a desultory light drying the mist. The mallorns, tall and feathered with blossoms, disbanded their march up the river and verdant pastures took their place, hugging the riverside, replacing the depressing water stumps and bog shrub that had become their habitual vista.

The day was young; a cool glare remained muted by soft cirrus. There was a silent loneliness gathering here. As the hours passed, the company grew ever more ruminative—not without some strains of unease. Poli's words seemed to have cast a shroud over all of them. Perhaps they would fall to Aurimag's machinnations?

There were no signs of roads, or inhabitants or grazing animals—just rock-strewn hills beginning to mount the river's flanks. Grasslands gave way to boulders and scree. The lands were old, untenanted by man or beast, shunned by the world, and growing somewhat desolate in the afternoon glow. Baus felt a hollowness in his guts, a signal that portended woe.

Westward the Lim snaked, winding a lustreless path amongst a wide white ravine, cut out in the shape of a ship's hull, pitched full of scree.

Boots crunched over the water-worn rocks; still the hills fled higher. Baus was amazed how high they soared so far inland. Studded outcrops glinted silver and white in the thinning light. Stunted mallorns crept up the slopes, clinging in small clots with ghost oak. Goats and unyoked wegmor now went roaming in small numbers.

The bleached distances grew hazy, showing several figures ahead. Baus spied a twain of wayfarers, trundling alongside an approaching wagon. They veered close to the river, possibly an unfavourable sign in this barren landscape.

The company halted. The encounter with the Wickles had left them somewhat hypersensitive to skulduggery. Curiosity overcame apprehension and Baus struck out with boldness, the seasoned wayfarer always . . .

His peers trailed back several paces. The locals ahead proved to be a group of fur-hooded men bundled in ragged bear-skins. They commanded a rickety cart that was drawn by a single wegmor. The wagon itself was half filled with odd-looking stumps and bunches of bundled firewood—possibly gathered from the sparse terrain to the north, but of this Baus could not be certain. He spied a set of axes and other arcane tools hidden in the back of the wagon, also a corked jug of mead amidst a sprawl of branches. The wegmor, tired and old, was equipped with a pair of sawn-off horns. Quietly the beast drank from the water while upriver, a faint way lanced its way up into hills, obviously the path the cart-riders had come down, disappearing amongst faint clefts.

Squinting into the sun, Baus gave them a jovial greeting. They only gave him a solemn scrutiny. The foremost: a broad-shouldered, black-eyed man, had a corded neck and ham-like hands. His partner, somewhat pug-faced and gangly, gazed on with sober concern while scratching his stubbled jowl.

Baus frowned. For the most part this twosome looked ill-formed.

"We are logcutters from a nearby village," declared the first man after a time. "We come to water our nag,"

"Logcutters, you say?" remarked Baus, raising an eyebrow. He motioned casually to the man's weird cargo. "I see no logs here—only miles of stumps and scree. Perhaps you might want to change your locale."

The remark elicited little humour. Winking at his partner, the former answered in bleak patois. "Your eyes are not trained as ours. We see the special qualities of wood, the *kumboyh*. There is singular energy in these trees growing along the Lim's periphery, peculiar to these parts only."

"Indeed," cried Baus, slightly put out.

"Aye, 'tis bog-root," explained his partner. "Imona, the wood carver of Aurenham, pays good sequals for us to scout out the bog-root cuts for her in these parts and she can craft her weather totems and communicate with the weather-demiurges."

"This sounds like an intricate science."

"'Tis a study of vast import," admitted the logcutter.

"You are men of obvious erudition beyond my ability," offered Baus deferentially. "I must yield to your expertise." A more slantwise peering upon the wagon proved that the eldritch waterlogged stumps akin to another Wicklish experiment—half plant, half fish curiosities—eerie, offensive things. But the gills had been closed and the flaps were near shorn to hardened crusts.

Baus shook his head sadly. The sweat and groggish breath of these two had begun to undermine his sense of goodwill.

"For the nonce," the first cutter rambled on with garrulous ease, "Nit and I gather faggots on our return leg to Xes to feed our fires."

"Xes, you say?" cried Baus. "I have heard of Xes before—a sister to Desenion. Your village then is nearby?"

"Up the hill and around a few bends—perhaps a league or more," the man motioned.

"This is good to know."

The husky man's companion swept a crabbed hand to the hills. "Just as notable as Tolnun, the village where I grew up."

Valere, Poli and Esling had chanced to catch up and appraised the locals with uncertainty.

Nit's jaw drooped when he caught sight of the Wickle. "A Wickle in your midst? Yebar! Look at the brown horns—the aberrant brow!"

Yebar's cry was one of strangled displeasure.

Esling's cheeks drooped. She fled in behind Baus, hunching in shame.

Baus stroked the Wickle's shoulders and consoled her with soft words. He turned to the woodcutters. "Mind your manners!" he cried. "Esling is a creature of impeccable valour. How is she of threat to you? Your loutishness reflects the insensitivity of a boor!"

The woodcutters grumbled but showed no sympathy. Pity and understanding dawned in Baus regarding the Wickles' fate—always being driven from the world, yet simultaneously yearning to be part of it.

"Do what you must," retorted the first woodcutter. "But guard your company well. I shall never trust a Wickle! Give her to me and I'll strip her of her hide and take the axe to her neck. Come Betsy!" he drawled at the nag. Coaxing the mare rudely along, he muttered, "Let us move on to our village."

"Wait!" cried Baus. "We seek Desenion. Where is it? Do you know of it?"

The small man flung a knotty fist up river. "There." Baus squinted in the haze and barely discerned the vestiges of some stone bridge, half ruined.

"'Tis is in that direction, stranger—across the ancient overpass and beyond the spur. Do not say we didn't do anything for you. But there you will find no comforts, or sympathy." The last sentence trailed off in a somewhat eerie growl.

Valere stepped in with impatience. "Explain yourself, if you would, sir!"

"The royal keep has been deserted for years. The folk fled the ghost citadel and sought asylum in Xes a long time ago—a story better for nighttime telling over mugs of ale."

"Though we lack the ale, we are all ears."

The log cutters mulishly hitched up their wegmor and made ready to go.

Valere uttered a sharp curse.

"My only other counsel is to mind the storks," muttered Yebar with a sardonic flavour.

Disliking the remark, Valere moved in to extract a compelling clarification. Likewise Baus unsheathed Lolispar, but the louts had turned away, offended by the display of iron and offered only mocking grunts. "Put away your toys before you hurt somebody." Yebar turned to his companion, but a telling glance from his crony had him hopping in the wagon. "The storks," he shouted back, "get cranky at times, so best be on your guard."

Nit laughed, his grin widening, but he showed no indication of shedding any light on his comrade's cryptic jibe. Laughing in unison, the two set about their business, sending the cart creaking up the dusty hill and casting sniggers back like old crotchety gulls.

Baus and his companions thought no more of the incident or the men's sinister admission. They pitched themselves on toward the bridge.

A mile later, they encountered the first line of stones, a ramp extending from the pebbly shore to the water itself. Several leaning pylons lay half submerged nearby. There were no storks here, only dark, lustreless waters, flowing steadily downriver. The bridge was somewhat low-spanning, an old structure marked with chalk-marmor ravaged and score-ribbed by time. Who made it? The ruined causeway remained enigmatic. Somewhere past the middle point the stone fell in jagged crumbles.

Baus stared out with despair. How to pass? Around the pylons the water gushed and looked deep. Slow bubbles began to form amid the columns of masonry. Sluggish waves rolled farther out. The water was shallower nearest the shoreline and noticeably cleaner, but emitted a listless purl and a dull sheen that struck the surface where late afternoon slanted obliquely.

Despite the impasse, the companions made brave steps up the ramp and around the vaulting stone to stare below.

They halted at the edge, looking forlornly across an empty strait of river . . . alas!—on the far shore the causeway continued: blocks of masonry tumbled onto a natural sandbar, forming crude stepping stones which they thought might allow them passage to the other side. From the tilted aspect of the blocks it appeared as if navigation was impossible. The pylons had been utterly destroyed—by what? Cannon blasts? A ship's weapons? What war vessel could ply these strange waters?

Baus glanced sideways. The river stretched like a long sheet far up the grey-clad valley. Leaning aside, he peered about to spy a blur of movement. An ostrich-like thing, twice his height, suddenly reared up out of the water like a monstrous balloon. Baus stumbled back. The bird harboured a pelican's beak, maroon wings, a pair of gangly legs, two ropy webbed feet and a stork's torso and a flamingo's bill. Some mutant hybrid of Wickle!

Staggering in shock, Baus saw four more of its kind lurking amid the toppled masonry. The gnashing beaks surged upward like scavenging thrush. The flock appeared to have been on some buckler-hunting mission—none were too pleased to be interrupted.

The first large, floating creature made a quick lunge for Baus. Almost immediately it drifted up, squawking and snapping its curved beak at his arms and flapping rusty wings with frightful power.

Baus tottered back, appalled at the size of the thing. The blue coxcomb flap was unnerving, no less a black baldish crown and wings with enough power to crush them all to death.

Baus instinctively grabbed for his weapon. Valere and Poli clamped themselves in fighters' positions and Valere backpedalled, clutching cutlass and mettle and calling out a rancorous yell. Poli skipped sideways to deliver a lynx-like sting in the maw with his halberd, but the stork snapped back and the weapon flipped out of Poli's grasp. The bird snapped the blade in two between the pincers of its beak.

Poli stood gaping, half-frozen. The feathered beast could snap metal as easily as wood and would do worse to flesh and bones.

The thing flapped within killing distance to snap off Poli's arm. Valere drove his sword through the crusty feathers and into the soft belly.

The stork screeched loudly and batted him aside with a swat of wing. The thing made efforts to maul Baus, essaying also to wing-smite Poli, now weaponless.

"Stop!" shrieked Esling. She threw herself between Baus and the giant bird. She held up a hand. The creature was held momentarily by her gaze. The four Wickles had flapped their way up amidst their winged peer, clinging to the edge of the stones. They regarded the men with glowering hostility. For an instant, there was a balance of power hung in check. The attacking bird jerked its head, gave a brief inspection of the Wickle, Esling. Eying the horns on her brow and the authority of her bearing, the leader seemed to pause, recognizing something there—a friend, or some quiet ally.

It settled on its talons, tipping its beak in attentive wonder, waiting for a signal. It ceased its aggression; no further violence was necessary.

As Baus skidded out of harm's way, Esling spoke words insisting that they cease their aggressions. He thrust Poli hobbling wincingly away from the murderous creature. Poli stooped to gather up the wreckage of his weapon and made a sad cry. Esling, undaunted, began to conduct colloquy with the stork, if such were possible. Baus, puzzled by the act, moved closer in an attempt to understand the language but felt no closer to comprehension. Obviously Wickle and Esling could converse in a form of a forest language. Esling waved Baus back with confidence. She could negotiate affairs with an ease of her own.

More truce-speakings ensued and the storks gradually bobbed back in neutral demeanour. They licked their bills and gave benign croaks. The giant leader withdrew its force; the four waded downriver where the currents were less taxing, shouldered by a small sandbar.

Esling consoled her new ally with waves and purrs and motioned her companions to come out of hiding.

Baus and his peers crept closer. They brushed off their garments. All were discomfited. The unassuming Wickle had voided what would have inevitably been a fatal skirmish.

Poli mourned the loss of his blade, but Baus informed him that it could be worse. The storks were wading not far distant. "What did you tell them?" he demanded.

Esling made a noncommittal gesture. "Nothing more than I would tell you. That I travel in the midst of good company—that we are bound to right the wrongs of the mages: the neomancers who fail to release the Wickles from their thraldom, along with the evil of Farling's Wall."

"A trove of assertions," remarked Valere.

"What of it?" Esling intoned. "Justice is more powerful than motive."

Valere harrumphed. "A very exalted statement for a Wickle."

"They are not molesters like Graeitch and they do not dwell in the Branx like my kin behind the wall. By rules of proximity the storks are exceptions. They are less ensorcelled by the wall."

"These creatures," Baus extrapolated, "have access beyond the wall? Are there more of them?

"I imagine so," mused Esling. "Do not worry about it! Silda and her peers have feral qualities, true, but they also retain partly human characteristics like myself. They know the words of truth over falseness—unlike your kind. I asked them to allow us passage across the bridge—they obliged."

"Quite a boon!" Valere grunted, pulling at his nose. "Seems you have brought about a single-handed miracle."

Baus flashed Esling an approving glance. "Good to know there are at least two such capable minds in our company, still—" His voice had become a hushed whisper. He turned his attention to the problem of crossing the river, more specifically, getting their hides down onto the sandbar.

Esling bunted him aside. "That's the hard way, Baus. Must you be so logical? You saved me from that lecher Coyod, yes, but I rescued you from Paiesmy and Loeitch—Now, I believe you owe me a favour!"

Baus gave Esling a sly nod. "While appearing factual, the remark is tainted with fallacy. I saved your hide from far worse than either Paiesmy or Loeitch. In the sake of all fairness, I acknowledge that your point may be somewhat persuasive and shall repay you by helping you down onto these rocks."

"Do not trouble yourself!" called Esling primly. "The Wickles will help us." She put finger to mouth, gave a loud whistle.

In short time, the four birds flew up from the water and landed with a thud before the company.

The men ducked to their knees, but after some amicable words, they lowered their necks and allowed the companions to climb up, agreeing, without fuss, to take them across the gap.

The outlaws were astounded by the courtesy and they hopped gladly up on the backs of the storks. The lead stork clacked its beak. With dignified ceremony, wings spread and the three were swept up over the river. The crew arrived unscathed on the other side of the causeway.

Amidst the sound of gratitude, the men bid leave of the Wickles which swung their proud necks and withdrew to their nesting grounds. The companions padded the rest of the way across the bridge and reached the hither shore, plunking themselves down in thankful heaps. The water lapped gently on the sand, tickling their ears and soothing their bared ankles. High overhead, the overcast massed as a single sheet of pale silver. Upriver, a great dome of the hills swept the landscape with an unsurpassed grandeur before it marched down to meet the river. An unbroken flagstone path led to Desenion, drowned in many places, wavering up the shoreline in curves and sweeps.

The explorers found the ancient royal path agreeable. But they followed it for perhaps two miles before the grey dusk sank deeper into crepuscular twilight.

From behind a horn of boulders appeared the first broken pier. A wharf was fitted with old stone posts. The dock and boardwalk seemed fixed with a timeless grandeur.

The company trudged closer to investigate. The desolate stone was carved with elegance. They failed to notice the wondrous castle nestled higher up in the wooded foreground at their back.

Moored amongst the weathered pilings, a coracle rocked in the water and was outfitted with a single cedar paddle.

Who commanded the craft? Why was it berthed here? The craft was obviously well-maintained—the mooring lines were fresh and someone had recently been about.

The facts begged mysteries and Baus knuckled his fist. He swept eyes unconsciously up the hill, intrigued by a sudden dull glint of stone. What was this?

Rushing up the knoll, he saw a magnificence as the sun peeked briefly from a rent of cloud. He indulged in a gasp: the dreamy, green-washed towers of Desenion were those that shimmered majestically, almost close enough to reach . . .

III

The castle was flanked with copses of mallorns and crafted of fabulous nephrite. Tarnished spear-tossers angled between agate merlons; emerald emblems hung in majestic profusion between the bulwarks and projections. The serpentine-hued walls shimmered dully and statue after statue lurked in eerie procession along the overgrown terrace, knee deep in rank gardens. Baus marvelled. The castle itself was cut into the side of the mountain. Battlements rose up in intricate intervals, sporting three octagonal towers guarding the central courtyard, one slightly higher than the others surmounted with a charcoal-coloured bulb like an age-old shallot. The iron gate, rusted with coxcomb traceries, swung ajar with an eerie promise.

A sharp aromatic waft caught Baus's senses—mallorn cones? Bristlebush?

In enthralled wonder the company advanced. Up the overgrown path they stumbled, looking from side to side, spying boulders chiselled in the forms of stags, wolves, storks and turtles. The statues were much weathered and difficult to distinguish facial features. A few smaller slabs were cut out in the shape of past rulers. A few broken war wagons with bronze wheels lay off to the side in the wild bushes.

The company gained the first flight of steps. They dragged their feet over the threshold and marched up spellbound. Some masonry was toppled and time-eaten. It seemed Desenion's forecourt was not what it used to be: a forsaken magnificence that had seen many years of decline.

The first section of wall was crumbling and graven with insignias. Weeds and shrubs growing from cracks in the flagstones. Some weatherworn coat of arms showed the word 'DESENION' inscribed in bold script.

Baus put hand to chin, guessing this lonely court had once been a place of festivity and pomp, a monarchy's pride with flowering shrubs and lady bowers, but now the grandeur had dwindled to a harshness, plunged in overgrowth and decay. A sprawling mallorn had taken residence in the forecourt's middle and its rooty appendages split the exquisite flags. Now a host of rude black ragbushes clustered about like hungry beggars, lurking in the shadows roguishly.

Baus's eyes ran up the vertiginous side of the central tower. He saw the sleek stone soft-plaqued with a green nephrite. The slenderness of the cylinder was contrasted by its tall, rude barren walls flecked with arrow holes like crows' eyes. The weatherworn stone cast a dull sheen in the dying light and long shadows began to play across the court, somewhat in the manner of pale bird's wings, spreading half way up the crenellated ramparts.

In silent wonder, they edged their way past a row of gloomy stables then a trio of darkened archways. Emerald stone rose high: a mixture of jade and onyx. A statue with a wren's nest on its crown stood high in the courtyard's centre beside an ancient stone well. They passed this and under another low arch and drew abreast of a forsaken court enclosed with less lofty walls. An adjoining tower, trailing with more disconsolate shadows, showed bleak scorings and chisel marks.

Baus studied the broken tower. Siege engine? Magic? Baus could not say. Perhaps this was the aftermath of the battle that Villuven raged. The back side of the tower was lime-grey crusted, with a lichenous verdigris, accounting for the pale greenish hue that they had seen from afar and kept the construction looking so forbidding.

Baus halted. The damp vapours exuding from the forest were depressing. The pulse in his chest began to beat at a disheartening pace. All this toil to get here for what?—a destination of emptiness—a fool's errand?

The golem was wrong about Desenion. Baus had hoped to find clues about Aurimag's whereabouts. Instead he had found only desolation. A bleak shiver ran through Baus's body. The thought of exploring this old keep was not at all appealing.

A sudden light flicked on in one of the tower's lower casements.

Baus turned in amazement. The flicker held some fugitive aspect—a strangeness of coincidence.

He sank back on his haunches while Valere gripped his sword. Across the buckled court they loped, drawing weapons; others followed.

They passed an arched oaken door and an ornamented lintel. They lifted their heads—in the window Baus spied a tiny figure tipped on a stool, huddled over an ornate, marquetry escritoire.

The man seemed to be fumbling for something—a map or parchment and a smoking torch.

Baus twisted his neck. Misgiving warned him of trouble. Who was the figure? He seemed familiar. He did not appear very ingenuous or dangerous, but one could never be too sure in these times. Even for a man so tiny, he wore a peaked green cap and a silver breastplate and purple hose and brown boots. He seemed to be mumbling something incoherent over the parchment, unintelligible words, despite the partially-opened casement.

Baus lowered his head and whispered his findings to the others; in fact, only Valere who became irked to find neither Poli nor Esling at his side.

The two had wandered off to test the lower tower door several paces down.

A clamour suddenly woke from within the keep. A clangour of bells!

Baus ducked. Idiots! Either Esling or Poli had triggered a raucous gonging.

The figure within the keep had disappeared. Now the portal sprang ajar. A small poniard shafted out, followed by an angry yell and a homunculus's head which came shafting out with cap drawn ever tightly over its ears.

Baus recognized the figure. Trimestrius! He loosed a gasp of dismay. So, the little prince had survived. So many moons ago—in Heagram's prison—he had his first acquaintance with the midget.

"Who are you?" the little figure called out in a shrill voice.

"A wayfarer; who are you?" Baus replied shortly.

The dwarf strode forward on miniature legs, menacing Esling with his dagger, "And who may you be, my eldritch little dabchick who harbours minatory horns?"

Esling crabbed back, grimacing distastefully as the dirk prodded her ribs and slitted her costume.

Baus gave a feral cry. "The maid is our guide. Save your pricks for jousts in the yard, if you do not want to feel my blade!"

"Guide, is it? Well, villains! 'Tis a private place and I urge you to depart. That's a Wickle if I've ever seen one, now take her away—wait, I know you, you varlet!"

The homunculus's eyes dimmed over with inhuman rage. A fathomless hate crept over the face as he seemed to recognize the gaunt lines of Baus's face and the confident curl of lip—a confirmed rascal with a golden gladius!

The dwarf jerked in dismay. The magical glint, flawlessly carved contours not normal on this earth seemed to jar a sensitive memory. "'Twas *you* who stole my precious Lolispar, you filthy, black-hearted knave! You dared to put my blade in your own belt-plunge me into that foul brine when I was at last free! Backstabber! Hardly can I believe my eyes! The reckless audacity of that act has plagued me for moons! Return me my heirloom and

684

weapon—at once!"

"Cease the bluster!" cautioned Baus. "All will be set in order in time. I did what I did for good reason. You should be thankful, little man, not a prisoner in a gaol, or worse, torn apart by snauzzerhounds."

"You think?" the homunculus brayed. He stormed forth and made angry sweeps to deal Baus a lethal wound, but Valere held up a foot and the little man tripped and the dagger flew wide, clanging off stone.

Valere scooped up the blade and examined it curiously. "Well, what a pretty blade." He kept his foot on the back of the dwarf's armour to stop him from rising. Baus advised his colleague to ease up on the harshness. "'Tis a long story, Valere, but I think this may be one in need of an explanation." He described his association with Trimestrius and the nature of events leading up to the prison breakout at Heagram and how he had shut the little prince up in his jar of brine.

"Well, that was an amusing turn of events!" chuckled Valere. "And you didn't bother to inform me of it earlier? Shame on you! I thought we were friends, Baus. I had no inkling there was so much intrigue involved in our time at the prison yard."

"There was."

"You laugh!" snorted Trimestrius coldly. "Wait until I am once again whole, you bullies—and then you will cry out while I laugh!"

"Mind your words, dwarf," called Valere, slightly miffed by the name-calling, "but I am not a bully. This occasion is one of import! Let us avail ourselves of this fine keep—then we shall set off for Aurimag's lair on the morrow. What do you think of that, my little armoured dawcock?"

Trimestrius, stunned by the announcement, lurched back on his heels. His eyes rolled in his sockets. "You would go to the blackguard's cave . . . alone?"

"Of course," announced Valere petulantly. "Who else do you see trailing on our heels?"

The homunculus reflected with awe. His brow seemed to glisten with a damp sweat. He licked his chops and padded menacingly to slap at the foppish little curls that thrust down from his midgetish crown. "Perhaps we might come to an agreement then, oaf. But I negotiate nothing—until my blade is returned!"

Baus tossed back the golden weapon. "Here, jackal! If the gaud means that much to you. The dagger has earned its weight in gold—'tis privy to magic, I think.”

“No understament,” snorted the dwarf. “The very edge of Lolispar is anointed with a rare and remarkable elixir—a mystical dust ground by the Sage Arkovorix on a fey eve. ’Twas in ages beyond memory. And it is back in my hands. What irony! Joyous it is to clasp its warmth against my bosom.”

Baus gave an easy shrug. “Well, note I do not conduct wars over inanimate objects.”

“Good to hear. And now an inquiry about your presence—”

“That is easy to detail. It starts with a certain brood of Wickles—”

Trimestrius gave the company an all-encompassing wave. “Come! I will fetch you garments and regalia and weapons for our journey. I appreciate the demonstration of good will by returning me my weapon, but I shall be on my guard. Once a knave, always a knave. I was just about to plod to Aurimag’s abode myself—for I have grievances with this lout. Ulisa will be arriving soon.”

Frowning at the unnatural presence of the Wickle, Trimestrius could not help but evince misgivings. He drew himself away from the doe-waif and led the four deep into his castle. They passed down a series of cresset-lit halls where the ceilings were lost in rich shadows and the walls were adorned with austere portraits of Desenion’s ancestors and old landscapes.

Baus was instantly stirred. The overt sanctity of the residence smacked of a stylish solemnity which seemed somewhat over-exalted.

The company crossed a wide gallery. They swung deep under a double archway and marched down a gloomy hall where they came face to face with a heavy, iron-bound door which ironically, took them back to the same chamber where Baus had first seen the homunculus.

They filed through the double-portal and Trimestrius cast a distrustful glance once again at the Wickle from which he did his best to keep a distance.

The chamber’s ceiling lofted to great heights: ’twas crisscrossed with ghost oak beams. It looked more like a place five hundred years old than a century. Mallorn pillars supported a domed roof; each column was pinned with a thousand gold insignias. Regalia of noble heritage rang everywhere. A weapons’ shelf occupied the far wall, glinting with a mass of scintillating swords, daggers and blades of all sizes. The blades, all burnished gold and gleaming, were tokens of craftsmanship, yet more than centuries old themselves, but looking as if forged yesterday. On the opposite wall hung a colourfully-woven tapestry—of Desenion's distinguished Coat of Arms. It featured a great griffon, a raptor, another mythical bird perched on high of the gleaming tower of Desenion's green stone.

Desenion! thought Baus. Despite the richness of its fixtures, the room's archaic splendour and heritage seemed tainted with a remote curse, bespeaking of tragedy that had somehow corrupted the walls and masonry.

Trimestrius hopped up on his chair and stabbed down a thumb at a place on the vellum scroll which he had been studying. "Look here! This marks the villain's abode," he proclaimed, showing a spot ticked off in green ink, set with skull and crossbones, "abreast the Lim, before it meets the Ul, where the brooding Brauvn forest meets the Branx. I was hoping to gain an advantage here through advance research, but I have been unsuccessful. Fiddle-fie! The region is shadowed by inscrutable pasts and disquieting creatures—a menagerie of Wickles, tasms, tengs, and other unruly things. The copses are impenetrable, infested with blights, phantom elms and haunted maulwoods—insects, orthovores, other frights. The encroaching forest, the Brauvn, borders the Branx as I mentioned, a mushroom-haunted hinterland, hunching far behind Farling's Wall where only the most malevolent and derelict linger."

Valere nodded with understanding. "We have some experience with this territory."

Trimestrius's lollipop mouth gave a sudden trill, but he silenced his emotions, uttering no further remark. A flapping tumult suddenly issued from the window.

All eyes turned. Baus gaped, appalled. An enormous shadow had descended over the window—and now in the courtyard—a monstrous set of outstretched wings floated down, forefronted by some huge globular eye. The bird, or *eye*, if it was one, hovered ingloriously alongside the pane, gazing in with a peculiar avidity, a look that would rival Guezzela, the hound girl. To everyone's amazement, the thing rotated its egg-like organ, jerked its body sideways and swung through the casement where the window was still ajar.

Baus stood in rooted dismay. The bird, of course, was far too immense to pass through the small slit and succeeded only in cracking the pane and barging through with thrusts of its powerful wings.

Trimestrius stared aghast. Baus's face crumpled in a rictus. The eye was almost as big as a beach ball and within the globular mass was positioned an ocular organ's spider-webbing with bloodshot streaks running.

The bird floated negligently to the escritoire where it hovered in complacent ease over Trimestrius's small frame. It seemed to teeter while the nobleman reeled back with dumb amazement. He pitched off his stool. Presently another small shape came through the window—a fluttering moth limned with golden light.

Trimestrius was beside himself with fury. He leaped aside, burst up onto his chair, stabbing jerkily in an attempt to pierce the winged creature. "Get this Wickle away! You are defiling my sanctum!"

The monster rose a step higher, out of the midget's reach. The nobleman shrilled a heady curse. "Fools! Skewer the beast! Why do you stand there like imbeciles?" He raised his sword, stabbed and slashed.

Baus implored, "We carry no blades, nor does Poli, whose weapon was snagged earlier by your wretched storks."

"They were not my storks. No matter! Harry the thing out of the window! Can you not see now why I oppose these weird creatures, these Wickles?"

"'Tis not a Wickle!" cried Esling, infuriated. "'Tis an eagle equipped with a single oleaginous eye. You can see. Look!"

"The Wickle speaks the truth," came a soft voice from behind the desk.

All turned eyes. The moth had changed shape—into a beautiful woman, three feet high, glowing with richly radiant aura and with arms raised now over her head.

By means of a rich enchantment, Ulisa had appeared in the moth's stead; but now she was limned with a golden nimbus radiating from toe to crown from every one of her pores. Luxuriously she stepped back, blooming to her full radiance, exuding an impressive energy.

"Ulisa?" sputtered Trimestrius. "Well, what happy luck! And a great fortuity. You would *know* this creature?"

She laughed. "I would!" Regally she marched forward.

Trimestrius gaped, still confused and bewildered by the sudden events. "What then?"

Ulisa flashed the prince a mirthful glance and the floating eagle-creature came down a notch with an imploring eye-blinking. "Kazzasius, why do you insist on maintaining such heights?"

The eye bobbed down with gentle ease. "I work my lustrous wings just enough to keep aloft, Ulisa. Really, I cannot think why you would want me to be so friendly in such circumstance," he said. "I am a monstrosity! Look for yourself! And yet you continue to deprive me of my only joy while encased in this freakish outfit! Which is simply: *surprise*! Now, dispense with the lecturing. How can I be forced to endure these indignities much longer in these tiresome days?"

"Enough of your complaints, Kazzasius," admonished Ulisa. "We all have our duties."

"Kazzasius?" shrilled Trimestrius. "Can it be you? The Kazzasius? I am hearing dream speech. Is it the Projector's name I hear with mine own ears?"

"One and only," asserted Kazzasius. "Chief Projector of Mismerion— lore-teller and wise person at your service!"

"But how?"

"Ah! The marvels of modern science—they go a million leagues, wouldn't you say, Ulisa?"

Ulisa affirmed the opinion.

"But this is highly irregular."

"The times on us are magical, Trimestrius, though hard."

"Very true," muttered the prince. "Now what of these Wickles?"

Ulisa gave a patient sigh. "I see you are busy with guests. You're not planning on making any expeditions to Aurimag's cave with these fellows, are you?" She tapped her fingers suggestively on the map laid out on the table.

Trimestrius shifted posture in a sulky fashion. Dropping his eyes, he muttered an unintelligible excuse.

The sorceress turned Baus a rather lugubrious inspection. "Well, it seems we have Baus, our fisherman. I see you are still alive, happily too." She gestured to his entourage with delight and merriment. "And your friends? You have to introduce us."

Baus crafted a debonair bow. "The pleasure is mine! Meet Valere and Poli, my sea chum and bodyguard, my excellent halberd-chopper . . . and Esling, my Wicklish friend and plucky minion, if not a sidekick. Comrades, meet Ulisa—esteemed Neomancer of the Mismerion Order!"

Poli made a curt bow. "Neomancer? I hope you are of more decency than this Aurimag fellow I keep hearing about."

Ulisa grinned a cool detachment. "I should think so. There was a time when Aurimag and I got along quite well—at least in the beginning, when we were instructor and pupil."

A flicker of mockery crossed Trimestrius face. "Instructor and pupil! What a lark! Aurimag is nothing more than a rotten traitor! He must be called to task for his hideous deeds! His heart is so black and cold that it shall be clipped by my blade!" He slashed headily. "This weapon is a singular core of retribution which will bring the knave to his knees, not a mere hack piece which this clown Baus has used in his recent forays, judging from all the dried blood."

Ulisa nodded keenly. "I see you have regained your long lost talisman."

"I have. Now in all capacities, I must replenish my mettle!" Flourishing the bodkin, he motioned toward the weapon stack. "Here, fisherman, take your choice of my weapons. This is a fine piece, crafted by my father's father's father, for example. One I freely furnish—in return for the wise, cooperative act of returning my talisman." He swaggered forward, motioned Baus to pluck a weapon of his choice.

"Go on, go on! Don't be timid! To me these weapons are universal boons, passed down by my father. Any shall do, and none shall disappoint."

"I don't doubt," mumbled Baus. "But what of my colleagues, Valere and Poli? They lack distinguished blades also."

"Let them select blades then—the redbeard included."

With stately dignity, Baus selected a sword of meticulous craftsmanship for himself—a finely-honed bronze blade carved of gold, which displayed the golden insignia of Desenion in its haft. Poli chose a weapon not dissimilar, likewise did Valere to replace his dented cutlass. Trimestrius outfitted them all with jewelled scabbards and belts of silver-gold clasps, thus completing the covenant. Valere took occasion to whet his blade on the nearby grindstone while Baus and Poli oiled their swords. Out the weapons slid from their sheaths with regal stealth.

Trimestrius stood back with hearty triumph. "That's better!" Addressing the company with a formal bearing, he spoke with a tone that Baus might have found grandiloquent. "By my own judgement and my peer Ulisa's high recommendation of you, I grant you these tokens! Treasure them and adore them! Guard these pieces with your life for they are heirlooms—all that remain of my father's heritage."

Baus acknowledged the honour. He roved about with Poli in a mock display of swordplay while Ulisa pussyfooted back from their clinking feints, examining the regal splendour of the chamber and its weaponry. Valere shouted quips at the fighters and offered pointers on the swordsmen's style.

Trimestrius clapped his hands,. He spoke in a quixotic recollection of the elder days. "Hearken! While vagabonds sport with the finest steel of Desenion, I, Prince of Desenion, remain an ensorcelled dwarf! Forsooth, now without proper subjects, I speak humbled but not cowed! History remains bleak for my kind and for Desenion! Years ago, I returned from service to Mismerion to visit my homeland—all in the hope of adhering to my father's wishes, regarding my future inheritance. But I arrived only to find my home blasted and laid waste by the cursed Villuven, of Owlen. My kindred were scattered across the lands, or dead. My parents, brave souls they were, Tirimes and fairest Hansa, were either deposed or executed. To this day, I know not of their fates. My sister, proud Mirkana, remains ever the cause of our virulent woe, refusing to wed our vindictive neighbour Viluven."

"You are a prince then?" inquired Valere, dumbstruck.

"That I am!" announced Trimestrius with a wave of pride. "And how misery falls so wickedly upon princes! I am an heir to this kingdom, but without a people!" He spread his palms, gestured about the gallery in futility.

The clangour of sword halted. Baus gave a quiet murmur. "And you still have royal kin then?"

Trimestrius gave a plaintive reply. "Yes, Mirkana is my sibling. She was my 'princess sister', destined to wed Arnin's father, but she refused. The lord was shamed. When he learned of her clandestine trysts kept with Rioulk of Buskerfield, he almost went mad. Now, none will return to Desenion for fear that Owlen's might will descend once more upon us and shatter our towers and blast our courtyards to dust should we rebuild. Ah, the demise of our kingdom!" Trimestrius's face darkened, a mask of bleak anguish.

"We all suffer mortifications," soothed Ulisa. "Fear not, Trimestrius, as time goes on, pain recedes. We must forge ahead. Let us lay siege to Aurimag's abode and have our vengeance!"

Trimestrius croaked out an excited chirrup. "Aye! We cannot sit about like chiplarks and sulk. Nor tinker here lamenting! Nor can we trot slapdash to Aurimag's hidey-hole! We must implement a cunning plan."

"That is true; have you one?"

Trimestrius's eyes bulged with craftiness. "Indubitably! My counsel is this; it weighs in at posting a lure or some trap of significance upon Aurimag's residence. Lay the blackguard low!—send him scrabbling back on his heels like a mewling crake!"

"Very good, Trimestrius, and you must elaborate on these brave traps! Have you such a specific lure in mind?"

Trimestrius nodded. "We must camouflage my coyote and bear engines and hide them at the threshold to Aurimag's cave. Then, when the scoundrel treads near—Blam!" He ploughed his tiny fist into a palm. "We merely tap the supporting chains of the device into the rock to preclude any scurrying off by the villain . . . A possibly bloody affair, but this strapping countryman here, Valere, looks quite disposed to the task."

Valere arched eyebrows in wry inquiry.

Ulisa seemed to warm to the idea. "Perhaps—but what if Aurimag does not emerge from this cave? He may decipher the trap beforehand and spring it prematurely."

"Then we must devise an alternate stratagem," snapped Trimestrius. "Who else is to engineer alleged plans, me alone?"

Valere complained: "While all of us bicker, I grow hungry. Is there not a crumb of food in this chill hall?"

Trimestrius nodded and Ulisa fabricated a discreet cough. The prince was impelled to manufacture some refreshments. He disappeared to fetch the provender. The larder, not far away, proved sparse, and the prince returned shortly bearing a small salver of chunks of malt bread and three mugs of wine for the starveling guests. Not surprisingly, Baus and his companions set on the food voraciously. Esling, dainty in her eating, took only finicky bites and small, wincing sips of wine.

Trimestrius watched the men's eating habits with disgust. "Are you trenchermen or boors! You call yourself gentlemen? Well—I must trust that the victual is at least ample?"

"'Tis. The wine—" Baus croaked, smacking lips between gulps "—is perhaps a trifle premature in its uncorking, but the bread, is otherwise divine."

Trimestrius's eyes strained to the beams. "And are you habitually such a frank talker when provided free provender?"

"When impelled," Baus answered in dignity. He gulped another draught and wiped his lips with the back of his hand then indulged in another teeth-

692

tearing of bread.

Trimestrius grimaced and began a sarcastic pacing about and inspection of his guests. Ulisa interrupted with a sharp announcement: "Kazzasius, come down! You and I bear news of Aurimag, which is to be relayed."

The prince gave his head a ridiculous shake. "What news can that monstrosity relay?"

"Listen and you will find out. We have affirmative knowledge that Aurimag is sequestered in his cave."

Trimestrius remained unmoved. "So? I could have told you this from the outset."

Kazzasius's eye swept about the room with astuteness and he dropped down a foot. He spoke politely, "I have embedded within my body a 'xenophone', a device with such technology that I can wield this wizardry to map out events within my matrix." His voice spoke with a strain of pride and richness. "The xenophone provides assistance and I trace our quarry. Like such and so. He demonstrated with blinks and flashes from his one eye. If you would like, Trimestrius, take seats with our guests and I shall provide a demonstration." The great eye bulged and showed a frosty beam which projected an indistinct image upon the floor.

All eyes turned to the stone. The eye continued in a professorial manner: "Observe the lack of colour in the depiction. Watch! The peculiarity remains illusive! The perturbations of the flux indicate an omni-presence of exceptionality. It allows neomancic exudations to dominate, the quality which Aurimag, amongst few, can wield."

Baus pushed up his brows. "So then, if this wretch is privy, what good is it to us? Is it enough for you to fabricate such lofty statements?"

"I think so," intervened Ulisa. "Let the Projector proceed."

Trimestrius forced a jeering laugh. "I could have spared you all the unnecessary trouble. As I said, I watched Aurimag leave his cave not two days ago."

Kazzasius hovered a foot lower, responding in precise hauteur. "Silence! That is old information. I shall shift the xenofilm within the device so as to simulate a crude depiction—of Aurimag and his comings and goings." The great eye luminesced—suddenly a projection of another chromatic image fell upon the floor.

All peered. The mosaic floor showed fragments and jumbles of colour from which the group struggled to extract meaning.

The image clarified. The scene depicted Baus and Poli, then Valere and Esling huddled about in a chamber like the one in which they now sat.

"There!—you see?" cried the eye, grinning with triumph, "notice how the fellow Baus and his companions remain standing in characteristic position. This indicates a stabilization. As you witness, each figure resides here at this hall at precisely this instant. The map indicates a new reality! The method stimulates the imagination and insinuates that we can trace the fisherman and his colleagues anywhere—so we can trace anybody, including the plights of his colleagues, all the way from Farling's Wall to Desenion."

"Very good, Kazzasius," sneered Trimestrius. "But what of the benefit? Is this such a great feat?"

Baus jerked his head back with disgust. "Why your sudden interest in me and my companions?"

Kazzasius declared with emphasis, "You alone have managed to outwit Aurimag, and members of our Circle have analyzed the information to the point of rigour. We have ascertained a metaphysical certainty that you can help us secure Aurimag's downfall. And are not taking pains to ignore it."

Baus muffled a dull cough. "Metaphysical certainty?"

"That is what I said."

"Pity," sighed Ulisa, "we had almost caught up with your company at Rastule glade, but by the time we arrived, the Wickles had all vanished. They were up in arms, tearing up the forest like a brood of many caged fiends. We did not know why. I barely escaped being mauled myself by some crazy, dizzy, half purplish frog-like bat invested with a slithering tongue, had not Kazzasius come rocketing out of the sky, driving it away."

"That would be Banaga," mused Baus, "or was it Eelrid? It's all a blur."

"It was Agulbeak," corrected Valere. Munching on his bread, he noted that Baus's memory was still shaky from riding the hub. "And so what of these fiends?"

"They are irrelevant," muttered Ulisa. "When I fluttered half lost into the Branx, I changed myself from firefly to a warbler and managed to trace Baus's path. The trail was lost—yet the Wickles were also lined up in a heap outside Farling's Wall. Baus had disappeared into the naked forest west of the Lim."

"True, and I thank you for your concern," intoned Baus sardonically. "But your efforts have proven dilatory. As it stands, my companions and I barely escaped the wrath of the Wickles. Some of us were given to ingesting spider broths and copulating with repulsive Wickles—not to mention many other disgusts."

"Some were nearly carried off by ape-armed golems too," added Esling wisely.

Ulisa clicked her tongue. "Enough. Kazzasius apologizes for these inconveniences. But I may remind you that the circumstances could be far worse. You escaped a nightmare. What then, Baus? Are you to curse the Wickles forever? I might also point out that you have your health and your sensibilities and suffer no further undue stress or damages."

"In corporeal essence only!" argued Baus casuistically. "Your accounting has not included some of the finer strains imposed on my spiritual being. These centss horrors of Wickles have frayed my nerves. Refine your argument, Ulisa. I sense a circumlocution here, even rhetoric. We all must share a common interest in this venture—evident enough, with the possible exception of Poli and Esling."

"Not true!" cried Esling. "I care not a whit for Aurimag or his history, but I care for Baus and thus become the mage's mutual enemy."

"A touching remark!" approved Baus. "So then, there remains only Poli to gainsay our common collusion."

The bully raved. "Both Valere and I must be added to the pool of neutral observers. Valere has harboured no quarrel with Aurimag in any shape or form."

Valere made a sour grimace. "That is not entirely true."

Baus made a gloating laugh, at which point Trimestrius joined in with Kazzasius and added his own sagacious arguments.

"Gentlemen!" cried out Ulisa. "Time is too short for arguments. Let us indulge in plans of action. We do not remain in this hall to fill air with superfluous babel. Let us brainstorm as one! I for one am thrilled to view so many brilliant intellects congregating in a small space with a likeness of mind and a vigour of spirit. The prince has offered a purposeful ploy—are there others? I fear his plan is too simplistic and must be discarded."

Poli raised a sullen hand. "If it is by cave you wish to enter, then why not drill a hole through the earth topside and pour liquid in and flush out the villain?"

Valere clapped Poli on the back. "An excellent scheme, Poli. We could also suck up a thousand cubits of water and spit it down the tube ourselves."

Poli resented the quip. "I do not applaud any jokes."

"Never mind," muttered Baus. "We could always smoke the villain out."

"How?"

Baus folded his fingers tent-like. "By launching a series of brands into his cave."

Kazzasius offered a sceptical murmur. "I think the scheme is a shade jejune. Aurimag is shrewder than that. He would recognize the ploy and seclude himself deeper in his cave. The cavern is vast!"

"What about the old fashioned way?" suggested Valere. "Chop and charge?"

"Too blunt and obvious," sneered Trimestrius.

Ulisa considered the puzzle from another angle. "The problem is somewhat intricate. Perchance we must rely on a more unanticipated method."

"Such as?"

"Take measures in our own hands," advised the shape-shifter. "We must travel to Aurimag's cave and simply wing it, scout the scenario as it comes."

"The idea prompts a certain conditional merit," mumbled Trimestrius.

"But first!" Ulisa cried. "Let us excise these reeking rags from the men! P-yew! I am dazed. As for the Wickle, her horrid jumpsuit must go. Trimestrius! I appoint you official proctor of this project. Hop to! Your ancestors' wardrobes are for the taking."

The prince gave a grudging acquiescence. Brandishing a beeswax candle, the nobleman conveyed the companions down to the Royal repository. The trip was like an experience in a ghost house, down a flight of sinister steps to a crypt-like gallery filled with glum airs and cool draughts.

Baus saw, in all the eeriness, a dozen figures lined in old dusty armour. In a cobwebbed corner stood a massive, ancient sideboard, where they discovered moth-eaten but serviceable clothes left by the prince's forebears.

The three picked out leather jerkins, tabards, black-laced breeches, peaked caps, jupons, woollen trousers, black belts, leather leggings, knee length boots and iron-shod cleats. An array of helmets were available, amongst breastplates, brassards, jambeau, gauntlets and sollerets—all from which Baus discovered a mesh of sturdy tarnished mail. He tried the mesh and was pleasantly surprised. An older, defensive covering—but selected from one of the less complex, armoured models made a quick pick while Valere acquired a silver-streaked mail of his own. Poli grabbed a black mesh no less grand than Valere's. Esling chose an old travelling costume worn by Trimestrius's mother—a purple travelling suit adorned with strips of silk and wool. The garment had been untouched by mice and still shone with its queenly dignity.

Acquiring their new outfits, the heroes made their way to the common room and grateful to be out of the gloom, they retired to a chamber on the upper floor designated by their host, set with conservative hangings, iron cressets, couches and a single large bed. A huge oil landscape of the Lim hung overtop of the headboard and made them feel somewhat at home.

Trimestrius left them to their habits. It had been a tiring day. All were wearied. Without much ado, Baus and Poli each took a half of the bed while Valere slapped himself on the couch. Esling made it her business to choose a settee by the wall but the long upholstered couch was not to her liking and she soon crawled into bed beside Baus, bunting Poli aside.

IV

The company struck out at dawn, cloaked and clad in their war gear. Gently they set their pace, the unlikely crew they were, clanking like lords down the footworn steps that stretched from courtyard to quay. As the first pangs of light lifted from the hills, they marched ceremoniously along the aged terrace of Desenion's harbourfront. The morning rays splashed polished gold, catching Desenion's riven watchtower and presaging some hope of fair weather. A chill wind blew and Baus felt somewhat homesick of heart as his mind wandered to his hometown of Heagram where might lie snow or frost at this time of year.

The river lay flat like a ribbon past the old marmor flood wall. The pier and the northern hills were lit up with a soft plum-rose. Behind rose the eastern downs and the bridge snaking its long way across the Lim, an umbral ribbon. The bridge ruins were akin to a caterpillar cleft in half. Ahead, a pebbly expanse shouldered the river, crowded by a dull smear of forest.

Trimestrius appeared invigorated and was pleased by the deployment of his new team. He deemed it a *heroes'* mission and sang songs and slogans to the occasion. Outfitted in the most dashing of his silver greaves, he looked as grand as any high Lord, the little prince in burnished glory marching with brisk economy, epaulettes shining and mail scrubbed.

Baus ambled less luxuriously, carrying whip and ferrule and other minor appurtenances which he deemed worthwhile, acquired at the expense of the Buskerfielders. Valere remained placid, composed to take up the rear, proud of his iron-sprung bear trap and the stout wood stakes strapped to his back by means of a complex leather baldric. Poli cast the captain a sullen look and he grumbled on about his hardship, carrying two coyote traps across his shoulders each with unusual weight. Esling, spry and cheery, trotted in radiant good nature at their heels.

The shapeshifter Ulisa darted in sweeps in the air. She enjoyed her freedom as a sparrowhawk might and seemed wont to fly more than walk. Kazzasius was of similar disposition—Ulisa's 'Eagle Eye', never remaining too far from her side. The distended eye looked horribly out of place, peering from its bloodshot view after flying all night. How the creature ate or slept, Baus could not guess.

The company trudged in single file. Whenever Esling strode too close to Trimestrius, he would brandish his weapon and wave a gauntleted hand as if to ward her off. Frightened, the Wickle retreated with fluttering brows. Dutifully she trotted at Baus's side, gazing up at him with eyes of adoration, a sentiment which Baus secretly found irking.

Stone domicile after stone domicile they passed, ruined, as well as ravaged clubhouses and fanes—the remains of Desenion's heritage. Sadly, they were the fruits of a crazed lord . . . Everywhere a moulder of masonry was overgrown with decay—but herein an implicit grandeur remained, not able to be quenched, still hinting of its former glory.

Trimestrius's eyes burned. His domain and people had been so ravaged it caused him pain to the point of vindictiveness.

The serpentine towers of Desenion faded from sight and soon they stood far away from the keep, entering the wood of crowded mallorn. The prince explained that the strip of forest along the Lim had once been his father's private hunting grounds, but the king was now dead or exiled and the deer, without culling, were monarchs of the domain. Farling's Wall was a league and more away through the wicked screen of foliage. He informed them that as the crow flies, Aurimag's cave was at least another day's march south— four leagues and a half west through Grimstol forest where the sylvan depths became the Brauvn.

The companions listened gravely to his counsel and evinced only mute shrugs and murmurs in return.

The river was seen in glimpses through the trees, a leaden slash of mystery as it slipped sibilantly over its marmor shelves. Boulders of strange designs appeared in its wake. At other times the Lim became a wide placid lake, showing little current, but moving through the lands with detached interest. Meanwhile the trees became denser, stretching taller and arching over the damp humus and then up to the yellowing sky. The clop of the company's boots were made softer by the closeness of the forest, becoming a murmur in the solemn fastness. To the ears of the flora, the clopping was an intrusion.

Struggling, the travellers navigated the gaps through the forest with difficulty and spied a company of two sleek dugout canoes making their way downriver. The wayfarers made no effort to signal these riders for the purposes of remaining indiscreet.

By midday, they had reached the hamlet of Lillenvir, a huddle of cottages of antique design set in stone with steep wooden gables. Standing on the opposite shore, they saw the village as a whole through the screen of phantom elm. Weathervanes and chimney pots were placed to top mica-sheathed roofs. The town, situated aback of a network of timber docks, was fashioned of twined logs.

Baus discerned amongst those structures, men: moving barrels of cargo and hauling lines. Stevedores transported loads to the canoes paddling up the river. Less upstanding dwellings ranged the shoreline. Baus saw glazed triangular panes and rattan siding, low domes looming in the periphery, framed with bands of cedar.

They paused no longer than was necessary to hike up the woodland trail and slogged it hard for an hour or so. They took little rest until they strode aside the wide blue lake nestled in a shallow valley. The lake's shimmer seemed dragged with catspaws; trim cottages and straw-thatched bungalows dotted the foreshore. Under Trimestrius's order, the avengers gave the dwellings wide berth. Baus saw that extended woodcutting had left the lands bare. Such denudation annoyed him. From the lake swelled up warm air, brushing the sumacs of their leaves, dropping petals of fine white flower to the turf. At last the terrain seemed easier to navigate and Baus picked up his feet, finally reaching the lake's terminus, where they found no more than a wet, soggy hinterland replete with leafy gendron and minatory mallorn. A whispering cascade fed the narrowing river, showing sections of rapids. Beautiful gendrons hugged the shoreline—like stately toadstools . . .

Climbing a steep set of slippery rocks, they heard the tinkle of rushing water.

Baus felt a cool spray of mist tickling the flush on his cheeks. A feeling of mystery pervaded this narrow band of land. Baus fell back, showing teeth, hoping that the remainder of the voyage entailed less sombre vistas.

Ulisa and Kazzasius still circled high, in an effort to reconnoitre the area. Yet Baus craned his neck and saw the distant bat-shaped kite of Kazzasius and the small dot whose blur was Ulisa.

As the forest thickened, the party travelled no farther than a half league before they halted abreast of a chalky white gauze hanging from selected mallorns. No paths or hope of traversing did the dense screen show.

Peering through a hoary gloom, Baus frowned. The queer whiteness or white stuff that enveloped the dour trees and fell in slow, snowflake-like rhythm, was disturbing.

700

He discovered that huge cocoons or 'pods' were flung haphazardly from branch to branch and presaged in some sense, a sign of eerie peril.

Moving several paces closer, he and Valere thought to discern threads of silky resins hanging from pod to pod like streamers. The powdery 'snow' fell from the boughs like dandelion fluff, bathing the forest in a creamy film of ivory-grey.

Baus pulled at his chin. What was this? In the distance he thought to spy glimpses of black, dead pools—the litters of deadheads clustered in glum knots. Islands?

'Twas hard to say. Unsettling slitherings oozed from the pores of the forest. Impossibly perched nests bobbed like so many sunflowers in mild gusts of air, movements which Trimestrius identified as 'spider' or 'caterpillar' infestations scourging the lands in colonies.

He gave a disgusted sneer, "We are best to skirt this haunt. To risk exposure to the insects is a senseless danger, withal, a reckless risk."

Valere muttered an agreement.

After a prolonged silence, Ulisa veered out of the sky and fell at their feet, eliciting gapes of astonishment as she transformed back to her womanly form. Kazzasius dropped down too, circling in awkward fashion. Ulisa confirmed that the white trunks were caterpillar spawn and they dwindled to a few stunted elm not a league distant. "Perhaps we can see the end of it in three or more miles. Until then, we must make do with this eeriness."

"The news is not heartening," grumbled Baus. "'Twas not a league earlier we had marched through clear forest." With effusive mutters, Baus and his allies dragged their feet away from the river and into the crabbed knot of mallorns. The trees grew more densely thick and their gaunt roots twisted about with prickly disquietude leaning athwart as if to block their passage. In similar manner, the ground grew disturbed, ruffled with the white material that encroached on their path and spread through the air in thin gauzy sheets.

The whiteness however, did fall away. The forest became a less tangible menace. They had reached the end of the domain—or so it seemed. The prince triumphantly announced that all was clear. They struck on with a tentative optimism, although Baus jokingly posed that the absence of birdsong in this quarter meant predators must be fiercer than the insectoids —a joke met with little humour.

The prophetic silence grew and only the thump of their boots and hearts punctuated the eerie stillness. Decayed moss, star-shaped leaves and ancient gnarly roots was their world.

Risking several glances back, Baus found the way behind looking much as the way ahead. He would hardly guess that they had even traversed a half league. The woods seemed to swallow all traces of their passage. With the realization, the companions tightened their stride, peering this way and that. The land was deceitful, suspicious: any entity could be hiding in the dank midsts.

Esling burrowed into Baus's ribs. Valere and Poli seemed to knit themselves together like a pair of pressed peas. The air grew darker and gloomier and weapons flashed into hands, with their eyes gleaming like candles in a grey world. Kazzasius found the strangling canopy oppressive and was forced to fly higher overhead, leaving the company and the spidery bog below. The Projector disappeared from sight while white streamers and silky white gauze again blew across their path. They grew dismayed and were denied also view of the fliers' passage.

The last tract of white wood receded, as too, the marsh. Crossing the faintest of trails, they bent back toward the river which curiously veered south, deeper into Grimstol. Trimestrius was at a loss to explain the deviance. He scratched his brow with fury. The path instilled a feeling of dread and Baus saw it angling alarmingly close to the deadheads which sprang up again, hung with similar white snow from tree to tree in ghastly splendour.

The troupe was within arm's reach of a glooping expanse of mud when all of a sudden a gigantic grey-green hump-backed shape slithered out of the slime to confront them.

Valere pitched his frame back in defense, clawing for his weapon.

The thing moved with uncanny speed, intercepting them—a huge monster akin to a tortoise.

Baus beetled back in dismay. He saw a grey-yellow glob of a head, a spiky lizard's tail, a leathery dome for a shell. It dragged its mass across their path, staring them down with impish eyes.

Baus gaped absurdly. Waiting for the turtle to resume its journey was an exercise in futility.

They were cut off from an escape. Because the trees were so thick, Esling and Ulisa had scampered to the side, exposed to assaults.

Baus considered his options. The turtle hunched itself ready to spring. Its scaly dome of a back was easily six feet across if it was an inch. Definitely not something to be trifled with, yet . . . there was something more stirringly human in the amphibian face than what ordinary glance would permit. Perhaps the doleful slant of eyes? The crooked glint of teeth?

Baus's brows twitched. The problem was not trivial. His mercurial mind came up with a plan. Skirting around the path, he plied an alternate course. But even as he chose that, the turtle waddled sideways, quick as a crab, blocking his path. The neck shot out several feet, thrusting a cannon-like neck with bulb-like eyes.

Baus swung back in stupefaction. How was it possible to move so fast?

He reached for his whip, snapping it out to wrap around the thing's neck. The creature uncoiled a length of glistening trachea and generated a vicious sideways tug that dragged Baus off his feet. He flew into the scum of the marshes, drenched with ooze.

Poli chuckled while Valere picked at his teeth wryly.

Baus raged to his feet, cursing and spitting, pitching sludge this way and that.

The creature stood waiting idly at the marshy shore for the outlaw's next move.

'Twas then that an enormous, gnarled creature suddenly came flying through the gaps in the trees. The bird had a dirty beak and dewlapped gums, gnashing under a fanned plume on a purple-black crown. It flapped furiously from somewhere in the deeps of the swamp—a creature akin to buzzard, but not.

Baus gazed helplessly at the creature as it landed atop a high deadhead very close to the swampy shore.

For a time, the bird did not move. All were stunned. It hung there motionless, like an archaic monument, sagging on its limb, content to survey the terrain, almost grinning at the turtle which, squatting with an expression of interest, received its slavering attention. Despite the disreputable appearance of the buzzard, it appeared lord of the domain. Beady eyes darted about in this lonely outpost of black muck and spider-haunted morass of the Brauvn.

Shaking the algae off his mail, Baus darted a canny glance at the turtle but both buzzard and turtle did not seem to budge. He thought the behaviour odd and sought to retrieve his whip. The creature jerked about with a defiant energy and lumbered forward, snapping teeth and driving Baus back into the marsh again with fully extensible neck.

Baus staggered, appalled as the green filth from its maw projected putrescence. He dodged the long neck with its gooey gums and barely escaped sharp teeth snapping inches from his face.

Valere sprang to action, giant sword arching to strike at the slimy neck, to lop off the head.

The blade, however, only clinked harmlessly off the armoured tail—which it whirled from nowhere to block the assault. No ordinary turtle was this. Unlike the ponderous shellbacks of the sea, this beast was probably a hybrid of gant-laxus and lepro-tort.

Baus padded back in revulsion.

The turtle revolved to face the two of them, displaying a maw of green teeth. Poli and Trimestrius teamed together, menacing it with halberd and sword.

Esling had shied back into the bush, hurling Wicklish words in its wake. The creature did not respond, seemingly immune to the Wickle language.

The thing swung its neck in an arrogant loop, taunting the passers-by with low croaks and sidestepping assault like a crab.

Baus sank into deep despair. Despite his obvious efforts to dissuade the turtle from violence, it seemed only to be more resolved to do just that: obstruct their passage and despatch them to the marsh.

Esling was perhaps more canny of this reality and watched from a distance, crying out, warning her allies at the last instant to beware the air above, but too late. The buzzard swooped, made a desperate snatch at Trimestrius's rucksack. Talons tore, ripping the sack off the prince's back and the scavenger uttered an unpleasant shriek.

Trimestrius flew a foot off the ground. He still held onto his pack with an oath-flinging rage.

Baus dodged the machination of the turtle's neck. He caught a glimpse of the crafty buzzard, almost twice his size, harrying Trimestrius with feathers flying and claws scratching.

The prince fabricated a blind thrust upward. Lolispar was slow to pierce it.

Esling sagged back. The Wickle was too horrified to act. Somehow, she sensed that serious bloodshed was about to erupt. Ravaged and thrown about like a cork, the prince was too short to achieve any striking victory, even as he stabbed with golden dagger at the bird.

Baus flourished his whip. The tail end came flicking up to lick at the buzzard's yellow legs.

The bird careened aside, eluding the leather flail, but raked at Baus's forearm, drawing blood with its outstretched claw.

Trimestrius lost his grip. He fell heavily to the earth. The buzzard dropped low, but the sack was clamped jealously in its claws. It flew back to its meagre perch, ruffling feathers as if nothing had happened.

The turtle found favour with the situation and passed between a maze of drowned roots, scraping belly over submerged rocks to slip back into the swamp and arrive at the base of the deadhead, glaring expectantly up at the buzzard.

All this occurred in a matter of seconds. The companions watched with open-mouthed wonder.

A wake of bubbles filtered to the surface near the island and the bubbles traced an arc where the turtle had reappeared.

The buzzard gave a pompous squawk. Tipping some food down form the sack on the turtle's head, the buzzard flicked beak and the reptile began to munch on the scraps as if a reward, leaving nothing left of Trimestrius's loaf and brace of fowl.

The prince was livid. Baus and Valere traded mirthless glares. The buzzard attacked the rest of the food with relish. A giggle came from Esling who had slunk out from behind a bottlegum with childlike impishness.

"What's so funny?" blurted out Trimestrius.

"These surely must be Wickles then?" growled Poli with disgust.

"Wickles, elderbeasts?" moaned Trimestrius. "What is the difference?! My delicious snacks, gone—with my incomparable wine! I declare these fiends to be heartless scavengers." He tore at the roots of his hair. "These robbers are in cahoots. Raiders of Wicklish design. And your chum is one of them!"

Baus twisted into a knot and showed his rebellious disagreement. "Little we can do, Prince tyrant, unless you fancy wading through the muck to retrieve what is yours."

Trimestrius grumbled an oath. Massaging his left arm which throbbed unmercifully at the buzzard's claw-hew, he searched about the woods to gather any possessions which may have dropped. "I'll make no attempt at retrieving anything. To waylay innocents plying between Lillenvir and

Ostgald is insufferable."

"Something must be done," said Baus. "There is a moral here."

"And what moral?"

"Never use a whip to coerce a reptile—it only leads to indignity and loss of lunch."

"A very droll maxim," observed Trimestrius with an angry grimace. "You should be a comic."

Baus bowed smilingly and infused the air with wry cheer. "You are too sober, Prince. Indeed your glum temperament will drag us into the doldrums. Lighten up! Levity is the key in times of trouble—"

Ulisa had arrived at that moment. In critical humour, she stared up at Trimestrius's ruffled cap and Baus's mud-streaked mail. "Well, well, what happened here?" Effervescing back to her regular self, she seemed mildly put out by the dishevelled appearance of her companions.

Baus crafted a negligent wave. "Nothing. A picayune misfortune which Trimestrius was unable to prevent."

Ulisa planted hands on hips, enjoining Esling to recount the tale.

Esling gave a brief account of events. Ulisa's face puckered into a smile when she heard about the buzzard and turtle. "Trimestrius, I see that you are irked. Perhaps I should refrain from flying so far afield and stick closer to the company."

Trimestrius hooked a fist up at Kazzasius who floated three feet over in leisure and amusement. "Why not induce this one-eyed mutant to come to our aid? Is there nothing of use for it? Beasts meanwhile gloat over my repast!"

The two rascal creatures indeed appeared to be enjoying their fare. The small bottle of wine had fallen from the height, smashing upon the tortoise's shell. The turtle lapped up the crumbs of the buzzard's falling scraps with ease.

The buzzard seemed apologetic for the inconvenience, as intimated by the series of squawking croaks. Trimestrius clutched beard with wrath and shook a gauntleted fist.

"What do you suggest then?" inquired Kazzasius.

"You could have flown across the morass," suggested Trimestrius of the Projector, "charged the deadhead, and extracted some sort of vengeance upon these gluttons. Those vile pigs have stolen our food. We have no lunch."

The great red-streaked eye gave a series of cautionary blinks. "I wholly eschew confrontation and I find your hints overreaching."

"Of course they are overreaching—what else should they be?"

"Listen!" clucked Kazzasius. "I conjure up a scene of a grimy tortoise champing on a wing of fowl and a foul-gummed buzzard tearing at my eye. Do you call this 'overreaching'? The xenophone tells me so. 'Tis a largely un-encouraging vision, and as I pointed out emphasize my role as 'scientist' over 'minion'."

Trimestrius grunted out a sour note. "This is a crass comparison. Must I involve Ulisa in the matter? Here, Ulisa!" But Kazzasius was already floating up in the air with offense. "Don't go sucking up to our shape-shifter! She can no more raise claws to a bird than harm a fly. She is a creature of the air herself."

Ulisa stood aside and nodded with a wise air. "Though your remarks are learned, Kazzasius, I find them somewhat over-simplified. Please let up on your assumptions."

Kazzasius flinched at the remark. The damage was done and the group was on its way, agreeing that to steer clear of redneck Wickles and to lead a wider path away from the deadheads was the wisest course. Ulisa posed thoughtful remarks upon the island and lingered behind with a pensive air. She crafted signals with her fingertips and made muttering references which Baus could barely distinguish. Momentarily she rubbed tiny hands and gave a quick clap, followed by a snap of fingers.

The giant turtle for a moment halted in its mastication, opened its grotesque beak and upended its victual in a huge yawning retch. The thing dropped like a stone into the mire, sinking out of sight. Ulisa gave a gleeful nod; her body continued to exude rich rosy glows, as if suspended in a bright airlessness. Baffled, the buzzard raised its crusted beak, twisted its crown in bemused wonder and suddenly cocked its head and inspected the tortoise's departure. Abruptly, it too seemed to lose interest in its lunch. Off it flew amid the maze of teetering deadheads, dodging and dashing, but smacked headfirst into a limbless trunk and disappeared from sight.

Baus nodded satisfaction and returned to join the others. From somewhere far away came a tinkling splash and then silence.

The matter was forgotten. The company resumed their quest down the root-riddled path without further incident.

Chris Turner

* * *

Before long the party had reached the shores of the river Lim and began to trek ever more doggedly westward toward Aurimag's cave. The sun had sunk to a ponderous globe on the horizon, partially hidden behind gaps in the trees. Now the river was fixed in a wan, metallic cast reflecting odd glimmers from its wake.

Baus lifted his gaze and stared at the spreading branches of tissel and bottlegums full of cones and acorns. A brooding watchfulness seemed to come over the forest in this eerie quarter.

A familiar emptiness began to strike Baus's belly—a feeling not dissimilar to those in the past. To embark upon an extensive foray in the coming of night with the possibility of danger, was a cheerless prospect.

This much Trimestrius agreed with and urged the company to take rest and indulge their cravings after they reached Aurimag's cave.

Poli set up a bleak moaning and Esling offered to ferret out foodstuffs to tide over the company until morning.

Baus substantiated Esling's competency in foraging. She scampered off with a willingness to find solace in the brush. The others were left staring into the shadows, fretting while Baus traded arguments with Trimestrius. The Wickle returned a quarter of an hour later laden with milkweed, brideswot and red mottled gurneyberries and troth-pods. The victual, while not substantial, allayed at least the brunt of hunger and they forced it down in gulps and grimaces, despite the bitterness of the herbs.

The sun sank gloomily west; thin amber rays trickled through the crooked boughs showing gnarled limbs in strange patterns. The ground became a dry carpet and hillier too, but the trees were often more numerous than could be counted. The infrequent green salamander fronds and rank bottlegum were somewhat comforting, no less the bogtooth bush.

The party hiked along the steep foot of a narrow hill for perhaps an hour before their heads drooped in fatigue. Below, the river purled in a swollen rush. A forgotten canyon was choked with asp and corkflower.

Trimestrius took pains to express his warnings of tumbling down into the defile.

Baus gazed down at the ravine. Black water gushed along splayed slabs of white marmor and after a quarter mile the water became surprisingly placid, more like a flat leaden pool—a course which a small punt might

708

traverse without portage.

Baus swung his haggard eyes to the far extremities of the woods. He fingered his sword—he felt danger was in the air as the sky dimmed to a deep purple.

No more than a few stones' throws away reared a trio of boulders: blue-lichened and fey. Clinging to the hillside the boulders were mounted with a teetering lintel, a slab so portentous as if to guard something within. Aurimag's doing, not unlikely! On top of the rise loomed a lone phantom elm—the same described by the hideous golem in Graietch's Honey Home —dangling precariously over the rise.

Trimestrius's heart missed a beat and he drew the company to a halt. His grimace was a knowing sneer and Baus's heart beat a shade faster. For a moment, the entrance seemed altogether too familiar a memory drawn from a vivid recollection of long ago. The phantom elm had withered with age. Its bulging roots sprawled over the mammoth stones like ropy vine; yet the sight was hauntingly familiar. 'Twas the same in his dreams, unquestionably the one envisaged from the golem's disgorged counsel. Moss and creepers piled over the lintel, down into the black gap of emptiness below like a beggar's hair. The dead, bone-grey limbs of the phantom elm were crooked and scraggly, perched with a handful of ravens whose steely eyes and ragged beaks showed testaments of omen.

Cawing bleak portent, the birds flew off at an unnatural pace.

Trimestrius motioned. "Aurimag's lair! To this very cave his minions dragged me a long time ago so that he could perform this hideous shrinking of my body!"

Baus shivered and was left with an unnameable apprehension as he studied the black cleft. The suspicions were fully confirmed—this was the same crevice which the golem had described in its ghastly, otherworldly whisper. How strange it was to be so near the place finally!—the eerie exudations and pulsing malice were disquieting at best even while shreds of daylight still graced the woods. Aurimag the neomancer, dwelt somewhere beyond the black mat—a chilling realization, and yet—gratifying.

But what other horrors lay await within that labyrinth?

Valere at last let his iron trap fall. "Well here we are!" he announced with verve. "I daresay, no better off than we were when we left Desenion."

Trimestrius pinched his brows into a frown and gestured to the trees. "We must plant our traps there and wait, seaman."

Valere gruntingly offered his tired advice. "Can we not simply enter the cave and be done with this exercise?"

"What, and be mauled by tree sprites?" growled Trimestrius. "If you wish death—go for it."

Valere barely restrained his annoyance. "Do you know when to jest and when not to?"

Poli chirped. "Tree goblins? What are those? How can we avoid them?"

"By steering clear of them!" laughed Valere.

"Silence! Your remarks are like hot air on the silence," grumbled Trimestrius.

"What can the goblins do to us?" asked Poli.

"Hurl one into a nesisphere perhaps?" chided the prince.

Poli waved off the omen. He was not much taken to n^{th} order devilry and Kazzasius, sensing something of the above, endorsed Trimestrius's admonitions. "The danger is real. Sprites of diseased intentions exist, warped nature that lie beyond the gap. Tossing their victims into a senseless void, they wait until the victims succumb to death by fright, or starvation."

Baus shuddered, appalled by the image.

"The sprites guard their domains ruthlessly—ministering all manners of punishments and terrors. I add, that these simplifications make Trimestrius's surmises seem like child's fables in comparison. Should any of us be caught in the webs of nth order sprites . . . we would be lucky to be ingested and excreted through their digestive roots into the earth."

Poli pinched nose in contempt, but was not wholly convinced. "You talk in fairy riddles, eagle. We have endured tribulations and disgusts by Wickles that you could never imagine."

"These are hardly comparable," lectured Ulisa. "Neomancers of the Circle, including Alvius, Maitor and Adelyheim, all agreed to the horror of Aurimag' conjurings. The magicians of the Circle will soon be arriving and vouch for Kazzasius's claim."

"From where do these neomancers come?" asked Esling.

"From Mismerion—to Aurimag's back door, so to speak," answered Ulisa truthfully. "We must wait here and draw on my colleagues' expertise."

Valere seconded the notion. "Better to wait for Adelyheim and Alvius, do you hear, Poli? Let's have no more of your gloomy talk. Baus and I have kept our covenant and you are alive thus far."

Poli gave a croak of derision, but Baus chided him. "True, Poli. It smarts me to hear you speak only of your rigours. I mirror Valere's own thinking. We were also subjected to vicissitude."

Ulisa advised the chatter to cease.

Dull amber was fast fading from the sky; the inky shadows in the forest stretched across the turf like streams. A whisper of funereal wind hissed through the woody eaves, investing the mallorns with spookiness.

Valere rigged the bear trap should anyone take ingress or egress from the cave. The prince advised him to descend with all speed and fulfil his task! Themselves, they would be saved a succession of awkward engagements and detestable blights when the perpetrator was ensnared.

Valere acknowledged the suggestion with pursed lips. Why was it he championing the perilous mission of initially installing the traps?

With a maximum of scepticism, the seaman crept down between the daunting boulders that framed the foot of the dark cleft, finding the ground soft, spongy, damp and spread with moss and decayed leaves.

He began hacking at the turf, implanting his bear trap with care, with its iron jaws set deep in the peat. Without undue peril the protruding barbs were covered with a quantity of soil and twigs to allay the magician's suspicion.

The trap was securely set and screened by detritus. Valere retreated to the hill's edge, grimacing from the odours that exuded from the cave's black mouth. He joined the others atop the hill where the phantom elm leaned so portentously. He rolled bow-legged over to Baus and crouched aside the grizzled trunk in a position of authority affording a bird's eye view of the cave and the mallorn-infested valley below.

Kazzasius circled overhead, reconnoitring the area with care. He now accompanied Ulisa in a flight of equal vigilance.

Dusk drew near and the companions stretched themselves behind the asp flower clumps, hoping that an opportunity would arrive: to bring Aurimag to his knees with no tragic repercussions to their own health.

CHAPTER 4

THE CAVE

OF

PASSIONS AND PUISSANCES

"The wise Neon watches his back; the wiser, incorporates a certain scope in his abode for an avenue of escape . . ."

—Old Lengish proverb

I

In a quandary, Aurimag felt his resolve slipping into penumbral territory. With the irritant Weavil out of his bottle roaming his cave at will, how best to recapture the imp and advance his puppet show thick on his mind?

Aurimag pulled back his loose black sleeves, swatting at his furrowed brow. He perspired under the most unbearable stress of the heat of the crucible; his mood not a great beacon of hope. He felt a contemptuous grin crawling across his face. He had only just visited Woisper, Salmeister and Graeitch, the last pawns in his revenge. The prisoners were safely sealed in their jars. The magician felt gladness and no inclination to meddle with the new seals on the cylinders. They might allow the occupants to somehow break free and cause him agitation.

Aurimag's lips parted in an aspect of shrewd reflection. To effect a performance by means of magical cords stretching through the glass—how that would entail a phenomenon of import! The actors would be immersed in their brine, puppets performing burlesques of excellence . . . enacting dramas on invisible strings through a cage of glass. An innovation beyond description!

Eagerly the magician set to work, devising strands of magical thread that could reach through the jar, attach themselves to the limbs of any of the occupants within. By no means a task of facility. In fact, sensitively intricate—as Aurimag was to discover some sweaty hours later, pushing himself awkwardly away from his workbench with a mixture of distaste and chagrin. To concoct the appendages of this sort involved a science beyond his understanding. He had kept no reference texts on the subject of parasynosis that might aid him in the construction of such strands.

The magician brooded. The scope of the enchantment remained a nebulous factor, so obscure likely that it precluded solution. He observed that if he could fashion such strings falling upon the lid, he could perhaps fabricate the *influence* of mastering puppets by psycho-magnetic force.

The scheme satisfied him to adequate degree and he ordered his simulacrum to fetch Woisper's and Salmeister's jars from the Vestuary. The golem disappeared. Aurimag thereafter set to devising an appropriate platform on which to host his remarkable puppets.

What joy! To consult his scrolls—a task of subsequent attention. He put finger to lip . . . coddled a smug grin. Leafing through the collation, he cried, "Ah, point of note!" It was an arcane rendition of a rare thaumaturgy—the '*Swangle Eruptor*' otherwise known as the '*Daisy Swingle*'—a spell so recklessly insidious that even the great Zossoke, Brown Neon of the 4rth Classification, had never committed it to papyrus.

Aurimag stared hours later at Woisper's rotund jar mounted on an impromptu stage of miniature configuration. The platform was expertly rigged—a complex mesh-weave of strangle-vine comprising a pleasing backdrop. It was devised to etch an impressive screen on the marmor wall.

Three parties appeared—Woisper, Graeitch and Salmeister—yet only one of himself, which allowed two of his pet 'ghosts' (another innovation) to command the shabby personalities of Salmeister, and inevitably Woisper, who was the main lead, while he, Aurimag, could control the infamous 'Graeitch'.

He laughed at the innovation. The sordid Wickle was to be Woisper's immediate but not penultimate 'bully'. The artistry had brought tears of laughter to his eyes. Salmeister lacked a bully puppet of his own, so the magician convinced himself to introduce another figure into the mixture—a blue schasm, which, though not his preferred choice, had inflicted Woisper with undue tribulation before Graeitch had become his intimate.

With two cylinders perched gaudily on the stage, Aurimag was provided an excellent vantage from which to dash from jar to jar, commanding the role of bully or 'spectator', such that with both neomancers and bullies controlled, actions could always be manipulated to the maximal interest of the 'bullies'.

In the dim hours of dawn Aurimag became exhausted of his sport. Without proper audience, the absence of Baus and Weavil, his two immediate enemies, had him drumming his fingers on his worktable, frowning in displeasure. Seven days had passed—without the return of his golem. Perhaps not an inordinate time—and yet? The creature was manufactured from a rich chemistry of mud slime with a purpose to a single-minded goal. Being of limited intelligence, the creature was equipped with a profound talisman in which to hasten its success—the *moolstone*. So . . . why had the wretched creature not returned?

Aurimag set to cleansing his cave to abate his misgivings—of serpents, leprolizards and bright-crakes . . .

* * *

The cave-purification was hitchless and the magician remained pleased to spy Salmeister out of the corner of his eye glaring. He recalled the earlier 'bully-puppet' performance and thought to provide a more permanent companion for Salmeister than the schasm. Weavil's capture would have to wait—though the poet would present a perfect housemate—a trickster so full of rude surprises that he should fulfil his purpose!

The magician gave a cryptic laugh. Slapping his shanks, he spent a deal of time speculating upon the scene of the two new 'peers' haranguing and bullying each other in their canister. How glad he would be when he caught the miniature Weavil!

His glee was short-lived. With lips compressed to slits, his thoughts travelled saturninely to Baus. Two of his new lines of simulacra had 'perished' in vitro, for lack of proper ministration. He had used the husks to feed his fires. It then occurred to him that it would be prudent to formulate another minion to capture the fisherman.

Aurimag pondered the idea. The complex undertaking was painstaking: he had no desire to prematurely creep about the eerie spaces of the forest. It was so full of marauders and perils as to make collecting the ingredients dangerous. Yet to gather the spores to act as seeds for REOGENESIS was essential. Were there any applicable constituents that he might collect in his cavern?

Aurimag's eyes teetered critically upon the mat which held the oval trap. Possibly the place below might comprise such entities as ghastly as the smells and exudations were.

Aurimag shivered. He felt revulsion at the thought of entering that black abysmal tunnel. Yet he gathered Petri dish and candle and snatched a key from the hook and unlatched the grate. Instantly a wash of sickening odours assailed his nostrils. The entire workroom was beset with a noisome reek. Half-gagging, Aurimag resisted the urge to slap shut the trap and abandon the enterprise completely. It might have been only spoiled milk or rancid meat that smelled so within, if not something more fetid. Something had likely died down there . . .

No matter. He crouched and hunched his way forward, setting foot down into the miasmal blackness. Still, even he could not permit himself to venture too many steps . . .

He snapped the trap shut. He latched the portal and flung the key scornfully back on its peg.

To formulate another simulacrum was the only recourse. The last specimen was occupied on an incidental mission to retrieve a new maid from Lillenvir. Loosing a menace on the village was a risky venture, but a useful ruse to allay singular suspicions of its earlier pilfering from Vishire. He had instructed the golem to cross the Lim by means of the coracle, stashed amidst chokeweed and bramble along the southern shore.

He had adopted a profitable method of recycling his maids, somewhat similar to urging a tired cow to give milk. Whenever one became dull or uninspiring, he had hypnotized the captive to forget her experiences before releasing her to the wild and always the golem arrived with a new substitute, blindfolded, while the other was returned, unharmed, to her native village.

The maids, at first, provided Aurimag with pleasure, but now he found them beneficial for additional purposes. A half pint of their blood mixed with his own comprised a salutary mix which showered the 'birthing' of his golems in their primitive tubs. Siphoning samples of blood every day, he astutely observed that the combination of male and female ichor to be an optimum formula for the golem's intelligence—a factor significantly increasing his success.

II

Meanwhile, clinging in a hole in the ceiling of Aurimag's cave, Weavil gnashed and fretted. The cranny that Weavil occupied offered little solace to his predicament. Compressed into a tight, beetle-like ball, very contrary to his dignity, he winced at the insane absurdity of the condition of his fate. His garments were torn and soiled and reeked of brine.

His eyelids fluttered as he sought to recall when he had last been in Heagram's prison. And before that? The last memory was of him and Baus stumbling through the dusky fair grounds one foggy evening in Heagram. Half soused, he struggled with a jangled memory of violence and confusion, a bewildering potpourri of faces and scenes, heated debates and truculent threats. A frightful shrinking, and his handsome young body was a miniature mockery of what it was and there was a spate of dialogue with a demented magician and his henchmen. A period of captivity—then a cold scramble through a dark shadowy world, a littered yard pocked with reeking fish, then—he was rudely scooped up into a black cylinder by a cold groping hand . . .

It seemed so many ages ago—in a hollow, insensate world, and feeling came over him of rancour. He recalled the experience with livid clarity: thrust in a jar, below an ocean of frights, endless moons after moon with only an opaque liquid pressing in on him, pasting his horizon with quietude and hopelessness . . .

Weavil jostled himself back to reality. The shivering feeling he thrust away. The green opaque world of soundless vertigo was still crowding his world—that flat hopeless plane of solitude and confinement.

A cool sweat glistened on Weavil's brow. He peered down to the worktable and saw a face which he only recalled with loathing.

The magician Nuzbek stood below, hand to chin, with gaunt face pressed in an arrogant scowl. The lout was garbed in moon cowl, a draping black gown, foppish black slippers. His eyes were cunning ferret's eyes and with a thin bony hand he was dropping three triangular rune-stones into a beaker of bubbling liquid, rich with pink colour. The liquid hissed, then sizzled; the magician's face showed a wary expressiveness. He looked older, this gaunt Nuzbek, more fractious and hypersensitive than what the poet remembered him. He shambled about on his slippers through the rude chamber like a ghoul, chanting and muttering monosyllables, pouring incessant liquids into beakers and combing through screeds and prodigious scripts, essaying to uncover some freakish, arcane sorcery.

The magician read from a favoured black tome; the leaves bulged with notes and side references. On and on the pages flipped.

A hundred cils Weavil would give to dash that pinch-faced dastard's brains to bits!

Yet drastic acts would have to be weighed against perils. A mallet or carboy would suffice, but it took no genius to realize that Nuzbek's power had grown since the days of his mediocre magic show back in Heagram . . .

He shifted weight back to his predicament. The air stank of balms and incenses and salt brick and disgusts. There was a sulphurous reek in the air, distillations, bromic exudations, macabre tinctures that the magician had been brewing with hasty malice, cultivating weird mixtures in his giant crucible like some earth-gnome who would add to his collection of flasks and ampoules strewn about his worktable with relish. 'Twas apparent that the magician placed regard for other creatures second to thaumaturgy—occultisms stemmed from death and decay—old mysteries whispered by diseased minds of men. The stenches and mists hinted of descents into madness, precious potentials of sorceric talent turned evil.

Weavil studied the grim face of his captor with caustic enmity. A bristle of stalagmites edged up from the floor like icicles—almost to his own height. Perhaps he could use one of these pillars as a launch-pad for an offence on the magician himself. The chamber contained a fearsome hotness owing to the presence of the crucible. The glowing cauldron, as big as a monastery bell, bloomed not fifteen paces away, choking with steam, cooking unwholesome things. The cavern walls were bare of adornments, composed of hard ropy rivulets of lava-like substance, perhaps from long ago.

The long cluttered workbench Aurimag coddled dominated the space. The knotted planks were corroded by spilled acids and elixirs, scabbed with black burns. A tubular mass of tinted glass, blues, greens and violets, occupied the main part of the table, the same which had aided the magician in the shrinking of Graeitch and Woisper long ago. Elsewhere ranged a set of corded candelabra, a host of frayed tomes and various miserable, grimed tubs. A group of brass chests and crates overflowed with gears, rotaries, flasks, bones, puppet pieces, ampoules, crystals and other imponderables. Mementos likely, thought Weavil, of times long past—as too, a sinister astrolabe, affixed to the far wall of the cavern, a source of disquiet, especially when it crafted peculiar clicks and gongs at unpredictable intervals.

Weavil gazed longingly at the limitless clutter. How long had Nuzbek been cooped up in this burrow? More importantly, where in the devil was he?

These questions had no answer. The days had passed and with grim animosity, Weavil sat ensconced like a cockroach, reciting old sea rhymes in his head to calm his nerves. Somehow he managed to snatch scraps of cheese and bits of leftover food stolen from the magician's larder while he was so absorbed in his endeavours that he did not hear the tiny scuff of feet. Such a despicable means to survive, Weavil brooded, yet a necessary means—scrabbling about on all fours like some mangy scavenger. But when shrunken to a size of a badger, hedged by a foe as Nuzbek, one could not be choosy . . .

Finally he could not sustain this undignified subterfuge for any longer and avowed to take matters into his own hands.

Swallowing a clot of phlegm, he thought of the prospect of discovery and quailed.

Weavil came to apprehend some of Nuzbek's patterns. 'Twas a rhythm complex and puzzling. Every so often, the magician would disappear, returning a time later, relaxed of face and flushed, with a jaunty step. Wherewith, he would gulp a goblet of mulled wine and consume a brace of fowl fried over his crucible. When the magician slept, which was sparingly, he did so in his private room off the main cavern hung with the bronze shields. Once, Weavil had spied him, following him up the precarious half-stair into the Bronze Room, disappearing beyond a thick, iron-ringed door which he could not bring himself to open for fear of being detected.

He had crouched, listening at a crack in the bottom jamb where the threshold met the stone and heard a thump and a bang: "So, my feisty little wench"—Nuzbek's voice came shafting through the crack—"Let's have no more of this snivelling and weeping. You are a rotten little princess!" Pressing an ear closer, Weavil had heard another wail and thump and a more sharp exclamation. "Hearken, witch! Let us have no more of these goose pimples and annoying sniggers. Let's have more sport! Yes, sport! Would you have me summon Hrigobr, my minion? He ministers only extreme rigour and is quite joyless."

Weavil retreated, riddled with fear. Here was a new dilemma—some glum hint of skulduggery in Nuzbek's midst. Equally as mystifying was the presence of the creature Graeitch, who now occupied a murky jug not dissimilar to his own in Nuzbek's Vestuary.

Weavil slunk sullenly back to his hidey-hole where he tried to sleep off his dilemma. He found the attempt hopeless. With one eye propped open, for fear of discovery, he tossed and turned.

He stuck out an eye, saw the walking marionette garbed in its brown baggy breeches. What a queer fellow! There was a black cloak draped around its mud body and a mauve hood coiled around its dead-looking face. To say that the 'marionette' bore a striking similarity to Nuzbek was pure understatement. The magician jocularly referred to the 'creature' as 'Hrigobr'—his puppet-golem facsimile of himself—to this, Weavil could not help but think of the intricacy of its construction.

Now, he saw the magician pace, and halt, hands clasped behind his back before the crucible. His temples were distorted and he muttered frightful things from texts too ancient to name. In between the stanzas Nuzbek blustered effusive gusts upon a strange cornet of his. The madman tipped the enchanted instrument to his ear, as if straining to hear some riddlish wisdom revealed by elemental forces.

An intellectual puzzle, thought Weavil. With lips compressed, he saw the magician sidle to the table, eyes distant and bulging over crabmarked screeds and cursive script. In a delirious tone, he tossed cryptic invocations such as '*oozasbar*' and '*inoredent*' at his marionette. The puppet appeared to stoop and glare with a corpse-like expression. It likewise seemed to understand something of its master's lunatic phraseology, for at times it would shamble out of the room on a given command and return later bearing a strange object or whispering new facts in the magician's ear.

All so strange was this that Weavil became more perplexed than ever. Nuzbek's behaviour was all too unnerving. Yet the magician's theme never varied—thrust, incant, sprinkle, gloat. The goals: delve into the spells of power for the purposes of darkness. Twice Weavil caught him committing a spectacular display—an emission of bright flame, of purple colour, a splattering of star-motes sent from his fingertips, the air singeing a tarp pinned to the far wall and leaving an electrical tinge in the air. Spurts of star-fire flew distances of five feet or more with alarming haste. Nuzbek hatched a lump of glowing coal into a trio of translucent balloons. These balloons floated on high, then he cradled them lovingly in his palms, juggling them about until they were a blur of luminescence. They floated again on high like birds, while he laughed ecstatically.

Weavil recalled the event and sagged back in dismay, afraid of this tortured madman and his abominable vessels of thaumaturgy nearby with their sinister light-patterns illuminating the gleam in his eye or the glint off his teeth. The magician had remained ignorant of the poet's presence up till now, cached in his ceiling. He had watched on with rising concern all the interesting events brewed and concoctions born. Spheres and cubes imprisoned an indigo egg with yellow fangs . . . suckerfish with bright marble wings all polished . . . a ghost carrack armed with lateen sail plying an imaginary sea . . . four huge battling gnats guarding eyes of carved cinnabar circling a slow-spinning mountain. All these fabrications were disturbing realities and brought Weavil a glimpse of a diseased mind. Filled with pangs of foreboding he cringed: the unearthly preambles into darker planes of existence indicated a much larger, eerier scheme in existence. All this was sequestered in Nuzbek's twisted brain. But what?

Weavil shuddered to imagine.

The magician chittered on to his 'puppet' about how he would flush out the little 'wedgebill' Weavil and how by means of a tube of putrescence sprayed through his abode, he would capture him. Weavil recoiled. Pulling a thrice-spell-soaked flaxhack gag over his own nostrils, he would remain immune to the taint, after which he would command a trio of wooly-woolies[*] to remove the acute unpleasantness from the air. ([*] Wooly-woolies: Invisible entities of green and brown classification, each of which owed Aurimag an indenture. Once the wooly-woolies were given as a 'sabbatical' gift from Kazzasius, though that was years ago.)

The disclosure rent Weavil with shivers. He crawled in panic. To be caught in one of Nuzbek's traps was insanely frightening. He recalled an incident, recently, when the magician had produced two jars and used the entombed neomancers (and Graeitch) as stage actors upon which to foist his disgusting and unseemly pranks.

With great swiftness, Weavil entertained wishes to ensure that he was not a participant.

Nuzbek trundled off whistling on one of his visits to the shield room, while Weavil crept out of his prickly crevice, swinging down upon the nearest stalagmite with courage.

With certain cautious indulgence, Weavil had gained Nuzbek's workbench, and now with calm agility, he snapped the top off one of the slow-burning candles. Hopping over to the wall, he stood aside the puppet stage where he had seen Nuzbek sit many times, often toying with a bone-shaped key hung on the wall. Carefully, the dwarf remained wary of the marionette's dull, vacant gaze. The thing refused to budge and it remained mindless of Weavil's motions or passage.

Weavil dragged aside the mat covering the trapdoor, a feat requiring significant effort. Weavil was surprised to see a tiny trickle of fluid dripping down the leg of Nuzbek's worktable.

What could it be? The liquid seeped around the edge of the hatch, disappeared in the blackness of the cracks with a tiny drip. Pursing his lips, Weavil watched with suspicion, fighting every wry compulsion to kick at the liquid, but he was revulsed at the alchemic greenness of it and thought to steer clear. But how could he if he wished to investigate the crevice? He thought to abandon his whole scheme completely!

But that would be defeat.

Weavil forced himself with great difficulty to open the rusty padlock. He dragged aside the iron clips and hefted the oval mesh, struggling to remain calm regarding the horrid stench wafting out from the darkness. The miasma was of such character to include fermented cabbage, rotting liver and worse things. A quick search revealed a spill rag draped atop one of Nuzbek's filthy tubs. Weavil tore a band of the rag to wrap about his nose. Nausea barely deserted him, but he gripped his candle and began a quaking descent into that dark hole, stopping only briefly to emit short breath-gasps as necessary. Grimacing with distaste, he hopped farther down into the rat hole . . .

Almost at once he plummeted several feet. The candle fell somewhere to his left—amidst a place of dankness and noisome roots. The flame flickered, nearly expired. Weavil scrambled to grab the dying flame. He coaxed it to life. Shaking with apprehension, the dwarf thrust the sputtering flame in front of his saucer-eyes and was astounded to find himself in a tunnel of sorts. 'Twas no ordinary corridor. There were numerous snake-like bends in the passageway that disappeared off into chilly distance. The walls were slime-clawed—most extraordinarily hewn, in relation to their labyrinthine quality.

Weavil knew he was in a maze of mystery: one step took him to a small cavern, another to a dead end which roused similar unease. The latter path, even widening, allowed him to at least walk upright—but barely. He took trembling steps to find he could just touch either wall with arms fully extended. Gingerly he moved like a sleepwalker, padding one foot after another along the pinched alleys, musty with age. He forced back the dread of what might live in some of those ponderous passages.

More twists came and went; they confounded Weavil's sense of direction. From where had he come? Various side ways had become constricted tunnels, many barely large enough for him to waddle through on all fours; the bulk of these were fraught with rank flows of air and unguessable reeks.

Weavil arduously marked off his passing by scraping a boot against the slimes—this way he could have an escape route if need be to retrace his steps in a manner of haste.

The slick walls became suddenly furred, with something of a moist green moss.

Weavil was repulsed. What was it?

Lichens? Fungus?

His sixth sense believed it some kind of underground spanglemoss. Either way, it mattered little. He daren't touch the stuff—such was an act of folly.

The minutes passed and Weavil grew more anxious descending lower, noticing a sinister set of vapours besetting his nostrils. What now? The passageway weaved. The tunnel seemed to breathe of its own accord, an unwholesome dankness. He mustered his resolve and found himself walking about in what seemed a rot-reeking corridor. Hell's hounds, what drake's bowel was this! Down, down he plunged—in a certainty of doom.

Peculiar things Weavil saw in that stretch of tunnel—many rope-like fibrils of brownish colour running infinitely long down the dark floor like some fibrous roots of an enormous, fantastic tree. Some were definite cables, no thicker than thumb width, but others fanned out to grow in slick numbers to the breadth of a man's wrist. The roots curved, twisted, switch-backed, reached upward and back, swivelled about every side chamber like rotten snakes.

For some odd reason, the strands chose to ignore specific tunnels.

Hand to chin, Weavil began to discern star- and fan-shaped creatures as if embedded in the mossy walls themselves. What were these? Sea cucumbers? Crinoids? Brittlestars? All were grey, green, and blue.

But impossible! There was no water down here!

Weavil caught his breath. The presence of an unknown tinkling reached his ears—'twas a jingling echo that crept through some dank slit in the twine-rooted floor.

Weavil put an ear to the ground. He recoiled at the dank sensation he felt. A jet of water on some sunless pool? An underground stream? Wild guesses! So much for his hunches— water didn't flow here . . .

Weavil's candle began to burn low in his hand. He saw a green stalagmite thrusting up, hindering his passage and casting shadows about the tunnel like mad fingers of doom.

Weavil crept on again, stumbling and staggering like a rat. More frightened than anything, he felt the presence of an underground stream possibly hinting of a confluence with a river *outside* the cave.

So, there was water . . . He leapt at the thought. He had passed below some river that may run on dry land. Water did not travel upwards which meant—

He abandoned this line of reasoning.

The passageway widened. Now he entered into a broad cavern—with domed, marmoric ceiling and three side passages. The rock ceiling was high. A grown man to stand in it, and peculiarly—the stench seemed only to escalate in intensity.

Weavil poked a finger to his lip. Indeed a sinister presence this stench—a source of quality which was likely due to the freakish moss which clung in clumps to the walls, and now possibly contained overtones of decayed flesh.

He raised his candle to his brow. Cautiously he followed a path leading into the cavern and lurid flickers cast disturbing shadows along the mossy walls, heralding monstrous shapes. The floor seemed to rear up between the stalagmites.

Weavil let loose a gasp.

A litter of brown, paper-thin roots had caked the entire floor of the chamber. They twined themselves spider-like to a central massive ropy trunk, sending tendrils attaching themselves to the gargantuan ghost oak, squat and hoary, sprawled heavily against the far wall. Weavil quailed. The dome-like roof of twining branches strained against the ceiling as if wanting to push up the whole cavern. The canopy ran the extent of the left wall, brooding, hulking, like some straddling cloak. The loglike roots hooked into the raised limestone floor. But here in this abysmal murk? How could a tree grow? Could such a phenomenon exist?

Weavil squinted with suspicion. Veins of dark magic seemed to lurk in this precinct. The tree limbs framed weirdly-fluted patterns among the fangish stalactites crusted like odd jewels above. Knots of eldritch wood protruded from the grey withered trunk like bone. Eyes peeked out of the bark, that seemed to watch him from all directions. The tree gave an odd shudder, then seemed to heave its leaveless and spidery bulk, dark and dead and possibly standing there deceased for centuries, and yet looking older still.

Weavil plucked at his nose. What a timeless mystery!

He crept closer to stare oppressively at the tree. A sequal he would give for the profound secrets this old goat. But better to try for the moon. What malignant force had betrayed it and stopped its growth?—or yet had teased it into germinating in this dank atmosphere?

So many things of an elder generation Weavil did not know. And hence, he stood witness to a sad and wondrous realm, some burrow of eerie mystery which the world above could hardly fathom.

Weavil pussyfooted closer and felt a jab of apprehension. Like a cub he felt lost in this dark grotto.

He tiptoed about on quiet feet, fashioning mousy movements as if his feet spurned the very rock on which he trod.

Water dripped from the rooty branches—plip-plop, like the tiny plink of raindrops in a quiet forest. But he was not cowed enough to deny himself a more scrupulous examination.

He poked his candle inside the first black passageway to his left and saw a rare sight. A fetor greeted his nose in a burrow crammed with bleached grey bones. Possibly other things dwelled there too: foul creatures that had stripped the unfortunate victims of their belongings —sandals, jewellery and antique beads.

Weavil quavered. A rusty dirk gleamed in the murk; though not definite; stuck to it was a tattered, rotting garment.

Why? Such glimpses could only foreshadow inquietude. He stepped back to the next passageway which seemed altogether eerier as it plunged down to quiet, empty depths.

A third passage rose up along a promising tunnel and exuded some sort of fresher vapours. Weavil breathed more easily.

For a heartbeat he felt indecision. Why cavil over unknowables? The last passage looked the most appealing. Why not take it, and leave this foul tree behind? He paused in indecision. Wait! He detected an odd tattered mass hanging from a low-lying oak branch arching deep into the cavern.

What could that sinister object be?

Weavil stole a wistful glance over his shoulder.

Nothing there. The gargantuan tree seemed to loom ever above him like an ancient sentinel. He stared up in the gloom, perceiving a hanging mat of hair, bone and fibre.

Weavil fought back a shiver. 'Twas perhaps a hide stretched upon the root branches nestled between stalagmite to stalagmite. He cautiously approached, seeing bones for sure—a series of them, for the candlelight twinkled and showed too much of that grisly matter for his tastes. A half eaten carcass or skeleton . . . Odd how these headless carcasses seemed to be suspended upside down on some withered shreds of their own flesh, as if they had been hung there purposefully with some kind of diseased intention.

He shuddered. What a crazy clothesline of trophies! The hides were disgusting, all drooping and dangling—the source of the ubiquitous stench, which remained no more a mystery, was the old rancid bits of bone, gristle and sinew. Why? How? Rags of bones do not dangle of their own accord.

Weavil thought to pitch himself quietly into the upward-winding tunnel, but paused to ponder the mystery. The carcasses were perhaps no higher than himself, and of girth comparable to a small brute beast of his size. Did the ragged tree somehow catch dwarves, perhaps intruders, and ensnare them in its boughs and perform some kind of horrid function upon them? Did Nuzbek perhaps pitch hapless victims down here in these catacombs?

Weavil shuddered at the thought. The tree's life was expired; the limbs were dead, gnarled as if from ages ago. What deviltry could occur in such a lifeless hulk? Weavil laughed. A tiny sound that was swallowed in the darkness. The limbs could no more snatch a living creature as fly to—

He glanced about with amazement. A sound? A groan?

His darker imagination contemplated climbing one of the stalagmites and touch one of the bleached bones dangling in the branches. The dismal thing waited for his examination, slowly twirling, with bones gleaming, tinkling like little fairy rattles.

He recoiled at his own morbidity. Quaint but terrifying! Was he insane? He had best be on his way.

Weavil crawled down the stalagmite to swing eager steps away from the monstrous tree. He had taken no more than a step when an exceedingly flesh-crawling voice, very baritone, struggled forth from a larynx of stone and wood.

He stopped short, frozen in inhuman panic.

The voice groaned forth again, words which Weavil seemed just barely to understand.

"Who goes there?" came the bellow again.

He cast darting glances left to right. Who had spoken? There was no response or signal to the inquiry.

He whirled in dismay. Fixing his attention on the ghost oak, he felt his poet's mouth sag. Surely it was not from the lopsided knotty wood gash that the eldritch voice came? The idea was too preposterous to imagine!—and yet . . . he cocked an eyebrow. More sounds—an echo? What dim sorcery was this? In a quavering voice, Weavil yelled out: "Show yourself! . . . 'Tis only Weavil! Whatever you are, spirit or sprite, be forthright. I am small, a simple creature, a casual good neighbour if you will. I intend only good wishes to this hall."

The tree responded in a dreary voice. "A do-gooder, eh?" The deep rumble almost shook the stone around them. "Then move your squeamish little hide over here, little rodent, so I can see you." Bark-like lips writhed in mocking synchrony. " . . . That's it!" The tree-bark lips worked in eccentric rhythm like some great earthworms moving. "Over here! I wish to see you better."

Weavil complied. The thought of offending this awesome tree was not on his wishlist.

The candle twitched in his hands—morbid flickers that scattered about the endless dark. It revealed two grainy knotholes for eyes, a glaring mouth that radiated forth from the base of the trunk. He pitched precariously back on his heels. He saw the orbs as pure jewels of mischief—beacons of mesmerization. The light seemed to twitch in its eyes. The face, or what Weavil recognized as such, comprised a lopsided tumble of features: a clown's mask of bark rivulets, two bevels for lips, a pair of eye knot-lumps and two broken-off twigs as ear knobs.

"Ah!" exhaled the tree. "What pygmy do I spy with my one good eye?" It rotated its knotty sight—orbs to better inspect Weavil's miniature body.

"No pygmy, sir tree, only Weavil, as I have mentioned."

"Weavil? Hmph! What kind of a name is that? I see that you have left dirty finger-marks on my coiffure. Very bad! And you would have nimble shanks—yes, nimble shanks, that is very good! Fingers as these may help me to ease the abominable itch on my left greesheckle. Great Gands! How the time has passed and pain goads my nerves!"

Weavil frowned in confusion. The tree did some harrumphing and twitching. "Yes! I shall very much like your service, you imp!" The uppermost branch began to flex and unflex.

Weavil stood transfixed. A delirious dread clutched his liver. But the tree thundered on: "The shreeks will not care to hear your complaints, little one—too moody they are, too busy, oh those bushy-tailed rotten pests! Mind you, I will teach them manners. Climb onto my mane and assuage these sensitive branch hairs—which for you, who are a spry thing, is nothing but a picayune task."

Weavil repudiated such a mission. "Not very efficiently could I do this deed."

Recovering from the shock, he could only lift eyes to the rooty maze of 'hair' spreading in every direction along the dripping ceiling. The tinkling skeletons lodged in the noxious reaches began to chime like ghastly bells. Weavil cringed. Skeletal clumps lodged bleakly and he balked at a climb through that ghastly net.

"Come, little bird! Time is not infinite."

In helpless tones Weavil announced: "Mayhap you are right, but like you, I have important errands which I must attend to."

The ghost oak shivered in annoyance. "Errands? What errands? Can they be as important as my greesheckle?"

"More so," Weavil remarked candidly. "If I knew what a greesheckle was. I refuse to enlarge on such thing as my errands. Such a request I may gladly oblige, after first securing a favour in return."

"A favour?" the tree growled. "What favour?" Its voice was like an old goat suffering an ague. Before Weavil could answer, the tree bawled out, "I would give you favours, varlet!— smacks and buffets. Not always have I been so sedentary! Once I could tramp my way through these passages like a young sapling! Each of my roots and hairs was part of a well-oiled machine!—Ah, I could travel through my corridors smartly like the most cunning weasel, sliding and grinding, teaching these filthy shreeks lessons and scares! Now they gnaw at my bones and plunge horrid things in my hair. At every corner the detestable things come to nibble at my toes; even now they might pounce in these corridors while I whine in my vainglory."

Weavil shook his head in conciliatory wonder. "Such uncouth beasts these shreeks are. I would be of mind to teach them their manners as you mentioned, if I had inclination."

The tree seemed pleased with the disclosure; it uttered an unearthly groan of impressive quality but which yet engulfed the chamber with shakes and shivers. Weavil groped around. The ripple was of such effect that he staggered and stumbled.

The tree intoned soberly, "Yes, dwarf, you are quite right; as time passes, my old gripes mean less than a hagwipple's teat. Well—what is it that you are wishing? Come now! Speak your mind and be done! Hags and hornblowers! You are an exasperating chit. Must I coax it from you? If I may pass the next hundred years untroubled by this wretched tingling in my left greesheckle, I would be overjoyed!"

Weavil was amazed and displeased at the tree's manner. "I for one, wish information."

"Specifically?"

Weavil spoke in a cautious tone, "At present, I seek the outside world, away from this gloom and dankness as I am in train of eluding a villainous oaf, more specifically, a deranged magician."

The tree seemed perplexed by the admission, but then some jog of memory seemed to recall the tenant above. "But why would you wish other than the beautiful serenity of *Twinelitch?*"

Weavil stared at the malign face in vexation. "The outside world is that delightful place where rosy sunlight fills the air, and fair valleys abound and where clever birds sing melodies all day long, where the breeze carries fallow scents and spring blossoms hustling over flowery fields."

"Very poetic but not my thing—I know nothing of those things. In fact, I confess it to be pure fiction. Your utopia is but a small fantasy, little man. Abandon it and come learn of the marvels of Twinelitch!"

"No, I will not," declared Weavil, and stated that other interests absorbed his attention.

The tree was irked with the remark and uttered a pompous expostulation. "Lout! Drabdrip! You must learn decorum in my abode! Would you insinuate that this underworld of mine, unseemly?"

"Nothing of the sort," assured Weavil. "I merely suggest an alternative to your perception." He hopped back several steps. "I only say in all honesty, that for one so gigantically large, it seems quite odd that you can't assuage your own woe with this greesheckle of yours. Not to mention that you can survive in an environment so dark and dank."

"Odd? I call it marvel, boy!" He grumbled out a magnificent triad. "Paragon!—Prodigy! Those are words to describe my mettle. As a young acorn I grew as *Finklerank*, carried as a seed by those rummaging shreeks who foraged me from some distant cranny. I needed no light to mollycoddle me like that fire stick you hold so fiercely in your hand. Cold drips I only need—and quietude—the chill hint of hidden, lightless waters—an abundance which exists in my domain!"

Weavil congratulated Finklerank. "Most inspiring!" Hopping from foot to foot, Weavil attempted to mollify Finklerank's consternation.

The tree grunted pridefully. He rippled his bark and seemed oblivious to the fact that he himself was some kind of ghost oak, or elm-sprite. "All my life I have grown! From seed to sapling, from middling to gargantuan—now I am in the process of *grimling*, for I have increased my lore and intelligence. In what medium? Nothing but this murksome dark! As Finklerank, I know no such things as light and heat! Only dampnesses, chills, seps, drips and draughts, mildews and vapours, chilblains, rats, moss, mice and shreeks . . ."

Weavil gulped.

The tree shouted, "If you would pursue such lofty goals as seeking this 'outside world' of yours, I would caution you to avoid it: for a fact I know that only one of the three tunnels shows a faint flicker—perhaps a path to lead you to a place of freedom—far away from the abysmal shreeks."

Weavil became suddenly animated. "This is profitable news! Humour me, old oak—which tunnel might bear me this light?"

The great tree regarded Weavil with zeal. "Do you think me such a mooncalf? The moment I inform you, you would be off down that corridor, scuttling like an eager beetle to win this 'outside' of yours!"

Weavil pinched lips in moody hauteur. "That would be a singularly gross thing to do, not to mention rude; furthermore, it denotes a certain lack of respect."

"Silence!" bawled the tree. "Either remedy my pang of greesheckle or feel my wrath!"

Weavil stamped his foot. "I shan't!"

The great eyes widened. "You would flout me? A rebellious imp you are. Perhaps you might eke out an hour or two in choosing one of my side tunnels, notably the wrong one, who is to say? But as to the other passages, would you take the risk? One might keep you safe from the shreeks for a while . . . another might bring you doom."

Weavil clenched his hand to chin. How to thwart this insatiable tree? He imposed several tremulous glances from one passage to another. "As you can see, I care not to grope amongst the corridors for shreeks or massage your coiffure with all its morbid clumps. I shall make my own way—trusting to my own fortune."

"That is a valiant hope!" roared the tree. "But how shall you succeed practically? You would defy me? Finklerank? Master of deep dark Twinelitch?"

"In a word, yes," replied Weavil with a small cough. "Now if you would excuse me, I must be off to my risk-taking."

"Insufferable cockatrice!" the ghost oak moaned. "You shall pay mightily for your insolence! Stand on guard—I service you a blight!"

Weavil stood his ground. He lifted a finger over his head. With a youthful flourish, he cried, "Stand down yourself, rot reek! Your vile threats do not scare me. Spare your groans and grumbles for others, for they shall not hinder me. You should accomplish nothing by browbeating me and infecting me with such bluster!"

"Miserable twit!" the tree groaned. "Prepare for a mishap!" From its barkish lips it erupted a peal of lunatic laughter that nearly swept Weavil off his feet. Cold and angry whooshes floated past Weavil's face and he clutched at his torso, essaying to scramble to the far end of the chamber before he was engulfed by the draughts. He sought the third tunnel but nearly lost his footing, pitching backwards in an attempt to scramble away, but looked dangerously deep down the second that yawned before him, concluding it was invariably his least favourite of the three.

He snatched up his hissing candle, preparing to flee up the most promising tunnel.

But the force of Finklerank's gusts prompted a chiming of the cursed skeletons hanging from his root-branches. The sounds remarkably symbolized 'mealtime' to certain unlovely creatures ravaging the niches below.

Weavil turned head in dismay, for a tumult of violence drifted from the deep-down bowels of the cavern. Rustlings, mewlings—the shuddering of a thousand padded feet—those were the reverbations that Weavil heard—squeakings of the most uncompromising kind, crawling, creeping, scrabbling . . .

Weavil scrambled on all fours. Lacking any semblance of sanity, he groped whimpering to the chamber's end.

From which corridor had the confusion come? None of the three seemed sanctuaries of safety.

The roar grew louder. Weavil struggled to his feet. He realized that his only chance was to flee the cavern before the horror came. The tumult spread not from the black yawning depths, but the tunnel of his own choosing!

Cursing, unnerved by the discovery, Weavil stood appalled, breathless. Hastily springing back toward the larger tunnel, he saw the manoeuvre gave Finklerank a chance to grope at him with an crooked bough. The branch hair whipped out to snatch his leg. Weavil gave Finklerank's trunk a wide berth.

The ghostly tree's roots piled overhead in wriggling masses. Just as the poet thought himself secure, a long branch wisped down to snatch at him. Bowed and slimy, the limb lashed down at Weavil's face.

Weavil gave a frightened yelp. Falling back, crouching, he was barely able to dodge another tentacle. Other limbs now writhed down to mimic the prior snatching. Finklerank intended to work Weavil over in this cramped hollow with those abominable feelers so abruptly invested with angry life.

A snaky limb latched onto Weavil's left ankle. He kicked at it, but he was dragged up by another and lifted brutally upside down in front of Finklerank's gloating face.

"There now, you miserable trickster! What do you think of that? No jokes now? Shall you scratch my left greesheckle, or shall I feed you to the shreeks?"

Weavil managed to wriggle about and emit a plaintive wail: "Comfort your own greesheckle, you creepy geezer. You seem to have gained some new miraculous dexterity—why not use it?"

The tree gave a brittle guffaw. "An excellent jibe!—your laconic jokes have become an inspiration!"

To Weavil's surprise, the oak gave a sudden lurch. Now its branches lifted in a kind of fearful synchrony. Three new shoots thrashed and stiffened, then went limp. In perplexity Weavil was tossed rudely to the floor, like some broken doll.

Shaking the daze out of his head, he scooped up his candle. He pumped his feet to safety. Finklerank stared at him from behind his sooty frame—on old eye gleamed with a malicious frustration. But the tree could not move. Why? Old age? Arthritis? Dotage? Weavil was at a loss to discover the tree's handicap. He wasted no time in thinking about it or scrambling up to the exit. A desperate dodge of a last feeble fibril was the last impression he had before he leaped past the threshold and dashed into the exit passageway.

Up the alley he bolted, appalled at the tangle of roots webbing the floor. They vibrated with menace. Feet pounding like hammers, he stumbled about with the roar of Finklerank's groans behind him in his blood-hammering ears. The background squeaking and chittering of a thousand scuttling creatures grew in strength.

He heaved on, scurrying in a psychotic frenzy. The roots littered the floor; essaying to flip him back into the cavern. Weavil quailed. The sounds of new pursuit ever gained.

His heart missed several beats. The sounds were growing stifling, of muffled bats or voles of some underground terror. They seemed to be attracted to his small candlelight . . .

Weavil fought back his horror and he resisted the urge to douse his flame—for without that he would be lost.

The horrific squeaking escalated to a kind of hoarse gibbering. Stench assailed his nostrils. Somewhere behind the wall of menace a reek was wafting up the tunnel. Not some theoretical concept—but a detestable miasma, unbuffered by any comfortable barrier of rock.

Weavil jerked about like a harried woodcock. He stole a look back down the tunnel and caught a glimpse of a large thing scrabbling down in the passage's down-twist.

What in—? Shrew? Murid? Gigantic vole? Weavil could not say. He let out a strangled yell. 'Twas all and none of this—a veritable ugly mutant. 'Twould take apart his limbs, at the very least.

The creature shambled forth on six legs, swivelling a poxy head in a weird way. Its skewed eyes assessed him with preternatural avidity.

Weavil stumbled ahead in blind terror. He had seen a pair of flapping ears, a grey and unwholesome elephantine body, a tubular head. A pelt of black bristly fur was shaped like a bulbous turtle and thrust out at him sickly; yellow fangs protruded from a fetid, dripping jowl —all ropy whiskers fanning a soot-black nose.

His feet felt like frozen stalks in a dark void. Whatever these things were, their noisome pad played on the dank stone like the soft beat of a drum. The threat propelled itself closer . . .

Weavil scudded up the passage, knee-melting fear nearly causing his heart to fail. In his reckless haste, he almost tripped and cracked his skull, but eluded one of the monsters, for it was lumbersome, and he was on his feet again, up the fated tunnel, grateful for marking the passageways beforehand.

He felt the thing's reek and its fellows' pink-noses twitching. Perhaps more than a half dozen flat splayed feet lay hinged to those furry bodies and pink-skinned underbellies.

Weavil choked back his revulsion. The creature snuffled inches from his heel! He ground out all thoughts of fear. He must not despair! A maniacal desire arose in him—to outwit the creatures, forge the last desperate feet to the hatch that led to Nuzbek's laboratory . . .

III

On top of the hill by the gnarly phantom elm the hour was old.

Baus shivered as chill vapours seeped from the nearby forest. He cast a quick glance around him, grimaced with distaste as the impenetrable mat of mallorns took form.

Crouched somewhat stomach-flat atop the knoll, he gazed intently down on the drop of boulders and shadow-ferns below. His first expectant hope was that a figure might emerge, but there was none. The eyes of his companions were glued to the cave mouth in similar manner.

The gibbous moon hung low in the sky. Its sallow luminosity, grinning like a yellow goblin, stretched across the ghost-naked trees, creating a false shield of security. An ambience, by no means comforting. Creeping over the forest, spider-leg shadows continued to spread their dull chill down the valley. Water-murmur drifted from the dark river; all was a blanket of eerie stillness punctuated by the odd remote hooting of an owl, or the scratch of tiny claws on bark.

Baus gave little attention to these distractions. He hunched in the darkness, intent on the cave.

Ulisa remained in her human form, her golden hair swept back, gleaming like a waterfall. Trimestrius grumbled as he fidgeted with his blade. Valere remained nursing his uncomfortable thoughts, yet seemingly indifferent to the plight upon them. Kazzasius hovered in the mist, unheedful of the chill and the unnatural conditions that were bestowed upon his person.

When asked about the arrival of reinforcements, Ulisa remarked rather plaintively that she was not at all surprised at Maitor's lack of punctuality. "That slackwit should never have been trusted to head the party. He should have been here yesterday."

Baus posed no comment. It was not his habit to indulge in internal strife. The company huddled in uneasy silence, passing in and out of what seemed sullen vigilance and strained drowsiness.

Roused some time later, Baus felt a heavy paw clapped on his shoulder. Valere's bearish form stared sardonically, looming over him. Trimestrius and Ulisa peered down into the valley. Gesticulating in low voices, they seemed excited by some creeping shape half hidden in the gloom below.

Peering past the nak-thistle, Baus saw a pallid form plodding its way toward the mouth of Aurimag's cave. Odd! This figure was dressed all in black, with a sickle-shaped cowl.

Aurimag? Baus crept closer to catch a better glimpse. The figure was shambling in an unnatural fashion, like a bent crow, carrying some queer cargo with a sack thrust over its head.

"How peculiar!" grumbled Trimestrius. "The mismatched cloak and domino smack of something of the thief." The prince's blue eyes sent darting glances down upon the figure. "Here, Aurimag returns from a foul errand—but who is his luckless comrade?"

Baus peered in misgiving. Trimestrius pressed his golden sword into his hand. "I shall carve the gizzard first. Who shall join me? How strong the knave must be to cart this cargo up that stout hill! Surely he must tire after so many miles?"

Poli murmured a dry remark: "Your magician appears to be hardly tasked."

Ulisa attempted to endorse the pirate's view. "The scoundrel likely has tapped into thaumaturgies of which we have no concept. His sequestered sabbatical has granted him powers. We must observe the dastard with care and make appropriate motions."

"All very well, Ulisa," Trimestrius mumbled, "But I am not a man to wait. It may be already too late to intercept—and if we dally . . . we miss the opportunity of winning past his wretched sprites and capitalizing on an element of surprise!"

Ulisa shook her head. "Trimestrius, 'tis an impulsive notion."

"And you are so eager to have us strung up like rats in the cage?" muttered Baus.

The prince's face became an urgent mask of ruddy impatience. "Wretch! Would you have us become procrastinators? Be quiet! Shall we wait and be foiled?"

Baus ran forked fingers through his beard. "I merely urge caution. My experience has taught me mindfulness."

Valere offered a dry endorsement, "You first, little prince. We shall scuttle after you gladly."

Trimestrius disliked the wry taunt. Scanning quickly, he decided that his plan was forward but that they should all at least advance upon the cave in the hopes of stumbling upon a clue or catching the reprobate off guard—even if it meant overwhelming him by force.

The plan was ambitious and Kazzasius spoke strong words against it. "Let us wait for Mismerion's reinforcements."

"No," sighed Ulisa. "I fear Trimestrius is right. Those people are unreliable, and you, Kazzasius, shall constitute part of this assault team. Your projectorial magic is nonpareil. Esling—who is neither equipped or versed in magic, shall be advised to watch our backs."

The Wickle was stung though there were nods of agreement. She clung to Baus who squirmed with frustration. Tears dribbled down her cheeks. She clutched her saviour while the others scrambled down the hill and the outlaw took her aside. "Do not cry, fair Wickle!" he consoled her. "You are the luckiest of all. Promise to never venture into that black hole. Do not imperil yourself with our mission. Fly from here if you sense trouble! Hesitate not— never look back!"

Esling shook her head with grief. "How can I? I will be heartbroken if I lose you, Baus. I know not these terrains!" Her chin dropped to her chest. She cast her idol a mournful look. The gaze was lovelorn and she mounted him an open-mouthed kiss.

Baus felt some embarrassment as he wiped away the kiss. Before she could react, he disappeared down the hillside, leaving Esling in tears.

Aurimag's cave loomed darkly to the side of the knoll. The magician was nowhere in sight. Evidently he had long disappeared into the cave and the group clustered around the portal like tense owls blinking in the chill. They were roused by their own nervous energy, shying from the ominous weight of the dolmenish stones that towered over them.

Edging closer, they saw that the dirt and thorn had been laboriously spread out but remained untouched. Whoever it was who had passed here had not taken Valere's bait. Like a huge lamprey's mouth the hole glared back, mocking them. Footprints encircled, indicating that figures had recently been here but were not fooled by the seaman's snare.

Valere let out a snarl. Certain misgivings coiled about Baus's innards. Was it wise to entertain the plan of breaching the cave?

The company shifted feet.

"Let's go. We have nothing to lose," muttered Trimestrius.

"Except maybe our lives?" suggested Baus.

Trimestrius paid no heed and hunkered down before the frightful group and shook his small blade. A damp odour of decay leaked from the chill interior. They caught wind of a tramping footfall receding—but accompanied by a distant and sinister thudding from the interior.

The sound was not encouraging. Trimestrius, nonetheless, crafted a prodding signal to follow him.

Ulisa followed, then Valere. The prince flourished his gladius and a pinch-lipped Poli hobbled after, squaring his shoulders, ready to slash out at any menace. The bird Kazzasius hovered a foot over the beleaguered Baus.

Baus's first impression was of a damp cloak shrouding him from all sides. The old, leavened smell of bats and mice hovered in the gloom. Predawn glimmers angled sharply in to illuminate a small patch of tunnel ahead. But it was long way ahead and a thin stretch of shadow promised eerie possibilities.

A familiar feeling of unpleasantness crawled on Baus's skin. To disturb the denizens of this warren was not a wise course . . .

Nevertheless, involuntarily the outlaw gulped down a rank breath before jerking his knees ahead.

Kazzasius hung at a spooky height. He bobbed over Baus's left shoulder like a gaunt bat. Its weird form cast a jagged shadow onto the stone.

Baus poked his sword about warily, testing the spaces to the side, distrustful of everything. He lifted eyes to see coal-dark rock rearing upward like anthills. Folded fangs of corded stalactites dripped cool drops on their heads. Cobwebs hung in the gloomy tangles.

Step by step, the troop advanced, hoping for a successful end to the venture. Clutching various weapons in their fingers, they were ready to slash out at an instant's notice.

The sides of the tunnel suddenly veered inwards. Now the black walls cordoned them off —two sets of thick portcullises barred each side, rusted grotesquely like animal meshes. In the gloom loomed a pair of gigantic grotesques, unspeakable in their malevolence, lurking behind the grates. They were trees made of some awful thaumaturgy, poised ready to spring, hanging in the heavy darkness like some quasi-ghouls. These were half elms—eldritch guardians of the nether realms, tense and unpredictable, half bursting at the seams, ready to rend. Their misshapen crowns were bark-crusted, yet with a thousand wire-like branch-streamers writhing and weaving in the air like octopi tentacles from their trunks and yearning to grab at any living being and crush the life out of them.

These appendages could not engage their prey. The grate was sound and only the pounding of the smaller-knit limbs was palpable on the metal, lancing through the mesh at them, flitting harmlessly out of reach—but should a passer-by pass too close . . . forsooth, Baus shuddered at the thought.

They had come to a sudden halt and were given time to eye-adjust to the gloom. Baus saw that the metallic odour and grittiness of the floor was reminiscent of blood mixed with ages of dust.

An observation hardly encouraging.

A disquieting inspection led the company to stumble on past the monsters. Trimestrius and Ulisa led the way, braving purposeful strides.

Some tentacles managed to squeeze through the grate and flick against Valere's and Poli's boots causing them fright. The snap of branchy-talons rebounding against the iron fell sharp on the stillness.

Dimly they could see the black-cloaked Aurimag still many paces ahead. Their eyes could not penetrate the foul murk but they could hear their quarry's unfailing plod somewhere in the black depths—also despondent whimpers, distinctly feminine, like some trapped animal.

Baus winced. The sounds were incongruous with the setting. A clanging smash suddenly rocked the leftmost grate.

Baus whirled. A haft of slimy tentacle came vaulting out of the gloom.

He pivoted in a whirling crouch, swinging blade, found a whiff of air brushing at his cheek where the portcullis bulged ajar and he felt the crush of a giantish branch near his face.

Just in sync a section of tentacle came slicing down—chopped by his sword an instant before it had come peeling out to wrap about his neck.

The member lay writhing on the stone like a centipede cloven in two.

The others stared in horror. Unconsciously, Baus reached to his side and grasped for the pouch of explosive that the Buskerfielder had given him. Almost at once, his eyes met those of the foremost elm sprite loitering in the gloom. The primitive, reptilian eyes crouched low on the trunk, old and evil, behind the straining mesh, too spectral to contemplate. Yet meeting them, Baus knew terror. In this realm it was a reason for swallowing the bile that shot up in his throat. He gripped his sword in gratitude and wrenched his devil-gripped gaze away.

The quarry stopped short somewhere ahead. It was aware at last of pursuit and snuffled in an odd, non-human way. Each of the company cast glances at his peers and felt a dread of unknowing. It seemed that Aurimag had some half human intelligence lurking up ahead in that darkness. Canny eyes scanned the darkness. An eerie moment passed. Poli sought to wrench his mail-clad shoulder about. Unwittingly, he elbow-chopped Baus in the mouth.

Baus flung a hand to his teeth, dropping the ferrule of explosive. The capsule went rolling up the corridor to wobble uncertainly within a foot of the shivering grate and the wavering tentacles.

Baus stifled a rancorous curse and gaped at the explosive. The glistening, yellow-grey tentacles were only inches away from the ferrule. There was no way to retrieve it.

"You idiot!" he hissed at Poli. "Look at what you've done!" He landed him a biff in the teeth.

Poli massaged his fattening lip, grinning dumbly. Baus realized there was nothing to do and strained eyes into the murk with frustation. He struggled to contain his anger. The capsule was lost. To retrieve the explosive meant moving within range of the deadly tentacles. Nobody was up for such a death wish.

He felt a wave of despair. Only the flare disc remained in his possession now, a weapon of much less impact.

The plodding footfall had resumed its course. Once more Baus kneed Poli along and Kazzasius lurked somewhere over his shoulder, flapping like a clownish goblin, with wings kicking up musty vapours from the floor.

A peculiar thing happened. A clammy wash spilled over the company and Baus, taking his next step, felt as if brushed with the slimy spray of a waterfall. Poli and he were plummeted into a lightless void. They thrashed about and kicked, but felt only a flicker of rufous light spill over them. They must have passed through a thin film of blackness!—wet, misty, cold and unreal—only just as suddenly to be plunged back into a dim, reddish light.

Baus blinked away his confusion. What happened? Where were they?

It seemed they were in a yawning cave, thick with stalactites. It was an awesome sight; 'twas an immense grotto equipped with a vast dome for a roof, the interior richly dressed with old bronze shields and eccentrically-wrought brass horns. The upper extent was entirely permeated with myriad stalactites. The floor was jutted with a profusion of stalagmites, housing strange, hourglass-shaped lamps lit by mysterious means. The lamps were the only source of illumination and provided the preternatural, beetle-red glow permeating the cave.

Baus peered about. He saw to his wonder that all the stalactites dripped with emerald water. The tunnel at their back was now replaced by twin pillars, handsomely carved by skilled hands, ornamented with the finest crafted spirals and volutes he had ever seen . . . Between the pillars, a black-holed portal gaped to the original tunnel. They had passed through some invisible field . . .

Kazzasius suddenly materialized from the void, wings working in just the same stunned wonder as Baus's legs. Valere, Trimestrius and Ulisa—had already stepped through the field and were shaking the daze out of their heads. The sprite-trap that Trimestrius had warned them about was gone . . . they had passed through a gateway and were now in the safety of Aurimag's sanctuary.

Baus caught a fluttery glimpse of a trailing cloak and a purple hood a stone's throw ahead. The figure seemed to be bent on escaping the company beyond the musty reaches of a leaden pool . . . weird! . . . Fast merging into the dim periphery, past the pool, smooth as a mirror, the figure clutched a desperate shape, a white-robed woman it seemed, sobbing and rocking in her captor's grip.

Trimestrius and Ulisa sprinted forward purposefully but Baus, Valere and Poli stood rooted like clams, casting each other perplexed glances. Finally they scrambled after under the shadow of the bronze-shielded walls.

As if from a dream, Baus found himself dodging a clotted mass of stalagmites that reared up like giant toes from the marmor floor. Amazed at the sheer mass of them—no less the cavern—he thought them reminiscent of the ribbed innards of a great drake. Rows of molars formed the endless grotto formations.

Baus's boots echoed like blacksmith hammers in the cavern's vastness. He passed over the chalky marmor with unease and bewilderment. The rufous beacons strapped to the stalagmites created a manageable glow and bronze shields and fantastic horns hung throughout reflecting the eerie light. The limpid, lead-green pools to their sides remained eerie, glistening anomalies.

The figure at last decided to halt before an ancient door. In a moment of hesitation, it flew within and clamped the door shut. Baus and Valere looked at each other and pulled Poli along. Ulisa raised her white-robed arms and fluttered her hands. Almost at once the door began to shatter, but a soft bugle brayed a sudden note. . .

Baus took a sharp breath. He staggered back. From where had the dismal noise come? From deep within the cavern, faraway and unknowable, another mournful echo drifted . . . Dwindling, the sound grew to a hollow drone and Baus held his breath. An orotund laugh suddenly emerged from the gloom.

The sound came from a tall thin figure who emerged from behind a vanguard of ancient stalagmites. The formations rose near to the ominous roof. The head was pinched, familiar, slightly thrown back, with the black crown hooded. The frame was bent stiffly on cocked knees, garbed in a set of dark black-grey robes. Each baggy fold carried some odd memory— as if the figure within had endured certain miracles of spellcraft not meant for mortal men.

Baus grew spellbound with incredulity. Aurimag? But how? Wasn't he just carrying some girl in a completely opposite direction?

Baus shook his head in wonder. He peered more closely upon the figure, startled to behold that the corpse-lit face and eerie expression was so studiously repulsive. It was marred with an even more macabre glint. Yet classically it was shrouded by that up-tilted, sickle moon cowl. The face was not so hale as the snorting voice and concealed the evil down-twitching mouth and the sardonic eyes that burned with angst. The man was horribly thin, emaciated even, and the brows and cheeks were filled with an incalculable hate.

The smirking figure called out a florid salutation: "Well! If it isn't my trusted friends, Baus and Valere! What a lucky day! And who is this? A newcomer—come to visit me in my humble little abode." He laughed aloud, lost his sinister aspect for a brief moment and skipped a step closer, holding forth palms in easy camaraderie. "Indeed a most unexpected surprise!—But pah! So rude of me not to have put on a pot of tea! You must forgive me my manners!"

Baus grabbed at his chin, marvelling. How could such a scarecrow of a villain appear in two places at a time?

The conundrum remained a mystery and Baus gave way to a tenuous scowl.

"Ah, Baus, you look well!" announced the neomancer with jocular emphasis. "I maunder. Like a book I read your flighty thoughts! You are so happy, like a skip-lark, hopping from branch to branch as you travel from hither to yon, now come to see me, but I am abashed and not worthy to see you. Never mind! We are at last rejoined! What fortuity! You haven't aged a day or sport an inkling of how much I have been at odds waiting for this opportunity to behold a dear friend in so fine a form!"

The dark magician paused, eager to relay his indulgent thoughts. "Ah, the nights! The nights I have lain awake imagining this moment!" He pranced closer, a bundle of brio, ready to pounce on Baus like a falcon. The face . . . too many fey lines in that countenance were carved of indicative diabolical thoughts streaming from a diseased mind.

"Likewise the same," Baus muttered cautiously.

The magician scrutinized the outlaw for a moment, then he turned his eyes to appraise Valere with similar ominous deliberation. "Well, Captain—you are certainly a striking figure in your fine accouterments—and your grimy-beard. So good to see you—after our brief but communal association in Heagram." He flicked a contemptuous gaze on Poli. "And who is this dabchick? . . . a hidebound bully if I've seen one. Regard the festering glare, the bulging muscles!"

Poli's response was only a sullen grunt. "Aye, rogue—we shall see who 'bulges'. I've heard plenty of your personality and sorcery. And with little commendation either."

"Well, tsk!" called Aurimag brusquely, shaking his head in mock resentment. "Defamation is no way to start off a good friendship!"

Ulisa planted fists on hips. "Enough of this idiot charade, Aurimag. Release the Hierarch, for I know you have him hidden somewhere in this foul den."

"Hush, Ulisa," chided Aurimag.

"I will not hush! Reckonings are to be administered, for which redemptive punishment will be exacted on your hide. Save yourself humiliation! Hand over the prisoners and then turn yourself in!"

Aurimag inspected the shape-shifter with amusement. "Ulisa . . . Ulisa . . . I suggest an alternate program. You shall become a doll, a permanent fixture in my nymphosium—a well oiled, perfumed, manicured and costumed doll, where you shall comprise its most unique concubine. You are quite a deal too miniature to take a premier role, but you shall fulfil an admirable one."

"Sacrilege!" Ulisa sputtered, barely controlling her rage. "You are a heretic! A blasphemer! A disgrace. You would speak insults to me even in your lowest degeneracy."

"Hush! My words are prophetic—I do not mean to brag."

Trimestrius called out an oath. "I defy your deeds, Aurimag! You are a blackguard, a cur, a vile deceiver and a misfit. You have no right to speak to Ulisa in this vulgar manner, nor will I permit it. I enjoin you to retract your statement. Now stand ready to feel the bite of my blade!"

Aurimag cupped his hand to his ear. "Hark? Do I hear a little bird tweeting? No, it must be a rat." He hopped a step closer, chuckled a jovial sound and turned his attention to Baus. "Well, master Baus! What do you think of this little exchange? A fol-de-rol? It seems like old times have caught up to us. Again—and on soft wings we celebrate our little reunion, and here I would bid you to indulge me in a small whim. To accept the leading role in my comic drama, 'Nalirthia'. There you will play a stunning role. 'Tis a play written in four parts—well five, if you consider the shocking incident at the end—but I will not talk of that. Nevertheless, it involves Ulisa too—but, I digress! The art of the playright sports a thousand intrigues! You must experience the drama for yourself. As for the lesser intellects in your company, like the vain and temperamental Trimestrius, you shall all be given distinct roles, as playthings in my amusing experiments—all directed to the pursuit of important, scientific advancement." Aurimag breathed a long sigh. "So hard are willing subjects to find these days!" He snuffled out a laugh, clasping his hands in a most peculiar manner while thrusting up an annoyed frown to the mighty winged creature whose incessant flapping had begun to irk him. "This monstrosity is ill-wrought. 'Tis hardly appropriate for a freak such as this to contaminate my venerated abode. Bridle the thing—or I shall prepare a brazier to sizzle its wings."

Kazzasius vented out an annoyed curse: "I'm afraid your arrogant piffle will do you little good! You know very well who I am—I am Kazzasius, the Projector—even as a globular eye, I demand respect, and urge you to arrest these silly jocularities and of yours and substitute them for a genial civility!"

Aurimag opened his mouth in a manner of awe. "Kazzasius! Can it be? Is it the Projector? The mighty projector is full of surprises? How your peers have made a rude display of you; dressing you in ludicrous garments, and endorsing your eerie, bombastic airs with yeas and nods. They fit you in a buffoon's clothes and let you truckle to dogma, and now you complain of my debonair airs?"

Kazzasius grunted a disparagement then was sullen, quietly objecting to the opinion.

"Really?" Aurimag cried a laugh, folding arms on his chest. "These wise people strip you of your dignity and your honour while you sit there and carp. They strip me of my manhood and my pride—and call it 'justice'? I have wandered far—to distant spheres! Roving eyes have never seen vistas darker and more fey than I! But in this same vein I am endowed with powers, which, as you shall see, will be instrumental in causing you woe!"

Ulisa stamped her heel. "Cease this braggadocio or yours. You are a broken crow. You are at disadvantage—by stronger minds than you admit. We shall break your arrogance! Now surrender to our justice, for we, as members of the Circle, will provide a dignified judgement. Consider this our final appeal!"

Aurimag gave a dull shrug. "Very well, if so it must be." He raised a hand to command some skullduggerish sorcery, but then a fierce anger gripped him and his eyes glowed with fire. "How you forget, you righteous hypocrite! While Woisper and the brutish Barbirius dragged me off to Mismerion's cloud tower to perform so many hideous deeds upon my body, you stood idly by."

"That was long ago—"

"Was it? You fail to recall? How coy, miss *Utilitarian*! Well perhaps a small fright shall jog your memory."

Ulisa sidestepped the sinister innuendo. "And where is the maid you sequestered here against her will?"

Aurimag's grin widened. "The maid! The wench's in a safe place. But your own safety I would think of first. Other things lurk in these crevices less tolerant than I." He gave a rich laugh.

Baus interrupted. "What of Weavil?"

Aurimag barked a trilling note. "The little brat is safe—what do you care?"

Baus was prompted to boldness. He clutched a rock behind his back and began to sidle surreptitiously around the magician's back. As he worked himself closer, Ulisa confronted him with fervid accusations.

Aurimag jerked about with displeasure. "So, dog!—you would think to brain me that easily? Drop that rock and curb your skulking; it is insulting!"

Baus halted—and looked up in bovine incomprehension. "Aren't you a little jittery, Aurimag? Jettison this paranoia of yours and I will drop this rock. I know that your golem has failed. Trapped by a twosome—or 'gruesome', I should say. 'Tis a failure on your part which shall mirror another very soon!"

Aurimag's lips drew back in a harsh scowl. "What do you know of such things? Ah, very well. A disappointment, my little golem in the form of a feckless experiment. For a moment I thought I had achieved something great . . ." Aurimag's expression relaxed into a gentle smile. "The thing is a drudge. I can manufacture more of them at will. ''Tis no great task—I stumbled upon the science writ in old scroll. It endorses the difference between you and me, your 'feeble' mind versus mine. To business!—I grow fatigued with all this pedestrian dialogue."

Baus ventured to reply with steel but Aurimag raised an obstinate hand. There was a strange warp that seemed to impinge on the air with his flutter of fingers. A bugle blew—from a place afar, and a sudden, plangent note.

Eyes darted in search of the noise, but answer could not be found.

Aurimag clapped his hands—twice, thrice. A sickly yellow glow suddenly pervaded the cavern. All peered with awe. Very suddenly the magician held forth a translucent, light-shimmering sphere that seemed to manifest out of thin air. Ulisa stared aghast. With a laughing sneer, Aurimag lobbed the sphere high. An opalescent wake of yellow luminescence was sent springing to the upper tier of stalactites tearing at the shadows.

"Now, dullards! Prepare to die—Confront my orb of woe!"

The globe grew larger, floating down like some gigantic balloon. The talisman exuded an obscene glow which appalled the company. It cast a spell-binding radiance, when suddenly, it appeared to alter shape . . .

Baus ducked low. Revulsion sickened the pit of his heart. A turbulent wind caught them in full force. The bubble grew, tore at the fabric of the enclosing air, then, in a whirl of shearing, a fairy castle came into being—a stone fabulous keep with bulbous towers protruding from its walls and sprouting a dozen lofty spires flown with gaudy banners.

Valere gave a bewildered shout. He drove his sword through the apparition but was instantly pitched off balance and thrown wide as the blade passed straight through. The ghost apparition achieved new levels of detail. The walls and battlements showed clown-like faces writhing within. The eyes were menacing, jubilant; their grimacing little smirks showed unnerving intent. Up the towers' flanks more figures appeared. The castle became a sudden lucid mass. Baus discerned a miniature gendarmerie spread toy-like in the courtyard. They were garbed in blue and green, armed with a sea of sharp pikes and glittering halberds.

Poli gaped. "What hellishness is this?"

Aurimag pointed a proud digit; he cried out in an imploring voice—a cantrap that threatened the company: "Behold an illusion even more rousing than even the pretentious Llonon! Is it illusion, or real? May his craven soul break under the spells of a hundred twisted Neons!" Aurimag laughed and without warning, sprang upon Ulisa.

Quick as a cat, she scrambled back under the cover of a stalagmite. "Hurry!" she called. "Search out Woisper! Liberate the Hierarch—" and then she raised her palms, letting her slender shape-shifter's body tentatively became a shimmering mass of motes. She blew out of existence, in favour of a white moth, invested with smart wings, dust-like antennae and a pair of tiny legs.

Aurimag guffawed, wise to her bewitchery. He sprinted forward like an ape, with an affected leer. He scooped up the delicate little insect in a palm and lobbed it up toward the glowing fairy keep. Without warning, Ulisa was caught by a half-naked ogre, no higher than eight inches, bursting forth from an emblazoned doorway and chasing the moth back and forth about the courtyard with vigour. Soldiers joined in the pursuit. The grounds were soon a mad knot of chaos.

Aurimag, pleased with the progression of events, clapped his hands. An evil wind came rattling through the keep, rustling flag and pennon. Ulisa was blown closer to the ogre's clutches.

The companions hissed. Aurimag nodded his head with delight. The net closed in and the ogre dragged Ulisa into the castle. The portal slammed shut and her indignant screams were lost in an empty corridor.

Baus blinked, apalled at her fate and launched himself at Aurimag. Sword sang; a dire tune whipped the air nearly lopping off the neomancer's head.

Aurimag crab-scuttled back in a facetious rage. He clapped his hands. Baus's sword was rendered moot—a fantastic, slippery mass of serpent slime. Aghast, he flung down the weapon. Valere's and Poli's blades were soon slimy masses too.

The outlaws all looked down in disgust and wonder. Blade and haft were gobbed with a thick oleaginous slime—sickly grey and reeking of what seemed snails.

Baus uttered a note of outrage. His fingers were gummy with the stuff and he tried to wipe it away furiously upon his mail. His fingers began to sting as if dipped in some vile acid.

He cried out a tormented note. Of all the blades, Lolispar was the only one that remained immune to Aurimag's spell.

But Trimestrius the prince knew no bounds of anger. He leaped up and menaced Aurimag, roaring a tribute to Desenion in quixotic ceremony.

Aurimag sidestepped the prince's charge and kneed the little midget in the groin. Trimestrius cried out while the magician fled behind a lichen-crusted stalagmite, dodging and grinning. Lolispar was in the prince's hand. It was swinging savage cuts, stabbing at the green-crusted rock. The neomancer bobbed back and forth in glee from the blind, corner-cracking stabs like a jester. The prince efforted, dripping oaths on his tongue. Unwittingly he allowed the rogue margin to slip away and draw a whip-stick from his gown. Aurimag tapped the prince lightly on the crown. His dervishing around the stalagmite came to an end.

The prince fell immobilized. Aurimag calmly emerged, with an expression of tolerant victory. His morbid face was a mat of aplomb and smug infallibility which struck Baus in the most pompous way. Baus, now faced with a nasty dilemma, snarled and shadowboxed him. Aurimag danced, turned to face the rest of the defenders—a trio of numb-limbed outlaws, including Poli and Valere.

They drew halting steps backward.

A sudden flapping of wings set the magician jigging. Aurimag glared, to behold Kazzasius hovering up some two feet above him, an eye glowing a distant cold white. An emblazoned spray of rainbow luminescence shot out, striking Aurimag in the face.

The neomancer sagged back, blinded, threatened by the unexpected thrust of spellcraft. The outlaws scrabbled forward, each trying to immobilize him but just out of reach as he regained his wits and shook the vision back into his skull. The three drew back. Aurimag pulled an amber-pulsing sphere from his cloak, an improved version of the glow pyramid. He launched it rather impassionedly at Valere. The seaman ducked, but the pulsing sphere bucked and warped—'twas the same the magician had used back in Heagram prison to effective result. It caught Valere on his shoulder mail and skidded off to strike Poli square in the chest.

Valere was knocked sideways but Poli was sent a-sprawl heavily on the dank rock.

For a few heavy seconds Poli thrashed and moaned in an obscene way; he quivered and lay slumped senselessly on the stone, motionless as a corpse.

Baus stood transfixed. The sobosphere had smote him cleanly in the chest, and now he was either dead or unconscious. The orb came floating back to the Aurimag's hand like some obedient pumpkin. The trajectory was like some enchanted boomerang, but it left a cold, pale, amber stream in its wake.

Baus jerked Valere aside, rummaged for his whip. The two stood their ground; each waited for Aurimag's next assault. None came. Poli was skewed astride a pool. The vapours were misting in green billows from proximity to the sobosphere. The neomancer laughed and launched the sphere again, but this time the target was not clear and the quivering form veered astray. Kazzasius threatened to blind him with another projectorial ray.

The sobosphere struck one of the creature's flapping wings. Feathers and skin went every which way and were scorched.

A great cracking light serrated the air and then a hot flash of incandescence as livid as tungsten tore at the surrounding space and Kazzasius's midsection became a blur of flame.

He let out a piercing shriek. The Projector plummeted in a ball of fire. A cloud of smoke drifted from the bird's body; a loud thud came upon Poli's mailed breast.

Aurimag loosed a dry cackle. Kazzasius's wing was now singed to a crisp and the magicker held out a placid hand to retrieve his weapon.

"Idiot pests!" he shouted. His tone spilled out vindictiveness from every pore. "You must cognize that my wrath is absolute and will have no surcease!"

With loose strides, he came hobbling after them with the force of a ghoul.

Baus faced down his terror; he flung back his whip, snapped it wickedly down in the neomancer's face.

Aurimag dodged the machination. He leered like a wolf. "It will take more than a toy weapon to thwart me. How do you like my 'Instant Fire'? A new addition to my arsenal." Lifting a crab-like hand, he threatened to launch a bolt of another fiery purulence.

Baus pre-empted his assault. He ducked under a stalagmite, seizing Poli's wrist and began dragging him back to the edge of the cave. Aurimag could muster no more damage at this juncture without leaping into the open.

Valere grabbed Poli's leg and they both pulled him to safety. The injured outlaw was breathing, but just. His face was gravelly, furrowed and scorched. A sunken chest showed black ringlets of his mail. They were singed and melted and seemed to weigh down on his breast.

Aurimag marched after them, fingers snapping with thaumaturgy sending purple flame every which way. A bolt landed abreast of Valere's boots, instantly besetting the seaman on fire.

Valere let out a crazy wail, dancing like a marionette. He desperately fought to extinguish the flames that threatened to consume his body. His leather pants crackled.

"Attend!" Aurimag thundered. "A jocular 'Impingement of Blinking Inflammatory'! So be warned!"

The seaman staggered sidewise, ready to tumble again. Baus struggled to stamp out the flames. His own life was in jeopardy, barely saved by the silver mesh padding his chest. It cushioned him from an nth order repercussion of Aurimag's 'Blinking Fire'.

Quelling the flames that ravaged Valere, Baus helped his companion desperately hop behind a stalagmite. Valere sought Baus's shoulder before he staggered up again. He tore weakly at the luggage on Poli's back, snatching at one of the coyote traps and armed it. He chucked it at the neomancer.

The trap crashed harmlessly to the side. Aurimag watched in hollow amusement. Valere growled in consternation and spat a bleak oath.

"Is this all you can do, you bumbling oaf?" cried Aurimag.

Valere shouted again: "Flee, Baus! We cannot defeat this megalomaniac on brawn alone. Grab your weapons, run; they are our only hope!"

Baus pitched back in doubt. "What weapons? They are caked in slime. What of Poli? We can't leave him here."

"We can do nothing for him at this time," wailed Valere. "Aurimag will kill us—with partiality."

"But we can't just abandon Poli!" protested Baus.

"We must!" Snarling, the seaman pulled Baus along. The two stumbled desperately toward the exit and Valere made a lunge for Poli's last coyote trap. Gracelessly the two were forced back toward the entrance—the same place where they had entered this dank hall of spell-haunted horror.

Brimming with exultation, the magician strolled casually to intercept them, passing within reach of the maimed Kazzasius. Baus realized with defeat that there was no rescuing the Projector or Poli.

How everything had gone so foully bad! Biting back his anguish, Baus felt the crushing reality of defeat he had never known. How a capsule of Tofax's explosive would be a godsend now! But no . . . it was lost, cached under the elm sprite's tentacle.

Misery played across Baus's expression. In these moments of sick despair, he felt a sagging defeat.

A sinister chittering of unwholesome character suddenly exploded from the back corridor, one enough to make a warrior's blood freeze.

Baus peered in loathing. The eeriness suddenly left his bones. Erupting from the far end of the cavern came a horde of squat brutish shapes emitting muffled squeals—a thumping bedlam followed and a palpitation of many heavy feet on dank stone. The tumult was defeaning followed by a rush of foul draughts, like rotting vegetables or rancid putrescences of the utmost unpleasantness.

The outlaw's mouth hung ajar. A horde of mammoth armadillo freaks had stormed into the cavern from the back hedge of stalagmites.

The hair on Baus's neck stood on end. How could such an obscene horror be happening? He felt a tortured shriek rise in his throat. What could the loathsome things be?

Baus's knees melted with fear. The things were black-matted, endowed with elephant ears and flappy pale legs, red, tubelike noses and yellow, impish two-pronged fangs. Each was enormous, at least his size and again. The brood appeared to be some sort of rodent, or cricetid, each uglier and more horrid than its peer.

The army bounded pell-mell after Aurimag, who had foolishly failed to detect the menace in time. Now he stood erect, deciding whether to confront the freaks or not. Baus was amazed at the indifference he exhibited. What was going on in his head? He only appeared irked by the intrusion rather than terrorized; the horde swarmed around him in growing numbers. To him they seemed only an intellectual curiosity.

Baus frowned in fascination. He could not help but stare in mute wonder. A shrew snapped forward with a fang lightly lacerating Aurimag's shin. The neomancer danced on one leg and called out a thaumaturgic expletive, which brought the sobosphere crashing upon the beast's skull. The creature slumped in lifeless agony.

Baus crouched behind a clammy stalagmite, spellbound, yet feeling a sickness to his stomach. How ineffectual he felt! In the fray he caught glimpses of another purple moon cowl bobbing its way toward the magician amongst the rampage of shrews. What was this? Another fiend? The cowl belonged to the same spare figure, struggling with equivalent energy to escape the shrews' manglings.

The figure bobbed inexorably, harbouring a great strength as exemplified by the way it tossed rodents as easily as flaxhack. In fact, Baus saw a remarkable resemblance to the neomancer himself, looking closer.

The similarity ended there. Aurimag was close by, less than a stone's throw, garbed in an almost mocking identical attire.

The magician raised his hand to project yet another bout of 'Blinking Fire'.

Baus's mind reeled. Two Aurimags?

How could this be? He squinted into the blackness. There was too much chaos to be sure. But the likeness could not be coincidence and he felt himself plunging into confusion. Even as the feeling hit, the unknown second figure had mysteriously disappeared, sliding into the shadows flanking the hoary stalactites. Monsters were reeling and foundering by the dozens, more shuffling in to replace the dead with grunts and snapping fangs.

Aurimag was now cornered. An army of armadillo-shaped horrors had him trapped.

The neomancer lifted a crooked finger. A blaze of purple fire stung the foremost creature in the flank. The murid twisted about, gnashing at its fiery pelt which had suddenly erupted in a blaze of flame. Flesh sizzled on the creature's hide. A cloud of bilious smoke rose up, mushroom-like. In a mad capering dance the shrew gnashed and gibbered, finally to toppled into a hissing pool aside Poli. The assault resulted in a quick drowning—and the fiend sank to the bottom of the pool in a charred, bubbling heap.

A vanguard of shrews now converged on the magician. He used the sobosphere and his fire digits to lay waste most of the throng. With an elegant ease, the magician repeated the tactic. But not far away, Baus spied two long-snouted shrews pulling at Poli's mail. Baus surged forward, but more enemies were gathering, obstructing his approach.

What to do? He jabbed and feinted. Another trio of beasts were having difficulty penetrating Trimestrius's sturdy armour. Even with all the gnashing and scrambling going on, he caught fervid glimpses of yet another figure scampering from the small spaces between pool to pool. Something was familiar about this tiny ragged shape that clawed its way up a black-blasted stalagmite. The figure only narrowly avoided a snapping of two fanged shrews.

A creature sprang upon the rock to molest the figure again. Half scared out of its wits, the shape knee-hugged its way up the column like a squirrel.

Baus croaked. Weavil?

The recognition brought a choking emotion to his chest. He was beset with a siege of emotions from the past. There was no getting to his friend, or Poli for that matter.

Aurimag was a jog away from the stalagmite and giant shrews were tearing about his shins in deadly numbers. They had taken complete command of the cavern—the place was in a vicious shambles, full of bristling, humpbacked fiends writhing in unguessable numbers . . . now, more were erupting from the dark hole at the end of the cavern.

Baus watched in sinking dismay: an old grey-furred goliath started dragging Poli away by the leg toward a dark passage. The fiend stared. With a glazed expression, it tossed round yellow horns and shaking slimy jowl—it must be some king of this horde. A stray blast from Aurimag's fire sent the thing writhing back in a ribbon-burst of flame.

With safety jeopardized, Valere scrambled for shelter. Certain of the black armadillo creatures cut off their escape and now they pulled aside, realizing that the pillared exitway was denied them.

Baus cast a sick, white-faced grimace upon the proposed avenue of escape. He saw it lost to rat shrews which piled in from all quarters and chewed at one another, displeased with their lack of success at securing fresh meat. Hopping on each other's backs, they gnawed each other's ears and noses and snapped at each other's jowls. A particularly loathsome creature tried to scramble through the unbroken gap between the pillars, but its scream alerted the menace within and the creature was sucked in the hole and swept into oblivion by the sprites. Several other would-be followers sniffed around the dark patch and withdrew from the opening in snuffling hate—the same which had swallowed their peer.

Baus shuddered. Their prospects of escape practically zero—and becoming dimmer.

The fright keep lingered close by and Valere motioned to it with a trembling hand. The luminous mass glittered like an abominable wraith, filling the entire area. It glowed with pale green and nacreous white, somehow violating the natural laws of a sane universe. Several creatures had been attracted to the luminescence and began to paw at it, but on contact, they fled back, shivering with pain. A visceral blight lanced out from the tallest tower blinding the shrews' sight and setting them a-chitter. The floating palace, it seemed, had devices of its own self protection.

The nearest predators seemed to catch the scent of Baus and Valere and shambled over on splayed feet.

Valere loosed a shard of loose marmor he had managed to snatch. The two scrambled off with unseemly haste.

Scrambling along the penumbral side of the cavern, Baus could only feel the horrid snuffling on his heels. A rancorous reek too horrid to describe shadowed them.

Outlaw and murid crossed the midnight pool and its guardian ring of stalagmites and Baus fingered the pocket knife in his pouch—the one won from Bardo, his last real weapon. He planned to use it wisely . . .

Skidding to a halt, Baus sent a vicious down-curving slash of tempered iron on the shrew's skull.

The blade caught flesh and it dragged and ripped on the creature's face—the blade slithered out, dragging out with it a wash of yellow ichor. The creature halted and a keen ghastly cry erupted from the its furred maw. Baus saw gum-fangs, a set of dripping teeth with thick saliva and a pair of ophidian eyes glaring down through its unfathomable terror. The left orb pulsed gore. Gruesome exultation shone on Baus's face; he readied himself for another strike. Almost gagging on the spot, he exhaled, sickened by the meat-rotty breath of the thing, but then he was buffed aside by a wet-whiskered nose.

Valere halted to defend himself. He yanked a coyote snare off his back and lifted the spring, projecting it backward at the pouncing shape.

The jaws snapped. The metal sent splashing gobs of yellow everywhere as the teeth clamped on a pipe-like snout. The thing yelped—romped about, thrashed like a fish and sent others of its kind toppling back into a pool. The maimed thing reared about like a tortured war wegmor and flopped over on its back, clawing frantically on the clamp of iron with front and back paws—teeth which refused to give.

A stalactite cracked. A spatter of purple stars fractured the air with discord.

Baus turned in satisfaction; he saw Aurimag go down under a nest of black shapes. The magician must be dead, he thought. But the magician rose up like a demon, eyes blazing tombfire. A flaring, purplish, balloonish fire coursed up and down his limbs like some column of liquid incandescence. The fire laid purple waste to the black humps which now surrounded him and coursed from the hole in a flood of death.

Baus shook his head with marvel. How was this possible? Here was an avatar of god-like endurance, more potent than any drake slayer, or sea-serpent spearer. 'Twas a miracle even more mystifying than Aurimag's enchanted flares and pyrotechnics. How could he withstand such assaults? More perplexing, how could the rodentine monsters be attracted to the fire like moths? The first wave of destruction had passed, and yet, the shrews came on again, pattering together again like army ants, regrouping with an alien force.

The action horrified Baus more than he could contemplate. Once more Aurimag's crooked fingers lifted in deathly wrath. Now pluming purple-lit flares filled the spaces between marmor and columns like giant fireworks, glowering and singeing flesh and rock alike. Aurimag's other hand sought his sobosphere. Digits quickly wrought swirling death in the throng. The magician struggled for his life; he was in a ring of foes threatening to clip his limbs and drag him under their flat, fetid feet.

The sobosphere struck again and again, pulsed as it beetled under a wash of foes. The glowing outersurface was clumped with gobs of flesh. Fur and hide had caught there and clung to its grinning face like a frying mesh of meat. Shrews died in the dozens with thin little shrieks coming from their dewlapped throats. Others went cringing down in a crush of death. An abysmal clamour rang through the cavern like the recoil of cannons.

Baus felt the pounding of blood in his brain like fire. He wasted no time on idle thoughts. Valere was on his knees, stunned by a close call with two bold shreeks colliding with each other and almost crushing the life out of him as they fell. The seaman was slow to rise. Baus saw another fiend tearing at his leather skullcap, hoping to gouge a fang into his brain.

Baus jerked forward, snapped the end of the whip into the attacker's face. The creature shrank back in revulsion, squatting on its hindquarters, hissing like a cat.

Baus looped fingers under Valere's armpits and dragged him to safety. The two sprang back through a nearby cage of stalagmites before further calamity could take them.

Seven paces to their left, an oval doorway showed a fleeting hope. Flanked by ornamental shields, the portal was topped by a tarnished, brass-coiled tuba.

A perfect hideaway!—Unfortunately the shrews had squeezed through the mesh and were now crowding them from either side.

Baus snapped his whip. The weapon hardly kept the beasts at bay, but it allowed Valere time to stagger through the portal and time for Baus to plough through. The opening led to some cramped subchamber.

The door was blocked. To each side appeared a thin marmor slab. Shot upright, the stone was white and smoothed with age. The two struggled to drag one of the weights across. Groaning with effort, they managed to slide it across.

They were in!

Not a second too soon.

A set of frightening weights slammed against the stone and slobbery mouths issued sucking sounds of resentment.

Baus made an enervated lunge. He gasped with sick fright as he drew the iron bar and sealed them in safety and fell to his knees in exhaustion.

IV

Baus scrambled on all fours to examine his surroundings. From underneath the door a crack showed baleful blips of light. Occasional dire sparks and flashes ensued, and an occasional painful yelp in the outside corridor.

Baus heard the restless patter of many feet. What foul deeds were transpiring in the corridor without?

He hopped closer, put his ear to stone. Several faint cries became palpable.

He glared about helplessly. The room he was encaged in was large enough for him and Valere to stand loosely with arms outstretched—but only barely. It was roughly rectangular, with grey stone and a close ceiling. A bloodlamp splayed glum rays across the floor. The drab interior stank of mice and bats. Shelves were etched in the rough marmor, scarred and pocked by hours of chipping and hammering. Sadly, there was no way out except in.

On reaching the end of the chamber, Baus sighed a long sigh as a resigned man while Valere wheezed and rubbed his aching joints.

A snatch of shelving dug deep into the farthest wall. Unlike the main cavern, this chamber was hewn from stone by artificial means. A hasty reconnaissance revealed nothing useful—a triple tier of ledges clogged with earthenware pottery, antique vases, a smattering of books, musical instruments, horns, drums, and several oddities.

Baus stepped back with perplexity, croaking: "Well, Weavil is alive—or what I thought was Weavil clambering up a stalagmite."

"Weavil?" Valere kicked at the shelves. His brows dipped; it had been a long time since he had heard of the poet, not since the sojourn at Heagram prison when Aurimag had recaptured him and stuffed him in a bottle.

"'Tis likely that Weavil's recent prankstering," mused Baus, "is responsible for all the infiltration of armadillos into Aurimag's cave."

"A bold speculation," Valere grunted. "But mattering little at this moment." A vase wobbled, toppled and smashed from the upper shelf. "The event has afforded us a stopgap to life. So what now?"

Baus gave an exhausted laugh. "Haste is our watchword, Valere! Already our enemies abound while our friends languish."

Valere peered about with disfavour. He was about to mutter a dour epithet, but desisted as something caught his eye. He had lost his leathern helm and his red mop of hair hung drably about his haggard cheeks. Rank sweat beaded his brow; his neck bulged—while Baus's black mail was splashed with yellow shrew's blood, owing to the gutted eye that had unceremoniously appeared before him.

A quick scan revealed another cramped shelf, higher and more dangerously poised than the other. The ledge was populated with two glassed jars—one whose girth was twice the other, yet both familiarly fitted to that in which the knee-high Weavil had been stuffed months ago.

Baus frowned, pulling at his chin. He made a wry mouth. He scrambled up on the first ledge, tugged at the heft of the larger tubular-shaped jar containing a twain of occupants. He yanked it and it came falling back to the floor.

The glass smacked but didn't break. The outlaws peered curiously. The cylinder held its shape. The occupant, or rather 'occupants' within, seemed stunned, or 'stricken' was more apt, like dopey groundhogs in a hole.

Baus hitched himself closer. Through the smoky depths, he discerned an old figure, brown-robed, pot-bellied and ashen-faced. The fellow had a wispy trail of beard, a pointed nose, a scratched cheek; possibly a magicker. Woisper?

Baus started. The figure appeared to move, garbed all in his brown-vest, cloak, hood, ermine-furred hose, low ankle boots . . .

Memories flooded back to Baus—had it been so long that he remembered seeing that figure? As for the other form in the jar, he thought to recognize an eldritch visage from the past, somewhere not long ago—a peculiar pig-like visage, with a rounded body, a mangy garb of red and black-checkered jacket . . .

Baus drew back, fighting nausea. Could it be the hobgoblin Graeitch? He clutched at his jaw and set the jar on its side, which looked impregnable.

Unscrewing the seal proved futile. Struck with an insight, he recognized it was hinged with brass clamps: part of the lid was stuck with an adhesive lock.

Team-wise he and Valere hefted the cylinder and they dashed it to the stone.

The glass did not crack. The canister thudded, rolled on the floor unscathed.

The two scratched their heads, gave each other questioning looks. They muttered their misgivings and took the jar again. The jar's occupants were greatly inconvenienced and swam about their brine with energetic movement, buoyed with chagrin.

With crafty energy, Baus lashed the end of his whip about the seal and advised Valere to grab hold of the whip's handle with diligence so the two could get the jar whirling about their heads.

A soft, humming gripped the air and the canister went flying with a bang. The glass smashed against the wall, then come rolling back to their feet—unmarred.

Baus's eyes bulged. Was the container invincible? It must be held by some impressive magical force?

Baus was about to abandon the scheme when the glass suddenly burst. The glass shattered inward, imploding into a thousand pieces, spewing forth a thick greenish slime and two dishevelled inhabitants.

For several heartbeats the two watched in fascination. The tiny, near comatose forms tried dazedly to rise to their feet. Both failed. Brine spewed from their nostrils.

The old wizard Woisper gave a grim shudder. His teeth chattered like eggs in a bowl. Finally, he gained his feet, pawing at his dripping robe, flinging off bits of broken glass. He staggered, began rubbing his body all over, as if trying to knead the malaise out of his bones. He was wobbly at first, but then looked to and fro from behind a set of fierce, green eyes. A dripping mat of ashen hair draped his long brooding face. An aristocratic nose hung loosely over a walrus type moustache, which collided dissonantly with his round, cherubic cheeks. His manner was gruff. From under his bowed legs squirmed a hog-like shape, groggily disposed and bent on extracting a revenge.

Baus's eyes met Valere's in a comic communion. They pushed ever closer to examine the perplexed crew.

Woisper kicked at the sopping Wickle. He burst forth a torrent of questions, barely intelligible.

Baus answered in a voice of cautious inquiry, "Who are we? We are nothing more than those who liberated you. I am Baus, and this is my confidant, Valere—we are important men of quality . . ."

Woisper seemed unconcerned with the designations. He tendered them a critical look and made a brief inspection, kicking once again at the sopping form under his feet. Underneath the long bedraggled cloak, the neomancer wore a padded, grey-breasted jacket which pretentiously contrasted with his darker outer garment. "If you would indulge me, perhaps you would care to elaborate on your presence, and as to where am I. You appear a rough-looking lot—bandits of some sort. But, if you liberated me—then thank you from the bottom of my heart. I am Woisper—wisest and eldest of the neomancers—from storm-brewed Mismerion. Are you squires—or serfs?—Without your service, I would be drowned, a wretch rolling in one of Aurimag's sealers."

"True—now that we have traded introductions, a word or two regarding remuneration would be proper. . ."

"Remuneration? 'Tis an ugly word."

Baus acknowledged the ingratitude with gritting teeth. He was about to tender curt words when the neomancer held up a hand. "Patience. This filth and gloom is no place to tender medallions or badges. For the time being, let us settle on an equitable agreement—" He reached in his robe to count out some coins but was accosted by a sudden rude and clumsy jostling from behind. "What?" he cried. "Again, this contemptible wretch!"

He lashed out at the Wickle and she tug-boated herself away, grunting and scratching like a badger. Suddenly in the dimness, there was a rank pause as she perceived the outlaws for who they were. She shrank back, a look of incredulity and anger pinching her face.

Valere detected the emotion and skipped forth with a grinning laugh. "Well, what have we here? A little piglet?" The seaman guffawed and reached to administer an ear-boxing slap. "Quite a little sow from the forest come jiggling out of her jar. Well, Graietch, how end ye in Aurimag's jar? Have you gotten on the bad side of our headstrong magician? Well, too bad!" He hefted her up by her hooves and began plucking out her eyebrows one by one.

Baus strolled over to pinch Graeitch pleasantly on the cheek. "Why this crackerjack fortune? Graeitch! How the pieces of the jigsaw puzzle fit together in one pleasant synchrony!"

"Curse your tongue! Unhand me! I am an important member of Rastule Glade. I am an honoured member of the League of Wise Women. My hooves are sharp and my magic is cogent. Now, stay back, beware, I shall skin you alive, ere the waxing moon!"

"Now, now, Graeitch—" smiled Baus. "None of your plangent boasts. 'Tis a poor way for friends to reopen a friendship."

"Friends?" she snorted.

Woisper barked out a disgusted chirp. "You would be friends with this repulsive swine?"

"Only under past compulsion," declared Baus blandly.

"How did you find me, you wretch?" shrilled Graeitch. "Was it that diseased magician's mad puppet that led you on my trail?"

Baus smiled indifferently. "Not entirely. Aurimag's golem did arrive at your Honey Home—but failed to make an impression. As far as your sisters go—well! They come under siege well . . . Nevertheless! I'm sure that matters are resolving themselves in quick time and they will send their warmest regards, were they capable."

Graeitch snuffled a grunt. "What did you do to them?"

Baus raised brows. "I did nothing. Paiesmy and Loeitch have hastened their own doom quite exclusively."

"Villains!" Graeitch screeched. "You shall pay for your mischief! When I retrieve my hornblort and my bottleroot—ah, watch out! My jingle-lace and scorpion bitters shall rinse your innards with fury! I shall feed you to Skmog—or better yet Mlog, my black tasm—I shall stuff you with spider stew that will bulge your insides!"

Valere uttered a gurgling croak. "Now, now, witch. It galls me to hear your malicious prattle." He ruffled his fingers under Graeitch's nose and snatched Baus's whip, which he instantly used to great effect upon Graeitch's hide.

After many howls on Graeitch's part, Baus continued to address her in a consoling tone. "In wise reflection, I must render this verdict. That I find you a creature of pitiful fortune. Yet, you are somewhat fortunate in that you have survived this far against Aurimag. He hasn't blasted you to oblivion with his golem. Fortuity knocks. Be forewarned! You may not be so lucky with us."

Woisper cried out in a husky quaver, "And what about me? I will skin this creature limb from limb. You cannot conceive of the disgusts and horrors this miserable creature has inflicted upon me. Slobbering, slurping, groping and squeezing—not to mention the indecent, lascivious exertions of a most horrid kind—"

Baus held up a hand. "We all know of Graeitch's prurience. So, let us move to matters of more importance."

"What could be more important than—" Graeitch, recovering from her outrage, twisted and flung oaths, kicking out her hooves which accomplished little, dangling from her hooves. Her tirade being done, Woisper managed to flutter his fingers in spellcraft and forestall the Wickle's aggressiveness.

The Wickle slumped. Valere let go of her rank hide and the pig-creature slid away with a thump, gathering herself in a corner.

Woisper issued a curt demand, "Where is that fiend Aurimag anyway? I see him nowhere about. Why do we remain confined in this dank chamber?"

"The answers are complex," explained Baus. "Giant shrews rage outside. They harbour fangs, dripping maws and foul breath, not to mention feet like mallets of doom. The neomancer is at large outside, outfitted with a baleful finger-fire."

"'Tis a gross order magic that I resent teaching him!" griped Woisper.

"Nevertheless, four of our companions are trapped on the hither side of this wall. They are presumed dead," announced Valere sullenly. "They include Poli and Trimestrius, Kazzasius the Projector and Ulisa the Utilitarian."

"Kazzasius and Ulisa? She too?" Woisper let out a grievous howl.

"I am afraid so," explained Baus sadly. "Ulisa, despite her shape-shifting ability, has been herded into a ghost keep of Aurimag's making—a floating sanctuary which hovers upon high like a toy and guards a savage ogre, some miniature colossus. The structure is unscalable. As a moth she was harried inside by the ogre who delivered her frights and disgusts. Kazzasius lies singed, a talonless one-eyed eagle at the foot of a patch of scorched stalagmites."

"Do not forget Trimestrius!" trumpeted Valere. "The prince lies frozen and insensate, incapacitated by Aurimag's sobosphere!"

"These words are replete with woe!" Woisper wailed. He raised his finger to the ceiling and called out a terrible ultimatum: "Aurimag! You are an abysmal traitor! Why did you not conform like the others? You have become an obstinate pest—but we shall end your tyranny very smartly. I shall personally see to your deposition and the mitigation of your outrages and disgusts once and for all!"

Valere nodded but felt an uneasy scepticism regarding the tenor of the boasts. "A high-minded ideal, old man. Yet somewhat pie in the sky."

"And why is that?"

Edging his way past, Baus suggested a stratagem, "We must combine our strengths, and confound your enemy with weaponry and magic."

"And how are we to do that?" The neomancer fidgeted his beard with disfavour. "Do you harbour weapons?"

Baus sidestepped the question. Some hummng and hawing later, he held up a long flayed whip, to which he gave an exaggerated snap.

Woisper seemed unimpressed. "So then? One whip. How can that deter the Spell of Fire?"

Baus motioned all-inclusively to his knife, dog-whistle, his tin capsule, and broken fire shell.

The magicker nodded thoughtfully but frowningly. "Indeed, indeed . . . the fire shell undoubtedly comprises a potent commixture of sulphur, glycerol, saltpetre and charcoal—a suitable melange of destructive puissance—but is it cogent?"

Baus nodded sombrely. Sensing some malicious presence, he motioned them all to silence. The lights from under the crack in the door had ceased. Aurimag's sobosphere was neither thudding nor rebounding like before against the walls.

The silence reigned auspiciously. It pervaded the other side of the slab with a threat and suspicion.

A lank haft of hose suddenly dipped beneath the slab.

Baus jerked back, brows raised in astonishment. The mouthpiece was a dead snake's crown fitted with a bony fang. From the serpent's mouth came a stream of viscous paste which instantly caused all to gag.

"A blight!" wailed Baus. He stomped on the snake's head, forced the mouth to pinch shut, squirting the effluvium back through the tube.

There was a loud cry of anguish on the other side. The backflow wafted out into the corridor and discharged itself upon the wielder. Baus recognized the voice of Aurimag in the form of a painful mutter.

Grunting satisfaction, Baus watched as the hose was retracted; the tread of angry feet came slowly clopping down the corridor, evincing more satisfied glee from Baus.

"Aurimag engineers fell magics which we must thwart. He will rain them down on us without restraint!"

"As shall I!" announced Woisper with vehemence. His face was a pyre of passion; a proud fervour glowed in his eyes which the others found disconcerting. "I am handicapped, yes—but I will thwart this gingerstamp, if it is the last thing I do. My reflexes are weak and he will think me feeble from exposure to this abominable Wickle, but I am crafty and knowledgeable and he is vain. That said," he chuckled, "I shall practice on this swine, splashing the same noxious substances which shall douse Aurimag!" The neomancer motioned meaningfully to Graeitch who still quivered in the corner.

"The idea sounds sensible," agreed Baus.

"It is that and more. Stand back!—I sprout water lilies from the lank mop of this Wickle's hair!"

Valere showed his white teeth. Baus crouched in a stance of wariness.

Raising hands high, the neomancer flitted fingers in a spidery way.

The Wickle's limbs went stiff as a sheet; her face blanched. She braced herself for a blight.

Graietch did not transmogrify. Instead she retained an auspicious glow and out of nowhere popped an angry parrot-headed shape from her ear; thumping up the wall on a green stalk, disappearing into the rocky ceiling.

Baus and Valere stood back in awe, glaring bleakly, each feeling a current of marvel.

Woisper scowled. "Ignore this side-effect. Attend! Watch now as I deal her a blight." Twirling index finger, the wizard sent a mournful ray to splash the wall. "I call this the 'Blight'—of the Zygote'!"

Baus showed teeth with anticipation.

An ominous creaking took place, and the chamber rocked. Baus reached hands out to the wall for stability; he thought to hear a small tumult like the tall mast straining against the fierce wind of a gale.

Valere ducked—a certain direness was in the air and he didn't want to be caught unawares.

The neomancer chewed on his beard, looking nonplussed. For a brief spell the magic seemed to have backfired. Woisper snickered and moved out from the shadow of the wall. Offered overhasty explanations, he finally planted his feet to deal his right leg a firm stamp, then to intone unearthly words:

"Diasma! Duma! Deurma! . . ."

A dolorous echo filled the room—now it diminished in the nothingness of blank air as a tormented ghost melded into the wall. A noticeable lack of companionability gripped the air, yet no malaise upon the Wickle. She squatted dazedly in her discontent. Baus sprang to his feet, thrust out an interrogating finger. "Time passes in waste. What is the problem with your magicking?"

Woisper crafted a pensive frown. "My magic is simply out of practice. A dirgeful vapour recently fled, what of it?" He dropped his chin in a rueful manner. "Fie on these diminutive n^{th} order subtremors—they defy my command!" Woisper shook a white fist and became adamant. "Watch!"

Peering about, all expected another comic interlude, but the blood in the wizard's face burned high and a lamp suddenly dimmed. A salamanderish thing leaped suddenly out of the far wall. The creature was graced of a green body and black slimy legs and it tramped straight for Baus.

Baus hopscotched back; he lifted a boot to thwart the creature but it passed clean through his shoe. Uttering a stammering gurgle, he leapt back and the thing rolled over, did a mournful somersault then shimmered out of existence.

There were long seconds of bewilderment before Graeitch began to assert herself in overweening way. Eyes strained—the Wickle snorted and with casual impertinence strode ever closer to Woisper, looking ready to pluck his nose.

Woisper sagged back, tossing incantations right and left. He looked toward Baus and Valere for succour. "Keep this filthy creature away from me! I will not stand for another string of ignominies!"

Baus made an impertinent leer. "Peace, Woisper! Regarding these magics of yours, I think they are well past their years."

"Mind your words!" Woisper boomed. "I will not be played down by untimely mishaps!"

Baus shrugged and forwarded another suggestion. "Of course, we could fling the Wickle into the hallway."

Woisper mused. "A simple plan, Baus, but how does it solve our dilemma with my temperamental magic?"

"It doesn't, but it forestalls the possibility of being hexed by this Wickle, should she have some trick up her sleeve."

"How's that?" demanded Woisper.

"By posting a line of defence, similar to the game of 'hopball'. A diversion, a buffer, as quite commonly unique as tactics to deflect further aggression."

Woisper sneered. "An innovation. I am unfamiliar with 'hopball'—yet still, I have an inkling of what the game involves."

"Precisely. Our enemy engages a diversion, with its main mass of opponents—those against Aurimag—he provides certain star players an opportunity to act with impunity." Baus held out his hands in a fashion to indicate Graeitch's participation in the matter which would entail a sense of appropriate reckoning.

Woisper's eyes glowed with keenness. "An excellent idea! Between the two of our excellent heads, we will wring out a successful conclusion to this abysmal affair!"

Valere rolled his eyes. But the crafty grin on Woisper's face began to fade. "Perhaps this swinish midget can help—" He turned to her with a harsh impatience. "What do you think of that, you little porker? You lead us the way out—or you suffer death right now." In such wise Graietch shrank back in glowering enmity. "In such service, Aurimag the knave, should he apply the Spell of Unblinking Fire—shall fail, or this repulsive hybrid will become the instant collateral damage!"

Baus gave a serene acknowledgement, to which Graeitch protested with fervour, and Woisper was obliged to unleash a punitive ray. "Silence, you pig! My decree is formal! Now, out in the corridor—at once, swine."

"Wait!" commanded Baus. "I myself must prepare for the blight before I hop senselessly into the wolf's den."

"Unorthodox, but wise planning!" Woisper forced his face into a sallow grimace. "Your plan?"

Baus peered balefully at the neomancer. "You are a magicker, cajole some puissance into your digits, gather some mojo to give me some lead time."

"Why don't you do some heavy lifting for a change?" cried Woisper with exasperation. "Clamping one's fists together into a knot to release a putrescence is not as easy as one may think."

"Nor is coming up with ideas to keep our skins from being flayed."

Clutching fingers, Woisper made loops and swirls in the air with a flourish of confidence. "To accomplish these weighty deeds, I require the assistance of Salmeister, my compeer, who is encased in the top jar on the far shelf."

Baus nodded placidly. "The deed is not impossible, but yet your sallow chum may have to wait. He lies entombed in a jar of his own bad doom! There is no time to get him. Aurimag foists tricks on our back door while beasts wander without, eager to gore us."

"No matter, we must free my good colleague or at least die in the process. You succeeded in emancipating me—why not him?"

"The logic is circular," said Baus. "Especially when we lie disarranged in filth with bolts of Unblinking Fire severing our limbs."

"A casuistic argument!" scoffed Woisper. "It appears that I must do all the work myself!"

"Then please do. Amass your blights. Aurimag is currently regrouping to mangle us!"

Graeitch gave a rankled squeal. "Must I sit here subjected to your vain babblings while shrunken and delivered blights?"

"Silence, you dour hag!" roared Woisper. "I shall not hear any of your dull roars. Consider yourself currently under prohibition of speech."

Graeitch politely refused to recognize such a command. Woisper raised fingers and glared. Graeitch shrank back. He clamped cold fingers about her lips and worked them roughly. He hopped back wildly to mutter a harsh syllable. Graeitch's lips suddenly fused together then faded from sight. There was only a craggy line where the mouth should be with a pig snout above, but no mouth to speak of.

Graeitch pitched back in stupefaction, mumbling gibberish through her quasi-mouth.

A strident voice shouted through the door. "Pay heed! Slide free the slab lest I unleash a purulence upon you. The discharge will chagrin you, comprised as it is of a rare toxin!"

Baus nodded blithely at the warning. On a sudden whim, he cupped his hands around his lips and feigned a sycophantic protest, "Of this we are well aware, Aurimag. Do not burden our time with rodomontade! We are in the process of profound reflection, after which we shall exit this chamber at our leisure."

"Accelerate the progress!" called the voice peremptorily. "I grow impatient with flagrant boasts."

"That is your problem."

Baus consulted Woisper and prompted the magicker to act with urgency.

Woisper's face flushed. "My emprise demands the inclusion of Salmeister, as I intimated."

"This caprice is irking!" sighed Baus. "Valere agrees . . . very well, help me release the varlet."

"Salmeister is not a varlet!" shouted Woisper. "He is my henchman, and friend."

"Crony, concomitant—it is all the same!"

Valere reached up to help Baus tug the last jar down from the shelf. Attaching whip to seal, the two conspirers got Salmeister's canister hurtling about the room with a ferocious velocity. Then the glass struck the walls and glass shattered in a most capricious way. A sallow-faced bonhomme splashed out, in a spectacular display of confusion.

Aurimag's voice called an admonitory command through the cracks. "What is all this disturbance in my reliquarium? I have valuable objects cached there. I detect the smashing of glass and the spilling of some liquids."

"Nothing to be concerned with," Baus reassured. "An antique vase accidentally slipped from the high shelf and is undergoing repair this instant."

An aggrieved cry stabbed out from behind the slab. "This is an irregular occurrence and displeases me most headily! These vases are priceless. My collectibles are not to be trifled with!"

"This is worthy of note, Aurimag, but for these reasons alone, we remain inculpable and must cite disclaimers."

"Butterfingers! Prepare to feel regret. My magic will blast you and all will tremble in its wake!"

"I harbour no doubt of that, Aurimag—now please, quiet down while we unhitch the slab."

"Do so immediately!" Aurimag cried. As he thrust his weight forward, they heard the door thud.

"Pay heed. You may break your limbs on stone that hard."

"Your advice falls on deaf ears! The shreeks have been despatched and lie deceased and crippled in the Bronze Hall. I have subjugated your cronies, Weavil and Poli, to indignities. They currently lie at my feet suffering pangs and contusions. Perform my wishes or they both die. Their lives can be shared for your surrender."

"So the bargain is forced on us," admitted Baus. "Do not harm them in any way and we will all exit."

"Briskly now! I grow fatigued with all this prolixity—but I warn you, any more harrowing breakages or mischief, coxcomb, and I will blast this door to $n+1^{th}$ oblivion— along with all your souls!"

"Muster your patience, Aurimag!" crooned Baus. "We are quaking with the thought. My colleague, Valere, and I are currently sliding the door at this moment which appears to be jammed."

"The concern is not mine!" rasped Aurimag. "Unjam it—and recall—your friends' lives hang in balance!"

Baus looked doubtfully around the confines with anguished distress. How long would Aurimag be fooled? He did not doubt for a second that the neomancer would shrink them all to homunculi.

Baus's gaze focused gloomily on Salmeister, who was now emerging from his torpor. The wizard was draped in voluminous garments, all tan and umber, dripping heavily of slime and glass from head to toe. The fluted golden circlet hung on his balding crown did little to exhibit his bearing. His face, sallow and moony, was distorted under a blood red glow of the lights. An untold misery was reflected in the face, augmented by an obtrusive squid-like thing that appeared to have latched itself onto his lower nostrils and cheek. The growth or epiphyte clung there about the lower portion of his face.

Valere crouched to inspect the dangling creature with curiosity. A flange seemed to have coiled thrice about the neomancer's neck, in the shape of an odd octopi-like tentacle. The blue and grey armature had latched insistently onto his visage and held his face in check, in a knotted grimace.

"What is the thing?" Valere cried out in jocular dismay.

Baus frowned. "Some sort of mollusc? Cephalopod? How should I know?"

"It's likely a schasm," remarked Woisper, frowning deeply and tugging at his chin. "These types of arparopods appear in two varieties—either the 'blue' or 'red'. This particular creature appears to belong to the 'blue' variety."

Baus nodded sagely. Squinting in interest, he stepped back to evaluate the parasite with a minimum of risk. After a discursive evaluation, he attempted to excise the creature with a knife.

To no avail. The creature was obdurate. He drew on Valere's aid—they put in significant exertions. Many grunts, heaves, groans, knife-thrusts, whip-snaps and boot-nudges later, Valere's fingers finally forked into the Salmeister's nostrils and Baus pulled with all his might to force the creature free.

Salmeister's physiognomy underwent significant marrings after the excising.

The schasm, thus detached from its host, sprang wildly back on itself to gain the top shelf. Baus's eyes grew wide. The creature spun forward with marvellous speed as it arched about the chamber on rubbery flanges. All the time it threatened to latch onto another host.

Baus stabbed out at it with his knife; Valere stomped with his war boots, but each failed to kill it, each fearing the thing would affix itself to their own breathing apparatuses.

Woisper ran cunningly about the room calling out cantraps and incantations, to no avail.

The schasm finally latched onto Graeitch's leg, and with a probing intensity, dug deep. Despite the Wickle's anguished attempts to prevent otherwise, she was the new host.

The schasm finally fixed itself to an area under her wet trousers—a few inches above the open hoof, sucking at the festering wound there delivered earlier by Weavil's teeth.

Salmeister wheezed out a hoarse laugh from sagging jowls. "Gratitude! How I abhorred that bloodsucking creature affixed to my sinuses." He pulled out a handkerchief and began massaging his beleaguered nose. "Well, where is that cursed Aurimag anyway? I shall rip his dawcock's larynx out. I shall cleft his limbs!—separate his eyes from his face!"

"Peace, Salmeister!" implored Woisper. "Everything is well. Aurimag is being dealt his just deserts. Here you shall find only the sternest of his enemies."

The sallow dwarf looked about the nest of faces, bewildered and rankled at the collection of allies and strangers.

"Who are you?"

"People who intend to launch a foray of assassination in short order," Woisper affirmed.

Salmeister evinced startled pleasure. "Good to hear," he growled. He rubbed his palms and peered unpleasantly upon Graeitch. "Who is this pig-like thing anyway? Am I to be confronted by hobgoblins so shortly after being mauled by a schasm?"

Woisper assured Salmeister that nothing was further from the truth. They were currently in the process of hatching plans to dispose of Aurimag. "Baus, will you bring Salmeister up to speed?"

Baus nodded. "The plan is—after the Wickle, this hobgoblin as you call her, runs interference, the magicians of our group, namely you and Woisper, shall rush in to zap your enemy with blue streaks while I, on the other hand, as supervisor of the operation, will act as rearguard, hopping importantly behind the front line, wreaking havoc with my purposeful blasts on this dog whistle!"

Salmeister frowned. "This plan seems simplistic, if not slapdash."

"'Tis nothing of the sort!" declared Baus. "Together, with your blue flames and my piercing notes, we will confound this pretender Aurimag! The plan stands! It allows Valere is allowed an angle of opportunity to subdue the villain before he can muster any peculiar spells."

Valere grinned unpleasantly.

Woisper fluttered fingers and tugged worriedly at his beard. "But suppose Valere flubs his task? While the idea seems outwardly plausible, I do doubt the efficacy of the whistle. I detect a note of casuistry in your scheme!"

"Stifle the pessimism!" called Baus. "I merely craft a reckless flourish of whip, emit an oratory blast, and Aurimag will be easily cowed." Baus emphasized the importance of the whip by demonstrating a series of looping flourishes and swings. "Once I have subdued the blackguard, we are in the rare position to inflict more drastic punishments. I have considered the angles from many vantages, both probable and improbable—now listen! We must hasten our industry. Aurimag plots wrathful countermeasures as you know unless we act fast. He only plots our complete annihilation. To counteract this possibility, I suggest we inflict roiling rigours of our own, particularly blights."

"The declaration seems indisputable," admitted Woisper hesitantly. "Yet what remains of our alternatives and what of our risks?—Never mind . . . We open the portal and bang! let us face this dire monster! I am ready—are you, Salmeister? What is that bloody mark on yur face?"

"Never mind," grumbled the sallow man. "I can discern old and rude spells rolling to memory."

"Excellent!" congratulated Woisper. "Salmeister, you are a gem in the rough. Baus, you may prise free the bar!"

Nodding perfunctorily, the outlaw yanked upon the door. A slab of putrid light fell upon the floor. Graeitch shrank back with loathing. What awaited her was not agreeable and Valere grabbed her by the snout and hurled her roughly through the portal.

The old wizard staggered in behind, his plump face set in a grimace while Salmeister shambled after in a similar humour. Valere was quick to follow while Baus tagged along at his back, nursing a sinking feeling that all was not to go as planned.

V

The scene was one of confusion. Baus jumped out of the jagged gap while Aurimag jerked sidewise from behind a stalagmite with a vile smirk on his face. Over charred huddles of shreeks he leaped with intent to destroy his enemies, his fingers dancing patterns to forge blights and rectify a grievous injustice long unresolved.

The seamen struck forth, Baus with his raised whip. Bodies of shreeks littered the marmor floor in the hundreds: the once desolate cavern was a sloppy graveyard of eerie, butchered corpses. The Wickle Graeitch was soon cornered in between Aurimag and Woisper. The creature hobbled on bent knees, confused in her process of attacking or fleeing. The two dwarfed sorcerers kept guard at her back.

Graeitch finally turned tail and fled off amidst the riddle of bodies.

Woisper bellowed, "Get back here, you miserable coward!" He trotted after the Wickle, fists in the air. He halted, stepped gingerly around bleeding shreeks. There was a foul number of them by the wall of shields. It was difficult not to cringe. "Back here, you hag!"

Graeitch ignored the order. More pressing things were in attendance. She leapt and scrabbled between gaps of carcasses, avoiding a quivering fang or two which twitched in death.

Graeitch found a cleft that seemed safe. The Wickle recoiled. A fiend reared up alive and snuffled at her face and she squealed and fled off toward the darker wall.

Aurimag meanwhile hopscotched his way through the mounds, hoping to locate Woisper, his eyes filled with hate.

Grey-haired Woisper lifted a cautionary hand. "Surrender, Aurimag! You cannot flee. 'Tis useless to struggle against us. Give up this lame struggle of yours. Your life hangs in balance."

"Silence, you oaf!" commanded Aurimag. "What do you know of 'choices' and 'balance', being such a feckless hypocrite? Doom awaits *you*!" His maniacal laugh rang through the cavern. A demented gleam showed in his eyes.

Words of incantations twanged from Aurimag's lips and Woisper followed up with sounds of his own: these came in a macabre question-answer of fiendish death. Baus thought the tumult akin to the voices of madmen, yet Aurimag's jabbers seemed the more sinister of the two. Fans of purple fire flared from both sets of fingers. The cavern burst in a heap of sick, frightful glows and sizzling starbursts sprayed about like flash lightning.

Baus turned to his colleagues. He caught a dismayed glimpse of Poli—within sight of Weavil and Trimestrius—they were slung up in dismal coils of twitch-vine upon a hedge of stalagmites. How had Poli been strung up with such soundness on those tall, glistening cones? Like Weavil and Trimestrius, his friend's face was a pale and lustreless mask of misery stretched in fright and marked with toothy depressions of shreeks. The creatures had had their play with him but he still lived. His wrists were swollen, his ankles bare, garments torn and skin soiled . . . but yet, he and his colleagues appeared remarkably alive.

Not far off, Kazzasius lay in a crumpled heap at the base of a stalagmite. Above floated the mysterious ghost keep. The glow, a ghastly lighthouse, green and grey, beat into the murk like some unholy beacon. Somewhere, the apparition had claimed Ulisa—and Baus felt sorrow, for the shape-shifter was a powerful ally.

In two expansive bounds, he gained the wall and snatched at the trio of swords glistening under Poli and Weavil's dangling feet. The weapons clanked and were clean of ooze and Baus guessed the shreeks had licked them dry. He hefted a blade, tossed it to Valere; together the two scrambled to hew their colleagues down from their posts.

The bodies fell in thuds. Poli managed a groggy mewling and Weavil stirred to life. Trimestrius lolled like some doll drowned in a pool, as he attempted to mutter intelligible syllables.

The captives were slashed free. Woisper ducked a crippling blaze from Aurimag's finger. Salmeister ran to comfort his colleague. "Keep up your dodging, Woisper! The 'Spell of Tensile Drag' is hungry for you."

In a flurry, Baus blew hard on his dog whistle. The shrilling had Aurimag clasping his ears. He bellowed out a command but Baus paid no heed.

The outlaw ducked hastily aside, avoiding Aurimag's death ray. Aurimag pitched the sobosphere.

Baus leaned aside. The orb shot past, taking out a shark-toothed stalactite. The spike came toppling down in a blaze of fire a few paces from his feet, setting flames to the hideous hides of shreeks.

The outlaw scrabbled away. The sobosphere was a dim grim pumpkin, a cannon shape of destruction, which came hurtling after him without mercy.

Baus's nostrils flared and he whirled his blade, caught the globe on his sword and deflected it off into the murk. The orb surged with an ominous 'twack', nearly bending his blade in two.

The projectile continued on a wild path, careening off into some bronze shields strung on the wall.

The globe spun a few times, traced a dizzying arc, then fell smoking on the floor between two humps of fallen shreeks. Somehow the bronze metal had defused the direness of its threat.

Aurimag gave a whistling call and the talisman came bobbing back, with new life, its amber gleam tracing a wake in its trail.

Baus's muscles knotted. With grim anticipation, he stood ready to face another onslaught, suddenly speculating that the power of the orb was undermined by the shields.

He swung his gaze from the sword to the bronze shields and tossed a sword to Valere. "Grab the shields. Quick! The metal offers us protection against Aurimag's fireball."

"How's that?" grunted Valere.

"Never mind, it just does!"

The captain wasted no time. He dragged three triangular shields down from the wall and threw one at Baus. Another he thrust into Poli's hand. "Up, if you wish to live!" cried Baus. "Shield your bodies!"

Poli dared to comply. With maddening slowness he raised the shield; a blaze of fire struck Valere from the side who absorbed the shock by luck with his raised shield. With weird impetus, the bolt caromed off the wall and zigzagged about the cave with harmless force. The seaman was knocked off his feet, but he struggled to outwit Aurimag, regaining his weapon and fanning it about his head for protection.

Baus crouched wide-eyed. He realized that not only did the bronze inhibit psychic intrusion, but it seemed also to resist the neomancer's blights.

Aurimag's grim smile curled about his lips. The ruddy murk was becoming too oppressive—not to mention the death-dealing environment was becoming unstable.

Poli put a feeble hand to his brow. "Leave me alone, Baus . . ." he wheezed. His laboured hiss sounded in Baus's ear. "You will fall to your doom—but kill the warlock at least— promise me."

"Have faith, you doomsayer—here, grab my arm!"

Poli struggled, but only crumpled to his knees. "Go!"

Weavil and Trimestrius could barely lift their shared shield. They could command an end each by gripping the leathern strap apiece. They hoisted the defence over their tiny forms, protecting themselves from Aurimag's fury of blights and curdles of flame.

Baus trained eyes warily upon Weavil's cloud-ridden face. Doubting if his friend could ever recognize him, he saw the straggly clumps of hair, the overlong moustache and beard. The gaunt folds and creases were too miserable to bear. The poet's earlier unique, jaunty self was gone.

Guilt overcame Baus. He and Valere frog-marched behind their shields, hopping forward with grim zeal. They hobbled together as a single vanguard, startling Aurimag whose lips were twisted sourly in an ugly grimace. He relaxed his vigil, at the same time allowing Woisper an opening of attack.

The mistake was a turning point.

Woisper slipped around the back of Aurimag and mumbled a cantrap while the smoke was streaming in from all sides. He mumbled fell spells while spreading an upturned hand. Swiftly, a looping curlicue of light launched itself banderole-like from his fingers.

Aurimag was grazed by a flashing ray on the throat. He cried out, barely dodging the impulse, before the blight struck a semi-comatose shreek which became an instant glowing mass.

The bray of horns suddenly chorused from afar.

Aurimag winced. It presaged the presence of foreign magics!

Aurimag cringed; grimacing with consternation. He disliked the turn of events and saw a nearby shreek carcass spurring to life, lofting on high and pitching him back on his heels. The dead form drifted aimlessly to become a buoyant mass of flesh in the air. The thing swirled in the air . . . slowly—like some colossal phantom. Up and up it spun—toward the luminous castle. The creature was a lifeless mass, rotating, with dead brain and a zombie set of eyes, staring sightlessly at the castle.

From the miniature central court came a storm of castle guard. The sounds rang stridently in the murk. A squadron of bells clanged. Armour clanked; weapons clinked. The liveried horde scurried up the parapets, wielding halberds and lofting pikes and mace, the men-at-arms' axes could not reach the sinister island of flesh—and so the defenders turned to chop at the new menace, bawling at the top of their lungs from their battlements.

Baus spied a particularly high window in one the towers. A tiny white insect strove to escape the net which whooshed about the nearby airs with purpose. 'Twas Ulisa and Ulisa's ogre was champing at the bit, clomping within the tower block, trying to capture its quarry. Evidently the Utilitarian had eluded its grasp thus far, but despite her cunning evasions, she was soon to be caught again.

Salmeister was struck with an innovation. He composed a thaumaturgical ode and his wrists gyrated; he spun forth a livid cry and a low mechanical rumble rose from ground to air.

His arms stretched akimbo, he did some strange acrobatic move and the giant floating shreek suddenly blinked in the dimness and its mouth opened in a curious grimace. The thing's lips worked with a disquieting mewling while the guardsmen stood appalled, straddling the wall like rats to stop from falling.

With a chuckling gloat, Woisper approved of Salmeister's jinx—it was a jinx straight from one of his earlier debacles that had earned him his cognomen, 'the Saturnine'.

The neomancer called out gutturals, at which point the shreek began to bob left and right senselessly, then faster. Now the shape-less thing hovered like an omen, nudging the castle with its brainless mass striking the central tower just below the window. A grinding crash rang through the keep.

The tower gave a spasmodic lurch. The hulk plummeted, imploding into a pile of rubble. Then dust and a million pieces of cracking masonry billowed, upsetting the ogre's plan.

The moth escaped the crash while the courtyard soldiers raged up and down the parapets, flinging up their weapons with disgust.

Aurimag loosed curses into the air. The sinister fright keep was no more; already the irksome moth was fluttering to safety. How could the pesky minx have escaped so easily?

He gasped in pure acrimony. The catastrophe was unimaginable!—all his planning was for naught if she escaped and avoided his spells and he found himself tumbling into a fit of doubt. He galvanized his fingers and administered rays to his foes, but further dog-whistling and creeping and skulking with bronze shields had him clutching his ears.

Woisper launched a rainbow beam. The swift, poignant luminescence arched toward Aurimag.

The magician was struck squarely in the chest.

With a cry, he fell and floated in the air. What senselessness was this? he thought. Ensnared in a configuration of 'Woisper's Spell of Buoyancy', now he felt himself bobbing out of control, caught in a horrific trap. He struggled and thrashed. Aurimag's upward progress was not checked. Countermeasures were not forthcoming, and like that of a runaway balloon, Aurimag was pricked by the cavern's needle-like nest of stalactites.

Aurimag's rising halted at par with the fright castle. Now he flailed arms and thrashed like a beached fish, raving in lunacy. Not two feet away fangs of rock crowded his horizon.

He pitched the sobosphere down amongst his foes. But he was unable to take proper aim. The orb weaved a helter-skelter path and clanged impotently off Valere's shield, then rebounded into a nearby pool.

The orb sank from sight and was gone. With ragged gasps, Aurimag clutched for dear life. He hoped to toss plumes, stars, effusions—anything to bombard his foes. To no avail. The purple radiances that were so effective up to this point splattered harmlessly off the walls, absorbed by shields and pools.

Stalactites toppled and now greenish waters boiled. About the cave a horrendous din rumbled while wreathy fogs billowed in insidious clouds.

Salmeister, prompted by his saturnine disposition, took liberty to project another definitive thaumaturgy upon his enemy—the frightful 'Mirth Flip and Spin', as it was known. The roiling rigour set Aurimag's teeth on edge and sent bells ringing in his ears, and he stopped short of breath.

Woisper did a little toe-tap. He sent up another ampoule of 'Discriminative Buoyancy', which trapped Aurimag and lofted him higher in the air, namely, brushing painfully against the projecting stalactites.

The villain, using his last energies, howled with bitterness and summoned the sobosphere which came bobbing back in a sick, wet amber trail.

Ulisa, alert to the new turn of events, dropped out of her mothlike guise and set up a thwarting spell. Aurimag was flummoxed. She summoned a sombre glow to coil about her body—a greenishly potent nimbus that made Aurimag mysteriously begin to heave the contents of his stomach.

Aurimag clutched at his sobosphere vainly. The contorted expression on his face bespoke of nausea and fright. His lips frothing, he felt an explosion wrack the upper cavern, sending a plume of hideous yellow flames mushrooming the upper reaches. From within the cloud, Baus saw the murky figure tumble. Glittering radiances fled like banshees. All quarters of the cavern became lit with an incandescent radiance as the dark magician toppled.

The air was stunned with shock. Stalactites toppled; stalagmites smashed and pools roiled while the atmosphere grew in thick sulphurous clouds . . .

Baus crouched for dear life, protecting his head. Hidden behind his shield, his eyes glimmered with rage and hate. He pitched his arm about him to protect himself from falling shards.

* * *

No one saw Aurimag fall in those moments of his demise. He made an almost soundless descent on a charred heap. His face was half smothered by smoke, blackened beyond repair. His breath came out in ragged gasps. Like a crushed animal, he felt his joints aching like fire. How he had survived the fall was a miracle—perhaps nothing but the pure luck of the giant shreek body he landed on—or a stroke of fate. The 'Spell of Amorphous Annihilation' had apparently thrust him into vorticular involution and had convolved upon itself, sending the energy bending inside an interdimensional rift of its own impetus, spraying back into an nth order whorl. In other terms the flux had saved him . . . but only delayed the doom that Woisper and Salmeister had set out for him. The shreek he toppled on was flattened beyond recognition, wreathed in yellow fogs.

Aurimag wasted no time. He struggled painfully to his feet, his body bloodied and racked with dozens of abrasions. The sobosphere lay covered in an inch of soot; amidst the rubble were fallen stalactites, bat dung and heaps of charred flesh. No matter—the orb's glower was still cogent. Impossibly the magician stooped to retrieve his talisman and limped off into the gloom.

How conditions had given him this small chance was beyond him! Gads, he was filthy. He wrapped the orb under the flaps of his tattered robe and muttered new curses. How this fiasco had played itself out wrongly! Valere and Baus and their sidekicks would pay! They had engineered this feat—'twas a doing far greater than any spell he had ever wrought.

Aurimag fought to control his anger. Revenge burned like a pyre, but still, he could hardly quench all hope—at least now he was alive and a glimmer had smitten him and given him an idea.

The vain, thoughtless cockerels! If they adored their chaos so much—well . . . then they would have it! . . .

Almost at once, he envisaged a final reckoning; a pleasurable revenge, sweet as curdled whey, as he wrought a cunning scheme . . .

He took some half crouching steps over to the mutilated carcass of a shreek and then to some dim place deeper within the cavern. He had made one last reconaissance and instruction to his golem which stood mutely by, curiously unmarred: fetch another maid, bring her to the nymphosium. The cretin abided, for the magician needed some object on which to project his wrath. But this was not his sole purpose. Fetching the maid, the husk had aided him in his struggle against the shreeks and returned to the 'nymphosium' staying out of harm's way until he directed it otherwise. Of course, the creature had not disobeyed. It was dumb enough to do what he said without argument and would squat there for an eternity until given another command.

Aurimag grinned the wry grin of his crooked nature.

On weak legs, he limped along the outer rim of the cavern, fog hiding his passage; he remained for the nonce undetected. Along the far, bronze wall he stumbled, half muttering to himself in fits. He shook his head, a miserable disgust took hold of him almost clouding his reason. He found the oaken door—and he pressed with all his strength.

The door sagged within. A slim, dark-eyed maid sat clenched on the edge of her bed. Shivering, hunched and terrified, she uttered a miserable cry. Here was a cowering beauty of such delicacy that Aurimag almost collapsed in wonder. She was dressed in saucy garments that caused him to lick his lips. Her white diaphanous tunic showed a thin satin sash wrapped about her waist; her soft golden breasts were plump and ripe; tiny slippers pushed at her dainty feet and a garnet of three braids pinned back the lustrous brown fan of the curls framing her face. She was a beauty and the only inhabitant of this cubicle besides the nearly-perfect golem upon which she cast horrified glances.

She attempted to flee, but the villain blocked her escape. He knew she could not defy him. He threw back his cowl and ordered the golem seize her—'twas a near simulacrum of himself and the maid looked from one copy to the other with a nail-clawing panic.

He grimaced. The behaviour suggested something demeaning of his personal mana. His minion could be excused from the contemptuous gaze, but not the maid who quivered before him, sobbing. Tiredly, he smoothed his charred chin and spoke in a tolerant voice. "Stay here, little pretty. Doom shall not be so horrid then." A pity to waste such a lacy creature on death and fate . . . Yet . . . he had no recourse—and now, no time for lusts. Taking his exit, he latched the door, and with his golem at his side, retraced his steps back to the place where he had tumbled along the smoggy corridor.

Shreeks were piled everywhere. The filthy litter choked his cavern like so many dead flies and caused him to gag with revulsion. Indeed, the aspect of the cavern was lamentable, but at least the monster he had landed on had protected him from a deathly fate.

He twitched with indecision. The entire left side of his face had been torn and ached with a horrible fury—but what could he do? He winced with the effort of moving as he struggled to stay alert to finish what he had planned.

Delivering his last instructions to the golem, he quit the minion's company and ducked behind a scorched stalagmite, leaving the mute to face his fate. He gasped with the hurt of his brain and the burn of his skin and attempted to collect his thoughts for the task ahead.

* * *

The smoke began to clear and Aurimag's simulacrum shambled out of the fumes, arms hanging limply at its sides like bird's wings. The face was unreadable—an unearthly creature sentenced to the gallows. The defenders saw a zombie-rich parody of unnatural creation ready to face its doom—but crafted of such flawless outer elegance that it fooled those who now beheld it.

Woisper and Salmeister surveyed the golem with vast suspicion. Their expressions were leaden and wrathful; both were ready to inflict ghastly revenge on who they thought their time-old enemy. Each failed to remark the unscathed appearance of the enemy's visage, so bent they were on fulfilling their fury. Baus watched in dry-mouthed wonder as the twain summoned spells and voiced fell words and conjurations as they lifted their fingers in vengeful tandem.

Salmeister tripped over Woisper's heels. The two impinged noxious blasts and flares and revolutions of retrograde buoyancies. The hateful gyrations were brutal to behold, multicoloured blasts of isohedrical projections. The golem stood defenceless. The mutinous magic gathered as the black-robed outer body gleamed a baleful glow—then, it shimmered— first a ribald red, then a sultry yellow, finally to culminate in a gangrenous green. The simulacrum burst into a thousand pieces, dissolving into a liquefying lead-coloured pool of slime . . .

Unbeknownst to the defenders, the crafty Aurimag had thence escaped to his vestibule. Now, untethering a candle from its broken blood lamp, he chanted stealthily a release spell.

The elm-sprites' disbanded.

The spell was broken and the filmy portal momentarily dissolved. Aurimag disappeared into the dying lamplight, chuckling, scrambling like a gleeful rat into the gap between the pillars.

VI

Crouching grimly in the dark niche, Aurimag looked out upon the wreckage of his Bronze Hall with dry-mouthed distaste. Many mixed emotions coursed through his heart. He surveyed the fruits of his labours with a crumple of a smile that crept over his charred visage like slow-moving lice.

How this bout of misfortune had turned to his favour! The destruction of the simulacrum had fooled the cretinous neomancers who thought him dead.

Aurimag allowed himself a gloating grin. The thought somehow appeased his rancour and led him to believe that the circumstances would play themselves out in better stead. Yet somewhere beneath all the chaos there was a blemish of doubt—forces were in play that did not seem to allow events to proceed so smoothly.

Aurimag frowned. Such thoughts were death knells for success. He staggered down the musty, bat-reeking corridor with glowering haste. The candle was no more than a feeble stub in his hand, causing timorous flickers to fleck into the gloom.

Pah! If he must struggle in this fetid reek, then so he must. He must exercise every caution lest his minions maul him.

The magician shuddered to think of the consequence of wandering too closely to his elm sprites. Drawn tight against the dank stone, the necro-horrors were only held back by the iron mesh separating a wayfarer from doom. The evil leering back at him was of the utmost vileness—ghoulish things cooked up in the bowel of some demon's nightmare. Arfenos and Darkus—two subterranean wraiths—demons, incubi—nightmares which had been rooted there for ages, if not longer, before he had even discovered the cave. Arfenos hulked like some huge colossus, a muscled insect in a sombre pall of murk: Darkus, only slightly smaller, lingered to his left, clamped like some goliath wretch. The fiend was rooted in its tomb-shell of rock and both the stalks of their beings plunged like stone snakes hundreds of cubits into the bedrock. Aurimag knew from physic probes that the trunks were greasy tangles of bone, rock and wood, that their branches were no more than ropy masses of filth that supported a nest of grey-brown worm-writhing twig limbs. Each trunk sported a misshapen crown; several knotty eyes peered with distaste; calculating brains behind the trunks nothing more than heavy masses of dispassion and festering evil.

Aurimag shuddered. The thought of the atrocities appalled him. Better to leave these things in the swamps and deeps—far away from mortal eyes, where they could instil their ultimate terror. Nonetheless, the horrors were hatched from the demon seeds of Morion; he could not move them, nor could he tame them. Now as he sought a second glimpse of the continuing corridor, a desultory flash of genius struck the magician full in the eyes. He could hear the two sprites' ancient evils tolling behind the knot-wrinkled brows . . .

Aurimag tore his gaze away and recalled a time in his youth while searching for a private domain, how his impressionable person had stumbled upon the remote fissure. The potential of the two evil monstrosities had sent a thrill of excitation coursing up his spine. He had cast them with a 'Spell of Long-lasting Torpor'—a mere tyro's cantrap, but enough to stymie the ghouls, which for six days, under the flickering glare of firebrands, he and his underworld imps had painstakingly installed the twin portcullises that stood now, which kept the guardians at bay.

Aurimag swallowed the bile at the back of his throat. The taste was bitter, and the thought of being caught by the twain with the grates raised . . . caused his throat to lump at the prospect.

Aurimag's fingers instinctively clutched at his candle. His light must not falter. His charcoal-burnt face gave a spasm. Flinching at the torment of his wounds, he felt his fingers tighten like claws around the base of his blood-wick. Retribution would come.

He shambled on like a ghost, ever gritting his teeth, on and on through the long murky corridor. Yet he remained undaunted by the shaking of the pales and the guardians' throaty roars as they visited trouble on the grates.

Aurimag observed one thing which piqued his interest. A glint of metal of an object trembling near the lopped off hank of a tentacle. What was this? A coin or medallion gleamed with a fulsome silver.

Aurimag stopped short. He bent his knees, squinting in the gloom.

A capsule-round and smooth, of two inches by two, lay perhaps a foot from the leftmost grate.

Why would a section of tentacle lie shorn on the stone next to Darkus's lair? Aurimag recalled not seeing the dissected member earlier on his pilgrimages . . .

One of the interlopers must have dropped the gewgaw, and the severed tree limb must be the feeble aftermath of a fending off of the creature's violence. Ha! Darkus must needs have his wings clipped! Aurimag chuckled.

On that note of satisfaction, he bent to peer at the object. How was it shiny! The exotic gleam was not explained as that of a simple ring, and yet it emitted a queer flux.

Aurimag chewed on his lip. Should he send out a questing hand to grab it?

The magician probed carefully for the mystery object and paused. A medallo? A mesometric? 'Twas within the grasp of Darkus's glistening tentacle . . . a risk . . .perhaps the most fractious of his monsters. Yet a tempting lure, also a foolhardy one.

The magician sneered. If he were cleverer than this minion, perhaps he could acquire the bauble—another challenge to secure the enigma without harm . . .

The ambition was arrogant but Aurimag's confidence was high—after foiling several enemies and escaping death. He skulked closer. The medallo shone with a fervour. He feigned a movement up the passage, then suddenly he sprang back, seizing the object. The tentacle snapped out but could not visit Aurimag's skin in time.

Aurimag loosed a shrill dry of triumph. Smug airs exuded from his being.

Round and warm to touch, the object was . . . definitely a medallo or ferrule of some sort. The candle sputtered—a flare not uncommon for this quality of burned-down wick. Beads of perspiration bulged on Aurimag's brow. The hot wax suddenly fizzled. A glob dropped from the flame upon the medallo's exterior.

Suddenly the object burst into a ball of molten flame.

Aurimag gave a shivering cry. He flung the capsule wide in agony, his fingers half-burned. He watched the mass explode into a bright ball of incandescence . . . unfortunately, astride Arfenos's grate.

Scrambling back was of no use. The magician was lifted with limbs of horror. Pain was his world—half blinded, he was unaware of the danger that he now faced. A flash, a snatch, a memory—some spook from a sick dream—His mind's eye faded . . .

And then, a thrashing tentacle uncoiled through the grate, wrapped thrice about his midsection and permitted no warning to Aurimag's fate. The neomancer felt himself dragged mercilessly through the hole and up into the boughs. He cried out one last feeble gasp . . .

VII

When the smoke had cleared, only a jungle of smashed bodies lay amidst the ruin of stalactites. Baus felt a singular weight lifted from his shoulders. Not solely from the vaporization of Aurimag, but a long end to a never-ending dream. There seemed to exist a fragile balance in the ontological fabric, yet a closure of finality. The poet Weavil had been freed; the company's mission had been realized and their fellowship was in good order, though doubtlessly changed. Only the retrieval of the pirates' gold remained a necessity, a stash carefully hidden in faraway Nosoheath. There would be, of course, the fruits of a festive reward, a singing of sea-chanteys long into the night with warm mugs of ale. Yet a hollowness of spirit remained in Baus's aura. Somehow he could not quite feel right, as if some piece of a larger puzzle lay missing, one terribly difficult to locate.

Baus shrugged off the uneasiness and swallowed the dryness in his mouth. He rubbed his cheeks, felt a stiffness to his joints. With every eerie step in this sinister cave, his muscles felt burdened with a plague.

He bent to minister to Poli, who was pitched roughly on the marmor, lying somewhat supine. The pirate was feverish, sweaty, and marginally improved. Valere was surly as usual but relieved as he paced the confines like an edgy fox; Woisper stood aside Salmeister, tugging at his beard while grumbling oaths.

An oppressive silence hung over the company. Sorceries had been committed here and the sun-deprived halls had never seen such past strife. The memory of unwholesome deeds lurked like wet sheets and eccentric plots and skulduggery reeked in the drab airs, like shadows of ghosts. The stench of death was overwhelming—shreek bodies lay everywhere, piled in macabre humps, glistening like some obscene toys in a madman's playground. Whole sections of hides had been ripped away, oozing ichor, sending stench-ridden vapours to the nostrils causing all sickness while they slashed about stalagmites that hung limply from their roots, battered like snauzzer teeth gone rotten, looking for clues as to their sudden appearance and a way out of the cavern. The magical 'Castle of Frights' had been torn asunder, now a barely-pulsing mass in the air. Half toppled masonry had given one last desperate shudder and given way, crumbling to dust and disembodied ghosts, disappearing from sight forever.

Baus could care less. The Utilitarian was herself again, picking her way through the grisly debris. She remained appalled at the wreckage, also the stink of the matted shreeks and disemboweled carcasses while seeking means to avoid those hides as best as she could. Woisper was in better spirits, speaking in complimentary terms to Salmeister whom he praised for his excellent spell-casting which had driven the final bolts in Aurimag's coffin.

The 'Saturnine' addressed Woisper with cordial grace. "What do you say, Woisper? You describe my 'Spell of Liquid Extinction', which is essentially a variation of 'The Unblinking Fire'—Aurimag's bane, so we see, and, to all purposes—the showiest of all thaumaturgies. 'Tis a modest example of my craft."

"'Tis, and a wise description," approved Woisper. He gave his index finger a twirl and manifested a luminous scrubbing tool to start stroking his ragged beard for comfort.

Trimestrius frowned, avoiding the beard-scrubbing magic and stooped near a puddle of gory slime. "A fitting conclusion to the knave—but somewhat foolishly premature."

Salmeister twitched his sallow cheeks. "What do you mean, Dwarf, by 'premature'?"

"It needs no explanation."

"Balderdash! Could the ending have been any better? We destroyed the villain. Now we are redeemed—you included—Aurimag is dead!"

Trimestrius uttered a choking laugh. "Redeemed?" He gestured at the slime which had once been Aurimag. "You call this 'redeemed'?—clawing our way out of these dank recesses with our fingers? Aurimag guards the key to the exit. Did you forget? Now he has the last laugh. If you recall, his bewitched horrors hound the tunnel-entrance—or were you too self-absorbed to consider that?"

Salmeister stepped back, scowling cynically; obviously he had not considered it.

Trimestrius flung aside his gauntlets and threw his hands bleakly in the air. "Well—at least we are at liberty to roam about these burrows safely. Perhaps we can find a tunnel or niche which will lead us the way out."

"Yes, 'tis as good an idea as any," intoned Ulisa.

Woisper nodded. "Well, we will let you lead on." A scorched and buckled shield suddenly up-ended in the ruddy murk.

All started. Trimestrius prodded his golden blade at the movement. From the darkness between a shreek carcass and the wall squirmed a tiny shape—a wobbly one, hidden under the leather-strap of a shield.

"Who is this?"

"Nevermind, who is this 'Aurimag'?" the tiny figure cried. He was doing as much as possible to eye-adjust to the ruddy gloom.

Trimestrius stared at him in stupefaction. "And who are you?"

"I am me—who else? Who are you?" There were moments of awkward silence.

Baus came up behind him to grip Weavil on the shoulder. Weavil recoiled.

"This is Trimestrius. Weavil, Aurimag is dead, aka 'Nuzbek'."

The poet's mouth opened and he peered up at his friend. Sweat glistened off his face. A variety of emotions smouldered in confusion, making his lips twitch, yet no words came.

Trimestrius frowned; he trotted off gloomily to search the cavern. Ulisa gathered her wits to explore the dark niches too, disliking Salmeister enough to forgo a reunion with Woisper. Meanwhile, Weavil stood blankly, recovering his wits.

"I gather the warlock is dead?" croaked the youth.

"Yes," said Baus.

"And good riddance!" grunted Poli, who was fluttering to life not far away. "I was starting to get doubtful at this juncture." He fell back, holding his ribs as a stab of torment gripped him. His face was candlewax pale and seemed contorted, as he experienced another crippling spasm of agony. "My head feels like a lead block, Baus—scratched by razor knives." He was wracked by a sudden coughing fit, which had him clutching direly at his chest.

Woisper leaned over his side and murmured sadly. "You are in a bad way, friend."

"True, but what can I do?" muttered Poli. With Valere's help, Baus tried to get him to his feet but it was tasking; they could hardly get him to stand for more than a few moments. Kazzasius was by far the worst of the crew. The old Hierarch eased himself down to assess the Projector's wing. "Is that really you, Kazzasius?"

"'Tis," mumbled the bird weakly. The left appendage was burnt to a grey crisp, but Kazzasius stirred and muttered a low whimper.

Woisper gave the bird a playful slap on its unscorched wing. "Well, my fellow! Consider yourself the recipient of a 3rd degree decoration! Heroism and daring are your encomiums! I order you to revive yourself, claim your position as an unsung hero!—this, based on a series of valorous deeds which I alone acclaim! Is that not right, Ulisa?" The wizard turned, but the Utilitarian had disappeared with Trimestrius to investigate the blackened portal from whence Aurimag had dragged his mysterious concubine. The old Hierarch was left frowning into his beard.

Weavil felt compelled to offer important information. "Sir, our efforts have been prodigious. Without the assistance of myself—the shreeks would have devoured us, or we would all be intimate with Aurimag's coloured jars—with the fiend gloating in our ears."

"Ostensibly true," mumbled the neomancer, "but what of it? I feel your mention of service is exaggerated."

"Not at all. I believe reconcilation is—"

"Any talk of reconciliation will be broached in due time. Your name is Weavil, you say? Well, in point of telling, Weavil—we must effect a revisiting of Mismerion!"

Weavil seemed nonplussed, if not galled.

Valere gave Woisper a dark look. "How will we perform this journey to 'Mismerion' when Trimestrius has told you of the presence of 'elm-sprites' blocking our path?"

"An inconvenient hitch, but—"

A flutter of movement roused the nearby shadows. All clutched weapons, waiting for a confrontation, but they relaxed when it was only Ulisa returning, leading a tall, quivering girl by the hand in a diaphanous gown.

The men's eyes raked over her slender body with desire. She was a wild-eyed, frightened maid clearly in shock, but they did not see this. She trembled with an unnameable dread and uttered small whimperings and her knees knocked together and her arms folded and unfolded about her pale, near-visible breasts.

The neomancers plied her with eager questions but she could only sob and shake her head in confusion and nervous exhaustion. "Snatched by a horror!" She held her face in her hands and gibbered out fits of nonsense about a terrible kidnapping and the terror of 'two sorcerers'. She described one vaguely as a lackwit mute, the other, an ill-tongued lecher— undoubtedly twins of some sort.

Salmeister gave a guffaw. "Obviously 'twas Aurimag and some varlet henchman of his." The information was received with sombre disfavour. The company could only imagine two villains as evil as Aurimag and they did not like the thought. Woisper and Ulisa managed to pry out that her name was Tatla, a weaver of Lillenvir. She had been wooed by some unprepossessing troubadour—some hobgoblin or deviant of sorts, obviously a trickster who had befriended her in an unorthodox way. It was during the last evening feast he kidnapped her. How? She had been bewitched by soothing melodies on his dopek. The kidnapper had further let her sip sweet aromatic drinks from the wineskin he held under his robe.

"What skulduggery is this?" Woisper shook his head with contempt. "Always a conniver, this Aurimag, to the end with his diseased tricks on enchanted instruments."

Ulisa turned a limp gaze upon Salmeister. "And how is this any different than your debaucheries? Recall the incident in the bower of Mismerion when you tried to seduce me."

Salmeister heaved his eyebrows sidewise and would offer no comment.

Ulisa comforted the maid. She asked her to kneel and rubbed her hands and forearms, then ran fingers up her spine and neck to warm off her trauma. She spoke soft words in her ear and somewhat eased the maid's terror.

Baus peeled off his undershirt and offered it to Tatla. She gratefully accepted and flashed Baus a humble smile. Ulisa assured her that she would be looked after and returned to her village soon enough, once they got out of this cursed cave. Now was the time to pool their knowledge! To collect their wits. An exit from the horror chamber was to be effected!

The group combed the warren, searching for exits and entrances. But nothing was forthcoming. All spoke with an exaggerated optimism and traded stories of their experiences up until the time of Aurimag's melting. Ulisa said she had been captured by the ogre's net and the vile creature had tried to shake her out of her guise and stuff her in a glass bottle. She had thrashed and flapped her wings and torn her tiny teeth across the mesh of net and luckily escaped. During the long chase up the tower, she had learned of the scares and rigours awaiting her at the ogre's clutches—she did not describe them. Ironically it had been Salmeister who had saved her, causing the tower to topple, and the sallow-faced man was quick to voice it.

Kazzasius had managed somehow to increase the coherency of his speech and claimed to have lain with his surviving wing curled in a trampled heap, to protect his one eye from the shrews' paws. By simple reflex he had miraculously survived: the shreeks were only interested in live prey, not dead ones, not dissimilar to the many depraved scavengers of the Drasla forests who haunt the wilds, hunting for the thrill of the capture of live prey. When he had finished his tale, his eye-body lolled back in exhaustion.

Baus scratched at his chin in cogitation. Raising eyebrows, he could not dispute that the Projector's theory, while imaginative, was still largely subjective and open to conjecture.

To support the supposition, Trimestrius launched volubly on a thesis describing his own long-winded tale lying stunned from the strike of Aurimag's magic stick, where he had survived only by remarkable means.

Baus congratulated the prince on his subtlety in eluding the neomancer in feigning death by following Kazzasius' example.

Trimestrius gruntingly acknowledged Baus's remark but remained cynical of the outlaw's praise. Weavil was eager to impress his own misadventure on the group and called out, "My plight was no less dangerous than Trimestrius's! 'Tis a reflection of the most harrowing horror! After a three-way dead end, I stumbled upon the shreeks. They tried to gnaw and hew me with their toenails but I barely escaped their lusts. I bravely endured loathsome stenches and grisly tricks, even their chittering, alas unwittingly I led them to Nuzbek's lair—from the rabbit hole to this workroom—if only for purposes of pure survival!"

Salmeister made a polite acknowledgement. "Weavil, I think all in all that your deeds likely saved us. To have such foresight is rare amongst even brave souls, for if not for your unwitting 'errors', we would be in some gruesome burlesque at this time, or quixotic ballet on Aurimag's stage."

"Too true," muttered Ulisa.

"A fact which reflects my own thinking!" announced Weavil. "Which is what I have been trying to impress upon Woisper's mind." His face had congested with a red heat that Woisper failed to notice.

Valere interrupted the debate to embellish his own details of heroic valour upon the eerie landscape. Poli, too, when the pain in his ribs was less acute. Meanwhile, Baus, cut into the bombast, describing his personal ordeal that involved keeping the shreeks at bay from gnawing his shins and his sea comrade's. Their weapons were defunct, and their only chance was to win free by cunning.

"Well-spoken!" cried Woisper.

Baus nodded, tendering thanks. After a careful inspection of the jangled facts, Weavil tossed back his head with annoyance. "So! The facts speak for themselves, do they, Baus? Your intent was never to rescue me at all—In fact, this whole charade was simply a pretext to engage in some grander scheme with the shape-shifter and the Projector—a superfluous venturing upon a quixotic magic-gathering!"

"Not entirely," Baus intoned. He scuffed his boots with dissatisfaction. "Do not plunge me into your melancholy. You are a free man and out of your stinking jar, so be thankful!"

"Baus speaks in earnest, Weavil," chided Ulisa. "The experiences of universal tribulation remain hopeful reminders of a life lived to its fullest, manifesting overall good. Let us draw dignity from these examples, withal, moral wisdom."

Weavil offered several caustic oaths to Ulisa's pedagogy and was reprimanded by the elder neomancers. Valere, while snickering, felt obliged to echo the opinion. Ulisa tipped brows in a quizzical amazement but remained detached. She launched on a lecture, ranging from a pedantic drone to a didactic hum and Baus drifted in and out of reverie, from which he was jerked alive by Valere's nudge, " . . . but we are forced to contend with non-trivial and possible visible quandaries—namely, how to escape Aurimag's cursed lair." She turned sharply to Weavil. "You say the passageway is blocked under Aurimag's workbench?"

"Barricaded, by some sort of spooks and sprites!" cried Weavil glumly.

"Sad news."

"'Tis abysmal," muttered Woisper.

"Blocked by a frightful tree sprite 'Finklerank' who haunts the realm," squawked Weavil. "He will permit none to pass, including myself, lest he tickle his left *greesheckle*."

"What is that?" cried Woisper in outrage. "Who is this Finklerank? I shall squeeze his neck from limbs with my magic!"

"He has no neck."

"Nevertheless, how dare he speak of his risible greesheckle to a shrunken adolescent!"

Weavil blinked. "I resent the categorization. As I adumbrated, Finklerank is a tree-some gnome or spirit—maybe both. I think it is a large beast of an earlier age, hinting of some enchantment, perhaps by this insidious Nuzbek. A sort of possessed oak, I gather."

"These are extreme creatures," announced Woisper with ceremony. "We shall have a look at this cursed 'gnome' of yours—we will thwart its dominion, tunnelling through this bare rock ourselves if we must." In a calmer voice, he muttered, "The latter may comprise a way out of this dungeon; In fact, I am all for leading it."

"Ambitious remarks," grunted Salmeister. "You are an enviable exemplar, if only as an inspirational lecturer."

"Thank you. You have also the talent of inspirationalism, Salmeister. Again, your remarks are always well-received."

"Enough of this prattle!" cried Ulisa.

The group marched down toward Aurimag's workchamber and all were prepared for a horror, if not residual blights, yet perhaps they would find other caverns. The company was bemused to discover a distraught-looking shape loitering amongst the clusters of stalagmites. The creature rocked back and forth, moaning a lament. 'Twas Graeitch, of course, uttering complaints through her swollen nostrils which had become inflamed and red from being the only possible orifice to imbibe any air.

Baus hunched himself closer with fascination. He was intrigued by the mouthless face and the swinish nostrils which seemed capable of snuffling out various insults at himself. The horrid schasm clasped so greedily to her leg, he gave wide berth.

None took pity on the wretch, except Ulisa, who helped the creature regain her mouth while Woisper marched truculently on to reconnoitre the chamber.

The company stumbled on and discovered further grim galleries—many appearing here and there as nothing more than stagnant lakes of dark empty life.

Woisper snuffled out a roar of dissatisfaction. Aurimag's workroom comprised a rectangular pit crudely-hewn with raked stone. It was in shambles. As Weavil had described, the place was rich with a broken-backed table, a monstrous crucible, an overturned tripod, some broken glass, various folios, strewn litter, smashed curios, sorcerous adjuncts, lumo-tubes, bone-rattles, puppets, prismatic shapes, crystals, zircon-carved amulets, tarnished cornets. The trap door lay wrenched ajar—which became clear that such passage was the source from where the infamous shreeks had emerged. It would never do for an exploration, Woisper saw, owing to its black reek. Even shrunken wizards with their blights and tricks could never brave those frightful depths.

Baus frowned. To think of delving down into that miserable hole was a plight inconceivable. How anything that large could have crawled up through that rabbit hole, was another matter; but then he had heard of oversized rats having squeezed through abominably small crannies to get to their prey.

The blood lamps had burnt low and now the Bronze room glimmered a baleful crimson. The wicks being almost spent, the cavern was now pitched in a new eeriness. Little food was about, save only crumbs and scraps. All at once the troupe was hungry. Valere pried open one of Aurimag's wine casks and they guzzled draughts of wine from beakers.

The old Hierarch leaned back, thinking to himself how clever he was to have discovered Aurimag's secret lair—and lucky to have vanquished him. He went to minister Kazzasius a draught of wine, but finding no mouth he stood back, perplexed.

"Do not worry, Hierarch," grated the Projector. "All this hullabaloo over a mere fisherman is absurd. For the purposes of saving our precious hides . . . ha, this ridiculous foray! Yes, a doughty soul is 'Baus the Bold', but it seems he has brought us more woe into the world than joy—which makes his cause saving our Circle somewhat nebulous. Yet our efforts have not been purposeless . . ."

"Where is Aurimag's puppet then?" demanded Weavil.

"The puppet is dead," Trimestrius declared.

"Your puppet," Weavil persisted, "resembles the rascal Aurimag—whom I saw earlier. He seems to have disappeared."

"Most odd," murmured Woipser.

Trimestrius waved Weavil a patronizing hand. "The 'puppet' you speak of is a canard of your imagination. Let it go. Likely a prop, perished in the fire."

"Possibly, but I don't cotton to the idea of being labelled a loon, sir Prince. Aurimag likely took it upon himself to conduct a dire ritual that was to cleanse—"

"To cleanse what?"

"Puppet, you say?" croaked Ulisa. "Could it be—?" She tilted back her head and swore; all saw a startled frown creeping across the shape-shifter's exquisite face. "Could it be? It makes no sense!"

Woisper gave a frustrated cry. "What makes no sense?"

"The villain Aurimag—he managed to craft an uncanny semblance of himself. Do you not see it? . . . no wonder he could be at two places at once. 'Tis no crafty conjuring at all. The gibberish that Tatla prattled on about—" She pulled her chin while squinting into the gloom. "You have been sequestered for some time now, Weavil—how many puppets did Aurimag have?"

Weavil frowned, becoming coy.

"Think! Much hinges on your answer."

"At least one, I think. Perhaps three. He birthed a particular ghastly prototype which ceased to function, so he burned it in his crucible. Gruesome affair! The thing shivered and moaned and rasped out something eldritch in an evil tongue which I could not help but think a weird spell of a bygone age. I watched it grimacing in its death throes, while I was hidden above his worktable, all the while the sadistic wretch remained busy fabricating more fiends."

Ulisa composed her thoughts in dry discomfort. "So there remains more of these simulacra that are unaccounted for?"

Woisper gave a rude laugh. "Why all the fuss, Ulisa? Aurimag is dead. Can you not see? Puppet or whatever they were, have perished. Even if they could have survived, what could they do without their master to pull their strings?"

Ulisa frowned and remained silent.

Woisper barreled on: "Salmeister and I watched Aurimag perish before our very own eyes. None can refute it."

"Perhaps," Ulisa declared, "but if Aurimag's mannequins existed, they could cause us harm now." She hunched and her expression grew dour. "Something chill still lives in the air and vexes me." She twisted her frame about in an abrupt manner and cried out, "Kazzasius! Can you confirm the state of Aurimag's existence?"

Kazzasius twitched a wing. A bloodshot eye jerked, shining a pale ray onto the nearby wall.

An embryonic image showed a kaleidoscopic mass flecked with miniscule motes of faded colour moving about at random.

"What is all this gibberish?" demanded Woisper.

Baus strained to perceive anything of significance in the pattern, but no glimmer of recognition.

The Projector murmured: "The flux indicates an extreme anomaly of nth order dispersal. Differences from the last projection show mixed analysis: a singular transmutation in the 9th valence—recall—I last composed a reading at Mismerion, and unless I am mistaken, Aurimag has ascended to the spirit realm."

Woisper gave a whistling expostulation. "There you see, a profitable analysis, Kazzasius! You are to be commended for your prognosis. Now, let us all drop the issue and drink more of this excellent wine!"

"By no means!" Ulisa called sharply. Barely had she managed to master her impatience before she was uttering another disturbing theory. "Woisper, this pronouncement lends no credence. The overweening Aurimag could easily be relegated to an $n\text{-}2^{th}$ sphere—one of limbo!"

Woisper made a conciliatory gesture. "Ulisa, your stubbornness is embarrassing. We all know that neomancers can only ascend to an nth order field after death, so Kazzasius's thesis can only be given more validity."

Ulisa's lips worked in an irked line. "Perhaps, but there are other ways to hide one's shade. Besides, your point about n^{th} order is flawed, Hierarch," she snapped. "I do not consider Aurimag a neomancer in any right."

Woisper absorbed the opinion without heat, but exhaled a vexed sigh.

The voices merged in a buzzing hum and Baus could not be convinced either way so he struck out on his own in a gloomy corridor. Struck with a further disturbing speculation, he reflected: what if Kazzasius's techno-tool were faulty?

Too distinct a possibility was it that the 'alternate' Aurimag was unaccounted for. A false analysis could propel belief down an avenue that a fake copy was what he had actually glimpsed fighting amongst the shreeks.

Baus's lips twitched and he paled. Perhaps the same copy had perished at the hands of Woisper and Salmeister, not the real Aurimag?

Baus allowed himself a heaving grunt. If Aurimag were not dead, then he could still be lurking about anywhere, ready to spring out like some hobgoblin. Yet there was no way to fully explain the discrepancy, nor was there any way in or out of the cavern, except through the filmy black orifice between the portentous pillars. 'Twas a corridor of nightmare he recalled where no one had come or gone since they had passed . . .

Baus shrugged off the memory . . . a sinister sentiment remained stuck under his skin. Was Aurimag dead? If so, where was the body? Something vaguely seemed out of place.

Baus was about to return and raise doubts, when a curious, heavy panting arose from the vestibule.

All whirled about to see a lanky, red-haired roustabout struggling out of the shadows with tiny candle in hand. In his other, the figure held a scrawny Wickle by the scruff of her neck. Her face was fair, her small budding horns peeked out on the tips of a gleaming brow and her lips were pinched. The down-turned scowl spoke of grievous affront.

Baus gave an outraged croak and ran forth, unsheathing his sword. "Here, you oaf! Unhand my ward." He advanced to strike. "Take your paws off the Wickle!"

Alvius mulishly swung around and shielded himself from the assailant's wrath by using the Wickle. "Who are you, you popinjay?"

"I am Baus the Bold, if it's any concern of yours." He flourished his gleaming weapon, advancing to take Esling into his custody. "The cognomen is not without its merit."

Alvius peevishly released the Wickle who ran to clasp Baus in a warm bear hug.

Woisper pulled back his hood, uttering a bemused snort. "So—if it's not another Wickle —and our Alchemist! How came you through the doom-dealing portal, Alvius? You are a weird one. Perhaps you are part demiurge . . . or part magician?"

"Neither," responded Alvius peevishly. "The tunnel was open; I merely stepped through —though I drew the shortest straw from a long line of contenders. Others of our Order await in the daylight on the other side."

"This is comforting to know." The Hierarch's crispness was not lost on anyone.

Weavil pressed closer and tossed a pebble between the pillars.

Seconds ticked by. Nothing happened. The pillars showed obscure carvings carved in its face. There came no grisly or horrific keening from the unbroken gap.

Perhaps the corridor was safe?

Baus was not convinced nor was Ulisa dissolved of her scepticism. She padded two feet closer and watched the hole with a scowling uncertainty before recoiling at the sight of a near dead shreek whose upturned face poked up at her with sudden ghoulish intent.

Weavil pushed forward with authority. "Only a soon-to-be cadaver, dear Lady. It is on its way to corpse-hood."

"I do not need assurances, sir Weavil. The way seems safe, a surprise which waxes entirely odd. How can this be?" Arching brows, she tugged at her nose. "I can hardly believe that Aurimag would leave his gate unguarded."

Salmeister gave a significant gesture. "The lout is dead; why do you question it? I opt for our immediate departure."

"No less I!" announced Woisper expansively. "Let us depart this foul burrow whose stench becomes ever more unbearable every second."

There were mutters of agreement and the party assembled to leave. The shape-shifter attended Tatla who still slumped catatonically in a nearby alcove.

Alvius scampered forth first, eager to relay his news to the waiting crew. However, Valere cradled Kazzasius in his arms while Baus steadied Poli so that he could ascend the last murky steps where, shivering at the threshold, he paused under the dim shadow to take one last look before ducking between the pillars. His last glance took in the ruin of broken stone and the hissing steam of pools. The cavern had a dim feeling, that of an incredibly unearthly presence that was enough to prompt twisted shudders: here the lair of a dark sorcerer driven to madness whose wracked spirit pervaded the lonely murks and the water-marked deeps.

The last of the blood lamps faded and the glimmer of redness finally dissipated, plunging them in thick, inky gloom.

The company passed beyond the heavy lintel toward the grate.

Graeitch had disappeared; likely she would never be seen again.

VIII

Baus crept heedfully through the black tunnel. He made two important observations. First: the peculiar way in which the elm-sprite on the right struggled to thrash through the grate, and, how its crony, the dark furrowed mass opposite the grate managed to remain contentedly composed. The thing clutched in its branches a single blurred bundle, completely inscrutable, being quick-juggled from one slimy limb to another. The 'limbs' comprised a loose classification, Baus thought. He observed a tightly-woven mesh and a tangle of flesh, whirling over a grotesque, gorgonish head. A moderate hole was gouged in the grate—two feet high by three feet wide.

Baus frowned. What could be the cause of this? A menace as this could plunge one of the larger tentacles through the orifice easily enough and snatch a person to doom.

Baus proceeded with alacrity to put as many hasty steps between himself and the monsters, likewise his peers.

The mystery was intriguing, but not of immediate interest. Valere and he helped drag Poli up the last stretch of stone corridor and a wash of pale light greeted them at the far end of the passage.

The seamen shambled out, eyes pinched against the blinding light. Menhir-like boulders reared to both sides of the opening as they remembered like sentinels and the sombre and watchful and eerie valley hung below like some weary shroud—mauve and russet woods showed drab thickets, thick in mist, through which snatches of black river could be seen.

A host of unfamiliar faces gathered about the cave mouth; they peered upon the newcomers with quiet introspection—eccentrics and misfits, judging from the look of them, thought Baus, with distinct, aristocratic noses and long faces and furrowed lines etched on their chins and cheeks. There was a hesitant air amongst them, an angular thrust of brows, a restless mannerism, which puzzled Baus at first. A long-bearded man was swathed from head to toe in a blue cape and cowl. He was stiff-necked and jerked aloft on light feet. Doubtless this was Ahrion the Astrologer. A dark-moustached, soft-featured *bonhomme* peered proudly from face to face—Maitor the Moralist who exuded a rich composure, a splendid attire in a double-breasted swallowtail jacket, and undoubtedly, a forced leader of the group. Another was a gangly, spare woman, comically-tall, dressed in a baggy yellow coverall—no doubt, Adelyheim the Healer. Finally a dumpy, augur-faced smiler, Onzo the Optimist, wore a soft subdued gown of fust-pink.

Maitor tottered forward with an air of urbane ceremony, greeting Woisper with subdued warmth. He almost tripped over the yet unsprung bear trap which Trimestrius had only warned him about at the last second.

Valere jumped to spring the trap with a mallorn root. The jaws clanged shut on a malign note, unnerving all.

Maitor's awkward carriage soon made itself obvious to the company, no less Woisper. The contrived pleasantries he proffered fell flat and no amusement was reflected in the iron-grey gaze of Woisper. Forsooth, the lukewarm and lackadaisical attitudes of the new company and their late-coming had made the Hierarch ever more irritated than normal.

Crisp words were traded between Hierarch and Moralist and Ulisa rushed to intervene. Valere entrusted the wounded Kazzasius into the Adelyheim's care. A brief diagnosis revealed severe wounds of wings and torso on the eye-bird and she hobbledehoyed to the forest to procure herbs for his remedying.

Woisper called the band together, addressing the elder members of the group in severe tones: "Friends, Colleagues: we are intact, as you can see—Salmeister, Ulisa and Alvius and myself. Fortunately, we have been spared of other tragedies, assisted in our endeavour by Baus the Bold and his comrades, who include the seaman Valere and his mate Poli whom you see before you in injured capacity. Aurimag is now dead. Yes. He has been smitten by Salmeister's magic—'twas a meritorious deed which was witnessed by all. In swift measure, Mismerion will be returned to her former glory!"

Onzo commended Woisper and gave the Hierarch a brief nod. "On other matters, which Ulisa has brought to my attention, I am speaking only in hindsight when I used the term 'fortunately. It appears that Salmeister and I were only 'lucky' to wind up this venture with our lives spared, if not for the relentless fortitude of Ulisa and the inestimable Projector, Kazzasius, now in the form of this omniscient eye, which you see before you. If not for these valorous souls, perhaps all of us might have perished!"

"To what do you allude?" cried Ahrion. "Are our efforts anything less than praiseworthy?"

"Your 'efforts'," hissed Woisper with a sardonic edge, "have been everything less than laudable."

"Indeed, they are dilatory," observed Salmeister.

Ahrion stormed forward with heat. He motioned to Maitor who had been slinking into the nearby trees, "I hold our Moralist completely responsible for this scandal!"

Woisper's heated gaze bore heavily upon the Astrologer. "Well, Maitor, what have you to say? And kind of you, Ahrion, to pin the blame." He fixed his attention on the Moralist and forwarded a cool question, "Well, what of it, Maitor?"

The Moralist jerked back with jutted chin. "The person known as Ahrion, speaks of facts of which he knows little. As for the other issues—Ulisa, with her well-meaning utilitarianism, has confounded us with her half-truths. On the insinuation of dilatoriness, one should peer no further than common error, not me."

Ulisa contracted into a peevish huff. "I deplore this pedantic fluff of yours, Maitor. Politely you hedge about a tenuous truth and make it sound as if I am to blame—'Miss Goody Two-shoes'. You were late! My orders on your date of arrival were specific."

Woisper held up a hand. "Peace. Dialectic investigation will take place at the appropriate time. Misconceptions will be revealed."

Baus listened patiently and noted the distrust amongst members of the Circle. Such low behaviour for a crew of intellectuals! he thought. Maitor had been remiss in his leadership, true. As punishment, he was relegated to stand guard at Aurimag's cave should looters ransack the villain's den whereby Alvius was obliged to accompany him.

The Moralist's remonstrations were long, no less Alvius's, but the Hierarch was adamant.

"Aurimag's thaumaturgical accessories may still be of use to us in the future," he emphasized. "They must be guarded against bandits."

Alvius projected an instant outcry. Why should I be coupled in punishment with Maitor? He was leader and by his edict we arrived today rather than yesterday." Woisper chopped peremptorily at the air with his fist. "The time for deeds has passed! We will return to Mismerion immediately. I wish only to reverse these awful dwarfish enchantments—they are categorically unbearable and have begun to rankle on my nerves!"

"The spell cannot be reversed!" called Weavil. "So did Aurimag advise me himself."

Woisper took two steps toward the midget in anger. "What? When was this uttered?"

"A deal of time ago—in Heagram, I recall—after I was transmogrified to my present condition," complained Weavil.

"Aurimag is a dotard!" roared Woisper. "Withal, he is dead! What would he know? Look at his pretended knowledge and what it has gained him. Nothing! Any spell can be thwarted —and so I shall thwart it."

"You are welcome to try."

Woisper became ever more livid. "With my folios and my excellent grasp of transfigurative magic," he continued, red-faced, "I shall nullify this abominable aberration!"

Weavil jigged about like a lark. "Happy news!" Trimestrius was no less ecstatic and the two swung arm in arm. Valere and Baus hitched themselves together and joined in. Ulisa and Adelyheim consoled Tatla who was weeping with the weirdness of it all. Pitying the girl, Woisper issued a gruff statement to the effect that the Astrologer should convey the girl at once to Lillenvir, along with Onzo who would act as guide.

The Optimist balked at the proposal.

Esling approached the Hierarch on diffident feet. "May I intrude a request, sir?"

"You may!" Woisper thundered. Looking at her with formal authority, he frowned.

"May I accompany you to Mismerion?"

The old man's eyes hardened. "Whatever for?"

When he saw her crestfallen expression his features softened. "Of course, child! Even if you are a Wickle, you are my colleague's friend—and any friend of Baus's, is a friend of mine!"

Esling bowed, gratified. She skipped away happily.

The company departed. This eerie section of forest was straining everyone's nerves and the wizened old wizard was first to lead. Gloomily left behind, Alvius and Maitor watched coldly as the crew of their Circle forged a crude path amongst the shrubbery and boulders and knots of mallorn. The troupe disappeared down the shore of the Lim, leaving Aurimag's cave and the minatory presence of phantom elm and skeleton vine behind. On the way, Onzo discovered a curious dugout hidden in reeds. Ahrion and he used it now to traverse the black waters; three trips were sufficient to carry the company across, while Ahrion and Onzo remained aboard to return Tatla downriver to Lillenvir.

The rest of the company slogged it aside the reeds and the river bracken. They followed looping trails and weaved amongst green-gummed stands of gamgkos and knotted old horlocks.

The company avoided the tree clusters jamming their way west and maintained a wide path on a barely-trod lumber trail through forests of spanglemoss and hissock.

The day went by slowly and talk was lengthy; Baus learned many facts about his new company—for example, Adelyheim was a healer, adept enough in her craft to heal Kazzasius and have him up and flying in jerks and fits. A miracle and Baus witnessed a mangled wing come to life. With healthy application of gum sap and a walworf leaf wrapped about the wing, she rubbed hands upon the singed area and Kazzasius's wing grew anew! Poli was remarkably cured too, thanks to Adelyheim's expert touches. The outlaw's concussion had abated and his ribs were intact; now he could at least limp without assistance.

Patches of blue sky peeked through the sprawling mallorns and caused the company melancholy. Baus thought about the past and the heavy burden left on their shoulders. Brown-dappled trunks reached everywhere and Woisper wheezed and puffed as he struggled, unused to the strenuous trek through brake and underbrush after an aqueous captivity. Mismerion's leader seemed disconnected from his surroundings; yet—he drew Baus and Valere about him and rambled on with cheer about the puissance of his spells and the efficacy of his thaumaturgy as it would liberate him from this blight of midget-dom. His lore was buried in the many wax-covered tomes and bone-engraved folios up top his moon tower.

Ulisa gave a pained chuckle. "Easy to speak of your spells, Woisper—when one is recently out of the frying pan. Perhaps not so easy to wield after being confined in a bottle for two years."

Woisper drew himself about with hauteur. "Mind your words, Ulisa. I am a neomancer, not a mouse. Aurimag's brine has encased me for years, true, and as resilient as I am to ensorcellment, this jinx was a bit much. I am no more a demiurge than a prodigy, but who could cast even the most twiddling enchantment under Aurimag's sinister shield? Did I see you escape your jar so easily? No—the magician saw to our demise. The devil incorporated the brine into the miniaturization process, knowing all the time we could not penetrate it. He engineered these traps with well-crafted cunning. This brings me to a discussion of how the villain hornswoggled us in the first place . . ?"

Salmeister mused, "Yes, how exactly did he kidnap you from your moon tower? Unlike Maitor, you are usually one endowed with caution."

Woisper gave him a mournful look. "Indeed, that is a bitter tale . . . and none need to remind me. Do you recall how we had appointed Aurimag 'junior under-steward' of Mismerion?"

"Yes. 'Twas after you and I had undressed him of his magics."

"Exactly. The delinquent came stumbling out of his shock after his rehabilitation, up the stairs to my tower, on his knees, penitent, pleading for an absolution from our strictures. Coddleswap! He claimed he was a 'changed man'. A reformer. What a conniver! I should have known better. Anything from the mouth of that blackguard was a lie, especially with all his crafty wheedling and supplicating at my doorstep for a higher position in the castle. What a ruse! Meanwhile, I remained engrossed in my most cogent spells[*] and he snatched a beaker, flung it in my eyes and he nearly took out my sight!" ([*] To many it was known that Woisper secretly worked on spells to make the sun shine when there was rain and bring glorious rainbows arching over Mismerion highest towers. His attempts to manifest the feat had failed, often producing eerie side effects such as eruptions from the soil: frogs, snakes, uncanny hybrids, mixed with brilliant bolts of lightning that slashed ice and rain at the windows.)

Ulisa brushed Woisper a questing glare. "How could you be so artless? You are the leader of our Order."

Woisper gave a moody nod. "True, but 'tis no mystery that Aurimag hoodwinked everyone. I was distracted from my game. What need I watch out over a wretch pillaged of his power?" His lips bit down in sardonic recollection. "Yet I should have known that the rascal was up to skulduggery. I did him injustice, true, despoiled him of his craft—and he didn't deserve it . . . but I was livid!" Tears came to the old neomancer's eyes, surprisingly, as if he only now were paying for his sins. "Deeds are unable to be amended. He had a brilliant mind, Aurimag, but a bigger ego . . . the misguided fool."

The old magicker stifled a tremulous sigh from escaping his lips. "Well—enough! What is done cannot be undone . . ."

The hours passed. In the afterglow the company marched under the low arches of gamgko in twilight mist, arriving at the village of Vishire, set back a pace of a secluded sycamore and honey-oak copse.

A well-trampled glade showed communal benches. There was a twain of fire pits, a stone well, and some collective pasture that dominated the hamlet. A twin guard of sky-tall oaks defended the glade's entrance, on whose branches lofted an impressive watchfort. The timbers were stained green and laced with fluttering white banners. A score of brick homes were tucked in behind the sycamores where Baus saw a small schoolhouse, repositories, low leaning wooden shacks. A pond glinted in the sunshine; the most distant domiciles gleamed flatly, set back from the shoreline rich with Fool's reed and aster. Patches of cleared land showed tidy strips along the waterfront—crops of flaxhack and winter wheat.

Folk were roaming about the glade, piling wood and cutting bush with axes. They tended fields, gathered berries, cooked boar on spits and a few heated a large cauldron of stew over a smoking fire.

The villagers suddenly stopped to stare at the newcomers. A trio of boys romping around a group of snickering girls stared in silence when they saw the company of dwarfs.

The impression was one of strained curiosity—who could these vagabonds be?—a gang of five strangely-garbed dwarves, a light-horned Wickle, three ragged seamen, a team of normal-sized eccentric neomancers and a weird flying eagle with eye—all certain to astound even the most flexible of folk.

The group passed the gathering unhindered where they halted before a rambling inn, the *Wandering Woodsman*. Its blackstone timbers and three storeys seemingly built marvellously around the trunk of an old honey oak. The structure was enormous. The trunk grew right through the middle, with sprawling limbs draped about its hatch-worked gables and spun down a gently-sloping roof to touch the white-panelled balconies and dormers that extended from the upper reaches.

The company moved on, limp of limb and fatigued beyond measure. They entered the foyer and inquired of a decent repast.

A burly attendant came briskly, listening to their orders with nodding complaisance and casting looks from one to the other with an air of urbane perplexity. The group was large—by all standards. After a careful appraisal, he assigned them a modest table set by an opaque window. Despite the early hour, the chamber was full of patrons and lit with carved-off wegmor-horn lamps and candelabra. Ornate stools brought special attention to their table on which the smaller members of the company could stand while the attendant passed them menus, asking for their dinner wishes. The choices were simple—braised lamb or roasted duck.

Woisper ordered all of the above, massively hungry, peering lordly over his menu plaque. Baus ordered likewise. The massive honey-oak's trunk was shorn of its limbs and its amber-lacquered bark was polished to a T with rich wax.

The attendant served them musk ale in ewers.

Baus remarked that the locals were dressed in green-dyed petticoats or cloaks strapped with leather bands. They seemed a gloomy folk with their sullen-peaked hats, drably embellished chest crests and limp plumes of feathers worn at the shoulders. The knot-eyed locals seemed a taciturn bunch, somewhat wooden-faced. They cast the newcomers guarded glances. More than a single mind seemed wondering of their presence and the grandness of their entrance. What curious errand had brought these strange wanderers out of the wilderness?

The residents did not seem to appreciate the intimidating look of Valere, Baus and Poli, whose war-weaponry and swords, which had not been worn for ages in these parts, was clearly aggressive. A few even guessed the accoutrements were clearly artifacts from old Desenion.

The seamen remained unconcerned. Over a too-heady tankard of mead, Woisper boasted of his plans for creating an invincible security about the 'Circle'. He helped himself to a heaping salver of roast mutton and poultry and declared somewhat volubly, "We will build a tightly-structured community of close-knit sorceries! We are to be a society of single-minded savants devoted to the exclusive pursuit of higher magics, vaporizing all traitors and scoundrels of our craft! Protocols will be enforced so grand that will shame the most cunning and canny of Neons!—"

As Woisper plodded on, his voice merged into a vast, rich drone . . .

Ulisa's expression remained dull. She caught the zealotish gleam in Woisper's eye and thought his scheme grandiose.

The waxy expressions of Woisper's entourage were not complimentary. Baus did not form any opinion, though he was more likely to agree with Ulisa. The Hierarch continued on in his railing oratory, seeming content for the time being to tear off a leg from his fowl or mouth a decree with a segment of lamb in his teeth. He smacked lips, wiped greasy fingers on paunch and chewed on his meat, while letting down his filthy hood. The Vishire folk did not disapprove of this supping, for they were hearty eaters. With mead frothing his beard, Woisper now ordered a large mug of mallorn whiskey for a toast and looked somewhat rakish in the bronze light. "Here, boy!" he called. "I require a goblet in which to slake my thirst, not a bathtub to wash my beard, like this vile cup of yours!"

The attendant bowed obsequiously and catered to the request and took back the large mug with a grudging politeness. Conversation turned to more practical matters whereby Woisper was asked about the missing presence of Barbirius. Here, Ulisa recounted the tale of the warmonger being no longer a resident of the castle and the harsh reception she had received at his War Mansion.

Woisper tossed a contemptuous grunt. He agreed that it was treachery. Tugging at his beard, he growled, "Barbirius is a bad egg—but what of Llonon—our illusionist? I would not have guessed he would be a sympathizer to this barbarian. Were he not so new to our coterie, I would think him incurably pliant! Gads! I guess we shall have to conduct serious words with the youth, or look for better recruits in the future."

Adelyheim foisted Woisper a lively rebuke: "Do not be so critical. Do you not think this a task better left for Maitor, our Moralist?"

Woisper snorted out stormy words. "Maitor is pedantically a naysayer. I will hear no more of him." The Hierarch, in his cups, motioned for more mead.

A husky barrel-shaped woodchopper chanced to blunder in at that moment, clearly out of sorts with the people before him and with the wild look of temper on him. He turned, menacing the neomancers with weapon and bared teeth.

Baus and Valere flinched, palms reaching for weapons. While his marble eyes swamg with anger and spleen, he hefted his double-headed axe and uttering a growl, let it fall on the table next to Woisper's mutton.

Woisper arched brows, remaining calm. There came a fierce accusation. An altercation brewed on the topic of 'maids' who had gone missing from Vishire. The Hierarch denied any such involvement. "Our troupe is indisputably innocent, please keep your angry hands away from our food."

The defence went unheard despite Ulisa's claims of having seen to the source of the abductions and as the woodsman swung wanton swipes, Baus and Valere were forced to arrest his chopping off Woisper's head, with blows and cuffs.

Quietly the woodsman was conveyed elsewhere and nursed his bruises at a far table with the outlaws eyeing their own minor wounds.

Woisper took pride in Baus and Valere's rough-dealing of the deranged woodcutter. "That was a loyal act, lads!" Hopping on the table, he put on a drunken show of delivering them glad slaps on the back. "Drake's breath!—that was choice sword-play. You are a pack of bold wolves, aren't you? I shall hire you as my personal guard!"

Baus coolly acknowledged the temporary engagement could be advantageous for both parties. A converging thought struck home; could Woisper be depended on for favours? Leaning backward, he casually asked, "Given our commission of several important services, recompense has crossed our minds, and has been promised at an earlier time which would be greatly appreciated."

Woisper gulped an egg-cupful of mead. "Recompense for what?" He grunted, his brow sober now. "'Tis it not enough to travel in the company of the illustrious 'Woisper'?"

"'Tis, but I emphasize that we are practical men who demand coin for services."

Woisper narrowed his eyes with shrewd calculation. "You are a crafty one, Baus. In my experience, 'practical men' are cunning men who rarely backtrack on matters of motive. So, speak! What is this favour?"

"A bagatelle, no more—a simple pardon from the disfavour of a certain figure of royalty."

"And who might this 'figure' be?"

"Arnin of Owlen."

"Arnin of Owlen?" Woisper nearly spat out his mead. "What have you done to anger the coxcomb?"

"Nothing much." Baus glanced guardedly at Valere. "We have smitten him with an insult, that's all—specifically Lolispar, and drawn blood."

Woisper's face went a ghastly white. "You fool!"

"'Tis a tragedy," Baus sighed. "One that I regret . . . all over a woman."

"It always is," sighed Woisper. He closed his eyes and clutched at his hair as Valere and Baus both recounted the roughhousing that had earned them their infamy several moons prior in the dark corridor of Sloe.

"You have committed an irreversible deed. Tsk tsk. Politics and the affairs of the nobility is not my territory."

Baus pinched lips in disappointment. He hunched his shoulders. Bleak-faced, he mumbled out a groan. Why was it always that it seemed his plans were coming to naught?

Conversation dwindled to desultory small talk and finally waned altogether. The group stayed the night at the inn and the neomancers ordered the attendant to arrange beds for them. Salmeister conjured up some gold coins with which he paid the innkeeper and Kazzasius continued to circle the village out of range of hunters' arrows, keeping lookout for the troupe . . .

IX

Before dawn's light the travellers left the tavern well-fed with a quick breakfast of flaxhack-mash, yamroot-pâté and mulled wine. They struck out to the edge of the common where a few villagers were wandering sleepy-eyed through a grey mist, gathering faggots and twigs from the nearby woods to rekindle their fires. Wool-cloaked farm-women went about their tasks, milking marbacks and gathering herbs for tea. Water-fetchers dragged wooden buckets from the communal well, catching well-earned yawns.

They skirted the open ground. Climbing a grassy knoll they saw the forest plain below them littered with cones and acorns slick with dew where dull crimson streaks hung eastward glimmering over aged oaks and dew-dripping canopies.

In the greenwood the travellers felt a lightness of heart. The plod of their footfall felt reassuring and they all pondered what awaited them at Mismerion. The damp turf was spongy under their boots which sank deep in spanglemoss.

The trail pressed on. The company seemed in a slow-moving dream. The dwarfs tracked ahead like a troop of eager children, but Baus and his crew, used to journeying overland, followed at a more leisurely pace, warming their aching limbs at the coming of dawn, aware only of the need for caution regarding incursions into uncharted territory. They had sombre experience in this regard.

Arms hung loosely to his sides; Baus reflected on the aftermath of Aurimag's demise. The fate of the magician weighed heavily on his mind, an ugly reminder of how easy it was to be tempted by power and sombre goals. With head cocked, he trudged through the first honey-coloured boughs and gnarly trunks to feel a strange sense of scepticism, somewhat void of feeling. Why? His spirits felt doused. By what? A man without a mission? A victim of false hopes? He had vanquished his most pressing foe.

A hollow victory at best. He gave a dubious grunt. He was still prey to feeling a petty criminal in the eyes of the law, a wolf's-head—with a price on his head.

His mood did not improve over the course of the day. He became taciturn and withdrawn, and his peers sensed it.Yet the edges of a plan were budding in his mind—but first Mismerion . . .

* * *

The path they trod led to wilder terrain, cluttered with fallen logs and false routes. The neomancers followed ghosts of trails, forded the chattering creeks that fed the Ul, tributary to the Lim, still many furlongs west. Through old forests and damp dells they shambled like dogged vagabonds. The trees were grizzled, portentous, tall-plumed and elder guardians of an arboreal kingdom; guarding long memories.

The company breasted the Ul, a narrow, sluggish, stony source of the Lim, starkly-framed with tall bull-weeds and low-lying gamgkos.

Late in the day the sun slanted gilded rays over willowy treetops, investing the dappled undergrowth with a dreamy luminescence. An old lichened bridge lurked in the weeds which Baus now saw was a carved old greystone structure thick with blocks of carved rhodochrosite.

Pulling at his chin, Baus saw the black water slide effortlessly underneath the stone. Green-shadowed arches sheltered the purling water—while yew and gendrons sprawled amidst remnants of ancient grandeur which remained memories of past glory. The bridge, however, promised safe passage across the river—to fabled Mismerion, where manors nestled on the far side on a shore hung in mist. Lofty roofs, sagging walls, grey marmor stonework—all were in need of great maintenance. The town of 'Old Mismerion' situated here, was long deserted, for reasons of the neomancers' tendencies of mystery and spells of dread.

The group crossed the bridge and Baus threaded his way through the copses and overgrown orchards with strange haste.

Halting for a breath, they found a blizzard of white blossoms falling from the trees. Some of the lower branches held fruit. Now Baus plucked an apple and suddenly he felt infused with an urgent compulsion to confide in his peers. The ideal moment was now.

"Friends, listen—for reasons of bravery and untold valour in a cause beyond the call of duty—Poli, Valere, Weavil, Esling—I wish to bequeath you a share of my wealth!"

"Wealth?" croaked Weavil.

Baus's closest comrades were still in the shadow of a gnarled tree when he spoke but he let them in anyway on his 'secret'—one that he had been cleverly concealing for many months.

His peers were dumbfounded and backed away despite the earnestness of his attestations —some secret stash buried some forty paces away from an old bearsbottom tree just shy of the pirate port, Nosoheath.

Weavil tersely rejected Baus's claim, insisting rudely that such jests were of poor taste. Baus assured the poet that everything was exact—that the hoard was actually real and marked with a conspicuous sign.

Esling was not savvy to the value of wealth and remained indifferent. Baus explained as best as possible that the validity of the treasure was indisputable—that its coins, gold and silver and gems were all glittering and ready for picking. But his delivery was perhaps lacking in convincing enthusiasm.

Valere sceptically demanded to know how he had single-handedly secured such a hoard with none the wiser.

Baus smiled, describing how he had snatched the pirates' gold by fortune from the traitor-thieves, Saul and Kribby. Zoren had slain the two thieves mercilessly and had dragged the bodies off into the swamp. The one remaining chest they had carried back to their ship was lost, but the other he, Baus, had buried in a hole by a singular bearsbottom tree. The cutthroats, unaware of the conniving involvement, had caught up with him in Nosoheath, and coerced him to accompany the band back to Dwiterin for the necessary 'clearing-up' of loose ends regarding the missing loot. Fortunately he had escaped.

Valere was unmoved by the revelation. "I know all this. So—is this how you carried it out? Why all the secrecy? Did you defer alerting us to this happy trove for the purposes of a surprise revelation?"

Baus explained that he believed that excessive bounty corrupt the amicable ties shared by bosom peers.

"Indeed!" Poli growled, turning an odious glare upon him. "It would have taken a bite out of some of the past indignities we suffered for sure."

Weavil agreed, demanding to know what quality of opulence was waiting in this fantastic place in Nosoheath. "I could care less about 'bonds' and 'boons' truth be told."

"All will be explained," Baus responded curtly.

"Nosoheath is a significant distance away!" complained Weavil.

"True, but what of it?"

"You forget my own miserable size makes it hard to trudge a hundred leagues from here!"

Baus emphasized that such a march might be salubrious for a person of his stature. "In fact, I suggest we let wisdom be our guide and that we recuperate our strengths at Mismerion."

"By no means!" argued Weavil. "I wish to receive my share of the wealth as quickly as possible."

Baus shrugged indifferently. "Have it as you like, Weavil."

In his heart Baus gathered confidence that the mission would bring good will and equitable fortune but a disappointment rang in his heart—that his peers did not understand his motives, as altruistic as he intended them.

The news gestated. Weavil, Poli and Valere became ever more excited on the subject of 'treasure' and continued to badger Baus into revealing more details about it such as: "What of the treasure's exact location? What of its extent, glitter, quality and value? And what of its transportability and resale?"

Baus replied that he did not know. Endless plans stirred in their brains.

He could hardly bear the respective expectations of it all and he shook his head finally at their crass self-interest.

The company grew silent. On the final leg to Mismerion, Weavil and Poli fretted over the weighty decisions involved in divvying up the treasure. Baus hung behind like a damp pillow. Somewhere in the back of his mind, he wished he had not told them so prematurely, and that there was no good to be gained from his retrieving the treasure himself . . . the quiet reality of an adventure winding down grew to full force.

Esling, sensing Baus's moroseness, tried to cajole him into better humour. To no avail. He remained sullen and uncommunicative.

At last they reached the castle, a stronghold glimmering with a thousand shades of grey and blue with its beguiling towers boasting ancient masonry and peaks configured of the most stylized umbrella and onion shapes. 'Twas a poignant reminder of Desenion that they had just quit. Part of Baus still resisted a full engagement with the old manner of his previous life, even with wealth. He concluded that he was face to face with a purposeless plodding after a picaresque set of misadventures. It gnawed at him, and laid him slightly low.

The last deep violet sky-streamers faded from the sky and Baus permitted himself a chuckle. Life was not morose! Events would go on regardless of his part in them and he would rise to meet the challenge . . .

The company arrived at the keep's weatherworn bailey, grimed and exhausted. Woisper gave a private blink to an invisible figure and tendered a salute to the leftmost iron raven that perched on the tall gatepost. The rough stone showed lustreless weather-stained façades replete with lichens. The raven seemed to flap its wing with approval and the gate creaked open with a groaning shriek.

The company passed within and the barbican was left behind. Woisper's head had not been soaked with so much brine to have forgotten the hallowed ritual of entry to Mismerion.

The company passed through the lonely courtyard and left the tangled, woolly bowers and orchards behind. They took small note of the ragged evergreens and the overgrown topiaries that had grown amongst the stony peripheries, no less the towered armoury that looked cracked and forlorn as if it had seen better days.

Woisper and Salmeister strode proudly on to the rain-worn steps of Mancer Hall. They breasted Mismerion's massive portal, the final outpost of the west. Forging another magic signal, they watched as the door slid back, and in they strode, clambering into the dusky interiors of Great Hall. They came nose to knee with Dious, their fusty undertaker, a pasty-faced steward much bald and greyed, and at his elbow, hunched the pawky Helaar—the Historian.

Helaar spoke in a casual tone: "Ah, Woisper! So good to see you at last! We were finally beginning to have few hopes of your return, to worry about your health—that you had abandoned us, or encountered some derivative misfortune. But, it seems you have proven us wrong!"

Woisper was not enlivened by Helaar's windy address, nor did he cast him no small frowning look of dripping sarcasm. "The hope, as you can see, Helaar, is unfounded."

Dious gave a crafty nod. "Ho so!—we are delighted at your presence, Hierarch. Even if it is at a two foot height instead of five—" he added jocularly.

Woisper disliked the jest. He gave Dious a truculent wave. "Make way, Dious—neither of you have lifted a baby finger to help me, nor so much as soiled a garment, and I am forbearing judgement, if not scorn."

Dious remained offended by the remark and attempted a formal accounting. "You must understand, Woisper, that we are too elderly to go gallivanting about the swamps and dells like you. We would catch our death of chills and frights!—not to mention injuries and blemishes of physical nature. We are members of Mismerion's elderly community—prone to fatigue and ailments!"

The Hierarch nodded gravely. "This is quite evident." A glowering gleam showed in his eye and he fluttered his fingers in a sinister way.

Helaar, hoping to steer the conversation down a more profitable avenue, spoke to Woisper in a slightly leering tone: "I see that you have returned with a host of travellers—and with our 'mystery agent' too, this Baus—as Dious has been maundering on of late."

Baus's dry grin slackened. He realized that the two stewards were hardly complimentariy of his address, nor sympathetic of his role.

"Your return means, of course," inquired Helaar cynically, "that we might rest assured that the magnificence of Mismerion shall be restored?"

"You can," announced Ulisa coolly. "Now, gentlemen, please regulate your quips to dull murmurs."

The steward made a cocky bow. "As you wish, esteemed Ulisa. We can accommodate your fabulous righteousness."

"Enough!" Woisper cried. "Where are my followers? I see only you two geriatrics, a quantity of dust and hairballs, and many grimy little lamps glowering here and there like glimmer bugs."

Dious offered him a look of rankled resentment. "There are no others in residence, as you see, Woisper. What do you imply? That absent from the castle many moons, you can shout at us like a pack of dogs with haughty bravado? The others are gone, as is evident."

Woisper arched his brows with stormy impatience. "Do not dodge me with your petty irrelevancies, Dious! I intend to minister alterations upon this demesne, starting this minute with your positions."

Helaar and Dious did not appreciate the volume of Woisper's voice and began to amend their statements about avoiding chills and frights. The Hierarch was deaf to their drivel and stomped from the hall. To his tower block on the bleaker part of the northern court he strode.

The hour was old. The first rays of moonlight shone upon the flagstones in cool nacreous bands. The eccentric towertops gleamed in the chill—the travellers were struck with a sense of dark wonder of Mismerion's battlements which seemed to gleam in a minatory way. There were, of course, evidences of instability within the new household, but this was to be expected, thought Baus. There would be no famous metamorphoses of Woisper's magic this night. Weavil's hope for augmentation was dashed too. The poet retired in the high chamber on the second floor with the rest of his fellow travellers, weary and worn. They all slept above Mancer Hall, nursing impatient thoughts.

Dious had given the companions fresh linens and Ulisa fetched them several compotes and teas to tide them over until morning, along with fresh garments. The company slept like children back from a long day's excursion . . .

X

Woisper was up at the crack of dawn in a most eager mood. He ordered Dious to fetch him his vat and a beat up tub. The Hierarch was not critical of battered, broken things—nor amazed at the disrepair of his unkempt workroom, but perplexed at his loss of memory of certain key spells and figments of lore required in the critical phases of his transformation back to his regular self. Nevertheless, other preparations were in order: fire-gathering, zaphost crystal-toning, flux-metering, and the boiling of much chloro-boxo in solutions of crystalmux.

By eight o'clock, the Mismerion crew were gathered in the number of a dozen up top Woisper's tower. They marvelled at the eye-bewildering array of tubes, alembics and apparatus that were spread wide on his worktable.

Baus scratched plaintively at his head; he regarded the coiled hoses, the bubbling beakers, the vitreous flasks and retorts, rods, wires, cables and pipes that abounded in all directions with a feeling of mixed horror and fascination. Weavil shared this bemusement—no less Esling. Trimestrius and Ulisa sat back with nonplussed expressions. Salmeister stood by with an austere frown while Ahrion and Onzo, recently arrived, stroked beards and jutted chins, having just come from Lillenvir after a successful completion of dropping off Tatla.

Valere and Poli were still sleeping, owing to significant exhaustion.

A square smoke-glazed vat allowed the space for a single, full-sized person, courtesy of Onzo. The vessel lay on the table's edge, looking somewhat awkwardly poised in relation to the ancillary apparatus so evidently eerie. At one end of the coiled maze hung a snake-like tube configured with a single decanting pipe which protruded obtrusively down to the tub, dripping sinister drops like a woodpecker's knock when striking the darker liquid within. The worktable was black-charred, as if it had seen much action in its lifetime.

Woisper cleared his throat. He swept the chicken mesh from the table. A bronze gargoyle remained hunched gloomily in the corner—some fetish of good luck—remaining the only item in the shadows, aside from an age-cracked bookcase, stocked with a hundred or more books of sorts of moth-eaten lore.

Baus could not altogether dismiss the feeling of woe, being cramped in this untidy burrow, which housed a time bomb in the form of an absent-minded wizard. The concern was real and conveyed a cloying premonition of disaster as if the chamber were about to explode with ill-wrought wizardry. In fact, the chamber reeked of experiments gone bad. Even the cool breeze drifting in through the casement seemed to spurn the space it was forced to occupy.

Oblivious to such trepidation, Woisper paced back and forth on his workbench, hands knit gently behind his back. He attempted to explain the essence of his experiments—but was somewhat impatiently disposed. His tone was highbrow, in need of some dumbing-down, and in the opinions of many, much in need of a translator. To the Hierarch the need for such explanations was unnecessary; indeed the science was essentially obvious—which any layman could understand with the simplest of examples: like his analogy, for instance, of the 'mesomatic improbables' and the 'causal field of manifestation'. He droned on: "I, unlike others, have isolated a conjoining field which governs the essential 'shrinking' of our unfortunate bodies. 'Tis focalized on a sphere, a node if you will have it, which ranges in symparitic variable to an nth order continuum, coincident with a certain horizon of synchronosis. The 'variable'—or lack of variable, has induced itself into our glands—those of myself, Ulisa, Salmeister, Trimestrius and Weavil. This has disabled the natural growth of our bodies, thus negating an acceptable size-per-mass gradient into its most opposite function —a descent into degradative midgetry! A reversal of the anomaly is immensely tasking; it violates the basic axioms of alchemy, which, for want of another term, forces me to employ a rather unorthodox methodology—an alchemic shift dedicated to the stabilization of important physical membranes."

Baus waved off the exegesis as if it required no mental energy. "The concept is jejune, Woisper, please move on with your lemma!"

"As you wish, Baus! Now, to action! Iso-embolisms are to be manifested and dwarfs to be undwarfed!"

Bouncing forward, Weavil introduced his own aspirations: "The emprise is to be undertaken with swift speed, diligence and care!"

"Indeed, indeed, Weavil!" uttered Woisper, stroking his chin and offering a condescending nod. He urged him to keep a tight lid on his outbursts and a respectful distance from the apparatus. "Sudden jolts or discords jar the sensitivity of my appliances." Weavil curled lips and the neomancer emphasized the concept with a sharp rap of his slide-rule upon a beaker. The unstoppered flask brimmed with a greenish liquid that was sinister to the eye. "Behold—my mimbo-gelatine!" Weavil frowned anew and Woisper sniffed the contents and recoiled with a wincing grimace. He added more chloro-boxo. Consulting his screeds, he withdrew another leather-bound compendium from the shelf, his fingers flitting over moth-eaten pages like butterflies. Baus saw the title which was labelled 'Temporal Volutes, Transmogrifications and Blights'. Clearly a volume the old wizard revered beyond measure which he took pride to read at length to the group.

"The fluxion admixtures of the causal variety is not to be confused with the layman's retrofix . . ."

All were amazed and perplexed. For a goodly period, Woisper continued to babble on, ornamenting his exposition with language that included qloacks, malomophic bloacks, jehisons, and ultimately gerhaks. Finally he halted with a finger piked in the air. A particular stanza seemed especially tuned to his sensibilities and squinting, he stamped a foot with authority, thus following a line of reasoning that aligned with a resigned, philosophic logic. The folio was snapped shut with a bang. "Now!" he intoned sharply. "Who shall be my first subject? Did some varlet pilfer my distillation pack?

"Nay, Woisper," soothed Ulisa. "Likely the pack perished in the blast you created two years ago. A similar pack was employed in the transformation of Kazzasius, don't you remember?—which was used as a supplement to abate the danger of formulosis." The Utilitarian's gaze went cloudy. "I entrusted the accessory to Helaar for cleaning in the depository, and for safe-keeping quite a while ago."

"Helaar, eh? Well, fetch the laggard then."

"The Historian sleeps; he would not like to be awakened."

"That matters little! Fetch him!" Woisper drew back a beaker with reptilian distaste. "Sluggard! Who else will hinder me? Better yet, what can we use in the pack's place?"

There were mutters but no answers came. In the interim Woisper employed Onzo as a guard to watch over the ghoulish-looking cucurbit that smoked gently in the background. The curved flask glowered with a fiendish green flame that disturbed even the most versed souls in alchemy, including Ahrion. The fanning network of pipes and hoses seemed pivotal to the Hierarch's enterprise, and he explained this in a bright voice and that it was not to be jostled in any wise.

Onzo, in all his eager impetuosity, accidentally bumped the alembic and sent an alarming oscillation careening obscenely through the pipes.

Woisper's face went white. The few smokes turned to virulent green, engulfing the alembic in a haze and sizzle.

Choking on the pungent fumes, Woisper boomed across the tabletop. "Bungling puppy! I said 'monitor' the flask, not worry it like a hopball. Now, wipe that cursed grin off your face."

Onzo complied.

Ahrion, scowling at the delay, voiced a complaint which Woisper riposted. Ahrion stormed again, "We have already suffered exotic implosions and blasts in this crampy-hole! Let's have no repeat performances or mishaps due to incompetent error!"

Woisper compressed his lips into a flat smile. "I do not want a reminder of that, Ahrion; now please, bridle your spleen and abide my earlier injunction—which is to stay out of harm's way."

Ahrion was rankled by the put down but resorted to retreating into a pall of peevish annoyance. Under Woisper's supervision, Ulisa monitored the instruments—a duty that Onzo was deposed of, since proven a bungler. Woisper framed ominous words to the effect that error was unacceptable at this juncture. "Now! Who will be the first to become whole again?" he blared.

Weavil instantly jigged forward in an amiable and cheerful mood. Hopping up on the tub, he forced Woisper to fastidiously place him in the vat. With strained patience Woisper bathed him in a dye of byke fusion and hue of chloro-boxo. Adding a flask of balsolo for good measure, he muttered an incantation that announced the preliminaries were essentially met—the rest of the procedure was to be taken with patience and forbearance—which indeed, was a delicate undertaking in its own. All retreated to a safe corner whereupon Woisper whisked about, murmuring pedagogic remarks, fussing with beakers, flasks, nodules, wires and fluoro-nuoros.

Ahrion suddenly jolted forward, alarmed at the sudden unorthodox bubbling which had precipitated itself in a twist of tubing. In conjunction with the fluoro-nuoros, the disturbance caused an important mixture of balsolo near the gear box to bubble over and cause further concern amongst the gathering. "I am no alchemist, Woisper, but this irregular displacement in this chloro-boxo is worrisome. I highly advise a strengthening of the balsolo, better diluted with tri-lorium in my opinion before the electrolysis is applied."

Woisper nodded fractiously, agreeing that such precaution might augment standard safety protocols. In a stuffy monotone, he added, "Operations of this sort, Ahrion, require a timed injection of a concentration unimpinged by the chattering of dilettantes and hobbyists."

Ahrion stepped back with slighted pride. Now Woisper entreated the Optimist to attach two crystalline nodes to the subject's right cranium. Aministering nodes to Weavil's spine and one to left arm and right leg, he explained that each minor ganglia was of lesser importance than the other. Weavil, still loitering in the vat, became increasingly apprehensive by this disclosure, carping that questionable connecting of wires running from his body to the gourdish-battery straddling the floor seemed unnecesary.

Woisper ignored the remark and consulted his screed for a final summation while Baus was not unperceptive to the possibility of calamity.

Crowing exuberantly, the Hierarch hit the mallet on his lubo-chime. A series of muttered syllables gonged; he blew into an angel horn and turned raven eyes upon Weavil.

Sparks flashed from Weavil's temples; bromidic fluid began to glisten in the vat a baleful red.

Weavil lurched. To everyone's astonishment, his body began to change, getting larger. First with a jolting spasm, then with a grimacing pang. There was a hint of rigour in his body, then a relaxation—of no more than a pinch of flux whereupon there came an eye-bulging enlargement, followed by a cracking of joints. His nose became larger, twisted askew like a scarecrow's, then appearing gnawed by a large predatory bird. Arms and leg seemed to grope, plunge, tangle, then become rigid. The poet thrashed, blossomed like a balloon, then suddenly he deflated, limbs flopping gracelessly in the tub until his clothes were seen bursting like wind-tossed pennants. Exposed at the seams, h was like a bare-naked baby. To the company's astonishment, the transformation had halted abruptly in mid step.

Woisper tugged perturbedly at his beard. "Why now?" He frowned, checking Weavil's smoking connectors.

The half-enlarged poet, sensing mishap, tore the electrodes from his scalp and grabbed strips of his former garb, seeking to cover his privates.

Baus stared with wonder at Weavil's newly-sized body. He took note that Weavil stood only 5' 4"—a far cry from his former 5' 9".

Folding fingers tentlike, the Hierarch spoke in frowning reservation. "It appears that Weavil has exhibited traits that are inappropriate for the metamorphosis. Therefore I must move on to another subject. Let the next subject come forward!"

Weavil groped, gaped, fighting lank-toothed, protesting vehemently to the abandonment of his enlargement. Woisper dismissed the remonstrations with brisk, clawed sweeps of arm. "To confirm my hypothesis, Weavil, I'll attempt another entirely different nodal tack."

Weavil hopped out of the vat with anger and indignity. He confronted Woisper. "Mountebank! Do you think you can get up and quit? Apply some more bloro-chloro or basolo, or splash more of this filthy liquid in the tub!"

Woisper shook his head with frowning annoyance. "Weavil, 'tis an unreal expectation. Now stand back. An overdose of electrolyte and a bad-mixing of chloro-boxo will only result in you sprouting horns and growing feathers or some such. Is that what you'd like? Yodelling like a pichbird?" Woisper gestured indulgently at Ulisa. "Look, here is a patient bystander. She will be the next incumbent. No—much better, Trimestrius—here, let him be the one to hop in the tub!"

Trimestrius ventured to do just that, then abruptly stopped in midstep. "Why the sudden change of mind from Ulisa to me?"

Woisper waved an easy hand, "Nothing. Ulisa is unusually accommodating—let her be the one serviced last."

Trimestrius was not so easily duped and called out, "You are a crafty dissembler, Woisper. In light of your last significant 'failure', you would conduct trials on another guinea pig—me, before engaging your 'precious' Ulisa. Is that not it?"

"Nonsense!" cried Woisper. "Balderdash. You are overwrought and distraught, Trimestrius. Now up into the tub like a proper prince!" Arching a fatherly hand as if to console a doubtful child, Woisper bared teeth suddenly finding a small body intruding itself between vat and beaker. "Weavil! If I tell you once, I'll tell you again, do not weasel your way into the tub! I shall be compelled to employ the Spell of Dismal Torpor which will be patty-cakes compared to the perils of re-aggrandization!"

"Enough of your hot wind! I must dispute that conclusion."

The Hierarch became instantly adamant and Weavil was forced to obey otherwise face chagrin. The poet slunk away sullenly down to Mancer Hall to fetch some better clothing.

The experiments continued. But with no more profitable results. Trimestrius, failing to achieve his former height, grew not a hair past 5' 4" similar to Weavil—nor did Salmeister, who remained a puny reminder of his past glory, stuck at an appalling 4' 9". When it came Ulisa's turn she insisted that a robe be drawn over her body to forestall her imminent nakedness while crouched so vulgarly in Woisper's tub. Woisper, chuckling, ordered Onzo to fetch an appropriate garment which he did. Ahrion urged Ulisa to reason, "Come, Ulisa! We are all adults here. There is no part of your anatomy that we have not already come into contact with."

Ulisa uttered a scalding croak. "I will not be exposed to filthy men like yourself, who peer down at me like a piece of candy."

Salmeister leaned over to Ahrion to say something ironic and Onzo returned at that moment with fresh white linen. He draped the fabric gently around Ulisa who self-consciously ducked back behind the rim of the tub angrily, flashing resentful looks at all male members of the company.

Woisper gave a tolerant nod and worked his magic as if nothing had ensued. He chanted a quatrain, letting the alembic drip its green dollops of elixir and sounding blasts into his angel horn.

There was a puff of magic—an odd booming here and there of drums like the sound of faraway thunder. Ulisa's body grew. Her exotic frame bloomed as nothing before. Clutching her blanket, she gave a cry of exultance, her eyes glowing, enraptured by her rapidly blossoming body.

She commanded the greatest success of experimentation—an impressive 5' 5". She stood beaming, six inches short of her true height. Indeed, Baus remarked attentively that she was never more breathtaking. Her sun-blond hair shone like liquid gold; her luxurious figure danced with a gleaming liveliness, and her pearl-lustrous skin was by far more suggestively enhanced in the intimacy of the surroundings with her slightly wet, if not bromidic blanket.

Woisper remarked upon the results with critical favour. "My technique is exact—so why the unoptimal growth?" He pulled at his tangled beard, clicking his tongue. "Ulisa, Trimestrius, and now the boy Weavil—all remain tallest of the bunch . . . yet they have been exposed to the least amount of Aurimag's brine for the least time—so what logic does this imply?" he muttered into his beard. "Salmeister who has been immersed for considerably longer has not enlarged himself beyond 5'—and myself?" He trailed off glumly, muttering a groan of displeasure which became a caw of rancour.

Baus, Esling and Onzo slunk out of the way as the Hierarch went on the rampage. He hurled in a pinch of powder and plunged himself into his work with absolute fervidity. Of the spectators, only three remained. Others had lost interest, fleeing uneasily elsewhere, or wandering off to eat. Now Woisper's grimace become a rictus as he attempted to effect his own augmentation. He reread his compendium, eased himself grimly into the vat, grumbled threats and maledictions while affixing wires to his cranium.

Stirring the electrolyte, he adjusted the pitch of his decanting pipe. Then the neomancer seemed to be having the most difficult time focussing on his task. For all the seriousness of the endeavour, it seemed inconceivable to be working under such pressure. The wire extending from Woisper's left temple was a mark short of its purpose and he began to pull at it with impatience which unwittingly caught the green chloro-boxo beaker. A brisk movement and the Hierarch reached to adjust the drip . . .

Baus called out a plangent warning. Not in time.

The beaker slid.

The Hierarch's ears were closed to advice. The flask tipped toward the battery on the floor—and it fell smashing, shattering in a wide spray of sparks.

An electrocuting flash jigged in and about Woisper's mouth. He jerked, writhed, twisted, flailed. Sharp electrical currents shot through his hair and teeth. He shook, shivered like a rag doll.

Baus leaped to save the man's life . . . he ripped the cerebral nodes free. Woisper collapsed in a smoking heap.

* * *

It was no surprise that the old Hierarch remained the shortest of the lot—an embarrassing 4' 7". He sneered at this failure, cursed with loathing, launched into a diatribe of abuse, pitching obscene catechisms left and right.

To little avail.

Whether it was the ineptitude of his thaumaturgy or the cogency of Aurimag's spell, Woisper was not to grow any taller.

Flinging the folio of 'Temporal Volutes' to the ground, he stamped the pages to dust and tipped the alembic to the floor where it crashed smashing into a jangled heap.

Baus, Esling and Onzo stood quietly before exiting the room.

In some karmic manner, it appeared that Aurimag had his last revenge, visiting a small, jocular restitution on his enemy, in the form of an exasperated failure . . .

* * *

On the following day further persistence on Woisper's part failed—as did other experiments. The fourth day his trials had concluded themselves, incurring similar results. Woisper declared that his enterprise should be abandoned.

Kazzasius the Projector was removed of the xenophone by arduous alchemic procedure and was somewhat restored to his real self, though he was displeased with the manner of his 're-integration'. If not for the agencies of Ulisa and Adelyheim's healing, he would have been far worse off.

Kazzasius retained a grossly bloodshot eye for the rest of his life, as if some droll reminder of his willingness to be an experimental subject at the whims of the neomancers. He complained loudly of this misfortune, though no one gave him sympathetic ears. Woisper was in sour reception of the grievances of late and seemed only marginally capable of offering anything beyond a grunt and gruff shrug. "Life treats us with strange umbrages, Kazzasius. We must make do with what we have and move on."

Kazzasius did not accept the maxim and began a rigorous research into restoring his former self. However, he was stymied. The subject of freak 'After-effects of blights' was explored to fervid degree; he even called upon Helaar and Dious to assist him in scouring the castle's dusty old library and the many leather-bound volumes for solutions. Cross-analyzing the multitudes of texts overflowing on the shelves was fruitless—as was further research which came to an unsatisfactory end.

XI

Amidst lonely excursions about the empty halls of Mismerion, Esling took liberty to explore the castle grounds. Better to solace her aching heart with fresh air and tranquility than shadows and dust. There was no groundskeeper on Mismerion's pleasances, only overgrown shrubbery. Yet there was a blooming flower garden which was tucked near an inner wall by the ever-leaning shadows of Ahrion's moss-covered cloud-tower which gave her some peace.

The garden was rich, dressed with poxy-eyed pansies, buttercups, red mallow-hocks, and dragon-winged weather-wisps. It showed promise of colourful possibilities. She asked herself: did the little plot grow by magic?

No answer was to come. Esling bent to sniff a cup of hollyhock and reviewed the nature of her aching heart. No reassurance did she feel, knowing that Baus, her heartache, to no surprise, was a figure so far removed from her life that all points of reflection seemed to bound inward on themselves; she felt ever more neglected by him and his secretive airs and solitude in this comfortless Mismerion. 'Twas a place of cold grandeur and gloomy shadows. Valere and Poli had become clownish ragabouts, no more comfort to her than a couple of jokesters and bumpkins. Weavil, needless to say, was a self-centered brat who let his tasteless jokes rule his temperament, not to mention his frowning cynicism which stemmed from the Wickle's close association with Baus. And Trimestrius? His ill love for Wickles was no secret to all.

Esling plucked a red flower from its stem and pressed it to her nose. She found herself dreaming, wandering, moving inward, very aloof . . .

She rambled aimlessly past the goblin-shrubbed hedge, past the weed-eaten fishpond, and several weathered grave markers. She kicked at the upturned proleweeds and bakers' thorn, loosing a despondent sigh.

Into the tall shadows of the weatherworn statues she stepped—their old sombre-faces peeked down on her with somewhat stern authority: first, Archokes the Great, then Kreo the II and then Zossaut the 'Brown' . . . Ah, what a bunch of old buzzards! she thought. From these forebears came the source of her abominable enchantment.

Squeezing through the ribs of the portcullis, she plodded her way under the cracked archway of the western bailey, sauntering to the open heath that lay to the west.

* * *

Ulisa's hours were spent mostly outdoors with Adelyheim. They were friends and traded stories and confided in each other with ease in the sunshine. The matters of spells and healings, potions and charms were regular points on their agenda, no less this afternoon, proving fair and cheerful.

The two neomancers sauntered on, patting each other on the shoulder from time to time, and feeling no compunction of leaving the castle and its eccentric brood of male persons behind. They roamed the spinneys far from the sunny side of the castle, keen on herb-gathering.

From behind a brown copse, they caught sight of the Wickle Esling. Ulisa was surprised and the newcomer's sudden appearance almost startled them. Meekly Esling approached, and with awkward pretence greeted the neomancers. A sudden storm of emotions broke surface and tears came to her eye and Ulisa and Adelyheim took her under their wing.

The shape-shifter discovered that the Wickle's wistful mood was the product of a matter not for from her suspicion, "Come join us," she invited cordially. "Adelyheim and I are on our way to the northern dells. We are to engage in a pilgrimage—seeking ox-fane, rose-twine, and felsasa. You must join us!—if you'd like."

Esling coyly shook her head. "Nay, ladies. I must decline. 'Twould be improper of me to impose on your healing excursion."

"Silly! You are far from improper—only too modest and mild of temperament."

"If you say so, my Lady. Yet I sojourn alone. With you, my grief would not be so bad; likely I would benefit from fresh air!" She warmed to walking with them and eventually accompanied them. "Bother these troubled halls of Mismerion and your associates. I keep bumping into your stewards—Helaar and Dious—those two bats seem purposely to haunt me like flies to the candle! But I would not criticize their hospitality at least. I would rather speak of another matter."

"What is that?"

"A wish—if I could only make it come true! . . . "

Adelyheim fluttered her fingers with delight. "And what wish wouldn't we want true? Do tell."

Esling shrugged. "I wish for what it would be like if only Baus returned my affection. He never does. He ignores me or speaks so condescendingly of me. Little does he remember that if it were not for me, he would be riding Graeitch's hub with teeth clenched and knuckles white, with a terrible ache in his bones! Alas. You know for yourself, you would be imprisoned under the shadow of Aurimag's tyranny, Ulisa, if it were not for his—"

The shape-shifter prompted Esling in gentle tones, "For his what—?"

Esling's voice crackled at the edges. "I have no desire to return to my kin, Ulisa, the fey forests, the dank enclaves and the threat of Farling's Wall. My kin are like furious beasts, yet sorely distressed. They hurt in their hearts. Strangle me, whip me, for sure if they find out what I've done. Yet I suffer from my own heart-sickness for Baus. Ah, what terrible fate! He can never love me—as long as I am a Wickle and wear this frightful doe's tail and budding horns, like a chicken's comb—they are things that make me look so much not like a lady!— I'm a *freak*." Esling's face pinched with a thousand unshed tears. "My wish is, can I not be human again? Is it not my birthright?"

Her appeal was so frank that neither of the two could not feel moved. They postponed their plans for the day and set their heads in order, trying to muster a plan for the Wickle.

While Adelyheim brewed herbs Ulisa conducted further research on the topic of reversals in the old library, searching for old references to spells that could aid Esling in her desire. The Healer gathered flowers in the garden, rare and pungent ones, and collected sweet nectars from the glades back of the castle.

In the early evening, Ulisa made use of Onzo's spell-tower to gaze at the sky and gather far-reaching wisdom from the northern stars. Adept in animal transformations, she harboured great skill in visioning, far beyond Woisper and Salmeister's ability. After a lengthy period, she was graced with a flash of supersight and whisked Esling to a far place beyond the old lych-gate, draped in spring blossoms and hung with flower vines. Wickle and shape-shifter journeyed for a day and a half to a hidden place two leagues west of the castle where at the foot of an old dagar mound, hot springs bubbled from the depths of a rocky pool. Together they chanted, and together they went on a visioning quest—of trance-dream, after which Ulisa began her treatments on Esling in the earth-warmed waters . . .

Three days passed.

Ulisa and the Wickle returned to the castle. Esling was much changed by her pilgrimage. The corrective liquids of Glesmere's pool had made her rubicund and radiant. Her face glowed with a healthy grace, while almost floating on her heels, the Wickle did appear more physically human, with Ulisa continuing to massage her brow and the budded temples. She summoned Adelyheim and the three journeyed north to a remote copse overgrown with asp-eye flower and wyre blossoms. The white and rose petals dispelled soft music in the air. Meanwhile Esling faced the sunshine in the nude so that the full radiance could stream down on her Wickle's body. The piping of flutes and melodies drifted from afar; whether they came from enchanted flowers or the enchantress's magic, Esling did not know.

In a circle of healers' energy, Ulisa and Adelyheim ringed the Wickle. With their eyes closed and lips pursed, the two healers sang old stanzas of therapeutic song. Hands pressed over Esling's head, they touched her fair hair, bathing her with soft energies, with the freshest spring nectars dowsed from deep in the earth's soils and the warmths and life-springing marvels were such that only those wise women knew.

Enchantment came to Esling's world. She knew euphoria. Her seraphic face glowed with lightness and heart-sprung love melted her heart. She was healed of bygone woes and macabre enchantments seeded from ages ago by manipulating magicians. Tears brimmed down Esling's dimpled cheeks. Jubilation shone in her heart and she was changed greatly, in ways she could not imagine. Her trembling fingers yearned to reach to her brow—she laughed in child's delight—for she found the skin soft and smooth, untainted of unladylike horns.

Placing a hesitating palm on her buttocks, she found there no ruffled appendage or animal-like fur to greet her touch!

Esling leaped back for joy, prancing like a kitten.

Ulisa admired Esling's rose-coloured hair and brushed it back with care and love. The graceful coltish energy of Esling the heroine was back—what a force to behold! A Wickle turned woman. 'Twas a great achievement in the world!

"There now!" laughed Ulisa. "You are as fine a maid as any to walk these lands. I attest to it. I shall christen you '*Lady Esling*'! Fine enough that a lass wanders in Mismerion. You are the surpassing beauty of the manor, Esling—as fair as any princess of Karsh, any gallant man can see, including that dimwitted Baus the Bold, who would be of greater idiocy not to take you for his own!"

Esling had a spurt of laughter. "If you could heal me like this, Ulisa, then you can transform the other Wickles! There are so many of them who need help to be rid of their horrid hybrid-ness."

Ulisa gave a remorseful sigh. "A worthy hope—but unfeasible."

"Why?" cried Esling.

Adelyheim mused: "I have oft journeyed in the forests, Esling. I've found the Wickles' plight sorrowful too. The truth: the world is unfair and we must accept it; the blight of the 'Wickles' is Woisper's doing, from days of old when he was folly-full and not as discerning of his deeds. The feat you ask is beyond even us, possibly even the entire might of the Mismerion Circle . . ."

Esling sagged. "But it's possible, isn't it?" she quavered. Her voice, caught by emotion, crackled dryly.

Ulisa cleared her throat: "No. But then again, past endeavours deemed impossible by others of lesser practicality, are fruitless. The effect of our magic, is small, like a small bubble breaking on the crests of an ocean. We could make a profound change on your form because your spirit is light and virtuous, and your 'animal' nature is small in comparison to others of your ilk."

Esling was shaken with emotion. Sensing her despair, Ulisa took her hand and gave it a plump squeeze. "Adelyheim and I will give you our solemn word that we will make efforts."

She sprang up, embraced them in her gratitude. "Thank you!" she cried.

"But I warn you, we are not miracle-workers," Ulisa laughed.

Esling wiped away the tears and she saw then that the cosmos was kind, and so felt renewed hope.

* * *

For nights and days, the companions kept to themselves in rooms of ancient fastness at Mismerion. All benefited in the respite. Valere and Poli were the happiest, provided with warmth and comfort. They ate hot meals and sipped mulled wine without the stress of frights of hostile forces. They were proclaimed heroes—bestowers of the Mismerion order.

Baus, however still brooded and did not participate in the festivities, nor did he notice the immediate transformation in Esling. The recognition came little by little. 'Twas in the early evening in the rosy-tinted glow in Mismerion's flower garden, when he caught a glimpse of her in the form of an evocative profile—seeing the angle of her forehead without horns, and the curve of her behind which seemed very unmarred by the swell of any animal's feature. When she finally made a point of cuddling up to him at night in the complete nakedness of warm human skin, he was amazed. Esling did become an attractive icon to him then . . .

Aside from the Wickle, Baus spent most of his time aloof, away from his peers, exploring the little-broached corridors of the castle. The shadow-draped alcoves and rooms were of immense interest. Some were lit by antique lamps and exuded a waft of soft magic; others were adorned with ancient, voluted pillars and faded ochre-pigmented friezes and tapestries hinting of a mystical antiquity beyond his guessing. He marvelled at the armoires, the sideboards, the settees, and particularly at many relics of the ancient past, imbued with an air of mystery and enchantment.

One a rainy afternoon, the outlaw discovered a large room in an out-of-the-way wing on the northern precinct. Hardly a room it was, but a great chamber—a depository, sprawling with mysterious adjuncts and curios of all sizes. He gaped and blinked. Cabinets abounded, with display cases, drawers, cubbyholes, an endless supply of curiosities and oddments— glowing wands, jewelled sceptres, translucent spheres, luminescent pipes, floating bottles, flasks of all sorts, iron-toothed astrolabes that hung conspicuously on the far wall. The devices were filigreed in brass and clicked with all kinds of singular energy. They seemed to violate the science of nature, similar to Aurimag's enchanted monstrosity hanging in his cave.

Baus seized hold of a charcoal-grey sceptre and made a few exploratory sweeps with it. It was in size comparable to the ganglestick, and was about to give it more air play when he was rudely interrupted by a strident voice that came shafting out of the shadows.

A luminous figure stood limned in the hallway. Ulisa. Somehow the figure defined authority and reason and did not take well to his meddling with adjuncts which did not belong to him. "Please replace the sceptre. Given your predisposition for misdemeanours, I think it unwise to tempt yourself with more chicanery."

Baus acquiesced and left without comment, failing to see the look of interest and attraction the shape-shifter had for him.

* * *

Weavil, the poet he was, had composed several odes to wile away his time. He was not accustomed to his not-so-fully-expanded stature and made an overt show of demonstrating his prowess, given more steam in the promise of his wealth. Those gathered gave indulgent smiles.

Valere and Poli had settled into a kind of smug lassitude. Both had taken the luxuries of Mismerion for granted—well-earned boons and rewards, simple recompense for their hardships. Neither was exempt from this mode of convenience, being of the mind 'as good as rich men'—so why exert any effort?

In down-filled beds they slept late into the day, taking breakfast at a time most convenient for them. When they awoke, they amused themselves with sports about the mukklewood forests, such as gallivanting on wild hunts, or arrowing pheasant and quail north of the keep.

A fortnight had bored them and Valere began to craft plans to head north to retrieve his treasure. With vast impatience Poli urged Baus to give up his dilly-dallying and join them on their mission. "We cannot sit here like dabchicks, pecking at seeds in a hay yard. We must retrieve the treasure!"

"In good time, in good time . . ." A long cogitation had Baus requesting an earnest discussion in Mancer Hall with his peers: "Poli, you may go, or stay here at the castle. I care not for the treasure; I have decided to forego a trip to Sarch."

Valere opened mouth and vaulted back in sudden shock. "What's this? The treasure is a hoax?"

"No, the treasure is as real."

"Then, what is your problem?"

"There is no problem."

An awkward silence ensued. Valere finally gave a brittle snort. "Of all your jokes, Baus, this is the worst."

"'Tis not a joke. Hear me out, seaman, for long have I considered the purpose of my life. 'Tis the open road that truly beckons me—'tis my heart's desire. No hoard shall keep me. I shall not be happy in its acquisition, no less by the promise of an un-besmirching of my honour in Heagram."

Poli looked at him with bovine incomprehension. "So—what are you saying? That you are tired of luxury and ease?"

"Not that. That I am off on another journey, far from Heagram," responded Baus distantly. "Perhaps, I shall open a small boot shop or even start up a haberdashery somewhere, if the opportunity wishes it."

"Quaint, very quaint," mumbled Valere jocularly.

"And yourselves?" inquired Baus in earnest. His smile had taken on an odd cast. "Will you join me? What of you, Weavil?"

Weavil gave a noncommittal grunt. "Out of the question—and forfeit the likes of wealth and convenience? You are mad! I have suffered enough to be wandering the wilds in the rain. Even if I must claw my way back to Nosoheath, I will do it—to divvy up this treasure of yours which is my rightful owing. I will return to Heagram as immediately as possible where I will unsully my name from the criminal cast it carries."

"That is a glad declaration."

Weavil was unimpressed with the sarcasm.

Poli made a rueful gesture. "I too, Baus, share affinity with Weavil, minus the unsullying of my name, of course, which was never tarnished to begin with. I am a rough-and-tumble type of man by nature—a sea rogue—a pirate and reaver by necessity. My lust for gold outmatches any urge to suffer the privations of the road, which are numerous, as our common experience attests."

Valere scoffed. "Well spoken, Poli! But it seems the bleak little surprises on the road are too much for you."

"For anyone," muttered Baus wistfully. He turned a sharp glance at the sea captain. "What of you, redbeard? I judge by your expression that you are not in accord with my plan?"

"Not at all," replied Valere, growling. "Truthfully, I rsent your minimalism and I am getting too old for adventure. With the luck of my kind, I shall be run through the first day on the road."

"Ah, you moan, old man," sighed Baus.

"I don't think so. With your treasure, though, I might purchase a small boat, perhaps a reasonably sized schooner at that, some craft of bearing, which I will ply to sea, live out a life there as I've always wanted. What else could I ever want, an old sea dog like me?" He spread his palms in frank disclaimer and Baus cast him a regretful look.

Somewhat peeved and resentful, Baus hung his head. His circle of friends was abandoning him. He felt crestfallen that not one seemed to share his vision. Ah, to fiery drakes with them! One would never have guessed that they would all drop their skirts like a circle of old women. And so, what of it? Cold knots gripped his shoulders. He asked himself, could he have expected much different?

"What of the price on your heads?" he muttered bleakly. "Are you not wolfs-heads?— Arnin will hunt you down to the ends of the earth."

"We are." Valere gave his head a firm shake. "But, there are many corners of this earth to hide in, none worse than the scummy den of Nosoheath. Even Illim Isle or Pirate's Point is better than there—and better than your prospect of traipsing all over hell's kitchen. As far as hideouts are concerned, Nosoheath and Heagram will serve for now. I shall fare tolerably, Baus, so shall Poli—if he has sense enough to follow me." He cast the youth a yellow glance and slapped him hard on the back.

Baus beseeched Esling. She returned his gaze with a spark of devotion.

Emotion caught in his throat. The ex-Wickle would not abandon him. To the ends of the earth she would travel at his side; he could never find a more gentle and loyal companion—at least, for the time being.

Wistfully he felt himself tumbling, slipping into state of remorse. He was perhaps deluded. He had lost three of his trusted comrades, Valere, Poli and Weavil, now also, the desire for a trouble-free existence, the easy quotidian pleasures of life: wealth, fame, power . . .

The light in Mancer Hall burned dim. The sun sank ever lower over the mukklewoods. As chance had it, Ulisa had borne witness to the whole conversation and had drifted in on quiet feet to offer words of wisdom. "Can I not persuade you, Baus, to stay at Mismerion? You are invited to study the neomancic arts—with me."

The sorceress struck a voluptuous figure in the grand light of the salon. Baus appreciated her, appraised her, unused to such tallness or such beauty or powerfully built aura; and yet a quickening in his blood brought a pang born of natural instinct. For long moments he warred with temptation.

Basking in the honour of apprenticeship with this beautiful neomancer, could entail many things, many quite sultry, each quite varied in their consequence.

A rare dilemma! Baus jeered gloomily to himself. To dally with this temptress—not an undesirable fantasy. Nay! Not at all. No man could disagree; yet a momentary tinge had him wavering, near capitulating to a more prosaic course of nature; the flash of caution caught in his throat and he straightened himself firmly.

Finding his voice, Baus spoke in an air of amicable formality. "No, Ulisa, I must demur. To stick to the open road is my course, as I've said—of this, I am certain, though I remain an outlaw. Woisper has reminded me, whispering in my ear, also of the pitfalls of magic and the lures of certain fatal women." His thought was interrupted by a returning misgiving—the malign fate like the rogue Aurimag, who had also been tempted by her charm and instruction . . . ending in doom. Yet ever was the promising vision dangling like a pleasant dream—particularly if remaining romantic acolyte to a beautiful sorceress.

Baus went on in a dispassionate voice: "The western hills are largely unknown to me; foolish of me to ignore them; forsooth, that will be my destination. I feel that the region is unpopulated, where I may find respite from this moody heart and casual ease for my restlessness which itches for a safe haven to shelter an outlaw such as me."

Ulisa retorted in mocking laugh, "How long will you last? This is a fine idealism, sir outlaw, but can you really live the life of a vagabond forever? Have you ever yet thought of the future?"

"What future?" Baus croaked cynically. He curled lips in a canny grin. "Let me say that, being bearer of Aurimag's ganglestick these past moons has been enough of a teaching for me—to better appreciate the experiences of dark obsession. My involvement with this villain, albeit a deluded one, has conveyed me a poignant truth . . ."

"What truth is that?" Ulisa demanded.

"Not to be enslaved by magical temptations of any sort. I become a miniature version of the magician himself."

Ulisa's lips pursed; a harsh thought took form to burst from her lips: "Is power so loathsome to you? Do you think you are as weak as the worm Aurimag? Why do you think that you would fail in the pursuit?"

"There is nothing to suggest that," Baus replied truthfully, "But—there is always chance of falling in his footsteps. A new thought arises—who was Aurimag before he became Aurimag? Was he just some ordinary person, a madman, a criminal, or lawless free-thinker like me, tempted by forces greater than himself. Or was he really just a misguided fool, as Woisper believes?"

Ulisa made no answer. She took her head in her hands. She shook her hair with sad exasperation.

"I seek not the path of magic, Ulisa—life already affords itself troubles enough." As his eyes rested on Esling a stray unease came over him. He wondered if the former Wickle could actually perceive his innermost feelings. Was she so innocent that she could not even see his desperate desire for Ulisa?

He hoped not.

He yanked himself from this reverie and turned his attention to the Utilitarian, who clutched his arm with a surprising strength. "You cannot leave the castle without performing a final divination," she ordered. "Stay here and learn of your path via a reading. You may be surprised. One reading shall disclose any truth of what lies in the future—and may suggest alternative paths."

Baus's dark eyes shifted. "How goes such a divination?"

Ulisa made a negligible gesture. "A simple procedure similar to Kazzasius—who entertained the prospect of a node inserted into a cerebral orifice—usually the sinuses—the rest is well—dependent on the subject."

Baus gave an unqualified croak. "Anything like the xenophone?"

Ulisa nodded briefly. "Something like that."

Baus coughed wryly. "I shall bypass such a divination, Ulisa. And so saying, well—" Eyes flashing, he caught sight of his chum Weavil slinking up the stairs. "Here Weavil, come here a moment!" he cried in a peevish tone. "Why are you yawning and so stricken with fatigue that you must leave? Come down here and listen to the words I have to impart."

Weavil brushed his colleague off. "Not at this moment. It is time for my regular bath and I am indisposed, as you can see. Can it not wait? Further conversations can be detained until the morrow."

Baus barked out a reprimand. "Hold your pretentiousness, Weavil. I may not be here for that conversation—you would forfeit saying goodbye to me on a sudden impulse for a bath? Would you reconsider my offer—of companionship along the road?"

"Absolutely not. I shall not be distracted from my immediate goals, which are to retrieve the treasure. You are a magnet for disaster!—a dark owl, hobgoblining about this world attracting confusion and disorder!"

Baus smiled. "I'm always glad of your opinion, Weavil." He gave a hostile, metallic snort. "But 'tis like the pot calling the kettle black, don't you think?"

"Don't carp at me, Baus—'tis not I who is the 'outlaw'. Everywhere you go, you bring shame and scandal. You will be hunted."

"So you say!—but did I ask for your opinion?"

Either way, bad words were traded and were unfortunate at this late time. Weavil went on to announce that the concept of his accompanying Baus was ridiculous. "Why should I suffer a gut-piercing and neck-hanging? I wish to retire in wealth and tranquility—in an appropriate peaceful mansion. You were always one to draw mishap to yourself. Look at you. Do you recall the shellames and yuyuks you shattered at Heagram fair, that imbroglio of evil that you began, with the run-in with the constables, and then Nuzbek . . . also my ruin? Aye! My personal woe attests to the fact that you are best steered clear of. My miniaturization and embottlement in a jar of caustic liquid has taught me much; indeed, left me grimly sensitive to stay away from you."

"So you articulate quite well," grunted Baus, giving his head a sullen jerk. "Perhaps you are not so far off in your judgements, Weavil . . . At this, I must concur." And so, the outlaw seemed further affirmed of a certain poignant truth about himself . . . that he was really a dark angel, perhaps born under an ill-fated conjunction, destined to walk a solitary path, seeking, wandering . . .

* * *

On the morn of the 12th of March, Baus and Esling left Mismerion by the old gravel road that led west to the hill station of Tatherlock some seven leagues distant. The journey was purportedly pleasant—across brakes, foothills and swales. The Nderian hills were not far away, and more momentous mountains were on the way. There would be camping and hostelry required, easy for a seasoned traveller as Baus.

Woisper wished the two well. Baus felt the brisk thrill of adventure quickening his blood. The thought of new territory, vistas and the unexpected—was a taste of the unordinary he yearned for, a fresh perspective in his new life.

There were moments of endearments and partings in Mancer Hall. Trimestrius had already embarked on a long journey with his peer Kazzasius to the seaside city of Aurenham. Last night they had set out to search for a bride for the young prince; Betrothed, Trimestrius was scheduled to return to Desenion and refound his rightful kingdom. Woisper had given the prince his best outfit, and best wishes, deliberating over whether he would relieve Alvius and Maitor of their tasking duty aside Aurimag's cave . . . Perhaps the old wizard would even let them stew over it for a while longer . . . Meanwhile, Baus recalled memories of his comrades, Valere and Poli, their swashbuckling exploits and misadventures o'er land and sea, slogging it through remote hinterlands, braving the elements and forest like bedraggled rats. There were many memories of bluster and joke-hurling, rodomontade, bravado and clashing swords. 'Twas none of the ordinary things—only bone-squelching fear, struggles, thiefdom, roguery, shipwrecks, palaces, rigours, frights and weirdnesses of all sorts stirred up in one pot of colour and ruckus that came to a head in a blinding flood of nostalgia . . .

Swallowing hard, Baus felt the lump in his throat ache; he embraced Valere and Poli with frank appraisal and looked them eye to eye and Baus felt an unwholesomely warm sting in his own.

In a final farewell, Woisper tendered him a small jingling of gold in a bulging sack. Baus was touched. To Esling, Ulisa proffered a necklace of power, and a silver-threaded rucksack filled with breads, cheeses and a handsome mix of good luck—'twas a fine amulet the necklace offered, gifted of excellent graces, and with it a bottle of the finest red wine fresh from Mismerion's cellars.

Woisper posed Baus a final warning: "Be wary of black unicorns, you rogue. And also wandering wizards and indomitable mistresses! Ha-ho. Of these, the latter shall be your ruin! Guard your Wickle well, covet her like a gem. She is a paragon, a valiant ally; you know you would be lost without her, and you'd be a fool to lose her, as any eye-roving young fool might. Follow the road to Tatherlock in earnest, straight to the hilltop! The path will lead you to the passes of Nderian, no less *destiny* if you have the mind for it. It will be anything more tender than the path which you have experienced."

Baus flashed him a grin and shook the weight from his shoulders. He gave a smart salute and a bow. Taking his leave of the castle, he tipped his hat to his colleagues, wrapped an arm about Esling. He skipped along the outer court to the gate, his jaunty companion in tow.

* * *

The sun was warm; the wind slackened and Baus loosed a sigh. Black mulberry and oxfane grew in numbers in the copse before him. A league out of Mismerion and pleasant spinneys surround him; abundant meadowlarks and cornflower dragonflies fluttered from shrub to shrub. The offhand murmur of the insects played pleasantly in his ears; he felt a sense of definite ease. No patrols of Arnin out this far. From the summit of a grassy knoll he looked west to spy the copper sheen of mounting Nderian hills glinting in a blaze of distance —also the bluer shades of the higher mounts dreamier still. There was a promise here—of mystery and exploit—a sky of deep azure, heralding good weather, wealth, and luck, and hopefully happier days . . .

Baus pondered the turn of fate. He whistled happy, forgotten songs and joked with Esling; his hand felt light on his sword and his heart airy, despite his inner being twinged with the ache of the missing-ness of his friends. There came to his mind no returning to Heagram—no gold or running fingers through a chest of it—only the *present*. An odd flash of Valere and Poli appeared in his mind, the two braves fast at his side, journeying, sword-swinging, backslapping and tackling the gloomy castles and the hair-raising foes they had come to know so well. A peaceful blur sang in his mind, an almost ordinary turn of memory . . .

Baus chuckled. How could it be so halcyon? Where were the rockgobblers on Heagram's dreary shore? Where the rude rejoinders on Harky the shoremaster's puggish lips? The snide insinuations of 'Captain Graves' and his crew of rat-brained Constables?

With a shrug and a leap, Baus gave a gusty chuckle and set his boots merrily to the west —away from the troubles of the past and frights of the chase, with Esling trotting schoolgirlishly behind him.

EPILOGUE

In another dimension, approaching n-$\frac{1}{2}^{th}$ order, a certain half-conscious form found himself spinning in a near airless void. The figure felt as if his insides were exploding—this, in the darkness of an obscure tunnel. That his viscera might splatter about the dank, dripping walls any second was a very real happening. How much more of it could he take?

He knew that any moment he could expire—specifically, the moment when he failed to twitch a muscle, or fend off the fiend which was slowly mastering him, ready to gobble his limbs. Inevitably the creature would maul him to death and slowly ingest him limb by limb, bone by bone, expectorating his pulp deep down into the stony veins of the earth.

Ah, what a fate!

A pale shaft of light wedged itself from a distant dark corridor. Aurimag felt his eyes stung smartly.

Daytime? What could this word mean in the desolate, futile oblivion of n-$\frac{1}{2}^{th}$ order?

The frail light was another sure sign of sanity though—perhaps a beacon penetrating the nebular gloom and illuminating the grim murk that he was in a position to *survive*. The hulking tormentor was Darkus: a monster thrice his own height, cursed with a whirl of waving tentacles and cold-hearted depravity seeking to empty his soul of life.

With desperate efforts Aurimag fought on, as much as this was painfully pitiful, akin to a man who clings to life as dearly as a rabid lust for vengeance.

The magician twitched, kicked; he blasphemed his captor as if he were about to lose his most precious gift—*life*. Better to preserve his existence than perish! he raved wildly. He must keep his wits! If he were to lose that edge, then he was finished and where then would be his mad, obsessive genius? To fade like the star in the last morning light was as dismal a prospect as it gets. His desire for revenge and power was fierce. Yes, power and resolve— they would only save him up to a point from this horror which had his life in balance, tossing him about like a child's ball from unearthly limb to unearthly limb . . .

Aurimag's sobosphere knocked against his thigh. Draped in the complex weaves of his cloak, the orb had failed to exert any damaging effect upon the elm sprite, Darkus; the adjunct's puissance had been eroded by its contact with that miserable bronze shield of Valere's before it had then stricken Kazzasius—or was it Poli?

It mattered not. Aurimag clamped bloodless lips to tongue.

The whip stick, however, was another matter. The magician had striven to access it perilously; fey luck had held him in a place of limbo! Cached in a deep fold of his robe, clinging leper-like to clammy skin, he could not reach it. It had been wrapped too tightly, lest a maligned movement stun his reason. Days after his capture, the elm-sprite had lobbed him carelessly, ignorant of the last loose lax toss . . .

And now, a writhing, glistening tentacle shot out—*missed*. The wild, corkscrewing of his body went unchecked and he fell several feet down the massive trunk which enabled him to grip the talisman, his whip stick.

A jarring jolt, and the ugliest lurch Aurimag had ever felt . . . then a looping branch caught hold of his ankle—Snap!—nearly breaking his neck.

Aurimag gritted his teeth with the pain, yet his euphoria knew no bound.

He tapped with the wand . . . Darkus's tentacles hung in a limp bundle; the glassy eyes hung ajar, staring at him, unfeeling, remorseless, knotting toward his peer, Arkenos, that grim hulk with expression of gleeful expectation behind the opposite grate.

The appraisal was obvious. The sibling had lost its prize. Now, its droopy lids dipped low in expectation that he might have the prize instead. Aurimag unravelled himself from the cold, slippery grip in the muted darkness, careful to avoid the lashing tentacles of his peer's.

His knees pressed uselessly against the trunk. He caught himself on the slimy twigs and knotty holes before he felt blood there, his own. Bruised limbs and muscles abounded, stiff as boards. Cold agony shot through Aurimag's body; he groaned with anguish as he jerked himself painfully to the floor.

He did not pause to reminisce over the frightful monster which towered above him. He hopped frantically through the jagged gap in the portcullis and crouched, peering, creeping, crouching on his hands and knees in this corridor of filth, all the while gulping stale lungfuls of air.

Brisk was his staggering . . . as he crab-scrambled up the tunnel before Arkenos could react . . .

The magician put a fevered hand to his temples. There was a throbbing there he never knew. He was out of harm's way, but wracked with a heady malaise that almost made him fall in drunken stupor. A strangled groan escaped his lips. To set torch and flame to this odious tunnel was his first inclination, but not a practical one. The miserable occupants within must perish meaningfully and with full knowledge of the agony pulsing through their sap. A strong desire forced Aurimag to recall certain conflagration was not uncommonly applied in the past to defeat elm-sprites . . . Yet even this was too kind. The destruction of the guardians would smoke out his cavern, destroy what was left of his valuables which he would need to salvage later to undermine old enemies. To clear the cave of shrew carcasses would be a staggering chore, but one better left to the lugubrious slaves he would employ in the future to hasten the task. As for n^{th} order abominations—those that had seized him, they would be cast into deeps so abysmal—

. . . but in due time, Aurimag cackled to himself, in a fashion that would not endanger his own life, or allow sad guardians a second chance to continue their mischief. One disastrous mistake and—well, suffice it to say, had already proven costly—another would be fatal.

Aurimag sank to his knees in gratitude somewhere half way up the tunnel. He quivered in joy. A pale light shone brighter than a beacon up ahead. The rush of daylight. Exhausted, but nearly lucid, he lay there panting in the clammy tunnel, pondering his next move.

For a long while he lay almost comatose, oblivious to the bat-reek and the mice dung—only to awaken to a foul pounding in his brain and the sudden desire to eat and drink ravenously. The dampness stole his will; cold fever pervaded his bones like a case of creeping rot. Now his joints popped like punky wood. The memory of Darkus swam evilly in his memory, a bewitching nightmare of horror.

How long had he lain stretched out on the stone in a half-tortured heap? He could not say.

Time had warped—become a contorted reality. He did not know that three days had passed, a total of ten days of torture in the ordinary dimension of men.

He twisted sickly to his feet. Almost crumpling again, only sheer will kept him continuing up the musty tunnel like a drunkard. He felt the brittle nature of his bones and the weakness of his age. Rheumy eyes followed the patch of growing light to mark out an exit . . .

Staggering out into a blaze of hot sunlight, he felt himself a pale, hunched figure. He blinked, stopped short. Through his blurred vision, he discerned a valley—green, pale, shrouded with mallorns, bottlegums and knob-kneed hissock.

A shadow flickered across his eyes—from the periphery, he saw a figure upon the brow of the hill.

He ducked back. The graceless action was unnecessary. New developments were in order. Neomancers had left some slack minions to guard the cave.

What prompted this? Did they harbour doubts of his death? Perhaps they wished to return later to rifle his collection?

Aurimag gurgled out a croak and felt loathing at the thought of recapture.

He risked another glance. A curling billow of smoke floated up toward the treetops, smelling of roast meat.

Hare? Fowl?

Aurimag licked his lips. A calculating smile crept over his ruined face. He recognized two of the figures—Alvius and Maitor—two of the 'fops' of the Circle. They lounged carelessly upon the ridge, expecting neither visitor nor harm. They were two idlers under the shade of the phantom elm.

Flames licked up and there was a slow-roasting over the crude spit. A small shelter was rigged off to the side, crafted of whittled mallorn. Aurimag frowned. Who would be the first to fall, Maitor or Alvius?

He began to laugh again. A froggish chortle squeezed itself from his larynx which was as raw as sandpaper. Gusmaye's ghost powder? The 'Spell of Unblinking Fire'? A knock of the whip stick? Any would suffice.

Coldness gleamed in his eyes. Retribution burned in his being like a black, torrid wave. He massaged his aching cheek with ever a twitching fervour.

With care and deliberation, he set to inching his way up the slope with the intent of snatching the roasting meat and despatching his enemies to n^{th} order.

But wait! The way was steep; scratching shrubs raked at his pasty skin. His garment was torn by stinging nettles. Any annoying number of twisted rocky niches might undermine him and send him spinning down with a broken ankle.

Half way up the slope, he halted. Spreading palms on an upthrust boulder, he winced with the sense of the effort. His fragile condition lent itself to no ambitious revenge.

A better idea came.

Why struggle when one need only lure pests into a cave and deal with them efficiently?

The magician was pleased with the ingenuity. He relaxed his wire-taut frame and rat-padded into the security of his hidey-hole to stick his head out once more. Cupping hands about his mouth, he gave a thin howl—half ululation, half cry of owl and hoar-wolf.

The sound surprised the sentries on the summit. They turned abruptly, stiffened, becoming pensive.

Aurimag reached for his white powder. Fingers curled about the whip stick as he paused to compose further plans. How easy to enslave two new minions! Hunt for sustenance would be quick and easy . . .then institute plans of revenge.

Aurimag grunted. Revenge was his reward. Almost could he taste the sweetness of revenge, for his chuckle was one of the ugliest philosophical irony. Of late, defeat had only shown its ugly maw, but with such genius as his, defeat would be thwarted, and then there would be much earth-shaking to come . . .

Aurimag peered grimly down toward the fading fastness of Mismerion. Far across the green-glimmering treetops, she existed as a lone keep of marvellous dimension where he would avenge himself of certain proud foes . . .

* * *

In a thicketed forest some eighty leagues away, three bedraggled shapes came blundering out of the forest, a blighted copse, trooping with ragged breaths down a potholed track. The trail, or road, if it could be so called, was easily witness to few visitors in these northern lands, evidenced by clumps of rank pikeweed and bilter-flower that edged indiscriminately from the forest. The lonely path snaked its way through crowding larch, mulberry and sea-beech, hinting of a trail more suited to those travelling at their own risk . . .

The hour was noon; the drab drizzle left the gloomy sky and the wayfaring trio suddenly came out of their sodden hollow, sopping like a coven of ruffled crows.

There was a sprightliness to the company's step, however, confident, given their condition, especially that of the junior member of the company whose jigging steps and prancing strides signified a mood of eager anticipation. Laughing and crooning, this figure announced in a quipping voice: "Let us predict that when the time comes all unpleasantness and inconvenience will be relieved!—that we might form an equal share amongst our merry fellowship!"

There were grumbles and grunts. The matted redbeard of their company gave a frosty retort: "I am an honest seaman; a four way split 'tis, Weavil, or 'tis none at all. How easily you forget our comrade Baus, so quickly."

"Comrade?" bawled the poet with a lip-curling grimace. "What smarmy comrade, redbeard? 'Tis 'Baus the Bold, Baus the Idealist', 'tis 'Baus the Avenger' . . . what others? Well—our sardonic 'saint' may never return from his travels—did you ever think of that?"

"I did. And your point being?"

"Better that we sub-allocate our friend's portion then to ourselves before calamity strikes his sensitive bones. The mathematics are simple—we line our pockets with extra cils—what better? The outlaw may at his own leisure acquire his full bounty by contacting us 'directly'."

"And how will 'the outlaw' accomplish that?—Ride on a magic carpet to scout us out with night vision?" mocked Valere.

"'Tis not our concern."

Poli stroked his chin. "The idea has some merit."

"In your mind perhaps, Poli," grunted Valere, "but I for one will not cheat our friend. He may yet return to Heagram when he finds out that gallivanting about the country is not all it is cut out to be. Some of you might appreciate that courtesy. Should any of us be captured by Arnin's men—well . . . 'tis better that we not flout protocol and let fortune have her way."

"A callow concept," scoffed Weavil. "I cannot wholly endorse it."

"Have it as you will, Weavil, but you must accept it, unless you wish to test swords with me?"

Weavil grimaced through his teeth.

Poli tipped back his black hunter's cap to stare critically at the poet. "You are forgetting, Poet, that Baus was largely responsible for liberating you—and us, ergo he should at least be allotted a partial share of the spoils."

Weavil gave Poli a spasmodic slap on the shoulder. "'Twas he who was 'largely responsible' for pitching me in Aurimag's cave in the first place, do you not remember?"

"What?" cried Poli. "Can I be hearing that Baus is to blame? I thought it was because of this cursed magician?"

"I shall explain!" asserted Weavil. "The 'magician' caught the two of us drunk many moons ago in the Heagram fairgrounds—this you know, after we had spoiled his side show and caused him prodigious inconvenience. He took us to his damaged tent. There, he performed disgusting things on us, particularly me, including the molestations which you have seen on my person. 'Performed' is a rather whimsical word actually. The villain could have easily picked either one of us to experiment on, yet he chose me, Weavil, 'the poet', owing to my comrade's narcissistic swaying of the situation to his advantage. Is this the 'glowingly infallible' Baus to whom you are so witlessly attached?"

Valere scowled, admitting that the scenario perhaps smacked of re-evaluation.

Weavil flapped his arms in vigorous exasperation. The conversation had ended. The threesome plodded on. Keeping their eyes attentive for a conspicuous 'bearsbottom', they looked for a trunk marked with a bearsbottom's 'secret' sign.

* * *

Within the hour the company did find such a sign. Loud were their groans when they counted out the forty paces from path to tree and discovered only a mound of earth next to a watery hole filled with mud. The companions gaped: they saw only an open chest, a broken case half tipped on its side, emptied of all its contents.

Poli gaped, knelt in the mud, gurgling in despair. Valere, bare-fisted, scoured the cold sludge, hunting for any stray jewels that may have slipped through the obvious thieves' pockets.

None were forthcoming. Weavil kicked at the chest with contemptuous rage. The chest rolled, skidded into the pool, rusted hinges and all, and the wood sagged like soft cheese. Not the least was a miserable groat or golden crown to be found in that mucky slime.

Valere stood motionless, slightly weak of leg. How had it come to this? In his brain many strained speculations ran.

Baus had possibly hidden the chest in ill fashion? The pirates had simply returned, spied the tree and its telltale mark and seized the wealth? All this work for nothing! The endless trudging of league on league. The options seemed innumerable. Perhaps Baus had been cack-brained enough not to conceal his presence from the scene and been seen burying the loot?

Either way, it did not matter and the Captain's conjectures were accompanied with a tearing of hair from everyone. Weavil's exaggerated shouts impinged on the quietude of the woods: "Back to where we started, eh redbeard? Baus the Bold! What a joke! Japing us with his suave jests and sense of jocularity!" Grimacing, the poet sucked in a gasp of damp air.

Poli loosed an oath. "It's all too complex, Weavil. We can't go blaming Baus yet. Just a bit of random luck, I think."

Weavil cawed. "Random luck! To what do you allude, dumbbrain? The scene is obvious; it strikes me as one of Baus's odious tricks . . ."

Valere shook his head with annoyance. "You think he came here and dug it up all on his own? Unlikely. Or gave us a false location? Look at the chest! It's legitimately smashed and pillaged—the same kind that Zoren's rogues use. I find your theories farfetched. Either way, this is what we have, Weavil, so let us suck it up and hump it back to Nosoheath. We must bear our losses." The captain tilted his head back and drained the last drops of larch whiskey in his pouch. He grimaced and followed up with a healthy belch very close to Weavil's face. "And that is for you, you little muckraker—so hump it up . . . both of you—Poli included!"

There was cursing and snarling. Poli groused at the crass stupidity of it all. He went back to his muck sifting and Weavil joined in too, and Valere clubbed Poli in the rear and sent Weavil flying, sliding to a similar fate into the rude disgusting water.

"There, you filthy lubbers! Heed my counsel. It looks like you've found your haven. Kismet has finally caught you up, eh? Well, what of it? 'Tis a case of paradoxical justice. To sea drakes with pirates' hoards! I've had enough of this. Nothing but a burdensome headache anyway. Out of these murks, I say, lads! Nosoheath's a shout and jog away, and Molly's fire crackles with a half-score of buxy-hipped skanks dancing, ready for the taking!"

Poli heaved a groan; the crew gathered themselves up to leave. Dragging themselves up the puddled path, they mumbled cursing words. Solitary tears of frustration dribbled down Weavil's cheeks though; Poli was racked with feelings he could not define . . . and yet, in short order, they were all laughing and shaking their heads at the fool's justice of it all . . .

About the Author

Chris is a prolific author of fantasy, adventure, and science fiction. His writing spans many genres: heroic fantasy, sword and sorcery and speculative fiction.

You can connect with Chris at:

http://innerskybooks.blogspot.com/